JOHN STEINBECK

JOHN STEINBECK

THE GRAPES OF WRATH
AND OTHER WRITINGS
1936–1941

The Long Valley
The Grapes of Wrath
The Log from the Sea of Cortez
The Harvest Gypsies

THE LIBRARY OF AMERICA

The paper used in this publication meets the
minimum requirements of the American National Standard for
Information Sciences—Permanence of Paper for Printed
Library Materials, ANSI Z39.48—1984.

Distributed to the trade in the United States
by Penguin Books USA Inc
and in Canada by Penguin Books Canada Ltd.

Library of Congress Catalog Number: 96–3725
For cataloging information, see end of Notes.
ISBN: 1–883011–15–9

First Printing
The Library of America—86

Manufactured in the United States of America

ROBERT DeMOTT
WROTE THE NOTES AND
ELAINE A. STEINBECK
WAS SPECIAL CONSULTANT FOR THIS VOLUME

Contents

THE LONG VALLEY

Contents

The Chrysanthemums

T HE HIGH grey-flannel fog of winter closed off the Salinas
Valley from the sky and from all the rest of the world.
On every side it sat like a lid on the mountains and made of
the great valley a closed pot. On the broad, level land floor
the gang plows bit deep and left the black earth shining like
metal where the shares had cut. On the foothill ranches across
the Salinas River, the yellow stubble fields seemed to be
bathed in pale cold sunshine, but there was no sunshine in
the valley now in December. The thick willow scrub along the
river flamed with sharp and positive yellow leaves.

It was a time of quiet and of waiting. The air was cold and
tender. A light wind blew up from the southwest so that the
farmers were mildly hopeful of a good rain before long; but
fog and rain do not go together.

Across the river, on Henry Allen's foothill ranch there was
little work to be done, for the hay was cut and stored and the
orchards were plowed up to receive the rain deeply when it
should come. The cattle on the higher slopes were becoming
shaggy and rough-coated.

Elisa Allen, working in her flower garden, looked down
across the yard and saw Henry, her husband, talking to two
men in business suits. The three of them stood by the tractor
shed, each man with one foot on the side of the little Fordson.
They smoked cigarettes and studied the machine as they
talked.

Elisa watched them for a moment and then went back to
her work. She was thirty-five. Her face was lean and strong
and her eyes were as clear as water. Her figure looked blocked
and heavy in her gardening costume, a man's black hat pulled
low down over her eyes, clodhopper shoes, a figured print
dress almost completely covered by a big corduroy apron with
four big pockets to hold the snips, the trowel and scratcher,
the seeds and the knife she worked with. She wore heavy
leather gloves to protect her hands while she worked.

She was cutting down the old year's chrysanthemum stalks
with a pair of short and powerful scissors. She looked down

5

toward the men by the tractor shed now and then. Her face was eager and mature and handsome; even her work with the scissors was over-eager, over-powerful. The chrysanthemum stems seemed too small and easy for her energy.

She brushed a cloud of hair out of her eyes with the back of her glove, and left a smudge of earth on her cheek in doing it. Behind her stood the neat white farm house with red geraniums close-banked around it as high as the windows. It was a hard-swept looking little house, with hard-polished windows, and a clean mud-mat on the front steps.

Elisa cast another glance toward the tractor shed. The strangers were getting into their Ford coupe. She took off a glove and put her strong fingers down into the forest of new green chrysanthemum sprouts that were growing around the old roots. She spread the leaves and looked down among the close-growing stems. No aphids were there, no sowbugs or snails or cutworms. Her terrier fingers destroyed such pests before they could get started.

Elisa started at the sound of her husband's voice. He had come near quietly, and he leaned over the wire fence that protected her flower garden from cattle and dogs and chickens.

"At it again," he said. "You've got a strong new crop coming."

Elisa straightened her back and pulled on the gardening glove again. "Yes. They'll be strong this coming year." In her tone and on her face there was a little smugness.

"You've got a gift with things," Henry observed. "Some of those yellow chrysanthemums you had this year were ten inches across. I wish you'd work out in the orchard and raise some apples that big."

Her eyes sharpened. "Maybe I could do it, too. I've a gift with things, all right. My mother had it. She could stick anything in the ground and make it grow. She said it was having planters' hands that knew how to do it."

"Well, it sure works with flowers," he said.

"Henry, who were those men you were talking to?"

"Why, sure, that's what I came to tell you. They were from the Western Meat Company. I sold those thirty head of three-year-old steers. Got nearly my own price, too."

"Good," she said. "Good for you."

"And I thought," he continued, "I thought how it's Saturday afternoon, and we might go into Salinas for dinner at a restaurant, and then to a picture show—to celebrate, you see."

"Good," she repeated. "Oh, yes. That will be good."

Henry put on his joking tone. "There's fights tonight. How'd you like to go to the fights?"

"Oh, no," she said breathlessly. "No, I wouldn't like fights."

"Just fooling, Elisa. We'll go to a movie. Let's see. It's two now. I'm going to take Scotty and bring down those steers from the hill. It'll take us maybe two hours. We'll go in town about five and have dinner at the Cominos Hotel. Like that?"

"Of course I'll like it. It's good to eat away from home."

"All right, then. I'll go get up a couple of horses."

She said, "I'll have plenty of time to transplant some of these sets, I guess."

She heard her husband calling Scotty down by the barn. And a little later she saw the two men ride up the pale yellow hillside in search of the steers.

There was a little square sandy bed kept for rooting the chrysanthemums. With her trowel she turned the soil over and over, and smoothed it and patted it firm. Then she dug ten parallel trenches to receive the sets. Back at the chrysanthemum bed she pulled out the little crisp shoots, trimmed off the leaves of each one with her scissors and laid it on a small orderly pile.

A squeak of wheels and plod of hoofs came from the road. Elisa looked up. The country road ran along the dense bank of willows and cottonwoods that bordered the river, and up this road came a curious vehicle, curiously drawn. It was an old spring-wagon, with a round canvas top on it like the cover of a prairie schooner. It was drawn by an old bay horse and a little grey-and-white burro. A big stubble-bearded man sat between the cover flaps and drove the crawling team. Underneath the wagon, between the hind wheels, a lean and rangy mongrel dog walked sedately. Words were painted on the canvas, in clumsy, crooked letters. "Pots, pans, knives, sisors, lawn mores, Fixed." Two rows of articles, and the triumphantly definitive "Fixed" below. The black paint had run down in little sharp points beneath each letter.

Elisa, squatting on the ground, watched to see the crazy, loose-jointed wagon pass by. But it didn't pass. It turned into the farm road in front of her house, crooked old wheels skirling and squeaking. The rangy dog darted from between the wheels and ran ahead. Instantly the two ranch shepherds flew out at him. Then all three stopped, and with stiff and quivering tails, with taut straight legs, with ambassadorial dignity, they slowly circled, sniffing daintily. The caravan pulled up to Elisa's wire fence and stopped. Now the newcomer dog, feeling out-numbered, lowered his tail and retired under the wagon with raised hackles and bared teeth.

The man on the wagon seat called out, "That's a bad dog in a fight when he gets started."

Elisa laughed. "I see he is. How soon does he generally get started?"

The man caught up her laughter and echoed it heartily. "Sometimes not for weeks and weeks," he said. He climbed stiffly down, over the wheel. The horse and the donkey drooped like unwatered flowers.

Elisa saw that he was a very big man. Although his hair and beard were greying, he did not look old. His worn black suit was wrinkled and spotted with grease. The laughter had disappeared from his face and eyes the moment his laughing voice ceased. His eyes were dark, and they were full of the brooding that gets in the eyes of teamsters and of sailors. The calloused hands he rested on the wire fence were cracked, and every crack was a black line. He took off his battered hat.

"I'm off my general road, ma'am," he said. "Does this dirt road cut over across the river to the Los Angeles highway?"

Elisa stood up and shoved the thick scissors in her apron pocket. "Well, yes, it does, but it winds around and then fords the river. I don't think your team could pull through the sand."

He replied with some asperity, "It might surprise you what them beasts can pull through."

"When they get started?" she asked.

He smiled for a second. "Yes. When they get started."

"Well," said Elisa, "I think you'll save time if you go back to the Salinas road and pick up the highway there."

He drew a big finger down the chicken wire and made it sing. "I ain't in any hurry, ma'am. I go from Seattle to San Diego and back every year. Takes all my time. About six months each way. I aim to follow nice weather."

Elisa took off her gloves and stuffed them in the apron pocket with the scissors. She touched the under edge of her man's hat, searching for fugitive hairs. "That sounds like a nice kind of a way to live," she said.

He leaned confidentially over the fence. "Maybe you noticed the writing on my wagon. I mend pots and sharpen knives and scissors. You got any of them things to do?"

"Oh, no," she said quickly. "Nothing like that." Her eyes hardened with resistance.

"Scissors is the worst thing," he explained. "Most people just ruin scissors trying to sharpen 'em, but I know how. I got a special tool. It's a little bobbit kind of thing, and patented. But it sure does the trick."

"No. My scissors are all sharp."

"All right, then. Take a pot," he continued earnestly, "a bent pot, or a pot with a hole. I can make it like new so you don't have to buy no new ones. That's a saving for you."

"No," she said shortly. "I tell you I have nothing like that for you to do."

His face fell to an exaggerated sadness. His voice took on a whining undertone. "I ain't had a thing to do today. Maybe I won't have no supper tonight. You see I'm off my regular road. I know folks on the highway clear from Seattle to San Diego. They save their things for me to sharpen up because they know I do it so good and save them money."

"I'm sorry," Elisa said irritably. "I haven't anything for you to do."

His eyes left her face and fell to searching the ground. They roamed about until they came to the chrysanthemum bed where she had been working. "What's them plants, ma'am?"

The irritation and resistance melted from Elisa's face. "Oh, those are chrysanthemums, giant whites and yellows. I raise them every year, bigger than anybody around here."

"Kind of a long-stemmed flower? Looks like a quick puff of colored smoke?" he asked.

"That's it. What a nice way to describe them."

"They smell kind of nasty till you get used to them," he said.

"It's a good bitter smell," she retorted, "not nasty at all."

He changed his tone quickly. "I like the smell myself."

"I had ten-inch blooms this year," she said.

The man leaned farther over the fence. "Look. I know a lady down the road a piece, has got the nicest garden you ever seen. Got nearly every kind of flower but no chrysanthemums. Last time I was mending a copper-bottom washtub for her (that's a hard job but I do it good), she said to me, 'If you ever run acrost some nice chrysantheums I wish you'd try to get me a few seeds.' That's what she told me."

Elisa's eyes grew alert and eager. "She couldn't have known much about chrysanthemums. You *can* raise them from seed, but it's much easier to root the little sprouts you see there."

"Oh," he said. "I s'pose I can't take none to her, then."

"Why yes you can," Elisa cried. "I can put some in damp sand, and you can carry them right along with you. They'll take root in the pot if you keep them damp. And then she can transplant them."

"She'd sure like to have some, ma'am. You say they're nice ones?"

"Beautiful," she said. "Oh, beautiful." Her eyes shone. She tore off the battered hat and shook out her dark pretty hair. "I'll put them in a flower pot, and you can take them right with you. Come into the yard."

While the man came through the picket gate Elisa ran excitedly along the geranium-bordered path to the back of the house. And she returned carrying a big red flower pot. The gloves were forgotten now. She kneeled on the ground by the starting bed and dug up the sandy soil with her fingers and scooped it into the bright new flower pot. Then she picked up the little pile of shoots she had prepared. With her strong fingers she pressed them into the sand and tamped around them with her knuckles. The man stood over her. "I'll tell you what to do," she said. "You remember so you can tell the lady."

"Yes, I'll try to remember."

"Well, look. These will take root in about a month. Then she must set them out, about a foot apart in good rich earth like this, see?" She lifted a handful of dark soil for him to look at. "They'll grow fast and tall. Now remember this: In July tell her to cut them down, about eight inches from the ground."

"Before they bloom?" he asked.

"Yes, before they bloom." Her face was tight with eagerness. "They'll grow right up again. About the last of September the buds will start."

She stopped and seemed perplexed. "It's the budding that takes the most care," she said hesitantly. "I don't know how to tell you." She looked deep into his eyes, searchingly. Her mouth opened a little, and she seemed to be listening. "I'll try to tell you," she said. "Did you ever hear of planting hands?"

"Can't say I have, ma'am."

"Well, I can only tell you what it feels like. It's when you're picking off the buds you don't want. Everything goes right down into your fingertips. You watch your fingers work. They do it themselves. You can feel how it is. They pick and pick the buds. They never make a mistake. They're with the plant. Do you see? Your fingers and the plant. You can feel that, right up your arm. They know. They never make a mistake. You can feel it. When you're like that you can't do anything wrong. Do you see that? Can you understand that?"

She was kneeling on the ground looking up at him. Her breast swelled passionately.

The man's eyes narrowed. He looked away self-consciously. "Maybe I know," he said. "Sometimes in the night in the wagon there——"

Elisa's voice grew husky. She broke in on him, "I've never lived as you do, but I know what you mean. When the night is dark—why, the stars are sharp-pointed, and there's quiet. Why, you rise up and up! Every pointed star gets driven into your body. It's like that. Hot and sharp and—lovely."

Kneeling there, her hand went out toward his legs in the greasy black trousers. Her hesitant fingers almost touched the cloth. Then her hand dropped to the ground. She crouched low like a fawning dog.

He said, "It's nice, just like you say. Only when you don't have no dinner, it ain't."

She stood up then, very straight, and her face was ashamed. She held the flower pot out to him and placed it gently in his arms. "Here. Put it in your wagon, on the seat, where you can watch it. Maybe I can find something for you to do."

At the back of the house she dug in the can pile and found two old and battered aluminum saucepans. She carried them back and gave them to him. "Here, maybe you can fix these."

His manner changed. He became professional. "Good as new I can fix them." At the back of his wagon he set a little anvil, and out of an oily tool box dug a small machine hammer. Elisa came through the gate to watch him while he pounded out the dents in the kettles. His mouth grew sure and knowing. At a difficult part of the work he sucked his under-lip.

"You sleep right in the wagon?" Elisa asked.

"Right in the wagon, ma'am. Rain or shine I'm dry as a cow in there."

"It must be nice," she said. "It must be very nice. I wish women could do such things."

"It ain't the right kind of a life for a woman."

Her upper lip raised a little, showing her teeth. "How do you know? How can you tell?" she said.

"I don't know, ma'am," he protested. "Of course I don't know. Now here's your kettles, done. You don't have to buy no new ones."

"How much?"

"Oh, fifty cents'll do. I keep my prices down and my work good. That's why I have all them satisfied customers up and down the highway."

Elisa brought him a fifty-cent piece from the house and dropped it in his hand. "You might be surprised to have a rival some time. I can sharpen scissors, too. And I can beat the dents out of little pots. I could show you what a woman might do."

He put his hammer back in the oily box and shoved the little anvil out of sight. "It would be a lonely life for a woman, ma'am, and a scarey life, too, with animals creeping under the wagon all night." He climbed over the singletree, steadying himself with a hand on the burro's white rump. He settled himself in the seat, picked up the lines. "Thank you kindly, ma'am," he said. "I'll do like you told me; I'll go back and catch the Salinas road."

"Mind," she called, "if you're long in getting there, keep the sand damp."

"Sand, ma'am? . . . Sand? Oh, sure. You mean around the chrysanthemums. Sure I will." He clucked his tongue. The beasts leaned luxuriously into their collars. The mongrel dog took his place between the back wheels. The wagon turned and crawled out the entrance road and back the way it had come, along the river.

Elisa stood in front of her wire fence watching the slow progress of the caravan. Her shoulders were straight, her head thrown back, her eyes half-closed, so that the scene came vaguely into them. Her lips moved silently, forming the words "Good-bye—good-bye." Then she whispered, "That's a bright direction. There's a glowing there." The sound of her whisper startled her. She shook herself free and looked about to see whether anyone had been listening. Only the dogs had heard. They lifted their heads toward her from their sleeping in the dust, and then stretched out their chins and settled asleep again. Elisa turned and ran hurriedly into the house.

In the kitchen she reached behind the stove and felt the water tank. It was full of hot water from the noonday cooking. In the bathroom she tore off her soiled clothes and flung them into the corner. And then she scrubbed herself with a little block of pumice, legs and thighs, loins and chest and arms, until her skin was scratched and red. When she had dried herself she stood in front of a mirror in her bedroom and looked at her body. She tightened her stomach and threw out her chest. She turned and looked over her shoulder at her back.

After a while she began to dress, slowly. She put on her newest underclothing and her nicest stockings and the dress which was the symbol of her prettiness. She worked carefully on her hair, penciled her eyebrows and rouged her lips.

Before she was finished she heard the little thunder of hoofs and the shouts of Henry and his helper as they drove the red steers into the corral. She heard the gate bang shut and set herself for Henry's arrival.

His step sounded on the porch. He entered the house calling, "Elisa, where are you?"

"In my room, dressing. I'm not ready. There's hot water for your bath. Hurry up. It's getting late."

When she heard him splashing in the tub, Elisa laid his dark suit on the bed, and shirt and socks and tie beside it. She stood his polished shoes on the floor beside the bed. Then she went to the porch and sat primly and stiffly down. She looked toward the river road where the willow-line was still yellow with frosted leaves so that under the high grey fog they seemed a thin band of sunshine. This was the only color in the grey afternoon. She sat unmoving for a long time. Her eyes blinked rarely.

Henry came banging out of the door, shoving his tie inside his vest as he came. Elisa stiffened and her face grew tight. Henry stopped short and looked at her. "Why—why, Elisa. You look so nice!"

"Nice? You think I look nice? What do you mean by 'nice'?"

Henry blundered on. "I don't know. I mean you look different, strong and happy."

"I am strong? Yes, strong. What do you mean 'strong'?"

He looked bewildered. "You're playing some kind of a game," he said helplessly. "It's a kind of a play. You look strong enough to break a calf over your knee, happy enough to eat it like a watermelon."

For a second she lost her rigidity. "Henry! Don't talk like that. You didn't know what you said." She grew complete again. "I'm strong," she boasted. "I never knew before how strong."

Henry looked down toward the tractor shed, and when he brought his eyes back to her, they were his own again. "I'll get out the car. You can put on your coat while I'm starting."

Elisa went into the house. She heard him drive to the gate and idle down his motor, and then she took a long time to put on her hat. She pulled it here and pressed it there. When

Henry turned the motor off she slipped into her coat and went out.

The little roadster bounced along on the dirt road by the river, raising the birds and driving the rabbits into the brush. Two cranes flapped heavily over the willow-line and dropped into the river-bed.

Far ahead on the road Elisa saw a dark speck. She knew.

She tried not to look as they passed it, but her eyes would not obey. She whispered to herself sadly, "He might have thrown them off the road. That wouldn't have been much trouble, not very much. But he kept the pot," she explained. "He had to keep the pot. That's why he couldn't get them off the road."

The roadster turned a bend and she saw the caravan ahead. She swung full around toward her husband so she could not see the little covered wagon and the mismatched team as the car passed them.

In a moment it was over. The thing was done. She did not look back.

She said loudly, to be heard above the motor, "It will be good, tonight, a good dinner."

"Now you're changed again," Henry complained. He took one hand from the wheel and patted her knee. "I ought to take you in to dinner oftener. It would be good for both of us. We get so heavy out on the ranch."

"Henry," she asked, "could we have wine at dinner?"

"Sure we could. Say! That will be fine."

She was silent for a while; then she said, "Henry, at those prize fights, do the men hurt each other very much?"

"Sometimes a little, not often. Why?"

"Well, I've read how they break noses, and blood runs down their chests. I've read how the fighting gloves get heavy and soggy with blood."

He looked around at her. "What's the matter, Elisa? I didn't know you read things like that." He brought the car to a stop, then turned to the right over the Salinas River bridge.

"Do any women ever go to the fights?" she asked.

"Oh, sure, some. What's the matter, Elisa? Do you want to

go? I don't think you'd like it, but I'll take you if you really want to go."

She relaxed limply in the seat. "Oh, no. No. I don't want to go. I'm sure I don't." Her face was turned away from him. "It will be enough if we can have wine. It will be plenty." She turned up her coat collar so he could not see that she was crying weakly—like an old woman.

The White Quail

T HE WALL opposite the fireplace in the living-room was a big dormer window stretching from the cushioned window seats almost to the ceiling—small diamond panes set in lead. From the window, preferably if you were sitting on the window seat, you could look across the garden and up the hill. There was a stretch of shady lawn under the garden oaks—around each oak there was a circle of carefully tended earth in which grew cinerarias, big ones with loads of flowers so heavy they bent the stems over, and ranging in color from scarlet to ultramarine. At the edge of the lawn, a line of fuchsias grew like little symbolic trees. In front of the fuchsias lay a shallow garden pool, the coping flush with the lawn for a very good reason.

Right at the edge of the garden, the hill started up, wild with cascara bushes and poison oak, with dry grass and live oak, very wild. If you didn't go around to the front of the house you couldn't tell it was on the very edge of the town.

Mary Teller, Mrs. Harry E. Teller, that is, knew the window and the garden were Right and she had a very good reason for knowing. Hadn't she picked out the place where the house and the garden would be years ago? Hadn't she seen the house and the garden a thousand times while the place was still a dry flat against the shoulder of a hill? For that matter, hadn't she, during five years, looked at every attentive man and wondered whether he and that garden would go together? She didn't think so much, "Would this man like such a garden?" but, "Would the garden like such a man?" For the garden was herself, and after all she had to marry some one she liked.

When she met Harry Teller, the garden seemed to like him. It may have surprised him a little when, after he had proposed and was waiting sulkily for his answer, as men do, Mary broke into a description of a big dormer window and a garden with a lawn and oak trees and cinerarias and then a wild hill.

He said, "Of course," rather perfunctorily.

Mary asked, "Do you think it's silly?"

He was waiting a little sullenly. "Of course not."

And then she remembered that he had proposed to her, and she accepted him, and let him kiss her. She said, "There will be a little cement pool flush with the lawn. Do you know why? Well, there are more birds on that hill than you'd ever think, yellowhammers and wild canaries and red-wing blackbirds, and of course sparrows and linnets, and lots of quail. Of course they'll be coming down to drink there, won't they?"

She was very pretty. He wanted to kiss her over and over, and she let him. "And fuchsias," she said. "Don't forget fuchsias. They're like little tropical Christmas trees. We'll have to have the lawn raked every day to keep the oak leaves clear."

He laughed at her. "You're a funny little bug. The lot isn't bought, and the house isn't built, and the garden isn't planted; and already you're worrying about oak leaves on the lawn. You're so pretty. You make me kind of—hungry."

That startled her a little. A little expression of annoyance crossed her face. But nevertheless she let him kiss her again, and then sent him home and went to her room, where she had a little blue writing desk and on it a copy-book to write things in. She took up a pen, of which the handle was a peacock feather, and she wrote, "Mary Teller" over and over again. Once or twice she wrote, "Mrs. Harry E. Teller."

II

The lot was bought and the house was built, and they were married. Mary drew a careful plan of the garden, and when the workmen were putting it in she didn't leave them alone for a moment. She knew to an inch where everything should be. And she drew the shape of the shallow pool for the cement workers, a kind of heart-shaped pool with no point at the bottom, with gradually sloping edges so the birds could drink easily.

Harry watched her with admiration. "Who could tell that such a pretty girl could have so much efficiency," he said.

That pleased her, too; and she was very happy, so that she

said, "You can plant some of the things you like in the garden, if you want."

"No, Mary, I like too much to see your own mind coming out in the garden. You do it all your own way."

She loved him for that; but after all, it was her garden. She had invented it, and willed it, and she had worked out the colors too, so carefully. It really wouldn't have been nice if, for instance, Harry had wanted some flowers that didn't go with the garden.

At last the green lawn was up, and the cinerarias around the oak trees bloomed in sunken pots. The little fuchsia trees had been moved in so carefully that not a leaf wilted.

The window seats behind the dormer windows were piled with cushions covered with bright, fadeless fabrics, for the sun shone in that window a good part of the day.

Mary waited until it was all done, all finished exactly as her mind had seen it; and then one evening when Harry came home from the office, she led him to the window seat. "You see," she said softly. "There it is, just the way I wanted it."

"It's beautiful," said Harry, "very beautiful."

"In a way I'm sad that it's done," she said. "But mostly I'm glad. We won't ever change it, will we, Harry? If a bush dies, we'll put another one just like it in the same place."

"Curious little bug," he said.

"Well, you see I've thought about it so long that it's part of me. If anything should be changed it would be like part of me being torn out."

He put out his hand to touch her, and then withdrew it. "I love you so much," he said, and then paused. "But I'm afraid of you, too."

She smiled quietly. "You? Afraid of me? What's there about me you can be afraid of?"

"Well, you're kind of untouchable. There's an inscrutability about you. Probably you don't even know it yourself. You're kind of like your own garden—fixed, and just so. I'm afraid to move around. I might disturb some of your plants."

Mary was pleased. "Dear," she said. "You let me do it. You made it my garden. Yes, you are dear." And she let him kiss her.

III

He was proud of her when people came in to dinner. She was so pretty, so cool and perfect. Her bowls of flowers were exquisite, and she talked about the garden modestly, hesitantly, almost as though she were talking about herself. Sometimes she took her guests into the garden. She pointed to a fuchsia tree. "I didn't know whether he would succeed," she said, just as though the plant were a person. "He ate a lot of plant food before he decided to come around." She smiled quietly to herself.

She was delightful when she worked in the garden. She wore a bright print dress, quite long in the skirt, and sleeveless. Somewhere she had found an old-fashioned sunbonnet. She wore good sturdy gloves to protect her hands. Harry liked to watch her going about with a bag and a big spoon, putting plant food about the roots of her flowers. He liked it, too, when they went out at night to kill slugs and snails. Mary held the flashlight while Harry did the actual killing, crushing the slugs and snails into oozy, bubbling masses. He knew it must be a disgusting business to her, but the light never wavered. "Brave girl," he thought. "She has a sturdiness in back of that fragile beauty." She made the hunts exciting too. "There's a big one, creeping and creeping," she would say. "He's after that big bloom. Kill him! Kill him quickly!" They came into the house after the hunts laughing happily.

Mary was worried about the birds. "They don't come down to drink," she complained. "Not many of them. I wonder what's keeping them away."

"Maybe they aren't used to it yet. They'll come later. Maybe there's a cat around."

Her face flushed and she breathed deeply. Her pretty lips tightened away from her teeth. "If there's a cat, I'll put out poisoned fish," she cried. "I won't have a cat after my birds!"

Harry had to soothe her. "I'll tell you what I'll do. I'll buy an air gun. Then if a cat comes, we can shoot it, and it won't kill the cat, but it'll hurt, and the cat won't come back."

"Yes," she said more calmly. "That might be better."

The living-room was very pleasant at night. The fire burned up in a sheet of flame. If there was a moon, Mary turned off the lights and then they sat looking through the window at the cool blue garden and the dark oak trees.

It was utterly calm and eternal out there. And then the garden ended and the dark thickets of the hill began.

"That's the enemy," Mary said one time. "That's the world that wants to get in, all rough and tangled and unkempt. But it can't get in because the fuchsias won't let it. That's what the fuchsias are there for, and they know it. The birds can get in. They live out in the wild, but they come to my garden for peace and for water." She laughed softly. "There's something profound in all that, Harry. I don't know quite what it is. The quail are beginning to come down now. At least a dozen were at the pool this evening."

He said, "I wish I could see the inside of your mind. It seems to flutter around, but it's a cool, collected mind. It's so—sure of itself."

Mary went to sit on his lap for a moment. "Not so awfully sure. You don't know, and I'm glad you don't."

IV

One night when Harry was reading his paper under the lamp, Mary jumped up. "I left my garden scissors outside," she said. "The dew will rust them."

Harry looked over his paper. "Can't I get them for you?"

"No, I'll go. You couldn't find them." She went out into the garden and found the shears, and then she looked in the window, into the living room. Harry was still reading his paper. The room was clear, like a picture, like the set of a play that was about to start. A curtain of fire waved up in the fireplace. Mary stood still and looked. There was the big, deep chair she had been sitting in a minute ago. What would she be doing if she hadn't come outside? Suppose only essence, only mind and sight had come, leaving Mary in the chair? She could almost see herself sitting there. Her round arms and long fingers were resting on the chair. Her delicate, sensitive face was in profile, looking reflectively into the firelight. "What is she thinking about?" Mary whispered. "I wonder what's going on in her mind. Will she get up? No, she's just sitting there. The neck of that dress is too wide, see how it slips sideways over the shoulder. But that's rather pretty. It looks careless, but neat and pretty. Now—she's smiling. She must be thinking something nice."

Suddenly Mary came to herself and realized what she had been doing. She was delighted. "There were two me's," she thought. "It was like having two lives, being able to see myself. That's wonderful. I wonder whether I can see it whenever I want to. I saw just what other people see when they look at me. I must tell Harry about that." But then a new picture formed; she saw herself explaining, trying to describe what had happened. She saw him looking over his paper with an intent, puzzled, almost pained look in his eyes. He tried so hard to understand when she told him things. He wanted to understand, and he never quite succeeded. If she told him about this vision tonight, he would ask questions. He would turn the thing over and over, trying to understand it, until finally he ruined it. He didn't want to spoil the things she told him, but he just couldn't help it. He needed too much light on things that light shriveled. No, she wouldn't tell him. She would want to come out and do it again, and she couldn't if he spoiled it for her.

Through the window she saw Harry put his paper down on his knee and look up at the door. She hurried in, showing him the shears to prove what she had gone for. "See, the rust was forming already. They'd've been all brown and nasty by morning."

He nodded and smiled at her. "It says in the paper we're going to have more trouble with that new loan bill. They put a lot of difficulties in our way. Somebody has to loan money when people want to borrow."

"I don't understand loans," she said. "Somebody told me your company had title to nearly every automobile in town."

He laughed. "Well, not all, but a good many of them, anyway. When times are a little bit hard, we make money."

"It sounds terrible," she observed. "It sounds like taking unfair advantage."

He folded the paper and put it on the table beside his chair. "No, I don't think it's unfair," he said. "The people must have the money, and we supply it. The law regulates the interest rate. We haven't anything to do with that."

She stretched her pretty arms and fingers on the chair, as she had seen them through the window. "I suppose it really isn't unfair," she said. "It just sounds as though you took advantage of people when they were down."

Harry looked seriously into the fire for a long time. Mary could see him, and she knew he was worrying about what she said. Well, it would do him no harm to see what business really was like. Things seemed righter when you did them than when you thought about them. A little mental housecleaning mightn't be a bad thing for Harry.

After a little, he looked over at her. "Dear, you don't think it's unfair practice, do you?"

"Why, I don't know anything about loans. How can I tell what is fair?"

Harry insisted, "But do you *feel* it's unfair? Are you ashamed of my business? I wouldn't like it if you were."

Suddenly Mary felt very glad and pleased. "I'm not ashamed, silly. Every one has a right to make a living. You do what you do well."

"You're sure, now?"

"Of course I'm sure, silly."

After she was in bed in her own little bedroom she heard a faint click and saw the door knob turn, and then turn slowly back. The door was locked. It was a signal; there were things Mary didn't like to talk about. The lock was an answer to a question, a clean, quick, decisive answer. It was peculiar about Harry, though. He always tried the door silently. It seemed as though he didn't want her to know he had tried it. But she always did know. He was sweet and gentle. It seemed to make him ashamed when he turned the knob and found the door locked.

Mary pulled the light chain, and when her eyes had become accustomed to the dark, she looked out the window at her garden in the half moonlight. Harry was sweet, and understanding, too. That time about the dog. He had come running into the house, really running. His face was so red and excited that Mary had a nasty shock. She thought there had been an accident. Later in the evening she had a headache from the shock. Harry had shouted, "Joe Adams—his Irish Terrier bitch had puppies. He's going to give me one!

Thoroughbred stock, red as strawberries!" He had really wanted one of the pups. It hurt Mary that he couldn't have one. But she was proud of his quick understanding of the situation. When she explained how a dog would—do things on the plants of her garden, or even dig in her flower beds, how, worst of all, a dog would keep the birds away from the pool, Harry understood. He might have trouble with complicated things, like that vision from the garden, but he understood about the dog. Later in the evening, when her head ached, he soothed her and patted Florida Water on her head. That was the curse of imagination. Mary had seen, actually seen the dog in her garden, and the dug holes, and ruined plants. It was almost as bad as though it actually happened. Harry was ashamed, but really he couldn't help it if she had such an imagination. Mary couldn't blame him, how could he have known?

v

Late in the afternoon, when the sun had gone behind the hill, there was a time Mary called the really-garden-time. Then the high school girl was in from school and had taken charge of the kitchen. It was almost a sacred time. Mary walked out into the garden and across the lawn to a folding chair half behind one of the lawn oaks. She could watch the birds drinking in the pool from there. She could really *feel* the garden. When Harry came home from the office, he stayed in the house and read his paper until she came in from the garden, star-eyed. It made her unhappy to be disturbed.

The summer was just breaking. Mary looked into the kitchen and saw that everything was all right there. She went through the living room and lighted the laid fire, and then she was ready for the garden. The sun had just dropped behind the hill, and the blue gauze of the evening had settled among the oaks.

Mary thought, "It's like millions of not quite invisible fairies coming into my garden. You can't see one of them, but the millions change the color of the air." She smiled to herself at the nice thought. The clipped lawn was damp and fresh with watering. The brilliant cinerarias threw little haloes of color into the air. The fuchsia trees were loaded with blooms. The buds, like little red Christmas tree ornaments, and the open blooms like ballet-skirted ladies. They were so *right*, the fuchsias, so absolutely right. And they discouraged the enemy on the other side, the brush and scrubby, untrimmed trees.

Mary walked across the lawn in the evening to her chair, and sat down. She could hear the birds gathering to come down to the pool. "Making up parties," she thought, "coming to my garden in the evening. How they must love it! How I would like to come to my garden for the first time. If I could be two people— 'Good evening, come into the garden, Mary.' 'Oh, isn't it lovely.' 'Yes, I like it, especially at this time. Quiet, now, Mary. Don't frighten the birds.' " She sat as still as a mouse. Her lips were parted with expectancy. In the brush the quail twittered sharply. A yellowhammer dropped to the edge of the pool. Two little flycatchers flickered out over the water and stood still in the air, beating their wings. And then the quail ran out, with funny little steps. They stopped and cocked their heads, to see whether it was safe. Their leader, a big fellow with a crest like a black question mark, sounded the bugle-like "All clear" call, and the band came down to drink.

And then it happened, the wonderful thing. Out of the brush ran a white quail. Mary froze. Yes, it was a quail, no doubt of it, and white as snow. Oh, this was wonderful! A shiver of pleasure, a bursting of pleasure swelled in Mary's breast. She held her breath. The dainty little white hen quail went to the other side of the pool, away from the ordinary quail. She paused and looked around, and then dipped her beak in the water.

"Why," Mary cried to herself, "she's like me!" A powerful ecstasy quivered in her body. "She's like the essence of me, an essence boiled down to utter purity. She must be the queen of the quail. She makes every lovely thing that ever happened to me one thing."

The white quail dipped her beak again and threw back her head to swallow.

The memories welled in Mary and filled her chest. Something sad, always something sad. The packages that came; untying the string was the ecstasy. The thing in the package was never quite——

The marvelous candy from Italy. "Don't eat it, dear. It's prettier than it's good." Mary never ate it, but looking at it was an ecstasy like this.

"What a pretty girl Mary is. She's like a gentian, so quiet." The hearing was an ecstasy like this.

"Mary dear, be very brave now. Your father has—passed away." The first moment of loss was an ecstasy like this.

The white quail stretched a wing backward and smoothed down the feathers with her beak. "This is the me that was everything beautiful. This is the center of me, my heart."

VI

The blue air became purple in the garden. The fuchsia buds blazed like little candles. And then a gray shadow moved out of the brush. Mary's mouth dropped open. She sat paralyzed with fear. A gray cat crept like death out of the brush, crept toward the pool and the drinking birds. Mary stared in horror. Her hand rose up to her tight throat. Then she broke the paralysis. She screamed terribly. The quail flew away on muttering wings. The cat bounded back into the brush. Still Mary screamed and screamed. Harry ran out of the house crying, "Mary! What is it, Mary?"

She shuddered when he touched her. She began to cry hysterically. He took her up in his arms and carried her into the house, and into her own room. She lay quivering on the bed. "What was it, dear? What frightened you?"

"It was a cat," she moaned. "It was creeping up on the birds." She sat up; her eyes blazed. "Harry, you must put out poison. Tonight you simply must put out some poison for that cat."

"Lie back, dear. You've had a shock."

"Promise me you'll put out poison." She looked closely at him and saw a rebellious light come into his eyes. "Promise."

"Dear," he apologized, "some dog might get it. Animals suffer terribly when they get poison."

"I don't care," she cried. "I don't want any animals in my garden, any kind."

"No," he said. "I won't do that. No, I can't do that. But I'll get up early in the morning. I'll take the new air gun and I'll shoot that cat so he'll never come back. The air gun shoots hard. It'll make a hurt the cat won't forget."

It was the first thing he had ever refused. She didn't know how to combat it; but her head ached, terribly. When it ached its worst he tried to make it up to her for refusing the poison. He kept a little pad soaked with Florida Water, and he patted it on her forehead. She wondered whether she should tell him about the white quail. He wouldn't believe it. But maybe if he knew how important it was, he might poison the cat. She waited until her nerves were calm before she told him. "Dear, there was a white quail in the garden."

"A white quail? Are you sure it wasn't a pigeon?"

There it was. Right from the first he spoiled it. "I know quail," she cried. "It was quite close to me. A white hen quail."

"That would be a thing to see," he said. "I never heard of one."

"But I tell you I saw it."

He dabbed at her forehead. "Well, I suppose it was an albino. No pigment in the feathers, something like that."

She was growing hysterical again. "You don't understand. That white quail was *me*, the secret me that no one can ever get at, the me that's way inside." Harry's face was contorted with the struggle to understand. "Can't you see, dear? The cat was after me. It was going to kill me. That's why I want to poison it." She studied his face. No, he didn't understand, he couldn't. Why had she told him? If she hadn't been so upset she never would have told him.

"I'll set my alarm clock," he assured her. "Tomorrow morning I'll give that cat something to remember."

At ten o'clock he left her alone. And when he had gone Mary got up and locked the door.

His alarm-clock bell awakened Mary in the morning. It was still dark in her room, but she could see the gray light of morning through the window. She heard Harry dressing quietly. He tiptoed past her door and went outside, closing the door silently for fear of awakening her. He carried the new shining air gun in his hand. The fresh gray morning air made him throw back his shoulders and step lightly over the damp lawn. He walked to the corner of the garden and lay down on his stomach in the wet grass.

The garden grew lighter. Already the quail were twittering metallically. The little brown band came to the edge of the brush and cocked their heads. Then the big leader called, "All's well," and his charges ran with quick steps to the pool. A moment later the white quail followed them. She went to the other side of the pool and dipped her beak and threw back her head. Harry raised the gun. The white quail tipped her head and looked toward him. The air gun spat with a vicious whisper. The quail flew off into the brush. But the white quail fell over and shuddered a moment, and lay still on the lawn.

Harry walked slowly over to her and picked her up. "I didn't mean to kill it," he said to himself. "I just wanted to scare it away." He looked at the white bird in his hand. Right in the head, right under the eye the BB shot had gone. Harry stepped to the line of fuchsias and threw the quail up into the brush. The next moment he put down the gun and crashed up through the undergrowth. He found the white quail, carried her far up the hill and buried her under a pile of leaves.

Mary heard him pass her door. "Harry, did you shoot the cat?"

"It won't ever come back," he said through the door.

"Well, I hope you killed it, but I don't want to hear the details."

Harry walked on into the living-room and sat down in a big chair. The room was still dusky, but through the big dormer window the garden glowed and the tops of the lawn oaks were afire with sunshine.

"What a skunk I am," Harry said to himself. "What a dirty skunk, to kill a thing she loved so much." He dropped his head and looked at the floor. "I'm lonely," he said. "Oh, Lord, I'm so lonely!"

Flight

ABOUT fifteen miles below Monterey, on the wild coast, the Torres family had their farm, a few sloping acres above a cliff that dropped to the brown reefs and to the hissing white waters of the ocean. Behind the farm the stone mountains stood up against the sky. The farm buildings huddled like little clinging aphids on the mountain skirts, crouched low to the ground as though the wind might blow them into the sea. The little shack, the rattling, rotting barn were grey-bitten with sea salt, beaten by the damp wind until they had taken on the color of the granite hills. Two horses, a red cow and a red calf, half a dozen pigs and a flock of lean, multicolored chickens stocked the place. A little corn was raised on the sterile slope, and it grew short and thick under the wind, and all the cobs formed on the landward sides of the stalks.

Mama Torres, a lean, dry woman with ancient eyes, had ruled the farm for ten years, ever since her husband tripped over a stone in the field one day and fell full length on a rattlesnake. When one is bitten on the chest there is not much that can be done.

Mama Torres had three children, two undersized black ones of twelve and fourteen, Emilio and Rosy, whom Mama kept fishing on the rocks below the farm when the sea was kind and when the truant officer was in some distant part of Monterey County. And there was Pepé, the tall smiling son of nineteen, a gentle, affectionate boy, but very lazy. Pepé had a tall head, pointed at the top, and from its peak, coarse black hair grew down like a thatch all around. Over his smiling little eyes Mama cut a straight bang so he could see. Pepé had sharp Indian cheek bones and an eagle nose, but his mouth was as sweet and shapely as a girl's mouth, and his chin was fragile and chiseled. He was loose and gangling, all legs and feet and wrists, and he was very lazy. Mama thought him fine and brave, but she never told him so. She said, "Some lazy cow must have got into thy father's family, else how could I have a son like thee." And she said, "When I carried thee, a sneaking lazy coyote came out of the brush and looked at me one day. That must have made thee so."

Pepé smiled sheepishly and stabbed at the ground with his knife to keep the blade sharp and free from rust. It was his inheritance, that knife, his father's knife. The long heavy blade folded back into the black handle. There was a button on the handle. When Pepé pressed the button, the blade leaped out ready for use. The knife was with Pepé always, for it had been his father's knife.

One sunny morning when the sea below the cliff was glinting and blue and the white surf creamed on the reef, when even the stone mountains looked kindly, Mama Torres called out the door of the shack, "Pepé, I have a labor for thee."

There was no answer. Mama listened. From behind the barn she heard a burst of laughter. She lifted her full long skirt and walked in the direction of the noise.

Pepé was sitting on the ground with his back against a box. His white teeth glistened. On either side of him stood the two black ones, tense and expectant. Fifteen feet away a redwood post was set in the ground. Pepé's right hand lay limply in his lap, and in the palm the big black knife rested. The blade was closed back into the handle. Pepé looked smiling at the sky.

Suddenly Emilio cried, "Ya!"

Pepé's wrist flicked like the head of a snake. The blade seemed to fly open in mid-air, and with a thump the point dug into the redwood post, and the black handle quivered. The three burst into excited laughter. Rosy ran to the post and pulled out the knife and brought it back to Pepé. He closed the blade and settled the knife carefully in his listless palm again. He grinned self-consciously at the sky.

"Ya!"

The heavy knife lanced out and sunk into the post again. Mama moved forward like a ship and scattered the play.

"All day you do foolish things with the knife, like a toy-baby," she stormed. "Get up on thy huge feet that eat up shoes. Get up!" She took him by one loose shoulder and hoisted at him. Pepé grinned sheepishly and came half-heartedly to his feet. "Look!" Mama cried. "Big lazy, you must catch the horse and put on him thy father's saddle. You must ride to Monterey. The medicine bottle is empty. There is no salt. Go thou now, Peanut! Catch the horse."

A revolution took place in the relaxed figure of Pepé. "To Monterey, me? Alone? *Sí*, Mama."

She scowled at him. "Do not think, big sheep, that you will buy candy. No, I will give you only enough for the medicine and the salt."

Pepé smiled. "Mama, you will put the hatband on the hat?"

She relented then. "Yes, Pepé. You may wear the hatband."

His voice grew insinuating, "And the green handkerchief, Mama?"

"Yes, if you go quickly and return with no trouble, the silk green handkerchief will go. If you make sure to take off the handkerchief when you eat so no spot may fall on it. . . ."

"*Sí*, Mama. I will be careful. I am a man."

"Thou? A man? Thou art a peanut."

He went into the rickety barn and brought out a rope, and he walked agilely enough up the hill to catch the horse.

When he was ready and mounted before the door, mounted on his father's saddle that was so old that the oaken frame showed through torn leather in many places, then Mama brought out the round black hat with the tooled leather band, and she reached up and knotted the green silk handkerchief about his neck. Pepé's blue denim coat was much darker than his jeans, for it had been washed much less often.

Mama handed up the big medicine bottle and the silver coins. "That for the medicine," she said, "and that for the salt. That for a candle to burn for the papa. That for *dulces* for the little ones. Our friend Mrs. Rodriguez will give you dinner and maybe a bed for the night. When you go to the church say only ten Paternosters and only twenty-five Ave Marias. Oh! I know, big coyote. You would sit there flapping your mouth over Aves all day while you looked at the candles and the holy pictures. That is not good devotion to stare at the pretty things."

The black hat, covering the high pointed head and black thatched hair of Pepé, gave him dignity and age. He sat the rangy horse well. Mama thought how handsome he was, dark and lean and tall. "I would not send thee now alone, thou little one, except for the medicine," she said softly. "It is not good to have no medicine, for who knows when the tooth-ache will come, or the sadness of the stomach. These things are."

"Adios, Mama," Pepé cried. "I will come back soon. You may send me often alone. I am a man."

"Thou art a foolish chicken."

He straightened his shoulders, flipped the reins against the horse's shoulder and rode away. He turned once and saw that they still watched him, Emilio and Rosy and Mama. Pepé grinned with pride and gladness and lifted the tough buckskin horse to a trot.

When he had dropped out of sight over a little dip in the road, Mama turned to the black ones, but she spoke to herself. "He is nearly a man now," she said. "It will be a nice thing to have a man in the house again." Her eyes sharpened on the children. "Go to the rocks now. The tide is going out. There will be abalones to be found." She put the iron hooks into their hands and saw them down the steep trail to the reefs. She brought the smooth stone *metate* to the doorway and sat grinding her corn to flour and looking occasionally at the road over which Pepé had gone. The noonday came and then the afternoon, when the little ones beat the abalones on a rock to make them tender and Mama patted the tortillas to make them thin. They ate their dinner as the red sun was plunging down toward the ocean. They sat on the doorsteps and watched the big white moon come over the mountain tops.

Mama said, "He is now at the house of our friend Mrs. Rodriguez. She will give him nice things to eat and maybe a present."

Emilio said, "Some day I too will ride to Monterey for medicine. Did Pepé come to be a man today?"

Mama said wisely, "A boy gets to be a man when a man is needed. Remember this thing. I have known boys forty years old because there was no need for a man."

Soon afterwards they retired, Mama in her big oak bed on one side of the room, Emilio and Rosy in their boxes full of straw and sheepskins on the other side of the room.

The moon went over the sky and the surf roared on the

rocks. The roosters crowed the first call. The surf subsided to a whispering surge against the reef. The moon dropped toward the sea. The roosters crowed again.

The moon was near down to the water when Pepé rode on a winded horse to his home flat. His dog bounced out and circled the horse yelping with pleasure. Pepé slid off the saddle to the ground. The weathered little shack was silver in the moonlight and the square shadow of it was black to the north and east. Against the east the piling mountains were misty with light; their tops melted into the sky.

Pepé walked wearily up the three steps and into the house. It was dark inside. There was a rustle in the corner.

Mama cried out from her bed. "Who comes? Pepé, is it thou?"

"*Sí*, Mama."

"Did you get the medicine?"

"*Sí*, Mama."

"Well, go to sleep, then. I thought you would be sleeping at the house of Mrs. Rodriguez." Pepé stood silently in the dark room. "Why do you stand there, Pepé? Did you drink wine?"

"*Sí*, Mama."

"Well, go to bed then and sleep out the wine."

His voice was tired and patient, but very firm. "Light the candle, Mama. I must go away into the mountains."

"What is this, Pepé? You are crazy." Mama struck a sulphur match and held the little blue burr until the flame spread up the stick. She set light to the candle on the floor beside her bed. "Now, Pepé, what is this you say?" She looked anxiously into his face.

He was changed. The fragile quality seemed to have gone from his chin. His mouth was less full than it had been, the lines of the lips were straighter, but in his eyes the greatest change had taken place. There was no laughter in them any more, nor any bashfulness. They were sharp and bright and purposeful.

He told her in a tired monotone, told her everything just as it had happened. A few people came into the kitchen of Mrs. Rodriguez. There was wine to drink. Pepé drank wine.

The little quarrel—the man started toward Pepé and then the knife—it went almost by itself. It flew, it darted before Pepé knew it. As he talked, Mama's face grew stern, and it seemed to grow more lean. Pepé finished. "I am a man now, Mama. The man said names to me I could not allow."

Mama nodded. "Yes, thou art a man, my poor little Pepé. Thou art a man. I have seen it coming on thee. I have watched you throwing the knife into the post, and I have been afraid." For a moment her face had softened, but now it grew stern again. "Come! We must get you ready. Go. Awaken Emilio and Rosy. Go quickly."

Pepé stepped over to the corner where his brother and sister slept among the sheepskins. He leaned down and shook them gently. "Come, Rosy! Come, Emilio! The mama says you must arise."

The little black ones sat up and rubbed their eyes in the candlelight. Mama was out of bed now, her long black skirt over her nightgown. "Emilio," she cried. "Go up and catch the other horse for Pepé. Quickly, now! Quickly." Emilio put his legs in his overalls and stumbled sleepily out the door.

"You heard no one behind you on the road?" Mama demanded.

"No, Mama. I listened carefully. No one was on the road."

Mama darted like a bird about the room. From a nail on the wall she took a canvas water bag and threw it on the floor. She stripped a blanket from her bed and rolled it into a tight tube and tied the ends with string. From a box beside the stove she lifted a flour sack half full of black stringy jerky. "Your father's black coat, Pepé. Here, put it on."

Pepé stood in the middle of the floor watching her activity. She reached behind the door and brought out the rifle, a long 38-56, worn shiny the whole length of the barrel. Pepé took it from her and held it in the crook of his elbow. Mama brought a little leather bag and counted the cartridges into his hand. "Only ten left," she warned. "You must not waste them."

Emilio put his head in the door. " *'Qui 'st 'l caballo*, Mama."

"Put on the saddle from the other horse. Tie on the blanket. Here, tie the jerky to the saddle horn."

Still Pepé stood silently watching his mother's frantic activity. His chin looked hard, and his sweet mouth was drawn and thin. His little eyes followed Mama about the room almost suspiciously.

Rosy asked softly, "Where goes Pepé?"

Mama's eyes were fierce. "Pepé goes on a journey. Pepé is a man now. He has a man's thing to do."

Pepé straightened his shoulders. His mouth changed until he looked very much like Mama.

At last the preparation was finished. The loaded horse stood outside the door. The water bag dripped a line of moisture down the bay shoulder.

The moonlight was being thinned by the dawn and the big white moon was near down to the sea. The family stood by the shack. Mama confronted Pepé. "Look, my son! Do not stop until it is dark again. Do not sleep even though you are tired. Take care of the horse in order that he may not stop of weariness. Remember to be careful with the bullets—there are only ten. Do not fill thy stomach with jerky or it will make thee sick. Eat a little jerky and fill thy stomach with grass. When thou comest to the high mountains, if thou seest any of the dark watching men, go not near to them nor try to speak to them. And forget not thy prayers." She put her lean hands on Pepé's shoulders, stood on her toes and kissed him formally on both cheeks, and Pepé kissed her on both cheeks. Then he went to Emilio and Rosy and kissed both of their cheeks.

Pepé turned back to Mama. He seemed to look for a little softness, a little weakness in her. His eyes were searching, but Mama's face remained fierce. "Go now," she said. "Do not wait to be caught like a chicken."

Pepé pulled himself into the saddle. "I am a man," he said.

It was the first dawn when he rode up the hill toward the little canyon which let a trail into the mountains. Moonlight and daylight fought with each other, and the two warring qualities made it difficult to see. Before Pepé had gone a hundred yards, the outlines of his figure were misty; and long before he entered the canyon, he had become a grey, indefinite shadow.

Mama stood stiffly in front of her doorstep, and on either

side of her stood Emilio and Rosy. They cast furtive glances at Mama now and then.

When the grey shape of Pepé melted into the hillside and disappeared, Mama relaxed. She began the high, whining keen of the death wail. "Our beautiful—our brave," she cried. "Our protector, our son is gone." Emilio and Rosy moaned beside her. "Our beautiful—our brave, he is gone." It was the formal wail. It rose to a high piercing whine and subsided to a moan. Mama raised it three times and then she turned and went into the house and shut the door.

Emilio and Rosy stood wondering in the dawn. They heard Mama whimpering in the house. They went out to sit on the cliff above the ocean. They touched shoulders. "When did Pepé come to be a man?" Emilio asked.

"Last night," said Rosy. "Last night in Monterey." The ocean clouds turned red with the sun that was behind the mountains.

"We will have no breakfast," said Emilio. "Mama will not want to cook." Rosy did not answer him. "Where is Pepé gone?" he asked.

Rosy looked around at him. She drew her knowledge from the quiet air. "He has gone on a journey. He will never come back."

"Is he dead? Do you think he is dead?"

Rosy looked back at the ocean again. A little steamer, drawing a line of smoke sat on the edge of the horizon. "He is not dead," Rosy explained. "Not yet."

Pepé rested the big rifle across the saddle in front of him. He let the horse walk up the hill and he didn't look back. The stony slope took on a coat of short brush so that Pepé found the entrance to a trail and entered it.

When he came to the canyon opening, he swung once in his saddle and looked back, but the houses were swallowed in the misty light. Pepé jerked forward again. The high shoulder of the canyon closed in on him. His horse stretched out its neck and sighed and settled to the trail.

It was a well-worn path, dark soft leaf-mould earth strewn with broken pieces of sandstone. The trail rounded the shoulder of the canyon and dropped steeply into the bed of the stream. In the shallows the water ran smoothly, glinting in the first morning sun. Small round stones on the bottom were as brown as rust with sun moss. In the sand along the edges of the stream the tall, rich wild mint grew, while in the water itself the cress, old and tough, had gone to heavy seed.

The path went into the stream and emerged on the other side. The horse sloshed into the water and stopped. Pepé dropped his bridle and let the beast drink of the running water.

Soon the canyon sides became steep and the first giant sentinel redwoods guarded the trail, great round red trunks bearing foliage as green and lacy as ferns. Once Pepé was among the trees, the sun was lost. A perfumed and purple light lay in the pale green of the underbrush. Gooseberry bushes and blackberries and tall ferns lined the stream, and overhead the branches of the redwoods met and cut off the sky.

Pepé drank from the water bag, and he reached into the flour sack and brought out a black string of jerky. His white teeth gnawed at the string until the tough meat parted. He chewed slowly and drank occasionally from the water bag. His little eyes were slumberous and tired, but the muscles of his face were hard set. The earth of the trail was black now. It gave up a hollow sound under the walking hoofbeats.

The stream fell more sharply. Little waterfalls splashed on the stones. Five-fingered ferns hung over the water and dripped spray from their fingertips. Pepé rode half over in his saddle, dangling one leg loosely. He picked a bay leaf from a tree beside the way and put it into his mouth for a moment to flavor the dry jerky. He held the gun loosely across the pommel.

Suddenly he squared in his saddle, swung the horse from the trail and kicked it hurriedly up behind a big redwood tree. He pulled up the reins tight against the bit to keep the horse from whinnying. His face was intent and his nostrils quivered a little.

A hollow pounding came down the trail, and a horseman rode by, a fat man with red cheeks and a white stubble beard. His horse put down its head and blubbered at the trail when it came to the place where Pepé had turned off. "Hold up!" said the man and he pulled up his horse's head.

When the last sound of the hoofs died away, Pepé came back into the trail again. He did not relax in the saddle any more. He lifted the big rifle and swung the lever to throw a shell into the chamber, and then he let down the hammer to half cock.

The trail grew very steep. Now the redwood trees were smaller and their tops were dead, bitten dead where the wind reached them. The horse plodded on; the sun went slowly overhead and started down toward the afternoon.

Where the stream came out of a side canyon, the trail left it. Pepé dismounted and watered his horse and filled up his water bag. As soon as the trail had parted from the stream, the trees were gone and only the thick brittle sage and manzanita and chaparral edged the trail. And the soft black earth was gone, too, leaving only the light tan broken rock for the trail bed. Lizards scampered away into the brush as the horse rattled over the little stones.

Pepé turned in his saddle and looked back. He was in the open now: he could be seen from a distance. As he ascended the trail the country grew more rough and terrible and dry. The way wound about the bases of great square rocks. Little grey rabbits skittered in the brush. A bird made a monotonous high creaking. Eastward the bare rock mountaintops were pale and powder-dry under the dropping sun. The horse plodded up and up the trail toward a little V in the ridge which was the pass.

Pepé looked suspiciously back every minute or so, and his eyes sought the tops of the ridges ahead. Once, on a white barren spur, he saw a black figure for a moment, but he looked quickly away, for it was one of the dark watchers. No one knew who the watchers were, nor where they lived, but it was better to ignore them and never to show interest in them. They did not bother one who stayed on the trail and minded his own business.

The air was parched and full of light dust blown by the breeze from the eroding mountains. Pepé drank sparingly from his bag and corked it tightly and hung it on the horn again. The trail moved up the dry shale hillside, avoiding rocks, dropping under clefts, climbing in and out of old water scars. When he arrived at the little pass he stopped and looked back for a long time. No dark watchers were to be seen now. The trail behind was empty. Only the high tops of the redwoods indicated where the stream flowed.

Pepé rode on through the pass. His little eyes were nearly closed with weariness, but his face was stern, relentless and manly. The high mountain wind coasted sighing through the pass and whistled on the edges of the big blocks of broken granite. In the air, a red-tailed hawk sailed over close to the ridge and screamed angrily. Pepé went slowly through the broken jagged pass and looked down on the other side.

The trail dropped quickly, staggering among broken rock. At the bottom of the slope there was a dark crease, thick with brush, and on the other side of the crease a little flat, in which a grove of oak trees grew. A scar of green grass cut across the flat. And behind the flat another mountain rose, desolate with dead rocks and starving little black bushes. Pepé drank from the bag again for the air was so dry that it encrusted his nostrils and burned his lips. He put the horse down the trail. The hooves slipped and struggled on the steep way, starting little stones that rolled off into the brush. The sun was gone behind the westward mountain now, but still it glowed brilliantly on the oaks and on the grassy flat. The rocks and the hillsides still sent up waves of the heat they had gathered from the day's sun.

Pepé looked up to the top of the next dry withered ridge. He saw a dark form against the sky, a man's figure standing on top of a rock, and he glanced away quickly not to appear curious. When a moment later he looked up again, the figure was gone.

Downward the trail was quickly covered. Sometimes the horse floundered for footing, sometimes set his feet and slid a little way. They came at last to the bottom where the dark chaparral was higher than Pepé's head. He held up his rifle on one side and his arm on the other to shield his face from the sharp brittle fingers of the brush.

Up and out of the crease he rode, and up a little cliff. The grassy flat was before him, and the round comfortable oaks. For a moment he studied the trail down which he had come, but there was no movement and no sound from it. Finally he rode out over the flat, to the green streak, and at the upper end of the damp he found a little spring welling out of the earth and dropping into a dug basin before it seeped out over the flat.

Pepé filled his bag first, and then he let the thirsty horse drink out of the pool. He led the horse to the clump of oaks, and in the middle of the grove, fairly protected from sight on all sides, he took off the saddle and the bridle and laid them on the ground. The horse stretched his jaws sideways and yawned. Pepé knotted the lead rope about the horse's neck and tied him to a sapling among the oaks, where he could graze in a fairly large circle.

When the horse was gnawing hungrily at the dry grass, Pepé went to the saddle and took a black string of jerky from the sack and strolled to an oak tree on the edge of the grove, from under which he could watch the trail. He sat down in the crisp dry oak leaves and automatically felt for his big black knife to cut the jerky, but he had no knife. He leaned back on his elbow and gnawed at the tough strong meat. His face was blank, but it was a man's face.

The bright evening light washed the eastern ridge, but the valley was darkening. Doves flew down from the hills to the spring, and the quail came running out of the brush and joined them, calling clearly to one another.

Out of the corner of his eye Pepé saw a shadow grow out of the bushy crease. He turned his head slowly. A big spotted wildcat was creeping toward the spring, belly to the ground, moving like thought.

Pepé cocked his rifle and edged the muzzle slowly around. Then he looked apprehensively up the trail and dropped the hammer again. From the ground beside him he picked an oak twig and threw it toward the spring. The quail flew up with a roar and the doves whistled away. The big cat stood up: for a long moment he looked at Pepé with cold yellow eyes, and then fearlessly walked back into the gulch.

The dusk gathered quickly in the deep valley. Pepé muttered his prayers, put his head down on his arm and went instantly to sleep.

The moon came up and filled the valley with cold blue light, and the wind swept rustling down from the peaks. The owls worked up and down the slopes looking for rabbits. Down in the brush of the gulch a coyote gabbled. The oak trees whispered softly in the night breeze.

Pepé started up, listening. His horse had whinnied. The moon was just slipping behind the western ridge, leaving the valley in darkness behind it. Pepé sat tensely gripping his rifle. From far up the trail he heard an answering whinny and the crash of shod hooves on the broken rock. He jumped to his feet, ran to his horse and led it under the trees. He threw on the saddle and cinched it tight for the steep trail, caught the unwilling head and forced the bit into the mouth. He felt the saddle to make sure the water bag and the sack of jerky were there. Then he mounted and turned up the hill.

It was velvet dark. The horse found the entrance to the trail where it left the flat, and started up, stumbling and slipping on the rocks. Pepé's hand rose up to his head. His hat was gone. He had left it under the oak tree.

The horse had struggled far up the trail when the first change of dawn came into the air, a steel greyness as light mixed thoroughly with dark. Gradually the sharp snaggled edge of the ridge stood out above them, rotten granite tortured and eaten by the winds of time. Pepé had dropped his reins on the horn, leaving direction to the horse. The brush grabbed at his legs in the dark until one knee of his jeans was ripped.

Gradually the light flowed down over the ridge. The starved brush and rocks stood out in the half light, strange and lonely in high perspective. Then there came warmth into the light. Pepé drew up and looked back, but he could see nothing in the darker valley below. The sky turned blue over the coming sun. In the waste of the mountainside, the poor dry brush grew only three feet high. Here and there, big outcroppings of unrotted granite stood up like mouldering houses. Pepé relaxed a little. He drank from his water bag and bit off a piece of jerky. A single eagle flew over, high in the light.

Without warning Pepé's horse screamed and fell on its side. He was almost down before the rifle crash echoed up from the valley. From a hole behind the struggling shoulder, a stream of bright crimson blood pumped and stopped and pumped and stopped. The hooves threshed on the ground.

Pepé lay half stunned beside the horse. He looked slowly down the hill. A piece of sage clipped off beside his head and another crash echoed up from side to side of the canyon. Pepé flung himself frantically behind a bush.

He crawled up the hill on his knees and one hand. His right hand held the rifle up off the ground and pushed it ahead of him. He moved with the instinctive care of an animal. Rapidly he wormed his way toward one of the big outcroppings of granite on the hill above him. Where the brush was high he doubled up and ran, but where the cover was slight he wriggled forward on this stomach, pushing the rifle ahead of him. In the last little distance there was no cover at all. Pepé poised and then he darted across the space and flashed around the corner of the rock.

He leaned panting against the stone. When his breath came easier he moved along behind the big rock until he came to a narrow split that offered a thin section of vision down the hill. Pepé lay on his stomach and pushed the rifle barrel through the slit and waited.

The sun reddened the western ridges now. Already the buzzards were settling down toward the place where the horse lay. A small brown bird scratched in the dead sage leaves directly in front of the rifle muzzle. The coasting eagle flew back toward the rising sun.

Pepé saw a little movement in the brush far below. His grip tightened on the gun. A little brown doe stepped daintily out on the trail and crossed it and disappeared into the brush again. For a long time Pepé waited. Far below he could see the little flat and the oak trees and the slash of green. Suddenly his eyes flashed back at the trail again. A quarter of a mile down there had been a quick movement in the chaparral. The rifle swung over. The front sight nestled in the v of the rear sight. Pepé studied for a moment and then raised the rear sight a notch. The little movement in the brush came again. The sight settled on it. Pepé squeezed the trigger. The explosion crashed down the mountain and up the other side, and came rattling back. The whole side of the slope grew still. No more movement. And then a white streak cut into the granite of the slit and a bullet whined away and a crash sounded up from below. Pepé felt a sharp pain in his right hand. A sliver of granite was sticking out from between his first and second knuckles and the point protruded from his palm. Carefully he pulled out the sliver of stone. The wound bled evenly and gently. No vein nor artery was cut.

Pepé looked into a little dusty cave in the rock and gathered a handful of spider web, and he pressed the mass into the cut, plastering the soft web into the blood. The flow stopped almost at once.

The rifle was on the ground. Pepé picked it up, levered a new shell into the chamber. And then he slid into the brush on his stomach. Far to the right he crawled, and then up the hill, moving slowly and carefully, crawling to cover and resting and then crawling again.

In the mountains the sun is high in its arc before it penetrates the gorges. The hot face looked over the hill and brought instant heat with it. The white light beat on the rocks and reflected from them and rose up quivering from the earth again, and the rocks and bushes seemed to quiver behind the air.

Pepé crawled in the general direction of the ridge peak, zig-zagging for cover. The deep cut between his knuckles began to throb. He crawled close to a rattlesnake before he saw it, and when it raised its dry head and made a soft beginning whirr, he backed up and took another way. The quick grey lizards flashed in front of him, raising a tiny line of dust. He found another mass of spider web and pressed it against his throbbing hand.

Pepé was pushing the rifle with his left hand now. Little drops of sweat ran to the ends of his coarse black hair and rolled down his cheeks. His lips and tongue were growing thick and heavy. His lips writhed to draw saliva into his mouth. His little dark eyes were uneasy and suspicious. Once when a grey lizard paused in front of him on the parched ground and turned its head sideways he crushed it flat with a stone.

When the sun slid past noon he had not gone a mile. He crawled exhaustedly a last hundred yards to a patch of high sharp manzanita, crawled desperately, and when the patch was reached he wriggled in among the tough gnarly trunks and dropped his head on his left arm. There was little shade in the meager brush, but there was cover and safety. Pepé went to sleep as he lay and the sun beat on his back. A few little birds hopped close to him and peered and hopped away. Pepé squirmed in his sleep and he raised and dropped his wounded hand again and again.

The sun went down behind the peaks and the cool evening came, and then the dark. A coyote yelled from the hillside, Pepé started awake and looked about with misty eyes. His hand was swollen and heavy; a little thread of pain ran up the inside of his arm and settled in a pocket in his armpit. He peered about and then stood up, for the mountains were black and the moon had not yet risen. Pepé stood up in the dark. The coat of his father pressed on his arm. His tongue was swollen until it nearly filled his mouth. He wriggled out of the coat and dropped it in the brush, and then he struggled up the hill, falling over rocks and tearing his way through the brush. The rifle knocked against stones as he went. Little dry avalanches of gravel and shattered stone went whispering down the hill behind him.

After a while the old moon came up and showed the jagged ridge top ahead of him. By moonlight Pepé traveled more easily. He bent forward so that his throbbing arm hung away from his body. The journey uphill was made in dashes and rests, a frantic rush up a few yards and then a rest. The wind coasted down the slope rattling the dry stems of the bushes.

The moon was at meridian when Pepé came at last to the sharp backbone of the ridge top. On the last hundred yards of the rise no soil had clung under the wearing winds. The way was on solid rock. He clambered to the top and looked down on the other side. There was a draw like the last below him, misty with moonlight, brushed with dry struggling sage and chaparral. On the other side the hill rose up sharply and at the top the jagged rotten teeth of the mountain showed against the sky. At the bottom of the cut the brush was thick and dark.

Pepé stumbled down the hill. His throat was almost closed with thirst. At first he tried to run, but immediately he fell and rolled. After that he went more carefully. The moon was just disappearing behind the mountains when he came to the bottom. He crawled into the heavy brush feeling with his fingers for water. There was no water in the bed of the stream, only damp earth. Pepé laid his gun down and scooped up a handful of mud and put it in his mouth, and then he spluttered and scraped the earth from his tongue with his finger, for the mud drew at his mouth like a poultice. He dug a hole in the stream bed with his fingers, dug a little basin to catch water; but before it was very deep his head fell forward on the damp ground and he slept.

The dawn came and the heat of the day fell on the earth, and still Pepé slept. Late in the afternoon his head jerked up. He looked slowly around. His eyes were slits of wariness. Twenty feet away in the heavy brush a big tawny mountain lion stood looking at him. Its long thick tail waved gracefully, its ears were erect with interest, not laid back dangerously. The lion squatted down on its stomach and watched him.

Pepé looked at the hole he had dug in the earth. A half inch of muddy water had collected in the bottom. He tore the sleeve from his hurt arm, with his teeth ripped out a little square, soaked it in the water and put it in his mouth. Over and over he filled the cloth and sucked it.

Still the lion sat and watched him. The evening came down but there was no movement on the hills. No birds visited the dry bottom of the cut. Pepé looked occasionally at the lion. The eyes of the yellow beast drooped as though he were about to sleep. He yawned and his long thin red tongue curled out. Suddenly his head jerked around and his nostrils quivered. His big tail lashed. He stood up and slunk like a tawny shadow into the thick brush.

A moment later Pepé heard the sound, the faint far crash of horses' hooves on gravel. And he heard something else, a high whining yelp of a dog.

Pepé took his rifle in his left hand and he glided into the brush almost as quietly as the lion had. In the darkening evening he crouched up the hill toward the next ridge. Only when the dark came did he stand up. His energy was short. Once it was dark he fell over the rocks and slipped to his knees on the steep slope, but he moved on and on up the hill, climbing and scrabbling over the broken hillside.

When he was far up toward the top, he lay down and slept for a little while. The withered moon, shining on his face, awakened him. He stood up and moved up the hill. Fifty yards away he stopped and turned back, for he had forgotten his rifle. He walked heavily down and poked about in the brush, but he could not find his gun. At last he lay down to rest. The pocket of pain in his armpit had grown more sharp. His arm seemed to swell out and fall with every heartbeat. There was no position lying down where the heavy arm did not press against his armpit.

With the effort of a hurt beast, Pepé got up and moved again toward the top of the ridge. He held his swollen arm away from his body with his left hand. Up the steep hill he dragged himself, a few steps and a rest, and a few more steps. At last he was nearing the top. The moon showed the uneven sharp back of it against the sky.

Pepé's brain spun in a big spiral up and away from him. He slumped to the ground and lay still. The rock ridge top was only a hundred feet above him.

The moon moved over the sky. Pepé half turned on his back. His tongue tried to make words, but only a thick hissing came from between his lips.

When the dawn came, Pepé pulled himself up. His eyes were sane again. He drew his great puffed arm in front of him and looked at the angry wound. The black line ran up from his wrist to his armpit. Automatically he reached in his pocket for the big black knife, but it was not there. His eyes searched the ground. He picked up a sharp blade of stone and scraped at the wound, sawed at the proud flesh and then squeezed the green juice out in big drops. Instantly he threw back his head and whined like a dog. His whole right side shuddered at the pain, but the pain cleared his head.

In the grey light he struggled up the last slope to the ridge and crawled over and lay down behind a line of rocks. Below him lay a deep canyon exactly like the last, waterless and desolate. There was no flat, no oak trees, not even heavy brush in the bottom of it. And on the other side a sharp ridge stood up, thinly brushed with starving sage, littered with broken granite. Strewn over the hill there were giant outcroppings, and on the top the granite teeth stood out against the sky.

The new day was light now. The flame of the sun came over the ridge and fell on Pepé where he lay on the ground. His coarse black hair was littered with twigs and bits of spider web.

His eyes had retreated back into his head. Between his lips the tip of his black tongue showed.

He sat up and dragged his great arm into his lap and nursed it, rocking his body and moaning in his throat. He threw back his head and looked up into the pale sky. A big black bird circled nearly out of sight, and far to the left another was sailing near.

He lifted his head to listen, for a familiar sound had come to him from the valley he had climbed out of; it was the crying yelp of hounds, excited and feverish, on a trail.

Pepé bowed his head quickly. He tried to speak rapid words but only a thick hiss came from his lips. He drew a shaky cross on his breast with his left hand. It was a long struggle to get to his feet. He crawled slowly and mechanically to the top of a big rock on the ridge peak. Once there, he arose slowly, swaying to his feet, and stood erect. Far below he could see the dark brush where he had slept. He braced his feet and stood there, black against the morning sky.

There came a ripping sound at his feet. A piece of stone flew up and a bullet droned off into the next gorge. The hollow crash echoed up from below. Pepé looked down for a moment and then pulled himself straight again.

His body jarred back. His left hand fluttered helplessly toward his breast. The second crash sounded from below. Pepé swung forward and toppled from the rock. His body struck and rolled over and over, starting a little avalanche. And when at last he stopped against a bush, the avalanche slid slowly down and covered up his head.

The Snake

IT WAS almost dark when young Dr. Phillips swung his sack to his shoulder and left the tide pool. He climbed up over the rocks and squashed along the street in his rubber boots. The street lights were on by the time he arrived at his little commercial laboratory on the cannery street of Monterey. It was a tight little building, standing partly on piers over the bay water and partly on the land. On both sides the big corrugated-iron sardine canneries crowded in on it.

Dr. Phillips climbed the wooden steps and opened the door. The white rats in their cages scampered up and down the wire, and the captive cats in their pens mewed for milk. Dr. Phillips turned on the glaring light over the dissection table and dumped his clammy sack on the floor. He walked to the glass cages by the window where the rattlesnakes lived, leaned over and looked in.

The snakes were bunched and resting in the corners of the cage, but every head was clear; the dusty eyes seemed to look at nothing, but as the young man leaned over the cage the forked tongues, black on the ends and pink behind, twittered out and waved slowly up and down. Then the snakes recognized the man and pulled in their tongues.

Dr. Phillips threw off his leather coat and built a fire in the tin stove; he set a kettle of water on the stove and dropped a can of beans into the water. Then he stood staring down at the sack on the floor. He was a slight young man with the mild, preoccupied eyes of one who looks through a microscope a great deal. He wore a short blond beard.

The draft ran breathily up the chimney and a glow of warmth came from the stove. The little waves washed quietly about the piles under the building. Arranged on shelves about the room were tier above tier of museum jars containing the mounted marine specimens the laboratory dealt in.

Dr. Phillips opened a side door and went into his bedroom, a book-lined cell containing an army cot, a reading light and an uncomfortable wooden chair. He pulled off his rubber boots and put on a pair of sheepskin slippers. When he went

back to the other room the water in the kettle was already
beginning to hum.

He lifted his sack to the table under the white light and
emptied out two dozen common starfish. These he laid out
side by side on the table. His preoccupied eyes turned to the
busy rats in the wire cages. Taking grain from a paper sack,
he poured it into the feeding troughs. Instantly the rats scrambled down from the wire and fell upon the food. A bottle of
milk stood on a glass shelf between a small mounted octopus
and a jellyfish. Dr. Phillips lifted down the milk and walked
to the cat cage, but before he filled the containers he reached
in the cage and gently picked out a big rangy alley tabby. He
stroked her for a moment and then dropped her in a small
black painted box, closed the lid and bolted it and then turned
on a petcock which admitted gas into the killing chamber.
While the short soft struggle went on in the black box he
filled the saucers with milk. One of the cats arched against his
hand and he smiled and petted her neck.

The box was quiet now. He turned off the petcock, for the
airtight box would be full of gas.

On the stove the pan of water was bubbling furiously about
the can of beans. Dr. Phillips lifted out the can with a big pair
of forceps, opened it, and emptied the beans into a glass dish.
While he ate he watched the starfish on the table. From between the rays little drops of milky fluid were exuding. He
bolted his beans and when they were gone he put the dish in
the sink and stepped to the equipment cupboard. From this
he took a microscope and a pile of little glass dishes. He filled
the dishes one by one with sea water from a tap and arranged
them in a line beside the starfish. He took out his watch and
laid it on the table under the pouring white light. The waves
washed with little sighs against the piles under the floor. He
took an eyedropper from a drawer and bent over the starfish.

At that moment there were quick soft steps on the wooden
stairs and a strong knocking at the door. A slight grimace of
annoyance crossed the young man's face as he went to open.
A tall, lean woman stood in the doorway. She was dressed in
a severe dark suit—her straight black hair, growing low on a
flat forehead, was mussed as though the wind had been
blowing it. Her black eyes glittered in the strong light.

She spoke in a soft throaty voice, "May I come in? I want to talk to you."

"I'm very busy just now," he said half-heartedly. "I have to do things at times." But he stood away from the door. The tall woman slipped in.

"I'll be quiet until you can talk to me."

He closed the door and brought the uncomfortable chair from the bedroom. "You see," he apologized, "the process is started and I must get to it." So many people wandered in and asked questions. He had little routines of explanations for the commoner processes. He could say them without thinking. "Sit here. In a few minutes I'll be able to listen to you."

The tall woman leaned over the table. With the eyedropper the young man gathered fluid from between the rays of the starfish and squirted it into a bowl of water, and then he drew some milky fluid and squirted it in the same bowl and stirred the water gently with the eyedropper. He began his little patter of explanation.

"When starfish are sexually mature they release sperm and ova when they are exposed at low tide. By choosing mature specimens and taking them out of the water, I give them a condition of low tide. Now I've mixed the sperm and eggs. Now I put some of the mixture in each one of these ten watch glasses. In ten minutes I will kill those in the first glass with menthol, twenty minutes later I will kill the second group and then a new group every twenty minutes. Then I will have arrested the process in stages, and I will mount the series on microscope slides for biologic study." He paused. "Would you like to look at this first group under the microscope?"

"No, thank you."

He turned quickly to her. People always wanted to look through the glass. She was not looking at the table at all, but at him. Her black eyes were on him, but they did not seem to see him. He realized why—the irises were as dark as the pupils, there was no color line between the two. Dr. Phillips was piqued at her answer. Although answering questions bored him, a lack of interest in what he was doing irritated him. A desire to arouse her grew in him.

"While I'm waiting the first ten minutes I have something

to do. Some people don't like to see it. Maybe you'd better step into that room until I finish."

"No," she said in her soft flat tone. "Do what you wish. I will wait until you can talk to me." Her hands rested side by side on her lap. She was completely at rest. Her eyes were bright but the rest of her was almost in a state of suspended animation. He thought, "Low metabolic rate, almost as low as a frog's, from the looks." The desire to shock her out of her inanition possessed him again.

He brought a little wooden cradle to the table, laid out scalpels and scissors and rigged a big hollow needle to a pressure tube. Then from the killing chamber he brought the limp dead cat and laid it in the cradle and tied its legs to hooks in the sides. He glanced sidewise at the woman. She had not moved. She was still at rest.

The cat grinned up into the light, its pink tongue stuck out between its needle teeth. Dr. Phillips deftly snipped open the skin at the throat; with a scalpel he slit through and found an artery. With flawless technique he put the needle in the vessel and tied it in with gut. "Embalming fluid," he explained. "Later I'll inject yellow mass into the veinous system and red mass into the arterial system—for bloodstream dissection—biology classes."

He looked around at her again. Her dark eyes seemed veiled with dust. She looked without expression at the cat's open throat. Not a drop of blood had escaped. The incision was clean. Dr. Phillips looked at his watch. "Time for the first group." He shook a few crystals of menthol into the first watch-glass.

The woman was making him nervous. The rats climbed about on the wire of their cage again and squeaked softly. The waves under the building beat with little shocks on the piles.

The young man shivered. He put a few lumps of coal in the stove and sat down. "Now," he said. "I haven't anything to do for twenty minutes." He noticed how short her chin was between lower lip and point. She seemed to awaken slowly, to come up out of some deep pool of consciousness. Her head raised and her dark dusty eyes moved about the room and then came back to him.

"I was waiting," she said. Her hands remained side by side on her lap. "You have snakes?"

"Why, yes," he said rather loudly. "I have about two dozen rattlesnakes. I milk out the venom and send it to the anti-venom laboratories."

She continued to look at him but her eyes did not center on him, rather they covered him and seemed to see in a big circle all around him. "Have you a male snake, a male rattlesnake?"

"Well, it just happens I know I have. I came in one morning and found a big snake in—in coition with a smaller one. That's very rare in captivity. You see, I do know I have a male snake."

"Where is he?"

"Why, right in the glass cage by the window there."

Her head swung slowly around but her two quiet hands did not move. She turned back toward him. "May I see?"

He got up and walked to the case by the window. On the sand bottom the knot of rattlesnakes lay entwined, but their heads were clear. The tongues came out and flickered a moment and then waved up and down feeling the air for vibrations. Dr. Phillips nervously turned his head. The woman was standing beside him. He had not heard her get up from the chair. He had heard only the splash of water among the piles and the scampering of the rats on the wire screen.

She said softly, "Which is the male you spoke of?"

He pointed to a thick, dusty grey snake lying by itself in one corner of the cage. "That one. He's nearly five feet long. He comes from Texas. Our Pacific coast snakes are usually smaller. He's been taking all the rats, too. When I want the others to eat I have to take him out."

The woman stared down at the blunt dry head. The forked tongue slipped out and hung quivering for a long moment. "And you're sure he's a male."

"Rattlesnakes are funny," he said glibly. "Nearly every generalization proves wrong. I don't like to say anything definite about rattlesnakes, but—yes—I can assure you he's a male."

Her eyes did not move from the flat head. "Will you sell him to me?"

"Sell him?" he cried. "Sell him to you?"

"You do sell specimens, don't you?"

"Oh—yes. Of course I do. Of course I do."

"How much? Five dollars? Ten?"

"Oh! Not more than five. But—do you know anything about rattlesnakes? You might be bitten."

She looked at him for a moment. "I don't intend to take him. I want to leave him here, but—I want him to be mine. I want to come here and look at him and feed him and to know he's mine." She opened a little purse and took out a five-dollar bill. "Here! Now he is mine."

Dr. Phillips began to be afraid. "You could come to look at him without owning him."

"I want to him to be mine."

"Oh, Lord!" he cried. "I've forgotten the time." He ran to the table. "Three minutes over. It won't matter much." He shook menthol crystals into the second watch-glass. And then he was drawn back to the cage where the woman still stared at the snake.

She asked, "What does he eat?"

"I feed them white rats, rats from the cage over there."

"Will you put him in the other cage? I want to feed him."

"But he doesn't need food. He's had a rat already this week. Sometimes they don't eat for three or four months. I had one that didn't eat for over a year."

In her low monotone she asked, "Will you sell me a rat?"

He shrugged his shoulders. "I see. You want to watch how rattlesnakes eat. All right. I'll show you. The rat will cost twenty-five cents. It's better than a bullfight if you look at it one way, and it's simply a snake eating his dinner if you look at it another." His tone had become acid. He hated people who made sport of natural processes. He was not a sportsman but a biologist. He could kill a thousand animals for knowledge, but not an insect for pleasure. He'd been over this in his mind before.

She turned her head slowly toward him and the beginning of a smile formed on her thin lips. "I want to feed my snake," she said. "I'll put him in the other cage." She had opened the top of the cage and dipped her hand in before he knew what she was doing. He leaped forward and pulled her back. The lid banged shut.

"Haven't you any sense," he asked fiercely. "Maybe he wouldn't kill you, but he'd make you damned sick in spite of what I could do for you."

"You put him in the other cage then," she said quietly.

Dr. Phillips was shaken. He found that he was avoiding the dark eyes that didn't seem to look at anything. He felt that it was profoundly wrong to put a rat into the cage, deeply sinful; and he didn't know why. Often he had put rats in the cage when someone or other had wanted to see it, but this desire tonight sickened him. He tried to explain himself out of it.

"It's a good thing to see," he said. "It shows you how a snake can work. It makes you have a respect for a rattlesnake. Then, too, lots of people have dreams about the terror of snakes making the kill. I think because it is a subjective rat. The person is the rat. Once you see it the whole matter is objective. The rat is only a rat and the terror is removed."

He took a long stick equipped with a leather noose from the wall. Opening the trap he dropped the noose over the big snake's head and tightened the thong. A piercing dry rattle filled the room. The thick body writhed and slashed about the handle of the stick as he lifted the snake out and dropped it in the feeding cage. It stood ready to strike for a time, but the buzzing gradually ceased. The snake crawled into a corner, made a big figure eight with its body and lay still.

"You see," the young man explained, "these snakes are quite tame. I've had them a long time. I suppose I could handle them if I wanted to, but everyone who does handle rattlesnakes gets bitten sooner or later. I just don't want to take the chance." He glanced at the woman. He hated to put in the rat. She had moved over in front of the new cage; her black eyes were on the stony head of the snake again.

She said, "Put in a rat."

Reluctantly he went to the rat cage. For some reason he was sorry for the rat, and such a feeling had never come to him before. His eyes went over the mass of swarming white bodies climbing up the screen toward him. "Which one?" he thought. "Which one shall it be?" Suddenly he turned angrily to the woman. "Wouldn't you rather I put in a cat? Then you'd see a real fight. The cat might even win, but if it did it might kill the snake. I'll sell you a cat if you like."

She didn't look at him. "Put in a rat," she said. "I want him to eat."

He opened the rat cage and thrust his hand in. His fingers found a tail and he lifted a plump, red-eyed rat out of the cage. It struggled up to try to bite his fingers and, failing, hung spread out and motionless from its tail. He walked quickly across the room, opened the feeding cage and dropped the rat in on the sand floor. "Now, watch it," he cried.

The woman did not answer him. Her eyes were on the snake where it lay still. Its tongue flicking in and out rapidly, tasted the air of the cage.

The rat landed on its feet, turned around and sniffed at its pink naked tail and then unconcernedly trotted across the sand, smelling as it went. The room was silent. Dr. Phillips did not know whether the water sighed among the piles or whether the woman sighed. Out of the corner of his eye he saw her body crouch and stiffen.

The snake moved out smoothly, slowly. The tongue flicked in and out. The motion was so gradual, so smooth that it didn't seem to be motion at all. In the other end of the cage the rat perked up in a sitting position and began to lick down the fine white hair on its chest. The snake moved on, keeping always a deep S curve in its neck.

The silence beat on the young man. He felt the blood drifting up in his body. He said loudly, "See! He keeps the striking curve ready. Rattlesnakes are cautious, almost cowardly animals. The mechanism is so delicate. The snake's dinner is to be got by an operation as deft as a surgeon's job. He takes no chances with his instruments."

The snake had flowed to the middle of the cage by now. The rat looked up, saw the snake and then unconcernedly went back to licking its chest.

"It's the most beautiful thing in the world," the young man said. His veins were throbbing. "It's the most terrible thing in the world."

The snake was close now. Its head lifted a few inches from

the sand. The head weaved slowly back and forth, aiming, getting distance, aiming. Dr. Phillips glanced again at the woman. He turned sick. She was weaving too, not much, just a suggestion.

The rat looked up and saw the snake. It dropped to four feet and back up, and then—the stroke. It was impossible to see, simply a flash. The rat jarred as though under an invisible blow. The snake backed hurriedly into the corner from which it had come, and settled down, its tongue working constantly.

"Perfect!" Dr. Phillips cried. "Right between the shoulder blades. The fangs must almost have reached the heart."

The rat stood still, breathing like a little white bellows. Suddenly it leaped in the air and landed on its side. Its legs kicked spasmodically for a second and it was dead.

The woman relaxed, relaxed sleepily.

"Well," the young man demanded, "it was an emotional bath, wasn't it?"

She turned her misty eyes to him. "Will he eat it now?" she asked.

"Of course he'll eat it. He didn't kill it for a thrill. He killed it because he was hungry."

The corners of the woman's mouth turned up a trifle again. She looked back at the snake. "I want to see him eat it."

Now the snake came out of its corner again. There was no striking curve in its neck, but it approached the rat gingerly, ready to jump back in case it attacked. It nudged the body gently with its blunt nose, and drew away. Satisfied that it was dead, the snake touched the body all over with its chin, from head to tail. It seemed to measure the body and to kiss it. Finally it opened its mouth and unhinged its jaws at the corners.

Dr. Phillips put his will against his head to keep it from turning toward the woman. He thought, "If she's opening her mouth, I'll be sick. I'll be afraid," He succeeded in keeping his eyes away.

The snake fitted its jaws over the rat's head and then with a slow peristaltic pulsing, began to engulf the rat. The jaws gripped and the whole throat crawled up, and the jaws gripped again.

Dr. Phillips turned away and went to his work table. "You've made me miss one of the series," he said bitterly.

"The set won't be complete." He put one of the watch glasses under a low-power microscope and looked at it, and then angrily he poured the contents of all the dishes into the sink. The waves had fallen so that only a wet whisper came up through the floor. The young man lifted a trapdoor at his feet and dropped the starfish down into the black water. He paused at the cat, crucified in the cradle and grinning comically into the light. Its body was puffed with embalming fluid. He shut off the pressure, withdrew the needle and tied the vein.

"Would you like some coffee?" he asked.

"No, thank you. I shall be going pretty soon."

He walked to her where she stood in front of the snake cage. The rat was swallowed, all except an inch of pink tail that stuck out of the snake's mouth like a sardonic tongue. The throat heaved again and the tail disappeared. The jaws snapped back into their sockets, and the big snake crawled heavily to the corner, made a big eight and dropped its head on the sand.

"He's asleep now," the woman said. "I'm going now. But I'll come back and feed my snake every little while. I'll pay for the rats. I want him to have plenty. And sometime—I'll take him away with me." Her eyes came out of their dusty dream for a moment. "Remember, he's mine. Don't take his poison. I want him to have it. Goodnight." She walked swiftly to the door and went out. He heard her footsteps on the stairs, but he could not hear her walk away on the pavement.

Dr. Phillips turned a chair around and sat down in front of the snake cage. He tried to comb out his thought as he looked at the torpid snake. "I've read so much about psychological sex symbols," he thought. "It doesn't seem to explain. Maybe I'm too much alone. Maybe I should kill the snake. If I knew—no, I can't pray to anything."

For weeks he expected her to return. "I will go out and leave her alone here when she comes," he decided. "I won't see the damned thing again."

She never came again. For months he looked for her when he walked about in the town. Several times he ran after some tall woman thinking it might be she. But he never saw her again—ever.

Breakfast

THIS THING fills me with pleasure. I don't know why, I can see it in the smallest detail. I find myself recalling it again and again, each time bringing more detail out of a sunken memory, remembering brings the curious warm pleasure.

It was very early in the morning. The eastern mountains were black-blue, but behind them the light stood up faintly colored at the mountain rims with a washed red, growing colder, greyer and darker as it went up and overhead until, at a place near the west, it merged with pure night.

And it was cold, not painfully so, but cold enough so that I rubbed my hands and shoved them deep into my pockets, and I hunched my shoulders up and scuffled my feet on the ground. Down in the valley where I was, the earth was that lavender grey of dawn. I walked along a country road and ahead of me I saw a tent that was only a little lighter grey than the ground. Beside the tent there was a flash of orange fire seeping out of the cracks of an old rusty iron stove. Grey smoke spurted up out of the stubby stovepipe, spurted up a long way before it spread out and dissipated.

I saw a young woman beside the stove, really a girl. She was dressed in a faded cotton skirt and waist. As I came close I saw that she carried a baby in a crooked arm and the baby was nursing, its head under her waist out of the cold. The mother moved about, poking the fire, shifting the rusty lids of the stove to make a greater draft, opening the oven door; and all the time the baby was nursing, but that didn't interfere with the mother's work, nor with the light quick gracefulness of her movements. There was something very precise and practiced in her movements. The orange fire flicked out of the cracks in the stove and threw dancing reflections on the tent.

I was close now and I could smell frying bacon and baking bread, the warmest, pleasantest odors I know. From the east the light grew swiftly. I came near to the stove and stretched my hands out to it and shivered all over when the warmth struck me. Then the tent flap jerked up and a young man came out and an older man followed him. They were dressed in new blue dungarees and in new dungaree coats with the brass buttons shining. They were sharp-faced men, and they looked much alike.

The younger had a dark stubble beard and the older had a grey stubble beard. Their heads and faces were wet, their hair dripped with water, and water stood out on their stiff beards and their cheeks shone with water. Together they stood looking quietly at the lightening east; they yawned together and looked at the light on the hill rims. They turned and saw me.

"Morning," said the older man. His face was neither friendly nor unfriendly.

"Morning, sir," I said.

"Morning," said the young man.

The water was slowly drying on their faces. They came to the stove and warmed their hands at it.

The girl kept to her work, her face averted and her eyes on what she was doing. Her hair was tied back out of her eyes with a string and it hung down her back and swayed as she worked. She set tin cups on a big packing box, set tin plates and knives and forks out too. Then she scooped fried bacon out of the deep grease and laid it on a big tin platter, and the bacon cricked and rustled as it grew crisp. She opened the rusty oven door and took out a square pan full of high big biscuits.

When the smell of that hot bread came out, both of the men inhaled deeply. The young man said softly, "Keerist!"

The elder man turned to me, "Had your breakfast?"

"No."

"Well, sit down with us, then."

That was the signal. We went to the packing case and squatted on the ground about it. The young man asked, "Picking cotton?"

"No."

"We had twelve days' work so far," the young man said.

The girl spoke from the stove. "They even got new clothes."

The two men looked down at their new dungarees and they both smiled a little.

The girl set out the platter of bacon, the brown high biscuits, a bowl of bacon gravy and a pot of coffee, and then she squatted down by the box too. The baby was still nursing, its head up under her waist out of the cold. I could hear the sucking noises it made.

We filled our plates, poured bacon gravy over our biscuits and sugared our coffee. The older man filled his mouth full and he chewed and chewed and swallowed. Then he said, "God Almighty, it's good," and he filled his mouth again.

The young man said, "We been eating good for twelve days."

We all ate quickly, frantically, and refilled our plates and ate quickly again until we were full and warm. The hot bitter coffee scalded our throats. We threw the last little bit with the grounds in it on the earth and refilled our cups.

There was color in the light now, a reddish gleam that made the air seem colder. The two men faced the east and their faces were lighted by the dawn, and I looked up for a moment and saw the image of the mountain and the light coming over it reflected in the older man's eyes.

Then the two men threw the grounds from their cups on the earth and they stood up together. "Got to get going," the older man said.

The younger turned to me. "'Fyou want to pick cotton, we could maybe get you on."

"No. I got to go along. Thanks for breakfast."

The older man waved his hand in a negative. "O.K. Glad to have you." They walked away together. The air was blazing with light at the eastern skyline. And I walked away down the country road.

That's all. I know, of course, some of the reasons why it was pleasant. But there was some element of great beauty there that makes the rush of warmth when I think of it.

The Raid

IT WAS DARK in the little California town when the two men stepped from the lunch car and strode arrogantly through the back streets. The air was full of the sweet smell of fermenting fruit from the packing plants. High over the corners, blue arc lights swung in the wind and put moving shadows of telephone wires on the ground. The old wooden buildings were silent and resting. The dirty windows dismally reflected the street lights.

The two men were about the same size, but one was much older than the other. Their hair was cropped, they wore blue jeans. The older man had on a peajacket, while the younger wore a blue turtle-neck sweater. As they swung down the dark street, footsteps echoed back loudly from the wooden buildings. The younger man began to whistle *Come to Me My Melancholy Baby*. He stopped abruptly. "I wish that damn tune would get out of my head. It's been going all day. It's an old tune, too."

His companion turned toward him. "You're scared, Root. Tell the truth. You're scared as hell."

They were passing under one of the blue street lights. Root's face put on its toughest look, the eyes squinted, the mouth went crooked and bitter. "No, I ain't scared." They were out of the light. His face relaxed again. "I wish I knew the ropes better. You been out before, Dick. You know what to expect. But I ain't ever been out."

"The way to learn is to do," Dick quoted sententiously. "You never really learn nothing from books."

They crossed a railroad track. A block tower up the line a little was starred with green lights. "It's awful dark," said Root. "I wonder if the moon will come up later. Usually does when it's so dark. You going to make the first speech, Dick?"

"No, you make it. I had more experience than you. I'll watch them while you talk and then I can smack them where I know they bite. Know what you're going to say?"

"Sure I do. I got it all in my head, every word. I wrote it out and learned it. I heard guys tell how they got up and couldn't think of a thing to say, and then all of a sudden they just started in like it was somebody else, and the words came out like water out of a hydrant. Big Mike Sheane said it was like that with him. But I wasn't taking no chances, so I wrote it out."

A train hooted mournfully, and in a moment it rounded a bend and pushed its terrible light down the track. The lighted coaches rattled past. Dick turned to watch it go by. "Not many people on that one," he said with satisfaction. "Didn't you say your old man worked on the railroad?"

Root tried to keep the bitterness out of his voice. "Sure, he works on the road. He's a brakeman. He kicked me out when he found out what I was doing. He was scared he'd lose his job. He couldn't see. I talked to him, but he just couldn't see. He kicked me right out." Root's voice was lonely. Suddenly he realized how he had weakened and how he sounded homesick. "That's the trouble with them," he went on harshly. "They can't see beyond their jobs. They can't see what's happening to them. They hang on to their chains."

"Save it," said Dick. "That's good stuff. Is that part of your speech?"

"No, but I guess I'll put it in if you say it's good."

The street lights were fewer now. A line of locust trees grew along the road, for the town was beginning to thin and the country took control. Along the unpaved road there were a few little houses with ill-kept gardens.

"Jesus! It's dark," Root said again. "I wonder if there'll be any trouble. It's a good night to get away if anything happens."

Dick snorted into the collar of his peajacket. They walked along in silence for a while.

"Do you think you'd try to get away, Dick?" Root asked.

"No, by God! It's against orders. If anything happens we got to stick. You're just a kid. I guess you'd run if I let you!"

Root blustered: "You think you're hell on wheels just because you been out a few times. You'd think you was a hundred to hear you talk."

"I'm dry behind the ears, anyway," said Dick.

Root walked with his head down. He said softly, "Dick, are

you sure you wouldn't run? Are you sure you could just stand there and take it?"

"Of course I'm sure. I've done it before. It's the orders, ain't it? Why, it's good publicity." He peered through the darkness at Root. "What makes you ask, kid? You scared you'll run? If you're scared you got no business here."

Root shivered. "Listen, Dick, you're a good guy. You won't tell nobody what I say, will you? I never been tried. How do I know what I'll do if somebody smacks me in the face with a club? How can anybody tell what he'd do? I don't think I'd run. I'd try not to run."

"All right, kid. Let it go at that. But you try running, and I'll turn your name in. We got no place for yellow bastards. You remember that, kid."

"Oh, lay off that kid stuff. You're running that in the ground."

The locust trees grew closer together as they went. The wind rustled gently in the leaves. A dog growled in one of the yards as the men went by. A light fog began to drift down through the air, and the stars were swallowed in it. "You sure you got everything ready?" Dick asked. "Got the lamps? Got the lit'ature? I left all that to you."

"I did it all this afternoon," said Root. "I didn't put the posters up yet, but I got them in a box out there."

"Got oil in the lamps?"

"They had plenty in. Say, Dick, I guess some bastard has squealed, don't you?"

"Sure. Somebody always squeals."

"Well, you didn't hear nothing about no raid, did you?"

"How the hell would I hear. You think they'd come and tell me they was going to knock my can off? Get hold of yourself, Root. You got the pants scared off you. You're going to make me nervous if you don't cut it out."

II

They approached a low, square building, black and heavy in the darkness. Their feet pounded on a wooden sidewalk. "Nobody here, yet," said Dick. "Let's open her up and get some light." They had come to a deserted store. The old show-windows were opaque with dirt. A Lucky Strike poster was stuck to the glass on one side while a big cardboard Coca-Cola lady stood like a ghost in the other. Dick threw open the double doors and walked in. He struck a match and lighted a kerosene lamp, got the chimney back in place, and set the lamp on an up-ended apple box. "Come on, Root, we got to get things ready."

The walls of the building were scabrous with streaked whitewash. A pile of dusty newspapers had been kicked into a corner. The two back windows were laced with cobwebs. Except for three apple boxes, there was nothing at all in the store.

Root walked to one of the boxes and took out a large poster bearing a portrait of a man done in harsh reds and blacks. He tacked the portrait to the whitewashed wall behind the lamp. Then he tacked another poster beside it, a large red symbol on a white background. Last he up-ended another apple box and piled leaflets and little paper-bound books on it. His footsteps were loud on the bare wooden floor. "Light the other lamp, Dick! It's too damned dark in here."

"Scared of the dark, too, kid?"

"No. The men will be here pretty soon. We want to have more light when they come. What time is it?"

Dick looked at his watch. "Quarter to eight. Some of the guys ought to be here pretty soon now." He put his hands in the breast pockets of his peajacket and stood loosely by the box of pamphlets. There was nothing to sit on. The black and red portrait stared harshly out at the room. Root leaned against the wall.

The light from one of the lamps yellowed, and the flame slowly sank down. Dick stepped over to it. "I thought you said there was plenty of oil. This one's dry."

"I thought there was plenty. Look! The other one's nearly full. We can pour some of that oil in this lamp."

"How we going to do that? We got to put them both out to pour the oil. You got any matches?"

Root felt through his pockets. "Only two."

"Now, you see? We got to hold this meeting with only one lamp. I should've looked things over this afternoon. I was busy in town, though. I thought I could leave it to you."

"Maybe we could quick pour some of this oil in a can and then pour it into the other lamp."

"Yeah, and then set the joint on fire. You're a hell of a helper."

Root leaned back against the wall again. "I wish they'd come. What time is it, Dick?"

"Five after eight."

"Well, what's keeping them? What are they waiting for? Did you tell them eight o'clock?"

"Oh! Shut up, kid. You'll get my goat pretty soon. I don't know what's keeping them. Maybe they got cold feet. Now shut up for a little while." He dug his hands into the pockets of his jacket again. "Got a cigarette, Root?"

"No."

It was very still. Nearer the center of the town, automobiles were moving; the mutter of their engines and an occasional horn sounded. A dog barked unexcitedly at one of the houses nearby. The wind ruffled the locust trees in whishing gusts.

"Listen, Dick! Do you hear voices? I think they're coming." They turned their heads and strained to listen.

"I don't hear nothing. You just thought you heard it."

Root walked to one of the dirty windows and looked out. Coming back, he paused at the pile of pamphlets and straightened them neatly. "What time is it now, Dick?"

"Keep still, will you? You'll drive me nuts. You got to have guts for this job. For God's sake show some guts."

"Well, I never been out before, Dick."

"Do you think anybody couldn't tell that? You sure make it plain enough."

The wind gusted sharply in the locust trees. The front doors clicked and one of them opened slowly, squeaking a little at the hinges. The breeze came in, ruffled the pile of dusty newspapers in the corner and sailed the posters out from the wall like curtains.

"Shut that door, Root. . . . No, leave it open. Then we can hear them coming better." He looked at his watch. "It's nearly half-past eight."

"Do you think they'll come? How long we going to wait, if they don't show up?"

The older man stared at the open door. "We ain't going to

leave here before nine-thirty at the earliest. We got orders to hold this meeting."

The night sounds came in more clearly through the open door—the dance of dry locust leaves on the road, the slow steady barking of the dog. On the wall the red and black portrait was menacing in the dim light. It floated out at the bottom again. Dick looked around at it. "Listen, kid," he said quietly. "I know you're scared. When you're scared, just take a look at him." He indicated the picture with his thumb. "He wasn't scared. Just remember about what he did."

The boy considered the portrait. "You suppose he wasn't ever scared?"

Dick reprimanded him sharply. "If he was, nobody ever found out about it. You take that for a lesson and don't go opening up for everybody to show them how you feel."

"You're a good guy, Dick. I don't know what I'll do when I get sent out alone."

"You'll be all right, kid. You got stuff in you. I can tell that. You just never been under fire."

Root glanced quickly at the door. "Listen! You hear some-body coming?"

"Lay off that stuff! When they get here, they'll get here."

"Well—let's close the door. It's kind of cold in here. Listen! There *is* somebody coming."

Quick footsteps sounded on the road, broke into a run and crossed the wooden sidewalk. A man in overalls and a painter's cap ran into the room. He was panting and winded. "You guys better scram," he said. "There's a raiding party coming. None of the boys is coming to the meeting. They was going to let you take it, but I wouldn't do that. Come on! Get your stuff together and get out. That party's on the way."

Root's face was pale and tight. He looked nervously at Dick. The older man shivered. He thrust his hands into his breast pockets and slumped his shoulders. "Thanks," he said. "Thanks for telling us. You run along. We'll be all right."

"The others was just going to leave you take it," the man said.

Dick nodded. "Sure, they can't see the future. They can't see beyond their nose. Run along now before you get caught."

"Well, ain't you guys coming? I'll help carry some of your stuff."

"We're going to stay," Dick said woodenly. "We got orders to stay. We got to take it."

The man was moving toward the door. He turned back. "Want me to stay with you?"

"No, you're a good guy. No need for you to stay. We could maybe use you some other time."

"Well, I did what I could."

III

Dick and Root heard him cross the wooden sidewalk and trot off into the darkness. The night resumed its sounds. The dead leaves scraped along the ground. The motors hummed from the centre of the town.

Root looked at Dick. He could see that the man's fists were doubled up in his breast pockets. The face muscles were stiff, but he smiled at the boy. The posters drifted out from the wall and settled back again.

"Scared, kid?"

Root bristled to deny it, and then gave it up. "Yes, I'm scared. Maybe I won't be no good at this."

"Take hold, kid!" Dick said fiercely. "You take hold!"

Dick quoted to him, " 'The men of little spirit must have an example of stead—steadfastness. The people at large must have an example of injustice.' There it is, Root. That's orders." He relapsed into silence. The barking dog increased his tempo.

"I guess that's them," said Root. "Will they kill us, do you think?"

"No, they don't very often kill anybody."

"But they'll hit us and kick us, won't they? They'll hit us in the face with sticks and break our nose. Big Mike, they broke his jaw in three places."

"Take hold, kid! You take hold! And listen to me; if some one busts you, it isn't him that's doing it, it's the System. And it isn't you he's busting. He's taking a crack at the Principle. Can you remember that?"

"I don't want to run, Dick. Honest to God I don't. If I start to run, you hold me, will you?"

Dick walked near and touched him on the shoulder. "You'll be all right. I can tell a guy that will stick."

"Well, hadn't we better hide the lit'ature so it won't all get burned?"

"No—somebody might put a book in his pocket and read it later. Then it would be doing some good. Leave the books there. And shut up now! Talking only makes it worse."

The dog had gone back to his slow, spiritless barking. A rush of wind brought a scurry of dead leaves in the open door. The portrait poster blew out and came loose at one corner. Root walked over and pinned it back. Somewhere in the town, an automobile squealed its brakes.

"Hear anything, Dick? Hear them coming yet?"

"No."

"Listen, Dick. Big Mike lay two days with his jaw broke before anybody'd help him."

The older man turned angrily on him. One doubled fist came out of his peajacket pocket. His eyes narrowed as he looked at the boy. He walked close and put an arm about his shoulders. "Listen to me close, kid," he said. "I don't know much, but I been through this mill before. I can tell you this for sure. When it comes—it won't hurt. I don't know why, but it won't. Even if they kill you it won't hurt." He dropped his arm and moved toward the front door. He looked out and listened in two directions before he came back into the room.

"Hear anything?"

"No. Not a thing."

"What—do you think is keeping them?"

"How do you suppose I'd know?"

Root swallowed thickly. "Maybe they won't come. Maybe it was all a lie that fella told us, just a joke."

"Maybe."

"Well, are—we going to wait all night to get our cans knocked off?"

Dick mimicked him. "Yes, we're going to wait all night to get our cans knocked off."

The wind sounded in one big fierce gust and then dropped away completely. The dog stopped barking. A train screamed for the crossing and went crashing by, leaving the night more silent than before. In a house nearby, an alarm clock went off. Dick said, "Somebody goes to work early. Night watchman, maybe." His voice was too loud in the stillness. The front door squeaked slowly shut.

"What time is it now, Dick?"

"Quarter-past nine."

"Jesus! Only that? I thought it was about morning. . . . Don't you wish they'd come and get it over, Dick? Listen, Dick!—I thought I heard voices."

They stood stiffly, listening. Their heads were bent forward. "You hear voices, Dick?"

"I think so. Like they're talking low."

The dog barked again, fiercely this time. A little quiet murmur of voices could be heard. "Look, Dick! I thought I saw somebody out the back window."

The older man chuckled uneasily. "That's so we can't get away. They got the place surrounded. Take hold, kid! They're coming now. Remember about it's not them, it's the System."

There came a rushing clatter of footsteps. The doors burst open. A crowd of men thronged in, roughly dressed men, wearing black hats. They carried clubs and sticks in their hands. Dick and Root stood erect, their chins out, their eyes dropped and nearly closed.

Once inside, the raiders were uneasy. They stood in a half-circle about the two men, scowling, waiting for some one to move.

Young Root glanced sidewise at Dick and saw that the older man was looking at him coldly, critically, as though he judged his deportment. Root shoved his trembling hands in his pockets. He forced himself forward. His voice was shrill with fright. "Comrades," he shouted, "you're just men like we are. We're all brothers——" A piece of two-by-four lashed out and struck him on the side of the head with a fleshy thump. Root went down to his knees and steadied himself with his hands.

The men stood still, glaring.

Root climbed slowly to his feet. His split ear spilled a red stream down his neck. The side of his face was mushy and purple. He got himself erect again. His breath burst passionately. His hands were steady now, his voice sure and strong.

His eyes were hot with an ecstasy. "Can't you see?" he shouted. "It's all for you. We're doing it for you. All of it. You don't know what you're doing."

"Kill the red rats!"

Some one giggled hysterically. And then the wave came. As he went down, Root caught a moment's glimpse of Dick's face smiling a tight, hard smile.

IV

He came near the surface several times, but didn't quite make it into consciousness. At last he opened his eyes and knew things. His face and head were heavy with bandages. He could only see a line of light between his puffed eyelids. For a time he lay, trying to think his way out. Then he heard Dick's voice near to him.

"You awake, kid?"

Root tried his voice and found that it croaked pretty badly. "I guess so."

"They sure worked out on your head. I thought you was gone. You was right about your nose. It ain't going to be very pretty."

"What'd they do to you, Dick?"

"Oh, they bust my arm and a couple of ribs. You got to learn to turn your face down to the ground. That saves your eyes." He paused and drew a careful breath. "Hurts some to breathe when you get a rib bust. We are lucky. The cops picked us up and took us in."

"Are we in jail, Dick?"

"Yeah! Hospital cell."

"What they got on the book?"

He heard Dick try to chuckle, and gasp when it hurt him. "Inciting to riot. We'll get six months, I guess. The cops got the lit'ature."

"You won't tell them I'm under age, will you, Dick?"

"No. I won't. You better shut up. Your voice don't sound so hot. Take it easy."

Root lay silent, muffled in a coat of dull pain. But in a moment he spoke again. "It didn't hurt, Dick. It was funny. I felt all full up—and good."

"You done fine, kid. You done as good as anybody I ever seen. I'll give you a blow to the committee. You just done fine."

Root struggled to get something straight in his head. "When they was busting me I wanted to tell them I didn't care."

"Sure, kid. That's what I told you. It wasn't them. It was the System. You don't want to hate them. They don't know no better."

Root spoke drowsily. The pain was muffling him under. "You remember in the Bible, Dick, how it says something like 'Forgive them because they don't know what they're doing'?"

Dick's reply was stern. "You lay off that religion stuff, kid." He quoted, " 'Religion is the opium of the people.' "

"Sure, I know," said Root. "But there wasn't no religion to it. It was just—I felt like saying that. It was just kind of the way I felt."

The Harness

PETER RANDALL was one of the most highly respected farmers of Monterey County. Once, before he was to make a little speech at a Masonic convention, the brother who introduced him referred to him as an example for young Masons of California to emulate. He was nearing fifty; his manner was grave and restrained, and he wore a carefully tended beard. From every gathering he reaped the authority that belongs to the bearded man. Peter's eyes were grave, too; blue and grave almost to the point of sorrowfulness. People knew there was force in him, but force held caged. Sometimes, for no apparent reason, his eyes grew sullen and mean, like the eyes of a bad dog; but that look soon passed, and the restraint and probity came back into his face. He was tall and broad. He held his shoulders back as though they were braced, and he sucked in his stomach like a soldier. Inasmuch as farmers are usually slouchy men, Peter gained an added respect because of his posture.

Concerning Peter's wife, Emma, people generally agreed that it was hard to see how such a little skin-and-bones woman could go on living, particularly when she was sick most of the time. She weighed eighty-seven pounds. At forty-five, her face was as wrinkled and brown as that of an old, old woman, but her dark eyes were feverish with a determination to live. She was a proud woman, who complained very little. Her father had been a thirty-third degree Mason and Worshipful Master of the Grand Lodge of California. Before he died he had taken a great deal of interest in Peter's Masonic career.

Once a year Peter went away for a week, leaving his wife alone on the farm. To neighbors who called to keep her company she invariably explained, "He's away on a business trip."

Each time Peter returned from a business trip, Emma was ailing for a month or two, and this was hard on Peter, for Emma did her own work and refused to hire a girl. When she was ill, Peter had to do the housework.

The Randall ranch lay across the Salinas River, next to the foothills. It was an ideal balance of bottom and upland. Forty-five acres of rich level soil brought from the cream of the country by the river in old times and spread out as flat as a board; and eighty acres of gentle upland for hay and orchard. The white farmhouse was as neat and restrained as its owners. The immediate yard was fenced, and in the garden, under Emma's direction, Peter raised button dahlias and immortelles, carnations and pinks.

From the front porch one could look down over the flat to the river with its sheath of willows and cottonwoods, and across the river to the beet fields, and past the fields to the bulbous dome of the Salinas courthouse. Often in the afternoon Emma sat in a rocking-chair on the front porch, until the breeze drove her in. She knitted constantly, looking up now and then to watch Peter working on the flat or in the orchard, or on the slope below the house.

The Randall ranch was no more encumbered with mortgage than any of the others in the valley. The crops, judiciously chosen and carefully tended, paid the interest, made a reasonable living and left a few hundred dollars every year toward paying off the principal. It was no wonder that Peter Randall was respected by his neighbors, and that his seldom spoken words were given attention even when they were about the weather or the way things were going. Let Peter say, "I'm going to kill a pig Saturday," and nearly every one of his hearers went home and killed a pig on Saturday. They didn't know why, but if Peter Randall was going to kill a pig, it seemed like a good, safe, conservative thing to do.

Peter and Emma were married for twenty-one years. They collected a houseful of good furniture, a number of framed pictures, vases of all shapes, and books of a sturdy type. Emma had no children. The house was unscarred, uncarved, unchalked. On the front and back porches footscrapers and thick cocoa-fiber mats kept dirt out of the house.

In the intervals between her illnesses, Emma saw to it that the house was kept up. The hinges of doors and cupboards were oiled, and no screws were gone from the catches. The furniture and woodwork were freshly varnished once a year. Repairs were usually made after Peter came home from his yearly business trips.

Whenever the word went around among the farms that

Emma was sick again, the neighbors waylaid the doctor as he drove by on the river road.

"Oh, I guess she'll be all right," he answered their questions. "She'll have to stay in bed for a couple of weeks."

The good neighbors took cakes to the Randall farm, and they tiptoed into the sickroom, where the little skinny bird of a woman lay in a tremendous walnut bed. She looked at them with her bright little dark eyes.

"Wouldn't you like the curtains up a little, dear?" they asked.

"No, thank you. The light worries my eyes."

"Is there anything we can do for you?"

"No, thank you. Peter does for me very well."

"Just remember, if there's anything you think of——"

Emma was such a tight woman. There was nothing you could do for her when she was ill, except to take pies and cakes to Peter. Peter would be in the kitchen, wearing a neat, clean apron. He would be filling a hot water bottle or making junket.

And so, one fall, when the news traveled that Emma was down, the farm-wives baked for Peter and prepared to make their usual visits.

Mrs. Chappell, the next farm neighbor, stood on the river road when the doctor drove by. "How's Emma Randall, doctor?"

"I don't think she's so very well, Mrs. Chappell. I think she's a pretty sick woman."

Because to Dr. Marn anyone who wasn't actually a corpse was well on the road to recovery, the word went about among the farms that Emma Randall was going to die.

It was a long, terrible illness. Peter himself gave enemas and carried bedpans. The doctor's suggestion that a nurse be employed met only beady, fierce refusal in the eyes of the patient; and, ill as she was, her demands were respected. Peter fed her and bathed her, and made up the great walnut bed. The bedroom curtains remained drawn.

It was two months before the dark, sharp bird eyes veiled, and the sharp mind retired into unconsciousness. And only then did a nurse come to the house. Peter was lean and sick himself, not far from collapse. The neighbors brought him cakes and pies, and found them uneaten in the kitchen when they called again.

Mrs. Chappell was in the house with Peter the afternoon Emma died. Peter became hysterical immediately. Mrs. Chappell telephoned the doctor, and then she called her husband to come and help her, for Peter was wailing like a crazy man, and beating his bearded cheeks with his fists. Ed Chappell was ashamed when he saw him.

Peter's beard was wet with his tears. His loud sobbing could be heard throughout the house. Sometimes he sat by the bed and covered his head with a pillow, and sometimes he paced the floor of the bedroom bellowing like a calf. When Ed Chappell self-consciously put a hand on his shoulder and said, "Come on, Peter, come on, now," in a helpless voice, Peter shook his hand off. The doctor drove out and signed the certificate.

When the undertaker came, they had a devil of a time with Peter. He was half mad. He fought them when they tried to take the body away. It was only after Ed Chappell and the undertaker held him down while the doctor stuck him with a hypodermic, that they were able to remove Emma.

The morphine didn't put Peter to sleep. He sat hunched in the corner, breathing heavily and staring at the floor.

"Who's going to stay with him?" the doctor asked. "Miss Jack?" to the nurse.

"I couldn't handle him, doctor, not alone."

"Will you stay, Chappell?"

"Sure, I'll stay."

"Well, look. Here are some triple bromides. If he gets going again, give him one of these. And if they don't work, here's some sodium amytal. One of these capsules will calm him down."

Before they went away, they helped the stupefied Peter into the sitting-room and laid him gently down on a sofa. Ed Chappell sat in an easy-chair and watched him. The bromides and a glass of water were on the table beside him.

The little sitting-room was clean and dusted. Only that morning Peter had swept the floor with pieces of damp newspaper. Ed built a little fire in the grate, and put on a couple of pieces of oak when the flames were well started. The dark had come early. A light rain spattered against the windows when the wind drove it. Ed trimmed the kerosene lamps and turned the flames low. In the grate the blaze snapped and crackled and the flames curled like hair over the oak. For a long time Ed sat in his easy-chair watching Peter where he lay drugged on the couch. At last Ed dozed off to sleep.

It was about ten o'clock when he awakened. He started up and looked toward the sofa. Peter was sitting up, looking at him. Ed's hand went out toward the bromide bottle, but Peter shook his head.

"No need to give me anything, Ed. I guess the doctor slugged me pretty hard, didn't he? I feel all right now, only a little dopey."

"If you'll just take one of these, you'll get some sleep."

"I don't want sleep." He fingered his draggled beard and then stood up. "I'll go out and wash my face, then I'll feel better."

Ed heard him running water in the kitchen. In a moment he came back into the living-room, still drying his face on a towel. Peter was smiling curiously. It was an expression Ed had never seen on him before, a quizzical, wondering smile. "I guess I kind of broke loose when she died, didn't I?" Peter said.

"Well—yes, you carried on some."

"It seemed like something snapped inside of me," Peter explained. "Something like a suspender strap. It made me all come apart. I'm all right, now, though."

Ed looked down at the floor and saw a little brown spider crawling, and stretched out his foot and stomped it.

Peter asked suddenly, "Do you believe in an after-life?"

Ed Chappell squirmed. He didn't like to talk about such things, for to talk about them was to bring them up in his mind and think about them. "Well, yes. I suppose if you come right down to it, I do."

"Do you believe that somebody that's—passed on—can look down and see what we're doing?"

"Oh, I don't know as I'd go that far—I don't know."

Peter went on as though he were talking to himself. "Even if she could see me, and I didn't do what she wanted, she ought to feel good because I did it when she was here. It ought to please her that she made a good man of me. If I wasn't a good man when she wasn't here, that'd prove she did it all, wouldn't it? I was a good man, wasn't I, Ed?"

"What do you mean, 'was'?"

"Well, except for one week a year I was good. I don't know what I'll do now. . . ." His face grew angry. "Except one thing." He stood up and stripped off his coat and his shirt. Over his underwear there was a web harness that pulled his shoulders back. He unhooked the harness and threw it off. Then he dropped his trousers, disclosing a wide elastic belt. He shucked this off over his feet, and then he scratched his stomach luxuriously before he put on his clothes again. He smiled at Ed, the strange, wondering smile, again. "I don't know how she got me to do things, but she did. She didn't seem to boss me, but she always made me do things. You know, I don't think I believe in an after-life. When she was alive, even when she was sick, I had to do things she wanted, but just the minute she died, it was—why like that harness coming off! I couldn't stand it. It was all over. I'm going to have to get used to going without that harness." He shook his finger in Ed's direction. "My stomach's going to stick out," he said positively. "I'm going to let it stick out. Why, I'm fifty years old."

Ed didn't like that. He wanted to get away. This sort of thing wasn't very decent. "If you'll just take one of these, you'll get some sleep," he said weakly.

Peter had not put his coat on. He was sitting on the sofa in an open shirt. "I don't want to sleep. I want to talk. I guess I'll have to put that belt and harness on for the funeral, but after that I'm going to burn them. Listen, I've got a bottle of whiskey in the barn. I'll go get it."

"Oh no," Ed protested quickly. "I couldn't drink now, not at a time like this."

Peter stood up. "Well, I could. You can sit and watch me if you want. I tell you, it's all over." He went out the door, leaving Ed Chappell unhappy and scandalized. It was only a moment before he was back. He started talking as he came through the doorway with the whiskey. "I only got one thing in my life, those trips. Emma was a pretty bright woman. She knew I'd've gone crazy if I didn't get away once a year. God, how she worked on my conscience when I came back!'' His voice lowered confidentially. "You know what I did on those trips?''

Ed's eyes were wide open now. Here was a man he didn't know, and he was becoming fascinated. He took the glass of whiskey when it was handed to him. "No, what did you do?''

Peter gulped his drink and coughed, and wiped his mouth with his hand. "I got drunk,'' he said. "I went to fancy houses in San Francisco. I was drunk for a week, and I went to a fancy house every night.'' He poured his glass full again. "I guess Emma knew, but she never said anything. I'd've *busted* if I hadn't got away.''

Ed Chappell sipped his whiskey gingerly. "She always said you went on business.''

Peter looked at his glass and drank it, and poured it full again. His eyes had begun to shine. "Drink your drink, Ed. I know you think it isn't right—so soon, but no one'll know but you and me. Kick up the fire. I'm not sad.''

Chappell went to the grate and stirred the glowing wood until lots of sparks flew up the chimney like little shining birds. Peter filled the glasses and retired to the sofa again. When Ed went back to the chair he sipped from his glass and pretended he didn't know it was filled up. His cheeks were flushing. It didn't seem so terrible, now, to be drinking. The afternoon and the death had receded into an indefinite past.

"Want some cake?'' Peter asked. "There's half a dozen cakes in the pantry.''

"No, I don't think I will thank you for some.''

"You know,'' Peter confessed, "I don't think I'll eat cake again. For ten years, every time Emma was sick, people sent cakes. It was nice of 'em, of course, only now cake means sickness to me. Drink your drink.''

Something happened in the room. Both men looked up, trying to discover what it was. The room was somehow different than it had been a moment before. Then Peter smiled sheepishly. "It was that mantel clock stopped. I don't think I'll start it any more. I'll get a little quick alarm clock that ticks fast. That clack-clack-clack is too mournful.'' He swallowed his whiskey. "I guess you'll be telling around that I'm crazy, won't you?''

Ed looked up from his glass, and smiled and nodded. "No, I will not. I can see pretty much how you feel about things. I didn't know you wore that harness and belt."

"A man ought to stand up straight," Peter said. "I'm a natural sloucher." Then he exploded: "I'm a natural fool! For twenty years I've been pretending I was a wise, good man— except for that one week a year." He said loudly, "Things have been dribbled to me. My life's been dribbled out to me. Here, let me fill your glass. I've got another bottle out in the barn, way down under a pile of sacks."

Ed held out his glass to be filled. Peter went on, "I thought how it would be nice to have my whole river flat in sweet peas. Think how it'd be to sit on the front porch and see all those acres of blue and pink, just solid. And when the wind came up over them, think of the big smell. A big smell that would almost knock you over."

"A lot of men have gone broke on sweet peas. 'Course you get a big price for the seed, but too many things can happen to your crop."

"I don't give a damn," Peter shouted. "I want a lot of everything. I want forty acres of color and smell. I want fat women, with breasts as big as pillows. I'm hungry, I tell you, I'm hungry for everything, for a lot of everything."

Ed's face became grave under the shouting. "If you'd just take one of these, you'd get some sleep."

Peter looked ashamed. "I'm all right. I didn't mean to yell like that. I'm not just thinking these things for the first time. I been thinking about them for years, the way a kid thinks of vacation. I was always afraid I'd be too old. Or that I'd go first and miss everything. But I'm only fifty, I've got plenty of vinegar left. I told Emma about the sweet peas, but she wouldn't let me. I don't know how she made me do things," he said wonderingly. "I can't remember. She had a way of doing it. But she's gone. I can feel she's gone just like that harness is gone. I'm going to slouch, Ed—slouch all over the place. I'm going to track dirt into the house. I'm going to get a big fat housekeeper—a big fat one from San Francisco. I'm going to have a bottle of brandy on the shelf all the time."

Ed Chappell stood up and stretched his arms over his head. "I guess I'll go home now, if you feel all right. I got to get some sleep. You better wind that clock, Peter. It don't do a clock any good to stand not running."

The day after the funeral Peter Randall went to work on his farm. The Chappells, who lived on the next place, saw the lamp in his kitchen long before daylight, and they saw his lantern cross the yard to the barn half an hour before they even got up.

Peter pruned his orchard in three days. He worked from first light until he couldn't see the twigs against the sky any more. Then he started to shape the big piece of river flat. He plowed and rolled and harrowed. Two strange men dressed in boots and riding breeches came out and looked at his land. They felt the dirt with their fingers and ran a post-hole digger deep down under the surface, and when they went away they took little paper bags of the dirt with them.

Ordinarily, before planting time, the farmers did a good deal of visiting back and forth. They sat on their haunches, picking up handsful of dirt and breaking little clods between their fingers. They discussed markets and crops, recalled other years when beans had done well in a good market, and other years when field peas didn't bring enough to pay for the seed hardly. After a great number of these discussions it usually happened that all the farmers planted the same things. There were certain men whose ideas carried weight. If Peter Randall or Clark DeWitt thought they would put in pink beans and barley, most of the crops would turn out to be pink beans and barley that year; for, since such men were respected and fairly successful, it was conceded that their plans must be based on something besides chance choice. It was generally believed but never stated that Peter Randall and Clark DeWitt had extra reasoning powers and special prophetic knowledge.

When the usual visits started, it was seen that a change had taken place in Peter Randall. He sat on his plow and talked pleasantly enough. He said he hadn't decided yet what to plant, but he said it in such a guilty way that it was plain he didn't intend to tell. When he had rebuffed a few inquiries, the visits to his place stopped and the farmers went over in a body to Clark DeWitt. Clark was putting in Chevalier barley. His decision dictated the major part of the planting in the vicinity.

But because the questions stopped, the interest did not. Men driving by the forty-five acre flat of the Randall place studied the field to try to figure out from the type of work what the crop was going to be. When Peter drove the seeder back and forth across the land no one came in, for Peter had made it plain that his crop was a secret.

Ed Chappell didn't tell on him, either. Ed was a little ashamed when he thought of that night; ashamed of Peter for breaking down, and ashamed of himself for having sat there and listened. He watched Peter narrowly to see whether his vicious intentions were really there or whether the whole conversation had been the result of loss and hysteria. He did notice that Peter's shoulders weren't back and that his stomach stuck out a little. He went to Peter's house and was relieved when he saw no dirt on the floor and when he heard the mantel clock ticking away.

Mrs. Chappell spoke often of the afternoon. "You'd've thought he lost his mind the way he carried on. He just howled. Ed stayed with him part of the night, until he quieted down. Ed had to give him some whiskey to get him to sleep. But," she said brightly, "hard work is the thing to kill sorrow. Peter Randall is getting up at three o'clock every morning. I can see the light in his kitchen window from my bedroom."

The pussywillows burst out in silver drops, and the little weeds sprouted up along the roadside. The Salinas River ran dark water, flowed for a month, and then subsided into green pools again. Peter Randall had shaped his land beautifully. It was smooth and black; no clod was larger than a small marble, and under the rains it looked purple with richness.

And then the little weak lines of green stretched out across the black field. In the dusk a neighbor crawled under the fence and pulled one of the tiny plants. "Some kind of legume," he told his friends. "Field peas, I guess. What did he want to be so quiet about it for? I asked him right out what he was planting, and he wouldn't tell me."

The word ran through the farms, "It's sweet peas. The whole God-damn' forty-five acres is in sweet peas!" Men called on Clark DeWitt then, to get his opinion.

His opinion was this: "People think because you can get twenty to sixty cents a pound for sweet peas you can get rich on them. But it's the most ticklish crop in the world. If the bugs don't get it, it might do good. And then come a hot day and bust the pods and lose your crop on the ground. Or it might come up a little rain and spoil the whole kaboodle. It's all right to put in a few acres and take a chance, but not the whole place. Peter's touched in the head since Emma died."

This opinion was widely distributed. Every man used it as his own. Two neighbors often said it to each other, each one repeating half of it. When too many people said it to Peter Randall he became angry. One day he cried, "Say, whose land is this? If I want to go broke, I've got a damn good right to, haven't I?" And that changed the whole feeling. Men remembered that Peter was a good farmer. Perhaps he had special knowledge. Why, that's who those two men in boots were— soil chemists! A good many of the farmers wished they'd put in a few acres of sweet peas.

They wished it particularly when the vines spread out, when they met each other across the rows and hid the dark earth from sight, when the buds began to form and it was seen the crop was rich. And then the blooms came; forty-five acres of color, forty-five acres of perfume. It was said that you could smell them in Salinas, four miles away. Busses brought the school children out to look at them. A group of men from a seed company spent all day looking at the vines and feeling the earth.

Peter Randall sat on his porch in a rocking-chair every afternoon. He looked down on the great squares of pink and blue, and on the mad square of mixed colors. When the afternoon breeze came up, he inhaled deeply. His blue shirt was open at the throat, as though he wanted to get the perfume down next his skin.

Men called on Clark DeWitt to get his opinion now. He said, "There's about ten things that can happen to spoil that crop. He's welcome to his sweet peas." But the men knew from Clark's irritation that he was a little jealous. They looked up over the fields of color to where Peter sat on his porch, and they felt a new admiration and respect for him.

Ed Chappell walked up the steps to him one afternoon. "You got a crop there, mister."

"Looks that way," said Peter.

"I took a look. Pods are setting fine."

Peter sighed. "Blooming's nearly over," he said. "I'll hate to see the petals drop off."

"Well, I'd be glad to see 'em drop. You'll make a lot of money, if nothing happens."

Peter took out a bandana handkerchief and wiped his nose, and jiggled it sideways to stop an itch. "I'll be sorry when the smell stops," he said.

Then Ed made his reference to the night of the death. One of his eyes drooped secretly. "Found somebody to keep house for you?"

"I haven't looked," said Peter. "I haven't had time." There were lines of worry about his eyes. But who wouldn't worry, Ed thought, when a single shower could ruin his whole year's crop.

If the year and the weather had been manufactured for sweet peas, they couldn't have been better. The fog lay close to the ground in the mornings when the vines were pulled. When the great piles of vines lay safely on spread canvasses, the hot sun shone down and crisped the pods for the threshers. The neighbors watched the long cotton sacks filling with round black seeds, and they went home and tried to figure out how much money Peter would make on his tremendous crop. Clark DeWitt lost a good part of his following. The men decided to find out what Peter was going to plant next year if they had to follow him around. How did he know, for instance, that this year'd be good for sweet peas? He *must* have some kind of special knowledge.

When a man from the upper Salinas Valley goes to San Francisco on business or for a vacation, he takes a room in the Ramona Hotel. This is a nice arrangement, for in the lobby he can usually find someone from home. They can sit in the soft chairs of the lobby and talk about the Salinas Valley.

Ed Chappell went to San Francisco to meet his wife's cousin who was coming out from Ohio for a trip. The train was not due until the next morning. In the lobby of the Ramona, Ed looked for someone from the Salinas Valley, but he could see only strangers sitting in the soft chairs. He went out to a moving picture show. When he returned, he looked again for someone from home, and still there were only strangers. For a moment he considered glancing over the register, but it was quite late. He sat down to finish his cigar before he went to bed.

There was a commotion at the door. Ed saw the clerk motion with his hand. A bellhop ran out. Ed squirmed around in his chair to look. Outside a man was being helped out of a taxicab. The bellhop took him from the driver and guided him in the door. It was Peter Randall. His eyes were glassy, and his mouth open and wet. He had no hat on his mussed hair. Ed jumped up and strode over to him.

"Peter!"

Peter was batting helplessly at the bellhop. "Let me alone," he explained. "I'm all right. You let me alone, and I'll give you two bits."

Ed called again, "Peter!"

The glassy eyes turned slowly to him, and then Peter fell into his arms. "My old friend," he cried. "Ed Chappell, my old, good friend. What you doing here? Come up to my room and have a drink."

Ed set him back on his feet. "Sure I will," he said. "I'd like a little night-cap."

"Night-cap, hell. We'll go out and see a show, or something."

Ed helped him into the elevator and got him to his room. Peter dropped heavily to the bed and struggled up to a sitting position. "There's a bottle of whiskey in the bathroom. Bring me a drink, too."

Ed brought out the bottle and the glasses. "What you doing, Peter, celebrating the crop? You must've made a pile of money."

Peter put out his palm and tapped it impressively with a forefinger. "Sure I made money—but it wasn't a bit better than gambling. It was just like straight gambling."

"But you got the money."

Peter scowled thoughtfully. "I might've lost my pants," he said. "The whole time, all the year, I been worrying. It was just like gambling."

"Well, you got it, anyway."

Peter changed the subject, then. "I been sick," he said. "I been sick right in the taxicab. I just came from a fancy house on Van Ness Avenue," he explained apologetically, "I just had to come up to the city. I'd'a busted if I hadn't come up and got some of the vinegar out of my system."

Ed looked at him curiously. Peter's head was hanging loosely between his shoulders. His beard was draggled and rough. "Peter—" Ed began, "the night Emma—passed on, you said you was going to—change things."

Peter's swaying head rose up slowly. He stared owlishly at Ed Chappell. "She didn't die dead," he said thickly. "She won't let me do things. She's worried me all year about those peas." His eyes were wondering. "I don't know how she does it." Then he frowned. His palm came out, and he tapped it again. "But you mark, Ed Chappell, I won't wear that harness, and I damn well won't ever wear it. You remember that." His head dropped forward again. But in a moment he looked up. "I been drunk," he said seriously. "I been to fancy houses." He edged out confidentially toward Ed. His voice dropped to a heavy whisper. "But it's all right, I'll fix it. When I get back, you know what I'm going to do? I'm going to put in electric lights. Emma always wanted electric lights." He sagged sideways on the bed.

Ed Chappell stretched Peter out and undressed him before he went to his own room.

The Vigilante

T HE GREAT SURGE of emotion, the milling and shouting of the people fell gradually to silence in the town park. A crowd of people still stood under the elm trees, vaguely lighted by a blue street light two blocks away. A tired quiet settled on the people; some members of the mob began to sneak away into the darkness. The park lawn was cut to pieces by the feet of the crowd.

Mike knew it was all over. He could feel the let-down in himself. He was as heavily weary as though he had gone without sleep for several nights, but it was a dream-like weariness, a grey comfortable weariness. He pulled his cap down over his eyes and moved away, but before leaving the park he turned for one last look.

In the center of the mob someone had lighted a twisted newspaper and was holding it up. Mike could see how the flame curled about the feet of the grey naked body hanging from the elm tree. It seemed curious to him that negroes turn a bluish grey when they are dead. The burning newspaper lighted the heads of the up-looking men, silent men and fixed; they didn't move their eyes from the hanged man.

Mike felt a little irritation at whoever it was who was trying to burn the body. He turned to a man who stood beside him in the near-darkness. "That don't do no good," he said.

The man moved away without replying.

The newspaper torch went out, leaving the park almost black by contrast. But immediately another twisted paper was lighted and held up against the feet. Mike moved to another watching man. "That don't do no good," he repeated. "He's dead now. They can't hurt him none."

The second man grunted but did not look away from the flaming paper. "It's a good job," he said. "This'll save the county a lot of money and no sneaky lawyers getting in."

"That's what I say," Mike agreed. "No sneaky lawyers. But it don't do no good to try to burn him."

The man continued staring toward the flame. "Well, it can't do much harm, either."

86

Mike filled his eyes with the scene. He felt that he was dull. He wasn't seeing enough of it. Here was a thing he would want to remember later so he could tell about it, but the dull tiredness seemed to cut the sharpness off the picture. His brain told him this was a terrible and important affair, but his eyes and his feelings didn't agree. It was just ordinary. Half an hour before, when he had been howling with the mob and fighting for a chance to help pull on the rope, then his chest had been so full that he had found he was crying. But now everything was dead, everything unreal; the dark mob was made up of stiff lay-figures. In the flamelight the faces were as expressionless as wood. Mike felt the stiffness, the unreality in himself, too. He turned away at last and walked out of the park.

The moment he left the outskirts of the mob a cold loneliness fell upon him. He walked quickly along the street wishing that some other man might be walking beside him. The wide street was deserted, empty, as unreal as the park had been. The two steel lines of the car tracks stretched glimmering away down the street under the electroliers, and the dark store windows reflected the midnight globes.

A gentle pain began to make itself felt in Mike's chest. He felt with his fingers; the muscles were sore. Then he remembered. He was in the front line of the mob when it rushed the closed jail door. A driving line forty men deep had crashed Mike against the door like the head of a ram. He had hardly felt it then, and even now the pain seemed to have the dull quality of loneliness.

Two blocks ahead the burning neon word BEER hung over the sidewalk. Mike hurried toward it. He hoped there would be people there, and talk, to remove this silence; and he hoped the men wouldn't have been to the lynching.

The bartender was alone in his little bar, a small, middle-aged man with a melancholy moustache and an expression like an aged mouse, wise and unkempt and fearful.

He nodded quickly as Mike came in. "You look like you been walking in your sleep," he said.

Mike regarded him with wonder. "That's just how I feel, too, like I been walking in my sleep."

"Well, I can give you a shot if you want."

Mike hesitated. "No—I'm kind of thirsty. I'll take a beer. . . . Was you there?"

The little man nodded his mouse-like head again. "Right at the last, after he was all up and it was all over. I figured a lot of the fellas would be thirsty, so I came back and opened up. Nobody but you so far. Maybe I was wrong."

"They might be along later," said Mike. "There's a lot of them still in the park. They cooled off, though. Some of them trying to burn him with newspapers. That don't do no good."

"Not a bit of good," said the little bartender. He twitched his thin moustache.

Mike knocked a few grains of celery salt into his beer and took a long drink. "That's good," he said. "I'm kind of dragged out."

The bartender leaned close to him over the bar, his eyes were bright. "Was you there all the time—to the jail and everything?"

Mike drank again and then looked through his beer and watched the beads of bubbles rising from the grains of salt in the bottom of the glass. "Everything," he said. "I was one of the first in the jail, and I helped pull on the rope. There's times when citizens got to take the law in their own hands. Sneaky lawyer comes along and gets some fiend out of it."

The mousy head jerked up and down. "You God-dam' right," he said. "Lawyers can get them out of anything. I guess the nigger was guilty all right."

"Oh, sure! Somebody said he even confessed."

The head came close over the bar again. "How did it start, mister? I was only there after it was all over, and then I only stayed a minute and then came back to open up in case any of the fellas might want a glass of beer."

Mike drained his glass and pushed it out to be filled. "Well, of course everybody knew it was going to happen. I was in a bar across from the jail. Been there all afternoon. A guy came in and says, 'What are we waiting for?' So we went across the street, and a lot more guys was there and a lot more come. We all stood there and yelled. Then the sheriff come out and made a speech, but we yelled him down. A guy with a twenty-two rifle went along the street and shot out the street lights.

Well, then we rushed the jail doors and bust them. The sheriff wasn't going to do nothing. It wouldn't do him no good to shoot a lot of honest men to save a nigger fiend.''

"And election coming on, too," the bartender put in.

"Well, the sheriff started yelling, 'Get the right man, boys, for Christ's sake get the right man. He's in the fourth cell down.'

"It was kind of pitiful," Mike said slowly. "The other prisoners was so scared. We could see them through the bars. I never seen such faces."

The bartender excitedly poured himself a small glass of whiskey and poured it down. "Can't blame 'em much. Suppose you was in for thirty days and a lynch mob came through. You'd be scared they'd get the wrong man."

"That's what I say. It was kind of pitiful. Well, we got to the nigger's cell. He just stood stiff with his eyes closed like he was dead drunk. One of the guys slugged him down and he got up, and then somebody else socked him and he went over and hit his head on the cement floor." Mike leaned over the bar and tapped the polished wood with his forefinger. " 'Course this is only my idea, but I think that killed him. Because I helped get his clothes off, and he never made a wiggle, and when we strung him up he didn't jerk around none. No, sir. I think he was dead all the time, after that second guy smacked him."

"Well, it's all the same in the end."

"No, it ain't. You like to do the thing right. He had it coming to him, and he should have got it." Mike reached into his trousers pocket and brought out a piece of torn blue denim. "That's a piece of the pants he had on."

The bartender bent close and inspected the cloth. He jerked his head up at Mike. "I'll give you a buck for it."

"Oh no, you won't!"

"All right. I'll give you two bucks for half of it."

Mike looked suspiciously at him. "What you want it for?"

"Here! Give me your glass! Have a beer on me. I'll pin it up on the wall with a little card under it. The fellas that come in will like to look at it."

Mike haggled the piece of cloth in two with his pocket knife and accepted two silver dollars from the bartender.

"I know a show card writer," the little man said. "Comes in every day. He'll print me up a nice little card to go under it." He looked wary. "Think the sheriff will arrest anybody?"

" 'Course not. What's he want to start any trouble for? There was a lot of votes in that crowd tonight. Soon as they all go away, the sheriff will come and cut the nigger down and clean up some."

The bartender looked toward the door. "I guess I was wrong about the fellas wanting a drink. It's getting late."

"I guess I'll get along home. I feel tired."

"If you go south, I'll close up and walk a ways with you. I live on south Eighth."

"Why, that's only two blocks from my house. I live on south Sixth. You must go right past my house. Funny I never saw you around."

The bartender washed Mike's glass and took off the long apron. He put on his hat and coat, walked to the door and switched off the red neon sign and the house lights. For a moment the two men stood on the sidewalk looking back toward the park. The city was silent. There was no sound from the park. A policeman walked along a block away, turning his flash into the store windows.

"You see?" said Mike. "Just like nothing happened."

"Well, if the fellas wanted a glass of beer they must have gone someplace else."

"That's what I told you," said Mike.

They swung along the empty street and turned south, out of the business district. "My name's Welch," the bartender said. "I only been in this town about two years."

The loneliness had fallen on Mike again. "It's funny—" he said, and then, "I was born right in this town, right in the house I live in now. I got a wife but no kids. Both of us born right in this town. Everybody knows us."

They walked on for a few blocks. The stores dropped behind and the nice houses with bushy gardens and cut lawns lined the street. The tall shade trees were shadowed on the sidewalk by the street lights. Two night dogs went slowly by, smelling at each other.

Welch said softly—"I wonder what kind of a fella he was— the nigger, I mean."

Mike answered out of his loneliness. "The papers all said he was a fiend. I read all the papers. That's what they all said."

"Yes, I read them, too. But it makes you wonder about him. I've known some pretty nice niggers."

Mike turned his head and spoke protestingly. "Well, I've knew some dam' fine niggers myself. I've worked right 'longside some niggers and they was as nice as any white man you could want to meet. —But not no fiends."

His vehemence silenced little Welch for a moment. Then he said, "You couldn't tell, I guess, what kind of a fella he was?"

"No—he just stood there stiff, with his mouth shut and his eyes tight closed and his hands right down at his sides. And then one of the guys smacked him. It's my idea he was dead when we took him out."

Welch sidled close on the walk. "Nice gardens along here. Must take a lot of money to keep them up." He walked even closer, so that his shoulder touched Mike's arm. "I never been to a lynching. How's it make you feel—afterwards?"

Mike shied away from the contact. "It don't make you feel nothing." He put down his head and increased his pace. The little bartender had nearly to trot to keep up. The street lights were fewer. It was darker and safer. Mike burst out, "Makes you feel kind of cut off and tired, but kind of satisfied, too. Like you done a good job—but tired and kind of sleepy." He slowed his steps. "Look, there's a light in the kitchen. That's where I live. My old lady's waiting up for me." He stopped in front of his little house.

Welch stood nervously beside him. "Come into my place when you want a glass of beer—or a shot. Open till midnight. I treat my friends right." He scampered away like an aged mouse.

Mike called, "Good night."

He walked around the side of his house and went in the back door. His thin, petulant wife was sitting by the open gas oven warming herself. She turned complaining eyes on Mike where he stood in the doorway.

Then her eyes widened and hung on his face. "You been with a woman," she said hoarsely. "What woman you been with?"

Mike laughed. "You think you're pretty slick, don't you? You're a slick one, ain't you? What makes you think I been with a woman?"

She said fiercely, "You think I can't tell by the look on your face that you been with a woman?"

"All right," said Mike. "If you're so slick and know-it-all, I won't tell you nothing. You can just wait for the morning paper."

He saw doubt come into the dissatisfied eyes. "Was it the nigger?" she asked. "Did they get the nigger? Everybody said they was going to."

"Find out for yourself if you're so slick. I ain't going to tell you nothing."

He walked through the kitchen and went into the bathroom. A little mirror hung on the wall. Mike took off his cap and looked at his face. "By God, she was right," he thought. "That's just exactly how I do feel."

Johnny Bear

T HE VILLAGE of Loma is built, as its name implies, on a low round hill that rises like an island out of the flat mouth of the Salinas Valley in central California. To the north and east of the town a black tule swamp stretches for miles, but to the south the marsh has been drained. Rich vegetable land has been the result of the draining, land so black with wealth that the lettuce and cauliflowers grow to giants.

The owners of the swamp to the north of the village began to covet the black land. They banded together and formed a reclamation district. I work for the company which took the contract to put a ditch through. The floating clam-shell digger arrived, was put together and started eating a ditch of open water through the swamp.

I tried living in the floating bunkhouse with the crew for a while, but the mosquitoes that hung in banks over the dredger and the heavy pestilential mist that sneaked out of the swamp every night and slid near to the ground drove me into the village of Loma, where I took a furnished room, the most dismal I have ever seen, in the house of Mrs. Ratz. I might have looked farther, but the idea of having my mail come in care of Mrs. Ratz decided me. After all, I only slept in the bare cold room. I ate my meals in the galley of the floating bunkhouse.

There aren't more than two hundred people in Loma. The Methodist church has the highest place on the hill; its spire is visible for miles. Two groceries, a hardware store, an ancient Masonic Hall and the Buffalo Bar comprise the public buildings. On the side of the hills are the small wooden houses of the population, and on the rich southern flats are the houses of the landowners, small yards usually enclosed by high walls of clipped cypress to keep out the driving afternoon winds.

There was nothing to do in Loma in the evening except to go to the saloon, an old board building with swinging doors and a wooden sidewalk awning. Neither prohibition nor repeal had changed its business, its clientele, or the quality of its whiskey. In the course of an evening every male inhabitant of Loma over fifteen years old came at least once to the Buffalo Bar, had a drink, talked a while and went home.

Fat Carl, the owner and bartender, greeted every newcomer with a phlegmatic sullenness which nevertheless inspired familiarity and affection. His face was sour, his tone downright unfriendly, and yet—I don't know how he did it. I know I felt gratified and warm when Fat Carl knew me well enough to turn his sour pig face to me and say with some impatience, "Well, what's it going to be?" He always asked that although he served only whiskey, and only one kind of whiskey. I have seen him flatly refuse to squeeze some lemon juice into it for a stranger. Fat Carl didn't like fumadiddles. He wore a big towel tied about his middle and he polished the glasses on it as he moved about. The floor was bare wood sprinkled with sawdust, the bar an old store counter, the chairs were hard and straight; the only decorations were the posters and cards and pictures stuck to the wall by candidates for county elections, salesmen and auctioneers. Some of these were many years old. The card of Sheriff Rittal still begged for re-election although Rittal had been dead for seven years.

The Buffalo Bar sounds, even to me, like a terrible place, but when you walked down the night street, over the wooden sidewalks, when the long streamers of swamp fog, like waving, dirty bunting, flapped in your face, when finally you pushed open the swinging doors of Fat Carl's and saw men sitting around talking and drinking, and Fat Carl coming along toward you, it seemed pretty nice. You couldn't get away from it.

There would be a game of the mildest kind of poker going on. Timothy Ratz, the husband of my landlady, would be playing solitaire, cheating pretty badly because he took a drink only when he got it out. I've seen him get it out five times in a row. When he won he piled the cards neatly, stood up and walked with great dignity to the bar. Fat Carl, with a glass half filled before he arrived, asked, "What'll it be?"

"Whiskey," said Timothy gravely.

In the long room, men from the farms and the town sat in the straight hard chairs or stood against the old counter. A soft, monotonous rattle of conversation went on except at times of elections or big prize fights, when there might be orations or loud opinions.

I hated to go out into the damp night, and to hear far off in the swamp the chuttering of the Diesel engine on the dredger and the clang of the bucket, and then to go to my own dismal room at Mrs. Ratz'.

Soon after my arrival in Loma I scraped an acquaintance with Mae Romero, a pretty half-Mexican girl. Sometimes in the evenings I walked with her down the south side of the hill, until the nasty fog drove us back into town. After I escorted her home I dropped in at the bar for a while.

I was sitting in the bar one night talking to Alex Hartnell, who owned a nice little farm. We were talking about black bass fishing, when the front doors opened and swung closed. A hush fell on the men in the room. Alex nudged me and said, "It's Johnny Bear." I looked around.

His name described him better than I can. He looked like a great, stupid, smiling bear. His black matted head bobbed forward and his long arms hung out as though he should have been on all fours and was only standing upright as a trick. His legs were short and bowed, ending with strange, square feet. He was dressed in dark blue denim, but his feet were bare; they didn't seem to be crippled or deformed in any way, but they were square, just as wide as they were long. He stood in the doorway, swinging his arms jerkily the way half-wits do. On his face there was a foolish happy smile. He moved forward and for all his bulk and clumsiness, he seemed to creep. He didn't move like a man, but like some prowling night animal. At the bar he stopped, his little bright eyes went about from face to face expectantly, and he asked, "Whiskey?"

Loma was not a treating town. A man might buy a drink for another if he were pretty sure the other would immediately buy one for him. I was surprised when one of the quiet men laid a coin on the counter. Fat Carl filled the glass. The monster took it and gulped the whiskey.

"What the devil——" I began. But Alex nudged me and said, "Sh."

There began a curious pantomime. Johnny Bear moved to the door and then he came creeping back. The foolish smile never left his face. In the middle of the room he crouched down on his stomach. A voice came from his throat, a voice that seemed familiar to me.

"But you are too beautiful to live in a dirty little town like this."

The voice rose to a soft throaty tone, with just a trace of accent in the words. "You just tell me that."

I'm sure I nearly fainted. The blood pounded in my ears. I flushed. It was my voice coming out of the throat of Johnny Bear, my words, my intonation. And then it was the voice of Mae Romero—exact. If I had not seen the crouching man on the floor I would have called to her. The dialogue went on. Such things sound silly when someone else says them. Johnny Bear went right on, or rather I should say I went right on. He said things and made sounds. Gradually the faces of the men turned from Johnny Bear, turned toward me, and they grinned at me. I could do nothing. I knew that if I tried to stop him I would have a fight on my hands, and so the scene went on, to a finish. When it was over I was cravenly glad Mae Romero had no brothers. What obvious, forced, ridiculous words had come from Johnny Bear. Finally he stood up, still smiling the foolish smile, and he asked again, "Whiskey?"

I think the men in the bar were sorry for me. They looked away from me and talked elaborately to one another. Johnny Bear went to the back of the room, crawled under a round cardtable, curled up like a dog and went to sleep.

Alex Hartnell was regarding me with compassion. "First time you ever heard him?"

"Yes, what in hell is he?"

Alex ignored my question for a moment. "If you're worrying about Mae's reputation, don't. Johnny Bear has followed Mae before."

"But how did he hear us? I didn't see him."

"No one sees or hears Johnny Bear when he's on business. He can move like no movement at all. Know what our young men do when they go out with girls? They take a dog along. Dogs are afraid of Johnny and they can smell him coming."

"But good God! Those voices——"

Alex nodded. "I know. Some of us wrote up to the university about Johnny, and a young man came down. He took a look and then he told us about Blind Tom. Ever hear of Blind Tom?"

"You mean the negro piano player? Yes, I've heard of him."

"Well, Blind Tom was a half-wit. He could hardly talk, but he could imitate anything he heard on the piano, long pieces. They tried him with fine musicians and he reproduced not only the music but every little personal emphasis. To catch him they made little mistakes, and he played the mistakes. He photographed the playing in the tiniest detail. The man says Johnny Bear is the same, only he can photograph words and voices. He tested Johnny with a long passage in Greek and Johnny did it exactly. He doesn't know the words he's saying, he just says them. He hasn't brains enough to make anything up, so you know that what he says is what he heard."

"But why does he do it? Why is he interested in listening if he doesn't understand?"

Alex rolled a cigarette and lighted it. "He isn't, but he loves whiskey. He knows if he listens in windows and comes here and repeats what he hears, someone will give him whiskey. He tries to palm off Mrs. Ratz' conversation in the store, or Jerry Noland arguing with his mother, but he can't get whiskey for such things."

I said, "It's funny somebody hasn't shot him while he was peeking in windows."

Alex picked at his cigarette. "Lots of people have tried, but you just don't see Johnny Bear, and you don't catch him. You keep your windows closed, and even then you talk in a whisper if you don't want to be repeated. You were lucky it was dark tonight. If he had seen you, he might have gone through the action too. You should see Johnny Bear screw up his face to look like a young girl. It's pretty awful."

I looked toward the sprawled figure under the table. Johnny Bear's back was turned to the room. The light fell on his black matted hair. I saw a big fly land on his head, and then I swear I saw the whole scalp shiver the way the skin of a horse shivers under flies. The fly landed again and the moving scalp shook it off. I shuddered too, all over.

Conversation in the room had settled to the bored monotone again. Fat Carl had been polishing a glass on his apron towel for the last ten minutes. A little group of men near me was discussing fighting dogs and fighting cocks, and they switched gradually to bullfighting.

Alex, beside me, said, "Come have a drink."

We walked to the counter. Fat Carl put out two glasses. "What'll it be?"

Neither of us answered. Carl poured out the brown whiskey. He looked sullenly at me and one of his thick, meaty eyelids winked at me solemnly. I don't know why, but I felt flattered. Carl's head twitched back toward the card table. "Got you, didn't he?"

I winked back at him. "Take a dog next time." I imitated his clipped sentences. We drank our whiskey and went back to our chairs. Timothy Ratz won a game of solitaire and piled his cards and moved up on the bar.

I looked back at the table under which Johnny Bear lay. He had rolled over on his stomach. His foolish, smiling face looked out at the room. His head moved and he peered all about, like an animal about to leave its den. And then he came sliding out and stood up. There was a paradox about his movement. He looked twisted and shapeless, and yet he moved with complete lack of effort.

Johnny Bear crept up the room toward the bar, smiling about at the men he passed. In front of the bar his insistent question arose. "Whiskey? Whiskey?" It was like a bird call. I don't know what kind of bird, but I've heard it—two notes on a rising scale, asking a question over and over, "Whiskey? Whiskey?"

The conversation in the room stopped, but no one came forward to lay money on the counter. Johnny smiled plaintively. "Whiskey?"

Then he tried to cozen them. Out of his throat an angry woman's voice issued. "I tell you it was all bone. Twenty cents a pound, and half bone." And then a man, "Yes, ma'am. I didn't know it. I'll give you some sausage to make it up."

Johnny Bear looked around expectantly. "Whiskey?" Still none of the men offered to come forward. Johnny crept to the front of the room and crouched. I whispered, "What's he doing?"

Alex said, "Sh. Looking through a window. Listen!"

A woman's voice came, a cold, sure voice, the words

clipped. "I can't quite understand it. Are you some kind of monster? I wouldn't have believed it if I hadn't seen you."

Another woman's voice answered her, a voice low and hoarse with misery. "Maybe I am a monster. I can't help it. I can't help it."

"You *must* help it," the cold voice broke in. "Why you'd be better dead."

I heard a soft sobbing coming from the thick smiling lips of Johnny Bear. The sobbing of a woman in hopelessness. I looked around at Alex. He was sitting stiffly, his eyes wide open and unblinking. I opened my mouth to whisper a question, but he waved me silent. I glanced about the room. All the men were stiff and listening. The sobbing stopped. "Haven't you ever felt that way, Emalin?"

Alex caught his breath sharply at the name. The cold voice announced, "Certainly not."

"Never in the night? Not ever—ever in your life?"

"If I had," the cold voice said, "if ever I had, I would cut that part of me away. Now stop your whining, Amy. I won't stand for it. If you don't get control of your nerves I'll see about having some medical treatment for you. Now go to your prayers."

Johnny Bear smiled on. "Whiskey?"

Two men advanced without a word and put down coins. Fat Carl filled two glasses and, when Johnny Bear tossed off one after the other, Carl filled one again. Everyone knew by that how moved he was. There were no drinks on the house at the Buffalo Bar. Johnny Bear smiled about the room and then he went out with that creeping gait of his. The doors folded together after him, slowly and without a sound.

Conversation did not spring up again. Everyone in the room seemed to have a problem to settle in his own mind. One by one they drifted out and the back-swing of the doors brought in little puffs of tule fog. Alex got up and walked out and I followed him.

The night was nasty with the evil-smelling fog. It seemed to cling to the buildings and to reach out with free arms into the air. I doubled my pace and caught up with Alex. "What was it?" I demanded. "What was it all about?"

For a moment I thought he wouldn't answer. But then he

stopped and turned to me. "Oh, damn it. Listen! Every town has its aristocrats, its family above reproach. Emalin and Amy Hawkins are our aristocrats, maiden ladies, kind people. Their father was a congressman. I don't like this. Johnny Bear shouldn't do it. Why! they feed him. Those men shouldn't give him whiskey. He'll haunt that house now. . . . Now he knows he can get whiskey for it."

I asked, "Are they relatives of yours?"

"No, but they're—why, they aren't like other people. They have the farm next to mine. Some Chinese farm it on shares. You see, it's hard to explain. The Hawkins women, they're symbols. They're what we tell our kids when we want to— well, to describe good people."

"Well," I protested, "nothing Johnny Bear said would hurt them, would it?"

"I don't know. I don't know what it means. I mean, I kind of know. Oh! Go on to bed. I didn't bring the Ford. I'm going to walk out home." He turned and hurried into that slow squirming mist.

I walked along to Mrs. Ratz' boarding house. I could hear the chuttering of the Diesel engine off in the swamp and the clang of the big steel mouth that ate its way through the ground. It was Saturday night. The dredger would stop at seven Sunday morning and rest until midnight Sunday. I could tell by the sound that everything was all right. I climbed the narrow stairs to my room. Once in bed I left the light burning for a while and stared at the pale insipid flowers on the wall-paper. I thought of those two voices speaking out of Johnny Bear's mouth. They were authentic voices, not reproductions. Remembering the tones, I could see the women who had spoken, the chill-voiced Emalin, and the loose, misery-broken face of Amy. I wondered what caused the misery. Was it just the lonely suffering of a middle-aged woman? It hardly seemed so to me, for there was too much fear in the voice. I went to sleep with the light on and had to get up later and turn it off.

About eight the next morning I walked down across the swamp to the dredger. The crew was busy bending some new wire to the drums and coiling the worn cable for removal. I looked over the job and at about eleven o'clock walked back to Loma. In front of Mrs. Ratz' boarding house Alex Hartnell sat in a model T Ford touring car. He called to me, "I was just going to the dredger to get you. I knocked off a couple of chickens this morning. Thought you might like to come out and help with them."

I accepted joyfully. Our cook was a good cook, a big pasty man; but lately I had found a dislike for him arising in me. He smoked Cuban cigarettes in a bamboo holder. I didn't like the way his fingers twitched in the morning. His hands were clean—floury like a miller's hands. I never knew before why they called them moth millers, those little flying bugs. Anyway I climbed into the Ford beside Alex and we drove down the hill to the rich land of the southwest. The sun shone brilliantly on the black earth. When I was little, a Catholic boy told me that the sun always shone on Sunday, if only for a moment, because it was God's day. I always meant to keep track to see if it were true. We rattled down to the level plain.

Alex shouted, "Remember about the Hawkinses?"

"Of course I remember."

He pointed ahead. "That's the house."

Little of the house could be seen, for a high thick hedge of cypress surrounded it. There must be a small garden inside the square too. Only the roof and the tops of the windows showed over the hedge. I could see that the house was painted tan, trimmed with dark brown, a combination favored for railroad stations and schools in California. There were two wicket gates in the front and side of the hedge. The barn was outside the green barrier to the rear of the house. The hedge was clipped square. It looked incredibly thick and strong.

"The hedge keeps the wind out," Alex shouted above the roar of the Ford.

"It doesn't keep Johnny Bear out," I said.

A shadow crossed his face. He waved at a whitewashed square building standing out in the field. "That's where the Chink share-croppers live. Good workers. I wish I had some like them."

At that moment from behind the corner of the hedge a horse and buggy appeared and turned into the road. The grey horse was old but well groomed, the buggy shiny and the harness polished. There was a big silver H on the outside of each blinder. It seemed to me that the check-rein was too short for such an old horse.

Alex cried, "There they are now, on their way to church."

We took off our hats and bowed to the women as they went by, and they nodded formally to us. I had a good look at them. It was a shock to me. They looked almost exactly as I thought they would. Johnny Bear was more monstrous even than I had known, if by the tone of voice he could describe the features of his people. I didn't have to ask which was Emalin and which was Amy. The clear straight eyes, the sharp sure chin, the mouth cut with the precision of a diamond, the stiff, curveless figure, that was Emalin. Amy was very like her, but so unlike. Her edges were soft. Her eyes were warm, her mouth full. There was a swell to her breast, and yet she did look like Emalin. But whereas Emalin's mouth was straight by nature, Amy *held* her mouth straight. Emalin must have been fifty or fifty-five and Amy about ten years younger. I had only a moment to look at them, and I never saw them again. It seems strange that I don't know anyone in the world better than those two women.

Alex was shouting, "You see what I meant about aristocrats?"

I nodded. It was easy to see. A community would feel kind of—safe, having women like that about. A place like Loma with its fogs, with its great swamp like a hideous sin, needed, really needed, the Hawkins women. A few years there might do things to a man's mind if those women weren't there to balance matters.

It was a good dinner. Alex's sister fried the chicken in butter and did everything else right. I grew more suspicious and uncharitable toward our cook. We sat around in the dining-room and drank really good brandy.

I said, "I can't see why you ever go into the Buffalo. That whiskey is——"

"I know," said Alex. "But the Buffalo is the mind of Loma. It's our newspaper, our theatre and our club."

This was so true that when Alex started the Ford and prepared to take me back I knew, and he knew, we would go for an hour or two to the Buffalo Bar.

We were nearly into town. The feeble lights of the car splashed about on the road. Another car rattled toward us. Alex swung across the road and stopped. "It's the doctor, Doctor Holmes," he explained. The oncoming car pulled up because it couldn't get around us. Alex called, "Say, Doc, I was going to ask you to take a look at my sister. She's got a swelling on her throat."

Doctor Holmes called back, "All right, Alex, I'll take a look. Pull out, will you? I'm in a hurry."

Alex was deliberate. "Who's sick, Doc?"

"Why, Miss Amy had a little spell. Miss Emalin phoned in and asked me to hurry. Get out of the way, will you?"

Alex squawked his car back and let the doctor by. We drove on. I was about to remark that the night was clear when, looking ahead, I saw the rags of fog creeping around the hill from the swamp side and climbing like slow snakes on the top of Loma. The Ford shuddered to a stop in front of the Buffalo. We went in.

Fat Carl moved toward us, wiping a glass on his apron. He reached under the bar for the nearby bottle. "What'll it be?"

"Whiskey."

For a moment a faint smile seemed to flit over the fat sullen face. The room was full. My dredger crew was there, all except the cook. He was probably on the scow, smoking his Cuban cigarettes in a bamboo holder. He didn't drink. That was enough to make me suspicious of him. Two deck hands and an engineer and three levermen were there. The levermen were arguing about a cutting. The old lumber adage certainly held for them: "Women in the woods and logging in the honky-tonk."

That was the quietest bar I ever saw. There weren't any fights, not much singing and no tricks. Somehow the sullen baleful eyes of Fat Carl made drinking a quiet, efficient business rather than a noisy game. Timothy Ratz was playing solitaire at one of the round tables. Alex and I drank our whiskey. No chairs were available, so we just stayed leaning against the bar, talking about sports and markets and adventures we had had or pretended we had—just a casual barroom conversation. Now and then we bought another drink. I guess we hung

around for a couple of hours. Alex had already said he was
going home, and I felt like it. The dredger crew trooped out,
for they had to start to work at midnight.

The doors unfolded silently, and Johnny Bear crept into the
room, swinging his long arms, nodding his big hairy head and
smiling foolishly about. His square feet were like cats' feet.

"Whiskey?" he chirruped. No one encouraged him. He got
out his wares. He was down on his stomach the way he had
been when he got me. Sing-song nasal words came out, Chinese I thought. And then it seemed to me that the same words
were repeated in another voice, slower and not nasally. Johnny
Bear raised his shaggy head and asked, "Whiskey?" He got to
his feet with effortless ease. I was interested. I wanted to see
him perform. I slid a quarter along the bar. Johnny gulped
his drink. A moment later I wished I hadn't. I was afraid to
look at Alex; for Johnny Bear crept to the middle of the room
and took that window pose of his.

The chill voice of Emalin said, "She's in here, doctor." I
closed my eyes against the looks of Johnny Bear, and the moment I did he went out. It was Emalin Hawkins who had
spoken.

I had heard the doctor's voice in the road, and it was his
veritable voice that replied, "Ah—you said a fainting fit?"

"Yes, doctor."

There was a little pause, and then the doctor's voice again,
very softly, "Why did she do it, Emalin?"

"Why did she do what?" There was almost a threat in the
question.

"I'm your doctor, Emalin. I was your father's doctor.
You've got to tell me things. Don't you think I've seen that
kind of a mark on the neck before? How long was she hanging
before you got her down?"

There was a longer pause then. The chill left the woman's
voice. It was soft, almost a whisper. "Two or three minutes.
Will she be all right, doctor?"

"Oh, yes, she'll come around. She's not badly hurt. Why
did she do it?"

The answering voice was even colder than it had been at
first. It was frozen. "I don't know, sir."

"You mean you won't tell me?"

"I mean what I say."

Then the doctor's voice went on giving directions for treatment, rest, milk and a little whiskey. "Above all, be gentle," he said. "Above everything, be gentle with her."

Emalin's voice trembled a little. "You would never—tell, doctor?"

"I'm your doctor," he said softly. "Of course I won't tell. I'll send down some sedatives tonight."

"Whiskey?" My eyes jerked open. There was the horrible Johnny Bear smiling around the room.

The men were silent, ashamed. Fat Carl looked at the floor. I turned apologetically to Alex, for I was really responsible. "I didn't know he'd do that," I said. "I'm sorry."

I walked out the door and went to the dismal room at Mrs. Ratz'. I opened the window and looked out into that coiling, pulsing fog. Far off in the marsh I heard the Diesel engine start slowly and warm up. And after a while I heard the clang of the big bucket as it went to work on the ditch.

The next morning one of those series of accidents so common in construction landed on us. One of the new wires parted on the in-swing and dropped the bucket on one of the pontoons, sinking it and the works in eight feet of ditch water. When we sunk a dead man and got a line out to it to pull us from the water, the line parted and clipped the legs neatly off one of the deck hands. We bound the stumps and rushed him to Salinas. And then little accidents happened. A leverman developed blood poisoning from a wire scratch. The cook finally justified my opinion by trying to sell a little can of marijuana to the engineer. Altogether there wasn't much peace in the outfit. It was two weeks before we were going again with a new pontoon, a new deck hand and a new cook.

The new cook was a sly, dark, little long-nosed man, with a gift for subtle flattery.

My contact with the social life of Loma had gone to pot, but when the bucket was clanging into the mud again and the big old Diesel was chuttering away in the swamp I walked out to Alex Hartnell's farm one night. Passing the Hawkins place, I peered in through one of the little wicket gates in the cypress hedge. The house was dark, more than dark because a low light glowed in one window. There was a gentle wind that night, blowing balls of fog like tumbleweeds along the ground. I walked in the clear a moment, and then was swallowed in a thick mist, and then was in the clear again. In the starlight I could see those big silver fog balls moving like elementals across the fields. I thought I heard a soft moaning in the Hawkins yard behind the hedge, and once when I came suddenly out of the fog I saw a dark figure hurrying along in the field, and I knew from the dragging footsteps that it was one of the Chinese field hands walking in sandals. The Chinese eat a great many things that have to be caught at night.

Alex came to the door when I knocked. He seemed glad to see me. His sister was away. I sat down by his stove and he brought out a bottle of that nice brandy. "I heard you were having some trouble," he said.

I explained the difficulty. "It seems to come in series. The men have it figured out that accidents come in groups of three, five, seven and nine."

Alex nodded. "I kind of feel that way myself."

"How are the Hawkins sisters?" I asked. "I thought I heard someone crying as I went by."

Alex seemed reluctant to talk about them, and at the same time eager to talk about them. "I stopped over about a week ago. Miss Amy isn't feeling very well. I didn't see her. I only saw Miss Emalin." Then Alex broke out, "There's something hanging over those people, something——"

"You almost seem to be related to them," I said.

"Well, their father and my father were friends. We called the girls Aunt Amy and Aunt Emalin. They can't do anything bad. It wouldn't be good for any of us if the Hawkins sisters weren't the Hawkins sisters."

"The community conscience?" I asked.

"The safe thing," he cried. "The place where a kid can get gingerbread. The place where a girl can get reassurance. They're proud, but they believe in things we hope are true. And they live as though—well, as though honesty really is the best policy and charity really is its own reward. We need them."

"I see."

"But Miss Emalin is fighting something terrible and—I don't think she's going to win."

"What do you mean?"

"I don't know what I mean. But I've thought I should shoot Johnny Bear and throw him in the swamp. I've really thought about doing it."

"It's not his fault," I argued. "He's just a kind of recording and reproducing device, only you use a glass of whiskey instead of a nickel."

We talked of some other things then, and after a while I walked back to Loma. It seemed to me that the fog was clinging to the cypress hedge of the Hawkins house, and it seemed to me that a lot of the fog balls were clustered about it and others were slowly moving in. I smiled as I walked along at the way a man's thought can rearrange nature to fit his thoughts. There was no light in the house as I went by.

A nice steady routine settled on my work. The big bucket cut out the ditch ahead of it. The crew felt the trouble was over too, and that helped, and the new cook flattered the men so successfully that they would have eaten fried cement. The personality of a cook has a lot more to do with the happiness of a dredger crew than his cooking has.

In the evening of the second day after my visit to Alex I walked down the wooden sidewalk trailing a streamer of fog behind me and went into the Buffalo Bar. Fat Carl moved toward me polishing the whiskey glass. I cried, "Whiskey," before he had a chance to ask what it would be. I took my glass and went to one of the straight chairs. Alex was not there. Timothy Ratz was playing solitaire and having a phenomenal run of luck. He got it out four times in a row and had a drink each time. More and more men arrived. I don't know what we would have done without the Buffalo Bar.

At about ten o'clock the news came. Thinking about such things afterwards, you never can remember quite what transpired. Someone comes in; a whisper starts; suddenly everyone knows what has happened, knows details. Miss Amy had committed suicide. Who brought in the story? I don't know. She had hanged herself. There wasn't much talk in the barroom about it. I could see the men were trying to get straight on it. It was a thing that didn't fit into their schemes. They stood in groups, talking softly.

The swinging doors opened slowly and Johnny Bear crept in, his great hairy head rolling, and that idiot smile on his face. His square feet slid quietly over the floor. He looked about and chirruped, "Whiskey? Whiskey for Johnny?"

Now those men really wanted to know. They were ashamed of wanting to know, but their whole mental system required the knowledge. Fat Carl poured out a drink. Timothy Ratz put down his cards and stood up. Johnny Bear gulped the whiskey. I closed my eyes.

The doctor's tone was harsh. "Where is she, Emalin?"

I've never heard a voice like that one that answered, cold control, layer and layer of control, but cold penetrated by the most awful heartbreak. It was a monotonous tone, emotionless, and yet the heartbreak got into the vibrations. "She's in here, doctor."

"H-m-m." A long pause. "She was hanging a long time."

"I don't know how long, doctor."

"Why did she do it, Emalin?"

The monotone again. "I don't—know, doctor."

A longer pause, and then, "H-m-m. Emalin, did you know she was going to have a baby?"

The chill voice cracked and a sigh came through. "Yes, doctor," very softly.

"If that was why you didn't find her for so long—— No, Emalin, I didn't mean that, poor dear."

The control was back in Emalin's voice. "Can you make out the certificate without mentioning——"

"Of course I can, sure I can. And I'll speak to the undertaker, too. You needn't worry."

"Thank you, doctor."

"I'll go and telephone now. I won't leave you here alone. Come into the other room, Emalin. I'm going to fix you a sedative. . . ."

"Whiskey? Whiskey for Johnny?" I saw the smile and the rolling hairy head. Fat Carl poured out another glass. Johnny Bear drank it and then crept to the back of the room and crawled under a table and went to sleep.

No one spoke. The men moved up to the bar and laid down their coins silently. They looked bewildered, for a system had fallen. A few minutes later Alex came into the silent room. He walked quickly over to me. "You've heard?" he asked softly.

"Yes."

"I've been afraid," he cried. "I told you a couple of nights ago. I've been afraid."

I said, "Did you know she was pregnant?"

Alex stiffened. He looked around the room and then back at me. "Johnny Bear?" he asked.

I nodded.

Alex ran his palm over his eyes. "I don't believe it." I was about to answer when I heard a little scuffle and looked to the back of the room. Johnny Bear crawled like a badger out of his hole and stood up and crept toward the bar.

"Whiskey?" He smiled expectantly at Fat Carl.

Then Alex stepped out and addressed the room. "Now you guys listen! This has gone far enough. I don't want any more of it." If he had expected opposition he was disappointed. I saw the men nodding to one another.

"Whiskey for Johnny?"

Alex turned on the idiot. "You ought to be ashamed. Miss Amy gave you food, and she gave you all the clothes you ever had."

Johnny smiled at him. "Whiskey?"

He got out his tricks. I heard the sing-song nasal language that sounded like Chinese. Alex looked relieved.

And then the other voice, slow, hesitant, repeating the words without the nasal quality.

Alex sprang so quickly that I didn't see him move. His fist splatted into Johnny Bear's smiling mouth. "I told you there was enough of it," he shouted.

Johnny Bear recovered his balance. His lips were split and bleeding, but the smile was still there. He moved slowly and without effort. His arms enfolded Alex as the tentacles of an anemone enfold a crab. Alex bent backward. Then I jumped and grabbed one of the arms and wrenched at it, and could not tear it loose. Fat Carl came rolling over the counter with a bung-starter in his hand. And he beat the matted head until the arms relaxed and Johnny Bear crumpled. I caught Alex and helped him to a chair. "Are you hurt?"

He tried to get his breath. "My back's wrenched, I guess," he said. "I'll be all right."

"Got your Ford outside? I'll drive you home."

Neither of us looked at the Hawkins place as we went by. I didn't lift my eyes off the road. I got Alex to his own dark house and helped him to bed and poured a hot brandy into him. He hadn't spoken all the way home. But after he was propped in the bed he demanded, "You don't think anyone noticed, do you? I caught him in time, didn't I?"

"What are you talking about? I don't know yet why you hit him."

"Well, listen," he said. "I'll have to stay close for a little while with this back. If you hear anyone say anything, you stop it, won't you? Don't let them say it."

"I don't know what you're talking about."

He looked into my eyes for a moment. "I guess I can trust you," he said. "That second voice—that was Miss Amy."

The Murder

THIS HAPPENED a number of years ago in Monterey County, in central California. The Cañon del Castillo is one of those valleys in the Santa Lucia range which lie between its many spurs and ridges. From the main Cañon del Castillo a number of little arroyos cut back into the mountains, oak-wooded canyons, heavily brushed with poison oak and sage. At the head of the canyon there stands a tremendous stone castle, buttressed and towered like those strongholds the Crusaders put up in the path of their conquests. Only a close visit to the castle shows it to be a strange accident of time and water and erosion working on soft, stratified sandstone. In the distance the ruined battlements, the gates, the towers, even the arrow slits, require little imagination to make out.

Below the castle, on the nearly level floor of the canyon, stand the old ranch house, a weathered and mossy barn and a warped feeding-shed for cattle. The house is deserted; the doors, swinging on rusted hinges, squeal and bang on nights when the wind courses down from the castle. Not many people visit the house. Sometimes a crowd of boys tramp through the rooms, peering into empty closets and loudly defying the ghosts they deny.

Jim Moore, who owns the land, does not like to have people about the house. He rides up from his new house, farther down the valley, and chases the boys away. He has put "No Trespassing" signs on his fences to keep curious and morbid people out. Sometimes he thinks of burning the old house down, but then a strange and powerful relation with the swinging doors, the blind and desolate windows, forbids the destruction. If he should burn the house he would destroy a great and important piece of his life. He knows that when he goes to town with his plump and still pretty wife, people turn and look at his retreating back with awe and some admiration.

Jim Moore was born in the old house and grew up in it. He knew every grained and weathered board of the barn, every smooth, worn manger-rack. His mother and father were both dead when he was thirty. He celebrated his majority by raising a beard. He sold the pigs and decided never to have any more. At last he bought a fine Guernsey bull to improve his stock, and he began to go to Monterey on Saturday nights, to get drunk and to talk with the noisy girls of the Three Star.

Within a year Jim Moore married Jelka Sepic, a Jugo-Slav girl, daughter of a heavy and patient farmer of Pine Canyon. Jim was not proud of her foreign family, of her many brothers and sisters and cousins, but he delighted in her beauty. Jelka had eyes as large and questioning as a doe's eyes. Her nose was thin and sharply faceted, and her lips were deep and soft. Jelka's skin always startled Jim, for between night and night he forgot how beautiful it was. She was so smooth and quiet and gentle, such a good housekeeper, that Jim often thought with disgust of her father's advice on the wedding day. The old man, bleary and bloated with festival beer, elbowed Jim in the ribs and grinned suggestively, so that his little dark eyes almost disappeared behind puffed and wrinkled lids.

"Don't be big fool, now," he said. "Jelka is Slav girl. He's not like American girl. If he is bad, beat him. If he's good too long, beat him too. I beat his mama. Papa beat my mama. Slav girl! He's not like a man that don't beat hell out of him."

"I wouldn't beat Jelka," Jim said.

The father giggled and nudged him again with his elbow. "Don't be big fool," he warned. "Sometime you see." He rolled back to the beer barrel.

Jim found soon enough that Jelka was not like American girls. She was very quiet. She never spoke first, but only answered his questions, and then with soft short replies. She learned her husband as she learned passages of Scripture. After they had been married a while, Jim never wanted for any habitual thing in the house but Jelka had it ready for him before he could ask. She was a fine wife, but there was no companionship in her. She never talked. Her great eyes followed him, and when he smiled, sometimes she smiled too, a distant and covered smile. Her knitting and mending and sewing were interminable. There she sat, watching her wise hands, and she seemed to regard with wonder and pride the little white hands that could do such nice and useful things. She was so much like an animal that sometimes Jim patted her head and neck under the same impulse that made him stroke a horse.

In the house Jelka was remarkable. No matter what time Jim came in from the hot dry range or from the bottom farm land, his dinner was exactly, steamingly ready for him. She watched while he ate, and pushed the dishes close when he needed them, and filled his cup when it was empty.

Early in the marriage he told her things that happened on the farm, but she smiled at him as a foreigner does who wishes to be agreeable even though he doesn't understand.

"The stallion cut himself on the barbed wire," he said.

And she replied, "Yes," with a downward inflection that held neither question nor interest.

He realized before long that he could not get in touch with her in any way. If she had a life apart, it was so remote as to be beyond his reach. The barrier in her eyes was not one that could be removed, for it was neither hostile nor intentional.

At night he stroked her straight black hair and her unbelievably smooth golden shoulders, and she whimpered a little with pleasure. Only in the climax of his embrace did she seem to have a life apart, fierce and passionate. And then immediately she lapsed into the alert and painfully dutiful wife.

"Why don't you ever talk to me?" he demanded. "Don't you want to talk to me?"

"Yes," she said. "What do you want me to say?" She spoke the language of his race out of a mind that was foreign to his race.

When a year had passed, Jim began to crave the company of women, the chattery exchange of small talk, the shrill pleasant insults, the shame-sharpened vulgarity. He began to go again to town, to drink and to play with the noisy girls of the Three Star. They liked him there for his firm, controlled face and for his readiness to laugh.

"Where's your wife?" they demanded.

"Home in the barn," he responded. It was a never-failing joke.

Saturday afternoons he saddled a horse and put a rifle in the scabbard in case he should see a deer. Always he asked, "You don't mind staying alone?"

"No. I don't mind."

At once he asked, "Suppose someone should come?"

Her eyes sharpened for a moment, and then she smiled. "I would send them away," she said.

"I'll be back about noon tomorrow. It's too far to ride in the night." He felt that she knew where he was going, but she never protested nor gave any sign of disapproval. "You should have a baby," he said.

Her face lighted up. "Some time God will be good," she said eagerly.

He was sorry for her loneliness. If only she visited with the other women of the canyon she would be less lonely, but she had no gift for visiting. Once every month or so she put horses to the buckboard and went to spend an afternoon with her mother, and with the brood of brothers and sisters and cousins who lived in her father's house.

"A fine time you'll have," Jim said to her. "You'll gabble your crazy language like ducks for a whole afternoon. You'll giggle with that big grown cousin of yours with the embarrassed face. If I could find any fault with you, I'd call you a damn foreigner." He remembered how she blessed the bread with the sign of the cross before she put it in the oven, how she knelt at the bedside every night, how she had a holy picture tacked to the wall in the closet.

One Saturday of a hot dusty June, Jim cut oats in the farm flat. The day was long. It was after six o'clock when the mower tumbled the last band of oats. He drove the clanking machine up into the barnyard and backed it into the implement shed, and there he unhitched the horses and turned them out to graze on the hills over Sunday. When he entered the kitchen Jelka was just putting his dinner on the table. He washed his hands and face and sat down to eat.

"I'm tired," he said, "but I think I'll go to Monterey anyway. There'll be a full moon."

Her soft eyes smiled.

"I'll tell you what I'll do," he said. "If you would like to go, I'll hitch up a rig and take you with me."

She smiled again and shook her head. "No, the stores would be closed. I would rather stay here."

"Well, all right, I'll saddle the horse then. I didn't think I was going. The stock's all turned out. Maybe I can catch a horse easy. Sure you don't want to go?"

"If it was early, and I could go to the stores—but it will be ten o'clock when you get there."

"Oh, no—well, anyway, on horseback I'll make it a little after nine."

Her mouth smiled to itself, but her eyes watched him for the development of a wish. Perhaps because he was tired from the long day's work, he demanded, "What are you thinking about?"

"Thinking about? I remember, you used to ask that nearly every day when we were first married."

"But what are you?" he insisted irritably.

"Oh—I'm thinking about the eggs under the black hen." She got up and went to the big calendar on the wall. "They will hatch tomorrow or maybe Monday."

It was almost dusk when he had finished shaving and putting on his blue serge suit and his new boots. Jelka had the dishes washed and put away. As Jim went through the kitchen he saw that she had taken the lamp to the table near the window, and that she sat beside it knitting a brown wool sock.

"Why do you sit there tonight?" he asked. "You always sit over here. You do funny things sometimes."

Her eyes arose slowly from her flying hands. "The moon," she said quietly. "You said it would be full tonight. I want to see the moon rise."

"But you're silly. You can't see it from that window. I thought you knew direction better than that."

She smiled remotely. "I will look out of the bedroom window, then."

Jim put on his black hat and went out. Walking through the dark empty barn, he took a halter from the rack. On the grassy sidehill he whistled high and shrill. The horses stopped feeding and moved slowly in towards him, and stopped twenty feet away. Carefully he approached his bay gelding and moved his hand from its rump along its side and up and over its neck. The halter-strap clicked in its buckle. Jim turned and led the horse back to the barn. He threw his saddle on and cinched it tight, put his silver-bound bridle over the stiff ears, buckled the throat latch, knotted the tie-rope about the gelding's neck and fastened the neat coil-end to the saddle string. Then he slipped the halter and led the horse to the house. A radiant crown of soft red light lay over the eastern hills. The full moon would rise before the valley had completely lost the daylight.

In the kitchen Jelka still knitted by the window. Jim strode to the corner of the room and took up his 30-30 carbine. As he rammed cartridges into the magazine, he said, "The moon glow is on the hills. If you are going to see it rise, you better go outside now. It's going to be a good red one at rising."

"In a moment," she replied, "when I come to the end here." He went to her and patted her sleek head.

"Good night. I'll probably be back by noon tomorrow." Her dusky black eyes followed him out of the door.

Jim thrust the rifle into his saddle-scabbard, and mounted and swung his horse down the canyon. On his right, from behind the blackening hills, the great red moon slid rapidly up. The double light of the day's last afterglow and the rising moon thickened the outlines of the trees and gave a mysterious new perspective to the hills. The dusty oaks shimmered and glowed, and the shade under them was black as velvet. A huge, long-legged shadow of a horse and half a man rode to the left and slightly ahead of Jim. From the ranches near and distant came the sound of dogs tuning up for a night of song. And the roosters crowed, thinking a new dawn had come too quickly. Jim lifted the gelding to a trot. The spattering hoof-steps echoed back from the castle behind him. He thought of blond May at the Three Star in Monterey. "I'll be late. Maybe someone else'll have her," he thought. The moon was clear of the hills now.

Jim had gone a mile when he heard the hoofbeats of a horse coming towards him. A horseman cantered up and pulled to a stop. "That you, Jim?"

"Yes. Oh, hello, George."

"I was just riding up to your place. I want to tell you—you know the springhead at the upper end of my land?"

"Yes, I know."

"Well, I was up there this afternoon. I found a dead camp-fire and a calf's head and feet. The skin was in the fire, half burned, but I pulled it out and it had your brand."

"The hell," said Jim. "How old was the fire?"

"The ground was still warm in the ashes. Last night, I guess. Look, Jim, I can't go up with you. I've got to go to town, but I thought I'd tell you, so you could take a look around."

Jim asked quietly, "Any idea how many men?"

"No. I didn't look close."

"Well, I guess I better go up and look. I was going to town too. But if there are thieves working, I don't want to lose any more stock. I'll cut up through your land if you don't mind, George."

"I'd go with you, but I've got to go to town. You got a gun with you?"

"Oh yes, sure. Here under my leg. Thanks for telling me."

"That's all right. Cut through any place you want. Good night." The neighbour turned his horse and cantered back in the direction from which he had come.

For a few moments Jim sat in the moonlight, looking down at his stilted shadow. He pulled his rifle from its scabbard, levered a cartridge into the chamber, and held the gun across the pommel of his saddle. He turned left from the road, went up the little ridge, through the oak grove, over the grassy hogback and down the other side into the next canyon.

In half an hour he had found the deserted camp. He turned over the heavy, leathery calf's head and felt its dusty tongue to judge by the dryness how long it had been dead. He lighted a match and looked at his brand on the half-burned hide. At last he mounted his horse again, rode over the bald grassy hills and crossed into his own land.

A warm summer wind was blowing on the hilltops. The moon, as it quartered up the sky, lost its redness and turned the colour of strong tea. Among the hills the coyotes were singing, and the dogs at the ranch houses below joined them with broken-hearted howling. The dark green oaks below and the yellow summer grass showed their colours in the moonlight.

Jim followed the sound of the cowbells to his herd, and found them eating quietly, and a few deer feeding with them. He listened for the sound of hoofbeats or the voices of men on the wind.

It was after eleven when he turned his horse towards home. He rounded the west tower of the sandstone castle, rode through the shadow and out into the moonlight again. Below, the roofs of his barn and house shone dully. The bedroom window cast back a streak of reflection.

The feeding horses lifted their heads as Jim came down through the pasture. Their eyes glinted redly when they turned their heads.

Jim had almost reached the corral fence—he heard a horse stamping in the barn. His hand jerked the gelding down. He listened. It came again, the stamping from the barn. Jim lifted his rifle and dismounted silently. He turned his horse loose and crept towards the barn.

In the blackness he could hear the grinding of the horse's teeth as it chewed hay. He moved along the barn until he came to the occupied stall. After a moment of listening he scratched a match on the butt of his rifle. A saddled and bridled horse was tied in the stall. The bit was slipped under the chin and the cinch loosened. The horse stopped eating and turned its head towards the light.

Jim blew out the match and walked quickly out of the barn. He sat on the edge of the horse trough and looked into the water. His thoughts came so slowly that he put them into words and said them under his breath.

"Shall I look through the window? No. My head would throw a shadow in the room."

He regarded the rifle in his hand. Where it had been rubbed and handled, the black gun finish had worn off, leaving the metal silvery.

At last he stood up with decision and moved towards the house. At the steps, an extended foot tried each board tenderly before he put his weight on it. The three ranch dogs came out from under the house and shook themselves, stretched and sniffed, wagged their tails and went back to bed.

The kitchen was dark, but Jim knew where every piece of furniture was. He put out his hand and touched the corner of the table, a chair back, the towel hanger, as he went along. He crossed the room so silently that even he could hear only his breath and the whisper of his trouser legs together, and the beating of his watch in his pocket. The bedroom door stood open and spilled a patch of moonlight on the kitchen floor. Jim reached the door at last and peered through.

The moonlight lay on the white bed. Jim saw Jelka lying on her back, one soft bare arm flung across her forehead and eyes. He could not see who the man was, for his head was turned away. Jim watched, holding his breath. Then Jelka twitched in her sleep and the man rolled his head and sighed—Jelka's cousin, her grown, embarrassed cousin.

Jim turned and quickly stole back across the kitchen and down the back steps. He walked up the yard to the water-trough again, and sat down on the edge of it. The moon was white as chalk, and it swam in the water, and lighted the straws and barley dropped by the horses' mouths. Jim could see the mosquito wigglers, tumbling up and down, end over end, in the water, and he could see a newt lying in the sun moss in the bottom of the trough.

He cried a few dry, hard, smothered sobs, and wondered why, for his thought was of the grassed hilltops and of the lonely summer wind whisking along.

His thought turned to the way his mother used to hold a bucket to catch the throat blood when his father killed a pig. She stood as far away as possible and held the bucket at arms'-length to keep her clothes from getting spattered.

Jim dipped his hand into the trough and stirred the moon to broken, swirling streams of light. He wetted his forehead with his damp hands and stood up. This time he did not move so quietly, but he crossed the kitchen on tiptoe and stood in the bedroom door. Jelka moved her arm and opened her eyes a little. Then the eyes sprang wide, then they glistened with moisture. Jim looked into her eyes; his face was empty of expression. A little drop ran out of Jelka's nose and lodged in the hollow of her upper lip. She stared back at him.

Jim cocked the rifle. The steel click sounded through the house. The man on the bed stirred uneasily in his sleep. Jim's hands were quivering. He raised the gun to his shoulder and held it tightly to keep from shaking. Over the sights he saw the little white square between the man's brows and hair. The front sight wavered a moment and then came to rest.

The gun crash tore the air. Jim, still looking down the barrel, saw the whole bed jolt under the blow. A small, black, bloodless hole was in the man's forehead. But behind, the hollow-point took brain and bone and splashed them on the pillow.

Jelka's cousin gurgled in his throat. His hands came crawling out from under the covers like big white spiders, and they walked for a moment, then shuddered and fell quiet.

Jim looked slowly back at Jelka. Her nose was running. Her eyes had moved from him to the end of the rifle. She whined softly, like a cold puppy.

Jim turned in panic. His boot heels beat on the kitchen floor, but outside, he moved slowly towards the water-trough again. There was a taste of salt in his throat, and his heart heaved painfully. He pulled his hat off and dipped his head into the water. Then he leaned over and vomited on the ground. In the house he could hear Jelka moving about. She whimpered like a puppy. Jim straightened up, weak and dizzy.

He walked tiredly through the corral and into the pasture. His saddled horse came at his whistle. Automatically he tightened the cinch, mounted and rode away, down the road to the valley. The squat black shadow traveled under him. The moon sailed high and white. The uneasy dogs barked monotonously.

At daybreak a buckboard and pair trotted up to the ranch yard, scattering the chickens. A deputy sheriff and a coroner sat in the seat. Jim Moore half reclined against his saddle in the wagon-box. His tired gelding followed behind. The deputy sheriff set the brake and wrapped the lines around it. The men dismounted.

Jim asked, "Do I have to go in? I'm too tired and wrought up to see it now."

The coroner pulled his lip and studied. "Oh, I guess not. We'll tend to things and look around."

Jim sauntered away towards the water-trough. "Say," he called, "kind of clean up a little, will you? You know."

The men went on into the house.

In a few minutes they emerged, carrying the stiffened body between them. It was wrapped up in a comforter. They eased it up into the wagon-box. Jim walked back towards them. "Do I have to go in with you now?"

"Where's your wife, Mr. Moore?" the deputy sheriff demanded.

"I don't know," he said wearily. "She's somewhere around."

"You're sure you didn't kill her too?"

"No. I didn't touch her. I'll find her and bring her in this afternoon. That is, if you don't want me to go in with you now."

"We've got your statement," the coroner said. "And by God, we've got eyes, haven't we, Will? Of course there's a technical charge of murder against you, but it'll be dismissed. Always is in this part of the country. Go kind of light on your wife, Mr. Moore."

"I won't hurt her," said Jim.

He stood and watched the buckboard jolt away. He kicked his feet reluctantly in the dust. The hot June sun showed its face over the hills and flashed viciously on the bedroom window.

Jim went slowly into the house, and brought out a nine-foot, loaded bull whip. He crossed the yard and walked into the barn. And as he climbed the ladder to the hayloft, he heard the high, puppy whimpering start.

When Jim came out of the barn again, he carried Jelka over his shoulder. By the water-trough he set her tenderly on the ground. Her hair was littered with bits of hay. The back of her shirtwaist was streaked with blood.

Jim wetted his bandana at the pipe and washed her bitten lips, and washed her face and brushed back her hair. Her dusty black eyes followed every move he made.

"You hurt me," she said. "You hurt me bad."

He nodded gravely. "Bad as I could without killing you."

The sun shone hotly on the ground. A few blowflies buzzed about, looking for the blood.

Jelka's thickened lips tried to smile. "Did you have any breakfast at all?"

"No," he said. "None at all."

"Well, then, I'll fry you up some eggs." She struggled painfully to her feet.

"Let me help you," he said. "I'll help you get your shirtwaist off. It's drying stuck to your back. It'll hurt."

"No. I'll do it myself." Her voice had a peculiar resonance in it. Her dark eyes dwelt warmly on him for a moment, and then she turned and limped into the house.

Jim waited, sitting on the edge of the water-trough. He saw the smoke start out of the chimney and sail straight up into the air. In a very few moments Jelka called him from the kitchen door.

"Come, Jim. Your breakfast."

Four fried eggs and four thick slices of bacon lay on a warmed plate for him. "The coffee will be ready in a minute," she said.

"Won't you eat?"

"No. Not now. My mouth's too sore."

He ate his eggs hungrily and then looked up at her. Her black hair was combed smooth. She had on a fresh white shirt-waist. "We're going to town this afternoon," he said. "I'm going to order lumber. We'll build a new house farther down the canyon."

Her eyes darted to the closed bedroom door and then back to him. "Yes," she said. "That will be good." And then, after a moment, "Will you whip me any more—for this?"

"No, not any more, for this."

Her eyes smiled. She sat down on a chair beside him, and Jim put out his hand and stroked her hair and the back of her neck.

Saint Katy the Virgin

IN P—— (as the French say), in the year 13——, there lived a bad man who kept a bad pig. He was a bad man because he laughed too much at the wrong times and at the wrong people. He laughed at the good brothers of M—— when they came to the door for a bit of whiskey or a piece of silver, and he laughed at tithe time. When Brother Clement fell in the mill pond and drowned because he would not drop the sack of salt he was carrying, the bad man, Roark, laughed until he had to go to bed for it. When you think of the low, nasty kind of laughter it was, you'll see what a bad man this Roark was, and you'll not be surprised that he didn't pay his tithes and got himself talked about for excommunication. You see, Roark didn't have the proper kind of a face for a laugh to come out of. It was a dark, tight face, and when he laughed it looked as though Roark's leg had just been torn off and his face was getting ready to scream about it. In addition he called people fools, which is unkind and unwise even if they are. Nobody knew what made Roark so bad except that he had been a traveler and seen bad things about the world.

You see the atmosphere the bad pig, Katy, grew up in, and maybe it's no wonder. There are books written how Katy came from a long line of bad pigs; how Katy's father was a chicken eater and everybody knew it, and how Katy's mother would make a meal out of her own litter if she was let. But that isn't true. Katy's mother and father were good modest pigs insofar as nature has provided pigs with equipment for modesty, which isn't far. But still, they had the spirit of modesty as a lot of people have.

Katy's mother had litter after litter of nice red hungry pigs, as normal and decent as you could wish. You must see that the badness of Katy wasn't anything she got by inheritance, so she must have picked it up from the man Roark.

There was Katy lying in the straw with her eyes squinted shut and her pink nose wrinkled, as fine and quiet a piglet as you ever saw, until the day when Roark went out to the sty to name the litter. "You'll be Brigid," he said, "and you're

Rory and—turn over you little devil!—you're Katy," and from that minute Katy was a bad pig, the worst pig, in fact, that was ever in the County of P——.

She began by stealing most of the milk; what dugs she couldn't suck on, she put her back against, so that poor Rory and Brigid and the rest turned out runts. Pretty soon, Katy was twice as big as her brothers and sisters and twice as strong. And for badness, can you equal this: one at a time, Katy caught Brigid and Rory and the rest and ate them. With such a start, you might expect almost any kind of a sin out of Katy; and sure enough, it wasn't long before she began eating chickens and ducks, until at last Roark interfered. He put her in a strong sty; at least it was strong on his side. After that, what chickens Katy ate she got from the neighbors.

You should have seen the face of Katy. From the beginning it was a wicked face. The evil yellow eyes of her would frighten you even if you had a stick to knock her on the nose with. She became the terror of the neighborhood. At night, Katy would go stealing out of a hole in her sty to raid hen roosts. Now and then even a child disappeared and was heard of no more. And Roark, who should have been ashamed and sad, grew fonder and fonder of Katy. He said she was the best pig he ever owned, and had more sense than any pig in the county.

After a while the whisper went around that it was a were-pig that wandered about in the night and bit people on the legs and rooted in gardens and ate ducks. Some even went so far as to say it was Roark himself who changed into a pig and stole through the hedges at night. That was the kind of reputation Roark had with his neighbors.

Well, Katy was a big pig now, and it came time for her to be bred. The boar was sterile from that day on and went about with a sad suspicious look on his face and was perplexed and distrustful. But Katy swelled up and swelled up until one night she had her litter. She cleaned them all up and licked them off the way you'd think motherhood had changed her ways. When she got them all dry and clean, she placed them in a row and ate every one of them. It was too much even for a bad man like Roark, for as everyone knows, a sow that will eat her own young is depraved beyond human ability to conceive wickedness.

Reluctantly Roark got ready to slaughter Katy. He was just getting the knife ready when along the path came Brother Colin and Brother Paul on their way collecting tithes. They were sent out from the Monastery of M—— and, while they didn't expect to get anything out of Roark, they thought they'd give him a try anyhow, the way a man will. Brother Paul was a thin, strong man, with a thin strong face and a sharp eye and unconditional piety written all over him, while Brother Colin was a short round man with a wide round face. Brother Paul looked forward to trying the graces of God in Heaven but Brother Colin was all for testing them on earth. The people called Colin a fine man and Paul a good man. They went tithing together, because what Brother Colin couldn't get by persuasion, Brother Paul dug out with threatenings and descriptions of the fires of Hell.

"Roark!" says Brother Paul, "we're out tithing. You won't go pickling your soul in sulphur the way you've been in the habit, will you?"

Roark stopped whetting the knife, and his eyes for evilness might have been Katy's own eyes. He started out to laugh, and then the beginning of it stuck in his throat. He got a look on his face like the look Katy had when she was for eating her litter. "I have a pig for you," said Roark, and he put the knife away.

The Brothers were amazed, for up to that time they'd got nothing out of Roark except the dog sic'd on them, and Roark laughing at the way they tripped over their skirts getting to the gate. "A pig?" said Brother Colin suspiciously. "What kind of a pig?"

"The pig that's in the sty alone there," said Roark, and his eyes seemed to turn yellow.

The Brothers hurried over to the sty and looked in. They noted the size of Katy and the fat on her, and they stared incredulously. Colin could think of nothing but the great hams she had and the bacon she wore about like a top coat. "We'll get a sausage for ourselves from this," he whispered. But Brother Paul was thinking of the praise from Father

Benedict when he heard they'd got a pig out of Roark. Paul turned away.

"When will you send this pig over?" he asked.

"I'll bring nothing," Roark cried. "It's your pig there. You take her with you or she will stay here."

The Brothers did not argue. They were too glad to get anything. Paul slipped a cord through the nose-ring of Katy and led her out of the sty; and for a moment Katy followed them as though she were a really good pig. As the three went through the gate, Roark called after them, "Her name is Katy," and the laugh that had been cooped up in his throat so long cackled out.

"It's a fine big sow," Brother Paul remarked uneasily.

Brother Colin was about to answer him, when something like a wolf trap caught him by the back of the leg. Colin yelled and spun about. There was Katy contentedly chewing up a piece of the calf of his leg, and the look on her face like the devil's own look. Katy chewed slowly and swallowed; then she started forward to get another piece of Brother Colin, but in that instant Brother Paul stepped forward and landed a fine big kick on the end of her snout. If there had been evil in Katy's face before, there were demons in her eyes then. She braced herself and growled down deep in her throat; she moved forward snorting and clicking her teeth like a bulldog. The Brothers didn't wait for her; they ran to a thorn tree beside the way and up they climbed with grunts and strainings until at last they were out of reach of the terrible Katy.

Roark had come down to his gate to see them off, and he stood there laughing the way they knew they'd get no help from him. Beneath them, on the ground, Katy paced back and forth; she pawed the ground and rooted out great pieces of turf to show her strength. Brother Paul threw a branch at her, and she tore it to pieces and ground the pieces into the earth under her sharp hooves, all the time looking up at them with her slanty yellow eyes and grinning to herself.

The two Brothers seated themselves miserably in the tree, their heads between their shoulders and their robes hugged tight. "Did you give her a good clout on the nose?" Brother Colin asked hopefully.

Brother Paul looked down at his foot and then at the tough leather snout of Katy. "The kick of my foot would knock down any pig but an elephant," he said.

"You cannot argue with a pig," Brother Colin suggested.

Katy strode ferociously about under the tree. For a long time the brothers sat in silence, moodily drawing their robes about their ankles. Brother Paul studied the problem with a disfiguring intensity. At last he observed: "You wouldn't say pigs had much the nature of a lion now, would you?"

"More the nature of the devil," Colin said wearily.

Paul sat straight up and scrutinized Katy with new interest. Then he held his crucifix out before him, and, in a terrible voice cried, "APAGE SATANAS!"

Katy shuddered as though a strong wind had struck her, but still she came on. "APAGE SATANAS!" Paul cried again and Katy was once more buffeted but unbeaten. A third time Brother Paul hurled the exorcism, but Katy had recovered from the first shock now. It had little effect except to singe a few dried leaves on the ground. Brother Paul turned discouraged eyes to Colin. "Nature of the devil," he announced sadly, "but not the Devil's own self, else that pig would have exploded."

Katy ground her teeth together with horrible pleasure.

"Before I got that idea about exorcising," Paul mused, "I was wondering about Daniel in the lion's den, and would the same thing work on a pig?"

Brother Colin regarded him apprehensively. "There may be some flaws in the nature of a lion," he argued. "Maybe lions are not so heretic as pigs. Every time there's a tight place for a pious man to get out of, there's a lion in it. Look at Daniel, look at Sampson, look at any number of martyrs just to stay in the religious list; and I could name many cases like Androcles that aren't religious at all. No, Brother, the lion is a beast especially made for saintliness and orthodoxy to cope with. If there's a lion in all those stories it must be because of all creatures, the lion is the least impervious to the force of religion. I think the lion must have been created as a kind of object lesson. It is a beast built for parables, surely. But the pig now—there is no record in my memory that a pig recognizes any force but a clout on the nose or a knife in the throat. Pigs in general, and this pig in particular, are the most headstrong and heretic of beasts."

"Still," Brother Paul went on, paying little attention to the lesson, "when you've got ammunition like the church in your hand, it would be a dirty shame not to give it a good try, be it on lion or on pig. The exorcism did not work, and that means nothing." He started to unwind the rope which served him for a girdle. Brother Colin regarded him with horror.

"Paul, lad," he cried, "Brother Paul, for the love of God, do not go down to that pig." But Paul paid him no attention. He unwound his girdle, and to the end of it tied the chain of his crucifix; then, leaning back until he was hanging by his knees, and the skirts of his robe about his head, Paul lowered the girdle like a fishing line and dangled the iron crucifix toward Katy.

As for Katy, she came forward stamping and champing, ready to snatch it and tread it under her feet. The face of Katy was a tiger's face. Just as she reached the cross, the sharp shadow of it fell on her face, and the cross itself was reflected in her yellow eyes. Katy stopped—paralyzed. The air, the tree, the earth shuddered in an expectant silence, while goodness fought with sin.

Then, slowly, two great tears squeezed out of the eyes of Katy, and before you could think, she was stretched prostrate on the ground, making the sign of the cross with her right hoof and mooing softly in anguish at the realization of her crimes.

Brother Paul dangled the cross a full minute before he hoisted himself back on the limb.

All this time Roark had been watching from his gate. From that day on, he was no longer a bad man; his whole life was changed in a moment. Indeed, he told the story over and over to anyone who would listen. Roark said he had never seen anything so grand and inspiring in his life.

Brother Paul rose and stood on the limb. He drew himself to his full height. Then, using his free hand for gestures, Brother Paul delivered the Sermon on the Mount in beautiful Latin to the groveling, moaning Katy under the tree. When he finished, there was complete and holy silence except for the sobs and sniffles of the repentant pig.

It is doubtful whether Brother Colin had the fiber of a true priest-militant in his nature. "Do—do you think it is safe to go down now?" he stammered.

For answer, Brother Paul broke a limb from the thorn trees and threw it at the recumbent sow. Katy sobbed aloud and raised a tear-stained countenance to them, a face from which all evil had departed; the yellow eyes were golden with repentance and the resulting anguish of grace. The Brothers scrambled out of the tree, put the cord through Katy's nose-ring again, and down the road they trudged with the redeemed pig trotting docilely behind them.

News that they were bringing home a pig from Roark caused such excitement that, on arriving at the gates of M——, Brothers Paul and Colin found a crowd of monks awaiting them. The Brotherhood squirmed about, feeling the fat sides of Katy and kneading her jowls. Suddenly an opening was broken in the ring, and Father Benedict paced through. His face wore such a smile that Colin was made sure of his sausage and Paul of his praise. Then, to the horror and consternation of everyone present, Katy waddled to a little font beside the chapel door, dipped her right hoof in holy water and crossed herself. It was a moment before anyone spoke. Then Father Benedict's stern voice rang out in anger. "Who was it converted this pig?"

Brother Paul stepped forward. "I did it, Father."

"You are a fool," said the Abbot.

"A fool? I thought you would be pleased, Father."

"You are a fool," Father Benedict repeated. "We can't slaughter this pig. This pig is a Christian."

"There is more rejoicing in heaven—" Brother Paul began to quote.

"Hush!" said the Abbot. "There are plenty of Christians. This year there's a great shortage of pigs."

It would take a whole volume to tell of the thousands of sick beds Katy visited, of the comfort she carried into palaces and cottages. She sat by beds of pain and her dear golden eyes brought relief to the sufferers. For a while it was thought that, because of her sex, she should leave the monastery and enter a nunnery, for the usual ribald tongues caused the usual scandal in the county. But, as the Abbot remarked, one need only look at Katy to be convinced of her purity.

The subsequent life of Katy was one long record of good deeds. It was not until one feast-day morning, however, that the Brothers began to suspect that their community harbored a saint. On the morning in question, while hymns of joy and thanksgiving sounded from a hundred pious mouths, Katy rose from her seat, strode to the altar, and, with a look of seraphic transport on her face, spun like a top on the tip of her tail for one hour and three-quarters. The assembled Brothers looked on with astonishment and admiration. This was a wonderful example of what a saintly life could accomplish.

From that time on M—— became a place of pilgrimage. Long lines of travelers wound into the valley and stopped at the taverns kept by the good Brothers. Daily at four o'clock, Katy emerged from the gates and blessed the multitudes. If any were afflicted with scrofula or trichina, she touched them and they were healed. Fifty years after her death to a day, she was added to the Calendar of the Elect.

The Proposition was put forward that she should be called Saint Katy the Virgin. However, a minority argued that Katy was not a virgin since she had, in her sinful days, produced a litter. The opposing party retorted that it made no difference at all. Very few virgins, so they said, were virgins.

To keep dissension out of the monastery, a committee presented the problem to a fair-minded and vastly learned barber, agreeing beforehand to be guided by his decision.

"It is a delicate question," said the barber. "You might say there are two kinds of virginity. Some hold that virginity consists in a little bit of tissue. If you have it, you are; if you haven't, you aren't. This definition is a grave danger to the basis of our religion since there is nothing to differentiate between the Grace of God knocking it out from the inside or the wickedness of man from the outside. On the other hand," he continued, "there is virginity by intent, and this definition admits the existence of a great many more virgins than the first does. But here again we get into trouble. When I was a much younger man, I went about in the evenings sometimes with a girl on my arm. Every one of them that ever walked with me was a virgin by intention, and if you take the second definition, you see, they still are."

The committee went away satisfied. Katy had without doubt been a virgin by intent.

In the chapel at M—— there is a gold-bound, jeweled reliquary, and inside, on a bed of crimson satin repose the bones of the Saint. People come great distances to kiss the little box, and such as do, go away leaving their troubles behind them. This holy relic has been found to cure female troubles and ringworm. There is a record left by a woman who visited the chapel to be cured of both. She deposes that she rubbed the reliquary against her cheek, and at the moment her face touched the holy object, a hair mole she had possessed from birth immediately vanished and has never returned.

The Red Pony

AT DAYBREAK Billy Buck emerged from the bunkhouse and stood for a moment on the porch looking up at the sky. He was a broad, bandy-legged little man with a walrus mustache, with square hands, puffed and muscled on the palms. His eyes were a contemplative, watery grey and the hair which protruded from under his Stetson hat was spiky and weathered. Billy was still stuffing his shirt into his blue jeans as he stood on the porch. He unbuckled his belt and tightened it again. The belt showed, by the worn shiny places opposite each hole, the gradual increase of Billy's middle over a period of years. When he had seen to the weather, Billy cleared each nostril by holding its mate closed with his forefinger and blowing fiercely. Then he walked down to the barn, rubbing his hands together. He curried and brushed two saddle horses in the stalls, talking quietly to them all the time; and he had hardly finished when the iron triangle started ringing at the ranch house. Billy stuck the brush and currycomb together and laid them on the rail, and went up to breakfast. His action had been so deliberate and yet so wasteless of time that he came to the house while Mrs. Tiflin was still ringing the triangle. She nodded her grey head to him and withdrew into the kitchen. Billy Buck sat down on the steps, because he was a cow-hand, and it wouldn't be fitting that he should go first into the dining-room. He heard Mr. Tiflin in the house, stamping his feet into his boots.

The high jangling note of the triangle put the boy Jody in motion. He was only a little boy, ten years old, with hair like dusty yellow grass and with shy polite grey eyes, and with a mouth that worked when he thought. The triangle picked him up out of sleep. It didn't occur to him to disobey the harsh note. He never had: no one he knew ever had. He brushed the tangled hair out of his eyes and skinned his nightgown off. In a moment he was dressed—blue chambray shirt and overalls. It was late in the summer, so of course there were no shoes to bother with. In the kitchen he waited until his mother got from in front of the sink and went back to the stove. Then he washed himself and brushed back his wet hair with his fingers. His mother turned sharply on him as he left the sink. Jody looked shyly away.

"I've got to cut your hair before long," his mother said. "Breakfast's on the table. Go on in, so Billy can come."

Jody sat at the long table which was covered with white oil-cloth washed through to the fabric in some places. The fried eggs lay in rows on their platter. Jody took three eggs on his plate and followed with three thick slices of crisp bacon. He carefully scraped a spot of blood from one of the egg yolks.

Billy Buck clumped in. "That won't hurt you," Billy explained. "That's only a sign the rooster leaves."

Jody's tall stern father came in then and Jody knew from the noise on the floor that he was wearing boots, but he looked under the table anyway, to make sure. His father turned off the oil lamp over the table, for plenty of morning light now came through the windows.

Jody did not ask where his father and Billy Buck were riding that day, but he wished he might go along. His father was a disciplinarian. Jody obeyed him in everything without questions of any kind. Now, Carl Tiflin sat down and reached for the egg platter.

"Got the cows ready to go, Billy?" he asked.

"In the lower corral," Billy said. "I could just as well take them in alone."

"Sure you could. But a man needs company. Besides your throat gets pretty dry." Carl Tiflin was jovial this morning.

Jody's mother put her head in the door. "What time do you think to be back, Carl?"

"I can't tell. I've got to see some men in Salinas. Might be gone till dark."

The eggs and coffee and big biscuits disappeared rapidly. Jody followed the two men out of the house. He watched them mount their horses and drive six old milk cows out of the corral and start over the hill toward Salinas. They were going to sell the old cows to the butcher.

When they had disappeared over the crown of the ridge Jody walked up the hill in back of the house. The dogs trotted around the house corner hunching their shoulders and

grinning horribly with pleasure. Jody patted their heads—
Doubletree Mutt with the big thick tail and yellow eyes, and
Smasher, the shepherd, who had killed a coyote and lost an
ear in doing it. Smasher's one good ear stood up higher than
a collie's ear should. Billy Buck said that always happened.
After the frenzied greeting the dogs lowered their noses to
the ground in a businesslike way and went ahead, looking
back now and then to make sure that the boy was coming.
They walked up through the chicken yard and saw the quail
eating with the chickens. Smasher chased the chickens a little
to keep in practice in case there should ever be sheep to herd.
Jody continued on through the large vegetable patch where
the green corn was higher than his head. The cow-pumpkins
were green and small yet. He went on to the sagebrush line
where the cold spring ran out of its pipe and fell into a round
wooden tub. He leaned over and drank close to the green
mossy wood where the water tasted best. Then he turned and
looked back on the ranch, on the low, whitewashed house
girded with red geraniums, and on the long bunkhouse by the
cypress tree where Billy Buck lived alone. Jody could see the
great black kettle under the cypress tree. That was where the
pigs were scalded. The sun was coming over the ridge now,
glaring on the whitewash of the houses and barns, making the
wet grass blaze softly. Behind him, in the tall sagebrush, the
birds were scampering on the ground, making a great noise
among the dry leaves; the squirrels piped shrilly on the side-
hills. Jody looked along at the farm buildings. He felt an uncertainty in the air, a feeling of change and of loss and of the
gain of new and unfamiliar things. Over the hillside two big
black buzzards sailed low to the ground and their shadows
slipped smoothly and quickly ahead of them. Some animal had
died in the vicinity. Jody knew it. It might be a cow or it
might be the remains of a rabbit. The buzzards overlooked
nothing. Jody hated them as all decent things hate them, but
they could not be hurt because they made away with carrion.

After a while the boy sauntered down hill again. The dogs
had long ago given him up and gone into the brush to do
things in their own way. Back through the vegetable garden
he went, and he paused for a moment to smash a green musk-
melon with his heel, but he was not happy about it. It was a

bad thing to do, he knew perfectly well. He kicked dirt over the ruined melon to conceal it.

Back at the house his mother bent over his rough hands, inspecting his fingers and nails. It did little good to start him clean to school for too many things could happen on the way. She sighed over the black cracks on his fingers, and then gave him his books and his lunch and started him on the mile walk to school. She noticed that his mouth was working a good deal this morning.

Jody started his journey. He filled his pockets with little pieces of white quartz that lay in the road, and every so often he took a shot at a bird or at some rabbit that had stayed sunning itself in the road too long. At the crossroads over the bridge he met two friends and the three of them walked to school together, making ridiculous strides and being rather silly. School had just opened two weeks before. There was still a spirit of revolt among the pupils.

It was four o'clock in the afternoon when Jody topped the hill and looked down on the ranch again. He looked for the saddle horses, but the corral was empty. His father was not back yet. He went slowly, then, toward the afternoon chores. At the ranch house, he found his mother sitting on the porch, mending socks.

"There's two doughnuts in the kitchen for you," she said. Jody slid to the kitchen, and returned with half of one of the doughnuts already eaten and his mouth full. His mother asked him what he had learned in school that day, but she didn't listen to his doughnut-muffled answer. She interrupted, "Jody, tonight see you fill the wood-box clear full. Last night you crossed the sticks and it wasn't only about half full. Lay the sticks flat tonight. And Jody, some of the hens are hiding eggs, or else the dogs are eating them. Look about in the grass and see if you can find any nests."

Jody, still eating, went out and did his chores. He saw the quail come down to eat with the chickens when he threw out the grain. For some reason his father was proud to have them come. He never allowed any shooting near the house for fear the quail might go away.

When the wood-box was full, Jody took his twenty-two rifle up to the cold spring at the brush line. He drank again and then aimed the gun at all manner of things, at rocks, at birds on the wing, at the big black pig kettle under the cypress tree, but he didn't shoot for he had no cartridges and wouldn't have until he was twelve. If his father had seen him aim the rifle in the direction of the house he would have put the cartridges off another year. Jody remembered this and did not point the rifle down the hill again. Two years was enough to wait for cartridges. Nearly all of his father's presents were given with reservations which hampered their value somewhat. It was good discipline.

The supper waited until dark for his father to return. When at last he came in with Billy Buck, Jody could smell the delicious brandy on their breaths. Inwardly he rejoiced, for his father sometimes talked to him when he smelled of brandy, sometimes even told things he had done in the wild days when he was a boy.

After supper, Jody sat by the fireplace and his shy polite eyes sought the room corners, and he waited for his father to tell what it was he contained, for Jody knew he had news of some sort. But he was disappointed. His father pointed a stern finger at him.

"You'd better go to bed, Jody. I'm going to need you in the morning."

That wasn't so bad. Jody liked to do the things he had to do as long as they weren't routine things. He looked at the floor and his mouth worked out a question before he spoke it. "What are we going to do in the morning, kill a pig?" he asked softly.

"Never you mind. You better get to bed."

When the door was closed behind him, Jody heard his father and Billy Buck chuckling and he knew it was a joke of some kind. And later, when he lay in bed, trying to make words out of the murmurs in the other room, he heard his father protest, "But, Ruth, I didn't give much for him."

Jody heard the hoot-owls hunting mice down by the barn, and he heard a fruit tree limb tap-tapping against the house. A cow was lowing when he went to sleep.

When the triangle sounded in the morning, Jody dressed more quickly even than usual. In the kitchen, while he washed his face and combed back his hair, his mother addressed him irritably. "Don't you go out until you get a good breakfast in you."

He went into the dining-room and sat at the long white table. He took a steaming hotcake from the platter, arranged two fried eggs on it, covered them with another hotcake and squashed the whole thing with his fork.

His father and Billy Buck came in. Jody knew from the sound on the floor that both of them were wearing flat-heeled shoes, but he peered under the table to make sure. His father turned off the oil lamp, for the day had arrived, and he looked stern and disciplinary, but Billy Buck didn't look at Jody at all. He avoided the shy questioning eyes of the boy and soaked a whole piece of toast in his coffee.

Carl Tiflin said crossly, "You come with us after breakfast!"

Jody had trouble with his food then, for he felt a kind of doom in the air. After Billy had tilted his saucer and drained the coffee which had slopped into it, and had wiped his hands on his jeans, the two men stood up from the table and went out into the morning light together, and Jody respectfully followed a little behind them. He tried to keep his mind from running ahead, tried to keep it absolutely motionless.

His mother called, "Carl! Don't you let it keep him from school."

They marched past the cypress, where a singletree hung from a limb to butcher the pigs on, and past the black iron kettle, so it was not a pig killing. The sun shone over the hill and threw long, dark shadows of the trees and buildings. They crossed a stubble-field to shortcut to the barn. Jody's father unhooked the door and they went in. They had been walking toward the sun on the way down. The barn was black as night in contrast and warm from the hay and from the beasts. Jody's father moved over toward the one box stall. "Come here!" he ordered. Jody could begin to see things now. He looked into the box stall and then stepped back quickly.

A red pony colt was looking at him out of the stall. Its tense ears were forward and a light of disobedience was in its eyes. Its coat was rough and thick as an airedale's fur and its mane was long and tangled. Jody's throat collapsed in on itself and cut his breath short.

"He needs a good currying," his father said, "and if I ever hear of you not feeding him or leaving his stall dirty, I'll sell him off in a minute."

Jody couldn't bear to look at the pony's eyes any more. He gazed down at his hands for a moment, and he asked very shyly, "Mine?" No one answered him. He put his hand out toward the pony. Its grey nose came close, sniffing loudly, and then the lips drew back and the strong teeth closed on Jody's fingers. The pony shook its head up and down and seemed to laugh with amusement. Jody regarded his bruised fingers. "Well," he said with pride—"Well, I guess he can bite all right." The two men laughed, somewhat in relief. Carl Tiflin went out of the barn and walked up a side-hill to be by himself, for he was embarrassed, but Billy Buck stayed. It was easier to talk to Billy Buck. Jody asked again—"Mine?"

Billy became professional in tone. "Sure! That is, if you look out for him and break him right. I'll show you how. He's just a colt. You can't ride him for some time."

Jody put out his bruised hand again, and this time the red pony let his nose be rubbed. "I ought to have a carrot," Jody said. "Where'd we get him, Billy?"

"Bought him at a sheriff's auction," Billy explained. "A show went broke in Salinas and had debts. The sheriff was selling off their stuff."

The pony stretched out his nose and shook the forelock from his wild eyes. Jody stroked the nose a little. He said softly, "There isn't a—saddle?"

Billy Buck laughed. "I'd forgot. Come along."

In the harness room he lifted down a little saddle of red morocco leather. "It's just a show saddle," Billy Buck said disparagingly. "It isn't practical for the brush, but it was cheap at the sale."

Jody couldn't trust himself to look at the saddle either, and he couldn't speak at all. He brushed the shining red leather with his fingertips, and after a long time he said, "It'll look pretty on him though." He thought of the grandest and prettiest things he knew. "If he hasn't a name already, I think I'll call him Gabilan Mountains," he said.

Billy Buck knew how he felt. "It's a pretty long name. Why

don't you just call him Gabilan? That means hawk. That would be a fine name for him." Billy felt glad. "If you will collect tail hair, I might be able to make a hair rope for you sometime. You could use it for a hackamore."

Jody wanted to go back to the box stall. "Could I lead him to school, do you think—to show the kids?"

But Billy shook his head. "He's not even halter-broke yet. We had a time getting him here. Had to almost drag him. You better be starting for school though."

"I'll bring the kids to see him here this afternoon," Jody said.

Six boys came over the hill half an hour early that afternoon, running hard, their heads down, their forearms working, their breath whistling. They swept by the house and cut across the stubble-field to the barn. And then they stood self-consciously before the pony, and then they looked at Jody with eyes in which there was a new admiration and a new respect. Before today Jody had been a boy, dressed in overalls and a blue shirt—quieter than most, even suspected of being a little cowardly. And now he was different. Out of a thousand centuries they drew the ancient admiration of the footman for the horseman. They knew instinctively that a man on a horse is spiritually as well as physically bigger than a man on foot. They knew that Jody had been miraculously lifted out of equality with them, and had been placed over them. Gabilan put his head out of the stall and sniffed them.

"Why'n't you ride him?" the boys cried. "Why'n't you braid his tail with ribbons like in the fair?" "When you going to ride him?"

Jody's courage was up. He too felt the superiority of the horseman. "He's not old enough. Nobody can ride him for a long time. I'm going to train him on the long halter. Billy Buck is going to show me how."

"Well, can't we even lead him around a little?"

"He isn't even halter broke," Jody said. He wanted to be completely alone when he took the pony out the first time. "Come and see the saddle."

They were speechless at the red morocco saddle, completely shocked out of comment. "It isn't much use in the brush,"

Jody explained. "It'll look pretty on him though. Maybe I'll ride bareback when I go into the brush."

"How you going to rope a cow without a saddle horn?"

"Maybe I'll get another saddle for every day. My father might want me to help him with the stock." He let them feel the red saddle, and showed them the brass chain throat-latch on the bridle and the big brass buttons at each temple where the headstall and brow band crossed. The whole thing was too wonderful. They had to go away after a little while, and each boy, in his mind, searched among his possessions for a bribe worthy of offering in return for a ride on the red pony when the time should come.

Jody was glad when they had gone. He took brush and currycomb from the wall, took down the barrier of the box stall and stepped cautiously in. The pony's eyes glittered, and he edged around into kicking position. But Jody touched him on the shoulder and rubbed his high arched neck as he had always seen Billy Buck do, and he crooned, "So-o-o Boy," in a deep voice. The pony gradually relaxed his tenseness. Jody curried and brushed until a pile of dead hair lay in the stall and until the pony's coat had taken on a deep red shine. Each time he finished he thought it might have been done better. He braided the mane into a dozen little pigtails, and he braided the forelock, and then he undid them and brushed the hair out straight again.

Jody did not hear his mother enter the barn. She was angry when she came, but when she looked in at the pony and at Jody working over him, she felt a curious pride rise up in her. "Have you forgot the wood-box?" she asked gently. "It's not far off from dark and there's not a stick of wood in the house, and the chickens aren't fed."

Jody quickly put up his tools. "I forgot, ma'am."

"Well, after this do your chores first. Then you won't forget. I expect you'll forget lots of things now if I don't keep an eye on you."

"Can I have carrots from the garden for him, ma'am?"

She had to think about that. "Oh—I guess so, if you only take the big tough ones."

"Carrots keep the coat good," he said, and again she felt the curious rush of pride.

Jody never waited for the triangle to get him out of bed after the coming of the pony. It became his habit to creep out of bed even before his mother was awake, to slip into his clothes and to go quietly down to the barn to see Gabilan. In the grey quiet mornings when the land and the brush and the houses and the trees were silver-gray and black like a photograph negative, he stole toward the barn, past the sleeping stones and the sleeping cypress tree. The turkeys, roosting in the tree out of coyotes' reach, clicked drowsily. The fields glowed with a grey frost-like light and in the dew the tracks of rabbits and of field mice stood out sharply. The good dogs came stiffly out of their little houses, hackles up and deep growls in their throats. Then they caught Jody's scent, and their stiff tails rose up and waved a greeting—Doubletree Mutt with the big thick tail, and Smasher, the incipient shepherd—then went lazily back to their warm beds.

It was a strange time and a mysterious journey, to Jody— an extension of a dream. When he first had the pony he liked to torture himself during the trip by thinking Gabilan would not be in his stall, and worse, would never have been there. And he had other delicious little self-induced pains. He thought how the rats had gnawed ragged holes in the red saddle, and how the mice had nibbled Gabilan's tail until it was stringy and thin. He usually ran the last little way to the barn. He unlatched the rusty hasp of the barn door and stepped in, and no matter how quietly he opened the door, Gabilan was always looking at him over the barrier of the box stall and Gabilan whinnied softly and stamped his front foot, and his eyes had big sparks of red fire in them like oakwood embers.

Sometimes, if the work horses were to be used that day, Jody found Billy Buck in the barn harnessing and currying. Billy stood with him and looked long at Gabilan and he told Jody a great many things about horses. He explained that they were terribly afraid for their feet, so that one must make a practice of lifting the legs and patting the hooves and ankles to remove their terror. He told Jody how horses love conversation. He must talk to the pony all the time, and tell him the reasons for everything. Billy wasn't sure a horse could understand everything that was said to him, but it was impossible to say how much was understood. A horse never kicked up a fuss if some one he liked explained things to him. Billy could give examples, too. He had known, for instance, a horse nearly dead beat with fatigue to perk up when told it was only a little farther to his destination. And he had known a horse paralyzed with fright to come out of it when his rider told him what it was that was frightening him. While he talked in the mornings, Billy Buck cut twenty or thirty straws into neat three-inch lengths and stuck them into his hatband. Then during the whole day, if he wanted to pick his teeth or merely to chew on something, he had only to reach up for one of them.

Jody listened carefully, for he knew and the whole country knew that Billy Buck was a fine hand with horses. Billy's own horse was a stringy cayuse with a hammer head, but he nearly always won the first prizes at the stock trials. Billy could rope a steer, take a double half-hitch about the horn with his riata, and dismount, and his horse would play the steer as an angler plays a fish, keeping a tight rope until the steer was down or beaten.

Every morning, after Jody had curried and brushed the pony, he let down the barrier of the stall, and Gabilan thrust past him and raced down the barn and into the corral. Around and around he galloped, and sometimes he jumped forward and landed on stiff legs. He stood quivering, stiff ears forward, eyes rolling so that the whites showed, pretending to be frightened. At last he walked snorting to the water-trough and buried his nose in the water up to the nostrils. Jody was proud then, for he knew that was the way to judge a horse. Poor horses only touched their lips to the water, but a fine spirited beast put his whole nose and mouth under, and only left room to breathe.

Then Jody stood and watched the pony, and he saw things he had never noticed about any other horse, the sleek, sliding flank muscles and the cords of the buttocks, which flexed like a closing fist, and the shine the sun put on the red coat. Having seen horses all his life, Jody had never looked at them very closely before. But now he noticed the moving ears which gave expression and even inflection of expression to the face. The pony talked with his ears. You could tell exactly how he

felt about everything by the way his ears pointed. Sometimes
they were stiff and upright and sometimes lax and sagging.
They went back when he was angry or fearful, and forward
when he was anxious and curious and pleased; and their exact
position indicated which emotion he had.

Billy Buck kept his word. In the early fall the training began.
First there was the halter-breaking, and that was the hardest
because it was the first thing. Jody held a carrot and coaxed
and promised and pulled on the rope. The pony set his feet
like a burro when he felt the strain. But before long he
learned. Jody walked all over the ranch leading him. Gradually
he took to dropping the rope until the pony followed him
unled wherever he went.

And then came the training on the long halter. That was
slower work. Jody stood in the middle of a circle, holding the
long halter. He clucked with his tongue and the pony started
to walk in a big circle, held in by the long rope. He clucked
again to make the pony trot, and again to make him gallop.
Around and around Gabilan went thundering and enjoying it
immensely. Then he called, "Whoa," and the pony stopped.
It was not long until Gabilan was perfect at it. But in many
ways he was a bad pony. He bit Jody in the pants and stomped
on Jody's feet. Now and then his ears went back and he aimed
a tremendous kick at the boy. Every time he did one of these
bad things, Gabilan settled back and seemed to laugh to himself.

Billy Buck worked at the hair rope in the evenings before
the fireplace. Jody collected tail hair in a bag, and he sat and
watched Billy slowly constructing the rope, twisting a few
hairs to make a string and rolling two strings together for a
cord, and then braiding a number of cords to make the rope.
Billy rolled the finished rope on the floor under his foot to
make it round and hard.

The long halter work rapidly approached perfection. Jody's
father, watching the pony stop and start and trot and gallop,
was a little bothered by it.

"He's getting to be almost a trick pony," he complained.
"I don't like trick horses. It takes all the—dignity out of a
horse to make him do tricks. Why, a trick horse is kind of like
an actor—no dignity, no character of his own." And his father

said, "I guess you better be getting him used to the saddle pretty soon."

Jody rushed for the harness-room. For some time he had been riding the saddle on a sawhorse. He changed the stirrup length over and over, and could never get it just right. Sometimes, mounted on the sawhorse in the harness-room, with collars and hames and tugs hung all about him, Jody rode out beyond the room. He carried his rifle across the pommel. He saw the fields go flying by, and he heard the beat of the galloping hoofs.

It was a ticklish job, saddling the pony the first time. Gabilan hunched and reared and threw the saddle off before the cinch could be tightened. It had to be replaced again and again until at last the pony let it stay. And the cinching was difficult, too. Day by day Jody tightened the girth a little more until at last the pony didn't mind the saddle at all.

Then there was the bridle. Billy explained how to use a stick of licorice for a bit until Gabilan was used to having something in his mouth. Billy explained, "Of course we could force-break him to everything, but he wouldn't be as good a horse if we did. He'd always be a little bit afraid, and he wouldn't mind because he wanted to."

The first time the pony wore the bridle he whipped his head about and worked his tongue against the bit until the blood oozed from the corners of his mouth. He tried to rub the headstall off on the manger. His ears pivoted about and his eyes turned red with fear and with general rambunctiousness. Jody rejoiced, for he knew that only a mean-souled horse does not resent training.

And Jody trembled when he thought of the time when he would first sit in the saddle. The pony would probably throw him off. There was no disgrace in that. The disgrace would come if he did not get right up and mount again. Sometimes he dreamed that he lay in the dirt and cried and couldn't make himself mount again. The shame of the dream lasted until the middle of the day.

Gabilan was growing fast. Already he had lost the long-leggedness of the colt; his mane was getting longer and blacker. Under the constant currying and brushing his coat lay as smooth and gleaming as orange-red lacquer. Jody oiled the hoofs and kept them carefully trimmed so they would not crack.

The hair rope was nearly finished. Jody's father gave him an old pair of spurs and bent in the side bars and cut down the strap and took up the chainlets until they fitted. And then one day Carl Tiflin said:

"The pony's growing faster than I thought. I guess you can ride him by Thanksgiving. Think you can stick on?"

"I don't know," Jody said shyly. Thanksgiving was only three weeks off. He hoped it wouldn't rain, for rain would spot the red saddle.

Gabilan knew and liked Jody by now. He nickered when Jody came across the stubble-field, and in the pasture he came running when his master whistled for him. There was always a carrot for him every time.

Billy Buck gave him riding instructions over and over. "Now when you get up there, just grab tight with your knees and keep your hands away from the saddle, and if you get throwed, don't let that stop you. No matter how good a man is, there's always some horse can pitch him. You just climb up again before he gets to feeling smart about it. Pretty soon, he won't throw you no more, and pretty soon he *can't* throw you no more. That's the way to do it."

"I hope it don't rain before," Jody said.

"Why not? Don't want to get throwed in the mud?"

That was partly it, and also he was afraid that in the flurry of bucking Gabilan might slip and fall on him and break his leg or his hip. He had seen that happen to men before, had seen how they writhed on the ground like squashed bugs, and he was afraid of it.

He practiced on the sawhorse how he would hold the reins in his left hand and a hat in his right hand. If he kept his hands thus busy, he couldn't grab the horn if he felt himself going off. He didn't like to think of what would happen if he did grab the horn. Perhaps his father and Billy Buck would never speak to him again, they would be so ashamed. The news would get about and his mother would be ashamed too. And in the school yard—it was too awful to contemplate.

He began putting his weight in a stirrup when Gabilan was

saddled, but he didn't throw his leg over the pony's back. That was forbidden until Thanksgiving.

Every afternoon he put the red saddle on the pony and cinched it tight. The pony was learning already to fill his stomach out unnaturally large while the cinching was going on, and then to let it down when the straps were fixed. Sometimes Jody led him up to the brush line and let him drink from the round green tub, and sometimes he led him up through the stubble-field to the hilltop from which it was possible to see the white town of Salinas and the geometric fields of the great valley, and the oak trees clipped by the sheep. Now and then they broke through the brush and came to little cleared circles so hedged in that the world was gone and only the sky and the circle of brush were left from the old life. Gabilan liked these trips and showed it by keeping his head very high and by quivering his nostrils with interest. When the two came back from an expedition they smelled of the sweet sage they had forced through.

Time dragged on toward Thanksgiving, but winter came fast. The clouds swept down and hung all day over the land and brushed the hilltops, and the winds blew shrilly at night. All day the dry oak leaves drifted down from the trees until they covered the ground, and yet the trees were unchanged.

Jody had wished it might not rain before Thanksgiving, but it did. The brown earth turned dark and the trees glistened. The cut ends of the stubble turned black with mildew; the haystacks grayed from exposure to the damp, and on the roofs the moss, which had been all summer as gray as lizards, turned a brilliant yellow-green. During the week of rain, Jody kept the pony in the box stall out of the dampness, except for a little time after school when he took him out for exercise and to drink at the water-trough in the upper corral. Not once did Gabilan get wet.

The wet weather continued until little new grass appeared. Jody walked to school dressed in a slicker and short rubber boots. At length one morning the sun came out brightly. Jody, at his work in the box stall, said to Billy Buck, "Maybe I'll leave Gabilan in the corral when I go to school today."

"Be good for him to be out in the sun," Billy assured him.

"No animal likes to be cooped up too long. Your father and me are going back on the hill to clean the leaves out of the spring." Billy nodded and picked his teeth with one of his little straws.

"If the rain comes, though—" Jody suggested.

"Not likely to rain today. She's rained herself out." Billy pulled up his sleeves and snapped his arm bands. "If it comes on to rain—why a little rain don't hurt a horse."

"Well, if it does come on to rain, you put him in, will you, Billy? I'm scared he might get cold so I couldn't ride him when the time comes."

"Oh sure! I'll watch out for him if we get back in time. But it won't rain today."

And so Jody, when he went to school left Gabilan standing out in the corral.

Billy Buck wasn't wrong about many things. He couldn't be. But he was wrong about the weather that day, for a little after noon the clouds pushed over the hills and the rain began to pour down. Jody heard it start on the schoolhouse roof. He considered holding up one finger for permission to go to the outhouse and, once outside, running for home to put the pony in. Punishment would be prompt both at school and at home. He gave it up and took ease from Billy's assurance that rain couldn't hurt a horse. When school was finally out, he hurried home through the dark rain. The banks at the sides of the road spouted little jets of muddy water. The rain slanted and swirled under a cold and gusty wind. Jody dog-trotted home, slopping through the gravelly mud of the road.

From the top of the ridge he could see Gabilan standing miserably in the corral. The red coat was almost black, and streaked with water. He stood head down with his rump to the rain and wind. Jody arrived running and threw open the barn door and led the wet pony in by his forelock. Then he found a gunny sack and rubbed the soaked hair and rubbed the legs and ankles. Gabilan stood patiently, but he trembled in gusts like the wind.

When he had dried the pony as well as he could, Jody went up to the horse and brought hot water down to the barn and soaked the grain in it. Gabilan was not very hungry. He nibbled at the hot mash, but he was not very much interested in it, and he still shivered now and then. A little steam rose from his damp back.

It was almost dark when Billy Buck and Carl Tiflin came home. "When the rain started we put up at Ben Herche's place, and the rain never let up all afternoon," Carl Tiflin explained. Jody looked reproachfully at Billy Buck and Billy felt guilty.

"You said it wouldn't rain," Jody accused him.

Billy looked away. "It's hard to tell, this time of year," he said, but his excuse was lame. He had no right to be fallible, and he knew it.

"The pony got wet, got soaked through."

"Did you dry him off?"

"I rubbed him with a sack and I gave him hot grain."

Billy nodded in agreement.

"Do you think he'll take cold, Billy?"

"A little rain never hurt anything," Billy assured him.

Jody's father joined the conversation then and lectured the boy a little. "A horse," he said, "isn't any lap-dog kind of thing." Carl Tiflin hated weakness and sickness, and he held a violent contempt for helplessness.

Jody's mother put a platter of steaks on the table and boiled potatoes and boiled squash, which clouded the room with their steam. They sat down to eat. Carl Tiflin still grumbled about weakness put into animals and men by too much coddling.

Billy Buck felt bad about his mistake. "Did you blanket him?" he asked.

"No. I couldn't find any blanket. I laid some sacks over his back."

"We'll go down and cover him up after we eat, then." Billy felt better about it then. When Jody's father had gone in to the fire and his mother was washing dishes, Billy found and lighted a lantern. He and Jody walked through the mud to the barn. The barn was dark and warm and sweet. The horses still munched their evening hay. "You hold the lantern!" Billy ordered. And he felt the pony's legs and tested the heat of the flanks. He put his cheek against the pony's grey muzzle and then he rolled up the eyelids to look at the eyeballs and he lifted the lips to see the gums, and he put his fingers inside the ears. "He don't seem so chipper," Billy said. "I'll give him a rub-down."

Then Billy found a sack and rubbed the pony's legs violently and he rubbed the chest and the withers. Gabilan was strangely spiritless. He submitted patiently to the rubbing. At last Billy brought an old cotton comforter from the saddle-room, and threw it over the pony's back and tied it at neck and chest with string.

"Now he'll be all right in the morning," Billy said.

Jody's mother looked up when he got back to the house. "You're late up from bed," she said. She held his chin in her hard hand and brushed the tangled hair out of his eyes and she said, "Don't worry about the pony. He'll be all right. Billy's as good as any horse doctor in the country."

Jody hadn't known she could see his worry. He pulled gently away from her and knelt down in front of the fireplace until it burned his stomach. He scorched himself through and then went in to bed, but it was a hard thing to go to sleep. He awakened after what seemed a long time. The room was dark but there was a greyness in the window like that which precedes the dawn. He got up and found his overalls and searched for the legs, and then the clock in the other room struck two. He laid his clothes down and got back into bed. It was broad daylight when he awakened again. For the first time he had slept through the ringing of the triangle. He leaped up, flung on his clothes and went out of the door still buttoning his shirt. His mother looked after him for a moment and then went quietly back to her work. Her eyes were brooding and kind. Now and then her mouth smiled a little but without changing her eyes at all.

Jody ran on toward the barn. Halfway there he heard the sound he dreaded, the hollow rasping cough of a horse. He broke into a sprint then. In the barn he found Billy Buck with the pony. Billy was rubbing its legs with his strong thick hands. He looked up and smiled gaily. "He just took a little cold," Billy said. "We'll have him out of it in a couple of days."

Jody looked at the pony's face. The eyes were half closed and the lids thick and dry. In the eye corners a crust of hard mucus stuck. Gabilan's ears hung loosely sideways and his head was low. Jody put out his hand, but the pony did not move close to it. He coughed again and his whole body constricted with the effort. A little stream of thin fluid ran from his nostrils.

Jody looked back at Billy Buck. "He's awful sick, Billy."

"Just a little cold, like I said," Billy insisted. "You go get some breakfast and then go back to school. I'll take care of him."

"But you might have to do something else. You might leave him."

"No, I won't. I won't leave him at all. Tomorrow's Saturday. Then you can stay with him all day." Billy had failed again, and he felt badly about it. He had to cure the pony now.

Jody walked up to the house and took his place listlessly at the table. The eggs and bacon were cold and greasy, but he didn't notice it. He ate his usual amount. He didn't even ask to stay home from school. His mother pushed his hair back when she took his plate. "Billy'll take care of the pony," she assured him.

He moped through the whole day at school. He couldn't answer any questions nor read any words. He couldn't even tell anyone the pony was sick, for that might make him sicker. And when school was finally out he started home in dread. He walked slowly and let the other boys leave him. He wished he might continue walking and never arrive at the ranch.

Billy was in the barn, as he had promised, and the pony was worse. His eyes were almost closed now, and his breath whistled shrilly past an obstruction in his nose. A film covered that part of the eyes that was visible at all. It was doubtful whether the pony could see any more. Now and then he snorted, to clear his nose, and by the action seemed to plug it tighter. Jody looked dispiritedly at the pony's coat. The hair lay rough and unkempt and seemed to have lost all of its old luster. Billy stood quietly beside the stall. Jody hated to ask, but he had to know.

"Billy, is he—is he going to get well?"

Billy put his fingers between the bars under the pony's jaw and felt about. "Feel here," he said and he guided Jody's fingers to a large lump under the jaw. "When that gets bigger, I'll open it up and then he'll get better."

Jody looked quickly away, for he had heard about that lump. "What is it the matter with him?"

Billy didn't want to answer, but he had to. He couldn't be wrong three times. "Strangles," he said shortly, "but don't you worry about that. I'll pull him out of it. I've seen them get well when they were worse than Gabilan is. I'm going to steam him now. You can help."

"Yes," Jody said miserably. He followed Billy into the grain room and watched him make the steaming bag ready. It was a long canvas nose bag with straps to go over a horse's ears. Billy filled it one-third full of bran and then he added a couple of handfuls of dried hops. On top of the dry substance he poured a little carbolic acid and a little turpentine. "I'll be mixing it all up while you run to the house for a kettle of boiling water," Billy said.

When Jody came back with the steaming kettle, Billy buckled the straps over Gabilan's head and fitted the bag tightly around his nose. Then through a little hole in the side of the bag he poured the boiling water on the mixture. The pony started away as a cloud of strong steam rose up, but then the soothing fumes crept through his nose and into his lungs, and the sharp steam began to clear out the nasal passages. He breathed loudly. His legs trembled in an ague, and his eyes closed against the biting cloud. Billy poured in more water and kept the steam rising for fifteen minutes. At last he set down the kettle and took the bag from Gabilan's nose. The pony looked better. He breathed freely, and his eyes were open wider than they had been.

"See how good it makes him feel," Billy said. "Now we'll wrap him up in the blanket again. Maybe he'll be nearly well by morning."

"I'll stay with him tonight," Jody suggested.

"No. Don't you do it. I'll bring my blankets down here and put them in the hay. You can stay tomorrow and steam him if he needs it."

The evening was falling when they went to the house for their supper. Jody didn't even realize that some one else had fed the chickens and filled the wood-box. He walked up past the house to the dark brush line and took a drink of water from the tub. The spring water was so cold that it stung his mouth and drove a shiver through him. The sky above the hills was still light. He saw a hawk flying so high that it caught the sun on its breast and shone like a spark. Two blackbirds were driving him down the sky, glittering as they attacked their enemy. In the west, the clouds were moving in to rain again.

Jody's father didn't speak at all while the family ate supper, but after Billy Buck had taken his blankets and gone to sleep in the barn, Carl Tiflin built a high fire in the fireplace and told stories. He told about the wild man who ran naked through the country and had a tail and ears like a horse, and he told about the rabbit-cats of Moro Cojo that hopped into the trees for birds. He revived the famous Maxwell brothers who found a vein of gold and hid the traces of it so carefully that they could never find it again.

Jody sat with his chin in his hands; his mouth worked nervously, and his father gradually became aware that he wasn't listening very carefully. "Isn't that funny?" he asked.

Jody laughed politely and said, "Yes, sir." His father was angry and hurt, then. He didn't tell any more stories. After a while, Jody took a lantern and went down to the barn. Billy Buck was asleep in the hay, and, except that his breath rasped a little in his lungs, the pony seemed to be much better. Jody stayed a little while, running his fingers over the red rough coat, and then he took up the lantern and went back to the house. When he was in bed, his mother came into the room.

"Have you enough covers on? It's getting winter."

"Yes, ma'am."

"Well, get some rest tonight." She hesitated to go out, stood uncertainly. "The pony will be all right," she said.

Jody was tired. He went to sleep quickly and didn't awaken until dawn. The triangle sounded, and Billy Buck came up from the barn before Jody could get out of the house.

"How is he?" Jody demanded.

Billy always wolfed his breakfast. "Pretty good. I'm going to open that lump this morning. Then he'll be better maybe."

After breakfast, Billy got out his best knife, one with a

needle point. He whetted the shining blade a long time on a little carborundum stone. He tried the point and the blade again and again on his calloused thumb-ball, and at last he tried it on his upper lip.

On the way to the barn, Jody noticed how the young grass was up and how the stubble was melting day by day into the new green crop of volunteer. It was a cold sunny morning.

As soon as he saw the pony, Jody knew he was worse. His eyes were closed and sealed shut with dried mucus. His head hung so low that his nose almost touched the straw of his bed. There was a little groan in each breath, a deep-seated, patient groan.

Billy lifted the weak head and made a quick slash with the knife. Jody saw the yellow pus run out. He held up the head while Billy swabbed out the wound with weak carbolic acid salve.

"Now he'll feel better," Billy assured him. "That yellow poison is what makes him sick."

Jody looked unbelieving at Billy Buck. "He's awful sick."

Billy thought a long time what to say. He nearly tossed off a careless assurance, but he saved himself in time. "Yes, he's pretty sick," he said at last. "I've seen worse ones get well. If he doesn't get pneumonia, we'll pull him through. You stay with him. If he gets worse, you can come and get me."

For a long time after Billy went away, Jody stood beside the pony, stroking him behind the ears. The pony didn't flip his head the way he had done when he was well. The groaning in his breathing was becoming more hollow.

Doubletree Mutt looked into the barn, his big tail waving provocatively, and Jody was so incensed at his health that he found a hard black clod on the floor and deliberately threw it. Doubletree Mutt went yelping away to nurse a bruised paw.

In the middle of the morning, Billy Buck came back and made another steam bag. Jody watched to see whether the pony improved this time as he had before. His breathing eased a little, but he did not raise his head.

The Saturday dragged on. Late in the afternoon Jody went to the house and brought his bedding down and made up a place to sleep in the hay. He didn't ask permission. He knew from the way his mother looked at him that she would let him do almost anything. That night he left a lantern burning on a wire over the box stall. Billy had told him to rub the pony's legs every little while.

At nine o'clock the wind sprang up and howled around the barn. And in spite of his worry, Jody grew sleepy. He got into his blankets and went to sleep, but the breathy groans of the pony sounded in his dreams. And in his sleep he heard a crashing noise which went on and on until it awakened him. The wind was rushing through the barn. He sprang up and looked down the lane of stalls. The barn door had blown open, and the pony was gone.

He caught the lantern and ran outside into the gale, and he saw Gabilan weakly shambling away into the darkness, head down, legs working slowly and mechanically. When Jody ran up and caught him by the forelock, he allowed himself to be led back and put into his stall. His groans were louder, and a fierce whistling came from his nose. Jody didn't sleep any more then. The hissing of the pony's breath grew louder and sharper.

He was glad when Billy Buck came in at dawn. Billy looked for a time at the pony as though he had never seen him before. He felt the ears and flanks. "Jody," he said, "I've got to do something you won't want to see. You run up to the house for a while."

Jody grabbed him fiercely by the forearm. "You're not going to shoot him?"

Billy patted his hand. "No. I'm going to open a little hole in his windpipe so he can breathe. His nose is filled up. When he gets well, we'll put a little brass button in the hole for him to breath through."

Jody couldn't have gone away if he had wanted to. It was awful to see the red hide cut, but infinitely more terrible to know it was being cut and not to see it. "I'll stay right here," he said bitterly. "You sure you got to?"

"Yes. I'm sure. If you stay, you can hold his head. If it doesn't make you sick, that is."

The fine knife came out again and was whetted again just as carefully as it had been the first time. Jody held the pony's head up and the throat taut, while Billy felt up and down for the right place. Jody sobbed once as the bright knife point disappeared into the throat. The pony plunged weakly away and then stood still, trembling violently. The blood ran thickly out and up the knife and across Billy's hand and into his shirt-sleeve. The sure square hand sawed out a round hole in the flesh, and the breath came bursting out of the hole, throwing a fine spray of blood. With the rush of oxygen, the pony took a sudden strength. He lashed out with his hind feet and tried to rear, but Jody held his head down while Billy mopped the new wound with carbolic salve. It was a good job. The blood stopped flowing and the air puffed out the hole and sucked it in regularly with a little bubbling noise.

The rain brought in by the night wind began to fall on the barn roof. Then the triangle rang for breakfast. "You go up and eat while I wait," Billy said. "We've got to keep this hole from plugging up."

Jody walked slowly out of the barn. He was too dispirited to tell Billy how the barn door had blown open and let the pony out. He emerged into the wet grey morning and sloshed up to the house, taking a perverse pleasure in splashing through all the puddles. His mother fed him and put dry clothes on. She didn't question him. She seemed to know he couldn't answer questions. But when he was ready to go back to the barn she brought him a pan of steaming meal. "Give him this," she said.

But Jody did not take the pan. He said, "He won't eat anything," and ran out of the house. At the barn, Billy showed him how to fix a ball of cotton on a stick, with which to swab out the breathing hole when it became clogged with mucus.

Jody's father walked into the barn and stood with them in front of the stall. At length he turned to the boy. "Hadn't you better come with me? I'm going to drive over the hill." Jody shook his head. "You better come on, out of this," his father insisted.

Billy turned on him angrily. "Let him alone. It's his pony, isn't it?"

Carl Tiflin walked away without saying another word. His feelings were badly hurt.

All morning Jody kept the wound open and the air passing in and out freely. At noon the pony lay wearily down on his side and stretched his nose out.

Billy came back. "If you're going to stay with him tonight, you better take a little nap," he said. Jody went absently out of the barn. The sky had cleared to a hard thin blue. Everywhere the birds were busy with worms that had come to the damp surface of the ground.

Jody walked to the brush line and sat on the edge of the mossy tub. He looked down at the house and at the old bunkhouse and at the dark cypress tree. The place was familiar, but curiously changed. It wasn't itself any more, but a frame for things that were happening. A cold wind blew out of the east now, signifying that the rain was over for a little while. At his feet Jody could see the little arms of new weeds spreading out over the ground. In the mud about the spring were thousands of quail tracks.

Doubletree Mutt came sideways and embarrassed up through the vegetable patch, and Jody, remembering how he had thrown the clod, put his arm about the dog's neck and kissed him on his wide black nose. Doubletree Mutt sat still, as though he knew some solemn thing was happening. His big tail slapped the ground gravely. Jody pulled a swollen tick out of Mutt's neck and popped it dead between his thumbnails. It was a nasty thing. He washed his hands in the cold spring water.

Except for the steady swish of the wind, the farm was very quiet. Jody knew his mother wouldn't mind if he didn't go in to eat his lunch. After a little while he went slowly back to the barn. Mutt crept into his own little house and whined softly to himself for a long time.

Billy Buck stood up from the box and surrendered the cotton swab. The pony still lay on his side and the wound in his throat bellowsed in and out. When Jody saw how dry and dead the hair looked, he knew at last that there was no hope for the pony. He had seen the dead hair before on dogs and on cows, and it was a sure sign. He sat heavily on the box and let down the barrier of the box stall. For a long time he kept his eyes on the moving wound, and at last he dozed, and the afternoon passed quickly. Just before dark his mother brought a deep dish of stew and left it for him and went away. Jody ate a little of it, and, when it was dark, he set the lantern on the floor by the pony's head so he could watch the wound and keep it open. And he dozed again until the night chill awakened him. The wind was blowing fiercely, bringing the north cold with it. Jody brought a blanket from his bed in the hay and wrapped himself in it. Gabilan's breathing was quiet at last; the hole in his throat moved gently. The owls flew through the hayloft, shrieking and looking for mice. Jody put his hands down on his head and slept. In his sleep he was aware that the wind had increased. He heard it slamming about the barn.

It was daylight when he awakened. The barn door had swung open. The pony was gone. He sprang up and ran out into the morning light.

The pony's tracks were plain enough, dragging through the frostlike dew on the young grass, tired tracks with little lines between them where the hoofs had dragged. They headed for the brush line halfway up the ridge. Jody broke into a run and followed them. The sun shone on the sharp white quartz that stuck through the ground here and there. As he followed the plain trail, a shadow cut across in front of him. He looked up and saw a high circle of black buzzards, and the slowly revolving circle dropped lower and lower. The solemn birds soon disappeared over the ridge. Jody ran faster then, forced on by panic and rage. The trail entered the brush at last and followed a winding route among the tall sage bushes.

At the top of the ridge Jody was winded. He paused, puffing noisily. The blood pounded in his ears. Then he saw what he was looking for. Below, in one of the little clearings in the brush, lay the red pony. In the distance, Jody could see the legs moving slowly and convulsively. And in a circle around him stood the buzzards, waiting for the moment of death they know so well.

Jody leaped forward and plunged down the hill. The wet ground muffled his steps and the brush hid him. When he arrived, it was all over. The first buzzard sat on the pony's head and its beak had just risen dripping with dark eye fluid. Jody plunged into the circle like a cat. The black brotherhood arose in a cloud, but the big one on the pony's head was too late. As it hopped along to take off, Jody caught its wing tip and pulled it down. It was nearly as big as he was. The free wing crashed into his face with the force of a club, but he hung on. The claws fastened on his leg and the wing elbows battered his head on either side. Jody groped blindly with his free hand. His fingers found the neck of the struggling bird. The red eyes looked into his face, calm and fearless and fierce; the naked head turned from side to side. Then the beak opened and vomited a stream of putrefied fluid. Jody brought up his knee and fell on the great bird. He held the neck to the ground with one hand while his other found a piece of sharp white quartz. The first blow broke the beak sideways and black blood spurted from the twisted, leathery mouth corners. He struck again and missed. The red fearless eyes still looked at him, impersonal and unafraid and detached. He struck again and again, until the buzzard lay dead, until its head was a red pulp. He was still beating the dead bird when Billy Buck pulled him off and held him tightly to calm his shaking.

Carl Tiflin wiped the blood from the boy's face with a red bandana. Jody was limp and quiet now. His father moved the buzzard with his toe. "Jody," he explained, "the buzzard didn't kill the pony. Don't you know that?"

"I know it," Jody said wearily.

It was Billy Buck who was angry. He had lifted Jody in his arms, and had turned to carry him home. But he turned back on Carl Tiflin. " 'Course he knows it," Billy said furiously. "Jesus Christ! man, can't you see how he'd feel about it?"

II. THE GREAT MOUNTAINS

In the humming heat of a midsummer afternoon the little boy Jody listlessly looked about the ranch for something to do. He had been to the barn, had thrown rocks at the swallows' nests under the eaves until every one of the little mud houses broke open and dropped its lining of straw and dirty feathers. Then at the ranch house he baited a rat trap with stale cheese and set it where Doubletree Mutt, that good big dog, would get his nose snapped. Jody was not moved by an impulse of cruelty; he was bored with the long hot afternoon. Doubletree Mutt put his stupid nose in the trap and got it smacked, and shrieked with agony and limped away with blood on his nostrils. No matter where he was hurt, Mutt limped. It was just a way he had. Once when he was young, Mutt got caught in a coyote trap, and always after that he limped, even when he was scolded.

When Mutt yelped, Jody's mother called from inside the house, "Jody! Stop torturing that dog and find something to do."

Jody felt mean then, so he threw a rock at Mutt. Then he took his slingshot from the porch and walked up toward the brush line to try to kill a bird. It was a good slingshot, with store-bought rubbers, but while Jody had often shot at birds, he had never hit one. He walked up through the vegetable patch, kicking his bare toes into the dust. And on the way he found the perfect slingshot stone, round and slightly flattened and heavy enough to carry through the air. He fitted it into the leather pouch of his weapon and proceeded to the brush line. His eyes narrowed, his mouth worked strenuously; for the first time that afternoon he was intent. In the shade of the sagebrush the little birds were working, scratching in the leaves, flying restlessly a few feet and scratching again. Jody pulled back the rubbers of the sling and advanced cautiously. One little thrush paused and looked at him and crouched, ready to fly. Jody sidled nearer, moving one foot slowly after the other. When he was twenty feet away, he carefully raised the sling and aimed. The stone whizzed; the thrush started up and flew right into it. And down the little bird went with a broken head. Jody ran to it and picked it up.

"Well, I got you," he said.

The bird looked much smaller dead than it had alive. Jody felt a little mean pain in his stomach, so he took out his pocket-knife and cut off the bird's head. Then he disemboweled it, and took off its wings; and finally he threw all the pieces into the brush. He didn't care about the bird, or its life, but he knew what older people would say if they had seen him kill it; he was ashamed because of their potential opinion. He decided to forget the whole thing as quickly as he could, and never to mention it.

The hills were dry at this season, and the wild grass was golden, but where the spring-pipe filled the round tub and the tub spilled over, there lay a stretch of fine green grass, deep and sweet and moist. Jody drank from the mossy tub and washed the bird's blood from his hands in cold water. Then he lay on his back in the grass and looked up at the dumpling summer clouds. By closing one eye and destroying perspective he brought them down within reach so that he could put up his fingers and stroke them. He helped the gentle wind push them down the sky; it seemed to him that they went faster for his help. One fat white cloud he helped clear to the mountain rims and pressed it firmly over, out of sight. Jody wondered what it was seeing, then. He sat up the better to look at the great mountains where they went piling back, growing darker and more savage until they finished with one jagged ridge, high up against the west. Curious secret mountains; he thought of the little he knew about them.

"What's on the other side?" he asked his father once.

"More mountains, I guess. Why?"

"And on the other side of them?"

"More mountains. Why?"

"More mountains on and on?"

"Well, no. At last you come to the ocean."

"But what's in the mountains?"

"Just cliffs and brush and rocks and dryness."

"Were you ever there?"

"No."

"Has anybody ever been there?"

"A few people, I guess. It's dangerous, with cliffs and things. Why, I've read there's more unexplored country in the mountains of Monterey County than any place in the United States." His father seemed proud that this should be so.

"And at last the ocean?"

"At last the ocean."

"But," the boy insisted, "but in between? No one knows?"

"Oh, a few people do, I guess. But there's nothing there

to get. And not much water. Just rocks and cliffs and greasewood. Why?"

"It would be good to go."

"What for? There's nothing there."

Jody knew something was there, something very wonderful
because it wasn't known, something secret and mysterious.
He could feel within himself that this was so. He said to his
mother, "Do you know what's in the big mountains?"

She looked at him and then back at the ferocious range,
and she said, "Only the bear, I guess."

"What bear?"

"Why the one that went over the mountain to see what he
could see."

Jody questioned Billy Buck, the ranch hand, about the possibility of ancient cities lost in the mountains, but Billy agreed
with Jody's father.

"It ain't likely," Billy said. "There'd be nothing to eat unless a kind of people that can eat rocks live there."

That was all the information Jody ever got, and it made the
mountains dear to him, and terrible. He thought often of the
miles of ridge after ridge until at last there was the sea. When
the peaks were pink in the morning they invited him among
them: and when the sun had gone over the edge in the evening and the mountains were a purple-like despair, then Jody
was afraid of them; then they were so impersonal and aloof
that their very imperturbability was a threat.

Now he turned his head toward the mountains of the east,
the Gabilans, and they were jolly mountains, with hill ranches
in their creases, and with pine trees growing on the crests.
People lived there, and battles had been fought against the
Mexicans on the slopes. He looked back for an instant at the
Great Ones and shivered a little at the contrast. The foothill
cup of the home ranch below him was sunny and safe. The
house gleamed with white light and the barn was brown and
warm. The red cows on the farther hill ate their way slowly
toward the north. Even the dark cypress tree by the bunkhouse was usual and safe. The chickens scratched about in the
dust of the farmyard with quick waltzing steps.

Then a moving figure caught Jody's eye. A man walked

slowly over the brow of the hill, on the road from Salinas, and he was headed toward the house. Jody stood up and moved down toward the house too, for if someone was coming, he wanted to be there to see. By the time the boy had got to the house the walking man was only halfway down the road, a lean man, very straight in the shoulders. Jody could tell he was old only because his heels struck the ground with hard jerks. As he approached nearer, Jody saw that he was dressed in blue jeans and in a coat of the same material. He wore clodhopper shoes and an old flat-brimmed Stetson hat. Over his shoulder he carried a gunny sack, lumpy and full. In a few moments he had trudged close enough so that his face could be seen. And his face was as dark as dried beef. A mustache, blue-white against the dark skin, hovered over his mouth, and his hair was white, too, where it showed at his neck. The skin of his face had shrunk back against the skull until it defined bone, not flesh, and made the nose and chin seem sharp and fragile. The eyes were large and deep and dark, with eyelids stretched tightly over them. Irises and pupils were one, and very black, but the eyeballs were brown. There were no wrinkles in the face at all. This old man wore a blue denim coat buttoned to the throat with brass buttons, as all men do who wear no shirts. Out of the sleeves came strong bony wrists and hands gnarled and knotted and hard as peach branches. The nails were flat and blunt and shiny.

The old man drew close to the gate and swung down his sack when he confronted Jody. His lips fluttered a little and a soft impersonal voice came from between them.

"Do you live here?"

Jody was embarrassed. He turned and looked at the house, and he turned back and looked toward the barn where his father and Billy Buck were. "Yes," he said, when no help came from either direction.

"I have come back," the old man said. "I am Gitano, and I have come back."

Jody could not take all this responsibility. He turned abruptly, and ran into the house for help, and the screen door banged after him. His mother was in the kitchen poking out the clogged holes of a colander with a hairpin, and biting her lower lip with concentration.

"It's an old man," Jody cried excitedly. "It's an old *paisano* man, and he says he's come back."

His mother put down the colander and stuck the hairpin behind the sink board. "What's the matter now?" she asked patiently.

"It's an old man outside. Come on out."

"Well, what does he want?" She untied the strings of her apron and smoothed her hair with her fingers.

"I don't know. He came walking."

His mother smoothed down her dress and went out, and Jody followed her. Gitano had not moved.

"Yes?" Mrs. Tiflin asked.

Gitano took off his old black hat and held it with both hands in front of him. He repeated, "I am Gitano, and I have come back."

"Come back? Back where?"

Gitano's whole straight body leaned forward a little. His right hand described the circle of the hills, the sloping fields and the mountains, and ended at his hat again. "Back to the rancho. I was born here, and my father, too."

"Here?" she demanded. "This isn't an old place."

"No, there," he said, pointing to the western ridge. "On the other side there, in a house that is gone."

At last she understood. "The old 'dobe that's washed almost away, you mean?"

"Yes, *señora*. When the rancho broke up they put no more lime on the 'dobe, and the rains washed it down."

Jody's mother was silent for a little, and curious homesick thoughts ran through her mind, but quickly she cleared them out. "And what do you want here now, Gitano?"

"I will stay here," he said quietly, "until I die."

"But we don't need an extra man here."

"I can not work hard any more, *señora*. I can milk a cow, feed chickens, cut a little wood; no more. I will stay here." He indicated the sack on the ground beside him. "Here are my things."

She turned to Jody. "Run down to the barn and call your father."

Jody dashed away, and he returned with Carl Tiflin and Billy Buck behind him. The old man was standing as he had been, but he was resting now. His whole body had sagged into a timeless repose.

"What is it?" Carl Tiflin asked. "What's Jody so excited about?"

Mrs. Tiflin motioned to the old man. "He wants to stay here. He wants to do a little work and stay here."

"Well, we can't have him. We don't need any more men. He's too old. Billy does everything we need."

They had been talking over him as though he did not exist, and now, suddenly, they both hesitated and looked at Gitano and were embarrassed.

He cleared his throat. "I am too old to work. I come back where I was born."

"You weren't born here," Carl said sharply.

"No. In the 'dobe house over the hill. It was all one rancho before you came."

"In the mud house that's all melted down?"

"Yes. I and my father. I will stay here now on the rancho."

"I tell you you won't stay," Carl said angrily. "I don't need an old man. This isn't a big ranch. I can't afford food and doctor bills for an old man. You must have relatives and friends. Go to them. It is like begging to come to strangers."

"I was born here," Gitano said patiently and inflexibly.

Carl Tiflin didn't like to be cruel, but he felt he must. "You can eat here tonight," he said. "You can sleep in the little room of the old bunkhouse. We'll give you your breakfast in the morning, and then you'll have to go along. Go to your friends. Don't come to die with strangers."

Gitano put on his black hat and stooped for the sack. "Here are my things," he said.

Carl turned away. "Come on, Billy, we'll finish down at the barn. Jody, show him the little room in the bunkhouse."

He and Billy turned back toward the barn. Mrs. Tiflin went into the house, saying over her shoulder, "I'll send some blankets down."

Gitano looked questioningly at Jody. "I'll show you where it is," Jody said.

There was a cot with a shuck mattress, an apple box holding a tin lantern, and a backless rocking-chair in the little room of the bunkhouse. Gitano laid his sack carefully on the floor and sat down on the bed. Jody stood shyly in the room, hesitating to go. At last he said,

"Did you come out of the big mountains?"

Gitano shook his head slowly. "No, I worked down the Salinas Valley."

The afternoon thought would not let Jody go. "Did you ever go into the big mountains back there?"

The old dark eyes grew fixed, and their light turned inward on the years that were living in Gitano's head. "Once—when I was a little boy. I went with my father."

"Way back, clear into the mountains?"

"Yes."

"What was there?" Jody cried. "Did you see any people or any houses?"

"No."

"Well, what was there?"

Gitano's eyes remained inward. A little wrinkled strain came between his brows.

"What did you see in there?" Jody repeated.

"I don't know," Gitano said. "I don't remember."

"Was it terrible and dry?"

"I don't remember."

In his excitement, Jody had lost his shyness. "Don't you remember anything about it?"

Gitano's mouth opened for a word, and remained open while his brain sought the word. "I think it was quiet—I think it was nice."

Gitano's eyes seemed to have found something back in the years, for they grew soft and a little smile seemed to come and go in them.

"Didn't you ever go back in the mountains again?" Jody insisted.

"No."

"Didn't you ever want to?"

But now Gitano's face became impatient. "No," he said in a tone that told Jody he didn't want to talk about it any more. The boy was held by a curious fascination. He didn't want to go away from Gitano. His shyness returned.

"Would you like to come down to the barn and see the stock?" he asked.

Gitano stood up and put on his hat and prepared to follow.

It was almost evening now. They stood near the watering trough while the horses sauntered in from the hillsides for an evening drink. Gitano rested his big twisted hands on the top rail of the fence. Five horses came down and drank, and then stood about, nibbling at the dirt or rubbing their sides against the polished wood of the fence. Long after they had finished drinking an old horse appeared over the brow of the hill and came painfully down. It had long yellow teeth; its hooves were flat and sharp as spades, and its ribs and hip-bones jutted out under its skin. It hobbled up to the trough and drank water with a loud sucking noise.

"That's old Easter," Jody explained. "That's the first horse my father ever had. He's thirty years old." He looked up into Gitano's old eyes for some response.

"No good any more," Gitano said.

Jody's father and Billy Buck came out of the barn and walked over.

"Too old to work," Gitano repeated. "Just eats and pretty soon dies."

Carl Tiflin caught the last words. He hated his brutality toward old Gitano, and so he became brutal again.

"It's a shame not to shoot Easter," he said. "It'd save him a lot of pains and rheumatism." He looked secretly at Gitano, to see whether he noticed the parallel, but the big bony hands did not move, nor did the dark eyes turn from the horse. "Old things ought to be put out of their misery," Jody's father went on. "One shot, a big noise, one big pain in the head maybe, and that's all. That's better than stiffness and sore teeth."

Billy Buck broke in. "They got a right to rest after they worked all of their life. Maybe they like to just walk around."

Carl had been looking steadily at the skinny horse. "You can't imagine now what Easter used to look like," he said softly. "High neck, deep chest, fine barrel. He could jump a five-bar gate in stride. I won a flat race on him when I was fifteen years old. I could of got two hundred dollars for him any time. You wouldn't think how pretty he was." He checked himself, for he hated softness. "But he ought to be shot now," he said.

"He's got a right to rest," Billy Buck insisted.

Jody's father had a humorous thought. He turned to Gitano. "If ham and eggs grew on a side-hill I'd turn you out to pasture too," he said. "But I can't afford to pasture you in my kitchen."

He laughed to Billy Buck about it as they went on toward the house. "Be a good thing for all of us if ham and eggs grew on the side-hills."

Jody knew how his father was probing for a place to hurt in Gitano. He had been probed often. His father knew every place in the boy where a word would fester.

"He's only talking," Jody said. "He didn't mean it about shooting Easter. He likes Easter. That was the first horse he ever owned."

The sun sank behind the high mountains as they stood there, and the ranch was hushed. Gitano seemed to be more at home in the evening. He made a curious sharp sound with his lips and stretched one of his hands over the fence. Old Easter moved stiffly to him, and Gitano rubbed the lean neck under the mane.

"You like him?" Jody asked softly.

"Yes—but he's no damn good."

The triangle sounded at the ranch house. "That's supper," Jody cried. "Come on up to supper."

As they walked up toward the house Jody noticed again that Gitano's body was as straight as that of a young man. Only by a jerkiness in his movements and by the scuffling of his heels could it be seen that he was old.

The turkeys were flying heavily into the lower branches of the cypress tree by the bunkhouse. A fat sleek ranch cat walked across the road carrying a rat so large that its tail dragged on the ground. The quail on the side-hills were still sounding the clear water call.

Jody and Gitano came to the back steps and Mrs. Tiflin looked out through the screen door at them.

"Come running, Jody. Come in to supper, Gitano."

Carl and Billy Buck had started to eat at the long oilcloth-covered table. Jody slipped into his chair without moving it, but Gitano stood holding his hat until Carl looked up and said, "Sit down, sit down. You might as well get your belly full before you go on." Carl was afraid he might relent and let the old man stay, and so he continued to remind himself that this couldn't be.

Gitano laid his hat on the floor and diffidently sat down. He wouldn't reach for food. Carl had to pass it to him. "Here, fill yourself up." Gitano ate very slowly, cutting tiny pieces of meat and arranging little pats of mashed potato on his plate.

The situation would not stop worrying Carl Tiflin. "Haven't you got any relatives in this part of the country?" he asked.

Gitano answered with some pride, "My brother-in-law is in Monterey. I have cousins there, too."

"Well, you can go and live there, then."

"I was born here," Gitano said in a gentle rebuke.

Jody's mother came in from the kitchen, carrying a large bowl of tapioca pudding.

Carl chuckled to her, "Did I tell you what I said to him? I said if ham and eggs grew on the side-hills I'd put him out to pasture, like old Easter."

Gitano stared unmoved at his plate.

"It's too bad he can't stay," said Mrs. Tiflin.

"Now don't you start anything," Carl said crossly.

When they had finished eating, Carl and Billy Buck and Jody went into the living-room to sit for a while, but Gitano, without a word of farewell or thanks, walked through the kitchen and out the back door. Jody sat and secretly watched his father. He knew how mean his father felt.

"This country's full of these old *paisanos*," Carl said to Billy Buck.

"They're damn good men," Billy defended them. "They can work older than white men. I saw one of them a hundred and five years old, and he could still ride a horse. You don't see any white men as old as Gitano walking twenty or thirty miles."

"Oh, they're tough, all right," Carl agreed. "Say, are you standing up for him too? Listen, Billy," he explained, "I'm having a hard enough time keeping this ranch out of the Bank of Italy without taking on anybody else to feed. You know that, Billy."

"Sure, I know," said Billy. "If you was rich, it'd be different."

"That's right, and it isn't like he didn't have relatives to go to. A brother-in-law and cousins right in Monterey. Why should I worry about him?"

Jody sat quietly listening, and he seemed to hear Gitano's gentle voice and its unanswerable, "But I was born here." Gitano was mysterious like the mountains. There were ranges back as far as you could see, but behind the last range piled up against the sky there was a great unknown country. And Gitano was an old man, until you got to the dull dark eyes. And in behind them was some unknown thing. He didn't ever say enough to let you guess what was inside, under the eyes. Jody felt himself irresistibly drawn toward the bunkhouse. He slipped from his chair while his father was talking and he went out the door without making a sound.

The night was very dark and far-off noises carried in clearly. The hamebells of a wood team sounded from way over the hill on the county road. Jody picked his way across the dark yard. He could see a light through the window of the little room of the bunkhouse. Because the night was secret he walked quietly up to the window and peered in. Gitano sat in the rocking-chair and his back was toward the window. His right arm moved slowly back and forth in front of him. Jody pushed the door open and walked in. Gitano jerked upright and, seizing a piece of deerskin, he tried to throw it over the thing in his lap, but the skin slipped away. Jody stood overwhelmed by the thing in Gitano's hand, a lean and lovely rapier with a golden basket hilt. The blade was like a thin ray of dark light. The hilt was pierced and intricately carved.

"What is it?" Jody demanded.

Gitano only looked at him with resentful eyes, and he picked up the fallen deerskin and firmly wrapped the beautiful blade in it.

Jody put out his hand. "Can't I see it?"

Gitano's eyes smoldered angrily and he shook his head.

"Where'd you get it? Where'd it come from?"

Now Gitano regarded him profoundly, as though he pondered. "I got it from my father."

"Well, where'd he get it?"

Gitano looked down at the long deerskin parcel in his hand. "I don' know."

"Didn't he ever tell you?"

"No."

"What do you do with it?"

Gitano looked slightly surprised. "Nothing. I just keep it."

"Can't I see it again?"

The old man slowly unwrapped the shining blade and let the lamplight slip along it for a moment. Then he wrapped it up again. "You go now. I want to go to bed." He blew out the lamp almost before Jody had closed the door.

As he went back toward the house, Jody knew one thing more sharply than he had ever known anything. He must never tell anyone about the rapier. It would be a dreadful thing to tell anyone about it, for it would destroy some fragile structure of truth. It was a truth that might be shattered by division.

On the way across the dark yard Jody passed Billy Buck. "They're wondering where you are," Billy said.

Jody slipped into the living-room, and his father turned to him. "Where have you been?"

"I just went out to see if I caught any rats in my new trap."

"It's time you went to bed," his father said.

Jody was first at the breakfast table in the morning. Then his father came in, and last, Billy Buck. Mrs. Tiflin looked in from the kitchen.

"Where's the old man, Billy?" she asked.

"I guess he's out walking," Billy said. "I looked in his room and he wasn't there."

"Maybe he started early to Monterey," said Carl. "It's a long walk."

"No," Billy explained. "His sack is in the little room."

After breakfast Jody walked down to the bunkhouse. Flies were flashing about in the sunshine. The ranch seemed especially quiet this morning. When he was sure no one was watching him, Jody went into the little room, and looked into Gitano's sack. An extra pair of long cotton underwear was there, an extra pair of jeans and three pairs of worn socks. Nothing else was in the sack. A sharp loneliness fell on Jody. He walked slowly back toward the house. His father stood on the porch talking to Mrs. Tiflin.

"I guess old Easter's dead at last," he said. "I didn't see him come down to water with the other horses."

In the middle of the morning Jess Taylor from the ridge ranch rode down.

"You didn't sell that old gray crowbait of yours, did you, Carl?"

"No, of course not. Why?"

"Well," Jess said. "I was out this morning early, and I saw a funny thing. I saw an old man on an old horse, no saddle, only a piece of rope for a bridle. He wasn't on the road at all. He was cutting right up straight through the brush. I think he had a gun. At least I saw something shine in his hand."

"That's old Gitano," Carl Tiflin said. "I'll see if any of my guns are missing." He stepped into the house for a second. "Nope, all here. Which way was he heading, Jess?"

"Well, that's the funny thing. He was heading straight back into the mountains."

Carl laughed. "They never get too old to steal," he said. "I guess he just stole old Easter."

"Want to go after him, Carl?"

"Hell no, just save me burying that horse. I wonder where he got the gun. I wonder what he wants back there."

Jody walked up through the vegetable patch, toward the brush line. He looked searchingly at the towering mountains—ridge after ridge after ridge until at last there was the ocean. For a moment he thought he could see a black speck crawling up the farthest ridge. Jody thought of the rapier and of Gitano. And he thought of the great mountains. A longing caressed him, and it was so sharp that he wanted to cry to get it out of his breast. He lay down in the green grass near the round tub at the brush line. He covered his eyes with his crossed arms and lay there a long time, and he was full of a nameless sorrow.

III. THE PROMISE

In a mid-afternoon of spring, the little boy Jody walked martially along the brush-lined road toward his home ranch. Banging his knee against the golden lard bucket he used for school lunch, he contrived a good bass drum, while his tongue fluttered sharply against his teeth to fill in snare drums and occasional trumpets. Some time back the other members of the squad that walked so smartly from the school had turned into the various little canyons and taken the wagon roads to their own home ranches. Now Jody marched seemingly alone, with high-lifted knees and pounding feet; but behind him there was a phantom army with great flags and swords, silent but deadly.

The afternoon was green and gold with spring. Underneath the spread branches of the oaks the plants grew pale and tall, and on the hills the feed was smooth and thick. The sage-brushes shone with new silver leaves and the oaks wore hoods of golden green. Over the hills there hung such a green odor that the horses on the flats galloped madly, and then stopped, wondering; lambs, and even old sheep jumped in the air unexpectedly and landed on stiff legs, and went on eating; young clumsy calves butted their heads together and drew back and butted again.

As the gray and silent army marched past, led by Jody, the animals stopped their feeding and their play and watched it go by.

Suddenly Jody stopped. The gray army halted, bewildered and nervous. Jody went down on his knees. The army stood in long uneasy ranks for a moment, and then, with a soft sigh of sorrow, rose up in a faint grey mist and disappeared. Jody had seen the thorny crown of a horny-toad moving under the dust of the road. His grimy hand went out and grasped the spiked halo and held firmly while the little beast struggled. Then Jody turned the horny-toad over, exposing its pale gold stomach. With a gentle forefinger he stroked the throat and chest until the horny-toad relaxed, until its eyes closed and it lay languorous and asleep.

Jody opened his lunch pail and deposited the first game inside. He moved on now, his knees bent slightly, his shoulders crouched; his bare feet were wise and silent. In his right hand there was a long gray rifle. The brush along the road stirred restively under a new and unexpected population of grey tigers and grey bears. The hunting was very good, for by the time Jody reached the fork of the road where the mail box stood on a post, he had captured two more horny-toads, four little grass lizards, a blue snake, sixteen yellow-winged grasshoppers and a brown damp newt from under a rock. This assortment scrabbled unhappily against the tin of the lunch bucket.

At the road fork the rifle evaporated and the tigers and bears melted from the hillsides. Even the moist and uncomfortable creatures in the lunch pail ceased to exist, for the little red metal flag was up on the mail box, signifying that some postal matter was inside. Jody set his pail on the ground and opened the letter box. There was a Montgomery Ward catalog and a copy of the *Salinas Weekly Journal*. He slammed the box, picked up his lunch pail and trotted over the ridge and down into the cup of the ranch. Past the barn he ran, and past the used-up haystack and the bunkhouse and the cypress tree. He banged through the front screen door of the ranch house calling, "Ma'am, ma'am, there's a catalog."

Mrs. Tiflin was in the kitchen spooning clabbered milk into a cotton bag. She put down her work and rinsed her hands under the tap. "Here in the kitchen, Jody. Here I am."

He ran in and clattered his lunch pail on the sink. "Here it is. Can I open the catalog, ma'am?"

Mrs. Tiflin took up the spoon again and went back to her cottage cheese. "Don't lose it, Jody. Your father will want to see it." She scraped the last of the milk into the bag. "Oh, Jody, your father wants to see you before you go to your chores." She waved a cruising fly from the cheese bag.

Jody closed the new catalog in alarm. "Ma'am?"

"Why don't you ever listen? I say your father wants to see you."

The boy laid the catalog gently on the sink board. "Do you—is it something I did?"

Mrs. Tiflin laughed. "Always a bad conscience. What did you do?"

"Nothing, ma'am," he said lamely. But he couldn't remember, and besides it was impossible to know what action might later be construed as a crime.

His mother hung the full bag on a nail where it could drip into the sink. "He just said he wanted to see you when you got home. He's somewhere down by the barn."

Jody turned and went out the back door. Hearing his mother open the lunch pail and then gasp with rage, a memory stabbed him and he trotted away toward the barn, conscientiously not hearing the angry voice that called him from the house.

Carl Tiflin and Billy Buck, the ranch hand, stood against the lower pasture fence. Each man rested one foot on the lowest bar and both elbows on the top bar. They were talking slowly and aimlessly. In the pasture half a dozen horses nibbled contentedly at the sweet grass. The mare, Nellie, stood backed up against the gate, rubbing her buttocks on the heavy post.

Jody sidled uneasily near. He dragged one foot to give an impression of great innocence and nonchalance. When he arrived beside the men he put one foot on the lowest fence rail, rested his elbows on the second bar and looked into the pasture too. The two men glanced sideways at him.

"I wanted to see you," Carl said in the stern tone he reserved for children and animals.

"Yes, sir," said Jody guiltily.

"Billy, here, says you took good care of the pony before it died."

No punishment was in the air. Jody grew bolder. "Yes, sir, I did."

"Billy says you have a good patient hand with horses."

Jody felt a sudden warm friendliness for the ranch hand.

Billy put in, "He trained that pony as good as anybody I ever seen."

Then Carl Tiflin came gradually to the point. "If you could have another horse would you work for it?"

Jody shivered. "Yes, sir."

"Well, look here, then. Billy says the best way for you to be a good hand with horses is to raise a colt."

"It's the *only* good way," Billy interrupted.

"Now, look here, Jody," continued Carl. "Jess Taylor, up to the ridge ranch, has a fair stallion, but it'll cost five dollars. I'll put up the money, but you'll have to work it out all summer. Will you do that?"

Jody felt that his insides were shriveling. "Yes, sir," he said softly.

"And no complaining? And no forgetting when you're told to do something?"

"Yes, sir."

"Well, all right, then. Tomorrow morning you take Nellie up to the ridge ranch and get her bred. You'll have to take care of her, too, till she throws the colt."

"Yes, sir."

"You better get to the chickens and the wood now."

Jody slid away. In passing behind Billy Buck he very nearly put out his hand to touch the blue-jeaned legs. His shoulders swayed a little with maturity and importance.

He went to his work with unprecedented seriousness. This night he did not dump the can of grain to the chickens so that they had to leap over each other and struggle to get it. No, he spread the wheat so far and so carefully that the hens couldn't find some of it at all. And in the house, after listening to his mother's despair over boys who filled their lunch pails with slimy, suffocated reptiles, and bugs, he promised never to do it again. Indeed, Jody felt that all such foolishness was lost in the past. He was far too grown up ever to put horny-toads in his lunch pail any more. He carried in so much wood and built such a high structure with it that his mother walked in fear of an avalanche of oak. When he was done, when he had gathered eggs that had remained hidden for weeks, Jody walked down again past the cypress tree, and past the bunk-house toward the pasture. A fat warty toad that looked out at him from under the watering trough had no emotional effect on him at all.

Carl Tiflin and Billy Buck were not in sight, but from a metallic ringing on the other side of the barn Jody knew that Billy Buck was just starting to milk a cow.

The other horses were eating toward the upper end of the pasture, but Nellie continued to rub herself nervously against the post. Jody walked slowly near, saying, "So, girl, so-o, Nellie." The mare's ears went back naughtily and her lips drew away from her yellow teeth. She turned her head around; her eyes were glazed and mad. Jody climbed to the top of the fence and hung his feet over and looked paternally down on the mare.

The evening hovered while he sat there. Bats and nighthawks flicked about. Billy Buck, walking toward the house carrying a full milk bucket, saw Jody and stopped. "It's a long time to wait," he said gently. "You'll get awful tired waiting."

"No I won't, Billy. How long will it be?"

"Nearly a year."

"Well, I won't get tired."

The triangle at the house rang stridently. Jody climbed down from the fence and walked to supper beside Billy Buck. He even put out his hand and took hold of the milk bucket to help carry it.

The next morning after breakfast Carl Tiflin folded a five-dollar bill in a piece of newspaper and pinned the package in the bib pocket of Jody's overalls. Billy Buck haltered the mare Nellie and led her out of the pasture.

"Be careful now," he warned. "Hold her up short here so she can't bite you. She's crazy as a coot."

Jody took hold of the halter leather itself and started up the hill toward the ridge ranch with Nellie skittering and jerking behind him. In the pasturage along the road the wild oat heads were just clearing their scabbards. The warm morning sun shone on Jody's back so sweetly that he was forced to take a serious stiff-legged hop now and then in spite of his maturity. On the fences the shiny blackbirds with red epaulets clicked their dry call. The meadowlarks sang like water, and the wild doves, concealed among the bursting leaves of the oaks, made a sound of restrained grieving. In the fields the rabbits sat sunning themselves, with only their forked ears showing above the grass heads.

After an hour of steady uphill walking, Jody turned into a narrow road that led up a steeper hill to the ridge ranch. He could see the red roof of the barn sticking up above the oak trees, and he could hear a dog barking unemotionally near the house.

Suddenly Nellie jerked back and nearly freed herself. From the direction of the barn Jody heard a shrill whistling scream and a splintering of wood, and then a man's voice shouting. Nellie reared and whinnied. When Jody held to the halter rope she ran at him with bared teeth. He dropped his hold and scuttled out of the way, into the brush. The high scream came from the oaks again, and Nellie answered it. With hoofs battering the ground the stallion appeared and charged down the hill trailing a broken halter rope. His eyes glittered feverishly. His stiff, erected nostrils were as red as flame. His black, sleek hide shone in the sunlight. The stallion came on so fast that he couldn't stop when he reached the mare. Nellie's ears went back; she whirled and kicked at him as he went by. The stallion spun around and reared. He struck the mare with his front hoof, and while she staggered under the blow, his teeth raked her neck and drew an ooze of blood.

Instantly Nellie's mood changed. She became coquettishly feminine. She nibbled his arched neck with her lips. She edged around and rubbed her shoulder against his shoulder. Jody stood half-hidden in the brush and watched. He heard the step of a horse behind him, but before he could turn, a hand caught him by the overall straps and lifted him off the ground. Jess Taylor sat the boy behind him on the horse.

"You might have got killed," he said. "Sundog's a mean devil sometimes. He busted his rope and went right through a gate."

Jody sat quietly, but in a moment he cried, "He'll hurt her, he'll kill her. Get him away!"

Jess chuckled. "She'll be all right. Maybe you'd better climb off and go up to the house for a little. You could get maybe a piece of pie up there."

But Jody shook his head. "She's mine, and the colt's going to be mine. I'm going to raise it up."

Jess nodded. "Yes, that's a good thing. Carl has good sense sometimes."

In a little while the danger was over. Jess lifted Jody down and then caught the stallion by its broken halter rope. And he rode ahead, while Jody followed, leading Nellie.

It was only after he had unpinned and handed over the five dollars, and after he had eaten two pieces of pie, that Jody started for home again. And Nellie followed docilely after him. She was so quiet that Jody climbed on a stump and rode her most of the way home.

The five dollars his father had advanced reduced Jody to peonage for the whole late spring and summer. When the hay was cut he drove a rake. He led the horse that pulled on the Jackson-fork tackle, and when the baler came he drove the circling horse that put pressure on the bales. In addition, Carl Tiflin taught him to milk and put a cow under his care, so that a new chore was added night and morning.

The bay mare Nellie quickly grew complacent. As she walked about the yellowing hillsides or worked at easy tasks, her lips were curled in a perpetual fatuous smile. She moved slowly, with the calm importance of an empress. When she was put to a team, she pulled steadily and unemotionally. Jody went to see her every day. He studied her with critical eyes and saw no change whatever.

One afternoon Billy Buck leaned the many-tined manure fork against the barn wall. He loosened his belt and tucked in his shirt-tail and tightened the belt again. He picked one of the little straws from his hatband and put it in the corner of his mouth. Jody, who was helping Doubletree Mutt, the big serious dog, to dig out a gopher, straightened up as the ranch hand sauntered out of the barn.

"Let's go up and have a look at Nellie," Billy suggested.

Instantly Jody fell into step with him. Doubletree Mutt watched them over his shoulder; then he dug furiously, growled, sounded little sharp yelps to indicate that the gopher was practically caught. When he looked over his shoulder again, and saw that neither Jody nor Billy was interested, he climbed reluctantly out of the hole and followed them up the hill.

The wild oats were ripening. Every head bent sharply under its load of grain, and the grass was dry enough so that it made a swishing sound as Jody and Billy stepped through it. Half-way up the hill they could see Nellie and the iron-grey gelding, Pete, nibbling the heads from the wild oats. When they approached, Nellie looked at them and backed her ears and bobbed her head up and down rebelliously. Billy walked to her and put his hand under her mane and patted her neck, until her ears came forward again and she nibbled delicately at his shirt.

Jody asked, "Do you think she's really going to have a colt?"

Billy rolled the lids back from the mare's eyes with his thumb and forefinger. He felt the lower lip and fingered the black, leathery teats. "I wouldn't be surprised," he said.

"Well, she isn't changed at all. It's three months gone."

Billy rubbed the mare's flat forehead with his knuckle while she grunted with pleasure. "I told you you'd get tired waiting. It'll be five months more before you can even see a sign, and it'll be at least eight months more before she throws the colt, about next January."

Jody sighed deeply. "It's a long time, isn't it?"

"And then it'll be about two years more before you can ride."

Jody cried out in despair, "I'll be grown up."

"Yep, you'll be an old man," said Billy.

"What color do you think the colt'll be?"

"Why, you can't ever tell. The stud is black and the dam is bay. Colt might be black or bay or gray or dappled. You can't tell. Sometimes a black dam might have a white colt."

"Well, I hope it's black, and a stallion."

"If it's a stallion, we'll have to geld it. Your father wouldn't let you have a stallion."

"Maybe he would," Jody said. "I could train him not to be mean."

Billy pursed his lips, and the little straw that had been in the corner of his mouth rolled down to the center. "You can't ever trust a stallion," he said critically. "They're mostly fighting and making trouble. Sometimes when they're feeling funny they won't work. They make the mares uneasy and kick hell out of the geldings. Your father wouldn't let you keep a stallion."

Nellie sauntered away, nibbling the drying grass. Jody skinned the grain from a grass stem and threw the handful into the air, so that each pointed, feathered seed sailed out like a dart. "Tell me how it'll be, Billy. Is it like when the cows have calves?"

"Just about. Mares are a little more sensitive. Sometimes you have to be there to help the mare. And sometimes if it's wrong, you have to——" he paused.

"Have to what, Billy?"

"Have to tear the colt to pieces to get it out, or the mare'll die."

"But it won't be that way this time, will it, Billy?"

"Oh, no. Nellie's thrown good colts."

"Can I be there, Billy? Will you be certain to call me? It's my colt."

"Sure, I'll call you. Of course I will."

"Tell me how it'll be."

"Why, you've seen the cows calving. It's almost the same. The mare starts groaning and stretching, and then, if it's a good right birth, the head and forefeet come out, and the front hoofs kick a hole just the way the calves do. And the colt starts to breathe. It's good to be there, 'cause if its feet aren't right maybe he can't break the sack, and then he might smother."

Jody whipped his leg with a bunch of grass. "We'll have to be there, then, won't we?"

"Oh, we'll be there, all right."

They turned and walked slowly down the hill toward the barn. Jody was tortured with a thing he had to say, although he didn't want to. "Billy," he began miserably, "Billy, you won't let anything happen to the colt, will you?"

And Billy knew he was thinking of the red pony, Gabilan, and of how it died of strangles. Billy knew he had been infallible before that, and now he was capable of failure. This knowledge made Billy much less sure of himself than he had been. "I can't tell," he said roughly. "All sorts of things might happen, and they wouldn't be my fault. I can't do everything." He felt badly about his lost prestige, and so he said, meanly, "I'll do everything I know, but I won't promise anything. Nellie's a good mare. She's thrown good colts before. She ought to this time." And he walked away from Jody and went into the saddle-room beside the barn, for his feelings were hurt.

Jody traveled often to the brushline behind the house. A rusty iron pipe ran a thin stream of spring water into an old green tub. Where the water spilled over and sank into the ground there was a patch of perpetually green grass. Even when the hills were brown and baked in the summer that little patch was green. The water whined softly into the trough all the year round. This place had grown to be a center-point for Jody. When he had been punished the cool green grass and the singing water soothed him. When he had been mean the biting acid of meanness left him at the brushline. When he sat in the grass and listened to the purling stream, the barriers set up in his mind by the stern day went down to ruin.

On the other hand, the black cypress tree by the bunkhouse was as repulsive as the water-tub was dear; for to this tree all the pigs came, sooner or later, to be slaughtered. Pig killing was fascinating, with the screaming and the blood, but it made Jody's heart beat so fast that it hurt him. After the pigs were scalded in the big iron tripod kettle and their skins were scraped and white, Jody had to go to the water-tub to sit in the grass until his heart grew quiet. The water-tub and the black cypress were opposites and enemies.

When Billy left him and walked angrily away, Jody turned up toward the house. He thought of Nellie as he walked, and of the little colt. Then suddenly he saw that he was under the black cypress, under the very singletree where the pigs were hung. He brushed his dry-grass hair off his forehead and hurried on. It seemed to him an unlucky thing to be thinking of his colt in the very slaughter place, especially after what Billy had said. To counteract any evil result of that bad conjunction he walked quickly past the ranch house, through the chicken yard, through the vegetable patch, until he came at last to the brushline.

He sat down in the green grass. The trilling water sounded in his ears. He looked over the farm buildings and across at the round hills, rich and yellow with grain. He could see Nellie feeding on the slope. As usual the water place eliminated time and distance. Jody saw a black, long-legged colt, butting against Nellie's flanks, demanding milk. And then he saw himself breaking a large colt to halter. All in a few moments the colt grew to be a magnificent animal, deep of chest, with a neck as high and arched as a sea-horse's neck, with a tail that tongued and rippled like black flame. This horse was terrible to everyone but Jody. In the schoolyard the boys begged rides, and Jody smilingly agreed. But no sooner were they mounted than the black demon pitched them off. Why, that was his name, Black Demon! For a moment the trilling water and the grass and the sunshine came back, and then . . .

Sometimes in the night the ranch people, safe in their beds, heard a roar of hoofs go by. They said, "It's Jody, on Demon. He's helping out the sheriff again." And then . . .

The golden dust filled the air in the arena at the Salinas Rodeo. The announcer called the roping contests. When Jody rode the black horse to the starting chute the other contestants shrugged and gave up first place, for it was well known that Jody and Demon could rope and throw and tie a steer a great deal quicker than any roping team of two men could. Jody was not a boy any more, and Demon was not a horse. The two together were one glorious individual. And then . . .

The President wrote a letter and asked them to help catch a bandit in Washington. Jody settled himself comfortably in the grass. The little stream of water whined into the mossy tub.

The year passed slowly on. Time after time Jody gave up his colt for lost. No change had taken place in Nellie. Carl Tiflin still drove her to a light cart, and she pulled on a hay rake and worked the Jackson-fork tackle when the hay was being put into the barn.

The summer passed, and the warm bright autumn. And then the frantic morning winds began to twist along the ground, and a chill came into the air, and the poison oak turned red. One morning in September, when he had finished his breakfast, Jody's mother called him into the kitchen. She was pouring boiling water into a bucket full of dry midlings and stirring the materials to a steaming paste.

"Yes, ma'am?" Jody asked.

"Watch how I do it. You'll have to do it after this every other morning."

"Well, what is it?"

"Why, it's warm mash for Nellie. It'll keep her in good shape."

Jody rubbed his forehead with a knuckle. "Is she all right?" he asked timidly.

Mrs. Tiflin put down the kettle and stirred the mash with a wooden paddle. "Of course she's all right, only you've got to take better care of her from now on. Here, take this breakfast out to her!"

Jody seized the bucket and ran, down past the bunkhouse, past the barn, with the heavy bucket banging against his knees. He found Nellie playing with the water in the trough, pushing waves and tossing her head so that the water slopped out on the ground.

Jody climbed the fence and set the bucket of steaming mash beside her. Then he stepped back to look at her. And she was changed. Her stomach was swollen. When she moved, her feet touched the ground gently. She buried her nose in the bucket and gobbled the hot breakfast. And when she had finished and had pushed the bucket around the ground with her nose a little, she stepped quietly over to Jody and rubbed her cheek against him.

Billy Buck came out of the saddle-room and walked over. "Starts fast when it starts, doesn't it?"

"Did it come all at once?"

"Oh, no, you just stopped looking for a while." He pulled her head around toward Jody. "She's goin' to be nice, too. See how nice her eyes are! Some mares get mean, but when they turn nice, they just love everything." Nellie slipped her head under Billy's arm and rubbed her neck up and down between his arms and his side. "You better treat her awful nice now," Billy said.

"How long will it be?" Jody demanded breathlessly.

The man counted in whispers on his fingers. "About three months," he said aloud. "You can't tell exactly. Sometimes it's eleven months to the day, but it might be two weeks early, or a month late, without hurting anything."

Jody looked hard at the ground. "Billy," he began nervously, "Billy, you'll call me when it's getting born, won't you? You'll let me be there, won't you?"

Billy bit the tip of Nellie's ear with his front teeth. "Carl says he wants you to start right at the start. That's the only way to learn. Nobody can tell you anything. Like my old man did with me about the saddle blanket. He was a government packer when I was your size, and I helped him some. One day I left a wrinkle in my saddle blanket and made a saddle-sore. My old man didn't give me hell at all. But the next morning he saddled me up with a forty-pound stock saddle. I had to lead my horse and carry that saddle over a whole

damn mountain in the sun. It darn near killed me, but I never
left no wrinkles in a blanket again. I couldn't. I never in my
life since then put on a blanket but I felt that saddle on my
back."

Jody reached up a hand and took hold of Nellie's mane.
"You'll tell me what to do about everything, won't you? I
guess you know everything about horses, don't you?"

Billy laughed. "Why I'm half horse myself, you see," he
said. "My ma died when I was born, and being my old man
was a government packer in the mountains, and no cows
around most of the time, why he just gave me mostly mare's
milk." He continued seriously, "And horses know that. Don't
you know it, Nellie?"

The mare turned her head and looked full into his eyes for
a moment, and this is a thing horses practically never do. Billy
was proud and sure of himself now. He boasted a little. "I'll
see you get a good colt. I'll start you right. And if you do like
I say, you'll have the best horse in the county."

That made Jody feel warm and proud, too; so proud that
when he went back to the house he bowed his legs and swayed
his shoulders as horsemen do. And he whispered, "Whoa, you
Black Demon, you! Steady down there and keep your feet on
the ground."

The winter fell sharply. A few preliminary gusty showers,
and then a strong steady rain. The hills lost their straw color
and blackened under the water, and the winter streams scrambled noisily down the canyons. The mushrooms and puffballs
popped up and the new grass started before Christmas.

But this year Christmas was not the central day to Jody.
Some undetermined time in January had become the axis day
around which the months swung. When the rains fell, he put
Nellie in a box stall and fed her warm food every morning
and curried her and brushed her.

The mare was swelling so greatly that Jody became alarmed.
"She'll pop wide open," he said to Billy.

Billy laid his strong square hand against Nellie's swollen
abdomen. "Feel here," he said quietly. "You can feel it move.
I guess it would surprise you if there were twin colts."

"You don't think so?" Jody cried. "You don't think it will be twins, do you, Billy?"

"No, I don't, but it does happen, sometimes."

During the first two weeks of January it rained steadily. Jody spent most of his time, when he wasn't in school, in the box stall with Nellie. Twenty times a day he put his hand on her stomach to feel the colt move. Nellie became more and more gentle and friendly to him. She rubbed her nose on him. She whinnied softly when he walked into the barn.

Carl Tiflin came to the barn with Jody one day. He looked admiringly at the groomed bay coat, and he felt the firm flesh over ribs and shoulders. "You've done a good job," he said to Jody. And this was the greatest praise he knew how to give. Jody was tight with pride for hours afterward.

The fifteenth of January came, and the colt was not born. And the twentieth came; a lump of fear began to form in Jody's stomach. "Is it all right?" he demanded of Billy.

"Oh, sure."

And again, "Are you sure it's going to be all right?"

Billy stroked the mare's neck. She swayed her head uneasily. "I told you it wasn't always the same time, Jody. You just have to wait."

When the end of the month arrived with no birth, Jody grew frantic. Nellie was so big that her breath came heavily, and her ears were close together and straight up, as though her head ached. Jody's sleep grew restless, and his dreams confused.

On the night of the second of February he awakened crying. His mother called to him, "Jody, you're dreaming. Wake up and start over again."

But Jody was filled with terror and desolation. He lay quietly a few moments, waiting for his mother to go back to sleep, and then he slipped his clothes on, and crept out in his bare feet.

The night was black and thick. A little misting rain fell. The cypress tree and the bunkhouse loomed and then dropped back into the mist. The barn door screeched as he opened it, a thing it never did in the daytime. Jody went to the rack and found a lantern and a tin box of matches. He lighted the wick and walked down the long straw-covered aisle to Nellie's stall. She was standing up. Her whole body weaved from side to side. Jody called to her, "So, Nellie, so-o, Nellie," but she did not stop her swaying nor look around. When he stepped into the stall and touched her on the shoulder she shivered under his hand. Then Billy Buck's voice came from the hayloft right above the stall.

"Jody, what are you doing?"

Jody started back and turned miserable eyes up toward the nest where Billy was lying in the hay. "Is she all right, do you think?"

"Why sure, I think so."

"You won't let anything happen, Billy, you're sure you won't?"

Billy growled down at him, "I told you I'd call you, and I will. Now you get back to bed and stop worrying that mare. She's got enough to do without you worrying her."

Jody cringed, for he had never heard Billy speak in such a tone. "I only thought I'd come and see," he said. "I woke up."

Billy softened a little then. "Well, you get to bed. I don't want you bothering her. I told you I'd get you a good colt. Get along now."

Jody walked slowly out of the barn. He blew out the lantern and set it in the rack. The blackness of the night, and the chilled mist struck him and enfolded him. He wished he believed everything Billy said as he had before the pony died. It was a moment before his eyes, blinded by the feeble lantern-flame, could make any form of the darkness. The damp ground chilled his bare feet. At the cypress tree the roosting turkeys chattered a little in alarm, and the two good dogs responded to their duty and came charging out, barking to frighten away the coyotes they thought were prowling under the tree.

As he crept through the kitchen, Jody stumbled over a chair. Carl called from his bedroom, "Who's there? What's the matter there?"

And Mrs. Tiflin said sleepily, "What's the matter, Carl?"

The next second Carl came out of the bedroom carrying a

candle, and found Jody before he could get into bed. "What are you doing out?"

Jody turned shyly away. "I was down to see the mare."

For a moment anger at being awakened fought with approval in Jody's father. "Listen," he said, finally, "there's not a man in this country that knows more about colts than Billy. You leave it to him."

Words burst out of Jody's mouth. "But the pony died——"

"Don't you go blaming that on him," Carl said sternly. "If Billy can't save a horse, it can't be saved."

Mrs. Tiflin called, "Make him clean his feet and go to bed, Carl. He'll be sleepy all day tomorrow."

It seemed to Jody that he had just closed his eyes to try to go to sleep when he was shaken violently by the shoulder. Billy Buck stood beside him, holding a lantern in his hand. "Get up," he said. "Hurry up." He turned and walked quickly out of the room.

Mrs. Tiflin called, "What's the matter? Is that you, Billy?"

"Yes, ma'am."

"Is Nellie ready?"

"Yes, ma'am."

"All right, I'll get up and heat some water in case you need it."

Jody jumped into his clothes so quickly that he was out the back door before Billy's swinging lantern was halfway to the barn. There was a rim of dawn on the mountain-tops, but no light had penetrated into the cup of the ranch yet. Jody ran frantically after the lantern and caught up to Billy just as he reached the barn. Billy hung the lantern to a nail on the stall-side and took off his blue denim coat. Jody saw that he wore only a sleeveless shirt under it.

Nellie was standing rigid and stiff. While they watched, she crouched. Her whole body was wrung with a spasm. The spasm passed. But in a few moments it started over again, and passed.

Billy muttered nervously, "There's something wrong." His bare hand disappeared. "Oh, Jesus," he said. "It's wrong."

The spasm came again, and this time Billy strained, and the

muscles stood out on his arm and shoulder. He heaved strongly, his forehead beaded with perspiration. Nellie cried with pain. Billy was muttering, "It's wrong. I can't turn it. It's way wrong. It's turned all around wrong."

He glared wildly toward Jody. And then his fingers made a careful, careful diagnosis. His cheeks were growing tight and grey. He looked for a long questioning minute at Jody standing back of the stall. Then Billy stepped to the rack under the manure window and picked up a horseshoe hammer with his wet right hand.

"Go outside, Jody," he said.

The boy stood still and stared dully at him.

"Go outside, I tell you. It'll be too late."

Jody didn't move.

Then Billy walked quickly to Nellie's head. He cried, "Turn your face away, damn you, turn your face."

This time Jody obeyed. His head turned sideways. He heard Billy whispering hoarsely in the stall. And then he heard a hollow crunch of bone. Nellie chuckled shrilly. Jody looked back in time to see the hammer rise and fall again on the flat forehead. Then Nellie fell heavily to her side and quivered for a moment.

Billy jumped to the swollen stomach; his big pocketknife was in his hand. He lifted the skin and drove the knife in. He sawed and ripped at the tough belly. The air filled with the sick odor of warm living entrails. The other horses reared back against their halter chains and squealed and kicked.

Billy dropped the knife. Both of his arms plunged into the terrible ragged hole and dragged out a big, white, dripping bundle. His teeth tore a hole in the covering. A little black head appeared through the tear, and little slick, wet ears. A gurgling breath was drawn, and then another. Billy shucked off the sac and found his knife and cut the string. For a moment he held the little black colt in his arms and looked at it. And then he walked slowly over and laid it in the straw at Jody's feet.

Billy's face and arms and chest were dripping red. His body shivered and his teeth chattered. His voice was gone; he spoke in a throaty whisper. "There's your colt. I promised. And there it is. I had to do it—had to." He stopped and looked over his shoulder into the box stall. "Go get hot water and a sponge," he whispered. "Wash him and dry him the way his mother would. You'll have to feed him by hand. But there's your colt, the way I promised."

Jody stared stupidly at the wet, panting foal. It stretched out its chin and tried to raise its head. Its blank eyes were navy blue.

"God damn you," Billy shouted, "will you go now for the water? *Will you go?*"

Then Jody turned and trotted out of the barn into the dawn. He ached from his throat to his stomach. His legs were stiff and heavy. He tried to be glad because of the colt, but the bloody face, and the haunted, tired eyes of Billy Buck hung in the air ahead of him.

The Leader of the People

O<small>N</small> S<small>ATURDAY</small> <small>AFTERNOON</small> Billy Buck, the ranch-hand, raked together the last of the old year's haystack and pitched small forkfuls over the wire fence to a few mildly interested cattle. High in the air small clouds like puffs of cannon smoke were driven eastward by the March wind. The wind could be heard whishing in the brush on the ridge crests, but no breath of it penetrated down into the ranch-cup.

The little boy, Jody, emerged from the house eating a thick piece of buttered bread. He saw Billy working on the last of the haystack. Jody tramped down scuffing his shoes in a way he had been told was destructive to good shoe-leather. A flock of white pigeons flew out of the black cypress tree as Jody passed, and circled the tree and landed again. A half-grown tortoise-shell cat leaped from the bunkhouse porch, galloped on stiff legs across the road, whirled and galloped back again. Jody picked up a stone to help the game along, but he was too late, for the cat was under the porch before the stone could be discharged. He threw the stone into the cypress tree and started the white pigeons on another whirling flight.

Arriving at the used-up haystack, the boy leaned against the barbed wire fence. "Will that be all of it, do you think?" he asked.

The middle-aged ranch-hand stopped his careful raking and stuck his fork into the ground. He took off his black hat and smoothed down his hair. "Nothing left of it that isn't soggy from ground moisture," he said. He replaced his hat and rubbed his dry leathery hands together.

"Ought to be plenty mice," Jody suggested.

"Lousy with them," said Billy. "Just crawling with mice."

"Well, maybe, when you get all through, I could call the dogs and hunt the mice."

"Sure, I guess you could," said Billy Buck. He lifted a forkful of the damp ground-hay and threw it into the air. Instantly three mice leaped out and burrowed frantically under the hay again.

Jody sighed with satisfaction. Those plump, sleek, arrogant mice were doomed. For eight months they had lived and multiplied in the haystack. They had been immune from cats, from traps, from poison and from Jody. They had grown smug in their security, overbearing and fat. Now the time of disaster had come; they would not survive another day.

Billy looked up at the top of the hills that surrounded the ranch. "Maybe you better ask your father before you do it," he suggested.

"Well, where is he? I'll ask him now."

"He rode up to the ridge ranch after dinner. He'll be back pretty soon."

Jody slumped against the fence post. "I don't think he'd care."

As Billy went back to his work he said ominously, "You'd better ask him anyway. You know how he is."

Jody did know. His father, Carl Tiflin, insisted upon giving permission for anything that was done on the ranch, whether it was important or not. Jody sagged farther against the post until he was sitting on the ground. He looked up at the little puffs of wind-driven cloud. "Is it like to rain, Billy?"

"It might. The wind's good for it, but not strong enough."

"Well, I hope it don't rain until after I kill those damn mice." He looked over his shoulder to see whether Billy had noticed the mature profanity. Billy worked on without comment.

Jody turned back and looked at the side-hill where the road from the outside world came down. The hill was washed with lean March sunshine. Silver thistles, blue lupins and a few poppies bloomed among the sage bushes. Halfway up the hill Jody could see Doubletree Mutt, the black dog, digging in a squirrel hole. He paddled for a while and then paused to kick bursts of dirt out between his hind legs, and he dug with an earnestness which belied the knowledge he must have had that no dog had ever caught a squirrel by digging in a hole.

Suddenly, while Jody watched, the black dog stiffened, and backed out of the hole and looked up the hill toward the cleft in the ridge where the road came through. Jody looked up too. For a moment Carl Tiflin on horseback stood out against the pale sky and then he moved down the road toward the house. He carried something white in his hand.

The boy started to his feet. "He's got a letter," Jody cried. He trotted away toward the ranch house, for the letter would probably be read aloud and he wanted to be there. He reached the house before his father did, and ran in. He heard Carl dismount from his creaking saddle and slap the horse on the side to send it to the barn where Billy would unsaddle it and turn it out.

Jody ran into the kitchen. "We got a letter!" he cried.

His mother looked up from a pan of beans. "Who has?"

"Father has. I saw it in his hand."

Carl strode into the kitchen then, and Jody's mother asked, "Who's the letter from, Carl?"

He frowned quickly. "How did you know there was a letter?"

She nodded her head in the boy's direction. "Big-Britches Jody told me."

Jody was embarrassed.

His father looked down at him contemptuously. "He *is* getting to be a Big-Britches," Carl said. "He's minding everybody's business but his own. Got his big nose into everything."

Mrs. Tiflin relented a little. "Well, he hasn't enough to keep him busy. Who's the letter from?"

Carl still frowned on Jody. "I'll keep him busy if he isn't careful." He held out a sealed letter. "I guess it's from your father."

Mrs. Tiflin took a hairpin from her head and slit open the flap. Her lips pursed judiciously. Jody saw her eyes snap back and forth over the lines. "He says," she translated, "he says he's going to drive out Saturday to stay for a little while. Why, this is Saturday. The letter must have been delayed." She looked at the postmark. "This was mailed day before yesterday. It should have been here yesterday." She looked up questioningly at her husband, and then her face darkened angrily. "Now what have you got that look on you for? He doesn't come often."

Carl turned his eyes away from her anger. He could be stern with her most of the time, but when occasionally her temper arose, he could not combat it.

"What's the matter with you?" she demanded again.

In his explanation there was a tone of apology Jody himself might have used. "It's just that he talks," Carl said lamely. "Just talks."

"Well, what of it? You talk yourself."

"Sure I do. But your father only talks about one thing."

"Indians!" Jody broke in excitedly. "Indians and crossing the plains!"

Carl turned fiercely on him. "You get out, Mr. Big-Britches! Go on, now! Get out!"

Jody went miserably out the back door and closed the screen with elaborate quietness. Under the kitchen window his shamed, downcast eyes fell upon a curiously shaped stone, a stone of such fascination that he squatted down and picked it up and turned it over in his hands.

The voices came clearly to him through the open kitchen window. "Jody's damn well right," he heard his father say. "Just Indians and crossing the plains. I've heard that story about how the horses got driven off about a thousand times. He just goes on and on, and he never changes a word in the things he tells."

When Mrs. Tiflin answered her tone was so changed that Jody, outside the window, looked up from his study of the stone. Her voice had become soft and explanatory. Jody knew how her face would have changed to match the tone. She said quietly, "Look at it this way, Carl. That was the big thing in my father's life. He led a wagon train clear across the plains to the coast, and when it was finished, his life was done. It was a big thing to do, but it didn't last long enough. Look!" she continued, "it's as though he was born to do that, and after he finished it, there wasn't anything more for him to do but think about it and talk about it. If there'd been any farther west to go, he'd have gone. He's told me so himself. But at last there was the ocean. He lives right by the ocean where he had to stop."

She had caught Carl, caught him and entangled him in her soft tone.

"I've seen him," he agreed quietly. "He goes down and stares off west over the ocean." His voice sharpened a little. "And then he goes up to the Horseshoe Club in Pacific Grove, and he tells people how the Indians drove off the horses."

She tried to catch him again. "Well, it's everything to him. You might be patient with him and pretend to listen."

Carl turned impatiently away. "Well, if it gets too bad, I can always go down to the bunkhouse and sit with Billy," he said irritably. He walked through the house and slammed the front door after him.

Jody ran to his chores. He dumped the grain to the chickens without chasing any of them. He gathered the eggs from the nests. He trotted into the house with the wood and interlaced it so carefully in the wood-box that two armloads seemed to fill it to overflowing.

His mother had finished the beans by now. She stirred up the fire and brushed off the stove-top with a turkey wing. Jody peered cautiously at her to see whether any rancor toward him remained. "Is he coming today?" Jody asked.

"That's what his letter said."

"Maybe I better walk up the road to meet him."

Mrs. Tiflin clanged the stove-lid shut. "That would be nice," she said. "He'd probably like to be met."

"I guess I'll just do it then."

Outside, Jody whistled shrilly to the dogs. "Come on up the hill," he commanded. The two dogs waved their tails and ran ahead. Along the roadside the sage had tender new tips. Jody tore off some pieces and rubbed them on his hands until the air was filled with the sharp wild smell. With a rush the dogs leaped from the road and yapped into the brush after a rabbit. That was the last Jody saw of them, for when they failed to catch the rabbit, they went back home.

Jody plodded on up the hill toward the ridge top. When he reached the little cleft where the road came through, the afternoon wind struck him and blew up his hair and ruffled his shirt. He looked down on the little hills and ridges below and then out at the huge green Salinas Valley. He could see the white town of Salinas far out in the flat and the flash of its windows under the waning sun. Directly below him, in an oak tree, a crow congress had convened. The tree was black with crows all cawing at once.

Then Jody's eyes followed the wagon road down from the ridge where he stood, and lost it behind a hill, and picked it up again on the other side. On that distant stretch he saw a cart slowly pulled by a bay horse. It disappeared behind the hill. Jody sat down on the ground and watched the place where the cart would reappear again. The wind sang on the hilltops and the puff-ball clouds hurried eastward.

Then the cart came into sight and stopped. A man dressed in black dismounted from the seat and walked to the horse's head. Although it was so far away, Jody knew he had un-hooked the check-rein, for the horse's head dropped forward. The horse moved on, and the man walked slowly up the hill beside it. Jody gave a glad cry and ran down the road toward them. The squirrels bumped along off the road, and a road-runner flirted its tail and raced over the edge of the hill and sailed out like a glider.

Jody tried to leap into the middle of his shadow at every step. A stone rolled under his foot and he went down. Around a little bend he raced, and there, a short distance ahead, were his grandfather and the cart. The boy dropped from his un-seemly running and approached at a dignified walk.

The horse plodded stumble-footedly up the hill and the old man walked beside it. In the lowering sun their giant shadows flickered darkly behind them. The grandfather was dressed in a black broadcloth suit and he wore kid congress gaiters and a black tie on a short, hard collar. He carried his black slouch hat in his hand. His white beard was cropped close and his white eyebrows overhung his eyes like moustaches. The blue eyes were sternly merry. About the whole face and figure there was a granite dignity, so that every motion seemed an impossible thing. Once at rest, it seemed the old man would be stone, would never move again. His steps were slow and certain. Once made, no step could ever be retraced; once headed in a direction, the path would never bend nor the pace increase nor slow.

When Jody appeared around the bend, Grandfather waved his hat slowly in welcome, and he called, "Why, Jody! Come down to meet me, have you?"

Jody sidled near and turned and matched his step to the old man's step and stiffened his body and dragged his heels a little. "Yes, sir," he said. "We got your letter only today."

"Should have been here yesterday," said Grandfather. "It certainly should. How are all the folks?"

"They're fine, sir." He hesitated and then suggested shyly, "Would you like to come on a mouse hunt tomorrow, sir?"

"Mouse hunt, Jody?" Grandfather chuckled. "Have the people of this generation come down to hunting mice? They aren't very strong, the new people, but I hardly thought mice would be game for them."

"No, sir. It's just play. The haystack's gone. I'm going to drive out the mice to the dogs. And you can watch, or even beat the hay a little."

The stern, merry eyes turned down on him. "I see. You don't eat them, then. You haven't come to that yet."

Jody explained, "The dogs eat them, sir. It wouldn't be much like hunting Indians, I guess."

"No, not much—but then later, when the troops were hunting Indians and shooting children and burning teepees, it wasn't much different from your mouse hunt."

They topped the rise and started down into the ranch cup, and they lost the sun from their shoulders. "You've grown," Grandfather said. "Nearly an inch, I should say."

"More," Jody boasted. "Where they mark me on the door, I'm up more than an inch since Thanksgiving even."

Grandfather's rich throaty voice said, "Maybe you're getting too much water and turning to pith and stalk. Wait until you head out, and then we'll see."

Jody looked quickly into the old man's face to see whether his feelings should be hurt, but there was no will to injure, no punishing nor putting-in-your-place light in the keen blue eyes. "We might kill a pig," Jody suggested.

"Oh, no! I couldn't let you do that. You're just humoring me. It isn't the time and you know it."

"You know Riley, the big boar, sir?"

"Yes. I remember Riley well."

"Well, Riley ate a hole into that same haystack, and it fell down on him and smothered him."

"Pigs do that when they can," said Grandfather.

"Riley was a nice pig, for a boar, sir. I rode him sometimes, and he didn't mind."

A door slammed at the house below them, and they saw Jody's mother standing on the porch waving her apron in welcome. And they saw Carl Tiflin walking up from the barn to be at the house for the arrival.

The sun had disappeared from the hills by now. The blue smoke from the house chimney hung in flat layers in the purpling ranch-cup. The puff-ball clouds, dropped by the falling wind, hung listlessly in the sky.

Billy Buck came out of the bunkhouse and flung a wash basin of soapy water on the ground. He had been shaving in mid-week, for Billy held Grandfather in reverence, and Grandfather said that Billy was one of the few men of the new generation who had not gone soft. Although Billy was in middle age, Grandfather considered him a boy. Now Billy was hurrying toward the house too.

When Jody and Grandfather arrived, the three were waiting for them in front of the yard gate.

Carl said, "Hello, sir. We've been looking for you."

Mrs. Tiflin kissed Grandfather on the side of his beard, and stood still while his big hand patted her shoulder. Billy shook hands solemnly, grinning under his straw moustache. "I'll put up your horse," said Billy, and he led the rig away.

Grandfather watched him go, and then, turning back to the group, he said as he had said a hundred times before, "There's a good boy. I knew his father, old Mule-tail Buck. I never knew why they called him Mule-tail except he packed mules."

Mrs. Tiflin turned and led the way into the house. "How long are you going to stay, Father? Your letter didn't say."

"Well, I don't know. I thought I'd stay about two weeks. But I never stay as long as I think I'm going to."

In a short while they were sitting at the white oilcloth table eating their supper. The lamp with the tin reflector hung over the table. Outside the dining-room windows the big moths battered softly against the glass.

Grandfather cut his steak into tiny pieces and chewed slowly. "I'm hungry," he said. "Driving out here got my appetite up. It's like when we were crossing. We all got so hungry every night we could hardly wait to let the meat get done. I could eat about five pounds of buffalo meat every night."

"It's moving around does it," said Billy. "My father was a government packer. I helped him when I was a kid. Just the two of us could about clean up a deer's ham."

"I knew your father, Billy," said Grandfather. "A fine man he was. They called him Mule-tail Buck. I don't know why except he packed mules."

"That was it," Billy agreed. "He packed mules."

Grandfather put down his knife and fork and looked around the table. "I remember one time we ran out of meat—" His voice dropped to a curious low sing-song, dropped into a tonal groove the story had worn for itself. "There was no buffalo, no antelope, not even rabbits. The hunters couldn't even shoot a coyote. That was the time for the leader to be on the watch. I was the leader, and I kept my eyes open. Know why? Well, just the minute the people began to get hungry they'd start slaughtering the team oxen. Do you believe that? I've heard of parties that just ate up their draft cattle. Started from the middle and worked toward the ends. Finally they'd eat the lead pair, and then the wheelers. The leader of a party had to keep them from doing that."

In some manner a big moth got into the room and circled the hanging kerosene lamp. Billy got up and tried to clap it between his hands. Carl struck with a cupped palm and caught the moth and broke it. He walked to the window and dropped it out.

"As I was saying," Grandfather began again, but Carl interrupted him. "You'd better eat some more meat. All the rest of us are ready for our pudding."

Jody saw a flash of anger in his mother's eyes. Grandfather picked up his knife and fork. "I'm pretty hungry, all right," he said. "I'll tell you about that later."

When supper was over, when the family and Billy Buck sat in front of the fireplace in the other room, Jody anxiously watched Grandfather. He saw the signs he knew. The bearded head leaned forward; the eyes lost their sternness and looked wonderingly into the fire; the big lean fingers laced themselves on the black knees. "I wonder," he began, "I just wonder whether I ever told you how those thieving Piutes drove off thirty-five of our horses."

"I think you did," Carl interrupted. "Wasn't it just before you went up into the Tahoe country?"

Grandfather turned quickly toward his son-in-law. "That's right. I guess I must have told you that story."

"Lots of times," Carl said cruelly, and he avoided his wife's eyes. But he felt the angry eyes on him, and he said, " 'Course I'd like to hear it again."

Grandfather looked back at the fire. His fingers unlaced and laced again. Jody knew how he felt, how his insides were collapsed and empty. Hadn't Jody been called a Big-Britches that very afternoon? He arose to heroism and opened himself to the term Big-Britches again. "Tell about Indians," he said softly.

Grandfather's eyes grew stern again. "Boys always want to hear about Indians. It was a job for men, but boys want to hear about it. Well, let's see. Did I ever tell you how I wanted each wagon to carry a long iron plate?"

Everyone but Jody remained silent. Jody said, "No. You didn't."

"Well, when the Indians attacked, we always put the wagons in a circle and fought from between the wheels. I thought that if every wagon carried a long plate with rifle holes, the men could stand the plates on the outside of the wheels when the wagons were in the circle and they would be protected. It would save lives and that would make up for the extra weight of the iron. But of course the party wouldn't do it. No party had done it before and they couldn't see why they should go to the expense. They lived to regret it, too."

Jody looked at his mother, and knew from her expression that she was not listening at all. Carl picked at a callus on his thumb and Billy Buck watched a spider crawling up the wall.

Grandfather's tone dropped into its narrative groove again. Jody knew in advance exactly what words would fall. The story droned on, speeded up for the attack, grew sad over the wounds, struck a dirge at the burials on the great plains. Jody sat quietly watching Grandfather. The stern blue eyes were detached. He looked as though he were not very interested in the story himself.

When it was finished, when the pause had been politely respected as the frontier of the story, Billy Buck stood up and stretched and hitched his trousers. "I guess I'll turn in," he said. Then he faced Grandfather. "I've got an old powder horn and a cap and ball pistol down to the bunkhouse. Did I ever show them to you?"

Grandfather nodded slowly. "Yes, I think you did, Billy. Reminds me of a pistol I had when I was leading the people across." Billy stood politely until the little story was done, and then he said, "Good night," and went out of the house.

Carl Tiflin tried to turn the conversation then. "How's the country between here and Monterey? I've heard it's pretty dry."

"It is dry," said Grandfather. "There's not a drop of water in the Laguna Seca. But it's a long pull from '87. The whole country was powder then, and in '61 I believe all the coyotes starved to death. We had fifteen inches of rain this year."

"Yes, but it all came too early. We could do with some now." Carl's eye fell on Jody. "Hadn't you better be getting to bed?"

Jody stood up obediently. "Can I kill the mice in the old haystack, sir?"

"Mice? Oh! Sure, kill them all off. Billy said there isn't any good hay left."

Jody exchanged a secret and satisfying look with Grandfather. "I'll kill every one tomorrow," he promised.

Jody lay in his bed and thought of the impossible world of Indians and buffaloes, a world that had ceased to be forever. He wished he could have been living in the heroic time, but he knew he was not of heroic timber. No one living now, save possibly Billy Buck, was worthy to do the things that had been done. A race of giants had lived then, fearless men, men of a staunchness unknown in this day. Jody thought of the wide plains and of the wagons moving across like centipedes. He thought of Grandfather on a huge white horse, marshaling the people. Across his mind marched the great phantoms, and they marched off the earth and they were gone.

He came back to the ranch for a moment, then. He heard the dull rushing sound that space and silence make. He heard one of the dogs, out in the doghouse, scratching a flea and bumping his elbow against the floor with every stroke. Then the wind arose again and the black cypress groaned and Jody went to sleep.

He was up half an hour before the triangle sounded for breakfast. His mother was rattling the stove to make the flames roar when Jody went through the kitchen. "You're up early," she said. "Where are you going?"

"Out to get a good stick. We're going to kill the mice to-day."

"Who is 'we'?"

"Why, Grandfather and I."

"So you've got him in it. You always like to have someone in with you in case there's blame to share."

"I'll be right back," said Jody. "I just want to have a good stick ready for after breakfast."

He closed the screen door after him and went out into the cool blue morning. The birds were noisy in the dawn and the ranch cats came down from the hill like blunt snakes. They had been hunting gophers in the dark, and although the four cats were full of gopher meat, they sat in a semi-circle at the back door and mewed piteously for milk. Doubletree Mutt and Smasher moved sniffing along the edge of the brush, performing the duty with rigid ceremony, but when Jody whistled, their heads jerked up and their tails waved. They plunged down to him, wriggling their skins and yawning. Jody patted their heads seriously, and moved on to the weathered scrap pile. He selected an old broom handle and a short piece of inch-square scrap wood. From his pocket he took a shoelace and tied the ends of the sticks loosely together to make a flail. He whistled his new weapon through the air and struck the ground experimentally, while the dogs leaped aside and whined with apprehension.

Jody turned and started down past the house toward the old haystack ground to look over the field of slaughter, but Billy Buck, sitting patiently on the back steps, called to him, "You better come back. It's only a couple of minutes till breakfast."

Jody changed his course and moved toward the house. He

leaned his flail against the steps. "That's to drive the mice out," he said. "I'll bet they're fat. I'll bet they don't know what's going to happen to them today."

"No, nor you either," Billy remarked philosophically, "nor me, nor anyone."

Jody was staggered by this thought. He knew it was true. His imagination twitched away from the mouse hunt. Then his mother came out on the back porch and struck the triangle, and all thoughts fell in a heap.

Grandfather hadn't appeared at the table when they sat down. Billy nodded at his empty chair. "He's all right? He isn't sick?"

"He takes a long time to dress," said Mrs. Tiflin. "He combs his whiskers and rubs up his shoes and brushes his clothes."

Carl scattered sugar on his mush. "A man that's led a wagon train across the plains has got to be pretty careful how he dresses."

Mrs. Tiflin turned on him. "Don't do that, Carl! Please don't!" There was more of threat than of request in her tone. And the threat irritated Carl.

"Well, how many times do I have to listen to the story of the iron plates, and the thirty-five horses? That time's done. Why can't he forget it, now it's done?" He grew angrier while he talked, and his voice rose. "Why does he have to tell them over and over? He came across the plains. All right! Now it's finished. Nobody wants to hear about it over and over."

The door into the kitchen closed softly. The four at the table sat frozen. Carl laid his mush spoon on the table and touched his chin with his fingers.

Then the kitchen door opened and Grandfather walked in. His mouth smiled tightly and his eyes were squinted. "Good morning," he said, and he sat down and looked at his mush dish.

Carl could not leave it there. "Did—did you hear what I said?"

Grandfather jerked a little nod.

"I don't know what got into me, sir. I didn't mean it. I was just being funny."

Jody glanced in shame at his mother, and he saw that she

was looking at Carl, and that she wasn't breathing. It was an awful thing that he was doing. He was tearing himself to pieces to talk like that. It was a terrible thing to him to retract a word, but to retract it in shame was infinitely worse.

Grandfather looked sidewise. "I'm trying to get right side up," he said gently. "I'm not being mad. I don't mind what you said, but it might be true, and I would mind that."

"It isn't true," said Carl. "I'm not feeling well this morning. I'm sorry I said it."

"Don't be sorry, Carl. An old man doesn't see things sometimes. Maybe you're right. The crossing is finished. Maybe it should be forgotten, now it's done."

Carl got up from the table. "I've had enough to eat. I'm going to work. Take your time, Billy!" He walked quickly out of the dining-room. Billy gulped the rest of his food and followed soon after. But Jody could not leave his chair.

"Won't you tell any more stories?" Jody asked.

"Why, sure I'll tell them, but only when—I'm sure people want to hear them."

"I like to hear them, sir."

"Oh! Of course you do, but you're a little boy. It was a job for men, but only little boys like to hear about it."

Jody got up from his place. "I'll wait outside for you, sir. I've got a good stick for those mice."

He waited by the gate until the old man came out on the porch. "Let's go down and kill the mice now," Jody called.

"I think I'll just sit in the sun, Jody. You go kill the mice."

"You can use my stick if you like."

"No, I'll just sit here a while."

Jody turned disconsolately away, and walked down toward the old haystack. He tried to whip up his enthusiasm with thoughts of the fat juicy mice. He beat the ground with his flail. The dogs coaxed and whined about him, but he could not go. Back at the house he could see Grandfather sitting on the porch, looking small and thin and black.

Jody gave up and went to sit on the steps at the old man's feet.

"Back already? Did you kill the mice?"

"No, sir. I'll kill them some other day."

The morning flies buzzed close to the ground and the ants

dashed about in front of the steps. The heavy smell of sage slipped down the hill. The porch boards grew warm in the sunshine.

Jody hardly knew when Grandfather started to talk. "I shouldn't stay here, feeling the way I do." He examined his strong old hands. "I feel as though the crossing wasn't worth doing." His eyes moved up the side-hill and stopped on a motionless hawk perched on a dead limb. "I tell those old stories, but they're not what I want to tell. I only know how I want people to feel when I tell them.

"It wasn't Indians that were important, nor adventures, nor even getting out here. It was a whole bunch of people made into one big crawling beast. And I was the head. It was westering and westering. Every man wanted something for himself, but the big beast that was all of them wanted only westering. I was the leader, but if I hadn't been there, someone else would have been the head. The thing had to have a head.

"Under the little bushes the shadows were black at white noonday. When we saw the mountains at last, we cried—all of us. But it wasn't getting here that mattered, it was movement and westering.

"We carried life out here and set it down the way those ants carry eggs. And I was the leader. The westering was as big as God, and the slow steps that made the movement piled up and piled up until the continent was crossed.

"Then we came down to the sea, and it was done." He stopped and wiped his eyes until the rims were red. "That's what I should be telling instead of stories."

When Jody spoke, Grandfather started and looked down at him. "Maybe I could lead the people some day," Jody said.

The old man smiled. "There's no place to go. There's the ocean to stop you. There's a line of old men along the shore hating the ocean because it stopped them."

"In boats I might, sir."

"No place to go, Jody. Every place is taken. But that's not the worst—no, not the worst. Westering has died out of the people. Westering isn't a hunger any more. It's all done. Your father is right. It is finished." He laced his fingers on his knee and looked at them.

Jody felt very sad. "If you'd like a glass of lemonade I could make it for you."

Grandfather was about to refuse, and then he saw Jody's face. "That would be nice," he said. "Yes, it would be nice to drink a lemonade."

Jody ran into the kitchen where his mother was wiping the last of the breakfast dishes. "Can I have a lemon to make a lemonade for Grandfather?"

His mother mimicked— "And another lemon to make a lemonade for you."

"No, ma'am. I don't want one."

"Jody! You're sick!" Then she stopped suddenly. "Take a lemon out of the cooler," she said softly. "Here, I'll reach the squeezer down to you."

THE GRAPES OF WRATH

Battle Hymn of the Republic

Julia Ward Howe, 1861

William Steffe, 1852

1. Mine eyes have seen the glo-ry of the com-ing of the
2. He has sound-ed forth the trum-pet that shall nev-er call re-
3. In the beau-ty of the lil-ies Christ was born a-cross the

Lord, He is tram-pling out the vin-tage where the grapes of
treat; He is sift-ing out the hearts of men be-fore His
sea   With a glo-ry in His bos-om that trans-fig-ures

wrath are stored; He hath loos'd the fateful lightning of His
judg-ment seat; Oh, be swift, my soul, to an-swer Him, be
you and me; As He died to make men ho-ly, let us

ter-ri-ble swift sword, His truth is march-ing on.
ju-bi-lent, my feet! Our God is march-ing on.
die to make men free, While God is march-ing on.

Glo-ry, glo-ry, hal-le-lu-jah! Glo-ry, glo-ry, hal-le-lu-jah!

Glo-ry, glo-ry, hal-le-lu-jah! His truth is march-ing on.

Chapter One

To the red country and part of the gray country of Oklahoma, the last rains came gently, and they did not cut the scarred earth. The plows crossed and recrossed the rivulet marks. The last rains lifted the corn quickly and scattered weed colonies and grass along the sides of the roads so that the gray country and the dark red country began to disappear under a green cover. In the last part of May the sky grew pale and the clouds that had hung in high puffs for so long in the spring were dissipated. The sun flared down on the growing corn day after day until a line of brown spread along the edge of each green bayonet. The clouds appeared, and went away, and in a while they did not try any more. The weeds grew darker green to protect themselves, and they did not spread any more. The surface of the earth crusted, a thin hard crust, and as the sky became pale, so the earth became pale, pink in the red country and white in the gray country.

In the water-cut gullies the earth dusted down in dry little streams. Gophers and ant lions started small avalanches. And as the sharp sun struck day after day, the leaves of the young corn became less stiff and erect; they bent in a curve at first, and then, as the central ribs of strength grew weak, each leaf tilted downward. Then it was June, and the sun shone more fiercely. The brown lines on the corn leaves widened and moved in on the central ribs. The weeds frayed and edged back toward their roots. The air was thin and the sky more pale; and every day the earth paled.

In the roads where the teams moved, where the wheels milled the ground and the hooves of the horses beat the ground, the dirt crust broke and the dust formed. Every moving thing lifted the dust into the air: a walking man lifted a thin layer as high as his waist, and a wagon lifted the dust as high as the fence tops, and an automobile boiled a cloud behind it. The dust was long in settling back again.

When June was half gone, the big clouds moved up out of Texas and the Gulf, high heavy clouds, rain-heads. The men in the fields looked up at the clouds and sniffed at them and

held wet fingers up to sense the wind. And the horses were
nervous while the clouds were up. The rain-heads dropped a
little spattering and hurried on to some other country. Behind
them the sky was pale again and the sun flared. In the dust
there were drop craters where the rain had fallen, and there
were clean splashes on the corn, and that was all.

A gentle wind followed the rain clouds, driving them on
northward, a wind that softly clashed the drying corn. A day
went by and the wind increased, steady, unbroken by gusts.
The dust from the roads fluffed up and spread out and fell on
the weeds beside the fields, and fell into the fields a little way.
Now the wind grew strong and hard and it worked at the rain
crust in the corn fields. Little by little the sky was darkened
by the mixing dust, and the wind felt over the earth, loosened
the dust, and carried it away. The wind grew stronger. The
rain crust broke and the dust lifted up out of the fields and
drove gray plumes into the air like sluggish smoke. The corn
threshed the wind and made a dry, rushing sound. The finest
dust did not settle back to earth now, but disappeared into
the darkening sky.

The wind grew stronger, whisked under stones, carried up
straws and old leaves, and even little clods, marking its course
as it sailed across the fields. The air and the sky darkened and
through them the sun shone redly, and there was a raw sting
in the air. During a night the wind raced faster over the land,
dug cunningly among the rootlets of the corn, and the corn
fought the wind with its weakened leaves until the roots were
freed by the prying wind and then each stalk settled wearily
sideways toward the earth and pointed the direction of the
wind.

The dawn came, but no day. In the gray sky a red sun
appeared, a dim red circle that gave a little light, like dusk;
and as that day advanced, the dusk slipped back toward darkness, and the wind cried and whimpered over the fallen corn.

Men and women huddled in their houses, and they tied
handkerchiefs over their noses when they went out, and wore
goggles to protect their eyes.

When the night came again it was black night, for the stars
could not pierce the dust to get down, and the window lights
could not even spread beyond their own yards. Now the dust

was evenly mixed with the air, an emulsion of dust and air. Houses were shut tight, and cloth wedged around doors and windows, but the dust came in so thinly that it could not be seen in the air, and it settled like pollen on the chairs and tables, on the dishes. The people brushed it from their shoulders. Little lines of dust lay at the door sills.

In the middle of that night the wind passed on and left the land quiet. The dust-filled air muffled sound more completely than fog does. The people, lying in their beds, heard the wind stop. They awakened when the rushing wind was gone. They lay quietly and listened deep into the stillness. Then the roosters crowed, and their voices were muffled, and the people stirred restlessly in their beds and wanted the morning. They knew it would take a long time for the dust to settle out of the air. In the morning the dust hung like fog, and the sun was as red as ripe new blood. All day the dust sifted down from the sky, and the next day it sifted down. An even blanket covered the earth. It settled on the corn, piled up on the tops of the fence posts, piled up on the wires; it settled on roofs, blanketed the weeds and trees.

The people came out of their houses and smelled the hot stinging air and covered their noses from it. And the children came out of the houses, but they did not run or shout as they would have done after a rain. Men stood by their fences and looked at the ruined corn, drying fast now, only a little green showing through the film of dust. The men were silent and they did not move often. And the women came out of the houses to stand beside their men—to feel whether this time the men would break. The women studied the men's faces secretly, for the corn could go, as long as something else remained. The children stood near by, drawing figures in the dust with bare toes, and the children sent exploring senses out to see whether men and women would break. The children peeked at the faces of the men and women, and then drew careful lines in the dust with their toes. Horses came to the watering troughs and nuzzled the water to clear the surface dust. After a while the faces of the watching men lost their bemused perplexity and became hard and angry and resistant. Then the women knew that they were safe and that there was no break. Then they asked, What'll we do? And the men replied, I don't know. But it was all right. The women knew it was all right, and the watching children knew it was all right. Women and children knew deep in themselves that no misfortune was too great to bear if their men were whole. The women went into the houses to their work, and the children began to play, but cautiously at first. As the day went forward the sun became less red. It flared down on the dust-blanketed land. The men sat in the doorways of their houses; their hands were busy with sticks and little rocks. The men sat still—thinking—figuring.

Chapter Two

A HUGE red transport truck stood in front of the little roadside restaurant. The vertical exhaust pipe muttered softly, and an almost invisible haze of steel-blue smoke hovered over its end. It was a new truck, shining red, and in twelve-inch letters on its sides—OKLAHOMA CITY TRANSPORT COMPANY. Its double tires were new, and a brass padlock stood straight out from the hasp on the big back doors. Inside the screened restaurant a radio played, quiet dance music turned low the way it is when no one is listening. A small outlet fan turned silently in its circular hole over the entrance, and flies buzzed excitedly about the doors and windows, butting the screens. Inside, one man, the truck driver, sat on a stool and rested his elbows on the counter and looked over his coffee at the lean and lonely waitress. He talked the smart listless language of the roadsides to her. "I seen him about three months ago. He had a operation. Cut somepin out. I forget what." And she— "Doesn't seem no longer ago than a week I seen him myself. Looked fine then. He's a nice sort of a guy when he ain't stinko." Now and then the flies roared softly at the screen door. The coffee machine spurted steam, and the waitress, without looking, reached behind her and shut it off.

Outside, a man walking along the edge of the highway crossed over and approached the truck. He walked slowly to the front of it, put his hand on the shiny fender, and looked at the *No Riders* sticker on the windshield. For a moment he was about to walk on down the road, but instead he sat on the running board on the side away from the restaurant. He was not over thirty. His eyes were very dark brown and there was a hint of brown pigment in his eyeballs. His cheek bones were high and wide, and strong deep lines cut down his cheeks, in curves beside his mouth. His upper lip was long, and since his teeth protruded, the lips stretched to cover them, for this man kept his lips closed. His hands were hard, with broad fingers and nails as thick and ridged as little clam shells. The space between thumb and forefinger and the hams of his hands were shiny with callus.

The man's clothes were new—all of them, cheap and new. His gray cap was so new that the visor was still stiff and the button still on, not shapeless and bulged as it would be when it had served for a while all the various purposes of a cap— carrying sack, towel, handkerchief. His suit was of cheap gray hardcloth and so new that there were creases in the trousers. His blue chambray shirt was stiff and smooth with filler. The coat was too big, the trousers too short, for he was a tall man. The coat shoulder peaks hung down on his arms, and even then the sleeves were too short and the front of the coat flapped loosely over his stomach. He wore a pair of new tan shoes of the kind called "army last," hobnailed and with half-circles like horseshoes to protect the edges of the heels from wear. This man sat on the running board and took off his cap and mopped his face with it. Then he put on the cap, and by pulling started the future ruin of the visor. His feet caught his attention. He leaned down and loosened the shoelaces, and did not tie the ends again. Over his head the exhaust of the Diesel engine whispered in quick puffs of blue smoke.

The music stopped in the restaurant and a man's voice spoke from the loudspeaker, but the waitress did not turn him off, for she didn't know the music had stopped. Her exploring fingers had found a lump under her ear. She was trying to see it in a mirror behind the counter without letting the truck driver know, and so she pretended to push a bit of hair to neatness. The truck driver said, "They was a big dance in Shawnee. I heard somebody got killed or somepin. You hear anything?" "No," said the waitress, and she lovingly fingered the lump under her ear.

Outside, the seated man stood up and looked over the cowl of the truck and watched the restaurant for a moment. Then he settled back on the running board, pulled a sack of tobacco and a book of papers from his side pocket. He rolled his cigarette slowly and perfectly, studied it, smoothed it. At last he lighted it and pushed the burning match into the dust at his feet. The sun cut into the shade of the truck as noon approached.

In the restaurant the truck driver paid his bill and put his two nickels' change in a slot machine. The whirling cylinders gave him no score. "They fix 'em so you can't win nothing," he said to the waitress.

And she replied, "Guy took the jackpot not two hours ago. Three-eighty he got. How soon you gonna be back by?"

He held the screen door a little open. "Week-ten days," he said. "Got to make a run to Tulsa, an' I never get back soon as I think."

She said crossly, "Don't let the flies in. Either go out or come in."

"So long," he said, and pushed his way out. The screen door banged behind him. He stood in the sun, peeling the wrapper from a piece of gum. He was a heavy man, broad in the shoulders, thick in the stomach. His face was red and his blue eyes long and slitted from having squinted always at sharp light. He wore army trousers and high laced boots. Holding the stick of gum in front of his lips he called through the screen, "Well, don't do nothing you don't want me to hear about." The waitress was turned toward a mirror on the back wall. She grunted a reply. The truck driver gnawed down the stick of gum slowly, opening his jaws and lips wide with each bite. He shaped the gum in his mouth, rolled it under his tongue while he walked to the big red truck.

The hitch-hiker stood up and looked across through the windows. "Could ya give me a lift, mister?"

The driver looked quickly back at the restaurant for a second. "Didn' you see the *No Riders* sticker on the win'shield?"

"Sure—I seen it. But sometimes a guy'll be a good guy even if some rich bastard makes him carry a sticker."

The driver, getting slowly into the truck, considered the parts of this answer. If he refused now, not only was he not a good guy, but he was forced to carry a sticker, was not allowed to have company. If he took in the hitch-hiker he was automatically a good guy and also he was not one whom any rich bastard could kick around. He knew he was being trapped, but he couldn't see a way out. And he wanted to be a good guy. He glanced again at the restaurant. "Scrunch down on the running board till we get around the bend," he said.

The hitch-hiker flopped down out of sight and clung to the door handle. The motor roared up for a moment, the gears clicked in, and the great truck moved away, first gear, second gear, third gear, and then a high whining pick-up and fourth gear. Under the clinging man the highway blurred dizzily by. It was a mile to the first turn in the road, then the truck slowed down. The hitch-hiker stood up, eased the door open, and slipped into the seat. The driver looked over at him, slitting his eyes, and he chewed as though thoughts and impressions were being sorted and arranged by his jaws before they were finally filed away in his brain. His eyes began at the new cap, moved down the new clothes to the new shoes. The hitch-hiker squirmed his back against the seat in comfort, took off his cap, and swabbed his sweating forehead and chin with it. "Thanks, buddy," he said. "My dogs was pooped out."

"New shoes," said the driver. His voice had the same quality of secrecy and insinuation his eyes had. "You oughtn' to take no walk in new shoes—hot weather."

The hiker looked down at the dusty yellow shoes. "Didn't have no other shoes," he said. "Guy got to wear 'em if he got no others."

The driver squinted judiciously ahead and built up the speed of the truck a little. "Goin' far?"

"Uh-uh! I'd a walked her if my dogs wasn't pooped out."

The questions of the driver had the tone of a subtle examination. He seemed to spread nets, to set traps with his questions. "Lookin' for a job?" he asked.

"No, my old man got a place, forty acres. He's a cropper, but we been there a long time."

The driver looked significantly at the fields along the road where the corn was fallen sideways and the dust was piled on it. Little flints shoved through the dusty soil. The driver said, as though to himself, "A forty-acre cropper and he ain't been dusted out and he ain't been tractored out?"

" 'Course I ain't heard lately," said the hitch-hiker.

"Long time," said the driver. A bee flew into the cab and buzzed in back of the windshield. The driver put out his hand and carefully drove the bee into an air stream that blew it out of the window. "Croppers going fast now," he said. "One cat' takes and shoves ten families out. Cat's all over hell now. Tear in and shove the croppers out. How's your old man hold on?" His tongue and his jaws became busy with the neglected gum, turned it and chewed it. With each opening of his mouth his tongue could be seen flipping the gum over.

"Well, I ain't heard lately. I never was no hand to write, nor my old man neither." He added quickly, "But the both of us can, if we want."

"Been doing a job?" Again the secret investigating casualness. He looked out over the fields, at the shimmering air, and gathering his gum into his cheek, out of the way, he spat out the window.

"Sure have," said the hitch-hiker.

"Thought so. I seen your hands. Been swingin' a pick or an ax or a sledge. That shines up your hands. I notice all stuff like that. Take a pride in it."

The hitch-hiker stared at him. The truck tires sang on the road. "Like to know anything else? I'll tell you. You ain't got to guess."

"Now don't get sore. I wasn't gettin' nosy."

"I'll tell you anything. I ain't hidin' nothin'."

"Now don't get sore. I just like to notice things. Makes the time pass."

"I'll tell you anything. Name's Joad, Tom Joad. Old man is ol' Tom Joad." His eyes rested broodingly on the driver.

"Don't get sore. I didn't mean nothin'."

"I don't mean nothin' neither," said Joad. "I'm just tryin' to get along without shovin' nobody around." He stopped and looked out at the dry fields, at the starved tree clumps hanging uneasily in the heated distance. From his side pocket he brought out his tobacco and papers. He rolled his cigarette down between his knees, where the wind could not get at it.

The driver chewed as rhythmically, as thoughtfully, as a cow. He waited to let the whole emphasis of the preceding passage disappear and be forgotten. At last, when the air seemed neutral again, he said, "A guy that never been a truck skinner don't know nothin' what it's like. Owners don't want us to pick up nobody. So we got to set here an' just skin her along 'less we want to take a chance of gettin' fired like I just done with you."

" 'Preciate it," said Joad.

"I've knew guys that done screwy things while they're drivin' trucks. I remember a guy use' to make up poetry. It passed the time." He looked over secretly to see whether Joad was interested or amazed. Joad was silent, looking into the distance ahead, along the road, along the white road that waved gently, like a ground swell. The driver went on at last, "I remember a piece of poetry this here guy wrote down. It was about him an' a couple other guys goin' all over the world drinkin' and raisin' hell and screwin' around. I wisht I could remember how that piece went. This guy had words in it that Jesus H. Christ wouldn't know what they meant. Part was like this: 'An' there we spied a nigger, with a trigger that was bigger than a elephant's proboscis or the whanger of a whale.' That proboscis is a nose-like. With a elephant it's his trunk. Guy showed me in a dictionary. Carried that dictionary all over hell with him. He'd look in it while he's pulled up gettin' his pie an' coffee." He stopped, feeling lonely in the long speech. His secret eyes turned on his passenger. Joad remained silent. Nervously the driver tried to force him into participation. "Ever know a guy that said big words like that?"

"Preacher," said Joad.

"Well, it makes you mad to hear a guy use big words. 'Course with a preacher it's all right because nobody would fool around with a preacher anyway. But this guy was funny. You didn't give a damn when he said a big word 'cause he just done it for ducks. He wasn't puttin' on no dog." The driver was reassured. He knew at least that Joad was listening. He swung the great truck viciously around a bend and the tires shrilled. "Like I was sayin'," he continued, "guy that drives a truck does screwy things. He got to. He'd go nuts just settin' here an' the road sneakin' under the wheels. Fella says once that truck skinners eats all the time—all the time in hamburger joints along the road."

"Sure seem to live there," Joad agreed.

"Sure they stop, but it ain't to eat. They ain't hardly ever hungry. They're just goddamn sick of goin'—get sick of it. Joints is the only place you can pull up, an' when you stop you got to buy somepin so you can sling the bull with the broad behind the counter. So you get a cup of coffee and a piece pie. Kind of gives a guy a little rest." He chewed his gum slowly and turned it with his tongue.

"Must be tough," said Joad with no emphasis.

The driver glanced quickly at him, looking for satire. "Well, it ain't no goddamn cinch," he said testily. "Looks easy, jus' settin' here till you put in your eight or maybe your ten or fourteen hours. But the road gets into a guy. He's got to do somepin. Some sings an' some whistles. Company won't let us have no radio. A few takes a pint along, but them kind don't stick long." He said the last smugly. "I don't never take a drink till I'm through."

"Yeah?" Joad asked.

"Yeah! A guy got to get ahead. Why, I'm thinkin' of takin' one of them correspondence school courses. Mechanical engineering. It's easy. Just study a few easy lessons at home. I'm thinkin' of it. Then I won't drive no truck. Then I'll tell other guys to drive trucks."

Joad took a pint of whisky from his side coat pocket. "Sure you won't have a snort?" His voice was teasing.

"No, by God. I won't touch it. A guy can't drink liquor all the time and study like I'm goin' to."

Joad uncorked the bottle, took two quick swallows, recorked it, and put it back in his pocket. The spicy hot smell of the whisky filled the cab. "You're all wound up," said Joad. "What's the matter—got a girl?"

"Well, sure. But I want to get ahead anyway. I been training my mind for a hell of a long time."

The whisky seemed to loosen Joad up. He rolled another cigarette and lighted it. "I ain't got a hell of a lot further to go," he said.

The driver went on quickly, "I don't need no shot," he said. "I train my mind all the time. I took a course in that two years ago." He patted the steering wheel with his right hand. "Suppose I pass a guy on the road. I look at him, an' after I'm past I try to remember ever'thing about him, kind a clothes an' shoes an' hat, an' how he walked an' maybe how tall an' what weight an' any scars. I do it pretty good. I can jus' make a whole picture in my head. Sometimes I think I ought to take a course to be a fingerprint expert. You'd be su'prised how much a guy can remember."

Joad took a quick drink from the flask. He dragged the last smoke from his raveling cigarette and then, with callused thumb and forefinger, crushed out the glowing end. He rubbed the butt to a pulp and put it out the window, letting the breeze suck it from his fingers. The big tires sang a high note on the pavement. Joad's dark quiet eyes became amused as he stared along the road. The driver waited and glanced uneasily over. At last Joad's long upper lip grinned up from his teeth and he chuckled silently, his chest jerked with the chuckles. "You sure took a hell of a long time to get to it, buddy."

The driver did not look over. "Get to what? How do you mean?"

Joad's lips stretched tight over his long teeth for a moment, and he licked his lips like a dog, two licks, one in each direction from the middle. His voice became harsh. "You know what I mean. You give me a goin'-over when I first got in. I seen you." The driver looked straight ahead, gripped the wheel so tightly that the pads of his palms bulged, and the backs of his hands paled. Joad continued, "You know where I come from." The driver was silent. "Don't you?" Joad insisted.

"Well—sure. That is—maybe. But it ain't none of my business. I mind my own yard. It ain't nothing to me." The words tumbled out now. "I don't stick my nose in nobody's business." And suddenly he was silent and waiting. And his hands were still white on the wheel. A grasshopper flipped through the window and lighted on top of the instrument panel, where it sat and began to scrape its wings with its angled jumping legs. Joad reached forward and crushed its hard skull-like head with his fingers, and he let it into the wind stream out the window. Joad chuckled again while he brushed the bits of broken insect from his fingertips. "You got me wrong, mister," he said. "I ain't keepin' quiet about it. Sure I been in McAlester. Been there four years. Sure these is the clothes they give me when I come out. I don't give a damn who knows it. An' I'm goin' to my old man's place so I don't have to lie to get a job."

The driver said, "Well—that ain't none of my business. I ain't a nosy guy."

"The hell you ain't," said Joad. "That big old nose of yours been stickin' out eight miles ahead of your face. You had that big nose goin' over me like a sheep in a vegetable patch."

The driver's face tightened. "You got me all wrong—" he began weakly.

Joad laughed at him. "You been a good guy. You give me a lift. Well, hell! I done time. So what! You want to know what I done time for, don't you?"

"That ain't none of my affair."

"Nothin' ain't none of your affair except skinnin' this here bull-bitch along, an' that's the least thing you work at. Now look. See that road up ahead?"

"Yeah."

"Well, I get off there. Sure, I know you're wettin' your pants to know what I done. I ain't a guy to let you down." The high hum of the motor dulled and the song of the tires dropped in pitch. Joad got out his pint and took another short drink. The truck drifted to a stop where a dirt road opened at right angles to the highway. Joad got out and stood beside the cab window. The vertical exhaust pipe puttered up its barely visible blue smoke. Joad leaned toward the driver. "Homicide," he said quickly. "That's a big word—means I killed a guy. Seven years. I'm sprung in four for keepin' my nose clean."

The driver's eyes slipped over Joad's face to memorize it. "I never asked you nothin' about it," he said. "I mind my own yard."

"You can tell about it in every joint from here to Texola." He smiled. "So long, fella. You been a good guy. But look, when you been in stir a little while, you can smell a question comin' from hell to breakfast. You telegraphed yours the first time you opened your trap." He spatted the metal door with the palm of his hand. "Thanks for the lift," he said. "So long." He turned away and walked into the dirt road.

For a moment the driver stared after him, and then he called, "Luck!" Joad waved his hand without looking around. Then the motor roared up and the gears clicked and the great red truck rolled heavily away.

Chapter Three

THE CONCRETE HIGHWAY was edged with a mat of tangled, broken, dry grass, and the grass heads were heavy with oat beards to catch on a dog's coat, and foxtails to tangle in a horse's fetlocks, and clover burrs to fasten in sheep's wool; sleeping life waiting to be spread and dispersed, every seed armed with an appliance of dispersal, twisting darts and parachutes for the wind, little spears and balls of tiny thorns, and all waiting for animals and for the wind, for a man's trouser cuff or the hem of a woman's skirt, all passive but armed with appliances of activity, still, but each possessed of the anlage of movement.

The sun lay on the grass and warmed it, and in the shade under the grass the insects moved, ants and ant lions to set traps for them, grasshoppers to jump into the air and flick their yellow wings for a second, sow bugs like little armadillos, plodding restlessly on many tender feet. And over the grass at the roadside a land turtle crawled, turning aside for nothing, dragging his high-domed shell over the grass. His hard legs and yellow-nailed feet threshed slowly through the grass, not really walking, but boosting and dragging his shell along. The barley beards slid off his shell, and the clover burrs fell on him and rolled to the ground. His horny beak was partly open, and his fierce, humorous eyes, under brows like fingernails, stared straight ahead. He came over the grass leaving a beaten trail behind him, and the hill, which was the highway embankment, reared up ahead of him. For a moment he stopped, his head held high. He blinked and looked up and down. At last he started to climb the embankment. Front clawed feet reached forward but did not touch. The hind feet kicked his shell along, and it scraped on the grass, and on the gravel. As the embankment grew steeper and steeper, the more frantic were the efforts of the land turtle. Pushing hind legs strained and slipped, boosting the shell along, and the horny head protruded as far as the neck could stretch. Little by little the shell slid up the embankment until at last a parapet cut straight across its line of march, the shoulder of the road, a concrete wall four inches high. As though they worked independently the hind legs pushed the shell against the wall. The head up-raised and peered over the wall to the broad smooth plain of cement. Now the hands, braced on top of the wall, strained and lifted, and the shell came slowly up and rested its front end on the wall. For a moment the turtle rested. A red ant ran into the shell, into the soft skin inside the shell, and sud-denly head and legs snapped in, and the armored tail clamped in sideways. The red ant was crushed between body and legs. And one head of wild oats was clamped into the shell by a front leg. For a long moment the turtle lay still, and then the neck crept out and the old humorous frowning eyes looked about and the legs and tail came out. The back legs went to work, straining like elephant legs, and the shell tipped to an angle so that the front legs could not reach the level cement plain. But higher and higher the hind legs boosted it, until at last the center of balance was reached, the front tipped down, the front legs scratched at the pavement, and it was up. But the head of wild oats was held by its stem around the front legs.

Now the going was easy, and all the legs worked, and the shell boosted along, waggling from side to side. A sedan driven by a forty-year-old woman approached. She saw the turtle and swung to the right, off the highway, the wheels screamed and a cloud of dust boiled up. Two wheels lifted for a moment and then settled. The car skidded back onto the road, and went on, but more slowly. The turtle had jerked into its shell, but now it hurried on, for the highway was burning hot.

And now a light truck approached, and as it came near, the driver saw the turtle and swerved to hit it. His front wheel struck the edge of the shell, flipped the turtle like a tiddly-wink, spun it like a coin, and rolled it off the highway. The truck went back to its course along the right side. Lying on its back, the turtle was tight in its shell for a long time. But at last its legs waved in the air, reaching for something to pull it over. Its front foot caught a piece of quartz and little by little the shell pulled over and flopped upright. The wild oat head fell out and three of the spearhead seeds stuck in the ground. And as the turtle crawled on down the embankment, its shell dragged dirt over the seeds. The turtle entered a dust road and jerked itself along, drawing a wavy shallow trench in the dust with its shell. The old humorous eyes looked ahead, and the horny beak opened a little. His yellow toe nails slipped a fraction in the dust.

Chapter Four

WHEN Joad heard the truck get under way, gear climbing up to gear and the ground throbbing under the rubber beating of the tires, he stopped and turned about and watched it until it disappeared. When it was out of sight he still watched the distance and the blue air-shimmer. Thoughtfully he took the pint from his pocket, unscrewed the metal cap, and sipped the whisky delicately, running his tongue inside the bottle neck, and then around his lips, to gather in any flavor that might have escaped him. He said experimentally, "There we spied a nigger—" and that was all he could remember. At last he turned about and faced the dusty side road that cut off at right angles through the fields. The sun was hot, and no wind stirred the sifted dust. The road was cut with furrows where dust had slid and settled back into the wheel tracks. Joad took a few steps, and the flourlike dust spurted up in front of his new yellow shoes, and the yellowness was disappearing under gray dust.

He leaned down and untied the laces, slipped off first one shoe and then the other. And he worked his damp feet comfortably in the hot dry dust until little spurts of it came up between his toes, and until the skin on his feet tightened with dryness. He took off his coat and wrapped his shoes in it and slipped the bundle under his arm. And at last he moved up the road, shooting the dust ahead of him, making a cloud that hung low to the ground behind him.

The right of way was fenced, two strands of barbed wire on willow poles. The poles were crooked and badly trimmed. Whenever a crotch came to the proper height the wire lay in it, and where there was no crotch the barbed wire was lashed to the post with rusty baling wire. Beyond the fence, the corn lay beaten down by wind and heat and drought, and the cups where leaf joined stalk were filled with dust.

Joad plodded along, dragging his cloud of dust behind him. A little bit ahead he saw the high-domed shell of a land turtle, crawling slowly along through the dust, its legs working stiffly and jerkily. Joad stopped to watch it, and his shadow fell on the turtle. Instantly head and legs were withdrawn and the short thick tail clamped sideways into the shell. Joad picked it up and turned it over. The back was brown-gray, like the dust, but the underside of the shell was creamy yellow, clean and smooth. Joad shifted his bundle high under his arm and stroked the smooth undershell with his finger, and he pressed it. It was softer than the back. The hard old head came out and tried to look at the pressing finger, and the legs waved wildly. The turtle wetted on Joad's hand and struggled uselessly in the air. Joad turned it back upright and rolled it up in his coat with his shoes. He could feel it pressing and struggling and fussing under his arm. He moved ahead more quickly now, dragging his heels a little in the fine dust.

Ahead of him, beside the road, a scrawny, dusty willow tree cast a speckled shade. Joad could see it ahead of him, its poor branches curving over the way, its load of leaves tattered and scraggly as a molting chicken. Joad was sweating now. His blue shirt darkened down his back and under his arms. He pulled at the visor of his cap and creased it in the middle, breaking its cardboard lining so completely that it could never look new again. And his steps took on new speed and intent toward the shade of the distant willow tree. At the willow he knew there would be shade, at least one hard bar of absolute shade thrown by the trunk, since the sun had passed its zenith. The sun whipped the back of his neck now and made a little humming in his head. He could not see the base of the tree, for it grew out of a little swale that held water longer than the level places. Joad speeded his pace against the sun, and he started down the declivity. He slowed cautiously, for the bar of absolute shade was taken. A man sat on the ground, leaning against the trunk of the tree. His legs were crossed and one bare foot extended nearly as high as his head. He did not hear Joad approaching, for he was whistling solemnly the tune of "Yes, Sir, That's My Baby." His extended foot swung slowly up and down in the tempo. It was not dance tempo. He stopped whistling and sang in an easy thin tenor:

> "Yes, sir, that's my Saviour,
>   Je—sus is my Saviour,
>   Je—sus is my Saviour now.

> On the level
> 'S not the devil,
> Jesus is my Saviour now."

Joad had moved into the imperfect shade of the molting leaves before the man heard him coming, stopped his song, and turned his head. It was a long head, bony, tight of skin, and set on a neck as stringy and muscular as a celery stalk. His eyeballs were heavy and protruding; the lids stretched to cover them, and the lids were raw and red. His cheeks were brown and shiny and hairless and his mouth full—humorous or sensual. The nose, beaked and hard, stretched the skin so tightly that the bridge showed white. There was no perspiration on the face, not even on the tall pale forehead. It was an abnormally high forehead, lined with delicate blue veins at the temples. Fully half of the face was above the eyes. His stiff gray hair was mussed back from his brow as though he had combed it back with his fingers. For clothes he wore overalls and a blue shirt. A denim coat with brass buttons and a spotted brown hat creased like a pork pie lay on the ground beside him. Canvas sneakers, gray with dust, lay near by where they had fallen when they were kicked off.

The man looked long at Joad. The light seemed to go far into his brown eyes, and it picked out little golden specks deep in the irises. The strained bundle of neck muscles stood out.

Joad stood still in the speckled shade. He took off his cap and mopped his wet face with it and dropped it and his rolled coat on the ground.

The man in the absolute shade uncrossed his legs and dug with his toes at the earth.

Joad said, "Hi. It's hotter'n hell on the road."

The seated man stared questioningly at him. "Now ain't you young Tom Joad—ol' Tom's boy?"

"Yeah," said Joad. "All the way. Goin' home now."

"You wouldn't remember me, I guess," the man said. He smiled and his full lips revealed great horse teeth. "Oh, no, you wouldn't remember. You was always too busy pullin' little girls' pigtails when I give you the Holy Sperit. You was all wropped up in yankin' that pigtail out by the roots. You maybe don't recollect, but I do. The two of you come to Jesus at once 'cause of that pigtail yankin'. Baptized both of you in the irrigation ditch at once. Fightin' an' yellin' like a couple a cats."

Joad looked at him with drooped eyes, and then he laughed. "Why, you're the preacher. You're the preacher. I jus' passed a recollection about you to a guy not an hour ago."

"I was a preacher," said the man seriously. "Reverend Jim Casy—was a Burning Busher. Used to howl out the name of Jesus to glory. And used to get an irrigation ditch so squirmin' full of repented sinners half of 'em like to drownded. But not no more," he sighed. "Just Jim Casy now. Ain't got the call no more. Got a lot of sinful idears—but they seem kinda sensible."

Joad said, "You're bound to get idears if you go thinkin' about stuff. Sure I remember you. You use ta give a good meetin'. I recollect one time you give a whole sermon walkin' around on your hands, yellin' your head off. Ma favored you more than anybody. An' Granma says you was just lousy with the spirit." Joad dug at his rolled coat and found the pocket and brought out his pint. The turtle moved a leg but he wrapped it up tightly. He unscrewed the cap and held out the bottle. "Have a little snort?"

Casy took the bottle and regarded it broodingly. "I ain't preachin' no more much. The sperit ain't in the people much no more; and worse'n that, the sperit ain't in me no more. 'Course now an' again the sperit gets movin' an' I rip out a meetin', or when folks sets out food I give 'em a grace, but my heart ain't in it. I on'y do it 'cause they expect it."

Joad mopped his face with his cap again. "You ain't too damn holy to take a drink, are you?" he asked.

Casy seemed to see the bottle for the first time. He tilted it and took three big swallows. "Nice drinkin' liquor," he said.

"Ought to be," said Joad. "That's fact'ry liquor. Cost a buck."

Casy took another swallow before he passed the bottle back. "Yes, sir!" he said. "Yes, sir!"

Joad took the bottle from him, and in politeness did not wipe the neck with his sleeve before he drank. He squatted on his hams and set the bottle upright against his coat roll.

His fingers found a twig with which to draw his thoughts on the ground. He swept the leaves from a square and smoothed the dust. And he drew angles and made little circles. "I ain't seen you in a long time," he said.

"Nobody seen me," said the preacher. "I went off alone, an' I sat and figured. The sperit's strong in me, on'y it ain't the same. I ain't so sure of a lot of things." He sat up straighter against the tree. His bony hand dug its way like a squirrel into his overall pocket, brought out a black, bitten plug of tobacco. Carefully he brushed off bits of straw and gray pocket fuzz before he bit off a corner and settled the quid into his cheek. Joad waved his stick in negation when the plug was held out to him. The turtle dug at the rolled coat. Casy looked over at the stirring garment. "What you got there—a chicken? You'll smother it."

Joad rolled the coat up more tightly. "An old turtle," he said. "Picked him up on the road. An old bulldozer. Thought I'd take 'im to my little brother. Kids like turtles."

The preacher nodded his head slowly. "Every kid got a turtle some time or other. Nobody can't keep a turtle though. They work at it and work at it, and at last one day they get out and away they go—off somewheres. It's like me. I wouldn' take the good ol' gospel that was just layin' there to my hand. I got to be pickin' at it an' workin' at it until I got it all tore down. Here I got the sperit sometimes an' nothin' to preach about. I got the call to lead the people, an' no place to lead 'em."

"Lead 'em around and around," said Joad. "Sling 'em in the irrigation ditch. Tell 'em they'll burn in hell if they don't think like you. What the hell you want to lead 'em someplace for? Jus' lead 'em." The straight trunk shade had stretched out along the ground. Joad moved gratefully into it and squatted on his hams and made a new smooth place on which to draw his thoughts with a stick. A thick-furred yellow shepherd dog came trotting down the road, head low, tongue lolling and dripping. Its tail hung limply curled, and it panted loudly. Joad whistled at it, but it only dropped its head an inch and trotted fast toward some definite destination. "Goin' someplace," Joad explained, a little piqued. "Goin' for home maybe."

The preacher could not be thrown from his subject. "Goin' someplace," he repeated. "That's right, he's goin' someplace. Me—I don't know where I'm goin'. Tell you what—I use ta get the people jumpin' an' talkin' in tongues, an' glory-shoutin' till they just fell down an' passed out. An' some I'd baptize to bring 'em to. An' then—you know what I'd do? I'd take one of them girls out in the grass, an' I'd lay with her. Done it ever' time. Then I'd feel bad, an' I'd pray an' pray, but it didn't do no good. Come the nex' time, them an' me was full of the sperit, I'd do it again. I figgered there just wasn't no hope for me, an' I was a damned ol' hypocrite. But I didn't mean to be."

Joad smiled and his long teeth parted and he licked his lips. "There ain't nothing like a good hot meetin' for pushin' 'em over," he said. "I done that myself."

Casy leaned forward excitedly. "You see," he cried, "I seen it was that way, an' I started thinkin'." He waved his bony big-knuckled hand up and down in a patting gesture. "I got to thinkin' like this—'Here's me preachin' grace. An' here's them people gettin' grace so hard they're jumpin' an' shout-in'. Now they say layin' up with a girl comes from the devil. But the more grace a girl got in her, the quicker she wants to go out in the grass.' An' I got to thinkin' how in hell, s'cuse me, how can the devil get in when a girl is so full of the Holy Spirit that it's spoutin' out of her nose an' ears. You'd think that'd be one time when the devil didn't stand a snowball's chance in hell. But there it was." His eyes were shining with excitement. He worked his cheeks for a moment and then spat into the dust, and the gob of spit rolled over and over, picking up dust until it looked like a round dry little pellet. The preacher spread out his hand and looked at his palm as though he were reading a book. "An' there's me," he went on softly. "There's me with all them people's souls in my han'—re-sponsible an' feelin' my responsibility—an' ever' time, I lay with one of them girls." He looked over at Joad and his face looked helpless. His expression asked for help.

Joad carefully drew the torso of a woman in the dirt, breasts, hips, pelvis. "I wasn't never a preacher," he said. "I never let nothin' get by when I could catch it. An' I never had no idears about it except I was goddamn glad when I got one."

"But you wasn't a preacher," Casy insisted. "A girl was just a girl to you. You could fuck 'em an' leave 'em. It wasn't nothin' to you. But to me they was holy vessels. I was savin' their souls. An' here with all that responsibility on me I'd just get 'em frothin' with the Holy Sperit, an' then I'd take 'em out an' screw 'em."

"Maybe I should of been a preacher," said Joad. He brought out his tobacco and papers and rolled a cigarette. He lighted it and squinted through the smoke at the preacher. "I been a long time without a girl," he said. "It's gonna take some catchin' up."

Casy continued, "It worried me till I couldn't get no sleep. Here I'd go to preachin' and I'd say, 'By God, this time I ain't gonna do it.' And right while I said it, I knowed I was."

"You should a got a wife," said Joad. "Preacher an' his wife stayed at our place one time. Jehovites they was. Slep' upstairs. Held meetin's in our barnyard. Us kids would listen. That preacher's missus took a godawful poundin' after ever' night meetin'."

"I'm glad you tol' me," said Casy. "I use to think it was jus' me. Finally it give me such pain I quit an' went off by myself an' give her a damn good thinkin' about." He doubled up his legs and scratched between his dry dusty toes. "I says to myself, 'What's gnawin' you? Is it the screwin'?' An' I says, 'No, it's the sin.' An' I says, 'Why is it that when a fella ought to be just about mule-ass proof against sin, an' all full up of Jesus, why is it that's the time a fella gets fingerin' his pants buttons?'" He laid two fingers down in his palm in rhythm, as though he gently placed each word there side by side. "I says, 'Maybe it ain't a sin. Maybe it's just the way folks is. Maybe we been whippin' the hell out of ourselves for nothin'.' An' I thought how some sisters took to beatin' theirselves with a three-foot shag of bobwire. An' I thought how maybe they liked to hurt themselves, an' maybe I liked to hurt myself. Well, I was layin' under a tree when I figured that out, and I went to sleep. And it come night, an' it was dark when I come to. They was a coyote squawkin' near by. Before I knowed it, I was sayin' out loud, 'The hell with it! There ain't no sin and there ain't no virtue. There's just stuff people do. It's all part of the same thing. And some of the things folks do is nice, and some ain't nice, but that's as far as any man got a right to say.' " He paused and looked up from the palm of his hand, where he had laid down the words.

Joad was grinning at him, but Joad's eyes were sharp and interested, too. "You give her a goin'-over," he said. "You figured her out."

Casy spoke again, and his voice rang with pain and confusion. "I says, 'What's this call, this sperit?' An' I says, 'It's love. I love people so much I'm fit to bust, sometimes.' An' I says, 'Don't you love Jesus?' Well, I thought an' thought, an' finally I says, 'No, I don't know nobody name' Jesus. I know a bunch of stories, but I only love people. An' sometimes I love 'em fit to bust, an' I want to make 'em happy, so I been preachin' somepin I thought would make 'em happy.' An' then—I been talkin' a hell of a lot. Maybe you wonder about me using bad words. Well, they ain't bad to me no more. They're jus' words folks use, an' they don't mean nothing bad with 'em. Anyways, I'll tell you one more thing I thought out; an' from a preacher it's the most unreligious thing, and I can't be a preacher no more because I thought it an' I believe it."

"What's that?" Joad asked.

Casy looked shyly at him. "If it hits you wrong, don't take no offense at it, will you?"

"I don't take no offense 'cept a bust in the nose," said Joad. "What did you figger?"

"I figgered about the Holy Sperit and the Jesus road. I figgered, 'Why do we got to hang it on God or Jesus? Maybe,' I figgered, 'maybe it's all men an' all women we love; maybe that's the Holy Sperit—the human sperit—the whole shebang. Maybe all men got one big soul ever'body's a part of.' Now I sat there thinkin' it, an' all of a sudden—I knew it. I knew it so deep down that it was true, and I still know it."

Joad's eyes dropped to the ground, as though he could not meet the naked honesty in the preacher's eyes. "You can't hold no church with idears like that," he said. "People would drive you out of the country with idears like that. Jumpin' an' yellin'. That's what folks like. Makes 'em feel swell. When Granma got to talkin' in tongues, you couldn't tie her down. She could knock over a full-growed deacon with her fist."

Casy regarded him broodingly. "Somepin I like to ast you," he said. "Somepin that been eatin' on me."

"Go ahead. I'll talk, sometimes."

"Well"—the preacher said slowly—"here's you that I baptized right when I was in the glory roof-tree. Got little hunks of Jesus jumpin' outa my mouth that day. You won't remember 'cause you was busy pullin' that pigtail."

"I remember," said Joad. "That was Susy Little. She bust my finger a year later."

"Well—did you take any good outa that baptizin'? Was your ways better?"

Joad thought about it. "No-o-o, can't say as I felt anything."

"Well—did you take any bad from it? Think hard."

Joad picked up the bottle and took a swig. "They wasn't nothing in it, good or bad. I just had fun." He handed the flask to the preacher.

He sighed and drank and looked at the low level of the whisky and took another tiny drink. "That's good," he said. "I got to worryin' about whether in messin' around maybe I done somebody a hurt."

Joad looked over toward his coat and saw the turtle, free of the cloth and hurrying away in the direction he had been following when Joad found him. Joad watched him for a moment and then got slowly to his feet and retrieved him and wrapped him in the coat again. "I ain't got no present for the kids," he said. "Nothin' but this ol' turtle."

"It's a funny thing," the preacher said. "I was thinkin' about ol' Tom Joad when you come along. Thinkin' I'd call in on him. I used to think he was a godless man but I liked him." He said confessingly, "But the only kind of men I ever really did like was godless men. How is Tom?"

"I don' know how he is. I ain't been home in four years."

"Didn't he write to you?"

Joad was embarrassed. "Well, Pa wasn't no hand to write for pretty, or to write for writin'. He'd sign up his name as nice as anybody, an' lick his pencil. But Pa never did write no letters. He always says what he couldn' tell a fella with his mouth wasn't worth leanin' on no pencil about."

"Been out travelin' around?" Casy asked.

Joad regarded him suspiciously. "Didn' you hear about me? I was in all the papers."

"No—I never. What?" He jerked one leg over the other and settled lower against the tree. The afternoon was advancing rapidly, and a richer tone was growing on the sun.

Joad said pleasantly, "Might's well tell you now an' get it over with. But if you was still preachin' I wouldn't tell, fear you get prayin' over me." He drained the last of the pint and flung it from him, and the flat brown bottle skidded lightly over the dust. "I been in McAlester them four years."

Casy swung around to him, and his brows lowered so that his tall forehead seemed even taller. "Ain't wantin' to talk about it, huh? I won't ask you no questions, if you done something bad——"

"I'd do what I done—again," said Joad. "I killed a guy in a fight. We was drunk at a dance. He got a knife in me, an' I killed him with a shovel that was layin' there. Knocked his head plumb to squash."

Casy's eyebrows resumed their normal level. "You ain't ashamed of nothin' then?"

"No," said Joad. "I ain't. I got seven years, account of he had a knife in me. Got out in four—parole."

"Then you ain't heard nothin' about your folks for four years?"

"Oh, I heard. Ma sent me a card two years ago, an' las' Christmus Granma sent a card. Jesus, the guys in the cell block laughed! Had a tree an' shiny stuff looks like snow. It says in po'try:

" 'Merry Christmus, purty child,
   Jesus meek an' Jesus mild,
   Underneath the Christmus tree
   There's a gif' for you from me.'

I guess Granma never read it. Prob'ly got it from a drummer an' picked out the one with the mos' shiny stuff on it. The guys in my cell block goddamn near died laughin'. Jesus Meek they called me after that. Granma never meant it funny;

she jus' figgered it was so purty she wouldn' bother to read
it. She lost her glasses the year I went up. Maybe she never
did find 'em."

"How they treat you in McAlester?" Casy asked.

"Oh, awright. You eat regular, an' get clean clothes, and
there's places to take a bath. It's pretty nice some ways. Makes
it hard not havin' no women." Suddenly he laughed. "They
was a guy paroled," he said. " 'Bout a month he's back for
breakin' parole. A guy ast him why he bust his parole. 'Well,
hell,' he says. 'They got no conveniences at my old man's
place. Got no 'lectric lights, got no shower baths. There ain't
no books, an' the food's lousy.' Says he come back where they
got a few conveniences an' he eats regular. He says it makes
him feel lonesome out there in the open havin' to think what
to do next. So he stole a car an' come back." Joad got out
his tobacco and blew a brown paper free of the pack and rolled
a cigarette. "The guy's right, too," he said. "Las' night,
thinkin' where I'm gonna sleep, I got scared. An' I got
thinkin' about my bunk, an' I wonder what the stir-bug I got
for a cell mate is doin'. Me an' some guys had a strang band
goin'. Good one. Guy said we ought to go on the radio. An'
this mornin' I didn' know what time to get up. Jus' laid there
waitin' for the bell to go off."

Casy chuckled. "Fella can get so he misses the noise of a
saw mill."

The yellowing, dusty, afternoon light put a golden color on
the land. The cornstalks looked golden. A flight of swallows
swooped overhead toward some waterhole. The turtle in
Joad's coat began a new campaign of escape. Joad creased the
visor of his cap. It was getting the long protruding curve of
a crow's beak now. "Guess I'll mosey along," he said. "I hate
to hit the sun, but it ain't so bad now."

Casy pulled himself together. "I ain't seen ol' Tom in a
bug's age," he said. "I was gonna look in on him anyways. I
brang Jesus to your folks for a long time, an' I never took up
a collection nor nothin' but a bite to eat."

"Come along," said Joad. "Pa'll be glad to see you. He
always said you got too long a pecker for a preacher." He
picked up his coat roll and tightened it snugly about his shoes
and turtle.

Casy gathered in his canvas sneakers and shoved his bare feet into them. "I ain't got your confidence," he said. "I'm always scared there's wire or glass under the dust. I don't know nothin' I hate so much as a cut toe."

They hesitated on the edge of the shade and then they plunged into the yellow sunlight like two swimmers hastening to get to shore. After a few fast steps they slowed to a gentle, thoughtful pace. The cornstalks threw gray shadows sideways now, and the raw smell of hot dust was in the air. The corn field ended and dark green cotton took its place, dark green leaves through a film of dust, and the bolls forming. It was spotty cotton, thick in the low places where water had stood, and bare on the high places. The plants strove against the sun. And distance, toward the horizon, was tan to invisibility. The dust road stretched out ahead of them, waving up and down. The willows of a stream lined across the west, and to the northwest a fallow section was going back to sparse brush. But the smell of burned dust was in the air, and the air was dry, so that mucus in the nose dried to a crust, and the eyes watered to keep the eyeballs from drying out.

Casy said, "See how good the corn come along until the dust got up. Been a dinger of a crop."

"Ever' year," said Joad. "Ever' year I can remember, we had a good crop comin', an' it never come. Grampa says she was good the first five plowin's, while the wild grass was still in her." The road dropped down a little hill and climbed up another rolling hill.

Casy said, "Ol' Tom's house can't be more'n a mile from here. Ain't she over that third rise?"

"Sure," said Joad. " 'Less somebody stole it, like Pa stole it."

"Your pa stole it?"

"Sure, got it a mile an' a half east of here an' drug it. Was a family livin' there, an' they moved away. Grampa an' Pa an' my brother Noah like to took the whole house, but she wouldn' come. They only got part of her. That's why she looks so funny on one end. They cut her in two an' drug her over with twelve head of horses and two mules. They was goin' back for the other half an' stick her together again, but before they got there Wink Manley come with his boys and stole the other half. Pa an' Grampa was pretty sore, but a little later them an' Wink got drunk together an' laughed their heads off about it. Wink, he says his house is at stud, an' if we'll bring our'n over an' breed 'em we'll maybe get a litter of crap houses. Wink was a great ol' fella when he was drunk. After that him an' Pa an' Grampa was friends. Got drunk together ever' chance they got."

"Tom's a great one," Casy agreed. They plodded dustily on down to the bottom of the draw, and then slowed their steps for the rise. Casy wiped his forehead with his sleeve and put on his flat-topped hat again. "Yes," he repeated, "Tom was a great one. For a godless man he was a great one. I seen him in meetin' sometimes when the sperit got into him just a little, an' I seen him take ten-twelve foot jumps. I tell you when ol' Tom got a dose of the Holy Sperit you got to move fast to keep from gettin' run down an' tromped. Jumpy as a stud horse in a box stall."

They topped the next rise and the road dropped into an old water-cut, ugly and raw, a ragged course, and freshet scars cutting into it from both sides. A few stones were in the crossing. Joad minced across in his bare feet. "You talk about Pa," he said. "Maybe you never seen Uncle John the time they baptized him over to Polk's place. Why, he got to plungin' an' jumpin'. Jumped over a feeny bush as big as a piana. Over he'd jump, an' back he'd jump, howlin' like a dog-wolf in moon time. Well, Pa seen him, an' Pa, he figgers he's the bes' Jesus-jumper in these parts. So Pa picks out a feeny bush 'bout twicet as big as Uncle John's feeny bush, and Pa lets out a squawk like a sow litterin' broken bottles, an' he takes a run at that feeny bush an' clears her an' bust his right leg. That took the sperit out of Pa. Preacher wants to pray it set, but Pa says, no, by God, he'd got his heart full of havin' a doctor. Well, they wasn't a doctor, but they was a travelin' dentist, an' he set her. Preacher give her a prayin' over anyways."

They plodded up the little rise on the other side of the water-cut. Now that the sun was on the wane some of its impact was gone, and while the air was hot, the hammering rays were weaker. The strung wire on crooked poles still edged the road. On the right-hand side a line of wire fence strung out across the cotton field, and the dusty green cotton was the same on both sides, dusty and dry and dark green.

Joad pointed to the boundary fence. "That there's our line. We didn't really need no fence there, but we had the wire, an' Pa kinda liked her there. Said it give him a feelin' that forty was forty. Wouldn't of had the fence if Uncle John didn' come drivin' in one night with six spools of wire in his wagon. He give 'em to Pa for a shoat. We never did know where he got that wire." They slowed for the rise, moving their feet in the deep soft dust, feeling the earth with their feet. Joad's eyes were inward on his memory. He seemed to be laughing inside himself. "Uncle John was a crazy bastard," he said. "Like what he done with that shoat." He chuckled and walked on.

Jim Casy waited impatiently. The story did not continue. Casy gave it a good long time to come out. "Well, what'd he do with that shoat?" he demanded at last, with some irritation.

"Huh? Oh! Well, he killed that shoat right there, an' he got Ma to light up the stove. He cut out pork chops an' put 'em in the pan, an' he put ribs an' a leg in the oven. He et chops till the ribs was done, an' he et ribs till the leg was done. An' then he tore into that leg. Cut off big hunks of her an' shoved 'em in his mouth. Us kids hung around slaverin', an' he give us some, but he wouldn' give Pa none. By an' by he et so much he throwed up an' went to sleep. While he's asleep us kids an' Pa finished off the leg. Well, when Uncle John woke up in the mornin' he slaps another leg in the oven. Pa says, 'John, you gonna eat that whole damn pig?' An' he says, 'I aim to, Tom, but I'm scairt some of her'll spoil 'fore I get her et, hungry as I am for pork. Maybe you better get a plate an' gimme back a couple rolls of wire.' Well, sir, Pa wasn't no fool. He jus' let Uncle John go on an' eat himself sick of pig, an' when he drove off he hadn't et much more'n half. Pa says, 'Whyn't you salt her down?' But not Uncle John; when he wants pig he wants a whole pig, an' when he's through, he don't want no pig hangin' around. So off he goes, and Pa salts down what's left."

Casy said, "While I was still in the preachin' sperit I'd a

made a lesson of that an' spoke it to you, but I don't do that no more. What you s'pose he done a thing like that for?"

"I dunno," said Joad. "He jus' got hungry for pork. Makes me hungry jus' to think of it. I had jus' four slices of roastin' pork in four years—one slice ever' Christmus."

Casy suggested elaborately, "Maybe Tom'll kill the fatted calf like for the prodigal in Scripture."

Joad laughed scornfully. "You don't know Pa. If he kills a chicken most of the squawkin' will come from Pa, not the chicken. He don't never learn. He's always savin' a pig for Christmus and then it dies in September of bloat or somepin so you can't eat it. When Uncle John wanted pork he et pork. He had her."

They moved over the curving top of the hill and saw the Joad place below them. And Joad stopped. "It ain't the same," he said. "Looka that house. Somepin's happened. They ain't nobody there." The two stood and stared at the little cluster of buildings.

Chapter Five

THE OWNERS of the land came onto the land, or more often a spokesman for the owners came. They came in closed cars, and they felt the dry earth with their fingers, and sometimes they drove big earth augers into the ground for soil tests. The tenants, from their sun-beaten dooryards, watched uneasily when the closed cars drove along the fields. And at last the owner men drove into the dooryards and sat in their cars to talk out of the windows. The tenant men stood beside the cars for a while, and then squatted on their hams and found sticks with which to mark the dust.

In the open doors the women stood looking out, and behind them the children—corn-headed children, with wide eyes, one bare foot on top of the other bare foot, and the toes working. The women and the children watched their men talking to the owner men. They were silent.

Some of the owner men were kind because they hated what they had to do, and some of them were angry because they hated to be cruel, and some of them were cold because they had long ago found that one could not be an owner unless one were cold. And all of them were caught in something larger than themselves. Some of them hated the mathematics that drove them, and some were afraid, and some worshiped the mathematics because it provided a refuge from thought and from feeling. If a bank or a finance company owned the land, the owner man said, The Bank—or the Company—needs—wants—insists—must have—as though the Bank or the Company were a monster, with thought and feeling, which had enslaved them. These last would take no responsibility for the banks or the companies because they were men and slaves, while the banks were machines and masters all at the same time. Some of the owner men were a little proud to be slaves to such cold and powerful masters. The owner men sat in the cars and explained. You know the land is poor. You've scrabbled at it long enough, God knows.

The squatting tenant men nodded and wondered and drew figures in the dust, and yes, they knew, God knows. If the dust only wouldn't fly. If the top would only stay on the soil, it might not be so bad.

The owner men went on leading to their point: You know the land's getting poorer. You know what cotton does to the land; robs it, sucks all the blood out of it.

The squatters nodded—they knew, God knew. If they could only rotate the crops they might pump blood back into the land.

Well, it's too late. And the owner men explained the workings and the thinkings of the monster that was stronger than they were. A man can hold land if he can just eat and pay taxes; he can do that.

Yes, he can do that until his crops fail one day and he has to borrow money from the bank.

But—you see, a bank or a company can't do that, because those creatures don't breathe air, don't eat side-meat. They breathe profits; they eat the interest on money. If they don't get it, they die the way you die without air, without side-meat. It is a sad thing, but it is so. It is just so.

The squatting men raised their eyes to understand. Can't we just hang on? Maybe the next year will be a good year. God knows how much cotton next year. And with all the wars—God knows what price cotton will bring. Don't they make explosives out of cotton? And uniforms? Get enough wars and cotton'll hit the ceiling. Next year, maybe. They looked up questioningly.

We can't depend on it. The bank—the monster has to have profits all the time. It can't wait. It'll die. No, taxes go on. When the monster stops growing, it dies. It can't stay one size.

Soft fingers began to tap the sill of the car window, and hard fingers tightened on the restless drawing sticks. In the doorways of the sun-beaten tenant houses, women sighed and then shifted feet so that the one that had been down was now on top, and the toes working. Dogs came sniffing near the owner cars and wetted on all four tires one after another. And chickens lay in the sunny dust and fluffed their feathers to get the cleansing dust down to the skin. In the little sties the pigs grunted inquiringly over the muddy remnants of the slops.

The squatting men looked down again. What do you want

us to do? We can't take less share of the crop—we're half starved now. The kids are hungry all the time. We got no clothes, torn an' ragged. If all the neighbors weren't the same, we'd be ashamed to go to meeting.

And at last the owner men came to the point. The tenant system won't work any more. One man on a tractor can take the place of twelve or fourteen families. Pay him a wage and take all the crop. We have to do it. We don't like to do it. But the monster's sick. Something's happened to the monster.

But you'll kill the land with cotton.

We know. We've got to take cotton quick before the land dies. Then we'll sell the land. Lots of families in the East would like to own a piece of land.

The tenant men looked up alarmed. But what'll happen to us? How'll we eat?

You'll have to get off the land. The plows'll go through the dooryard.

And now the squatting men stood up angrily. Grampa took up the land, and he had to kill the Indians and drive them away. And Pa was born here, and he killed weeds and snakes. Then a bad year came and he had to borrow a little money. An' we was born here. There in the door—our children born here. And Pa had to borrow money. The bank owned the land then, but we stayed and we got a little bit of what we raised.

We know that—all that. It's not us, it's the bank. A bank isn't like a man. Or an owner with fifty thousand acres, he isn't like a man either. That's the monster.

Sure, cried the tenant men, but it's our land. We measured it and broke it up. We were born on it, and we got killed on it, died on it. Even if it's no good, it's still ours. That's what makes it ours—being born on it, working it, dying on it. That makes ownership, not a paper with numbers on it.

We're sorry. It's not us. It's the monster. The bank isn't like a man.

Yes, but the bank is only made of men.

No, you're wrong there—quite wrong there. The bank is something else than men. It happens that every man in a bank hates what the bank does, and yet the bank does it. The bank is something more than men, I tell you. It's the monster. Men made it, but they can't control it.

The tenants cried, Grampa killed Indians, Pa killed snakes for the land. Maybe we can kill banks—they're worse than Indians and snakes. Maybe we got to fight to keep our land, like Pa and Grampa did.

And now the owner men grew angry. You'll have to go.

But it's ours, the tenant men cried. We——

No. The bank, the monster owns it. You'll have to go.

We'll get our guns, like Grampa when the Indians came. What then?

Well—first the sheriff, and then the troops. You'll be stealing if you try to stay, you'll be murderers if you kill to stay. The monster isn't men, but it can make men do what it wants.

But if we go, where'll we go? How'll we go? We got no money.

We're sorry, said the owner men. The bank, the fifty-thousand-acre owner can't be responsible. You're on land that isn't yours. Once over the line maybe you can pick cotton in the fall. Maybe you can go on relief. Why don't you go on west to California? There's work there, and it never gets cold. Why, you can reach out anywhere and pick an orange. Why, there's always some kind of crop to work in. Why don't you go there? And the owner men started their cars and rolled away.

The tenant men squatted down on their hams again to mark the dust with a stick, to figure, to wonder. Their sunburned faces were dark, and their sun-whipped eyes were light. The women moved cautiously out of the doorways toward their men, and the children crept behind the women, cautiously, ready to run. The bigger boys squatted beside their fathers, because that made them men. After a time the women asked, What did he want?

And the men looked up for a second, and the smolder of pain was in their eyes. We got to get off. A tractor and a superintendent. Like factories.

Where'll we go? the women asked.

We don't know. We don't know.

And the women went quickly, quietly back into the houses and herded the children ahead of them. They knew that a man so hurt and so perplexed may turn in anger, even on people he loves. They left the men alone to figure and to wonder in the dust.

After a time perhaps the tenant man looked about—at the pump put in ten years ago, with a goose-neck handle and iron flowers on the spout, at the chopping block where a thousand chickens had been killed, at the hand plow lying in the shed, and the patent crib hanging in the rafters over it.

The children crowded about the women in the houses. What we going to do, Ma? Where we going to go?

The women said, We don't know, yet. Go out and play. But don't go near your father. He might whale you if you go near him. And the women went on with the work, but all the time they watched the men squatting in the dust—perplexed and figuring.

The tractors came over the roads and into the fields, great crawlers moving like insects, having the incredible strength of insects. They crawled over the ground, laying the track and rolling on it and picking it up. Diesel tractors, puttering while they stood idle; they thundered when they moved, and then settled down to a droning roar. Snub-nosed monsters, raising the dust and sticking their snouts into it, straight down the country, across the country, through fences, through door-yards, in and out of gullies in straight lines. They did not run on the ground, but on their own roadbeds. They ignored hills and gulches, water courses, fences, houses.

The man sitting in the iron seat did not look like a man; gloved, goggled, rubber dust mask over nose and mouth, he was a part of the monster, a robot in the seat. The thunder of the cylinders sounded through the country, became one with the air and the earth, so that earth and air muttered in sympathetic vibration. The driver could not control it—straight across country it went, cutting through a dozen farms and straight back. A twitch at the controls could swerve the cat', but the driver's hands could not twitch because the monster that built the tractor, the monster that sent the tractor out, had somehow got into the driver's hands, into his brain and muscle, had goggled him and muzzled him—goggled his mind, muzzled his speech, goggled his perception, muzzled his protest. He could not see the land as it was, he could not smell the land as it smelled; his feet did not stamp the clods or feel the warmth and power of the earth. He sat in an iron seat and stepped on iron pedals. He could not cheer or beat or curse or encourage the extension of his power, and because of this he could not cheer or whip or curse or encourage himself. He did not know or own or trust or beseech the land. If a seed dropped did not germinate, it was no skin off his ass. If the young thrusting plant withered in drought or drowned in a flood of rain, it was no more to the driver than to the tractor.

He loved the land no more than the bank loved the land. He could admire the tractor—its machined surfaces, its surge of power, the roar of its detonating cylinders; but it was not his tractor. Behind the tractor rolled the shining disks, cutting the earth with blades—not plowing but surgery, pushing the cut earth to the right where the second row of disks cut it and pushed it to the left; slicing blades shining, polished by the cut earth. And pulled behind the disks, the harrows combing with iron teeth so that the little clods broke up and the earth lay smooth. Behind the harrows, the long seeders—twelve curved iron penes erected in the foundry, orgasms set by gears, raping methodically, raping without passion. The driver sat in his iron seat and he was proud of the straight lines he did not will, proud of the tractor he did not own or love, proud of the power he could not control. And when that crop grew, and was harvested, no man had crumbled a hot clod in his fingers and let the earth sift past his fingertips. No man had touched the seed, or lusted for the growth. Men ate what they had not raised, had no connection with the bread. The land bore under iron, and under iron gradually died; for it was not loved or hated, it had no prayers or curses.

At noon the tractor driver stopped sometimes near a tenant house and opened his lunch: sandwiches wrapped in waxed paper, white bread, pickle, cheese, Spam, a piece of pie branded like an engine part. He ate without relish. And tenants not yet moved away came out to see him, looked curiously while the goggles were taken off, and the rubber dust mask, leaving white circles around the eyes and a large white circle around nose and mouth. The exhaust of the tractor puttered on, for fuel is so cheap it is more efficient to leave the engine running than to heat the Diesel nose for a new start.

Curious children crowded close, ragged children who ate their fried dough as they watched. They watched hungrily the un-wrapping of the sandwiches, and their hunger-sharpened noses smelled the pickle, cheese, and Spam. They didn't speak to the driver. They watched his hand as it carried food to his mouth. They did not watch him chewing; their eyes followed the hand that held the sandwich. After a while the tenant who could not leave the place came out and squatted in the shade beside the tractor.

"Why, you're Joe Davis's boy!"

"Sure," the driver said.

"Well, what you doing this kind of work for—against your own people?"

"Three dollars a day. I got damn sick of creeping for my dinner—and not getting it. I got a wife and kids. We got to eat. Three dollars a day, and it comes every day."

"That's right," the tenant said. "But for your three dollars a day fifteen or twenty families can't eat at all. Nearly a hun-dred people have to go out and wander on the roads for your three dollars a day. Is that right?"

And the driver said, "Can't think of that. Got to think of my own kids. Three dollars a day, and it comes every day. Times are changing, mister, don't you know? Can't make a living on the land unless you've got two, five, ten thousand acres and a tractor. Crop land isn't for little guys like us any more. You don't kick up a howl because you can't make Fords, or because you're not the telephone company. Well, crops are like that now. Nothing to do about it. You try to get three dollars a day someplace. That's the only way."

The tenant pondered. "Funny thing how it is. If a man owns a little property, that property is him, it's part of him, and it's like him. If he owns property only so he can walk on it and handle it and be sad when it isn't doing well, and feel fine when the rain falls on it, that property is him, and some way he's bigger because he owns it. Even if he isn't successful he's big with his property. That is so."

And the tenant pondered more. "But let a man get prop-erty he doesn't see, or can't take time to get his fingers in, or can't be there to walk on it—why, then the property is the man. He can't do what he wants, he can't think what he wants. The property is the man, stronger than he is. And he is small, not big. Only his possessions are big—and he's the servant of his property. That is so, too."

The driver munched the branded pie and threw the crust away. "Times are changed, don't you know? Thinking about stuff like that don't feed the kids. Get your three dollars a day, feed your kids. You got no call to worry about anybody's kids but your own. You get a reputation for talking like that, and you'll never get three dollars a day. Big shots won't give you three dollars a day if you worry about anything but your three dollars a day."

"Nearly a hundred people on the road for your three dollars. Where will we go?"

"And that reminds me," the driver said, "you better get out soon. I'm going through the dooryard after dinner."

"You filled in the well this morning."

"I know. Had to keep the line straight. But I'm going through the dooryard after dinner. Got to keep the lines straight. And—well, you know Joe Davis, my old man, so I'll tell you this. I got orders wherever there's a family not moved out—if I have an accident—you know, get too close and cave the house in a little—well, I might get a couple of dollars. And my youngest kid never had no shoes yet."

"I built it with my hands. Straightened old nails to put the sheathing on. Rafters are wired to the stringers with baling wire. It's mine. I built it. You bump it down—I'll be in the window with a rifle. You even come too close and I'll pot you like a rabbit."

"It's not me. There's nothing I can do. I'll lose my job if I don't do it. And look—suppose you kill me? They'll just hang you, but long before you're hung there'll be another guy on the tractor, and he'll bump the house down. You're not killing the right guy."

"That's so," the tenant said. "Who gave you orders? I'll go after him. He's the one to kill."

"You're wrong. He got his orders from the bank. The bank told him, 'Clear those people out or it's your job.'"

"Well, there's a president of the bank. There's a board of directors. I'll fill up the magazine of the rifle and go into the bank."

The driver said, "Fellow was telling me the bank gets orders from the East. The orders were, 'Make the land show profit or we'll close you up.' "

"But where does it stop? Who can we shoot? I don't aim to starve to death before I kill the man that's starving me."

"I don't know. Maybe there's nobody to shoot. Maybe the thing isn't men at all. Maybe, like you said, the property's doing it. Anyway I told you my orders."

"I got to figure," the tenant said. "We all got to figure. There's some way to stop this. It's not like lightning or earthquakes. We've got a bad thing made by men, and by God that's something we can change." The tenant sat in his doorway, and the driver thundered his engine and started off, tracks falling and curving, harrows combing, and the phalli of the seeder slipping into the ground. Across the dooryard the tractor cut, and the hard, foot-beaten ground was seeded field, and the tractor cut through again; the uncut space was ten feet wide. And back he came. The iron guard bit into the house-corner, crumbled the wall, and wrenched the little house from its foundation so that it fell sideways, crushed like a bug. And the driver was goggled and a rubber mask covered his nose and mouth. The tractor cut a straight line on, and the air and the ground vibrated with its thunder. The tenant man stared after it, his rifle in his hand. His wife was beside him, and the quiet children behind. And all of them stared after the tractor.

Chapter Six

THE REVEREND CASY and young Tom stood on the hill and looked down on the Joad place. The small unpainted house was mashed at one corner, and it had been pushed off its foundations so that it slumped at an angle, its blind front windows pointing at a spot of sky well above the horizon. The fences were gone and the cotton grew in the dooryard and up against the house, and the cotton was about the shed barn. The outhouse lay on its side, and the cotton grew close against it. Where the dooryard had been pounded hard by the bare feet of children and by stamping horses' hooves and by the broad wagon wheels, it was cultivated now, and the dark green, dusty cotton grew. Young Tom stared for a long time at the ragged willow beside the dry horse trough, at the concrete base where the pump had been. "Jesus!" he said at last. "Hell musta popped here. There ain't nobody livin' there." At last he moved quickly down the hill, and Casy followed him. He looked into the barn shed, deserted, a little ground straw on the floor, and at the mule stall in the corner. And as he looked in, there was a skittering on the floor and a family of mice faded in under the straw. Joad paused at the entrance to the tool-shed leanto, and no tools were there—a broken plow point, a mess of hay wire in the corner, an iron wheel from a hayrake and a rat-gnawed mule collar, a flat gallon oil can crusted with dirt and oil, and a pair of torn overalls hanging on a nail. "There ain't nothin' left," said Joad. "We had pretty nice tools. There ain't nothin' left."

Casy said, "If I was still a preacher I'd say the arm of the Lord had struck. But now I don't know what happened. I been away. I didn't hear nothin'." They walked toward the concrete well-cap, walked through cotton plants to get to it, and the bolls were forming on the cotton, and the land was cultivated.

"We never planted here," Joad said. "We always kept this clear. Why, you can't get a horse in now without he tromps the cotton." They paused at the dry watering trough, and the proper weeds that should grow under a trough were gone and the old thick wood of the trough was dry and cracked. On the well-cap the bolts that had held the pump stuck up, their threads rusty and the nuts gone. Joad looked into the tube of the well and spat and listened. He dropped a clod down the well and listened. "She was a good well," he said. "I can't hear water." He seemed reluctant to go to the house. He dropped clod after clod down the well. "Maybe they're all dead," he said. "But somebody'd a told me. I'd a got word some way."

"Maybe they left a letter or something to tell in the house. Would they of knowed you was comin' out?"

"I don' know," said Joad. "No, I guess not. I didn' know myself till a week ago."

"Le's look in the house. She's all pushed out a shape. Something knocked the hell out of her." They walked slowly toward the sagging house. Two of the supports of the porch roof were pushed out so that the roof flopped down on one end. And the house-corner was crushed in. Through a maze of splintered wood the room at the corner was visible. The front door hung open inward, and a low strong gate across the front door hung outward on leather hinges.

Joad stopped at the step, a twelve-by-twelve timber. "Doorstep's here," he said. "But they're gone—or Ma's dead." He pointed to the low gate across the front door. "If Ma was anywheres about, that gate'd be shut an' hooked. That's one thing she always done—seen that gate was shut." His eyes were warm. "Ever since the pig got in over to Jacobs' an' et the baby. Milly Jacobs was jus' out in the barn. She come in while the pig was still eatin' it. Well, Milly Jacobs was in a family way, an' she went ravin'. Never did get over it. Touched ever since. But Ma took a lesson from it. She never lef' that pig gate open 'less she was in the house herself. Never did forget. No—they're gone—or dead." He climbed to the split porch and looked into the kitchen. The windows were broken out, and throwing rocks lay on the floor, and the floor and walls sagged steeply away from the door, and the sifted dust was on the boards. Joad pointed to the broken glass and the rocks. "Kids," he said. "They'll go twenty miles to bust a window. I done it myself. They know when a house is empty, they know. That's the fust thing kids do when folks move out." The kitchen was empty of furniture, stove gone and the round stovepipe hole in the wall showing light. On the sink shelf lay an old beer opener and a broken fork with its wooden handle gone. Joad slipped cautiously into the room, and the floor groaned under his weight. An old copy of the Philadelphia *Ledger* was on the floor against the wall, its pages yellow and curling. Joad looked into the bedroom—no bed, no chairs, nothing. On the wall a picture of an Indian girl in color, labeled Red Wing. A bed slat leaning against the wall, and in one corner a woman's high button shoe, curled up at the toe and broken over the instep. Joad picked it up and looked at it. "I remember this," he said. "This was Ma's. It's all wore out now. Ma liked them shoes. Had 'em for years. No, they've went—an' took ever'thing."

The sun had lowered until it came through the angled end windows now, and it flashed on the edges of the broken glass. Joad turned at last and went out and crossed the porch. He sat down on the edge of it and rested his bare feet on the twelve-by-twelve step. The evening light was on the fields, and the cotton plants threw long shadows on the ground, and the molting willow tree threw a long shadow.

Casy sat down beside Joad. "They never wrote you nothin'?" he asked.

"No. Like I said, they wasn't people to write. Pa could write, but he wouldn'. Didn't like to. It give him the shivers to write. He could work out a catalogue order as good as the nex' fella, but he wouldn' write no letters just for ducks." They sat side by side, staring off into the distance. Joad laid his rolled coat on the porch beside him. His independent hands rolled a cigarette, smoothed it and lighted it, and he inhaled deeply and blew the smoke out through his nose. "Somepin's wrong," he said. "I can't put my finger on her. I got an itch that somepin's wronger'n hell. Just this house pushed aroun' an' my folks gone."

Casy said, "Right over there the ditch was, where I done the baptizin'. You wasn't mean, but you was tough. Hung onto that little girl's pigtail like a bulldog. We baptize' you both in the name of the Holy Ghos', and still you hung on. Ol' Tom says, 'Hol' 'im under water.' So I shove your head down till you start to bubblin' before you'd let go a that pigtail. You wasn't mean, but you was tough. Sometimes a tough kid grows up with a big jolt of the sperit in him.''

A lean gray cat came sneaking out of the barn and crept through the cotton plants to the end of the porch. It leaped silently up to the porch and crept low-belly toward the men. It came to a place between and behind the two, and then it sat down, and its tail stretched out straight and flat to the floor, and the last inch of it flicked. The cat sat and looked off into the distance where the men were looking.

Joad glanced around at it. "By God! Look who's here. Somebody stayed." He put out his hand, but the cat leaped away out of reach and sat down and licked the pads of its lifted paw. Joad looked at it, and his face was puzzled. "I know what's the matter," he cried. "That cat jus' made me figger what's wrong."

"Seems to me there's lots wrong," said Casy.

"No, it's more'n jus' this place. Whyn't that cat jus' move in with some neighbors—with the Rances. How come nobody ripped some lumber off this house? Ain't been nobody here for three-four months, an' nobody's stole no lumber. Nice planks on the barn shed, plenty good planks on the house, winda frames—an' nobody's took 'em. That ain't right. That's what was botherin' me, an' I couldn't catch hold of her."

"Well, what's that figger out for you?" Casy reached down and slipped off his sneakers and wriggled his long toes on the step.

"I don' know. Seems like maybe there ain't any neighbors. If there was, would all them nice planks be here? Why, Jesus Christ! Albert Rance took his family, kids an' dogs an' all, into Oklahoma City one Christmus. They was gonna visit with Albert's cousin. Well, folks aroun' here thought Albert moved away without sayin' nothin'—figgered maybe he got debts or some woman's squarin' off at him. When Albert come back a week later there wasn't a thing lef' in his house—stove was gone, beds was gone, winda frames was gone, an' eight feet of plankin' was gone off the south side of the house so you could look right through her. He come drivin' home just as Muley Graves was goin' away with three doors an' the well pump. Took Albert two weeks drivin' aroun' the neighbors' 'fore he got his stuff back."

Casy scratched his toes luxuriously. "Didn't nobody give him an argument? All of 'em jus' give the stuff up?"

"Sure. They wasn't stealin' it. They thought he lef' it, an' they jus' took it. He got all of it back—all but a sofa pilla, velvet with a pitcher of an Injun on it. Albert claimed Grampa got it. Claimed Grampa got Injun blood, that's why he wants that pitcher. Well, Grampa did get her, but he didn't give a damn about the pitcher on it. He jus' liked her. Used to pack her aroun' an' he'd put her wherever he was gonna sit. He never would give her back to Albert. Says, 'If Albert wants this pilla so bad, let him come an' get her. But he better come shootin', 'cause I'll blow his goddamn stinkin' head off if he comes messin' aroun' my pilla.' So finally Albert give up an' made Grampa a present of that pilla. It give Grampa idears, though. He took to savin' chicken feathers. Says he's gonna have a whole damn bed of feathers. But he never got no feather bed. One time Pa got mad at a skunk under the house. Pa slapped that skunk with a two-by-four, and Ma burned all Grampa's feathers so we could live in the house." He laughed. "Grampa's a tough ol' bastard. Jus' set on that Injun pilla an' says, 'Let Albert come an' get her. Why,' he says, 'I'll take that squirt and wring 'im out like a pair of drawers.'"

The cat crept close between the men again, and its tail lay flat and its whiskers jerked now and then. The sun dropped low toward the horizon and the dusty air was red and golden. The cat reached out a gray questioning paw and touched Joad's coat. He looked around. "Hell, I forgot the turtle. I ain't gonna pack it all over hell." He unwrapped the land turtle and pushed it under the house. But in a moment it was out, headed southwest as it had been from the first. The cat leaped at it and struck at its straining head and slashed at its moving feet. The old, hard, humorous head was pulled in, and the thick tail slapped in under the shell, and when the cat grew tired of waiting for it and walked off, the turtle headed on southwest again.

Young Tom Joad and the preacher watched the turtle go— waving its legs and boosting its heavy, high-domed shell along toward the southwest. The cat crept along behind for a while, but in a dozen yards it arched its back to a strong taut bow and yawned, and came stealthily back toward the seated men.

"Where the hell you s'pose he's goin'?" said Joad. "I seen turtles all my life. They're always goin' someplace. They always seem to want to get there." The gray cat seated itself between and behind them again. It blinked slowly. The skin over its shoulders jerked forward under a flea, and then slipped slowly back. The cat lifted a paw and inspected it, flicked its claws out and in again experimentally, and licked its pads with a shell-pink tongue. The red sun touched the horizon and spread out like a jellyfish, and the sky above it seemed much brighter and more alive than it had been. Joad unrolled his new yellow shoes from his coat, and he brushed his dusty feet with his hand before he slipped them on.

The preacher, staring off across the fields, said, "Somebody's comin'. Look! Down there, right through the cotton."

Joad looked where Casy's finger pointed. "Comin' afoot," he said. "Can't see 'im for the dust he raises. Who the hell's comin' here?" They watched the figure approaching in the evening light, and the dust it raised was reddened by the setting sun. "Man," said Joad. The man drew closer, and as he walked past the barn, Joad said, "Why, I know him. You know him—that's Muley Graves." And he called, "Hey, Muley! How ya?"

The approaching man stopped, startled by the call, and then he came on quickly. He was a lean man, rather short. His movements were jerky and quick. He carried a gunny sack in his hand. His blue jeans were pale at knee and seat, and he wore an old black suit coat, stained and spotted, the sleeves torn loose from the shoulders in back, and ragged holes worn through at the elbows. His black hat was as stained as his coat, and the band, torn half free, flopped up and down as he walked. Muley's face was smooth and unwrinkled, but it wore the truculent look of a bad child, the mouth held tight and small, the little eyes half scowling, half petulant.

"You remember Muley," Joad said softly to the preacher.

"Who's that?" the advancing man called. Joad did not answer. Muley came close, very close, before he made out the faces. "Well, I'll be damned," he said. "It's Tommy Joad. When'd you get out, Tommy?" He dropped his sack to the ground.

"Two days ago," said Joad. "Took a little time to hitchhike home. An' look here what I find. Where's my folks, Muley? What's the house all smashed up for, an' cotton planted in the dooryard?"

"By God, it's lucky I come by!" said Muley. " 'Cause ol' Tom worried himself. When they was fixin' to move I was settin' in the kitchen there. I jus' tol' Tom I wan't gonna move, by God. I tol' him that, an' Tom says, 'I'm worryin' myself about Tommy. S'pose he comes home an' they ain't nobody here. What'll he think?' I says, 'Whyn't you write down a letter?' An' Tom says, 'Maybe I will. I'll think about her. But if I don't, you keep your eye out for Tommy if you're still aroun'.' 'I'll be aroun',' I says. 'I'll be aroun' till hell freezes over. There ain't nobody can run a guy name of Graves outa this country.' An' they ain't done it, neither."

Joad said impatiently, "Where's my folks? Tell about you standin' up to 'em later, but where's my folks?"

"Well, they was gonna stick her out when the bank come to tractorin' off the place. Your grampa stood out here with a rifle, an' he blowed the headlights off that cat', but she come on just the same. Your grampa didn't wanta kill the guy drivin' that cat', an' that was Willy Feeley, an' Willy knowed it, so he jus' come on, an' bumped the hell outa the house. Ol' Tom jas' stood there a-cussin', but it didn't do him no good. When he sees that cat' come a-bustin' through the house, an' give her a shake like a dog shakes a rat—well, it took somepin outa Tom. Kinda got into 'im. He ain't been the same ever since."

"Where is my folks?" Joad spoke angrily.

"What I'm tellin' you. Took three trips with your Uncle John's wagon. Took the stove an' the pump an' the beds. You should a seen them beds go out with all them kids an' your granma an' grampa settin' up against the headboard, an' your brother Noah settin' there smokin' a cigareet, an' spittin' la-de-da over the side of the wagon." Joad opened his mouth to speak. "They're all at your Uncle John's," Muley said quickly.

"Oh! All at John's. Well, what they doin' there? Now stick to her for a second, Muley. Jus' stick to her. In jus' a minute you can go on your own way. What they doin' there?"

"Well, they been choppin' cotton, all of 'em, even the kids an' your grampa. Gettin' money together so they can shove on west. Gonna buy a car and shove on west where it's easy livin'. There ain't nothin' here. Fifty cents a clean acre for choppin' cotton, an' folks beggin' for the chance to chop."

"An' they ain't gone yet?"

"No," said Muley. "Not that I know. Las' I heard was four days ago when I seen your brother Noah out shootin' jack-rabbits, an' he says they're aimin' to go in about two weeks. John got his notice he got to get off. You jus' go on about eight miles to John's place. You'll find your folks piled in John's house like gophers in a winter burrow."

"O.K." said Joad. "Now you can ride on your own way. You ain't changed a bit, Muley. If you want to tell about somepin off northwest, you point your nose straight south-east."

Muley said truculently, "You ain't changed neither. You was a smart-aleck kid, an' you're still a smart aleck. You ain't tellin' me how to skin my life, by any chancet?"

Joad grinned. "No, I ain't. If you wanta drive your head into a pile a broken glass, there ain't nobody can tell you different. You know this here preacher, don't you, Muley? Rev. Casy."

"Why, sure, sure. Didn't look over. Remember him well." Casy stood up and the two shook hands. "Glad to see you again," said Muley. "You ain't been aroun' for a hell of a long time."

"I been off a-askin' questions," said Casy. "What happened here? Why they kickin' folks off the lan'?"

Muley's mouth snapped shut so tightly that a little parrot's beak in the middle of his upper lip stuck down over his under lip. He scowled. "Them sons-a-bitches," he said. "Them dirty sons-a-bitches. I tell ya, men, I'm stayin'. They ain't gettin' rid a me. If they throw me off, I'll come back, an' if they figger I'll be quiet underground, why, I'll take a couple-three of the sons-a-bitches along for company." He patted a heavy weight in his side coat pocket. "I ain't a-goin'. My pa come here fifty years ago. An' I ain't a-goin'."

Joad said, "What's the idear of kickin' the folks off?"

"Oh! They talked pretty about it. You know what kinda years we been havin'. Dust comin' up an' spoilin' ever'thing so a man didn't get enough crop to plug up an ant's ass. An' ever'body got bills at the grocery. You know how it is. Well, the folks that owns the lan' says, 'We can't afford to keep no tenants.' An' they says, 'The share a tenant gets is jus' the margin a profit we can't afford to lose.' An' they says, 'If we put all our lan' in one piece we can jus' hardly make her pay.' So they tractored all the tenants off a the lan'. All 'cept me, an' by God I ain't goin'. Tommy, you know me. You knowed me all your life."

"Damn right," said Joad, "all my life."

"Well, you know I ain't a fool. I know this land ain't much good. Never was much good 'cept for grazin'. Never should a broke her up. An' now she's cottoned damn near to death. If on'y they didn' tell me I got to get off, why, I'd prob'y be in California right now a-eatin' grapes an' a-pickin' an orange when I wanted. But them sons-a-bitches says I got to get off—an', Jesus Christ, a man can't, when he's tol' to!"

"Sure," said Joad. "I wonder Pa went so easy. I wonder Grampa didn' kill nobody. Nobody never tol' Grampa where to put his feet. An' Ma ain't nobody you can push aroun', neither. I seen her beat the hell out of a tin peddler with a live chicken one time 'cause he give her a argument. She had the chicken in one han', an' the ax in the other, about to cut its head off. She aimed to go for that peddler with the ax, but she forgot which han' was which, an' she takes after him with the chicken. Couldn' even eat that chicken when she got done. They wasn't nothing but a pair a legs in her han'. Grampa throwed his hip outa joint laughin'. How'd my folks go so easy?"

"Well, the guy that come aroun' talked nice as pie. 'You got to get off. It ain't my fault.' 'Well,' I says, 'whose fault is it? I'll go an' I'll nut the fella.' 'It's the Shawnee Lan' an' Cattle Company. I jus' got orders.' 'Who's the Shawnee Lan' an' Cattle Company?' 'It ain't nobody. It's a company.' Got a fella crazy. There wasn't nobody you could lay for. Lot a the folks jus' got tired out lookin' for somepin to be mad at—but not me. I'm mad at all of it. I'm stayin'."

A large red drop of sun lingered on the horizon and then dripped over and was gone, and the sky was brilliant over the spot where it had gone, and a torn cloud, like a bloody rag, hung over the spot of its going. And dusk crept over the sky from the eastern horizon, and darkness crept over the land from the east. The evening star flashed and glittered in the dusk. The gray cat sneaked away toward the open barn shed and passed inside like a shadow.

Joad said, "Well, we ain't gonna walk no eight miles to Uncle John's place tonight. My dogs is burned up. How's it if we go to your place, Muley? That's on'y about a mile."

"Won't do no good." Muley seemed embarrassed. "My wife an' the kids an' her brother all took an' went to California. They wasn't nothin' to eat. They wasn't as mad as me, so they went. Bought an ol' Chevy an' took what they could. Fella came a-passin' out han'bills say good wages in California. So they went. They wasn't nothin' to eat here."

The preacher stirred nervously. "You should of went too. You shouldn't of broke up the fambly."

"I couldn'," said Muley Graves. "Somepin jus' wouldn' let me."

"Well, by God, I'm hungry," said Joad. "Four solemn years I been eatin' right on the minute. My guts is yellin' bloody murder. What you gonna eat, Muley? How you been gettin' your dinner?"

Muley said ashamedly, "For a while I et frogs an' squirrels an' prairie dogs sometimes. Had to do it. But now I got some wire nooses on the tracks in the dry stream brush. Get rabbits, an' sometimes a prairie chicken. Skunks get caught, an' coons, too." He reached down, picked up his sack, and emptied it on the porch. Two cottontails and a jackrabbit fell out and rolled over limply, soft and furry.

"God Awmighty," said Joad, "it's more'n four years sence I've et fresh-killed meat."

Casy picked up one of the cottontails and held it in his hand. "You sharin' with us, Muley Graves?" he asked.

Muley fidgeted in embarrassment. "I ain't got no choice in the matter." He stopped on the ungracious sound of his own words. "That ain't like I mean it. That ain't. I mean"—he stumbled—"what I mean, if a fella's got somepin to eat an' another fella's hungry—why, the first fella ain't got no choice. I mean, s'pose I pick up my rabbits an' go off somewheres an' eat 'em. See?"

"I see," said Casy. "I can see that. Muley sees somepin

there, Tom. Muley's got a-holt of somepin, an' it's too big for him, an' it's too big for me."

Young Tom rubbed his hands together. "Who got a knife? Le's get at these here miserable rodents. Le's get at 'em."

Muley reached in his pants pocket and produced a large horn-handled pocket knife. Tom Joad took it from him, opened a blade, and smelled it. He drove the blade again and again into the ground and smelled it again, wiped it on his trouser leg, and felt the edge with his thumb.

Muley took a quart bottle of water out of his hip pocket and set it on the porch. "Go easy on that there water," he said. "That's all there is. This here well's filled in."

Tom took up a rabbit in his hand. "One of you go get some bale wire outa the barn. We'll make a fire with some a this broken plank from the house." He looked at the dead rabbit. "There ain't nothin' so easy to get ready as a rabbit," he said. He lifted the skin of the back, slit it, put his fingers in the hole, and tore the skin off. It slipped off like a stocking, slipped off the body to the neck, and off the legs to the paws. Joad picked up the knife again and cut off head and feet. He laid the skin down, slit the rabbit along the ribs, shook out the intestines onto the skin, and then threw the mess off into the cotton field. And the clean-muscled little body was ready. Joad cut off the legs and cut the meaty back into two pieces. He was picking up the second rabbit when Casy came back with a snarl of bale wire in his hand. "Now build up a fire and put some stakes up," said Joad. "Jesus Christ, I'm hungry for these here creatures!" He cleaned and cut up the rest of the rabbits and strung them on the wire. Muley and Casy tore splintered boards from the wrecked house-corner and started a fire, and they drove a stake into the ground on each side to hold the wire.

Muley came back to Joad. "Look out for boils on that jackrabbit," he said. "I don't like to eat no jackrabbit with boils." He took a little cloth bag from his pocket and put it on the porch.

Joad said, "The jack was clean as a whistle—Jesus God, you got salt too? By any chance you got some plates an' a tent in your pocket?" He poured salt in his hand and sprinkled it over the pieces of rabbit strung on the wire.

The fire leaped and threw shadows on the house, and the dry wood crackled and snapped. The sky was almost dark now and the stars were out sharply. The gray cat came out of the barn shed and trotted miaowing toward the fire, but, nearly there, it turned and went directly to one of the little piles of rabbit entrails on the ground. It chewed and swallowed, and the entrails hung from its mouth.

Casy sat on the ground beside the fire, feeding it broken pieces of board, pushing the long boards in as the flame ate off their ends. The evening bats flashed into the firelight and out again. The cat crouched back and licked its lips and washed its face and whiskers.

Joad held up his rabbit-laden wire between his two hands and walked to the fire. "Here, take one end, Muley. Wrap your end around that stake. That's good, now! Let's tighten her up. We ought to wait till the fire's burned down, but I can't wait." He made the wire taut, then found a stick and slipped the pieces of meat along the wire until they were over the fire. And the flames licked up around the meat and hardened and glazed the surfaces. Joad sat down by the fire, but with his stick he moved and turned the rabbit so that it would not become sealed to the wire. "This here is a party," he said. "Yes, sir, this sure as hell is a party. Salt, Muley's got, an' water an' rabbits. I wish he got a pot of hominy in his pocket. That's all I wish."

Muley said over the fire, "You fellas'd think I'm touched, the way I live."

"Touched, nothin'," said Joad. "If you're touched, I wisht ever'body was touched."

Muley continued, "Well, sir, it's a funny thing. Somepin went an' happened to me when they tol' me I had to get off the place. Fust I was gonna go in an' kill a whole flock a people. Then all my folks all went away out west. An' I got wanderin' aroun'. Jus' walkin' aroun'. Never went far. Slep' wherever I was. I was gonna sleep here tonight. That's why I come. I'd tell myself, 'I'm lookin' after things so when all the folks come back it'll be all right.' But I knowed that wan't true. There ain't nothin' to look after. The folks ain't never comin' back. I'm jus' wanderin' aroun' like a damn ol' graveyard ghos'."

"Fella gets use' to a place, it's hard to go," said Casy. "Fella gets use' to a way a thinkin', it's hard to leave. I ain't a preacher no more, but all the time I find I'm prayin', not even thinkin' what I'm doin'."

Joad turned the pieces of meat over on the wire. The juice was dripping now, and every drop, as it fell in the fire, shot up a spurt of flame. The smooth surface of the meat was crinkling up and turning a faint brown. "Smell her," said Joad. "Jesus, look down an' jus' smell her!"

Muley went on, "Like a damn ol' graveyard ghos'. I been goin' aroun' the places where stuff happened. Like there's a place over by our forty; in a gully they's a bush. Fust time I ever laid with a girl was there. Me fourteen an' stampin' an' jerkin' an' snortin' like a buck deer, randy as a billy goat. So I went there an' I laid down on the groun', an' I seen it all happen again. An' there's the place down by the barn where Pa got gored to death by a bull. An' his blood is right in that groun', right now. Mus' be. Nobody never washed it out. An' I put my han' on that groun' where my own pa's blood is part of it." He paused uneasily. "You fellas think I'm touched?"

Joad turned the meat, and his eyes were inward. Casy, feet drawn up, stared into the fire. Fifteen feet back from the men the fed cat was sitting, the long gray tail wrapped neatly around the front feet. A big owl shrieked as it went overhead, and the firelight showed its white underside and the spread of its wings.

"No," said Casy. "You ain't touched. You're lonely—but you ain't touched."

Muley's tight little face was rigid. "I put my han' right on the groun' where that blood is still. An' I seen my pa with a hole through his ches', an' I felt him shiver up against me like he done, an' I seen him kind of settle back an' reach with his han's an' his feet. An' I seen his eyes all milky with hurt, an' then he was still an' his eyes so clear—lookin' up. An' me a little kid settin' there, not cryin' nor nothin,' jus' settin' there." He shook his head sharply. Joad turned the meat over and over. "An' I went in the room where Joe was born. Bed wasn't there, but it was the room. An' all them things is true, an' they're right in the place they happened. Joe come to life right there. He give a big ol' gasp an' then he let out a squawk you could hear a mile, an' his granma standin' there says, 'That's a daisy, that's a daisy,' over an' over. An' her so proud she bust three cups that night."

Joad cleared his throat. "Think we better eat her now."

"Let her get good an' done, good an' brown, awmost black," said Muley irritably. "I wanta talk. I ain't talked to nobody. If I'm touched, I'm touched, an' that's the end of it. Like a ol' graveyard ghos' goin' to neighbors' houses in the night. Peters', Jacobs', Rance's, Joad's; an' the houses all dark, standin' like miser'ble ratty boxes, but they was good parties an' dancin'. An' there was meetin's and shoutin' glory. They was weddin's, all in them houses. An' then I'd want to go in town an' kill folks. 'Cause what'd they take when they tractored the folks off the lan'? What'd they get so their 'margin a profit' was safe? They got Pa dyin' on the groun', an' Joe yellin' his first breath, an' me jerkin' like a billy goat under a bush in the night. What'd they get? God knows the lan' ain't no good. Nobody been able to make a crop for years. But them sons-a-bitches at their desks, they jus' chopped folks in two for their margin a profit. They jus' cut 'em in two. Place where folks live is them folks. They ain't whole, out lonely on the road in a piled-up car. They ain't alive no more. Them sons-a-bitches killed 'em." And he was silent, his thin lips still moving, his chest still panting. He sat and looked down at his hands in the firelight. "I—I ain't talked to nobody for a long time," he apologized softly. "I been sneakin' aroun' like a ol' graveyard ghos'."

Casy pushed the long boards into the fire and the flames licked up around them and leaped up toward the meat again. The house cracked loudly as the cooler night air contracted the wood. Casy said quietly, "I gotta see them folks that's gone out on the road. I got a feelin' I got to see them. They gonna need help no preacher can give 'em. Hope of heaven when their lives ain't lived? Holy Sperit when their own sperit is downcast an' sad? They gonna need help. They got to live before they can afford to die."

Joad cried nervously, "Jesus Christ, le's eat this meat 'fore it's smaller'n a cooked mouse! Look at her. Smell her." He leaped to his feet and slid the pieces of meat along the wire until they were clear of the fire. He took Muley's knife from his pocket and sawed through a piece of meat until it was free of the wire. "Here's for the preacher," he said.

"I tol' you I ain't no preacher."

"Well, here's for the man, then." He cut off another piece. "Here, Muley, if you ain't too goddamn upset to eat. This here's jackrabbit. Tougher'n a bull-bitch." He sat back and clamped his long teeth on the meat and tore out a great bite and chewed it. "Jesus Christ! Hear her crunch!" And he tore out another bite ravenously.

Muley still sat regarding his meat. "Maybe I oughtn' to a-talked like that," he said. "Fella should maybe keep stuff like that in his head."

Casy looked over, his mouth full of rabbit. He chewed, and his muscled throat convulsed in swallowing. "Yes, you should talk," he said. "Sometimes a sad man can talk the sadness right out through his mouth. Sometimes a killin' man can talk the murder right out of his mouth an' not do no murder. You done right. Don't you kill nobody if you can help it." And he bit out another hunk of rabbit. Joad tossed the bones in the fire and jumped up and cut more off the wire. Muley was eating slowly now, and his nervous little eyes went from one to the other of his companions. Joad ate scowling like an animal, and a ring of grease formed around his mouth.

For a long time Muley looked at him, almost timidly. He put down the hand that held the meat. "Tommy," he said.

Joad looked up and did not stop gnawing the meat. "Yeah?" he said, around a mouthful.

"Tommy, you ain't mad with me talkin' about killin' people? You ain't huffy, Tom?"

"No," said Tom. "I ain't huffy. It's jus' somepin that happened."

"Ever'body knowed it wasn't no fault of yours," said Muley. "Ol' man Turnbull said he was gonna get you when ya come out. Says nobody can kill one a his boys. All the folks hereabouts talked him outa it, though."

"We was drunk," Joad said softly. "Drunk at a dance. I don' know how she started. An' then I felt that knife go in me, an' that sobered me up. Fust thing I see is Herb comin' for me again with his knife. They was this here shovel leanin' against the schoolhouse, so I grabbed it an' smacked 'im over the head. I never had nothing against Herb. He was a nice fella. Come a-bullin' after my sister Rosasharn when he was a little fella. No, I liked Herb.''

"Well, ever'body tol' his pa that, an' finally cooled 'im down. Somebody says they's Hatfield blood on his mother's side in ol' Turnbull, an' he's got to live up to it. I don't know about that. Him an' his folks went on to California six months ago.''

Joad took the last of the rabbit from the wire and passed it around. He settled back and ate more slowly now, chewed evenly, and wiped the grease from his mouth with his sleeve. And his eyes, dark and half closed, brooded as he looked into the dying fire. "Ever'body's goin' west," he said. "I got me a parole to keep. Can't leave the state.''

"Parole?" Muley asked. "I heard about them. How do they work?''

"Well, I got out early, three years early. They's stuff I gotta do, or they send me back in. Got to report ever' so often.''

"How they treat ya there in McAlester? My woman's cousin was in McAlester an' they give him hell.''

"It ain't so bad," said Joad. "Like ever'place else. They give ya hell if ya raise hell. You get along O.K. les' some guard gets it in for ya. Then you catch plenty hell. I got along O.K. Minded my own business, like any guy would. I learned to write nice as hell. Birds an' stuff like that, too; not just word writin'. My ol' man'll be sore when he sees me whip out a bird in one stroke. Pa's gonna be mad when he sees me do that. He don't like no fancy stuff like that. He don't even like word writin'. Kinda scares 'im, I guess. Ever' time Pa seen writin', somebody took somepin away from 'im.''

"They didn' give you no beatin's or nothin' like that?''

"No, I jus' tended my own affairs. 'Course you get god-damn good an' sick a-doin' the same thing day after day for four years. If you done somepin you was ashamed of, you might think about that. But, hell, if I seen Herb Turnbull comin' for me with a knife right now, I'd squash him down with a shovel again.''

"Anybody would," said Muley. The preacher stared into the fire, and his high forehead was white in the settling dark.

The flash of little flames picked out the cords of his neck. His hands, clasped about his knees, were busy pulling knuckles.

Joad threw the last bones into the fire and licked his fingers and then wiped them on his pants. He stood up and brought the bottle of water from the porch, took a sparing drink, and passed the bottle before he sat down again. He went on, "The thing that give me the mos' trouble was, it didn' make no sense. You don't look for no sense when lightnin' kills a cow, or it comes up a flood. That's jus' the way things is. But when a bunch of men take an' lock you up four years, it ought to have some meaning. Men is supposed to think things out. Here they put me in, an' keep me an' feed me four years. That ought to either make me so I won't do her again or else punish me so I'll be afraid to do her again"—he paused— "but if Herb or anybody else come for me, I'd do her again. Do her before I could figure her out. Specially if I was drunk. That sort of senselessness kind a worries a man."

Muley observed, "Judge says he give you a light sentence 'cause it wasn't all your fault."

Joad said, "They's a guy in McAlester—lifer. He studies all the time. He's sec'etary of the warden—writes the warden's letters an' stuff like that. Well, he's one hell of a bright guy an' reads law an' all stuff like that. Well, I talked to him one time about her, 'cause he reads so much stuff. An' he says it don't do no good to read books. Says he's read ever'thing about prisons now, an' in the old times; an' he says she makes less sense to him now than she did before he starts readin'. He says it's a thing that started way to hell an' gone back, an' nobody seems to be able to stop her, an' nobody got sense enough to change her. He says for God's sake don't read about her because he says for one thing you'll jus' get messed up worse, an' for another you won't have no respect for the guys that work the gover'ments."

"I ain't got a hell of a lot of respec' for 'em now," said Muley. "On'y kind a gover'ment we got that leans on us fellas is the 'safe margin a profit.' There's one thing that got me stumped, an' that's Willy Feeley—drivin' that cat', an' gonna be a straw boss on lan' his own folks used to farm. That worries me. I can see how a fella might come from some other place an' not know no better, but Willy belongs. Worried me so I went up to 'im and ast 'im. Right off he got mad. 'I got two little kids,' he says. 'I got a wife an' my wife's mother. Them people got to eat.' Gets madder'n hell. 'Fust an' on'y thing I got to think about is my own folks,' he says. 'What happens to other folks is their look-out,' he says. Seems like he's 'shamed, so he gets mad."

Jim Casy had been staring at the dying fire, and his eyes had grown wider and his neck muscles stood higher. Suddenly he cried, "I got her! If ever a man got a dose of the sperit, I got her! Got her all of a flash!" He jumped to his feet and paced back and forth, his head swinging. "Had a tent one time. Drawed as much as five hundred people ever' night. That's before either you fellas seen me." He stopped and faced them. "Ever notice I never took no collections when I was preachin' out here to folks—in barns an' in the open?"

"By God, you never," said Muley. "People around here got so use' to not givin' you money they got to bein' a little mad when some other preacher come along an' passed the hat. Yes, sir!"

"I took somepin to eat," said Casy. "I took a pair a pants when mine was wore out, an' a ol' pair a shoes when I was walkin' through to the groun', but it wasn't like when I had the tent. Some days there I'd take in ten or twenty dollars. Wasn't happy that-a-way, so I give her up, an' for a time I was happy. I think I got her now. I don' know if I can say her. I guess I won't try to say her—but maybe there's a place for a preacher. Maybe I can preach again. Folks out lonely on the road, folks with no lan', no home to go to. They got to have some kind of home. Maybe—" He stood over the fire. The hundred muscles of his neck stood out in high relief, and the firelight went deep into his eyes and ignited red embers. He stood and looked at the fire, his face tense as though he were listening, and the hands that had been active to pick, to handle, to throw ideas, grew quiet, and in a moment crept into his pockets. The bats flittered in and out of the dull firelight, and the soft watery burble of a night hawk came from across the fields.

Tom reached quietly into his pocket and brought out his tobacco, and he rolled a cigarette slowly and looked over it at the coals while he worked. He ignored the whole speech of the preacher, as though it were some private thing that should not be inspected. He said, "Night after night in my bunk I figgered how she'd be when I come home again. I figgered maybe Grampa or Granma'd be dead, an' maybe there'd be some new kids. Maybe Pa'd not be so tough. Maybe Ma'd set back a little an' let Rosasharn do the work. I knowed it wouldn't be the same as it was. Well, we'll sleep here I guess, an' come daylight we'll get on to Uncle John's. Leastwise I will. You think you're comin' along, Casy?"

The preacher still stood looking into the coals. He said slowly, "Yeah, I'm goin' with you. An' when your folks start out on the road I'm goin' with them. An' where folks are on the road, I'm gonna be with them."

"You'd be welcome," said Joad. "Ma always favored you. Said you was a preacher to trust. Rosasharn wasn't growed up then." He turned his head. "Muley, you gonna walk on over with us?" Muley was looking toward the road over which they had come. "Think you'll come along, Muley?" Joad repeated.

"Huh? No. I don't go no place, an' I don't leave no place. See that glow over there, jerkin' up an' down? That's prob'ly the super'ntendent of this stretch a cotton. Somebody maybe seen our fire."

Tom looked. The glow of light was nearing over the hill. "We ain't doin' no harm," he said. "We'll jus' set here. We ain't doin' nothin'."

Muley cackled. "Yeah! We're doin' somepin just' bein' here. We're trespassin'. We can't stay. They been tryin' to catch me for two months. Now you look. If that's a car comin' we go out in the cotton an' lay down. Don't have to go far. Then by God let 'em try to fin' us! Have to look up an' down ever' row. Jus' keep your head down."

Joad demanded, "What's come over you, Muley? You wasn't never no run-an'-hide fella. You was mean."

Muley watched the approaching lights. "Yeah!" he said. "I was mean like a wolf. Now I'm mean like a weasel. When you're huntin' somepin you're a hunter, an' you're strong. Can't nobody beat a hunter. But when you get hunted— that's different. Somepin happens to you. You ain't strong; maybe you're fierce, but you ain't strong. I been hunted now

for a long time. I ain't a hunter no more. I'd maybe shoot a
fella in the dark, but I don't maul nobody with a fence stake
no more. It don't do no good to fool you or me. That's how
it is."

"Well, you go out an' hide," said Joad. "Leave me an' Casy
tell these bastards a few things." The beam of light was closer
now, and it bounced into the sky and then disappeared, and
then bounced up again. All three men watched.

Muley said, "There's one more thing about bein' hunted.
You get to thinkin' about all the dangerous things. If you're
huntin' you don't think about 'em, an' you ain't scared. Like
you says to me, if you get in any trouble they'll sen' you back
to McAlester to finish your time."

"That's right," said Joad. "That's what they tol' me, but
settin' here restin' or sleepin' on the groun'—that ain't gettin'
in no trouble. That ain't doin' nothin' wrong. That ain't like
gettin' drunk or raisin' hell."

Muley laughed. "You'll see. You jus' set here, an' the car'll
come. Maybe it's Willy Feeley, an' Willy's a deputy sheriff
now. 'What you doin' trespassin' here?' Willy says. Well, you
always did know Willy was full a shit, so you says, 'What's it
to you?' Willy gets mad an' says, 'You get off or I'll take you
in.' An' you ain't gonna let no Feeley push you aroun' 'cause
he's mad an' scared. He's made a bluff an' he got to go on
with it, an' here's you gettin' tough an' you got to go
through—oh, hell, it's a lot easier to lay out in the cotton an'
let 'em look. It's more fun, too, 'cause they're mad an' can't
do nothin', an' you're out there a-laughin' at 'em. But you
jus' talk to Willy or any boss, an' you slug hell out of 'em an'
they'll take you in an' run you back to McAlester for three
years."

"You're talkin' sense," said Joad. "Ever' word you say is
sense. But, Jesus, I hate to get pushed around! I lots rather
take a sock at Willy."

"He got a gun," said Muley. "He'll use it 'cause he's a
deputy. Then he either got to kill you or you got to get his
gun away an' kill him. Come on, Tommy. You can easy tell
yourself you're foolin' them lyin' out like that. An' it all just
amounts to what you tell yourself." The strong lights angled
up into the sky now, and the even drone of a motor could be

heard. "Come on, Tommy. Don't have to go far, jus' fourteen-fifteen rows over, an' we can watch what they do."

Tom got to his feet. "By God, you're right!" he said. "I ain't got a thing in the worl' to win, no matter how it comes out."

"Come on, then, over this way." Muley moved around the house and out into the cotton field about fifty yards. "This is good," he said. "Now lay down. You on'y got to pull your head down if they start the spotlight goin'. It's kinda fun." The three men stretched out at full length and propped themselves on their elbows. Muley sprang up and ran toward the house, and in a few moments he came back and threw a bundle of coats and shoes down. "They'd of taken 'em along just to get even," he said. The lights topped the rise and bore down on the house.

Joad asked, "Won't they come out here with flashlights an' look aroun' for us? I wisht I had a stick."

Muley giggled. "No, they won't. I tol' you I'm mean like a weasel. Willy done that one night an' I clipped 'im from behint with a fence stake. Knocked him colder'n a wedge. He tol' later how five guys come at him."

The car drew up to the house and a spotlight snapped on. "Duck," said Muley. The bar of cold white light swung over their heads and crisscrossed the field. The hiding men could not see any movement, but they heard a car door slam and they heard voices. "Scairt to get in the light," Muley whispered. "Once-twice I've took a shot at the headlights. That keeps Willy careful. He got somebody with 'im tonight." They heard footsteps on wood, and then from inside the house they saw the glow of a flashlight. "Shall I shoot through the house?" Muley whispered. "They couldn't see where it come from. Give 'em somepin to think about."

"Sure, go ahead," said Joad.

"Don't do it," Casy whispered. "It won't do no good. Jus' a waste. We got to get thinkin' about doin' stuff that means somepin."

A scratching sound came from near the house. "Puttin' out the fire," Muley whispered. "Kickin' dust over it." The car doors slammed, the headlights swung around and faced the road again. "Now duck!" said Muley. They dropped their heads and the spotlight swept over them and crossed and re-crossed the cotton field, and then the car started and slipped away and topped the rise and disappeared.

Muley sat up. "Willy always tries that las' flash. He done it so often I can time 'im. An' he still thinks it's cute."

Casy said, "Maybe they left some fellas at the house. They'd catch us when we come back."

"Maybe. You fellas wait here. I know this game." He walked quietly away, and only a slight crunching of clods could be heard from his passage. The two waiting men tried to hear him, but he had gone. In a moment he called from the house, "They didn't leave nobody. Come on back." Casy and Joad struggled up and walked back toward the black bulk of the house. Muley met them near the smoking dust pile which had been their fire. "I didn' think they'd leave no-body," he said proudly. "Me knockin' Willy over an' takin' a shot at the lights once-twice keeps 'em careful. They ain't sure who it is, an' I ain't gonna let 'em catch me. I don't sleep near no house. If you fellas wanta come along, I'll show you where to sleep, where there ain't nobody gonna stumble over ya."

"Lead off," said Joad. "We'll folla you. I never thought I'd be hidin' out on my old man's place."

Muley set off across the fields, and Joad and Casy followed him. They kicked the cotton plants as they went. "You'll be hidin' from lots of stuff," said Muley. They marched in single file across the fields. They came to a water-cut and slid easily down to the bottom of it.

"By God, I bet I know," cried Joad. "Is it a cave in the bank?"

"That's right. How'd you know?"

"I dug her," said Joad. "Me an' my brother Noah dug her. Lookin' for gold we says we was, but we was jus' diggin' caves like kids always does." The walls of the water-cut were above their heads now. "Ought to be pretty close," said Joad. "Seems to me I remember her pretty close."

Muley said, "I've covered her with bresh. Nobody couldn't find her." The bottom of the gulch leveled off, and the footing was sand.

Joad settled himself on the clean sand. "I ain't gonna sleep in no cave," he said. "I'm gonna sleep right here." He rolled his coat and put it under his head.

Muley pulled at the covering brush and crawled into his cave. "I like it in here," he called. "I feel like nobody can come at me."

Jim Casy sat down on the sand beside Joad.

"Get some sleep," said Joad. "We'll start for Uncle John's at daybreak."

"I ain't sleepin'," said Casy. "I got too much to puzzle with." He drew up his feet and clasped his legs. He threw back his head and looked at the sharp stars. Joad yawned and brought one hand back under his head. They were silent, and gradually the skittering life of the ground, of holes and burrows, of the brush, began again; the gophers moved, and the rabbits crept to green things, the mice scampered over clods, and the winged hunters moved soundlessly overhead.

Chapter Seven

IN THE TOWNS, on the edges of the towns, in fields, in vacant lots, the used-car yards, the wreckers' yards, the garages with blazoned signs—Used Cars, Good Used Cars. Cheap transportation, three trailers. '27 Ford, clean. Checked cars, guaranteed cars. Free radio. Car with 100 gallons of gas free. Come in and look. Used Cars. No overhead.

A lot and a house large enough for a desk and chair and a blue book. Sheaf of contracts, dog-eared, held with paper clips, and a neat pile of unused contracts. Pen—keep it full, keep it working. A sale's been lost 'cause a pen didn't work.

Those sons-of-bitches over there ain't buying. Every yard gets 'em. They're lookers. Spend all their time looking. Don't want to buy no cars; take up your time. Don't give a damn for your time. Over there, them two people—no, with the kids. Get 'em in a car. Start 'em at two hundred and work down. They look good for one and a quarter. Get 'em rolling. Get 'em out in a jalopy. Sock it to 'em! They took our time.

Owners with rolled-up sleeves. Salesmen, neat, deadly, small intent eyes watching for weaknesses.

Watch the woman's face. If the woman likes it we can screw the old man. Start 'em on that Cad'. Then you can work 'em down to that '26 Buick. 'F you start on the Buick, they'll go for a Ford. Roll up your sleeves an' get to work. This ain't gonna last forever. Show 'em that Nash while I get the slow leak pumped up on that '25 Dodge. I'll give you a Hymie when I'm ready.

What you want is transportation, ain't it? No baloney for you. Sure the upholstery is shot. Seat cushions ain't turning no wheels over.

Cars lined up, noses forward, rusty noses, flat tires. Parked close together.

Like to get in to see that one? Sure, no trouble. I'll pull her out of the line.

Get 'em under obligation. Make 'em take up your time. Don't let 'em forget they're takin' your time. People are nice, mostly. They hate to put you out. Make 'em put you out, an' then sock it to 'em.

Cars lined up, Model T's, high and snotty, creaking wheel, worn bands. Buicks, Nashes, De Sotos.

Yes, sir. '22 Dodge. Best goddamn car Dodge ever made. Never wear out. Low compression. High compression got lots a sap for a while, but the metal ain't made that'll hold it for long. Plymouths, Rocknes, Stars.

Jesus, where'd that Apperson come from, the Ark? And a Chalmers and a Chandler—ain't made 'em for years. We ain't sellin' cars—rolling junk. Goddamn it, I got to get jalopies. I don't want nothing for more'n twenty-five, thirty bucks. Sell 'em for fifty, seventy-five. That's a good profit. Christ, what cut do you make on a new car? Get jalopies. I can sell 'em fast as I get 'em. Nothing over two hundred fifty. Jim, corral that old bastard on the sidewalk. Don't know his ass from a hole in the ground. Try him on that Apperson. Say, where is that Apperson? Sold? If we don't get some jalopies we got nothing to sell.

Flags, red and white, white and blue—all along the curb. Used Cars. Good Used Cars.

Today's bargain—up on the platform. Never sell it. Makes folks come in, though. If we sold that bargain at that price we'd hardly make a dime. Tell 'em it's jus' sold. Take out that yard battery before you make delivery. Put in that dumb cell. Christ, what they want for six bits? Roll up your sleeves—pitch in. This ain't gonna last. If I had enough jalopies I'd retire in six months.

Listen, Jim, I heard that Chevvy's rear end. Sounds like bustin' bottles. Squirt in a couple quarts of sawdust. Put some in the gears, too. We got to move that lemon for thirty-five dollars. Bastard cheated me on that one. I offer ten an' he jerks me to fifteen, an' then the son-of-a-bitch took the tools out. God Almighty! I wisht I had five hundred jalopies. This ain't gonna last. He don't like the tires? Tell 'im they got ten thousand in 'em, knock off a buck an' a half.

Piles of rusty ruins against the fence, rows of wrecks in back, fenders, grease-black wrecks, blocks lying on the ground and a pig weed growing up through the cylinders. Brake rods, exhausts, piled like snakes. Grease, gasoline.

See if you can't find a spark plug that ain't cracked. Christ, if I had fifty trailers at under a hundred I'd clean up. What the hell is he kickin' about? We sell 'em, but we don't push 'em home for him. That's good! Don't push 'em home. Get that one in the Monthly, I bet. You don't think he's a prospect? Well, kick 'im out. We got too much to do to bother with a guy that can't make up his mind. Take the right front tire off the Graham. Turn that mended side down. The rest looks swell. Got tread an' everything.

Sure! There's fifty thousan' in that ol' heap yet. Keep plenty oil in. So long. Good luck.

Lookin' for a car? What did you have in mind? See anything attracts you? I'm dry. How about a little snort a good stuff? Come on, while your wife's lookin' at that La Salle. You don't want no La Salle. Bearings shot. Uses too much oil. Got a Lincoln '24. There's a car. Run forever. Make her into a truck.

Hot sun on rusted metal. Oil on the ground. People are wandering in, bewildered, needing a car.

Wipe your feet. Don't lean on that car, it's dirty. How do you buy a car? What does it cost? Watch the children, now. I wonder how much for this one? We'll ask. It don't cost money to ask. We can ask, can't we? Can't pay a nickel over seventy-five, or there won't be enough to get to California.

God, if I could only get a hundred jalopies. I don't care if they run or not.

Tires, used, bruised tires, stacked in tall cylinders; tubes, red, gray, hanging like sausages.

Tire patch? Radiator cleaner? Spark intensifier? Drop this little pill in your gas tank and get ten extra miles to the gallon. Just paint it on—you got a new surface for fifty cents. Wipers, fan belts, gaskets? Maybe it's the valve. Get a new valve stem. What can you lose for a nickel?

All right, Joe. You soften 'em up an' shoot 'em in here. I'll close 'em, I'll deal 'em or I'll kill 'em. Don't send in no bums. I want deals.

Yes, sir, step in. You got a buy there. Yes, sir! At eighty bucks you got a buy.

I can't go no higher than fifty. The fella outside says fifty.

Fifty. Fifty? He's nuts. Paid seventy-eight fifty for that little

number. Joe, you crazy fool, you tryin' to bust us? Have to
can that guy. I might take sixty. Now look here, mister, I ain't
got all day. I'm a business man but I ain't out to stick nobody.
Got anything to trade?

Got a pair of mules I'll trade.

Mules! Hey, Joe, hear this? This guy wants to trade mules.
Didn't nobody tell you this is the machine age? They don't
use mules for nothing but glue no more.

Fine big mules—five and seven years old. Maybe we better
look around.

Look around! You come in when we're busy, an' take up
our time an' then walk out! Joe, did you know you was talkin'
to pikers?

I ain't a piker. I got to get a car. We're goin' to California.
I got to get a car.

Well, I'm a sucker. Joe says I'm a sucker. Says if I don't
quit givin' my shirt away I'll starve to death. Tell you what
I'll do—I can get five bucks apiece for them mules for dog
feed.

I wouldn't want them to go for dog feed.

Well, maybe I can get ten or seven maybe. Tell you what
we'll do. We'll take your mules for twenty. Wagon goes with
'em, don't it? An' you put up fifty, an' you can sign a contract
to send the rest at ten dollars a month.

But you said eighty.

Didn't you never hear about carrying charges and insurance? That just boosts her a little. You'll get her all paid up
in four-five months. Sign your name right here. We'll take care
of ever'thing.

Well, I don't know——

Now, look here. I'm givin' you my shirt, an' you took all
this time. I might a made three sales while I been talkin' to
you. I'm disgusted. Yeah, sign right there. All right, sir. Joe,
fill up the tank for this gentleman. We'll even give him gas.

Jesus, Joe, that was a hot one! What'd we give for that
jalopy? Thirty bucks—thirty-five wasn't it? I got that team,
an' if I can't get seventy-five for that team, I ain't a business
man. An' I got fifty cash an' a contract for forty more. Oh, I
know they're not all honest, but it'll surprise you how many
kick through with the rest. One guy come through with a

hundred two years after I wrote him off. I bet you this guy sends the money. Christ, if I could only get five hundred ja- lopies! Roll up your sleeves, Joe. Go out an' soften 'em, an' send 'em in to me. You get twenty on that last deal. You ain't doing bad.

Limp flags in the afternoon sun. Today's Bargain. '29 Ford pickup, runs good.

What do you want for fifty bucks—a Zephyr?

Horsehair curling out of seat cushions, fenders battered and hammered back. Bumpers torn loose and hanging. Fancy Ford roadster with little colored lights at fender guide, at ra- diator cap, and three behind. Mud aprons, and a big die on the gear-shift lever. Pretty girl on tire cover, painted in color and named Cora. Afternoon sun on the dusty windshields.

Christ, I ain't had time to go out an' eat! Joe, send a kid for a hamburger.

Spattering roar of ancient engines.

There's a dumb-bunny lookin' at that Chrysler. Find out if he got any jack in his jeans. Some a these farm boys is sneaky. Soften 'em up an' roll 'em in to me, Joe. You're doin' good.

Sure, we sold it. Guarantee? We guaranteed it to be an automobile. We didn't guarantee to wet-nurse it. Now listen here, you—you bought a car, an' now you're squawkin'. I don't give a damn if you don't make payments. We ain't got your paper. We turn that over to the finance company. They'll get after you, not us. We don't hold no paper. Yeah? Well you jus' get tough an' I'll call a cop. No, we did not switch the tires. Run 'im outa here, Joe. He bought a car, an' now he ain't satisfied. How'd you think if I bought a steak an' et half an' try to bring it back? We're runnin' a business, not a charity ward. Can ya imagine that guy, Joe? Say—looka there! Got a Elk's tooth! Run over there. Let 'em glance over that '36 Pon- tiac. Yeah.

Square noses, round noses, rusty noses, shovel noses, and the long curves of streamlines, and the flat surfaces before streamlining. Bargains Today. Old monsters with deep up- holstery—you can cut her into a truck easy. Two-wheel trail- ers, axles rusty in the hard afternoon sun. Used Cars. Good Used Cars. Clean, runs good. Don't pump oil.

Christ, look at 'er! Somebody took nice care of 'er.

Cadillacs, La Salles, Buicks, Plymouths, Packards, Chevvies, Fords, Pontiacs. Row on row, headlights glinting in the afternoon sun. Good Used Cars.

Soften 'em up, Joe. Jesus, I wisht I had a thousand jalopies! Get 'em ready to deal, an' I'll close 'em.

Goin' to California? Here's jus' what you need. Looks shot, but they's thousan's of miles in her.

Lined up side by side. Good Used Cars. Bargains. Clean, runs good.

Chapter Eight

THE SKY grayed among the stars, and the pale, late quarter-moon was insubstantial and thin. Tom Joad and the preacher walked quickly along a road that was only wheel tracks and beaten caterpillar tracks through a cotton field. Only the unbalanced sky showed the approach of dawn, no horizon to the west, and a line to the east. The two men walked in silence and smelled the dust their feet kicked into the air.

"I hope you're dead sure of the way," Jim Casy said. "I'd hate to have the dawn come an' us be way to hell an' gone somewhere." The cotton field scurried with waking life, the quick flutter of morning birds feeding on the ground, the scamper over the clods of disturbed rabbits. The quiet thudding of the men's feet in the dust, the squeak of crushed clods under their shoes, sounded against the secret noises of the dawn.

Tom said, "I could shut my eyes an' walk right there. On'y way I can go wrong is think about her. Jus' forget about her, an' I'll go right there. Hell, man, I was born right aroun' in here. I run aroun' here when I was a kid. They's a tree over there—look, you can jus' make it out. Well, once my old man hung up a dead coyote in that tree. Hung there till it was all sort of melted, an' then dropped off. Dried up, like. Jesus, I hope Ma's cookin' somepin. My belly's caved."

"Me too," said Casy. "Like a little eatin' tobacca? Keeps ya from gettin' too hungry. Been better if we didn' start so damn early. Better if it was light." He paused to gnaw off a piece of plug. "I was sleepin' nice."

"That crazy Muley done it," said Tom. "He got me clear jumpy. Wakes me up an' says, ' 'By, Tom. I'm goin' on. I got places to go.' An' he says, 'Better get goin' too, so's you'll be offa this lan' when the light comes.' He's gettin' screwy as a gopher, livin' like he does. You'd think Injuns was after him. Think he's nuts?"

"Well, I dunno. You seen that car come las' night when we had a little fire. You seen how the house was smashed. They's somepin purty mean goin' on. 'Course Muley's crazy, all right. Creepin' aroun' like a coyote; that's boun' to make him crazy. He'll kill somebody purty soon an' they'll run him down with dogs. I can see it like a prophecy. He'll get worse an' worse. Wouldn' come along with us, you say?"

"No," said Joad. "I think he's scared to see people now. Wonder he come up to us. We'll be at Uncle John's place by sunrise." They walked along in silence for a time, and the late owls flew over toward the barns, the hollow trees, the tank houses, where they hid from daylight. The eastern sky grew fairer and it was possible to see the cotton plants and the graying earth. "Damn' if I know how they're all sleepin' at Uncle John's. He on'y got one room an' a cookin' leanto, an' a little bit of a barn. Must be a mob there now."

The preacher said, "I don't recollect that John had a fambly. Just a lone man, ain't he? I don't recollect much about him."

"Lonest goddamn man in the world," said Joad. "Crazy kind of son-of-a-bitch, too—somepin like Muley, on'y worse in some ways. Might see 'im anywheres—at Shawnee, drunk, or visitin' a widow twenty miles away, or workin' his place with a lantern. Crazy. Ever'body thought he wouldn't live long. A lone man like that don't live long. But Uncle John's older'n Pa. Jus' gets stringier an' meaner ever' year. Meaner'n Grampa."

"Look a the light comin'," said the preacher. "Silvery-like. Didn' John never have no fambly?"

"Well, yes, he did, an' that'll show you the kind a fella he is—set in his ways. Pa tells about it. Uncle John, he had a young wife. Married four months. She was in a family way, too, an' one night she gets a pain in her stomick, an' she says, 'You better go for a doctor.' Well, John, he's settin' there, an' he says, 'You just got a stomickache. You et too much. Take a dose a pain killer.' In the night she wakes him up an' he gives her another dose a pain killer. 'You crowd up ya stomick an' ya get a stomickache,' he says. Nex' noon she's outa her head, an' she dies at about four in the afternoon."

"What was it?" Casy asked. "Poisoned from somepin she et?"

"No, somepin jus' bust in her. Ap—appendick or somepin.

Well, Uncle John, he's always been a easy-goin' fella, an' he takes it hard. Takes it for a sin. For a long time he won't have nothin' to say to nobody. Just walks aroun' like he don't see nothin', an' he prays some. Took 'im two years to come out of it, an' then he ain't the same. Sort of wild. Made a damn nuisance of hisself. Ever' time one of us kids got worms or a gutache Uncle John brings a doctor out. Pa finally tol' him he got to stop. Kids all the time gettin' a gutache. He figures it's his fault his woman died. Funny fella. He's all the time makin' it up to somebody—givin' kids stuff, droppin' a sack a meal on somebody's porch. Give away about ever'thing he got, an' still he ain't very happy. Gets walkin' around alone at night sometimes. He's a good farmer, though. Keeps his lan' nice."

"Poor fella," said the preacher. "Poor lonely fella. Did he go to church much when his woman died?"

"No, he didn'. Never wanted to get close to folks. Wanted to be off alone. I never seen a kid that wasn't crazy about him. He'd come to our house in the night sometimes, an' we knowed he come 'cause jus' as sure as he come there'd be a pack a gum in the bed right beside ever' one of us. We thought he was Jesus Christ Awmighty."

The preacher walked along, head down. He didn't answer. And the light of the coming morning made his forehead seem to shine, and his hands, swinging beside him, flicked into the light and out again.

Tom was silent too, as though he had said too intimate a thing and was ashamed. He quickened his pace and the preacher kept step. They could see a little into gray distance ahead now. A snake wriggled slowly from the cotton rows into the road. Tom stopped short of it and peered. "Gopher snake," he said. "Let him go." They walked around the snake and went on their way. A little color came into the eastern sky, and almost immediately the lonely dawn light crept over the land. Green appeared on the cotton plants and the earth was gray-brown. The faces of the men lost their grayish shine. Joad's face seemed to darken with the growing light. "This is the good time," Joad said softly. "When I was a kid I used to get up an' walk around by myself when it was like this. What's that ahead?"

A committee of dogs had met in the road, in honor of a bitch. Five males, shepherd mongrels, collie mongrels, dogs whose breeds had been blurred by a freedom of social life, were engaged in complimenting the bitch. For each dog sniffed daintily and then stalked to a cotton plant on stiff legs, raised a hind foot ceremoniously and wetted, then went back to smell. Joad and the preacher stopped to watch, and suddenly Joad laughed joyously. "By God!" he said. "By God!" Now all dogs met and hackles rose, and they all growled and stood stiffly, each waiting for the others to start a fight. One dog mounted and, now that it was accomplished, the others gave way and watched with interest, and their tongues were out, and their tongues dripped. The two men walked on. "By God!" Joad said. "I think that up-dog is our Flash. I thought he'd be dead. Come, Flash!" He laughed again. "What the hell, if somebody called me, I wouldn' hear him neither. 'Minds me of a story they tell about Willy Feeley when he was a young fella. Willy was bashful, awful bashful. Well, one day he takes a heifer over to Graves' bull. Ever'body was out but Elsie Graves, and Elsie wasn't bashful at all. Willy, he stood there turnin' red an' he couldn' even talk. Elsie says, 'I know what you come for; the bull's out in back a the barn.' Well, they took the heifer out there an' Willy an' Elsie sat on the fence to watch. Purty soon Willy got feelin' purty fly. Elsie looks over an' says, like she don't know, 'What's a matter, Willy?' Willy's so randy he can't hardly set still. 'By God,' he says, 'by God, I wisht I was a-doin' that!' Elsie says, 'Why not, Willy? It's your heifer.' "

The preacher laughed softly. "You know," he said, "it's a nice thing not bein' a preacher no more. Nobody use' ta tell stories when I was there, or if they did I couldn' laugh. An' I couldn' cuss. Now I cuss all I want, any time I want, an' it does a fella good to cuss if he wants to."

A redness grew up out of the eastern horizon, and on the ground birds began to chirp, sharply. "Look!" said Joad. "Right ahead. That's Uncle John's tank. Can't see the win'mill, but there's his tank. See it against the sky?" He speeded his walk. "I wonder if all the folks are there." The hulk of the tank stood above a rise. Joad, hurrying, raised a cloud of dust about his knees. "I wonder if Ma—" They saw the tank legs now, and the house, a square little box, un-painted and bare, and the barn, low-roofed and huddled. Smoke was rising from the tin chimney of the house. In the yard was a litter, piled furniture, the blades and motor of the windmill, bedsteads, chairs, tables. "Holy Christ, they're fixin' to go!" Joad said. A truck stood in the yard, a truck with high sides, but a strange truck, for while the front of it was a sedan, the top had been cut off in the middle and the truck bed fitted on. And as they drew near, the men could hear pound-ing from the yard, and as the rim of the blinding sun came up over the horizon, it fell on the truck, and they saw a man and the flash of his hammer as it rose and fell. And the sun flashed on the windows of the house. The weathered boards were bright. Two red chickens on the ground flamed with reflected light.

"Don't yell," said Tom. "Let's creep up on 'em, like," and he walked so fast that the dust rose as high as his waist. And then he came to the edge of the cotton field. Now they were in the yard proper, earth beaten hard, shiny hard, and a few dusty crawling weeds on the ground. And Joad slowed as though he feared to go on. The preacher, watching him, slowed to match his step. Tom sauntered forward, sidled em-barrassedly toward the truck. It was a Hudson Super-Six se-dan, and the top had been ripped in two with a cold chisel. Old Tom Joad stood in the truck bed and he was nailing on the top rails of the truck sides. His grizzled, bearded face was low over his work, and a bunch of six-penny nails stuck out of his mouth. He set a nail and his hammer thundered it in. From the house came the clash of a lid on the stove and the wail of a child. Joad sidled up to the truck bed and leaned against it. And his father looked at him and did not see him. His father set another nail and drove it in. A flock of pigeons started from the deck of the tank house and flew around and settled again and strutted to the edge to look over; white pigeons and blue pigeons and grays, with iridescent wings.

Joad hooked his fingers over the lowest bar of the truck side. He looked up at the aging, graying man on the truck. He wet his thick lips with his tongue, and he said softly, "Pa."

"What do you want?" old Tom mumbled around his mouthful of nails. He wore a black, dirty slouch hat and a blue work shirt over which was a buttonless vest; his jeans were held up by a wide harness-leather belt with a big square brass buckle, leather and metal polished from years of wearing; and his shoes were cracked and the soles swollen and boat-shaped from years of sun and wet and dust. The sleeves of his shirt were tight on his forearms, held down by the bulging powerful muscles. Stomach and hips were lean, and legs, short, heavy, and strong. His face, squared by a bristling pepper and salt beard, was all drawn down to the forceful chin, a chin thrust out and built out by the stubble beard which was not so grayed on the chin, and gave weight and force to its thrust. Over old Tom's unwhiskered cheek bones the skin was as brown as meerschaum, and wrinkled in rays around his eye-corners from squinting. His eyes were brown, black-coffee brown, and he thrust his head forward when he looked at a thing, for his bright dark eyes were failing. His lips, from which the big nails protruded, were thin and red.

He held his hammer suspended in the air, about to drive a set nail, and he looked over the truck side at Tom, looked resentful at being interrupted. And then his chin drove forward and his eyes looked at Tom's face, and then gradually his brain became aware of what he saw. The hammer dropped slowly to his side, and with his left hand he took the nails from his mouth. And he said wonderingly, as though he told himself the fact, "It's Tommy—" And then, still informing himself, "It's Tommy come home." His mouth opened again, and a look of fear came into his eyes. "Tommy," he said softly, "you ain't busted out? You ain't got to hide?" He listened tensely.

"Naw," said Tom. "I'm paroled. I'm free. I got my papers." He gripped the lower bars of the truck side and looked up.

Old Tom laid his hammer gently on the floor and put his nails in his pocket. He swung his leg over the side and dropped lithely to the ground, but once beside his son he seemed embarrassed and strange. "Tommy," he said, "we are goin' to California. But we was gonna write you a letter an' tell you." And he said, incredulously, "But you're back. You can go with us. You can go!" The lid of a coffee pot slammed in the house. Old Tom looked over his shoulder. "Le's supprise 'em," he said, and his eyes shone with excitement. "Your ma got a bad feelin' she ain't never gonna see you no more. She got that quiet look like when somebody died. Almost she don't want to go to California, fear she'll never see you no more." A stove lid clashed in the house again. "Le's surprise 'em," old Tom repeated. "Le's go in like you never been away. Le's jus' see what your ma says." At last he touched Tom, but touched him on the shoulder, timidly, and instantly took his hand away. He looked at Jim Casy.

Tom said, "You remember the preacher, Pa. He come along with me."

"He been in prison too?"

"No, I met 'im on the road. He been away."

Pa shook hands gravely. "You're welcome here, sir."

Casy said, "Glad to be here. It's a thing to see when a boy comes home. It's a thing to see."

"Home," Pa said.

"To his folks," the preacher amended quickly. "We stayed at the other place last night."

Pa's chin thrust out, and he looked back down the road for a moment. Then he turned to Tom. "How'll we do her?" he began excitedly. "S'pose I go in an' say, 'Here's some fellas want some breakfast,' or how'd it be if you jus' come in an' stood there till she seen you? How'd that be?" His face was alive with excitement.

"Don't le's give her no shock," said Tom. "Don't le's scare her none."

Two rangy shepherd dogs trotted up pleasantly, until they caught the scent of strangers, and then they backed cautiously away, watchful, their tails moving slowly and tentatively in the air, but their eyes and noses quick for animosity or danger. One of them, stretching his neck, edged forward, ready to run, and little by little he approached Tom's legs and sniffed loudly at them. Then he backed away and watched Pa for some kind of signal. The other pup was not so brave. He looked about for something that could honorably divert his attention, saw a red chicken go mincing by, and ran at it. There was the squawk of an outraged hen, a burst of red feathers, and the hen ran off, flapping stubby wings for speed. The pup looked proudly back at the men, and then flopped down in the dust and beat its tail contentedly on the ground.

"Come on," said Pa, "come on in now. She got to see you. I got to see her face when she sees you. Come on. She'll yell breakfast in a minute. I heard her slap the salt pork in the pan a good time ago." He led the way across the fine-dusted ground. There was no porch on this house, just a step and then the door; a chopping block beside the door, its surface matted and soft from years of chopping. The graining in the sheathing wood was high, for the dust had cut down the softer wood. The smell of burning willow was in the air, and, as the three men neared the door, the smell of frying side-meat and the smell of high brown biscuits and the sharp smell of coffee rolling in the pot. Pa stepped up into the open doorway and stood there blocking it with his wide short body. He said, "Ma, there's a coupla fellas jus' come along the road, an' they wonder if we could spare a bite."

Tom heard his mother's voice, the remembered cool, calm drawl, friendly and humble. "Let 'em come," she said. "We got a-plenty. Tell 'em they got to wash their han's. The bread is done. I'm jus' takin' up the side-meat now." And the sizzle of the angry grease came from the stove.

Pa stepped inside, clearing the door, and Tom looked in at his mother. She was lifting the curling slices of pork from the frying pan. The oven door was open, and a great pan of high brown biscuits stood waiting there. She looked out the door, but the sun was behind Tom, and she saw only a dark figure outlined by the bright yellow sunlight. She nodded pleasantly. "Come in," she said. "Jus' lucky I made plenty bread this morning."

Tom stood looking in. Ma was heavy, but not fat; thick with child-bearing and work. She wore a loose Mother Hubbard of gray cloth in which there had once been colored flowers, but the color was washed out now, so that the small flowered pattern was only a little lighter gray than the background. The dress came down to her ankles, and her strong, broad, bare feet moved quickly and deftly over the floor. Her thin, steel-gray hair was gathered in a sparse wispy knot at the back of her head. Strong, freckled arms were bare to the elbow, and her hands were chubby and delicate, like those of a plump

little girl. She looked out into the sunshine. Her full face was
not soft; it was controlled, kindly. Her hazel eyes seemed to
have experienced all possible tragedy and to have mounted
pain and suffering like steps into a high calm and a super-
human understanding. She seemed to know, to accept, to welcome her position, the citadel of the family, the strong place
that could not be taken. And since old Tom and the children
could not know hurt or fear unless she acknowledged hurt
and fear, she had practiced denying them in herself. And since,
when a joyful thing happened, they looked to see whether joy
was on her, it was her habit to build up laughter out of inadequate materials. But better than joy was calm. Imperturbability could be depended upon. And from her great and
humble position in the family she had taken dignity and a
clean calm beauty. From her position as healer, her hands had
grown sure and cool and quiet; from her position as arbiter
she had become as remote and faultless in judgment as a goddess. She seemed to know that if she swayed the family shook,
and if she ever really deeply wavered or despaired the family
would fall, the family will to function would be gone.

She looked out into the sunny yard, at the dark figure of a
man. Pa stood near by, shaking with excitement. "Come in,"
he cried. "Come right in, mister." And Tom a little shame-
facedly stepped over the doorsill.

She looked up pleasantly from the frying pan. And then her
hand sank slowly to her side and the fork clattered to the
wooden floor. Her eyes opened wide, and the pupils dilated.
She breathed heavily through her open mouth. She closed her
eyes. "Thank God," she said. "Oh, thank God!" And suddenly her face was worried. "Tommy, you ain't wanted? You
didn' bust loose?"

"No, Ma. Parole. I got the papers here." He touched his
breast.

She moved toward him lithely, soundlessly in her bare feet,
and her face was full of wonder. Her small hand felt his arm,
felt the soundness of his muscles. And then her fingers went
up to his cheek as a blind man's fingers might. And her joy
was nearly like sorrow. Tom pulled his underlip between his
teeth and bit it. Her eyes went wonderingly to his bitten lip,
and she saw the little line of blood against his teeth and the

trickle of blood down his lip. Then she knew, and her control came back, and her hand dropped. Her breath came out explosively. "Well!" she cried. "We come mighty near to goin' on without ya. An' we was wonderin' how in the worl' you could ever find us." She picked up the fork and combed the boiling grease and brought out a dark curl of crisp pork. And she set the pot of tumbling coffee on the back of the stove.

Old Tom giggled, "Fooled ya, huh, Ma? We aimed to fool ya, and we done it. Jus' stood there like a hammered sheep. Wisht Grampa'd been here to see. Looked like somebody'd beat ya between the eyes with a sledge. Grampa would a whacked 'imself so hard he'd a throwed his hip out—like he done when he seen Al take a shot at that grea' big airship the army got. Tommy, it come over one day, half a mile big, an' Al gets the thirty-thirty and blazes away at her. Grampa yells, 'Don't shoot no fledglin's, Al; wait till a growed-up one goes over,' an' then he whacked 'imself an' throwed his hip out."

Ma chuckled and took down a heap of tin plates from a shelf.

Tom asked, "Where is Grampa? I ain't seen the ol' devil."

Ma stacked the plates on the kitchen table and piled cups beside them. She said confidentially, "Oh, him an' Granma sleeps in the barn. They got to get up so much in the night. They was stumblin' over the little fellas."

Pa broke in, "Yeah, ever' night Grampa'd get mad. Tumble over Winfield, an' Winfield'd yell, an' Grampa'd get mad an' wet his drawers, an' that'd make him madder, an' purty soon ever'body in the house'd be yellin' their head off." His words tumbled out between chuckles. "Oh, we had lively times. One night when ever'body was yellin' an' a-cussin', your brother Al, he's a smart aleck now, he says, 'Goddamn it, Grampa, why don't you run off an' be a pirate?' Well, that made Grampa so goddamn mad he went for his gun. Al had ta sleep out in the fiel' that night. But now Granma an' Grampa both sleeps in the barn."

Ma said, "They can jus' get up an' step outside when they feel like it. Pa, run on out an' tell 'em Tommy's home. Grampa's a favorite of him."

"A course," said Pa. "I should of did it before." He went out the door and crossed the yard, swinging his hands high.

Tom watched him go, and then his mother's voice called his attention. She was pouring coffee. She did not look at him. "Tommy," she said hesitantly, timidly.

"Yeah?" His timidity was set off by hers, a curious embarrassment. Each one knew the other was shy, and became more shy in the knowledge.

"Tommy, I got to ask you—you ain't mad?"

"Mad, Ma?"

"You ain't poisoned mad? You don't hate nobody? They didn' do nothin' in that jail to rot you out with crazy mad?"

He looked sidewise at her, studied her, and his eyes seemed to ask how she could know such things. "No-o-o," he said. "I was for a little while. But I ain't proud like some fellas. I let stuff run off'n me. What's a matter, Ma?"

Now she was looking at him, her mouth open, as though to hear better, her eyes digging to know better. Her face looked for the answer that is always concealed in language. She said in confusion, "I knowed Purty Boy Floyd. I knowed his ma. They was good folks. He was full a hell, sure, like a good boy oughta be." She paused and then her words poured out. "I don' know all like this—but I know it. He done a little bad thing an' they hurt 'im, caught 'im an' hurt him so he was mad, an' the nex' bad thing he done was mad, an' they hurt 'im again. An' purty soon he was mean-mad. They shot at him like a varmint, an' he shot back, an' then they run him like a coyote, an' him a-snappin' an' a-snarlin', mean as a lobo. An' he was mad. He wasn't no boy or no man no more, he was jus' a walkin' chunk a mean-mad. But the folks that knowed him didn' hurt 'im. He wasn' mad at them. Finally they run him down an' killed 'im. No matter how they say it in the paper how he was bad—that's how it was." She paused and she licked her dry lips, and her whole face was an aching question. "I got to know, Tommy. Did they hurt you so much? Did they make you mad like that?"

Tom's heavy lips were pulled tight over his teeth. He looked down at his big flat hands. "No," he said. "I ain't like that." He paused and studied the broken nails, which were ridged like clam shells. "All the time in stir I kep' away from stuff like that. I ain' so mad."

She sighed, "Thank God!" under her breath.

He looked up quickly. "Ma, when I seen what they done to our house——"

She came near to him then, and stood close; and she said passionately, "Tommy, don't you go fightin' 'em alone. They'll hunt you down like a coyote. Tommy, I got to thinkin' an' dreamin' an' wonderin'. They say there's a hun'erd thousand of us shoved out. If we was all mad the same way, Tommy—they wouldn't hunt nobody down——" She stopped.

Tommy, looking at her, gradually drooped his eyelids, until just a short glitter showed through his lashes. "Many folks feel that way?" he demanded.

"I don' know. They're jus' kinda stunned. Walk aroun' like they was half asleep."

From outside and across the yard came an ancient creaking bleat. "Pu-raise Gawd fur vittory! Pu-raise Gawd fur vittory!"

Tom turned his head and grinned. "Granma finally heard I'm home. Ma," he said, "you never was like this before!"

Her face hardened and her eyes grew cold. "I never had my house pushed over," she said. "I never had my fambly stuck out on the road. I never had to sell—ever'thing— Here they come now." She moved back to the stove and dumped the big pan of bulbous biscuits on two tin plates. She shook flour into the deep grease to make gravy, and her hand was white with flour. For a moment Tom watched her, and then he went to the door.

Across the yard came four people. Grampa was ahead, a lean, ragged, quick old man, jumping with quick steps and favoring his right leg—the side that came out of joint. He was buttoning his fly as he came, and his old hands were having trouble finding the buttons, for he had buttoned the top button into the second buttonhole, and that threw the whole sequence off. He wore dark ragged pants and a torn blue shirt, open all the way down, and showing long gray underwear, also unbuttoned. His lean white chest, fuzzed with white hair, was visible through the opening in his underwear. He gave up the fly and left it open and fumbled with the underwear buttons, then gave the whole thing up and hitched his brown suspenders. His was a lean excitable face with little bright eyes as evil as a frantic child's eyes. A cantankerous, complaining, mischievous, laughing face. He fought and argued, told dirty stories. He was as lecherous as always. Vicious and cruel and impatient, like a frantic child, and the whole structure overlaid with amusement. He drank too much when he could get it, ate too much when it was there, talked too much all the time.

Behind him hobbled Granma, who had survived only because she was as mean as her husband. She had held her own with a shrill ferocious religiosity that was as lecherous and as savage as anything Grampa could offer. Once, after a meeting, while she was still speaking in tongues, she fired both barrels of a shotgun at her husband, ripping one of his buttocks nearly off, and after that he admired her and did not try to torture her as children torture bugs. As she walked she hiked her Mother Hubbard up to her knees, and she bleated her shrill terrible war cry: "Pu-raise Gawd fur vittory."

Granma and Grampa raced each other to get across the broad yard. They fought over everything, and loved and needed the fighting.

Behind them, moving slowly and evenly, but keeping up, came Pa and Noah—Noah the first-born, tall and strange, walking always with a wondering look on his face, calm and puzzled. He had never been angry in his life. He looked in wonder at angry people, wonder and uneasiness, as normal people look at the insane. Noah moved slowly, spoke seldom, and then so slowly that people who did not know him often thought him stupid. He was not stupid, but he was strange. He had little pride, no sexual urges. He worked and slept in a curious rhythm that nevertheless sufficed him. He was fond of his folks, but never showed it in any way. Although an observer could not have told why, Noah left the impression of being misshapen, his head or his body or his legs or his mind; but no misshapen member could be recalled. Pa thought he knew why Noah was strange, but Pa was ashamed, and never told. For on the night when Noah was born, Pa, frightened at the spreading thighs, alone in the house, and horrified at the screaming wretch his wife had become, went mad with apprehension. Using his hands, his strong fingers for forceps, he had pulled and twisted the baby. The midwife, arriving late, had found the baby's head pulled out of shape, its neck stretched, its body warped; and she had pushed the head back and molded the body with her hands. But Pa always remembered, and was ashamed. And he was kinder to Noah than to the others. In Noah's broad face, eyes too far apart, and long fragile jaw, Pa thought he saw the twisted, warped skull of the baby. Noah could do all that was required of him, could read and write, could work and figure, but he didn't seem to care; there was a listlessness in him toward things people wanted and needed. He lived in a strange silent house and looked out of it through calm eyes. He was a stranger to all the world, but he was not lonely.

The four came across the yard, and Grampa demanded, "Where is he? Goddamn it, where is he?" And his fingers fumbled for his pants button, and forgot and strayed into his pocket. And then he saw Tom standing in the door. Grampa stopped and he stopped the others. His little eyes glittered with malice. "Lookut him," he said. "A jailbird. Ain't been no Joads in jail for a hell of a time." His mind jumped. "Got no right to put 'im in jail. He done just what I'd do. Sons-a-bitches got not right." His mind jumped again. "An' ol' Turnbull, stinkin' skunk, braggin' how he'll shoot ya when ya come out. Says he got Hatfield blood. Well, I sent word to him. I says, 'Don't fuck around with no Joad. Maybe I got McCoy blood for all I know.' I says, 'You lay your sights any-wheres near Tommy an' I'll take it an' I'll ram it up your ass,' I says. Scairt 'im, too."

Granma, not following the conversation, bleated, "Pu-raise Gawd fur vittory."

Grampa walked up and slapped Tom on the chest, and his eyes grinned with affection and pride. "How are ya, Tommy?"

"O.K." said Tom. "How ya keepin' yaself?"

"Full a piss an' vinegar," said Grampa. His mind jumped. "Jus' like I said, they ain't a gonna keep no Joad in jail. I says, 'Tommy'll come a-bustin' outa that jail like a bull through a corral fence.' An' you done it. Get outa my way, I'm hungry." He crowded past, sat down, loaded his plate with pork and two big biscuits and poured the thick gravy over the whole mess, and before the others could get in, Grampa's mouth was full.

Tom grinned affectionately at him. "Ain't he a heller?" he

said. And Grampa's mouth was so full that he couldn't even splutter, but his mean little eyes smiled, and he nodded his head violently.

Granma said proudly, "A wicketer, cussin'er man never lived. He's goin' to hell on a poker, praise Gawd! Wants to drive the truck!" she said spitefully. "Well, he ain't goin' ta."

Grampa choked, and a mouthful of paste sprayed into his lap, and he coughed weakly.

Granma smiled up at Tom. "Messy, ain't he?" she observed brightly.

Noah stood on the step, and he faced Tom, and his wide-set eyes seemed to look around him. His face had little expression. Tom said, "How ya, Noah?"

"Fine," said Noah. "How a' you?" That was all, but it was a comfortable thing.

Ma waved the flies away from the bowl of gravy. "We ain't got room to set down," she said. "Jus' get yaself a plate an' set down wherever ya can. Out in the yard or someplace."

Suddenly Tom said, "Hey! Where's the preacher? He was right here. Where'd he go?"

Pa said, "I seen him, but he's gone."

And Granma raised a shrill voice, "Preacher? You got a preacher? Go git him. We'll have a grace." She pointed at Grampa. "Too late for him—he's et. Go git the preacher."

Tom stepped out on the porch. "Hey, Jim! Jim Casy!" he called. He walked out in the yard. "Oh, Casy!" The preacher emerged from under the tank, sat up, and then stood up and moved toward the house. Tom asked, "What was you doin', hidin'?"

"Well, no. But a fella shouldn' butt his head in where a fambly got fambly stuff. I was jus' settin' a-thinkin'."

"Come on in an' eat," said Tom. "Granma wants a grace."

"But I ain't a preacher no more," Casy protested.

"Aw, come on. Give her a grace. Won't do you no harm, an' she likes 'em." They walked into the kitchen together.

Ma said quietly, "You're welcome."

And Pa said, "You're welcome. Have some breakfast."

"Grace fust," Granma clamored. "Grace fust."

Grampa focused his eyes fiercely until he recognized Casy. "Oh, that preacher," he said. "Oh, he's all right. I always liked him since I seen him—" He winked so lecherously that Granma thought he had spoken and retorted, "Shut up, you sinful ol' goat."

Casy ran his fingers through his hair nervously. "I got to tell you, I ain't a preacher no more. If me jus' bein' glad to be here an' bein' thankful for people that's kind and generous, if that's enough—why, I'll say that kinda grace. But I ain't a preacher no more."

"Say her," said Granma. "An' get in a word about us goin' to California." The preacher bowed his head, and the others bowed their heads. Ma folded her hands over her stomach and bowed her head. Granma bowed so low that her nose was nearly in her plate of biscuit and gravy. Tom, leaning against the wall, a plate in his hand, bowed stiffly, and Grampa bowed his head sidewise, so that he could keep one mean and merry eye on the preacher. And on the preacher's face there was a look not of prayer, but of thought; and in his tone not supplication, but conjecture.

"I been thinkin'," he said. "I been in the hills, thinkin', almost you might say like Jesus went into the wilderness to think His way out of a mess of troubles."

"Pu-raise Gawd!" Granma said, and the preacher glanced over at her in surprise.

"Seems like Jesus got all messed up with troubles, and He couldn't figure nothin' out, an' He got to feelin' what the hell good is it all, an' what's the use fightin' an' figurin'. Got tired, got good an' tired, an' His sperit all wore out. Jus' about come to the conclusion, the hell with it. An' so He went off into the wilderness."

"A—men," Granma bleated. So many years she had timed her responses to the pauses. And it was so many years since she had listened to or wondered at the words used.

"I ain't sayin' I'm like Jesus," the preacher went on. "But I got tired like Him, an' I got mixed up like Him, an' I went into the wilderness like Him, without no campin' stuff. Nighttime I'd lay on my back an' look up at the stars; morning I'd set an' watch the sun come up; midday I'd look out from a hill at the rollin' dry country; evenin' I'd foller the sun down. Sometimes I'd pray like I always done. On'y I couldn' figure what I was prayin' to or for. There was the hills, an' there was me, an' we wasn't separate no more. We was one thing. An' there was me an' the hills an' there was the stars an' the black sky, an' we was all one thing. An' that one thing was holy.''

"Hallelujah," said Granma, and she rocked a little, back and forth, trying to catch hold of an ecstasy.

"An' I got thinkin', on'y it wasn't thinkin', it was deeper down than thinkin'. I got thinkin' how we was holy when we was one thing, an' mankin' was holy when it was one thing. An' it on'y got unholy when one mis'able little fella got the bit in his teeth an' run off his own way, kickin' an' draggin' an' fightin'. Fella like that bust the holiness. But when they're all workin' together, not one fella for another fella, but one fella kind of harnessed to the whole shebang—that's right, that's holy. An' then I got thinkin' I don't even know what I mean by holy.'' He paused, but the bowed heads stayed down, for they had been trained like dogs to rise at the "amen" signal. "I can't say no grace like I use' ta say. I'm glad of the holiness of breakfast. I'm glad there's love here. That's all.'' The heads stayed down. The preacher looked around. "I've got your breakfast cold," he said; and then he remembered. "Amen," he said, and all the heads rose up.

"A—men," said Granma, and she fell to her breakfast, and broke down the soggy biscuits with her hard old toothless gums. Tom ate quickly, and Pa crammed his mouth. There was no talk until the food was gone, the coffee drunk; only the crunch of chewed food and the slup of coffee cooled in transit to the tongue. Ma watched the preacher as he ate, and her eyes were questioning, probing and understanding. She watched him as though he were suddenly a spirit, not human any more, a voice out of the ground.

The men finished and put down their plates, and drained the last of their coffee; and then the men went out, Pa and the preacher and Noah and Grampa and Tom, and they walked over to the truck, avoiding the litter of furniture, the wooden bedsteads, the windmill machinery, the old plow. They walked to the truck and stood beside it. They touched the new pine side-boards.

Tom opened the hood and looked at the big greasy engine. And Pa came up beside him. He said, "Your brother Al looked her over before we bought her. He says she's all right."

"What's he know? He's just a squirt," said Tom.

"He worked for a company. Drove truck last year. He knows quite a little. Smart aleck like he is. He knows. He can tinker an engine, Al can."

Tom asked, "Where's he now?"

"Well," said Pa, "he's a-billygoatin' aroun' the country. Tom-cattin' hisself to death. Smart-aleck sixteen-year-older, an' his nuts is just a-eggin' him on. He don't think of nothin' but girls and engines. A plain smart aleck. Ain't been in nights for a week."

Grampa, fumbling with his chest, had succeeded in buttoning the buttons of his blue shirt into the buttonholes of his underwear. His fingers felt that something was wrong, but did not care enough to find out. His fingers went down to try to figure out the intricacies of the buttoning of his fly. "I was worse," he said happily. "I was much worse. I was a heller, you might say. Why, they was a camp meetin' right in Sallisaw when I was a young fella a little bit older'n Al. He's just a squirt, an' punkin-soft. But I was older. An' we was to this here camp meetin'. Five hunderd folks there, an' a proper sprinklin' of young heifers."

"You look like a heller yet, Grampa," said Tom.

"Well, I am, kinda. But I ain't nowheres near the fella I was. Jus' let me get out to California where I can pick me an orange when I want it. Or grapes. There's a thing I ain't never had enough of. Gonna get me a whole big bunch a grapes off a bush, or whatever, an' I'm gonna squash 'em on my face an' let 'em run offen my chin."

Tom asked, "Where's Uncle John? Where's Rosasharn? Where's Ruthie an' Winfield? Nobody said nothin' about them yet."

Pa said, "Nobody asked. John gone to Sallisaw with a load a stuff to sell: pump, tools, chickens, an' all the stuff we brung over. Took Ruthie an' Winfield with 'im. Went 'fore daylight."

"Funny I never saw him," said Tom.

"Well, you come down from the highway, didn' you? He took the back way, by Cowlington. An' Rosasharn, she's nestin' with Connie's folks. By God! You don't even know Rosasharn's married to Connie Rivers. You 'member Connie.

Nice young fella. An' Rosasharn's due 'bout three-four-five months now. Swellin' up right now. Looks fine."

"Jesus!" said Tom. "Rosasharn was just a little kid. An' now she's gonna have a baby. So damn much happens in four years if you're away. When ya think to start out west, Pa?"

"Well, we got to take this stuff in an' sell it. If Al gets back from his squirtin' aroun', I figgered he could load the truck an' take all of it in, an' maybe we could start out tomorra or day after. We ain't got so much money, an' a fella says it's damn near two thousan' miles to California. Quicker we get started, surer it is we get there. Money's a-dribblin' out all the time. You got any money?"

"On'y a couple dollars. How'd you get money?"

"Well," said Pa, "we sol' all the stuff at our place, an' the whole bunch of us chopped cotton, even Grampa."

"Sure did," said Grampa.

"We put ever'thing together—two hunderd dollars. We give seventy-five for this here truck, an' me an' Al cut her in two an' built on this here back. Al was gonna grind the valves, but he's too busy fuckin' aroun' to get down to her. We'll have maybe a hunderd an' fifty when we start. Damn ol' tires on this here truck ain't gonna go far. Got a couple of wore out spares. Pick stuff up along the road, I guess."

The sun, driving straight down, stung with its rays. The shadows of the truck bed were dark bars on the ground, and the truck smelled of hot oil and oilcloth and paint. The few chickens had left the yard to hide in the tool shed from the sun. In the sty the pigs lay panting, close to the fence where a thin shadow fell, and they complained shrilly now and then. The two dogs were stretched in the red dust under the truck, panting, their dripping tongues covered with dust. Pa pulled his hat low over his eyes and squatted down on his hams. And, as though this were his natural position of thought and observation, he surveyed Tom critically, the new but aging cap, the suit, and the new shoes.

"Did you spen' your money for them clothes?" he asked. "Them clothes are jus' gonna be a nuisance to ya."

"They give 'em to me," said Tom. "When I come out they give 'em to me." He took off his cap and looked at it with some admiration, then wiped his forehead with it and put it on rakishly and pulled at the visor.

Pa observed, "Them's a nice-lookin' pair a shoes they give ya."

"Yeah," Joad agreed. "Purty for nice, but they ain't no shoes to go walkin' aroun' in on a hot day." He squatted beside his father.

Noah said slowly, "Maybe if you got them side-boards all true on, we could load up this stuff. Load her up so maybe if Al comes in——"

"I can drive her, if that's what you want," Tom said. "I drove truck at McAlester."

"Good," said Pa, and then his eyes stared down the road. "If I ain't mistaken, there's a young smart aleck draggin' his tail home right now," he said. "Looks purty wore out, too."

Tom and the preacher looked up the road. And randy Al, seeing he was being noticed, threw back his shoulders, and he came into the yard with a swaying strut like that of a rooster about to crow. Cockily, he walked close before he recognized Tom; and when he did, his boasting face changed, and admiration and veneration shone in his eyes, and his swagger fell away. His stiff jeans, with the bottoms turned up eight inches to show his heeled boots, his three-inch belt with copper figures on it, even the red arm bands on his blue shirt and the rakish angle of his Stetson hat could not build him up to his brother's stature; for his brother had killed a man, and no one would ever forget it. Al knew that even he had inspired some admiration among boys of his own age because his brother had killed a man. He had heard in Sallisaw how he was pointed out: "That's Al Joad. His brother killed a fella with a shovel."

And now Al, moving humbly near, saw that his brother was not a swaggerer as he had supposed. Al saw the dark brooding eyes of his brother, and the prison calm, the smooth hard face trained to indicate nothing to a prison guard, neither resistance nor slavishness. And instantly Al changed. Unconsciously he became like his brother, and his handsome face brooded, and his shoulders relaxed. He hadn't remembered how Tom was.

Tom said, "Hello, Al. Jesus, you're growin' like a bean! I wouldn't of knowed you."

Al, his hand ready if Tom should want to shake it, grinned self-consciously. Tom stuck out his hand and Al's hand jerked out to meet it. And there was liking between these two. "They tell me you're a good hand with a truck," said Tom.

And Al, sensing that his brother would not like a boaster, said, "I don't know nothin' much about it."

Pa said, "Been smart-alecking aroun' the country. You look wore out. Well, you got to take a load of stuff into Sallisaw to sell."

Al looked at his brother Tom. "Care to ride in?" he said as casually as he could.

"No, I can't," said Tom. "I'll help aroun' here. We'll be— together on the road."

Al tried to control his question. "Did—did you bust out? Of jail?"

"No," said Tom. "I got paroled."

"Oh." And Al was a little disappointed.

Chapter Nine

I<small>N THE LITTLE HOUSES</small> the tenant people sifted their belongings and the belongings of their fathers and of their
grandfathers. Picked over their possessions for the journey to
the west. The men were ruthless because the past had been
spoiled, but the women knew how the past would cry to them
in the coming days. The men went into the barns and the
sheds.

That plow, that harrow, remember in the war we planted
mustard? Remember a fella wanted us to put in that rubber
bush they call guayule? Get rich, he said. Bring out those
tools—get a few dollars for them. Eighteen dollars for that
plow, plus freight—Sears Roebuck.

Harness, carts, seeders, little bundles of hoes. Bring 'em
out. Pile 'em up. Load 'em in the wagon. Take 'em to town.
Sell 'em for what you can get. Sell the team and the wagon,
too. No more use for anything.

Fifty cents isn't enough to get for a good plow. That seeder
cost thirty-eight dollars. Two dollars isn't enough. Can't haul
it all back— Well, take it, and a bitterness with it. Take the
well pump and the harness. Take halters, collars, hames, and
tugs. Take the little glass brow-band jewels, roses red under
glass. Got those for the bay gelding. 'Member how he lifted
his feet when he trotted?

Junk piled up in a yard.

Can't sell a hand plow any more. Fifty cents for the weight
of the metal. Disks and tractors, that's the stuff now.

Well, take it—all junk—and give me five dollars. You're not
buying only junk, you're buying junked lives. And more—
you'll see—you're buying bitterness. Buying a plow to plow
your own children under, buying the arms and spirits that
might have saved you. Five dollars, not four. I can't haul 'em
back— Well, take 'em for four. But I warn you, you're buying
what will plow your own children under. And you won't see.
You can't see. Take 'em for four. Now, what'll you give for
the team and wagon? Those fine bays, matched they are,
matched in color, matched the way they walk, stride to stride.

In the stiff pull—straining hams and buttocks, split-second timed together. And in the morning, the light on them, bay light. They look over the fence sniffing for us, and the stiff ears swivel to hear us, and the black forelocks! I've got a girl. She likes to braid the manes and forelocks, puts little red bows on them. Likes to do it. Not any more. I could tell you a funny story about that girl and that off bay. Would make you laugh. Off horse is eight, near is ten, but might of been twin colts the way they work together. See? The teeth. Sound all over. Deep lungs. Feet fair and clean. How much? Ten dollars? For both? And the wagon— Oh, Jesus Christ! I'd shoot 'em for dog feed first. Oh, take 'em! Take 'em quick, mister. You're buying a little girl plaiting the forelocks, taking off her hair ribbon to make bows, standing back, head cocked, rubbing the soft noses with her cheek. You're buying years of work, toil in the sun; you're buying a sorrow that can't talk. But watch it, mister. There's a premium goes with this pile of junk and the bay horses—so beautiful—a packet of bitterness to grow in your house and to flower, some day. We could have saved you, but you cut us down, and soon you will be cut down and there'll be none of us to save you.

And the tenant men came walking back, hands in their pockets, hats pulled down. Some bought a pint and drank it fast to make the impact hard and stunning. But they didn't laugh and they didn't dance. They didn't sing or pick the guitars. They walked back to the farms, hands in pockets and heads down, shoes kicking the red dust up.

Maybe we can start again, in the new rich land—in California, where the fruit grows. We'll start over.

But you can't start. Only a baby can start. You and me— why, we're all that's been. The anger of a moment, the thousand pictures, that's us. This land, this red land, is us; and the flood years and the dust years and the drought years are us. We can't start again. The bitterness we sold to the junk man— he got it all right, but we have it still. And when the owner men told us to go, that's us; and when the tractor hit the house, that's us until we're dead. To California or any place— every one a drum major leading a parade of hurts, marching with our bitterness. And some day—the armies of bitterness will all be going the same way. And they'll all walk together, and there'll be a dead terror from it.

The tenant men scuffed home to the farms through the red dust.

When everything that could be sold was sold, stoves and bedsteads, chairs and tables, little corner cupboards, tubs and tanks, still there were piles of possessions; and the women sat among them, turning them over and looking off beyond and back, pictures, square glasses, and here's a vase.

Now you know well what we can take and what we can't take. We'll be camping out—a few pots to cook and wash in, and mattresses and comforts, lantern and buckets, and a piece of canvas. Use that for a tent. This kerosene can. Know what that is? That's the stove. And clothes—take all the clothes. And—the rifle? Wouldn't go out naked of a rifle. When shoes and clothes and food, when even hope is gone, we'll have the rifle. When grampa came—did I tell you?—he had pepper and salt and a rifle. Nothing else. That goes. And a bottle for water. That just about fills us. Right up the sides of the trailer, and the kids can set in the trailer, and granma on a mattress. Tools, a shovel and saw and wrench and pliers. An ax, too. We had that ax forty years. Look how she's wore down. And ropes, of course. The rest? Leave it—or burn it up.

And the children came.

If Mary takes that doll, that dirty rag doll, I got to take my Injun bow. I got to. An' this roun' stick—big as me. I might need this stick. I had this stick so long—a month, or maybe a year. I got to take it. And what's it like in California?

The women sat among the doomed things, turning them over and looking past them and back. This book. My father had it. He liked a book. *Pilgrim's Progress.* Used to read it. Got his name in it. And his pipe—still smells rank. And this picture—an angel. I looked at that before the fust three come—didn't seem to do much good. Think we could get this china dog in? Aunt Sadie brought it from the St. Louis Fair. See? Wrote right on it. No, I guess not. Here's a letter my brother wrote the day before he died. Here's an old-time hat. These feathers—never got to use them. No, there isn't room.

How can we live without our lives? How will we know it's us without our past? No. Leave it. Burn it.

They sat and looked at it and burned it into their memories. How'll it be not to know what land's outside the door? How if you wake up in the night and know—and *know* the willow tree's not there? Can you live without the willow tree? Well, no, you can't. The willow tree is you. The pain on that mattress there—that dreadful pain—that's you.

And the children—if Sam takes his Injun bow an' his long roun' stick, I get to take two things. I choose the fluffy pilla. That's mine.

Suddenly they were nervous. Got to get out quick now. Can't wait. We can't wait. And they piled up the goods in the yards and set fire to them. They stood and watched them burning, and then frantically they loaded up the cars and drove away, drove in the dust. The dust hung in the air for a long time after the loaded cars had passed.

Chapter Ten

WHEN THE TRUCK had gone, loaded with implements, with heavy tools, with beds and springs, with every movable thing that might be sold, Tom hung around the place. He mooned into the barn shed, into the empty stalls, and he walked into the implement leanto and kicked the refuse that was left, turned a broken mower tooth with his foot. He visited places he remembered—the red bank where the swallows nested, the willow tree over the pig pen. Two shoats grunted and squirmed at him through the fence, black pigs, sunning and comfortable. And then his pilgrimage was over, and he went to sit on the doorstep where the shade was lately fallen. Behind him Ma moved about in the kitchen, washing children's clothes in a bucket; and her strong freckled arms dripped soapsuds from the elbows. She stopped her rubbing when he sat down. She looked at him a long time, and at the back of his head when he turned and stared out at the hot sunlight. And then she went back to her rubbing.

She said, "Tom, I hope things is all right in California."

He turned and looked at her. "What makes you think they ain't?" he asked.

"Well—nothing. Seems too nice, kinda. I seen the han'bills fellas pass out, an' how much work they is, an' high wages an' all; an' I seen in the paper how they want folks to come an' pick grapes an' oranges an' peaches. That'd be nice work, Tom, pickin' peaches. Even if they wouldn't let you eat none, you could maybe snitch a little ratty one sometimes. An' it'd be nice under the trees, workin' in the shade. I'm scared of stuff so nice. I ain't got faith. I'm scared somepin ain't so nice about it."

Tom said, "Don't roust your faith bird-high an' you won't do no crawlin' with the worms."

"I know that's right. That's Scripture, ain't it?"

"I guess so," said Tom. "I never could keep Scripture straight sence I read a book name' *The Winning of Barbara Worth.*"

Ma chuckled lightly and scrounged the clothes in and out

of the bucket. And she wrung out overalls and shirts, and the muscles of her forearms corded out. "Your Pa's pa, he quoted Scripture all the time. He got it all roiled up, too. It was the *Dr. Miles' Almanac* he got mixed up. Used to read ever' word in that almanac out loud—letters from folks that couldn't sleep or had lame backs. An' later he'd give them people for a lesson, an' he'd say, 'That's a par'ble from Scripture.' Your Pa an' Uncle John troubled 'im some about it when they'd laugh." She piled wrung clothes like cord wood on the table. "They say it's two thousan' miles where we're goin'. How far ya think that is, Tom? I seen it on a map, big mountains like on a post card, an' we're goin' right through 'em. How long ya s'pose it'll take to go that far, Tommy?"

"I dunno," he said. "Two weeks, maybe ten days if we got luck. Look, Ma, stop your worryin'. I'm a-gonna tell you somepin about bein' in the pen. You can't go thinkin' when you're gonna be out. You'd go nuts. You got to think about that day, an' then the nex' day, about the ball game Sat'dy. That's what you got to do. Ol' timers does that. A new young fella gets buttin' his head on the cell door. He's thinkin' how long it's gonna be. Whyn't you do that? Jus' take ever' day."

"That's a good way," she said, and she filled up her bucket with hot water from the stove, and she put in dirty clothes and began punching them down into the soapy water. "Yes, that's a good way. But I like to think how nice it's gonna be, maybe, in California. Never cold. An' fruit ever'place, an' people just bein' in the nicest places, little white houses in among the orange trees. I wonder—that is, if we all get jobs an' all work—maybe we can get one of them little white houses. An' the little fellas go out an' pick oranges right off the tree. They ain't gonna be able to stand it, they'll get to yellin' so."

Tom watched her working, and his eyes smiled. "It done you good jus' thinkin' about it. I knowed a fella from California. He didn't talk like us. You'd of knowed he come from some far-off place jus' the way he talked. But he says they's too many folks lookin' for work right there now. An' he says the folks that pick the fruit live in dirty ol' camps an' don't hardly get enough to eat. He says wages is low an' hard to get any."

A shadow crossed her face. "Oh, that ain't so," she said.

"Your father got a han'bill on yella paper, tellin' how they need folks to work. They wouldn' go to that trouble if they wasn't plenty work. Costs 'em good money to get them han'bills out. What'd they want ta lie for, an' costin' 'em money to lie?"

Tom shook his head. "I don' know, Ma. It's kinda hard to think why they done it. Maybe—" He looked out at the hot sun, shining on the red earth.

"Maybe what?"

"Maybe it's nice, like you says. Where'd Grampa go? Where'd the preacher go?"

Ma was going out of the house, her arms loaded high with the clothes. Tom moved aside to let her pass. "Preacher says he's gonna walk aroun'. Grampa's asleep here in the house. He comes in here in the day an' lays down sometimes." She walked to the line and began to drape pale blue jeans and blue shirts and long gray underwear over the wire.

Behind him Tom heard a shuffling step, and he turned to look in. Grampa was emerging from the bedroom, and as in the morning, he fumbled with the buttons of his fly. "I heerd talkin'," he said. "Sons-a-bitches won't let a ol' fella sleep. When you bastards get dry behin' the ears, you'll maybe learn to let a ol' fella sleep." His furious fingers managed to flip open the only two buttons on his fly that had been buttoned. And his hand forgot what it had been trying to do. His hand reached in and contentedly scratched under the testicles. Ma came in with wet hands, and her palms puckered and bloated from hot water and soap.

"Thought you was sleepin'. Here, let me button you up." And though he struggled, she held him and buttoned his underwear and his shirt and his fly. "You go aroun' a sight," she said, and let him go.

And he spluttered angrily, "Fella's come to a nice—to a nice—when somebody buttons 'em. I want ta be let be to button my own pants."

Ma said playfully, "They don't let people run aroun' with their clothes unbutton' in California."

"They don't, hey! Well, I'll show 'em. They think they're gonna show me how to act out there? Why, I'll go aroun' a-hangin' out if I wanta!"

Ma said, "Seems like his language gets worse ever' year. Showin' off, I guess."

The old man thrust out his bristly chin, and he regarded Ma with his shrewd, mean, merry eyes. "Well, sir," he said, "we'll be a-startin' 'fore long now. An', by God, they's grapes out there, just a-hangin' over inta the road. Know what I'm a-gonna do? I'm gonna pick me a wash tub full a grapes, an' I'm gonna set in 'em, an' scrooge aroun', an' let the juice run down my pants."

Tom laughed. "By God, if he lives to be two hundred you never will get Grampa house broke," he said. "You're all set on goin', ain't you, Grampa?"

The old man pulled out a box and sat down heavily on it. "Yes, sir," he said. "An' goddamn near time, too. My brother went on out there forty years ago. Never did hear nothin' about him. Sneaky son-of-a-bitch, he was. Nobody loved him. Run off with a single-action Colt of mine. If I ever run across him or his kids, if he got any out in California, I'll ask 'em for that Colt. But if I know 'im, an' he got any kids, he cuckoo'd 'em, an' somebody else is a-raisin' 'em. I sure will be glad to get out there. Got a feelin' it'll make a new fella outa me. Go right to work in the fruit."

Ma nodded. "He means it, too," she said. "Worked right up to three months ago, when he throwed his hip out the last time."

"Damn right," said Grampa.

Tom looked outward from his seat on the doorstep. "Here comes that preacher, walkin' aroun' from the back side a the barn."

Ma said, "Curiousest grace I ever heerd, that he give this mornin'. Wasn't hardly no grace at all. Jus' talkin', but the sound of it was like a grace."

"He's a funny fella," said Tom. "Talks funny all the time. Seems like he's talkin' to hisself, though. He ain't tryin' to put nothin' over."

"Watch the look in his eye," said Ma. "He looks baptized. Got that look they call lookin' through. He sure looks baptized. An' a-walkin' with his head down, a-starin' at nothin' on the groun'. There *is* a man that's baptized." And she was silent, for Casy had drawn near the door.

"You gonna get sun-shook, walkin' around like that," said Tom.

Casy said, "Well, yeah—maybe." He appealed to them all suddenly, to Ma and Grampa and Tom. "I got to get goin' west. I got to go. I wonder if I kin go along with you folks." And then he stood, embarrassed by his own speech.

Ma looked to Tom to speak, because he was a man, but Tom did not speak. She let him have the chance that was his right, and then she said, "Why, we'd be proud to have you. 'Course I can't say right now; Pa says all the men'll talk tonight and figger when we gonna start. I guess maybe we better not say till all the men come. John an' Pa an' Noah an' Tom an' Grampa an' Al an' Connie, they're gonna figger soon's they get back. But if they's room I'm pretty sure we'll be proud to have ya."

The preacher sighed. "I'll go anyways," he said. "Somepin's happening. I went up an' I looked, an' the houses is all empty, an' the lan' is empty, an' this whole country is empty. I can't stay here no more. I got to go where the folks is goin'. I'll work in the fiel's, an' maybe I'll be happy."

"An' you ain't gonna preach?" Tom asked.

"I ain't gonna preach."

"An' you ain't gonna baptize?" Ma asked.

"I ain't gonna baptize. I'm gonna work in the fiel's, in the green fiel's, an' I'm gonna be near to folks. I ain't gonna try to teach 'em nothin'. I'm gonna try to learn. Gonna learn why the folks walks in the grass, gonna hear 'em talk, gonna hear 'em sing. Gonna listen to kids eatin' mush. Gonna hear husban' an' wife a-poundin' the mattress in the night. Gonna eat with 'em an' learn." His eyes were wet and shining. "Gonna lay in the grass, open an' honest with anybody that'll have me. Gonna cuss an' swear an' hear the poetry of folks talkin'. All that's holy, all that's what I didn' understan'. All them things is the good things."

Ma said, "A-men."

The preacher sat humbly down on the chopping block beside the door. "I wonder what they is for a fella so lonely."

Tom coughed delicately. "For a fella that don't preach no more—" he began.

"Oh, I'm a talker!" said Casy. "No gettin' away from that.

But I ain't preachin'. Preachin' is tellin' folks stuff. I'm askin' 'em. That ain't preachin', is it?"

"I don' know," said Tom. "Preachin's a kinda tone a voice, an' preachin's a way a lookin' at things. Preachin's bein' good to folks when they wanna kill ya for it. Las' Christmus in McAlester, Salvation Army come an' done us good. Three solid hours a cornet music, an' we set there. They was bein' nice to us. But if one of us tried to walk out, we'd a-drawed solitary. That's preachin'. Doin' good to a fella that's down an' can't smack ya in the puss for it. No, you ain't no preacher. But don't you blow no cornets aroun' here."

Ma threw some sticks into the stove. "I'll get you a bit now, but it ain't much."

Grampa brought his box outside and sat on it and leaned against the wall, and Tom and Casy leaned back against the house wall. And the shadow of the afternoon moved out from the house.

In the late afternoon the truck came back, bumping and rattling through the dust, and there was a layer of dust in the bed, and the hood was covered with dust, and the headlights were obscured with a red film. The sun was setting when the truck came back, and the earth was bloody in its setting light. Al sat bent over the wheel, proud and serious and efficient, and Pa and Uncle John, as befitted the heads of the clan, had the honor seats beside the driver. Standing in the truck bed, holding onto the bars of the sides, rode the others, twelve-year-old Ruthie and ten-year-old Winfield, grime-faced and wild, their eyes tired but excited, their fingers and the edges of their mouths black and sticky from licorice whips, whined out of their father in town. Ruthie, dressed in a real dress of pink muslin that came below her knees, was a little serious in her young-ladiness. But Winfield was still a trifle of a snot-nose, a little of a brooder back of the barn, and an inveterate collector and smoker of snipes. And whereas Ruthie felt the might, the responsibility, and the dignity of her developing breasts, Winfield was kid-wild and calfish. Beside them, clinging lightly to the bars, stood Rose of Sharon, and she balanced, swaying on the balls of her feet, and took up the road shock in her knees and hams. For Rose of Sharon was pregnant and careful. Her hair, braided and wrapped around her head, made an ash-blond crown. Her round soft face, which had been voluptuous and inviting a few months ago, had already put on the barrier of pregnancy, the self-sufficient smile, the knowing perfection-look; and her plump body—full soft breasts and stomach, hard hips and buttocks that had swung so freely and provocatively as to invite slapping and stroking— her whole body had become demure and serious. Her whole thought and action were directed inward on the baby. She balanced on her toes now, for the baby's sake. And the world was pregnant to her; she thought only in terms of reproduction and of motherhood. Connie, her nineteen-year-old husband, who had married a plump, passionate hoyden, was still frightened and bewildered at the change in her; for there were no more cat fights in bed, biting and scratching with muffled giggles and final tears. There was a balanced, careful, wise creature who smiled shyly but very firmly at him. Connie was proud and fearful of Rose of Sharon. Whenever he could, he put a hand on her or stood close, so that his body touched her at hip and shoulder, and he felt that this kept a relation that might be departing. He was a sharp-faced, lean young man of a Texas strain, and his pale blue eyes were sometimes dangerous and sometimes kindly, and sometimes frightened. He was a good hard worker and would make a good husband. He drank enough, but not too much; fought when it was required of him; and never boasted. He sat quietly in a gathering and yet managed to be there and to be recognized.

Had he not been fifty years old, and so one of the natural rulers of the family, Uncle John would have preferred not to sit in the honor place beside the driver. He would have liked Rose of Sharon to sit there. This was impossible, because she was young and a woman. But Uncle John sat uneasily, his lonely haunted eyes were not at ease, and his thin strong body was not relaxed. Nearly all the time the barrier of loneliness cut Uncle John off from people and from appetites. He ate little, drank nothing, and was celibate. But underneath, his appetites swelled into pressures until they broke through. Then he would eat of some craved food until he was sick; or he would drink jake or whisky until he was a shaken paralytic with red wet eyes; or he would raven with lust for some whore in Sallisaw. It was told of him that once he went clear to Shawnee and hired three whores in one bed, and snorted and rutted on their unresponsive bodies for an hour. But when one of his appetites was sated, he was sad and ashamed and lonely again. He hid from people, and by gifts tried to make up to all people for himself. Then he crept into houses and left gum under pillows for children; then he cut wood and took no pay. Then he gave away any possession he might have: a saddle, a horse, a new pair of shoes. One could not talk to him then, for he ran away, or if confronted hid within himself and peeked out of frightened eyes. The death of his wife, followed by months of being alone, had marked him with guilt and shame and had left an unbreaking loneliness on him.

But there were things he could not escape. Being one of the heads of the family, he had to govern; and now he had to sit on the honor seat beside the driver.

The three men on the seat were glum as they drove toward home over the dusty road. Al, bending over the wheel, kept shifting eyes from the road to the instrument panel, watching the ammeter needle, which jerked suspiciously, watching the oil gauge and the heat indicator. And his mind was cataloguing weak points and suspicious things about the car. He listened to the whine, which might be the rear end, dry; and he listened to tappets lifting and falling. He kept his hand on the gear lever, feeling the turning gears through it. And he had let the clutch out against the brake to test for slipping clutch plates. He might be a musking goat sometimes, but this was his responsibility, this truck, its running, and its maintenance. If something went wrong it would be his fault, and while no one would say it, everyone, and Al most of all, would know it was his fault. And so he felt it, watched it, and listened to it. And his face was serious and responsible. And everyone respected him and his responsibility. Even Pa, who was the leader, would hold a wrench and take orders from Al.

They were all tired on the truck. Ruthie and Winfield were tired from seeing too much movement, too many faces, from fighting to get licorice whips; tired from the excitement of having Uncle John secretly slip gum into their pockets.

And the men in the seat were tired and angry and sad, for they had got eighteen dollars for every movable thing from the farm: the horses, the wagon, the implements, and all the furniture from the house. Eighteen dollars. They had assailed the buyer, argued; but they were routed when his interest seemed to flag and he had told them he didn't want the stuff at any price. Then they were beaten, believed him, and took two dollars less than he had first offered. And now they were weary and frightened because they had gone against a system they did not understand and it had beaten them. They knew the team and the wagon were worth much more. They knew the buyer man would get much more, but they didn't know how to do it. Merchandising was a secret to them.

Al, his eyes darting from road to panel board, said, "That fella, he ain't a local fella. Didn' talk like a local fella. Clothes was different, too."

And Pa explained, "When I was in the hardware store I talked to some men I know. They say there's fellas comin' in jus' to buy up the stuff us fellas got to sell when we get out. They say these new fellas is cleaning up. But there ain't nothin' we can do about it. Maybe Tommy should of went. Maybe he could of did better."

John said, "But the fella wasn't gonna take it at all. We couldn' haul it back."

"These men I know told about that," said Pa. "Said the buyer fellas always done that. Scairt folks that way. We jus' don' know how to go about stuff like that. Ma's gonna be disappointed. She'll be mad an' disappointed."

Al said, "When ya think we're gonna go, Pa?"

"I dunno. We'll talk her over tonight an' decide. I'm sure glad Tom's back. That makes me feel good. Tom's a good boy."

Al said, "Pa, some fellas was talkin' about Tom, an' they says he's parole'. An' they says that means he can't go outside the State, or if he goes, an' they catch him, they send 'im back for three years."

Pa looked startled. "They said that? Seem like fellas that knowed? Not jus' blowin' off?"

"I don' know," said Al. "They was just a-talkin' there, an' I didn' let on he's my brother. I jus' stood an' took it in."

Pa said, "Jesus Christ, I hope that ain't true! We need Tom. I'll ask 'im about that. We got trouble enough without they chase the hell out of us. I hope it ain't true. We got to talk that out in the open."

Uncle John said, "Tom, he'll know."

They fell silent while the truck battered along. The engine was noisy, full of little clashings, and the brake rods banged. There was a wooden creaking from the wheels, and a thin jet of steam escaped through a hole in the top of the radiator cap. The truck pulled a high whirling column of red dust behind it. They rumbled up the last little rise while the sun was still half-face above the horizon, and they bore down on the house as it disappeared. The brakes squealed when they stopped, and the sound printed in Al's head—no lining left.

Ruthie and Winfield climbed yelling over the side walls and dropped to the ground. They shouted, "Where is he? Where's Tom?" And then they saw him standing beside the door, and they stopped, embarrassed, and walked slowly toward him and looked shyly at him.

And when he said, "Hello, how you kids doin'?" they replied softly, "Hello! All right." And they stood apart and watched him secretly, the great brother who had killed a man and been in prison. They remembered how they had played prison in the chicken coop and fought for the right to be prisoner.

Connie Rivers lifted the high tail-gate out of the truck and got down and helped Rose of Sharon to the ground; and she accepted it nobly, smiling her wise, self-satisfied smile, mouth tipped at the corners a little fatuously.

Tom said, "Why, it's Rosasharn. I didn' know you was comin' with them."

"We was walkin'," she said. "The truck come by an' picked us up." And then she said, "This is Connie, my husband." And she was grand, saying it.

The two shook hands, sizing each other up, looking deeply into each other; and in a moment each was satisfied, and Tom said, "Well, I see you been busy."

She looked down. "You do not see, not yet."

"Ma tol' me. When's it gonna be?"

"Oh, not for a long time! Not till nex' winter."

Tom laughed. "Gonna get 'im bore in a orange ranch, huh? In one a them white houses with orange trees all aroun'."

Rose of Sharon felt her stomach with both her hands. "You do not see," she said, and she smiled her complacent smile and went into the house. The evening was hot, and the thrust of light still flowed up from the western horizon. And without any signal the family gathered by the truck, and the congress, the family government, went into session.

The film of evening light made the red earth lucent, so that its dimensions were deepened, so that a stone, a post, a building had greater depth and more solidity than in the daytime light; and these objects were curiously more individual—a post was more essentially a post, set off from the earth it stood in and the field of corn it stood out against. And plants were individuals, not the mass of crop; and the ragged willow tree was itself, standing free of all other willow trees. The earth contributed a light to the evening. The front of the gray, paintless house, facing the west, was luminous as the moon is. The gray dusty truck, in the yard before the door, stood out magically in this light, in the overdrawn perspective of a stereopticon.

The people too were changed in the evening, quieted. They seemed to be a part of an organization of the unconscious. They obeyed impulses which registered only faintly in their thinking minds. Their eyes were inward and quiet, and their eyes, too, were lucent in the evening, lucent in dusty faces.

The family met at the most important place, near the truck. The house was dead, and the fields were dead; but this truck was the active thing, the living principle. The ancient Hudson, with bent and scarred radiator screen, with grease in dusty globules at the worn edges of every moving part, with hub caps gone and caps of red dust in their places—this was the new hearth, the living center of the family; half passenger car and half truck, high-sided and clumsy.

Pa walked around the truck, looking at it, and then he squatted down in the dust and found a stick to draw with. One foot was flat to the ground, the other rested on the ball and slightly back, so that one knee was higher than the other. Left forearm rested on the lower, left, knee; the right elbow on the right knee, and the right fist cupped for the chin. Pa squatted there, looking at the truck, his chin in his cupped fist. And Uncle John moved toward him and squatted down beside him. Their eyes were brooding. Grampa came out of the house and saw the two squatting together, and he jerked over and sat on the running board of the truck, facing them. That was the nucleus. Tom and Connie and Noah strolled in and squatted, and the line was a half-circle with Grampa in the opening. And then Ma came out of the house, and Granma with her, and Rose of Sharon behind, walking daintily. They took their places behind the squatting men; they stood up and put their hands on their hips. And the children, Ruthie and Winfield, hopped from foot to foot beside the women; the children squidged their toes in the red dust, but they made no sound. Only the preacher was not there. He, out of delicacy, was sitting on the ground behind the house. He was a good preacher and knew his people.

The evening light grew softer, and for a while the family sat and stood silently. Then Pa, speaking to no one, but to the group, made his report. "Got skinned on the stuff we sold. The fella knowed we couldn't wait. Got eighteen dollars only."

Ma stirred restively, but she held her peace.

Noah, the oldest son, asked, "How much, all added up, we got?"

Pa drew figures in the dust and mumbled to himself for a moment. "Hunderd fifty-four," he said. "But Al here says we gonna need better tires. Says these here won't last."

This was Al's first participation in the conference. Always he had stood behind with the women before. And now he made his report solemnly. "She's old an' she's ornery," he said gravely. "I gave the whole thing a good goin'-over 'fore we bought her. Didn' listen to the fella talkin' what a hell of a bargain she was. Stuck my finger in the differential an' they wasn't no sawdust. Opened the gear box an' they wasn't no sawdust. Test' her clutch an' rolled her wheels for line. Went under her an' her frame ain't splayed none. She never been rolled. Seen they was a cracked cell in her battery an' made the fella put in a good one. The tires ain't worth a damn, but they're a good size. Easy to get. She'll ride like a bull calf, but she ain't shootin' no oil. Reason I says buy her is she was a pop'lar car. Wreckin' yards is full a Hudson Super-Sixes, an' you can buy parts cheap. Could a got a bigger, fancier car for the same money, but parts too hard to get, an' too dear. That's how I figgered her anyways." The last was his submission to the family. He stopped speaking and waited for their opinions.

Grampa was still the titular head, but he no longer ruled. His position was honorary and a matter of custom. But he did have the right of first comment, no matter how silly his old mind might be. And the squatting men and the standing women waited for him. "You're all right, Al," Grampa said. "I was a squirt jus' like you, a-fartin' aroun' like a dog-wolf. But when they was a job, I done it. You've growed up good." He finished in the tone of a benediction, and Al reddened a little with pleasure.

Pa said, "Sounds right-side-up to me. If it was horses we wouldn' have to put the blame on Al. But Al's the on'y automobile fella here."

Tom said, "I know some. Worked some in McAlester. Al's right. He done good." And now Al was rosy with the compliment. Tom went on, "I'd like to say—well, that preacher— he wants to go along." He was silent. His words lay in the group, and the group was silent. "He's a nice fella," Tom added. "We've knowed him a long time. Talks a little wild sometimes, but he talks sensible." And he relinquished the proposal to the family.

The light was going gradually. Ma left the group and went into the house, and the iron clang of the stove came from the house. In a moment she walked back to the brooding council.

Grampa said, "They was two ways a thinkin'. Some folks use' ta figger that a preacher was poison luck."

Tom said, "This fella says he ain't a preacher no more."

Grampa waved his hand back and forth. "Once a fella's a preacher, he's always a preacher. That's somepin you can't get shut of. They was some folks figgered it was a good respectable thing to have a preacher along. Ef somebody died, preacher buried 'em. Weddin' come due, or overdue, an' there's your preacher. Baby come, an' you got a christener right under the roof. Me, I always said they was preachers *an'* preachers. Got to pick 'em. I kinda like this fella. He ain't stiff."

Pa dug his stick into the dust and rolled it between his

fingers so that it bored a little hole. "They's more to this than is he lucky, or is he a nice fella," Pa said. "We got to figger close. It's a sad thing to figger close. Le's see, now. There's Grampa an' Granma—that's two. An' me an' John an' Ma—that's five. An' Noah an' Tommy an' Al—that's eight. Rosasharn an' Connie is ten, an' Ruthie an' Winfiel' is twelve. We got to take the dogs 'cause what'll we do else? Can't shoot a good dog, an' there ain't nobody to give 'em to. An' that's fourteen."

"Not countin' what chickens is left, an' two pigs," said Noah.

Pa said, "I aim to get those pigs salted down to eat on the way. We gonna need meat. Carry the salt kegs right with us. But I'm wonderin' if we can all ride, an' the preacher too. An' kin we feed a extra mouth?" Without turning his head he asked, "Kin we, Ma?"

Ma cleared her throat. "It ain't kin we? It's will we?" she said firmly. "As far as 'kin,' we can't do nothin', not go to California or nothin'; but as far as 'will,' why, we'll do what we will. An' as far as 'will'—it's a long time our folks been here and east before, an' I never heerd tell of no Joads or no Hazletts, neither, ever refusin' food an' shelter or a lift on the road to anybody that asked. They's been mean Joads, but never that mean."

Pa broke in, "But s'pose there just ain't room?" He had twisted his neck to look up at her, and he was ashamed. Her tone had made him ashamed. "S'pose we jus' can't all get in the truck?"

"There ain't room now," she said. "There ain't room for more'n six, an' twelve is goin' sure. One more ain't gonna hurt; an' a man, strong an' healthy, ain't never no burden. An' any time when we got two pigs an' over a hunderd dollars, an' we wonderin' if we kin feed a fella—" She stopped, and Pa turned back, and his spirit was raw from the whipping.

Granma said, "A preacher is a nice thing to be with us. He give a nice grace this morning."

Pa looked at the face of each one for dissent, and then he said, "Want to call 'im over, Tommy? If he's goin', he ought ta be here."

Tom got up from his hams and went toward the house, calling, "Casy—oh, Casy!"

A muffled voice replied from behind the house. Tom walked to the corner and saw the preacher sitting back against the wall, looking at the flashing evening star in the light sky. "Calling me?" Casy asked.

"Yeah. We think long as you're goin' with us, you ought to be over with us, helpin' to figger things out."

Casy got to his feet. He knew the government of families, and he knew he had been taken into the family. Indeed his position was eminent, for Uncle John moved sideways, leaving space between Pa and himself for the preacher. Casy squatted down like the others, facing Grampa enthroned on the running board.

Ma went to the house again. There was a screech of a lantern hood and the yellow light flashed up in the dark kitchen. When she lifted the lid of the big pot, the smell of boiling side-meat and beet greens came out the door. They waited for her to come back across the darkening yard, for Ma was powerful in the group.

Pa said, "We got to figger when to start. Sooner the better. What we got to do 'fore we go is get them pigs slaughtered an' in salt, an' pack our stuff an' go. Quicker the better, now."

Noah agreed, "If we pitch in, we kin get ready tomorrow, an' we kin go bright the nex' day."

Uncle John objected, "Can't chill no meat in the heat a the day. Wrong time a year for slaughterin'. Meat'll be sof' if it don' chill."

"Well, le's do her tonight. She'll chill tonight some. Much as she's gonna. After we eat, le's get her done. Got salt?"

Ma said, "Yes. Got plenty salt. Got two nice kegs, too."

"Well, le's get her done, then," said Tom.

Grampa began to scrabble about, trying to get a purchase to arise. "Gettin' dark," he said. "I'm gettin' hungry. Come time we get to California I'll have a big bunch a grapes in my han' all the time, a-nibblin' off it all the time, by God!" He got up, and the men arose.

Ruthie and Winfield hopped excitedly about in the dust, like crazy things. Ruthie whispered hoarsely to Winfield,

"Killin' pigs *and* goin' to California. Killin' pigs *and* goin'—all the same time."

And Winfield was reduced to madness. He stuck his finger against his throat, made a horrible face, and wobbled about, weakly shrilling, "I'm a ol' pig. Look! I'm a ol' pig. Look at the blood, Ruthie!" And he staggered and sank to the ground, and waved arms and legs weakly.

But Ruthie was older, and she knew the tremendousness of the time. "*And* goin' to California," she said again. And she knew this was the great time in her life so far.

The adults moved toward the lighted kitchen through the deep dusk, and Ma served them greens and side-meat in tin plates. But before Ma ate, she put the big round wash tub on the stove and started the fire to roaring. She carried buckets of water until the tub was full, and then around the tub she clustered the buckets, full of water. The kitchen became a swamp of heat, and the family ate hurriedly, and went out to sit on the doorstep until the water should get hot. They sat looking out at the dark, at the square of light the kitchen lantern threw on the ground outside the door, with a hunched shadow of Grampa in the middle of it. Noah picked his teeth thoroughly with a broom straw. Ma and Rose of Sharon washed up the dishes and piled them on the table.

And then, all of a sudden, the family began to function. Pa got up and lighted another lantern. Noah, from a box in the kitchen, brought out the bow-bladed butchering knife and whetted it on a worn little carborundum stone. And he laid the scraper on the chopping block, and the knife beside it. Pa brought two sturdy sticks, each three feet long, and pointed the ends with the ax, and he tied strong ropes, double half-hitched, to the middle of the sticks.

He grumbled, "Shouldn't of sold those singletrees—all of 'em."

The water in the pots steamed and rolled.

Noah asked, "Gonna take the water down there or bring the pigs up here?"

"Pigs up here," said Pa. "You can't spill a pig and scald yourself like you can hot water. Water about ready?"

"Jus' about," said Ma.

"Aw right. Noah, you an' Tom an' Al come along. I'll carry the light. We'll slaughter down there an' bring 'em up here."

Noah took his knife, and Al the ax, and the four men moved down on the sty, their legs flickering in the lantern light. Ruthie and Winfield skittered along, hopping over the ground. At the sty Pa leaned over the fence, holding the lantern. The sleepy young pigs struggled to their feet, grunting suspiciously. Uncle John and the preacher walked down to help.

"All right," said Pa. "Stick 'em, an' we'll run 'em up and bleed an' scald at the house." Noah and Tom stepped over the fence. They slaughtered quickly and efficiently. Tom struck twice with the blunt head of the ax; and Noah, leaning over the felled pigs, found the great artery with his curving knife and released the pulsing streams of blood. Then over the fence with the squealing pigs. The preacher and Uncle John dragged one by the hind legs, and Tom and Noah the other. Pa walked along with the lantern, and the black blood made two trails in the dust.

At the house, Noah slipped his knife between tendon and bone of the hind legs; the pointed sticks held the legs apart, and the carcasses were hung from the two-by-four rafters that stuck out from the house. Then the men carried the boiling water and poured it over the black bodies. Noah slit the bodies from end to end and dropped the entrails out on the ground. Pa sharpened two more sticks to hold the bodies open to the air, while Tom with the scrubber and Ma with a dull knife scraped the skins to take out the bristles. Al brought a bucket and shoveled the entrails into it, and dumped them on the ground away from the house, and two cats followed him, mewing loudly, and the dogs followed him, growling lightly at the cats.

Pa sat on the doorstep and looked at the pigs hanging in the lantern light. The scraping was done now, and only a few drops of blood continued to fall from the carcasses into the black pool on the ground. Pa got up and went to the pigs and felt them with his hand, and then he sat down again. Granma and Grampa went toward the barn to sleep, and Grampa carried a candle lantern in his hand. The rest of the family sat quietly about the doorstep, Connie and Al and Tom on the ground, leaning their backs against the house wall, Uncle John on a box, Pa in the doorway. Only Ma and Rose of Sharon continued to move about. Ruthie and Winfield were sleepy now, but fighting it off. They quarreled sleepily out in the darkness. Noah and the preacher squatted side by side, facing the house. Pa scratched himself nervously, and took off his hat and ran his fingers through his hair. "Tomorra we'll get that pork salted early in the morning, an' then we'll get the truck loaded, all but the beds, an' nex' morning off we'll go." No one answered him. "Hardly is a day's work in all that," he said uneasily.

Tom broke in, "We'll be moonin' aroun' all day, lookin' for somepin to do." The group stirred uneasily. "We could get ready by daylight an' go," Tom suggested. Pa rubbed his knee with his hand. And the restiveness spread to all of them.

Noah said, "Prob'ly wouldn' hurt that meat to git her right down in salt. Cut her up, she'd cool quicker anyways."

It was Uncle John who broke over the edge, his pressures too great. "What we hangin' aroun' for? I want to get shut of this. Now we're goin', why don't we go?"

And the revulsion spread to the rest. "Whyn't we go? Get sleep on the way." And a sense of hurry crept into them.

Pa said, "They say it's two thousan' miles. That's a hell of a long ways. We oughta go. Noah, you an' me can get that meat cut up an' we can put all the stuff in the truck."

Ma put her head out of the door. "How about if we forgit somepin, not seein' it in the dark?"

"We could look 'round after daylight," said Noah. They sat still then, thinking about it. But in a moment Noah got up and began to sharpen the bow-bladed knife on his little worn stone. "Ma," he said, "git that table cleared." And he stepped to a pig, cut a line down one side of the backbone and began peeling the meat forward, off the ribs.

Pa stood up excitedly. "We got to get the stuff together," he said. "Come on, you fellas."

Now that they were committed to going, the hurry infected all of them. Noah carried the slabs of meat into the kitchen and cut it into small salting blocks, and Ma patted the coarse salt in, laid it piece by piece in the kegs, careful that no two pieces touched each other. She laid the slabs like bricks, and pounded salt in the spaces. And Noah cut up the side-meat and he cut up the legs. Ma kept her fire going, and as Noah cleaned the ribs and the spines and leg bones of all the meat he could, she put them in the oven to roast for gnawing purposes.

In the yard and in the barn the circles of lantern light moved about, and the men brought together all the things to be taken, and piled them by the truck. Rose of Sharon brought out all the clothes the family possessed: the overalls, the thick-soled shoes, the rubber boots, the worn best suits, the sweaters and sheepskin coats. And she packed these tightly into a wooden box and got into the box and tramped them down. And then she brought out the print dresses and shawls, the black cotton stockings and the children's clothes—small overalls and cheap print dresses—and she put these in the box and tramped them down.

Tom went to the tool shed and brought what tools were left to go, a hand saw and a set of wrenches, a hammer and a box of assorted nails, a pair of pliers and a flat file and a set of rat-tail files.

And Rose of Sharon brought out the big piece of tarpaulin and spread it on the ground behind the truck. She struggled through the door with the mattresses, three double ones and a single. She piled them on the tarpaulin and brought armloads of folded ragged blankets and piled them up.

Ma and Noah worked busily at the carcasses, and the smell of roasting pork bones came from the stove. The children had fallen by the way in the late night. Winfield lay curled up in the dust outside the door; and Ruthie, sitting on a box in the kitchen where she had gone to watch the butchering, had dropped her head back against the wall. She breathed easily in her sleep, and her lips were parted over her teeth.

Tom finished with the tools and came into the kitchen with his lantern, and the preacher followed him. "God in a buckboard," Tom said, "smell that meat! An' listen to her crackle."

Ma laid the bricks of meat in a keg and poured salt around and over them and covered the layer with salt and patted it down. She looked up at Tom and smiled a little at him, but her eyes were serious and tired. "Be nice to have pork bones for breakfas'," she said.

The preacher stepped beside her. "Leave me salt down this meat," he said. "I can do it. There's other stuff for you to do."

She stopped her work then and inspected him oddly, as though he suggested a curious thing. And her hands were crusted with salt, pink with fluid from the fresh pork. "It's women's work," she said finally.

"It's all work," the preacher replied. "They's too much of it to split it up to men's or women's work. You got stuff to do. Leave me salt the meat."

Still for a moment she stared at him, and then she poured water from a bucket into the tin wash basin and she washed her hands. The preacher took up the blocks of pork and patted on the salt while she watched him. And he laid them in the kegs as she had. Only when he had finished a layer and covered it carefully and patted down the salt was she satisfied. She dried her bleached and bloated hands.

Tom said, "Ma, what stuff we gonna take from here?"

She looked quickly about the kitchen. "The bucket," she said. "All the stuff to eat with: plates an' the cups, the spoons an' knives an' forks. Put all them in that drawer, an' take the drawer. The big fry pan an' the big stew kettle, the coffee pot. When it gets cool, take the rack outa the oven. That's good over a fire. I'd like to take the wash tub, but I guess there ain't room. I'll wash clothes in the bucket. Don't do no good to take little stuff. You can cook little stuff in a big kettle, but you can't cook big stuff in a little pot. Take the bread pans, all of 'em. They fit down inside each other." She stood and looked about the kitchen. "You jus' take that stuff I tol' you, Tom. I'll fix up the rest, the big can a pepper an' the salt an' the nutmeg an' the grater. I'll take all that stuff jus' at the last." She picked up a lantern and walked heavily into the bedroom, and her bare feet made no sound on the floor.

The preacher said, "She looks tar'd."

"Women's always tar'd," said Tom. "That's just the way women is, 'cept at meetin' once an' again."

"Yeah, but tar'der'n that. Real tar'd, like she's sick-tar'd."

Ma was just through the door, and she heard his words. Slowly her relaxed face tightened, and the lines disappeared from the taut muscular face. Her eyes sharpened and her shoulders straightened. She glanced about the stripped room. Nothing was left in it except trash. The mattresses which had been on the floor were gone. The bureaus were sold. On the floor lay a broken comb, an empty talcum powder can, and a few dust mice. Ma set her lantern on the floor. She reached behind one of the boxes that had served as chairs and brought out a stationery box, old and soiled and cracked at the corners. She sat down and opened the box. Inside were letters, clippings, photographs, a pair of earrings, a little gold signet ring, and a watch chain braided of hair and tipped with gold swivels. She touched the letters with her fingers, touched them lightly, and she smoothed a newspaper clipping on which there was an account of Tom's trial. For a long time she held the box, looking over it, and her fingers disturbed the letters and then lined them up again. She bit her lower lip, thinking, remembering. And at last she made up her mind. She picked out the ring, the watch charm, the earrings, dug under the pile and found one gold cuff link. She took a letter from an envelope and dropped the trinkets in the envelope. She folded the envelope over and put it in her dress pocket. Then gently and tenderly she closed the box and smoothed the top carefully with her fingers. Her lips parted. And then she stood up, took her lantern, and went back into the kitchen. She lifted the stove lid and laid the box gently among the coals. Quickly the heat browned the paper. A flame licked up and over the box. She replaced the stove lid and instantly the fire sighed up and breathed over the box.

Out in the dark yard, working in the lantern light, Pa and Al loaded the truck. Tools on the bottom, but handy to reach in case of a breakdown. Boxes of clothes next, and kitchen utensils in a gunny sack; cutlery and dishes in their box. Then the gallon bucket tied on behind. They made the bottom of the load as even as possible, and filled the spaces between boxes with rolled blankets. Then over the top they laid the mattresses, filling the truck in level. And last they spread the big tarpaulin over the load and Al made holes in the edge, two feet apart, and inserted little ropes, and tied it down to the side-bars of the truck.

"Now, if it rains," he said, "we'll tie it to the bar above, an' the folks can get underneath, out of the wet. Up front we'll be dry enough."

And Pa applauded. "That's a good idear."

"That ain't all," Al said. "First chance I git I'm gonna fin' a long plank an' make a ridge pole, an' put the tarp over that. An' then it'll be covered in, an' the folks'll be outa the sun, too."

And Pa agreed, "That's a good idear. Whyn't you think a that before?"

"I ain't had time," said Al.

"Ain't had time? Why, Al, you had time to coyote all over the country. God knows where you been this las' two weeks."

"Stuff a fella got to do when he's leavin' the country," said Al. And then he lost some of his assurance. "Pa," he asked. "You glad to be goin', Pa?"

"Huh? Well—sure. Leastwise—yeah. We had hard times here. 'Course it'll be all different out there—plenty work, an' ever'thing nice an' green, an' little white houses an' oranges growin' aroun'."

"Is it all oranges ever'where?"

"Well, maybe not ever'where, but plenty places."

The first gray of daylight began in the sky. And the work was done—the kegs of pork ready, the chicken coop ready to go on top. Ma opened the oven and took out the pile of roasted bones, crisp and brown, with plenty of gnawing meat left. Ruthie half awakened, and slipped down from the box, and slept again. But the adults stood around the door, shivering a little and gnawing at the crisp pork.

"Guess we oughta wake up Granma an' Grampa," Tom said. "Gettin' along on toward day."

Ma said, "Kinda hate to, till the las' minute. They need the sleep. Ruthie an' Winfield ain't hardly got no real rest neither."

"Well, they kin all sleep on top a the load," said Pa. "It'll be nice an' comf'table there."

Suddenly the dogs started up from the dust and listened. And then, with a roar, went barking off into the darkness.

"Now what in hell is that?" Pa demanded. In a moment they heard a voice speaking reassuringly to the barking dogs and the barking lost its fierceness. Then footsteps, and a man approached. It was Muley Graves, his hat pulled low.

He came near timidly. "Morning, folks," he said.

"Why, Muley." Pa waved the ham bone he held. "Step in an' get some pork for yourself, Muley."

"Well, no," said Muley. "I ain't hungry, exactly."

"Oh, get it, Muley, get it. Here!" And Pa stepped into the house and brought out a hand of spareribs.

Muley took them. "I wasn't aiming to eat none a your stuff," he said. "I was jus' walkin' aroun', an' I thought how you'd be goin', an' I'd maybe say good-by."

"Goin' in a little while now," said Pa. "You'd a missed us if you'd come an hour later. All packed up—see?"

"All packed up." Muley looked at the loaded truck. "Sometimes I wisht I'd go an' fin' my folks."

Ma asked, "Did you hear from 'em out in California?"

"No," said Muley, "I ain't heard. But I ain't been to look in the post office. I oughta go in sometimes."

Pa said, "Al, go down, wake up Granma, Grampa. Tell 'em to come an' eat. We're goin' before long." And as Al sauntered toward the barn, "Muley, ya wanta squeeze in with us an' go? We'd try to make room for ya."

Muley took a bite of meat from the edge of a rib bone and chewed it. "Sometimes I think I might. But I know I won't," he said. "I know perfectly well the las' minute I'd run an' hide like a damn ol' graveyard ghos'."

Noah said, "You gonna die out in the fiel' some day, Muley."

"I know. I thought about that. Sometimes it seems pretty lonely, an' sometimes it seems all right, an' sometimes it seems good. It don't make no difference. But if ya come acrost my folks—that's really what I come to say—if ya come on any my folks in California, tell 'em I'm well. Tell 'em I'm doin' all right. Don't let on I'm livin' this way. Tell 'em I'll come to 'em soon's I git the money."

Ma asked, "An' will ya?"

"No," Muley said softly. "No, I won't. I can't go away. I got to stay now. Time back I might of went. But not now.

Fella gits to thinkin', an' he gits to knowin'. I ain't never goin'."

The light of the dawn was a little sharper now. It paled the lanterns a little. Al came back with Grampa struggling and limping by his side. "He wasn't sleepin'," Al said. "He was settin' out back of the barn. They's somepin wrong with 'im."

Grampa's eyes had dulled, and there was none of the old meanness in them. "Ain't nothin' the matter with me," he said. "I jus' ain't a-goin'."

"Not goin'?" Pa demanded. "What you mean you ain't a-goin'? Why, here we're all packed up, ready. We got to go. We got no place to stay."

"I ain't sayin' for you to stay," said Grampa. "You go right on along. Me—I'm stayin'. I give her a goin'-over all night mos'ly. This here's my country. I b'long here. An' I don't give a goddamn if they's oranges an' grapes crowdin' a fella outa bed even. I ain't a-goin'. This country ain't no good, but it's my country. No, you all go ahead. I'll jus' stay right here where I b'long."

They crowded near to him. Pa said, "You can't, Grampa. This here lan' is goin' under the tractors. Who'd cook for you? How'd you live? You can't stay here. Why, with nobody to take care of you, you'd starve."

Grampa cried, "Goddamn it, I'm a ol' man, but I can still take care a myself. How's Muley here get along? I can get along as good as him. I tell ya I ain't goin', an' ya can lump it. Take Granma with ya if ya want, but ya ain't takin' me, an' that's the end of it."

Pa said helplessly, "Now listen to me, Grampa. Jus' listen to me, jus' a minute."

"Ain't a-gonna listen. I tol' ya what I'm a-gonna do."

Tom touched his father on the shoulder. "Pa, come in the house. I wanta tell ya somepin." And as they moved toward the house, he called, "Ma—come here a minute, will ya?"

In the kitchen one lantern burned and the plate of pork bones was still piled high. Tom said, "Listen, I know Grampa got the right to say he ain't goin', but he can't stay. We know that."

"Sure he can't stay," said Pa.

"Well, look. If we got to catch him an' tie him down, we

li'ble to hurt him, an' he'll git so mad he'll hurt himself. Now we can't argue with him. If we could get him drunk it'd be all right. You got any whisky?"

"No," said Pa. "There ain't a drop a' whisky in the house. An' John got no whisky. He never has none when he ain't drinkin'."

Ma said, "Tom, I got a half a bottle soothin' sirup I got for Winfiel' when he had them earaches. Think that might work? Use ta put Winfiel' ta sleep when his earache was bad."

"Might," said Tom. "Get it, Ma. We'll give her a try anyways."

"I throwed it out on the trash pile," said Ma. She took the lantern and went out, and in a moment she came back with a bottle half full of black medicine.

Tom took it from her and tasted it. "Don' taste bad," he said. "Make up a cup a black coffee, good an' strong. Le's see—says one teaspoon. Better put in a lot, coupla tablespoons."

Ma opened the stove and put a kettle inside, down next to the coals, and she measured water and coffee into it. "Have to give it to 'im in a can," she said. "We got the cups all packed."

Tom and his father went back outside. "Fella got a right to say what he's gonna do. Say, who's eatin' spareribs?" said Grampa.

"We've et," said Tom. "Ma's fixin' you a cup a coffee an' some pork."

He went into the house, and he drank his coffee and ate his pork. The group outside in the growing dawn watched him quietly, through the door. They saw him yawn and sway, and they saw him put his arms on the table and rest his head on his arms and go to sleep.

"He was tar'd anyways," said Tom. "Leave him be."

Now they were ready. Granma, giddy and vague, saying, "What's all this? What you doin' now, so early?" But she was dressed and agreeable. And Ruthie and Winfield were awake, but quiet with the pressure of tiredness and still half dreaming. The light was sifting rapidly over the land. And the movement of the family stopped. They stood about, reluctant to make the first active move to go. They were afraid, now that the time had come—afraid in the same way Grampa was afraid. They saw the shed take shape against the light, and they saw the lanterns pale until they no longer cast their circles of yellow light. The stars went out, few by few, toward the west. And still the family stood about like dream walkers, their eyes focused panoramically, seeing no detail, but the whole dawn, the whole land, the whole texture of the country at once.

Only Muley Graves prowled about restlessly, looking through the bars into the truck, thumping the spare tires hung on the back of the truck. And at last Muley approached Tom. "You goin' over the State line?" he asked. "You gonna break your parole?"

And Tom shook himself free of the numbness. "Jesus Christ, it's near sunrise," he said loudly. "We got to get goin'." And the others came out of their numbness and moved toward the truck.

"Come on," Tom said. "Le's get Grampa on." Pa and Uncle John and Tom and Al went into the kitchen where Grampa slept, his forehead down on his arms, and a line of drying coffee on the table. They took him under the elbows and lifted him to his feet, and he grumbled and cursed thickly, like a drunken man. Out the door they boosted him, and when they came to the truck Tom and Al climbed up, and, leaning over, hooked their hands under his arms and lifted him gently up, and laid him on top of the load. Al untied the tarpaulin, and they rolled him under and put a box under the tarp beside him, so that the weight of the heavy canvas would not be upon him.

"I got to get that ridge pole fixed," Al said. "Do her tonight when we stop." Grampa grunted and fought weakly against awakening, and when he was finally settled he went deeply to sleep again.

Pa said, "Ma, you an' Granma set in with Al for a while. We'll change aroun' so it's easier, but you start out that way." They got into the cab, and then the rest swarmed up on top of the load, Connie and Rose of Sharon, Pa and Uncle John, Ruthie and Winfield, Tom and the preacher. Noah stood on the ground, looking up at the great load of them sitting on top of the truck.

Al walked around, looking underneath at the springs.

"Holy Jesus," he said, "them springs is flat as hell. Lucky I blocked under 'em."

Noah said, "How about the dogs, Pa?"

"I forgot the dogs," Pa said. He whistled shrilly, and one bouncing dog ran in, but only one. Noah caught him and threw him up on the top, where he sat rigid and shivering at the height. "Got to leave the other two," Pa called. "Muley, will you look after 'em some? See they don't starve?"

"Yeah," said Muley. "I'll like to have a couple dogs. Yeah! I'll take 'em."

"Take them chickens, too," Pa said.

Al got into the driver's seat. The starter whirred and caught, and whirred again. And then the loose roar of the six cylinders and a blue smoke behind. "So long, Muley," Al called.

And the family called, "Good-by, Muley."

Al slipped in the low gear and let in the clutch. The truck shuddered and strained across the yard. And the second gear took hold. They crawled up the little hill, and the red dust arose about them. "Chr-ist, what a load!" said Al. "We ain't makin' no time on this trip."

Ma tried to look back, but the body of the load cut off her view. She straightened her head and peered straight ahead along the dirt road. And a great weariness was in her eyes.

The people on top of the load did look back. They saw the house and the barn and a little smoke still rising from the chimney. They saw the windows reddening under the first color of the sun. They saw Muley standing forlornly in the dooryard looking after them. And then the hill cut them off. The cotton fields lined the road. And the truck crawled slowly through the dust toward the highway and the west.

Chapter Eleven

T HE HOUSES were left vacant on the land, and the land was vacant because of this. Only the tractor sheds of corrugated iron, silver and gleaming, were alive; and they were alive with metal and gasoline and oil, the disks of the plows shining. The tractors had lights shining, for there is no day and night for a tractor and the disks turn the earth in the darkness and they glitter in the daylight. And when a horse stops work and goes into the barn there is a life and a vitality left, there is a breathing and a warmth, and the feet shift on the straw, and the jaws champ on the hay, and the ears and the eyes are alive. There is a warmth of life in the barn, and the heat and smell of life. But when the motor of a tractor stops, it is as dead as the ore it came from. The heat goes out of it like the living heat that leaves a corpse. Then the corrugated iron doors are closed and the tractor man drives home to town, perhaps twenty miles away, and he need not come back for weeks or months, for the tractor is dead. And this is easy and efficient. So easy that the wonder goes out of work, so efficient that the wonder goes out of land and the working of it, and with the wonder the deep understanding and the relation. And in the tractor man there grows the contempt that comes only to a stranger who has little understanding and no relation. For nitrates are not the land, nor phosphates; and the length of fiber in the cotton is not the land. Carbon is not a man, nor salt nor water nor calcium. He is all these, but he is much more, much more; and the land is so much more than its analysis. That man who is more than his chemistry, walking on the earth, turning his plow point for a stone, dropping his handles to slide over an outcropping, kneeling in the earth to eat his lunch; that man who is more than his elements knows the land that is more than its analysis. But the machine man, driving a dead tractor on land he does not know and love, understands only chemistry; and he is contemptuous of the land and of himself. When the corrugated iron doors are shut, he goes home, and his home is not the land.

The doors of the empty houses swung open, and drifted back and forth in the wind. Bands of little boys came out from the towns to break the windows and to pick over the debris, looking for treasures. And here's a knife with half the blade gone. That's a good thing. And—smells like a rat died here. And look what Whitey wrote on the wall. He wrote that in the toilet in school, too, an' teacher made 'im wash it off.

When the folks first left, and the evening of the first day came, the hunting cats slouched in from the fields and mewed on the porch. And when no one came out, the cats crept through the open doors and walked mewing through the empty rooms. And then they went back to the fields and were wild cats from then on, hunting gophers and field mice, and sleeping in ditches in the daytime. When the night came, the bats, which had stopped at the doors for fear of light, swooped into the houses and sailed about through the empty rooms, and in a little while they stayed in dark room corners during the day, folded their wings high, and hung head-down among the rafters, and the smell of their droppings was in the empty houses.

And the mice moved in and stored weed seeds in corners, in boxes, in the backs of drawers in the kitchens. And weasels came in to hunt the mice, and the brown owls flew shrieking in and out again.

Now there came a little shower. The weeds sprang up in front of the doorstep, where they had not been allowed, and grass grew up through the porch boards. The houses were vacant, and a vacant house falls quickly apart. Splits started up the sheathing from the rusted nails. A dust settled on the floors, and only mouse and weasel and cat tracks disturbed it.

On a night the wind loosened a shingle and flipped it to the ground. The next wind pried into the hole where the shingle had been, lifted off three, and the next, a dozen. The midday sun burned through the hole and threw a glaring spot on the floor. The wild cats crept in from the fields at night, but they did not mew at the doorstep any more. They moved like shadows of a cloud across the moon, into the rooms to hunt the mice. And on windy nights the doors banged, and the ragged curtains fluttered in the broken windows.

Chapter Twelve

Highway 66 is the main migrant road. 66—the long concrete path across the country, waving gently up and down on the map, from Mississippi to Bakersfield—over the red lands and the gray lands, twisting up into the mountains, crossing the Divide and down into the bright and terrible desert, and across the desert to the mountains again, and into the rich California valleys.

66 is the path of a people in flight, refugees from dust and shrinking land, from the thunder of tractors and shrinking ownership, from the desert's slow northward invasion, from the twisting winds that howl up out of Texas, from the floods that bring no richness to the land and steal what little richness is there. From all of these the people are in flight, and they come into 66 from the tributary side roads, from the wagon tracks and the rutted country roads. 66 is the mother road, the road of flight.

Clarksville and Ozark and Van Buren and Fort Smith on 62, and there's an end of Arkansas. And all the roads into Oklahoma City, 66 down from Tulsa, 270 up from McAlester. 81 from Wichita Falls south, from Enid north. Edmond, McLoud, Purcell. 66 out of Oklahoma City; El Reno and Clinton, going west on 66. Hydro, Elk City, and Texola; and there's an end to Oklahoma. 66 across the Panhandle of Texas. Shamrock and McLean, Conway and Amarillo, the yellow. Wildorado and Vega and Boise, and there's an end of Texas. Tucumcari and Santa Rosa and into the New Mexican mountains to Albuquerque, where the road comes down from Santa Fe. Then down the gorged Rio Grande to Los Lunas and west again on 66 to Gallup, and there's the border of New Mexico.

And now the high mountains. Holbrook and Winslow and Flagstaff in the high mountains of Arizona. Then the great plateau rolling like a ground swell. Ashfork and Kingman and stone mountains again, where water must be hauled and sold. Then out of the broken sun-rotted mountains of Arizona to the Colorado, with green reeds on its banks, and that's the end of Arizona. There's California just over the river, and a pretty town to start it. Needles, on the river. But the river is a stranger in this place. Up from Needles and over a burned range, and there's the desert. And 66 goes on over the terrible desert, where the distance shimmers and the black center mountains hang unbearably in the distance. At last there's Barstow, and more desert until at last the mountains rise up again, the good mountains, and 66 winds through them. Then suddenly a pass, and below the beautiful valley, below orchards and vineyards and little houses, and in the distance a city. And, oh, my God, it's over.

The people in flight streamed out on 66, sometimes a single car, sometimes a little caravan. All day they rolled slowly along the road, and at night they stopped near water. In the day ancient leaky radiators sent up columns of steam, loose connecting rods hammered and pounded. And the men driving the trucks and the overloaded cars listened apprehensively. How far between towns? It is a terror between towns. If something breaks—well, if something breaks we camp right here while Jim walks to town and gets a part and walks back and—how much food we got?

Listen to the motor. Listen to the wheels. Listen with your ears and with your hands on the steering wheel; listen with the palm of your hand on the gear-shift lever; listen with your feet on the floor boards. Listen to the pounding old jalopy with all your senses; for a change of tone, a variation of rhythm may mean—a week here? That rattle—that's tappets. Don't hurt a bit. Tappets can rattle till Jesus comes again without no harm. But that thudding as the car moves along—can't hear that—just kind of feel it. Maybe oil isn't gettin' someplace. Maybe a bearing's startin' to go. Jesus, if it's a bearing, what'll we do? Money's goin' fast.

And why's the son-of-a-bitch heat up so hot today? This ain't no climb. Le's look. God Almighty, the fan belt's gone! Here, make a belt outa this little piece a rope. Le's see how long—there. I'll splice the ends. Now take her slow—slow, till we can get to a town. That rope belt won't last long.

'F we can on'y get to California where the oranges grow before this here ol' jug blows up. 'F we on'y can.

And the tires—two layers of fabric worn through. On'y a

four-ply tire. Might get a hunderd miles more outa her if we don't hit a rock an' blow her. Which'll we take—a hunderd, maybe, miles, or maybe spoil the tube? Which? A hunderd miles. Well, that's somepin you got to think about. We got tube patches. Maybe when she goes she'll only spring a leak. How about makin' a boot? Might get five hunderd more miles. Le's go on till she blows.

We got to get a tire, but, Jesus, they want a lot for a ol' tire. They look a fella over. They know he got to go on. They know he can't wait. And the price goes up.

Take it or leave it. I ain't in business for my health. I'm here a-sellin' tires. I ain't givin' 'em away. I can't help what happens to you. I got to think what happens to me.

How far's the nex' town?

I seen forty-two cars a you fellas go by yesterday. Where you all come from? Where all of you goin'?

Well, California's a big State.

It ain't that big. The whole United States ain't that big. It ain't that big. It ain't big enough. There ain't room enough for you an' me, for your kind an' my kind, for rich and poor together all in one country, for thieves and honest men. For hunger and fat. Whyn't you go back where you come from?

This is a free country. Fella can go where he wants.

That's what *you* think! Ever hear of the border patrol on the California line? Police from Los Angeles—stopped you bastards, turned you back. Says, if you can't buy no real estate we don't want you. Says, got a driver's license? Le's see it. Tore it up. Says you can't come in without no driver's license.

It's a free country.

Well, try to get some freedom to do. Fella says you're jus' as free as you got jack to pay for it.

In California they got high wages. I got a han'bill here tells about it.

Horseshit! I seen folks comin' back. Somebody's kiddin' you. You want that tire or don't ya?

Got to take it, but, Jesus, mister, it cuts into our money! We ain't got much left.

Well, I ain't no charity. Take her along.

Got to, I guess. Let's look her over. Open her up, look a'

the casing—you son-of-a-bitch, you said the casing was good. She's broke damn near through.

The hell she is. Well—by George! How come I didn' see that?

You did see it, you son-of-a-bitch. You wanta charge us four bucks for a busted casing. I'd like to take a sock at you.

Now keep your shirt on. I didn' see it, I tell you. Here— tell ya what I'll do. I'll give ya this one for three-fifty.

You'll take a flying fuck at the moon! We'll try to make the nex' town.

Think we can make it on that tire?

Got to. I'll go on the rim before I'd give that son-of-a-bitch a dime.

What do ya think a guy in business is? Like he says, he ain't in it for his health. That's what business is. What'd you think it was? Fella's got— See that sign 'longside the road there? Service Club. Luncheon Tuesday, Colmado Hotel? Welcome, brother. That's a Service Club. Fella had a story. Went to one of them meetings an' told the story to all them business men. Says, when I was a kid my ol' man give me a haltered heifer an' says take her down an' git her serviced. An' the fella says, I done it, an' ever' time since then when I hear a business man talkin' about service, I wonder who's gettin' screwed. Fella in business got to lie an' cheat, but he calls it somepin else. That's what's important. You go steal that tire an' you're a thief, but he tried to steal your four dollars for a busted tire. They call that sound business.

Danny in the back seat wants a cup a water.

Have to wait. Got no water here.

Listen—that the rear end?

Can't tell.

Sound telegraphs through the frame.

There goes a gasket. Got to go on. Listen to her whistle. Find a nice place to camp an' I'll jerk the head off. But, God Almighty, the food's gettin' low, the money's gettin' low. When we can't buy no more gas—what then?

Danny in the back seat wants a cup a water. Little fella's thirsty.

Listen to that gasket whistle.

Chee-rist! There she went. Blowed tube an' casing all to hell. Have to fix her. Save that casing to make boots; cut 'em out an' stick 'em inside a weak place.

Cars pulled up beside the road, engine heads off, tires mended. Cars limping along 66 like wounded things, panting and struggling. Too hot, loose connections, loose bearings, rattling bodies.

Danny wants a cup of water.

People in flight along 66. And the concrete road shone like a mirror under the sun, and in the distance the heat made it seem that there were pools of water in the road.

Danny wants a cup a water.

He'll have to wait, poor little fella. He's hot. Nex' service station. *Service* station, like the fella says.

Two hundred and fifty thousand people over the road. Fifty thousand old cars—wounded, steaming. Wrecks along the road, abandoned. Well, what happened to them? What happened to the folks in that car? Did they walk? Where are they? Where does the courage come from? Where does the terrible faith come from?

And here's a story you can hardly believe, but it's true, and it's funny and it's beautiful. There was a family of twelve and they were forced off the land. They had no car. They built a trailer out of junk and loaded it with their possessions. They pulled it to the side of 66 and waited. And pretty soon a sedan picked them up. Five of them rode in the sedan and seven on the trailer, and a dog on the trailer. They got to California in two jumps. The man who pulled them fed them. And that's true. But how can such courage be, and such faith in their own species? Very few things would teach such faith.

The people in flight from the terror behind—strange things happen to them, some bitterly cruel and some so beautiful that the faith is refired forever.

Chapter Thirteen

T HE ANCIENT overloaded Hudson creaked and grunted to the highway at Sallisaw and turned west, and the sun was blinding. But on the concrete road Al built up his speed because the flattened springs were not in danger any more. From Sallisaw to Gore is twenty-one miles and the Hudson was doing thirty-five miles an hour. From Gore to Warner thirteen miles; Warner to Checotah fourteen miles; Checotah a long jump to Henrietta—thirty-four miles, but a real town at the end of it. Henrietta to Castle nineteen miles, and the sun was overhead, and the red fields, heated by the high sun, vibrated the air.

Al, at the wheel, his face purposeful, his whole body listening to the car, his restless eye jumping from the road to the instrument panel. Al was one with his engine, every nerve listening for weaknesses, for the thumps or squeals, hums and chattering that indicate a change that may cause a breakdown. He had become the soul of the car.

Granma, beside him on the seat, half slept, and whimpered in her sleep, opened her eyes to peer ahead, and then dozed again. And Ma sat beside Granma, one elbow out the window, and the skin reddening under the fierce sun. Ma looked ahead too, but her eyes were flat and did not see the road or the fields, the gas stations, the little eating sheds. She did not glance at them as the Hudson went by.

Al shifted himself on the broken seat and changed his grip on the steering wheel. And he sighed, "Makes a racket, but I think she's awright. God knows what she'll do if we got to climb a hill with the load we got. Got any hills 'tween here an' California, Ma?"

Ma turned her head slowly and her eyes came to life. "Seems to me they's hills," she said. " 'Course I dunno. But seems to me I heard they's hills an' even mountains. Big ones."

Granma drew a long whining sigh in her sleep.

Al said, "We'll burn right up if we got climbin' to do. Have to throw out some a' this stuff. Maybe we shouldn' a brang that preacher."

"You'll be glad a that preacher 'fore we're through," said Ma. "That preacher'll help us." She looked ahead at the gleaming road again.

Al steered with one hand and put the other on the vibrating gear-shift lever. He had difficulty in speaking. His mouth formed the words silently before he said them aloud. "Ma—" She looked slowly around at him, her head swaying a little with the car's motion. "Ma, you scared a goin'? You scared a goin' to a new place?"

Her eyes grew thoughtful and soft. "A little," she said. "Only it ain't like scared so much. I'm jus' a settin' here waitin'. When somepin happens that I got to do somepin— I'll do it."

"Ain't you thinkin' what's it gonna be like when we get there? Ain't you scared it won't be nice like we thought?"

"No," she said quickly. "No, I ain't. You can't do that. I can't do that. It's too much—livin' too many lives. Up ahead they's a thousan' lives we might live, but when it comes, it'll on'y be one. If I go ahead on all of 'em, it's too much. You got to live ahead 'cause you're so young, but—it's jus' the road goin' by for me. An' it's jus' how soon they gonna wanta eat some more pork bones." Her face tightened. "That's all I can do. I can't do no more. All the rest'd get upset if I done any more'n that. They all depen' on me jus' thinkin' about that."

Granma yawned shrilly and opened her eyes. She looked wildly about. "I got to git out, praise Gawd," she said.

"First clump a brush," said Al. "They's one up ahead."

"Brush or no brush, I got to git out, I tell ya." And she began to whine, "I got to git out. I got to git out."

Al speeded up, and when he came to the low brush he pulled up short. Ma threw the door open and half pulled the struggling old lady out beside the road and into the bushes. And Ma held her so Granma would not fall when she squatted.

On top of the truck the others stirred to life. Their faces were shining with sunburn they could not escape. Tom and Casy and Noah and Uncle John let themselves wearily down.

Ruthie and Winfield swarmed down the side-boards and went off into the bushes. Connie helped Rose of Sharon gently down. Under the canvas, Grampa was awake, his head sticking out, but his eyes were drugged and watery and still senseless. He watched the others, but there was little recognition in his watching.

Tom called to him, "Want to come down, Grampa?"

The old eyes turned listlessly to him. "No," said Grampa. For a moment the fierceness came into his eyes. "I ain't a-goin', I tell you. Gonna stay like Muley." And then he lost interest again. Ma came back, helping Granma up the bank to the highway.

"Tom," she said. "Get that pan a bones, under the canvas in back. We got to eat somepin." Tom got the pan and passed it around, and the family stood by the roadside, gnawing the crisp particles from the pork bones.

"Sure lucky we brang these along," said Pa. "Git so stiff up there can't hardly move. Where's the water?"

"Ain't it up with you?" Ma asked. "I set out that gallon jug."

Pa climbed the sides and looked under the canvas. "It ain't here. We must a forgot it."

Thirst set in instantly. Winfield moaned, "I wanta drink. I wanta drink." The men licked their lips, suddenly conscious of their thirst. And a little panic started.

Al felt the fear growing. "We'll get water first service station we come to. We need some gas too." The family swarmed up the truck sides; Ma helped Granma in and got in beside her. Al started the motor and they moved on.

Castle to Paden twenty-five miles and the sun passed the zenith and started down. And the radiator cap began to jiggle up and down and steam started to whish out. Near Paden there was a shack beside the road and two gas pumps in front of it; and beside a fence, a water faucet and a hose. Al drove in and nosed the Hudson up to the hose. As they pulled in, a stout man, red of face and arms, got up from a chair behind the gas pumps and moved toward them. He wore brown corduroys, and suspenders and a polo shirt; and he had a cardboard sun helmet, painted silver, on his head. The sweat beaded on his nose and under his eyes and formed streams in the wrinkles of his neck. He strolled toward the truck, looking truculent and stern.

"You folks aim to buy anything? Gasoline or stuff?" he asked.

Al was out already, unscrewing the steaming radiator cap with the tips of his fingers, jerking his hand away to escape the spurt when the cap should come loose. He looked over at the fat man. "Need some gas, mister."

"Got any money?"

"Sure. Think we're beggin'?"

The truculence left the fat man's face. "Well, that's all right, folks. He'p yourself to water." And he hastened to explain. "Road is full a people, come in, use water, dirty up the toilet, an' then, by God, they'll steal stuff an' don't buy nothin'. Got no money to buy with. Come beggin' a gallon gas to move on."

Tom dropped angrily to the ground and moved toward the fat man. "We're payin' our way," he said fiercely. "You got no call to give us a goin'-over. We ain't asked you for nothin'."

"I ain't," the fat man said quickly. The sweat began to soak through his short-sleeved polo shirt. "Jus' he'p yourself to water, and go use the toilet if you want."

Winfield had got the hose. He drank from the end and then turned the stream over his head and face, and emerged dripping. "It ain't cool," he said.

"I don' know what the country's comin' to," the fat man continued. His complaint had shifted now and he was no longer talking to or about the Joads. "Fifty-sixty cars a folks go by ever' day, folks all movin' west with kids an' househol' stuff. Where they goin'? What they gonna do?"

"Doin' the same as us," said Tom. "Goin' someplace to live. Tryin' to get along. That's all."

"Well, I don' know what the country's comin' to. I jus' don' know. Here's me tryin' to get along, too. Think any them big new cars stops here? No, sir! They go on to them yella-painted company stations in town. They don't stop no place like this. Most folks stops here ain't got nothin'."

Al flipped the radiator cap and it jumped into the air with a head of steam behind it, and a hollow bubbling sound came out of the radiator. On top of the truck, the suffering hound dog crawled timidly to the edge of the load and looked over, whimpering, toward the water. Uncle John climbed up and lifted him down by the scruff of the neck. For a moment the dog staggered on stiff legs, and then he went to lap the mud under the faucet. In the highway the cars whizzed by, glistening in the heat, and the hot wind of their going fanned into the service-station yard. Al filled the radiator with the hose.

"It ain't that I'm tryin' to git trade outa rich folks," the fat man went on. "I'm jus' tryin' to git trade. Why, the folks that stops here begs gasoline an' they trades for gasoline. I could show you in my back room the stuff they'll trade for gas an' oil: beds an' baby buggies an' pots an' pans. One family traded a doll their kid had for a gallon. An' what'm I gonna do with the stuff, open a junk shop? Why, one fella wanted to gimme his shoes for a gallon. An' if I was that kinda fella I bet I could git—" He glanced at Ma and stopped.

Jim Casy had wet his head, and the drops still coursed down his high forehead, and his muscled neck was wet, and his shirt was wet. He moved over beside Tom. "It ain't the people's fault," he said. "How'd you like to sell the bed you sleep on for a tankful a gas?"

"I know it ain't their fault. Ever' person I talked to is on the move for a damn good reason. But what's the country comin' to? That's what I wanta know. What's it comin' to? Fella can't make a livin' no more. Folks can't make a livin' farmin'. I ask you, what's it comin' to? I can't figure her out. Ever'body I ask, they can't figure her out. Fella wants to trade his shoes so he can git a hunderd miles on. I can't figure her out." He took off his silver hat and wiped his forehead with his palm. And Tom took off his cap and wiped his forehead with it. He went to the hose and wet the cap through and squeezed it and put it on again. Ma worked a tin cup out through the side bars of the truck, and she took water to Granma and to Grampa on top of the load. She stood on the bars and handed the cup to Grampa, and he wet his lips, and then shook his head and refused more. The old eyes looked up at Ma in pain and bewilderment for a moment before the awareness receded again.

Al started the motor and backed the truck to the gas pump.

"Fill her up. She'll take about seven," said Al. "We'll give her six so she don't spill none."

The fat man put the hose in the tank. "No, sir," he said. "I jus' don't know what the country's comin' to. Relief an' all."

Casy said, "I been walkin' aroun' in the country. Ever'-body's askin' that. What we comin' to? Seems to me we don't never come to nothin'. Always on the way. Always goin' and goin'. Why don't folks think about that? They's movement now. People moving. We know why, an' we know how. Movin' 'cause they got to. That's why folks always move. Movin' 'cause they want somepin better'n what they got. An' that's the on'y way they'll ever git it. Wantin' it an' needin' it, they'll go out an' git it. It's bein' hurt that makes folks mad to fightin'. I been walkin' aroun' the country, an' hearin' folks talk like you."

The fat man pumped the gasoline and the needle turned on the pump dial, recording the amount. "Yeah, but what's it comin' to? That's what I want ta know."

Tom broke in irritably, "Well, you ain't never gonna know. Casy tries to tell ya an' you jest ast the same thing over. I seen fellas like you before. You ain't askin' nothin'; you're jus' singin' a kinda song. 'What we comin' to?' You don' wanta know. Country's movin' aroun', goin' places. They's folks dyin' all aroun'. Maybe you'll die pretty soon, but you won't know nothin'. I seen too many fellas like you. You don't want to know nothin'. Just sing yourself to sleep with a song— 'What we comin' to?'" He looked at the gas pump, rusted and old, and at the shack behind it, built of old lumber, the nail holes of its first use still showing through the paint that had been brave, the brave yellow paint that had tried to imitate the big company stations in town. But the paint couldn't cover the old nail holes and the old cracks in the lumber, and the paint could not be renewed. The imitation was a failure and the owner had known it was a failure. And inside the open door of the shack Tom saw the oil barrels, only two of them, and the candy counter with stale candies and licorice whips turning brown with age, and cigarettes. He saw the broken chair and the fly screen with a rusted hole in it. And the lit-tered yard that should have been graveled, and behind, the corn field drying and dying in the sun. Beside the house the little stock of used tires and retreaded tires. And he saw for the first time the fat man's cheap washed pants and his cheap polo shirt and his paper hat. He said, "I didn' mean to sound off at ya, mister. It's the heat. You ain't got nothin'. Pretty soon you'll be on the road yourse'f. And it ain't tractors'll put you there. It's them pretty yella stations in town. Folks is movin'," he said ashamedly. "An' you'll be movin', mister."

The fat man's hand slowed on the pump and stopped while Tom spoke. He looked worriedly at Tom. "How'd you know?" he asked helplessly. "How'd you know we was already talkin' about packin' up an' movin' west?"

Casy answered him. "It's ever'body," he said. "Here's me that used to give all my fight against the devil 'cause I figgered the devil was the enemy. But they's somepin worse'n the devil got hold a the country, an' it ain't gonna let go till it's chopped loose. Ever see one a them Gila monsters take hold, mister? Grabs hold, an' you chop him in two an' his head hangs on. Chop him at the neck an' his head hangs on. Got to take a screw-driver an' pry his head apart to git him loose. An' while he's layin' there, poison is drippin' an' drippin' into the hole he's made with his teeth." He stopped and looked sideways at Tom.

The fat man stared hopelessly straight ahead. His hand started turning the crank slowly. "I dunno what we're comin' to," he said softly.

Over by the water hose, Connie and Rose of Sharon stood together, talking secretly. Connie washed the tin cup and felt the water with his finger before he filled the cup again. Rose of Sharon watched the cars go by on the highway. Connie held out the cup to her. "This water ain't cool, but it's wet," he said.

She looked at him and smiled secretly. She was all secrets now she was pregnant, secrets and little silences that seemed to have meanings. She was pleased with herself, and she complained about things that didn't really matter. And she demanded services of Connie that were silly, and both of them knew they were silly. Connie was pleased with her too, and filled with wonder that she was pregnant. He liked to think he was in on the secrets she had. When she smiled slyly, he smiled slyly too, and they exchanged confidences in whispers. The world had drawn close around them, and they were in the center of it, or rather Rose of Sharon was in the center of it with Connie making a small orbit about her. Everything they said was a kind of secret.

She drew her eyes from the highway. "I ain't very thirsty," she said daintily. "But maybe I *ought* to drink."

And he nodded, for he knew well what she meant. She took the cup and rinsed her mouth and spat and then drank the cupful of tepid water. "Want another?" he asked.

"Jus' a half." And so he filled the cup just half, and gave it to her. A Lincoln Zephyr, silvery and low, whisked by. She turned to see where the others were and saw them clustered about the truck. Reassured, she said, "How'd you like to be goin' along in that?"

Connie sighed, "Maybe—after." They both knew what he meant. "An' if they's plenty work in California, we'll git our own car. But them"—he indicated the disappearing Zephyr— "them kind costs as much as a good size house. I ruther have the house."

"I like to have the house *an'* one a them," she said. "But 'course the house would be first because—" And they both knew what she meant. They were terribly excited about the pregnancy.

"You feel awright?" he asked.

"Tar'd. Jus' tar'd ridin' in the sun."

"We *got* to do that or we won't never get to California."

"I know," she said.

The dog wandered, sniffing, past the truck, trotted to the puddle under the hose again and lapped at the muddy water. And then he moved away, nose down and ears hanging. He sniffed his way among the dusty weeds beside the road, to the edge of the pavement. He raised his head and looked across, and then started over. Rose of Sharon screamed shrilly. A big swift car whisked near, tires squealed. The dog dodged help-lessly, and with a shriek, cut off in the middle, went under the wheels. The big car slowed for a moment and faces looked back, and then it gathered greater speed and disappeared. And the dog, a blot of blood and tangled, burst intestines, kicked slowly in the road.

Rose of Sharon's eyes were wide. "D'you think it'll hurt?" she begged. "Think it'll hurt?"

Connie put his arm around her. "Come set down," he said. "It wasn't nothin'."

"But I felt it hurt. I felt it kinda jar when I yelled."

"Come set down. It wasn't nothin'. It won't hurt." He led her to the side of the truck away from the dying dog and sat her down on the running board.

Tom and Uncle John walked out to the mess. The last quiver was going out of the crushed body. Tom took it by the legs and dragged it to the side of the road. Uncle John looked embarrassed, as though it were his fault. "I ought ta tied him up," he said.

Pa looked down at the dog for a moment and then he turned away. "Le's get outa here," he said. "I don' know how we was gonna feed 'im anyways. Just as well, maybe."

The fat man came from behind the truck. "I'm sorry, folks," he said. "A dog jus' don' last no time near a highway. I had three dogs run over in a year. Don't keep none, no more." And he said, "Don't you folks worry none about it. I'll take care of 'im. Bury 'im out in the corn field."

Ma walked over to Rose of Sharon, where she sat, still shuddering, on the running board. "You all right, Rosasharn?" she asked. "You feelin' poorly?"

"I—I seen that. Give me a start."

"I heard ya yip," said Ma. "Git yourself laced up, now."

"You suppose it might of hurt?"

"No," said Ma. "'F you go to greasin' yourself an' feelin' sorry, an' tuckin' yourself in a swalla's nest, it might. Rise up now, an' he'p me get Granma comf'table. Forget that baby for a minute. He'll take care a hisself."

"Where is Granma?" Rose of Sharon asked.

"I dunno. She's aroun' here somewheres. Maybe in the outhouse."

The girl went toward the toilet, and in a moment she came out, helping Granma along. "She went to sleep in there," said Rose of Sharon.

Granma grinned. "It's nice in there," she said. "They got a patent toilet in there an' the water comes down. I like it in there," she said contentedly. "Would of took a good nap if I wasn't woke up."

"It ain't a nice place to sleep," said Rose of Sharon, and she helped Granma into the car. Granma settled herself happily. "Maybe it ain't nice for purty, but it's nice for nice," she said.

Tom said, "Le's go. We got to make miles."

Pa whistled shrilly. "Now where'd them kids go?" He whistled again, putting his fingers in his mouth.

In a moment they broke from the corn field, Ruthie ahead and Winfield trailing her. "Eggs!" Ruthie cried. "I got sof' eggs." She rushed close, with Winfield close behind. "Look!" A dozen soft, grayish-white eggs were in her grubby hand. And as she held up her hand, her eyes fell upon the dead dog beside the road. "Oh!" she said. Ruthie and Winfield walked slowly toward the dog. They inspected him.

Pa called to them, "Come on, you, 'less you want to git left."

They turned solemnly and walked to the truck. Ruthie looked once more at the gray reptile eggs in her hand, and then she threw them away. They climbed up the side of the truck. "His eyes was still open," said Ruthie in a hushed tone.

But Winfield gloried in the scene. He said boldly, "His guts was just strowed all over—all over"—he was silent for a moment—"strowed—all—over," he said, and then he rolled over quickly and vomited down the side of the truck. When he sat up again his eyes were watery and his nose running. "It ain't like killin' pigs," he said in explanation.

Al had the hood of the Hudson up, and he checked the oil level. He brought a gallon can from the floor of the front seat and poured a quantity of cheap black oil into the pipe and checked the level again.

Tom came beside him. "Want I should take her a piece?" he asked.

"I ain't tired," said Al.

"Well, you didn' get no sleep las' night. I took a snooze this morning. Get up there on top. I'll take her."

"Awright," Al said reluctantly. "But watch the oil gauge

pretty close. Take her slow. An' I been watchin' for a short.
Take a look a the needle now an' then. 'F she jumps to
discharge it's a short. An' take her slow, Tom. She's overloaded."

Tom laughed. "I'll watch her," he said. "You can res' easy."

The family piled on top of the truck again. Ma settled herself beside Granma in the seat, and Tom took his place and
started the motor. "Sure is loose," he said, and he put it in
gear and pulled away down the highway.

The motor droned along steadily and the sun receded down
the sky in front of them. Granma slept steadily, and even Ma
dropped her head forward and dozed. Tom pulled his cap over
his eyes to shut out the blinding sun.

Paden to Meeker is thirteen miles; Meeker to Harrah is
fourteen miles; and then Oklahoma City—the big city. Tom
drove straight on. Ma waked up and looked at the streets as
they went through the city. And the family, on top of the
truck, stared about at the stores, at the big houses, at the
office buildings. And then the buildings grew smaller and the
stores smaller. The wrecking yards and hot-dog stands, the
out-city dance halls.

Ruthie and Winfield saw it all, and it embarrassed them with
its bigness and its strangeness, and it frightened them with the
fine-clothed people they saw. They did not speak of it to each
other. Later—they would, but not now. They saw the oil derricks in the town, on the edge of the town; oil derricks black,
and the smell of oil and gas in the air. But they didn't exclaim.
It was so big and so strange it frightened them.

In the street Rose of Sharon saw a man in a light suit. He
wore white shoes and a flat straw hat. She touched Connie
and indicated the man with her eyes, and then Connie and
Rose of Sharon giggled softly to themselves, and the giggles
got the best of them. They covered their mouths. And it felt
so good that they looked for other people to giggle at. Ruthie
and Winfield saw them giggling and it looked such fun that
they tried to do it too—but they couldn't. The giggles
wouldn't come. But Connie and Rose of Sharon were breathless and red with stifling laughter before they could stop. It
got so bad that they had only to look at each other to start
over again.

The outskirts were wide spread. Tom drove slowly and carefully in the traffic, and then they were on 66—the great western road, and the sun was sinking on the line of the road. The windshield was bright with dust. Tom pulled his cap lower over his eyes, so low that he had to tilt his head back to see out at all. Granma slept on, the sun on her closed eyelids, and the veins on her temples were blue, and the little bright veins on her cheeks were wine-colored, and the old brown marks on her face turned darker.

Tom said, "We stay on this road right straight through."

Ma had been silent for a long time. "Maybe we better fin' a place to stop 'fore sunset," she said. "I got to get some pork a-boilin' an' some bread made. That takes time."

"Sure," Tom agreed. "We ain't gonna make this trip in one jump. Might's well stretch ourselves."

Oklahoma City to Bethany is fourteen miles.

Tom said, "I think we better stop 'fore the sun goes down. Al got to build that thing on the top. Sun'll kill the folks up there."

Ma had been dozing again. Her head jerked upright. "Got to get some supper a-cookin'," she said. And she said, "Tom, your pa tol' me about you crossin' the State line——"

He was a long time answering. "Yeah? What about it, Ma?"

"Well, I'm scairt about it. It'll make you kinda runnin' away. Maybe they'll catch ya."

Tom held his hand over his eyes to protect himself from the lowering sun. "Don't you worry," he said. "I figgered her out. They's lots a fellas out on parole an' they's more goin' in all the time. If I get caught for anything else out west, well, then they got my pitcher an' my prints in Washington. They'll sen' me back. But if I don't do no crimes, they won't give a damn."

"Well, I'm a-scairt about it. Sometimes you do a crime, an' you don't even know it's bad. Maybe they got crimes in California we don't even know about. Maybe you gonna do somepin an' it's all right, an' in California it ain't all right."

"Be jus' the same if I wasn't on parole," he said. "On'y if I get caught I get a bigger jolt'n other folks. Now you quit a-worryin'," he said. "We got plenty to worry about 'thout you figgerin' out things to worry about."

"I can't he'p it," she said. "Minute you cross the line you done a crime."

"Well, tha's better'n stickin' aroun' Sallisaw an' starvin' to death," he said. "We better look out for a place to stop."

They went through Bethany and out on the other side. In a ditch, where a culvert went under the road, an old touring car was pulled off the highway and a little tent was pitched beside it, and smoke came out of a stove pipe through the tent. Tom pointed ahead. "There's some folks campin'. Looks like as good a place as we seen." He slowed his motor and pulled to a stop beside the road. The hood of the old touring car was up, and a middle-aged man stood looking down at the motor. He wore a cheap straw sombrero, a blue shirt, and a black, spotted vest, and his jeans were stiff and shiny with dirt. His face was lean, the deep cheek-lines great furrows down his face so that his cheek bones and chin stood out sharply. He looked up at the Joad truck and his eyes were puzzled and angry.

Tom leaned out of the window. "Any law 'gainst folks stoppin' here for the night?"

The man had seen only the truck. His eyes focused down on Tom. "I dunno," he said. "We on'y stopped here 'cause we couldn' git no further."

"Any water here?"

The man pointed to a service-station shack about a quarter of a mile ahead. "They's water there they'll let ya take a bucket of."

Tom hesitated. "Well, ya 'spose we could camp down 'longside?"

The lean man looked puzzled. "We don't own it," he said. "We on'y stopped here 'cause this goddamn ol' trap wouldn' go no further."

Tom insisted. "Anyways you're here an' we ain't. You got a right to say if you wan' neighbors or not."

The appeal to hospitality had an instant effect. The lean face broke into a smile. "Why, sure, come on off the road. Proud to have ya." And he called, "Sairy, there's some folks goin' ta stay with us. Come on out an' say how d'ya do. Sairy ain't well," he added. The tent flaps opened and a wizened woman came out—a face wrinkled as a dried leaf and eyes that seemed to flame in her face, black eyes that seemed to look out of a well of horror. She was small and shuddering. She held herself upright by a tent flap, and the hand holding onto the canvas was a skeleton covered with wrinkled skin.

When she spoke her voice had a beautiful low timbre, soft and modulated, and yet with ringing overtones. "Tell 'em welcome," she said. "Tell 'em good an' welcome."

Tom drove off the road and brought his truck into the field and lined it up with the touring car. And people boiled down from the truck; Ruthie and Winfield too quickly, so that their legs gave way and they shrieked at the pins and needles that ran through their limbs. Ma went quickly to work. She untied the three-gallon bucket from the back of the truck and approached the squealing children. "Now you go git water— right down there. Ask nice. Say, 'Please, kin we git a bucket a water?' and say, 'Thank you.' An' carry it back together helpin', an' don't spill none. An' if you see stick wood to burn, bring it on." The children stamped away toward the shack.

By the tent a little embarrassment had set in, and social intercourse had paused before it started. Pa said, "You ain't Oklahomy folks?"

And Al, who stood near the car, looked at the license plates. "Kansas," he said.

The lean man said, "Galena, or right about there. Wilson, Ivy Wilson."

"We're Joads," said Pa. "We come from right near Sallisaw."

"Well, we're proud to meet you folks," said Ivy Wilson. "Sairy, these is Joads."

"I knowed you wasn't Oklahomy folks. You talk queer, kinda—that ain't no blame, you understan'."

"Ever'body says words different," said Ivy. "Arkansas folks says 'em different, and Oklahomy folks says 'em different. And we seen a lady from Massachusetts, an' she said 'em differentest of all. Couldn' hardly make out what she was sayin'."

Noah and Uncle John and the preacher began to unload the truck. They helped Grampa down and sat him on the ground and he sat limply, staring ahead of him. "You sick, Grampa?" Noah asked.

"You goddamn right," said Grampa weakly. "Sicker'n hell."

Sairy Wilson walked slowly and carefully toward him. "How'd you like ta come in our tent?" she asked. "You kin lay down on our mattress an' rest."

He looked up at her, drawn by her soft voice. "Come on now," she said. "You'll git some rest. We'll he'p you over."

Without warning Grampa began to cry. His chin wavered and his old lips tightened over his mouth and he sobbed hoarsely. Ma rushed over to him and put her arms around him. She lifted him to his feet, her broad back straining, and she half lifted, half helped him into the tent.

Uncle John said, "He must be good an' sick. He ain't never done that before. Never seen him blubberin' in my life." He jumped up on the truck and tossed a mattress down.

Ma came out of the tent and went to Casy. "You been aroun' sick people," she said. "Grampa's sick. Won't you go take a look at him?"

Casy walked quickly to the tent and went inside. A double mattress was on the ground, the blankets spread neatly; and a little tin stove stood on iron legs, and the fire in it burned unevenly. A bucket of water, a wooden box of supplies, and a box for a table, that was all. The light of the setting sun came pinkly through the tent walls. Sairy Wilson knelt on the ground, beside the mattress, and Grampa lay on his back. His eyes were open, staring upward, and his cheeks were flushed. He breathed heavily.

Casy took the skinny old wrist in his fingers. "Feeling kinda tired, Grampa?" he asked. The staring eyes moved toward his voice but did not find him. The lips practiced a speech but did not speak it. Casy felt the pulse and he dropped the wrist and put his hand on Grampa's forehead. A struggle began in the old man's body, his legs moved restlessly and his hands stirred. He said a whole string of blurred sounds that were not words, and his face was red under the spiky white whiskers.

Sairy Wilson spoke softly to Casy. "Know what's wrong?"

He looked up at the wrinkled face and the burning eyes. "Do you?"

"I—think so."

"What?" Casy asked.

"Might be wrong. I wouldn' like to say."

Casy looked back at the twitching red face. "Would you say—maybe—he's workin' up a stroke?"

"I'd say that," said Sairy. "I seen it three times before."

From outside came the sounds of camp-making, wood chopping, and the rattle of pans. Ma looked through the flaps. "Granma wants to come in. Would she better?"

The preacher said, "She'll jus' fret if she don't."

"Think he's awright?" Ma asked.

Casy shook his head slowly. Ma looked quickly down at the struggling old face with blood pounding through it. She drew outside and her voice came through. "He's awright, Granma. He's jus' takin' a little res'."

And Granma answered sulkily, "Well, I want ta see him. He's a tricky devil. He wouldn't never let ya know." And she came scurrying through the flaps. She stood over the mattress and looked down. "What's the matter'th you?" she demanded of Grampa. And again his eyes reached toward her voice and his lips writhed. "He's sulkin'," said Granma. "I tol' you he was tricky. He was gonna sneak away this mornin' so he wouldn't have to come. An' then his hip got a-hurtin'," she said disgustedly. "He's jus' sulkin'. I seen him when he wouldn' talk to nobody before."

Casy said gently, "He ain't sulkin', Granma. He's sick."

"Oh!" She looked down at the old man again. "Sick bad, you think?"

"Purty bad, Granma."

For a moment she hesitated uncertainly. "Well," she said quickly, "why ain't you prayin'? You're a preacher, ain't you?"

Casy's strong fingers blundered over to Grampa's wrist and clasped around it. "I tol' you, Granma. I ain't a preacher no more."

"Pray anyway," she ordered. "You know all the stuff by heart."

"I can't," said Casy. "I don' know what to pray for or who to pray to."

Granma's eyes wandered away and came to rest on Sairy. "He won't pray," she said. "D'I ever tell ya how Ruthie prayed when she was a little skinner? Says, 'Now I lay me down to sleep. I pray the Lord my soul to keep. An' when she got there the cupboard was bare, an' so the poor dog got none. Amen.' That's jus' what she done." The shadow of someone walking between the tent and the sun crossed the canvas.

Grampa seemed to be struggling; all his muscles twitched. And suddenly he jarred as though under a heavy blow. He lay still and his breath was stopped. Casy looked down at the old man's face and saw that it was turning a blackish purple. Sairy touched Casy's shoulder. She whispered, "His tongue, his tongue, his tongue."

Casy nodded. "Get in front a Granma." He pried the tight jaws apart and reached into the old man's throat for the tongue. And as he lifted it clear, a rattling breath came out, and a sobbing breath was indrawn. Casy found a stick on the ground and held down the tongue with it, and the uneven breath rattled in and out.

Granma hopped about like a chicken. "Pray," she said. "Pray, you. Pray, I tell ya." Sairy tried to hold her back. "Pray, goddamn you!" Granma cried.

Casy looked up at her for a moment. The rasping breath came louder and more unevenly. "Our Father who art in Heaven, hallowed be Thy name——"

"Glory!" shouted Granma.

"Thy kingdom come, Thy will be done—on earth—as it is in Heaven."

"Amen."

A long gasping sigh came from the open mouth, and then a crying release of air.

"Give us this day—our daily bread—and forgive us——" The breathing had stopped. Casy looked down into Grampa's eyes and they were clear and deep and penetrating, and there was a knowing serene look in them.

"Hallelujah!" said Granma. "Go on."

"Amen," said Casy.

Granma was still then. And outside the tent all the noise had stopped. A car whished by on the highway. Casy still knelt on the floor beside the mattress. The people outside were listening, standing quietly intent on the sounds of dying. Sairy took Granma by the arm and led her outside, and Granma moved with dignity and held her head high. She walked for the family and held her head straight for the family. Sairy took her to a mattress lying on the ground and sat her down on it. And Granma looked straight ahead, proudly, for she was on show now. The tent was still, and at last Casy spread the tent flaps with his hands and stepped out.

Pa asked softly, "What was it?"

"Stroke," said Casy. "A good quick stroke."

Life began to move again. The sun touched the horizon and flattened over it. And along the highway there came a long line of huge freight trucks with red sides. They rumbled along, putting a little earthquake in the ground, and the standing exhaust pipes sputtered blue smoke from the Diesel oil. One man drove each truck, and his relief man slept in a bunk high up against the ceiling. But the trucks never stopped; they thundered day and night and the ground shook under their heavy march.

The family became a unit. Pa squatted down on the ground, and Uncle John beside him. Pa was the head of the family now. Ma stood behind him. Noah and Tom and Al squatted, and the preacher sat down, and then reclined on his elbow. Connie and Rose of Sharon walked at a distance. Now Ruthie and Winfield, clattering up with a bucket of water held between them, felt the change, and they slowed up and set down the bucket and moved quietly to stand with Ma.

Granma sat proudly, coldly, until the group was formed, until no one looked at her, and then she lay down and covered her face with her arm. The red sun set and left a shining twilight on the land, so that faces were bright in the evening and eyes shone in reflection of the sky. The evening picked up light where it could.

Pa said, "It was in Mr. Wilson's tent."

Uncle John nodded. "He loaned his tent."

"Fine friendly folks," Pa said softly.

Wilson stood by his broken car, and Sairy had gone to the mattress to sit beside Granma, but Sairy was careful not to touch her.

Pa called, "Mr. Wilson!" The man scuffed near and squatted down, and Sairy came and stood beside him. Pa said, "We're thankful to you folks."

"We're proud to help," said Wilson.

"We're beholden to you," said Pa.

"There's no beholden in a time of dying," said Wilson, and Sairy echoed him, "Never no beholden."

Al said, "I'll fix your car—me an' Tom will." And Al looked proud that he could return the family's obligation.

"We could use some help." Wilson admitted the retiring of the obligation.

Pa said, "We got to figger what to do. They's laws. You got to report a death, an' when you do that, they either take forty dollars for the undertaker or they take him for a pauper."

Uncle John broke in, "We never did have no paupers."

Tom said, "Maybe we got to learn. We never got booted off no land before, neither."

"We done it clean," said Pa. "There can't no blame be laid on us. We never took nothin' we couldn' pay; we never suffered no man's charity. When Tom here got in trouble we could hold up our heads. He only done what any man would a done."

"Then what'll we do?" Uncle John asked.

"We go in like the law says an' they'll come out for him. We on'y got a hunderd an' fifty dollars. They take forty to bury Grampa an' we won't get to California—or else they'll bury him a pauper." The men stirred restively, and they studied the darkening ground in front of their knees.

Pa said softly, "Grampa buried his pa with his own hand, done it in dignity, an' shaped the grave nice with his own shovel. That was a time when a man had the right to be buried by his own son an' a son had the right to bury his own father."

"The law says different now," said Uncle John.

"Sometimes the law can't be foller'd no way," said Pa. "Not in decency, anyways. They's lots a times you can't. When Floyd was loose an' goin' wild, law said we got to give him up—an' nobody give him up. Sometimes a fella got to sift the law. I'm sayin' now I got the right to bury my own pa. Anybody got somepin to say?"

The preacher rose high on his elbow. "Law changes," he said, "but 'got to's' go on. You got the right to do what you got to do."

Pa turned to Uncle John. "It's your right too, John. You got any word against?"

"No word against," said Uncle John. "On'y it's like hidin' him in the night. Grampa's way was t'come out a-shootin'."

Pa said ashamedly, "We can't do like Grampa done. We got to get to California 'fore our money gives out."

Tom broke in, "Sometimes fellas workin' dig up a man an' then they raise hell an' figger he been killed. The gov'ment's got more interest in a dead man than a live one. They'll go hell-scrapin' tryin' to fin' out who he was and how he died. I offer we put a note of writin' in a bottle an' lay it with Grampa, tellin' who he is an' how he died, an' why he's buried here."

Pa nodded agreement. "Tha's good. Wrote out in a nice han'. Be not so lonesome too, knowin' his name is there with 'im, not jus' a old fella lonesome underground. Any more stuff to say?" The circle was silent.

Pa turned his head to Ma. "You'll lay 'im out?"

"I'll lay 'im out," said Ma. "But who's to get supper?"

Sairy Wilson said, "I'll get supper. You go right ahead. Me an' that big girl of yourn."

"We sure thank you," said Ma. "Noah, you get into them kegs an' bring out some nice pork. Salt won't be deep in it yet, but it'll be right nice eatin'."

"We got a half sack a potatoes," said Sairy.

Ma said, "Gimme two half-dollars." Pa dug in his pocket and gave her the silver. She found the basin, filled it full of water, and went into the tent. It was nearly dark in there. Sairy came in and lighted a candle and stuck it upright on a box and then she went out. For a moment Ma looked down at the dead old man. And then in pity she tore a strip from her own apron and tied up his jaw. She straightened his limbs, folded his hands over his chest. She held his eyelids down and laid a silver piece on each one. She buttoned his shirt and washed his face.

Sairy looked in, saying, "Can I give you any help?"

Ma looked slowly up. "Come in," she said. "I like to talk to ya."

"That's a good big girl you got," said Sairy. "She's right in peelin' potatoes. What can I do to help?"

"I was gonna wash Grampa all over," said Ma, "but he got no other clo'es to put on. An' 'course your quilt's spoilt. Can't never get the smell a death from a quilt. I seen a dog growl an' shake at a mattress my ma died on, an' that was two years later. We'll wrop 'im in your quilt. We'll make it up to you. We got a quilt for you."

Sairy said, "You shouldn' talk like that. We're proud to help. I ain't felt so—safe in a long time. People needs—to help."

Ma nodded. "They do," she said. She looked long into the old whiskery face, with its bound jaw and silver eyes shining in the candlelight. "He ain't gonna look natural. We'll wrop him up."

"The ol' lady took it good."

"Why, she's so old," said Ma, "maybe she don't even rightly know what happened. Maybe she won't really truly know for quite a while. Besides, us folks takes a pride holdin' in. My pa used to say, 'Anybody can break down. It takes a man not to.' We always try to hold in." She folded the quilt neatly about Grampa's legs and around his shoulders. She brought the corner of the quilt over his head like a cowl and pulled it down over his face. Sairy handed her half-a-dozen big safety pins, and she pinned the quilt neatly and tightly about the long package. And at last she stood up. "It won't be a bad burying," she said. "We got a preacher to see him in, an' his folks is all aroun'." Suddenly she swayed a little, and Sairy went to her and steadied her. "It's sleep—" Ma said in a shamed tone. "No, I'm awright. We been so busy gettin' ready, you see."

"Come out in the air," Sairy said.

"Yeah, I'm all done here." Sairy blew out the candle and the two went out.

A bright fire burned in the bottom of the little gulch. And Tom, with sticks and wire, had made supports from which two kettles hung and bubbled furiously, and good steam poured out under the lids. Rose of Sharon knelt on the ground out of range of the burning heat, and she had a long spoon in her hand. She saw Ma come out of the tent, and she stood up and went to her.

"Ma," she said. "I got to ask."

"Scared again?" Ma asked. "Why, you can't get through nine months without sorrow."

"But will it—hurt the baby?"

Ma said, "They used to be a sayin', 'A chile born outa sorrow'll be a happy chile.' Isn't that so, Mis' Wilson?"

"I heard it like that," said Sairy. "An' I heard the other: 'Born outa too much joy'll be a doleful boy.'"

"I'm all jumpy inside," said Rose of Sharon.

"Well, we ain't none of us jumpin' for fun," said Ma. "You jes' keep watchin' the pots."

On the edge of the ring of firelight the men had gathered. For tools they had a shovel and a mattock. Pa marked out the ground—eight feet long and three feet wide. The work went on in relays. Pa chopped the earth with the mattock and then Uncle John shoveled it out. Al chopped and Tom shoveled, Noah chopped and Connie shoveled. And the hole drove down, for the work never diminished in speed. The shovels of dirt flew out of the hole in quick spurts. When Tom was shoulder deep in the rectangular pit, he said, "How deep, Pa?"

"Good an' deep. A couple feet more. You get out now, Tom, and get that paper wrote."

Tom boosted himself out of the hole and Noah took his place. Tom went to Ma, where she tended the fire. "We got any paper an' pen, Ma?"

Ma shook her head slowly, "No-o. That's one thing we didn' bring." She looked toward Sairy. And the little woman walked quickly to her tent. She brought back a Bible and a half pencil. "Here," she said. "They's a clear page in front. Use that an' tear it out." She handed book and pencil to Tom.

Tom sat down in the firelight. He squinted his eyes in concentration, and at last wrote slowly and carefully on the end paper in big clear letters: "This here is William James Joad, dyed of a stroke, old old man. His fokes bured him becaws they got no money to pay for funerls. Nobody kilt him. Jus a stroke an he dyed." He stopped. "Ma, listen to this here." He read it slowly to her.

"Why, that soun's nice," she said. "Can't you stick on somepin from Scripture so it'll be religious? Open up an' git a-sayin' somepin outa Scripture."

"Got to be short," said Tom. "I ain't got much room lef' on the page."

Sairy said, "How 'bout 'God have mercy on his soul'?"

"No," said Tom. "Sounds too much like he was hung. I'll copy somepin." He turned the pages and read, mumbling his lips, saying the words under his breath. "Here's a good short one," he said. "'An' Lot said unto them, Oh, not so, my Lord.'"

"Don't mean nothin'," said Ma. "Long's you're gonna put one down, it might's well mean somepin."

Sairy said, "Turn to Psalms, over further. You kin always get somepin outa Psalms."

Tom flipped the pages and looked down the verses. "Now here *is* one," he said. "This here's a nice one, just blowed full a religion: 'Blessed is he whose transgression is forgiven, whose sin is covered.' How's that?"

"That's real nice," said Ma. "Put that one in."

Tom wrote it carefully. Ma rinsed and wiped a fruit jar and handed it to him. Tom tore the leaf carefully from the Bible and rolled it and put it in the fruit jar and he screwed the lid down tight on it. "Maybe the preacher ought to wrote it," he said.

Ma said, "No, the preacher wan't no kin." She took the jar from him and went into the dark tent. She unpinned the covering and slipped the fruit jar in under the thin cold hands and pinned the comforter tight again. And then she went back to the fire.

The men came from the grave, their faces shining with perspiration. "Awright," said Pa. He and John and Noah and Al went into the tent, and they came out carrying the long, pinned bundle between them. They carried it to the grave. Pa leaped into the hole and received the bundle in his arms and laid it gently down. Uncle John put out a hand and helped Pa out of the hole. Pa asked, "How about Granma?"

"I'll see," Ma said. She walked to the mattress and looked down at the old woman for a moment. Then she went back to the grave. "Sleepin'," she said. "Maybe she'd hold it against me, but I ain't a-gonna wake her up. She's tar'd."

Pa said, "Where at's the preacher? We oughta have a prayer."

Tom said, "I seen him walkin' down the road. He don't like to pray no more."

"Don't like to pray?"

"No," said Tom. "He ain't a preacher no more. He figgers it ain't right to fool people actin' like a preacher when he ain't a preacher. I bet he went away so nobody wouldn' ast him."

Casy had come quietly near, and he heard Tom speaking. "I didn' run away," he said. "I'll he'p you folks, but I won't fool ya."

Pa said, "Won't you say a few words? Ain't none of our folks ever been buried without a few words."

"I'll say 'em," said the preacher.

Connie led Rose of Sharon to the graveside, she reluctant. "You got to," Connie said. "It ain't decent not to. It'll jus' be a little."

The firelight fell on the grouped people, showing their faces and their eyes, dwindling on their dark clothes. All the hats were off now. The light danced, jerking over the people.

Casy said, "It'll be a short one." He bowed his head, and the others followed his lead. Casy said solemnly, "This here ol' man jus' lived a life an' jus' died out of it. I don' know whether he was good or bad, but that don't matter much. He was alive, an' that's what matters. An' now he's dead, an' that don't matter. Heard a fella tell a poem one time, an' he says 'All that lives is holy.' Got to thinkin', an' purty soon it means more than the words says. An' I wouldn' pray for a ol' fella that's dead. He's awright. He got a job to do, but it's all laid out for 'im an' there's on'y one way to do it. But us, we got a job to do, an' they's a thousan' ways, an' we don' know which one to take. An' if I was to pray, it'd be for the folks that don' know which way to turn. Grampa here, he got the easy straight. An' now cover 'im up and let 'im get to his work." He raised his head.

Pa said, "Amen," and the others muttered, "A-men." Then Pa took the shovel, half filled it with dirt, and spread it gently into the black hole. He handed the shovel to Uncle John, and John dropped in a shovelful. Then the shovel went from hand to hand until every man had his turn. When all had taken their duty and their right, Pa attacked the mound of loose dirt and hurriedly filled the hole. The women moved back to the fire to see to supper. Ruthie and Winfield watched, absorbed.

Ruthie said solemnly, "Grampa's down under there." And Winfield looked at her with horrified eyes. And then he ran away to the fire and sat on the ground and sobbed to himself.

Pa half filled the hole, and then he stood panting with the effort while Uncle John finished it. And John was shaping up the mound when Tom stopped him. "Listen," Tom said. "'F we leave a grave, they'll have it open in no time. We got to hide it. Level her off an' we'll strew dry grass. We got to do that."

Pa said, "I didn' think a that. It ain't right to leave a grave unmounded."

"Can't he'p it," said Tom. "They'd dig 'im right up, an' we'd get it for breakin' the law. You know what I get if I break the law."

"Yeah," Pa said. "I forgot that." He took the shovel from John and leveled the grave. "She'll sink, come winter," he said.

"Can't he'p that," said Tom. "We'll be a long ways off by winter. Tromp her in good, an' we'll strew stuff over her."

When the pork and potatoes were done the families sat about on the ground and ate, and they were quiet, staring into the fire. Wilson, tearing a slab of meat with his teeth, sighed with contentment. "Nice eatin' pig," he said.

"Well," Pa explained, "we had a couple shoats, an' we thought we might's well eat 'em. Can't get nothin' for them. When we get kinda use' ta movin' an' Ma can set up bread, why, it'll be pretty nice, seein' the country an' two kags a' pork right in the truck. How long you folks been on the road?"

Wilson cleared his teeth with his tongue and swallowed. "We ain't been lucky," he said. "We been three weeks from home."

"Why, God Awmighty, we aim to be in California in ten days or less."

Al broke in, "I dunno, Pa. With that load we're packin',

we maybe ain't never gonna get there. Not if they's mountains to go over."

They were silent about the fire. Their faces were turned downward and their hair and foreheads showed in the firelight. Above the little dome of the firelight the summer stars shone thinly, and the heat of the day was gradually withdrawing. On her mattress, away from the fire, Granma whimpered softly like a puppy. The heads of all turned in her direction.

Ma said, "Rosasharn, like a good girl go lay down with Granma. She needs somebody now. She's knowin', now."

Rose of Sharon got to her feet and walked to the mattress and lay beside the old woman, and the murmur of their soft voices drifted to the fire. Rose of Sharon and Granma whispered together on the mattress.

Noah said, "Funny thing is—losin' Grampa ain't made me feel no different than I done before. I ain't no sadder than I was."

"It's just the same thing," Casy said. "Grampa an' the old place, they was jus' the same thing."

Al said, "It's a goddamn shame. He been talkin' what he's gonna do, how he gonna squeeze grapes over his head an' let the juice run in his whiskers, an' all stuff like that."

Casy said, "He was foolin', all the time. I think he knowed it. He knowed it. You fellas can make some kinda new life, but Grampa, his life was over an' he knowed it. An' Grampa didn' die tonight. He died the minute you took 'im off the place."

"You sure a that?" Pa cried. "Why no!"

"Oh, he was breathin'," Casy went on, "but he was dead. He was that place, an' he knowed it."

Uncle John said, "Did you know he was a-dyin'?"

"Yeah," said Casy. "I knowed it."

John gazed at him, and a horror grew in his face. "An' you didn' tell nobody?"

"What good?" Casy asked.

"We—we might of did somepin."

"What?"

"I don' know, but——"

"No," Casy said, "you couldn' a done nothin'. Your way was fixed an' Grampa didn' have no part in it. He didn' suffer none. Not after fust thing this mornin'. He's jus' stayin' with the lan'. He couldn' leave it."

Uncle John sighed deeply.

Wilson said, "We hadda leave my brother Will." The heads turned toward him. "Him an' me had forties side by side. He's older'n me. Neither one ever drove a car. Well, we went in an' we sol' ever'thing. Will, he bought a car, an' they give him a kid to show 'im how to use it. So the afternoon 'fore we're gonna start, Will an' Aunt Minnie go a-practicin'. Will, he comes to a bend in the road an' he yells 'Whoa' an' yanks back, an' he goes through a fence. An' he yells 'Whoa, you bastard' an' tromps down on the gas an' goes over into a gulch. An' there he was. Didn't have nothin' more to sell an' didn't have no car. But it were his own damn fault, praise God. He's so damn mad he won't come along with us, jus' set there a-cussin' an' a-cussin'."

"What's he gonna do?"

"I dunno. He's too mad to figger. An' we couldn' wait. On'y had eighty-five dollars to go on. We couldn' set an' cut it up, but we et it up anyways. Didn' go a hunderd mile when a tooth in the rear end bust, an' cost thirty dollars to get her fix', an' then we got to get a tire, an' then a spark plug cracked, an' Sairy got sick. Had ta stop ten days. An' now the goddamn car is bust again, an' money's gettin' low. I dunno when we'll ever get to California. 'F I could on'y fix a car, but I don' know nothin' about 'em."

Al asked importantly, "What's the matter?"

"Well, she jus' won't run. Starts an' farts an' stops. In a minute she'll start again, an' then 'fore you can git her goin', she peters out again."

"Runs a minute an' then dies?"

"Yes, sir. An' I can't keep her a-goin' no matter how much gas I give her. Got worse an' worse, an' now I cain't get her a-movin' a-tall."

Al was very proud and very mature, then. "I think you got a plugged gas line. I'll blow her out for ya."

And Pa was proud too. "He's a good hand with a car," Pa said.

"Well, I'll sure thank ya for a han'. I sure will. Makes a fella kinda feel—like a little kid, when he can't fix nothin'. When we get to California I aim to get me a nice car. Maybe she won't break down."

Pa said, "When we get there. Gettin' there's the trouble."

"Oh, but she's worth it," said Wilson. "Why, I seen han'bills how they need folks to pick fruit, an' good wages. Why, jus' think how it's gonna be, under them shady trees a-pickin' fruit an' takin' a bite ever' once in a while. Why, hell, they don't care how much you eat 'cause they got so much. An' with them good wages, maybe a fella can get hisself a little piece a land an' work out for extra cash. Why, hell, in a couple years I bet a fella could have a place of his own."

Pa said, "We seen them han'bills. I got one right here." He took out his purse and from it took a folded orange hand-bill. In black type it said, "Pea Pickers Wanted in California. Good Wages All Season. 800 Pickers Wanted."

Wilson looked at it curiously. "Why, that's the one I seen. The very same one. You s'pose—maybe they got all eight hunderd awready?"

Pa said, "This is jus' one little part a California. Why, that's the secon' biggest State we got. S'pose they did get all them eight hunderd. They's plenty places else. I rather pick fruit anyways. Like you says, under them trees an' pickin' fruit— why, even the kids'd like to do that."

Suddenly Al got up and walked to the Wilsons' touring car. He looked in for a moment and then came back and sat down.

"You can't fix her tonight," Wilson said.

"I know. I'll get to her in the morning."

Tom had watched his young brother carefully. "I was thinkin' somepin like that myself," he said.

Noah asked, "What you two fellas talkin' about?"

Tom and Al were silent, each waiting for the other. "You tell 'em," Al said finally.

"Well, maybe it's no good, an' maybe it ain't the same thing Al's thinking. Here she is, anyways. We got a overload, but Mr. an' Mis' Wilson ain't. If some of us folks could ride with them an' take some a their light stuff in the truck, we wouldn't break no springs an' we could git up hills. An' me an' Al both knows about a car, so we could keep that car a-rollin'. We'd keep together on the road an' it'd be good for ever'body."

Wilson jumped up. "Why, sure. Why, we'd be proud. We certain'y would. You hear that, Sairy?"

"It's a nice thing," said Sairy. "Wouldn' be a burden on you folks?"

"No, by God," said Pa. "Wouldn't be no burden at all. You'd be helpin' us."

Wilson settled back uneasily. "Well, I dunno."

"What's a matter, don' you wanta?"

"Well, ya see—I on'y got 'bout thirty dollars lef', an' I won't be no burden."

Ma said, "You won't be no burden. Each'll help each, an' we'll all git to California. Sairy Wilson he'ped lay Grampa out," and she stopped. The relationship was plain.

Al cried, "That car'll take six easy. Say me to drive, an' Rosasharn an' Connie and Granma. Then we take the big light stuff an' pile her on the truck. An' we'll trade off ever' so often." He spoke loudly, for a load of worry was lifted from him.

They smiled shyly and looked down at the ground. Pa fingered the dusty earth with his fingertips. He said, "Ma favors a white house with oranges growin' around. They's a big pitcher on a calendar she seen."

Sairy said, "If I get sick again, you got to go on an' get there. We ain't a-goin' to burden."

Ma looked carefully at Sairy, and she seemed to see for the first time the pain-tormented eyes and the face that was haunted and shrinking with pain. And Ma said, "We gonna see you get through. You said yourself, you can't let help go unwanted."

Sairy studied her wrinkled hands in the firelight. "We got to get some sleep tonight." She stood up.

"Grampa—it's like he's dead a year," Ma said.

The families moved lazily to their sleep, yawning luxuriously. Ma sloshed the tin plates off a little and rubbed the grease free with a flour sack. The fire died down and the stars descended. Few passenger cars went by on the highway now, but the transport trucks thundered by at intervals and put little earthquakes in the ground. In the ditch the cars were barely visible under the starlight. A tied dog howled at the service station down the road. The families were quiet and sleeping, and the field mice grew bold and scampered about among the mattresses. Only Sairy Wilson was awake. She stared into the sky and braced her body firmly against pain.

Chapter Fourteen

THE WESTERN LAND, nervous under the beginning change. The Western States, nervous as horses before a thunder storm. The great owners, nervous, sensing a change, knowing nothing of the nature of the change. The great owners, striking at the immediate thing, the widening government, the growing labor unity; striking at new taxes, at plans; not knowing these things are results, not causes. Results, not causes; results, not causes. The causes lie deep and simply—the causes are a hunger in a stomach, multiplied a million times; a hunger in a single soul, hunger for joy and some security, multiplied a million times; muscles and mind aching to grow, to work, to create, multiplied a million times. The last clear definite function of man—muscles aching to work, minds aching to create beyond the single need—this is man. To build a wall, to build a house, a dam, and in the wall and house and dam to put something of Manself, and to Manself take back something of the wall, the house, the dam; to take hard muscles from the lifting, to take the clear lines and form from conceiving. For man, unlike any other thing organic or inorganic in the universe, grows beyond his work, walks up the stairs of his concepts, emerges ahead of his accomplishments. This you may say of man—when theories change and crash, when schools, philosophies, when narrow dark alleys of thought, national, religious, economic, grow and disintegrate, man reaches, stumbles forward, painfully, mistakenly sometimes. Having stepped forward, he may slip back, but only half a step, never the full step back. This you may say and know it and know it. This you may know when the bombs plummet out of the black planes on the market place, when prisoners are stuck like pigs, when the crushed bodies drain filthily in the dust. You may know it in this way. If the step were not being taken, if the stumbling-forward ache were not alive, the bombs would not fall, the throats would not be cut. Fear the time when the bombs stop falling while the bombers live—for every bomb is proof that the spirit has not died. And fear the time when the strikes stop while the great owners live—for every little beaten strike is proof that the step is being taken. And this you can know—fear the time when Manself will not suffer and die for a concept, for this one quality is the foundation of Manself, and this one quality is man, distinctive in the universe.

The Western States nervous under the beginning change. Texas and Oklahoma, Kansas and Arkansas, New Mexico, Arizona, California. A single family moved from the land. Pa borrowed money from the bank, and now the bank wants the land. The land company—that's the bank when it has land— wants tractors, not families on the land. Is a tractor bad? Is the power that turns the long furrows wrong? If this tractor were ours it would be good—not mine, but ours. If our tractor turned the long furrows of our land, it would be good. Not my land, but ours. We could love that tractor then as we have loved this land when it was ours. But this tractor does two things—it turns the land and turns us off the land. There is little difference between this tractor and a tank. The people are driven, intimidated, hurt by both. We must think about this.

One man, one family driven from the land; this rusty car creaking along the highway to the west. I lost my land, a single tractor took my land. I am alone and I am bewildered. And in the night one family camps in a ditch and another family pulls in and the tents come out. The two men squat on their hams and the women and children listen. Here is the node, you who hate change and fear revolution. Keep these two squatting men apart; make them hate, fear, suspect each other. Here is the anlage of the thing you fear. This is the zygote. For here "I lost my land" is changed; a cell is split and from its splitting grows the thing you hate—"We lost *our* land." The danger is here, for two men are not as lonely and perplexed as one. And from this first "we" there grows a still more dangerous thing: "I have a little food" plus "I have none." If from this problem the sum is "We have a little food," the thing is on its way, the movement has direction. Only a little multiplication now, and this land, this tractor are ours. The two men squatting in a ditch, the little fire, the side-meat stewing in a single pot, the silent, stone-eyed women; behind, the children listening with their souls to words their minds do not understand. The night draws down. The baby has a cold. Here, take this blanket. It's wool. It was my mother's blanket—take it for the baby. This is the thing to bomb. This is the beginning—from "I" to "we."

If you who own the things people must have could understand this, you might preserve yourself. If you could separate causes from results, if you could know that Paine, Marx, Jefferson, Lenin, were results, not causes, you might survive. But that you cannot know. For the quality of owning freezes you forever into "I," and cuts you off forever from the "we."

The Western States are nervous under the beginning change. Need is the stimulus to concept, concept to action. A half-million people moving over the country; a million more restive, ready to move; ten million more feeling the first nervousness.

And tractors turning the multiple furrows in the vacant land.

Chapter Fifteen

ALONG 66 the hamburger stands—Al & Susy's Place—Carl's Lunch—Joe & Minnie—Will's Eats. Board-and-bat shacks. Two gasoline pumps in front, a screen door, a long bar, stools, and a foot rail. Near the door three slot machines, showing through the glass the wealth in nickels three bars will bring. And beside them, the nickel phonograph with records piled up like pies, ready to swing out to the turntable and play dance music, "Ti-pi-ti-pi-tin," "Thanks for the Memory," Bing Crosby, Benny Goodman. At one end of the counter a covered case; candy cough drops, caffeine sulphate called Sleepless, No-Doze; candy, cigarettes, razor blades, aspirin, Bromo-Seltzer, Alka-Seltzer. The walls decorated with posters, bathing girls, blondes with big breasts and slender hips and waxen faces, in white bathing suits, and holding a bottle of Coca-Cola and smiling—see what you get with a Coca-Cola. Long bar, and salts, peppers, mustard pots, and paper napkins. Beer taps behind the counter, and in back the coffee urns, shiny and steaming, with glass gauges showing the coffee level. And pies in wire cages and oranges in pyramids of four. And little piles of Post Toasties, corn flakes, stacked up in designs.

The signs on cards, picked out with shining mica: Pies Like Mother Used to Make. Credit Makes Enemies, Let's Be Friends. Ladies May Smoke But Be Careful Where You Lay Your Butts. Eat Here and Keep Your Wife for a Pet. IITYWYBAD?

Down at one end the cooking plates, pots of stew, potatoes, pot roast, roast beef, gray roast pork waiting to be sliced.

Minnie or Susy or Mae, middle-aging behind the counter, hair curled and rouge and powder on a sweating face. Taking orders in a soft low voice, calling them to the cook with a screech like a peacock. Mopping the counter with circular strokes, polishing the big shining coffee urns. The cook is Joe or Carl or Al, hot in a white coat and apron, beady sweat on white forehead, below the white cook's cap; moody, rarely speaking, looking up for a moment at each new entry. Wiping the griddle, slapping down the hamburger. He repeats Mae's orders gently, scrapes the griddle, wipes it down with burlap. Moody and silent.

Mae is the contact, smiling, irritated, near to outbreak; smiling while her eyes look on past—unless for truck drivers. There's the backbone of the joint. Where the trucks stop, that's where the customers come. Can't fool truck drivers, they know. They bring the custom. They know. Give 'em a stale cup a coffee an' they're off the joint. Treat 'em right an' they come back. Mae really smiles with all her might at truck drivers. She bridles a little, fixes her back hair so that her breasts will lift with her raised arms, passes the time of day and indicates great things, great times, great jokes. Al never speaks. He is no contact. Sometimes he smiles a little at a joke, but he never laughs. Sometimes he looks up at the vivaciousness in Mae's voice, and then he scrapes the griddle with a spatula, scrapes the grease into an iron trough around the plate. He presses down a hissing hamburger with his spatula. He lays the split buns on the plate to toast and heat. He gathers up stray onions from the plate and heaps them on the meat and presses them in with the spatula. He puts half the bun on top of the meat, paints the other half with melted butter, with thin pickle relish. Holding the bun on the meat, he slips the spatula under the thin pad of meat, flips it over, lays the buttered half on top, and drops the hamburger on a small plate. Quarter of a dill pickle, two black olives beside the sandwich. Al skims the plate down the counter like a quoit. And he scrapes his griddle with the spatula and looks moodily at the stew kettle.

Cars whisking by on 66. License plates. Mass., Tenn., R.I., N.Y., Vt., Ohio. Going west. Fine cars, cruising at sixty-five.

There goes one of them Cords. Looks like a coffin on wheels.

But, Jesus, how they travel!

See that La Salle? Me for that. I ain't a hog. I go for a La Salle.

'F ya goin' big, what's a matter with a Cad'? Jus' a little bigger, little faster.

I'd take a Zephyr myself. You ain't ridin' no fortune, but you got class an' speed. Give me a Zephyr.

Well, sir, you may get a laugh outa this—I'll take a Buick-Puick. That's good enough.

But, hell, that costs in the Zephyr class an' it ain't got the sap.

I don' care. I don' want nothin' to do with nothing of Henry Ford's. I don' like 'im. Never did. Got a brother worked in the plant. Oughta hear him tell.

Well, a Zephyr got sap.

The big cars on the highway. Languid, heat-raddled ladies, small nucleuses about whom revolve a thousand accouterments: creams, ointments to grease themselves, coloring matter in phials—black, pink, red, white, green, silver—to change the color of hair, eyes, lips, nails, brows, lashes, lids. Oils, seeds, and pills to make the bowels move. A bag of bottles, syringes, pills, powders, fluids, jellies to make their sexual intercourse safe, odorless, and unproductive. And this apart from clothes. What a hell of a nuisance!

Lines of weariness around the eyes, lines of discontent down from the corners of the mouth, breasts lying heavily in little hammocks, stomach and thighs straining against cases of rubber. And the mouths panting, the eyes sullen, disliking sun and wind and earth, resenting food and weariness, hating time that rarely makes them beautiful and always makes them old.

Beside them, little pot-bellied men in light suits and panama hats; clean, pink men with puzzled, worried eyes, with restless eyes. Worried because formulas do not work out; hungry for security and yet sensing its disappearance from the earth. In their lapels the insignia of lodges and service clubs, places where they can go and, by a weight of numbers of little worried men, reassure themselves that business is noble and not the curious ritualized thievery they know it is; that business men are intelligent in spite of the records of their stupidity; that they are kind and charitable in spite of the principles of sound business; that their lives are rich instead of the thin tiresome routines they know; and that a time is coming when they will not be afraid any more.

And these two, going to California; going to sit in the lobby of the Beverly-Wilshire Hotel and watch people they envy go by, to look at mountains—mountains, mind you, and great trees—he with his worried eyes and she thinking how the sun will dry her skin. Going to look at the Pacific Ocean, and I'll bet a hundred thousand dollars to nothing at all, he will say, "It isn't as big as I thought it would be." And she will envy plump young bodies on the beach. Going to California really to go home again. To say, "Joan Crawford was at the table next to us at the Trocadero. She's really a mess, but she does wear nice clothes." And he, "I talked to good sound business men out there. They don't see a chance till we get rid of that fellow in the White House." And, "I got it from a man in the know. —— —— has syphilis, you know—she was in that Warner picture. Man said she'd slept her way into pictures. Well, she got what she was looking for." But the worried eyes are never calm, and the pouting mouth is never glad. The big car cruising along at sixty.

I want a cold drink.

Well, there's something up ahead. Want to stop?

Do you think it would be clean?

Clean as you're going to find in this God-forsaken country.

Well, maybe the bottled soda will be all right.

The great car squeals and pulls to a stop. The fat worried man helps his wife out.

Mae looks at and past them as they enter. Al looks up from his griddle, and down again. Mae knows. They'll drink a five-cent soda and crab that it ain't cold enough. The woman will use six paper napkins and drop them on the floor. The man will choke and try to put the blame on Mae. The woman will sniff as though she smelled rotting meat and they will go out again and tell forever afterward that the people in the West are sullen. And Mae, when she is alone with Al, has a name for them. She calls them shitheels.

Truck drivers. That's the stuff.

Here's a big transport comin'. Hope they stop; take away the taste of them shitheels. When I worked in that hotel in Albuquerque, Al, the way they steal—ever' darn thing. An' the bigger the car they got, the more they steal—towels, silver, soap dishes. I can't figger it.

And Al, morosely, Where ya think they get them big cars and stuff? Born with 'em? You won't never have nothin'.

The transport truck, a driver and relief. How 'bout stoppin' for a cup a Java? I know this dump.

How's the schedule?

Oh, we're ahead!

Pull up, then. They's a ol' war horse in here that's a kick. Good Java, too.

The truck pulls up. Two men in khaki riding trousers, boots, short jackets, and shiny-visored military caps. Screen door—slam.

H'ya, Mae?

Well, if it ain't Big Bill the Rat! When'd you get back on this run?

Week ago.

The other man puts a nickel in the phonograph, watches the disk slip free and the turntable rise up under it. Bing Crosby's voice—golden. "Thanks for the memory, of sunburn at the shore— You might have been a headache, but you never were a bore—" And the truck driver sings for Mae's ears, you might have been a haddock but you never was a whore—

Mae laughs. Who's ya frien', Bill? New on this run, ain't he?

The other puts a nickel in the slot machine, wins four slugs, and puts them back. Walks to the counter.

Well, what's it gonna be?

Oh, cup a Java. Kinda pie ya got?

Banana cream, pineapple cream, chocolate cream—an' apple.

Make it apple. Wait— Kind is that big thick one?

Mae lifts it out and sniffs it. Banana cream.

Cut off a hunk; make it a big hunk.

Man at the slot machine says, Two all around.

Two it is. Seen any new etchin's lately, Bill?

Well, here's one.

Now, you be careful front of a lady.

Oh, this ain't bad. Little kid comes in late ta school. Teacher says, "Why ya late?" Kid says, "Had a take a heifer down—get 'er bred." Teacher says, "Couldn't your ol' man do it?" Kid says, "Sure he could, but not as good as the bull."

Mae squeaks with laughter, harsh screeching laughter. Al, slicing onions carefully on a board, looks up and smiles, and then looks down again. Truck drivers, that's the stuff. Gonna leave a quarter each for Mae. Fifteen cents for pie an' coffee an' a dime for Mae. An' they ain't tryin' to make her, neither.

Sitting together on the stools, spoons sticking up out of the coffee mugs. Passing the time of day. And Al, rubbing down his griddle, listening but making no comment. Bing Crosby's voice stops. The turntable drops down and the record swings into its place in the pile. The purple light goes off. The nickel, which has caused all this mechanism to work, has caused Crosby to sing and an orchestra to play—this nickel drops from between the contact points into the box where the profits go. This nickel, unlike most money, has actually done a job of work, has been physically responsible for a reaction.

Steam spurts from the valve of the coffee urn. The compressor of the ice machine chugs softly for a time and then stops. The electric fan in the corner waves its head slowly back and forth, sweeping the room with a warm breeze. On the highway, on 66, the cars whiz by.

They was a Massachusetts car stopped a while ago, said Mae.

Big Bill grasped his cup around the top so that the spoon stuck up between his first and second fingers. He drew in a snort of air with the coffee, to cool it. "You ought to be out on 66. Cars from all over the country. All headin' west. Never seen so many before. Sure some honeys on the road."

"We seen a wreck this mornin'," his companion said. "Big car. Big Cad', a special job and a honey, low, cream-color, special job. Hit a truck. Folded the radiator right back into the driver. Must a been doin' ninety. Steerin' wheel went right on through the guy an' lef' him a-wigglin' like a frog on a hook. Peach of a car. A honey. You can have her for peanuts now. Drivin' alone, the guy was."

Al looked up from his work. "Hurt the truck?"

"Oh, Jesus Christ! Wasn't a truck. One of them cut-down cars full a stoves an' pans an' mattresses an' kids an' chickens. Goin' west, you know. This guy come by us doin' ninety— r'ared up on two wheels just to pass us, an' a car's comin' so he cuts in an' whangs this here truck. Drove like he's blin' drunk. Jesus, the air was full a bed clothes an' chickens an' kids. Killed one kid. Never seen such a mess. We pulled up.

Ol' man that's drivin' the truck, he jus' stan's there lookin' at that dead kid. Can't get a word out of 'im. Jus' rum-dumb. God Almighty, the road is full a them families goin' west. Never seen so many. Gets worse all a time. Wonder where the hell they all come from?"

"Wonder where they all go to," said Mae. "Come here for gas sometimes, but they don't hardly never buy nothin' else. People says they steal. We ain't got nothin' layin' around. They never stole nothin' from us."

Big Bill, munching his pie, looked up the road through the screened window. "Better tie your stuff down. I think you got some of 'em comin' now."

A 1926 Nash sedan pulled wearily off the highway. The back seat was piled nearly to the ceiling with sacks, with pots and pans, and on the very top, right up against the ceiling, two boys rode. On the top of the car, a mattress and a folded tent; tent poles tied along the running board. The car pulled up to the gas pumps. A dark-haired, hatchet-faced man got slowly out. And the two boys slid down from the load and hit the ground.

Mae walked around the counter and stood in the door. The man was dressed in gray wool trousers and a blue shirt, dark blue with sweat on the back and under the arms. The boys in overalls and nothing else, ragged patched overalls. Their hair was light, and it stood up evenly all over their heads, for it had been roached. Their faces were streaked with dust. They went directly to the mud puddle under the hose and dug their toes into the mud.

The man asked, "Can we git some water, ma'am?"

A look of annoyance crossed Mae's face. "Sure, go ahead." She said softly over her shoulder, "I'll keep my eye on the hose." She watched while the man slowly unscrewed the radiator cap and ran the hose in.

A woman in the car, a flaxen-haired woman, said, "See if you can't git it here."

The man turned off the hose and screwed on the cap again. The little boys took the hose from him and they upended it and drank thirstily. The man took off his dark, stained hat and stood with a curious humility in front of the screen. "Could you see your way to sell us a loaf of bread, ma'am?"

Mae said, "This ain't a grocery store. We got bread to make san'widges."

"I know, ma'am." His humility was insistent. "We need bread and there ain't nothin' for quite a piece, they say."

"'F we sell bread we gonna run out." Mae's tone was faltering.

"We're hungry," the man said.

"Whyn't you buy a san'widge? We got nice san'widges, hamburgs."

"We'd sure admire to do that, ma'am. But we can't. We got to make a dime do all of us." And he said embarrassedly, "We ain't got but a little."

Mae said, "You can't get no loaf a bread for a dime. We only got fifteen-cent loafs."

From behind her Al growled, "God Almighty, Mae, give 'em bread."

"We'll run out 'fore the bread truck comes."

"Run out, then, goddamn it," said Al. And he looked sullenly down at the potato salad he was mixing.

Mae shrugged her plump shoulders and looked to the truck drivers to show them what she was up against.

She held the screen door open and the man came in, bringing a smell of sweat with him. The boys edged in behind him and they went immediately to the candy case and stared in— not with craving or with hope or even with desire, but just with a kind of wonder that such things could be. They were alike in size and their faces were alike. One scratched his dusty ankle with the toe nails of his other foot. The other whispered some soft message and then they straightened their arms so that their clenched fists in the overall pockets showed through the thin blue cloth.

Mae opened a drawer and took out a long waxpaper-wrapped loaf. "This here is a fifteen-cent loaf."

The man put his hat back on his head. He answered with inflexible humility, "Won't you—can't you see your way to cut off ten cents' worth?"

Al said snarlingly, "Goddamn it, Mae. Give 'em the loaf."

The man turned toward Al. "No, we want ta buy ten cents' worth of it. We got it figgered awful close, mister, to get to California."

Mae said resignedly, "You can have this for ten cents."

"That'd be robbin' you, ma'am."

"Go ahead—Al says to take it." She pushed the waxpapered loaf across the counter. The man took a deep leather pouch from his rear pocket, untied the strings, and spread it open. It was heavy with silver and with greasy bills.

"May soun' funny to be so tight," he apologized. "We got a thousan' miles to go, an' we don' know if we'll make it." He dug in the pouch with a forefinger, located a dime, and pinched in for it. When he put it down on the counter he had a penny with it. He was about to drop the penny back into the pouch when his eye fell on the boys frozen before the candy counter. He moved slowly down to them. He pointed in the case at big long sticks of striped peppermint. "Is them penny candy, ma'am?"

Mae moved down and looked in. "Which ones?"

"There, them stripy ones."

The little boys raised their eyes to her face and they stopped breathing; their mouths were partly opened, their half-naked bodies were rigid.

"Oh—them. Well, no—them's two for a penny."

"Well, gimme two then, ma'am." He placed the copper cent carefully on the counter. The boys expelled their held breath softly. Mae held the big sticks out.

"Take 'em," said the man.

They reached timidly, each took a stick, and they held them down at their sides and did not look at them. But they looked at each other, and their mouth corners smiled rigidly with embarrassment.

"Thank you, ma'am." The man picked up the bread and went out the door, and the little boys marched stiffly behind him, the red-striped sticks held tightly against their legs. They leaped like chipmunks over the front seat and onto the top of the load, and they burrowed back out of sight like chipmunks.

The man got in and started his car, and with a roaring motor and a cloud of blue oily smoke the ancient Nash climbed up on the highway and went on its way to the west.

From inside the restaurant the truck drivers and Mae and Al stared after them.

Big Bill wheeled back. "Them wasn't two-for-a-cent candy," he said.

"What's that to you?" Mae said fiercely.

"Them was nickel apiece candy," said Bill.

"We got to get goin'," said the other man. "We're droppin' time." They reached in their pockets. Bill put a coin on the counter and the other man looked at it and reached again and put down a coin. They swung around and walked to the door.

"So long," said Bill.

Mae called, "Hey! Wait a minute. You got change."

"You go to hell," said Bill, and the screen door slammed.

Mae watched them get into the great truck, watched it lumber off in low gear, and heard the shift up the whining gears to cruising ratio. "Al—" she said softly.

He looked up from the hamburger he was patting thin and stacking between waxed papers. "What ya want?"

"Look there." She pointed at the coins beside the cups— two half-dollars. Al walked near and looked, and then he went back to his work.

"Truck drivers," Mae said reverently, "an' after them shit-heels."

Flies struck the screen with little bumps and droned away. The compressor chugged for a time and then stopped. On 66 the traffic whizzed by, trucks and fine streamlined cars and jalopies; and they went by with a vicious whiz. Mae took down the plates and scraped the pie crusts into a bucket. She found her damp cloth and wiped the counter with circular sweeps. And her eyes were on the highway, where life whizzed by.

Al wiped his hands on his apron. He looked at a paper pinned to the wall over the griddle. Three lines of marks in columns on the paper. Al counted the longest line. He walked along the counter to the cash register, rang "No Sale," and took out a handful of nickels.

"What ya doin'?" Mae asked.

"Number three's ready to pay off," said Al. He went to the third slot machine and played his nickels in, and on the fifth spin of the wheels the three bars came up and the jack pot dumped out into the cup. Al gathered up the big handful of coins and went back of the counter. He dropped them in the drawer and slammed the cash register. Then he went back to his place and crossed out the line of dots. "Number three gets more play'n the others," he said. "Maybe I ought to shift 'em around." He lifted a lid and stirred the slowly simmering stew.

"I wonder what they'll do in California?" said Mae.

"Who?"

"Them folks that was just in."

"Christ knows," said Al.

"S'pose they'll get work?"

"How the hell would I know?" said Al.

She stared eastward along the highway. "Here comes a transport, double. Wonder if they stop? Hope they do." And as the huge truck came heavily down from the highway and parked, Mae seized her cloth and wiped the whole length of the counter. And she took a few swipes at the gleaming coffee urn too, and turned up the bottle-gas under the urn. Al brought out a handful of little turnips and started to peel them. Mae's face was gay when the door opened and the two uniformed truck drivers entered.

"Hi, sister!"

"I won't be a sister to no man," said Mae. They laughed and Mae laughed. "What'll it be, boys?"

"Oh, a cup a Java. What kinda pie ya got?"

"Pineapple cream an' banana cream an' chocolate cream an' apple."

"Give me apple. No, wait—what's that big thick one?"

Mae picked up the pie and smelled it. "Pineapple cream," she said.

"Well, chop out a hunk a that."

The cars whizzed viciously by on 66.

Chapter Sixteen

JOADS AND WILSONS crawled westward as a unit: El Reno and Bridgeport, Clinton, Elk City, Sayre, and Texola. There's the border, and Oklahoma was behind. And this day the cars crawled on and on, through the Panhandle of Texas. Shamrock and Alanreed, Groom and Yarnell. They went through Amarillo in the evening, drove too long, and camped when it was dusk. They were tired and dusty and hot. Granma had convulsions from the heat, and she was weak when they stopped.

That night Al stole a fence rail and made a ridge pole on the truck, braced at both ends. That night they ate nothing but pan biscuits, cold and hard, held over from breakfast. They flopped down on the mattresses and slept in their clothes. The Wilsons didn't even put up their tent.

Joads and Wilsons were in flight across the Panhandle, the rolling gray country, lined and cut with old flood scars. They were in flight out of Oklahoma and across Texas. The land turtles crawled through the dust and the sun whipped the earth, and in the evening the heat went out of the sky and the earth sent up a wave of heat from itself.

Two days the families were in flight, but on the third the land was too huge for them and they settled into a new technique of living; the highway became their home and movement their medium of expression. Little by little they settled into the new life. Ruthie and Winfield first, then Al, then Connie and Rose of Sharon, and, last, the older ones. The land rolled like great stationary ground swells. Wildorado and Vega and Boise and Glenrio. That's the end of Texas. New Mexico and the mountains. In the far distance, waved up against the sky, the mountains stood. And the wheels of the cars creaked around, and the engines were hot, and the steam spurted around the radiator caps. They crawled to the Pecos river, and crossed at Santa Rosa. And they went on for twenty miles.

Al Joad drove the touring car, and his mother sat beside him, and Rose of Sharon beside her. Ahead the truck crawled.

The hot air folded in waves over the land, and the mountains shivered in the heat. Al drove listlessly, hunched back in the seat, his hand hooked easily over the cross-bar of the steering wheel; his gray hat, peaked and pulled to an incredibly cocky shape, was low over one eye; and as he drove, he turned and spat out the side now and then.

Ma, beside him, had folded her hands in her lap, had retired into a resistance against weariness. She sat loosely, letting the movement of the car sway her body and her head. She squinted her eyes ahead at the mountains. Rose of Sharon was braced against the movement of the car, her feet pushed tight against the floor, and her right elbow hooked over the door. And her plump face was tight against the movement, and her head jiggled sharply because her neck muscles were tight. She tried to arch her whole body as a rigid container to preserve her fetus from shock. She turned her head toward her mother.

"Ma," she said. Ma's eyes lighted up and she drew her attention toward Rose of Sharon. Her eyes went over the tight, tired, plump face, and she smiled. "Ma," the girl said, "when we get there, all you gonna pick fruit an' kinda live in the country, ain't you?"

Ma smiled a little satirically. "We ain't there yet," she said. "We don't know what it's like. We got to see."

"Me an' Connie don't want to live in the country no more," the girl said. "We got it all planned up what we gonna do."

For a moment a little worry came on Ma's face. "Ain't you gonna stay with us—with the family?" she asked.

"Well, we talked all about it, me an' Connie. Ma, we wanna live in a town." She went on excitedly, "Connie gonna get a job in a store or maybe a fact'ry. An' he's gonna study at home, maybe radio, so he can git to be a expert an' maybe later have his own store. An' we'll go to pitchers whenever. An' Connie says I'm gonna have a *doctor* when the baby's born; an' he says we'll see how times is, an' maybe I'll go to a hospiddle. An' we'll have a car, little car. An' after he studies at night, why—it'll be nice, an' he tore a page outa *Western Love Stories*, an' he's gonna send off for a course, 'cause it don't cost nothin' to send off. Says right on that clipping. I seen it. An', why—they even get you a job when you take that course—radios, it is—nice clean work, and a future. An' we'll live in town an' go to pitchers whenever, an'—well, I'm gonna have a 'lectric iron, an' the baby'll have all new stuff. Connie says all new stuff—white an'— Well, you seen in the catalogue all the stuff they got for a baby. Maybe right at first while Connie's studyin' at home it won't be so easy, but—well, when the baby comes, maybe he'll be all done studyin' an' we'll have a place, little bit of a place. We don't want nothin' fancy, but we want it nice for the baby—" Her face glowed with excitement. "An' I thought—well, I thought maybe we could all go in town, an' when Connie gets his store—maybe Al could work for him."

Ma's eyes had never left the flushing face. Ma watched the structure grow and followed it. "We don' want you to go 'way from us," she said. "It ain't good for folks to break up."

Al snorted, "Me work for Connie? How about Connie comes a-workin' for me? He thinks he's the on'y son-of-a-bitch can study at night?"

Ma suddenly seemed to know it was all a dream. She turned her head forward again and her body relaxed, but the little smile stayed around her eyes. "I wonder how Granma feels today," she said.

Al grew tense over the wheel. A little rattle had developed in the engine. He speeded up and the rattle increased. He retarded his spark and listened, and then he speeded up for a moment and listened. The rattle increased to a metallic pounding. Al blew his horn and pulled the car to the side of the road. Ahead the truck pulled up and then backed slowly. Three cars raced by, westward, and each one blew its horn and the last driver leaned out and yelled, "Where the hell ya think you're stoppin'?"

Tom backed the truck close, and then he got out and walked to the touring car. From the back of the loaded truck heads looked down. Al retarded his spark and listened to his idling motor. Tom asked, "What's a matter, Al?"

Al speeded the motor. "Listen to her." The rattling pound was louder now.

Tom listened. "Put up your spark an' idle," he said. He opened the hood and put his head inside. "Now speed her."

He listened for a moment and then closed the hood. "Well, I guess you're right, Al," he said.

"Con-rod bearing, ain't it?"

"Sounds like it," said Tom.

"I kep' plenty oil in," Al complained.

"Well, it jus' didn' get to her. Drier'n a bitch monkey now. Well, there ain't nothin' to do but tear her out. Look, I'll pull ahead an' find a flat place to stop. You come ahead slow. Don't knock the pan out of her."

Wilson asked, "Is it bad?"

"Purty bad," said Tom, and walked back to the truck and moved slowly ahead.

Al explained, "I don' know what made her go out. I give her plenty of oil." Al knew the blame was on him. He felt his failure.

Ma said, "It ain't your fault. You done ever'thing right." And then she asked a little timidly, "Is it terrible bad?"

"Well, it's hard to get at, an' we got to get a new con-rod or else some babbitt in this one." He sighed deeply. "I sure am glad Tom's here. I never fitted no bearing. Hope to Jesus Tom did."

A huge red billboard stood beside the road ahead, and it threw a great oblong shadow. Tom edged the truck off the road and across the shallow roadside ditch, and he pulled up in the shadow. He got out and waited until Al came up.

"Now go easy," he called. "Take her slow or you'll break a spring too."

Al's face went red with anger. He throttled down his motor. "Goddamn it," he yelled, "I didn't burn that bearin' out! What d'ya mean, I'll bust a spring too?"

Tom grinned. "Keep all four feet on the groun'," he said. "I didn' mean nothin'. Jus' take her easy over this ditch."

Al grumbled as he inched the touring car down, and up the other side. "Don't you go givin' nobody no idear I burned out that bearin'." The engine clattered loudly now. Al pulled into the shade and shut down the motor.

Tom lifted the hood and braced it. "Can't even start on her before she cools off," he said. The family piled down from the cars and clustered about the touring car.

Pa asked, "How bad?" And he squatted on his hams.

Tom turned to Al. "Ever fitted one?"

"No," said Al, "I never. 'Course I had pans off."

Tom said, "Well, we got to tear the pan off an' get the rod out, an' we got to get a new part an' hone her an' shim her an' fit her. Good day's job. Got to go back to that las' place for a part, Santa Rosa. Albuquerque's about seventy-five miles on— Oh, Jesus, tomorra's Sunday! We can't get nothin' tomorra." The family stood silently. Ruthie crept close and peered into the open hood, hoping to see the broken part. Tom went on softly, "Tomorra's Sunday. Monday we'll get the thing an' prob'ly won't get her fitted 'fore Tuesday. We ain't got the tools to make it easy. Gonna be a job." The shadow of a buzzard slid across the earth, and the family all looked up at the sailing black bird.

Pa said, "What I'm scairt of is we'll run outa money so we can't git there 't all. Here's all us eatin', an' got to buy gas an' oil. 'F we run outa money, I don' know what we gonna do."

Wilson said, "Seems like it's my fault. This here goddamn wreck's give me trouble right along. You folks been nice to us. Now you jus' pack up an' get along. Me an' Sairy'll stay, an' we'll figger some way. We don't aim to put you folks out none."

Pa said slowly, "We ain't a-gonna do it. No, sir. We got almost a kin bond. Grampa, he died in your tent."

Sairy said tiredly, "We been nothin' but trouble, nothin' but trouble."

Tom slowly made a cigarette, and inspected it and lighted it. He took off his ruined cap and wiped his forehead. "I got an idear," he said. "Maybe nobody gonna like it, but here she is: The nearer to California our folks get, the quicker they's gonna be money rollin' in. Now this here car'll go twicet as fast as that truck. Now here's my idear. You take out some a that stuff in the truck, an' then all you folks but me an' the preacher get in an' move on. Me an' Casy'll stop here an' fix this here car an' then we drive on, day an' night, an' we'll catch up, or if we don't meet on the road, you'll be a-workin' anyways. An' if you break down, why, jus' camp 'longside the road till we come. You can't be no worse off, an' if you get through, why, you'll all be a-workin', an' stuff'll be easy. Casy can give me a lif' with this here car, an' we'll come a-sailin'.''

The gathered family considered it. Uncle John dropped to his hams beside Pa.

Al said, "Won't ya need me to give ya a han' with that conrod?"

"You said your own se'f you never fixed one."

"That's right," Al agreed. "All ya got to have is a strong back. Maybe the preacher don' wanta stay."

"Well—whoever—I don' care," said Tom.

Pa scratched the dry earth with his forefinger. "I kind a got a notion Tom's right," he said. "It ain't goin' ta do no good all of us stayin' here. We can get fifty, a hunderd miles on 'fore dark."

Ma said worriedly, "How you gonna find us?"

"We'll be on the same road," said Tom. "Sixty-six right on through. Come to a place name' Bakersfiel'. Seen it on the map I got. You go straight on there."

"Yeah, but when we get to California an' spread out sideways off this road—?"

"Don't you worry," Tom reassured her. "We're gonna find ya. California ain't the whole world."

"Looks like an awful big place on the map," said Ma.

Pa appealed for advice. "John, you see any reason why not?"

"No," said John.

"Mr. Wilson, it's your car. You got any objections if my boy fixes her an' brings her on?"

"I don' see none," said Wilson. "Seems like you folks done ever'thing for us awready. Don' see why I cain't give your boy a han'.''

"You can be workin', layin' in a little money, if we don' ketch up with ya," said Tom. "An' s'pose we all jus' lay aroun' here. There ain't no water here, an' we can't move this here car. But s'pose you all git out there an' git to work. Why, you'd have money, an' maybe a house to live in. How about it, Casy? Wanna stay with me an' gimme a lif'?"

"I wanna do what's bes' for you folks," said Casy. "You took me in, carried me along. I'll do whatever."

"Well, you'll lay on your back an' get grease in your face if you stay here," Tom said.

"Suits me awright."

Pa said, "Well, if that's the way she's gonna go, we better get a-shovin'. We can maybe squeeze in a hunderd miles 'fore we stop."

Ma stepped in front of him. "I ain't a-gonna go."

"What you mean, you ain't gonna go? You got to go. You got to look after the family." Pa was amazed at the revolt.

Ma stepped to the touring car and reached in on the floor of the back seat. She brought out a jack handle and balanced it in her hand easily. "I ain't a-gonna go," she said.

"I tell you, you got to go. We made up our mind."

And now Ma's mouth set hard. She said softly, "On'y way you gonna get me to go is whup me." She moved the jack handle gently again. "An' I'll shame you, Pa. I won't take no whuppin', cryin' an' a-beggin'. I'll light into you. An' you ain't so sure you can whup me anyways. An' if ya do get me, I swear to God I'll wait till you got your back turned, or you're settin' down, an' I'll knock you belly-up with a bucket. I swear to Holy Jesus' sake I will."

Pa looked helplessly about the group. "She sassy," he said. "I never seen her so sassy." Ruthie giggled shrilly.

The jack handle flicked hungrily back and forth in Ma's hand. "Come on," said Ma. "You made up your mind. Come on an' whup me. Jus' try it. But I ain't a-goin'; or if I do, you ain't never gonna get no sleep, 'cause I'll wait an' I'll wait, an' jus' the minute you take sleep in your eyes, I'll slap ya with a stick a stove wood."

"So goddamn sassy," Pa murmured. "An' she ain't young, neither."

The whole group watched the revolt. They watched Pa, waiting for him to break into fury. They watched his lax hands to see the fists form. And Pa's anger did not rise, and his hands hung limply at his sides. And in a moment the group knew that Ma had won. And Ma knew it too.

Tom said, "Ma, what's eatin' on you? What ya wanna do this-a-way for? What's the matter'th you anyways? You gone johnrabbit on us?"

Ma's face softened, but her eyes were still fierce. "You done this 'thout thinkin' much," Ma said. "What we got lef' in the worl'? Nothin' but us. Nothin' but the folks. We come out an' Grampa, he reached for the shovel-shelf right off. An' now, right off, you wanna bust up the folks——"

Tom cried, "Ma, we was gonna catch up with ya. We wasn't gonna be gone long."

Ma waved the jack handle. "S'pose we was camped, and you went on by. S'pose we got on through, how'd we know where to leave the word, an' how'd you know where to ask?" She said, "We got a bitter road. Granma's sick. She's up there on the truck a-pawin' for a shovel herself. She's jus' tar'd out. We got a long bitter road ahead."

Uncle John said, "But we could be makin' some money. We could have a little bit saved up, come time the other folks got there."

The eyes of the whole family shifted back to Ma. She was the power. She had taken control. "The money we'd make wouldn't do no good," she said. "All we got is the family unbroke. Like a bunch a cows, when the lobos are ranging, stick all together. I ain't scared while we're all here, all that's alive, but I ain't gonna see us bust up. The Wilsons here is with us, an' the preacher is with us. I can't say nothin' if they want to go, but I'm a-goin' cat-wild with this here piece a bar-arn if my own folks busts up." Her tone was cold and final.

Tom said soothingly, "Ma, we can't all camp here. Ain't no water here. Ain't even much shade here. Granma, she needs shade."

"All right," said Ma. "We'll go along. We'll stop first place they's water an' shade. An'—the truck'll come back an' take you in town to get your part, an' it'll bring you back. You ain't goin' walkin' along in the sun, an' I ain't havin' you out all alone, so if you get picked up there ain't nobody of your folks to he'p ya."

Tom drew his lips over his teeth and then snapped them open. He spread his hands helplessly and let them flop against his sides. "Pa," he said, "if you was to rush her one side an' me the other an' then the res' pile on, an' Granma jump down on top, maybe we can get Ma 'thout more'n two-three of us gets killed with that there jack handle. But if you ain't willin' to get your head smashed, I guess Ma's went an' filled her flush. Jesus Christ, one person with their mind made up can shove a lot of folks aroun'! You win, Ma. Put away that jack handle 'fore you hurt somebody."

Ma looked in astonishment at the bar of iron. Her hand trembled. She dropped her weapon on the ground, and Tom, with elaborate care, picked it up and put it back in the car. He said, "Pa, you jus' got set back on your heels. Al, you drive the folks on an' get 'em camped, an' then you bring the truck back here. Me an' the preacher'll get the pan off. Then, if we can make it, we'll run in Santa Rosa an' try an' get a con-rod. Maybe we can, seein' it's Sat'dy night. Get jumpin' now so we can go. Lemme have the monkey wrench an' pliers outa the truck." He reached under the car and felt the greasy pan. "Oh, yeah, lemme have a can, that ol' bucket, to catch the oil. Got to save that." Al handed over the bucket and Tom set it under the car and loosened the oil cap with a pair of pliers. The black oil flowed down his arm while he unscrewed the cap with his fingers, and then the black stream ran silently into the bucket. Al had loaded the family on the truck by the time the bucket was half full. Tom, his face already smudged with oil, looked out between the wheels. "Get back fast!" he called. And he was loosening the pan bolts as the truck moved gently across the shallow ditch and crawled away. Tom turned each bolt a single turn, loosening them evenly to spare the gasket.

The preacher knelt beside the wheels. "What can I do?"

"Nothin', not right now. Soon's the oil's out an' I get these here bolts loose, you can he'p me drop the pan off." He squirmed away under the car, loosening the bolts with a wrench and turning them out with his fingers. He left the bolts on each end loosely threaded to keep the pan from dropping. "Ground's still hot under here," Tom said. And then, "Say, Casy, you been awful goddamn quiet the las' few days. Why, Jesus! When I first come up with you, you was makin' a speech ever' half-hour or so. An' here you ain't said ten words the las' couple days. What's a matter—gettin' sour?"

Casy was stretched out on his stomach, looking under the car. His chin, bristly with sparse whiskers, rested on the back of one hand. His hat was pushed back so that it covered the back of his neck. "I done enough talkin' when I was a preacher to las' the rest a my life," he said.

"Yeah, but you done some talkin' sence, too."

"I'm all worried up," Casy said. "I didn' even know it when I was a-preachin' aroun', but I was doin' consid'able tom-cattin' aroun'. If I ain't gonna preach no more, I got to get married. Why, Tommy, I'm a-lustin' after the flesh."

"Me too," said Tom. "Say, the day I come outa McAlester I was smokin'. I run me down a girl, a hoor girl, like she was a rabbit. I won't tell ya what happened. I wouldn' tell nobody what happened."

Casy laughed. "I know what happened. I went a-fastin' into the wilderness one time, an' when I come out the same damn thing happened to me."

"Hell it did!" said Tom. "Well, I saved my money anyway, an' I give that girl a run. Thought I was nuts. I should a paid her, but I on'y got five bucks to my name. She said she didn' want no money. Here, roll in under here an' grab a-holt. I'll tap her loose. Then you turn out that bolt an' I turn out my end, an' we let her down easy. Careful that gasket. See, she comes off in one piece. They's on'y four cylinders to these here ol' Dodges. I took one down one time. Got main bearings big as a cantaloupe. Now—let her down—hold it. Reach up an' pull down that gasket where it's stuck—easy now. There!" The greasy pan lay on the ground between them, and a little oil still lay in the wells. Tom reached into one of the front wells and picked out some broken pieces of babbitt. "There she is," he said. He turned the babbitt in his fingers. "Shaft's up. Look in back an' get the crank. Turn her over till I tell you."

Casy got to his feet and found the crank and fitted it. "Ready?"

"Ready—now easy—little more—little more—right there."

Casy kneeled down and looked under again. Tom rattled the connecting-rod bearing against the shaft. "There she is."

"What ya s'pose done it?" Casy asked.

"Oh, hell, I don' know! This buggy been on the road thirteen years. Says sixty-thousand miles on the speedometer. That means a hunderd an' sixty, an' God knows how many

times they turned the numbers back. Gets hot—maybe somebody let the oil get low—jus' went out." He pulled the cotter-
pins and put his wrench on a bearing bolt. He strained and
the wrench slipped. A long gash appeared on the back of his
hand. Tom looked at it—the blood flowed evenly from the
wound and met the oil and dripped into the pan.

"That's too bad," Casy said. "Want I should do that an'
you wrap up your han'?"

"Hell, no! I never fixed no car in my life 'thout cuttin'
myself. Now it's done I don't have to worry no more." He
fitted the wrench again. "Wisht I had a crescent wrench," he
said, and he hammered the wrench with the butt of his hand
until the bolts loosened. He took them out and laid them
with the pan bolts in the pan, and the cotter-pins with them.
He loosened the bearing bolts and pulled out the piston. He
put piston and connecting-rod in the pan. "There, by God!"
He squirmed free from under the car and pulled the pan out
with him. He wiped his hand on a piece of gunny sacking and
inspected the cut. "Bleedin' like a son-of-a-bitch," he said.
"Well, I can stop that." He urinated on the ground, picked
up a handful of the resulting mud, and plastered it over the
wound. Only for a moment did the blood ooze out, and then
it stopped. "Bes' damn thing in the worl' to stop bleedin',"
he said.

"Han'ful a spider web'll do it too," said Casy.

"I know, but there ain't no spider web, an' you can always
get piss." Tom sat on the running board and inspected the
broken bearing. "Now if we can on'y find a '25 Dodge an'
get a used con-rod an' some shims, maybe we'll make her all
right. Al must a gone a hell of a long ways."

The shadow of the billboard was sixty feet out by now. The
afternoon lengthened away. Casy sat down on the running
board and looked westward. "We gonna be in high mountains
pretty soon," he said, and he was silent for a few moments.
Then, "Tom!"

"Yeah?"

"Tom, I been watchin' the cars on the road, them we
passed an' them that passed us. I been keepin' track."

"Track a what?"

"Tom, they's hunderds a families like us all a-goin' west. I watched. There ain't none of 'em goin' east—hunderds of 'em. Did you notice that?"

"Yeah, I noticed."

"Why—it's like—it's like they was runnin' away from soldiers. It's like a whole country is movin'."

"Yeah," Tom said. "They is a whole country movin'. We're movin' too."

"Well—s'pose all these here folks an' ever'body—s'pose they can't get no jobs out there?"

"Goddamn it!" Tom cried. "How'd I know? I'm jus' puttin' one foot in front a the other. I done it at Mac for four years, jus' marchin' in cell an' out cell an' in mess an' out mess. Jesus Christ, I thought it'd be somepin different when I come out! Couldn' think a nothin' in there, else you go stir happy, an' now can't think a nothin'." He turned on Casy. "This here bearing went out. We didn' know it was goin', so we didn' worry none. Now she's out an' we'll fix her. An' by Christ that goes for the rest of it! I ain't gonna worry. I can't do it. This here little piece of iron an' babbitt. See it? Ya see it? Well, that's the only goddamn thing in the world I got on my mind. I wonder where the hell Al is."

Casy said, "Now look, Tom. Oh, what the hell! So goddamn hard to say anything."

Tom lifted the mud pack from his hand and threw it on the ground. The edge of the wound was lined with dirt. He glanced over to the preacher. "You're fixin' to make a speech," Tom said. "Well, go ahead. I like speeches. Warden used to make speeches all the time. Didn't do us no harm an' he got a hell of a bang out of it. What you tryin' to roll out?"

Casy picked the backs of his long knotty fingers. "They's stuff goin' on and they's folks doin' things. Them people layin' one foot down in front of the other, like you says, they ain't thinkin' where they're goin', like you says—but they're all layin' 'em down the same direction, jus' the same. An' if ya listen, you'll hear a movin', an' a sneakin', an' a rustlin', an'—an' a res'lessness. They's stuff goin' on that the folks doin' it don't know nothin' about—yet. They's gonna come somepin outa all these folks goin' wes'—outa all their farms lef' lonely. They's comin' a thing that's gonna change the whole country."

Tom said, "I'm still layin' my dogs down one at a time."

"Yeah, but when a fence comes up at ya, ya gonna climb that fence."

"I climb fences when I got fences to climb," said Tom.

Casy sighed. "It's the bes' way. I gotta agree. But they's different kinda folks. They's folks like me that climbs fences that ain't even strang up yet—an' can't he'p it."

"Ain't that Al a-comin'?" Tom asked.

"Yeah. Looks like."

Tom stood up and wrapped the connecting-rod and both halves of the bearing in the piece of sack. "Wanta make sure I get the same," he said.

The truck pulled alongside the road and Al leaned out the window.

Tom said, "You was a hell of a long time. How far'd you go?"

Al sighed. "Got the rod out?"

"Yeah." Tom held up the sack. "Babbitt jus' broke down."

"Well, it wasn't no fault of mine," said Al.

"No. Where'd you take the folks?"

"We had a mess," Al said. "Granma got to bellerin', an' that set Rosasharn off an' she bellered some. Got her head under a mattress an' bellered. But Granma, she was just layin' back her jaw an' bayin' like a moonlight houn' dog. Seems like Granma ain't got no sense no more. Like a little baby. Don' speak to nobody, don' seem to reco'nize nobody. Jus' talks on like she's talkin' to Grampa."

"Where'd ya leave 'em?" Tom insisted.

"Well, we come to a camp. Got shade an' got water in pipes. Costs half a dollar a day to stay there. But ever'body's so goddamn tired an' wore out an' mis'able, they stayed there. Ma says they got to 'cause Granma's so tired an' wore out. Got Wilson's tent up an' got our tarp for a tent. I think Granma gone nuts."

Tom looked toward the lowering sun. "Casy," he said, "somebody got to stay with this car or she'll get stripped. You jus' as soon?"

"Sure. I'll stay."

Al took a paper bag from the seat. "This here's some bread an' meat Ma sent, an' I got a jug a water here."

"She don't forget nobody," said Casy.

Tom got in beside Al. "Look," he said. "We'll get back jus' as soon's we can. But we can't tell how long."

"I'll be here."

"Awright. Don't make no speeches to yourself. Get goin', Al." The truck moved off in the late afternoon. "He's a nice fella," Tom said. "He thinks about stuff all the time."

"Well, hell—if you been a preacher, I guess you got to. Pa's all mad about it costs fifty cents jus' to camp under a tree. He can't see that noways. Settin' a-cussin'. Says nex' thing they'll sell ya a little tank a air. But Ma says they gotta be near shade an' water 'cause a Granma." The truck rattled along the highway, and now that it was unloaded, every part of it rattled and clashed. The side-board of the bed, the cut body. It rode hard and light. Al put it up to thirty-eight miles an hour and the engine clattered heavily and a blue smoke of burning oil drifted up through the floor boards.

"Cut her down some," Tom said. "You gonna burn her right down to the hub caps. What's eatin' on Granma?"

"I don' know. 'Member the las' couple days she's been airy-nary, sayin' nothin' to nobody? Well, she's yellin' an' talkin' plenty now, on'y she's talkin' to Grampa. Yellin' at him. Kinda scary, too. You can almos' see 'im a-settin' there grinnin' at her the way he always done, a-fingerin' hisself an' grinnin'. Seems like she sees him a-settin' there, too. She's jus' givin' him hell. Say, Pa, he give me twenty dollars to hand you. He don' know how much you gonna need. Ever see Ma stand up to 'im like she done today?"

"Not I remember. I sure did pick a nice time to get paroled. I figgered I was gonna lay aroun' an' get up late an' eat a lot when I come home. I was goin' out an' dance, an' I was gonna go tom-cattin'—an' here I ain't had time to do none of them things."

Al said, "I forgot. Ma give me a lot a stuff to tell you. She says don't drink nothin', an' don' get in no arguments, an' don't fight nobody. 'Cause she says she's scairt you'll get sent back."

"She got plenty to get worked up about 'thout me givin' her no trouble," said Tom.

"Well, we could get a couple beers, can't we? I'm jus' a-ravin' for a beer."

"I dunno," said Tom. "Pa'd crap a litter of lizards if we buy beers."

"Well, look, Tom. I got six dollars. You an' me could get a couple pints an' go down the line. Nobody don't know I got that six bucks. Christ, we could have a hell of a time for ourselves."

"Keep ya jack," Tom said. "When we get out to the coast you an' me'll take her an' we'll raise hell. Maybe when we're workin'—" He turned in the seat. "I didn' think you was a fella to go down the line. I figgered you was talkin' 'em out of it."

"Well, hell, I don't know nobody here. If I'm gonna ride aroun' much, I'm gonna get married. I'm gonna have me a hell of a time when we get to California."

"Hope so," said Tom.

"You ain't sure a nothin' no more."

"No, I ain't sure a nothin'."

"When ya killed that fella—did—did ya ever dream about it or anything? Did it worry ya?"

"No."

"Well, didn' ya never think about it?"

"Sure. I was sorry 'cause he was dead."

"Ya didn't take no blame to yourself?"

"No. I done my time, an' I done my own time."

"Was it—awful bad—there?"

Tom said nervously, "Look, Al. I done my time, an' now it's done. I don' wanna do it over an' over. There's the river up ahead, an' there's the town. Let's jus' try an' get a con-rod an' the hell with the res' of it."

"Ma's awful partial to you," said Al. "She mourned when you was gone. Done it all to herself. Kinda cryin' down inside of her throat. We could tell what she was thinkin' about, though."

Tom pulled his cap down low over his eyes. "Now look here, Al. S'pose we talk 'bout some other stuff."

"I was jus' tellin' ya what Ma done."

"I know—I know. But—I ruther not. I ruther jus'—lay one foot down in front a the other."

Al relapsed into an insulted silence. "I was jus' tryin' to tell ya," he said, after a moment.

Tom looked at him, and Al kept his eyes straight ahead. The lightened truck bounced noisily along. Tom's long lips drew up from his teeth and he laughed softly. "I know you was, Al. Maybe I'm kinda stir-nuts. I'll tell ya about it some-time maybe. Ya see, it's jus' somepin you wanta know. Kinda interestin'. But I got a kind a funny idear the bes' thing'd be if I forget about it for a while. Maybe in a little while it won't be that way. Right now when I think about it my guts gets all droopy an' nasty feelin'. Look here, Al, I'll tell ya one thing—the jail house is jus' a kind a way a drivin' a guy slowly nuts. See? An' they go nuts, an' you see 'em an' hear 'em, an' pretty soon you don' know if you're nuts or not. When they get to screamin' in the night sometimes you think it's you doin' the screamin'—an' sometimes it is."

Al said, "Oh! I won't talk about it no more, Tom."

"Thirty days is all right," Tom said. "An' a hunderd an' eighty days is all right. But over a year—I dunno. There's somepin about it that ain't like nothin' else in the worl'. Somepin screwy about it, somepin screwy about the whole idear a lockin' people up. Oh, the hell with it! I don' wanna talk about it. Look a the sun a-flashin' on them windas."

The truck drove to the service-station belt, and there on the right-hand side of the road was a wrecking yard—an acre lot surrounded by a high barbed-wire fence, a corrugated iron shed in front with used tires piled up by the doors, and price-marked. Behind the shed there was a little shack built of scrap, scrap lumber and pieces of tin. The windows were windshields built into the walls. In the grassy lot the wrecks lay, cars with twisted, stove-in noses, wounded cars lying on their sides with the wheels gone. Engines rusting on the ground and against the shed. A great pile of junk; fenders and truck sides, wheels and axles; over the whole lot a spirit of decay, of mold and rust; twisted iron, half-gutted engines, a mass of derelicts.

Al drove the truck up on the oily ground in front of the shed. Tom got out and looked into the dark doorway. "Don't see nobody," he said, and he called, "Anybody here?"

"Jesus, I hope they got a '25 Dodge."

Behind the shed a door banged. A specter of a man came through the dark shed. Thin, dirty, oily skin tight against stringy muscles. One eye was gone, and the raw, uncovered socket squirmed with eye muscles when his good eye moved. His jeans and shirt were thick and shiny with old grease, and his hands cracked and lined and cut. His heavy, pouting underlip hung out sullenly.

Tom asked, "You the boss?"

The one eye glared. "I work for the boss," he said sullenly. "Whatcha want?"

"Got a wrecked '25 Dodge? We need a con-rod."

"I don't know. If the boss was here he could tell ya—but he ain't here. He's went home."

"Can we look an' see?"

The man blew his nose into the palm of his hand and wiped his hand on his trousers. "You from hereabouts?"

"Come from east—goin' west."

"Look aroun' then. Burn the goddamn place down, for all I care."

"Looks like you don't love your boss none."

The man shambled close, his one eye flaring. "I hate 'im," he said softly. "I hate the son-of-a-bitch! Gone home now. Gone home to his house." The words fell stumbling out. "He got a way—he got a way a-pickin' a fella an' a-tearin' a fella. He—the son-of-a-bitch. Got a girl nineteen, purty. Says to me, 'How'd ya like ta marry her?' Says that right to me. An' tonight—says, 'They's a dance; how'd ya like to go?' Me, he says it to me!" Tears formed in his eye and tears dripped from the corner of the red eye socket. "Some day, by God—some day I'm gonna have a pipe wrench in my pocket. When he says them things he looks at my eye. An' I'm gonna, I'm gonna jus' take his head right down off his neck with that wrench, little piece at a time." He panted with his fury. "Little piece at a time, right down off'n his neck."

The sun disappeared behind the mountains. Al looked into the lot at the wrecked cars. "Over there, look, Tom! That there looks like a '25 or '26."

Tom turned to the one-eyed man. "Mind if we look?"

"Hell, no! Take any goddamn thing you want."

They walked, threading their way among the dead auto-mobiles, to a rusting sedan, resting on flat tires.

"Sure it's a '25," Al cried. "Can we yank off the pan, mister?"

Tom kneeled down and looked under the car. "Pan's off awready. One rod's been took. Looks like one gone." He wriggled under the car. "Get a crank an' turn her over, Al." He worked the rod against the shaft. "Purty much froze with grease." Al turned the crank slowly. "Easy," Tom called. He picked a splinter of wood from the ground and scraped the cake of grease from the bearing and the bearing bolts.

"How is she for tight?" Al asked.

"Well, she's a little loose, but not bad."

"Well, how is she for wore?"

"Got plenty shim. Ain't been all took up. Yeah, she's O.K. Turn her over easy now. Get her down, easy—there! Run over the truck an' get some tools."

The one-eyed man said, "I'll get you a box a tools." He shuffled off among the rusty cars and in a moment he came back with a tin box of tools. Tom dug out a socket wrench and handed it to Al.

"You take her off. Don' lose no shims an' don' let the bolts get away, an' keep track a the cotter-pins. Hurry up. The light's gettin' dim."

Al crawled under the car. "We oughta get us a set a socket wrenches," he called. "Can't get in no place with a monkey wrench."

"Yell out if you want a hand," Tom said.

The one-eyed man stood helplessly by. "I'll help ya if ya want," he said. "Know what that son-of-a-bitch done? He come by an' he got on white pants. An' he says, 'Come on, le's go out to my yacht.' By God, I'll whang him some day!" He breathed heavily. "I ain't been out with a woman sence I los' my eye. An' he says stuff like that." And big tears cut channels in the dirt beside his nose.

Tom said impatiently, "Whyn't you roll on? Got no guards to keep ya here."

"Yeah, that's easy to say. Ain't so easy to get a job—not for a one-eye' man."

Tom turned on him. "Now look-a-here, fella. You got that

eye wide open. An' ya dirty, ya stink. Ya jus' askin' for it. Ya like it. Lets ya feel sorry for yaself. 'Course ya can't get no woman with that empty eye flappin' aroun'. Put somepin over it an' wash ya face. You ain't hittin' nobody with no pipe wrench."

"I tell ya, a one-eye' fella got a hard row," the man said. "Can't see stuff the way other fellas can. Can't see how far off a thing is. Ever'thing's jus' flat."

Tom said, "Ya full a shit. Why, I knowed a one-legged whore one time. Think she was takin' two-bits in a alley? No, by God! She's gettin' half a dollar extra. She says, 'How many one-legged women you slep' with? None!' she says. 'O.K.,' she says. 'You got somepin pretty special here, an' it's gonna cos' ya half a buck extry.' An' by God, she was gettin' 'em, too, an' the fellas comin' out thinkin' they're pretty lucky. She says she's good luck. An' I knowed a hump-back in—in a place I was. Make his whole livin' lettin' folks rub his hump for luck. Jesus Christ, an' all you got is one eye gone."

The man said stumblingly, "Well, Jesus, ya see somebody edge away from ya, an' it gets into ya."

"Cover it up then, goddamn it. Ya stickin' it out like a cow's ass. Ya like to feel sorry for yaself. There ain't nothin' the matter with you. Buy yaself some white pants. Ya gettin' drunk an' cryin' in ya bed, I bet. Need any help, Al?"

"No," said Al. "I got this here bearin' loose. Jus' tryin' to work the piston down."

"Don' bang yaself," said Tom.

The one-eyed man said softly, "Think—somebody'd like—me?"

"Why, sure," said Tom. "Tell 'em ya dong's growed sence you los' your eye."

"Where at you fellas goin'?"

"California. Whole family. Gonna get work out there."

"Well, ya think a fella like me could get work? Black patch on my eye?"

"Why not? You ain't no cripple."

"Well—could I catch a ride with you fellas?"

"Christ, no. We're so goddamn full now we can't move. You get out some other way. Fix up one a these here wrecks an' go out by yaself."

"Maybe I will, by God," said the one-eyed man.

There was a clash of metal. "I got her," Al called.

"Well, bring her out, let's look at her." Al handed him the piston and connecting-rod and the lower half of the bearing.

Tom wiped the babbitt surface and sighted along it sideways. "Looks O.K. to me," he said. "Say, by God, if we had a light we could get this here in tonight."

"Say, Tom," Al said, "I been thinkin'. We got no ring clamps. Gonna be a job gettin' them rings in, specially underneath."

Tom said, "Ya know, a fella tol' me one time ya wrap some fine brass wire aroun' the ring to hol' her."

"Yeah, but how ya gonna get the wire off?"

"Ya don't get her off. She melts off an' don't hurt nothin'."

"Copper wire'd be better."

"It ain't strong enough," said Tom. He turned to the one-eyed man. "Got any fine brass wire?"

"I dunno. I think they's a spool somewheres. Where d'ya think a fella could get one a them black patches one-eye' fellas wear?"

"I don' know," said Tom. "Le's see if you can fin' that wire."

In the iron shed they dug through boxes until they found the spool. Tom set the rod in a vise and carefully wrapped the wire around the piston rings, forcing them deep into their slots, and where the wire was twisted he hammered it flat; and then he turned the piston and tapped the wire all around until it cleared the piston wall. He ran his finger up and down to make sure that the rings and wire were flush with the wall. It was getting dark in the shed. The one-eyed man brought a flashlight and shone its beam on the work.

"There she is!" said Tom. "Say—what'll ya take for that light?"

"Well, it ain't much good. Got fifteen cents' a new batteries. You can have her for—oh, thirty-five cents."

"O.K. An' what we owe ya for this here con-rod an' piston?"

The one-eyed man rubbed his forehead with a knuckle, and a line of dirt peeled off. "Well, sir, I jus' dunno. If the boss was here, he'd go to a parts book an' he'd find out how much is a new one, an' while you was workin', he'd be findin' out how bad you're hung up, an' how much jack ya got, an' then he'd—well, say it's eight bucks in the part book—he'd make a price a five bucks. An' if you put up a squawk, you'd get it for three. You say it's all me, but, by God, he's a son-of-a-bitch. Figgers how bad ya need it. I seen him git more for a ring gear than he give for the whole car."

"Yeah! But how much am I gonna give you for this here?"

"'Bout a buck, I guess.'"

"Awright, an' I'll give ya a quarter for this here socket wrench. Make it twice as easy." He handed over the silver. "Thank ya. An' cover up that goddamn eye."

Tom and Al got into the truck. It was deep dusk. Al started the motor and turned on the lights. "So long," Tom called. "See ya maybe in California." They turned across the highway and started back.

The one-eyed man watched them go, and then he went through the iron shed to his shack behind. It was dark inside. He felt his way to the mattress on the floor, and he stretched out and cried in his bed, and the cars whizzing by on the highway only strengthened the walls of his loneliness.

Tom said, "If you'd tol' me we'd get this here thing an' get her in tonight, I'd a said you was nuts."

"We'll get her in awright," said Al. "You got to do her, though. I'd be scared I'd get her too tight an' she'd burn out, or too loose an' she'd hammer out."

"I'll stick her in," said Tom. "If she goes out again, she goes out. I got nothin' to lose."

Al peered into the dusk. The lights made no impression on the gloom; but ahead, the eyes of a hunting cat flashed green in reflection of the lights. "You sure give that fella hell," Al said. "Sure did tell him where to lay down his dogs."

"Well, goddamn it, he was askin' for it! Jus' a pattin' hisself 'cause he got one eye, puttin' all the blame on his eye. He's a lazy, dirty son-of-a-bitch. Maybe he can snap out of it if he knowed people was wise to him."

Al said, "Tom, it wasn't nothin' I done burned out that bearin'."

Tom was silent for a moment, then, "I'm gonna take a fall

outa you, Al. You jus' scrabblin' ass over tit, fear somebody gonna pin some blame on you. I know what's a matter. Young fella, all full a piss an' vinegar. Wanta be a hell of a guy all the time. But, goddamn it, Al, don' keep ya guard up when nobody ain't sparrin' with ya. You gonna be all right."

Al did not answer him. He looked straight ahead. The truck rattled and banged over the road. A cat whipped out from the side of the road and Al swerved to hit it, but the wheels missed and the cat leaped into the grass.

"Nearly got him," said Al. "Say, Tom. You heard Connie talkin' how he's gonna study nights? I been thinkin' maybe I'd study nights too. You know, radio or television or Diesel engines. Fella might get started that-a-way."

"Might," said Tom. "Find out how much they gonna sock ya for the lessons, first. An' figger out if you're gonna study 'em. There was fellas takin' them mail lessons in McAlester. I never knowed one of 'em that finished up. Got sick of it an' left 'em slide."

"God Awmighty, we forgot to get somepin to eat."

"Well, Ma sent down plenty; preacher couldn' eat it all. Be some lef'. I wonder how long it'll take us to get to California."

"Christ, I don' know. Jus' plug away at her."

They fell into silence, and the dark came and the stars were sharp and white.

Casy got out of the back seat of the Dodge and strolled to the side of the road when the truck pulled up. "I never expected you so soon," he said.

Tom gathered the parts in the piece of sacking on the floor. "We was lucky," he said. "Got a flashlight, too. Gonna fix her right up."

"You forgot to take your dinner," said Casy.

"I'll get it when I finish. Here, Al, pull off the road a little more an' come hol' the light for me." He went directly to the Dodge and crawled under on his back. Al crawled under on his belly and directed the beam of the flashlight. "Not in my eyes. There, put her up." Tom worked the piston up into the cylinder, twisting and turning. The brass wire caught a little on the cylinder wall. With a quick push he forced it past the rings. "Lucky she's loose or the compression'd stop her. I think she's gonna work all right."

"Hope that wire don't clog the rings," said Al.

"Well, that's why I hammered her flat. She won't roll off. I think she'll jus' melt out an' maybe give the walls a brass plate."

"Think she might score the walls?"

Tom laughed. "Jesus Christ, them walls can take it. She's drinkin' oil like a gopher hole awready. Little more ain't gonna hurt none." He worked the rod down over the shaft and tested the lower half. "She'll take some shim." He said, "Casy!"

"Yeah."

"I'm takin' up this here bearing now. Get out to that crank an' turn her over slow when I tell ya." He tightened the bolts. "Now. Over slow!" And as the angular shaft turned, he worked the bearing against it. "Too much shim," Tom said. "Hold it, Casy." He took out the bolts and removed thin shims from each side and put the bolts back. "Try her again, Casy!" And he worked the rod again. "She's a lit-tle bit loose yet. Wonder if she'd be too tight if I took out more shim. I'll try her." Again he removed the bolts and took out another pair of the thin strips. "Now try her, Casy."

"That looks good," said Al.

Tom called, "She any harder to turn, Casy?"

"No, I don't think so."

"Well, I think she's snug here. I hope to God she is. Can't hone no babbitt without tools. This here socket wrench makes her a hell of a lot easier."

Al said, "Boss a that yard gonna be purty mad when he looks for that size socket an' she ain't there."

"That's his screwin'," said Tom. "We didn' steal her." He tapped the cotter-pins in and bent the ends out. "I think that's good. Look, Casy, you hold the light while me an' Al get this here pan up."

Casy knelt down and took the flashlight. He kept the beam on the working hands as they patted the gasket gently in place and lined the holes with the pan bolts. The two men strained at the weight of the pan, caught the end bolts, and then set in the others; and when they were all engaged, Tom took them up little by little until the pan settled evenly in against the gasket, and he tightened hard against the nuts.

"I guess that's her," Tom said. He tightened the oil tap, looked carefully up at the pan, and took the light and searched the ground. "There she is. Le's get the oil back in her."

They crawled out and poured the bucket of oil back in the crank case. Tom inspected the gasket for leaks.

"O.K., Al. Turn her over," he said. Al got into the car and stepped on the starter. The motor caught with a roar. Blue smoke poured from the exhaust pipe. "Throttle down!" Tom shouted. "She'll burn oil till that wire goes. Gettin' thinner now." And as the motor turned over, he listened carefully. "Put up the spark an' let her idle." He listened again. "O.K., Al. Turn her off. I think we done her. Where's that meat now?"

"You make a darn good mechanic," Al said.

"Why not? I worked in the shop a year. We'll take her good an' slow for a couple hunderd miles. Give her a chance to work in."

They wiped their grease-covered hands on bunches of weeds and finally rubbed them on their trousers. They fell hungrily on the boiled pork and swigged the water from the bottle.

"I like to starved," said Al. "What we gonna do now, go on to the camp?"

"I dunno," said Tom. "Maybe they'd charge us a extry half-buck. Le's go on an' talk to the folks—tell 'em we're fixed. Then if they wanta sock us extry—we'll move on. The folks'll wanta know. Jesus, I'm glad Ma stopped us this afternoon. Look around with the light, Al. See we don't leave nothin'. Get that socket wrench in. We may need her again."

Al searched the ground with the flashlight. "Don't see nothin'."

"All right. I'll drive her. You bring the truck, Al." Tom started the engine. The preacher got in the car. Tom moved slowly, keeping the engine at a low speed, and Al followed in the truck. He crossed the shallow ditch, crawling in low gear. Tom said, "These here Dodges can pull a house in low gear. She's sure ratio'd down. Good thing for us—I wanta break that bearin' in easy."

On the highway the Dodge moved along slowly. The 12-volt headlights threw a short blob of yellowish light on the pavement.

Casy turned to Tom. "Funny how you fellas can fix a car. Jus' light right in an' fix her. I couldn't fix no car, not even now when I seen you do it."

"Got to grow into her when you're a little kid," Tom said. "It ain't jus' knowin'. It's more'n that. Kids now can tear down a car 'thout even thinkin' about it."

A jackrabbit got caught in the lights and he bounced along ahead, cruising easily, his great ears flopping with every jump. Now and then he tried to break off the road, but the wall of darkness thrust him back. Far ahead bright headlights appeared and bore down on them. The rabbit hesitated, faltered, then turned and bolted toward the lesser lights of the Dodge. There was a small soft jolt as he went under the wheels. The oncoming car swished by.

"We sure squashed him," said Casy.

Tom said, "Some fellas like to hit 'em. Gives me a little shakes ever' time. Car sounds O.K. Them rings must a broke loose by now. She ain't smokin' so bad."

"You done a nice job," said Casy.

A small wooden house dominated the camp ground, and on the porch of the house a gasoline lantern hissed and threw its white glare in a great circle. Half a dozen tents were pitched near the house, and cars stood beside the tents. Cooking for the night was over, but the coals of the campfires still glowed on the ground by the camping places. A group of men had gathered to the porch where the lantern burned, and their faces were strong and muscled under the harsh white light, light that threw black shadows of their hats over their foreheads and eyes and made their chins seem to jut out. They sat on the steps, and some stood on the ground, resting their elbows on the porch floor. The proprietor, a sullen lanky man, sat in a chair on the porch. He leaned back against the wall, and he drummed his fingers on his knee. Inside the house a kerosene lamp burned, but its thin light was blasted by the hissing glare of the gasoline lantern. The gathering of men surrounded the proprietor.

Tom drove the Dodge to the side of the road and parked. Al drove through the gate in the truck. "No need to take her in," Tom said. He got out and walked through the gate to the white glare of the lantern.

The proprietor dropped his front chair legs to the floor and leaned forward. "You men wanta camp here?"

"No," said Tom. "We got folks here. Hi, Pa."

Pa, seated on the bottom step, said, "Thought you was gonna be all week. Get her fixed?"

"We was pig lucky," said Tom. "Got a part 'fore dark. We can get goin' fust thing in the mornin'."

"That's a pretty nice thing," said Pa. "Ma's worried. Ya Granma's off her chump."

"Yeah, Al tol' me. She any better now?"

"Well, anyways she's a-sleepin'."

The proprietor said, "If you wanta pull in here an' camp it'll cost you four bits. Get a place to camp an' water an' wood. An' nobody won't bother you."

"What the hell," said Tom. "We can sleep in the ditch right beside the road, an' it won't cost nothin'."

The owner drummed his knee with his fingers. "Deputy sheriff comes on by in the night. Might make it tough for ya. Got a law against sleepin' out in this State. Got a law about vagrants."

"If I pay you a half a dollar I ain't a vagrant, huh?"

"That's right."

Tom's eyes glowed angrily. "Deputy sheriff ain't your brother-'n-law by any chance?"

The owner leaned forward. "No, he ain't. An' the time ain't come yet when us local folks got to take no shit from you goddamn bums, neither."

"It don't trouble you none to take our four bits. An' when'd we get to be bums? We ain't asked ya for nothin'. All of us bums, huh? Well, we ain't askin' no nickels from you for the chance to lay down an' rest."

The men on the porch were rigid, motionless, quiet. Expression was gone from their faces; and their eyes, in the shadows under their hats, moved secretly up to the face of the proprietor.

Pa growled, "Come off it, Tom."

"Sure, I'll come off it."

The circle of men were quiet, sitting on the steps, leaning on the high porch. Their eyes glittered under the harsh light of the gas lantern. Their faces were hard in the hard light, and they were very still. Only their eyes moved from speaker to speaker, and their faces were expressionless and quiet. A lamp bug slammed into the lantern and broke itself, and fell into the darkness.

In one of the tents a child wailed in complaint, and a woman's soft voice soothed it and then broke into a low song, "Jesus loves you in the night. Sleep good, sleep good. Jesus watches in the night. Sleep, oh, sleep, oh."

The lantern hissed on the porch. The owner scratched in the V of his open shirt, where a tangle of white chest hair showed. He was watchful and ringed with trouble. He watched the men in the circle, watched for some expression. And they made no move.

Tom was silent for a long time. His dark eyes looked slowly up at the proprietor. "I don't wanta make no trouble," he said. "It's a hard thing to be named a bum. I ain't afraid," he said softly. "I'll go for you an' your deputy with my mitts—here now, or jump Jesus. But there ain't no good in it."

The men stirred, changed positions, and their glittering eyes moved slowly upward to the mouth of the proprietor, and their eyes watched for his lips to move. He was reassured. He felt that he had won, but not decisively enough to charge in. "Ain't you got half a buck?" he asked.

"Yeah, I got it. But I'm gonna need it. I can't set it out jus' for sleepin'."

"Well, we all got to make a livin'."

"Yeah," Tom said. "On'y I wisht they was some way to make her 'thout takin' her away from somebody else."

The men shifted again. And Pa said, "We'll get movin' smart early. Look, mister. We paid. This here fella is part a our folks. Can't he stay? We paid."

"Half a dollar a car," said the proprietor.

"Well, he ain't got no car. Car's out in the road."

"He came in a car," said the proprietor. "Ever'body'd leave their car out there an' come in an' use my place for nothin'."

Tom said, "We'll drive along the road. Meet ya in the morning. We'll watch for ya. Al can stay an' Uncle John can come with us—" He looked at the proprietor. "That awright with you?"

He made a quick decision, with a concession in it. "If the same number stays that come an' paid—that's awright."

Tom brought out his bag of tobacco, a limp gray rag by now, with a little damp tobacco dust in the bottom of it. He made a lean cigarette and tossed the bag away. "We'll go along pretty soon," he said.

Pa spoke generally to the circle. "It's dirt hard for folks to tear up an' go. Folks like us that had our place. We ain't shif'less. Till we got tractored off, we was people with a farm."

A young thin man, with eyebrows sunburned yellow, turned his head slowly. "Croppin'?" he asked.

"Sure we was sharecroppin'. Use' ta own the place."

The young man faced forward again. "Same as us," he said.

"Lucky for us it ain't gonna las' long," said Pa. "We'll get out west an' we'll get work an' we'll get a piece a growin' land with water."

Near the edge of the porch a ragged man stood. His black coat dripped torn streamers. The knees were gone from his dungarees. His face was black with dust, and lined where sweat had washed through. He swung his head toward Pa. "You folks must have a nice little pot a money."

"No, we ain't got no money," Pa said. "But they's plenty of us to work, an' we're all good men. Get good wages out there an' we'll put 'em together. We'll make out."

The ragged man stared while Pa spoke, and then he laughed, and his laughter turned to a high whinnying giggle. The circle of faces turned to him. The giggling got out of control and turned into coughing. His eyes were red and watering when he finally controlled the spasms. "You goin' out there—oh, Christ!" The giggling started again. "You goin' out an' get—good wages—oh, Christ!" He stopped and said slyly, "Pickin' oranges maybe? Gonna pick peaches?"

Pa's tone was dignified. "We gonna take what they got. They got lots a stuff to work in." The ragged man giggled under his breath.

Tom turned irritably. "What's so goddamn funny about that?"

The ragged man shut his mouth and looked sullenly at the porch boards. "You folks all goin' to California, I bet."

"I tol' you that," said Pa. "You didn' guess nothin'."

The ragged man said slowly, "Me—I'm comin' back. I been there."

The faces turned quickly toward him. The men were rigid. The hiss of the lantern dropped to a sigh and the proprietor lowered the front chair legs to the porch, stood up, and pumped the lantern until the hiss was sharp and high again. He went back to his chair, but he did not tilt back again. The ragged man turned toward the faces. "I'm goin' back to starve. I ruther starve all over at oncet."

Pa said, "What the hell you talkin' about? I got a han'bill says they got good wages, an' little while ago I seen a thing in the paper says they need folks to pick fruit."

The ragged man turned to Pa. "You got any place to go, back home?"

"No," said Pa. "We're out. They put a tractor past the house."

"You wouldn' go back then?"

" 'Course not."

"Then I ain't gonna fret you," said the ragged man.

" 'Course you ain't gonna fret me. I got a han'bill says they need men. Don't make no sense if they don't need men. Costs money for them bills. They wouldn' put 'em out if they didn' need men."

"I don' wanna fret you."

Pa said angrily, "You done some jackassin'. You ain't gonna shut up now. My han'bill says they need men. You laugh an' say they don't. Now, which one's a liar?"

The ragged man looked down into Pa's angry eyes. He looked sorry. "Han'bill's right," he said. "They need men."

"Then why the hell you stirrin' us up laughin'?"

" 'Cause you don't know what kind a men they need."

"What you talkin' about?"

The ragged man reached a decision. "Look," he said. "How many men they say they want on your han'bill?"

"Eight hunderd, an' that's in one little place."

"Orange color han'bill?"

"Why—yes."

"Give the name a the fella—says so and so, labor contractor?"

Pa reached in his pocket and brought out the folded handbill. "That's right. How'd you know?"

"Look," said the man. "It don't make no sense. This fella wants eight hundred men. So he prints up five thousand of them things an' maybe twenty thousan' people sees 'em. An' maybe two-three thousan' folks gets movin' account a this here han'bill. Folks that's crazy with worry."

"But it don't make no sense!" Pa cried.

"Not till you see the fella that put out this here bill. You'll see him, or somebody that's workin' for him. You'll be a-campin' by a ditch, you an' fifty other famblies. An' he'll come in. He'll look in your tent an' see if you got anything lef' to eat. An' if you got nothin', he says, 'Wanna job?' An' you'll say, 'I sure do, mister. I'll sure thank you for a chance to do some work.' An' he'll say, 'I can use you.' An' you'll say, 'When do I start?' An' he'll tell you where to go, an' what time, an' then he'll go on. Maybe he needs two hunderd men, so he talks to five hunderd, an' they tell other folks, an' when you get to the place, they's a thousan' men. This here fella says, 'I'm payin' twenty cents an hour.' An' maybe half a the men walk off. But they's still five hunderd that's so goddamn hungry they'll work for nothin' but biscuits. Well, this here fella's got a contract to pick them peaches or—chop that cotton. You see now? The more fellas he can get, an' the hungrier, less he's gonna pay. An' he'll get a fella with kids if he can, 'cause—hell, I says I wasn't gonna fret ya." The circle of faces looked coldly at him. The eyes tested his words. The ragged man grew self-conscious. "I says I wasn't gonna fret ya, an' here I'm a-doin' it. You gonna go on. You ain't goin' back." The silence hung on the porch. And the light hissed, and a halo of moths swung around and around the lantern. The ragged man went on nervously, "Lemme tell ya what to do when ya meet that fella says he got work. Lemme tell ya. Ast him what he's gonna pay. Ast him to write down what he's gonna pay. Ast him that. I tell you men you're gonna get fucked if you don't."

The proprietor leaned forward in his chair, the better to see the ragged dirty man. He scratched among the gray hairs on his chest. He said coldly, "You sure you ain't one of these here troublemakers? You sure you ain't a labor faker?"

And the ragged man cried, "I swear to God I ain't!"

"They's plenty of 'em," the proprietor said. "Goin' aroun' stirrin' up trouble. Gettin' folks mad. Chiselin' in. They's plenty of 'em. Time's gonna come when we string 'em all up, all them troublemakers. We gonna run 'em outa the country. Man wants to work, O.K. If he don't—the hell with him. We ain't gonna let him stir up trouble."

The ragged man drew himself up. "I tried to tell you fellas," he said. "Somepin it took me a year to find out. Took two kids dead, took my wife dead to show me. But I can't tell you. I should of knew that. Nobody couldn't tell me, neither. I can't tell ya about them little fellas layin' in the tent with their bellies puffed out an' jus' skin on their bones, an' shiverin' an' whinin' like pups, an' me runnin' aroun' tryin' to get work—not for money, not for wages!" he shouted. "Jesus Christ, jus' for a cup a flour an' a spoon a lard. An' then the coroner come. 'Them children died a heart failure,' he said. Put it on his paper. Shiverin', they was, an' their bellies stuck out like a pig bladder."

The circle was quiet, and mouths were open a little. The men breathed shallowly, and watched.

The ragged man looked around at the circle, and then he turned and walked quickly away into the darkness. The dark swallowed him, but his dragging footsteps could be heard a long time after he had gone, footsteps along the road; and a car came by on the highway, and its lights showed the ragged man shuffling along the road, his head hanging down and his hands in the black coat pockets.

The men were uneasy. One said, "Well—gettin' late. Got to get to sleep."

The proprietor said, "Prob'ly shif'less. They's so goddamn many shif'less fellas on the road now." And then he was quiet. And he tipped his chair back against the wall again and fingered his throat.

Tom said, "Guess I'll go see Ma for a minute, an' then we'll shove along a piece." The Joad men moved away.

Pa said, "S'pose he's tellin' the truth—that fella?"

The preacher answered, "He's tellin' the truth, awright. The truth for him. He wasn't makin' nothin' up."

"How about us?" Tom demanded. "Is that the truth for us?"

"I don' know," said Casy.

"I don' know," said Pa.

They walked to the tent, tarpaulin spread over a rope. And it was dark inside, and quiet. When they came near, a grayish mass stirred near the door and arose to person height. Ma came out to meet them.

"All sleepin'," she said. "Granma finally dozed off." Then she saw it was Tom. "How'd you get here?" she demanded anxiously. "You ain't had no trouble?"

"Got her fixed," said Tom. "We're ready to go when the rest is."

"Thank the dear God for that," Ma said. "I'm just a-twit-terin' to go on. Wanta get where it's rich an' green. Wanta get there quick."

Pa cleared his throat. "Fella was jus' sayin'——"

Tom grabbed his arm and yanked it. "Funny what he says," Tom said. "Says they's lots a folks on the way."

Ma peered through the darkness at them. Inside the tent Ruthie coughed and snorted in her sleep. "I washed 'em up," Ma said. "Fust water we got enough of to give 'em a goin'-over. Lef' the buckets out for you fellas to wash too. Can't keep nothin' clean on the road."

"Ever'body in?" Pa asked.

"All but Connie an' Rosasharn. They went off to sleep in the open. Says it's too warm in under cover."

Pa observed querulously, "That Rosasharn is gettin' awful scary an' nimsy-mimsy."

"It's her fust," said Ma. "Her an' Connie sets a lot a store by it. You done the same thing."

"We'll go now," Tom said. "Pull off the road a little piece ahead. Watch out for us ef we don't see you. Be off right-han' side."

"Al's stayin'?"

"Yeah. Leave Uncle John come with us. 'Night, Ma."

They walked away through the sleeping camp. In front of

one tent a low fitful fire burned, and a woman watched a kettle that cooked early breakfast. The smell of the cooking beans was strong and fine.

"Like to have a plate a them," Tom said politely as they went by.

The woman smiled. "They ain't done or you'd be welcome," she said. "Come aroun' in the daybreak."

"Thank you, ma'am," Tom said. He and Casy and Uncle John walked by the porch. The proprietor still sat in his chair, and the lantern hissed and flared. He turned his head as the three went by. "Ya runnin' outa gas," Tom said.

"Well, time to close up anyways."

"No more half-bucks rollin' down the road, I guess," Tom said.

The chair legs hit the floor. "Don't you go a-sassin' me. I 'member you. You're one of these here troublemakers."

"Damn right," said Tom. "I'm bolshevisky."

"They's too damn many of you kinda guys aroun'."

Tom laughed as they went out the gate and climbed into the Dodge. He picked up a clod and threw it at the light. They heard it hit the house and saw the proprietor spring to his feet and peer into the darkness. Tom started the car and pulled into the road. And he listened closely to the motor as it turned over, listened for knocks. The road spread dimly under the weak lights of the car.

Chapter Seventeen

T HE CARS of the migrant people crawled out of the side roads onto the great cross-country highway, and then took the migrant way to the West. In the daylight they scuttled like bugs to the westward; and as the dark caught them, they clustered like bugs near to shelter and to water. And because they were lonely and perplexed, because they had all come from a place of sadness and worry and defeat, and because they were all going to a new mysterious place, they huddled together; they talked together; they shared their lives, their food, and the things they hoped for in the new country. Thus it might be that one family camped near a spring, and another camped for the spring and for company, and a third because two families had pioneered the place and found it good. And when the sun went down, perhaps twenty families and twenty cars were there.

In the evening a strange thing happened: the twenty families became one family, the children were the children of all. The loss of home became one loss, and the golden time in the West was one dream. And it might be that a sick child threw despair into the hearts of twenty families, of a hundred people; that a birth there in a tent kept a hundred people quiet and awestruck through the night and filled a hundred people with the birth-joy in the morning. A family which the night before had been lost and fearful might search its goods to find a present for a new baby. In the evening, sitting about the fires, the twenty were one. They grew to be units of the camps, units of the evenings and the nights. A guitar unwrapped from a blanket and tuned—and the songs, which were all of the people, were sung in the nights. Men sang the words, and women hummed the tunes.

Every night a world created, complete with furniture—friends made and enemies established; a world complete with braggarts and with cowards, with quiet men, with humble men, with kindly men. Every night relationships that make a world, established; and every morning the world torn down like a circus.

At first the families were timid in the building and tumbling worlds, but gradually the technique of building worlds became their technique. Then leaders emerged, then laws were made, then codes came into being. And as the worlds moved westward they were more complete and better furnished, for their builders were more experienced in building them.

The families learned what rights must be observed—the right of privacy in the tent; the right to keep the past black hidden in the heart; the right to talk and to listen; the right to refuse help or to accept, to offer help or to decline it; the right of son to court and daughter to be courted; the right of the hungry to be fed; the rights of the pregnant and the sick to transcend all other rights.

And the families learned, although no one told them, what rights are monstrous and must be destroyed: the right to intrude upon privacy, the right to be noisy while the camp slept, the right of seduction or rape, the right of adultery and theft and murder. These rights were crushed, because the little worlds could not exist for even a night with such rights alive.

And as the worlds moved westward, rules became laws, although no one told the families. It is unlawful to shit near the camp; it is unlawful in any way to foul the drinking water; it is unlawful to eat good rich food near one who is hungry, unless he is asked to share.

And with the laws, the punishments—and there were only two—a quick and murderous fight or ostracism; and ostracism was the worst. For if one broke the laws his name and face went with him, and he had no place in any world, no matter where created.

In the worlds, social conduct became fixed and rigid, so that a man must say "Good morning" when asked for it, so that a man might have a willing girl if he stayed with her, if he fathered her children and protected them. But a man might not have one girl one night and another the next, for this would endanger the worlds.

The families moved westward, and the technique of building the worlds improved so that the people could be safe in their worlds; and the form was so fixed that a family acting in the rules knew it was safe in the rules.

There grew up government in the worlds, with leaders, with

elders. A man who was wise found that his wisdom was needed in every camp; a man who was a fool could not change his folly with his world. And a kind of insurance developed in these nights. A man with food fed a hungry man, and thus insured himself against hunger. And when a baby died a pile of silver coins grew at the door flap, for a baby must be well buried, since it has had nothing else of life. An old man may be left in a potter's field, but not a baby.

A certain physical pattern is needed for the building of a world—water, a river bank, a stream, a spring, or even a faucet unguarded. And there is needed enough flat land to pitch the tents, a little brush or wood to build the fires. If there is a garbage dump not too far off, all the better; for there can be found equipment—stove tops, a curved fender to shelter the fire, and cans to cook in and to eat from.

And the worlds were built in the evening. The people, moving in from the highways, made them with their tents and their hearts and their brains.

In the morning the tents came down, the canvas was folded, the tent poles tied along the running board, the beds put in place on the cars, the pots in their places. And as the families moved westward, the technique of building up a home in the evening and tearing it down with the morning light became fixed; so that the folded tent was packed in one place, the cooking pots counted in their box. And as the cars moved westward, each member of the family grew into his proper place, grew into his duties; so that each member, old and young, had his place in the car; so that in the weary, hot evenings, when the cars pulled into the camping places, each member had his duty and went to it without instruction: children to gather wood, to carry water; men to pitch the tents and bring down the beds; women to cook the supper and to watch while the family fed. And this was done without command. The families, which had been units of which the boundaries were a house at night, a farm by day, changed their boundaries. In the long hot light, they were silent in the cars moving slowly westward; but at night they integrated with any group they found.

Thus they changed their social life—changed as in the whole universe only man can change. They were not farm men any more, but migrant men. And the thought, the planning, the long staring silence that had gone out to the fields, went now to the roads, to the distance, to the West. That man whose mind had been bound with acres lived with narrow concrete miles. And his thought and his worry were not any more with rainfall, with wind and dust, with the thrust of the crops. Eyes watched the tires, ears listened to the clattering motors, and minds struggled with oil, with gasoline, with the thinning rubber between air and road. Then a broken gear was tragedy. Then water in the evening was the yearning, and food over the fire. Then health to go on was the need and strength to go on, and spirit to go on. The wills thrust westward ahead of them, and fears that had once apprehended drought or flood now lingered with anything that might stop the westward crawling.

The camps became fixed—each a short day's journey from the last.

And on the road the panic overcame some of the families, so that they drove night and day, stopped to sleep in the cars, and drove on to the West, flying from the road, flying from movement. And these lusted so greatly to be settled that they set their faces into the West and drove toward it, forcing the clashing engines over the roads.

But most of the families changed and grew quickly into the new life. And when the sun went down——

Time to look out for a place to stop.

And—there's some tents ahead.

The car pulled off the road and stopped, and because others were there first, certain courtesies were necessary. And the man, the leader of the family, leaned from the car.

Can we pull up here an' sleep?

Why, sure, be proud to have you. What State you from?

Come all the way from Arkansas.

They's Arkansas people down that fourth tent.

That so?

And the great question, How's the water?

Well, she don't taste so good, but they's plenty.

Well, thank ya.

No thanks to me.

But the courtesies had to be. The car lumbered over the

ground to the end tent, and stopped. Then down from the
car the weary people climbed, and stretched stiff bodies. Then
the new tent sprang up; the children went for water and the
older boys cut brush or wood. The fires started and supper
was put on to boil or to fry. Early comers moved over, and
States were exchanged, and friends and sometimes relatives
discovered.

Oklahoma, huh? What county?

Cherokee.

Why, I got folks there. Know the Allens? They's Allens all
over Cherokee. Know the Willises?

Why, sure.

And a new unit was formed. The dusk came, but before the
dark was down the new family was of the camp. A word had
been passed with every family. They were known people—
good people.

I knowed the Allens all my life. Simon Allen, ol' Simon,
had trouble with his first wife. She was part Cherokee. Purty
as a black colt.

Sure, an' young Simon, he married a Rudolph, didn' he?
That's what I thought. They went to live in Enid an' done
well—real well.

Only Allen that ever done well. Got a garage.

When the water was carried and the wood cut, the children
walked shyly, cautiously among the tents. And they made elaborate acquaintanceship gestures. A boy stopped near another
boy and studied a stone, picked it up, examined it closely, spat
on it, and rubbed it clean and inspected it until he forced the
other to demand, What you got there?

And casually, Nothin'. Jus' a rock.

Well, what you lookin' at it like that for?

Thought I seen gold in it.

How'd you know? Gold ain't gold, it's black in a rock.

Sure, ever'body knows that.

I bet it's fool's gold, an' you figgered it was gold.

That ain't so, 'cause Pa, he's foun' lots a gold an' he tol'
me how to look.

How'd you like to pick up a big ol' piece a gold?

Sa-a-ay! I'd git the bigges' old son-a-bitchin' piece a candy
you ever seen.

I ain't let to swear, but I do, anyways.

Me too. Le's go to the spring.

And young girls found each other and boasted shyly of their popularity and their prospects. The women worked over the fire, hurrying to get food to the stomachs of the family—pork if there was money in plenty, pork and potatoes and onions. Dutch-oven biscuits or cornbread, and plenty of gravy to go over it. Side-meat or chops and a can of boiled tea, black and bitter. Fried dough in drippings if money was slim, dough fried crisp and brown and the drippings poured over it.

Those families which were very rich or very foolish with their money ate canned beans and canned peaches and packaged bread and bakery cake; but they ate secretly, in their tents, for it would not have been good to eat such fine things openly. Even so, children eating their fried dough smelled the warming beans and were unhappy about it.

When supper was over and the dishes dipped and wiped, the dark had come, and then the men squatted down to talk.

And they talked of the land behind them. I don' know what it's coming to, they said. The country's spoilt.

It'll come back though, on'y we won't be there.

Maybe, they thought, maybe we sinned some way we didn't know about.

Fella says to me, gov'ment fella, an' he says, she's gullied up on ya. Gov'ment fella. He says, if ya plowed 'cross the contour, she won't gully. Never did have no chance to try her. An' the new super' ain't plowin' 'cross the contour. Runnin' a furrow four miles long that ain't stoppin' or goin' aroun' Jesus Christ Hisself.

And they spoke softly of their homes: They was a little coolhouse under the win'mill. Use' ta keep milk in there ta cream up, an' watermelons. Go in there midday when she was hotter'n a heifer, an' she'd be jus' as cool, as cool as you'd want. Cut open a melon in there an' she'd hurt your mouth, she was so cool. Water drippin' down from the tank.

They spoke of their tragedies: Had a brother Charley, hair as yella as corn, an' him a growed man. Played the 'cordeen nice too. He was harrowin' one day an' he went up to clear his lines. Well, a rattlesnake buzzed an' them horses bolted an' the harrow went over Charley, an' the points dug into his guts an' his stomach, an' they pulled his face off an'—God Almighty!

They spoke of the future: Wonder what it's like out there?

Well, the pitchers sure do look nice. I seen one where it's hot an' fine, an' walnut trees an' berries; an' right behind, close as a mule's ass to his withers, they's a tall up mountain covered with snow. That was a pretty thing to see.

If we can get work it'll be fine. Won't have no cold in the winter. Kids won't freeze on the way to school. I'm gonna take care my kids don't miss no more school. I can read good, but it ain't no pleasure to me like with a fella that's used to it.

And perhaps a man brought out his guitar to the front of his tent. And he sat on a box to play, and everyone in the camp moved slowly in toward him, drawn in toward him. Many men can chord a guitar, but perhaps this man was a picker. There you have something—the deep chords beating, beating, while the melody runs on the strings like little foot-steps. Heavy hard fingers marching on the frets. The man played and the people moved slowly in on him until the circle was closed and tight, and then he sang "Ten-Cent Cotton and Forty-Cent Meat." And the circle sang softly with him. And he sang "Why Do You Cut Your Hair, Girls?" And the circle sang. He wailed the song, "I'm Leaving Old Texas," that eerie song that was sung before the Spaniards came, only the words were Indian then.

And now the group was welded to one thing, one unit, so that in the dark the eyes of the people were inward, and their minds played in other times, and their sadness was like rest, like sleep. He sang the "McAlester Blues" and then, to make up for it to the older people, he sang "Jesus Calls Me to His Side." The children drowsed with the music and went into the tents to sleep, and the singing came into their dreams.

And after a while the man with the guitar stood up and yawned. Good night, folks, he said.

And they murmured, Good night to you.

And each wished he could pick a guitar, because it is a gra-cious thing. Then the people went to their beds, and the camp was quiet. And the owls coasted overhead, and the coyotes gabbled in the distance, and into the camp skunks walked, looking for bits of food—waddling, arrogant skunks, afraid of nothing.

The night passed, and with the first streak of dawn the women came out of the tents, built up the fires, and put the coffee to boil. And the men came out and talked softly in the dawn.

When you cross the Colorado river, there's the desert, they say. Look out for the desert. See you don't get hung up. Take plenty water, case you get hung up.

I'm gonna take her at night.

Me too. She'll cut the living Jesus outa you.

The families ate quickly, and the dishes were dipped and wiped. The tents came down. There was a rush to go. And when the sun arose, the camping place was vacant, only a little litter left by the people. And the camping place was ready for a new world in a new night.

But along the highway the cars of the migrant people crawled out like bugs, and the narrow concrete miles stretched ahead.

Chapter Eighteen

THE JOAD FAMILY moved slowly westward, up into the mountains of New Mexico, past the pinnacles and pyramids of the upland. They climbed into the high country of Arizona, and through a gap they looked down on the Painted Desert. A border guard stopped them.

"Where you going?"

"To California," said Tom.

"How long you plan to be in Arizona?"

"No longer'n we can get acrost her."

"Got any plants?"

"No plants."

"I ought to look your stuff over."

"I tell you we ain't got no plants."

The guard put a little sticker on the windshield.

"O.K. Go ahead, but you better keep movin'."

"Sure. We aim to."

They crawled up the slopes, and the low twisted trees covered the slopes. Holbrook, Joseph City, Winslow. And then the tall trees began, and the cars spouted steam and labored up the slopes. And there was Flagstaff, and that was the top of it all. Down from Flagstaff over the great plateaus, and the road disappeared in the distance ahead. The water grew scarce, water was to be bought, five cents, ten cents, fifteen cents a gallon. The sun drained the dry rocky country, and ahead were jagged broken peaks, the western wall of Arizona. And now they were in flight from the sun and the drought. They drove all night, and came to the mountains in the night. And they crawled the jagged ramparts in the night, and their dim lights flickered on the pale stone walls of the road. They passed the summit in the dark and came slowly down in the late night, through the shattered stone debris of Oatman; and when the daylight came they saw the Colorado river below them. They drove to Topock, pulled up at the bridge while a guard washed off the windshield sticker. Then across the bridge and into the broken rock wilderness. And although they were dead weary and the morning heat was growing, they stopped.

Pa called, "We're there—we're in California!" They looked dully at the broken rock glaring under the sun, and across the river the terrible ramparts of Arizona.

"We got the desert," said Tom. "We got to get to the water and rest."

The road runs parallel to the river, and it was well into the morning when the burning motors came to Needles, where the river runs swiftly among the reeds.

The Joads and Wilsons drove to the river, and they sat in the cars looking at the lovely water flowing by, and the green reeds jerking slowly in the current. There was a little encampment by the river, eleven tents near the water, and the swamp grass on the ground. And Tom leaned out of the truck window. "Mind if we stop here a piece?"

A stout woman, scrubbing clothes in a bucket, looked up. "We don't own it, mister. Stop if you want. They'll be a cop down to look you over." And she went back to her scrubbing in the sun.

The two cars pulled to a clear place on the swamp grass. The tents were passed down, the Wilson tent set up, the Joad tarpaulin stretched over its rope.

Winfield and Ruthie walked slowly down through the willows to the reedy place. Ruthie said, with soft vehemence, "California. This here's California an' we're right in it!"

Winfield broke a tule and twisted it free, and he put the white pulp in his mouth and chewed it. They walked into the water and stood quietly, the water about the calves of their legs.

"We got the desert yet," Ruthie said.

"What's the desert like?"

"I don't know. I seen pitchers once says a desert. They was bones ever'place."

"Man bones?"

"Some, I guess, but mos'ly cow bones."

"We gonna get to see them bones?"

"Maybe. I don' know. Gonna go 'crost her at night. That's what Tom said. Tom says we get the livin' Jesus burned outa us if we go in daylight."

"Feels nicet an' cool," said Winfield, and he squidged his toes in the sand of the bottom.

They heard Ma calling, "Ruthie! Winfiel'! You come back." They turned and walked slowly back through the reeds and the willows.

The other tents were quiet. For a moment, when the cars came up, a few heads had stuck out between the flaps, and then were withdrawn. Now the family tents were up and the men gathered together.

Tom said, "I'm gonna go down an' take a bath. That's what I'm gonna do—before I sleep. How's Granma sence we got her in the tent?"

"Don' know," said Pa. "Couldn' seem to wake her up." He cocked his head toward the tent. A whining, babbling voice came from under the canvas. Ma went quickly inside.

"She woke up, awright," said Noah. "Seems like all night she was a-croakin' up on the truck. She's all outa sense."

Tom said, "Hell! She's wore out. If she don't get some res' pretty soon, she ain' gonna las'. She's jes' wore out. Anybody comin' with me? I'm gonna wash, an' I'm gonna sleep in the shade—all day long." He moved away, and the other men followed him. They took off their clothes in the willows and then they walked into the water and sat down. For a long time they sat, holding themselves with heels dug into the sand, and only their heads stuck out of the water.

"Jesus, I needed this," Al said. He took a handful of sand from the bottom and scrubbed himself with it. They lay in the water and looked across at the sharp peaks called Needles, and at the white rock mountains of Arizona.

"We come through them," Pa said in wonder.

Uncle John ducked his head under the water. "Well, we're here. This here's California, an' she don't look so prosperous."

"Got the desert yet," said Tom. "An' I hear she's a son-of-a-bitch."

Noah asked, "Gonna try her tonight?"

"What ya think, Pa?" Tom asked.

"Well, I don' know. Do us good to get a little res', 'specially Granma. But other ways, I'd kinda like to get acrost her an' get settled into a job. On'y got 'bout forty dollars left. I'll feel better when we're all workin', an' a little money comin' in."

Each man sat in the water and felt the tug of the current. The preacher let his arms and hands float on the surface. The bodies were white to the neck and wrists, and burned dark brown on hands and faces, with V's of brown at the collar bones. They scratched themselves with sand.

And Noah said lazily, "Like to jus' stay here. Like to lay here forever. Never get hungry an' never get sad. Lay in the water all life long, lazy as a brood sow in the mud."

And Tom, looking at the ragged peaks across the river and the Needles downstream: "Never seen such tough mountains. This here's a murder country. This here's the bones of a country. Wonder if we'll ever get in a place where folks can live 'thout fightin' hard scrabble an' rocks. I seen pitchers of a country flat an' green, an' with little houses like Ma says, white. Ma got her heart set on a white house. Get to thinkin' they ain't no such country. I seen pitchers like that."

Pa said, "Wait till we get to California. You'll see nice country then."

"Jesus Christ, Pa! This here *is* California."

Two men dressed in jeans and sweaty blue shirts came through the willows and looked toward the naked men. They called, "How's the swimmin'?"

"Dunno," said Tom. "We ain't tried none. Sure feels good to set here, though."

"Mind if we come in an' set?"

"She ain't our river. We'll len' you a little piece of her."

The men shucked off their pants, peeled their shirts, and waded out. The dust coated their legs to the knee; their feet were pale and soft with sweat. They settled lazily into the water and washed listlessly at their flanks. Sun-bitten, they were, a father and a boy. They grunted and groaned with the water.

Pa asked politely, "Goin' west?"

"Nope. We come from there. Goin' back home. We can't make no livin' out there."

"Where's home?" Tom asked.

"Panhandle, come from near Pampa."

Pa asked, "Can you make a livin' there?"

"Nope. But at leas' we can starve to death with folks we know. Won't have a bunch a fellas that hates us to starve with."

Pa said, "Ya know, you're the second fella talked like that. What makes 'em hate you?"

"Dunno," said the man. He cupped his hands full of water and rubbed his face, snorting and bubbling. Dusty water ran out of his hair and streaked his neck.

"I like to hear some more 'bout this," said Pa.

"Me too," Tom added. "Why these folks out west hate ya?"

The man looked sharply at Tom. "You jus' goin' wes'?"

"Jus' on our way."

"You ain't never been in California?"

"No, we ain't."

"Well, don' take my word. Go see for yourself."

"Yeah," Tom said, "but a fella kind a likes to know what he's gettin' into."

"Well, if you truly wanta know, I'm a fella that's asked questions an' give her some thought. She's a nice country. But she was stole a long time ago. You git acrost the desert an' come into the country aroun' Bakersfield. An' you never seen such purty country—all orchards an' grapes, purtiest country you ever seen. An' you'll pass lan' flat an' fine with water thirty feet down, and that lan's layin' fallow. But you can't have none of that lan'. That's a Lan' and Cattle Company. An' if they don't want ta work her, she ain't gonna git worked. You go in there an' plant you a little corn, an' you'll go to jail!"

"Good lan', you say? An' they ain't workin' her?"

"Yes, sir. Good lan' an' they ain't! Well, sir, that'll get you a little mad, but you ain't seen nothin'. People gonna have a look in their eye. They gonna look at you an' their face says, 'I don't like you, you son-of-a-bitch.' Gonna be deputy sheriffs, an' they'll push you aroun'. You camp on the roadside, an' they'll move you on. You gonna see in people's face how they hate you. An'—I'll tell you somepin. They hate you 'cause they're scairt. They know a hungry fella gonna get food even if he got to take it. They know that fallow lan's a sin an' somebody' gonna take it. What the hell! You never been called 'Okie' yet."

Tom said, "Okie? What's that?"

"Well, Okie use' ta mean you was from Oklahoma. Now it means you're a dirty son-of-a-bitch. Okie means you're scum. Don't mean nothing itself, it's the way they say it. But I can't tell you nothin'. You got to go there. I hear there's three hunderd thousan' of our people there—an' livin' like hogs, 'cause ever'thing in California is owned. They ain't nothin' left. An' them people that owns it is gonna hang on to it if they got ta kill ever'body in the worl' to do it. An' they're scairt, an' that makes 'em mad. You got to see it. You got to hear it. Purtiest goddamn country you ever seen, but they ain't nice to you, them folks. They're so scairt an' worried they ain't even nice to each other."

Tom looked down into the water, and he dug his heels into the sand. "S'pose a fella got work an' saved, couldn' he get a little lan'?"

The older man laughed and he looked at his boy, and his silent boy grinned almost in triumph. And the man said, "You ain't gonna get no steady work. Gonna scrabble for your dinner ever' day. An' you gonna do her with people lookin' mean at you. Pick cotton, an' you gonna be sure the scales ain't honest. Some of 'em is, an' some of 'em ain't. But you gonna think all the scales is crooked, an' you don' know which ones. Ain't nothin' you can do about her anyways."

Pa asked slowly, "Ain't—ain't it nice out there at all?"

"Sure, nice to look at, but you can't have none of it. They's a grove of yella oranges—an' a guy with a gun that got the right to kill you if you touch one. They's a fella, newspaper fella near the coast, got a million acres——"

Casy looked up quickly, "Million acres? What in the worl' can he do with a million acres?"

"I dunno. He jus' got it. Runs a few cattle. Got guards ever'place to keep folks out. Rides aroun' in a bullet-proof car. I seen pitchers of him. Fat, sof' fella with little mean eyes an' a mouth like a ass-hole. Scairt he's gonna die. Got a million acres an' scairt of dyin'."

Casy demanded, "What in hell can he do with a million acres? What's he want a million acres for?"

The man took his whitening, puckering hands out of the water and spread them, and he tightened his lower lip and bent his head down to one shoulder. "I dunno," he said. "Guess he's crazy. Mus' be crazy. Seen a pitcher of him. He looks crazy. Crazy an' mean."

"Say he's scairt to die?" Casy asked.

"That's what I heard."

"Scairt God'll get him?"

"I dunno. Jus' scairt."

"What's he care?" Pa said. "Don't seem like he's havin' no fun."

"Grampa wasn't scairt," Tom said. "When Grampa was havin' the most fun, he come clostest to gettin' kil't. Time Grampa an' another fella whanged into a bunch a Navajo in the night. They was havin' the time a their life, an' same time you wouldn' give a gopher for their chance."

Casy said, "Seems like that's the way. Fella havin' fun, he don't give a damn; but a fella mean an' lonely an' old an' disappointed—he's scared of dyin'!"

Pa asked, "What's he disappointed about if he got a million acres?"

The preacher smiled, and he looked puzzled. He splashed a floating water bug away with his hand. "If he needs a million acres to make him feel rich, seems to me he needs it 'cause he feels awful poor inside hisself, and if he's poor in hisself, there ain't no million acres gonna make him feel rich, an' maybe he's disappointed that nothin' he can do'll make him feel rich—not rich like Mis' Wilson was when she give her tent when Grampa died. I ain't tryin' to preach no sermon, but I never seen nobody that's busy as a prairie dog collectin' stuff that wasn't disappointed." He grinned. "Does kinda soun' like a sermon, don't it?"

The sun was flaming fiercely now. Pa said, "Better scrunch down under water. She'll burn the living Jesus outa you." And he reclined and let the gently moving water flow around his neck. "If a fella's willin' to work hard, can't he cut her?" Pa asked.

The man sat up and faced him. "Look, mister. I don' know ever'thing. You might go out there an' fall into a steady job, an' I'd be a liar. An' then, you might never get no work, an' I didn' warn ya. I can tell ya mos' of the folks is purty mis'able." He lay back in the water. "A fella don' know ever'thing," he said.

Pa turned his head and looked at Uncle John. "You never was a fella to say much," Pa said. "But I'll be goddamned if you opened your mouth twicet sence we lef' home. What you think 'bout this here?"

Uncle John scowled. "I don't think nothin' about it. We're a-goin' there, ain't we? None of this here talk gonna keep us from goin' there. When we get there, we'll get there. When we get a job we'll work, an' when we don't get a job we'll set on our ass. This here talk ain't gonna do no good no way."

Tom lay back and filled his mouth with water, and he spurted it into the air and he laughed. "Uncle John don't talk much, but he talks sense. Yes, by God! He talks sense. We goin' on tonight, Pa?"

"Might's well. Might's well get her over."

"Well, I'm goin' up in the brush an' get some sleep then." Tom stood up and waded to the sandy shore. He slipped his clothes on his wet body and winced under the heat of the cloth. The others followed him.

In the water, the man and his boy watched the Joads disappear. And the boy said, "Like to see 'em in six months. Jesus!"

The man wiped his eye corners with his forefinger. "I shouldn' of did that," he said. "Fella always wants to be a wise guy, wants to tell folks stuff."

"Well, Jesus, Pa! They asked for it."

"Yeah, I know. But like that fella says, they're a-goin' anyways. Nothin' won't be changed from what I tol' 'em, 'cept they'll be mis'able 'fore they hafta."

Tom walked in among the willows, and he crawled into a cave of shade to lie down. And Noah followed him.

"Gonna sleep here," Tom said.

"Tom!"

"Yeah?"

"Tom, I ain't a-goin' on."

Tom sat up. "What you mean?"

"Tom, I ain't a-gonna leave this here water. I'm a-gonna walk on down this here river."

"You're crazy," Tom said.

"Get myself a piece a line. I'll catch fish. Fella can't starve beside a nice river."

Tom said, "How 'bout the fam'ly? How 'bout Ma?"

"I can't he'p it. I can't leave this here water." Noah's wide-set eyes were half closed. "You know how it is, Tom. You know how the folks are nice to me. But they don't really care for me."

"You're crazy."

"No, I ain't. I know how I am. I know they're sorry. But— Well, I ain't a-goin'. You tell Ma—Tom."

"Now you look-a-here," Tom began.

"No. It ain't no use. I was in that there water. An' I ain't a-gonna leave her. I'm a-gonna go now, Tom—down the river. I'll catch fish an' stuff, but I can't leave her. I can't." He crawled back out of the willow cave. "You tell Ma, Tom." He walked away.

Tom followed him to the river bank. "Listen, you goddamn fool——"

"It ain't no use," Noah said. "I'm sad, but I can't he'p it. I got to go." He turned abruptly and walked downstream along the shore. Tom started to follow, and then he stopped. He saw Noah disappear into the brush, and then appear again, following the edge of the river. And he watched Noah growing smaller on the edge of the river, until he disappeared into the willows at last. And Tom took off his cap and scratched his head. He went back to his willow cave and lay down to sleep.

Under the spread tarpaulin Granma lay on a mattress, and Ma sat beside her. The air was stiflingly hot, and the flies buzzed in the shade of the canvas. Granma was naked under a long piece of pink curtain. She turned her old head restlessly from side to side, and she muttered and choked. Ma sat on the ground beside her, and with a piece of cardboard drove the flies away and fanned a stream of moving hot air over the tight old face. Rose of Sharon sat on the other side and watched her mother.

Granma called imperiously, "Will! Will! You come here, Will." And her eyes opened and she looked fiercely about. "Tol' him to come right here," she said. "I'll catch him. I'll take the hair off'n him." She closed her eyes and rolled her head back and forth and muttered thickly. Ma fanned with the cardboard.

Rose of Sharon looked helplessly at the old woman. She said softly, "She's awful sick."

Ma raised her eyes to the girl's face. Ma's eyes were patient, but the lines of strain were on her forehead. Ma fanned and fanned the air, and her piece of cardboard warned off the flies. "When you're young, Rosasharn, ever'thing that happens is a thing all by itself. It's a lonely thing. I know, I 'member, Rosasharn." Her mouth loved the name of her daughter. "You're gonna have a baby, Rosasharn, and that's somepin to you lonely and away. That's gonna hurt you, an' the hurt'll be lonely hurt, an' this here tent is alone in the worl', Rosasharn." She whipped the air for a moment to drive a buzzing blow fly on, and the big shining fly circled the tent twice and zoomed out into the blinding sunlight. And Ma went on, "They's a time of change, an' when that comes, dyin' is a piece of all dyin', and bearin' is a piece of all bearin', an' bearin' an' dyin' is two pieces of the same thing. An' then things ain't lonely any more. An' then a hurt don't hurt so bad, 'cause it ain't a lonely hurt no more, Rosasharn. I wisht I could tell you so you'd know, but I can't." And her voice was so soft, so full of love, that tears crowded into Rose of Sharon's eyes, and flowed over her eyes and blinded her.

"Take an' fan Granma," Ma said, and she handed the cardboard to her daughter. "That's a good thing to do. I wisht I could tell you so you'd know."

Granma, scowling her brows down over her closed eyes, bleated, "Will! You're dirty! You ain't never gonna get clean." Her little wrinkled claws moved up and scratched her cheek. A red ant ran up the curtain cloth and scrambled over the folds of loose skin on the old lady's neck. Ma reached quickly and picked it off, crushed it between thumb and forefinger, and brushed her fingers on her dress.

Rose of Sharon waved the cardboard fan. She looked up at Ma. "She—?" And the words parched in her throat.

"Wipe your feet, Will—you dirty pig!" Granma cried.

Ma said, "I dunno. Maybe if we can get her where it ain't so hot, but I dunno. Don't worry yourself, Rosasharn. Take your breath in when you need it, an' let it go when you need to."

A large woman in a torn black dress looked into the tent. Her eyes were bleared and indefinite, and the skin sagged to her jowls and hung down in little flaps. Her lips were loose, so that the upper lip hung like a curtain over her teeth, and her lower lip, by its weight, folded outward, showing her lower gums. "Mornin', ma'am," she said. "Mornin', an' praise God for victory."

Ma looked around. "Mornin'," she said.

The woman stooped into the tent and bent her head over Granma. "We heerd you got a soul here ready to join her Jesus. Praise God!"

Ma's face tightened and her eyes grew sharp. "She's tar'd, tha's all," Ma said. "She's wore out with the road an' the heat. She's jus' wore out. Get a little res', an' she'll be well."

The woman leaned down over Granma's face, and she seemed almost to sniff. Then she turned to Ma and nodded quickly, and her lips jiggled and her jowls quivered. "A dear soul gonna join her Jesus," she said.

Ma cried, "That ain't so!"

The woman nodded, slowly, this time, and put a puffy hand on Granma's forehead. Ma reached to snatch the hand away, and quickly restrained herself. "Yes, it's so, sister," the woman said. "We got six in Holiness in our tent. I'll go git 'em, an' we'll hol' a meetin'—a prayer an' grace. Jehovites, all. Six, countin' me. I'll go git 'em out."

Ma stiffened. "No—no," she said. "No, Granma's tar'd. She couldn't stan' a meetin'."

The woman said, "Couldn't stan' grace? Couldn' stan' the sweet breath of Jesus? What you talkin' about, sister?"

Ma said, "No, not here. She's too tar'd."

The woman looked reproachfully at Ma. "Ain't you believers, ma'am?"

"We always been Holiness," Ma said, "but Granma's tar'd, an' we been a-goin' all night. We won't trouble you."

"It ain't no trouble, an' if it was, we'd want ta do it for a soul a-soarin' to the Lamb."

Ma arose to her knees. "We thank ya," she said coldly. "We ain't gonna have no meetin' in this here tent."

The woman looked at her for a long time. "Well, we ain't a-gonna let a sister go away 'thout a little praisin'. We'll git the meetin' goin' in our own tent, ma'am. An' we'll forgive ya for your hard heart."

Ma settled back again and turned her face to Granma, and her face was still set and hard. "She's tar'd," Ma said. "She's on'y tar'd." Granma swung her head back and forth and muttered under her breath.

The woman walked stiffly out of the tent. Ma continued to look down at the old face.

Rose of Sharon fanned her cardboard and moved the hot air in a stream. She said, "Ma!"

"Yeah?"

"Whyn't ya let 'em hol' a meetin'?"

"I dunno," said Ma. "Jehovites is good people. They're howlers an' jumpers. I dunno. Somepin jus' come over me. I didn' think I could stan' it. I'd jus' fly all apart."

From some little distance there came the sound of the beginning meeting, a sing-song chant of exhortation. The words were not clear, only the tone. The voice rose and fell, and went higher at each rise. Now a response filled in the pause, and the exhortation went up with a tone of triumph, and a growl of power came into the voice. It swelled and paused, and a growl came into the response. And now gradually the sentences of exhortation shortened, grew sharper, like commands; and into the responses came a complaining note. The rhythm quickened. Male and female voices had been one tone, but now in the middle of a response one woman's voice went up and up in a wailing cry, wild and fierce, like the cry of a beast; and a deeper woman's voice rose up beside it, a baying voice, and a man's voice traveled up the scale in the howl of a wolf. The exhortation stopped, and only the feral howling came from the tent, and with it a thudding sound on the earth. Ma shivered. Rose of Sharon's breath was panting and short, and the chorus of howls went on so long it seemed that lungs must burst.

Ma said, "Makes me nervous. Somepin happened to me."

Now the high voice broke into hysteria, the gabbling

screams of a hyena, the thudding became louder. Voices cracked and broke, and then the whole chorus fell to a sobbing, grunting undertone, and the slap of flesh and the thuddings on the earth; and the sobbing changed to a little whining, like that of a litter of puppies at a food dish.

Rose of Sharon cried softly with nervousness. Granma kicked the curtain off her legs, which lay like gray, knotted sticks. And Granma whined with the whining in the distance. Ma pulled the curtain back in place. And then Granma sighed deeply and her breathing grew steady and easy, and her closed eyelids ceased their flicking. She slept deeply, and snored through her half-open mouth. The whining from the distance was softer and softer until it could not be heard at all any more.

Rose of Sharon looked at Ma, and her eyes were blank with tears. "It done good," said Rose of Sharon. "It done Granma good. She's a-sleepin'."

Ma's head was down, and she was ashamed. "Maybe I done them good people wrong. Granma is asleep."

"Whyn't you ast our preacher if you done a sin?" the girl asked.

"I will—but he's a queer man. Maybe it's him made me tell them people they couldn' come here. That preacher, he's gettin' roun' to thinkin' that what people does is right to do." Ma looked at her hands, and then she said, "Rosasharn, we got to sleep. 'F we're gonna go tonight, we got to sleep." She stretched out on the ground beside the mattress.

Rose of Sharon asked, "How about fannin' Granma?"

"She's asleep now. You lay down an' rest."

"I wonder where at Connie is?" the girl complained. "I ain't seen him around for a long time."

Ma said, "Sh! Get some rest."

"Ma, Connie gonna study nights an' get to be somepin."

"Yeah. You tol' me about that. Get some rest."

The girl lay down on the edge of Granma's mattress. "Connie's got a new plan. He's thinkin' all a time. When he gets all up on 'lectricity he gonna have his own store, an' then guess what we gonna have?"

"What?"

"Ice—all the ice you want. Gonna have a ice box. Keep it full. Stuff don't spoil if you got ice."

"Connie's thinkin' all a time," Ma chuckled. "Better get some rest now."

Rose of Sharon closed her eyes. Ma turned over on her back and crossed her hands under her head. She listened to Granma's breathing and to the girl's breathing. She moved a hand to start a fly from her forehead. The camp was quiet in the blinding heat, but the noises of hot grass—of crickets, the hum of flies—were a tone that was close to silence. Ma sighed deeply and then yawned and closed her eyes. In her half-sleep she heard footsteps approaching, but it was a man's voice that started her awake.

"Who's in here?"

Ma sat up quickly. A brown-faced man bent over and looked in. He wore boots and khaki pants and a khaki shirt with epaulets. On a Sam Browne belt a pistol holster hung, and a big silver star was pinned to his shirt at the left breast. A loose-crowned military cap was on the back of his head. He beat on the tarpaulin with his hand, and the tight canvas vibrated like a drum.

"Who's in here?" he demanded again.

Ma asked, "What is it you want, mister?"

"What you think I want? I want to know who's in here."

"Why, they's jus' us three in here. Me an' Granma an' my girl."

"Where's your men?"

"Why, they went down to clean up. We was drivin' all night."

"Where'd you come from?"

"Right near Sallisaw, Oklahoma."

"Well, you can't stay here."

"We aim to get out tonight an' cross the desert, mister."

"Well, you better. If you're here tomorra this time I'll run you in. We don't want none of you settlin' down here."

Ma's face blackened with anger. She got slowly to her feet. She stooped to the utensil box and picked out the iron skillet. "Mister," she said, "you got a tin button an' a gun. Where I come from, you keep your voice down." She advanced on him with the skillet. He loosened the gun in the holster. "Go ahead," said Ma. "Scarin' women. I'm thankful the men folks ain't here. They'd tear ya to pieces. In my country you watch your tongue."

The man took two steps backward. "Well, you ain't in your country now. You're in California, an' we don't want you goddamn Okies settlin' down."

Ma's advance stopped. She looked puzzled. "Okies?" she said softly. "Okies."

"Yeah, Okies! An' if you're here when I come tomorra, I'll run ya in." He turned and walked to the next tent and banged on the canvas with his hand. "Who's in here?" he said.

Ma went slowly back under the tarpaulin. She put the skillet in the utensil box. She sat down slowly. Rose of Sharon watched her secretly. And when she saw Ma fighting with her face, Rose of Sharon closed her eyes and pretended to be asleep.

The sun sank low in the afternoon, but the heat did not seem to decrease. Tom awakened under his willow, and his mouth was parched and his body was wet with sweat, and his head was dissatisfied with his rest. He staggered to his feet and walked toward the water. He peeled off his clothes and waded into the stream. And the moment the water was about him, his thirst was gone. He lay back in the shallows and his body floated. He held himself in place with his elbows in the sand, and looked at his toes, which bobbed above the surface.

A pale skinny little boy crept like an animal through the reeds and slipped off his clothes. And he squirmed into the water like a muskrat, and pulled himself along like a muskrat, only his eyes and nose above the surface. Then suddenly he saw Tom's head and saw that Tom was watching him. He stopped his game and sat up.

Tom said, "Hello."

" 'Lo!"

"Looks like you was playin' mushrat."

"Well, I was." He edged gradually away toward the bank; he moved casually, and then he leaped out, gathered his clothes with a sweep of his arms, and was gone among the willows.

Tom laughed quietly. And then he heard his name called shrilly. "Tom, oh, Tom!" He sat up in the water and whistled through his teeth, a piercing whistle with a loop on the end. The willows shook, and Ruthie stood looking at him.

"Ma wants you," she said. "Ma wants you right away."

"Awright." He stood up and strode through the water to the shore; and Ruthie looked with interest and amazement at his naked body.

Tom, seeing the direction of her eyes, said, "Run on now. Git!" And Ruthie ran. Tom heard her calling excitedly for Winfield as she went. He put the hot clothes on his cool, wet body and he walked slowly up through the willows toward the tent.

Ma had started a fire of dry willow twigs, and she had a pan of water heating. She looked relieved when she saw him.

"What's a matter, Ma?" he asked.

"I was scairt," she said. "They was a policeman here. He says we can't stay here. I was scairt he talked to you. I was scairt you'd hit him if he talked to you."

Tom said, "What'd I go an' hit a policeman for?"

Ma smiled. "Well—he talked so bad—I nearly hit him myself."

Tom grabbed her arm and shook her roughly and loosely, and he laughed. He sat down on the ground, still laughing. "My God, Ma. I knowed you when you was gentle. What's come over you?"

She looked serious. "I don' know, Tom."

"Fust you stan' us off with a jack handle, and now you try to hit a cop." He laughed softly, and he reached out and patted her bare foot tenderly. "A ol' hell-cat," he said.

"Tom."

"Yeah?"

She hesitated a long time. "Tom, this here policeman—he called us—Okies. He says, 'We don' want you goddamn Okies settlin' down.'"

Tom studied her, and his hand still rested gently on her bare foot. "Fella tol' about that," he said. "Fella tol' how they say it." He considered, "Ma, would you say I was a bad fella? Oughta be locked up—like that?"

"No," she said. "You been tried— No. What you ast me for?"

"Well, I dunno. I'd a took a sock at that cop."

Ma smiled with amusement. "Maybe I oughta ast you that, 'cause I nearly hit 'im with a skillet."

"Ma, why'd he say we couldn' stop here?"

"Jus' says they don' want no damn Okies settlin' down. Says he's gonna run us in if we're here tomorra."

"But we ain't use' ta gettin' shoved aroun' by no cops."

"I tol' him that," said Ma. "He says we ain't home now. We're in California, and they do what they want."

Tom said uneasily, "Ma, I got somepin to tell ya. Noah— he went on down the river. He ain't a-goin' on."

It took a moment for Ma to understand. "Why?" she asked softly.

"I don' know. Says he got to. Says he got to stay. Says for me to tell you."

"How'll he eat?" she demanded.

"I don' know. Says he'll catch fish."

Ma was silent a long time. "Family's fallin' apart," she said. "I don' know. Seems like I can't think no more. I jus' can't think. They's too much."

Tom said lamely, "He'll be awright, Ma. He's a funny kind a fella."

Ma turned stunned eyes toward the river. "I jus' can't seem to think no more."

Tom looked down the line of tents and he saw Ruthie and Winfield standing in front of a tent in decorous conversation with someone inside. Ruthie was twisting her skirt in her hands, while Winfield dug a hole in the ground with his toe. Tom called, "You, Ruthie!" She looked up and saw him and trotted toward him, with Winfield behind her. When she came up, Tom said, "You go get our folks. They're sleepin' down the willows. Get 'em. An' you, Winfiel'. You tell the Wilsons we're gonna get rollin' soon as we can." The children spun around and charged off.

Tom said, "Ma, how's Granma now?"

"Well, she got a sleep today. Maybe she's better. She's still a-sleepin'."

"Tha's good. How much pork we got?"

"Not very much. Quarter hog."

"Well, we got to fill that other kag with water. Got to take water along." They could hear Ruthie's shrill cries for the men down in the willows.

Ma shoved willow sticks into the fire and made it crackle up about the black pot. She said, "I pray God we gonna get some res'. I pray Jesus we gonna lay down in a nice place."

The sun sank toward the baked and broken hills to the west. The pot over the fire bubbled furiously. Ma went under the tarpaulin and came out with an apronful of potatoes, and she dropped them into the boiling water. "I pray God we gonna be let to wash some clothes. We ain't never been dirty like this. Don't even wash potatoes 'fore we boil 'em. I wonder why? Seems like the heart's took out of us."

The men came trooping up from the willows, and their eyes were full of sleep, and their faces were red and puffed with daytime sleep.

Pa said, "What's a matter?"

"We're goin'," said Tom. "Cop says we got to go. Might's well get her over. Get a good start an' maybe we'll be through her. Near three hunderd miles where we're goin'."

Pa said, "I thought we was gonna get a rest."

"Well, we ain't. We got to go. Pa," Tom said, "Noah ain't a-goin'. He walked on down the river."

"Ain't goin'? What the hell's the matter with him?" And then Pa caught himself. "My fault," he said miserably. "That boy's all my fault."

"No."

"I don't wanta talk about it no more," said Pa. "I can't— my fault."

"Well, we got to go," said Tom.

Wilson walked near for the last words. "We can't go, folks," he said. "Sairy's done up. She got to res'. She ain't gonna git acrost that desert alive."

They were silent at his words; then Tom said, "Cop says he'll run us in if we're here tomorra."

Wilson shook his head. His eyes were glazed with worry, and a paleness showed through his dark skin. "Jus' hafta do 'er, then. Sairy can't go. If they jail us, why, they'll hafta jail us. She got to res' an' get strong."

Pa said, "Maybe we better wait an' all go together."

"No," Wilson said. "You been nice to us; you been kin', but you can't stay here. You got to get on an' get jobs and work. We ain't gonna let you stay."

Pa said excitedly, "But you ain't got nothing."

Wilson smiled. "Never had nothin' when you took us up. This ain't none of your business. Don't you make me git mean. You got to go, or I'll get mean an' mad."

Ma beckoned Pa into the cover of the tarpaulin and spoke softly to him.

Wilson turned to Casy. "Sairy wants you should go see her."

"Sure," said the preacher. He walked to the Wilson tent, tiny and gray, and he slipped the flaps aside and entered. It was dusky and hot inside. The mattress lay on the ground, and the equipment was scattered about, as it had been unloaded in the morning. Sairy lay on the mattress, her eyes wide and bright. He stood and looked down at her, his large head bent and the stringy muscles of his neck tight along the sides. And he took off his hat and held it in his hand.

She said, "Did my man tell ya we couldn' go on?"

"Tha's what he said."

Her low, beautiful voice went on, "I wanted us to go. I knowed I wouldn' live to the other side, but he'd be acrost anyways. But he won't go. He don' know. He thinks it's gonna be all right. He don' know."

"He says he won't go."

"I know," she said. "An' he's stubborn. I ast you to come to say a prayer."

"I ain't a preacher," he said softly. "My prayers ain't no good."

She moistened her lips. "I was there when the ol' man died. You said one then."

"It wasn't no prayer."

"It was a prayer," she said.

"It wasn't no preacher's prayer."

"It was a good prayer. I want you should say one for me."

"I don' know what to say."

She closed her eyes for a minute and then opened them

again. "Then say one to yourself. Don't use no words to it. That'd be awright."

"I got no God," he said.

"You got a God. Don't make no difference if you don' know what he looks like." The preacher bowed his head. She watched him apprehensively. And when he raised his head again she looked relieved. "That's good," she said. "That's what I needed. Somebody close enough—to pray."

He shook his head as though to awaken himself. "I don' understan' this here," he said.

And she replied, "Yes—you know, don't you?"

"I know," he said, "I know, but I don't understan'. Maybe you'll res' a few days an' then come on."

She shook her head slowly from side to side. "I'm jus' pain covered with skin. I know what it is, but I won't tell him. He'd be too sad. He wouldn' know what to do anyways. Maybe in the night, when he's a-sleepin'—when he waked up, it won't be so bad."

"You want I should stay with you an' not go on?"

"No," she said. "No. When I was a little girl I use' ta sing. Folks roun' about use' ta say I sung as nice as Jenny Lind. Folks use' ta come an' listen when I sung. An'—when they stood—an' me a-singin', why, me an' them was together more'n you could ever know. I was thankful. There ain't so many folks can feel so full up, so close, an' them folks standin' there an' me a-singin'. Thought maybe I'd sing in theaters, but I never done it. An' I'm glad. They wasn't nothin' got in between me an' them. An'—that's why I wanted you to pray. I wanted to feel that clostness, oncet more. It's the same thing, singin' an' prayin', jus' the same thing. I wisht you could a-heerd me sing."

He looked down at her, into her eyes. "Good-by," he said.

She shook her head slowly back and forth and closed her lips tight. And the preacher went out of the dusky tent into the blinding light.

The men were loading up the truck, Uncle John on top, while the others passed equipment up to him. He stowed it carefully, keeping the surface level. Ma emptied the quarter of a keg of salt pork into a pan, and Tom and Al took both little barrels to the river and washed them. They tied them to the running boards and carried water in buckets to fill them. Then over the tops they tied canvas to keep them from slopping the water out. Only the tarpaulin and Granma's mattress were left to be put on.

Tom said, "With the load we'll take, this ol' wagon'll boil her head off. We got to have plenty water."

Ma passed the boiled potatoes out and brought the half sack from the tent and put it with the pan of pork. The family ate standing, shuffling their feet and tossing the hot potatoes from hand to hand until they cooled.

Ma went to the Wilson tent and stayed for ten minutes, and then she came out quietly. "It's time to go," she said.

The men went under the tarpaulin. Granma still slept, her mouth wide open. They lifted the whole mattress gently and passed it up on top of the truck. Granma drew up her skinny legs and frowned in her sleep, but she did not awaken.

Uncle John and Pa tied the tarpaulin over the cross-piece, making a little tight tent on top of the load. They lashed it down to the side-bars. And then they were ready. Pa took out his purse and dug two crushed bills from it. He went to Wilson and held them out. "We want you should take this, an' "—he pointed to the pork and potatoes—"an' that."

Wilson hung his head and shook it sharply. "I ain't a-gonna do it," he said. "You ain't got much."

"Got enough to get there," said Pa. "We ain't left it all. We'll have work right off."

"I ain't a-gonna do it," Wilson said. "I'll git mean if you try."

Ma took the two bills from Pa's hand. She folded them neatly and put them on the ground and placed the pork pan over them. "That's where they'll be," she said. "If you don' get 'em, somebody else will." Wilson, his head still down, turned and went to his tent; he stepped inside and the flaps fell behind him.

For a few moments the family waited, and then, "We got to go," said Tom. "It's near four, I bet."

The family climbed on the truck, Ma on top, beside Granma. Tom and Al and Pa in the seat, and Winfield on Pa's lap. Connie and Rose of Sharon made a nest against the cab. The preacher and Uncle John and Ruthie were in a tangle on the load.

Pa called, "Good-by, Mister and Mis' Wilson." There was no answer from the tent. Tom started the engine and the truck lumbered away. And as they crawled up the rough road toward Needles and the highway, Ma looked back. Wilson stood in front of his tent, staring after them, and his hat was in his hand. The sun fell full on his face. Ma waved her hand at him, but he did not respond.

Tom kept the truck in second gear over the rough road, to protect the springs. At Needles he drove into a service station, checked the worn tires for air, checked the spares tied to the back. He had the gas tank filled, and he bought two five-gallon cans of gasoline and a two-gallon can of oil. He filled the radiator, begged a map, and studied it.

The service-station boy, in his white uniform, seemed uneasy until the bill was paid. He said, "You people sure have got nerve."

Tom looked up from the map. "What you mean?"

"Well, crossin' in a jalopy like this."

"You been acrost?"

"Sure, plenty, but not in no wreck like this."

Tom said, "If we broke down maybe somebody'd give us a han'."

"Well, maybe. But folks are kind of scared to stop at night. I'd hate to be doing it. Takes more nerve than I've got."

Tom grinned. "It don't take no nerve to do somepin when there ain't nothin' else you can do. Well, thanks. We'll drag on." And he got in the truck and moved away.

The boy in white went into the iron building where his helper labored over a book of bills. "Jesus, what a hard-looking outfit!"

"Them Okies? They're all hard-lookin'."

"Jesus, I'd hate to start out in a jalopy like that."

"Well, you and me got sense. Them goddamn Okies got no sense and no feeling. They ain't human. A human being wouldn't live like they do. A human being couldn't stand it to be so dirty and miserable. They ain't a hell of a lot better than gorillas."

"Just the same I'm glad I ain't crossing the desert in no Hudson Super-Six. She sounds like a threshing machine."

The other boy looked down at his book of bills. And a big drop of sweat rolled down his finger and fell on the pink bills. "You know, they don't have much trouble. They're so goddamn dumb they don't know it's dangerous. And, Christ Almighty, they don't know any better than what they got. Why worry?"

"I'm not worrying. Just thought if it was me, I wouldn't like it."

"That's 'cause you know better. They don't know any better." And he wiped the sweat from the pink bill with his sleeve.

The truck took the road and moved up the long hill, through the broken, rotten rock. The engine boiled very soon and Tom slowed down and took it easy. Up the long slope, winding and twisting through dead country, burned white and gray, and no hint of life in it. Once Tom stopped for a few moments to let the engine cool, and then he traveled on. They topped the pass while the sun was still up, and looked down on the desert—black cinder mountains in the distance, and the yellow sun reflected on the gray desert. The little starved bushes, sage and greasewood, threw bold shadows on the sand and bits of rock. The glaring sun was straight ahead. Tom held his hand before his eyes to see at all. They passed the crest and coasted down to cool the engine. They coasted down the long sweep to the floor of the desert, and the fan turned over to cool the water in the radiator. In the driver's seat, Tom and Al and Pa, and Winfield on Pa's knee, looked into the bright descending sun, and their eyes were stony, and their brown faces were damp with perspiration. The burnt land and the black, cindery hills broke the even distance and made it terrible in the reddening light of the setting sun.

Al said, "Jesus, what a place. How'd you like to walk acrost her?"

"People done it," said Tom. "Lots a people done it; an' if they could, we could."

"Lots must a died," said Al.

"Well, we ain't come out exac'ly clean."

Al was silent for a while, and the reddening desert swept past. "Think we'll ever see them Wilsons again?" Al asked.

Tom flicked his eyes down to the oil gauge. "I got a hunch nobody ain't gonna see Mis' Wilson for long. Jus' a hunch I got."

Winfield said, "Pa, I wanta get out."

Tom looked over at him. "Might's well let ever'body out 'fore we settle down to drivin' tonight." He slowed the car and brought it to a stop. Winfield scrambled out and urinated at the side of the road. Tom leaned out. "Anybody else?"

"We're holdin' our water up here," Uncle John called.

Pa said, "Winfiel', you crawl up on top. You put my legs to sleep a-settin' on 'em." The little boy buttoned his overalls and obediently crawled up the back board and on his hands and knees crawled over Granma's mattress and forward to Ruthie.

The truck moved on into the evening, and the edge of the sun struck the rough horizon and turned the desert red.

Ruthie said, "Wouldn' leave you set up there, huh?"

"I didn' want to. It wasn't so nice as here. Couldn' lie down."

"Well, don' you bother me, a-squawkin' an' a-talkin'," Ruthie said, " 'cause I'm goin' to sleep, an' when I wake up, we gonna be there! 'Cause Tom said so! Gonna seem funny to see pretty country."

The sun went down and left a great halo in the sky. And it grew very dark under the tarpaulin, a long cave with light at each end—a flat triangle of light.

Connie and Rose of Sharon leaned back against the cab, and the hot wind tumbling through the tent struck the backs of their heads, and the tarpaulin whipped and drummed above them. They spoke together in low tones, pitched to the drumming canvas, so that no one could hear them. When Connie spoke he turned his head and spoke into her ear, and she did the same to him. She said, "Seems like we wasn't never gonna do nothin' but move. I'm so tar'd."

He turned his head to her ear. "Maybe in the mornin'. How'd you like to be alone now?" In the dusk his hand moved out and stroked her hip.

She said, "Don't. You'll make me crazy as a loon. Don't do that." And she turned her head to hear his response.

"Maybe—when ever'body's asleep."

"Maybe," she said. "But wait till they get to sleep. You'll make me crazy, an' maybe they won't get to sleep."

"I can't hardly stop," he said.

"I know. Me neither. Le's talk about when we get there; an' you move away 'fore I get crazy."

He shifted away a little. "Well, I'll get to studyin' nights right off," he said. She sighed deeply. "Gonna get one a them books that tells about it an' cut the coupon, right off."

"How long, you think?" she asked.

"How long what?"

"How long 'fore you'll be makin' big money an' we got ice?"

"Can't tell," he said importantly. "Can't really rightly tell. Fella oughta be studied up pretty good 'fore Christmus."

"Soon's you get studied up we could get ice an' stuff, I guess."

He chuckled. "It's this here heat," he said. "What you gonna need ice roun' Christmus for?"

She giggled. "Tha's right. But I'd like ice any time. Now don't. You'll get me crazy!"

The dusk passed into dark and the desert stars came out in the soft sky, stars stabbing and sharp, with few points and rays to them, and the sky was velvet. And the heat changed. While the sun was up, it was a beating, flailing heat, but now the heat came from below, from the earth itself, and the heat was thick and muffling. The lights of the truck came on, and they illuminated a little blur of highway ahead, and a strip of desert on either side of the road. And sometimes eyes gleamed in the lights far ahead, but no animal showed in the lights. It was pitch dark under the canvas now. Uncle John and the preacher were curled in the middle of the truck, resting on their elbows, and staring out the back triangle. They could see the two bumps that were Ma and Granma against the outside. They could see Ma move occasionally, and her dark arm moving against the outside.

Uncle John talked to the preacher. "Casy," he said, "you're a fella oughta know what to do."

"What to do about what?"

"I dunno," said Uncle John.

Casy said, "Well, that's gonna make it easy for me!"

"Well, you been a preacher."

"Look, John, ever'body takes a crack at me 'cause I been a preacher. A preacher ain't nothin' but a man."

"Yeah, but—he's—a *kind* of a man, else he wouldn' be a preacher. I wanna ast you—well, you think a fella could bring bad luck to folks?"

"I dunno," said Casy. "I dunno."

"Well—see—I was married—fine, good girl. An' one night she got a pain in her stomach. An' she says, 'You better get a doctor.' An' I says, 'Hell, you jus' et too much.'" Uncle John put his hand on Casy's knee and he peered through the darkness at him. "She give me a *look*. An' she groaned all night, an' she died the next afternoon." The preacher mumbled something. "You see," John went on, "I kil't her. An' sence then I tried to make it up—mos'ly to kids. An' I tried to be good, an' I can't. I get drunk, an' I go wild."

"Ever'body goes wild," said Casy. "I do too."

"Yeah, but you ain't got a sin on your soul like me."

Casy said gently, "Sure I got sins. Ever'body got sins. A sin is somepin you ain't sure about. Them people that's sure about ever'thing an' ain't got no sin—well, with that kind a son-of-a-bitch, if I was God I'd kick their ass right outa heaven! I couldn' stand 'em!"

Uncle John said, "I got a feelin' I'm bringin' bad luck to my own folks. I got a feelin' I oughta go away an' let 'em be. I ain't comf'table bein' like this."

Casy said quickly, "I know this—a man got to do what he got to do. I can't tell you. I don't think they's luck or bad luck. On'y one thing in this worl' I'm sure of, an' that's I'm sure nobody got a right to mess with a fella's life. He got to do it all hisself. Help him, maybe, but not tell him what to do."

Uncle John said disappointedly, "Then you don' know?"

"I don' know."

"You think it was a sin to let my wife die like that?"

"Well," said Casy, "for anybody else it was a mistake, but if you think it was a sin—then it's a sin. A fella builds his own sins right up from the groun'."

"I got to give that a goin'-over," said Uncle John, and he rolled on his back and lay with his knees pulled up.

The truck moved on over the hot earth, and the hours passed. Ruthie and Winfield went to sleep. Connie loosened a blanket from the load and covered himself and Rose of Sharon with it, and in the heat they struggled together, and held their breaths. And after a time Connie threw off the blanket and the hot tunneling wind felt cool on their wet bodies.

On the back of the truck Ma lay on the mattress beside Granma, and she could not see with her eyes, but she could feel the struggling body and the struggling heart; and the sobbing breath was in her ear. And Ma said over and over, "All right. It's gonna be all right." And she said hoarsely, "You know the family got to get acrost. You know that."

Uncle John called, "You all right?"

It was a moment before she answered. "All right. Guess I dropped off to sleep." And after a time Granma was still, and Ma lay rigid beside her.

The night hours passed, and the dark was in against the truck. Sometimes cars passed them, going west and away; and sometimes great trucks came up out of the west and rumbled eastward. And the stars flowed down in a slow cascade over the western horizon. It was near midnight when they neared Daggett, where the inspection station is. The road was flood-lighted there, and a sign illuminated, "KEEP RIGHT AND STOP." The officers loafed in the office, but they came out and stood under the long covered shed when Tom pulled in. One officer put down the license number and raised the hood.

Tom asked, "What's this here?"

"Agricultural inspection. We got to look over your stuff. Got any vegetables or seeds?"

"No," said Tom.

"Well, we got to look over your stuff. You got to unload."

Now Ma climbed heavily down from the truck. Her face was swollen and her eyes were hard. "Look, mister. We got a sick ol' lady. We got to get her to a doctor. We can't wait." She seemed to fight with hysteria. "You can't make us wait."

"Yeah? Well, we got to look you over."

"I swear we ain't got any thing!" Ma cried. "I swear it. An' Granma's awful sick."

"You don't look so good yourself," the officer said.

Ma pulled herself up the back of the truck, hoisted herself with huge strength. "Look," she said.

The officer shot a flashlight beam up on the old shrunken face. "By God, she is," he said. "You swear you got no seeds or fruits or vegetables, no corn, no oranges?"

"No, no. I swear it!"

"Then go ahead. You can get a doctor in Barstow. That's only eight miles. Go on ahead."

Tom climbed in and drove on.

The officer turned to his companion. "I couldn' hold 'em."

"Maybe it was a bluff," said the other.

"Oh, Jesus, no! You should of seen that ol' woman's face. That wasn't no bluff."

Tom increased his speed to Barstow, and in the little town he stopped, got out, and walked around the truck. Ma leaned out. "It's awright," she said. "I didn' wanta stop there, fear we wouldn' get acrost."

"Yeah! But how's Granma?"

"She's awright—awright. Drive on. We got to get acrost." Tom shook his head and walked back.

"Al," he said, "I'm gonna fill her up, an' then you drive some." He pulled to an all-night gas station and filled the tank and the radiator, and filled the crank case. Then Al slipped under the wheel and Tom took the outside, with Pa in the middle. They drove away into the darkness and the little hills near Barstow were behind them.

Tom said, "I don' know what's got into Ma. She's flighty as a dog with a flea up his ass. Wouldn' a took long to look over the stuff. An' she says Granma's sick; an' now she says Granma's awright. I can't figger her out. She ain't right. S'pose she wore her brains out on the trip."

Pa said, "Ma's almost like she was when she was a girl. She was a wild one then. She wasn' scairt of nothin'. I thought havin' all the kids an' workin' took it out a her, but I guess it ain't. Christ! When she got that jack handle back there, I tell you I wouldn' wanna be the fella took it away from her."

"I dunno what's got into her," Tom said. "Maybe she's jus' tar'd out."

Al said, "I won't be doin' no weepin' an' a-moanin' to get through. I got this goddamn car on my soul."

Tom said, "Well, you done a damn good job a pickin'. We ain't had hardly no trouble with her at all."

All night they bored through the hot darkness, and jack-rabbits scuttled into the lights and dashed away in long jolting leaps. And the dawn came up behind them when the lights of Mojave were ahead. And the dawn showed high mountains to the west. They filled the water and oil at Mojave and crawled into the mountains, and the dawn was about them.

Tom said, "Jesus, the desert's past! Pa, Al, for Christ sakes! The desert's past!"

"I'm too goddamn tired to care," said Al.

"Want me to drive?"

"No, wait awhile."

They drove through Tehachapi in the morning glow, and the sun came up behind them, and then—suddenly they saw the great valley below them. Al jammed on the brake and stopped in the middle of the road, and, "Jesus Christ! Look!" he said. The vineyards, the orchards, the great flat valley, green and beautiful, the trees set in rows, and the farm houses.

And Pa said, "God Almighty!" The distant cities, the little towns in the orchard land, and the morning sun, golden on the valley. A car honked behind them. Al pulled to the side of the road and parked.

"I want ta look at her." The grain fields golden in the morning, and the willow lines, the eucalyptus trees in rows.

Pa sighed, "I never knowed they was anything like her." The peach trees and the walnut groves, and the dark green patches of oranges. And red roofs among the trees, and barns—rich barns. Al got out and stretched his legs.

He called, "Ma—come look. We're there!"

Ruthie and Winfield scrambled down from the car, and then they stood, silent and awestruck, embarrassed before the great valley. The distance was thinned with haze, and the land grew softer and softer in the distance. A windmill flashed in the sun, and its turning blades were like a little heliograph, far away. Ruthie and Winfield looked at it, and Ruthie whispered, "It's California."

Winfield moved his lips silently over the syllables. "There's fruit," he said aloud.

Casy and Uncle John, Connie and Rose of Sharon climbed down. And they stood silently. Rose of Sharon had started to brush her hair back, when she caught sight of the valley and her hand dropped slowly to her side.

Tom said, "Where's Ma? I want Ma to see it. Look, Ma! Come here, Ma." Ma was climbing slowly, stiffly, down the back board. Tom looked at her. "My God, Ma, you sick?" Her face was stiff and putty-like, and her eyes seemed to have sunk deep into her head, and the rims were red with weariness. Her feet touched the ground and she braced herself by holding the truck-side.

Her voice was a croak. "Ya say we're acrost?"

Tom pointed to the great valley. "Look!"

She turned her head, and her mouth opened a little. Her fingers went to her throat and gathered a little pinch of skin and twisted gently. "Thank God!" she said. "The fambly's here." Her knees buckled and she sat down on the running board.

"You sick, Ma?"

"No, jus' tar'd."

"Didn' you get no sleep?"

"No."

"Was Granma bad?"

Ma looked down at her hands, lying together like tired lovers in her lap. "I wisht I could wait an' not tell you. I wisht it could be all—nice."

Pa said, "Then Granma's bad."

Ma raised her eyes and looked over the valley. "Granma's dead."

They looked at her, all of them, and Pa asked, "When?"

"Before they stopped us las' night."

"So that's why you didn' want 'em to look."

"I was afraid we wouldn' get acrost," she said. "I tol' Granma we couldn' he'p her. The fambly had ta get acrost. I tol' her, tol' her when she was a-dyin'. We couldn' stop in the desert. There was the young ones—an' Rosasharn's baby. I tol' her." She put up her hands and covered her face for a moment. "She can get buried in a nice green place," Ma said softly. "Trees aroun' an' a nice place. She got to lay her head down in California."

The family looked at Ma with a little terror at her strength.

Tom said, "Jesus Christ! You layin' there with her all night long!"

"The fambly hadda get acrost," Ma said miserably.

Tom moved close to put his hand on her shoulder.

"Don' touch me," she said. "I'll hol' up if you don' touch me. That'd get me."

Pa said, "We got to go on now. We got to go on down."

Ma looked up at him. "Can—can I set up front? I don' wanna go back there no more—I'm tar'd. I'm awful tar'd."

They climbed back on the load, and they avoided the long stiff figure covered and tucked in a comforter, even the head covered and tucked. They moved to their places and tried to keep their eyes from it—from the hump on the comfort that would be the nose, and the steep cliff that would be the jut of the chin. They tried to keep their eyes away, and they could not. Ruthie and Winfield, crowded in a forward corner as far away from the body as they could get, stared at the tucked figure.

And Ruthie whispered, "Tha's Granma, an' she's dead."

Winfield nodded solemnly. "She ain't breathin' at all. She's awful dead."

And Rose of Sharon said softly to Connie, "She was a-dyin' right when we——"

"How'd we know?" he reassured her.

Al climbed on the load to make room for Ma in the seat. And Al swaggered a little because he was sorry. He plumped down beside Casy and Uncle John. "Well, she was ol'. Guess her time was up," Al said. "Ever'body got to die." Casy and Uncle John turned eyes expressionlessly on him and looked at him as though he were a curious talking bush. "Well, ain't they?" he demanded. And the eyes looked away, leaving Al sullen and shaken.

Casy said in wonder, "All night long, an' she was alone." And he said, "John, there's a woman so great with love—she scares me. Makes me afraid an' mean."

John asked, "Was it a sin? Is they any part of it you might call a sin?"

Casy turned on him in astonishment, "A sin? No, there ain't no part of it that's a sin."

"I ain't never done nothin' that wasn't part sin," said John, and he looked at the long wrapped body.

Tom and Ma and Pa got into the front seat. Tom let the truck roll and started on compression. And the heavy truck moved, snorting and jerking and popping down the hill. The sun was behind them, and the valley golden and green before them. Ma shook her head slowly from side to side. "It's purty," she said. "I wisht they could of saw it."

"I wisht so too," said Pa.

Tom patted the steering wheel under his hand. "They was too old," he said. "They wouldn't of saw nothin' that's here. Grampa would a been a-seein' the Injuns an' the prairie country when he was a young fella. An' Granma would a remembered an' seen the first home she lived in. They was too ol'. Who's really seein' it is Ruthie an' Winfiel'."

Pa said, "Here's Tommy talkin' like a growed-up man, talkin' like a preacher almos'."

And Ma smiled sadly. "He is. Tommy's growed way up— way up so I can't get aholt of 'im sometimes."

They popped down the mountain, twisting and looping, losing the valley sometimes, and then finding it again. And the hot breath of the valley came up to them, with hot green smells on it, and with resinous sage and tarweed smells. The crickets crackled along the road. A rattlesnake crawled across the road and Tom hit it and broke it and left it squirming.

Tom said, "I guess we got to go to the coroner, wherever he is. We got to get her buried decent. How much money might be lef', Pa?"

" 'Bout forty dollars," said Pa.

Tom laughed. "Jesus, are we gonna start clean! We sure ain't bringin' nothin' with us." He chuckled a moment, and then his face straightened quickly. He pulled the visor of his cap down low over his eyes. And the truck rolled down the mountain into the great valley.

Chapter Nineteen

ONCE California belonged to Mexico and its land to Mexicans; and a horde of tattered feverish Americans poured in. And such was their hunger for land that they took the land—stole Sutter's land, Guerrero's land, took the grants and broke them up and growled and quarreled over them, those frantic hungry men; and they guarded with guns the land they had stolen. They put up houses and barns, they turned the earth and planted crops. And these things were possession, and possession was ownership.

The Mexicans were weak and fed. They could not resist, because they wanted nothing in the world as ferociously as the Americans wanted land.

Then, with time, the squatters were no longer squatters, but owners; and their children grew up and had children on the land. And the hunger was gone from them, the feral hunger, the gnawing, tearing hunger for land, for water and earth and the good sky over it, for the green thrusting grass, for the swelling roots. They had these things so completely that they did not know about them any more. They had no more the stomach-tearing lust for a rich acre and a shining blade to plow it, for seed and a windmill beating its wings in the air. They arose in the dark no more to hear the sleepy birds' first chittering, and the morning wind around the house while they waited for the first light to go out to the dear acres. These things were lost, and crops were reckoned in dollars, and land was valued by principal plus interest, and crops were bought and sold before they were planted. Then crop failure, drought, and flood were no longer little deaths within life, but simple losses of money. And all their love was thinned with money, and all their fierceness dribbled away in interest until they were no longer farmers at all, but little shopkeepers of crops, little manufacturers who must sell before they can make. Then those farmers who were not good shopkeepers lost their land to good shopkeepers. No matter how clever, how loving a man might be with earth and growing things, he could not survive if he were not also a good shopkeeper. And as time went on, the business men had the farms, and the farms grew larger, but there were fewer of them.

Now farming became industry, and the owners followed Rome, although they did not know it. They imported slaves, although they did not call them slaves: Chinese, Japanese, Mexicans, Filipinos. They live on rice and beans, the business men said. They don't need much. They wouldn't know what to do with good wages. Why, look how they live. Why, look what they eat. And if they get funny—deport them.

And all the time the farms grew larger and the owners fewer. And there were pitifully few farmers on the land any more. And the imported serfs were beaten and frightened and starved until some went home again, and some grew fierce and were killed or driven from the country. And the farms grew larger and the owners fewer.

And the crops changed. Fruit trees took the place of grain fields, and vegetables to feed the world spread out on the bottoms: lettuce, cauliflower, artichokes, potatoes—stoop crops. A man may stand to use a scythe, a plow, a pitchfork; but he must crawl like a bug between the rows of lettuce, he must bend his back and pull his long bag between the cotton rows, he must go on his knees like a penitent across a cauliflower patch.

And it came about that owners no longer worked on their farms. They farmed on paper; and they forgot the land, the smell, the feel of it, and remembered only that they owned it, remembered only what they gained and lost by it. And some of the farms grew so large that one man could not even conceive of them any more, so large that it took batteries of bookkeepers to keep track of interest and gain and loss; chemists to test the soil, to replenish; straw bosses to see that the stooping men were moving along the rows as swiftly as the material of their bodies could stand. Then such a farmer really became a storekeeper, and kept a store. He paid the men, and sold them food, and took the money back. And after a while he did not pay the men at all, and saved bookkeeping. These farms gave food on credit. A man might work and feed himself; and when the work was done, he might find that he owed money to the company. And the owners not only did not work the farms any more, many of them had never seen the farms they owned.

And then the dispossessed were drawn west—from Kansas, Oklahoma, Texas, New Mexico; from Nevada and Arkansas families, tribes, dusted out, tractored out. Carloads, caravans, homeless and hungry; twenty thousand and fifty thousand and a hundred thousand and two hundred thousand. They streamed over the mountains, hungry and restless—restless as ants, scurrying to find work to do—to lift, to push, to pull, to pick, to cut—anything, any burden to bear, for food. The kids are hungry. We got no place to live. Like ants scurrying for work, for food, and most of all for land.

We ain't foreign. Seven generations back Americans, and beyond that Irish, Scotch, English, German. One of our folks in the Revolution, an' they was lots of our folks in the Civil War—both sides. Americans.

They were hungry, and they were fierce. And they had hoped to find a home, and they found only hatred. Okies—the owners hated them because the owners knew they were soft and the Okies strong, that they were fed and the Okies hungry; and perhaps the owners had heard from their grandfathers how easy it is to steal land from a soft man if you are fierce and hungry and armed. The owners hated them. And in the towns, the storekeepers hated them because they had no money to spend. There is no shorter path to a storekeeper's contempt, and all his admirations are exactly opposite. The town men, little bankers, hated Okies because there was nothing to gain from them. They had nothing. And the laboring people hated Okies because a hungry man must work, and if he must work, if he has to work, the wage payer automatically gives him less for his work; and then no one can get more.

And the dispossessed, the migrants, flowed into California, two hundred and fifty thousand, and three hundred thousand. Behind them new tractors were going on the land and the tenants were being forced off. And new waves were on the way, new waves of the dispossessed and the homeless, hardened, intent, and dangerous.

And while the Californians wanted many things, accumulation, social success, amusement, luxury, and a curious banking security, the new barbarians wanted only two things—land and food; and to them the two were one. And whereas the wants of the Californians were nebulous and undefined, the wants of the Okies were beside the roads, lying there to be seen and coveted: the good fields with water to be dug for, the good green fields, earth to crumble experimentally in the hand, grass to smell, oaten stalks to chew until the sharp sweetness was in the throat. A man might look at a fallow field and know, and see in his mind that his own bending back and his own straining arms would bring the cabbages into the light, and the golden eating corn, the turnips and carrots.

And a homeless hungry man, driving the roads with his wife beside him and his thin children in the back seat, could look at the fallow fields which might produce food but not profit, and that man could know how a fallow field is a sin and the unused land a crime against the thin children. And such a man drove along the roads and knew temptation at every field, and knew the lust to take these fields and make them grow strength for his children and a little comfort for his wife. The temptation was before him always. The fields goaded him, and the company ditches with good water flowing were a goad to him.

And in the south he saw the golden oranges hanging on the trees, the little golden oranges on the dark green trees; and guards with shotguns patrolling the lines so a man might not pick an orange for a thin child, oranges to be dumped if the price was low.

He drove his old car into a town. He scoured the farms for work. Where can we sleep the night?

Well, there's Hooverville on the edge of the river. There's a whole raft of Okies there.

He drove his old car to Hooverville. He never asked again, for there was a Hooverville on the edge of every town.

The rag town lay close to water; and the houses were tents, and weed-thatched enclosures, paper houses, a great junk pile. The man drove his family in and became a citizen of Hooverville—always they were called Hooverville. The man put up his own tent as near to water as he could get; or if he had no tent, he went to the city dump and brought back cartons and built a house of corrugated paper. And when the rains came the house melted and washed away. He settled in Hooverville and he scoured the countryside for work, and the little money he had went for gasoline to look for work. In the evening the men gathered and talked together. Squatting on their hams they talked of the land they had seen.

There's thirty thousan' acres, out west of here. Layin' there. Jesus, what I could do with that, with five acres of that! Why, hell, I'd have ever'thing to eat.

Notice one thing? They ain't no vegetables nor chickens nor pigs at the farms. They raise one thing—cotton, say, or peaches, or lettuce. 'Nother place'll be all chickens. They buy the stuff they could raise in the dooryard.

Jesus, what I could do with a couple pigs!

Well, it ain't yourn, an' it ain't gonna be yourn.

What we gonna do? The kids can't grow up this way.

In the camps the word would come whispering, There's work at Shafter. And the cars would be loaded in the night, the highways crowded—a gold rush for work. At Shafter the people would pile up, five times too many to do the work. A gold rush for work. They stole away in the night, frantic for work. And along the roads lay the temptations, the fields that could bear food.

That's owned. That ain't our'n.

Well, maybe we could get a little piece of her. Maybe—a little piece. Right down there—a patch. Jimson weed now. Christ, I could git enough potatoes off'n that little patch to feed my whole family!

It ain't our'n. It got to have Jimson weeds.

Now and then a man tried; crept on the land and cleared a piece, trying like a thief to steal a little richness from the earth. Secret gardens hidden in the weeds. A package of carrot seeds and a few turnips. Planted potato skins, crept out in the evening secretly to hoe in the stolen earth.

Leave the weeds around the edge—then nobody can see what we're a-doin'. Leave some weeds, big tall ones, in the middle.

Secret gardening in the evenings, and water carried in a rusty can.

And then one day a deputy sheriff: Well, what you think you're doin'?

I ain't doin' no harm.

I had my eye on you. This ain't your land. You're trespassing.

The land ain't plowed, an' I ain't hurtin' it none.

You goddamned squatters. Pretty soon you'd think you owned it. You'd be sore as hell. Think you owned it. Get off now.

And the little green carrot tops were kicked off and the turnip greens trampled. And then the Jimson weed moved back in. But the cop was right. A crop raised—why, that makes ownership. Land hoed and the carrots eaten—a man might fight for land he's taken food from. Get him off quick! He'll think he owns it. He might even die fighting for the little plot among the Jimson weeds.

Did ya see his face when we kicked them turnips out? Why, he'd kill a fella soon's he'd look at him. We got to keep these here people down or they'll take the country. They'll take the country.

Outlanders, foreigners.

Sure, they talk the same language, but they ain't the same. Look how they live. Think any of us folks'd live like that? Hell, no!

In the evenings, squatting and talking. And an excited man: Whyn't twenty of us take a piece of lan'? We got guns. Take it an' say, "Put us off if you can." Whyn't we do that?

They'd jus' shoot us like rats.

Well, which'd you ruther be, dead or here? Under groun' or in a house all made of gunny sacks? Which'd you ruther for your kids, dead now or dead in two years with what they call malnutrition? Know what we et all week? Biled nettles an' fried dough! Know where we got the flour for the dough? Swep' the floor of a boxcar.

Talking in the camps, and the deputies, fat-assed men with guns slung on fat hips, swaggering through the camps: Give 'em somepin to think about. Got to keep 'em in line or Christ only knows what they'll do! Why, Jesus, they're as dangerous as niggers in the South! If they ever get together there ain't nothin' that'll stop 'em.

Quote: In Lawrenceville a deputy sheriff evicted a squatter, and the squatter resisted, making it necessary for the officer to use force. The eleven-year-old son of the squatter shot and killed the deputy with a .22 rifle.

Rattlesnakes! Don't take chances with 'em, an' if they argue, shoot first. If a kid'll kill a cop, what'll the men do? Thing is, get tougher'n they are. Treat 'em rough. Scare 'em.

What if they won't scare? What if they stand up and take it and shoot back? These men were armed when they were children. A gun is an extension of themselves. What if they won't scare? What if some time an army of them marches on the land as the Lombards did in Italy, as the Germans did on Gaul and the Turks did on Byzantium? They were land-hungry, ill-armed hordes too, and the legions could not stop them. Slaughter and terror did not stop them. How can you frighten a man whose hunger is not only in his own cramped stomach but in the wretched bellies of his children? You can't scare him—he has known a fear beyond every other.

In Hooverville the men talking: Grampa took his lan' from the Injuns.

Now, this ain't right. We're a-talkin' here. This here you're talkin' about is stealin'. I ain't no thief.

No? You stole a bottle of milk from a porch night before last. An' you stole some copper wire and sold it for a piece of meat.

Yeah, but the kids was hungry.

It's stealin', though.

Know how the Fairfiel' ranch was got? I'll tell ya. It was all gov'ment lan', an' could be took up. Ol' Fairfiel', he went into San Francisco to the bars, an' he got him three hunderd stew bums. Them bums took up the lan'. Fairfiel' kep' 'em in food an' whisky, an' then when they'd proved the lan', ol' Fairfiel' took it from 'em. He used to say the lan' cost him a pint of rotgut an acre. Would you say that was stealin'?

Well, it wasn't right, but he never went to jail for it.

No, he never went to jail for it. An' the fella that put a boat in a wagon an' made his report like it was all under water 'cause he went in a boat—he never went to jail neither. An' the fellas that bribed congressmen and the legislatures never went to jail neither.

All over the State, jabbering in the Hoovervilles.

And then the raids—the swoop of armed deputies on the squatters' camps. Get out. Department of Health orders. This camp is a menace to health.

Where we gonna go?

That's none of our business. We got orders to get you out of here. In half an hour we set fire to the camp.

They's typhoid down the line. You want ta spread it all over?

We got orders to get you out of here. Now get! In half an hour we burn the camp.

In half an hour the smoke of paper houses, of weed-thatched huts, rising to the sky, and the people in their cars rolling over the highways, looking for another Hooverville.

And in Kansas and Arkansas, in Oklahoma and Texas and New Mexico, the tractors moved in and pushed the tenants out.

Three hundred thousand in California and more coming. And in California the roads full of frantic people running like ants to pull, to push, to lift, to work. For every manload to lift, five pairs of arms extended to lift it; for every stomachful of food available, five mouths open.

And the great owners, who must lose their land in an up-heaval, the great owners with access to history, with eyes to read history and to know the great fact: when property ac-cumulates in too few hands it is taken away. And that com-panion fact: when a majority of the people are hungry and cold they will take by force what they need. And the little screaming fact that sounds through all history: repression works only to strengthen and knit the repressed. The great owners ignored the three cries of history. The land fell into fewer hands, the number of the dispossessed increased, and every effort of the great owners was directed at repression. The money was spent for arms, for gas to protect the great holdings, and spies were sent to catch the murmuring of re-volt so that it might be stamped out. The changing econ-omy was ignored, plans for the change ignored; and only means to destroy revolt were considered, while the causes of revolt went on.

The tractors which throw men out of work, the belt lines

which carry loads, the machines which produce, all were increased; and more and more families scampered on the highways, looking for crumbs from the great holdings, lusting after the land beside the roads. The great owners formed associations for protection and they met to discuss ways to intimidate, to kill, to gas. And always they were in fear of a principal—three hundred thousand—if they ever move under a leader—the end. Three hundred thousand, hungry and miserable; if they ever know themselves, the land will be theirs and all the gas, all the rifles in the world won't stop them. And the great owners, who had become through the might of their holdings both more and less than men, ran to their destruction, and used every means that in the long run would destroy them. Every little means, every violence, every raid on a Hooverville, every fat-assed deputy swaggering through a ragged camp put off the day a little and cemented the inevitability of the day.

The men squatted on their hams, sharp-faced men, lean from hunger and hard from resisting it, sullen eyes and hard jaws. And the rich land was around them.

D'ja hear about the kid in that fourth tent down?

No, I jus' come in.

Well, that kid's been a-cryin' in his sleep an' a-rollin' in his sleep. Them folks thought he got worms. So they give him a blaster, an' he died. It was what they call black-tongue the kid had. Comes from not gettin' good things to eat.

Poor little fella.

Yeah, but them folks can't bury him. Got to go to the county stone orchard.

Well, hell.

And hands went into pockets and little coins came out. In front of the tent a little heap of silver grew. And the family found it there.

Our people are good people; our people are kind people. Pray God some day kind people won't all be poor. Pray God some day a kid can eat.

And the associations of owners knew that some day the praying would stop.

And there's the end.

Chapter Twenty

THE FAMILY, on top of the load, the children and Connie and Rose of Sharon and the preacher were stiff and cramped. They had sat in the heat in front of the coroner's office in Bakersfield while Pa and Ma and Uncle John went in. Then a basket was brought out and the long bundle lifted down from the truck. And they sat in the sun while the examination went on, while the cause of death was found and the certificate signed.

Al and Tom strolled along the street and looked in store windows and watched the strange people on the sidewalks.

And at last Pa and Ma and Uncle John came out, and they were subdued and quiet. Uncle John climbed up on the load. Pa and Ma got in the seat. Tom and Al strolled back and Tom got under the steering wheel. He sat there silently, waiting for some instruction. Pa looked straight ahead, his dark hat pulled low. Ma rubbed the side of her mouth with her fingers, and her eyes were far away and lost, dead with weariness.

Pa sighed deeply. "They wasn't nothin' else to do," he said.

"I know," said Ma. "She would a liked a nice funeral, though. She always wanted one."

Tom looked sideways at them. "County?" he asked.

"Yeah," Pa shook his head quickly, as though to get back to some reality. "We didn' have enough. We couldn' of done it." He turned to Ma. "You ain't to feel bad. We couldn' no matter how hard we tried, no matter what we done. We jus' didn' have it; embalming, an' a coffin an' a preacher, an' a plot in a graveyard. It would of took ten times what we got. We done the bes' we could."

"I know," Ma said. "I jus' can't get it outa my head what store she set by a nice funeral. Got to forget it." She sighed deeply and rubbed the side of her mouth. "That was a purty nice fella in there. Awful bossy, but he was purty nice."

"Yeah," Pa said. "He give us the straight talk, awright."

Ma brushed her hair back with her hand. Her jaw tightened. "We got to git," she said. "We got to find a place to stay. We got to get work an' settle down. No use a-lettin' the little fellas go hungry. That wasn't never Granma's way. She always et a good meal at a funeral."

"Where we goin'?" Tom asked.

Pa raised his hat and scratched among his hair. "Camp," he said. "We ain't gonna spen' what little's lef' till we get work. Drive out in the country."

Tom started the car and they rolled through the streets and out toward the country. And by a bridge they saw a collection of tents and shacks. Tom said, "Might's well stop here. Find out what's doin', an' where at the work is." He drove down a steep dirt incline and parked on the edge of the encampment.

There was no order in the camp; little gray tents, shacks, cars were scattered about at random. The first house was nondescript. The south wall was made of three sheets of rusty corrugated iron, the east wall a square of moldy carpet tacked between two boards, the north wall a strip of roofing paper and a strip of tattered canvas, and the west wall six pieces of gunny sacking. Over the square frame, on untrimmed willow limbs, grass had been piled, not thatched, but heaped up in a low mound. The entrance, on the gunny-sack side, was cluttered with equipment. A five-gallon kerosene can served for a stove. It was laid on its side, with a section of rusty stovepipe thrust in one end. A wash boiler rested on its side against the wall; and a collection of boxes lay about, boxes to sit on, to eat on. A Model T Ford sedan and a two-wheel trailer were parked beside the shack, and about the camp there hung a slovenly despair.

Next to the shack there was a little tent, gray with weathering, but neatly, properly set up; and the boxes in front of it were placed against the tent wall. A stovepipe stuck out of the door flap, and the dirt in front of the tent had been swept and sprinkled. A bucketful of soaking clothes stood on a box. The camp was neat and sturdy. A Model A roadster and a little home-made bed trailer stood beside the tent.

And next there was a huge tent, ragged, torn in strips and the tears mended with pieces of wire. The flaps were up, and inside four wide mattresses lay on the ground. A clothes line strung along the side bore pink cotton dresses and several pairs of overalls. There were forty tents and shacks, and beside each habitation some kind of automobile. Far down the line a few children stood and stared at the newly arrived truck, and they moved cautiously toward it, little boys in overalls and bare feet, their hair gray with dust.

Tom stopped the truck and looked at Pa. "She ain't very purty," he said. "Want to go somewheres else?"

"Can't go nowheres else till we know where we're at," Pa said. "We got to ast about work."

Tom opened the door and stepped out. The family climbed down from the load and looked curiously at the camp. Ruthie and Winfield, from the habit of the road, took down the bucket and walked toward the willows, where there would be water; and the line of children parted for them and closed after them.

The flaps of the first shack parted and a woman looked out. Her gray hair was braided, and she wore a dirty, flowered Mother Hubbard. Her face was wizened and dull, deep gray pouches under blank eyes, and a mouth slack and loose.

Pa said, "Can we jus' pull up anywheres an' camp?"

The head was withdrawn inside the shack. For a moment there was quiet and then the flaps were pushed aside and a bearded man in shirt sleeves stepped out. The woman looked out after him, but she did not come into the open.

The bearded man said, "Howdy, folks," and his restless dark eyes jumped to each member of the family, and from them to the truck to the equipment.

Pa said, "I jus' ast your woman if it's all right to set our stuff anywheres."

The bearded man looked at Pa intently, as though he had said something very wise that needed thought. "Set down anywheres, here in this place?" he asked.

"Sure. Anybody own this place, that we got to see 'fore we can camp?"

The bearded man squinted one eye nearly closed and studied Pa. "You wanta camp here?"

Pa's irritation arose. The gray woman peered out of the burlap shack. "What you think I'm a-sayin'?" Pa said.

"Well, if you wanta camp here, why don't ya? I ain't a-stoppin' you."

Tom laughed. "He got it."

Pa gathered his temper. "I jus' wanted to know does anybody own it? Do we got to pay?"

The bearded man thrust out his jaw. "Who owns it?" he demanded.

Pa turned away. "The hell with it," he said. The woman's head popped back in the tent.

The bearded man stepped forward menacingly. "Who owns it?" he demanded. "Who's gonna kick us outa here? You tell *me*."

Tom stepped in front of Pa. "You better go take a good long sleep," he said. The bearded man dropped his mouth open and put a dirty finger against his lower gums. For a moment he continued to look wisely, speculatively at Tom, and then he turned on his heel and popped into the shack after the gray woman.

Tom turned on Pa. "What the hell was that?" he asked.

Pa shrugged his shoulders. He was looking across the camp. In front of a tent stood an old Buick, and the head was off. A young man was grinding the valves, and as he twisted back and forth, back and forth, on the tool, he looked up at the Joad truck. They could see that he was laughing to himself. When the bearded man had gone, the young man left his work and sauntered over.

"H'are ya?" he said, and his blue eyes were shiny with amusement. "I seen you just met the Mayor."

"What the hell's the matter with 'im?" Tom demanded.

The young man chuckled. "He's jus' nuts like you an' me. Maybe he's a little nutser'n me, I don' know."

Pa said, "I jus' ast him if we could camp here."

The young man wiped his greasy hands on his trousers. "Sure. Why not? You folks jus' come acrost?"

"Yeah," said Tom. "Jus' got in this mornin'."

"Never been in Hooverville before?"

"Where's Hooverville?"

"This here's her."

"Oh!" said Tom. "We jus' got in."

Winfield and Ruthie came back, carrying a bucket of water between them.

Ma said, "Le's get the camp up. I'm tuckered out. Maybe

we can all rest." Pa and Uncle John climbed up on the truck to unload the canvas and the beds.

Tom sauntered to the young man, and walked beside him back to the car he had been working on. The valve-grinding brace lay on the exposed block, and a little yellow can of valve-grinding compound was wedged on top of the vacuum tank. Tom asked, "What the hell was the matter'th that ol' fella with the beard?"

The young man picked up his brace and went to work, twisting back and forth, grinding valve against valve seat. "The Mayor? Chris' knows. I guess maybe he's bull-simple."

"What's 'bull-simple'?"

"I guess cops push 'im aroun' so much he's still spinning."

Tom asked, "Why would they push a fella like that aroun'?"

The young man stopped his work and looked in Tom's eyes. "Chris' knows," he said. "You jus' come. Maybe you can figger her out. Some fellas says one thing, an' some says another thing. But you jus' camp in one place a little while, an' you see how quick a deputy sheriff shoves you along." He lifted a valve and smeared compound on the seat.

"But what the hell for?"

"I tell ya I don' know. Some says they don' want us to vote; keep us movin' so we can't vote. An' some says so we can't get on relief. An' some says if we set in one place we'd get organized. I don' know why. I on'y know we get rode all the time. You wait, you'll see."

"We ain't no bums," Tom insisted. "We're lookin' for work. We'll take any kind a work."

The young man paused in fitting the brace to the valve slot. He looked in amazement at Tom. "Lookin' for work?" he said. "So you're lookin' for work. What ya think ever'body else is lookin' for? Di'monds? What you think I wore my ass down to a nub lookin' for?" He twisted the brace back and forth.

Tom looked about at the grimy tents, the junk equipment, at the old cars, the lumpy mattresses out in the sun, at the blackened cans on fire-blackened holes where the people cooked. He asked quietly, "Ain't they no work?"

"I don' know. Mus' be. Ain't no crop right here now.

Grapes to pick later, an' cotton to pick later. We're a-movin' on, soon's I get these here valves groun'. Me an' my wife an' my kid. We heard they was work up north. We're shovin' north, up aroun' Salinas.''

Tom saw Uncle John and Pa and the preacher hoisting the tarpaulin on the tent poles and Ma on her knees inside, brushing off the mattresses on the ground. A circle of quiet children stood to watch the new family get settled, quiet children with bare feet and dirty faces. Tom said, ''Back home some fellas come through with han'bills—orange ones. Says they need lots a people out here to work the crops.''

The young man laughed. ''They say they's three hunderd thousan' us folks here, an' I bet ever' dam' fam'ly seen them han'bills.''

''Yeah, but if they don' need folks, what'd they go to the trouble puttin' them things out for?''

''Use your head, why don'cha?''

''Yeah, but I wanta know.''

''Look,'' the young man said. ''S'pose you got a job a work, an' there's jus' one fella wants the job. You got to pay 'im what he asts. But s'pose they's a hunderd men.'' He put down his tool. His eyes hardened and his voice sharpened. ''S'pose they's a hunderd men wants that job. S'pose them men got kids, an' them kids is hungry. S'pose a lousy dime'll buy a box a mush for them kids. S'pose a nickel'll buy at leas' somepin for them kids. An' you got a hunderd men. Jus' offer 'em a nickel—why, they'll kill each other fightin' for that nickel. Know what they was payin', las' job I had? Fifteen cents an hour. Ten hours for a dollar an' a half, an' ya can't stay on the place. Got to burn gasoline gettin' there.'' He was panting with anger, and his eyes blazed with hate. ''That's why them han'bills was out. You can print a hell of a lot of han'bills with what ya save payin' fifteen cents an hour for fiel' work.''

Tom said, ''That's stinkin'.''

The young man laughed harshly. ''You stay out here a little while, an' if you smell any roses, you come let me smell, too.''

''But they is work,'' Tom insisted. ''Christ Almighty, with all this stuff a-growin': orchards, grapes, vegetables—I seen it. They got to have men. I seen all that stuff.''

A child cried in the tent beside the car. The young man went into the tent and his voice came softly through the canvas. Tom picked up the brace, fitted it in the slot of the valve, and ground away, his hand whipping back and forth. The child's crying stopped. The young man came out and watched Tom. "You can do her," he said. "Damn good thing. You'll need to."

"How 'bout what I said?" Tom resumed. "I seen all the stuff growin'."

The young man squatted on his heels. "I'll tell ya," he said quietly. "They's a big son-of-a-bitch of a peach orchard I worked in. Takes nine men all the year roun'." He paused impressively. "Takes three thousan' men for two weeks when them peaches is ripe. Got to have 'em or them peaches'll rot. So what do they do? They send out han'bills all over hell. They need three thousan', an' they get six thousan'. They get them men for what they wanta pay. If ya don' wanta take what they pay, goddamn it, they's a thousan' men waitin' for your job. So ya pick, an' ya pick, an' then she's done. Whole part a the country's peaches. All ripe together. When ya get 'em picked, ever' goddamn one is picked. There ain't another damn thing in that part a the country to do. An' then them owners don' want you there no more. Three thousan' of you. The work's done. You might steal, you might get drunk, you might jus' raise hell. An' besides, you don' look nice, livin' in ol' tents; an' it's a pretty country, but you stink it up. They don' want you aroun'. So they kick you out, they move you along. That's how it is."

Tom, looking down toward the Joad tent, saw his mother, heavy and slow with weariness, build a little trash fire and put the cooking pots over the flame. The circle of children drew closer, and the calm wide eyes of the children watched every move of Ma's hands. An old, old man with a bent back came like a badger out of a tent and snooped near, sniffing the air as he came. He laced his arms behind him and joined the children to watch Ma. Ruthie and Winfield stood near to Ma and eyed the strangers belligerently.

Tom said angrily, "Them peaches got to be picked right now, don't they? Jus' when they're ripe?"

" 'Course they do."

"Well, s'pose them people got together an' says, 'Let 'em rot.' Wouldn' be long 'fore the price went up, by God!"

The young man looked up from the valves, looked sardonically at Tom. "Well, you figgered out somepin, didn' you. Come right outa your own head."

"I'm tar'd," said Tom. "Drove all night. I don't wanta start no argument. An' I'm so goddamn tar'd I'd argue easy. Don' be smart with me. I'm askin' you."

The young man grinned. "I didn' mean it. You ain't been here. Folks figgered that out. An' the folks with the peach orchard figgered her out too. Look, if the folks gets together, they's a leader—got to be—fella that does the talkin'. Well, first time this fella opens his mouth they grab 'im an' stick 'im in jail. An' if they's another leader pops up, why, they stick 'im in jail."

Tom said, "Well, a fella eats in jail anyways."

"His kids don't. How'd you like to be in an' your kids starvin' to death?"

"Yeah," said Tom slowly. "Yeah."

"An' here's another thing. Ever hear a' the blacklist?"

"What's that?"

"Well, you jus' open your trap about us folks gettin' together, an' you'll see. They take your pitcher an' send it all over. Then you can't get work nowhere. An' if you got kids——"

Tom took off his cap and twisted it in his hands. "So we take what we can get, huh, or we starve; an' if we yelp we starve."

The young man made a sweeping circle with his hand, and his hand took in the ragged tents and the rusty cars.

Tom looked down at his mother again, where she sat scraping potatoes. And the children had drawn closer. He said, "I ain't gonna take it. Goddamn it, I an' my folks ain't no sheep. I'll kick the hell outa somebody."

"Like a cop?"

"Like anybody."

"You're nuts," said the young man. "They'll pick you right off. You got no name, no property. They'll find you in a ditch, with the blood dried on your mouth an' your nose. Be one little line in the paper—know what it'll say? 'Vagrant foun' dead.' An' that's all. You'll see a lot of them little lines, 'Vagrant foun' dead.' "

Tom said, "They'll be somebody else foun' dead right 'longside of this here vagrant."

"You're nuts," said the young man. "Won't be no good in that."

"Well, what you doin' about it?" He looked into the grease-streaked face. And a veil drew down over the eyes of the young man.

"Nothin'. Where you from?"

"Us? Right near Sallisaw, Oklahoma."

"Jus' get in?"

"Jus' today."

"Gonna be aroun' here long?"

"Don't know. We'll stay wherever we can get work. Why?"

"Nothin'." And the veil came down again.

"Got to sleep up," said Tom. "Tomorra we'll go out lookin' for work."

"You kin try."

Tom turned away and moved toward the Joad tent.

The young man took up the can of valve compound and dug his finger into it. "Hi!" he called.

Tom turned. "What you want?"

"I wanta tell ya." He motioned with his finger, on which a blob of compound stuck. "I jus' wanta tell ya. Don' go lookin' for no trouble. 'Member how that bull-simple guy looked?"

"Fella in the tent up there?"

"Yeah—looked dumb—no sense?"

"What about him?"

"Well, when the cops come in, an' they come in all a time, that's how you wanta be. Dumb—don't know nothin'. Don't understan' nothin'. That's how the cops like us. Don't hit no cops. That's jus' suicide. Be bull-simple."

"Let them goddamn cops run over me, an' me do nothin'?"

"No, looka here. I'll come for ya tonight. Maybe I'm wrong. There's stools aroun' all a time. I'm takin' a chancet, an' I got a kid, too. But I'll come for ya. An' if ya see a cop, why, you're a goddamn dumb Okie, see?"

"Tha's awright if we're doin' anythin'," said Tom.

"Don' you worry. We're doin' somepin, on'y we ain't stickin' our necks out. A kid starves quick. Two-three days for a kid." He went back to his job, spread the compound on a valve seat, and his hand jerked rapidly back and forth on the brace, and his face was dull and dumb.

Tom strolled slowly back to his camp. "Bull-simple," he said under his breath.

Pa and Uncle John came toward the camp, their arms loaded with dry willow sticks, and they threw them down by the fire and squatted on their hams. "Got her picked over pretty good," said Pa. "Had ta go a long ways for wood." He looked up at the circle of staring children. "Lord God Almighty!" he said. "Where'd you come from?" All of the children looked self-consciously at their feet.

"Guess they smelled the cookin'," said Ma. "Winfiel', get out from under foot." She pushed him out of her way. "Got ta make us up a little stew," she said. "We ain't et nothin' cooked right sence we come from home. Pa, you go up to the store there an' get me some neck meat. Make a nice stew here." Pa stood up and sauntered away.

Al had the hood of the car up, and he looked down at the greasy engine. He looked up when Tom approached. "You sure look happy as a buzzard," Al said.

"I'm jus' gay as a toad in spring rain," said Tom.

"Looka the engine," Al pointed. "Purty good, huh?"

Tom peered in. "Looks awright to me."

"Awright? Jesus, she's wonderful. She ain't shot no oil nor nothin'." He unscrewed a spark plug and stuck his forefinger in the hole. "Crusted up some, but she's dry."

Tom said, "You done a nice job a pickin'. That what ya want me to say?"

"Well, I sure was scairt the whole way, figgerin' she'd bust down an' it'd be my fault."

"No, you done good. Better get her in shape, 'cause tomorra we're goin' out lookin' for work."

"She'll roll," said Al. "Don't you worry none about that." He took out a pocket knife and scraped the points of the spark plug.

Tom walked around the side of the tent, and he found Casy sitting on the earth, wisely regarding one bare foot. Tom sat down heavily beside him. "Think she's gonna work?"

"What?" asked Casy.

"Them toes of yourn."

"Oh! Jus' settin' here a-thinkin'."

"You always get good an' comf'table for it," said Tom.

Casy waggled his big toe up and his second toe down, and he smiled quietly. "Hard enough for a fella to think 'thout kinkin' hisself up to do it."

"Ain't heard a peep outa you for days," said Tom. "Thinkin' all the time?"

"Yeah, thinkin' all the time."

Tom took off his cloth cap, dirty now, and ruinous, the visor pointed as a bird's beak. He turned the sweat band out and removed a long strip of folded newspaper. "Sweat so much she's shrank," he said. He looked at Casy's waving toes. "Could ya come down from your thinkin' an' listen a minute?"

Casy turned his head on the stalk-like neck. "Listen all the time. That's why I been thinkin'. Listen to people a-talkin', an' purty soon I hear the way folks are feelin'. Goin' on all the time. I hear 'em an' feel 'em; an' they're beating their wings like a bird in a attic. Gonna bust their wings on a dusty winda tryin' ta get out."

Tom regarded him with widened eyes, and then he turned and looked at a gray tent twenty feet away. Washed jeans and shirts and a dress hung to dry on the tent guys. He said softly, "That was about what I was gonna tell ya. An' you seen awready."

"I seen," Casy agreed. "They's a army of us without no harness." He bowed his head and ran his extended hand slowly up his forehead and into his hair. "All along I seen it," he said. "Ever' place we stopped I seen it. Folks hungry for side-meat, an' when they get it, they ain't fed. An' when they'd get so hungry they couldn' stan' it no more, why, they'd ast me to pray for 'em, an' sometimes I done it." He clasped his hands around drawn-up knees and pulled his legs in. "I use ta think that'd cut 'er," he said. "Use ta rip off a prayer an' all the troubles'd stick to that prayer like flies on flypaper, an' the prayer'd go a-sailin' off, a-takin' them troubles along. But it don' work no more."

Tom said, "Prayer never brought in no side-meat. Takes a shoat to bring in pork."

"Yeah," Casy said. "An' Almighty God never raised no wages. These here folks want to live decent and bring up their kids decent. An' when they're old they wanta set in the door an' watch the downing sun. An' when they're young they wanta dance an' sing an' lay together. They wanta eat an' get drunk and work. An' that's it—they wanta jus' fling their god-damn muscles aroun' an' get tired. Christ! What'm I talkin' about?"

"I dunno," said Tom. "Sounds kinda nice. When ya think you can get ta work an' quit thinkin' a spell? We got to get work. Money's 'bout gone. Pa give five dollars to get a painted piece of board stuck up over Granma. We ain't got much lef'."

A lean brown mongrel dog came sniffing around the side of the tent. He was nervous and flexed to run. He sniffed close before he was aware of the two men, and then looking up he saw them, leaped sideways, and fled, ears back, bony tail clamped protectively. Casy watched him go, dodging around a tent to get out of sight. Casy sighed. "I ain't doin' nobody no good," he said. "Me or nobody else. I was thinkin' I'd go off alone by myself. I'm a-eatin' your food an' a-takin' up room. An' I ain't give you nothin'. Maybe I could get a steady job an' maybe pay back some a the stuff you've give me."

Tom opened his mouth and thrust his lower jaw forward, and he tapped his lower teeth with a dried piece of mustard stalk. His eyes stared over the camp, over the gray tents and the shacks of weed and tin and paper. "Wisht I had a sack a Durham," he said. "I ain't had a smoke in a hell of a time. Use ta get tobacco in McAlester. Almost wisht I was back." He tapped his teeth again and suddenly he turned on the preacher. "Ever been in a jail house?"

"No," said Casy. "Never been."

"Don't go away right yet," said Tom. "Not right yet."

"Quicker I get lookin' for work—quicker I'm gonna find some."

Tom studied him with half-shut eyes and he put on his cap again. "Look," he said, "this ain't no lan' of milk an' honey like the preachers say. They's a mean thing here. The folks here is scared of us people comin' west; an' so they got cops out tryin' to scare us back."

"Yeah," said Casy. "I know. What you ask about me bein' in jail for?"

Tom said slowly, "When you're in jail—you get to kinda—sensin' stuff. Guys ain't let to talk a hell of a lot together—two maybe, but not a crowd. An' so you get kinda sensy. If somepin's gonna bust—if say a fella's goin' stir-bugs an' take a crack at a guard with a mop handle—why, you know it 'fore it happens. An' if they's gonna be a break or a riot, nobody don't have to tell ya. You're sensy about it. You know."

"Yeah?"

"Stick aroun'," said Tom. "Stick aroun' till tomorra anyways. Somepin's gonna come up. I was talkin' to a kid up the road. An' he's bein' jus' as sneaky an' wise as a dog coyote, but he's too wise. Dog coyote a-mindin' his own business an' innocent an' sweet, jus' havin' fun an' no harm—well, they's a hen roost clost by."

Casy watched him intently, started to ask a question, and then shut his mouth tightly. He waggled his toes slowly and, releasing his knees, pushed out his foot so he could see it. "Yeah," he said, "I won't go right yet."

Tom said, "When a bunch a folks, nice quiet folks, don't know nothin' about nothin'—somepin's goin' on."

"I'll stay," said Casy.

"An' tomorra we'll go out in the truck an' look for work."

"Yeah!" said Casy, and he waved his toes up and down and studied them gravely. Tom settled back on his elbow and closed his eyes. Inside the tent he could hear the murmur of Rose of Sharon's voice and Connie's answering.

The tarpaulin made a dark shadow and the wedge-shaped light at each end was hard and sharp. Rose of Sharon lay on a mattress and Connie squatted beside her. "I oughta help Ma," Rose of Sharon said. "I tried, but ever' time I stirred about I threwed up."

Connie's eyes were sullen. "If I'd of knowed it would be like this I wouldn' of came. I'd a studied nights 'bout tractors back home an' got me a three-dollar job. Fella can live awful nice on three dollars a day, an' go to the pitcher show ever' night, too."

Rose of Sharon looked apprehensive. "You're gonna study nights 'bout radios," she said. He was long in answering. "Ain't you?" she demanded.

"Yeah, sure. Soon's I get on my feet. Get a little money."

She rolled up on her elbow. "You ain't givin' it up!"

"No—no—'course not. But—I didn' know they was places like this we got to live in."

The girl's eyes hardened. "You got to," she said quietly.

"Sure. Sure, I know. Got to get on my feet. Get a little money. Would a been better maybe to stay home an' study 'bout tractors. Three dollars a day they get, an' pick up extra money, too." Rose of Sharon's eyes were calculating. When he looked down at her he saw in her eyes a measuring of him, a calculation of him. "But I'm gonna study," he said. "Soon's I get on my feet."

She said fiercely, "We got to have a house 'fore the baby comes. We ain't gonna have this baby in no tent."

"Sure," he said. "Soon's I get on my feet." He went out of the tent and looked down at Ma, crouched over the brush fire. Rose of Sharon rolled on her back and stared at the top of the tent. And then she put her thumb in her mouth for a gag and she cried silently.

Ma knelt beside the fire, breaking twigs to keep the flame up under the stew kettle. The fire flared and dropped and flared and dropped. The children, fifteen of them, stood silently and watched. And when the smell of the cooking stew came to their noses, their noses crinkled slightly. The sunlight glistened on hair tawny with dust. The children were embarrassed to be there, but they did not go. Ma talked quietly to a little girl who stood inside the lusting circle. She was older than the rest. She stood on one foot, caressing the back of her leg with a bare instep. Her arms were clasped behind her. She watched Ma with steady small gray eyes. She suggested, "I could break up some bresh if you want me, ma'am."

Ma looked up from her work. "You wanta get ast to eat, huh?"

"Yes, ma'am," the girl said steadily.

Ma slipped the twigs under the pot and the flame made a puttering sound. "Didn' you have no breakfast?"

"No, ma'am. They ain't no work hereabouts. Pa's in tryin' to sell some stuff to git gas so's we can git 'long."

Ma looked up. "Didn' none of these here have no breakfast?"

The circle of children shifted nervously and looked away from the boiling kettle. One small boy said boastfully, "I did—me an' my brother did—an' them two did, 'cause I seen 'em. We et good. We're a-goin' south tonight."

Ma smiled. "Then you ain't hungry. They ain't enough here to go around."

The small boy's lip stuck out. "We et good," he said, and he turned and ran and dived into a tent. Ma looked after him so long that the oldest girl reminded her.

"The fire's down, ma'am. I can keep it up if you want."

Ruthie and Winfield stood inside the circle, comporting themselves with proper frigidity and dignity. They were aloof, and at the same time possessive. Ruthie turned cold and angry eyes on the little girl. Ruthie squatted down to break up the twigs for Ma.

Ma lifted the kettle lid and stirred the stew with a stick. "I'm sure glad some of you ain't hungry. That little fella ain't, anyways."

The girl sneered. "Oh, him! He was a-braggin'. He's always a-braggin'. High an' mighty. If he don't have no supper— know what he done? Las' night, come out an' says they got chicken to eat. Well, sir, I looked in whilst they was a-eatin' an' it was fried dough jus' like ever'body else."

"Oh!" And Ma looked down toward the tent where the small boy had gone. She looked back at the little girl. "How long you been in California?" she asked.

"Oh, 'bout six months. We lived in a gov'ment camp a while, an' then we went north, an' when we come back it was full up. That's a nice place to live, you bet."

"Where's that?" Ma asked. And she took the sticks from Ruthie's hand and fed the fire. Ruthie glared with hatred at the older girl.

"Over by Weedpatch. Got nice toilets an' baths, an' you kin wash clothes in a tub, an' they's water right handy, good drinkin' water; an' nights the folks plays music an' Sat'dy night they give a dance. Oh, you never seen anything so nice. Got a place for kids to play, an' them toilets with paper. Pull down a little jigger an' the water comes right in the toilet, an' they ain't no cops let to come look in your tent any time they want, an' the fella runs the camp is so polite, comes a-visitin' an' talks an' ain't high an' mighty. I wisht we could go live there again."

Ma said, "I never heard about it. I sure could use a wash tub, I tell you."

The girl went on excitedly, "Why, God Awmighty, they got hot water right in pipes, an' you get in under a shower bath an' it's warm. You never seen such a place."

Ma said, "All full now, ya say?"

"Yeah. Las' time we ast it was."

"Mus' cost a lot," said Ma.

"Well, it costs, but if you ain't got the money, they let you work it out—couple hours a week, cleanin' up, an' garbage cans. Stuff like that. An' nights they's music an' folks talks together an' hot water right in the pipes. You never seen nothin' so nice."

Ma said, "I sure wisht we could go there."

Ruthie had stood all she could. She blurted fiercely, "Granma died right on top a the truck." The girl looked questioningly at her. "Well, she did," Ruthie said. "An' the cor'ner got her." She closed her lips tightly and broke up a little pile of sticks.

Winfield blinked at the boldness of the attack. "Right on the truck," he echoed. "Cor'ner stuck her in a big basket."

Ma said, "You shush now, both of you, or you got to go away." And she fed twigs into the fire.

Down the line Al had strolled to watch the valve-grinding job. "Looks like you're 'bout through," he said.

"Two more."

"Is they any girls in this here camp?"

"I got a wife," said the young man. "I got no time for girls."

"I always got time for girls," said Al. "I got no time for nothin' else."

"You get a little hungry an' you'll change."

Al laughed. "Maybe. But I ain't never changed that notion yet."

"Fella I talked to while ago, he's with you, ain't he?"

"Yeah! My brother Tom. Better not fool with him. He killed a fella."

"Did? What for?"

"Fight. Fella got a knife in Tom. Tom busted 'im with a shovel."

"Did, huh? What'd the law do?"

"Let 'im off 'cause it was a fight," said Al.

"He don't look like a quarreler."

"Oh, he ain't. But Tom don't take nothin' from nobody." Al's voice was very proud. "Tom, he's quiet. But—look out!"

"Well—I talked to 'im. He didn' soun' mean."

"He ain't. Jus' as nice as pie till he's roused, an' then— look out." The young man ground at the last valve. "Like me to he'p you get them valves set an' the head on?"

"Sure, if you got nothin' else to do."

"Oughta get some sleep," said Al. "But, hell, I can't keep my han's out of a tore-down car. Jus' got to git in."

"Well, I'd admire to git a hand," said the young man. "My name's Floyd Knowles."

"I'm Al Joad."

"Proud to meet ya."

"Me too," said Al. "Gonna use the same gasket?"

"Got to," said Floyd.

Al took out his pocket knife and scraped at the block. "Jesus!" he said. "They ain't nothin' I love like the guts of a engine."

"How 'bout girls?"

"Yeah, girls too! Wisht I could tear down a Rolls an' put her back. I looked under the hood of a Cad' 16 one time an', God Awmighty, you never seen nothin' so sweet in your life! In Sallisaw—an' here's this 16 a-standin' in front of a restaurant, so I lifts the hood. An' a guy comes out an' says, 'What the hell you doin'?' I says, 'Jus' lookin'. Ain't she swell?' An' he jus' stands there. I don' think he ever looked in her before. Jus' stands there. Rich fella in a straw hat. Got a stripe' shirt on, an' eye glasses. We don' say nothin'. Jus' look. An' purty soon he says, 'How'd you like to drive her?'"

Floyd said, "The hell!"

"Sure—'How'd you like to drive her?' Well, hell, I got on jeans—all dirty. I says, 'I'd get her dirty.' 'Come on!' he says. 'Jus' take her roun' the block.' Well, sir, I set in that seat an' I took her roun' the block eight times, an', oh, my God Almighty!"

"Nice?" Floyd asked.

"Oh, Jesus!" said Al. "If I could of tore her down why—I'd a give—anythin'."

Floyd slowed his jerking arm. He lifted the last valve from its seat and looked at it. "You better git use' ta a jalopy," he said, " 'cause you ain't gonna drive no 16." He put his brace down on the running board and took up a chisel to scrape the crust from the block. Two stocky women, bare-headed and bare-footed, went by carrying a bucket of milky water between them. They limped against the weight of the bucket, and neither one looked up from the ground. The sun was half down in afternoon.

Al said, "You don't like nothin' much."

Floyd scraped harder with the chisel. "I been here six months," he said. "I been scrabblin' over this here State tryin' to work hard enough and move fast enough to get meat an' potatoes for me an' my wife an' my kid. I've run myself like a jackrabbit an'—I can't quite make her. There just ain't quite enough to eat no matter what I do. I'm gettin' tired, that's all. I'm gettin' tired way past where sleep rests me. An' I jus' don' know what to do."

"Ain't there no steady work for a fella?" Al asked.

"No, they ain't no steady work." With his chisel he pushed the crust off the block, and he wiped the dull metal with a greasy rag.

A rusty touring car drove down into the camp and there were four men in it, men with brown hard faces. The car drove slowly through the camp. Floyd called to them, "Any luck?"

The car stopped. The driver said, "We covered a hell of a lot a ground. They ain't a hand's work in this here county. We gotta move."

"Where to?" Al called.

"God knows. We worked this here place over." He let in his clutch and moved slowly down the camp.

Al looked after them. "Wouldn' it be better if one fella went alone? Then if they was one piece a work, a fella'd get it."

Floyd put down the chisel and smiled sourly. "You ain't learned," he said. "Takes gas to get roun' the country. Gas costs fifteen cents a gallon. Them four fellas can't take four cars. So each of 'em puts in a dime an' they get gas. You got to learn."

"Al!"

Al looked down at Winfield standing importantly beside him. "Al, Ma's dishin' up stew. She says come git it."

Al wiped his hands on his trousers. "We ain't et today," he said to Floyd. "I'll come give you a han' when I eat."

"No need 'less you wanta."

"Sure, I'll do it." He followed Winfield toward the Joad camp.

It was crowded now. The strange children stood close to the stew pot, so close that Ma brushed them with her elbows as she worked. Tom and Uncle John stood beside her.

Ma said helplessly, "I dunno what to do. I got to feed the fambly. What'm I gonna do with these here?" The children stood stiffly and looked at her. Their faces were blank, rigid, and their eyes went mechanically from the pot to the tin plate she held. Their eyes followed the spoon from pot to plate, and when she passed the steaming plate up to Uncle John, their eyes followed it up. Uncle John dug his spoon into the stew, and the banked eyes rose up with the spoon. A piece of potato went into John's mouth and the banked eyes were on his face, watching to see how he would react. Would it be good? Would he like it?

And then Uncle John seemed to see them for the first time. He chewed slowly. "You take this here," he said to Tom. "I ain't hungry."

"You ain't et today," Tom said.

"I know, but I got a stomickache. I ain't hungry."

Tom said quietly, "You take that plate inside the tent an' you eat it."

"I ain't hungry," John insisted. "I'd still see 'em inside the tent."

Tom turned on the children. "You git," he said. "Go on now, git." The bank of eyes left the stew and rested wondering on his face. "Go on now, git. You ain't doin' no good. There ain't enough for you."

Ma ladled stew into the tin plates, very little stew, and she laid the plates on the ground. "I can't send 'em away," she said. "I don' know what to do. Take your plates an' go inside. I'll let 'em have what's lef'. Here, take a plate in to Rosasharn." She smiled up at the children. "Look," she said, "you little fellas go an' get you each a flat stick an' I'll put what's lef' for you. But they ain't to be no fightin'." The group broke up with a deadly, silent swiftness. Children ran to find sticks, they ran to their own tents and brought spoons. Before Ma had finished with the plates they were back, silent and wolfish. Ma shook her head. "I dunno what to do. I can't rob the fambly. I got to feed the fambly. Ruthie, Winfiel', Al," she cried fiercely. "Take your plates. Hurry up. Git in the tent quick." She looked apologetically at the waiting children. "There ain't enough," she said humbly. "I'm a-gonna set this here kettle out, an' you'll all get a little tas', but it ain't gonna do you no good." She faltered, "I can't he'p it. Can't keep it from you." She lifted the pot and set it down on the ground. "Now wait. It's too hot," she said, and she went into the tent quickly so she would not see. Her family sat on the ground, each with his plate; and outside they could hear the children digging into the pot with their sticks and their spoons and their pieces of rusty tin. A mound of children smothered the pot from sight. They did not talk, did not fight or argue; but there was a quiet intentness in all of them, a wooden fierceness. Ma turned her back so she couldn't see. "We can't do that no more," she said. "We got to eat alone." There was the sound of scraping at the kettle, and then the mound of children broke and the children walked away and left the scraped kettle on the ground. Ma looked at the empty plates. "Didn' none of you get nowhere near enough."

Pa got up and left the tent without answering. The preacher smiled to himself and lay back on the ground, hands clasped behind his head. Al got to his feet. "Got to help a fella with a car."

Ma gathered the plates and took them outside to wash. "Ruthie," she called, "Winfiel'. Go get me a bucket a water right off." She handed them the bucket and they trudged off toward the river.

A strong broad woman walked near. Her dress was streaked with dust and splotched with car oil. Her chin was held high with pride. She stood a short distance away and regarded Ma belligerently. At last she approached. "Afternoon," she said coldly.

"Afternoon," said Ma, and she got up from her knees and pushed a box forward. "Won't you set down?"

The woman walked near. "No, I won't set down."

Ma looked questioningly at her. "Can I he'p you in any way?"

The woman set her hands on her hips. "You kin he'p me by mindin' your own children an' lettin' mine alone."

Ma's eyes opened wide. "I ain't done nothin'—" she began.

The woman scowled at her. "My little fella come back smellin' of stew. You give it to 'im. He tol' me. Don' you go a-boastin' an' a-braggin' 'bout havin' stew. Don' you do it. I got 'nuf troubles 'thout that. Come in ta me, he did, an' says, 'Whyn't we have stew?'" Her voice shook with fury.

Ma moved close. "Set down," she said. "Set down an' talk a piece."

"No, I ain't gonna set down. I'm tryin' to feed my folks, an' you come along with your stew."

"Set down," Ma said. "That was 'bout the las' stew we're gonna have till we get work. S'pose you was cookin' a stew an' a bunch a little fellas stood aroun' moonin', what'd you do? We didn't have enough, but you can't keep it when they look at ya like that."

The woman's hands dropped from her hips. For a moment her eyes questioned Ma, and then she turned and walked quickly away, and she went into a tent and pulled the flaps down behind her. Ma stared after her, and then she dropped to her knees again beside the stack of tin dishes.

Al hurried near. "Tom," he called. "Ma, is Tom inside?"

Tom stuck his head out. "What you want?"

"Come on with me," Al said excitedly.

They walked away together. "What's a matter with you?" Tom asked.

"You'll find out. Jus' wait." He led Tom to the torn-down car. "This here's Floyd Knowles," he said.

"Yeah, I talked to him. How ya?"

"Jus' gettin' her in shape," Floyd said.

Tom ran his finger over the top of the block. "What kinda bugs is crawlin' on you, Al?"

"Floyd jus' tol' me. Tell 'im, Floyd."

Floyd said, "Maybe I shouldn', but—yeah, I'll tell ya. Fella come through an' he says they's gonna be work up north."

"Up north?"

"Yeah—place called Santa Clara Valley, way to hell an' gone up north."

"Yeah? Kinda work?"

"Prune pickin', an' pears an' cannery work. Says it's purty near ready."

"How far?" Tom demanded.

"Oh, Christ knows. Maybe two hundred miles."

"That's a hell of a long ways," said Tom. "How we know they's gonna be work when we get there?"

"Well, we don' know," said Floyd. "But they ain't nothin' here, an' this fella says he got a letter from his brother, an' he's on his way. He says not to tell nobody, they'll be too many. We oughta get out in the night. Oughta get there an' get some work lined up."

Tom studied him. "Why we gotta sneak away?"

"Well, if ever'body gets there, ain't gonna be work for no-body."

"It's a hell of a long ways," Tom said.

Floyd sounded hurt. "I'm jus' givin' you the tip. You don' have to take it. Your brother here he'ped me, an' I'm givin' you the tip."

"You sure there ain't no work here?"

"Look, I been scourin' aroun' for three weeks all over hell, an' I ain't had a bit a work, not a single han'-holt. 'F you wanta look aroun' an' burn up gas lookin', why, go ahead. I ain't beggin' you. More that goes, the less chance I got."

Tom said, "I ain't findin' fault. It's jus' such a hell of a long ways. An' we kinda hoped we could get work here an' rent a house to live in."

Floyd said patiently, "I know ya jus' got here. They's stuff ya got to learn. If you'd let me tell ya, it'd save ya somepin. If ya don' let me tell ya, then ya got to learn the hard way. You ain't gonna settle down 'cause they ain't no work to settle ya. An' your belly ain't gonna let ya settle down. Now—that's straight."

"Wisht I could look aroun' first," Tom said uneasily.

A sedan drove through the camp and pulled up at the next tent. A man in overalls and a blue shirt climbed out. Floyd called to him, "Any luck?"

"There ain't a han'-turn of work in the whole darn country, not till cotton pickin'." And he went into the ragged tent.

"See?" said Floyd.

"Yeah, I see. But two hunderd miles, Jesus!"

"Well, you ain't settlin' down no place for a while. Might's well make up your mind to that."

"We better go," Al said.

Tom asked, "When is they gonna be work aroun' here?"

"Well, in a month the cotton'll start. If you got plenty money you can wait for the cotton."

Tom said, "Ma ain't a-gonna wanta move. She's all tar'd out."

Floyd shrugged his shoulders. "I ain't a-tryin' to push ya north. Suit yaself. I jus' tol' ya what I heard." He picked the oily gasket from the running board and fitted it carefully on the block and pressed it down. "Now," he said to Al, " 'f you want to give me a han' with that engine head."

Tom watched while they set the heavy head gently down over the head bolts and dropped it evenly. "Have to talk about it," he said.

Floyd said, "I don't want nobody but your folks to know about it. Jus' you. An' I wouldn't of tol' you if ya brother didn' he'p me out here."

Tom said, "Well, I sure thank ya for tellin' us. We got to figger it out. Maybe we'll go."

Al said, "By God, I think I'll go if the res' goes or not. I'll hitch there."

"An' leave the fambly?" Tom asked.

"Sure. I'd come back with my jeans plumb fulla jack. Why not?"

"Ma ain't gonna like no such thing," Tom said. "An' Pa, he ain't gonna like it neither."

Floyd set the nuts and screwed them down as far as he could with his fingers. "Me an' my wife come out with our folks," he said. "Back home we wouldn' of thought of goin' away. Wouldn' of thought of it. But, hell, we was all up north a piece and I come down here, an' they moved on, an' now God knows where they are. Been lookin' an' askin' about 'em ever since." He fitted his wrench to the engine-head bolts and turned them down evenly, one turn to each nut, around and around the series.

Tom squatted down beside the car and squinted his eyes up the line of tents. A little stubble was beaten into the earth between the tents. "No, sir," he said, "Ma ain't gonna like you goin' off."

"Well, seems to me a lone fella got more chance of work."

"Maybe, but Ma ain't gonna like it at all."

Two cars loaded with disconsolate men drove down into the camp. Floyd lifted his eyes, but he didn't ask them about their luck. Their dusty faces were sad and resistant. The sun was sinking now, and the yellow sunlight fell on the Hoover-ville and on the willows behind it. The children began to come out of the tents, to wander about the camp. And from the tents the women came and built their little fires. The men gathered in squatting groups and talked together.

A new Chevrolet coupé turned off the highway and headed down into the camp. It pulled to the center of the camp. Tom said, "Who's this? They don't belong here."

Floyd said, "I dunno—cops, maybe."

The car door opened and a man got out and stood beside the car. His companion remained seated. Now all the squatting men looked at the newcomers and the conversation was still. And the women building their fires looked secretly at the shiny car. The children moved closer with elaborate circu-itousness, edging inward in long curves.

Floyd put down his wrench. Tom stood up. Al wiped his hands on his trousers. The three strolled toward the Chev-rolet. The man who had got out of the car was dressed in khaki trousers and a flannel shirt. He wore a flat-brimmed Stetson hat. A sheaf of papers was held in his shirt pocket by a little fence of fountain pens and yellow pencils; and from his hip pocket protruded a notebook with metal covers. He moved to one of the groups of squatting men, and they looked up at him, suspicious and quiet. They watched him and did not move; the whites of their eyes showed beneath the irises, for they did not raise their heads to look. Tom and Al and Floyd strolled casually near.

The man said, "You men want to work?" Still they looked quietly, suspiciously. And men from all over the camp moved near.

One of the squatting men spoke at last. "Sure we wanta work. Where's at's work?"

"Tulare County. Fruit's opening up. Need a lot of pickers."

Floyd spoke up. "You doin' the hiring?"

"Well, I'm contracting the land."

The men were in a compact group now. An overalled man took off his black hat and combed back his long black hair with his fingers. "What you payin'?" he asked.

"Well, can't tell exactly, yet. 'Bout thirty cents, I guess."

"Why can't you tell? You took the contract, didn' you?"

"That's true," the khaki man said. "But it's keyed to the price. Might be a little more, might be a little less."

Floyd stepped out ahead. He said quietly, "I'll go, mister. You're a contractor, an' you got a license. You jus' show your license, an' then you give us an order to go to work, an' where, an' when, an' how much we'll get, an' you sign that, an' we'll all go."

The contractor turned, scowling. "You telling me how to run my own business?"

Floyd said, "'F we're workin' for you, it's our business too."

"Well, you ain't telling me what to do. I told you I need men."

Floyd said angrily, "You didn' say how many men, an' you didn' say what you'd pay."

"Goddamn it, I don't know yet."

"If you don' know, you got no right to hire men."

"I got a right to run my business my own way. If you men want to sit here on your ass, O.K. I'm out getting men for Tulare County. Going to need a lot of men."

Floyd turned to the crowd of men. They were standing up now, looking quietly from one speaker to the other. Floyd said, "Twicet now I've fell for that. Maybe he needs a thousan' men. He'll get five thousan' there, an' he'll pay fifteen cents an hour. An' you poor bastards'll have to take it 'cause you'll be hungry. 'F he wants to hire men, let him hire 'em an' write it out an' say what he's gonna pay. Ast ta see his license. He ain't allowed to contract men without a license."

The contractor turned to the Chevrolet and called, "Joe!" His companion looked out and then swung the car door open and stepped out. He wore riding breeches and laced boots. A heavy pistol holster hung on a cartridge belt around his waist. On his brown shirt a deputy sheriff's star was pinned. He walked heavily over. His face was set to a thin smile. "What you want?" The holster slid back and forth on his hip.

"Ever see this guy before, Joe?"

The deputy asked "Which one?"

"This fella." The contractor pointed to Floyd.

"What'd he do?" The deputy smiled at Floyd.

"He's talkin' red, agitating trouble."

"Hm-m-m." The deputy moved slowly around to see Floyd's profile, and the color slowly flowed up Floyd's face.

"You see?" Floyd cried. "If this guy's on the level, would he bring a cop along?"

"Ever see 'im before?" the contractor insisted.

"Hmm, seems like I have. Las' week when that used-car lot was busted into. Seems like I seen this fella hangin' aroun'. Yep! I'd swear it's the same fella." Suddenly the smile left his face. "Get in the car," he said, and he unhooked the strap that covered the butt of his automatic.

Tom said, "You got nothin' on him."

The deputy swung around. " 'F you'd like to go in too, you jus' open your trap once more. They was two fellas hangin' around that lot."

"I wasn't even in the State las' week," Tom said.

"Well, maybe you're wanted someplace else. You keep your trap shut."

The contractor turned back to the men. "You fellas don't want ta listen to these goddamn reds. Troublemakers—they'll

get you in trouble. Now I can use all of you in Tulare
County."

The men didn't answer.

The deputy turned back to them. "Might be a good idear
to go," he said. The thin smile was back on his face. "Board
of Health says we got to clean out this camp. An' if it gets
around that you got reds out here—why, somebody might git
hurt. Be a good idear if all you fellas moved on to Tulare.
They isn't a thing to do aroun' here. That's jus' a friendly way
a telling you. Be a bunch a guys down here, maybe with pick
handles, if you ain't gone."

The contractor said, "I told you I need men. If you don't
want to work—well, that's your business."

The deputy smiled. "If they don't want to work, they ain't
a place for 'em in this county. We'll float 'em quick."

Floyd stood stiffly beside the deputy, and Floyd's thumbs
were hooked over his belt. Tom stole a look at him, and then
stared at the ground.

"That's all," the contractor said. "There's men needed in
Tulare County; plenty of work."

Tom looked slowly up at Floyd's hands, and he saw the
strings at the wrists standing out under the skin. Tom's own
hands came up, and his thumbs hooked over his belt.

"Yeah, that's all. I don't want one of you here by tomorra
morning."

The contractor stepped into the Chevrolet.

"Now, you," the deputy said to Floyd, "you get in that
car." He reached a large hand up and took hold of Floyd's
left arm. Floyd spun and swung with one movement. His fist
splashed into the large face, and in the same motion he was
away, dodging down the line of tents. The deputy staggered
and Tom put out his foot for him to trip over. The deputy
fell heavily and rolled, reaching for his gun. Floyd dodged in
and out of sight down the line. The deputy fired from the
ground. A woman in front of a tent screamed and then looked
at a hand which had no knuckles. The fingers hung on strings
against her palm, and the torn flesh was white and bloodless.
Far down the line Floyd came in sight, sprinting for the willows. The deputy, sitting on the ground, raised his gun again

and then, suddenly, from the group of men, the Reverend Casy stepped. He kicked the deputy in the neck and then stood back as the heavy man crumpled into unconsciousness.

The motor of the Chevrolet roared and it streaked away, churning the dust. It mounted to the highway and shot away. In front of her tent, the woman still looked at her shattered hand. Little droplets of blood began to ooze from the wound. And a chuckling hysteria began in her throat, a whining laugh that grew louder and higher with each breath.

The deputy lay on his side, his mouth open against the dust.

Tom picked up his automatic, pulled out the magazine and threw it into the brush, and he ejected the live shell from the chamber. "Fella like that ain't got no right to a gun," he said; and he dropped the automatic to the ground.

A crowd had collected around the woman with the broken hand, and her hysteria increased, a screaming quality came into her laughter.

Casy moved close to Tom. "You got to git out," he said. "You go down in the willas an' wait. He didn' see me kick 'im, but he seen you stick out your foot."

"I don' wanta go," Tom said.

Casy put his head close. He whispered, "They'll fingerprint you. You broke parole. They'll send you back."

Tom drew in his breath quietly. "Jesus! I forgot."

"Go quick," Casy said. " 'Fore he comes to."

"Like to have his gun," Tom said.

"No. Leave it. If it's awright to come back, I'll give ya four high whistles."

Tom strolled away casually, but as soon as he was away from the group he hurried his steps, and he disappeared among the willows that lined the river.

Al stepped over to the fallen deputy. "Jesus," he said admiringly, "you sure flagged 'im down!"

The crowd of men had continued to stare at the unconscious man. And now in the great distance a siren screamed up the scale and dropped, and it screamed again, nearer this time. Instantly the men were nervous. They shifted their feet for a moment and then they moved away, each one to his own tent. Only Al and the preacher remained.

Casy turned to Al. "Get out," he said. "Go on, get out—to the tent. You don't know nothin'."

"Yeah? How 'bout you?"

Casy grinned at him. "Somebody got to take the blame. I got no kids. They'll jus' put me in jail, an' I ain't doin' nothin' but set aroun'."

Al said, "Ain't no reason for——"

"Go on now," Casy said sharply. "You get outa this."

Al bristled. "I ain't takin' orders."

Casy said softly, "If you mess in this your whole fambly, all your folks, gonna get in trouble. I don' care about you. But your ma and your pa, they'll get in trouble. Maybe they'll send Tom back to McAlester."

Al considered it for a moment. "O.K.," he said, and he started away.

"Wait," Casy called. "Look, if they take me, you look aroun' an' when it's safe you give four high whistles. Then Tom'll know he can come back."

Al turned away again. "O.K.," he said. "I think you're a damn fool, though."

"Sure," said Casy. "Why not?"

The siren screamed again and again, and always it came closer. Casy knelt beside the deputy and turned him over. The man groaned and fluttered his eyes, and he tried to see. Casy wiped the dust off his lips. The families were in the tents now, and the flaps were down, and the setting sun made the air red and the gray tents bronze.

Tires squealed on the highway and an open car came swiftly into the camp. Four men, armed with rifles, piled out. Casy stood up and walked to them.

"What the hell's goin' on here?"

Casy said, "I knocked out your man there."

One of the armed men went to the deputy. He was conscious now, trying weakly to sit up.

"Now what happened here?"

"Well," Casy said, "he got tough an' I hit 'im, and he started shootin'—hit a woman down the line. So I hit 'im again."

"Well, what'd you do in the first place?"

"I talked back," said Casy.

"Get in that car."

"Sure," said Casy, and he climbed into the back seat and sat down. Two men helped the hurt deputy to his feet. He felt his neck gingerly. Casy said, "They's a woman down the row like to bleed to death from his bad shootin'."

"We'll see about that later. Mike, is this the fella that hit you?"

The dazed man stared sickly at Casy. "Don't look like him."

"It was me, all right," Casy said. "You got smart with the wrong fella."

Mike shook his head slowly. "You don't look like the right fella to me. By God, I'm gonna be sick!"

Casy said, "I'll go 'thout no trouble. You better see how bad that woman's hurt."

"Where's she?"

"That tent over there."

The leader of the deputies walked to the tent, rifle in hand. He spoke through the tent walls, and then went inside. In a moment he came out and walked back. And he said, a little proudly, "Jesus, what a mess a .45 does make! They got a tourniquet on. We'll send a doctor out."

Two deputies sat on either side of Casy. The leader sounded his horn. There was no movement in the camp. The flaps were down tight, and the people in their tents. The engine started and the car swung around and pulled out of the camp. Between his guards Casy sat proudly, his head up and the stringy muscles of his neck prominent. On his lips there was a faint smile and on his face a curious look of conquest.

When the deputies had gone, the people came out of the tents. The sun was down now, and the gentle blue evening light was in the camp. To the east the mountains were still yellow with sunlight. The women went back to the fires that had died. The men collected to squat together and to talk softly.

Al crawled from under the Joad tarpaulin and walked toward the willows to whistle for Tom. Ma came out and built her little fire of twigs.

"Pa," she said, "we ain't gonna have much. We et so late."

Pa and Uncle John stuck close to the camp, watching Ma peeling potatoes and slicing them raw into a frying pan of deep grease. Pa said, "Now what the hell made the preacher do that?"

Ruthie and Winfield crept close and crouched down to hear the talk.

Uncle John scratched the earth deeply with a long rusty nail. "He knowed about sin. I ast him about sin, an' he tol' me; but I don' know if he's right. He says a fella's sinned if he thinks he's sinned." Uncle John's eyes were tired and sad. "I been secret all my days," he said. "I done things I never tol' about."

Ma turned from the fire. "Don' go tellin', John," she said. "Tell 'em to God. Don' go burdenin' other people with your sins. That ain't decent."

"They're a-eatin' on me," said John.

"Well, don' tell 'em. Go down the river an' stick your head under an' whisper 'em in the stream."

Pa nodded his head slowly at Ma's words. "She's right," he said. "It gives a fella relief to tell, but it jus' spreads out his sin."

Uncle John looked up to the sun-gold mountains, and the mountains were reflected in his eyes. "I wisht I could run it down," he said. "But I can't. She's a-bitin' in my guts."

Behind him Rose of Sharon moved dizzily out of the tent. "Where's Connie?" she asked irritably. "I ain't seen Connie for a long time. Where'd he go?"

"I ain't seen him," said Ma. "If I see 'im, I'll tell 'im you want 'im."

"I ain't feelin' good," said Rose of Sharon. "Connie shouldn' of left me."

Ma looked up to the girl's swollen face. "You been a-cryin'," she said.

The tears started freshly in Rose of Sharon's eyes.

Ma went on firmly, "You git aholt on yaself. They's a lot of us here. You git aholt on yaself. Come here now an' peel some potatoes. You're feelin' sorry for yaself."

The girl started to go back in the tent. She tried to avoid Ma's stern eyes, but they compelled her and she came slowly toward the fire. "He shouldn' of went away," she said, but the tears were gone.

"You got to work," Ma said. "Set in the tent an' you'll get

feelin' sorry about yaself. I ain't had time to take you in han'. I will now. You take this here knife an' get to them potatoes."

The girl knelt down and obeyed. She said fiercely, "Wait'll I see 'im. I'll tell 'im."

Ma smiled slowly. "He might smack you. You got it comin' with whinin' aroun' an' candyin' yaself. If he smacks some sense in you I'll bless 'im." The girl's eyes blazed with resentment, but she was silent.

Uncle John pushed his rusty nail deep into the ground with his broad thumb. "I got to tell," he said.

Pa said, "Well, tell then, goddamn it! Who'd ya kill?"

Uncle John dug with his thumb into the watch pocket of his blue jeans and scooped out a folded dirty bill. He spread it out and showed it. "Fi' dollars," he said.

"Steal her?" Pa asked.

"No, I had her. Kept her out."

"She was yourn, wasn't she?"

"Yeah, but I didn't have no right to keep her out."

"I don't see much sin in that," Ma said. "It's yourn."

Uncle John said slowly, "It ain't only the keepin' her out. I kep' her out to get drunk. I knowed they was gonna come a time when I got to get drunk, when I'd get to hurtin' inside so I got to get drunk. Figgered time wasn' yet, an' then—the preacher went an' give 'imself up to save Tom."

Pa nodded his head up and down and cocked his head to hear. Ruthie moved closer, like a puppy, crawling on her elbows, and Winfield followed her. Rose of Sharon dug at a deep eye in a potato with the point of her knife. The evening light deepened and became more blue.

Ma said, in a sharp matter-of-fact tone, "I don' see why him savin' Tom got to get you drunk."

John said sadly, "Can't say her. I feel awful. He done her so easy. Jus' stepped up there an' says, 'I done her.' An' they took 'im away. An' I'm a-gonna get drunk."

Pa still nodded his head. "I don't see why you got to tell," he said. "If it was me, I'd jus' go off an' get drunk if I had to."

"Come a time when I could a did somepin an' took the big sin off my soul," Uncle John said sadly. "An' I slipped up. I didn' jump on her, an'—an' she got away. Lookie!" he said. "You got the money. Gimme two dollars."

Pa reached reluctantly into his pocket and brought out the leather pouch. "You ain't gonna need no seven dollars to get drunk. You don't need to drink champagny water."

Uncle John held out his bill. "You take this here an' gimme two dollars. I can get good an' drunk for two dollars. I don' want no sin of waste on me. I'll spend whatever I got. Always do."

Pa took the dirty bill and gave Uncle John two silver dollars. "There ya are," he said. "A fella got to do what he got to do. Nobody don' know enough to tell 'im."

Uncle John took the coins. "You ain't gonna be mad? You know I got to?"

"Christ, yes," said Pa. "You know what you got to do."

"I wouldn' be able to get through this night no other way," he said. He turned to Ma. "You ain't gonna hold her over me?"

Ma didn't look up. "No," she said softly. "No—you go 'long."

He stood up and walked forlornly away in the evening. He walked up to the concrete highway and across the pavement to the grocery store. In front of the screen door he took off his hat, dropped it into the dust, and ground it with his heel in self-abasement. And he left his black hat there, broken and dirty. He entered the store and walked to the shelves where the whisky bottles stood behind wire netting.

Pa and Ma and the children watched Uncle John move away. Rose of Sharon kept her eyes resentfully on the potatoes.

"Poor John," Ma said. "I wondered if it would a done any good if—no—I guess not. I never seen a man so drove."

Ruthie turned on her side in the dust. She put her head close to Winfield's head and pulled his ear against her mouth. She whispered, "I'm gonna get drunk." Winfield snorted and pinched his mouth tight. The two children crawled away, holding their breath, their faces purple with the pressure of their giggles. They crawled around the tent and leaped up and ran squealing away from the tent. They ran to the willows, and once concealed, they shrieked with laughter. Ruthie crossed her eyes and loosened her joints; she staggered about, tripping loosely, with her tongue hanging out. "I'm drunk," she said.

"Look," Winfield cried. "Looka me, here's me, an' I'm Uncle John." He flapped his arms and puffed, he whirled until he was dizzy.

"No," said Ruthie. "Here's the way. Here's the way. *I'm* Uncle John. I'm awful drunk."

Al and Tom walked quietly through the willows, and they came on the children staggering crazily about. The dusk was thick now. Tom stopped and peered. "Ain't that Ruthie an' Winfiel'? What the hell's the matter with 'em?" They walked nearer. "You crazy?" Tom asked.

The children stopped, embarrassed. "We was—jus' playin'," Ruthie said.

"It's a crazy way to play," said Al.

Ruthie said pertly, "It ain't no crazier'n a lot of things."

Al walked on. He said to Tom, "Ruthie's workin' up a kick in the pants. She been workin' it up a long time. 'Bout due for it."

Ruthie mushed her face at his back, pulled out her mouth with her forefingers, slobbered her tongue at him, outraged him in every way she knew, but Al did not turn back to look at her. She looked at Winfield again to start the game, but it had been spoiled. They both knew it.

"Le's go down the water an' duck our heads," Winfield suggested. They walked down through the willows, and they were angry at Al.

Al and Tom went quietly in the dusk. Tom said, "Casy shouldn' of did it. I might of knew, though. He was talkin' how he ain't done nothin' for us. He's a funny fella, Al. All the time thinkin'."

"Comes from bein' a preacher," Al said. "They get all messed up with stuff."

"Where ya s'pose Connie was a-goin'?"

"Goin' to take a crap, I guess."

"Well, he was goin' a hell of a long way."

They walked among the tents, keeping close to the walls. At Floyd's tent a soft hail stopped them. They came near to the tent flap and squatted down. Floyd raised the canvas a little. "You gettin' out?"

Tom said, "I don' know. Think we better?"

Floyd laughed sourly. "You heard what that bull said. They'll burn ya out if ya don't. 'F you think that guy's gonna take a beatin' 'thout gettin' back, you're nuts. The pool-room boys'll be down here tonight to burn us out."

"Guess we better git, then," Tom said. "Where you a-goin'?"

"Why, up north, like I said."

Al said, "Look, a fella tol' me 'bout a gov'ment camp near here. Where's it at?"

"Oh, I think that's full up."

"Well, where's it at?"

"Go south on 99 'bout twelve-fourteen miles, an' turn east to Weedpatch. It's right near there. But I think she's full up."

"Fella says it's nice," Al said.

"Sure, she's nice. Treat ya like a man 'stead of a dog. Ain't no cops there. But she's full up."

Tom said, "What I can't understan's why that cop was so mean. Seemed like he was aimin' for trouble; seemed like he's pokin' a fella to make trouble."

Floyd said, "I don' know about here, but up north I knowed one a them fellas, an' he was a nice fella. He tol' me up there the deputies got to take guys in. Sheriff gets seventy-five cents a day for each prisoner, an' he feeds 'em for a quarter. If he ain't got prisoners, he don't make no profit. This fella says he didn' pick up nobody for a week, an' the sheriff tol' 'im he better bring in guys or give up his button. This fella today sure looks like he's out to make a pinch one way or another."

"We got to get on," said Tom. "So long, Floyd."

"So long. Prob'ly see you. Hope so."

"Good-by," said Al. They walked through the dark gray camp to the Joad tent.

The frying pan of potatoes was hissing and spitting over the fire. Ma moved the thick slices about with a spoon. Pa sat near by, hugging his knees. Rose of Sharon was sitting under the tarpaulin.

"It's Tom!" Ma cried. "Thank God."

"We got to get outa here," said Tom.

"What's the matter now?"

"Well, Floyd says they'll burn the camp tonight."

"What the hell for?" Pa asked. "We ain't done nothin'."

"Nothin' 'cept beat up a cop," said Tom.

"Well, we never done it."

"From what that cop said, they wanta push us along."

Rose of Sharon demanded, "You seen Connie?"

"Yeah," said Al. "Way to hell an' gone up the river. He's goin' south."

"Was—was he goin' away?"

"I don' know."

Ma turned on the girl. "Rosasharn, you been talkin' an' actin' funny. What'd Connie say to you?"

Rose of Sharon said sullenly, "Said it would a been a good thing if he stayed home an' studied up tractors."

They were very quiet. Rose of Sharon looked at the fire and her eyes glistened in the firelight. The potatoes hissed sharply in the frying pan. The girl sniffled and wiped her nose with the back of her hand.

Pa said, "Connie wasn' no good. I seen that a long time. Didn' have no guts, jus' too big for his balls."

Rose of Sharon got up and went into the tent. She lay down on the mattress and rolled over on her stomach and buried her head in her crossed arms.

"Wouldn' do no good to catch 'im, I guess," Al said.

Pa replied, "No. If he ain't no good, we don' want him."

Ma looked into the tent, where Rose of Sharon lay on her mattress. Ma said, "Sh. Don' say that."

"Well, he ain't no good," Pa insisted. "All the time a-sayin' what he's a-gonna do. Never doin' nothin'. I didn' wanta say nothin' while he's here. But now he's run out——"

"Sh!" Ma said softly.

"Why, for Christ's sake? Why do I got to shush? He run out, didn' he?"

Ma turned over the potatoes with her spoon, and the grease boiled and spat. She fed twigs to the fire, and the flames laced up and lighted the tent. Ma said, "Rosasharn gonna have a little fella an' that baby is half Connie. It ain't good for a baby to grow up with folks a-sayin' his pa ain't no good."

"Better'n lyin' about it," said Pa.

"No, it ain't," Ma interrupted. "Make out like he's dead.

You wouldn' say no bad things about Connie if he's dead."

Tom broke in, "Hey, what is this? We ain't sure Connie's gone for good. We got no time for talkin'. We got to eat an' get on our way."

"On our way? We jus' come here." Ma peered at him through the firelighted darkness.

He explained carefully, "They gonna burn the camp tonight, Ma. Now you know I ain't got it in me to stan' by an' see our stuff burn up, nor Pa ain't got it in him, nor Uncle John. We'd come up a-fightin', an' I jus' can't afford to be took in an' mugged. I nearly got it today, if the preacher hadn' jumped in."

Ma had been turning the frying potatoes in the hot grease. Now she took her decision. "Come on!" she cried. "Le's eat this stuff. We got to go quick." She set out the tin plates.

Pa said, "How 'bout John?"

"Where is Uncle John?" Tom asked.

Pa and Ma were silent for a moment, and then Pa said, "He went to get drunk."

"Jesus!" Tom said. "What a time he picked out! Where'd he go?"

"I don' know," said Pa.

Tom stood up. "Look," he said, "you all eat an' get the stuff loaded. I'll go look for Uncle John. He'd of went to the store 'crost the road."

Tom walked quickly away. The little cooking fires burned in front of the tents and the shacks, and the light fell on the faces of ragged men and women, on crouched children. In a few tents the light of kerosene lamps shone through the canvas and placed shadows of people hugely on the cloth.

Tom walked up the dusty road and crossed the concrete highway to the little grocery store. He stood in front of the screen door and looked in. The proprietor, a little gray man with an unkempt mustache and watery eyes, leaned on the counter reading a newspaper. His thin arms were bare and he wore a long white apron. Heaped around and in back of him were mounds, pyramids, walls of canned goods. He looked up when Tom came in, and his eyes narrowed as though he aimed a shotgun.

"Good evening," he said. "Run out of something?"

"Run out of my uncle," said Tom. "Or he run out, or something."

The gray man looked puzzled and worried at the same time. He touched the tip of his nose tenderly and waggled it around to stop an itch. "Seems like you people always lost somebody," he said. "Ten times a day or more somebody comes in here an' says, 'If you see a man named so an' so, an' looks like so an' so, will you tell 'im we went up north?' Somepin like that all the time."

Tom laughed. "Well, if you see a young snot-nose name' Connie, looks a little bit like a coyote, tell 'im to go to hell. We've went south. But he ain't the fella I'm lookin' for. Did a fella 'bout sixty years ol', black pants, sort of grayish hair, come in here an' get some whisky?"

The eyes of the gray man brightened. "Now he sure did. I never seen anything like it. He stood out front an' he dropped his hat an' stepped on it. Here, I got his hat here." He brought the dusty broken hat from under the counter.

Tom took it from him. "That's him, all right."

"Well, sir, he got couple pints of whisky an' he didn' say a thing. He pulled the cork an' tipped up the bottle. I ain't got a license to drink here. I says, 'Look, you can't drink here. You got to go outside.' Well, sir! He jus' stepped outside the door, an' I bet he didn't tilt up that pint more'n four times till it was empty. He throwed it away an' he leaned in the door. Eyes kinda dull. He says, 'Thank you, sir,' an' he went on. I never seen no drinkin' like that in my life."

"Went on? Which way? I got to get him."

"Well, it so happens I can tell you. I never seen such drinkin', so I looked out after him. He went north; an' then a car come along an' lighted him up, an' he went down the bank. Legs was beginnin' to buckle a little. He got the other pint open awready. He won't be far—not the way he was goin'."

Tom said, "Thank ya. I got to find him."

"You want ta take his hat?"

"Yeah! Yeah! He'll need it. Well, thank ya."

"What's the matter with him?" the gray man asked. "He wasn't takin' pleasure in his drink."

"Oh, he's kinda—moody. Well, good night. An' if you see that squirt Connie, tell 'im we've went south."

"I got so many people to look out for an' tell stuff to, I can't ever remember 'em all."

"Don't put yourself out too much," Tom said. He went out the screen door carrying Uncle John's dusty black hat. He crossed the concrete road and walked along the edge of it. Below him in the sunken field, the Hooverville lay; and the little fires flickered and the lanterns shone through the tents. Somewhere in the camp a guitar sounded, slow chords, struck without any sequence, practice chords. Tom stopped and listened, and then he moved slowly along the side of the road, and every few steps he stopped to listen again. He had gone a quarter of a mile before he heard what he listened for. Down below the embankment the sound of a thick, tuneless voice, singing drably. Tom cocked his head, the better to hear.

And the dull voice sang, "I've give my heart to Jesus, so Jesus take me home. I've give my soul to Jesus, so Jesus is my home." The song trailed off to a murmur, and then stopped. Tom hurried down from the embankment, toward the song. After a while he stopped and listened again. And the voice was close this time, the same slow, tuneless singing, "Oh, the night that Maggie died, she called me to her side, an' give to me them ol' red flannel drawers that Maggie wore. They was baggy at the knees——"

Tom moved cautiously forward. He saw the black form sitting on the ground, and he stole near and sat down. Uncle John tilted the pint and the liquor gurgled out of the neck of the bottle.

Tom said quietly, "Hey, wait! Where do I come in?"

Uncle John turned his head. "Who you?"

"You forgot me awready? You had four drinks to my one."

"No, Tom. Don' try fool me. I'm all alone here. You ain't been here."

"Well, I'm sure here now. How 'bout givin' me a snort?"

Uncle John raised the pint again and the whisky gurgled. He shook the bottle. It was empty. "No more," he said. "Wanta die so bad. Wanta die awful. Die a little bit. Got to. Like sleepin'. Die a little bit. So tar'd. Tar'd. Maybe—don' wake up no more." His voice crooned off. "Gonna wear a crown—a golden crown."

Tom said, "Listen here to me, Uncle John. We're gonna move on. You come along, an' you can go right to sleep up on the load."

John shook his head. "No. Go on. Ain't goin'. Gonna res' here. No good goin' back. No good to nobody—jus' a-draggin' my sins like dirty drawers 'mongst nice folks. No. Ain't goin'."

"Come on. We can't go 'less you go."

"Go ri' 'long. I ain't no good. I ain't no good. Jus' a-draggin' my sins, a-dirtyin' ever'body."

"You got no more sin'n anybody else."

John put his head close, and he winked one eye wisely. Tom could see his face dimly in the starlight. "Nobody don' know my sins, nobody but Jesus. He knows."

Tom got down on his knees. He put his hand on Uncle John's forehead, and it was hot and dry. John brushed his hand away clumsily.

"Come on," Tom pleaded. "Come on now, Uncle John."

"Ain't goin' go. Jus' tar'd. Gon' res' ri' here. Ri' here."

Tom was very close. He put his fist against the point of Uncle John's chin. He made a small practice arc twice, for distance; and then, with his shoulder in the swing, he hit the chin a delicate perfect blow. John's chin snapped up and he fell backwards and tried to sit up again. But Tom was kneeling over him and as John got one elbow up Tom hit him again. Uncle John lay still on the ground.

Tom stood up and, bending, he lifted the loose sagging body and boosted it over his shoulder. He staggered under the loose weight. John's hanging hands tapped him on the back as he went, slowly, puffing up the bank to the highway. Once a car came by and lighted him with the limp man over his shoulder. The car slowed for a moment and then roared away.

Tom was panting when he came back to the Hooverville, down from the road and to the Joad truck. John was coming to; he struggled weakly. Tom set him gently down on the ground.

Camp had been broken while he was gone. Al passed the

bundles up on the truck. The tarpaulin lay ready to bind over the load.

Al said, "He sure got a quick start."

Tom apologized. "I had to hit 'im a little to make 'im come. Poor fella."

"Didn' hurt 'im?" Ma asked.

"Don' think so. He's a-comin' out of it."

Uncle John was weakly sick on the ground. His spasms of vomiting came in little gasps.

Ma said, "I lef' a plate a potatoes for you, Tom."

Tom chuckled. "I ain't just in the mood right now."

Pa called, "Awright, Al. Sling up the tarp."

The truck was loaded and ready. Uncle John had gone to sleep. Tom and Al boosted and pulled him up on the load while Winfield made a vomiting noise behind the truck and Ruthie plugged her mouth with her hand to keep from squealing.

"Awready," Pa said.

Tom asked, "Where's Rosasharn?"

"Over there," said Ma. "Come on, Rosasharn. We're a-goin'."

The girl sat still, her chin sunk on her breast. Tom walked over to her. "Come on," he said.

"I ain't a-goin'." She did not raise her head.

"You got to go."

"I want Connie. I ain't a-goin' till he comes back."

Three cars pulled out of the camp, up the road to the highway, old cars loaded with the camps and the people. They clanked up to the highway and rolled away, their dim lights glancing along the road.

Tom said, "Connie'll find us. I lef' word up at the store where we'd be. He'll find us."

Ma came up and stood beside him. "Come on, Rosasharn. Come on, honey," she said gently.

"I wanta wait."

"We can't wait." Ma leaned down and took the girl by the arm and helped her to her feet.

"He'll find us," Tom said. "Don' you worry. He'll find us." They walked on either side of the girl.

"Maybe he went to get them books to study up," said Rose of Sharon. "Maybe he was a-gonna surprise us."

Ma said, "Maybe that's jus' what he done." They led her to the truck and helped her up on top of the load, and she crawled under the tarpaulin and disappeared into the dark cave.

Now the bearded man from the weed shack came timidly to the truck. He waited about, his hands clutched behind his back. "You gonna leave any stuff a fella could use?" he asked at last.

Pa said, "Can't think of nothin'. We ain't got nothin' to leave."

Tom asked, "Ain't ya gettin' out?"

For a long time the bearded man stared at him. "No," he said at last.

"But they'll burn ya out."

The unsteady eyes dropped to the ground. "I know. They done it before."

"Well, why the hell don't ya get out?"

The bewildered eyes looked up for a moment, and then down again, and the dying firelight was reflected redly. "I don' know. Takes so long to git stuff together."

"You won't have nothin' if they burn ya out."

"I know. You ain't leavin' nothin' a fella could use?"

"Cleaned out, slick," said Pa. The bearded man vaguely wandered away. "What's a matter with him?" Pa demanded.

"Cop-happy," said Tom. "Fella was sayin'—he's bull-simple. Been beat over the head too much."

A second little caravan drove past the camp and climbed to the road and moved away.

"Come on, Pa. Let's go. Look here, Pa. You an' me an' Al ride in the seat. Ma can get on the load. No. Ma, you ride in the middle. Al"—Tom reached under the seat and brought out a big monkey wrench—"Al, you get up behind. Take this here. Jus' in case. If anybody tries to climb up—let 'im have it."

Al took the wrench and climbed up the back board, and he settled himself cross-legged, the wrench in his hand. Tom pulled the iron jack handle from under the seat and laid it on the floor, under the brake pedal. "Awright," he said. "Get in the middle, Ma."

Pa said, "I ain't got nothin' in my han'."

"You can reach over an' get the jack handle," said Tom. "I hope to Jesus you don' need it." He stepped on the starter and the clanking flywheel turned over, the engine caught and died, and caught again. Tom turned on the lights and moved out of the camp in low gear. The dim lights fingered the road nervously. They climbed up to the highway and turned south. Tom said, "They comes a time when a man gets mad."

Ma broke in, "Tom—you tol' me—you promised me you wasn't like that. You promised."

"I know, Ma. I'm a-tryin'. But them deputies— Did you ever see a deputy that didn' have a fat ass? An' they waggle their ass an' flop their gun aroun'. Ma," he said, "if it was the law they was workin' with, why, we could take it. But it *ain't* the law. They're a-workin' away at our spirits. They're a-tryin' to make us cringe an' crawl like a whipped bitch. They tryin' to break us. Why, Jesus Christ, Ma, they comes a time when the on'y way a fella can keep his decency is by takin' a sock at a cop. They're workin' on our decency."

Ma said, "You promised, Tom. That's how Pretty Boy Floyd done. I knowed his ma. They hurt him."

"I'm a-tryin', Ma. Honest to God, I am. You don' want me to crawl like a beat bitch, with my belly on the groun', do you?"

"I'm a-prayin'. You got to keep clear, Tom. The fambly's breakin' up. You got to keep clear."

"I'll try, Ma. But when one a them fat asses gets to workin' me over, I got a big job tryin'. If it was the law, it'd be different. But burnin' the camp ain't the law."

The car jolted along. Ahead, a little row of red lanterns stretched across the highway.

"Detour, I guess," Tom said. He slowed the car and stopped it, and immediately a crowd of men swarmed about the truck. They were armed with pick handles and shotguns. They wore trench helmets and some American Legion caps. One man leaned in the window, and the warm smell of whisky preceded him.

"Where you think you're goin'?" He thrust a red face near to Tom's face.

Tom stiffened. His hand crept down to the floor and felt for the jack handle. Ma caught his arm and held it powerfully.

Tom said, "Well—" and then his voice took on a servile whine. "We're strangers here," he said. "We heard about they's work in a place called Tulare."

"Well, goddamn it, you're goin' the wrong way. We ain't gonna have no goddamn Okies in this town."

Tom's shoulders and arms were rigid, and a shiver went through him. Ma clung to his arm. The front of the truck was surrounded by the armed men. Some of them, to make a military appearance, wore tunics and Sam Browne belts.

Tom whined, "Which way is it at, mister?"

"You turn right around an' head north. An' don't come back till the cotton's ready."

Tom shivered all over. "Yes, sir," he said. He put the car in reverse, backed around and turned. He headed back the way he had come. Ma released his arm and patted him softly. And Tom tried to restrain his hard smothered sobbing.

"Don' you mind," Ma said. "Don' you mind."

Tom blew his nose out the window and wiped his eyes on his sleeve. "The sons-of-bitches——"

"You done good," Ma said tenderly. "You done jus' good."

Tom swerved into a side dirt road, ran a hundred yards, and turned off his lights and motor. He got out of the car, carrying the jack handle.

"Where you goin'?" Ma demanded.

"Jus' gonna look. We ain't goin' north." The red lanterns moved up the highway. Tom watched them cross the entrance of the dirt road and continue on. In a few moments there came the sounds of shouts and screams, and then a flaring light arose from the direction of the Hooverville. The light grew and spread, and from the distance came a crackling sound. Tom got in the truck again. He turned around and ran up the dirt road without lights. At the highway he turned south again, and he turned on his lights.

Ma asked timidly, "Where we goin', Tom?"

"Goin' south," he said. "We couldn' let them bastards push us aroun'. We couldn'. Try to get aroun' the town 'thout goin' through it."

"Yeah, but where we goin'?" Pa spoke for the first time. "That's what I wanta know."

"Gonna look for that gov'ment camp," Tom said. "A fella

said they don' let no fat-ass deputies in there. Ma—I got to get away from 'em. I'm scairt I'll kill one."

"Easy, Tom." Ma soothed him. "Easy, Tommy. You done good once. You can do it again."

"Yeah, an' after a while I won't have no decency lef'."

"Easy," she said. "You got to have patience. Why, Tom—us people will go on livin' when all them people is gone. Why, Tom, we're the people that live. They ain't gonna wipe us out. Why, we're the people—we go on."

"We take a beatin' all the time."

"I know." Ma chuckled. "Maybe that makes us tough. Rich fellas come up an' they die, an' their kids ain't no good, an' they die out. But, Tom, we keep a-comin'. Don' you fret none, Tom. A different time's comin'."

"How do you know?"

"I don' know how."

They entered the town and Tom turned down a side street to avoid the center. By the street lights he looked at his mother. Her face was quiet and a curious look was in her eyes, eyes like the timeless eyes of a statue. Tom put out his right hand and touched her on the shoulder. He had to. And then he withdrew his hand. "Never heard you talk so much in my life," he said.

"Wasn't never so much reason," she said.

He drove through the side streets and cleared the town, and then he crossed back. At an intersection the sign said "99." He turned south on it.

"Well, anyways they never shoved us north," he said. "We still go where we want, even if we got to crawl for the right."

The dim lights felt along the broad black highway ahead.

Chapter Twenty-One

THE MOVING, questing people were migrants now. Those families which had lived on a little piece of land, who had lived and died on forty acres, had eaten or starved on the produce of forty acres, had now the whole West to rove in. And they scampered about, looking for work; and the highways were streams of people, and the ditch banks were lines of people. Behind them more were coming. The great highways streamed with moving people. There in the Middle- and Southwest had lived a simple agrarian folk who had not changed with industry, who had not farmed with machines or known the power and danger of machines in private hands. They had not grown up in the paradoxes of industry. Their senses were still sharp to the ridiculousness of the industrial life.

And then suddenly the machines pushed them out and they swarmed on the highways. The movement changed them; the highways, the camps along the road, the fear of hunger and the hunger itself, changed them. The children without dinner changed them, the endless moving changed them. They were migrants. And the hostility changed them, welded them, united them—hostility that made the little towns group and arm as though to repel an invader, squads with pick handles, clerks and storekeepers with shotguns, guarding the world against their own people.

In the West there was panic when the migrants multiplied on the highways. Men of property were terrified for their property. Men who had never been hungry saw the eyes of the hungry. Men who had never wanted anything very much saw the flare of want in the eyes of the migrants. And the men of the towns and of the soft suburban country gathered to defend themselves; and they reassured themselves that they were good and the invaders bad, as a man must do before he fights. They said, These goddamned Okies are dirty and ignorant. They're degenerate, sexual maniacs. These goddamned Okies are thieves. They'll steal anything. They've got no sense of property rights.

And the latter was true, for how can a man without property know the ache of ownership? And the defending people said, They bring disease, they're filthy. We can't have them in the schools. They're strangers. How'd you like to have your sister go out with one of 'em?

The local people whipped themselves into a mold of cruelty. Then they formed units, squads, and armed them—armed them with clubs, with gas, with guns. We own the country. We can't let these Okies get out of hand. And the men who were armed did not own the land, but they thought they did. And the clerks who drilled at night owned nothing, and the little storekeepers possessed only a drawerful of debts. But even a debt is something, even a job is something. The clerk thought, I get fifteen dollars a week. S'pose a goddamn Okie would work for twelve? And the little storekeeper thought, How could I compete with a debtless man?

And the migrants streamed in on the highways and their hunger was in their eyes, and their need was in their eyes. They had no argument, no system, nothing but their numbers and their needs. When there was work for a man, ten men fought for it—fought with a low wage. If that fella'll work for thirty cents, I'll work for twenty-five.

If he'll take twenty-five, I'll do it for twenty.

No, me, I'm hungry. I'll work for fifteen. I'll work for food. The kids. You ought to see them. Little boils, like, comin' out, an' they can't run aroun'. Give 'em some windfall fruit, an' they bloated up. Me. I'll work for a little piece of meat.

And this was good, for wages went down and prices stayed up. The great owners were glad and they sent out more handbills to bring more people in. And wages went down and prices stayed up. And pretty soon now we'll have serfs again.

And now the great owners and the companies invented a new method. A great owner bought a cannery. And when the peaches and the pears were ripe he cut the price of fruit below the cost of raising it. And as cannery owner he paid himself a low price for the fruit and kept the price of canned goods up and took his profit. And the little farmers who owned no canneries lost their farms, and they were taken by the great owners, the banks, and the companies who also owned the canneries. As time went on, there were fewer farms. The little farmers moved into town for a while and exhausted their credit, exhausted their friends, their relatives. And then they too went on the highways. And the roads were crowded with men ravenous for work, murderous for work.

And the companies, the banks worked at their own doom and they did not know it. The fields were fruitful, and starving men moved on the roads. The granaries were full and the children of the poor grew up rachitic, and the pustules of pellagra swelled on their sides. The great companies did not know that the line between hunger and anger is a thin line. And money that might have gone to wages went for gas, for guns, for agents and spies, for blacklists, for drilling. On the highways the people moved like ants and searched for work, for food. And the anger began to ferment.

Chapter Twenty-Two

IT WAS LATE when Tom Joad drove along a country road looking for the Weedpatch camp. There were few lights in the countryside. Only a sky glare behind showed the direction of Bakersfield. The truck jiggled slowly along and hunting cats left the road ahead of it. At a crossroad there was a little cluster of white wooden buildings.

Ma was sleeping in the seat and Pa had been silent and withdrawn for a long time.

Tom said, "I don' know where she is. Maybe we'll wait till daylight an' ast somebody." He stopped at a boulevard signal and another car stopped at the crossing. Tom leaned out. "Hey, mister. Know where the big camp is at?"

"Straight ahead."

Tom pulled across into the opposite road. A few hundred yards, and then he stopped. A high wire fence faced the road, and a wide-gated driveway turned in. A little way inside the gate there was a small house with a light in the window. Tom turned in. The whole truck leaped into the air and crashed down again.

"Jesus!" Tom said. "I didn' even see that hump."

A watchman stood up from the porch and walked to the car. He leaned on the side. "You hit her too fast," he said. "Next time you'll take it easy."

"What is it, for God's sake?"

The watchman laughed. "Well, a lot of kids play in here. You tell folks to go slow and they're liable to forget. But let 'em hit that hump once and they don't forget."

"Oh! Yeah. Hope I didn' break nothin'. Say—you got any room here for us?"

"Got one camp. How many of you?"

Tom counted on his fingers. "Me an' Pa an' Ma, Al an' Rosasharn an' Uncle John an' Ruthie an' Winfiel'. Them last is kids."

"Well, I guess we can fix you. Got any camping stuff?"

"Got a big tarp an' beds."

The watchman stepped up on the running board. "Drive

down the end of that line an' turn right. You'll be in Number
Four Sanitary Unit."

"What's that?"

"Toilets and showers and wash tubs."

Ma demanded, "You got wash tubs—running water?"

"Sure."

"Oh! Praise God," said Ma.

Tom drove down the long dark row of tents. In the sanitary
building a low light burned. "Pull in here," the watchman
said. "It's a nice place. Folks that had it just moved out."

Tom stopped the car. "Right there?"

"Yeah. Now you let the others unload while I sign you up.
Get to sleep. The camp committee'll call on you in the morning and get you fixed up."

Tom's eyes drew down. "Cops?" he asked.

The watchman laughed. "No cops. We got our own cops.
Folks here elect their own cops. Come along."

Al dropped off the truck and walked around. "Gonna stay
here?"

"Yeah," said Tom. "You an' Pa unload while I go to the
office."

"Be kinda quiet," the watchman said. "They's a lot of folks
sleeping."

Tom followed through the dark and climbed the office steps
and entered a tiny room containing an old desk and a chair.
The guard sat down at the desk and took out a form.

"Name?"

"Tom Joad."

"That your father?"

"Yeah."

"His name?"

"Tom Joad, too."

The questions went on. Where from, how long in the State,
what work done. The watchman looked up. "I'm not nosy.
We got to have this stuff."

"Sure," said Tom.

"Now—got any money?"

"Little bit."

"You ain't destitute?"

"Got a little. Why?"

"Well, the camp site costs a dollar a week, but you can work it out, carrying garbage, keeping the camp clean—stuff like that."

"We'll work it out," said Tom.

"You'll see the committee tomorrow. They'll show you how to use the camp and tell you the rules."

Tom said, "Say—what is this? What committee is this, anyways?"

The watchman settled himself back. "Works pretty nice. There's five sanitary units. Each one elects a Central Committee man. Now that committee makes the laws. What they say goes."

"S'pose they get tough," Tom said.

"Well, you can vote 'em out jus' as quick as you vote 'em in. They've done a fine job. Tell you what they did—you know the Holy Roller preachers all the time follow the people around, preachin' an' takin' up collections? Well, they wanted to preach in this camp. And a lot of the older folks wanted them. So it was up to the Central Committee. They went into meeting and here's how they fixed it. They say, 'Any preacher can preach in this camp. Nobody can take up a collection in this camp.' And it was kinda sad for the old folks, 'cause there hasn't been a preacher in since."

Tom laughed and then he asked, "You mean to say the fellas that runs the camp is jus' fellas—campin' here?"

"Sure. And it works."

"You said about cops——"

"Central Committee keeps order an' makes rules. Then there's the ladies. They'll call on your ma. They keep care of kids an' look after the sanitary units. If your ma isn't working, she'll look after kids for the ones that is working, an' when she gets a job—why, there'll be others. They sew, and a nurse comes out an' teaches 'em. All kinds of things like that."

"You mean to say they ain't no fat-ass cops?"

"No, sir. No cop can come in here without a warrant."

"Well, s'pose a fella is jus' mean, or drunk an' quarrelsome. What then?"

The watchman stabbed the blotter with a pencil. "Well, the first time the Central Committee warns him. And the second time they really warn him. The third time they kick him out of the camp."

"God Almighty, I can't hardly believe it! Tonight the deputies an' them fellas with the little caps, they burned the camp out by the river."

"They don't get in here," the watchman said. "Some nights the boys patrol the fences, 'specially dance nights."

"Dance nights? Jesus Christ!"

"We got the best dances in the county every Saturday night."

"Well, for Christ's sake! Why ain't they more places like this?"

The watchman looked sullen. "You'll have to find that out yourself. Go get some sleep."

"Good night," said Tom. "Ma's gonna like this place. She ain't been treated decent for a long time."

"Good night," the watchman said. "Get some sleep. This camp wakes up early."

Tom walked down the street between the rows of tents. His eyes grew used to the starlight. He saw that the rows were straight and that there was no litter about the tents. The ground of the street had been swept and sprinkled. From the tents came the snores of sleeping people. The whole camp buzzed and snorted. Tom walked slowly. He neared Number Four Sanitary Unit and he looked at it curiously, an unpainted building, low and rough. Under a roof, but open at the sides, the rows of wash trays. He saw the Joad truck standing near by, and went quietly toward it. The tarpaulin was pitched and the camp was quiet. As he drew near a figure moved from the shadow of the truck and came toward him.

Ma said softly, "That you, Tom?"

"Yeah."

"Sh!" she said. "They're all asleep. They was tar'd out."

"You ought to be asleep too," Tom said.

"Well, I wanted to see ya. Is it awright?"

"It's nice," Tom said. "I ain't gonna tell ya. They'll tell ya in the mornin'. Ya gonna like it."

She whispered, "I heard they got hot water."

"Yeah. Now you get to sleep. I don' know when you slep' las'."

She begged, "What ain't you a-gonna tell me?"

"I ain't. You get to sleep."

Suddenly she seemed girlish. "How can I sleep if I got to think about what you ain't gonna tell me?"

"No, you don't," Tom said. "First thing in the mornin' you get on your other dress an' then—you'll find out."

"I can't sleep with nothin' like that hangin' over me."

"You got to," Tom chuckled happily. "You jus' got to."

"Good night," she said softly; and she bent down and slipped under the dark tarpaulin.

Tom climbed up over the tail-board of the truck. He lay down on his back on the wooden floor and he pillowed his head on his crossed hands, and his forearms pressed against his ears. The night grew cooler. Tom buttoned his coat over his chest and settled back again. The stars were clear and sharp over his head.

It was still dark when he awakened. A small clashing noise brought him up from sleep. Tom listened and heard again the squeak of iron on iron. He moved stiffly and shivered in the morning air. The camp still slept. Tom stood up and looked over the side of the truck. The eastern mountains were blue-black, and as he watched, the light stood up faintly behind them, colored at the mountain rims with a washed red, then growing colder, grayer, darker, as it went up overhead, until at a place near the western horizon it merged with pure night. Down in the valley the earth was the lavender-gray of dawn.

The clash of iron sounded again. Tom looked down the line of tents, only a little lighter gray than the ground. Beside a tent he saw a flash of orange fire seeping from the cracks in an old iron stove. Gray smoke spurted up from a stubby smoke-pipe.

Tom climbed over the truck side and dropped to the ground. He moved slowly toward the stove. He saw a girl working about the stove, saw that she carried a baby on her crooked arm, and that the baby was nursing, its head up under the girl's shirtwaist. And the girl moved about, poking the fire, shifting the rusty stove lids to make a better draft, opening the oven door; and all the time the baby sucked, and the mother shifted it deftly from arm to arm. The baby didn't interfere with her work or with the quick gracefulness of her movements. And the orange fire licked out of the stove cracks and threw flickering reflections on the tent.

Tom moved closer. He smelled frying bacon and baking bread. From the east the light grew swiftly. Tom came near to the stove and stretched out his hands to it. The girl looked at him and nodded, so that her two braids jerked.

"Good mornin'," she said, and she turned the bacon in the pan.

The tent flap jerked up and a young man came out and an older man followed him. They were dressed in new blue dungarees and in dungaree coats, stiff with filler, the brass buttons shining. They were sharp-faced men, and they looked much alike. The younger man had a dark stubble beard and the older man a white stubble beard. Their heads and faces were wet, their hair dripped, water stood in drops on their stiff beards. Their cheeks shone with dampness. Together they stood looking quietly into the lightening east. They yawned together and watched the light on the hill rims. And then they turned and saw Tom.

"Mornin'," the older man said, and his face was neither friendly nor unfriendly.

"Mornin'," said Tom.

And, "Mornin'," said the younger man.

The water slowly dried on their faces. They came to the stove and warmed their hands at it.

The girl kept to her work. Once she set the baby down and tied her braids together in back with a string, and the two braids jerked and swung as she worked. She set tin cups on a big packing box, set tin plates and knives and forks out. Then she scooped bacon from the deep grease and laid it on a tin platter, and the bacon cricked and rustled as it grew crisp. She opened the rusty oven door and took out a square pan full of big high biscuits.

When the smell of the biscuits struck the air both of the men inhaled deeply. The younger said, "Kee-rist!" softly.

Now the older man said to Tom, "Had your breakfast?"

"Well, no, I ain't. But my folks is over there. They ain't up. Need the sleep."

"Well, set down with us, then. We got plenty—thank God!"

"Why, thank ya," Tom said. "Smells so darn good I couldn' say no."

"Don't she?" the younger man asked. "Ever smell anything so good in ya life?" They marched to the packing box and squatted around it.

"Workin' around here?" the young man asked.

"Aim to," said Tom. "We jus' got in las' night. Ain't had no chance to look aroun'."

"We had twelve days' work," the young man said.

The girl, working by the stove, said, "They even got new clothes." Both men looked down at their stiff blue clothes, and they smiled a little shyly. The girl set out the platter of bacon and the brown, high biscuits and a bowl of bacon gravy and a pot of coffee, and then she squatted down by the box too. The baby still nursed, its head up under the girl's shirt-waist.

They filled their plates, poured bacon gravy over the biscuits, and sugared their coffee.

The older man filled his mouth full, and he chewed and chewed and gulped and swallowed. "God Almighty, it's good!" he said, and he filled his mouth again.

The younger man said, "We been eatin' good for twelve days now. Never missed a meal in twelve days—none of us. Workin' an' gettin' our pay an' eatin'." He fell to again, almost frantically, and refilled his plate. They drank the scalding coffee and threw the grounds to the earth and filled their cups again.

There was color in the light now, a reddish gleam. The father and son stopped eating. They were facing to the east and their faces were lighted by the dawn. The image of the mountain and the light coming over it were reflected in their eyes. And then they threw the grounds from their cups to the earth, and they stood up together.

"Got to git goin'," the older man said.

The younger turned to Tom. "Lookie," he said. "We're layin' some pipe. 'F you wanta walk over with us, maybe we could get you on."

Tom said, "Well, that's mighty nice of you. An' I sure thank ya for the breakfast."

"Glad to have you," the older man said. "We'll try to git you workin' if you want."

"Ya goddamn right I want," Tom said. "Jus' wait a minute. I'll tell my folks." He hurried to the Joad tent and bent over and looked inside. In the gloom under the tarpaulin he saw the lumps of sleeping figures. But a little movement started among the bedclothes. Ruthie came wriggling out like a snake, her hair down over her eyes and her dress wrinkled and twisted. She crawled carefully out and stood up. Her gray eyes were clear and calm from sleep, and mischief was not in them. Tom moved off from the tent and beckoned her to follow, and when he turned, she looked up at him.

"Lord God, you're growin' up," he said.

She looked away in sudden embarrassment. "Listen here," Tom said. "Don't you wake nobody up, but when they get up, you tell 'em I got a chancet at a job, an' I'm a-goin' for it. Tell Ma I et breakfas' with some neighbors. You hear that?"

Ruthie nodded and turned her head away, and her eyes were little girl's eyes. "Don't you wake 'em up," Tom cautioned. He hurried back to his new friends. And Ruthie cautiously approached the sanitary unit and peeked in the open doorway.

The two men were waiting when Tom came back. The young woman had dragged a mattress out and put the baby on it while she cleaned up the dishes.

Tom said, "I wanted to tell my folks where-at I was. They wasn't awake." The three walked down the street between the tents.

The camp had begun to come to life. At the new fires the women worked, slicing meat, kneading the dough for the morning's bread. And the men were stirring about the tents and about the automobiles. The sky was rosy now. In front of the office a lean old man raked the ground carefully. He so dragged his rake that the tine marks were straight and deep.

"You're out early, Pa," the young man said as they went by.

"Yep, yep. Got to make up my rent."

The three went out the gate.

"Rent, hell!" the young man said. "He was drunk last

Sat'dy night. Sung in his tent all night. Committee give him work for it." They walked along the edge of the oiled road; a row of walnut trees grew beside the way. The sun shoved its edge over the mountains.

Tom said, "Seems funny. I've et your food, an' I ain't tol' you my name—nor you ain't mentioned yours. I'm Tom Joad."

The older man looked at him, and then he smiled a little. "You ain't been out here long?"

"Hell, no! Jus' a couple days."

"I knowed it. Funny, you git outa the habit a mentionin' your name. They's so goddamn many. Jist fellas. Well, sir—I'm Timothy Wallace, an' this here's my boy Wilkie."

"Proud to know ya," Tom said. "You been out here long?"

"Ten months," Wilkie said. "Got here right on the tail a the floods las' year. Jesus! We had *a* time, *a* time! Goddamn near starve' to death." Their feet rattled on the oiled road. A truckload of men went by, and each man was sunk into himself. Each man braced himself in the truck bed and scowled down.

"Goin' out for the Gas Company," Timothy said. "They got a nice job of it."

"I could of took our truck," Tom suggested.

"No." Timothy leaned down and picked up a green walnut. He tested it with his thumb and then shied it at a blackbird sitting on a fence wire. The bird flew up, let the nut sail under it, and then settled back on the wire and smoothed its shining black feathers with its beak.

Tom asked, "Ain't you got no car?"

Both Wallaces were silent, and Tom, looking at their faces, saw that they were ashamed.

Wilkie said, "Place we work at is on'y a mile up the road."

Timothy said angrily, "No, we ain't got no car. We sol' our car. Had to. Run outa food, run outa ever'thing. Couldn' git no job. Fellas come aroun' ever' week, buyin' cars. Come aroun', an' if you're hungry, why, they'll buy your car. An' if you're hungry enough, they don't hafta pay nothin' for it. An'—we was hungry enough. Give us ten dollars for her." He spat into the road.

Wilkie said quietly, "I was in Bakersfiel' las' week. I seen her—a settin' in a use'-car lot—settin' right there, an' seventy-five dollars was the sign on her."

"We had to," Timothy said. "It was either us let 'em steal our car or us steal somepin from them. We ain't had to steal yet, but, goddamn it, we been close!"

Tom said, "You know, 'fore we lef' home, we heard they was plenty work out here. Seen han'bills askin' folks to come out."

"Yeah," Timothy said. "We seen 'em too. An' they ain't much work. An' wages is comin' down all a time. I git so goddamn tired jus' figgerin' how to eat."

"You got work now," Tom suggested.

"Yeah, but it ain't gonna las' long. Workin' for a nice fella. Got a little place. Works 'longside of us. But, hell—it ain't gonna las' no time."

Tom said, "Why in hell you gonna git me on? I'll make it shorter. What you cuttin' your own throat for?"

Timothy shook his head slowly. "I dunno. Got no sense, I guess. We figgered to get us each a hat. Can't do it, I guess. There's the place, off to the right there. Nice job, too. Gettin' thirty cents an hour. Nice frien'ly fella to work for."

They turned off the highway and walked down a graveled road, through a small kitchen orchard; and behind the trees they came to a small white farm house, a few sheds, and a barn; behind the barn a vineyard and a field of cotton. As the three men walked past the house a screen door banged, and a stocky sunburned man came down the back steps. He wore a paper sun helmet, and he rolled up his sleeves as he came across the yard. His heavy sunburned eyebrows were drawn down in a scowl. His cheeks were sunburned a beef red.

"Mornin', Mr. Thomas," Timothy said.

"Morning." The man spoke irritably.

Timothy said, "This here's Tom Joad. We wondered if you could see your way to put him on?"

Thomas scowled at Tom. And then he laughed shortly, and his brows still scowled. "Oh, sure! I'll put him on. I'll put everybody on. Maybe I'll get a hundred men on."

"We jus' thought—" Timothy began apologetically.

Thomas interrupted him. "Yes, I been thinkin' too." He

swung around and faced them. "I've got some things to tell you. I been paying you thirty cents an hour—that right?"

"Why, sure, Mr. Thomas—but——"

"And I been getting thirty cents' worth of work." His heavy hard hands clasped each other.

"We try to give a good day of work."

"Well, goddamn it, this morning you're getting twenty-five cents an hour, and you take it or leave it." The redness of his face deepened with anger.

Timothy said, "We've give you good work. You said so yourself."

"I know it. But it seems like I ain't hiring my own men any more." He swallowed. "Look," he said. "I got sixty-five acres here. Did you ever hear of the Farmers' Association?"

"Why, sure."

"Well, I belong to it. We had a meeting last night. Now, do you know who runs the Farmers' Association? I'll tell you. The Bank of the West. That bank owns most of this valley, and it's got paper on everything it don't own. So last night the member from the bank told me, he said, 'You're paying thirty cents an hour. You'd better cut it down to twenty-five.' I said, 'I've got good men. They're worth thirty.' And he says, 'It isn't that,' he says. 'The wage is twenty-five now. If you pay thirty, it'll only cause unrest. And by the way,' he says, 'you going to need the usual amount for a crop loan next year?'" Thomas stopped. His breath was panting through his lips. "You see? The wage is twenty-five cents—and like it."

"We done good work," Timothy said helplessly.

"Ain't you got it yet? Mr. Bank hires two thousand men an' I hire three. I've got paper to meet. Now if you can figure some way out, by Christ, I'll take it! They got me."

Timothy shook his head. "I don' know what to say."

"You wait here." Thomas walked quickly to the house. The door slammed after him. In a moment he was back, and he carried a newspaper in his hand. "Did you see this? Here, I'll read it: 'Citizens, angered at red agitators, burn squatters' camp. Last night a band of citizens, infuriated at the agitation going on in a local squatters' camp, burned the tents to the ground and warned agitators to get out of the country.'"

Tom began, "Why, I—" and then he closed his mouth and was silent.

Thomas folded the paper carefully and put it in his pocket. He had himself in control again. He said quietly, "Those men were sent out by the Association. Now I'm giving 'em away. And if they ever find out I told, I won't have a farm next year."

"I jus' don't know what to say," Timothy said. "If they was agitators, I can see why they was mad."

Thomas said, "I watched it a long time. There's always red agitators just before a pay cut. Always. Goddamn it, they got me trapped. Now, what are you going to do? Twenty-five cents?"

Timothy looked at the ground. "I'll work," he said.

"Me too," said Wilkie.

Tom said, "Seems like I walked into somepin. Sure, I'll work. I got to work."

Thomas pulled a bandanna out of his hip pocket and wiped his mouth and chin. "I don't know how long it can go on. I don't know how you men can feed a family on what you get now."

"We can while we work," Wilkie said. "It's when we don't git work."

Thomas looked at his watch. "Well, let's go out and dig some ditch. By God," he said, "I'm a-gonna tell you. You fellas live in that government camp, don't you?"

Timothy stiffened. "Yes, sir."

"And you have dances every Saturday night?"

Wilkie smiled. "We sure do."

"Well, look out next Saturday night."

Suddenly Timothy straightened. He stepped close. "What you mean? I belong to the Central Committee. I got to know."

Thomas looked apprehensive. "Don't you ever tell I told."

"What is it?" Timothy demanded.

"Well, the Association don't like the government camps. Can't get a deputy in there. The people make their own laws, I hear, and you can't arrest a man without a warrant. Now if there was a big fight and maybe shooting—a bunch of deputies could go in and clean out the camp."

Timothy had changed. His shoulders were straight and his eyes cold. "What you mean?"

"Don't you ever tell where you heard," Thomas said uneasily. "There's going to be a fight in the camp Saturday night. And there's going to be deputies ready to go in."

Tom demanded, "Why, for God's sake? Those folks ain't bothering nobody."

"I'll tell you why," Thomas said. "Those folks in the camp are getting used to being treated like humans. When they go back to the squatters' camps they'll be hard to handle." He wiped his face again. "Go on out to work now. Jesus, I hope I haven't talked myself out of my farm. But I like you people."

Timothy stepped in front of him and put out a hard lean hand, and Thomas took it. "Nobody won't know who tol'. We thank you. They won't be no fight."

"Go on to work," Thomas said. "And it's twenty-five cents an hour."

"We'll take it," Wilkie said, "from you."

Thomas walked away toward the house. "I'll be out in a piece," he said. "You men get to work." The screen door slammed behind him.

The three men walked out past the little white-washed barn, and along a field edge. They came to a long narrow ditch with sections of concrete pipe lying beside it.

"Here's where we're a-workin'," Wilkie said.

His father opened the barn and passed out two picks and three shovels. And he said to Tom, "Here's your beauty."

Tom hefted the pick. "Jumping Jesus! If she don't feel good!"

"Wait'll about 'leven o'clock," Wilkie suggested. "See how good she feels then."

They walked to the end of the ditch. Tom took off his coat and dropped it on the dirt pile. He pushed up his cap and stepped into the ditch. Then he spat on his hands. The pick arose into the air and flashed down. Tom grunted softly. The pick rose and fell, and the grunt came at the moment it sank into the ground and loosened the soil.

Wilkie said, "Yes, sir, Pa, we got here a first-grade muckstick man. This here boy been married to that there little digger."

Tom said, "I put in time (*umph*). Yes, sir, I sure did (*umph*).

Put in my years (*umph!*). Kinda like the feel (*umph!*)." The soil loosened ahead of him. The sun cleared the fruit trees now and the grape leaves were golden green on the vines. Six feet along and Tom stepped aside and wiped his forehead. Wilkie came behind him. The shovel rose and fell and the dirt flew out to the pile beside the lengthening ditch.

"I heard about this here Central Committee," said Tom. "So you're one of 'em."

"Yes, sir," Timothy replied. "And it's a responsibility. All them people. We're doin' our best. An' the people in the camp a-doin' their best. I wisht them big farmers wouldn' plague us so. I wisht they wouldn'."

Tom climbed back into the ditch and Wilkie stood aside. Tom said, "How 'bout this fight (*umph!*) at the dance, he tol' about (*umph*)? What they wanta do that for?"

Timothy followed behind Wilkie, and Timothy's shovel beveled the bottom of the ditch and smoothed it ready for the pipe. "Seems like they got to drive us," Timothy said. "They're scairt we'll organize, I guess. An' maybe they're right. This here camp is a organization. People there look out for theirselves. Got the nicest strang band in these parts. Got a little charge account in the store for folks that's hungry. Fi' dollars—you can git that much food an' the camp'll stan' good. We ain't never had no trouble with the law. I guess the big farmers is scairt of that. Can't throw us in jail—why, it scares 'em. Figger maybe if we can gove'n ourselves, maybe we'll do other things."

Tom stepped clear of the ditch and wiped the sweat out of his eyes. "You hear what that paper said 'bout agitators up north a Bakersfiel'?"

"Sure," said Wilkie. "They do that all a time."

"Well, I was there. They wasn't no agitators. What they call reds. What the hell is these reds anyways?"

Timothy scraped a little hill level in the bottom of the ditch. The sun made his white bristle beard shine. "They's a lot a fellas wanta know what reds is." He laughed. "One of our boys foun' out." He patted the piled earth gently with his shovel. "Fella named Hines—got 'bout thirty thousan' acres, peaches and grapes—got a cannery an' a winery. Well, he's all a time talkin' about 'them goddamn reds.' 'Goddamn reds is

drivin' the country to ruin,' he says, an' 'We got to drive these
here red bastards out.' Well, they were a young fella jus' come
out west here, an' he's listenin' one day. He kinda scratched
his head an' he says, 'Mr. Hines, I ain't been here long. What
is these goddamn reds?' Well, sir, Hines says, 'A red is any
son-of-a-bitch that wants thirty cents an hour when we're
payin' twenty-five!' Well, this young fella he thinks about her,
an' he scratches his head, an' he says, 'Well, Jesus, Mr. Hines.
I ain't a son-of-a-bitch, but if that's what a red is—why, I
want thirty cents an hour. Ever'body does. Hell, Mr. Hines,
we're all reds.' " Timothy drove his shovel along the ditch
bottom, and the solid earth shone where the shovel cut it.

Tom laughed. "Me too, I guess." His pick arced up and
drove down, and the earth cracked under it. The sweat rolled
down his forehead and down the sides of his nose, and it
glistened on his neck. "Damn it," he said, "a pick is a nice
tool (*umph*), if you don' fight it (*umph*). You an' the pick
(*umph*) workin' together (*umph*)."

In line, the three men worked, and the ditch inched along,
and the sun shone hotly down on them in the growing
morning.

When Tom left her, Ruthie gazed in at the door of the
sanitary unit for a while. Her courage was not strong without
Winfield to boast for. She put a bare foot in on the concrete
floor, and then withdrew it. Down the line a woman came
out of a tent and started a fire in a tin camp stove. Ruthie
took a few steps in that direction, but she could not leave.
She crept to the entrance of the Joad tent and looked in. On
one side, lying on the ground, lay Uncle John, his mouth
open and his snores bubbling spittily in his throat. Ma and Pa
were covered with a comfort, their heads in, away from the
light. Al was on the far side from Uncle John, and his arm
was flung over his eyes. Near the front of the tent Rose of
Sharon and Winfield lay, and there was the space where Ruthie
had been, beside Winfield. She squatted down and peered in.
Her eyes remained on Winfield's tow head; and as she looked,
the little boy opened his eyes and stared out at her, and his
eyes were solemn. Ruthie put her finger to her lips and beckoned with her other hand. Winfield rolled his eyes over to

Rose of Sharon. Her pink flushed face was near to him, and her mouth was open a little. Winfield carefully loosened the blanket and slipped out. He crept out of the tent cautiously and joined Ruthie. "How long you been up?" he whispered.

She led him away with elaborate caution, and when they were safe, she said, "I never been to bed. I was up all night."

"You was not," Winfield said. "You're a dirty liar."

"Awright," she said. "If I'm a liar I ain't gonna tell you nothin' that happened. I ain't gonna tell how the fella got killed with a stab knife an' how they was a bear come in an' took off a little chile."

"They wasn't no bear," Winfield said uneasily. He brushed up his hair with his fingers and he pulled down his overalls at the crotch.

"All right—they wasn't no bear," she said sarcastically. "An' they ain't no white things made outa dish-stuff, like in the catalogues."

Winfield regarded her gravely. He pointed to the sanitary unit. "In there?" he asked.

"I'm a dirty liar," Ruthie said. "It ain't gonna do me no good to tell stuff to you."

"Le's go look," Winfield said.

"I already been," Ruthie said. "I already set on 'em. I even pee'd in one."

"You never neither," said Winfield.

They went to the unit building, and that time Ruthie was not afraid. Boldly she led the way into the building. The toilets lined one side of the large room, and each toilet had its compartment with a door in front of it. The porcelain was gleaming white. Hand basins lined another wall, while on the third wall were four shower compartments.

"There," said Ruthie. "Them's the toilets. I seen 'em in the catalogue." The children drew near to one of the toilets. Ruthie, in a burst of bravado, boosted her skirt and sat down. "I tol' you I been here," she said. And to prove it, there was a tinkle of water in the bowl.

Winfield was embarrassed. His hand twisted the flushing lever. There was a roar of water. Ruthie leaped into the air and jumped away. She and Winfield stood in the middle of the room and looked at the toilet. The hiss of water continued in it.

"You done it," Ruthie said. "You went an' broke it. I seen you."

"I never. Honest I never."

"I seen you," Ruthie said. "You jus' ain't to be trusted with no nice stuff."

Winfield sunk his chin. He looked up at Ruthie and his eyes filled with tears. His chin quivered. And Ruthie was instantly contrite.

"Never you mind," she said. "I won't tell on you. We'll pretend like she was already broke. We'll pretend we ain't even been in here." She led him out of the building.

The sun lipped over the mountain by now, shone on the corrugated-iron roofs of the five sanitary units, shone on the gray tents and on the swept ground of the streets between the tents. And the camp was waking up. The fires were burning in camp stoves, in the stoves made of kerosene cans and of sheets of metal. The smell of smoke was in the air. Tent flaps were thrown back and people moved about in the streets. In front of the Joad tent Ma stood looking up and down the street. She saw the children and came over to them.

"I was worryin'," Ma said. "I didn' know where you was."

"We was jus' lookin'," Ruthie said.

"Well, where's Tom? You seen him?"

Ruthie became important. "Yes, ma'am. Tom, he got me up an' he tol' me what to tell you." She paused to let her importance be apparent.

"Well—what?" Ma demanded.

"He said tell you—" She paused again and looked to see that Winfield appreciated her position.

Ma raised her hand, the back of it toward Ruthie. "What?"

"He got work," said Ruthie quickly. "Went out to work." She looked apprehensively at Ma's raised hand. The hand sank down again, and then it reached out for Ruthie. Ma embraced Ruthie's shoulders in a quick convulsive hug, and then released her.

Ruthie stared at the ground in embarrassment, and changed

the subject. "They got toilets over there," she said. "White ones."

"You been in there?" Ma demanded.

"Me an' Winfiel'," she said; and then, treacherously, "Winfiel', he bust a toilet."

Winfield turned red. He glared at Ruthie. "She pee'd in one," he said viciously.

Ma was apprehensive. "Now what did you do? You show me." She forced them to the door and inside. "Now what'd you do?"

Ruthie pointed. "It was a-hissin' and a-swishin'. Stopped now."

"Show me what you done," Ma demanded.

Winfield went reluctantly to the toilet. "I didn' push it hard," he said. "I jus' had aholt of this here, an'—" The swish of water came again. He leaped away.

Ma threw back her head and laughed, while Ruthie and Winfield regarded her resentfully. "Tha's the way she works," Ma said. "I seen them before. When you finish, you push that."

The shame of their ignorance was too great for the children. They went out the door, and they walked down the street to stare at a large family eating breakfast.

Ma watched them out of the door. And then she looked about the room. She went to the shower closets and looked in. She walked to the wash basins and ran her finger over the white porcelain. She turned the water on a little and held her finger in the stream, and jerked her hand away when the water came hot. For a moment she regarded the basin, and then, setting the plug, she filled the bowl a little from the hot faucet, a little from the cold. And then she washed her hands in the warm water, and she washed her face. She was brushing water through her hair with her fingers when a step sounded on the concrete floor behind her. Ma swung around. An elderly man stood looking at her with an expression of righteous shock.

He said harshly, "How you come in here?"

Ma gulped, and she felt the water dripping from her chin and soaking through her dress. "I didn' know," she said apologetically. "I thought this here was for folks to use."

The elderly man frowned on her. "For men folks," he said sternly. He walked to the door and pointed to a sign on it: MEN. "There," he said. "That proves it. Didn' you see that?"

"No," Ma said in shame, "I never seen it. Ain't they a place where I can go?"

The man's anger departed. "You jus' come?" he asked more kindly.

"Middle of the night," said Ma.

"Then you ain't talked to the Committee?"

"What committee?"

"Why, the Ladies' Committee."

"No, I ain't."

He said proudly, "The Committee'll call on you purty soon an' fix you up. We take care of folks that jus' come in. Now, if you want a ladies' toilet, you jus' go on the other side of the building. That side's yourn."

Ma said uneasily, "Ya say a ladies' committee—comin' to my tent?"

He nodded his head. "Purty soon, I guess."

"Thank ya," said Ma. She hurried out, and half ran to the tent.

"Pa," she called. "John, git up! You, Al. Git up an' git washed." Startled sleepy eyes looked out at her. "All of you," Ma cried. "You git up an' git your face washed. An' comb your hair."

Uncle John looked pale and sick. There was a red bruised place on his chin.

Pa demanded, "What's the matter?"

"The Committee," Ma cried. "They's a committee—a ladies' committee a-comin' to visit. Git up now, an' git washed. An' while we was a-sleepin' an' a-snorin', Tom's went out an' got work. Git up, now."

They came sleepily out of the tent. Uncle John staggered a little, and his face was pained.

"Git over to that house and wash up," Ma ordered. "We got to get breakfus' an' be ready for the Committee." She went to a little pile of split wood in the camp lot. She started a fire and put up her cooking irons. "Pone," she said to herself. "Pone an' gravy. That's quick. Got to be quick." She talked on to herself, and Ruthie and Winfield stood by, wondering.

The smoke of the morning fires arose all over the camp, and the mutter of talk came from all sides.

Rose of Sharon, unkempt and sleepy-eyed, crawled out of the tent. Ma turned from the cornmeal she was measuring in fistfuls. She looked at the girl's wrinkled dirty dress, at her frizzled uncombed hair. "You got to clean up," she said briskly. "Go right over and clean up. You got a clean dress. I washed it. Git your hair combed. Git the seeds out a your eyes." Ma was excited.

Rose of Sharon said sullenly, "I don' feel good. I wisht Connie would come. I don't feel like doin' nothin' 'thout Connie."

Ma turned full around on her. The yellow cornmeal clung to her hands and wrists. "Rosasharn," she said sternly, "you git upright. You jus' been mopin' enough. They's a ladies' committee a-comin', an' the fambly ain't gonna be frawny when they get here."

"But I don' feel good."

Ma advanced on her, mealy hands held out. "Git," Ma said. "They's times when how you feel got to be kep' to your-self."

"I'm a-goin' to vomit," Rose of Sharon whined.

"Well, go an' vomit. 'Course you're gonna vomit. Ever'-body does. Git it over an' then you clean up, an' you wash your legs an' put on them shoes of yourn." She turned back to her work. "An' braid your hair," she said.

A frying pan of grease sputtered over the fire, and it splashed and hissed when Ma dropped the pone in with a spoon. She mixed flour with grease in a kettle and added water and salt and stirred the gravy. The coffee began to turn over in the gallon can, and the smell of coffee rose from it.

Pa wandered back from the sanitary unit, and Ma looked critically up. Pa said, "Ya say Tom's got work?"

"Yes, sir. Went out 'fore we was awake. Now look in that box an' get you some clean overhalls an' a shirt. An', Pa, I'm awful busy. You git in Ruthie an' Winfiel's ears. They's hot water. Will you do that? Scrounge aroun' in their ears good, an' their necks. Get 'em red an' shinin'."

"Never seen you so bubbly," Pa said.

Ma cried, "This here's the time the fambly got to get decent. Comin' acrost they wasn't no chancet. But now we can. Th'ow your dirty overhalls in the tent an' I'll wash 'em out."

Pa went inside the tent, and in a moment he came out with pale blue, washed overalls and shirt on. And he led the sad and startled children toward the sanitary unit.

Ma called after him, "Scrounge aroun' good in their ears."

Uncle John came to the door of the men's side and looked out, and then he went back and sat on the toilet a long time and held his aching head in his hands.

Ma had taken up a panload of brown pone and was dropping spoons of dough in the grease for a second pan when a shadow fell on the ground beside her. She looked over her shoulder. A little man dressed all in white stood behind her—a man with a thin, brown, lined face and merry eyes. He was lean as a picket. His white clean clothes were frayed at the seams. He smiled at Ma. "Good morning," he said.

Ma looked at his white clothes and her face hardened with suspicion. "Mornin'," she said.

"Are you Mrs. Joad?"

"Yes."

"Well, I'm Jim Rawley. I'm camp manager. Just dropped by to see if everything's all right. Got everything you need?"

Ma studied him suspiciously. "Yes," she said.

Rawley said, "I was asleep when you came last night. Lucky we had a place for you." His voice was warm.

Ma said simply, "It's nice. 'Specially them wash tubs."

"You wait till the women get to washing. Pretty soon now. You never heard such a fuss. Like a meeting. Know what they did yesterday, Mrs. Joad? They had a chorus. Singing a hymn tune and rubbing the clothes all in time. That was something to hear, I tell you."

The suspicion was going out of Ma's face. "Must a been nice. You're the boss?"

"No," he said. "The people here worked me out of a job. They keep the camp clean, they keep order, they do everything. I never saw such people. They're making clothes in the meeting hall. And they're making toys. Never saw such people."

Ma looked down at her dirty dress. "We ain't clean yet," she said. "You jus' can't keep clean a-travelin'."

"Don't I know it," he said. He sniffed the air. "Say—is that your coffee smells so good?"

Ma smiled. "Does smell nice, don't it? Outside it always smells nice." And she said proudly, "We'd take it in honor 'f you'd have some breakfus' with us."

He came to the fire and squatted on his hams, and the last of Ma's resistance went down. "We'd be proud to have ya," she said. "We ain't got much that's nice, but you're welcome."

The little man grinned at her. "I had my breakfast. But I'd sure like a cup of that coffee. Smells so good."

"Why—why, sure."

"Don't hurry yourself."

Ma poured a tin cup of coffee from the gallon can. She said, "We ain't got sugar yet. Maybe we'll get some today. If you need sugar, it won't taste good."

"Never use sugar," he said. "Spoils the taste of good coffee."

"Well, I like a little sugar," said Ma. She looked at him suddenly and closely, to see how he had come so close so quickly. She looked for motive on his face, and found nothing but friendliness. Then she looked at the frayed seams on his white coat, and she was reassured.

He sipped the coffee. "I guess the ladies'll be here to see you this morning."

"We ain't clean," Ma said. "They shouldn't be comin' till we get cleaned up a little."

"But they know how it is," the manager said. "They came in the same way. No, sir. The committees are good in this camp because they do know." He finished his coffee and stood up. "Well, I got to go on. Anything you want, why, come over to the office. I'm there all the time. Grand coffee. Thank you." He put the cup on the box with the others, waved his hand, and walked down the line of tents. And Ma heard him speaking to the people as he went.

Ma put down her head and she fought with a desire to cry.

Pa came back leading the children, their eyes still wet with pain at the ear-scrounging. They were subdued and shining. The sunburned skin on Winfield's nose was scrubbed off.

"There," Pa said. "Got dirt an' two layers a skin. Had to almost lick 'em to make 'em stan' still."

Ma appraised them. "They look nice," she said. "He'p ya-self to pone an' gravy. We got to get stuff outa the way an' the tent in order."

Pa served plates for the children and for himself. "Wonder where Tom got work?"

"I dunno."

"Well, if he can, we can."

Al came excitedly to the tent. "What a place!" he said. He helped himself and poured coffee. "Know what a fella's doin'? He's buildin' a house trailer. Right over there, back a them tents. Got beds an' a stove—ever'thing. Jus' live in her. By God, that's the way to live! Right where you stop—tha's where you live."

Ma said, "I ruther have a little house. Soon's we can, I want a little house."

Pa said, "Al—after we've et, you an' me an' Uncle John'll take the truck an' go out lookin' for work."

"Sure," said Al. "I like to get a job in a garage if they's any jobs. Tha's what I really like. An' get me a little ol' cut-down Ford. Paint her yella an' go a-kyoodlin' aroun'. Seen a purty girl down the road. Give her a big wink, too. Purty as hell, too."

Pa said sternly, "You better get you some work 'fore you go a-tom-cattin'."

Uncle John came out of the toilet and moved slowly near. Ma frowned at him.

"You ain't washed—" she began, and then she saw how sick and weak and sad he looked. "You go on in the tent an' lay down," she said. "You ain't well."

He shook his head. "No," he said. "I sinned, an' I got to take my punishment." He squatted down disconsolately and poured himself a cup of coffee.

Ma took the last pones from the pan. She said casually, "The manager of the camp come an' set an' had a cup a coffee."

Pa looked over slowly. "Yeah? What's he want awready?"

"Jus' come to pass the time," Ma said daintily. "Jus' set

down an' had coffee. Said he didn' get good coffee so often, an' smelt our'n."

"What'd he want?" Pa demanded again.

"Didn' want nothin'. Come to see how we was gettin' on."

"I don' believe it," Pa said. "He's probably a-snootin' an' a-smellin' aroun'."

"He was not!" Ma cried angrily. "I can tell a fella that's snootin' aroun' quick as the nex' person."

Pa tossed his coffee grounds out of his cup.

"You got to quit that," Ma said. "This here's a clean place."

"You see she don't get so goddamn clean a fella can't live in her," Pa said jealously. "Hurry up, Al. We're goin' out lookin' for a job."

Al wiped his mouth with his hand. "I'm ready," he said.

Pa turned to Uncle John. "You a-comin'?"

"Yes, I'm a-comin'."

"You don't look so good."

"I ain't so good, but I'm comin'."

Al got in the truck. "Have to get gas," he said. He started the engine. Pa and Uncle John climbed in beside him and the truck moved away down the street.

Ma watched them go. And then she took a bucket and went to the wash trays under the open part of the sanitary unit. She filled her bucket with hot water and carried it back to her camp. And she was washing the dishes in the bucket when Rose of Sharon came back.

"I put your stuff on a plate," Ma said. And then she looked closely at the girl. Her hair was dripping and combed, and her skin was bright and pink. She had put on the blue dress printed with little white flowers. On her feet she wore the heeled slippers of her wedding. She blushed under Ma's gaze. "You had a bath," Ma said.

Rose of Sharon spoke huskily. "I was in there when a lady come in an' done it. Know what you do? You get in a little stall-like, an' you turn handles, an' water comes a-floodin' down on you—hot water or col' water, jus' like you want it—an' I done it!"

"I'm a-goin' to myself," Ma cried. "Jus' soon as I get finish' here. You show me how."

"I'm a-gonna do it ever' day," the girl said. "An' that lady—she seen me, an' she seen about the baby, an'—know what she said? Said they's a nurse comes ever' week. An' I'm to go see that nurse an' she'll tell me jus' what to do so's the baby'll be strong. Says all the ladies here do that. An' I'm a-gonna do it." The words bubbled out. "An'—know what—? Las' week they was a baby borned an' the whole camp give a party, an' they give clothes, an' they give stuff for the baby—even give a baby buggy—wicker one. Wasn't new, but they give it a coat a pink paint, an' it was jus' like new. An' they give the baby a name, an' had a cake. Oh, Lord!" She subsided, breathing heavily.

Ma said, "Praise God, we come home to our own people. I'm a-gonna have a bath."

"Oh, it's nice," the girl said.

Ma wiped the tin dishes and stacked them. She said, "We're Joads. We don't look up to nobody. Grampa's grampa, he fit in the Revolution. We was farm people till the debt. And then—them people. They done somepin to us. Ever' time they come seemed like they was a-whippin' me—all of us. An' in Needles, that police. He done somepin to me, made me feel mean. Made me feel ashamed. An' now I ain't ashamed. These folks is our folks—is our folks. An' that manager, he come an' set an' drank coffee, an' he says, 'Mrs. Joad' this, an' 'Mrs. Joad' that—an' 'How you gettin' on, Mrs. Joad?'" She stopped and sighed. "Why, I feel like people again." She stacked the last dish. She went into the tent and dug through the clothes box for her shoes and a clean dress. And she found a little paper package with her earrings in it. As she went past Rose of Sharon, she said, "If them ladies comes, you tell 'em I'll be right back." She disappeared around the side of the sanitary unit.

Rose of Sharon sat down heavily on a box and regarded her wedding shoes, black patent leather and tailored black bows. She wiped the toes with her finger and wiped her finger on the inside of her skirt. Leaning down put a pressure on her growing abdomen. She sat up straight and touched herself with exploring fingers, and she smiled a little as she did it.

Along the road a stocky woman walked, carrying an apple box of dirty clothes toward the wash tubs. Her face was brown

with sun, and her eyes were black and intense. She wore a
great apron, made from a cotton bag, over her gingham dress,
and men's brown oxfords were on her feet. She saw that Rose
of Sharon caressed herself, and she saw the little smile on the
girl's face.

"So!" she cried, and she laughed with pleasure. "What you
think it's gonna be?"

Rose of Sharon blushed and looked down at the ground,
and then peeked up, and the little shiny black eyes of the
woman took her in. "I don' know," she mumbled.

The woman plopped the apple box on the ground. "Got a
live tumor," she said, and she cackled like a happy hen.
"Which'd you ruther?" she demanded.

"I dunno—boy, I guess. Sure—boy."

"You jus' come in, didn' ya?"

"Las' night—late."

"Gonna stay?"

"I don' know. 'F we can get work, guess we will."

A shadow crossed the woman's face, and the little black eyes
grew fierce. " 'F you can git work. That's what we all say."

"My brother got a job already this mornin'."

"Did, huh? Maybe you're lucky. Look out for luck. You
can't trus' luck." She stepped close. "You can only git one
kind a luck. Cain't have more. You be a good girl," she said
fiercely. "You be good. If you got sin on you—you better
watch out for that there baby." She squatted down in front
of Rose of Sharon. "They's scandalous things goes on in this
here camp," she said darkly. "Ever' Sat'dy night they's dancin', an' not only squar' dancin', neither. They's some does
clutch-an'-hug dancin'! I seen 'em."

Rose of Sharon said guardedly, "I like dancin', squar' dancin'." And she added virtuously, "I never done that other
kind."

The brown woman nodded her head dismally. "Well, some
does. An' the Lord ain't lettin' it get by, neither; an' don' you
think He is."

"No, ma'am," the girl said softly.

The woman put one brown wrinkled hand on Rose of Sharon's knee, and the girl flinched under the touch. "You let me
warn you now. They ain't but a few deep down Jesus-lovers

lef'. Ever' Sat'dy night when that there strang ban' starts up
an' should be a-playin' hymnody, they're a-reelin'—yes, sir, a-
reelin'. I seen 'em. Won' go near, myself, nor I don' let my
kin go near. They's clutch-an'-hug, I tell ya." She paused for
emphasis and then said, in a hoarse whisper, "They do more.
They give a stage play oncet." She backed away and cocked
her head to see how Rose of Sharon would take such a rev-
elation.

"Actors?" the girl said in awe.

"No, sir!" the woman exploded. "Not *actors*, not them
already damn' people. Our own kinda folks. Our own people.
An' they was little children didn' know no better, in it, an'
they was pertendin' to be stuff they wasn't. I didn' go near.
But I hearn 'em talkin' what they was a-doin'. The devil was
jus' a-struttin' through this here camp."

Rose of Sharon listened, her eyes and mouth open. "Oncet
in school we give a Chris' chile play—Christmus."

"Well—I ain' sayin' tha's bad or good. They's good folks
thinks a Chris' chile is awright. But—well, I wouldn' care to
come right out flat an' say so. But this here wasn' no Chris'
chile. This here was sin an' delusion an' devil stuff. Struttin'
an' paradin' an' speakin' like they're somebody they ain't. An'
dancin' an' clutchin' an' a-huggin'."

Rose of Sharon sighed.

"An' not jus' a few, neither," the brown woman went on.
"Gettin' so's you can almos' count the deep-down lamb-
blood folks on your toes. An' don' you think them sinners is
puttin' nothin' over on God, neither. No, sir, He's a-chalkin'
'em up sin by sin, an' He's drawin' His line an' addin' 'em
up sin by sin. God's a-watchin', an' I'm a-watchin'. He's
awready smoked two of 'em out."

Rose of Sharon panted, "Has?"

The brown woman's voice was rising in intensity. "I seen
it. Girl a-carryin' a little one, jes' like you. An' she play-acted,
an' she hug-danced. And"—the voice grew bleak and ominous—"she thinned out and she skinnied out, an'—she
dropped that baby, dead."

"Oh, my!" The girl was pale.

"Dead and bloody. 'Course nobody wouldn' speak to her
no more. She had a go away. Can't tech sin 'thout catchin'

it. No, sir. An' they was another, done the same thing. An' she skinnied out, an'—know what? One night she was gone. An' two days, she's back. Says she was visitin'. But—she ain't got no baby. Know what I think? I think the manager, he took her away to drop her baby. He don' believe in sin. Tol' me hisself. Says the sin is bein' hungry. Says the sin is bein' cold. Says—I tell ya, he tol' me hisself—can't see God in them things. Says them girls skinnied out 'cause they didn' git 'nough food. Well, I fixed him up." She rose to her feet and stepped back. Her eyes were sharp. She pointed a rigid fore-finger in Rose of Sharon's face. "I says, 'Git back!' I says. I says, 'I knowed the devil was rampagin' in this here camp. Now I know who the devil is. Git back, Satan,' I says. An', by Chris', he got back! Tremblin' he was, an' sneaky. Says, 'Please!' Says, 'Please don' make the folks unhappy.' I says, 'Unhappy? How 'bout their soul? How 'bout them dead ba-bies an' them poor sinners ruint 'count of play-actin'?' He jes' looked, an' he give a sick grin an' went away. He knowed when he met a real testifier to the Lord. I says, 'I'm a-helpin' Jesus watch the goin's-on. An' you an' them other sinners ain't gittin' away with it.'" She picked up her box of dirty clothes. "You take heed. I warned you. You take heed a that pore chile in your belly an' keep outa sin." And she strode away titanically, and her eyes shone with virtue.

Rose of Sharon watched her go, and then she put her head down on her hands and whimpered into her palms. A soft voice sounded beside her. She looked up, ashamed. It was the little white-clad manager. "Don't worry," he said. "Don't you worry."

Her eyes blinded with tears. "But I done it," she cried. "I hug-danced. I didn' tell her. I done it in Sallisaw. Me an' Connie."

"Don't worry," he said.

"She says I'll drop the baby."

"I know she does. I kind of keep my eye on her. She's a good woman, but she makes people unhappy."

Rose of Sharon sniffled wetly. "She knowed two girls los' their baby right in this here camp."

The manager squatted down in front of her. "Look!" he said. "Listen to me. I know them too. They were too hungry and too tired. And they worked too hard. And they rode on a truck over bumps. They were sick. It wasn't their fault."

"But she said——"

"Don't worry. That woman likes to make trouble."

"But she says you was the devil."

"I know she does. That's because I won't let her make people miserable." He patted her shoulder. "Don't you worry. She doesn't know." And he walked quickly away.

Rose of Sharon looked after him; his lean shoulders jerked as he walked. She was still watching his slight figure when Ma came back, clean and pink, her hair combed and wet, and gathered in a knot. She wore her figured dress and the old cracked shoes; and the little earrings hung in her ears.

"I done it," she said. "I stood in there an' let warm water come a-floodin' an' a-flowin' down over me. An' they was a lady says you can do it ever' day if you want. An'—did them ladies' committee come yet?"

"Uh-uh!" said the girl.

"An' you jus' set there an' didn' redd up the camp none!" Ma gathered up the tin dishes as she spoke. "We got to get in shape," she said. "Come on, stir! Get that sack and kinda sweep along the groun'." She picked up the equipment, put the pans in their box and the box in the tent. "Get them beds neat," she ordered. "I tell ya I ain't never felt nothin' so nice as that water."

Rose of Sharon listlessly followed orders. "Ya think Connie'll be back today?"

"Maybe—maybe not. Can't tell."

"You sure he knows where-at to come?"

"Sure."

"Ma—ya don' think—they could a killed him when they burned—?"

"Not him," Ma said confidently. "He can travel when he wants—jackrabbit-quick an' fox-sneaky."

"I wisht he'd come."

"He'll come when he comes."

"Ma——"

"I wisht you'd get to work."

"Well, do you think dancin' an' play-actin' is sins an'll make me drop the baby?"

Ma stopped her work and put her hands on her hips. "Now what you talkin' about? You ain't done no play-actin'."

"Well, some folks here done it, an' one girl, she dropped her baby—dead—an' bloody, like it was a judgment."

Ma stared at her. "Who tol' you?"

"Lady that come by. An' that little fella in white clothes, he come by an' he says that ain't what done it."

Ma frowned. "Rosasharn," she said, "you stop pickin' at yourself. You're jest a-teasin' yourself up to cry. I don' know what's come at you. Our folks ain't never did that. They took what come to 'em dry-eyed. I bet it's that Connie give you all them notions. He was jes' too big for his overhalls." And she said sternly, "Rosasharn, you're jest one person, an' they's a lot of other folks. You git to your proper place. I knowed people built theirself up with sin till they figgered they was big mean shucks in the sight a the Lord."

"But, Ma——"

"No. Jes' shut up an' git to work. You ain't big enough or mean enough to worry God much. An' I'm gonna give you the back a my han' if you don' stop this pickin' at yourself." She swept the ashes into the fire hole and brushed the stones on its edge. She saw the committee coming along the road. "Git workin'," she said. "Here's the ladies comin'. Git a-workin' now, so's I can be proud." She didn't look again, but she was conscious of the approach of the committee.

There could be no doubt that it was the committee; three ladies, washed, dressed in their best clothes: a lean woman with stringy hair and steel-rimmed glasses, a small stout lady with curly gray hair and a small sweet mouth, and a mammoth lady, big of hock and buttock, big of breast, muscled like a dray-horse, powerful and sure. And the committee walked down the road with dignity.

Ma managed to have her back turned when they arrived. They stopped, wheeled, stood in a line. And the great woman boomed, "Mornin', Mis' Joad, ain't it?"

Ma whirled around as though she had been caught off guard. "Why, yes—yes. How'd you know my name?"

"We're the committee," the big woman said. "Ladies' Committee of Sanitary Unit Number Four. We got your name in the office."

Ma flustered, "We ain't in very good shape yet. I'd be proud to have you ladies come an' set while I make up some coffee."

The plump committee woman said, "Give our names, Jessie. Mention our names to Mis' Joad. Jessie's the Chair," she explained.

Jessie said formally, "Mis' Joad, this here's Annie Littlefield an' Ella Summers, an' I'm Jessie Bullitt."

"I'm proud to make your acquaintance," Ma said. "Won't you set down? They ain't nothin' to set on yet," she added. "But I'll make up some coffee."

"Oh, no," said Annie formally. "Don't put yaself out. We jes' come to call an' see how you was, an' try to make you feel at home."

Jessie Bullitt said sternly, "Annie, I'll thank you to remember I'm Chair."

"Oh! Sure, sure. But next week I am."

"Well, you wait'll next week then. We change ever' week," she explained to Ma.

"Sure you wouldn' like a little coffee?" Ma asked helplessly.

"No, thank you." Jessie took charge. "We gonna show you 'bout the sanitary unit fust, an' then if you wanta, we'll sign you up in the Ladies' Club an' give you duty. 'Course you don' have to join."

"Does—does it cost much?"

"Don't cost nothing but work. An' when you're knowed, maybe you can be 'lected to this committee," Annie interrupted. "Jessie, here, is on the committee for the whole camp. She's a big committee lady."

Jessie smiled with pride. " 'Lected unanimous," she said. "Well, Mis' Joad, I guess it's time we tol' you 'bout how the camp runs."

Ma said, "This here's my girl, Rosasharn."

"How do," they said.

"Better come 'long too."

The huge Jessie spoke, and her manner was full of dignity and kindness, and her speech was rehearsed.

"You shouldn' think we're a-buttin' into your business, Mis' Joad. This here camp got a lot of stuff ever'body uses. An' we got rules we made ourself. Now we're a-goin' to the unit. That there, ever'body uses, an' ever'body got to take care of it." They strolled to the roofed section where the wash trays were, twenty of them. Eight were in use, the women bending over, scrubbing the clothes, and the piles of wrung-out clothes were heaped on the clean concrete floor. "Now you can use these here any time you want," Jessie said. "The on'y thing is, you got to leave 'em clean."

The women who were washing looked up with interest. Jessie said loudly, "This here's Mis' Joad an' Rosasharn, come to live." They greeted Ma in a chorus, and Ma made a dumpy little bow at them and said, "Proud to meet ya."

Jessie led the committee into the toilet and shower room.

"I been here awready," Ma said. "I even took a bath."

"That's what they're for," Jessie said. "An' they's the same rule. You got to leave 'em clean. Ever' week they's a new committee to swab out oncet a day. Maybe you'll git on that committee. You got to bring your own soap."

"We got to get some soap," Ma said. "We're all out."

Jessie's voice became almost reverential. "You ever used this here kind?" she asked, and pointed to the toilets.

"Yes, ma'am. Right this mornin'."

Jessie sighed. "Tha's good."

Ella Summers said, "Jes' las' week——"

Jessie interrupted sternly, "Mis' Summers—I'll tell."

Ella gave ground. "Oh, awright."

Jessie said, "Las' week, when you was Chair, you done it all. I'll thank you to keep out this week."

"Well, tell what that lady done," Ella said.

"Well," said Jessie, "it ain't this committee's business to go a-blabbin', but I won't pass no names. Lady come in las' week, an' she got in here 'fore the committee got to her, an' she had her ol' man's pants in the toilet, an' she says, 'It's too low, an' it ain't big enough. Bust your back over her,' she says. 'Why couldn' they stick her higher?'" The committee smiled superior smiles.

Ella broke in, "Says, 'Can't put 'nough in at oncet.'" And Ella weathered Jessie's stern glance.

Jessie said, "We got our troubles with toilet paper. Rule says you can't take none away from here." She clicked her tongue sharply. "Whole camp chips in for toilet paper." For a moment she was silent, and then she confessed. "Number Four is usin' more than any other. Somebody's a-stealin' it. Come up in general ladies' meetin'. 'Ladies' side, Unit Number Four is usin' too much.' Come right up in meetin'!"

Ma was following the conversation breathlessly. "Stealin' it—what for?"

"Well," said Jessie, "we had trouble before. Las' time they was three little girls cuttin' paper dolls out of it. Well, we caught them. But this time we don't know. Hardly put a roll out 'fore it's gone. Come right up in meetin'. One lady says we oughta have a little bell that rings ever' time the roll turns oncet. Then we could count how many ever'body takes." She shook her head. "I jes' don' know," she said. "I been worried all week. Somebody's a-stealin' toilet paper from Unit Four."

From the doorway came a whining voice, "Mis' Bullitt." The committee turned. "Mis' Bullitt, I hearn what you says." A flushed, perspiring woman stood in the doorway. "I couldn' git up in meetin', Mis' Bullitt. I jes' couldn'. They'd a-laughed or somepin."

"What you talkin' about?" Jessie advanced.

"Well, we-all—maybe—it's us. But we ain't a-stealin', Mis' Bullitt."

Jessie advanced on her, and the perspiration beaded out on the flustery confessor. "We can't he'p it, Mis' Bullitt."

"Now you tell what you're tellin'," Jessie said. "This here unit's suffered a shame 'bout that toilet paper."

"All week, Mis' Bullitt. We couldn' he'p it. You know I got five girls."

"What they been a-doin' with it?" Jessie demanded ominously.

"Jes' usin' it. Hones', jes' usin' it."

"They ain't got the right! Four-five sheets is enough. What's the matter'th 'em?"

The confessor bleated, "Skitters. All five of 'em. We been low on money. They et green grapes. They all five got the howlin' skitters. Run out ever' ten minutes." She defended them, "But they ain't stealin' it."

Jessie sighed. "You should a tol'," she said. "You got to tell. Here's Unit Four been sufferin' shame 'cause you never tol'. Anybody can git the skitters."

The meek voice whined, "I jes' can't keep 'em from eatin' them green grapes. An' they're a-gettin' worse all a time."

Ella Summers burst out, "The Aid. She oughta git the Aid."

"Ella Summers," Jessie said, "I'm a-tellin' you for the las' time, you ain't the Chair." She turned back to the raddled little woman. "Ain't you got no money, Mis' Joyce?"

She looked ashamedly down. "No, but we might git work any time."

"Now you hol' up your head," Jessie said. "That ain't no crime. You jes' waltz right over t' the Weedpatch store an' git you some grocteries. The camp got twenty dollars' credit there. You git yourself fi' dollars' worth. An' you kin pay it back to the Central Committee when you git work. Mis' Joyce, you knowed that," she said sternly. "How come you let your girls git hungry?"

"We ain't never took no charity," Mrs. Joyce said.

"This ain't charity, an' you know it," Jessie raged. "We had all that out. They ain't no charity in this here camp. We won't have no charity. Now you waltz right over an' git you some grocteries, an' you bring the slip to me."

Mrs. Joyce said timidly, "S'pose we can't never pay? We ain't had work for a long time."

"You'll pay if you can. If you can't, that ain't none of our business, an' it ain't your business. One fella went away, an' two months later he sent back the money. You ain't got the right to let your girls git hungry in this here camp."

Mrs. Joyce was cowed. "Yes, ma'am," she said.

"Git you some cheese for them girls," Jessie ordered. "That'll take care a them skitters."

"Yes, ma'am." And Mrs. Joyce scuttled out of the door.

Jessie turned in anger on the committee. "She got no right to be stiff-necked. She got no right, not with our own people."

Annie Littlefield said, "She ain't been here long. Maybe she don't know. Maybe she's took charity one time-another. No," Annie said, "don't you try to shut me up, Jessie. I got a right to pass speech." She turned half to Ma. "If a body's ever took charity, it makes a burn that don't come out. This ain't charity, but if you ever took it, you don't forget it. I bet Jessie ain't ever done it."

"No, I ain't," said Jessie.

"Well, I did," Annie said. "Las' winter; an' we was a-starvin'—me an' Pa an' the little fellas. An' it was a-rainin'. Fella tol' us to go to the Salvation Army." Her eyes grew fierce. "We was hungry—they made us crawl for our dinner. They took our dignity. They—I hate 'em! An'—maybe Mis' Joyce took charity. Maybe she didn' know this ain't charity. Mis' Joad, we don't allow nobody in this camp to build their-self up that-a-way. We don't allow nobody to give nothing to another person. They can give it to the camp, an' the camp can pass it out. We won't have no charity!" Her voice was fierce and hoarse. "I hate 'em," she said. "I ain't never seen my man beat before, but them—them Salvation Army done it to 'im."

Jessie nodded. "I heard," she said softly, "I heard. We got to take Mis' Joad aroun'."

Ma said, "It sure is nice."

"Le's go to the sewin' room," Annie suggested. "Got two machines. They's a-quiltin', an' they're makin' dresses. You might like ta work over there."

When the committee called on Ma, Ruthie and Winfield faded imperceptibly back out of reach.

"Whyn't we go along an' listen?" Winfield asked.

Ruthie gripped his arm. "No," she said. "We got washed for them sons-a-bitches. I ain't goin' with 'em."

Winfield said, "You tol' on me 'bout the toilet. I'm a-gonna tell what you called them ladies."

A shadow of fear crossed Ruthie's face. "Don' do it. I tol' 'cause I knowed you didn' really break it."

"You did not," said Winfield.

Ruthie said, "Le's look aroun'." They strolled down the line of tents, peering into each one, gawking self-consciously. At the end of the unit there was a level place on which a croquet court had been set up. Half a dozen children played seriously. In front of a tent an elderly lady sat on a bench and watched. Ruthie and Winfield broke into a trot. "Leave us play," Ruthie cried. "Leave us get in."

The children looked up. A pig-tailed little girl said, "Nex' game you kin."

"I wanta play now," Ruthie cried.

"Well, you can't. Not till nex' game."

Ruthie moved menacingly out on the court. "I'm a-gonna play." The pig-tails gripped her mallet tightly. Ruthie sprang at her, slapped her, pushed her, and wrested the mallet from her hands. "I says I was gonna play," she said triumphantly.

The elderly lady stood up and walked onto the court. Ruthie scowled fiercely and her hands tightened on the mallet. The lady said, "Let her play—like you done with Ralph las' week."

The children laid their mallets on the ground and trooped silently off the court. They stood at a distance and looked on with expressionless eyes. Ruthie watched them go. Then she hit a ball and ran after it. "Come on, Winfiel'. Get a stick," she called. And then she looked in amazement. Winfield had joined the watching children, and he too looked at her with expressionless eyes. Defiantly she hit the ball again. She kicked up a great dust. She pretended to have a good time. And the children stood and watched. Ruthie lined up two balls and hit both of them, and she turned her back on the watching eyes, and then turned back. Suddenly she advanced on them, mallet in hand. "You come an' play," she demanded. They moved silently back at her approach. For a moment she stared at them, and then she flung down the mallet and ran crying for home. The children walked back on the court.

Pigtails said to Winfield, "You can git in the nex' game."

The watching lady warned them, "When she comes back an' wants to be decent, you let her. You was mean yourself, Amy." The game went on, while in the Joad tent Ruthie wept miserably.

The truck moved along the beautiful roads, past orchards where the peaches were beginning to color, past vineyards with the clusters pale and green, under lines of walnut trees whose branches spread half across the road. At each entrance-gate Al slowed; and at each gate there was a sign: "No help wanted. No trespassing."

Al said, "Pa, they's boun' to be work when them fruits gets

ready. Funny place—they tell ya they ain't no work 'fore you ask 'em." He drove slowly on.

Pa said, "Maybe we could go in anyways an' ask if they know where they's any work. Might do that."

A man in blue overalls and a blue shirt walked along the edge of the road. Al pulled up beside him. "Hey, mister," Al said. "Know where they's any work?"

The man stopped and grinned, and his mouth was vacant of front teeth. "No," he said. "Do you? I been walkin' all week, an' I can't tree none."

"Live in that gov'ment camp?" Al asked.

"Yeah!"

"Come on, then. Git up back, an' we'll all look." The man climbed over the side-boards and dropped in the bed.

Pa said, "I ain't got no hunch we'll find work. Guess we got to look, though. We don't even know where-at to look."

"Shoulda talked to the fellas in the camp," Al said. "How you feelin', Uncle John?"

"I ache," said Uncle John. "I ache all over, an' I got it comin'. I oughta go away where I won't bring down punishment on my own folks."

Pa put his hand on John's knee. "Look here," he said, "don' you go away. We're droppin' folks all the time— Grampa an' Granma dead, Noah an' Connie—run out, an' the preacher—in jail."

"I got a hunch we'll see that preacher agin," John said.

Al fingered the ball on the gear-shift lever. "You don' feel good enough to have no hunches," he said. "The hell with it. Le's go back an' talk, an' find out where they's some work. We're jus' huntin' skunks under water." He stopped the truck and leaned out the window and called back, "Hey! Lookie! We're a-goin' back to the camp an' try an' see where they's work. They ain't no use burnin' gas like this."

The man leaned over the truck side. "Suits me," he said. "My dogs is wore clean up to the ankle. An' I ain't even got a nibble."

Al turned around in the middle of the road and headed back.

Pa said, "Ma's gonna be purty hurt, 'specially when Tom got work so easy."

"Maybe he never got none," Al said. "Maybe he jus' went lookin', too. I wisht I could get work in a garage. I'd learn that stuff quick, an' I'd like it."

Pa grunted, and they drove back toward the camp in silence.

When the committee left, Ma sat down on a box in front of the Joad tent, and she looked helplessly at Rose of Sharon. "Well—" she said, "well—I ain't been so perked up in years. *Wasn't* them ladies nice?"

"I get to work in the nursery," Rose of Sharon said. "They tol' me. I can find out all how to do for babies, an' then I'll know."

Ma nodded in wonder. "Wouldn' it be nice if the menfolks all got work?" she asked. "Them a-workin', an' a little money comin' in?" Her eyes wandered into space. "Them a-workin', an' us a-workin' here, an' all them nice people. Fust thing we get a little ahead I'd get me a little stove—nice one. They don' cost much. An' then we'd get a tent, big enough, an' maybe secon'-han' springs for the beds. An' we'd use this here tent jus' to eat under. An' Sat'dy night we'll go to the dancin'. They says you can invite folks if you want. I wisht we had some frien's to invite. Maybe the men'll know somebody to invite."

Rose of Sharon peered down the road. "That lady that says I'll lose the baby—" she began.

"Now you stop that," Ma warned her.

Rose of Sharon said softly, "I seen her. She's a-comin' here, I think. Yeah! Here she comes. Ma, don' let her——"

Ma turned and looked at the approaching figure.

"Howdy," the woman said. "I'm Mis' Sandry—Lisbeth Sandry. I seen your girl this mornin'."

"Howdy do," said Ma.

"Are you happy in the Lord?"

"Pretty happy," said Ma.

"Are you saved?"

"I been saved." Ma's face was closed and waiting.

"Well, I'm glad," Lisbeth said. "The sinners is awful strong aroun' here. You come to a awful place. They's wicketness all around about. Wicket people, wicket goin's-on that a lamb'-

blood Christian jes' can't hardly stan'. They's sinners all around us."

Ma colored a little, and shut her mouth tightly. "Seems to me they's nice people here," she said shortly.

Mrs. Sandry's eyes stared. "Nice!" she cried. "You think they're nice when they's dancin' an' huggin'? I tell ya, ya eternal soul ain't got a chancet in this here camp. Went out to a meetin' in Weedpatch las' night. Know what the preacher says? He says, 'They's wicketness in that camp.' He says, 'The poor is tryin' to be rich.' He says, 'They's dancin' an' huggin' when they should be wailin' an' moanin' in sin.' That's what he says. 'Ever'body that ain't here is a black sinner,' he says. I tell you it made a person feel purty good to hear 'im. An' we knowed we was safe. We ain't danced."

Ma's face was red. She stood up slowly and faced Mrs. Sandry. "Git!" she said. "Git out now, 'fore I git to be a sinner a-tellin' you where to go. Git to your wailin' an' moanin'."

Mrs. Sandry's mouth dropped open. She stepped back. And then she became fierce. "I thought you was Christians."

"So we are," Ma said.

"No, you ain't. You're hell-burnin' sinners, all of you! An' I'll mention it in meetin', too. I can see your black soul a-burnin'. I can see that innocent chile in that there girl's belly a-burnin'."

A low wailing cry escaped from Rose of Sharon's lips. Ma stooped down and picked up a stick of wood.

"Git!" she said coldly. "Don' you never come back. I seen your kind before. You'd take the little pleasure, wouldn' you?" Ma advanced on Mrs. Sandry.

For a moment the woman backed away and then suddenly she threw back her head and howled. Her eyes rolled up, her shoulders and arms flopped loosely at her side, and a string of thick ropy saliva ran from the corner of her mouth. She howled again and again, long deep animal howls. Men and women ran up from the other tents, and they stood near—frightened and quiet. Slowly the woman sank to her knees and the howls sank to a shuddering, bubbling moan. She fell sideways and her arms and legs twitched. The white eyeballs showed under the open eyelids.

A man said softly, "The sperit. She got the sperit." Ma stood looking down at the twitching form.

The little manager strolled up casually. "Trouble?" he asked. The crowd parted to let him through. He looked down at the woman. "Too bad," he said. "Will some of you help get her back to her tent?" The silent people shuffled their feet. Two men bent over and lifted the woman, one held her under the arms and the other took her feet. They carried her away, and the people moved slowly after them. Rose of Sharon went under the tarpaulin and lay down and covered her face with a blanket.

The manager looked at Ma, looked down at the stick in her hand. He smiled tiredly. "Did you clout her?" he asked.

Ma continued to stare after the retreating people. She shook her head slowly. "No—but I would a. Twicet today she worked my girl up."

The manager said, "Try not to hit her. She isn't well. She just isn't well." And he added softly, "I wish she'd go away, and all her family. She brings more trouble on the camp than all the rest together."

Ma got herself in hand again. "If she comes back, I might hit her. I ain't sure. I won't let her worry my girl no more."

"Don't worry about it, Mrs. Joad," he said. "You won't ever see her again. She works over the newcomers. She won't ever come back. She thinks you're a sinner."

"Well, I am," said Ma.

"Sure. Everybody is, but not the way she means. She isn't well, Mrs. Joad."

Ma looked at him gratefully, and she called, "You hear that, Rosasharn? She ain't well. She's crazy." But the girl did not raise her head. Ma said, "I'm warnin' you, mister. If she comes back, I ain't to be trusted. I'll hit her."

He smiled wryly. "I know how you feel," he said. "But just try not to. That's all I ask—just try not to." He walked slowly away toward the tent where Mrs. Sandry had been carried.

Ma went into the tent and sat down beside Rose of Sharon. "Look up," she said. The girl lay still. Ma gently lifted the blanket from her daughter's face. "That woman's kinda crazy," she said. "Don't you believe none of them things."

Rose of Sharon whispered in terror, "When she said about burnin', I—felt burnin'."

"That ain't true," said Ma.

"I'm tar'd out," the girl whispered. "I'm tar'd a things happenin'. I wanta sleep. I wanta sleep."

"Well, you sleep, then. This here's a nice place. You can sleep."

"But she might come back."

"She won't," said Ma. "I'm a-gonna set right outside, an' I won't let her come back. Res' up now, 'cause you got to get to work in the nu'sery purty soon."

Ma struggled to her feet and went to sit in the entrance to the tent. She sat on a box and put her elbows on her knees and her chin in her cupped hands. She saw the movement in the camp, heard the voices of the children, the hammering on an iron rim; but her eyes were staring ahead of her.

Pa, coming back along the road, found her there, and he squatted near her. She looked slowly over at him. "Git work?" she asked.

"No," he said, ashamed. "We looked."

"Where's Al and John and the truck?"

"Al's fixin' somepin. Had ta borry some tools. Fella says Al got to fix her there."

Ma said sadly, "This here's a nice place. We could be happy here awhile."

"If we could get work."

"Yeah! If you could get work."

He felt her sadness, and studied her face. "What you a-mopin' about? If it's sech a nice place why have you got to mope?"

She gazed at him, and she closed her eyes slowly. "Funny, ain't it. All the time we was a-movin' an' shovin', I never thought none. An' now these here folks been nice to me, been awful nice; an' what's the first thing I do? I go right back over the sad things—that night Grampa died an' we buried him. I was all full up of the road, and bumpin' and movin', an' it wasn't so bad. But I come out here, an' it's worse now. An' Granma—an' Noah walkin' away like that! Walkin' away jus' down the river. Them things was part of all, an' now they come a-flockin' back. Granma a pauper, an' buried a pauper. That's sharp now. That's awful sharp. An' Noah walkin' away down the river. He don' know what's there. He jus' don' know. An' we don' know. We ain't never gonna know if he's alive or dead. Never gonna know. An' Connie sneakin' away. I didn' give 'em brain room before, but now they're a-flockin' back. An' I oughta be glad 'cause we're in a nice place." Pa watched her mouth while she talked. Her eyes were closed. "I can remember how them mountains was, sharp as ol' teeth beside the river where Noah walked. I can remember how the stubble was on the groun' where Grampa lies. I can remember the choppin' block back home with a feather caught on it, all criss-crossed with cuts, an' black with chicken blood."

Pa's voice took on her tone. "I seen the ducks today," he said. "Wedgin' south—high up. Seems like they're awful dinky. An' I seen the blackbirds a-settin' on the wires, an' the doves was on the fences." Ma opened her eyes and looked at him. He went on, "I seen a little whirlwin', like a man a-spinnin' acrost a fiel'. An' the ducks drivin' on down, wedgin' on down to the southward."

Ma smiled. "Remember?" she said. "Remember what we'd always say at home? 'Winter's a-comin' early,' we said, when the ducks flew. Always said that, an' winter come when it was ready to come. But we always said, 'She's a-comin' early.' I wonder what we meant."

"I seen the blackbirds on the wires," said Pa. "Settin' so close together. An' the doves. Nothin' sets so still as a dove—on the fence wires—maybe two, side by side. An' this little whirlwin'—big as a man, an' dancin' off acrost a fiel'. Always did like the little fellas, big as a man."

"Wisht I wouldn't think how it is home," said Ma. "It ain't our home no more. Wisht I'd forget it. An' Noah."

"He wasn't ever right—I mean—well, it was my fault."

"I tol' you never to say that. Wouldn' a lived at all, maybe."

"But I should a knowed more."

"Now stop," said Ma. "Noah was strange. Maybe he'll have a nice time by the river. Maybe it's better so. We can't do no worryin'. This here is a nice place, an' maybe you'll get work right off."

Pa pointed at the sky. "Look—more ducks. Big bunch. An' Ma, 'Winter's a-comin' early.'"

She chuckled. "They's things you do, an' you don' know why."

"Here's John," said Pa. "Come on an' set, John."

Uncle John joined them. He squatted down in front of Ma. "We didn' get nowheres," he said. "Jus' run aroun'. Say, Al wants to see ya. Says he got to git a tire. Only one layer a cloth lef', he says."

Pa stood up. "I hope he can git her cheap. We ain't got much lef'. Where is Al?"

"Down there, go the nex' cross-street an' turn right. Says gonna blow out an' spoil a tube if we don' get a new one." Pa strolled away, and his eyes followed the giant V of ducks down the sky.

Uncle John picked a stone from the ground and dropped it from his palm and picked it up again. He did not look at Ma. "They ain't no work," he said.

"You didn' look all over," Ma said.

"No, but they's signs out."

"Well, Tom musta got work. He ain't been back."

Uncle John suggested, "Maybe he went away—like Connie, or like Noah."

Ma glanced sharply at him, and then her eyes softened. "They's things you know," she said. "They's stuff you're sure of. Tom's got work, an' he'll come in this evenin'. That's true." She smiled in satisfaction. "Ain't he a fine boy!" she said. "Ain't he a good boy!"

The cars and trucks began to come into the camp, and the men trooped by toward the sanitary unit. And each man carried clean overalls and shirt in his hand.

Ma pulled herself together. "John, you go find Pa. Get to the store. I want beans an' sugar an'—a piece of fryin' meat an' carrots an'—tell Pa to get somepin nice—anything—but nice—for tonight. Tonight—we'll have—somepin nice."

Chapter Twenty-Three

THE MIGRANT PEOPLE, scuttling for work, scrabbling to live, looked always for pleasure, dug for pleasure, manufactured pleasure, and they were hungry for amusement. Sometimes amusement lay in speech, and they climbed up their lives with jokes. And it came about in the camps along the roads, on the ditch banks beside the streams, under the sycamores, that the story teller grew into being, so that the people gathered in the low firelight to hear the gifted ones. And they listened while the tales were told, and their participation made the stories great.

I was a recruit against Geronimo——

And the people listened, and their quiet eyes reflected the dying fire.

Them Injuns was cute—slick as snakes, an' quiet when they wanted. Could go through dry leaves, an' make no rustle. Try to do that sometime.

And the people listened and remembered the crash of dry leaves under their feet.

Come the change of season an' the clouds up. Wrong time. Ever hear of the army doing anything right? Give the army ten chances, an' they'll stumble along. Took three regiments to kill a hundred braves—always.

And the people listened, and their faces were quiet with listening. The story tellers, gathering attention into their tales, spoke in great rhythms, spoke in great words because the tales were great, and the listeners became great through them.

They was a brave on a ridge, against the sun. Knowed he stood out. Spread his arms an' stood. Naked as morning, an' against the sun. Maybe he was crazy. I don' know. Stood there, arms spread out; like a cross he looked. Four hunderd yards. An' the men—well, they raised their sights an' they felt the wind with their fingers; an' then they jus' lay there an' couldn' shoot. Maybe that Injun knowed somepin. Knowed we couldn' shoot. Jes' laid there with the rifles cocked, an' didn' even put 'em to our shoulders. Lookin' at him. Headband, one feather. Could see it, an' naked as the sun. Long time we laid there an' looked, an' he never moved. An' then the captain got mad. "Shoot, you crazy bastards, shoot!" he yells. An' we jus' laid there. "I'll give you to a five-count, an' then mark you down," the captain says. Well, sir—we put up our rifles slow, an' ever' man hoped somebody'd shoot first. I ain't never been so sad in my life. An' I laid my sights on his belly, 'cause you can't stop a Injun no other place—an'—then. Well, he jest plunked down an' rolled. An' we went up. An' he wasn' big—he'd looked so grand—up there. All tore to pieces an' little. Ever see a cock pheasant, stiff and beautiful, ever' feather drawed an' painted, an' even his eyes drawed in pretty? An' bang! You pick him up—bloody an' twisted, an' you spoiled him—you spoiled somepin better'n you; an' eatin' him don't never make it up to you, 'cause you spoiled somepin in yaself, an' you can't never fix it up.

And the people nodded, and perhaps the fire spurted a little light and showed their eyes looking in on themselves.

Against the sun, with his arms out. An' he looked big—as God.

And perhaps a man balanced twenty cents between food and pleasure, and he went to a movie in Marysville or Tulare, in Ceres or Mountain View. And he came back to the ditch camp with his memory crowded. And he told how it was:

They was this rich fella, an' he makes like he's poor, an' they's this rich girl, an' she purtends like she's poor too, an' they meet in a hamburg' stan'.

Why?

I don't know why—that's how it was.

Why'd they purtend like they's poor?

Well, they're tired of bein' rich.

Horseshit!

You want to hear this, or not?

Well, go on then. Sure, I wanta hear it, but if I was rich I'd git so many pork chops—I'd cord 'em up aroun' me like wood, an' I'd eat my way out. Go on.

Well, they each think the other one's poor. An' they git arrested an' they git in jail, an' they don' git out 'cause the other one'd find out the first one is rich. An' the jail keeper, he's mean to 'em 'cause he thinks they're poor. Oughta see how he looks when he finds out. Jes' nearly faints, that's all.

What they git in jail for?

Well, they git caught at some kind a radical meetin' but they ain't radicals. They jes' happen to be there. An' they don't each one wanta marry fur money, ya see.

So the sons-of-bitches start lyin' to each other right off.

Well, in the pitcher it was like they was doin' good. They're nice to people, you see.

I was to a show oncet that was me, an' more'n me; an' my life, an' more'n my life, so ever'thing was bigger.

Well, I git enough sorrow. I like to git away from it.

Sure—if you can believe it.

So they got married, an' then they foun' out, an' all them people that's treated 'em mean. They was a fella had been uppity, an' he nearly fainted when this fella come in with a plug hat on. Jes' nearly fainted. An' they was a newsreel with them German soldiers kickin' up their feet—funny as hell.

And always, if he had a little money, a man could get drunk. The hard edges gone, and the warmth. Then there was no loneliness, for a man could people his brain with friends, and he could find his enemies and destroy them. Sitting in a ditch, the earth grew soft under him. Failures dulled and the future was no threat. And hunger did not skulk about, but the world was soft and easy, and a man could reach the place he started for. The stars came down wonderfully close and the sky was soft. Death was a friend, and sleep was death's brother. The old times came back—dear and warm. A girl with pretty feet, who danced one time at home. A horse—a long time ago. A horse and a saddle. And the leather was carved. When was that? Ought to find a girl to talk to. That's nice. Might lay with her, too. But warm here. And the stars down so close, and sadness and pleasure so close together, really the same thing. Like to stay drunk all the time. Who says it's bad? Who dares to say it's bad? Preachers—but they got their own kinda drunkenness. Thin, barren women, but they're too miserable to know. Reformers—but they don't bite deep enough into living to know. No—the stars are close and dear and I have joined the brotherhood of the worlds. And everything's holy—everything, even me.

A harmonica is easy to carry. Take it out of your hip pocket, knock it against your palm to shake out the dirt and pocket fuzz and bits of tobacco. Now it's ready. You can do anything with a harmonica: thin reedy single tone, or chords, or melody with rhythm chords. You can mold the music with curved hands, making it wail and cry like bagpipes, making it full and round like an organ, making it as sharp and bitter as the reed pipes of the hills. And you can play and put it back in your pocket. It is always with you, always in your pocket. And as you play, you learn new tricks, new ways to mold the tone with your hands, to pinch the tone with your lips, and no one teaches you. You feel around—sometimes alone in the shade at noon, sometimes in the tent door after supper when the women are washing up. Your foot taps gently on the ground. Your eyebrows rise and fall in rhythm. And if you lose it or break it, why, it's no great loss. You can buy another for a quarter.

A guitar is more precious. Must learn this thing. Fingers of the left hand must have callus caps. Thumb of the right hand a horn of callus. Stretch the left-hand fingers, stretch them like a spider's legs to get the hard pads on the frets.

This was my father's box. Wasn't no bigger'n a bug first time he give me C chord. An' when I learned as good as him, he hardly never played no more. Used to set in the door, an' listen an' tap his foot. I'm tryin' for a break, an' he'd scowl mean till I get her, an' then he'd settle back easy, an' he'd nod. "Play," he'd say. "Play nice." It's a good box. See how the head is wore. They's many a million songs wore down that wood an' scooped her out. Some day she'll cave in like a egg. But you can't patch her nor worry her no way or she'll lose tone. Play her in the evening, an' they's a harmonica player in the nex' tent. Makes it pretty nice together.

The fiddle is rare, hard to learn. No frets, no teacher.

Jes' listen to a ol' man an' try to pick it up. Won't tell how to double. Says it's a secret. But I watched. Here's how he done it.

Shrill as a wind, the fiddle, quick and nervous and shrill.

She ain't much of a fiddle. Give two dollars for her. Fella says they's fiddles four hundred years old, and they git mellow like whisky. Says they'll cost fifty-sixty thousan' dollars. I don' know. Soun's like a lie. Harsh ol' bastard, ain't she? Wanta dance? I'll rub up the bow with plenty rosin. Man! Then she'll squawk. Hear her a mile.

These three in the evening, harmonica and fiddle and guitar. Playing a reel and tapping out the tune, and the big deep strings of the guitar beating like a heart, and the harmonica's sharp chords and the skirl and squeal of the fiddle. People have to move close. They can't help it. "Chicken Reel" now, and the feet tap and a young lean buck takes three quick steps, and his arms hang limp. The square closes up and the dancing starts, feet on the bare ground, beating dull, strike with your heels. Hands 'round and swing. Hair falls down, and panting breaths. Lean to the side now.

Look at that Texas boy, long legs loose, taps four times for ever' damn step. Never seen a boy swing aroun' like that. Look at him swing that Cherokee girl, red in her cheeks an' her toe points out. Look at her pant, look at her heave. Think she's tired? Think she's winded? Well, she ain't. Texas boy got his hair in his eyes, mouth's wide open, can't get air, but he pats four times for ever' darn step, an' he'll keep a-going' with the Cherokee girl.

The fiddle squeaks and the guitar bongs. Mouth-organ man is red in the face. Texas boy and the Cherokee girl, pantin' like dogs an' a-beatin' the groun'. Ol' folks stan' a-pattin' their han's. Smilin' a little, tappin' their feet.

Back home—in the schoolhouse, it was. The big moon sailed off to the westward. An' we walked, him an' me—a little ways. Didn' talk 'cause our throats was choked up. Didn' talk none at all. An' purty soon they was a haycock. Went right to it and laid down there. Seein' the Texas boy an' that girl a-steppin' away into the dark—think nobody seen 'em go. Oh, God! I wisht I was a-goin' with that Texas boy. Moon'll be up 'fore long. I seen that girl's ol' man move out to stop 'em, an' then he didn'. He knowed. Might as well stop the fall from comin', and might as well stop the sap from movin' in the trees. An' the moon'll be up 'fore long.

Play more—play the story songs—"As I Walked through the Streets of Laredo."

The fire's gone down. Be a shame to build her up. Little ol' moon'll be up 'fore long.

Beside an irrigation ditch a preacher labored and the people cried. And the preacher paced like a tiger, whipping the people with his voice, and they groveled and whined on the ground. He calculated them, gauged them, played on them, and when they were all squirming on the ground he stooped down and of his great strength he picked each one up in his arms and shouted, Take 'em, Christ! and threw each one in the water. And when they were all in, waist deep in the water, and looking with frightened eyes at the master, he knelt down on the bank and he prayed for them; and he prayed that all men and women might grovel and whine on the ground. Men and women, dripping, clothes sticking tight, watched; then gurgling and sloshing in their shoes they walked back to the camp, to the tents, and they talked softly in wonder:

We been saved, they said. We're washed white as snow. We won't never sin again.

And the children, frightened and wet, whispered together: We been saved. We won't sin no more.

Wisht I knowed what all the sins was, so I could do 'em.

The migrant people looked humbly for pleasure on the roads.

Chapter Twenty-Four

O N SATURDAY MORNING the wash tubs were crowded. The women washed dresses, pink ginghams and flowered cottons, and they hung them in the sun and stretched the cloth to smooth it. When afternoon came the whole camp quickened and the people grew excited. The children caught the fever and were more noisy than usual. About mid-afternoon child bathing began, and as each child was caught, subdued, and washed, the noise on the playground gradually subsided. Before five, the children were scrubbed and warned about getting dirty again; and they walked about, stiff in clean clothes, miserable with carefulness.

At the big open-air dance platform a committee was busy. Every bit of electric wire had been requisitioned. The city dump had been visited for wire, every tool box had contributed friction tape. And now the patched, spliced wire was strung out to the dance floor, with bottle necks as insulators. This night the floor would be lighted for the first time. By six o'clock the men were back from work or from looking for work, and a new wave of bathing started. By seven, dinners were over, men had on their best clothes: freshly washed overalls, clean blue shirts, sometimes the decent blacks. The girls were ready in their print dresses, stretched and clean, their hair braided and ribboned. The worried women watched the families and cleaned up the evening dishes. On the platform the string band practiced, surrounded by a double wall of children. The people were intent and excited.

In the tent of Ezra Huston, chairman, the Central Committee of five men went into meeting. Huston, a tall spare man, wind-blackened, with eyes like little blades, spoke to his committee, one man from each sanitary unit.

"It's goddamn lucky we got the word they was gonna try to bust up the dance!" he said.

The tubby little representative from Unit Three spoke up. "I think we oughta squash the hell out of 'em, an' show 'em."

"No," said Huston. "That's what they want. No, sir. If they can git a fight goin', then they can run in the cops an' say we ain't orderly. They tried it before—other places." He turned to the sad dark boy from Unit Two. "Got the fellas together to go roun' the fences an' see nobody sneaks in?"

The sad boy nodded. "Yeah! Twelve. Tol' 'em not to hit nobody. Jes' push 'em out ag'in."

Huston said, "Will you go out an' find Willie Eaton? He's chairman a the entertainment, ain't he?"

"Yeah."

"Well, tell 'im we wanta see 'im."

The boy went out, and he returned in a moment with a stringy Texas man. Willie Eaton had a long fragile jaw and dust-colored hair. His arms and legs were long and loose, and he had the gray sunburned eyes of the Panhandle. He stood in the tent, grinning, and his hands pivoted restlessly on his wrists.

Huston said, "You heard about tonight?"

Willie grinned. "Yeah!"

"Did anything 'bout it?"

"Yeah!"

"Tell what you done."

Willie Eaton grinned happily. "Well, sir, ordinary ent'tainment committee is five. I got twenty more—all good strong boys. They're a-gonna be a-dancin' an' a-keepin' their eyes open an' their ears open. First sign—any talk or argament, they close in tight. Worked her out purty nice. Can't even see nothing. Kinda move out, an' the fella will go out with 'em."

"Tell 'em they ain't to hurt the fellas."

Willie laughed gleefully. "I tol' 'em," he said.

"Well, tell 'em so they know."

"They know. Got five men out to the gate lookin' over the folks that comes in. Try to spot 'em 'fore they git started."

Huston stood up. His steel-colored eyes were stern. "Now you look here, Willie. We don't want them fellas hurt. They's gonna be deputies out by the front gate. If you blood 'em up, why—them deputies'll git you."

"Got that there figgered out," said Willie. "Take 'em out the back way, into the fiel'. Some a the boys'll see they git on their way."

"Well, it soun's awright," Huston said worriedly. "But don't you let nothing happen, Willie. You're responsible.

Don' you hurt them fellas. Don' you use no stick nor no knife or arn, or nothing like that."

"No, sir," said Willie. "We won't mark 'em."

Huston was suspicious. "I wisht I knowed I could trus' you, Willie. If you got to sock 'em, sock 'em where they won't bleed."

"Yes, sir!" said Willie.

"You sure of the fellas you picked?"

"Yes, sir."

"Awright. An' if she gits outa han', I'll be in the right-han' corner, this way on the dance floor."

Willie saluted in mockery and went out.

Huston said, "I dunno. I jes' hope Willie's boys don't kill nobody. What the hell the deputies want to hurt the camp for? Why can't they let us be?"

The sad boy from Unit Two said, "I lived out at Sunlan' Lan' an' Cattle Company's place. Honest to God, they got a cop for ever' ten people. Got one water faucet for 'bout two hundred people."

The tubby man said, "Jesus, God, Jeremy. You ain't got to tell me. I was there. They got a block of shacks—thirty-five of 'em in a row, an' fifteen deep. An' they got ten crappers for the whole shebang. An', Christ, you could smell 'em a mile. One of them deputies give me the lowdown. We was settin' aroun', an' he says, 'Them goddamn gov'ment camps,' he says. 'Give people hot water, an' they gonna want hot water. Give 'em flush toilets, an' they gonna want 'em.' He says, 'You give them goddamn Okies stuff like that an' they'll want 'em.' An' he says, 'They hol' red meetin's in them gov'ment camps. All figgerin' how to git on relief,' he says."

Huston asked, "Didn' nobody sock him?"

"No. They was a little fella, an' he says, 'What you mean, relief?'

" 'I mean relief—what us taxpayers put in an' you goddamn Okies takes out.'

" 'We pay sales tax an' gas tax an' tobacco tax,' this little guy says. An' he says, 'Farmers get four cents a cotton poun' from the gov'ment—ain't that relief?' An' he says,

'Railroads an' shippin' companies draws subsidies—ain't that relief?'

" 'They're doin' stuff got to be done,' this deputy says.

" 'Well,' the little guy says, 'how'd your goddamn crops get picked if it wasn't for us?' " The tubby man looked around.

"What'd the deputy say?" Huston asked.

"Well, the deputy got mad. An' he says, 'You goddamn reds is all the time stirrin' up trouble,' he says. 'You better come along with me.' So he takes this little guy in, an' they give him sixty days in jail for vagrancy."

"How'd they do that if he had a job?" asked Timothy Wallace.

The tubby man laughed. "You know better'n that," he said. "You know a vagrant is anybody a cop don't like. An' that's why they hate this here camp. No cops can get in. This here's United States, not California."

Huston sighed. "Wisht we could stay here. Got to be goin' 'fore long. I like this here. Folks gits along nice; an', God Awmighty, why can't they let us do it 'stead of keepin' us miserable an' puttin' us in jail? I swear to God they gonna push us into fightin' if they don't quit a-worryin' us." Then he calmed his voice. "We jes' got to keep peaceful," he reminded himself. "The committee got no right to fly off'n the handle."

The tubby man from Unit Three said, "Anybody that thinks this committee got all cheese an' crackers ought to jes' try her. They was a fight in my unit today—women. Got to callin' names, an' then got to throwin' garbage. Ladies' Committee couldn' handle it, an' they come to me. Want me to bring the fight in this here committee. I tol' 'em they got to handle women trouble theirselves. This here committee ain't gonna mess with no garbage fights."

Huston nodded. "You done good," he said.

And now the dusk was falling, and as the darkness deepened the practicing of the string band seemed to grow louder. The lights flashed on and two men inspected the patched wire to the dance floor. The children crowded thickly about the musicians. A boy with a guitar sang the "Down Home Blues," chording delicately for himself, and on his second chorus three harmonicas and a fiddle joined him. From the tents the people streamed toward the platform, men in their clean blue denim and women in their ginghams. They came near to the platform and then stood quietly waiting, their faces bright and intent under the light.

Around the reservation there was a high wire fence, and along the fence, at intervals of fifty feet, the guards sat in the grass and waited.

Now the cars of the guests began to arrive, small farmers and their families, migrants from other camps. And as each guest came through the gate he mentioned the name of the camper who had invited him.

The string band took a reel tune up and played loudly, for they were not practicing any more. In front of their tents the Jesus-lovers sat and watched, their faces hard and contemptuous. They did not speak to one another, they watched for sin, and their faces condemned the whole proceeding.

At the Joad tent Ruthie and Winfield had bolted what little dinner they had, and then they started for the platform. Ma called them back, held up their faces with a hand under each chin, and looked into their nostrils, pulled their ears and looked inside, and sent them to the sanitary unit to wash their hands once more. They dodged around the back of the building and bolted for the platform, to stand among the children, close-packed about the band.

Al finished his dinner and spent half an hour shaving with Tom's razor. Al had a tight-fitting wool suit and a striped shirt, and he bathed and washed and combed his straight hair back. And when the washroom was vacant for a moment, he smiled engagingly at himself in the mirror, and he turned and tried to see himself in profile when he smiled. He slipped his purple arm-bands on and put on his tight coat. And he rubbed up his yellow shoes with a piece of toilet paper. A late bather came in, and Al hurried out and walked recklessly toward the platform, his eye peeled for girls. Near the dance floor he saw a pretty blond girl sitting in front of a tent. He sidled near and threw open his coat to show his shirt.

"Gonna dance tonight?" he asked.

The girl looked away and did not answer.

"Can't a fella pass a word with you? How 'bout you an' me dancin'?" And he said nonchalantly, "I can waltz."

The girl raised her eyes shyly, and she said, "That ain't nothin'—anybody can waltz."

"Not like me," said Al. The music surged, and he tapped one foot in time. "Come on," he said.

A very fat woman poked her head out of the tent and scowled at him. "You git along," she said fiercely. "This here girl's spoke for. She's a-gonna be married, an' her man's a-comin' for her."

Al winked rakishly at the girl, and he tripped on, striking his feet to the music and swaying his shoulders and swinging his arms. And the girl looked after him intently.

Pa put down his plate and stood up. "Come on, John," he said; and he explained to Ma, "We're a-gonna talk to some fellas about gettin' work." And Pa and Uncle John walked toward the manager's house.

Tom worked a piece of store bread into the stew gravy on his plate and ate the bread. He handed his plate to Ma, and she put it in the bucket of hot water and washed it and handed it to Rose of Sharon to wipe. "Ain't you goin' to the dance?" Ma asked.

"Sure," said Tom. "I'm on a committee. We're gonna entertain some fellas."

"Already on a committee?" Ma said. "I guess it's 'cause you got work."

Rose of Sharon turned to put the dish away. Tom pointed at her. "My God, she's a-gettin' big," he said.

Rose of Sharon blushed and took another dish from Ma. "Sure she is," Ma said.

"An' she's gettin' prettier," said Tom.

The girl blushed more deeply and hung her head. "You stop it," she said, softly.

" 'Course she is," said Ma. "Girl with a baby always gets prettier."

Tom laughed. "If she keeps a-swellin' like this, she gonna need a wheelbarra to carry it."

"Now you stop," Rose of Sharon said, and she went inside the tent, out of sight.

Ma chuckled, "You shouldn' ought to worry her."

"She likes it," said Tom.

"I know she likes it, but it worries her, too. And she's a-mournin' for Connie."

"Well, she might's well give him up. He's prob'ly studyin' to be President of the United States by now."

"Don't worry her," Ma said. "She ain't got no easy row to hoe."

Willie Eaton moved near, and he grinned and said, "You Tom Joad?"

"Yeah."

"Well, I'm Chairman the Entertainment Committee. We gonna need you. Fella tol' me 'bout you."

"Sure, I'll play with you," said Tom. "This here's Ma."

"Howdy," said Willie.

"Glad to meet ya."

Willie said, "Gonna put you on the gate to start, an' then on the floor. Want ya to look over the guys when they come in, an' try to spot 'em. You'll be with another fella. Then later I want ya to dance an' watch."

"Yeah! I can do that awright," said Tom.

Ma said apprehensively, "They ain't no trouble?"

"No, ma'am," Willie said. "They ain't gonna be no trouble."

"None at all," said Tom. "Well, I'll come 'long. See you at the dance, Ma." The two young men walked quickly away toward the main gate.

Ma piled the washed dishes on a box. "Come on out," she called, and when there was no answer, "Rosasharn, you come out."

The girl stepped from the tent, and she went on with the dish-wiping.

"Tom was on'y jollyin' ya."

"I know. I didn't mind; on'y I hate to have folks look at me."

"Ain't no way to he'p that. Folks gonna look. But it makes folks happy to see a girl in a fambly way—makes folks sort of giggly an' happy. Ain't you a-goin' to the dance?"

"I was—but I don' know. I wisht Connie was here." Her voice rose. "Ma, I wisht he was here. I can't hardly stan' it."

Ma looked closely at her. "I know," she said. "But, Rosa-sharn—don' shame your folks."

"I don' aim to, Ma."

"Well, don't you shame us. We got too much on us now, without no shame."

The girl's lip quivered. "I—I ain' goin' to the dance. I couldn'—Ma—he'p me!" She sat down and buried her head in her arms.

Ma wiped her hands on the dish towel and she squatted down in front of her daughter, and she put her two hands on Rose of Sharon's hair. "You're a good girl," she said. "You always was a good girl. I'll take care a you. Don't you fret." She put an interest in her tone. "Know what you an' me's gonna do? We're a-goin' to that dance, an' we're a-gonna set there an' watch. If anybody says to come dance—why, I'll say you ain't strong enough. I'll say you're poorly. An' you can hear the music an' all like that."

Rose of Sharon raised her head. "You won't let me dance?"

"No, I won't."

"An' don' let nobody touch me."

"No, I won't."

The girl sighed. She said desperately, "I don' know what I'm a-gonna do, Ma. I jus' don' know. I don' know."

Ma patted her knee. "Look," she said. "Look here at me. I'm a-gonna tell ya. In a little while it ain't gonna be so bad. In a little while. An' that's true. Now come on. We'll go get washed up, an' we'll put on our nice dress an' we'll set by the dance." She led Rose of Sharon toward the sanitary unit.

Pa and Uncle John squatted with a group of men by the porch of the office. "We nearly got work today," Pa said. "We was jus' a few minutes late. They awready got two fellas. An', well, sir, it was a funny thing. They's a straw boss there, an' he says, 'We jus' got some two-bit men. 'Course we could use twenty-cent men. We can use a lot a twenty-cent men. You go to your camp an' say we'll put a lot a fellas on for twenty cents.'"

The squatting men moved nervously. A broad-shouldered man, his face completely in the shadow of a black hat, spatted his knee with his palm. "I know it, goddamn it!" he cried.

"An' they'll git men. They'll git hungry men. You can't feed your fam'ly on twenty cents an hour, but you'll take anything. They got you goin' an' comin'. They jes' auction a job off. Jesus Christ, pretty soon they're gonna make us pay to work."

"We would of took her," Pa said. "We ain't had no job. We sure would a took her, but they was them guys in there, an' the way they looked, we was scairt to take her."

Black Hat said, "Get crazy thinkin'! I been workin' for a fella, an' he can't pick his crop. Cost more jes' to pick her than he can git for her, an' he don' know what to do."

"Seems to me—" Pa stopped. The circle was silent for him. "Well—I jus' thought, if a fella had a acre. Well, my woman she could raise a little truck an' a couple pigs an' some chickens. An' us men could get out an' find work, an' then go back. Kids could maybe go to school. Never seen sech schools as out here."

"Our kids ain't happy in them schools," Black Hat said.

"Why not? They're pretty nice, them schools."

"Well, a raggedy kid with no shoes, an' them other kids with socks on, an' nice pants, an' them a-yellin' 'Okie.' My boy went to school. Had a fight evr' day. Done good, too. Tough little bastard. Ever' day he got to fight. Come home with his clothes tore an' his nose bloody. An' his ma'd whale him. Made her stop that. No need ever'body beatin' the hell outa him, poor little fella. Jesus! He give some a them kids a goin'-over, though—them nice-pants sons-a-bitches. I dunno. I dunno."

Pa demanded, "Well, what the hell am I gonna do? We're outa money. One of my boys got a short job, but that won't feed us. I'm a-gonna go an' take twenty cents. I got to."

Black Hat raised his head, and his bristled chin showed in the light, and his stringy neck where the whiskers lay flat like fur. "Yeah!" he said bitterly. "You'll do that. An' I'm a two-bit man. You'll take my job for twenty cents. An' then I'll git hungry an' I'll take my job back for fifteen. Yeah! You go right on an' do her."

"Well, what the hell can I do?" Pa demanded. "I can't starve so's you can get two bits."

Black Hat dipped his head again, and his chin went into the shadow. "I dunno," he said. "I jes' dunno. It's bad enough to work twelve hours a day an' come out jes' a little bit hungry, but we got to figure all a time, too. My kid ain't gettin' enough to eat. I can't think all the time, goddamn it! It drives a man crazy." The circle of men shifted their feet nervously.

Tom stood at the gate and watched the people coming in to the dance. A floodlight shone down into their faces. Willie Eaton said, "Jes' keep your eyes open. I'm sendin' Jule Vitela over. He's half Cherokee. Nice fella. Keep your eyes open. An' see if you can pick out the ones."

"O.K.," said Tom. He watched the farm families come in, the girls with braided hair and the boys polished for the dance. Jule came and stood beside him.

"I'm with you," he said.

Tom looked at the hawk nose and the high brown cheek bones and the slender receding chin. "They says you're half Injun. You look all Injun to me."

"No," said Jule. "Jes' half. Wisht I was a full-blood. I'd have my lan' on the reservation. Them full-bloods got it pretty nice, some of 'em."

"Look a them people," Tom said.

The guests were moving in through the gateway, families from the farms, migrants from the ditch camps. Children straining to be free and quiet parents holding them back.

Jule said, "These here dances done funny things. Our people got nothing, but jes' because they can ast their frien's to come here to the dance, sets 'em up an' makes 'em proud. An' the folks respects 'em 'count of these here dances. Fella got a little place where I was a-workin'. He come to a dance here. I ast him myself, an' he come. Says we got the only decent dance in the county, where a man can take his girls an' his wife. Hey! Look."

Three young men were coming through the gate—young working men in jeans. They walked close together. The guard at the gate questioned them, and they answered and passed through.

"Look at 'em careful," Jule said. He moved to the guard. "Who ast them three?" he asked.

"Fella named Jackson, Unit Four."

Jule came back to Tom. "I think them's our fellas."

"How ya know?"

"I dunno how. Jes' got a feelin'. They're kinda scared. Foller 'em an' tell Willie to look 'em over, an' tell Willie to check with Jackson, Unit Four. Get him to see if they're all right. I'll stay here."

Tom strolled after the three young men. They moved toward the dance floor and took their positions quietly on the edge of the crowd. Tom saw Willie near the band and signaled him.

"What cha want?" Willie asked.

"Them three—see—there?"

"Yeah."

"They say a fella name' Jackson, Unit Four, ast 'em."

Willie craned his neck and saw Huston and called him over. "Them three fellas," he said. "We better get Jackson, Unit Four, an' see if he ast 'em."

Huston turned on his heel and walked away; and in a few moments he was back with a lean and bony Kansan. "This here's Jackson," Huston said. "Look, Jackson, see them three young fellas—?"

"Yeah."

"Well, did you ast 'em?"

"No."

"Ever see 'em before?"

Jackson peered at them. "Sure. Worked at Gregorio's with 'em."

"So they knowed your name."

"Sure. I worked right beside 'em."

"Awright," Huston said. "Don't you go near 'em. We ain't gonna th'ow 'em out if they're nice. Thanks, Mr. Jackson."

"Good work," he said to Tom. "I guess them's the fellas."

"Jule picked 'em out," said Tom.

"Hell, no wonder," said Willie. "His Injun blood smelled 'em. Well, I'll point 'em out to the boys."

A sixteen-year-old boy came running through the crowd. He stopped, panting, in front of Huston. "Mista Huston," he said. "I been like you said. They's a car with six men parked down by the euc'lyptus trees, an' they's one with four men up that north-side road. I ast 'em for a match. They got guns. I seen 'em."

Huston's eyes grew hard and cruel. "Willie," he said, "you sure you got ever'thing ready?"

Willie grinned happily. "Sure have, Mr. Huston. Ain't gonna be no trouble."

"Well, don't hurt 'em. 'Member now. If you kin, quiet an' nice, I kinda like to see 'em. Be in my tent."

"I'll see what we kin do," said Willie.

Dancing had not formally started, but now Willie climbed onto the platform. "Choose up your squares," he called. The music stopped. Boys and girls, young men and women, ran about until eight squares were ready on the big floor, ready and waiting. The girls held their hands in front of them and squirmed their fingers. The boys tapped their feet restlessly. Around the floor the old folks sat, smiling slightly, holding the children back from the floor. And in the distance the Jesus-lovers sat with hard condemning faces and watched the sin.

Ma and Rose of Sharon sat on a bench and watched. And as each boy asked Rose of Sharon as partner, Ma said, "No, she ain't well." And Rose of Sharon blushed and her eyes were bright.

The caller stepped to the middle of the floor and held up his hands. "All ready? Then let her go!"

The music snarled out "Chicken Reel," shrill and clear, fiddle skirling, harmonicas nasal and sharp, and the guitars booming on the bass strings. The caller named the turns, the squares moved. And they danced forward and back, hands 'round, swing your lady. The caller, in a frenzy, tapped his feet, strutted back and forth, went through the figures as he called them.

"Swing your ladies an' a dol ce do. Join han's roun' an' away we go." The music rose and fell, and the moving shoes beating in time on the paltform sounded like drums. "Swing to the right an' a swing to lef'; break, now—break—back to—back," the caller sang the high vibrant monotone. Now the girls' hair lost the careful combing. Now perspiration stood out on the foreheads of the boys. Now the experts showed the tricky inter-steps. And the old people on the edge of the floor took up the rhythm, patted their hands softly, and tapped their feet; and they smiled gently and then caught one another's eyes and nodded.

Ma leaned her head close to Rose of Sharon's ear. "Maybe you wouldn' think it, but your Pa was as nice a dancer as I ever seen, when he was young." And Ma smiled. "Makes me think of ol' times," she said. And on the faces of the watchers the smiles were of old times.

"Up near Muskogee twenty years ago, they was a blin' man with a fiddle——"

"I seen a fella oncet could slap his heels four times in one jump."

"Swedes up in Dakota—know what they do sometimes? Put pepper on the floor. Gits up the ladies' skirts an' makes 'em purty lively—lively as a filly in season. Swedes do that sometimes."

In the distance, the Jesus-lovers watched their restive children. "Look on sin," they said. "Them folks is ridin' to hell on a poker. It's a shame the godly got to see it." And their children were silent and nervous.

"One more roun' an' then a little res'," the caller chanted. "Hit her hard, 'cause we're gonna stop soon." And the girls were damp and flushed, and they danced with open mouths and serious reverent faces, and the boys flung back their long hair and pranced, pointed their toes, and clicked their heels. In and out the squares moved, crossing, backing, whirling, and the music shrilled.

Then suddenly it stopped. The dancers stood still, panting with fatigue. And the children broke from restraint, dashed on the floor, chased one another madly, ran, slid, stole caps, and pulled hair. The dancers sat down, fanning themselves with their hands. The members of the band got up and stretched themselves and sat down again. And the guitar players worked softly over their strings.

Now Willie called, "Choose again for another square, if you can." The dancers scrambled to their feet and new dancers plunged forward for partners. Tom stood near the three young men. He saw them force their way through, out on the floor, toward one of the forming squares. He waved his hand at Willie, and Willie spoke to the fiddler. The fiddler squawked his bow across the strings. Twenty young men lounged slowly across the floor. The three reached the square. And one of them said, "I'll dance with this here."

A blond boy looked up in astonishment. "She's my partner."

"Listen, you little son-of-a-bitch——"

Off in the darkness a shrill whistle sounded. The three were walled in now. And each one felt the grip of hands. And then the wall of men moved slowly off the platform.

Willie yelped, "Le's go!" The music shrilled out, the caller intoned the figures, the feet thudded on the platform.

A touring car drove to the entrance. The driver called, "Open up. We hear you got a riot."

The guard kept his position. "We got no riot. Listen to that music. Who are you?"

"Deputy sheriffs."

"Got a warrant?"

"We don't need a warrant if there's a riot."

"Well, we got no riots here," said the gate guard.

The men in the car listened to the music and the sound of the caller, and then the car pulled slowly away and parked in a crossroad and waited.

In the moving squad each of the three young men was pinioned, and a hand was over each mouth. When they reached the darkness the group opened up.

Tom said, "That sure was did nice." He held both arms of his victim from behind.

Willie ran over to them from the dance floor. "Nice work," he said. "On'y need six now. Huston wants to see these here fellers."

Huston himself emerged from the darkness. "These the ones?"

"Sure," said Jule. "Went right up an' started it. But they didn' even swing once."

"Let's look at 'em." The prisoners were swung around to face him. Their heads were down. Huston put a flashlight beam in each sullen face. "What did you wanta do it for?" he asked. There was no answer. "Who the hell tol' you to do it?"

"Goddarn it, we didn' do nothing. We was jes' gonna dance."

"No, you wasn't," Jule said. "You was gonna sock that kid."

Tom said, "Mr. Huston, jus' when these here fellas moved in, somebody give a whistle."

"Yeah, I know! The cops come right to the gate." He turned back. "We ain't gonna hurt you. Now who tol' you to come bus' up our dance?" He waited for a reply. "You're our own folks," Huston said sadly. "You belong with us. How'd you happen to come? We know all about it," he added.

"Well, goddamn it, a fella got to eat."

"Well, who sent you? Who paid you to come?"

"We ain't been paid."

"An' you ain't gonna be. No fight, no pay. Ain't that right?"

One of the pinioned men said, "Do what you want. We ain't gonna tell nothing."

Huston's head sank down for a moment, and then he said softly, "O.K. Don't tell. But looka here. Don't knife your own folks. We're tryin' to get along, havin' fun an' keepin' order. Don't tear all that down. Jes' think about it. You're jes' harmin' yourself.

"Awright, boys, put 'em over the back fence. An' don't hurt 'em. They don't know what they're doin'."

The squad moved slowly toward the rear of the camp, and Huston looked after them.

Jule said, "Le's jes' take one good kick at their ass."

"No, you don't!" Willie cried. "I said we wouldn'."

"Jes' one nice little kick," Jule pleaded. "Jes' loft 'em over the fence."

"No, sir," Willie insisted.

"Listen, you," he said, "we're lettin' you off this time. But you take back the word. If'n ever this here happens again, we'll jes' natcherally kick the hell outa whoever comes; we'll bust ever' bone in their body. Now you tell your boys that. Huston says you're our kinda folks—maybe. I'd hate to think it."

They neared the fence. Two of the seated guards stood up and moved over. "Got some fellas goin' home early," said Willie. The three men climbed over the fence and disappeared into the darkness.

And the squad moved quickly back toward the dance floor. And the music of "Ol' Dan Tucker" skirled and whined from the string band.

Over near the office the men still squatted and talked, and the shrill music came to them.

Pa said, "They's change a-comin'. I don' know what. Maybe we won't live to see her. But she's a-comin'. They's a res'less feelin'. Fella can't figger nothin' out, he's so nervous."

And Black Hat lifted his head up again, and the light fell on his bristly whiskers. He gathered some little rocks from the ground and shot them like marbles, with his thumb. "I don' know. She's a-comin' awright, like you say. Fella tol' me what happened in Akron, Ohio. Rubber companies. They got mountain people in 'cause they'd work cheap. An' these here mountain people up an' joined the union. Well, sir, hell jes' popped. All them storekeepers and legioners an' people like that, they get drillin' an' yellin', 'Red!' An' they're gonna run the union right outa Akron. Preachers git a-preachin' about it, an' papers a-yowlin', an' they's pick handles put out by the rubber companies, an' they're a-buyin' gas. Jesus, you'd think them mountain boys was reg'lar devils!" He stopped and found some more rocks to shoot. "Well, sir—it was las' March, an' one Sunday five thousan' of them mountain men had a turkey shoot outside a town. Five thousan' of 'em jes' marched through town with their rifles. An' they had their turkey shoot, an' then they marched back. An' that's all they done. Well, sir, they ain't been no trouble sence then. These here citizens committees give back the pick handles, an' the storekeepers keep their stores, an' nobody been clubbed nor tarred an' feathered, an' nobody been killed." There was a long silence, and then Black Hat said, "They're gettin' purty mean out here. Burned that camp an' beat up folks. I been thinkin'. All our folks got guns. I been thinkin' maybe we ought to git up a turkey shootin' club an' have meetin's ever' Sunday."

The men looked up at him, and then down at the ground, and their feet moved restlessly and they shifted their weight from one leg to the other.

Chapter Twenty-Five

THE SPRING is beautiful in California. Valleys in which the fruit blossoms are fragrant pink and white waters in a shallow sea. Then the first tendrils of the grapes, swelling from the old gnarled vines, cascade down to cover the trunks. The full green hills are round and soft as breasts. And on the level vegetable lands are the mile-long rows of pale green lettuce and the spindly little cauliflowers, the gray-green unearthly artichoke plants.

And then the leaves break out on the trees, and the petals drop from the fruit trees and carpet the earth with pink and white. The centers of the blossoms swell and grow and color: cherries and apples, peaches and pears, figs which close the flower in the fruit. All California quickens with produce, and the fruit grows heavy, and the limbs bend gradually under the fruit so that little crutches must be placed under them to support the weight.

Behind the fruitfulness are men of understanding and knowledge and skill, men who experiment with seed, endlessly developing the techniques for greater crops of plants whose roots will resist the million enemies of the earth: the molds, the insects, the rusts, the blights. These men work carefully and endlessly to perfect the seed, the roots. And there are the men of chemistry who spray the trees against pests, who sulphur the grapes, who cut out disease and rots, mildews and sicknesses. Doctors of preventive medicine, men at the borders who look for fruit flies, for Japanese beetle, men who quarantine the sick trees and root them out and burn them, men of knowledge. The men who graft the young trees, the little vines, are the cleverest of all, for theirs is a surgeon's job, as tender and delicate; and these men must have surgeons' hands and surgeons' hearts to slit the bark, to place the grafts, to bind the wounds and cover them from the air. These are great men.

Along the rows, the cultivators move, tearing the spring grass and turning it under to make a fertile earth, breaking the ground to hold the water up near the surface, ridging the ground in little pools for the irrigation, destroying the weed roots that may drink the water away from the trees.

And all the time the fruit swells and the flowers break out in long clusters on the vines. And in the growing year the warmth grows and the leaves turn dark green. The prunes lengthen like little green bird's eggs, and the limbs sag down against the crutches under the weight. And the hard little pears take shape, and the beginning of the fuzz comes out on the peaches. Grape blossoms shed their tiny petals and the hard little beads become green buttons, and the buttons grow heavy. The men who work in the fields, the owners of the little orchards, watch and calculate. The year is heavy with produce. And men are proud, for of their knowledge they can make the year heavy. They have transformed the world with their knowledge. The short, lean wheat has been made big and productive. Little sour apples have grown large and sweet, and that old grape that grew among the trees and fed the birds its tiny fruit has mothered a thousand varieties, red and black, green and pale pink, purple and yellow; and each variety with its own flavor. The men who work in the experimental farms have made new fruits: nectarines and forty kinds of plums, walnuts with paper shells. And always they work, selecting, grafting, changing, driving themselves, driving the earth to produce.

And first the cherries ripen. Cent and a half a pound. Hell, we can't pick 'em for that. Black cherries and red cherries, full and sweet, and the birds eat half of each cherry and the yellowjackets buzz into the holes the birds made. And on the ground the seeds drop and dry with black shreds hanging from them.

The purple prunes soften and sweeten. My God, we can't pick them and dry and sulphur them. We can't pay wages, no matter what wages. And the purple prunes carpet the ground. And first the skins wrinkle a little and swarms of flies come to feast, and the valley is filled with the odor of sweet decay. The meat turns dark and the crop shrivels on the ground.

And the pears grow yellow and soft. Five dollars a ton. Five dollars for forty fifty-pound boxes; trees pruned and sprayed, orchards cultivated—pick the fruit, put it in boxes, load the trucks, deliver the fruit to the cannery—forty boxes for five dollars. We can't do it. And the yellow fruit falls heavily to the ground and splashes on the ground. The yellowjackets dig into the soft meat, and there is a smell of ferment and rot.

Then the grapes—we can't make good wine. People can't buy good wine. Rip the grapes from the vines, good grapes, rotten grapes, wasp-stung grapes. Press stems, press dirt and rot.

But there's mildew and formic acid in the vats.

Add sulphur and tannic acid.

The smell from the ferment is not the rich odor of wine, but the smell of decay and chemicals.

Oh, well. It has alcohol in it, anyway. They can get drunk.

The little farmers watched debt creep up on them like the tide. They sprayed the trees and sold no crop, they pruned and grafted and could not pick the crop. And the men of knowledge have worked, have considered, and the fruit is rotting on the ground, and the decaying mash in the wine vats is poisoning the air. And taste the wine—no grape flavor at all, just sulphur and tannic acid and alcohol.

This little orchard will be a part of a great holding next year, for the debt will have choked the owner.

This vineyard will belong to the bank. Only the great owners can survive, for they own the canneries too. And four pears peeled and cut in half, cooked and canned, still cost fifteen cents. And the canned pears do not spoil. They will last for years.

The decay spreads over the State, and the sweet smell is a great sorrow on the land. Men who can graft the trees and make the seed fertile and big can find no way to let the hungry people eat their produce. Men who have created new fruits in the world cannot create a system whereby their fruits may be eaten. And the failure hangs over the State like a great sorrow.

The works of the roots of the vines, of the trees, must be destroyed to keep up the price, and this is the saddest, bitterest thing of all. Carloads of oranges dumped on the ground. The people came for miles to take the fruit, but this could not be. How would they buy oranges at twenty cents a dozen if they could drive out and pick them up? And men with hoses squirt kerosene on the oranges, and they are angry at the crime, angry at the people who have come to take the fruit.

A million people hungry, needing the fruit—and kerosene sprayed over the golden mountains.

And the smell of rot fills the country.

Burn coffee for fuel in the ships. Burn corn to keep warm, it makes a hot fire. Dump potatoes in the rivers and place guards along the banks to keep the hungry people from fishing them out. Slaughter the pigs and bury them, and let the putrescence drip down into the earth.

There is a crime here that goes beyond denunciation. There is a sorrow here that weeping cannot symbolize. There is a failure here that topples all our success. The fertile earth, the straight tree rows, the sturdy trunks, and the ripe fruit. And children dying of pellagra must die because a profit cannot be taken from an orange. And coroners must fill in the certificates—died of malnutrition—because the food must rot, must be forced to rot.

The people come with nets to fish for potatoes in the river, and the guards hold them back; they come in rattling cars to get the dumped oranges, but the kerosene is sprayed. And they stand still and watch the potatoes float by, listen to the screaming pigs being killed in a ditch and covered with quicklime, watch the mountains of oranges slop down to a putrefying ooze; and in the eyes of the people there is the failure; and in the eyes of the hungry there is a growing wrath. In the souls of the people the grapes of wrath are filling and growing heavy, growing heavy for the vintage.

Chapter Twenty-Six

I<small>N THE</small> W<small>EEDPATCH</small> <small>CAMP</small>, on an evening when the long, barred clouds hung over the set sun and inflamed their edges, the Joad family lingered after their supper. Ma hesitated before she started to do the dishes.

"We got to do somepin," she said. And she pointed at Winfield. "Look at 'im," she said. And when they stared at the little boy, "He's a-jerkin' an' a-twistin' in his sleep. Lookut his color." The members of the family looked at the earth again in shame. "Fried dough," Ma said. "One month we been here. An' Tom had five days' work. An' the rest of you scrabblin' out ever' day, an' no work. An' scairt to talk. An' the money gone. You're scairt to talk it out. Ever' night you jus' eat, an' then you get wanderin' away. Can't bear to talk it out. Well, you got to. Rosasharn ain't far from due, an' lookut her color. You got to talk it out. Now don't none of you get up till we figger somepin out. One day' more grease an' two days' flour, an' ten potatoes. You set here an' get busy!"

They looked at the ground. Pa cleaned his thick nails with his pocket knife. Uncle John picked at a splinter on the box he sat on. Tom pinched his lower lip and pulled it away from his teeth.

He released his lip and said softly, "We been a-lookin', Ma. Been walkin' out sence we can't use the gas no more. Been goin' in ever' gate, walkin' up to ever' house, even when we knowed they wasn't gonna be nothin'. Puts a weight on ya. Goin' out lookin' for somepin you know you ain't gonna find."

Ma said fiercely, "You ain't got the right to get discouraged. This here fambly's goin' under. You jus' ain't got the right."

Pa inspected his scraped nail. "We gotta go," he said. "We didn' wanta go. It's nice here, an' folks is nice here. We're feared we'll have to go live in one a them Hoovervilles."

"Well, if we got to, we got to. First thing is, we got to eat."

Al broke in. "I got a tankful a gas in the truck. I didn' let nobody get into that."

Tom smiled. "This here Al got a lot of sense along with he's randy-pandy."

"Now you figger," Ma said. "I ain't watchin' this here fambly starve no more. One day' more grease. That's what we got. Come time for Rosasharn to lay in, she got to be fed up. You figger!"

"This here hot water an' toilets—" Pa began.

"Well, we can't eat no toilets."

Tom said, "They was a fella come by today lookin' for men to go to Marysville. Pickin' fruit."

"Well, why don' we go to Marysville?" Ma demanded.

"I dunno," said Tom. "Didn' seem right, somehow. He was so anxious. Wouldn' say how much the pay was. Said he didn' know exactly."

Ma said, "We're a-goin' to Marysville. I don' care what the pay is. We're a-goin'."

"It's too far," said Tom. "We ain't got the money for gasoline. We couldn' get there. Ma, you say we got to figger. I ain't done nothin' but figger the whole time."

Uncle John said, "Feller says they's cotton a-comin' in up north, near a place called Tulare. That ain't very far, the feller says."

"Well, we got to git goin', an' goin' quick. I ain't a-settin' here no longer, no matter how nice." Ma took up her bucket and walked toward the sanitary unit for hot water.

"Ma gets tough," Tom said. "I seen her a-gettin' mad quite a piece now. She jus' boils up."

Pa said with relief, "Well, she brang it into the open, anyways. I been layin' at night a-burnin' my brains up. Now we can talk her out, anyways."

Ma came back with her bucket of steaming water. "Well," she demanded, "figger anything out?"

"Jus' workin' her over," said Tom. "Now s'pose we jus' move up north where that cotton's at. We been over this here country. We know they ain't nothin' here. S'pose we pack up an' shove north. Then when the cotton's ready, we'll be there. I kinda like to get my han's aroun' some cotton. You got a full tank, Al?"

"Almos'—'bout two inches down."

"Should get us up to that place."

Ma poised a dish over the bucket. "Well?" she demanded.

Tom said, "You win. We'll move on, I guess. Huh, Pa?"

"Guess we got to," Pa said.

Ma glanced at him. "When?"

"Well—no need waitin'. Might's well go in the mornin'."

"We got to go in the mornin'. I tol' you what's lef'."

"Now, Ma, don' think I don' wanta go. I ain't had a good gutful to eat in two weeks. 'Course I filled up, but I didn' take no good from it."

Ma plunged the dish into the bucket. "We'll go in the mornin'," she said.

Pa sniffled. "Seems like times is changed," he said sarcastically. "Time was when a man said what we'd do. Seems like women is tellin' now. Seems like it's purty near time to get out a stick."

Ma put the clean dripping tin dish out on a box. She smiled down at her work. "You get your stick, Pa," she said. "Times when they's food an' a place to set, then maybe you can use your stick an' keep your skin whole. But you ain't a-doin' your job, either a-thinkin' or a-workin'. If you was, why, you could use your stick, an' women folks'd sniffle their nose an' creep-mouse aroun'. But you jus' get you a stick now an' you ain't lickin' no woman you're a-fightin', 'cause I got a stick all laid out too."

Pa grinned with embarrassment. "Now it ain't good to have the little fellas hear you talkin' like that," he said.

"You get some bacon inside the little fellas 'fore you come tellin' what else is good for 'em," said Ma.

Pa got up in disgust and moved away, and Uncle John followed him.

Ma's hands were busy in the water, but she watched them go, and she said proudly to Tom, "He's all right. He ain't beat. I was scairt he wouldn' get mad. He's good an' mad. Look how he walks a-heelin' down with his feet. He's like as not to take a smack at me."

Tom laughed. "You jus' a-treadin' him on?"

"Sure," said Ma. "Take a man, he can get worried an' worried, an' it eats out his liver, an' purty soon he'll jus' lay down and die with his heart et out. But if you can take an' make 'im mad, why, he'll be awright. Pa, he didn' say nothin', but he's mad now. He'll show me now. He's awright."

Al got up. "I'm gonna walk down the row," he said.

"Better see the truck's ready to go," Tom warned him.

"She's ready."

"If she ain't, I'll turn Ma on ya."

"She's ready." Al strolled jauntily along the row of tents.

Tom sighed. "I'm a-gettin' tired, Ma. How 'bout makin' me mad?"

"You got more sense, Tom. I don' need to make you mad. I got to lean on you. Them others—they're kinda strangers, all but you. You won't give up, Tom."

The joke fell from him. "I don' like it," he said. "I wanta go out like Al. An' I wanta get mad like Pa, an' I wanta get drunk like Uncle John."

Ma shook her head. "You can't, Tom. I know. I knowed from the time you was a little fella. You can't. They's some folks that's just theirself an' nothin' more. There's Al—he's jus' a young fella after a girl. You wasn't never like that, Tom."

"Sure I was," said Tom. "Still am."

"No you ain't. Ever'thing you do is more'n you. When they sent you up to prison I knowed it. You're spoke for."

"Now, Ma—cut it out. It ain't true. It's all in your head."

She stacked the knives and forks on top of the plates. "Maybe. Maybe it's in my head. Rosasharn, you wipe up these here an' put 'em away."

The girl got breathlessly to her feet and her swollen middle hung out in front of her. She moved sluggishly to the box and picked up a washed dish.

Tom said, "Gettin' so tightful it's a-pullin' her eyes wide."

"Don't you go a-jollyin'," said Ma. "She's doin' good. You go 'long an' say goo'-by to anybody you wan'."

"O.K.," he said. "I'm gonna see how far it is up there."

Ma said to the girl, "He ain't sayin' stuff like that to make you feel bad. Where's Ruthie an' Winfiel'?"

"They snuck off after Pa. I seen 'em."

"Well, leave 'em go."

Rose of Sharon moved sluggishly about her work. Ma inspected her cautiously. "You feelin' pretty good? Your cheeks is kinda saggy."

"I ain't had milk like they said I ought."

"I know. We jus' didn' have no milk."

Rose of Sharon said dully, "Ef Connie hadn' went away, we'd a had a little house by now, with him studyin' an' all. Would a got milk like I need. Would a had a nice baby. This here baby ain't gonna be no good. I ought a had milk." She reached in her apron pocket and put something into her mouth.

Ma said, "I seen you nibblin' on somepin. What you eatin'?"

"Nothin'."

"Come on, what you nibblin' on?"

"Jus' a piece a slack lime. Foun' a big hunk."

"Why, tha's jus' like eatin' dirt."

"I kinda feel like I wan' it."

Ma was silent. She spread her knees and tightened her skirt. "I know," she said at last. "I et coal oncet when I was in a fambly way. Et a big piece a coal. Granma says I shouldn'. Don' you say that about the baby. You got no right even to think it."

"Got no husban'! Got no milk!"

Ma said, "If you was a well girl, I'd take a whang at you. Right in the face." She got up and went inside the tent. She came out and stood in front of Rose of Sharon, and she held out her hand. "Look!" The small gold earrings were in her hand. "These is for you."

The girl's eyes brightened for a moment, and then she looked aside. "I ain't pierced."

"Well, I'm a-gonna pierce ya." Ma hurried back into the tent. She came back with a cardboard box. Hurriedly she threaded a needle, doubled the thread and tied a series of knots in it. She threaded a second needle and knotted the thread. In the box she found a piece of cork.

"It'll hurt. It'll hurt."

Ma stepped to her, put the cork in back of the ear lobe and pushed the needle through the ear, into the cork.

The girl twitched. "It sticks. It'll hurt."

"No more'n that."

"Yes, it will."

"Well, then. Le's see the other ear first." She placed the cork and pierced the other ear.

"It'll hurt."

"Hush!" said Ma. "It's all done."

Rose of Sharon looked at her in wonder. Ma clipped the needles off and pulled one knot of each thread through the lobes.

"Now," she said. "Ever' day we'll pull one knot, and in a couple weeks it'll be all well an' you can wear 'em. Here— they're your'n now. You can keep 'em."

Rose of Sharon touched her ears tenderly and looked at the tiny spots of blood on her fingers. "It didn' hurt. Jus' stuck a little."

"You oughta been pierced long ago," said Ma. She looked at the girl's face, and she smiled in triumph. "Now get them dishes all done up. Your baby gonna be a good baby. Very near let you have a baby without your ears was pierced. But you're safe now."

"Does it mean somepin?"

"Why, 'course it does," said Ma. " 'Course it does."

Al strolled down the street toward the dancing platform. Outside a neat little tent he whistled softly, and then moved along the street. He walked to the edge of the grounds and sat down in the grass.

The clouds over the west had lost the red edging now, and the cores were black. Al scratched his legs and looked toward the evening sky.

In a few moments a blond girl walked near; she was pretty and sharp-featured. She sat down in the grass beside him and did not speak. Al put his hand on her waist and walked his fingers around.

"Don't," she said. "You tickle."

"We're goin' away tomorra," said Al.

She looked at him, startled. "Tomorra? Where?"

"Up north," he said lightly.

"Well, we're gonna git married, ain't we?"

"Sure, sometime."

"You said purty soon!" she cried angrily.

"Well, soon is when soon comes."

"You promised." He walked his fingers around farther. "Git away," she cried. "You said we was."

"Well, sure we are."

"An' now you're goin' away."

Al demanded, "What's the matter with you? You in a fambly way?"

"No, I ain't."

Al laughed. "I jus' been wastin' my time, huh?"

Her chin shot out. She jumped to her feet. "You git away from me, Al Joad. I don' wanta see you no more."

"Aw, come on. What's the matter?"

"You think you're jus'—hell on wheels."

"Now wait a minute."

"You think I got to go out with you. Well, I don't! I got lots a chances."

"Now wait a minute."

"No, sir—you git away."

Al lunged suddenly, caught her by the ankle, and tripped her. He grabbed her when she fell and held her and put his hand over her angry mouth. She tried to bite his palm, but he cupped it out over her mouth, and he held her down with his other arm. And in a moment she lay still, and in another moment they were giggling together in the dry grass.

"Why, we'll be a-comin' back purty soon," said Al. "An' I'll have a pocketful a jack. We'll go down to Hollywood an' see the pitchers."

She was lying on her back. Al bent over her. And he saw the bright evening star reflected in her eyes, and he saw the black cloud reflected in her eyes. "We'll go on the train," he said.

"How long ya think it'll be?" she asked.

"Oh, maybe a month," he said.

The evening dark came down and Pa and Uncle John squatted with the heads of families out by the office. They studied the night and the future. The little manager, in his white clothes, frayed and clean, rested his elbows on the porch rail. His face was drawn and tired.

Huston looked up at him. "You better get some sleep, mister."

"I guess I ought. Baby born last night in Unit Three. I'm getting to be a good midwife."

"Fella oughta know," said Huston. "Married fella got to know."

Pa said, "We're a-gittin' out in the mornin'."

"Yeah? Which way you goin'?"

"Thought we'd go up north a little. Try to get in the first cotton. We ain't had work. We're outa food."

"Know if they's any work?" Huston asked.

"No, but we're sure they ain't none here."

"They will be, a little later," Huston said. "We'll hold on."

"We hate to go," said Pa. "Folks been so nice here—an' the toilets an' all. But we got to eat. Got a tank of gas. That'll get us a little piece up the road. We had a bath ever' day here. Never was so clean in my life. Funny thing—use ta be I on'y got a bath ever' week an' I never seemed to stink. But now if I don't get one ever' day I stink. Wonder if takin' a bath so often makes that?"

"Maybe you couldn't smell yourself before," the manager said.

"Maybe. I wisht we could stay."

The little manager held his temples between his palms. "I think there's going to be another baby tonight," he said.

"We gonna have one in our fambly 'fore long," said Pa. "I wisht we could have it here. I sure wisht we could."

Tom and Willie and Jule the half-breed sat on the edge of the dance floor and swung their feet.

"I got a sack of Durham," Jule said. "Like a smoke?"

"I sure would," said Tom. "Ain't had a smoke for a hell of a time." He rolled the brown cigarette carefully, to keep down the loss of tobacco.

"Well, sir, we'll be sorry to see you go," said Willie. "You folks is good folks."

Tom lighted his cigarette. "I been thinkin' about it a lot. Jesus Christ, I wisht we could settle down."

Jule took back his Durham. "It ain't nice," he said. "I got a little girl. Thought when I come out here she'd get some schoolin'. But hell, we ain't in one place hardly long enough. Jes' gits goin' an' we got to drag on."

"I hope we don't get in no more Hoovervilles," said Tom. "I was really scairt, there."

"Deputies push you aroun'?"

"I was scairt I'd kill somebody," said Tom. "Was on'y there a little while, but I was a-stewin' aroun' the whole time. Depity come in an' picked up a frien', jus' because he talked outa turn. I was jus' stewin' all the time."

"Ever been in a strike?" Willie asked.

"No."

"Well, I been a-thinkin' a lot. Why don' them depities get in here an' raise hell like ever' place else? Think that little guy in the office is a-stoppin' 'em? No, sir."

"Well, what is?" Jule asked.

"I'll tell ya. It's 'cause we're all a-workin' together. Depity can't pick on one fella in this camp. He's pickin' on the whole darn camp. An' he don't dare. All we got to do is give a yell an' they's two hunderd men out. Fella organizin' for the union was a-talkin' out on the road. He says we could do that any place. Jus' stick together. They ain't raisin' hell with no two hunderd men. They're pickin' on one man."

"Yeah," said Jule, "an' suppose you got a union? You got to have leaders. They'll jus' pick up your leaders, an' where's your union?"

"Well," said Willie, "we got to figure her out some time. I been out here a year, an' wages is goin' right on down. Fella can't feed his fam'ly on his work now, an' it's gettin' worse all the time. It ain't gonna do no good to set aroun' an' starve. I don' know what to do. If a fella owns a team a horses, he don't raise no hell if he got to feed 'em when they ain't workin'. But if a fella got men workin' for him, he jus' don't give a damn. Horses is a hell of a lot more worth than men. I don' understan' it."

"Gits so I don' wanta think about it," said Jule. "An' I got to think about it. I got this here little girl. You know how purty she is. One week they give her a prize in this camp 'cause she's so purty. Well, what's gonna happen to her? She's gettin' spindly. I ain't gonna stan' it. She's so purty. I'm gonna bust out."

"How?" Willie asked. "What you gonna do—steal some stuff an' git in jail? Kill somebody an' git hung?"

"I don' know," said Jule. "Gits me nuts thinkin' about it. Gits me clear nuts."

"I'm a-gonna miss them dances," Tom said. "Them was some of the nicest dances I ever seen. Well, I'm gonna turn in. So long. I'll be seein' you someplace." He shook hands.

"Sure will," said Jule.

"Well, so long." Tom moved away into the darkness.

In the darkness of the Joad tent Ruthie and Winfield lay on their mattress, and Ma lay beside them. Ruthie whispered, "Ma!"

"Yeah? Ain't you asleep yet?"

"Ma—they gonna have croquet where we're goin'?"

"I don' know. Get some sleep. We want to get an early start."

"Well, I wisht we'd stay here where we're sure we got croquet."

"Sh!" said Ma.

"Ma, Winfiel' hit a kid tonight."

"He shouldn' of."

"I know. I tol' 'im, but he hit the kid right in the nose an', Jesus, how the blood run down!"

"Don' talk like that. It ain't a nice way to talk."

Winfield turned over. "That kid says we was Okies," he said in an outraged voice. "He says he wasn't no Okie 'cause he come from Oregon. Says we was goddamn Okies. I socked him."

"Sh! You shouldn'. He can't hurt you callin' names."

"Well, I won't let 'im," Winfield said fiercely.

"Sh! Get some sleep."

Ruthie said, "You oughta seen the blood run down—all over his clothes."

Ma reached a hand from under the blanket and snapped Ruthie on the cheek with her finger. The little girl went rigid for a moment, and then dissolved into sniffling, quiet crying.

In the sanitary unit Pa and Uncle John sat in adjoining compartments. "Might's well get in a good las' one," said Pa. "It's sure nice. 'Member how the little fellas was so scairt when they flushed 'em the first time?"

"I wasn't so easy myself," said Uncle John. He pulled his overalls neatly up around his knees. "I'm gettin' bad," he said. "I feel sin."

"You can't sin none," said Pa. "You ain't got no money. Jus' sit tight. Cos' you at leas' two bucks to sin, an' we ain't got two bucks amongst us."

"Yeah! But I'm a-thinkin' sin."

"Awright. You can think sin for nothin'."

"It's jus' as bad," said Uncle John.

"It's a whole hell of a lot cheaper," said Pa.

"Don't you go makin' light of sin."

"I ain't. You jus' go ahead. You always gets sinful jus' when hell's a-poppin'."

"I know it," said Uncle John. "Always was that way. I never tol' half the stuff I done."

"Well, keep it to yaself."

"These here nice toilets gets me sinful."

"Go out in the bushes then. Come on, pull up ya pants an' le's get some sleep." Pa pulled his overall straps in place and snapped the buckle. He flushed the toilet and watched thoughtfully while the water whirled in the bowl.

It was still dark when Ma roused her camp. The low night lights shone through the open doors of the sanitary unit. From the tents along the road came the assorted snores of the campers.

Ma said, "Come on, roll out. We got to be on our way. Day's not far off." She raised the screechy shade of the lantern and lighted the wick. "Come on, all of you."

The floor of the tent squirmed into slow action. Blankets and comforts were thrown back and sleepy eyes squinted blindly at the light. Ma slipped on her dress over the underclothes she wore to bed. "We got no coffee," she said. "I got a few biscuits. We can eat 'em on the road. Jus' get up now, an' we'll load the truck. Come on now. Don't make no noise. Don' wanta wake the neighbors."

It was a few moments before they were fully aroused. "Now don' you get away," Ma warned the children. The family dressed. The men pulled down the tarpaulin and loaded up the truck. "Make it nice an' flat," Ma warned them. They piled the mattress on top of the load and bound the tarpaulin in place over its ridge pole.

"Awright, Ma," said Tom. "She's ready."

Ma held a plate of cold biscuits in her hand. "Awright. Here. Each take one. It's all we got."

Ruthie and Winfield grabbed their biscuits and climbed up on the load. They covered themselves with a blanket and went back to sleep, still holding the cold hard biscuits in their hands. Tom got into the driver's seat and stepped on the starter. It buzzed a little, and then stopped.

"Goddamn you, Al!" Tom cried. "You let the battery run down."

Al blustered, "How the hell was I gonna keep her up if I ain't got gas to run her?"

Tom chuckled suddenly. "Well, I don' know how, but it's your fault. You got to crank her."

"I tell you it ain't my fault."

Tom got out and found the crank under the seat. "It's my fault," he said.

"Gimme that crank." Al seized it. "Pull down the spark so she don't take my arm off."

"O.K. Twist her tail."

Al labored at the crank, around and around. The engine caught, spluttered, and roared as Tom choked the car delicately. He raised the spark and reduced the throttle.

Ma climbed in beside him. "We woke up ever'body in the camp," she said.

"They'll go to sleep again."

Al climbed in on the other side. "Pa 'n' Uncle John got up top," he said. "Goin' to sleep again."

Tom drove toward the main gate. The watchman came out of the office and played his flashlight on the truck. "Wait a minute."

"What ya want?"

"You checkin' out?"

"Sure."

"Well, I got to cross you off."

"O.K."

"Know which way you're goin'?"

"Well, we're gonna try up north."

"Well, good luck," said the watchman.

"Same to you. So long."

The truck edged slowly over the big hump and into the road. Tom retraced the road he had driven before, past Weed-patch and west until he came to 99, then north on the great paved road, toward Bakersfield. It was growing light when he came into the outskirts of the city.

Tom said, "Ever' place you look is restaurants. An' them places all got coffee. Lookit that all-nighter there. Bet they got ten gallons a coffee in there, all hot!"

"Aw, shut up," said Al.

Tom grinned over at him. "Well, I see you got yaself a girl right off."

"Well, what of it?"

"He's mean this mornin', Ma. He ain't good company."

Al said irritably, "I'm goin' out on my own purty soon. Fella can make his way lot easier if he ain't got a fambly."

Tom said, "You'd have yaself a fambly in nine months. I seen you playin' aroun'."

"Ya crazy," said Al. "I'd get myself a job in a garage an' I'd eat in restaurants——"

"An' you'd have a wife an' kid in nine months."

"I tell ya I wouldn'."

Tom said, "You're a wise guy, Al. You gonna take some beatin' over the head."

"Who's gonna do it?"

"They'll always be guys to do it," said Tom.

"You think jus' because you——"

"Now you jus' stop that," Ma broke in.

"I done it," said Tom. "I was a-badgerin' him. I didn' mean no harm, Al. I didn' know you liked that girl so much."

"I don't like no girls much."

"Awright, then, you don't. You ain't gonna get no argument out of me."

The truck came to the edge of the city. "Look a them hot-dog stan's—hunderds of 'em," said Tom.

Ma said, "Tom! I got a dollar put away. You wan' coffee bad enough to spen' it?"

"No, Ma. I'm jus' foolin'."

"You can have it if you wan' it bad enough."

"I wouldn' take it."

Al said, "Then shut up about coffee."

Tom was silent for a time. "Seems like I got my foot in it all the time," he said. "There's the road we run up that night."

"I hope we don't never have nothin' like that again," said Ma. "That was a bad night."

"I didn' like it none either."

The sun rose on their right, and the great shadow of the truck ran beside them, flicking over the fence posts beside the road. They ran on past the rebuilt Hooverville.

"Look," said Tom. "They got new people there. Looks like the same place."

Al came slowly out of his sullenness. "Fella tol' me some a them people been burned out fifteen-twenty times. Says they jus' go hide down the willows an' then they come out an' build 'em another weed shack. Jus' like gophers. Got so use' to it they don't even get mad no more, this fella says. They jus' figger it's like bad weather."

"Sure was bad weather for me that night," said Tom. They moved up the wide highway. And the sun's warmth made them shiver. "Gettin' snappy in the mornin'," said Tom. "Winter's on the way. I jus' hope we can get some money 'fore it comes. Tent ain't gonna be nice in the winter."

Ma sighed, and then she straightened her head. "Tom," she said, "we gotta have a house in the winter. I tell ya we got to. Ruthie's awright, but Winfiel' ain't so strong. We got to have a house when the rains come. I heard it jus' rains cats aroun' here."

"We'll get a house, Ma. You res' easy. You gonna have a house."

"Jus' so's it's got a roof an' a floor. Jus' to keep the little fellas off'n the groun'."

"We'll try, Ma."

"I don' wanna worry ya now."

"We'll try, Ma."

"I jus' get panicky sometimes," she said. "I jus' lose my spunk."

"I never seen you when you lost it."

"Nights I do, sometimes."

There came a harsh hissing from the front of the truck. Tom grabbed the wheel tight and he thrust the brake down to the floor. The truck bumped to a stop. Tom sighed. "Well, there she is." He leaned back in the seat. Al leaped out and ran to the right front tire.

"Great big nail," he called.

"We got any tire patch?"

"No," said Al. "Used it all up. Got patch, but no glue stuff."

Tom turned and smiled sadly at Ma. "You shouldn' a tol' about that dollar," he said. "We'd a fixed her some way." He got out of the car and went to the flat tire.

Al pointed to a big nail protruding from the flat casing. "There she is!"

"If they's one nail in the county, we run over it."

"Is it bad?" Ma called.

"No, not bad, but we got to fix her."

The family piled down from the top of the truck. "Puncture?" Pa asked, and then he saw the tire and was silent.

Tom moved Ma from the seat and got the can of tire patch from underneath the cushion. He unrolled the rubber patch and took out the tube of cement, squeezed it gently. "She's almos' dry," he said. "Maybe they's enough. Awright, Al. Block the back wheels. Le's get her jacked up."

Tom and Al worked well together. They put stones behind the wheels, put the jack under the front axle, and lifted the weight off the limp casing. They ripped off the casing. They found the hole, dipped a rag in the gas tank and washed the tube around the hole. And then, while Al held the tube tight over his knee, Tom tore the cement tube in two and spread the little fluid thinly on the rubber with his pocket knife. He scraped the gum delicately. "Now let her dry while I cut a patch." He trimmed and beveled the edge of the blue patch. Al held the tube tight while Tom put the patch tenderly in place. "There! Now bring her to the running board while I tap her with a hammer." He pounded the patch carefully, then stretched the tube and watched the edges of the patch. "There she is! She's gonna hold. Stick her on the rim an' we'll pump her up. Looks like you keep your buck, Ma."

Al said, "I wisht we had a spare. We got to get us a spare,

Tom, on a rim an' all pumped up. Then we can fix a puncture at night."

"When we get money for a spare we'll get us some coffee an' side-meat instead," Tom said.

The light morning traffic buzzed by on the highway, and the sun grew warm and bright. A wind, gentle and sighing, blew in puffs from the southwest, and the mountains on both sides of the great valley were indistinct in a pearly mist.

Tom was pumping at the tire when a roadster, coming from the north, stopped on the other side of the road. A brown-faced man dressed in a light gray business suit got out and walked across to the truck. He was bareheaded. He smiled, and his teeth were very white against his brown skin. He wore a massive gold wedding ring on the third finger of his left hand. A little gold football hung on a slender chain across his vest.

"Morning," he said pleasantly.

Tom stopped pumping and looked up. "Mornin'."

The man ran his fingers through his coarse, short, graying hair. "You people looking for work?"

"We sure are, mister. Lookin' even under boards."

"Can you pick peaches?"

"We never done it," Pa said.

"We can do anything," Tom said hurriedly. "We can pick anything there is."

The man fingered his gold football. "Well, there's plenty of work for you about forty miles north."

"We'd sure admire to get it," said Tom. "You tell us how to get there, an' we'll go a-lopin'."

"Well, you go north to Pixley, that's thirty-five or -six miles, and you turn east. Go about six miles. Ask anybody where the Hooper ranch is. You'll find plenty of work there."

"We sure will."

"Know where there's other people looking for work?"

"Sure," said Tom. "Down at the Weedpatch camp they's plenty lookin' for work."

"I'll take a run down there. We can use quite a few. Remember now, turn east at Pixley and keep straight east to the Hooper ranch."

"Sure," said Tom. "An' we thank ya, mister. We need work awful bad."

"All right. Get along as soon as you can." He walked back across the road, climbed into his open roadster, and drove away south.

Tom threw his weight on the pump. "Twenty apiece," he called. "One—two—three—four—" At twenty Al took the pump, and then Pa and then Uncle John. The tire filled out and grew plump and smooth. Three times around, the pump went. "Let 'er down an' le's see," said Tom.

Al released the jack and lowered the car. "Got plenty," he said. "Maybe a little too much."

They threw the tools into the car. "Come on, le's go," Tom called. "We're gonna get some work at last."

Ma got in the middle again. Al drove this time.

"Now take her easy. Don't burn her up, Al."

They drove on through the sunny morning fields. The mist lifted from the hilltops and they were clear and brown, with black-purple creases. The wild doves flew up from the fences as the truck passed. Al unconsciously increased his speed.

"Easy," Tom warned him. "She'll blow up if you crowd her. We got to get there. Might even get in some work today."

Ma said excitedly, "With four men a-workin' maybe I can get some credit right off. Fust thing I'll get is coffee, 'cause you been wanting that, an' then some flour an' bakin' powder an' some meat. Better not get no side-meat right off. Save that for later. Maybe Sat'dy. An' soap. Got to get soap. Wonder where we'll stay." She babbled on. "An' milk. I'll get some milk 'cause Rosasharn, she ought to have milk. The lady nurse says that."

A snake wriggled across the warm highway. Al zipped over and ran it down and came back to his own lane.

"Gopher snake," said Tom. "You oughtn't to done that."

"I hate 'em," said Al gaily. "Hate all kinds. Give me the stomach-quake."

The forenoon traffic on the highway increased, salesmen in shiny coupés with the insignia of their companies painted on the doors, red and white gasoline trucks dragging clinking chains behind them, great square-doored vans from wholesale grocery houses, delivering produce. The country was rich along the roadside. There were orchards, heavy leafed in their prime, and vineyards with the long green crawlers carpeting the ground between the rows. There were melon patches and grain fields. White houses stood in the greenery, roses growing over them. And the sun was gold and warm.

In the front seat of the truck Ma and Tom and Al were overcome with happiness. "I ain't really felt so good for a long time," Ma said. " 'F we pick plenty peaches we might get a house, pay rent even, for a couple months. We got to have a house."

Al said, "I'm a-gonna save up. I'll save up an' then I'm a-goin' in a town an' get me a job in a garage. Live in a room an' eat in restaurants. Go to the movin' pitchers ever' damn night. Don' cost much. Cowboy pitchers." His hands tightened on the wheel.

The radiator bubbled and hissed steam. "Did you fill her up?" Tom asked.

"Yeah. Wind's kinda behind us. That's what makes her boil."

"It's a awful nice day," Tom said. "Use' ta work there in McAlester an' think all the things I'd do. I'd go in a straight line way to hell an' gone an' never stop nowheres. Seems like a long time ago. Seems like it's years ago I was in. They was a guard made it tough. I was gonna lay for 'im. Guess that's what makes me mad at cops. Seems like ever' cop got his face. He use' ta get red in the face. Looked like a pig. Had a brother out west, they said. Use' ta get fellas paroled to his brother, an' then they had to work for nothin'. If they raised a stink, they'd get sent back for breakin' parole. That's what the fellers said."

"Don' think about it," Ma begged him. "I'm a-gonna lay in a lot a stuff to eat. Lot a flour an' lard."

"Might's well think about it," said Tom. "Try to shut it out, an' it'll whang back at me. They was a screwball. Never tol' you 'bout him. Looked like Happy Hooligan. Harmless kinda fella. Always was gonna make a break. Fellas all called him Hooligan." Tom laughed to himself.

"Don' think about it," Ma begged.

"Go on," said Al. "Tell about the fella."

"It don't hurt nothin', Ma," Tom said. "This fella was always gonna break out. Make a plan, he would; but he couldn' keep it to hisself an' purty soon ever'body knowed it, even the warden. He'd make his break an' they'd take 'im by the han' an' lead 'im back. Well, one time he drawed a plan where he's goin' over. 'Course he showed it aroun', an' ever'body kep' still. An' he hid out, an' ever'body kep' still. So he's got himself a rope somewheres, an' he goes over the wall. They's six guards outside with a great big sack, an' Hooligan comes quiet down the rope an' they jus' hol' the sack out an' he goes right inside. They tie up the mouth an' take 'im back inside. Fellas laughed so hard they like to died. But it busted Hooligan's spirit. He jus' cried an' cried, an' moped aroun' an' got sick. Hurt his feelin's so bad. Cut his wrists with a pin an' bled to death 'cause his feelin's was hurt. No harm in 'im at all. They's all kinds a screwballs in stir."

"Don' talk about it," Ma said. "I knowed Purty Boy Floyd's ma. He wan't a bad boy. Jus' got drove in a corner."

The sun moved up toward noon and the shadow of the truck grew lean and moved in under the wheels.

"Mus' be Pixley up the road," Al said. "Seen a sign a little back." They drove into the little town and turned eastward on a narrower road. And the orchards lined the way and made an aisle.

"Hope we can find her easy," Tom said.

Ma said, "That fella said the Hooper ranch. Said anybody'd tell us. Hope they's a store near by. Might get some credit, with four men workin'. I could get a real nice supper if they'd gimme some credit. Make up a big stew maybe."

"An' coffee," said Tom. "Might even get me a sack a Durham. I ain't had no tobacca of my own for a long time."

Far ahead the road was blocked with cars, and a line of white motorcycles was drawn up along the roadside. "Mus' be a wreck," Tom said.

As they drew near a State policeman, in boots and Sam Browne belt, stepped around the last parked car. He held up his hand and Al pulled to a stop. The policeman leaned confidentially on the side of the car. "Where you going?"

Al said, "Fella said they was work pickin' peaches up this way."

"Want to work, do you?"

"Damn right," said Tom.

"O.K. Wait here a minute." He moved to the side of the

road and called ahead. "One more. That's six cars ready. Better take this batch through."

Tom called, "Hey! What's the matter?"

The patrol man lounged back. "Got a little trouble up ahead. Don't you worry. You'll get through. Just follow the line."

There came the splattering blast of motorcycles starting. The line of cars moved on, with the Joad truck last. Two motorcycles led the way, and two followed.

Tom said uneasily, "I wonder what's a matter."

"Maybe the road's out," Al suggested.

"Don' need four cops to lead us. I don' like it."

The motorcycles ahead speeded up. The line of old cars speeded up. Al hurried to keep in back of the last car.

"These here is our own people, all of 'em," Tom said. "I don' like this."

Suddenly the leading policemen turned off the road into a wide graveled entrance. The old cars whipped after them. The motorcycles roared their motors. Tom saw a line of men standing in the ditch beside the road, saw their mouths open as though they were yelling, saw their shaking fists and their furious faces. A stout woman ran toward the cars, but a roaring motorcycle stood in her way. A high wire gate swung open. The six old cars moved through and the gate closed behind them. The four motorcycles turned and sped back in the direction from which they had come. And now that the motors were gone, the distant yelling of the men in the ditch could be heard. Two men stood beside the graveled road. Each one carried a shotgun.

One called, "Go on, go on. What the hell are you waiting for?" The six cars moved ahead, turned a bend and came suddenly on the peach camp.

There were fifty little square, flat-roofed boxes, each with a door and a window, and the whole group in a square. A water tank stood high on one edge of the camp. And a little grocery store stood on the other side. At the end of each row of square houses stood two men armed with shotguns and wearing big silver stars pinned to their shirts.

The six cars stopped. Two bookkeepers moved from car to car. "Want to work?"

Tom answered, "Sure, but what is this?"

"That's not your affair. Want to work?"

"Sure we do."

"Name?"

"Joad."

"How many men?"

"Four."

"Women?"

"Two."

"Kids?"

"Two."

"Can all of you work?"

"Why—I guess so."

"O.K. Find house sixty-three. Wages five cents a box. No bruised fruit. All right, move along now. Go to work right away."

The cars moved on. On the door of each square red house a number was painted. "Sixty," Tom said. "There's sixty. Must be down that way. There, sixty-one, sixty-two— There she is."

Al parked the truck close to the door of the little house. The family came down from the top of the truck and looked about in bewilderment. Two deputies approached. They looked closely into each face.

"Name?"

"Joad," Tom said impatiently. "Say, what is this here?"

One of the deputies took out a long list. "Not here. Ever see these here? Look at the license. Nope. Ain't got it. Guess they're O.K."

"Now you look here. We don't want no trouble with you. Jes' do your work and mind your own business and you'll be all right." The two turned abruptly and walked away. At the end of the dusty street they sat down on two boxes and their position commanded the length of the street.

Tom stared after them. "They sure do wanta make us feel at home."

Ma opened the door of the house and stepped inside. The floor was splashed with grease. In the one room stood a rusty tin stove and nothing more. The tin stove rested on four bricks and its rusty stovepipe went up through the roof. The room smelled of sweat and grease. Rose of Sharon stood be-side Ma. "We gonna live here?"

Ma was silent for a moment. "Why, sure," she said at last. "It ain't so bad once we wash it out. Get her mopped."

"I like the tent better," the girl said.

"This got a floor," Ma suggested. "This here wouldn' leak when it rains." She turned to the door. "Might as well un-load," she said.

The men unloaded the truck silently. A fear had fallen on them. The great square of boxes was silent. A woman went by in the street, but she did not look at them. Her head was sunk and her dirty gingham dress was frayed at the bottom in little flags.

The pall had fallen on Ruthie and Winfield. They did not dash away to inspect the place. They stayed close to the truck, close to the family. They looked forlornly up and down the dusty street. Winfield found a piece of baling wire and he bent it back and forth until it broke. He made a little crank of the shortest piece and turned it around and around in his hands.

Tom and Pa were carrying the mattresses into the house when a clerk appeared. He wore khaki trousers and a blue shirt and a black necktie. He wore silver-bound eyeglasses, and his eyes, through the thick lenses, were weak and red, and the pupils were staring little bull's eyes. He leaned forward to look at Tom.

"I want to get you checked down," he said. "How many of you going to work?"

Tom said, "They's four men. Is this here hard work?"

"Picking peaches," the clerk said. "Piece work. Give five cents a box."

"Ain't no reason why the little fellas can't help?"

"Sure not, if they're careful."

Ma stood in the doorway. "Soon's I get settled down I'll come out an' help. We got nothin' to eat, mister. Do we get paid right off?"

"Well, no, not money right off. But you can get credit at the store for what you got coming."

"Come on, let's hurry," Tom said. "I wanta get some meat an' bread in me tonight. Where de we go, mister?"

"I'm going out there now. Come with me."

Tom and Pa and Al and Uncle John walked with him down the dusty street and into the orchard, in among the peach trees. The narrow leaves were beginning to turn a pale yellow. The peaches were little globes of gold and red on the branches. Among the trees were piles of empty boxes. The pickers scurried about, filling their buckets from the branches, putting the peaches in the boxes, carrying the boxes to the checking station; and at the stations, where the piles of filled boxes waited for the trucks, clerks waited to check against the names of the pickers.

"Here's four more," the guide said to a clerk.

"O.K. Ever picked before?"

"Never did," said Tom.

"Well, pick careful. No bruised fruit, no windfalls. Bruise your fruit an' we won't check 'em. There's some buckets."

Tom picked up a three-gallon bucket and looked at it. "Full a holes on the bottom."

"Sure," said the near-sighted clerk. "That keeps people from stealing them. All right—down in that section. Get going."

The four Joads took their buckets and went into the orchard. "They don't waste no time," Tom said.

"Christ Awmighty," Al said. "I ruther work in a garage."

Pa had followed docilely into the field. He turned suddenly on Al. "Now you jus' quit it," he said. "You been a-hankerin' an' a-complainin' an' a-bullblowin'. You get to work. You ain't so big I can't lick you yet."

Al's face turned red with anger. He started to bluster.

Tom moved near to him. "Come on, Al," he said quietly. "Bread an' meat. We got to get 'em."

They reached for the fruit and dropped them in the buckets. Tom ran at his work. One bucket full, two buckets. He dumped them in a box. Three buckets. The box was full. "I jus' made a nickel," he called. He picked up the box and walked hurriedly to the station. "Here's a nickel's worth," he said to the checker.

The man looked into the box, turned over a peach or two. "Put it over there. That's out," he said. "I told you not to bruise them. Dumped 'em outa the bucket, didn't you? Well, every damn peach is bruised. Can't check that one. Put 'em in easy or you're working for nothing."

"Why—goddamn it——"

"Now go easy. I warned you before you started."

Tom's eyes drooped sullenly. "O.K.," he said. "O.K." He went quickly back to the others. "Might's well dump what you got," he said. "Yours is the same as mine. Won't take 'em."

"Now, what the hell!" Al began.

"Got to pick easier. Can't drop 'em in the bucket. Got to lay 'em in."

They started again, and this time they handled the fruit gently. The boxes filled more slowly. "We could figger somepin out, I bet," Tom said. "If Ruthie an' Winfiel' or Rosasharn jus' put 'em in the boxes, we could work out a system." He carried his newest box to the station. "Is this here worth a nickel?"

The checker looked them over, dug down several layers. "That's better," he said. He checked the box in. "Just take it easy."

Tom hurried back. "I got a nickel," he called. "I got a nickel. On'y got to do that there twenty times for a dollar."

They worked on steadily through the afternoon. Ruthie and Winfield found them after a while. "You got to work," Pa told them. "You got to put the peaches careful in the box. Here, now, one at a time."

The children squatted down and picked the peaches out of the extra bucket, and a line of buckets stood ready for them. Tom carried the full boxes to the station. "That's seven," he said. "That's eight. Forty cents we got. Get a nice piece of meat for forty cents."

The afternoon passed. Ruthie tried to go away. "I'm tar'd," she whined. "I got to rest."

"You got to stay right where you're at," said Pa.

Uncle John picked slowly. He filled one bucket to two of Tom's. His pace didn't change.

In mid-afternoon Ma came trudging out. "I would a come before, but Rosasharn fainted," she said. "Jes' fainted away."

"You been eatin' peaches," she said to the children. "Well,

they'll blast you out." Ma's stubby body moved quickly. She abandoned her bucket quickly and picked into her apron. When the sun went down they had picked twenty boxes.

Tom set the twentieth box down. "A buck," he said. "How long do we work?"

"Work till dark, long as you can see."

"Well, can we get credit now? Ma oughta go in an' buy some stuff to eat."

"Sure. I'll give you a slip for a dollar now." He wrote on a strip of paper and handed it to Tom.

He took it to Ma. "Here you are. You can get a dollar's worth of stuff at the store."

Ma put down her bucket and straightened her shoulders. "Gets you, the first time, don't it?"

"Sure. We'll all get used to it right off. Roll on in an' get some food."

Ma said, "What'll you like to eat?"

"Meat," said Tom. "Meat an' bread an' a big pot a coffee with sugar in. Great big piece a meat."

Ruthie wailed, "Ma, we're tar'd."

"Better come along in, then."

"They was tar'd when they started," Pa said. "Wild as rabbits they're a-gettin'. Ain't gonna be no good at all 'less we can pin 'em down."

"Soon's we get set down, they'll go to school," said Ma. She trudged away, and Ruthie and Winfield timidly followed her.

"We got to work ever' day?" Winfield asked.

Ma stopped and waited. She took his hand and walked along holding it. "It ain't hard work," she said. "Be good for you. An' you're helpin' us. If we all work, purty soon we'll live in a nice house. We all got to help."

"But I got so tar'd."

"I know. I got tar'd too. Ever'body gets wore out. Got to think about other stuff. Think about when you'll go to school."

"I don't wanta go to no school. Ruthie don't, neither. Them kids that goes to school, we seen 'em, Ma. Snots! Calls us Okies. We seen 'em. I ain't a-goin'."

Ma looked pityingly down on his straw hair. "Don' give us

no trouble right now," she begged. "Soon's we get on our feet, you can be bad. But not now. We got too much, now."

"I et six of them peaches," Ruthie said.

"Well, you'll have the skitters. An' it ain't close to no toilet where we are."

The company's store was a large shed of corrugated iron. It had no display window. Ma opened the screen door and went in. A tiny man stood behind the counter. He was completely bald, and his head was blue-white. Large, brown eyebrows covered his eyes in such a high arch that his face seemed surprised and a little frightened. His nose was long and thin, and curved like a bird's beak, and his nostrils were blocked with light brown hair. Over the sleeves of his blue shirt he wore black sateen sleeve protectors. He was leaning on his elbows on the counter when Ma entered.

"Afternoon," she said.

He inspected her with interest. The arch over his eyes became higher. "Howdy."

"I got a slip here for a dollar."

"You can get a dollar's worth," he said, and he giggled shrilly. "Yes, sir. A dollar's worth. One dollar's worth." He waved his hand at the stock. "Any of it." He pulled his sleeve protectors up neatly.

"Thought I'd get a piece of meat."

"Got all kinds," he said. "Hamburg, like to have some hamburg? Twenty cents a pound, hamburg."

"Ain't that awful high? Seems to me hamburg was fifteen las' time I got some."

"Well," he giggled softly, "yes, it's high, an' same time it ain't high. Time you go on in town for a couple poun's of hamburg, it'll cos' you 'bout a gallon gas. So you see it ain't really high here, 'cause you got no gallon a gas."

Ma said sternly, "It didn' cos' you no gallon a gas to get it out here."

He laughed delightedly. "You're lookin' at it bass-ackwards," he said. "We ain't a-buyin' it, we're a-sellin' it. If we was buyin' it, why, that'd be different."

Ma put two fingers to her mouth and frowned with thought. "It looks all full a fat an' gristle."

"I ain't guaranteein' she won't cook down," the storekeeper said. "I ain't guaranteein' I'd eat her myself; but they's lots of stuff I wouldn' do."

Ma looked up at him fiercely for a moment. She controlled her voice. "Ain't you got some cheaper kind a meat?"

"Soup bones," he said. "Ten cents a pound."

"But them's jus' bones."

"Them's jes' bones," he said. "Make nice soup. Jes' bones."

"Got any boilin' beef?"

"Oh, yeah! Sure. That's two bits a poun'."

"Maybe I can't get no meat," Ma said. "But they want meat. They said they wanted meat."

"Ever'body wants meat—needs meat. That hamburg is purty nice stuff. Use the grease that comes out a her for gravy. Purty nice. No waste. Don't throw no bone away."

"How—how much is side-meat?"

"Well, now you're gettin' into fancy stuff. Christmas stuff. Thanksgivin' stuff. Thirty-five cents a poun'. I could sell you turkey cheaper, if I had some turkey."

Ma sighed. "Give me two pounds hamburg."

"Yes, ma'am." He scooped the pale meat on a piece of waxed paper. "An' what else?"

"Well, some bread."

"Right here. Fine big loaf, fifteen cents."

"That there's a twelve-cent loaf."

"Sure, it is. Go right in town an' get her for twelve cents. Gallon a gas. What else can I sell you, potatoes?"

"Yes, potatoes."

"Five pounds for a quarter."

Ma moved menacingly toward him. "I heard enough from you. I know what they cost in town."

The little man clamped his mouth tight. "Then go git 'em in town."

Ma looked at her knuckles. "What is this?" she asked softly. "You own this here store?"

"No. I jus' work here."

"Any reason you got to make fun? That help you any?" She regarded her shiny wrinkled hands. The little man was silent. "Who owns this here store?"

"Hooper Ranches, Incorporated, ma'am."

"An' they set the prices?"

"Yes, ma'am."

She looked up, smiling a little. "Ever'body comes in talks like me, is mad?"

He hesitated for a moment. "Yes, ma'am."

"An' that's why you make fun?"

"What cha mean?"

"Doin' a dirty thing like this. Shames ya, don't it? Got to act flip, huh?" Her voice was gentle. The clerk watched her, fascinated. He didn't answer. "That's how it is," Ma said finally. "Forty cents for meat, fifteen for bread, quarter for potatoes. That's eighty cents. Coffee?"

"Twenty cents the cheapest, ma'am."

"An' that's the dollar. Seven of us workin, an' that's supper." She studied her hand. "Wrap 'em up," she said quickly.

"Yes, ma'am," he said. "Thanks." He put the potatoes in a bag and folded the top carefully down. His eyes slipped to Ma, and then hid in his work again. She watched him, and she smiled a little.

"How'd you get a job like this?" she asked.

"A fella got to eat," he began; and then, belligerently, "A fella got a right to eat."

"What fella?" Ma asked.

He placed the four packages on the counter. "Meat," he said. "Potatoes, bread, coffee. One dollar, even." She handed him her slip of paper and watched while he entered the name and the amount in a ledger. "There," he said. "Now we're all even."

Ma picked up her bags. "Say," she said. "We got no sugar for the coffee. My boy Tom, he wants sugar. Look!" she said. "They're a-workin' out there. You let me have some sugar an' I'll bring the slip in later."

The little man looked away—took his eyes as far from Ma as he could. "I can't do it," he said softly. "That's the rule. I can't. I'd get in trouble. I'd get canned."

"But they're a-workin' out in the field now. They got more'n a dime comin'. Gimme ten cents' of sugar. Tom, he wanted sugar in his coffee. Spoke about it."

"I can't do it, ma'am. That's the rule. No slip, no groceries. The manager, he talks about that all the time. No, I can't do it. No, I can't. They'd catch me. They always catch fellas. Always. I can't."

"For a dime?"

"For anything, ma'am." He looked pleadingly at her. And then his face lost its fear. He took ten cents from his pocket and rang it up in the cash register. "There," he said with relief. He pulled a little bag from under the counter, whipped it open and scooped some sugar into it, weighed the bag, and added a little more sugar. "There you are," he said. "Now it's all right. You bring in your slip an' I'll get my dime back."

Ma studied him. Her hand went blindly out and put the little bag of sugar on the pile in her arm. "Thanks to you," she said quietly. She started for the door, and when she reached it, she turned about. "I'm learnin' one thing good," she said. "Learnin' it all a time, ever' day. If you're in trouble or hurt or need—go to poor people. They're the only ones that'll help—the only ones." The screen door slammed behind her.

The little man leaned his elbows on the counter and looked after her with his surprised eyes. A plump tortoise-shell cat leaped up on the counter and stalked lazily near to him. It rubbed sideways against his arms, and he reached out with his hand and pulled it against his cheek. The cat purred loudly, and the tip of its tail jerked back and forth.

Tom and Al and Pa and Uncle John walked in from the orchard when the dusk was deep. Their feet were a little heavy against the road.

"You wouldn' think jus' reachin' up an' pickin'd get you in the back," Pa said.

"Be awright in a couple days," said Tom. "Say, Pa, after we eat I'm a-gonna walk out an' see what all that fuss is outside the gate. It's been a-workin' on me. Wanta come?"

"No," said Pa. "I like to have a little while to jus' work an' not think about nothin'. Seems like I jus' been beatin' my brains to death for a hell of a long time. No, I'm gonna set awhile, an' then go to bed."

"How 'bout you, Al?"

Al looked away. "Guess I'll look aroun' in here, first," he said.

"Well, I know Uncle John won't come. Guess I'll go her alone. Got me all curious."

Pa said, "I'll get a hell of a lot curiouser 'fore I'll do anything about it—with all them cops out there."

"Maybe they ain't there at night," Tom suggested.

"Well, I ain't gonna find out. An' you better not tell Ma where you're a-goin'. She'll jus' squirt her head off worryin'."

Tom turned to Al. "Ain't you curious?"

"Guess I'll jus' look aroun' this here camp," Al said.

"Lookin' for girls, huh?"

"Mindin' my own business," Al said acidly.

"I'm still a-goin'," said Tom.

They emerged from the orchard into the dusty street between the red shacks. The low yellow light of kerosene lanterns shone from some of the doorways, and inside, in the half-gloom, the black shapes of people moved about. At the end of the street a guard still sat, his shotgun resting against his knee.

Tom paused as he passed the guard. "Got a place where a fella can get a bath, mister?"

The guard studied him in the half-light. At last he said, "See that water tank?"

"Yeah."

"Well, there's a hose over there."

"Any warm water?"

"Say, who in hell you think you are, J. P. Morgan?"

"No," said Tom. "No, I sure don't. Good night, mister."

The guard grunted contemptuously. "Hot water, for Christ's sake. Be wantin' tubs next." He stared glumly after the four Joads.

A second guard came around the end house. "'S'matter, Mack?"

"Why, them goddamn Okies. 'Is they warm water?' he says."

The second guard rested his gun butt on the ground. "It's them gov'ment camps," he said. "I bet that fella been in a gov'ment camp. We ain't gonna have no peace till we wipe them camps out. They'll be wantin' clean sheets, first thing we know."

Mack asked, "How is it out at the main gate—hear anything?"

"Well, they was out there yellin' all day. State police got it in hand. They're runnin' the hell outa them smart guys. I heard they's a long lean son-of-a-bitch spark-pluggin' the thing. Fella says they'll get him tonight, an' then she'll go to pieces."

"We won't have no job if it comes too easy," Mack said.

"We'll have a job, all right. These goddamn Okies! You got to watch 'em all the time. Things get a little quiet, we can always stir 'em up a little."

"Have trouble when they cut the rate here, I guess."

"We sure will. No, you needn' worry about us havin' work—not while Hooper's snubbin' close."

The fire roared in the Joad house. Hamburger patties splashed and hissed in the grease, and the potatoes bubbled. The house was full of smoke, and the yellow lantern light threw heavy black shadows on the walls. Ma worked quickly about the fire while Rose of Sharon sat on a box resting her heavy abdomen on her knees.

"Feelin' better now?" Ma asked.

"Smell a cookin' gets me. I'm hungry, too."

"Go set in the door," Ma said. "I got to have that box to break up anyways."

The men trooped in. "Meat, by God!" said Tom. "And coffee. I smell her. Jesus, I'm hungry! I et a lot of peaches, but they didn' do no good. Where can we wash, Ma?"

"Go down to the water tank. Wash down there. I jus' sent Ruthie an' Winfiel' to wash." The men went out again.

"Go on now, Rosasharn," Ma ordered. "Either you set in the door or else on the bed. I got to break that box up."

The girl helped herself up with her hands. She moved heavily to one of the mattresses and sat down on it. Ruthie and Winfield came in quietly, trying by silence and by keeping close to the wall to remain obscure.

Ma looked over at them. "I got a feelin' you little fellas is lucky they ain't much light," she said. She pounced at Winfield and felt his hair. "Well, you got wet, anyway, but I bet you ain't clean."

"They wasn't no soap," Winfield complained.

"No, that's right. I couldn' buy no soap. Not today. Maybe we can get soap tomorra." She went back to the stove, laid out the plates, and began to serve the supper. Two patties apiece and a big potato. She placed three slices of bread on each plate. When the meat was all out of the frying pan she poured a little of the grease on each plate. The men came in again, their faces dripping and their hair shining with water.

"Leave me at her," Tom cried.

They took the plates. They ate silently, wolfishly, and wiped up the grease with the bread. The children retired into the corner of the room, put their plates on the floor, and knelt in front of the food like little animals.

Tom swallowed the last of his bread. "Got any more, Ma?"

"No," she said. "That's all. You made a dollar, an' that's a dollar's worth."

"That?"

"They charge extry out here. We got to go in town when we can."

"I ain't full," said Tom.

"Well, tomorra you'll get in a full day. Tomorra night—we'll have plenty."

Al wiped his mouth on his sleeve. "Guess I'll take a look around," he said.

"Wait, I'll go with you." Tom followed him outside. In the darkness Tom went close to his brother. "Sure you don' wanta come with me?"

"No. I'm gonna look aroun' like I said."

"O.K.," said Tom. He turned away and strolled down the street. The smoke from the houses hung low to the ground, and the lanterns threw their pictures of doorways and windows into the street. On the doorsteps people sat and looked out into the darkness. Tom could see their heads turn as their eyes followed him down the street. At the street end the dirt road continued across a stubble field, and the black lumps of haycocks were visible in the starlight. A thin blade of moon was low in the sky toward the west, and the long cloud of the milky way trailed clearly overhead. Tom's feet sounded softly on the dusty road, a dark path against the yellow stubble. He put his hands in his pockets and trudged along toward the main gate. An embankment came close to the road. Tom could hear the whisper of water against the grasses in the irrigation ditch. He climbed up the bank and looked down on the dark water, and saw the stretched reflections of the stars. The State road was ahead. Car lights swooping past showed where it was. Tom set out again toward it. He could see the high wire gate in the starlight.

A figure stirred beside the road. A voice said, "Hello—who is it?"

Tom stopped and stood still. "Who are you?"

A man stood up and walked near. Tom could see the gun in his hand. Then a flashlight played on his face. "Where you think you're going?"

"Well, I thought I'd take a walk. Any law against it?"

"You better walk some other way."

Tom asked, "Can't I even get out of here?"

"Not tonight you can't. Want to walk back, or shall I whistle some help an' take you?"

"Hell," said Tom, "it ain't nothin' to me. If it's gonna cause a mess, I don't give a darn. Sure, I'll go back."

The dark figure relaxed. The flash went off. "Ya see, it's for your own good. Them crazy pickets might get you."

"What pickets?"

"Them goddamn reds."

"Oh," said Tom. "I didn' know 'bout them."

"You seen 'em when you come, didn' you?"

"Well, I seen a bunch a guys, but they was so many cops I didn' know. Thought it was a accident."

"Well, you better git along back."

"That's O.K. with me, mister." He swung about and started back. He walked quietly along the road a hundred yards, and then he stopped and listened. The twittering call of a raccoon sounded near the irrigation ditch and, very far away, the angry howl of a tied dog. Tom sat down beside the road and listened. He heard the high soft laughter of a night hawk and the stealthy movement of a creeping animal in the stubble. He inspected the skyline in both directions, dark frames both ways, nothing to show against. Now he stood up and walked slowly to the right of the road, off into the stubble field, and he walked bent down, nearly as low as the haycocks. He moved slowly and stopped occasionally to listen. At last he came to the wire fence, five strands of taut barbed wire. Beside the fence he lay on his back, moved his head under the lowest strand, held the wire up with his hands and slid himself under, pushing against the ground with his feet.

He was about to get up when a group of men walked by on the edge of the highway. Tom waited until they were far ahead before he stood up and followed them. He watched the side of the road for tents. A few automobiles went by. A stream cut across the fields, and the highway crossed it on a small concrete bridge. Tom looked over the side of the bridge. In the bottom of the deep ravine he saw a tent and a lantern was burning inside. He watched it for a moment, saw the shadows of people against the canvas walls. Tom climbed a fence and moved down into the ravine through brush and dwarf willows; and in the bottom, beside a tiny stream, he found a trail. A man sat on a box in front of the tent.

"Evenin'," Tom said.

"Who are you?"

"Well—I guess, well—I'm jus' goin' past."

"Know anybody here?"

"No. I tell you I was jus' goin' past."

A head stuck out of the tent. A voice said, "What's the matter?"

"Casy!" Tom cried. "Casy! For Chris' sake, what you doin' here?"

"Why, my God, it's Tom Joad! Come on in, Tommy. Come on in."

"Know him, do ya?" the man in front asked.

"Know him? Christ, yes. Knowed him for years. I come west with him. Come on in, Tom." He clutched Tom's elbow and pulled him into the tent.

Three other men sat on the ground, and in the center of the tent a lantern burned. The men looked up suspiciously. A dark-faced, scowling man held out his hand. "Glad to meet ya," he said. "I heard what Casy said. This the fella you was tellin' about?"

"Sure. This is him. Well, for God's sake! Where's your folks? What you doin' here?"

"Well," said Tom, "we heard they was work this-a-way. An' we come, an' a bunch a State cops run us into this here ranch an' we been a-pickin' peaches all afternoon. I seen a bunch a fellas yellin'. They wouldn' tell me nothin', so I come out here to see what's goin' on. How'n hell'd you get here, Casy?"

The preacher leaned forward and the yellow lantern light fell on his high pale forehead. "Jail house is a kinda funny place," he said. "Here's me, been a-goin' into the wilderness like Jesus to try find out somepin. Almost got her sometimes, too. But it's in the jail house I really got her." His eyes were sharp and merry. "Great big ol' cell, an' she's full all a time. New guys come in, and guys go out. An' 'course I talked to all of 'em."

" 'Course you did," said Tom. "Always talk. If you was up on the gallows you'd be passin' the time a day with the hangman. Never seen sech a talker."

The men in the tent chuckled. A wizened little man with a wrinkled face slapped his knee. "Talks all the time," he said. "Folks kinda likes to hear 'im, though."

"Use' ta be a preacher," said Tom. "Did he tell that?"

"Sure, he told."

Casy grinned. "Well, sir," he went on, "I begin gettin' at things. Some a them fellas in the tank was drunks, but mostly they was there 'cause they stole stuff; an' mostly it was stuff they needed an' couldn' get no other way. Ya see?" he asked.

"No," said Tom.

"Well, they was nice fellas, ya see. What made 'em bad was they needed stuff. An' I begin to see, then. It's need that makes all the trouble. I ain't got it worked out. Well, one day they give us some beans that was sour. One fella started yellin', an' nothin' happened. He yelled his head off. Trusty come along an' looked in an' went on. Then another fella yelled. Well, sir, then we all got yellin'. And we all got on the same tone, an' I tell ya, it jus' seemed like that tank bulged an' give and swelled up. By God! Then somepin happened! They come a-runnin', and they give us some other stuff to eat—give it to us. Ya see?"

"No," said Tom.

Casy put his chin down on his hands. "Maybe I can't tell you," he said. "Maybe you got to find out. Where's your cap?"

"I come out without it."

"How's your sister?"

"Hell, she's big as a cow. I bet she got twins. Gonna need wheels under her stomach. Got to holdin' it with her han's, now. You ain' tol' me what's goin' on."

The wizened man said, "We struck. This here's a strike."

"Well, fi' cents a box ain't much, but a fella can eat."

"Fi' cents?" the wizened man cried. "Fi' cents! They payin' you fi' cents?"

"Sure. We made a buck an' a half."

A heavy silence fell in the tent. Casy stared out the entrance, into the dark night. "Lookie, Tom," he said at last. "We come to work there. They says it's gonna be fi' cents. They was a hell of a lot of us. We got there an' they says they're payin' two an' a half cents. A fella can't even eat on that, an' if he got kids— So we says we won't take it. So they druv us off. An' all the cops in the worl' come down on us. Now they're payin' you five. When they bust this here strike—ya think they'll pay five?"

"I dunno," Tom said. "Payin' five now."

"Lookie," said Casy. "We tried to camp together, an' they druv us like pigs. Scattered us. Beat the hell outa fellas. Druv us like pigs. They run you in like pigs, too. We can't las' much longer. Some people ain't et for two days. You goin' back tonight?"

"Aim to," said Tom.

"Well—tell the folks in there how it is, Tom. Tell 'em they're starvin' us an' stabbin' theirself in the back. 'Cause sure as cowflops she'll drop to two an' a half jus' as soon as they clear us out."

"I'll tell 'em," said Tom. "I don' know how. Never seen so many guys with guns. Don' know if they'll even let a fella talk. An' folks don' pass no time of day. They jus' hang down their heads an' won't even give a fella a howdy."

"Try an' tell 'em, Tom. They'll get two an' a half, jus' the minute we're gone. You know what two an' a half is—that's one ton of peaches picked an' carried for a dollar." He dropped his head. "No—you can't do it. You can't get your food for that. Can't eat for that."

"I'll try to get to tell the folks."

"How's your ma?"

"Purty good. She liked that gov'ment camp. Baths an' hot water."

"Yeah—I heard."

"It was pretty nice there. Couldn' find no work, though. Had a leave."

"I'd like to go to one," said Casy. "Like to see it. Fella says they ain't no cops."

"Folks is their own cops."

Casy looked up excitedly. "An' was they any trouble? Fightin', stealin', drinkin'?"

"No," said Tom.

"Well, if a fella went bad—what then? What'd they do?"

"Put 'im outa the camp."

"But they wasn' many?"

"Hell, no," said Tom. "We was there a month, an' on'y one."

Casy's eyes shone with excitement. He turned to the other men. "Ya see?" he cried. "I tol' you. Cops cause more trouble than they stop. Look, Tom. Try an' get the folks in there to come on out. They can do it in a couple days. Them peaches is ripe. Tell 'em."

"They won't," said Tom. "They're a-gettin' five, an' they don' give a damn about nothin' else."

"But jus' the minute they ain't strikebreakin' they won't get no five."

"I don' think they'll swalla that. Five they're a-gettin'. Tha's all they care about."

"Well, tell 'em anyways."

"Pa wouldn' do it," Tom said. "I know 'im. He'd say it wasn't none of his business."

"Yes," Casy said disconsolately. "I guess that's right. Have to take a beatin' 'fore he'll know."

"We was outa food," Tom said. "Tonight we had meat. Not much, but we had it. Think Pa's gonna give up his meat on account a other fellas? An' Rosasharn oughta get milk.

Think Ma's gonna wanta starve that baby jus' 'cause a bunch a fellas is yellin' outside a gate?''

Casy said sadly, ''I wisht they could see it. I wisht they could see the on'y way they can depen' on their meat— Oh, the hell! Get tar'd sometimes. God-awful tar'd. I knowed a fella. Brang 'im in while I was in the jail house. Been tryin' to start a union. Got one started. An' then them vigilantes bust it up. An' know what? Them very folks he been tryin' to help tossed him out. Wouldn' have nothin' to do with 'im. Scared they'd get saw in his comp'ny. Says, 'Git out. You're a danger on us.' Well, sir, it hurt his feelin's purty bad. But then he says, 'It ain't so bad if you know.' He says, 'French Revolution— all them fellas that figgered her out got their heads chopped off. Always that way,' he says. 'Jus' as natural as rain. You ain't doin' it for fun no way. Doin' it 'cause you have to. 'Cause it's you. Look a Washington,' he says. 'Fit the Revolution, an' after, them sons-a-bitches turned on him. An' Lincoln the same. Same folks yellin' to kill 'em. Natural as rain.' ''

''Don't soun' like no fun,'' said Tom.

''No, it don't. This fella in jail, he says, 'Anyways, you do what you can. An',' he says, 'the on'y thing you got to look at is that ever' time they's a little step fo'ward, she may slip back a little, but she never slips clear back. You can prove that,' he says, 'an' that makes the whole thing right. An' that means they wasn't no waste even if it seemed like they was.' ''

''Talkin','' said Tom. ''Always talkin'. Take my brother Al. He's out lookin' for a girl. He don't care 'bout nothin' else. Couple days he'll get him a girl. Think about it all day an' do it all night. He don't give a damn 'bout steps up or down or sideways.''

''Sure,'' said Casy. ''Sure. He's jus' doin' what he's got to do. All of us like that.''

The man seated outside pulled the tent flap wide. ''God-damn it, I don' like it,'' he said.

Casy looked out at him. ''What's the matter?''

''I don' know. I jus' itch all over. Nervous as a cat.''

''Well, what's the matter?''

''I don' know. Seems like I hear somepin, an' then I listen an' they ain't nothin' to hear.''

"You're jus' jumpy," the wizened man said. He got up and went outside. And in a second he looked into the tent. "They's a great big ol' black cloud a-sailin' over. Bet she's got thunder. That's what's itchin' him—'lectricity." He ducked out again. The other two men stood up from the ground and went outside.

Casy said softly, "All of 'em's itchy. Them cops been sayin' how they're gonna beat the hell outa us an' run us outa the county. They figger I'm a leader 'cause I talk so much."

The wizened face looked in again. "Casy, turn out that lantern an' come outside. They's somepin."

Casy turned the screw. The flame drew down into the slots and popped and went out. Casy groped outside and Tom followed him. "What is it?" Casy asked softly.

"I dunno. Listen!"

There was a wall of frog sounds that merged with silence. A high, shrill whistle of crickets. But through this background came other sounds—faint footsteps from the road, a crunch of clods up on the bank, a little swish of brush down the stream.

"Can't really tell if you hear it. Fools you. Get nervous," Casy reassured them. "We're all nervous. Can't really tell. You hear it, Tom?"

"I hear it," said Tom. "Yeah, I hear it. I think they's guys comin' from ever' which way. We better get outa here."

The wizened man whispered, "Under the bridge span—out that way. Hate to leave my tent."

"Le's go," said Casy.

They moved quietly along the edge of the stream. The black span was a cave before them. Casy bent over and moved through. Tom behind. Their feet slipped into the water. Thirty feet they moved, and their breathing echoed from the curved ceiling. Then they came out on the other side and straightened up.

A sharp call, "There they are!" Two flashlight beams fell on the men, caught them, blinded them. "Stand where you are." The voices came out of the darkness. "That's him. That shiny bastard. That's him."

Casy stared blindly at the light. He breathed heavily.

"Listen," he said. "You fellas don' know what you're doin'. You're helpin' to starve kids."

"Shut up, you red son-of-a-bitch."

A short heavy man stepped into the light. He carried a new white pick handle.

Casy went on, "You don' know what you're a-doin'."

The heavy man swung with the pick handle. Casy dodged down into the swing. The heavy club crashed into the side of his head with a dull crunch of bone, and Casy fell sideways out of the light.

"Jesus, George. I think you killed him."

"Put the light on him," said George. "Serve the son-of-a-bitch right." The flashlight beam dropped, searched and found Casy's crushed head.

Tom looked down at the preacher. The light crossed the heavy man's legs and the white new pick handle. Tom leaped silently. He wrenched the club free. The first time he knew he had missed and struck a shoulder, but the second time his crushing blow found the head, and as the heavy man sank down, three more blows found his head. The lights danced about. There were shouts, the sound of running feet, crashing through brush. Tom stood over the prostrate man. And then a club reached his head, a glancing blow. He felt the stroke like an electric shock. And then he was running along the stream, bending low. He heard the splash of footsteps following him. Suddenly he turned and squirmed up into the brush, deep into a poison-oak thicket. And he lay still. The footsteps came near, the light beams glanced along the stream bottom. Tom wriggled up through the thicket to the top. He emerged in an orchard. And still he could hear the calls, the pursuit in the stream bottom. He bent low and ran over the cultivated earth; the clods slipped and rolled under his feet. Ahead he saw the bushes that bounded the field, bushes along the edges of an irrigation ditch. He slipped through the fence, edged in among vines and blackberry bushes. And then he lay still, panting hoarsely. He felt his numb face and nose. The nose was crushed, and a trickle of blood dripped from his chin. He lay still on his stomach until his mind came back. And then he crawled slowly over the edge of the ditch. He bathed his face in the cool water, tore off the tail of his blue shirt and dipped it and held it against his torn cheek and nose. The water stung and burned.

The black cloud had crossed the sky, a blob of dark against the stars. The night was quiet again.

Tom stepped into the water and felt the bottom drop from under his feet. He threshed the two strokes across the ditch and pulled himself heavily up the other bank. His clothes clung to him. He moved and made a slopping noise; his shoes squished. Then he sat down, took off his shoes and emptied them. He wrung the bottoms of his trousers, took off his coat and squeezed the water from it.

Along the highway he saw the dancing beams of the flashlights, searching the ditches. Tom put on his shoes and moved cautiously across the stubble field. The squishing noise no longer came from his shoes. He went by instinct toward the other side of the stubble field, and at last he came to the road. Very cautiously he approached the square of houses.

Once a guard, thinking he heard a noise, called, "Who's there?"

Tom dropped and froze to the ground, and the flashlight beam passed over him. He crept silently to the door of the Joad house. The door squalled on its hinges. And Ma's voice, calm and steady and wide awake:

"What's that?"

"Me. Tom."

"Well, you better get some sleep. Al ain't in yet."

"He must a foun' a girl."

"Go on to sleep," she said softly. "Over under the window."

He found his place and took off his clothes to the skin. He lay shivering under his blanket. And his torn face awakened from its numbness, and his whole head throbbed.

It was an hour more before Al came in. He moved cautiously near and stepped on Tom's wet clothes.

"Sh!" said Tom.

Al whispered, "You awake? How'd you get wet?"

"Sh," said Tom. "Tell you in the mornin'."

Pa turned on his back, and his snoring filled the room with gasps and snorts.

"You're col'," Al said.

"Sh. Go to sleep." The little square of the window showed gray against the black of the room.

Tom did not sleep. The nerves of his wounded face came back to life and throbbed, and his cheek bone ached, and his broken nose bulged and pulsed with pain that seemed to toss him about, to shake him. He watched the little square window, saw the stars slide down over it and drop from sight. At intervals he heard the footsteps of the watchmen.

At last the roosters crowed, far away, and gradually the window lightened. Tom touched his swollen face with his fingertips, and at his movement Al groaned and murmured in his sleep.

The dawn came finally. In the houses, packed together, there was a sound of movement, a crash of breaking sticks, a little clatter of pans. In the graying gloom Ma sat up suddenly. Tom could see her face, swollen with sleep. She looked at the window, for a long moment. And then she threw the blanket off and found her dress. Still sitting down, she put it over her head and held her arms up and let the dress slide down to her waist. She stood up and pulled the dress down around her ankles. Then, in bare feet, she stepped carefully to the window and looked out, and while she stared at the growing light, her quick fingers unbraided her hair and smoothed the strands and braided them up again. Then she clasped her hands in front of her and stood motionless for a moment. Her face was lighted sharply by the window. She turned, stepped carefully among the mattresses, and found the lantern. The shade screeched up, and she lighted the wick.

Pa rolled over and blinked at her. She said, "Pa, you got more money?"

"Huh? Yeah. Paper wrote for sixty cents."

"Well, git up an' go buy some flour an' lard. Quick, now."

Pa yawned. "Maybe the store ain't open."

"Make 'em open it. Got to get somepin in you fellas. You got to get out to work."

Pa struggled into his overalls and put on his rusty coat. He went sluggishly out the door, yawning and stretching.

The children awakened and watched from under their blanket, like mice. Pale light filled the room now, but colorless light, before the sun. Ma glanced at the mattresses. Uncle John was awake, Al slept heavily. Her eyes moved to Tom. For a moment she peered at him, and then she moved quickly to him. His face was puffed and blue, and the blood was dried black on his lips and chin. The edges of the torn cheek were gathered and tight.

"Tom," she whispered, "what's the matter?"

"Sh!" he said. "Don't talk loud. I got in a fight."

"Tom!"

"I couldn' help it, Ma."

She knelt down beside him. "You in trouble?"

He was a long time answering. "Yeah," he said. "In trouble. I can't go out to work. I got to hide."

The children crawled near on their hands and knees, staring greedily. "What's the matter'th him, Ma?"

"Hush!" Ma said. "Go wash up."

"We got no soap."

"Well, use water."

"What's the matter'th Tom?"

"Now you hush. An' don't you tell nobody."

They backed away and squatted down against the far wall, knowing they would not be inspected.

Ma asked, "Is it bad?"

"Nose busted."

"I mean the trouble?"

"Yeah. Bad!"

Al opened his eyes and looked at Tom. "Well, for Chris' sake! What was you in?"

"What's a matter?" Uncle John asked.

Pa clumped in. "They was open all right." He put a tiny bag of flour and his package of lard on the floor beside the stove. " 'S'a matter?" he asked.

Tom braced himself on one elbow for a moment, and then he lay back. "Jesus, I'm weak. I'm gonna tell ya once. So I'll tell all of ya. How 'bout the kids?"

Ma looked at them, huddled against the wall. "Go wash ya face."

"No," Tom said. "They got to hear. They got to know. They might blab if they don' know."

"What the hell is this?" Pa demanded.

"I'm a-gonna tell. Las' night I went out to see what all the yellin' was about. An' I come on Casy."

"The preacher?"

"Yeah, Pa. The preacher, on'y he was a-leadin' the strike. They come for him."

Pa demanded, "Who come for him?"

"I dunno. Same kinda guys that turned us back on the road that night. Had pick handles." He paused. "They killed 'im. Busted his head. I was standin' there. I went nuts. Grabbed the pick handle." He looked bleakly back at the night, the darkness, the flashlights, as he spoke. "I—I clubbed a guy."

Ma's breath caught in her throat. Pa stiffened. "Kill 'im?" he asked softly.

"I—don't know. I was nuts. Tried to."

Ma asked, "Was you saw?"

"I dunno. I dunno. I guess so. They had the lights on us."

For a moment Ma stared into his eyes. "Pa," she said, "break up some boxes. We got to get breakfas'. You got to go to work. Ruthie, Winfiel'. If anybody asts you—Tom is sick—you hear? If you tell—he'll—get sent to jail. You hear?"

"Yes, ma'am."

"Keep your eye on 'em, John. Don' let 'em talk to nobody." She built the fire as Pa broke the boxes that had held the goods. She made her dough, put a pot of coffee to boil. The light wood caught and roared its flame in the chimney.

Pa finished breaking the boxes. He came near to Tom. "Casy—he was a good man. What'd he wanta mess with that stuff for?"

Tom said dully, "They come to work for fi' cents a box."

"That's what we're a-gettin'."

"Yeah. What we was a-doin' was breakin' strike. They give them fellas two an' a half cents."

"You can't eat on that."

"I know," Tom said wearily. "That's why they struck. Well, I think they bust that strike las' night. We'll maybe be gettin' two an' a half cents today."

"Why, the sons-a-bitches——"

"Yeah! Pa. You see? Casy was still a—good man. Goddamn

it, I can't get that pitcher outa my head. Him layin' there—
head jus' crushed flat an' oozin'. Jesus!" He covered his eyes
with his hand.

"Well, what we gonna do?" Uncle John asked.

Al was standing up now. "Well, by God, I know what I'm
gonna do. I'm gonna get out of it."

"No, you ain't, Al," Tom said. "We need you now. I'm the
one. I'm a danger now. Soon's I get on my feet I got to go."

Ma worked at the stove. Her head was half turned to hear.
She put grease in the frying pan, and when it whispered with
heat, she spooned the dough into it.

Tom went on, "You got to stay, Al. You got to take care a
the truck."

"Well, I don' like it."

"Can't help it, Al. It's your folks. You can help 'em. I'm a
danger to 'em."

Al grumbled angrily. "I don' know why I ain't let to get
me a job in a garage."

"Later, maybe." Tom looked past him, and he saw Rose of
Sharon lying on the mattress. Her eyes were huge—opened
wide. "Don' worry," he called to her. "Don' you worry.
Gonna get you some milk today." She blinked slowly, and
didn't answer him.

Pa said, "We got to know, Tom. Think ya killed this fella?"

"I don' know. It was dark. An' somebody smacked me. I
don' know. I hope so. I hope I killed the bastard."

"Tom!" Ma called. "Don' talk like that."

From the street came the sound of many cars moving
slowly. Pa stepped to the window and looked out. "They's a
whole slew a new people comin' in," he said.

"I guess they bust the strike, awright," said Tom. "I guess
you'll start at two an' a half cents."

"But a fella could work at a run, an' still he couldn' eat."

"I know," said Tom. "Eat win'fall peaches. That'll keep ya
up."

Ma turned the dough and stirred the coffee. "Listen to
me," she said. "I'm gettin' cornmeal today. We're a-gonna
eat cornmeal mush. An' soon's we get enough for gas, we're
movin' away. This ain't a good place. An' I ain't gonna have
Tom out alone. No, sir."

"Ya can't do that, Ma. I tell you I'm jus' a danger to ya."

Her chin was set. "That's what we'll do. Here, come eat this here, an' then get out to work. I'll come out soon's I get washed up. We got to make some money."

They ate the fried dough so hot that it sizzled in their mouths. And they tossed the coffee down and filled their cups and drank more coffee.

Uncle John shook his head over his plate. "Don't look like we're a-gonna get shet of this here. I bet it's my sin."

"Oh, shut up!" Pa cried. "We ain't got the time for your sin. Come on now. Le's get out to her. Kids, you come he'p. Ma's right. We got to go outa here."

When they were gone, Ma took a plate and a cup to Tom. "Better eat a little somepin."

"I can't, Ma. I'm so darn sore I couldn' chew."

"You better try."

"No, I can't, Ma."

She sat down on the edge of his mattress. "You got to tell me," she said. "I got to figger how it was. I got to keep straight. What was Casy a-doin'? Why'd they kill 'im?"

"He was jus' standin' there with the lights on 'im."

"What'd he say? Can ya 'member what he says?"

Tom said, "Sure. Casy said, 'You got no right to starve people.' An' then this heavy fella called him a red son-of-a-bitch. An' Casy says, 'You don' know what you're a-doin'.' An' then this guy smashed 'im."

Ma looked down. She twisted her hands together. "Tha's what he said—'You don' know what you're doin''?"

"Yeah!"

Ma said, "I wisht Granma could a heard."

"Ma—I didn' know what I was a-doin', no more'n when you take a breath. I didn' even know I was gonna do it."

"It's awright. I wisht you didn' do it. I wisht you wasn' there. But you done what you had to do. I can't read no fault on you." She went to the stove and dipped a cloth in the heating dishwater. "Here," she said. "Put that there on your face."

He laid the warm cloth over his nose and cheek, and winced at the heat. "Ma, I'm a-gonna go away tonight. I can't go puttin' this on you folks."

Ma said angrily, "Tom! They's a whole lot I don' un'er-stan'. But goin' away ain't gonna ease us. It's gonna bear us down." And she went on, "They was the time when we was on the lan'. They was a boundary to us then. Ol' folks died off, an' little fellas come, an' we was always one thing—we was the fambly—kinda whole and clear. An' now we ain't clear no more. I can't get straight. They ain't nothin' keeps us clear. Al—he's a-hankerin' an' a-jibbitin' to go off on his own. An' Uncle John is jus' a-draggin' along. Pa's lost his place. He ain't the head no more. We're crackin' up, Tom. There ain't no fambly now. An' Rosasharn—" She looked around and found the girl's wide eyes. "She gonna have her baby an' they won't be no fambly. I don' know. I been a-tryin' to keep her goin'. Winfiel'—what's he gonna be, this-a-way? Gettin' wild, an' Ruthie too—like animals. Got nothin' to trus'. Don' go, Tom. Stay an' help."

"O.K.," he said tiredly. "O.K. I shouldn', though. I know it."

Ma went to her dishpan and washed the tin plates and dried them. "You didn' sleep."

"No."

"Well, you sleep. I seen your clothes was wet. I'll hang 'em by the stove to dry." She finished her work. "I'm goin' now. I'll pick. Rosasharn, if anybody comes, Tom's sick, you hear? Don' let nobody in. You hear?" Rose of Sharon nodded. "We'll come back at noon. Get some sleep, Tom. Maybe we can get outa here tonight." She moved swiftly to him. "Tom, you ain't gonna slip out?"

"No, Ma."

"You sure? You won't go?"

"No, Ma. I'll be here."

"Awright. 'Member, Rosasharn." She went out and closed the door firmly behind her.

Tom lay still—and then a wave of sleep lifted him to the edge of unconsciousness and dropped him slowly back and lifted him again.

"You—Tom!"

"Huh? Yeah!" He started awake. He looked over at Rose of Sharon. Her eyes were blazing with resentment. "What you want?"

"You killed a fella!"

"Yeah. Not so loud! You wanta rouse somebody?"

"What da I care?" she cried. "That lady tol' me. She says what sin's gonna do. She tol' me. What chance I got to have a nice baby? Connie's gone, an' I ain't gettin' good food. I ain't gettin' milk." Her voice rose hysterically. "An' now you kill a fella. What chance that baby got to get bore right? I know—gonna be a freak—a freak! I never done no dancin'."

Tom got up. "Sh!" he said. "You're gonna get folks in here."

"I don' care. I'll have a freak! I didn' dance no hug-dance."

He went near to her. "Be quiet."

"You get away from me. It ain't the first fella you killed, neither." Her face was growing red with hysteria. Her words blurred. "I don' wanta look at you." She covered her head with her blanket.

Tom heard the choked, smothered cries. He bit his lower lip and studied the floor. And then he went to Pa's bed. Under the edge of the mattress the rifle lay, a lever-action Winchester .38, long and heavy. Tom picked it up and dropped the lever to see that a cartridge was in the chamber. He tested the hammer on half-cock. And then he went back to his mattress. He laid the rifle on the floor beside him, stock up and barrel pointing down. Rose of Sharon's voice thinned to a whimper. Tom lay down again and covered himself, covered his bruised cheek with the blanket and made a little tunnel to breathe through. He sighed, "Jesus, oh, Jesus!"

Outside, a group of cars went by, and voices sounded.

"How many men?"

"Jes' us—three. Whatcha payin'?"

"You go to house twenty-five. Number's right on the door."

"O.K., mister. Whatcha payin'?"

"Two and a half cents."

"Why, goddamn it, a man can't make his dinner!"

"That's what we're payin'. There's two hundred men coming from the South that'll be glad to get it."

"But, Jesus, mister!"

"Go on now. Either take it or go on along. I got no time to argue."

"But——"

"Look. I didn' set the price. I'm just checking you in. If you want it, take it. If you don't, turn right around and go along."

"Twenty-five, you say?"

"Yes, twenty-five."

Tom dozed on his mattress. A stealthy sound in the room awakened him. His hand crept to the rifle and tightened on the grip. He drew back the covers from his face. Rose of Sharon was standing beside his mattress.

"What you want?" Tom demanded.

"You sleep," she said. "You jus' sleep off. I'll watch the door. They won't nobody get in."

He studied her face for a moment. "O.K.," he said, and he covered his face with the blanket again.

In the beginning dusk Ma came back to the house. She paused on the doorstep and knocked and said, "It's me," so that Tom would not be worried. She opened the door and entered, carrying a bag. Tom awakened and sat up on his mattress. His wound had dried and tightened so that the un-broken skin was shiny. His left eye was drawn nearly shut. "Anybody come while we was gone?" Ma asked.

"No," he said. "Nobody. I see they dropped the price."

"How'd you know?"

"I heard folks talkin' outside."

Rose of Sharon looked dully up at Ma.

Tom pointed at her with his thumb. "She raised hell, Ma. Thinks all the trouble is aimed right smack at her. If I'm gonna get her upset like that I oughta go 'long."

Ma turned on Rose of Sharon. "What you doin'?"

The girl said resentfully, "How'm I gonna have a nice baby with stuff like this?"

Ma said, "Hush! You hush now. I know how you're a-feelin', an' I know you can't he'p it, but you jus' keep your mouth shut."

She turned back to Tom. "Don't pay her no mind, Tom. It's awful hard, an' I 'member how it is. Ever'thing is a-shootin' right at you when you're gonna have a baby, an' ever'thing anybody says is a insult, an' ever'thing's against you. Don't pay no mind. She can't he'p it. It's jus' the way she feels."

"I don' wanta hurt her."

"Hush! Jus' don' talk." She set her bag down on the cold stove. "Didn' hardly make nothin'," she said. "I tol' you, we're gonna get outa here. Tom, try an' wrassle me some wood. No—you can't. Here, we got on'y this one box lef'. Break it up. I tol' the other fellas to pick up some sticks on the way back. Gonna have mush an' a little sugar on."

Tom got up and stamped the last box to small pieces. Ma carefully built her fire in one end of the stove, conserving the flame under one stove hole. She filled a kettle with water and put it over the flame. The kettle rattled over the direct fire, rattled and wheezed.

"How was it pickin' today?" Tom asked.

Ma dipped a cup into her bag of cornmeal. "I don' wanta talk about it. I was thinkin' today how they use' to be jokes. I don' like it, Tom. We don't joke no more. When they's a joke, it's a mean bitter joke, an' they ain't no fun in it. Fella says today, 'Depression is over. I seen a jackrabbit, an' they wasn't nobody after him.' An' another fella says, 'That ain't the reason. Can't afford to kill jackrabbits no more. Catch 'em and milk 'em an' turn 'em loose. One you seen prob'ly gone dry.' That's how I mean. Ain't really funny, not funny like that time Uncle John converted an Injun an' brang him home, an' that Injun et his way clean to the bottom of the bean bin, an' then backslid with Uncle John's whisky. Tom, put a rag with col' water on your face."

The dusk deepened. Ma lighted the lantern and hung it on a nail. She fed the fire and poured cornmeal gradually into the hot water. "Rosasharn," she said, "can you stir the mush?"

Outside there was a patter of running feet. The door burst open and banged against the wall. Ruthie rushed in. "Ma!" she cried. "Ma. Winfiel' got a fit!"

"Where? Tell me!"

Ruthie panted, "Got white an' fell down. Et so many peaches he skittered hisself all day. Jus' fell down. White!"

"Take me!" Ma demanded. "Rosasharn, you watch that mush."

She went out with Ruthie. She ran heavily up the street behind the little girl. Three men walked toward her in the dusk, and the center man carried Winfield in his arms. Ma ran up to them. "He's mine," she cried. "Give 'im to me."

"I'll carry 'im for you, ma'am."

"No, here, give 'im to me." She hoisted the little boy and turned back; and then she remembered herself. "I sure thank ya," she said to the men.

"Welcome, ma'am. The little fella's purty weak. Looks like he got worms."

Ma hurried back, and Winfield was limp and relaxed in her arms. Ma carried him into the house and knelt down and laid him on a mattress. "Tell me. What's the matter?" she demanded. He opened his eyes dizzily and shook his head and closed his eyes again.

Ruthie said, "I tol' ya, Ma. He skittered all day. Ever' little while. Et too many peaches."

Ma felt his head. "He ain't fevered. But he's white and drawed out."

Tom came near and held the lantern down. "I know," he said. "He's hungered. Got no strength. Get him a can a milk an' make him drink it. Make 'im take milk on his mush."

"Winfiel'," Ma said. "Tell how ya feel."

"Dizzy," said Winfield, "jus' a-whirlin' dizzy."

"You never seen sech skitters," Ruthie said importantly.

Pa and Uncle John and Al came into the house. Their arms were full of sticks and bits of brush. They dropped their loads by the stove. "Now what?" Pa demanded.

"It's Winfiel'. He needs some milk."

"Christ Awmighty! We all need stuff!"

Ma said, "How much'd we make today?"

"Dollar forty-two."

"Well, you go right over'n get a can a milk for Winfiel'."

"Now why'd he have to get sick?"

"I don't know why, but he is. Now you git!" Pa went grumbling out the door. "You stirrin' that mush?"

"Yeah." Rose of Sharon speeded up the stirring to prove it.

Al complained, "God Awmighty, Ma! Is mush all we get after workin' till dark?"

"Al, you know we got to git. Take all we got for gas. You know."

"But, God Awmighty, Ma! A fella needs meat if he's gonna work."

"Jus' you sit quiet," she said. "We got to take the bigges' thing an' whup it fust. An' you know what that thing is."

Tom asked, "Is it about me?"

"We'll talk when we've et," said Ma. "Al, we got enough gas to go a ways, ain't we?"

" 'Bout a quarter tank," said Al.

"I wisht you'd tell me," Tom said.

"After. Jus' wait."

"Keep a-stirrin' that mush, you. Here, lemme put on some coffee. You can have sugar on your mush or in your coffee. They ain't enough for both."

Pa came back with one tall can of milk. " 'Leven cents," he said disgustedly.

"Here!" Ma took the can and stabbed it open. She let the thick stream out into a cup, and handed it to Tom. "Give that to Winfiel'."

Tom knelt beside the mattress. "Here, drink this."

"I can't. I'd sick it all up. Leave me be."

Tom stood up. "He can't take it now, Ma. Wait a little."

Ma took the cup and set it on the window ledge. "Don't none of you touch that," she warned. "That's for Winfiel'."

"I ain't had no milk," Rose of Sharon said sullenly. "I oughta have some."

"I know, but you're still on your feet. This here little fella's down. Is that mush good an' thick?"

"Yeah. Can't hardly stir it no more."

"Awright, le's eat. Now here's the sugar. They's about one spoon each. Have it on ya mush or in ya coffee."

Tom said, "I kinda like salt an' pepper on mush."

"Salt her if you like," Ma said. "The pepper's out."

The boxes were all gone. The family sat on the mattresses to eat their mush. They served themselves again and again, until the pot was nearly empty. "Save some for Winfiel'," Ma said.

Winfield sat up and drank his milk, and instantly he was ravenous. He put the mush pot between his legs and ate what was left and scraped at the crust on the sides. Ma poured the rest of the canned milk in a cup and sneaked it to Rose of Sharon to drink secretly in a corner. She poured the hot black coffee into the cups and passed them around.

"Now will you tell what's goin' on?" Tom asked. "I wanta hear."

Pa said uneasily, "I wisht Ruthie an' Winfiel' didn' hafta hear. Can't they go outside?"

Ma said, "No. They got to act growed up, even if they ain't. They's no help for it. Ruthie—you an' Winfiel' ain't ever to say what you hear, else you'll jus' break us to pieces."

"We won't," Ruthie said. "We're growed up."

"Well, jus' be quiet, then." The cups of coffee were on the floor. The short thick flame of the lantern, like a stubby butterfly's wing, cast a yellow gloom on the walls.

"Now tell," said Tom.

Ma said, "Pa, you tell."

Uncle John slupped his coffee. Pa said, "Well, they dropped the price like you said. An' they was a whole slew a new pickers so goddamn hungry they'd pick for a loaf a bread. Go for a peach, an' somebody'd get it first. Gonna get the whole crop picked right off. Fellas runnin' to a new tree. I seen fights—one fella claims it's his tree, 'nother fella wants to pick off'n it. Brang these here folks from as far's El Centro. Hungrier'n hell. Work all day for a piece a bread. I says to the checker, 'We can't work for two an' a half cents a box,' an' he says, 'Go on, then, quit. These fellas can.' I says, 'Soon's they get fed up they won't.' An' he says, 'Hell, we'll have these here peaches in 'fore they get fed up.'" Pa stopped.

"She was a devil," said Uncle John. "They say they's two hunderd more men comin' in tonight."

Tom said, "Yeah! But how about the other?"

Pa was silent for a while. "Tom," he said, "looks like you done it."

"I kinda thought so. Couldn' see. Felt like it."

"Seems like the people ain't talkin' 'bout much else," said Uncle John. "They got posses out, an' they's fellas talkin' up a lynchin'—'course when they catch the fella."

Tom looked over at the wide-eyed children. They seldom blinked their eyes. It was as though they were afraid something might happen in the split second of darkness. Tom said, "Well—this fella that done it, he on'y done it after they killed Casy."

Pa interrupted, "That ain't the way they're tellin' it now. They're sayin' he done it fust."

Tom's breath sighed out, "Ah-h!"

"They're workin' up a feelin' against us folks. That's what I heard. All them drum-corpse fellas an' lodges an' all that. Say they're gonna get this here fella."

"They know what he looks like?" Tom asked.

"Well—not exactly—but the way I heard it, they think he got hit. They think—he'll have——"

Tom put his hand up slowly and touched his bruised cheek.

Ma cried, "It ain't so, what they say!"

"Easy, Ma," Tom said. "They got it cold. Anything them drum-corpse fellas say is right if it's against us."

Ma peered through the ill light, and she watched Tom's face, and particularly his lips. "You promised," she said.

"Ma, I—maybe this fella oughta go away. If—this fella done somepin wrong, maybe he'd think, 'O.K. Le's get the hangin' over. I done wrong an' I got to take it.' But this fella didn' do nothin' wrong. He don' feel no worse'n if he killed a skunk."

Ruthie broke in, "Ma, me an' Winfiel' knows. He don' have to go this-fella'in' for us."

Tom chuckled. "Well, this fella don' want no hangin', 'cause he'd do it again. An' same time, he don't aim to bring trouble down on his folks. Ma—I got to go."

Ma covered her mouth with her fingers and coughed to clear her throat. "You can't," she said. "They wouldn' be no way to hide out. You couldn' trus' nobody. But you can trus' us. We can hide you, an' we can see you get to eat while your face gets well."

"But, Ma——"

She got to her feet. "You ain't goin'. We're a-takin' you. Al, you back the truck against the door. Now, I got it figgered out. We'll put one mattress on the bottom, an' then Tom gets quick there, an' we take another mattress an' sort of fold it so it makes a cave, an' he's in the cave; and then we sort of wall it in. He can breathe out the end, ya see. Don't argue. That's what we'll do."

Pa complained, "Seems like the man ain't got no say no more. She's jus' a heller. Come time we get settled down, I'm a-gonna smack her."

"Come that time, you can," said Ma. "Roust up, Al. It's dark enough."

Al went outside to the truck. He studied the matter and backed up near the steps.

Ma said, "Quick now. Git that mattress in!"

Pa and Uncle John flung it over the end gate. "Now that one." They tossed the second mattress up. "Now—Tom, you jump up there an' git under. Hurry up."

Tom climbed quickly, and dropped. He straightened one mattress and pulled the second on top of him. Pa bent it upwards, stood it sides up, so that the arch covered Tom. He could see out between the side-boards of the truck. Pa and Al and Uncle John loaded quickly, piled the blankets on top of Tom's cave, stood the buckets against the sides, spread the last mattress behind. Pots and pans, extra clothes, went in loose, for their boxes had been burned. They were nearly finished loading when a guard moved near, carrying his shotgun across his crooked arm.

"What's goin' on here?" he asked.

"We're goin' out," said Pa.

"What for?"

"Well—we got a job offered—good job."

"Yeah? Where's it at?"

"Why—down by Weedpatch."

"Let's have a look at you." He turned a flashlight in Pa's face, in Uncle John's, and in Al's. "Wasn't there another fella with you?"

Al said, "You mean that hitch-hiker? Little short fella with a pale face?"

"Yeah. I guess that's what he looked like."

"We jus' picked him up on the way in. He went away this mornin' when the rate dropped."

"What did he look like again?"

"Short fella. Pale face."

"Was he bruised up this mornin'?"

"I didn' see nothin'," said Al. "Is the gas pump open?"

"Yeah, till eight."

"Git in," Al cried. "If we're gonna get to Weedpatch 'fore mornin' we gotta ram on. Gettin' in front, Ma?"

"No, I'll set in back," she said. "Pa, you set back here too. Let Rosasharn set in front with Al an' Uncle John."

"Give me the work slip, Pa," said Al. "I'll get gas an' change if I can."

The guard watched them pull along the street and turn left to the gasoline pumps.

"Put in two," said Al.

"You ain't goin' far."

"No, not far. Can I get change on this here work slip?"

"Well—I ain't supposed to."

"Look, mister," Al said. "We got a good job offered if we get there tonight. If we don't, we miss out. Be a good fella."

"Well, O.K. You sign her over to me."

Al got out and walked around the nose of the Hudson. "Sure I will," he said. He unscrewed the water cap and filled the radiator.

"Two, you say?"

"Yeah, two."

"Which way you goin'?"

"South. We got a job."

"Yeah? Jobs is scarce—reg'lar jobs."

"We got a frien'," Al said. "Job's all waitin' for us. Well, so long." The truck swung around and bumped over the dirt street into the road. The feeble headlights jiggled over the way, and the right headlight blinked on and off from a bad connection. At every jolt the loose pots and pans in the truck-bed jangled and crashed.

Rose of Sharon moaned softly.

"Feel bad?" Uncle John asked.

"Yeah! Feel bad all a time. Wisht I could set still in a nice place. Wisht we was home an' never come. Connie wouldn' a went away if we was home. He would a studied up an' got someplace." Neither Al nor Uncle John answered her. They were embarrassed about Connie.

At the white painted gate to the ranch a guard came to the side of the truck. "Goin' out for good?"

"Yeah," said Al. "Goin' north. Got a job."

The guard turned his flashlight on the truck, turned it up into the tent. Ma and Pa looked stonily down into the glare. "O.K." The guard swung the gate open. The truck turned left and moved toward 101, the great north-south highway.

"Know where we're a-goin'?" Uncle John asked.

"No," said Al. "Jus' goin', an' gettin' goddamn sick of it."

"I ain't so tur'ble far from my time," Rose of Sharon said threateningly. "They better be a nice place for me."

The night air was cold with the first sting of frost. Beside the road the leaves were beginning to drop from the fruit trees. On the load, Ma sat with her back against the truck side, and Pa sat opposite, facing her.

Ma called, "You all right, Tom?"

His muffled voice came back, "Kinda tight in here. We all through the ranch?"

"You be careful," said Ma. "Might git stopped."

Tom lifted up one side of his cave. In the dimness of the truck the pots jangled. "I can pull her down quick," he said. "'Sides, I don' like gettin' trapped in here." He rested up on his elbow. "By God, she's gettin' cold, ain't she?"

"They's clouds up," said Pa. "Fellas says it's gonna be an early winter."

"Squirrels a-buildin' high, or grass seeds?" Tom asked. "By God, you can tell weather from anythin'. I bet you could find a fella could tell weather from a old pair of underdrawers."

"I dunno," Pa said. "Seems like it's gittin' on winter to me. Fella'd have to live here a long time to know."

"Which way we a-goin'?" Tom asked.

"I dunno. Al, he turned off lef'. Seems like he's goin' back the way we come."

Tom said, "I can't figger what's best. Seems like if we get on the main highway they'll be more cops. With my face this-a-way, they'd pick me right up. Maybe we oughta keep to back roads."

Ma said, "Hammer on the back. Get Al to stop."

Tom pounded the front board with his fist; the truck pulled to a stop on the side of the road. Al got out and walked to the back. Ruthie and Winfield peeked out from under their blanket.

"What ya want?" Al demanded.

Ma said, "We got to figger what to do. Maybe we better keep on the back roads. Tom says so."

"It's my face," Tom added. "Anybody'd know. Any cop'd know me."

"Well, which way you wanta go? I figgered north. We been south."

"Yeah," said Tom, "but keep on back roads."

Al asked, "How 'bout pullin' off an' catchin' some sleep, goin' on tomorra?"

Ma said quickly, "Not yet. Le's get some distance fust."

"O.K." Al got back in his seat and drove on.

Ruthie and Winfield covered up their heads again. Ma called, "Is Winfiel' all right?"

"Sure, he's awright," Ruthie said. "He been sleepin'."

Ma leaned back against the truck side. "Gives ya a funny feelin' to be hunted like. I'm gittin' mean."

"Ever'body's gittin' mean," said Pa. "Ever'body. You seen that fight today. Fella changes. Down that gov'ment camp we wasn' mean."

Al turned right on a graveled road, and the yellow lights shuddered over the ground. The fruit trees were gone now, and cotton plants took their place. They drove on for twenty miles through the cotton, turning, angling on the country roads. The road paralleled a bushy creek and turned over a concrete bridge and followed the stream on the other side. And then, on the edge of the creek the lights showed a long line of red boxcars, wheelless; and a big sign on the edge of the road said, "Cotton Pickers Wanted." Al slowed down. Tom peered between the side-bars of the truck. A quarter of a mile past the boxcars Tom hammered on the car again. Al stopped beside the road and got out again.

"Now what ya want?"

"Shut off the engine an' climb up here," Tom said.

Al got into the seat, drove off into the ditch, cut lights and engine. He climbed over the tail gate. "Awright," he said.

Tom crawled over the pots and knelt in front of Ma. "Look," he said. "It says they want cotton pickers. I seen that sign. Now I been tryin' to figger how I'm gonna stay with you, an' not make no trouble. When my face gets well, maybe it'll be awright, but not now. Ya see them cars back there. Well, the pickers live in them. Now maybe they's work there. How about if you get work there an' live in one of them cars?"

"How 'bout you?" Ma demanded.

"Well, you seen that crick, all full a brush. Well, I could hide in that brush an' keep outa sight. An' at night you could bring me out somepin to eat. I seen a culvert, little ways back. I could maybe sleep in there."

Pa said, "By God, I'd like to get my hands on some cotton! There's work I un'erstan'."

"Them cars might be a purty place to stay," said Ma. "Nice an' dry. You think they's enough brush to hide in, Tom?"

"Sure. I been watchin'. I could fix up a little place, hide away. Soon's my face gets well, why, I'd come out."

"You gonna scar purty bad," said Ma.

"Hell! Ever'body got scars."

"I picked four hunderd poun's oncet," Pa said. "'Course it was a good heavy crop. If we all pick, we could get some money."

"Could get some meat," said Al. "What'll we do right now?"

"Go back there, an' sleep in the truck till mornin'," Pa said. "Git work in the mornin'. I can see them bolls even in the dark."

"How 'bout Tom?" Ma asked.

"Now you jus' forget me, Ma. I'll take me a blanket. You look out on the way back. They's a nice culvert. You can bring me some bread or potatoes, or mush, an' just leave it there. I'll come get it."

"Well!"

"Seems like good sense to me," said Pa.

"It is good sense," Tom insisted. "Soon's my face gets a little better, why, I'll come out an' go to pickin'."

"Well, awright," Ma agreed. "But don' you take no chancet. Don' you let nobody see you for a while."

Tom crawled to the back of the truck. "I'll jus' take this here blanket. You look for that culvert on the way back, Ma."

"Take care," she begged. "You take care."

"Sure," said Tom. "Sure I will." He climbed the tail board, stepped down the bank. "Good night," he said.

Ma watched his figure blur with the night and disappear into the bushes beside the stream. "Dear Jesus, I hope it's awright," she said.

Al asked, "You want I should go back now?"

"Yeah," said Pa.

"Go slow," said Ma. "I wanta be sure an' see that culvert he said about. I got to see that."

Al backed and filled on the narrow road, until he had reversed his direction. He drove slowly back to the line of box-cars. The truck lights showed the cat-walks up to the wide car doors. The doors were dark. No one moved in the night. Al shut off his lights.

"You and Uncle John climb up back," he said to Rose of Sharon. "I'll sleep in the seat here."

Uncle John helped the heavy girl to climb up over the tail board. Ma piled the pots in a small space. The family lay wedged close together in the back of the truck.

A baby cried, in long jerking cackles, in one of the boxcars. A dog trotted out, sniffing and snorting, and moved slowly around the Joad truck. The tinkle of moving water came from the streambed.

Chapter Twenty-Seven

Cotton Pickers Wanted—placards on the road, hand-bills out, orange-colored handbills—Cotton Pickers Wanted.

Here, up this road, it says.

The dark green plants stringy now, and the heavy bolls clutched in the pod. White cotton spilling out like popcorn.

Like to get our hands on the bolls. Tenderly, with the fingertips.

I'm a good picker.

Here's the man, right here.

I aim to pick some cotton.

Got a bag?

Well, no, I ain't.

Cost ya a dollar, the bag. Take it out o' your first hunderd and fifty. Eighty cents a hunderd first time over the field. Ninety cents second time over. Get your bag there. One dollar. 'F you ain't got the buck, we'll take it out of your first hunderd and fifty. That's fair, and you know it.

Sure it's fair. Good cotton bag, last all season. An' when she's wore out, draggin', turn 'er aroun', use the other end. Sew up the open end. Open up the wore end. And when both ends is gone, why, that's nice cloth! Makes a nice pair a summer drawers. Makes nightshirts. And well, hell—a cotton bag's a nice thing.

Hang it around your waist. Straddle it, drag it between your legs. She drags light at first. And your fingertips pick out the fluff, and the hands go twisting into the sack between your legs. Kids come along behind; got no bags for the kids—use a gunny sack or put it in your ol' man's bag. She hangs heavy, some, now. Lean forward, hoist 'er along. I'm a good hand with cotton. Finger-wise, boll-wise. Jes' move along talkin', an' maybe singin' till the bag gets heavy. Fingers go right to it. Fingers know. Eyes see the work—and don't see it.

Talkin' across the rows——

They was a lady back home, won't mention no names—had a nigger kid all of a sudden. Nobody knowed before. Never did hunt out the nigger. Couldn' never hold up her head no more. But I started to tell—she was a good picker.

Now the bag is heavy, boost it along. Set your hips and tow it along, like a work horse. And the kids pickin' into the old man's sack. Good crop here. Gets thin in the low places, thin and stringy. Never seen no cotton like this here California cotton. Long fiber, bes' damn cotton I ever seen. Spoil the lan' pretty soon. Like a fella wants to buy some cotton lan'— Don' buy her, rent her. Then when she's cottoned on down, move someplace new.

Lines of people moving across the fields. Finger-wise. Inquisitive fingers snick in and out and find the bolls. Hardly have to look.

Bet I could pick cotton if I was blind. Got a feelin' for a cotton boll. Pick clean, clean as a whistle.

Sack's full now. Take her to the scales. Argue. Scale man says you got rocks to make weight. How 'bout him? His scales is fixed. Sometimes he's right, you got rocks in the sack. Sometimes you're right, the scales is crooked. Sometimes both; rocks an' crooked scales. Always argue, always fight. Keeps your head up. An' his head up. What's a few rocks? Jus' one, maybe. Quarter pound? Always argue.

Back with the empty sack. Got our own book. Mark in the weight. Got to. If they know you're markin', then they don't cheat. But God he'p ya if ya don' keep your own weight.

This is good work. Kids runnin' aroun'. Heard 'bout the cotton-pickin' machine?

Yeah, I heard.

Think it'll ever come?

Well, if it comes—fella says it'll put han' pickin' out.

Come night. All tired. Good pickin', though. Got three dollars, me an' the ol' woman an' the kids.

The cars move to the cotton fields. The cotton camps set up. The screened high trucks and trailers are piled high with white fluff. Cotton clings to the fence wires, and cotton rolls in little balls along the road when the wind blows. And clean white cotton, going to the gin. And the big, lumpy bales standing, going to the compress. And cotton clinging to your clothes and stuck to your whiskers. Blow your nose, there's cotton in your nose.

Hunch along now, fill up the bag 'fore dark. Wise fingers seeking in the bolls. Hips hunching along, dragging the bag. Kids are tired, now in the evening. They trip over their feet in the cultivated earth. And the sun is going down.

Wisht it would last. It ain't much money, God knows, but I wisht it would last.

On the highway the old cars piling in, drawn by the handbills.

Got a cotton bag?

No.

Cost ya a dollar, then.

If they was on'y fifty of us, we could stay awhile, but they's five hunderd. She won't last hardly at all. I knowed a fella never did git his bag paid out. Ever' job he got a new bag, an' ever' fiel' was done 'fore he got his weight.

Try for God's sake ta save a little money! Winter's comin' fast. They ain't no work at all in California in the winter. Fill up the bag 'fore it's dark. I seen that fella put two clods in.

Well, hell. Why not? I'm jus' balancin' the crooked scales.

Now here's my book, three hunderd an' twelve poun's.

Right!

Jesus, he never argued! His scales mus' be crooked. Well, that's a nice day anyways.

They say a thousan' men are on their way to this field. We'll be fightin' for a row tomorra. We'll be snatchin' cotton, quick.

Cotton Pickers Wanted. More men picking, quicker to the gin.

Now into the cotton camp.

Side-meat tonight, by God! We got money for side-meat! Stick out a han' to the little fella, he's wore out. Run in ahead an' git us four poun' of side-meat. The ol' woman'll make some nice biscuits tonight, ef she ain't too tired.

Chapter Twenty-Eight

THE BOXCARS, twelve of them, stood end to end on a little flat beside the stream. There were two rows of six each, the wheels removed. Up to the big sliding doors slatted planks ran for cat-walks. They made good houses, water-tight and draftless, room for twenty-four families, one family in each end of each car. No windows, but the wide doors stood open. In some of the cars a canvas hung down in the center of the car, while in others only the position of the door made the boundary.

The Joads had one end of an end car. Some previous occupant had fitted up an oil can with a stovepipe, had made a hole in the wall for the stovepipe. Even with the wide door open, it was dark in the ends of the car. Ma hung the tarpaulin across the middle of the car.

"It's nice," she said. "It's almost nicer than anything we had 'cept the gov'ment camp."

Each night she unrolled the mattresses on the floor, and each morning rolled them up again. And every day they went into the fields and picked the cotton, and every night they had meat. On a Saturday they drove into Tulare, and they bought a tin stove and new overalls for Al and Pa and Winfield and Uncle John, and they bought a dress for Ma and gave Ma's best dress to Rose of Sharon.

"She's so big," Ma said. "Jus' a waste of good money to get her a new dress now."

The Joads had been lucky. They got in early enough to have a place in the boxcars. Now the tents of the late-comers filled the little flat, and those who had the boxcars were oldtimers, and in a way aristocrats.

The narrow stream slipped by, out of the willows, and back into the willows again. From each car a hard-beaten path went down to the stream. Between the cars the clothes lines hung, and every day the lines were covered with drying clothes.

In the evening they walked back from the fields, carrying their folded cotton bags under their arms. They went into the store which stood at the crossroads, and there were many pickers in the store, buying their supplies.

"How much today?"

"We're doin' fine. We made three and a half today. Wisht she'd keep up. Them kids is gettin' to be good pickers. Ma's worked 'em up a little bag for each. They couldn' tow a growed-up bag. Dump into ours. Made bags outa a couple old shirts. Work fine."

And Ma went to the meat counter, her forefinger pressed against her lips, blowing on her finger, thinking deeply. "Might get some pork chops," she said. "How much?"

"Thirty cents a pound, ma'am."

"Well, lemme have three poun's. An' a nice piece a boilin' beef. My girl can cook it tomorra. An' a bottle a milk for my girl. She dotes on milk. Gonna have a baby. Nurse-lady tol' her to eat lots a milk. Now, le's see, we got potatoes."

Pa came close, carrying a can of sirup in his hands. "Might get this here," he said. "Might have some hotcakes."

Ma frowned. "Well—well, yes. Here, we'll take this here. Now—we got plenty lard."

Ruthie came near, in her hands two large boxes of Cracker Jack, in her eyes a brooding question, which on a nod or a shake of Ma's head might become tragedy or joyous excitement. "Ma?" She held up the boxes, jerked them up and down to make them attractive.

"Now you put them back——"

The tragedy began to form in Ruthie's eyes. Pa said, "They're on'y a nickel apiece. Them little fellas worked good today."

"Well——" The excitement began to steal into Ruthie's eyes. "Awright."

Ruthie turned and fled. Halfway to the door she caught Winfield and rushed him out the door, into the evening.

Uncle John fingered a pair of canvas gloves with yellow leather palms, tried them on and took them off and laid them down. He moved gradually to the liquor shelves, and he stood studying the labels on the bottles. Ma saw him. "Pa," she said, and motioned with her head toward Uncle John.

Pa lounged over to him. "Gettin' thirsty, John?"

"No, I ain't."

"Jus' wait till cotton's done," said Pa. "Then you can go on a hell of a drunk."

" 'Tain't sweatin' me none," Uncle John said. "I'm workin' hard an' sleepin' good. No dreams nor nothin'."

"Jus' seen you sort of droolin' out at them bottles."

"I didn' hardly see 'em. Funny thing. I wanta buy stuff. Stuff I don't need. Like to git one a them safety razors. Thought I'd like to have some a them gloves over there. Awful cheap."

"Can't pick no cotton with gloves," said Pa.

"I know that. An' I don't need no safety razor, neither. Stuff settin' out there, you jus' feel like buyin' it whether you need it or not."

Ma called, "Come on. We got ever'thing." She carried a bag. Uncle John and Pa each took a package. Outside Ruthie and Winfield were waiting, their eyes strained, their cheeks puffed and full of Cracker Jack.

"Won't eat no supper, I bet," Ma said.

People streamed toward the boxcar camp. The tents were lighted. Smoke poured from the stovepipes. The Joads climbed up their cat-walk and into their end of the boxcar. Rose of Sharon sat on a box beside the stove. She had a fire started, and the tin stove was wine-colored with heat. "Did ya get milk?" she demanded.

"Yeah. Right here."

"Give it to me. I ain't had any sence noon."

"She thinks it's like medicine."

"That nurse-lady says so."

"You got potatoes ready?"

"Right there—peeled."

"We'll fry 'em," said Ma. "Got pork chops. Cut up them potatoes in the new fry pan. And th'ow in a onion. You fellas go out an' wash, an' bring in a bucket a water. Where's Ruthie an' Winfiel'? They oughta wash. They each got Cracker Jack," Ma told Rose of Sharon. "Each got a whole box."

The men went out to wash in the stream. Rose of Sharon sliced the potatoes into the frying pan and stirred them about with the knife point.

Suddenly the tarpaulin was thrust aside. A stout perspiring face looked in from the other end of the car. "How'd you all make out, Mis' Joad?"

Ma swung around. "Why, evenin', Mis' Wainwright. We done good. Three an' a half. Three fifty-seven, exact."

"We done four dollars."

"Well," said Ma. " 'Course they's more *of* you."

"Yeah. Jonas is growin' up. Havin' pork chops, I see."

Winfield crept in through the door. "Ma!"

"Hush a minute. Yes, my men jus' loves pork chops."

"I'm cookin' bacon," said Mrs. Wainwright. "Can you smell it cookin'?"

"No—can't smell it over these here onions in the pota-toes."

"She's burnin'!" Mrs. Wainwright cried, and her head jerked back.

"Ma," Winfield said.

"What? You sick from Cracker Jack?"

"Ma—Ruthie tol'."

"Tol' what?"

" 'Bout Tom."

Ma stared. "Tol'?" Then she knelt in front of him. "Win-fiel', who'd she tell?"

Embarrassment seized Winfield. He backed away. "Well, she on'y tol' a little bit."

"Winfiel'! Now you tell what she said."

"She—she didn' eat all her Cracker Jack. She kep' some, an' she et jus' one piece at a time, slow, like she always done, an' she says, 'Bet you wisht you had some lef'."

"Winfiel'!" Ma demanded. "You tell now." She looked back nervously at the curtain. "Rosasharn, you go over an' talk to Mis' Wainwright so she don' listen."

"How 'bout these here potatoes?"

"I'll watch 'em. Now you go. I don' want her listenin' at that curtain." The girl shuffled heavily down the car and went around the side of the hung tarpaulin.

Ma said, "Now, Winfiel', you tell."

"Like I said, she et jus' one little piece at a time, an' she bust some in two so it'd las' longer."

"Go on, hurry up."

"Well, some kids come aroun', an' 'course they tried to get some, but Ruthie, she jus' nibbled an' nibbled, an' wouldn' give 'em none. So they got mad. An' one kid grabbed her Cracker Jack box."

"Winfiel', you tell quick about the other."

"I am," he said. "So Ruthie got mad an' chased 'em, an' she fit one, an' then she fit another, an' then one big girl up an' licked her. Hit 'er a good one. So then Ruthie cried, an' she said she'd git her big brother, an' he'd kill that big girl. An' that big girl said, Oh, yeah? Well, she got a big brother too." Winfield was breathless in his telling. "So then they fit, an' that big girl hit Ruthie a good one, an' Ruthie said her brother'd kill that big girl's brother. An' that big girl said how about if her brother kil't our brother. An' then—an' then, Ruthie said our brother already kil't two fellas. An'—an'— that big girl said, 'Oh, yeah? You're jus' a little smarty liar.' An' Ruthie said, Oh, yeah? Well, our brother's a-hidin' right now from killin' a fella, an' he can kill that big girl's brother too. An' then they called names an' Ruthie throwed a rock, an' that big girl chased her, an' I come home."

"Oh, my!" Ma said wearily. "Oh! My dear sweet Lord Jesus asleep in a manger! What we goin' to do now?" She put her forehead in her hand and rubbed her eyes. "What we gonna do now?" A smell of burning potatoes came from the roaring stove. Ma moved automatically and turned them.

"Rosasharn!" Ma called. The girl appeared around the curtain. "Come watch this here supper. Winfiel', you go out an' you fin' Ruthie an' bring her back here."

"Gonna whup her, Ma?" he asked hopefully.

"No. This here you couldn' do nothin' about. Why, I wonder, did she haf' to do it? No. It won't do no good to whup her. Run now, an' find her an' bring her back."

Winfield ran for the car door, and he met the three men tramping up the cat-walk, and he stood aside while they came in.

Ma said softly, "Pa, I got to talk to you. Ruthie tol' some kids how Tom's a-hidin'."

"What?"

"She tol'. Got in a fight an' tol'."

"Why, the little bitch!"

"No, she didn' know what she was a-doin'. Now look, Pa. I want you to stay here. I'm goin' out an' try to fin' Tom an' tell him. I got to tell 'im to be careful. You stick here, Pa, an' kinda watch out for things. I'll take 'im some dinner."

"Awright," Pa agreed.

"Don' you even mention to Ruthie what she done. I'll tell her."

At that moment Ruthie came in, with Winfield behind her. The little girl was dirtied. Her mouth was sticky, and her nose still dripped a little blood from her fight. She looked shamed and frightened. Winfield triumphantly followed her. Ruthie looked fiercely about, but she went to a corner of the car and put her back in the corner. Her shame and fierceness were blended.

"I tol' her what she done," Winfield said.

Ma was putting two chops and some fried potatoes on a tin plate. "Hush, Winfiel'," she said. "They ain't no need to hurt her feelings no more'n what they're hurt."

Ruthie's body hurtled across the car. She grabbed Ma around the middle and buried her head in Ma's stomach, and her strangled sobs shook her whole body. Ma tried to loosen her, but the grubby fingers clung tight. Ma brushed the hair on the back of her head gently, and she patted her shoulders. "Hush," she said. "You didn' know."

Ruthie raised her dirty, tear-stained, bloody face. "They stoled my Cracker Jack!" she cried. "That big son-of-a-bitch of a girl, she belted me—" She went off into hard crying again.

"Hush!" Ma said. "Don' talk like that. Here. Let go. I'm a-goin' now."

"Whyn't ya whup her, Ma? If she didn't git snotty with her Cracker Jack 'twouldn' a happened. Go on, give her a whup."

"You jus' min' your business, mister," Ma said fiercely. "You'll git a whup yourself. Now leggo, Ruthie."

Winfield retired to a rolled mattress, and he regarded the family cynically and dully. And he put himself in a good position of defense, for Ruthie would attack him at the first opportunity, and he knew it. Ruthie went quietly, heart-brokenly to the other side of the car.

Ma put a sheet of newspaper over the tin plate. "I'm a-goin' now," she said.

"Ain't you gonna eat nothin' yourself?" Uncle John demanded.

"Later. When I come back. I wouldn' want nothin' now."
Ma walked to the open door; she steadied herself down the
steep, cleated cat-walk.

On the stream side of the boxcars, the tents were pitched
close together, their guy ropes crossing one another, and the
pegs of one at the canvas line of the next. The lights shone
through the cloth, and all the chimneys belched smoke. Men
and women stood in the doorways talking. Children ran feverishly about. Ma moved majestically down the line of tents.
Here and there she was recognized as she went by. "Evenin',
Mis' Joad."

"Evenin'."

"Takin' somepin out, Mis' Joad?"

"They's a frien'. I'm takin' back some bread."

She came at last to the end of the line of tents. She stopped
and looked back. A glow of light was on the camp, and the
soft overtone of a multitude of speakers. Now and then a
harsher voice cut through. The smell of smoke filled the air.
Someone played a harmonica softly, trying for an effect, one
phrase over and over.

Ma stepped in among the willows beside the stream. She
moved off the trail and waited, silently, listening to hear any
possible follower. A man walked down the trail toward the
camp, boosting his suspenders and buttoning his jeans as he
went. Ma sat very still, and he passed on without seeing her.
She waited five minutes and then she stood up and crept on
up the trail beside the stream. She moved quietly, so quietly
that she could hear the murmur of the water above her soft
steps on the willow leaves. Trail and stream swung to the left
and then to the right again until they neared the highway. In
the gray starlight she could see the embankment and the black
round hole of the culvert where she always left Tom's food.
She moved forward cautiously, thrust her package into the
hole, and took back the empty tin plate which was left there.
She crept back among the willows, forced her way into a
thicket, and sat down to wait. Through the tangle she could
see the black hole of the culvert. She clasped her knees and
sat silently. In a few moments the thicket crept to life again.

The field mice moved cautiously over the leaves. A skunk padded heavily and unself-consciously down the trail, carrying a faint effluvium with him. And then a wind stirred the willows delicately, as though it tested them, and a shower of golden leaves coasted down to the ground. Suddenly a gust boiled in and racked the trees, and a cricking downpour of leaves fell. Ma could feel them on her hair and on her shoulders. Over the sky a plump black cloud moved, erasing the stars. The fat drops of rain scattered down, splashing loudly on the fallen leaves, and the cloud moved on and unveiled the stars again. Ma shivered. The wind blew past and left the thicket quiet, but the rushing of the trees went on down the stream. From back at the camp came the thin penetrating tone of a violin feeling about for a tune.

Ma heard a stealthy step among the leaves far to her left, and she grew tense. She released her knees and straightened her head, the better to hear. The movement stopped, and after a long moment began again. A vine rasped harshly on the dry leaves. Ma saw a dark figure creep into the open and draw near to the culvert. The black round hole was obscured for a moment, and then the figure moved back. She called softly, "Tom!" The figure stood still, so still, so low to the ground that it might have been a stump. She called again, "Tom, oh, Tom!" Then the figure moved.

"That you, Ma?"

"Right over here." She stood up and went to meet him.

"You shouldn' of came," he said.

"I got to see you, Tom. I got to talk to you."

"It's near the trail," he said. "Somebody might come by."

"Ain't you got a place, Tom?"

"Yeah—but if—well, s'pose somebody seen you with me—whole fambly'd be in a jam."

"I got to, Tom."

"Then come along. Come quiet." He crossed the little stream, wading carelessly through the water, and Ma followed him. He moved through the brush, out into a field on the other side of the thicket, and along the plowed ground. The blackening stems of the cotton were harsh against the ground, and a few fluffs of cotton clung to the stems. A quarter of a mile they went along the edge of the field, and then he turned into the brush again. He approached a great mound of wild blackberry bushes, leaned over and pulled a mat of vines aside. "You got to crawl in," he said.

Ma went down on her hands and knees. She felt sand under her, and then the black inside of the mound no longer touched her, and she felt Tom's blanket on the ground. He arranged the vines in place again. It was lightless in the cave.

"Where are you, Ma?"

"Here. Right here. Talk soft, Tom."

"Don't worry. I been livin' like a rabbit some time."

She heard him unwrap his tin plate.

"Pork chops," she said. "And fry potatoes."

"God Awmighty, an' still warm."

Ma could not see him at all in the blackness, but she could hear him chewing, tearing at the meat and swallowing.

"It's a pretty good hide-out," he said.

Ma said uneasily, "Tom—Ruthie tol' about you." She heard him gulp.

"Ruthie? What for?"

"Well, it wasn' her fault. Got in a fight, an' says her brother'll lick that other girl's brother. You know how they do. An' she tol' that her brother killed a man an' was hidin'."

Tom was chuckling. "With me I was always gonna get Uncle John after 'em, but he never would do it. That's jus' kid talk, Ma. That's awright."

"No, it ain't," Ma said. "Them kids'll tell it aroun' an' then the folks'll hear, an' they'll tell aroun', an' pretty soon, well, they liable to get men out to look, jus' in case. Tom, you got to go away."

"That's what I said right along. I was always scared somebody'd see you put stuff in that culvert, an' then they'd watch."

"I know. But I wanted you near. I was scared for you. I ain't seen you. Can't see you now. How's your face?"

"Gettin' well quick."

"Come clost, Tom. Let me feel it. Come clost." He crawled near. Her reaching hand found his head in the blackness and her fingers moved down to his nose, and then over his left cheek. "You got a bad scar, Tom. An' your nose is all crooked."

"Maybe tha's a good thing. Nobody wouldn't know me, maybe. If my prints wasn't on record, I'd be glad." He went back to his eating.

"Hush," she said. "Listen!"

"It's the wind, Ma. Jus' the wind." The gust poured down the stream, and the trees rustled under its passing.

She crawled close to his voice. "I wanta touch ya again, Tom. It's like I'm blin', it's so dark. I wanta remember, even if it's on'y my fingers that remember. You got to go away, Tom."

"Yeah! I knowed it from the start."

"We made purty good," she said. "I been squirrelin' money away. Hol' out your han', Tom. I got seven dollars here."

"I ain't gonna take ya money," he said. "I'll get 'long all right."

"Hol' out ya han', Tom. I ain't gonna sleep none if you got no money. Maybe you got to take a bus, or somepin. I want you should go a long ways off, three-four hunderd miles."

"I ain't gonna take it."

"Tom," she said sternly. "You take this money. You hear me? You got no right to cause me pain."

"You ain't playin' it fair," he said.

"I thought maybe you could go to a big city. Los Angeles, maybe. They wouldn' never look for you there."

"Hm-m," he said. "Lookie, Ma. I been all day an' all night hidin' alone. Guess who I been thinkin' about? Casy! He talked a lot. Used ta bother me. But now I been thinkin' what he said, an' I can remember—all of it. Says one time he went out in the wilderness to find his own soul, an' he foun' he didn' have no soul that was his'n. Says he foun' he jus' got a little piece of a great big soul. Says a wilderness ain't no good, 'cause his little piece of a soul wasn't no good 'less it was with the rest, an' was whole. Funny how I remember. Didn' think I was even listenin'. But I know now a fella ain't no good alone."

"He was a good man," Ma said.

Tom went on, "He spouted out some Scripture once, an' it didn' soun' like no hell-fire Scripture. He tol' it twicet, an' I remember it. Says it's from the Preacher."

"How's it go, Tom?"

"Goes, 'Two are better than one, because they have a good reward for their labor. For if they fall, the one will lif' up his fellow, but woe to him that is alone when he falleth, for he hath not another to help him up.' That's part of her."

"Go on," Ma said. "Go on, Tom."

"Jus' a little bit more. 'Again, if two lie together, then they have heat: but how can one be warm alone? And if one prevail against him, two shall withstand him, and a three-fold cord is not quickly broken.'"

"An' that's Scripture?"

"Casy said it was. Called it the Preacher."

"Hush—listen."

"On'y the wind, Ma. I know the wind. An' I got to thinkin', Ma—most of the preachin' is about the poor we shall have always with us, an' if you got nothin', why, jus' fol' your hands an' to hell with it, you gonna git ice cream on gol' plates when you're dead. An' then this here Preacher says two get a better reward for their work."

"Tom," she said. "What you aimin' to do?"

He was quiet for a long time. "I been thinkin' how it was in that gov'ment camp, how our folks took care a theirselves, an' if they was a fight they fixed it theirself; an' they wasn't no cops wagglin' their guns, but they was better order than them cops ever give. I been a-wonderin' why we can't do that all over. Throw out the cops that ain't our people. All work together for our own thing—all farm our own lan'."

"Tom," Ma repeated, "what you gonna do?"

"What Casy done," he said.

"But they killed him."

"Yeah," said Tom. "He didn' duck quick enough. He wasn' doing nothin' against the law, Ma. I been thinkin' a hell of a lot, thinkin' about our people livin' like pigs, an' the good rich lan' layin' fallow, or maybe one fella with a million acres, while a hunderd thousan' good farmers is starvin'. An' I been wonderin' if all our folks got together an' yelled, like them fellas yelled, only a few of 'em at the Hooper ranch——"

Ma said, "Tom, they'll drive you, an' cut you down like they done to young Floyd."

"They gonna drive me anyways. They drivin' all our people."

"You don't aim to kill nobody, Tom?"

"No. I been thinkin', long as I'm a outlaw anyways, maybe I could— Hell, I ain't thought it out clear, Ma. Don' worry me now. Don' worry me."

They sat silent in the coal-black cave of vines. Ma said, "How'm I gonna know 'bout you? They might kill ya an' I wouldn' know. They might hurt ya. How'm I gonna know?"

Tom laughed uneasily, "Well, maybe like Casy says, a fella ain't got a soul of his own, but on'y a piece of a big one— an' then——"

"Then what, Tom?"

"Then it don' matter. Then I'll be all aroun' in the dark. I'll be ever'where—wherever you look. Wherever they's a fight so hungry people can eat, I'll be there. Wherever they's a cop beatin' up a guy, I'll be there. If Casy knowed, why, I'll be in the way guys yell when they're mad an'—I'll be in the way kids laugh when they're hungry an' they know supper's ready. An' when our folks eat the stuff they raise an' live in the houses they build—why, I'll be there. See? God, I'm talkin' like Casy. Comes of thinkin' about him so much. Seems like I can see him sometimes."

"I don' un'erstan'," Ma said. "I don' really know."

"Me neither," said Tom. "It's jus' stuff I been thinkin' about. Get thinkin' a lot when you ain't movin' aroun'. You got to get back, Ma."

"You take the money then."

He was silent for a moment. "Awright," he said.

"An', Tom, later—when it's blowed over, you'll come back. You'll find us?"

"Sure," he said. "Now you better go. Here, gimme your han'." He guided her toward the entrance. Her fingers clutched his wrist. He swept the vines aside and followed her out. "Go up to the field till you come to a sycamore on the edge, an' then cut acrost the stream. Good-by."

"Good-by," she said, and she walked quickly away. Her eyes were wet and burning, but she did not cry. Her footsteps were loud and careless on the leaves as she went through the brush. And as she went, out of the dim sky the rain began to fall, big drops and few, splashing on the dry leaves heavily. Ma stopped and stood still in the dripping thicket. She turned about—took three steps back toward the mound of vines; and then she turned quickly and went back toward the boxcar camp. She went straight out to the culvert and climbed up on the road. The rain had passed now, but the sky was overcast. Behind her on the road she heard footsteps, and she turned nervously. The blinking of a dim flashlight played on the road. Ma turned back and started for home. In a moment a man caught up with her. Politely, he kept his light on the ground and did not play it in her face.

"Evenin'," he said.

Ma said, "Howdy."

"Looks like we might have a little rain."

"I hope not. Stop the pickin'. We need the pickin'."

"I need the pickin' too. You live at the camp there?"

"Yes, sir." Their footsteps beat on the road together.

"I got twenty acres of cotton. Little late, but it's ready now. Thought I'd go down and try to get some pickers."

"You'll get 'em awright. Season's near over."

"Hope so. My place is only a mile up that way."

"Six of us," said Ma. "Three men an' me an' two little fellas."

"I'll put out a sign. Two miles—this road."

"We'll be there in the mornin'."

"I hope it don't rain."

"Me too," said Ma. "Twenty acres won' las' long."

"The less it lasts the gladder I'll be. My cotton's late. Didn' get it in till late."

"What you payin', mister?"

"Ninety cents."

"We'll pick. I hear fellas say nex' year it'll be seventy-five or even sixty."

"That's what I hear."

"They'll be trouble," said Ma.

"Sure. I know. Little fella like me can't do anything. The Association sets the wage, and we got to mind. If we don't— we ain't got a farm. Little fella gets crowded all the time."

They came to the camp. "We'll be there," Ma said. "Not much pickin' lef'." She went to the end boxcar and climbed the cleated walk. The low light of the lantern made gloomy shadows in the car. Pa and Uncle John and an elderly man squatted against the car wall.

"Hello," Ma said. "Evenin', Mr. Wainwright."

He raised a delicately chiseled face. His eyes were deep under the ridges of his brows. His hair was blue-white and fine. A patina of silver beard covered his jaws and chin. "Evenin', ma'am," he said.

"We got pickin' tomorra," Ma observed. "Mile north. Twenty acres."

"Better take the truck, I guess," Pa said. "Get in more pickin'."

Wainwright raised his head eagerly. "S'pose we can pick?"

"Why, sure. I walked a piece with the fella. He was comin' to get pickers."

"Cotton's nearly gone. Purty thin, these here seconds. Gonna be hard to make a wage on the seconds. Got her pretty clean the fust time."

"Your folks could maybe ride with us," Ma said. "Split the gas."

"Well—that's frien'ly of you, ma'am."

"Saves us both," said Ma.

Pa said, "Mr. Wainwright—he's got a worry he come to us about. We was a-talkin' her over."

"What's the matter?"

Wainwright looked down at the floor. "Our Aggie," he said. "She's a big girl—near sixteen, an' growed up."

"Aggie's a pretty girl," said Ma.

"Listen 'im out," Pa said.

"Well, her an' your boy Al, they're a-walkin' out ever' night. An' Aggie's a good healthy girl that oughta have a husban', else she might git in trouble. We never had no trouble in our family. But what with us bein' so poor off, now, Mis' Wainwright an' me, we got to worryin'. S'pose she got in trouble?"

Ma rolled down a mattress and sat on it. "They out now?" she asked.

"Always out," said Wainwright. "Ever' night."

"Hm. Well, Al's a good boy. Kinda figgers he's a dung-hill

rooster these days, but he's a good steady boy. I couldn' want for a better boy."

"Oh, we ain't complainin' about Al as a fella! We like him. But what scares Mis' Wainwright an' me—well, she's a growed-up woman-girl. An' what if we go away, or you go away, an' we find out Aggie's in trouble? We ain't had no shame in our family."

Ma said softly, "We'll try an' see that we don't put no shame on you."

He stood up quickly. "Thank you, ma'am. Aggie's a growed-up woman-girl. She's a good girl—jes' as nice an' good. We'll sure thank you, ma'am, if you'll keep shame from us. It ain't Aggie's fault. She's growed up."

"Pa'll talk to Al," said Ma. "Or if Pa won't, I will."

Wainwright said, "Good night, then, an' we sure thank ya." He went around the end of the curtain. They could hear him talking softly in the other end of the car, explaining the result of his embassy.

Ma listened a moment, and then, "You fellas," she said. "Come over an' set here."

Pa and Uncle John got heavily up from their squats. They sat on the mattress beside Ma.

"Where's the little fellas?"

Pa pointed to a mattress in the corner. "Ruthie, she jumped Winfiel' an' bit 'im. Made 'em both lay down. Guess they're asleep. Rosasharn, she went to set with a lady she knows."

Ma sighed. "I foun' Tom," she said softly. "I—sent 'im away. Far off."

Pa nodded slowly. Uncle John dropped his chin on his chest. "Couldn' do nothin' else," Pa said. "Think he could, John?"

Uncle John looked up. "I can't think nothin' out," he said. "Don't seem like I'm hardly awake no more."

"Tom's a good boy," Ma said; and then she apologized, "I didn' mean no harm a-sayin' I'd talk to Al."

"I know," Pa said quietly. "I ain't no good any more. Spen' all my time a-thinkin' how it use' ta be. Spen' all my time thinkin' of home, an' I ain't never gonna see it no more."

"This here's purtier—better lan'," said Ma.

"I know. I never even see it, thinkin' how the willow's los' its leaves now. Sometimes figgerin' to mend that hole in the south fence. Funny! Woman takin' over the fambly. Woman sayin' we'll do this here, an' we'll go there. An' I don' even care."

"Woman can change better'n a man," Ma said soothingly. "Woman got all her life in her arms. Man got it all in his head. Don' you mind. Maybe—well, maybe nex' year we can get a place."

"We got nothin', now," Pa said. "Comin' a long time— no work, no crops. What we gonna do then? How we gonna git stuff to eat? An' I tell you Rosasharn ain't so far from due. Git so I hate to think. Go diggin' back to a ol' time to keep from thinkin'. Seems like our life's over an' done."

"No, it ain't," Ma smiled. "It ain't, Pa. An' that's one more thing a woman knows. I noticed that. Man, he lives in jerks— baby born an' a man dies, an' that's a jerk—gets a farm an' loses his farm, an' that's a jerk. Woman, it's all one flow, like a stream, little eddies, little waterfalls, but the river, it goes right on. Woman looks at it like that. We ain't gonna die out. People is goin' on—changin' a little, maybe, but goin' right on."

"How can you tell?" Uncle John demanded. "What's to keep ever'thing from stoppin'; all the folks from jus' gittin' tired an' layin' down?"

Ma considered. She rubbed the shiny back of one hand with the other, pushed the fingers of her right hand between the fingers of her left. "Hard to say," she said. "Ever'thing we do—seems to me is aimed right at goin' on. Seems that way to me. Even gettin' hungry—even bein' sick; some die, but the rest is tougher. Jus' try to live the day, jus' the day."

Uncle John said, "If on'y she didn' die that time——"

"Jus' live the day," Ma said. "Don' worry yaself."

"They might be a good year nex' year, back home," said Pa.

Ma said, "Listen!"

There were creeping steps on the cat-walk, and then Al came in past the curtain. "Hullo," he said. "I thought you'd be sleepin' by now."

"Al," Ma said. "We're a-talkin'. Come set here."

"Sure—O.K. I wanta talk too. I'll hafta be goin' away pretty soon now."

"You can't. We need you here. Why you got to go away?"

"Well, me an' Aggie Wainwright, we figgers to get married, an' I'm gonna git a job in a garage, an' we'll have a rent' house for a while, an'—" He looked up fiercely. "Well, we are, an' they ain't nobody can stop us!"

They were staring at him. "Al," Ma said at last, "we're glad. We're awful glad."

"You are?"

"Why, 'course we are. You're a growed man. You need a wife. But don' go right now, Al."

"I promised Aggie," he said. "We got to go. We can't stan' this no more."

"Jus' stay till spring," Ma begged. "Jus' till spring. Won't you stay till spring? Who'd drive the truck?"

"Well——"

Mrs. Wainwright put her head around the curtain. "You heard yet?" she demanded.

"Yeah! Jus' heard."

"Oh, my! I wisht—I wisht we had a cake. I wisht we had—a cake or somepin."

"I'll set on some coffee an' make up some pancakes," Ma said. "We got sirup."

"Oh, my!" Mrs. Wainwright said. "Why—well. Look, I'll bring some sugar. We'll put sugar in them pancakes."

Ma broke twigs into the stove, and the coals from the dinner cooking started them blazing. Ruthie and Winfield came out of their bed like hermit crabs from shells. For a moment they were careful; they watched to see whether they were still criminals. When no one noticed them, they grew bold. Ruthie hopped all the way to the door and back on one foot, without touching the wall.

Ma was pouring flour into a bowl when Rose of Sharon climbed the cat-walk. She steadied herself and advanced cautiously. "What's a matter?" she asked.

"Why, it's news!" Ma cried. "We're gonna have a little party 'count a Al an' Aggie Wainwright is gonna get married."

Rose of Sharon stood perfectly still. She looked slowly at Al, who stood there flustered and embarrassed.

Mrs. Wainwright shouted from the other end of the car, "I'm puttin' a fresh dress on Aggie. I'll be right over."

Rose of Sharon turned slowly. She went back to the wide door, and she crept down the cat-walk. Once on the ground, she moved slowly toward the stream and the trail that went beside it. She took the way Ma had gone earlier—into the willows. The wind blew more steadily now, and the bushes whished steadily. Rose of Sharon went down on her knees and crawled deep into the brush. The berry vines cut her face and pulled at her hair, but she didn't mind. Only when she felt the bushes touching her all over did she stop. She stretched out on her back. And she felt the weight of the baby inside of her.

In the lightless car, Ma stirred, and then she pushed the blanket back and got up. At the open door of the car the gray starlight penetrated a little. Ma walked to the door and stood looking out. The stars were paling in the east. The wind blew softly over the willow thickets, and from the little stream came the quiet talking of the water. Most of the camp was still asleep, but in front of one tent a little fire burned, and people were standing about it, warming themselves. Ma could see them in the light of the new dancing fire as they stood facing the flames, rubbing their hands; and then they turned their backs and held their hands behind them. For a long moment Ma looked out, and she held her hands clasped in front of her. The uneven wind whisked up and passed, and a bite of frost was in the air. Ma shivered and rubbed her hands to-gether. She crept back and fumbled for the matches beside the lantern. The shade screeched up. She lighted the wick, watched it burn blue for a moment and then put up its yellow, delicately curved ring of light. She carried the lantern to the stove and set it down while she broke the brittle dry willow twigs into the fire box. In a moment the fire was roaring up the chimney.

Rose of Sharon rolled heavily over and sat up. "I'll git right up," she said.

"Whyn't you lay a minute till it warms?" Ma asked.

"No, I'll git."

Ma filled the coffee pot from the bucket and set it on the

stove, and she put on the frying pan, deep with fat, to get hot for the pones. "What's over you?" she said softly.

"I'm a-goin' out," Rose of Sharon said.

"Out where?"

"Goin' out to pick cotton."

"You can't," Ma said. "You're too far along."

"No, I ain't. An' I'm a-goin'."

Ma measured coffee into the water. "Rosasharn, you wasn't to the pancakes las' night." The girl didn't answer. "What you wanta pick cotton for?" Still no answer. "Is it 'cause of Al an' Aggie?" This time Ma looked closely at her daughter. "Oh. Well, you don' need to pick."

"I'm goin'."

"Awright, but don' you strain yourself."

"Git up, Pa! Wake up, git up!"

Pa blinked and yawned. "Ain't slep' out," he moaned. "Musta been on to eleven o'clock when we went down."

"Come on, git up, all a you, an' wash."

The inhabitants of the car came slowly to life, squirmed up out of the blankets, writhed into their clothes. Ma sliced salt pork into her second frying pan. "Git out an' wash," she commanded.

A light sprang up in the other end of the car. And there came the sound of the breaking of twigs from the Wainwright end. "Mis' Joad," came the call. "We're gettin' ready. We'll be ready."

Al grumbled, "What we got to be up so early for?"

"It's on'y twenty acres," Ma said. "Got to get there. Ain't much cotton lef'. Got to be there 'fore she's picked." Ma rushed them dressed, rushed the breakfast into them. "Come on, drink your coffee," she said. "Got to start."

"We can't pick no cotton in the dark, Ma."

"We can *be* there when it gets light."

"Maybe it's wet."

"Didn' rain enough. Come on now, drink your coffee. Al, soon's you're through, better get the engine runnin'."

She called, "You near ready, Mis' Wainwright?"

"Jus' eatin'. Be ready in a minute."

Outside, the camp had come to life. Fires burned in front of the tents. The stovepipes from the boxcars spurted smoke.

Al tipped up his coffee and got a mouthful of grounds. He went down the cat-walk spitting them out.

"We're awready, Mis' Wainwright," Ma called. She turned to Rose of Sharon. "You shouldn' come."

"I'm a-goin' out."

"Lemme look 't your eyes." Ma stared into the girl's nervous bright eyes. "You ain't goin'," she said. "You got to stay."

The girl set her jaw. "I'm a-goin'," she said. "Ma, I got to go."

"Well, you got no cotton sack. You can't pull no sack."

"I'll pick into your sack."

"I wisht you wouldn'."

"I'm a-goin'."

Ma sighed. "I'll keep my eye on you. Wisht we could have a doctor." Rose of Sharon moved nervously about the car. She put on a light coat and took it off. "Take a blanket," Ma said. "Then if you wanta res', you can keep warm." They heard the truck motor roar up behind the boxcar. "We gonna be first out," Ma said exultantly. "Awright, get your sacks. Ruthie, don' you forget them shirts I fixed for you to pick in."

Wainwrights and Joads climbed into the truck in the dark. The dawn was coming, but it was slow and pale.

"Turn lef'," Ma told Al. "They'll be a sign out where we're goin'." They drove along the dark road. And other cars followed them, and behind, in the camp, the cars were being started, the families piling in; and the cars pulled out on the highway and turned left.

A piece of cardboard was tied to a mailbox on the right-hand side of the road, and on it, printed with blue crayon, "Cotton Pickers Wanted." Al turned into the entrance and drove out to the barnyard. And the barnyard was full of cars already. An electric globe on the end of the white barn lighted a group of men and women standing near the scales, their bags rolled under their arms. Some of the women wore the bags over their shoulders and crossed in front.

"We ain't so early as we thought," said Al. He pulled the truck against a fence and parked. The families climbed down and went to join the waiting group, and more cars came in from the road and parked, and more families joined the group. Under the light on the barn end, the owner signed them in.

"Hawley?" he said. "H-a-w-l-e-y? How many?"

"Four. Will——"

"Will."

"Benton——"

"Benton."

"Amelia——"

"Amelia."

"Claire——"

"Claire. Who's next? Carpenter? How many?"

"Six."

He wrote them in the book, with a space left for the weights. "Got your bags? I got a few. Cost you a dollar." And the cars poured into the yard. The owner pulled his sheep-lined leather jacket up around his throat. He looked at the driveway apprehensively. "This twenty isn't gonna take long to pick with all these people," he said.

Children were climbing into the big cotton trailer, digging their toes into the chicken-wire sides. "Git off there," the owner cried. "Come on down. You'll tear that wire loose." And the children climbed slowly down, embarrassed and si-lent. The gray dawn came. "I'll have to take a tare for dew," the owner said. "Change it when the sun comes out. All right, go out when you want. Light enough to see."

The people moved quickly out into the cotton field and took their rows. They tied the bags to their waists and they slapped their hands together to warm stiff fingers that had to be nimble. The dawn colored over the eastern hills, and the wide line moved over the rows. And from the highway the cars still moved in and parked in the barnyard until it was full, and they parked along the road on both sides. The wind blew briskly across the field. "I don't know how you all found out," the owner said. "There must be a hell of a grapevine. The twenty won't last till noon. What name? Hume? How many?"

The line of people moved out across the field, and the strong steady west wind blew their clothes. Their fingers flew to the spilling bolls, and flew to the long sacks growing heavy behind them.

Pa spoke to the man in the row to his right. "Back home we might get rain out of a wind like this. Seems a little mite frosty for rain. How long you been out here?" He kept his eyes down on his work as he spoke.

His neighbor didn't look up. "I been here nearly a year."

"Would you say it was gonna rain?"

"Can't tell, an' that ain't no insult, neither. Folks that lived here all their life can't tell. If the rain can git in the way of a crop, it'll rain. Tha's what they say out here."

Pa looked quickly at the western hills. Big gray clouds were coasting over the ridge, riding the wind swiftly. "Them looks like rain-heads," he said.

His neighbor stole a squinting look. "Can't tell," he said. And all down the line of rows the people looked back at the clouds. And then they bent lower to their work, and their hands flew to the cotton. They raced at the picking, raced against time and cotton weight, raced against the rain and against each other—only so much cotton to pick, only so much money to be made. They came to the other side of the field and ran to get a new row. And now they faced into the wind, and they could see the high gray clouds moving over the sky toward the rising sun. And more cars parked along the roadside, and new pickers came to be checked in. The line of people moved frantically across the field, weighed at the end, marked their cotton, checked the weights into their own books, and ran for new rows.

At eleven o'clock the field was picked and the work was done. The wire-sided trailers were hooked on behind wire-sided trucks, and they moved out to the highway and drove away to the gin. The cotton fluffed out through the chicken wire and little clouds of cotton blew through the air, and rags of cotton caught and waved on the weeds beside the road. The pickers clustered disconsolately back to the barnyard and stood in line to be paid off.

"Hume, James. Twenty-two cents. Ralph, thirty cents. Joad, Thomas, ninety cents. Winfield, fifteen cents." The money lay in rolls, silver and nickels and pennies. And each man looked in his own book as he was being paid. "Wainwright, Agnes, thirty-four cents. Tobin, sixty-three cents." The line moved past slowly. The families went back to their cars, silently. And they drove slowly away.

Joads and Wainwrights waited in the truck for the driveway

to clear. And as they waited, the first drops of rain began to fall. Al put his hand out of the cab to feel them. Rose of Sharon sat in the middle, and Ma on the outside. The girl's eyes were lusterless again.

"You shouldn' of came," Ma said. "You didn' pick more'n ten-fifteen pounds." Rose of Sharon looked down at her great bulging belly, and she didn't reply. She shivered suddenly and held her head high. Ma, watching her closely, unrolled her cotton bag, spread it over Rose of Sharon's shoulders, and drew her close.

At last the way was clear. Al started his motor and drove out into the highway. The big infrequent drops of rain lanced down and splashed on the road, and as the truck moved along, the drops became smaller and closer. Rain pounded on the cab of the truck so loudly that it could be heard over the pounding of the old worn motor. On the truck bed the Wainwrights and Joads spread their cotton bags over their heads and shoulders.

Rose of Sharon shivered violently against Ma's arm, and Ma cried, "Go faster, Al. Rosasharn got a chill. Gotta get her feet in hot water."

Al speeded the pounding motor, and when he came to the boxcar camp, he drove down close to the red cars. Ma was spouting orders before they were well stopped. "Al," she commanded, "you an' John an' Pa go into the willows an' c'lect all the dead stuff you can. We got to keep warm."

"Wonder if the roof leaks."

"No, I don' think so. Be nice an' dry, but we got to have wood. Got to keep warm. Take Ruthie an' Winfiel' too. They can get twigs. This here girl ain't well." Ma got out, and Rose of Sharon tried to follow, but her knees buckled and she sat down heavily on the running board.

Fat Mrs. Wainwright saw her. "What's a matter? Her time come?"

"No, I don' think so," said Ma. "Got a chill. Maybe took col'. Gimme a han', will you?" The two women supported Rose of Sharon. After a few steps her strength came back—her legs took her weight.

"I'm awright, Ma," she said. "It was jus' a minute there."

The older women kept hands on her elbows. "Feet in hot

water," Ma said wisely. They helped her up the cat-walk and into the boxcar.

"You rub her," Mrs. Wainwright said. "I'll get a far' goin'." She used the last of the twigs and built up a blaze in the stove. The rain poured now, scoured at the roof of the car.

Ma looked up at it. "Thank God we got a tight roof," she said. "Them tents leaks, no matter how good. Jus' put on a little water, Mis' Wainwright."

Rose of Sharon lay still on a mattress. She let them take off her shoes and rub her feet. Mrs. Wainwright bent over her. "You got pain?" she demanded.

"No. Jus' don' feel good. Jus' feel bad."

"I got pain killer an' salts," Mrs. Wainwright said. "You're welcome to 'em if you want 'em. Perfec'ly welcome."

The girl shivered violently. "Cover me up, Ma. I'm col'." Ma brought all the blankets and piled them on top of her. The rain roared down on the roof.

Now the wood-gatherers returned, their arms piled high with sticks and their hats and coats dripping. "Jesus, she's wet," Pa said. "Soaks you in a minute."

Ma said, "Better go back an' get more. Burns up awful quick. Be dark purty soon." Ruthie and Winfield dripped in and threw their sticks on the pile. They turned to go again. "You stay," Ma ordered. "Stan' up close to the fire an' get dry."

The afternoon was silver with rain, the roads glittered with water. Hour by hour the cotton plants seemed to blacken and shrivel. Pa and Al and Uncle John made trip after trip into the thickets and brought back loads of dead wood. They piled it near the door, until the heap of it nearly reached the ceiling, and at last they stopped and walked toward the stove. Streams of water ran from their hats to their shoulders. The edges of their coats dripped and their shoes squished as they walked.

"Awright, now, get off them clothes," Ma said. "I got some nice coffee for you fellas. An' you got dry overhalls to put on. Don' stan' there."

The evening came early. In the boxcars the families huddled together, listening to the pouring water on the roofs.

Chapter Twenty-Nine

O VER the high coast mountains and over the valleys the gray clouds marched in from the ocean. The wind blew fiercely and silently, high in the air, and it swished in the brush, and it roared in the forests. The clouds came in brokenly, in puffs, in folds, in gray crags; and they piled in together and settled low over the west. And then the wind stopped and left the clouds deep and solid. The rain began with gusty showers, pauses and downpours; and then gradually it settled to a single tempo, small drops and a steady beat, rain that was gray to see through, rain that cut midday light to evening. And at first the dry earth sucked the moisture down and blackened. For two days the earth drank the rain, until the earth was full. Then puddles formed, and in the low places little lakes formed in the fields. The muddy lakes rose higher, and the steady rain whipped the shining water. At last the mountains were full, and the hillsides spilled into the streams, built them to freshets, and sent them roaring down the canyons into the valleys. The rain beat on steadily. And the streams and the little rivers edged up to the bank sides and worked at willows and tree roots, bent the willows deep in the current, cut out the roots of cottonwoods and brought down the trees. The muddy water whirled along the bank sides and crept up the banks until at last it spilled over, into the fields, into the orchards, into the cotton patches where the black stems stood. Level fields became lakes, broad and gray, and the rain whipped up the surfaces. Then the water poured over the highways, and cars moved slowly, cutting the water ahead, and leaving a boiling muddy wake behind. The earth whispered under the beat of the rain, and the streams thundered under the churning freshets.

When the first rain started, the migrant people huddled in their tents, saying, It'll soon be over, and asking, How long's it likely to go on?

And when the puddles formed, the men went out in the rain with shovels and built little dikes around the tents. The beating rain worked at the canvas until it penetrated and sent streams down. And then the little dikes washed out and the water came inside, and the streams wet the beds and the blankets. The people sat in wet clothes. They set up boxes and put planks on the boxes. Then, day and night, they sat on the planks.

Beside the tents the old cars stood, and water fouled the ignition wires and water fouled the carburetors. The little gray tents stood in lakes. And at last the people had to move. Then the cars wouldn't start because the wires were shorted; and if the engines would run, deep mud engulfed the wheels. And the people waded away, carrying their wet blankets in their arms. They splashed along, carrying the children, carrying the very old, in their arms. And if a barn stood on high ground, it was filled with people, shivering and hopeless.

Then some went to the relief offices, and they came sadly back to their own people.

They's rules—you got to be here a year before you can git relief. They say the gov'ment is gonna help. They don' know when.

And gradually the greatest terror of all came along.

They ain't gonna be no kinda work for three months.

In the barns, the people sat huddled together; and the terror came over them, and their faces were gray with terror. The children cried with hunger, and there was no food.

Then the sickness came, pneumonia, and measles that went to the eyes and to the mastoids.

And the rain fell steadily, and the water flowed over the highways, for the culverts could not carry the water.

Then from the tents, from the crowded barns, groups of sodden men went out, their clothes slopping rags, their shoes muddy pulp. They splashed out through the water, to the towns, to the country stores, to the relief offices, to beg for food, to cringe and beg for food, to beg for relief, to try to steal, to lie. And under the begging, and under the cringing, a hopeless anger began to smolder. And in the little towns pity for the sodden men changed to anger, and anger at the hungry people changed to fear of them. Then sheriffs swore in deputies in droves, and orders were rushed for rifles, for tear gas, for ammunition. Then the hungry men crowded the alleys behind the stores to beg for bread, to beg for rotting vegetables, to steal when they could.

Frantic men pounded on the doors of the doctors; and the doctors were busy. And sad men left word at country stores for the coroner to send a car. The coroners were not too busy. The coroners' wagons backed up through the mud and took out the dead.

And the rain pattered relentlessly down, and the streams broke their banks and spread out over the country.

Huddled under sheds, lying in wet hay, the hunger and the fear bred anger. Then boys went out, not to beg, but to steal; and men went out weakly, to try to steal.

The sheriffs swore in new deputies and ordered new rifles; and the comfortable people in tight houses felt pity at first, and then distaste, and finally hatred for the migrant people.

In the wet hay of leaking barns babies were born to women who panted with pneumonia. And old people curled up in corners and died that way, so that the coroners could not straighten them. At night frantic men walked boldly to hen roosts and carried off the squawking chickens. If they were shot at, they did not run, but splashed sullenly away; and if they were hit, they sank tiredly in the mud.

The rain stopped. On the fields the water stood, reflecting the gray sky, and the land whispered with moving water. And the men came out of the barns, out of the sheds. They squatted on their hams and looked out over the flooded land. And they were silent. And sometimes they talked very quietly.

No work till spring. No work.

And if no work—no money, no food.

Fella had a team of horses, had to use 'em to plow an' cultivate an' mow, wouldn' think a turnin' 'em out to starve when they wasn't workin'.

Them's horses—we're men.

The women watched the men, watched to see whether the break had come at last. The women stood silently and watched. And where a number of men gathered together, the fear went from their faces, and anger took its place. And the women sighed with relief, for they knew it was all right—the break had not come; and the break would never come as long as fear could turn to wrath.

Tiny points of grass came through the earth, and in a few days the hills were pale green with the beginning year.

Chapter Thirty

I N THE BOXCAR CAMP the water stood in puddles, and the rain splashed in the mud. Gradually the little stream crept up the bank toward the low flat where the boxcars stood.

On the second day of the rain Al took the tarpaulin down from the middle of the car. He carried it out and spread it over the nose of the truck, and he came back into the car and sat down on his mattress. Now, without the separation, the two families in the car were one. The men sat together, and their spirits were damp. Ma kept a little fire going in the stove, kept a few twigs burning, and she conserved her wood. The rain poured down on the nearly flat roof of the boxcar.

On the third day the Wainwrights grew restless. "Maybe we better go 'long," Mrs. Wainwright said.

And Ma tried to keep them. "Where'd you go an' be sure of a tight roof?"

"I dunno, but I got a feelin' we oughta go along." They argued together, and Ma watched Al.

Ruthie and Winfield tried to play for a while, and then they too relapsed into sullen inactivity, and the rain drummed down on the roof.

On the third day the sound of the stream could be heard above the drumming rain. Pa and Uncle John stood in the open door and looked out on the rising stream. At both ends of the camp the water ran near to the highway, but at the camp it looped away so that the highway embankment surrounded the camp at the back and the stream closed it in on the front. And Pa said, "How's it look to you, John? Seems to me if that crick comes up, she'll flood us."

Uncle John opened his mouth and rubbed his bristling chin. "Yeah," he said. "Might at that."

Rose of Sharon was down with a heavy cold, her face flushed and her eyes shining with fever. Ma sat beside her with a cup of hot milk. "Here," she said. "Take this here. Got bacon grease in it for strength. Here, drink it!"

Rose of Sharon shook her head weakly. "I ain't hungry."

Pa drew a curved line in the air with his finger. "If we was all to get our shovels an' throw up a bank, I bet we could keep her out. On'y have to go from up there down to there."

"Yeah," Uncle John agreed. "Might. Dunno if them other fellas'd wanta. They'd maybe ruther move somewheres else."

"But these here cars is dry," Pa insisted. "Couldn' find no dry place as good as this. You wait." From the pile of brush in the car he picked a twig. He ran down the cat-walk, splashed through the mud to the stream and he set his twig upright on the edge of the swirling water. In a moment he was back in the car. "Jesus, ya get wet through," he said.

Both men kept their eyes on the little twig on the water's edge. They saw the water move slowly up around it and creep up the bank. Pa squatted down in the doorway. "Comin' up fast," he said. "I think we oughta go talk to the other fellas. See if they'll help ditch up. Got to git outa here if they won't." Pa looked down the long car to the Wainwright end. Al was with them, sitting beside Aggie. Pa walked into their precinct. "Water's risin'," he said. "How about if we throwed up a bank? We could do her if ever'body helped."

Wainwright said, "We was jes' talkin'. Seems like we oughta be gettin' outa here."

Pa said, "You been aroun'. You know what chancet we got a gettin' a dry place to stay."

"I know. But jes' the same——"

Al said, "Pa, if they go, I'm a-goin' too."

Pa looked startled. "You can't, Al. The truck— We ain't fit to drive that truck."

"I don' care. Me an' Aggie got to stick together."

"Now you wait," Pa said. "Come on over here." Wainwright and Al got to their feet and approached the door. "See?" Pa said, pointing. "Jus' a bank from there an' down to there." He looked at his stick. The water swirled about it now, and crept up the bank.

"Be a lot a work, an' then she might come over anyways," Wainwright protested.

"Well, we ain't doin' nothin', might's well be workin'. We ain't gonna find us no nice place to live like this. Come on, now. Le's go talk to the other fellas. We can do her if ever'-body helps."

Al said, "If Aggie goes, I'm a-goin' too."

Pa said, "Look, Al, if them fellas won't dig, then we'll all hafta go. Come on, le's go talk to 'em." They hunched their shoulders and ran down the cat-walk to the next car and up the walk into its open door.

Ma was at the stove, feeding a few sticks to the feeble flame. Ruthie crowded close beside her. "I'm hungry," Ruthie whined.

"No, you ain't," Ma said. "You had good mush."

"Wisht I had a box a Cracker Jack. There ain't nothin' to do. Ain't no fun."

"They'll be fun," Ma said. "You jus' wait. Be fun purty soon. Git a house an' a place, purty soon."

"Wisht we had a dog," Ruthie said.

"We'll have a dog; have a cat, too."

"Yella cat?"

"Don't bother me," Ma begged. "Don't go plaguin' me now, Ruthie. Rosasharn's sick. Jus' you be a good girl a little while. They'll be fun." Ruthie wandered, complaining, away.

From the mattress where Rose of Sharon lay covered up there came a quick sharp cry, cut off in the middle. Ma whirled and went to her. Rose of Sharon was holding her breath and her eyes were filled with terror.

"What is it?" Ma cried. The girl expelled her breath and caught it again. Suddenly Ma put her hand under the covers. Then she stood up. "Mis' Wainwright," she called. "Oh, Mis' Wainwright!"

The fat little woman came down the car. "Want me?"

"Look!" Ma pointed at Rose of Sharon's face. Her teeth were clamped on her lower lip and her forehead was wet with perspiration, and the shining terror was in her eyes.

"I think it's come," Ma said. "It's early."

The girl heaved a great sigh and relaxed. She released her lip and closed her eyes. Mrs. Wainwright bent over her.

"Did it kinda grab you all over—quick? Open up an' answer me." Rose of Sharon nodded weakly. Mrs. Wainwright turned to Ma. "Yep," she said. "It's come. Early, ya say?"

"Maybe the fever brang it."

"Well, she oughta be up on her feet. Oughta be walkin' aroun'."

"She can't," Ma said. "She ain't got the strength."

"Well, she oughta." Mrs. Wainwright grew quiet and stern with efficiency. "I he'ped with lots," she said. "Come on, le's close that door, nearly. Keep out the draf'." The two women pushed on the heavy sliding door, boosted it along until only a foot was open. "I'll git our lamp, too," Mrs. Wainwright said. Her face was purple with excitement. "Aggie," she called. "You take care of these here little fellas."

Ma nodded, "Tha's right. Ruthie! You an' Winfiel' go down with Aggie. Go on now."

"Why?" they demanded.

" 'Cause you got to. Rosasharn gonna have her baby."

"I wanta watch, Ma. Please let me."

"Ruthie! You git now. You git quick." There was no argument against such a tone. Ruthie and Winfield went reluctantly down the car. Ma lighted the lantern. Mrs. Wainwright brought her Rochester lamp down and set it on the floor, and its big circular flame lighted the boxcar brightly.

Ruthie and Winfield stood behind the brush pile and peered over. "Gonna have a baby, an' we're a-gonna see," Ruthie said softly. "Don't you make no noise now. Ma won't let us watch. If she looks this-a-way, you scrunch down behin' the brush. Then we'll see."

"There ain't many kids seen it," Winfield said.

"There ain't no kids seen it," Ruthie insisted proudly. "On'y us."

Down by the mattress, in the bright light of the lamp, Ma and Mrs. Wainwright held conference. Their voices were raised a little over the hollow beating of the rain. Mrs. Wainwright took a paring knife from her apron pocket and slipped it under the mattress. "Maybe it don't do no good," she said apologetically. "Our folks always done it. Don't do no harm, anyways."

Ma nodded. "We used a plow point. I guess anything sharp'll work, long as it can cut birth pains. I hope it ain't gonna be a long one."

"You feelin' awright now?"

Rose of Sharon nodded nervously. "Is it a-comin'?"

"Sure," Ma said. "Gonna have a nice baby. You jus' got to help us. Feel like you could get up an' walk?"

"I can try."

"That's a good girl," Mrs. Wainwright said. "That *is* a good girl. We'll he'p you, honey. We'll walk with ya." They helped her to her feet and pinned a blanket over her shoulders. Then Ma held her arm from one side, and Mrs. Wainwright from the other. They walked her to the brush pile and turned slowly and walked her back, over and over; and the rain drummed deeply on the roof.

Ruthie and Winfield watched anxiously. "When's she gonna have it?" he demanded.

"Sh! Don't draw 'em. We won't be let to look."

Aggie joined them behind the brush pile. Aggie's lean face and yellow hair showed in the lamplight, and her nose was long and sharp in the shadow of her head on the wall.

Ruthie whispered, "You ever saw a baby bore?"

"Sure," said Aggie.

"Well, when's she gonna have it?"

"Oh, not for a long, long time."

"Well, how long?"

"Maybe not 'fore tomorrow mornin'."

"Shucks!" said Ruthie. "Ain't no good watchin' now, then. Oh! Look!"

The walking women had stopped. Rose of Sharon had stiffened, and she whined with pain. They laid her down on the mattress and wiped her forehead while she grunted and clenched her fists. And Ma talked softly to her. "Easy," Ma said. "Gonna be all right—all right. Jus' grip ya han's. Now, then, take your lip outa your teeth. Tha's good—tha's good." The pain passed on. They let her rest awhile, and then helped her up again, and the three walked back and forth, back and forth between the pains.

Pa stuck his head in through the narrow opening. His hat dripped with water. "What ya shut the door for?" he asked. And then he saw the walking women.

Ma said, "Her time's come."

"Then—then we couldn' go 'f we wanted to."

"No."

"Then we got to buil' that bank."

"You got to."

Pa sloshed through the mud to the stream. His marking

stick was four inches down. Twenty men stood in the rain. Pa cried, "We got to build her. My girl got her pains." The men gathered around him.

"Baby?"

"Yeah. We can't go now."

A tall man said, "It ain't our baby. We kin go."

"Sure," Pa said. "You can go. Go on. Nobody's stoppin' you. They's only eight shovels." He hurried to the lowest part of the bank and drove his shovel into the mud. The shovelful lifted with a sucking sound. He drove it again, and threw the mud into the low place on the stream bank. And beside him the other men ranged themselves. They heaped the mud up in a long embankment, and those who had no shovels cut live willow whips and wove them in a mat and kicked them into the bank. Over the men came a fury of work, a fury of battle. When one man dropped his shovel, another took it up. They had shed their coats and hats. Their shirts and trousers clung tightly to their bodies, their shoes were shapeless blobs of mud. A shrill scream came from the Joad car. The men stopped, listened uneasily, and then plunged to work again. And the little levee of earth extended until it connected with the highway embankment on either end. They were tired now, and the shovels moved more slowly. And the stream rose slowly. It edged above the place where the first dirt had been thrown.

Pa laughed in triumph. "She'd come over if we hadn' a built up!" he cried.

The stream rose slowly up the side of the new wall, and tore at the willow mat. "Higher!" Pa cried. "We got to git her higher!"

The evening came, and the work went on. And now the men were beyond weariness. Their faces were set and dead. They worked jerkily, like machines. When it was dark the women set lanterns in the car doors, and kept pots of coffee handy. And the women ran one by one to the Joad car and wedged themselves inside.

The pains were coming close now, twenty minutes apart. And Rose of Sharon had lost her restraint. She screamed fiercely under the fierce pains. And the neighbor women looked at her and patted her gently and went back to their own cars.

Ma had a good fire going now, and all her utensils, filled with water, sat on the stove to heat. Every little while Pa looked in the car door. "All right?" he asked.

"Yeah! I think so," Ma assured him.

As it grew dark, someone brought out a flashlight to work by. Uncle John plunged on, throwing mud on top of the wall.

"You take it easy," Pa said. "You'll kill yaself."

"I can't he'p it. I can't stan' that yellin'. It's like—it's like when——"

"I know," Pa said. "But jus' take it easy."

Uncle John blubbered, "I'll run away. By God, I got to work or I'll run away."

Pa turned from him. "How's she stan' on the last marker?"

The man with the flashlight threw the beam on the stick. The rain cut whitely through the light. "Comin' up."

"She'll come up slower now," Pa said. "Got to flood purty far on the other side."

"She's comin' up, though."

The women filled the coffee pots and set them out again. And as the night went on, the men moved slower and slower, and they lifted their heavy feet like draft horses. More mud on the levee, more willows interlaced. The rain fell steadily. When the flashlight turned on faces, the eyes showed staring, and the muscles on the cheeks were welted out.

For a long time the screams continued from the car, and at last they were still.

Pa said, "Ma'd call me if it was bore." He went on shoveling the mud sullenly.

The stream eddied and boiled against the bank. Then, from up the stream there came a ripping crash. The beam of the flashlight showed a great cottonwood toppling. The men stopped to watch. The branches of the tree sank into the water and edged around with the current while the stream dug out the little roots. Slowly the tree was freed, and slowly it edged down the stream. The weary men watched, their mouths hanging open. The tree moved slowly down. Then a branch caught on a stump, snagged and held. And very slowly the roots swung around and hooked themselves on the new embankment. The water piled up behind. The tree moved and tore the bank. A little stream slipped through. Pa threw himself forward and jammed mud in the break. The water piled against the tree. And then the bank washed quickly down, washed around ankles, around knees. The men broke and ran, and the current worked smoothly into the flat, under the cars, under the automobiles.

Uncle John saw the water break through. In the murk he could see it. Uncontrollably his weight pulled him down. He went to his knees, and the tugging water swirled about his chest.

Pa saw him go. "Hey! What's the matter?" He lifted him to his feet. "You sick? Come on, the cars is high."

Uncle John gathered his strength. "I dunno," he said apologetically. "Legs give out. Jus' give out." Pa helped him along toward the cars.

When the dike swept out, Al turned and ran. His feet moved heavily. The water was about his calves when he reached the truck. He flung the tarpaulin off the nose and jumped into the car. He stepped on the starter. The engine turned over and over, and there was no bark of the motor. He choked the engine deeply. The battery turned the sodden motor more and more slowly, and there was no cough. Over and over, slower and slower. Al set the spark high. He felt under the seat for the crank and jumped out. The water was higher than the running board. He ran to the front end. Crank case was under water now. Frantically he fitted the crank and twisted around and around, and his clenched hand on the crank splashed in the slowly flowing water at each turn. At last his frenzy gave out. The motor was full of water, the battery fouled by now. On slightly higher ground two cars were started and their lights on. They floundered in the mud and dug their wheels down until finally the drivers cut off the motors and sat still, looking into the headlight beams. And the rain whipped white streaks through the lights. Al went slowly around the truck, reached in, and turned off the ignition.

When Pa reached the cat-walk, he found the lower end floating. He stepped it down into the mud, under water. "Think ya can make it awright, John?" he asked.

"I'll be awright. Jus' go on."

Pa cautiously climbed the cat-walk and squeezed himself

in the narrow opening. The two lamps were turned low. Ma sat on the mattress beside Rose of Sharon, and Ma fanned her still face with a piece of cardboard. Mrs. Wainwright poked dry brush into the stove, and a dank smoke edged out around the lids and filled the car with a smell of burning tissue. Ma looked up at Pa when he entered, and then quickly down.

"How—is she?" Pa asked.

Ma did not look up at him again. "Awright, I think. Sleepin'."

The air was fetid and close with the smell of the birth. Uncle John clambered in and held himself upright against the side of the car. Mrs. Wainwright left her work and came to Pa. She pulled him by the elbow toward the corner of the car. She picked up a lantern and held it over an apple box in the corner. On a newspaper lay a blue shriveled little mummy.

"Never breathed," said Mrs. Wainwright softly. "Never was alive."

Uncle John turned and shuffled tiredly down the car to the dark end. The rain whished softly on the roof now, so softly that they could hear Uncle John's tired sniffling from the dark.

Pa looked up at Mrs. Wainwright. He took the lantern from her hand and put it on the floor. Ruthie and Winfield were asleep on their own mattress, their arms over their eyes to cut out the light.

Pa walked slowly to Rose of Sharon's mattress. He tried to squat down, but his legs were too tired. He knelt instead. Ma fanned her square of cardboard back and forth. She looked at Pa for a moment, and her eyes were wide and staring, like a sleepwalker's eyes.

Pa said, "We—done—what we could."

"I know."

"We worked all night. An' a tree cut out the bank."

"I know."

"You can hear it under the car."

"I know. I heard it."

"Think she's gonna be all right?"

"I dunno."

"Well—couldn' we—of did nothin'?"

Ma's lips were stiff and white. "No. They was on'y one thing to do—ever—an' we done it."

"We worked till we dropped, an' a tree— Rain's lettin' up some." Ma looked at the ceiling, and then down again. Pa went on, compelled to talk. "I dunno how high she'll rise. Might flood the car."

"I know."

"You know ever'thing."

She was silent, and the cardboard moved slowly back and forth.

"Did we slip up?" he pleaded. "Is they anything we could of did?"

Ma looked at him strangely. Her white lips smiled in a dreaming compassion. "Don't take no blame. Hush! It'll be awright. They's changes—all over."

"Maybe the water—maybe we'll have to go."

"When it's time to go—we'll go. We'll do what we got to do. Now hush. You might wake her."

Mrs. Wainwright broke twigs and poked them in the sodden, smoking fire.

From outside came the sound of an angry voice. "I'm goin' in an' see the son-of-a-bitch myself."

And then, just outside the door, Al's voice, "Where you think you're goin'?"

"Goin' in to see that bastard Joad."

"No, you ain't. What's the matter'th you?"

"If he didn't have that fool idear about the bank, we'd a got out. Now our car is dead."

"You think ours is burnin' up the road?"

"I'm a-goin' in."

Al's voice was cold. "You're gonna fight your way in."

Pa got slowly to his feet and went to the door. "Awright, Al. I'm comin' out. It's awright, Al." Pa slid down the cat-walk. Ma heard him say, "We got sickness. Come on down here."

The rain scattered lightly on the roof now, and a new-risen breeze blew it along in sweeps. Mrs. Wainwright came from the stove and looked down at Rose of Sharon. "Dawn's a-comin' soon, ma'am. Whyn't you git some sleep? I'll set with her."

"No," Ma said. "I ain't tar'd."

"In a pig's eye," said Mrs. Wainwright. "Come on, you lay down awhile."

Ma fanned the air slowly with her cardboard. "You been frien'ly," she said. "We thank you."

The stout woman smiled. "No need to thank. Ever'body's in the same wagon. S'pose we was down. You'd a give us a han'."

"Yes," Ma said, "we would."

"Or anybody."

"Or anybody. Use' ta be the fambly was fust. It ain't so now. It's anybody. Worse off we get, the more we got to do."

"We couldn' a saved it."

"I know," said Ma.

Ruthie sighed deeply and took her arm from over her eyes. She looked blindly at the lamp for a moment, and then turned her head and looked at Ma. "Is it bore?" she demanded. "Is the baby out?"

Mrs. Wainwright picked up a sack and spread it over the apple box in the corner.

"Where's the baby?" Ruthie demanded.

Ma wet her lips. "They ain't no baby. They never was no baby. We was wrong."

"Shucks!" Ruthie said. Winfield stirred uneasily.

Ma said, "Hush now an' go to sleep. You wake up Winfiel'."

Ruthie yawned. "I wisht it had a been a baby."

Mrs. Wainwright sat down beside Ma and took the cardboard from her and fanned the air. Ma folded her hands in her lap, and her tired eyes never left the face of Rose of Sharon, sleeping in exhaustion. "Come on," Mrs. Wainwright said. "Jus' lay down. You'll be right beside her. Why, you'd wake up if she took a deep breath, even."

"Awright, I will." Ma stretched out on the mattress beside the sleeping girl. And Mrs. Wainwright sat on the floor and kept watch.

Pa and Al and Uncle John sat in the car doorway and watched the steely dawn come. The rain had stopped, but the sky was deep and solid with cloud. As the light came, it was reflected on the water. The men could see the current of the stream, slipping swiftly down, bearing black branches of trees, boxes, boards. The water swirled into the flat where the boxcars stood. There was no sign of the embankment left. On the flat the current stopped. The edges of the flood were lined with yellow foam. Pa leaned out the door and placed a twig on the cat-walk, just above the water line. The men watched the water slowly climb to it, lift it gently and float it away. Pa placed another twig an inch above the water and settled back to watch.

"Think it'll come inside the car?" Al asked.

"Can't tell. They's a hell of a lot of water got to come down from the hills yet. Can't tell. Might start up to rain again."

Al said, "I been a-thinkin'. If she come in, ever'thing'll get soaked."

"Yeah."

"Well, she won't come up more'n three-four feet in the car 'cause she'll go over the highway an' spread out first."

"How you know?" Pa asked.

"I took a sight on her, off the end of the car." He held his hand. " 'Bout this far up she'll come."

"Awright," Pa said. "What about it? We won't be here."

"We got to be here. Truck's here. Take a week to get the water out of her when the flood goes down."

"Well—what's your idear?"

"We can tear out the side-boards of the truck an' build a kinda platform in here to pile our stuff an' to set up on."

"Yeah? How'll we cook—how'll we eat?"

"Well, it'll keep our stuff dry."

The light grew stronger outside, a gray metallic light. The second little stick floated away from the cat-walk. Pa placed another one higher up. "Sure climbin'," he said. "I guess we better do that."

Ma turned restlessly in her sleep. Her eyes started wide open. She cried sharply in warning, "Tom! Oh, Tom! Tom!"

Mrs. Wainwright spoke soothingly. The eyes flicked closed again and Ma squirmed under her dream. Mrs. Wainwright got up and walked to the doorway. "Hey!" she said softly. "We ain't gonna git out soon." She pointed to the corner of the car where the apple box was. "That ain't doin' no good.

Jus' cause trouble an' sorra. Couldn' you fellas kinda—take it out an' bury it?"

The men were silent. Pa said at last, "Guess you're right. Jus' cause sorra. 'Gainst the law to bury it."

"They's lots a things 'gainst the law that we can't he'p doin'."

"Yeah."

Al said, "We oughta git them truck sides tore off 'fore the water comes up much more."

Pa turned to Uncle John. "Will you take an' bury it while Al an' me git that lumber in?"

Uncle John said sullenly, "Why do I got to do it? Why don't you fellas? I don' like it." And then, "Sure. I'll do it. Sure, I will. Come on, give it to me." His voice began to rise. "Come on! Give it to me."

"Don' wake 'em up," Mrs. Wainwright said. She brought the apple box to the doorway and straightened the sack decently over it.

"Shovel's standin' right behin' you," Pa said.

Uncle John took the shovel in one hand. He slipped out the doorway into the slowly moving water, and it rose nearly to his waist before he struck bottom. He turned and settled the apple box under his other arm.

Pa said, "Come on, Al. Le's git that lumber in."

In the gray dawn light Uncle John waded around the end of the car, past the Joad truck; and he climbed the slippery bank to the highway. He walked down the highway, past the boxcar flat, until he came to a place where the boiling stream ran close to the road, where the willows grew along the road side. He put his shovel down, and holding the box in front of him, he edged through the brush until he came to the edge of the swift stream. For a time he stood watching it swirl by, leaving its yellow foam among the willow stems. He held the apple box against his chest. And then he leaned over and set the box in the stream and steadied it with his hand. He said fiercely, "Go down an' tell 'em. Go down in the street an' rot an' tell 'em that way. That's the way you can talk. Don' even know if you was a boy or a girl. Ain't gonna find out. Go on down now, an' lay in the street. Maybe they'll know then." He guided the box gently out into the current and let it go.

It settled low in the water, edged sideways, whirled around, and turned slowly over. The sack floated away, and the box, caught in the swift water, floated quickly away, out of sight, behind the brush. Uncle John grabbed the shovel and went rapidly back to the boxcars. He sloshed down into the water and waded to the truck, where Pa and Al were working, taking down the one-by-six planks.

Pa looked over at him. "Get it done?"

"Yeah."

"Well, look," Pa said. "If you'll he'p Al, I'll go down the store an' get some stuff to eat."

"Get some bacon," Al said. "I need some meat."

"I will," Pa said. He jumped down from the truck and Uncle John took his place.

When they pushed the planks into the car door, Ma awakened and sat up. "What you doin'?"

"Gonna build up a place to keep outa the wet."

"Why?" Ma asked. "It's dry in here."

"Ain't gonna be. Water's comin' up."

Ma struggled up to her feet and went to the door. "We got to git outa here."

"Can't," Al said. "All our stuff's here. Truck's here. Ever'thing we got."

"Where's Pa?"

"Gone to get stuff for breakfas'."

Ma looked down at the water. It was only six inches down from the floor by now. She went back to the mattress and looked at Rose of Sharon. The girl stared back at her.

"How you feel?" Ma asked.

"Tar'd. Jus' tar'd out."

"Gonna get some breakfas' into you."

"I ain't hungry."

Mrs. Wainwright moved beside Ma. "She looks all right. Come through it fine."

Rose of Sharon's eyes questioned Ma, and Ma tried to avoid the question. Mrs. Wainwright walked to the stove.

"Ma."

"Yeah? What you want?"

"Is—it—all right?"

Ma gave up the attempt. She kneeled down on the mattress.

"You can have more," she said. "We done ever'thing we knowed."

Rose of Sharon struggled and pushed herself up. "Ma!"

"You couldn' he'p it."

The girl lay back again, and covered her eyes with her arms. Ruthie crept close and looked down in awe. She whispered harshly, "She sick, Ma? She gonna die?"

" 'Course not. She's gonna be awright. Awright."

Pa came in with his armload of packages. "How is she?"

"Awright," Ma said. "She's gonna be awright."

Ruthie reported to Winfield. "She ain't gonna die. Ma says so."

And Winfield, picking his teeth with a splinter in a very adult manner, said, "I knowed it all the time."

"How'd you know?"

"I won't tell," said Winfield, and he spat out a piece of the splinter.

Ma built the fire up with the last twigs and cooked the bacon and made gravy. Pa had brought store bread. Ma scowled when she saw it. "We got any money lef'?"

"Nope," said Pa. "But we was so hungry."

"An' you got store bread," Ma said accusingly.

"Well, we was awful hungry. Worked all night long."

Ma sighed. "Now what we gonna do?"

As they ate, the water crept up and up. Al gulped his food and he and Pa built the platform. Five feet wide, six feet long, four feet above the floor. And the water crept to the edge of the doorway, seemed to hesitate a long time, and then moved slowly inward over the floor. And outside, the rain began again, as it had before, big heavy drops splashing on the water, pounding hollowly on the roof.

Al said, "Come on now, let's get the mattresses up. Let's put the blankets up, so they don't git wet." They piled their possessions up on the platform, and the water crept over the floor. Pa and Ma, Al and Uncle John, each at a corner, lifted Rose of Sharon's mattress, with the girl on it, and put it on top of the pile.

And the girl protested, "I can walk. I'm awright." And the water crept over the floor, a thin film of it. Rose of Sharon whispered to Ma, and Ma put her hand under the blanket and felt her breast and nodded.

In the other end of the boxcar, the Wainwrights were pounding, building a platform for themselves. The rain thickened, and then passed away.

Ma looked down at her feet. The water was half an inch deep on the car floor by now. "You, Ruthie—Winfiel'!" she called distractedly. "Come get on top of the pile. You'll get cold." She saw them safely up, sitting awkwardly beside Rose of Sharon. Ma said suddenly, "We got to git out."

"We can't," Pa said. "Like Al says, all our stuff's here. We'll pull off the boxcar door an' make more room to set on."

The family huddled on the platforms, silent and fretful. The water was six inches deep in the car before the flood spread evenly over the embankment and moved into the cotton field on the other side. During that day and night the men slept soddenly, side by side on the boxcar door. And Ma lay close to Rose of Sharon. Sometimes Ma whispered to her and sometimes sat up quietly, her face brooding. Under the blanket she hoarded the remains of the store bread.

The rain had become intermittent now—little wet squalls and quiet times. On the morning of the second day Pa splashed through the camp and came back with ten potatoes in his pockets. Ma watched him sullenly while he chopped out part of the inner wall of the car, built a fire, and scooped water into a pan. The family ate the steaming boiled potatoes with their fingers. And when this last food was gone, they stared at the gray water; and in the night they did not lie down for a long time.

When the morning came they awakened nervously. Rose of Sharon whispered to Ma.

Ma nodded her head. "Yes," she said. "It's time for it." And then she turned to the car door, where the men lay. "We're a-gettin' outa here," she said savagely, "gettin' to higher groun'. An' you're comin' or you ain't comin', but I'm takin' Rosasharn an' the little fellas outa here."

"We can't!" Pa said weakly.

"Awright, then. Maybe you'll pack Rosasharn to the high-

way, anyways, an' then come back. It ain't rainin' now, an'
we're a-goin'."

"Awright, we'll go," Pa said.

Al said, "Ma, I ain't goin'."

"Why not?"

"Well—Aggie—why, her an' me——"

Ma smiled. " 'Course," she said. "You stay here, Al. Take
care of the stuff. When the water goes down—why, we'll come
back. Come quick, 'fore it rains again," she told Pa. "Come
on, Rosasharn. We're goin' to a dry place."

"I can walk."

"Maybe a little, on the road. Git your back bent, Pa."

Pa slipped into the water and stood waiting. Ma helped
Rose of Sharon down from the platform and steadied her
across the car. Pa took her in his arms, held her as high as he
could, and pushed his way carefully through the deep water,
around the car, and to the highway. He set her down on her
feet and held onto her. Uncle John carried Ruthie and followed. Ma slid down into the water, and for a moment her
skirts billowed out around her.

"Winfiel', set on my shoulder. Al—we'll come back soon's
the water's down. Al—" She paused. "If—if Tom comes—
tell him we'll be back. Tell him be careful. Winfiel'! Climb on
my shoulder—there! Now, keep your feet still." She staggered
off through the breast-high water. At the highway embankment they helped her up and lifted Winfield from her shoulder.

They stood on the highway and looked back over the sheet
of water, the dark red blocks of the cars, the trucks and automobiles deep in the slowly moving water. And as they stood,
a little misting rain began to fall.

"We got to git along," Ma said. "Rosasharn, you feel like
you could walk?"

"Kinda dizzy," the girl said. "Feel like I been beat."

Pa complained, "Now we're a-goin', where we goin'?"

"I dunno. Come on, give your han' to Rosasharn." Ma
took the girl's right arm to steady her, and Pa her left. "Goin'
someplace where it's dry. Got to. You fellas ain't had dry
clothes on for two days." They moved slowly along the highway. They could hear the rushing of the water in the stream

beside the road. Ruthie and Winfield marched together, splashing their feet against the road. They went slowly along the road. The sky grew darker and the rain thickened. No traffic moved along the highway.

"We got to hurry," Ma said. "If this here girl gits good an' wet—I don' know what'll happen to her."

"You ain't said where-at we're a-hurryin' to," Pa reminded her sarcastically.

The road curved along beside the stream. Ma searched the land and the flooded fields. Far off the road, on the left, on a slight rolling hill a rain-blackened barn stood. "Look!" Ma said. "Look there! I bet it's dry in that barn. Le's go there till the rain stops."

Pa sighed. "Prob'ly get run out by the fella owns it."

Ahead, beside the road, Ruthie saw a spot of red. She raced to it. A scraggly geranium gone wild, and there was one rain-beaten blossom on it. She picked the flower. She took a petal carefully off and stuck it on her nose. Winfield ran up to see.

"Lemme have one?" he said.

"No, sir! It's all mine. I foun' it." She stuck another red petal on her forehead, a little bright-red heart.

"Come on, Ruthie! Lemme have one. Come on, now." He grabbed at the flower in her hand and missed it, and Ruthie banged him in the face with her open hand. He stood for a moment, surprised, and then his lips shook and his eyes welled.

The others caught up. "Now what you done?" Ma asked. "Now what you done?"

"He tried to grab my fl'ar."

Winfield sobbed, "I—on'y wanted one—to—stick on my nose."

"Give him one, Ruthie."

"Leave him find his own. This here's mine."

"Ruthie! You give him one."

Ruthie heard the threat in Ma's tone, and changed her tactics. "Here," she said with elaborate kindness. "I'll stick on one for you." The older people walked on. Winfield held his nose near to her. She wet a petal with her tongue and jabbed it cruelly on his nose. "You little son-of-a-bitch," she said softly. Winfield felt for the petal with his fingers, and pressed it down on his nose. They walked quickly after the others. Ruthie felt how the fun was gone. "Here," she said. "Here's some more. Stick some on your forehead."

From the right of the road there came a sharp swishing. Ma cried, "Hurry up. They's a big rain. Le's go through the fence here. It's shorter. Come on, now! Bear on, Rosasharn." They half dragged the girl across the ditch, helped her through the fence. And then the storm struck them. Sheets of rain fell on them. They plowed through the mud and up the little incline. The black barn was nearly obscured by the rain. It hissed and splashed, and the growing wind drove it along. Rose of Sharon's feet slipped and she dragged between her supporters.

"Pa! Can you carry her?"

Pa leaned over and picked her up. "We're wet through anyways," he said. "Hurry up. Winfiel'—Ruthie! Run on ahead."

They came panting up to the rain-soaked barn and staggered into the open end. There was no door in this end. A few rusty farm tools lay about, a disk plow and a broken cultivator, an iron wheel. The rain hammered on the roof and curtained the entrance. Pa gently set Rose of Sharon down on an oily box. "God Awmighty!" he said.

Ma said, "Maybe they's hay inside. Look, there's a door." She swung the door on its rusty hinges. "They is hay," she cried. "Come on in, you."

It was dark inside. A little light came in through the cracks between the boards.

"Lay down, Rosasharn," Ma said. "Lay down an' res'. I'll try to figger some way to dry you off."

Winfield said, "Ma!" and the rain roaring on the roof drowned his voice. "*Ma!*"

"What is it? What you want?"

"Look! In the corner."

Ma looked. There were two figures in the gloom; a man who lay on his back, and a boy sitting beside him, his eyes wide, staring at the newcomers. As she looked, the boy got slowly up to his feet and came toward her. His voice croaked. "You own this here?"

"No," Ma said. "Jus' come in outa the wet. We got a sick

girl. You got a dry blanket we could use an' get her wet clothes off?"

The boy went back to the corner and brought a dirty comfort and held it out to Ma.

"Thank ya," she said. "What's the matter'th that fella?"

The boy spoke in a croaking monotone. "Fust he was sick—but now he's starvin'."

"What?"

"Starvin'. Got sick in the cotton. He ain't et for six days."

Ma walked to the corner and looked down at the man. He was about fifty, his whiskery face gaunt, and his open eyes were vague and staring. The boy stood beside her. "Your pa?" Ma asked.

"Yeah! Says he wasn' hungry, or he jus' et. Give me the food. Now he's too weak. Can't hardly move."

The pounding of the rain decreased to a soothing swish on the roof. The gaunt man moved his lips. Ma knelt beside him and put her ear close. His lips moved again.

"Sure," Ma said. "You jus' be easy. He'll be awright. You jus' wait'll I get them wet clo'es off'n my girl."

Ma went back to the girl. "Now slip 'em off," she said. She held the comfort up to screen her from view. And when she was naked, Ma folded the comfort about her.

The boy was at her side again explaining, "I didn' know. He said he et, or he wasn' hungry. Las' night I went an' bust a winda an' stoled some bread. Made 'im chew 'er down. But he puked it all up, an' then he was weaker. Got to have soup or milk. You folks got money to git milk?"

Ma said, "Hush. Don' worry. We'll figger somepin out."

Suddenly the boy cried, "He's dyin', I tell you! He's starvin' to death, I tell you."

"Hush," said Ma. She looked at Pa and Uncle John standing helplessly gazing at the sick man. She looked at Rose of Sharon huddled in the comfort. Ma's eyes passed Rose of Sharon's eyes, and then came back to them. And the two women looked deep into each other. The girl's breath came short and gasping.

She said "Yes."

Ma smiled. "I knowed you would. I knowed!" She looked down at her hands, tight-locked in her lap.

Rose of Sharon whispered, "Will—will you all—go out?" The rain whisked lightly on the roof.

Ma leaned forward and with her palm she brushed the tousled hair back from her daughter's forehead, and she kissed her on the forehead. Ma got up quickly. "Come on, you fellas," she called. "You come out in the tool shed."

Ruthie opened her mouth to speak. "Hush," Ma said. "Hush and git." She herded them through the door, drew the boy with her; and she closed the squeaking door.

For a minute Rose of Sharon sat still in the whispering barn. Then she hoisted her tired body up and drew the comfort about her. She moved slowly to the corner and stood looking down at the wasted face, into the wide, frightened eyes. Then slowly she lay down beside him. He shook his head slowly from side to side. Rose of Sharon loosened one side of the blanket and bared her breast. "You got to," she said. She squirmed closer and pulled his head close. "There!" she said. "There." Her hand moved behind his head and supported it. Her fingers moved gently in his hair. She looked up and across the barn, and her lips came together and smiled mysteriously.

THE LOG FROM
THE SEA OF CORTEZ

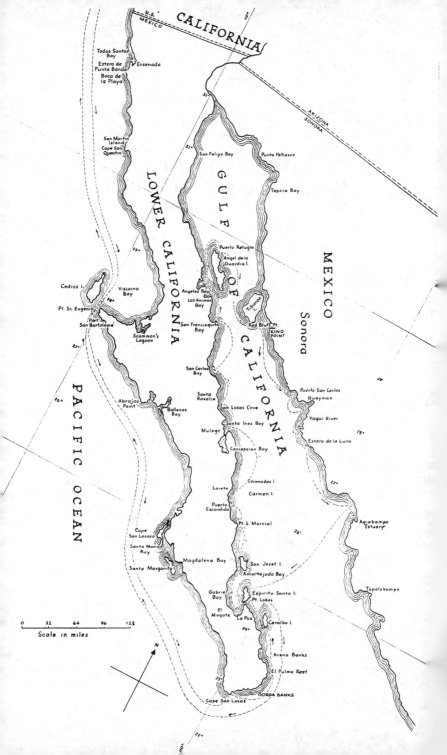

Contents

About Ed Ricketts

JUST about dusk one day in April 1948 Ed Ricketts stopped work in the laboratory in Cannery Row. He covered his instruments and put away his papers and filing cards. He rolled down the sleeves of his wool shirt and put on the brown coat which was slightly small for him and frayed at the elbows.

He wanted a steak for dinner and he knew just the market in New Monterey where he could get a fine one, well hung and tender.

He went out into the street that is officially named Ocean View Avenue and is known as Cannery Row. His old car stood at the gutter, a beat-up sedan. The car was tricky and hard to start. He needed a new one but could not afford it at the expense of other things.

Ed tinkered away at the primer until the ancient rusty motor coughed and broke into a bronchial chatter which indicated that it was running. Ed meshed the jagged gears and moved away up the street.

He turned up the hill where the road crosses the Southern Pacific Railways track. It was almost dark, or rather that kind of mixed light and dark which makes it very difficult to see. Just before the crossing the road takes a sharp climb. Ed shifted to second gear, the noisiest gear, to get up the hill. The sound of his motor and gears blotted out every other sound. A corrugated iron warehouse was on his left, obscuring any sight of the right of way.

The Del Monte Express, the evening train from San Francisco, slipped around from behind the warehouse and crashed into the old car. The cow-catcher buckled in the side of the automobile and pushed and ground and mangled it a hundred yards up the track before the train stopped.

Ed was conscious when they got him out of the car and laid him on the grass. A crowd had collected of course—people from the train and more from the little houses that hug the track.

In almost no time a doctor was there. Ed's skull had a

crooked look and his eyes were crossed. There was blood around his mouth, and his body was twisted, distorted— wrong, as though seen under an untrue lens.

The doctor got down on one knee and leaned over. The ring of people was silent.

Ed asked, "How bad is it?"

"I don't know," the doctor said. "How do you feel?"

"I don't feel much of anything," Ed said.

Because the doctor knew him and knew what kind of a man he was, he said, "That's shock, of course."

"Of course!" Ed said, and his eyes began to glaze.

They edged him onto a stretcher and took him to the hospital. Section hands pried his old car off the cow-catcher and pushed it aside, and the Del Monte Express moved slowly into the station at Pacific Grove, which is the end of the line.

Several doctors had come in and more were phoning, wanting to help because they all loved him. The doctors knew it was very serious, so they gave him ether and opened him up to see how bad it was. When they finished they knew it was hopeless. Ed was all messed up—spleen broken, ribs shattered, lungs punctured, concussion of the skull. It might have been better to let him go out under the ether, but the doctors could not give up, any more than could the people gathered in the waiting room of the hospital. Men who knew better began talking about miracles and how anything could happen. They reminded each other of cases of people who had got well when there was no reason to suppose they could. The surgeons cleaned Ed's insides as well as possible and closed him up. Every now and then one of the doctors would go out to the waiting room, and it was like facing a jury. There were lots of people out there, sitting waiting, and their eyes all held a stone question.

The doctors said things like, "Doing as well as can be expected" and "We won't be able to tell for some time but he seems to be making progress." They talked more than was necessary, and the people sitting there didn't talk at all. They just stared, trying to get adjusted.

The switchboard was loaded with calls from people who wanted to give blood.

The next morning Ed was conscious but very tired and

groggy from ether and morphine. His eyes were washed out and he spoke with great difficulty. But he did repeat his first question.

"How bad is it?"

The doctor who was in the room caught himself just as he was going to say some soothing nonsense, remembering that Ed was his friend and that Ed loved true things and knew a lot of true things too, so the doctor said, "Very bad."

Ed didn't ask again. He hung on for a couple of days because his vitality was very great. In fact he hung on so long that some of the doctors began to believe the things they had said about miracles when they knew such a chance to be nonsense. They noted a stronger heartbeat. They saw improved color in his cheeks below the bandages. Ed hung on so long that some people from the waiting room dared to go home to get some sleep.

And then, as happens so often with men of large vitality, the energy and the color and the pulse and the breathing went away silently and quickly, and he died.

By that time the shock in Monterey had turned to dullness. He was dead and had to be got rid of. People wanted to get rid of him quickly and with dignity so they could think about him and restore him again.

On a small rise not far from the Great Tide Pool near Lighthouse Point there is a small chapel and crematory. Ed's closed coffin was put in that chapel for part of an afternoon.

Naturally no one wanted flowers, but the greatest fear was that someone might say a speech or make a remark about him—good or bad. Luckily it was all over so quickly that the people who ordinarily make speeches were caught unprepared.

A large number of people drifted into the chapel, looked for a few moments at the coffin, and then walked away. No one wanted company. Everyone wanted to be alone. Some went to the beach by the Great Tide Pool and sat in the coarse sand and blindly watched the incoming tide creeping around the rocks and tumbling in over the seaweed.

A kind of anesthesia settled on the people who knew Ed Ricketts. There was not sorrow really but rather puzzled questions—what are we going to do? how can we rearrange our lives now? Everyone who knew him turned inward. It was a strange thing—quiet and strange. We were lost and could not find ourselves.

It is going to be difficult to write down the things about Ed Ricketts that must be written, hard to separate entities. And anyone who knew him would find it difficult. Maybe some of the events are imagined. And perhaps some very small happenings may have grown out of all proportion in the mind. And then there is the personal impact. I am sure that many people, seeing this account, will be sure to say, "Why, that's not true. That's not the way he was at all. He was this way and this." And the speaker may go on to describe a person this writer did not know at all. But no one who knew him will deny the force and influence of Ed Ricketts. Everyone near him was influenced by him, deeply and permanently. Some he taught how to think, others how to see or hear. Children on the beach he taught how to look for and find beautiful animals in worlds they had not suspected were there at all. He taught everyone without seeming to.

Nearly everyone who knew him has tried to define him. Such things were said of him as, "He was half-Christ and half-goat." He was a great teacher and a great lecher—an immortal who loved women. Surely he was an original and his character was unique, but in such a way that everyone was related to him, one in this way and another in some different way. He was gentle but capable of ferocity, small and slight but strong as an ox, loyal and yet untrustworthy, generous but gave little and received much. His thinking was as paradoxical as his life. He thought in mystical terms and hated and distrusted mysticism. He was an individualist who studied colonial animals with satisfaction.

We have all tried to define Ed Ricketts with little success. Perhaps it would be better to put down the mass of material from our memories, anecdotes, quotations, events. Of course some of the things will cancel others, but that is the way he was. The essence lies somewhere. There must be some way of finding it.

Finally there is another reason to put Ed Ricketts down on paper. He will not die. He haunts the people who knew him.

He is always present even in the moments when we feel his loss the most.

One night soon after his death a number of us were drinking beer in the laboratory. We laughed and told stories about Ed, and suddenly one of us said in pain, "We'll have to let him go! We'll have to release him and let him go." And that was true not for Ed but for ourselves. We can't keep him, and still he will not go away.

Maybe if I write down everything I can remember about him, that will lay the ghost. It is worth trying anyway. It will have to be true or it can't work. It must be no celebration of his virtues, because, as was said of another man, he had the faults of his virtues. There can be no formula. The simplest and best way will be just to remember—as much as I can.

The statistics on Ed Ricketts would read: Born in Chicago, played in the streets, went to public school, studied biology at the University of Chicago. Opened a small commercial laboratory in Pacific Grove, California. Moved to Cannery Row in Monterey. Degrees—Bachelor of Science only; clubs, none; honors, none. Army service—both World Wars. Killed by a train at the age of fifty-two. Within that frame he went a long way and burned a deep scar.

I was sitting in a dentist's waiting room in New Monterey, hoping the dentist had died. I had a badly aching tooth and not enough money to have a good job done on it. My main hope was that the dentist could stop the ache without charging too much and without finding too many other things wrong.

The door to the slaughterhouse opened and a slight man with a beard came out. I didn't look at him closely because of what he held in his hand, a bloody molar with a surprisingly large piece of jawbone sticking to it. He was cursing gently as he came through the door. He held the reeking relic out to me and said, "Look at that god-damned thing." I was already looking at it. "That came out of me," he said.

"Seems to be more jaw than tooth," I said.

"He got impatient, I guess. I'm Ed Ricketts."

"I'm John Steinbeck. Does it hurt?"

"Not much. I've heard of you."

"I've heard of you, too. Let's have a drink."

That was the first time I ever saw him. I had heard that there was an interesting man in town who ran a commercial laboratory, had a library of good music, and interests wider than invertebratology. I had wanted to come across him for some time.

We did not think of ourselves as poor then. We simply had no money. Our food was fairly plentiful, what with fishing and planning and a minimum of theft. Entertainment had to be improvised without benefit of currency. Our pleasures consisted in conversation, walks, games, and parties with people of our own financial nonexistence. A real party was dressed with a gallon of thirty-nine-cent wine, and we could have a hell of a time on that. We did not know any rich people, and for that reason we did not like them and were proud and glad we didn't live *that* way.

We had been timid about meeting Ed Ricketts because he was rich people by our standards. This meant that he could depend on a hundred to a hundred and fifty dollars a month and he had an automobile. To us this was fancy, and we didn't see how anyone could go through that kind of money. But we learned.

Knowing Ed Ricketts was instant. After the first moment I knew him, and for the next eighteen years I knew him better than I knew anyone, and perhaps I did not know him at all. Maybe it was that way with all of his friends. He was different from anyone and yet so like that everyone found himself in Ed, and that might be one of the reasons his death had such an impact. It wasn't Ed who had died but a large and important part of oneself.

When I first knew him, his laboratory was an old house in Cannery Row which he had bought and transformed to his purposes. The entrance was a kind of showroom with mounted marine specimens in glass jars on shelves around the walls. Next to this room was a small office, where for some reason the rattlesnakes were kept in cages between the safe and the filing cabinets. The top of the safe was piled high with stationery and filing cards. Ed loved paper and cards. He never ordered small amounts but huge supplies of it.

On the side of the building toward the ocean were two

more rooms, one with cages for white rats—hundreds of white rats, and reproducing furiously. This room used to get pretty smelly if it was not cleaned with great regularity—which it never was. The other rear room was set up with microscopes and slides and the equipment for making and mounting and baking the delicate microorganisms which were so much a part of the laboratory income. In the basement there was a big stockroom with jars and tanks for preserving the larger animals, and also the equipment for embalming and injecting the cats, dogfish, frogs, and other animals that were used by dissection classes.

This little house was called Pacific Biological Laboratories, Inc., as strange an operation as ever outraged the corporate laws of California. When, after Ed's death, the corporation had to be liquidated, it was impossible to find out who owned the stock, how much of it there was, or what it was worth. Ed kept the most careful collecting notes on record, but sometimes he would not open a business letter for weeks.

How the business ran for twenty years no one knows, but it did run even though it staggered a little sometimes. At times it would spurt ahead with system and efficiency and then wearily collapse for several months. Orders would pile up on the desk. Once during a weary period someone sent Ed a cheesecake by parcel post. He thought it was preserved material of some kind, and when he finally opened it three months later we could not have identified it had it not been that a note was enclosed which said, "Eat this cheesecake at once. It's very delicate."

Often the desk was piled so high with unopened letters that they slid tiredly to the floor. Ed believed completely in the theory that a letter unanswered for a week usually requires no answer, but he went even farther. A letter unopened for a month does not require opening.

Every time some definite statement like that above is set down I think of exceptions. Ed carried on a large and varied correspondence with a number of people. He answered letters quickly and at length, using a typewriter with elite type to save space. The purchase of a typewriter was a long process with him, for much of the type had to be changed from business signs to biologic signs, and he also liked to have some foreign-language signs on his typewriter, tilde for Spanish, accents and cedilla for French, umlaut for German. He rarely used them but he liked to have them.

The days of the laboratory can be split into two periods. The era before the fire and that afterwards. The fire was interesting in many respects.

One night something went wrong with the electric current on the whole water front. Where 220 volts were expected and prepared for, something like two thousand volts suddenly came through. Since in the subsequent suits the electric company was found blameless by the courts, this must be set down to an act of God. What happened was that a large part of Cannery Row burst into flames in a moment. By the time Ed awakened, the laboratory was a sheet of fire. He grabbed his typewriter, rushed to the basement, and got his car out just in time, and just before the building was about ready to crash into its own basement. He had no pants but he had transportation and printing. He always admired his choice. The scientific library, accumulated with such patience and some of it irreplaceable, was gone. All the fine equipment, the microscopes, the museum jars, the stock—everything was gone. Besides typewriter and automobile, only one thing was saved.

Ed had a remarkably fine safe. It was so good that he worried for fear some misguided and romantic burglar might think there was something of value in it and, trying to open it, might abuse and injure its beautiful mechanism. Consequently he not only never locked the safe but contrived a wood block so that it could not be locked. Also, he pasted a note above the combination, assuring all persons that the safe was not locked. Then it developed that there was nothing to put in the safe anyway. Thus the safe became the repository of foods which might attract the flies of Cannery Row, and there were clouds of them drawn to the refuse of the fish canneries but willing to come to other foods. And it must be said that no fly was ever able to negotiate the safe.

But to get back to the fire. After the ashes had cooled, there was the safe lying on its side in the basement where it had fallen when the floor above gave way. It must have been an excellent safe, for when we opened it we found half a pineapple pie, a quarter of a pound of Gorgonzola cheese, and an open can of sardines—all of them except the sardines in good condition. The sardines were a little dry. Ed admired that safe and used to refer to it with affection. He would say that if there *had* been valuable things in the safe it would surely have protected them. "Think how delicate Gorgonzola is," he said. "It couldn't have been very hot inside that safe. The cheese is still delicious."

In spite of a great erudition, or perhaps because of it, Ed had some naive qualities. After the fire there were a number of suits against the electric company, based on the theory, later proved wrong, that if the fires were caused by error or negligence on the part of the company, the company should pay for the damage.

Pacific Biological Laboratories, Inc., was one of the plaintiffs in this suit. Ed went over to Superior Court in Salinas to testify. He told the truth as clearly and as fully as he could. He loved true things and believed in them. Then he became fascinated by the trial and the jury and he spent much time in court, inspecting the legal system with the same objective care he would have lavished on a new species of marine animal.

Afterwards he said calmly and with a certain wonder, "You see how easy it is to be completely wrong about a simple matter. It was always my conviction—or better, my impression—that the legal system was designed to arrive at the truth in matters of human and property relationships. You see, I had forgotten or never considered one thing. Each side wants to win, and that factor warps any original intent to the extent that the objective truth of the matter disappears in emphasis. Now you take the case of this fire," he went on. "Both sides wanted to win, and neither had any interest in, indeed both sides seemed to have a kind of abhorrence for, the truth." It was an amazing discovery to him and one that required thinking out. Because he loved true things, he thought everyone did. The fact that it was otherwise did not sadden him. It simply interested him. And he set about rebuilding his laboratory and replacing his books with an antlike methodicalness.

Ed's use of words was unorthodox and, until you knew him, somewhat startling. Once, in getting a catalogue ready, he wanted to advise the trade that he had plenty of hagfish available. Now the hagfish is a most disgusting animal both in appearance and texture, and some of its habits are nauseating. It is a perfect animal horror. But Ed did not feel this, because the hagfish has certain functions which he found fascinating. In his catalogue he wrote, "Available in some quantities, delightful and beautiful hagfish."

He admired worms of all kinds and found them so desirable that, searching around for a pet name for a girl he loved, he called her "Wormy." She was a little huffy until she realized that he was using not the adjective but a diminutive of the noun. His use of this word meant that he found her pretty, interesting, and desirable. But still it always sounded to the girl like an adjective.

Ed loved food, and many of the words he used were eating words. I have heard him refer to a girl, a marine animal, and a plain song as "delicious."

His mind had no horizons. He was interested in everything. And there were very few things he did not like. Perhaps it would be well to set down the things he did not like. Maybe they would be some kind of key to his personality, although it is my conviction that there is no such key.

Chief among his hatreds was old age. He hated it in other people and did not even conceive of it in himself. He hated old women and would not stay in a room with them. He said he could smell them. He had a remarkable sense of smell. He could smell a mouse in a room, and I have seen him locate a rattlesnake in the brush by smell.

He hated women with thin lips. "If the lips are thin—where will there be any fullness?" he would say. His observation was certainly physical and open to verification, and he seemed to believe in its accuracy and so do I, but with less vehemence.

He loved women too much to take any nonsense from the thin-lipped ones. But if a girl with thin lips painted on fuller ones with lipstick, he was satisfied. "Her intentions are correct," he said. "There is a psychic fullness, and sometimes that can be very fine."

He hated hot soup and would pour cold water into the most beautifully prepared bisque.

He unequivocally hated to get his head wet. Collecting animals in the tide pools, he would be soaked by the waves to his eyebrows, but his head was invariably covered and safe. In the shower he wore an oilskin sou'wester—a ridiculous sight.

He hated one professor whom he referred to as "old jingle ballicks." It never developed why he hated "old jingle ballicks."

He hated pain inflicted without good reason. Driving through the streets one night, he saw a man beating a red setter with a rake handle. Ed stopped the car and attacked the man with a monkey wrench and would have killed him if the man had not run away.

Although slight in build, when he was angry Ed had no fear and could be really dangerous. On an occasion one of our cops was pistol-whipping a drunk in the middle of the night. Ed attacked the cop with his bare hands, and his fury was so great that the cop released the drunk.

This hatred was only for reasonless cruelty. When the infliction of pain was necessary, he had little feeling about it. Once during the depression we found we could buy a live sheep for three dollars. This may seem incredible now but it was so. It was a great deal of food and even for those days a great bargain. Then we had the sheep and none of us could kill it. But Ed cut its throat with no emotion whatever, and even explained to the rest of us who were upset that bleeding to death is quite painless if there is no fear involved. The pain of opening a vein is slight if the instrument is sharp, and he had opened the jugular with a scalpel and had not frightened the animal, so that our secondary or empathic pain was probably much greater than that of the sheep.

His feeling for psychic pain in normal people also was philosophic. He would say that nearly everything that can happen to people not only does happen but has happened for a million years. "Therefore," he would say, "for everything that can happen there is a channel or mechanism in the human to take care of it—a channel worn down in prehistory and transmitted in the genes."

He disliked time intensely unless it was part of an observation or an experiment. He was invariably and consciously late for appointments. He said he had once worked for a railroad where his whole life had been regulated by a second hand and that he had then conceived his disgust, a disgust for exactness in time. To my knowledge, that is the only time he ever spoke of the railroad experience. If you asked him to dinner at seven, he might get there at nine. On the other hand, if a good low collecting tide was at 6:53, he would be in the tide pool at 6:52.

The farther I get into this the more apparent it becomes to me that no rule was final. He himself was not conscious of any rules of behavior in himself, although he observed behavior patterns in other people with delight.

For many years he wore a beard, not large, and slightly pointed, which accentuated his half-goat, half-Christ appearance. He had started wearing the beard because some girl he wanted thought he had a weak chin. He didn't have a weak chin, but as long as she thought so he cultivated his beard. This was probably during the period of the prognathous Arrow Collar men in the advertising pages. Many girls later he was still wearing the beard because he was used to it. He kept it until the Army made him shave it off in the Second World War. His beard sometimes caused a disturbance. Small boys often followed Ed, baaing like sheep. He developed a perfect defense against this. He would turn and baa back at them, which invariably so embarrassed the boys that they slipped shyly away.

Ed had a strange and courteous relationship with dogs, although he never owned one or wanted to. Passing a dog on the street, he greeted it with dignity and, when driving, often tipped his hat and smiled and waved at dogs on the sidewalk. And damned if they didn't smile back at him. Cats, on the other hand, did not arouse any enthusiasm in him. However, he always remembered one cat with admiration. It was in the old days before the fire when Ed's father was still alive and doing odd jobs about the laboratory. The cat in question took a dislike to Ed's father and developed a spite tactic which charmed Ed. The cat would climb up on a shelf and pee on Ed's father when he went by—the cat did it not once but many times.

Ed regarded his father with affection. "He has one quality of genius," Ed would say. "He is always wrong. If a man makes a million decisions and judgments at random, it is perhaps mathematically tenable to suppose that he will be right

half the time and wrong half the time. But you take my father—he is wrong all of the time about everything. That is a
matter not of luck but of selection. That requires genius."

Ed's father was a rather silent, shy, but genial man who took
so many aspirins for headaches that he had developed a
chronic acetanilide poisoning and the quaint dullness that
goes with it. For many years he worked in the basement stockroom, packing specimens to be shipped and even mounting
some of the larger and less delicate forms. His chief pride,
however, was a human fetus which he had mounted in a museum jar. It was to have been the lone child of a Negress and
a Chinese. When the mother succumbed to a lover's quarrel
and a large dose of arsenic administered by person or persons
unknown, the autopsy revealed her secret, and her secret was
acquired by Pacific Biological. It was much too far advanced
to be of much value for study so Ed's father inherited it. He
crossed its little legs in a Buddha pose, arranged its hands in
an attitude of semi-prayer, and fastened it securely upright in
the museum jar. It was rather a startling figure, for while it
had negroid features, the preservative had turned it to a pale
ivory color. It was Dad Ricketts' great pride. Children and
many adults made pilgrimages to the basement to see it. It
became famous in Cannery Row.

One day an Italian woman blundered into the basement.
Although she did not speak any English, Dad Ricketts naturally thought she had come to see his prize. He showed it to
her; whereupon, to his amazement and embarrassment, she
instantly undressed to show him her fine scar from a Caesarian
section.

Cats were a not inconsiderable source of income to Pacific
Biological Laboratories, Inc. They were chloroformed, the
blood drained, and embalming fluid and color mass injected
in the venous and arterial systems. These finished cats were
sold to schools for study of anatomy.

When an order came in for, say, twenty-five cats, there was
only one way to get them, since the ASPCA will not allow
the raising of cats for laboratory purposes. Ed would circulate
the word among the small boys of the neighborhood that
twenty-five cents apiece would be paid for cats. It saddened
Ed a little to see how venially warped the cat-loving small boys

of Monterey were. They sold their own cats, their aunts' cats, their neighbors' cats. For a few days there would be scurrying footsteps and soft thumps as cats in gunny sacks were secretly deposited in the basement. Then guileless and innocent-faced little catacides would collect their quarters and rush for Wing Chong's grocery for pop and cap pistols. No matter what happened, Wing Chong made some small profit.

Once a lady who liked cats very much, if they were the better sort of cats, remarked to Ed, "Of course I realize that these things are necessary. I am very broad-minded. But, thank heaven, you do not get pedigreed cats."

Ed reassured her by saying, "Madam, that's about the only kind I do get. Alley cats are too quick and intelligent. I get the sluggish stupid cats of the rich and indulgent. You can look through the basement and see whether I have yours— yet." That friendship based on broad-mindedness did not flourish.

If there were a complaint and a recognition Ed always gave the cat back. Once two small boys who had obviously read about the oldest cheat in the world worked it twice on Ed before he realized it. One of them sold the cat and collected, the other came in crying and got the cat back. They should have got another cat the third time. If they had been clever and patient they would have made a fortune, but even Ed recognized a bright yellow cat with a broken tail the third time he bought it.

Everyone, so Ed said, has at least one biologic theory, and some people develop many. Ed was very tolerant of these flights of theoretic fancy. A strange group flowed through the laboratory.

There were, for instance, the people who suddenly discovered parallels in nature, like the man who conceived the thought that tuna, which is called commercially "Chicken of the Sea," might be related to chickens, because, as he said, "Their eyes look alike." Ed's reply to this man was that he rarely liked to make a positive statement, but in this case he was willing to venture the conviction that there was no very close relation between chickens and tunas.

One day there came into the laboratory a young Chinese,

dressed in the double-breasted height of fashion, smelling of lily of the valley, and bringing a mysterious air with him. He was about twenty-three and his speech was that of an American high-school boy. He suggested darkly that he would like to see Ed alone. Ed happily joined the mystery and indicated that I was his associate and the sharer of his secrets. We found ourselves speaking in heavy, pregnant whispers.

Our visitor asked, "Have you got any cat blood?"

"No, not right now," Ed replied. "It is true I do draw off the blood when I inject cats. What do you want it for?"

Our visitor said tightly, "I'm making an experiment." Then, to prove that we could trust his judgment and experience, he flipped his lapel to show the badge of a detective correspondence school. And he drew out his diploma to back up the badge. We were delighted with him. But he would not explain what he needed the cat blood for. Ed promised that he would save some blood from the next series of cats. We all nodded mysteriously back and forth and our visitor left quietly, walking on his toes.

Mysteries were constant at the laboratory. A thing happened one night which I later used as a short story. I wrote it just as it happened. I don't know what it means and do not even answer the letters asking what its philosophic intent is. It just happened. Very briefly, this is the incident. A woman came in one night wanting to buy a male rattlesnake. It happened that we had one and knew it was a male because it had recently copulated with another snake in the cage. The woman paid for the snake and then insisted that it be fed. She paid for a white rat to be given it. Ed put the rat in the cage. The snake struck and killed it and then unhinged its jaws preparatory to swallowing it. The frightening thing was that the woman, who had watched the process closely, moved her jaws and stretched her mouth just as the snake was doing. After the rat was swallowed, she paid for a year's supply of rats and said she would come back. But she never did come back. What happened or why I have no idea. Whether the woman was driven by a sexual, a religious, a zoophilic, or a gustatory impulse we never could figure. When I wrote the story just as it happened there were curious reactions. One librarian wrote that it was not only a bad story but the worst story she had ever read. A number of orders came in for snakes. I was denounced by a religious group for having a perverted imagination, and one man found symbolism of Moses smiting the rock in the account.

I shall mention only a few other of the mysteries. There was the persecution with flowers, for example. Someone who must have been watching the laboratory waited until we were out on several occasions and then placed a line of white flowers across the doorstep. This happened a number of times and seems to have been meant as a hex. Such a curse is practiced by some northern Indians to bring death to anyone who steps over the flowers. But who put them there and whether that was the intention we never found out.

During the time when the Klan was spreading its sheets all over the nation the laboratory got its share of attention. Small red cards with the printed words, "We are watching *you*, K.K.K.," were slipped under the door on several occasions.

Mysteries had a bad effect on Ed Ricketts. He hated all thoughts and manifestations of mysticism with an intensity which argued a basic and undefeatable belief in them. He refused to have his fortune told or his palm read even in fun. The play with a Ouija board drove him into a nervous rage. Ghost stories made him so angry that he would leave a room where one was being told.

In the course of time Ed's father died. There was an intercom phone between the basement and the upstairs office. Once after his father's death Ed admitted to me that he had a waking nightmare that the intercom phone would ring, that he would lift the receiver and hear his father's voice on the other end. He had dreamed of this, and it was becoming an obsession with him. I suggested that someone might play a practical joke and that it might be a good idea to disconnect the phone. This he did instantly, but he went further and removed both phones. "It would be worse disconnected," he said. "I couldn't stand that."

I think that if anyone had played such a joke, Ed would have been very ill from shock. The white flowers bothered him a great deal.

I have said that his mind had no horizons, but that is untrue. He forbade his mind to think of metaphysical or extra-physical matters, and his mind refused to obey him.

Life on Cannery Row was curious and dear and outrageous. Across the street from Pacific Biological was Monterey's largest, most genteel and respected whorehouse. It was owned and operated by a very great woman who was beloved and trusted by all who came in contact with her except those few whose judgment was twisted by a limited virtue. She was a large-hearted woman and a law-abiding citizen in every way except one—she did violate the nebulous laws against prostitution. But since the police didn't seem to care, she felt all right about it and even made little presents in various directions.

During the depression Madam paid the grocery bills for most of the destitute families on Cannery Row. When the Chamber of Commerce collected money for any cause and businessmen were assessed at ten dollars, Madam was always nicked for a hundred. The same was true for any mendicant charity. She halfway paid for the widows and orphans of policemen and firemen. She was expected to and did contribute ten times the ordinary amount toward any civic brainstorm of citizens who pretended she did not exist. Also, she was a wise and tolerant pushover for any hard-luck story. Everyone put the bee on her. Even when she knew it was a fake she dug down.

Ed Ricketts maintained relations of respect and friendliness with Madam. He did not patronize the house. His sex life was far too complicated for that. But Madam brought many of her problems to him, and he gave her the best of his thinking and his knowledge, both scientific and profane.

There seems to be a tendency toward hysteria among girls in such a house. I do not know whether hysterically inclined types enter the business or whether the business produces hysteria. But often Madam would send a girl over to the laboratory to talk to Ed. He would listen with great care and concern to her troubles, which were rarely complicated, and then he would talk soothingly to her and play some of his favorite music to her on his phonograph. The girl usually went back reinforced with his strength. He never moralized in any way. He would be more likely to examine the problem carefully, with calm and clarity, and to lift the horrors out of it by easy examination. Suddenly the girl would discover that she was not alone, that many other people had the same problems—in a word that her misery was not unique. And then she usually felt better about it.

There was a tacit but strong affection between Ed and Madam. She did not have a license to sell liquor to be taken out. Quite often Ed would run out of beer so late at night that everything except Madam's house was closed. There followed a ritual which was thoroughly enjoyed by both parties. Ed would cross the street and ask Madam to sell him some beer. She invariably refused, explaining every time that she did not have a license. Ed would shrug his shoulders, apologize for asking, and go back to the lab. Ten minutes later there would be soft footsteps on the stairs and a little thump in front of the door and then running slippered steps down again. Ed would wait a decent interval and then go to the door. And on his doorstep, in a paper bag, would be six bottles of ice-cold beer. He would never mention it to Madam. That would have been breaking the rules of the game. But he repaid her with hours of his time when she needed his help. And his help was not inconsiderable.

Sometimes, as happens even in the soundest whorehouse, there would be a fight on a Saturday night—one of those things which are likely to occur when love and wine come together. It was only sensible that Madam would not want to bother the police or a doctor with her little problem. Then her good friend Ed would patch up cut faces and torn ears and split mouths. He was a good operator and there were never any complaints. And naturally no one ever mentioned the matter since he was not a doctor of medicine and had no license to practice anything except philanthropy. Madam and Ed had the greatest respect for each other. "She's one hell of a woman," he said. "I wish good people could be as good."

Just as Madam was the target for every tired heist, so Ed was the fall guy for any illicit scheme that could be concocted by the hustling instincts of some of the inhabitants of Cannery Row. The people of the Row really loved Ed, but this affection did not forbid them from subjecting him to any outrageous scheming that occurred to them. In nearly all cases he knew the game before the play had even started and his hand would be in his pocket before the intricate gambit had come to a request. But he would cautiously wait out the pitch before he brought out the money. "It gives them so much pleasure to earn it," he would say.

He never gave much. He never *had* much. But in spite of his wide experience in chicanery, now and then he would be startled into admiration by some particularly audacious or imaginative approach to the problem of a touch.

One evening while he was injecting small dogfish in the basement, one of his well-known clients came to him with a face of joy.

"I am a happy man," the hustler proclaimed, and went on to explain how he had arrived at the true philosophy of rest and pleasure.

"You think I've got nothing, Eddie," the man lectured him. "But you don't know from my simple outsides what I've got inside."

Ed moved restlessly, waiting for the trap.

"I've got peace of mind, Eddie. I've got a place to sleep, not a palace but comfortable. I'm not hungry very often. And best of all I've got friends. I guess I'm gladdest of all for my friends."

Ed braced himself. Here it comes, he thought.

"Why, Ed," the client continued, "some nights I just lay in my bed and thank God for my blessings. What does a man need, Eddie—a few things like food and shelter and a few little tiny vices, like liquor and women—and tobacco—"

Ed could feel it moving in on him. "No liquor," he said.

"I ain't drinking," the client said with dignity, "didn't you hear?"

"How much?" Ed asked.

"Only a dime, Eddie boy. I need a couple of sacks of tobacco. I don't mind using the brown papers on the sacks. I *like* the brown papers."

Ed gave him a quarter. He was delighted. "Where else in the world could you find a man who would lavish care and thought and art and emotion on a lousy dime?" he said. He felt that it had been worth more than a quarter, but he did not tell his client so.

On another occasion Ed was on his way across the street to Wing Chong's grocery for a couple of quarts of beer. Another of his clients was sitting comfortably in the gutter in front of the store. He glanced casually at the empty quart bottles Ed carried in his hand.

"Say Doc," he said, "I'm having a little trouble peeing. What's a good diuretic?"

Ed fell into that hole. "I never needed to think beyond beer," he said.

The man looked at the bottles in Ed's hand and raised his shoulders in a gesture of helplessness. And only then did Ed realize that he had been had. "Oh, come on in," he said, and he bought beer for both of them.

Afterward he said admiringly, "Can you imagine the trouble he went to for that beer? He had to look up the word diuretic, and then he had to plan to be there just when I went over for beer. And he had to read my mind quite a bit. If any part of his plan failed, it all failed. I think it is remarkable."

The only part of it that was not remarkable was planning to be there when Ed went for beer. He went for beer pretty often. Sometimes when he overbought and the beer got warm, he took it back and Wing Chong exchanged it for cold beer.

The various hustlers who lived by their wits and some work in the canneries when they had time were an amazing crew. Ed never got over his admiration for them.

"They have worked out my personality and my resistances to a fine mathematical point," he would say. "They know me better than I know myself, and I am not uncomplicated. Over and over, their analysis of my possible reaction is accurate."

He was usually delighted when one of these minor triumphs took place. It never cost him much. He always tried to figure out in advance what the attack on his pocket would be. At least he always knew the end. Every now and then the audacity and freedom of thought and invention of his loving enemy would leave him with a sense of wonder.

Now and then he hired some of the boys to collect animals

for him and paid them a fixed price, so much for frogs, so much for snakes or cats.

One of his collectors we will call Al. That was not his name. An early experience with Al gave Ed a liking for his inventiveness. Ed needed cats and needed them quickly. And Al got them and got them quickly—all fine mature cats and, only at the end of the operation did Ed discover, all tomcats. For a long time Al held out his method but finally he divulged it in secret. Since Al has long since gone to his maker and will need no more cats, his secret can be told.

"I made a double trap," he said, "a little cage inside a big cage. Then in the little cage I put a nice lady cat in a loving condition. And, Eddie, sometimes I'd catch as many as ten tomcats in one night. Why, hell, Ed, that exact same kind of trap catches me every Saturday night. That's where I got the idea."

Al was such a good collector that after a while he began to do odd jobs around the lab. Ed taught him to inject dogfish and to work the ball mill for mixing color mass and to preserve some of the less delicate animals. Al became inordinately proud of his work and began to use a mispronounced scientific vocabulary and put on a professorial air that delighted Ed. He got to trusting Al although he knew Al's persistent alcoholic history.

Once when a large number of dogfish came in Ed left them for Al to inject while he went to a party. It was a late party. Ed returned to find all the lights on in the basement. The place was a wreck. Broken glass littered the floor, a barrel of formaldehyde was tipped over and spilled, museum jars were stripped from the shelves and broken. A whirlwind had gone through. Al was not there but Al's pants were, and also an automobile seat which was never explained.

In a white fury Ed began to sweep up the broken glass. He was well along when Al entered, wearing a long overcoat and a pair of high rubber boots. Ed's rage was terrible. He advanced on Al.

"You son-of-a-bitch!" he cried. "I should think you could stay sober until you finished work!"

Al held up his hand with senatorial dignity. "You go right

ahead, Eddie," he said. "You call me anything you want, and I forgive you."

"Forgive me?" Ed screamed. He was near to murder.

Al silenced him with a sad and superior gesture. "I deserve it, Eddie," he said. "Go ahead—call me lots of names. I only regret that they will not hurt my feelings."

"What in hell are you talking about?" Ed demanded uneasily.

Al turned and parted the tails of his overcoat. He was completely naked except for the rubber boots.

"Eddie boy," he said, "I have been out calling socially in this condition. Now, Eddie, if I could do that, I must be pretty insensitive. Nothing you can call me is likely to get under my thick skin. And I forgive you."

Ed's anger disappeared in pure wonder. And afterward he said, "If that Al had turned the pure genius of his unique mind to fields other than cadging drinks, there is no limit to what he might have done." And then he continued, "But no. He has chosen a difficult and crowded field and he is a success in it. Any other career, international banking for instance, might have been too easy for Al."

Al was married, but his wife and family did not exercise a restraining influence on him. His wife finally used the expedient of putting Al in jail when he was on one of his beauties.

Al said one time, "When they hire a new cop in Monterey they give him a test. They send him down Cannery Row, and if he can't pick me up he don't get the job."

Al detested the old red stone Salinas jail. It was gloomy and unsanitary, he said. But then the county built a beautiful new jail, and the first time Al made sixty days he was gone seventy-five. He came back to Monterey enthusiastic.

"Eddie," he said, "they got radios in the cells. And that new sheriff's a pushover at euchre. When my time was up the sheriff owed me eighty-six bucks. I couldn't run out on the game. A sheriff can make it tough on a man. It took me fifteen days to lose it back so it wouldn't look too obvious. But you can't win from a sheriff, Eddie—not if you expect to go back."

Al went back often until his wife finally tumbled to the fact that Al preferred jail to home life. She visited Ed for advice. She was a red-eyed, unkempt little woman with a runny nose.

"I work hard and try to make ends meet," she said bitterly. "And all the time Al's over in Salinas taking his ease in the new jail. I can't let him go to jail any more. He likes it." She was all frayed from having Al's children and supporting them.

For once Ed had no answer. "I don't know what you can do," he said. "I'm stumped. You could kill him—but then you wouldn't have any fun any more."

A complicated social structure existed on Cannery Row. One had to know or there were likely to be errors in procedure and protocol. You could not speak to one of the girls from Madam's if you met her on the street. You might have talked to her all night, but it was bad manners to greet her outside.

From the windows of the laboratory Ed and I watched a piece of social cruelty which has never been bettered in Scarsdale. Across the street in the lot between the whorehouse and Wing Chong's grocery, there were a number of rusty pipes, a boiler or two, and some great timbers, all thrown there by the canneries. A number of the free company of Cannery Row slept in the big pipes, and when the sun was warm they would come out to sit like lizards on the timbers. There they held social commerce. They borrowed dimes back and forth, shared tobacco, and if anyone brought a pint of liquor into sight, it meant that he not only wanted to share it but intended to. They were a fairly ragged set of men, their clothing of blue denim almost white at knees and buttocks from pure erosion. They were, as Ed said, the Lotus Eaters of our era, successful in their resistance against the nervousness and angers and frustrations of our time.

Ed regarded these men with the admiration he had for any animal, family, or species that was successful in survival and happiness factors.

We had many discussions about these men. Ed held that one couldn't tell from a quick look how successful a species is.

"Consider now," he would say, "if you look superficially, you would say that the local banker or the owner of a cannery or even the mayor of Monterey is the successful and surviving individual. But consider their ulcers, consider the heart trouble, the blood pressure in that group. And then consider the bums over there—cirrhosis of the liver I will grant will have its toll, but not the other things." He would cluck his tongue in admiration. "It is a rule in paleontology," he would say, "that over-armor, and/or over-ornamentation are symptoms of extinction in a species. You have only to consider the great reptiles, the mammoth, etc. Now those bums have no armor and practically no ornament, except here and there a pair of red and yellow sleeve garters. In our whole time pattern those men may be the ones who will deliver our species from the enemies within and without which attack it."

But much as he liked the bums, he was grieved at their social cruelty toward George, the pimp of the whorehouse.

George was well built, a snappy dresser, and very polite. He had complete extra-legal police powers over the girls in the house and an arguable access to any or all of them. He might even treat a friend. He had dark wavy hair, a good salary, he ate in the house, and he clipped several of the girls for their money. In other words, he was rich. He was a good bouncer with an enviable reputation for in-fighting, and—when the problem grew more confused—a triumphant record of eye-gouging, booting, and kneeing. In a word, one would have thought him a happy man—one would, unless one knew the true soul of George, as we came to.

George was lonely. He wanted the company of men, the camaraderie and warmth and roughness and good feeling and arguments of men. He got very tired of a woman's world of perfumes and periods, of hysterics and noisy mysteries and permanents. Perhaps he had no one to boast to of his superiority over women, and it bothered him.

We watched him try to associate with the bums sitting on the timber in the sun, and they would have none of him. They considered a pimp as abysmally beneath them socially. When George wandered up through the weeds and sat with the boys they would turn away from him. They did not insult him or tell him to go away, but they would not associate with him. If an argument was going on when he arrived, it would stop and a painful silence would take its place.

George recognized his ostracism and he was sad and hang-dog about it. We, watching from the window, could see it in his wilting posture and his fawning gestures. We could hear it in his too loud laughter at a mildly amusing joke. Ed shook his head over this injustice. He had hoped for better from the boys.

"I don't know why I thought they would be better," he said. "Of course, being bums does give them advantages, but why should I expect them to be above all smallness just because they are bums? I guess it was just a romantic hopefulness." And he said, "I knew a man who believed all whores were honest just because they were whores. Time and again he got rolled—once a girl even stole his clothes, but he would not give up his conviction. It had become an article of faith, and you can't give such a thing up because it is yourself. I must re-examine my feeling about the boys," he said.

We watched George fall back, in his craven loneliness, on bribery. He bought whisky and passed it around. He loaned money like a crazy man. The bums accepted George's bribes but they would not accept George.

Ed Ricketts did not ordinarily meddle in the affairs of his neighbors but he brooded about George.

One afternoon he confronted the boys on the timber. "Why don't you be nice to him?" he said. "He's a lonely man. He wants to be friends with you. You are putting a mark on him that may warp and sour his whole life. He won't be any good to anyone. I wouldn't be surprised if you were responsible for his death."

To which Whitey No. 2 (there were two Whiteys, known as Whitey No. 1 and Whitey No. 2) replied, "Now, Doc, you're not asking us to associate with a pimp, are you? Nobody likes a pimp."

It must be noted that when the hustlers spoke to Ed formally he was Doc. When they hustled him, he was Ed, Eddie, or Eddie boy.

I don't think that Ed had any idea how accurate his prediction was. But not very long after this George killed himself with an ice pick in the kitchen of the whorehouse. And when Ed berated the boys for having been one of the causes of his death, Whitey No. 1 echoed Whitey No. 2's words.

"Hell, we can't help it, Doc. You just can't be friendly with a pimp."

Ed mused sadly, "I find it rather hard to believe that the boys were moved by any moral consideration. It must have been an unscalable social barrier that no argument could overleap." And he said, "White chicks will kill a black chick every time. But I do hope it isn't as simple as that."

Ed's association with Wing Chong, the Chinese grocer, and later, after Wing Chong's death, with his son, was one of mutual respect. Ed could always get credit and for long periods of time. And sometimes he needed it. Once we tried to compute how many gallons of beer had crossed the street in the years of our association, but we soon gave up as the figures mounted. We didn't even want to know.

Ed had many friends, and in addition he attracted some people from the lunatic fringe, like the Chinese detective and the snake woman. There were others who used him as a source of information.

One afternoon the phone rang and a woman's voice asked, "Dr. Ricketts, can you tell me the name of a tropical fish with so many spines on the dorsal fin and so many on the ventral? The name begins with an L."

"Not offhand," said Ed, "but I'll be glad to look it up for you if you want to call back in half an hour." He went to work, saying, "Lovely voice—fine throaty voice."

Twenty minutes later the phone rang again and the fine throaty voice said, "Dr. Ricketts, never mind. I worked it out from the horizontals."

He never did meet the puzzle-worker with the throaty voice.

In appearance and temperament Ed was a remarkably unmilitary man, but in spite of this he was drafted for service in both World Wars. One would have thought that his complete individuality and his uniqueness of approach to all problems would have caused him to go crazy in the organized mediocrity of the Army. Actually the exact opposite was true. He was a successful soldier. In spite of itself, the Army—at least that part of it which sheltered him—was gradually warped in his favor and for his comfort. He was quite happy in the Army in both wars.

He described his military experience in the first World War

to me with satisfaction. "I was young then," he said, "and I am amazed that I showed such good sense. I have often thought," he went on, "that if any big company like General Motors or Standard Oil should start a private army, no public army would stand a chance against it. A private company is organized to do something or to produce something, profit or gold or steel. It has a direction. But a public army is made up of millions of individuals all working for themselves. Some want promotions, some want to steal, some want personal power or glory, and some want simply to get out. Very few have any interest in winning a war."

He told me about his first war experience. "I gave it a good deal of thought before I decided what to be," he said. "As I said, I was young then, but I have always admired my choice. Literacy was not terribly high in 1917, and it was comparatively easy for me to become company clerk without any danger of being driven into officer's training school. I definitely did not want to be an officer. No one wanted the job of company clerk.

"People are singularly blind," he continued. "It escaped the greed and self-interest of the other men that the company clerk makes out the passes and that if the captain and lieutenants happen to have hobbies like golf or women, this duty and even the selections are left in the hands of an efficient company clerk." He sighed with pleasure. He had enjoyed the Army. "In almost no time," he said, "the rumor got about that I liked whisky. It became quite common knowledge. And do you know, when I was demobilized I had over three hundred pints left, and that in a time of prohibition, if you will remember."

A little venom crept into his voice. "You know," he said in an outraged tone, "there was one christing son-of-a-bitch who complained to the captain about me. Can you imagine that? He put it on a moral basis. He didn't drink. I wonder why non-drinkers are so often vicious."

"What happened?" I asked.

"He was a silly man," Ed said. "He didn't get a single pass for eighteen months. He wrote complaint after complaint. He was a very silly man."

"But how about the complaints?"

"If he had given it any thought he would have realized that complaints go through the hands of the company clerk." He chuckled. "I guess I should not bear a grudge," he said, "but I still don't like that man. Word got about—you know how rumors move in the Army. Anyway, the word got out that the good, kind company clerk was being persecuted. I guess the poor fellow had a rough time of it—from latrines to kitchen police to the brig. I think it ruined his whole military career. I'm pretty sure it ruined his stomach. A very silly man."

I have always felt that drafting Ed in the Second World War was spiteful on the part of the draft board. He was one week under forty-six when his call came, and his birthday had passed when he was examined. I think there were people in Monterey who were jealous of him. He was really not good soldier material from any point of view. He wore a beard, which is frowned on by Army psychiatrists. The doctor who examined him came from the interview puzzled and worried, but he passed Ed, and the Army made him shave off his beard.

He did not resent being drafted because he remembered the first war with such pleasure.

"I thought that with my subsequent experience and maturity I might be all right," he said.

Because of his long laboratory experience they put him in charge of the venereal disease section of the induction center at Monterey. This job had its compensations. He could go home every night and he had complete charge of an inexhaustible medicine chest. He was still in no danger of being hustled off to officer's training school. Ed didn't want to command men. He wanted to associate with them. His commanding officer had a hobby—whether golf or women I do not know, but it was strong enough so that he let Ed do all the work.

Ed liked that and did a very good job with his section. Possibly because of the medicine chest a little group of passionate admirers clung to him and protected him and defended him against any possible charge that Ed didn't get to work before ten in the morning and sometimes went away for long weekends.

Quite early in his second hitch in the Army Ed got tired of the sameness of laboratory alcohol and grapefruit juice. With his unlimited medicine chest, he began to experiment. Now another rumor crept about the Presidio of Monterey that a fabulous drink had been invented. It had a strange effect. No one had tasted or felt anything quite like it. It was called "Ricketts' Folly." It was said that the commanding officer of the unit, and he a major at that, after two drinks of it had marched smartly and with no hint of stagger right into a wall, and that he had made a short heroic speech as he slid to the ground.

After Ed was safely and honorably discharged I asked him about the drink that had achieved a notoriety as far east as Chicago and that was discussed with hushed respect on the beachheads of the Pacific.

"Well, actually it was very simple," he said. "Its components were not complicated and it *was* delicious. I never could figure why it had such a curious and sometimes humorous effect. It was nothing but alcohol, codeine, and grenadine. It was a pretty drink too. You know," he said, "it made every other kind of liquor seem kind of weak and flabby."

This account of Ed Ricketts goes seesawing back and forth chronologically and in every other way. I did not intend when I started to departmentalize him, but now that seems to be a good method. He was so complex and many-faceted that perhaps the best method will be to go from one facet of him to another so that from all the bits a whole picture may build itself for me as well as for others.

Ed had more fun than nearly anyone I have ever known, and he had deep sorrows also, which will be treated later. As long as we are on the subject of drinking I will complete that department.

Ed loved to drink, and he loved to drink just about anything. I don't think I ever saw him in the state called drunkenness, but twice he told me he had no memory of getting home to the laboratory at all. And even on those nights one would have had to know him well to be aware that he was affected at all. Evidences of drinking were subtle. He smiled a little more broadly. His voice became a little higher in pitch, and he would dance a few steps on tiptoe, a curious pigeon-footed mouse step. He liked every drink that contained alcohol and, except for coffee which he often laced with whisky, he disliked every drink that did not contain alcohol. He once estimated that it had been twelve years since he had tasted water without some benign addition.

At one time when bad teeth and a troublesome love affair were running concurrently, he got a series of stomach-aches which were diagnosed as a developing ulcer. The doctor put him on a milk diet and ordered him off all alcohol. A sullen sadness fell on the laboratory. It was a horrid time. For a few days Ed was in a state of dismayed shock. Then his anger rose at the cruelty of a fate that could do this to him. He merely disliked and distrusted water, but he had an active and fierce hatred for milk. He found the color unpleasant and the taste ugly. He detested its connotations.

For a few days he forced a little milk into his stomach, complaining bitterly the while, and then he went back to see the doctor. He explained his dislike for the taste of milk, giving as its basis some pre-memory shock amounting to a trauma. He thought this dislike for milk might have driven him into the field of marine biology since no marine animals but whales and their family of sea cows give milk and he had never had the least interest in any of the Cetaceans. He said that he was afraid the cure for his stomach-aches was worse than the disease and finally he asked if it would be all right to add a few drops of aged rum to the milk just to kill its ugly taste. The doctor perhaps knew he was fighting a losing battle. He gave in on the few drops of rum.

We watched the cure with fascination as day by day the ratio changed until at the end of a month Ed was adding a few drops of milk to the rum. But his stomach-aches had disappeared. He never liked milk, but after this he always spoke of it with admiration as a specific for ulcers.

There were great parties at the laboratory, some of which went on for days. There would come a time in our poverty when we needed a party. Then we would gather together the spare pennies. It didn't take very many of them. There was a wine sold in Monterey for thirty-nine cents a gallon. It was not a delicate-tasting wine and sometimes curious things were found in the sludge on the bottom of the jug, but it was adequate. It added a gaiety to a party and it never killed anyone. If four couples got together and each brought a gallon, the party could go on for some time and toward the end of it Ed would be smiling and doing his tippy-toe mouse dance.

Later, when we were not so poor, we drank beer or, as Ed preferred it, a sip of whisky and a gulp of beer. The flavors, he said, complemented each other.

Once on my birthday there was a party at the laboratory that lasted four days. We really needed a party. It was fairly large, and no one went to bed except for romantic purposes. Early in the morning at the end of the fourth day a benign exhaustion had settled on the happy group. We spoke in whispers because our vocal chords had long since been burned out in song.

Ed carefully placed half a quart of beer on the floor beside his bed and sank back for a nap. In a moment he was asleep. He had consumed perhaps five gallons since the beginning of the party. He slept for about twenty minutes, then stirred, and without opening his eyes groped with his hand for the beer bottle. He found it, sat up, and took a deep drink of it. He smiled sweetly and waved two fingers in the air in a kind of benediction.

"There's nothing like that first taste of beer," he said.

Not only did Ed love liquor. He went further. He had a deep suspicion of anyone who did not. If a non-drinker shut up and minded his own business and did not make an issue of his failing, Ed could be kind to him. But alas, a laissez-faire attitude is very uncommon in teetotalers. The moment one began to spread his poison Ed experienced a searing flame of scorn and rage. He believed that anyone who did not like to drink was either sick and/or crazy or had in him some obscure viciousness. He believed that the soul of a non-drinker was dried up and shrunken, that the virtuous pose of the non-drinker was a cover for some nameless and disgusting practice.

He had somewhat the same feeling for those who did not or pretended they did not love sex, but this field will be explored later.

If pressed, Ed would name you the great men, great minds, great hearts and imaginations in the history of the world, and he could not discover one of them who was a teetotaler. He would even try to recall one single man or woman of much ability who did not drink and like liquor, and he could never light on a single name. In all such discussions the name of Shaw was offered, and in answer Ed would simply laugh, but in his laughter there would be no admiration for that abstemious old gentleman.

Ed's interest in music was passionate and profound. He thought of it as deeply akin to creative mathematics. His taste in music was not strange but very logical. He loved the chants of the Gregorian mode and the whole library of the plain song with their angelic intricacies. He loved the masses of William Byrd and Palestrina. He listened raptly to Buxtehude, and he once told me that he thought the *Art of the Fugue* of Bach might be the greatest of all music up to our time. Always "up to our time." He never considered anything finished or completed but always continuing, one thing growing on and out of another. It is probable that his critical method was the outgrowth of his biologic training and observation.

He loved the secular passion of Monteverde, and the sharpness of Scarlatti. His was a very broad appreciation and a curiosity that dug for music as he dug for his delicious worms in a mud flat. He listened to music with his mouth open as though he wanted to receive the tones even in his throat. His forefinger moved secretly at his side in rhythm.

He could not sing, could not carry a tune or reproduce a true note with his voice, but he could hear true notes. It was a matter of sorrow to him that he could not sing.

Once we bought sets of tuning forks and set them in rubber to try to reteach ourselves the forgotten mathematical scale. And Ed's ear was very aware in recognition although he could not make his voice come even near to imitating the pitch. I never heard him whistle. I wonder whether he could. He would try to hum melodies, stumbling over the notes, and then he would smile helplessly when his ear told him how badly he was doing it.

He thought of music as something incomparably concrete and dear. Once, when I had suffered an overwhelming emotional upset, I went to the laboratory to stay with him. I was dull and speechless with shock and pain. He used music on me like medicine. Late in the night when he should have been

asleep, he played music for me on his great phonograph—
even when I was asleep he played it, knowing that its soothing
would get into my dark confusion. He played the curing and
reassuring plain songs, remote and cool and separate, and then
gradually he played the sure patterns of Bach, until I was ready
for more personal thought and feeling again, until I could
bear to come back to myself. And when that time came, he
gave me Mozart. I think it was as careful and loving medi-
cation as has ever been administered.

Ed's reading was very broad. Of course he read greatly in
his own field of marine invertebratology. But he read hugely
otherwise. I do not know where he found the time. I can
judge his liking only by the things he went back to—translations of Li Po and Tu Fu, that greatest of all love poetry, the
Black Marigolds—and *Faust*, most of all *Faust*. Just as he
thought the *Art of the Fugue* might be the greatest music up
to our time, he considered *Faust* the greatest writing that had
been done. He enlarged his scientific German so that he could
read Faust and hear the sounds of the words as they were
written and taste their meanings. Ed's mind seems to me to
have been a timeless mind, not modern and not ancient. He
loved to read Layamon aloud and Beowulf, making the words
sound as fresh as though they had been written yesterday.

He had no religion in the sense of creed or dogma. In fact
he distrusted all formal religions, suspecting them of having
been fouled with economics and power and politics. He did
not believe in any God as recognized by any group or cult.
Probably his God could have been expressed by the mathematical symbol for an expanding universe. Surely he did not
believe in an after life in any sense other than chemical. He
was suspicious of promises of an after life, believing them to
be sops to our fear or hope artificially supplied.

Economics and politics he observed with the same interested detachment he applied to the ecological relationships
and balances in a tide pool.

For a time after the Russian Revolution he watched the
Soviet with the pleased interest of a terrier seeing its first frog.
He thought there might be some new thing in Russia, some
human progression that might be like a mutation in the nature
of the species. But when the Revolution was accomplished and

the experiments ceased and the Soviets steadied and moved inexorably toward power and the perpetuation of power through applied ignorance and dogmatic control of the creative human spirit, he lost interest in the whole thing. Now and then he would take a sampling to verify his conclusions as to the direction. His last hope for that system vanished when he wrote to various Russian biologists, asking for information from their exploration of the faunal distribution on the Arctic Sea. He then discovered that they not only did not answer, they did not even get his letters. He felt that any restriction or control of knowledge or conclusion was a dreadful sin, a violation of first principles. He lost his interest in Marxian dialectics when he could not verify in observable nature. He watched with a kind of amused contempt while the adepts warped the world to fit their pattern. And when he read the conclusions of Lysenko, he simply laughed without comment.

Very many conclusions Ed and I worked out together through endless discussion and reading and observation and experiment. We worked together, and so closely that I do not now know in some cases who started which line of speculation since the end thought was the product of both minds. I do not know whose thought it was.

We had a game which we playfully called speculative metaphysics. It was a sport consisting of lopping off a piece of observed reality and letting it move up through the speculative process like a tree growing tall and bushy. We observed with pleasure how the branches of thought grew away from the trunk of external reality. We believed, as we must, that the laws of thought parallel the laws of things. In our game there was no stricture of rightness. It was an enjoyable exercise on the instruments of our minds, improvisations and variations on a theme, and it gave the same delight and interest that discovered music does. No one can say, "This music is the only music," nor would we say, "This thought is the only thought," but rather, "This is *a* thought, perhaps well or ill formed, but *a* thought which is a real thing in nature."

Once a theme was established we subjected observable nature to it. The following is an example of our game—one developed quite a long time ago.

We thought that perhaps our species thrives best and most creatively in a state of semi-anarchy, governed by loose rules and half-practiced mores. To this we added the premise that over-integration in human groups might parallel the law in paleontology that over-armor or over-ornamentation are symptoms of decay and disappearance. Indeed, we thought, over-integration *might be* the symptom of human decay. We thought: there is no creative unit in the human save the individual working alone. In pure creativeness, in art, in music, in mathematics, there are no true collaborations. The creative principle is a lonely and an individual matter. Groups can correlate, investigate, and build, but we could not think of any group that has ever created or invented anything. Indeed, the first impulse of the group seems to be to destroy the creation and the creator. But integration, or the designed group, seems to be highly vulnerable.

Now with this structure of speculation we would slip examples on the squares of the speculative graphing paper.

Consider, we would say, the Third Reich or the Politburo-controlled Soviet. The sudden removal of twenty-five key men from either system could cripple it so thoroughly that it would take a long time to recover, if it ever could. To preserve itself in safety such a system must destroy or remove all opposition as a danger to itself. But opposition is creative and restriction is non-creative. The force that feeds growth is therefore cut off. Now, the tendency to integration must constantly increase. And this process of integration must destroy all tendencies toward improvisation, must destroy the habit of creation, since this is sand in the bearings of the system. The system then must, if our speculation is accurate, grind to a slow and heavy stop. Thought and art must be forced to disappear and a weighty traditionalism take its place. Thus we would play with thinking. A too greatly integrated system or society is in danger of destruction since the removal of one unit may cripple the whole.

Consider the blundering anarchic system of the United States, the stupidity of some of its lawmakers, the violent reaction, the slowness of its ability to change. Twenty-five key men destroyed could make the Soviet Union stagger, but we could lose our congress, our president, and our general staff and nothing much would have happened. We would go right on. In fact we might be better for it.

That is an example of the game we played. Always our thinking was prefaced with, "It might be so!" Often a whole night would draw down to a moment while we pursued the fireflies of our thinking.

Ed spoke sometimes of a period he valued in his life. It was after he had left home and entered the University of Chicago. He had not liked his home life very well. The rules that he had known were silly from his early childhood were finally removed.

"Adults, in their dealing with children, are insane," he said. "And children know it too. Adults lay down rules they would not think of following, speak truths they do not believe. And yet they expect children to obey the rules, believe the truths, and admire and respect their parents for this nonsense. Children must be very wise and secret to tolerate adults at all. And the greatest nonsense of all that adults expect children to believe is that people learn by experience. No greater lie was ever revered. And its falseness is immediately discerned by children since their parents obviously have not learned anything by experience. Far from learning, adults simply become set in a maze of prejudices and dreams and sets of rules whose origins they do not know and would not dare inspect for fear the whole structure might topple over on them. I think children instinctively know this," Ed said. "Intelligent children learn to conceal their knowledge and keep free of this howling mania."

When he left home, he was free at last, and he remembered his first freedom with a kind of glory. His freedom was not one of idleness.

"I don't know when I slept," he said. "I don't think there was time to sleep. I tended furnaces in the early morning. Then I went to class. I had lab all afternoon, then tended furnaces in the early evening. I had a job in a little store in the evening and got some studying done then, until midnight. Well, then I was in love with a girl whose husband worked nights, and naturally I didn't sleep much from midnight until morning. Then I got up and tended furnaces and went to class. What a time," he said, "what a fine time that was."

It is necessary in any kind of picture of Ed Ricketts to give some account of his sex life since that was by far his greatest drive. His life was saturated with sex and he was to a very great extent preoccupied with it. He gave it a monumental amount of thought and time and analysis. It will be no violation to discuss this part of his life since he had absolutely no shyness about discussing it himself.

To begin with, he was a hyper-thyroid. His metabolic rate was abnormally high. He had to eat at very frequent intervals or his body revolted with pain and anger. He was, during the time I knew him, and, I gather, from the very beginning, as concupiscent as a bull terrier. His sexual output and preoccupation was or purported to be prodigious. I do not know beyond doubt about the actual output. That is hearsay but well authenticated; but certainly his preoccupation with sexual matters was very great.

As far as women were concerned, he was completely without what is generally called "honor." It was not that he was dishonorable. The word simply had no meaning for him if it implied abstemiousness. Any man who left a wife in his care and expected him not to try for her was just a fool. He was compelled to try. The woman might reject him, and he would not be unreasonably importunate, but certainly he would not fail for lack of trying.

When I first met him he was engaged in a scholarly and persistent way in the process of deflowering a young girl. This was a long and careful affair. He not only was interested in a sexual sense, but he had also an active interest in the psychic and physical structure of virginity. There was, I believe, none of the usual sense of triumph at overcoming or being first. Ed's physical basis was a pair of very hot pants, but his secondary motive was an active and highly intellectual interest in the state of virginity and the change involved in abandoning that state. His knowledge of anatomy was large, but, as he was wont to say, the variation in structure is delightfully large, even leaving out abnormalities, and this variation gives a constant interest and surprise to a function which is basically pleasant anyway.

The resistance of this particular virgin was surprising. He did not know whether it was based on some block, or on the old-fashioned reluctance of a normal girl toward defloration, or, as he thought possible, on a distaste for himself personally. He inspected each of these possibilities with patient care. And since he had no shyness about himself, it did not occur to him to have any reluctance about discussing his project with his friends and acquaintances. It is perhaps a fortunate thing that this particular virgin did not hear the discussions. They might have embarrassed her, a matter that did not occur to Ed. Many years later, when she heard about the whole thing, she was of the opinion that she might still be a virgin if she had heard herself so intimately discussed. But by then, it was fortunately, she agreed, far too late.

One thing is certain. Ed did not like his sex uncomplicated. If a girl were unattached and without problems as well as willing, his interest was not large. But if she had a husband or seven children or a difficulty with the law or some whimsical neuroticism in the field of love, Ed was charmed and instantly active. If he could have found a woman who was not only married, but a mother, in prison, and one of Siamese twins, he would have been delighted.

It will be impossible to put down much anecdote concerning his activities. The more interesting affairs were discussed with such freedom, not only by Ed but by any number of amateur referees, that they acquired a certain local fame. This may be perfectly acceptable as confirmed gossip, but in print the protagonists might be inclined to consider the histories libelous, and they surely are.

His taste in women was catholic as long as there were complications and no thin lips. Complexion, color of hair and eyes, shape or size, seemed to make no difference to him. He was singularly open to suggestion.

Ordinarily Ed was able to view his fellow humans with the clear sight of objectivity only slightly warped by like or dislike. He could give the best and most valuable advice based on great knowledge and understanding. However, when the strong winds of love shook him, all this was changed. Then his objectivity was likely to blow sky-high.

The object of his affection herself contributed very little to his picture of her. She was only the physical frame on which he draped a woman. She was like those large faceless dolls on which clothes are made. He built his own woman on this form, created her from the ground up, invented her appearance and built her mind, furnished her with talents and sensitivenesses which were not only astonishing but downright untrue. Then the woman in process was likely to come with surprise to the conclusion that she loved poetry she had never heard of, and could not understand if she had, that she breathed shallowly over music the existence of which was equally unknown to her. She became beautiful but not necessarily in any way that was familiar to her. And her thoughts—these would be likely to surprise her most of all, since she might not have been aware that she had any thoughts at all.

I cannot think of this tendency of Ed's as self-delusion. He simply manufactured the woman he wanted, rather like that enlightened knight in the Welsh tale who made a wife entirely out of flowers. Sometimes the building process went on for quite a long time, and when it was completed everyone—even Ed—was quite confused. But at other times the force of his structure changed the raw material until the girl actually became what he thought her to be. I remember one very sharp example of this.

One of our friends was a sardine fisherman who had an interesting and profitable avocation. The sardine season continues only part of the year, leaving some months of idleness, which is the financial downfall of most fisherman. Our friend, however, was never idle and never broke. He managed, booked, protected, disciplined, and robbed a string of women—never many, rarely over five. He was successful and happy in his hobby. He was our friend and we saw a good deal of him.

This story is to illustrate the force and reasonableness of Ed's woman-building. I don't know how he got confused in this matter but he did, and the subsequent history bears out my belief in his success.

Our friend, in a moment of playfulness, brought one of his clients to a party, a small but unfragile blonde of endurance and experience. Ed met her and in a lapse of reason made an error about her. He went to considerable effort to get her away from her protector. He had an idea that she was not only inexperienced but quite shy—this last probably because she barely had acquired the power of speech and did not trust it as a means of communication. Ed thought her beautiful and young and virginal. He took her away on a vacation. He rebuilt her in his mind. And he tried to seduce her, he tried manfully, persuasively, philosophically, to seduce her. But he had built too well. In some way he had convinced her that she was what he had mistaken her for and she resisted his advances with maidenly fiber and consistency. At the end of a month he had to give up. He never did get to bed with her. But he took up so much of her time that she had to work very hard to make a stake for our friend when the sardine season was over.

In Ed's ecstasy he was able to make true things which lacked a certain scientific verification. One of his loves, one of his greatest, lasted a number of years. Every night he wrote a letter to his love, sometimes three lines, sometimes ten pages of his small, careful typing. He told me that she did the same, that she wrote to him every day, and he believed it. And I know beyond any doubt that in five years he received from her not more than eight childish scribbled notes. And he truly believed that she wrote to him every day.

Ed's scientific notebooks were very interesting. Among his collecting notes and zoological observations there would be the most outspoken and indelicate observation from another kind of collecting. After his death I had to go through these notebooks before turning them over to Hopkins Marine Station, a branch of Stanford University, as Ed's will directed. I was sorry I had to remove a number, a great number, of the entries from the notebooks. I did not do this because they lacked interest, but it occurred to me that a student delving into Ed's notes for information on invertebratology could emerge with blackmail material on half the female population of Monterey. Ed simply had no reticence about such things. I removed the notes but did not destroy them. They have an interest, I think, above the personalities mentioned. In some future time the women involved may lovingly remember the incidents.

In the back of his car Ed carried an ancient blanket that once had been red but that had faded to a salmon pink from use and exposure. It was a battle-scarred old blanket, veteran of many spreadings on hill and beach. Grass seeds and bits of seaweed were pounded and absorbed into the wool itself. I do not think Ed would have started his car in the evening without his blanket in the back seat.

Before love struck and roiled his vision like a stirred pool, Ed had a fine and appraising eye for a woman. He would note with enthusiasm a well-lipped mouth, a swelling breast, a firm yet cushioned bottom, but he also inquired into other subtleties—the padded thumb, shape of foot, length and structure of finger and toe, plump-lobed ear and angle of teeth, thigh and set of hip and movement in walking too. He regarded these things with joy and thanksgiving. He always was pleased that love and women were what they were or what he imagined them.

But for all of Ed's pleasures and honesties there was a transcendent sadness in his love—something he missed or wanted, a searching that sometimes approached panic. I don't know what it was he wanted that was never there, but I know he always looked for it and never found it. He sought for it and listened for it and looked for it and smelled for it in love. I think he found some of it in music. It was like a deep and endless nostalgia—a thirst and passion for "going home."

He was walled off a little, so that he worked at his philosophy of "breaking through," of coming out through the back of the mirror into some kind of reality which would make the day world dreamlike. This thought obsessed him. He found the symbols of "breaking through" in *Faust*, in Gregorian music, and in the sad, drunken poetry of Li Po. Of the *Art of the Fugue* he would say, "Bach nearly made it. Hear now how close he comes, and hear his anger when he cannot. Every time I hear it I believe that this time he will come crashing through into the light. And he never does—not quite."

And of course it was he himself who wanted so desperately to break through into the light.

We worked and thought together very closely for a number of years so that I grew to depend on his knowledge and on his patience in research. And then I went away to another part of the country but it didn't make any difference. Once a week or once a month would come a fine long letter so much in the style of his speech that I could hear his voice over the neat page full of small elite type. It was as though I hadn't been away at all. And sometimes now when the postman comes I look before I think for that small type on an envelope.

Ed was deeply pleased with the little voyage which is described in the latter part of this book, and he was pleased with the manner of setting it down. Often he would read it to remember a mood or a joke.

His scientific interest was essentially ecological and holistic. His mind always tried to enlarge the smallest picture. I remember his saying, "You know, at first view you would think the rattlesnake and the kangaroo rat were the greatest of enemies since the snake hunts and feeds on the rat. But in a larger sense they must be the best of friends. The rat feeds the snake and the snake selects out the slow and weak and generally thins the rat people so that both species can survive. It is quite possible that neither species could exist without the other." He was pleased with commensal animals, particularly with groups of several species contributing to the survival of all. He seemed as pleased with such things as though they had been created for him.

With any new food or animal he looked, felt, smelled, and tasted. Once in a tide pool we were discussing the interesting fact that nudibranchs, although beautiful and brightly colored and tasty-looking and soft and unweaponed, are never eaten by other animals which should have found them irresistible. He reached under water and picked up a lovely orange-colored nudibranch and put it in his mouth. And instantly he made a horrible face and spat and retched, but he had found out why fishes let these living tidbits completely alone.

On another occasion he tasted a species of free-swimming anemone and got his tongue so badly stung by its nettle cells that he could hardly close his mouth for twenty-four hours. But he would have done the same thing the next day if he had wanted to know.

Although small and rather slight, Ed was capable of prodigies of strength and endurance. He could drive for many hours to arrive at a good collecting ground for a favorable low tide, then work like a fury turning over rocks while the tide was out, then drive back to preserve his catch. He could carry heavy burdens over soft and unstable sand with no show of weariness. He had enormous resistance. It took a train to kill him. I think nothing less could have done it.

His sense of smell was very highly developed. He smelled all food before he ate it, not only the whole dish but each forkful. He invariably smelled each animal as he took it from the tide pool. He spoke of the smells of different animals, and some moods and even thoughts had characteristic odors to him—undoubtedly conditioned by some experience good or bad. He referred often to the smells of people, how individual each one was, and how it was subject to change. He delighted in his sense of smell in love.

With his delicate olfactory equipment, one would have thought that he would be disgusted by so-called ugly odors, but this was not true. He could pick over decayed tissue or lean close to the fetid viscera of a cat with no repulsion. I have seen him literally crawl into the carcass of a basking shark to take its liver in the dark of its own body so that no light might touch it. And this is as horrid an odor as I know.

Ed loved fine tools and instruments, and conversely he had a bitter dislike for bad ones. Often he spoke with contempt of "consumer goods"—things made to catch the eye, to delight the first impression with paint and polish, things made to sell rather than to use. On the other hand, the honest workmanship of a good miscroscope gave him great pleasure. Once I brought him from Sweden a set of the finest scalpels, surgical scissors, and delicate forceps. I remember his joy in them.

His laboratory practice was immaculate and his living quarters were not clean. It was his custom to say that most people paid too much for things they didn't really want, paid too much in effort and time and thought. "If a swept floor gives you enough pleasure and reward to pay for sweeping it, then sweep it," he said. "But if you do not see it dirty or clean, then it is paying too much to sweep it."

I think he set down his whole code or procedure once in a time of stress. He found himself quite poor and with three children to take care of. In a very scholarly manner, he told the children how they must proceed.

"We must remember three things," he said to them. "I will tell them to you in the order of their importance. Number one and first in importance, we must have as much fun as we can with what we have. Number two, we must eat as well as we can, because if we don't we won't have the health and strength to have as much fun as we might. And number three and third and last in importance, we must keep the house reasonably in order, wash the dishes, and such things. But we will not let the last interfere with the other two."

Ed's feeling for clothes was interesting. He wore Bass moccasins, buckskin-colored and quite expensive. He loved thick soft wool socks and wool shirts that would scratch the hell out of anyone else. But outside of those he had no interest. His clothing was fairly ragged, particularly at elbows and knees. He had one necktie hanging in his closet, a wrinkled old devil of a yellow tint, but no one ever saw him wear it. His clothes he just came by, and the coats were not likely to fit him at all. He was not in the least embarrassed by his clothes. He went everywhere in the same costume. And always he seemed strangely neat. Such was his sense of inner security that he did not seem ill dressed. Often people around him appeared over-dressed. The only time he ever wore a hat was when there was some chance of getting his head wet, and then it was likely to be an oilskin sou'wester. But whatever else he wore or did not wear, there was invariably pinned to his shirt pocket a twenty-power Bausch and Lomb magnifying glass on a little roller chain. He used the glass constantly. It was a very close part of him—one of his techniques of seeing.

Always the paradox is there. He loved nice things and did not care about them. He loved to bathe and yet when the water heater in the laboratory broke down he bathed in cold water for over a year before he got around to having it fixed. I finally mended his leaking toilet tank with a piece of chewing gum which I imagine is still there. A broken window was stuffed with newspaper for several years and never was repaired.

He liked comfort and the chairs in the lab were stiff and miserable. His bed was a redwood box laced with hemp rope on which a thin mattress was thrown. And this bed was not big enough for two. Ladies complained bitterly about his bed, which was not only narrow and uncomfortable but gave out shrieks of protest at the slightest movement.

I used the laboratory and Ed himself in a book called *Cannery Row*. I took it to him in typescript to see whether he would resent it and to offer to make any changes he would suggest. He read it through carefully, smiling, and when he had finished he said, "Let it go that way. It is written in kindness. Such a thing can't be bad."

But it was bad in several ways neither of us foresaw. As the book began to be read, tourists began coming to the laboratory, first a few and then in droves. People stopped their cars and stared at Ed with that glassy look that is used on movie stars. Hundreds of people came into the lab to ask questions and peer around. It became a nuisance to him. But in a way he liked it too. For as he said, "Some of the callers were women and some of the women were very nice looking." However, he was glad when the little flurry of publicity or notoriety was over.

It never occurred to me to ask Ed much about his family background or his life as a boy. I suppose it would be easy to find out. When he was alive there were too many other things to talk about, and now—it doesn't matter. Of course I have heard him asked the usual question about his name. Ricketts. He said, "No, I was not named after the disease—one of my relatives is responsible for its naming."

When the book *Studs Lonigan* came out, Ed read it twice very quickly. "This is a true book," he said. "I was born and grew up in this part of Chicago. I played in these streets. I know them all. I know the people. This is a true book." And, of course, to Ed a thing that was true was beautiful. He followed the whole series of Farrell's books after that and only after the locale moved to New York did he lose interest. He did not know true things about New York.

One of the most amusing things that ever happened in Pacific Biological Laboratories was our attempt to help with the war effort against Japan and the complete fiasco that resulted.

When we came back from the collecting trip which is recorded in the latter part of this book, we went to work on the thousands of animals we had gathered. Our project had been to lay the basis for a new faunal geography rather than a search for new species. We needed a great amount of supplementary information regarding the distribution of species on both sides of the Pacific Ocean and among the Pacific Islands, since many species are widely placed.

By this time Pearl Harbor had been attacked and we were at war with Japan. But even if we had not been, there were difficulties. Soon after the First World War a great number of the islands of the Pacific were mandated to Japan by the League of Nations. And Japan's first act had been to draw a bamboo curtain over these islands and over the whole area. No foreigner had been permitted to land on them in twenty years for any purpose whatever.

These islands had not been well known in a zoologic sense before the mandate and nothing had been heard from them since—so we thought.

We sent out the usual letters to universities, requesting information that might be available concerning these curtained islands. The replies delighted us. There was a great deal of information available.

What had happened is this. Japan had certainly cut off the islands from the world, but, perhaps with the future war in view, Japan had wanted to make a survey of her new possessions in the matter of food supply from the ocean. The Japanese eat many more sea products than we do. Who better to send to make this survey than certain eminent Japanese zoologists who were internationally known?

What followed is truly comic opera. The zoologists did make the survey—very secretly. Then afterwards, since they were good scientists and specialists, what was more natural than that they should study their specialties together with the ecological theater? And then, being thoroughly good men, they completed their zoologic survey.

Now a careful zoologic survey notes not only the animals but their neighbor animals—friends and enemies and the conditions under which they live. Such conditions would include weather, wave shock, tidal range, currents, salinity, reefs, headlands, winds, nature of coast and nature of bottom, and any interesting phenomena which might interfere with or promote the occurrence, normal growth, and happiness of the animals in question. Such matters might be mentioned as the discharge into tide pools of by-products of new chemical plants which would change the ecological balance.

Having finished their sea-food reports to the Japanese government, the zoologists with even more loving care wrote their papers on the specialties. And then, what was more natural than that they should send these papers to their colleagues around the world? Japan was not at war. They knew their brother zoologists would be interested and many of the Japanese had studied at Harvard, at Hopkins, at California Institute of Technology—in fact at all of the American universities. They had friends all over the world who would appreciate and applaud their work in pure science.

When these surveys began to arrive Ed and I suddenly lost our interest in the animals. Here under our hands were detailed studies of the physical make-up of one of the least-known areas of the world and one which was in the hands of our enemy. With excitement we realized that if we were ever going to go island-hopping toward Japan, which seemed reasonable, here was all the information needed if we were to make beach landings—depth, tide, currents, reefs, nature of coast, etc. We did not know whether we were alone in our discovery. We wondered whether our naval or military intelligence knew of the existence of these reports. Often a very obvious thing may lie unnoticed. It seemed to us that if our intelligence services did not know, they should, and we were quite willing to take the chance of duplication.

We drafted a letter to the Navy Department in Washington, explaining the material, its possible use, and how we had come upon it.

Six weeks later we received a form letter thanking us for our patriotism. I seem to remember that the letter was mimeographed. Ed was philosophical about it, but I, who did not have his military experience and cynicism, got mad. I wrote to the Secretary of the Navy, at that time the Honorable Frank Knox, again telling the story of the island material. And then after the letter was sealed, in a moment of angry impudence, I wrote "Personal" on the envelope.

Nothing happened for two months. I was away when it did happen. Ed told me about it later. One afternoon a tight-lipped man in civilian clothes came into the laboratory and identified himself as a lieutenant commander of Naval Intelligence.

"We have had a communication from you," he said sternly.

"Oh, yes," Ed said. "We're glad you are here."

The officer interrupted him. "Do you speak or read Japanese?" he asked suspiciously.

"No, I don't," Ed said.

"Does your partner speak or read Japanese?"

"No—why do you ask?"

"Then what is this information you claim to have about the Pacific islands?"

Only then did Ed understand him. "But they're in English—the papers are all in English!" he cried.

"How in English?"

"The men, the Japanese zoologists, wrote them in English. They had studied here. English is becoming the scientific language of the world."

This thought, Ed said, really made quite a struggle to get in, but it failed.

"Why don't they write in Japanese?" the commander demanded.

"I don't know." Ed was getting tired. "The fact remains that they write English—sometimes quaint English but English."

That word tore it, just as my "Personal" on the envelope probably tore it in Washington.

The lieutenant commander looked grim. "Quaint!" he said. "You will hear from us."

But we never did. And I have always wondered whether they had the information or got it. I wonder whether some of the soldiers whose landing craft grounded a quarter of a mile from the beach and who had to wade ashore under fire had the feeling that bottom and tidal range either were not known or were ignored. I don't know.

Ed shook his head after he told me about the visit of the officer. "I never learn," he said. "I really fell into that one. And I should know better. And I used to be a company clerk." Then he told me about the Navy tests at Bremerton.

The tests were designed to develop some bottom material or paint which would repel barnacles. The outlay of money was considerable—big concrete tanks were built and samples of paints, metal salts, poisons, tars, were immersed to see what material barnacles would be most likely to stay away from.

"Now," Ed said, "a friend of mine who teaches at the University of Washington is one of the world's specialists in barnacles. My friend happens to be a woman. She heard of the tests and offered her services to the Navy. A very patriotic woman as well as a damn good scientist.

"There were two strikes against her," Ed said. "One, she was a woman, and two, she was a professor. The Navy was gallant but adamant. She was thanked and informed that the Navy was not interested in theory. This was hard-boiled realism, and practical men—not theoreticians—would see it through."

Ed grinned at me. "You know," he said, "at the end of three months there wasn't a single barnacle on any of the test materials, not even on the guide materials, the untouched wood and steel. My friend heard of this and visited the station again. She was shy about imposing theory. But she saw what was wrong very quickly.

"The Navy is hard-boiled but it is clean," Ed said. "Bremerton water, on the other hand, is very dirty—you know, harbor stuff, oil and algae, decayed fish and even some human residue. The Navy didn't like that filth so the water was filtered before it went to the tanks. The filters got the water clean," said Ed, "but it also removed all of the barnacle larvae." He laughed. "I wonder whether she ever told them," he said.

Thus was our impertinent attempt to change the techniques of warfare put in its place. But we won.

I became associated in the business of the laboratory in the simplest of ways. A number of years ago Ed had gradually got into debt until the interest on his loan from the bank was bleeding the laboratory like a cat in the basement. Rather sadly he prepared to liquidate the little business and give up his independence—the right to sleep late and work late, the right to make his own decisions. While the lab was not run efficiently, it could make enough to support him, but it could not also pay the bank interest.

At that time I had some money put away and I took up the bank loans and lowered the interest to a vanishing point. I knew the money would vanish anyway. To secure the loan I received stock in the corporation—the most beautiful stock, and the mortgage on the property. I didn't understand much of the transaction but it allowed the laboratory to operate for another ten years. Thus I became a partner in the improbable business. I must say I brought no efficiency to bear on it. The fact that the institution survived at all is a matter that must be put down to magic. I can find no other reasonable explanation. It had no right to survive. A board of directors' meeting differed from any other party only in that there was more beer. A stern business discussion had a way of slipping into a consideration of a unified field hypothesis.

Our trip to the Gulf of Lower California was a marvel of bumbling efficiency. We went where we intended, got what we wanted, and did the work on it. It had been our intention to continue the work with a survey of the Aleutian chain of islands when the war closed that area to us.

At the time of Ed's death our plans were completed, tickets bought, containers and collecting equipment ready for a long collecting trip to the Queen Charlotte Islands, which reach so deep into the Pacific Ocean. There was one deep bay with a long and narrow opening where we thought we might observe some changes in animal forms due to a specialized life and a long period of isolation. Ed was to have started within a month and I was to have joined him there. Maybe someone else will study that little island sea. The light has gone out of it for me.

Now I am coming near to the close of this account. I have not put down Ed's relations with his wives or with his three children. There isn't time, and besides I did not know much about these things.

As I have said, no one who knew Ed will be satisfied with this account. They will have known innumerable other Eds. I imagine that there were as many Eds as there were friends of Ed. And I wonder whether there can be any parallel thinking on his nature and the reason for his impact on the people who knew him. I wonder whether I can make any kind of generalization that would be satisfactory.

I have tried to isolate and inspect the great talent that was in Ed Ricketts, that made him so loved and needed and makes him so missed now that he is dead. Certainly he was an interesting and charming man, but there was some other quality which far exceeded these. I have thought that it might be his ability to receive, to receive anything from anyone, to receive gracefully and thankfully and to make the gift seem very fine. Because of this everyone felt good in giving to Ed—a present, a thought, anything.

Perhaps the most overrated virtue in our list of shoddy virtues is that of giving. Giving builds up the ego of the giver, makes him superior and higher and larger than the receiver. Nearly always, giving is a selfish pleasure, and in many cases it is a downright destructive and evil thing. One has only to remember some of our wolfish financiers who spend two-thirds of their lives clawing fortunes out of the guts of society and the latter third pushing it back. It is not enough to suppose that their philanthropy is a kind of frightened restitution, or that their natures change when they have enough. Such a nature never has enough and natures do not change that readily. I think that the impulse is the same in both cases. For giving can bring the same sense of superiority as getting does, and philanthropy may be another kind of spiritual avarice.

It is so easy to give, so exquisitely rewarding. Receiving, on the other hand, if it be well done, requires a fine balance of self-knowledge and kindness. It requires humility and tact and great understanding of relationships. In receiving you cannot appear, even to yourself, better or stronger or wiser than the giver, although you must be wiser to do it well.

It requires a self-esteem to receive—not self-love but just a pleasant acquaintance and liking for oneself.

Once Ed said to me, "For a very long time I didn't like myself." It was not said in self-pity but simply as an unfortunate fact. "It was a very difficult time," he said, "and very painful. I did not like myself for a number of reasons, some of them valid and some of them pure fancy. I would hate to have to go back to that. Then gradually," he said, "I discovered with surprise and pleasure that a number of people did like me. And I thought, if they can like me, why cannot I like myself? Just thinking it did not do it, but slowly I learned to like myself and then it was all right."

This was not said in self-love in its bad connotation but in self-knowledge. He meant literally that he had learned to accept and like the person "Ed" as he liked other people. It gave him a great advantage. Most people do not like themselves at all. They distrust themselves, put on masks and pomposities. They quarrel and boast and pretend and are jealous because they do not like themselves. But mostly they do not even know themselves well enough to form a true liking. They cannot see themselves well enough to form a true liking, and since we automatically fear and dislike strangers, we fear and dislike our stranger-selves.

Once Ed was able to like himself he was released from the secret prison of self-contempt. Then he did not have to prove superiority any more by any of the ordinary methods, including giving. He could receive and understand and be truly glad, not competitively glad.

Ed's gift for receiving made him a great teacher. Children brought shells to him and gave him information about the shells. And they had to learn before they could tell him.

In conversation you found yourself telling him things— thoughts, conjectures, hypotheses—and you found a pleased surprise at yourself for having arrived at something you were not aware that you could think or know. It gave you such a good sense of participation with him that you could present him with this wonder.

Then Ed would say, "Yes, that's so. That's the way it might be and besides—" and he would illuminate it but not so that he took it away from you. He simply accepted it.

Although his creativeness lay in receiving, that does not mean that he kept things as property. When you had something from him it was not something that was his that he tore away from himself. When you had a thought from him or a piece of music or twenty dollars or a steak dinner, it was not his—it was yours already, and his was only the head and hand that steadied it in position toward you. For this reason no one was ever cut off from him. Association with him was deep participation with him, never competition.

I wish we could all be so. If we could learn even a little to like ourselves, maybe our cruelties and angers might melt away. Maybe we would not have to hurt one another just to keep our ego-chins above water.

There it is. That's all I can set down about Ed Ricketts. I don't know whether any clear picture has emerged. Thinking back and remembering has not done what I hoped it might. It has not laid the ghost.

The picture that remains is a haunting one. It is the time just before dusk. I can see Ed finishing his work in the laboratory. He covers his instruments and puts his papers away. He rolls down the sleeves of his wool shirt and puts on his old brown coat. I see him go out and get in his beat-up old car and slowly drive away in the evening.

I guess I'll have that with me all my life.

Sea of Cortez

T HE DESIGN of a book is the pattern of a reality controlled and shaped by the mind of the writer. This is completely understood about poetry or fiction, but it is too seldom realized about books of fact. And yet the impulse which drives a man to poetry will send another man into the tide pools and force him to try to report what he finds there. Why is an expedition to Tibet undertaken, or a sea bottom dredged? Why do men, sitting at the microscope, examine the calcareous plates of a sea-cucumber, and, finding a new arrangement and number, feel an exaltation and give the new species a name, and write about it possessively? It would be good to know the impulse truly, not to be confused by the "services to science" platitudes or the other little mazes into which we entice our minds so that they will not know what we are doing.

We have a book to write about the Gulf of California. We could do one of several things about its design. But we have decided to let it form itself: its boundaries a boat and a sea; its duration a six weeks' charter time; its subject everything we could see and think and even imagine; its limits—our own without reservation.

We made a trip into the Gulf; sometimes we dignified it by calling it an expedition. Once it was called the Sea of Cortez, and that is a better-sounding and a more exciting name. We stopped in many little harbors and near barren coasts to collect and preserve the marine invertebrates of the littoral. One of the reasons we gave ourselves for this trip—and when we used this reason, we called the trip an expedition—was to observe the distribution of invertebrates, to see and to record their kinds and numbers, how they lived together, what they ate, and how they reproduced. That plan was simple, straightforward, and only a part of the truth. But we did tell the truth to ourselves. We were curious. Our curiosity was not limited, but was as wide and horizonless as that of Darwin or Agassiz or Linnaeus or Pliny. We wanted to see everything our eyes would accommodate, to think what we could, and, out of our seeing and thinking, to build some kind of structure in modeled imitation of the observed reality. We knew that what we would see and record and construct would be warped, as all knowledge patterns are warped, first, by the collective pressure and stream of our time and race, second by the thrust of our individual personalities. But knowing this, we might not fall into too many holes—we might maintain some balance between our warp and the separate thing, the external reality. The oneness of these two might take its contribution from both. For example: the Mexican sierra has "XVII–15–IX" spines in the dorsal fin. These can easily be counted. But if the sierra strikes hard on the line so that our hands are burned, if the fish sounds and nearly escapes and finally comes in over the rail, his colors pulsing and his tail beating the air, a whole new relational externality has come into being—an entity which is more than the sum of the fish plus the fisherman. The only way to count the spines of the sierra unaffected by this second relational reality is to sit in a laboratory, open an evil-smelling jar, remove a stiff colorless fish from formalin solution, count the spines, and write the truth "D. XVII–15–IX." There you have recorded a reality which cannot be assailed—probably the least important reality concerning either the fish or yourself.

It is good to know what you are doing. The man with his pickled fish has set down one truth and has recorded in his experience many lies. The fish is not that color, that texture, that dead, nor does he smell that way.

Such things we had considered in the months of planning our expedition and we were determined not to let a passion for unassailable little truths draw in the horizons and crowd the sky down on us. We knew that what seemed to us true could be only relatively true anyway. There is no other kind of observation. The man with his pickled fish has sacrificed a great observation about himself, the fish, and the focal point, which is his thought on both the sierra and himself.

We suppose this was the mental provisioning of our expedition. We said, "Let's go wide open. Let's see what we see, record what we find, and not fool ourselves with conventional scientific strictures. We could not observe a completely objective Sea of Cortez anyway, for in that lonely and uninhabited Gulf our boat and ourselves would change it the moment we entered. By going there, we would bring a new factor to the Gulf. Let us consider that factor and not be betrayed by this myth of permanent objective reality. If it exists at all, it is only available in pickled tatters or in distorted flashes. Let us go," we said, "into the Sea of Cortez, realizing that we become forever a part of it; that our rubber boots slogging through a flat of eel-grass, that the rocks we turn over in a tide pool, make us truly and permanently a factor in the ecology of the region. We shall take something away from it, but we shall leave something too." And if we seem a small factor in a huge pattern, nevertheless it is of relative importance. We take a tiny colony of soft corals from a rock in a little water world. And that isn't terribly important to the tide pool. Fifty miles away the Japanese shrimp boats are dredging with overlapping scoops, bringing up tons of shrimps, rapidly destroying the species so that it may never come back, and with the species destroying the ecological balance of the whole region. That isn't very important in the world. And thousands of miles away the great bombs are falling and the stars are not moved thereby. None of it is important or all of it is.

We determined to go doubly open so that in the end we could, if we wished, describe the sierra thus: "D. XVII–15–IX; A. II–15–IX," but also we could see the fish alive and swimming, feel it plunge against the lines, drag it threshing over the rail, and even finally eat it. And there is no reason why either approach should be inaccurate. Spine-count description need not suffer because another approach is also used. Perhaps out of the two approaches, we thought, there might emerge a picture more complete and even more accurate than either alone could produce. And so we went.

I

How does one organize an expedition: what equipment is taken, what sources read; what are the little dangers and the large ones? No one has ever written this. The information is not available. The design is simple, as simple as the design of a well-written book. Your expedition will be enclosed in the physical framework of start, direction, ports of call, and return. These you can forecast with some accuracy; and in the better-known parts of the world it is possible to a degree to know what the weather will be in a given season, how high and low the tides, and the hours of their occurrence. One can know within reason what kind of boat to take, how much food will be necessary for a given crew for a given time, what medicines are usually needed—all this subject to accident, of course.

We had read what books were available about the Gulf and they were few and in many cases confused. The *Coast Pilot* had not been adequately corrected for some years. A few naturalists with specialties had gone into the Gulf and, in the way of specialists, had seen nothing they hadn't wanted to. Clavigero, a Jesuit of the eighteenth century, had seen more than most and reported what he saw with more accuracy than most. There were some romantic accounts by young people who had gone into the Gulf looking for adventure and, of course, had found it. The same romantic drive aimed at the stockyards would not be disappointed. From the information available, a few facts did emerge. The Sea of Cortez, or the Gulf of California, is a long, narrow, highly dangerous body of water. It is subject to sudden and vicious storms of great intensity. The months of March and April are usually quite calm and dependable and the March–April tides of 1940 were particularly good for collecting in the littoral.

The maps of the region were self-possessed and confident about headlands, coastlines, and depth, but at the edge of the Coast they become apologetic—laid in lagoons with dotted lines, supposed and presumed their boundaries. The *Coast Pilot* spoke as heatedly as it ever does about mirage and treachery of light. Going back from the *Coast Pilot* to Clavigero, we found more visual warnings in his accounts of ships broken up and scattered, of wrecks and wayward currents; of fifty miles of sea more dreaded than any other. The *Coast Pilot*, like an elderly scientist, cautious and restrained, on one side— and the old monk, setting down ships and men lost, and starvation on the inhospitable coasts.

In time of peace in the modern world, if one is thoughtful and careful, it is rather more difficult to be killed or maimed in the outland places of the globe than it is in the streets of our great cities, but the atavistic urge toward danger persists and its satisfaction is called adventure. However, your adventurer feels no gratification in crossing Market Street in San Francisco against the traffic. Instead he will go to a good deal of trouble and expense to get himself killed in the South Seas. In reputedly rough water, he will go in a canoe; he will invade deserts without adequate food and he will expose his tolerant and uninoculated blood to strange viruses. This is adventure. It is possible that his ancestor, wearying of the humdrum attacks of the saber-tooth, longed for the good old days of pterodactyl and triceratops.

We had no urge toward adventure. We planned to collect marine animals in a remote place on certain days and at certain hours indicated on the tide charts. To do this we had, in so far as we were able, to avoid adventure. Our plans, supplies, and equipment had to be more, not less, than adequate; and none of us was possessed of the curious boredom within ourselves which makes adventurers or bridge-players.

Our first problem was to charter a boat. It had to be sturdy and big enough to go to sea, comfortable enough to live on for six weeks, roomy enough to work on, and shallow enough so that little bays could be entered. The purse-seiners of Monterey were ideal for the purpose. They are dependable work boats with comfortable quarters and ample storage room. Furthermore, in March and April the sardine season is over and they are tied up. It would be easy, we thought, to charter such a boat; there must have been nearly a hundred of them anchored in back of the breakwater. We went to the pier and spread the word that we were looking for such a boat for charter. The word spread all right, but we were not overwhelmed with offers. In fact, no boat was offered. Only gradually did we discover the state of mind of the boat owners.

They were uneasy about our project. Italians, Slavs, and some Japanese, they were primarily sardine fishers. They didn't even approve of fishermen who fished for other kinds of fish. They frankly didn't believe in the activities of the land—road-building and manufacturing and brick-laying. This was not a matter of ignorance on their part, but of intensity. All the directionalism of thought and emotion that man was capable of went into sardine-fishing; there wasn't room for anything else. An example of this occurred later when we were at sea. Hitler was invading Denmark and moving up towards Norway; there was no telling when the invasion of England might begin; our radio was full of static and the world was going to hell. Finally in all the crackle and noise of the short-wave one of our men made contact with another boat. The conversation went like this:

"This is the *Western Flyer*. Is that you, Johnny?"

"Yeah, that you, Sparky?"

"Yeah, this is Sparky. How much fish you got?"

"Only fifteen tons; we lost a school today. How much fish you got?"

"We're not fishing."

"Why not?"

"Aw, we're going down in the Gulf to collect starfish and bugs and stuff like that."

"Oh, yeah? Well, O.K., Sparky, I'll clear the wave length."

"Wait, Johnny. You say you only got fifteen tons?"

"That's right. If you talk to my cousin, tell him, will you?"

"Yeah, I will, Johnny. *Western Flyer's* all clear now."

Hitler marched into Denmark and into Norway, France had fallen, the Maginot Line was lost—we didn't know it, but we knew the daily catch of every boat within four hundred miles. It was simply a directional thing; a man has only so much. And so it was with the chartering of a boat. The owners were not distrustful of us; they didn't even listen to us because they couldn't quite believe we existed. We were obviously ridiculous.

Now the time was growing short and we began to worry. Finally one boat owner who was in financial difficulty offered his boat at a reasonable price and we were ready to accept when suddenly he raised the price out of question and bolted.

He was horrified at what he had done. He raised the price, not to cheat us, but to get out of going.

The boat problem was growing serious when Anthony Berry sailed into Monterey Bay on the *Western Flyer*. The idea was no shock to Tony Berry; he had chartered to the government for salmon tagging in Alaskan waters and was used to nonsense. Besides, he was an intelligent and tolerant man. He knew that he had idiosyncrasies and that some of his friends had. He was willing to let us do any crazy thing that we wanted so long as we (1) paid a fair price, (2) told him where to go, (3) did not insist that he endanger the boat, (4) got back on time, and (5) didn't mix him up in our nonsense. His boat was not busy and he was willing to go. He was a quiet young man, very serious and a good master. He knew some navigation—a rare thing in the fishing fleet—and he had a natural caution which we admired. His boat was new and comfortable and clean, the engines in fine condition. We took the *Western Flyer* on charter.

She was seventy-six feet long with a twenty-five-foot beam; her engine, a hundred and sixty-five horsepower direct reversible Diesel, drove her at ten knots. Her deckhouse had a wheel forward, then combination master's room and radio room, then bunkroom, very comfortable, and behind that the galley. After the galley, a large hatch gave into the fish-hold, and after the hatch were the big turn-table and roller of the purse-seiner. She carried a twenty-foot skiff and a ten-foot skiff. Her engine was a thing of joy, spotlessly clean, the moving surfaces shining and damp with oil and the green paint fresh and new on the housings. The engine-room floor was clean and all the tools polished and hung in their places. One look into the engine-room inspired confidence in the master. We had seen other engines in the fishing fleet and this perfection on the *Western Flyer* was by no means a general thing.

As crew we signed Tex Travis, engineer, and Sparky Enea and Tiny Colletto, seamen. All three were a little reluctant to go, for the whole thing was crazy. None of us had been into the Gulf, although the master had been as far as Cape San Lucas, and the Gulf has a really bad name. It was a thoughtful crew who agreed to go with us.

We could never tell when the change of attitude toward us

came, but it came very rapidly. Perhaps it was because Tony Berry was known as a cautious man who would not indulge in nonsense, or perhaps it was pure relief that at last it had been settled. All of a sudden we were overwhelmed with help. We had offers from men to go with us without pay. Sparky was offered a certain price for his job that was more than he would get from us. All he had to do was turn over his job and sit in Monterey and spend the money. But Sparky refused. Our project had become honorable. We had more help than we could use and advice enough to move the navies of the world.

We did not know what our crew thought of the expedition but later, in the field, they became good collectors—a little emotional sometimes, as when Tiny, in outrage at being pinched, declared a war of extermination on the whole Sally Lightfoot species, but on the whole collectors of taste and quickness.

The charter was signed with dignity and reverence. It is impossible to be light-hearted in the face of a ship's charter, for the law has foreseen or remembered the most doleful and arbitrary acts of God and has set them down as possibilities, but in the tone of inevitabilities. Thus, you read what you or the others must do in the case of wreck, or sunken rocks; of death at sea in its most painful and astonishing aspects; of injury to plank and keel; of water shortage and mutiny. Next to marriage settlement or sentence of death, a ship's charter is as portentous a document as has ever been written. Penalties are set down against both parties, and if on some morning the rising sun should find your ship in the middle of the Mojave Desert you have only to look again at the charter to find the blame assigned and the penalty indicated. It took us several hours to get over the solemn feeling the charter put on us. We thought we might live better lives and pay our debts, and one at least of us contemplated for one holy, horrified moment a vow of chastity.

But the charter was signed and food began to move into the *Western Flyer*. It is amazing how much food seven people need to exist for six weeks. Cases of spaghetti, cases and cases of peaches and pineapple, of tomatoes, whole Romano cheeses, canned milk in coveys, flour and cornmeal, gallons of olive oil, tomato paste, crackers, cans of butter and jam, catsup and rice, beans and bacon and canned meats, vegetables and soups in cans; truckloads of food. And all this food was stored eagerly and happily by the crew. It disappeared into cupboards, under little hatches in the galley floor, and many cases went below.

We had done a good deal of collecting, but largely in temperate zones. The equipment for collecting, preserving, and storing specimens was selected on the basis of experience in other waters and of anticipation of difficulties imposed by a hot humid country. In some cases we were right, in others very wrong.

In a small boat, the library should be compact and available. We had constructed a strong, steel-reinforced wooden case, the front of which hinged down to form a desk. This case holds about twenty large volumes and has two filing cases, one for separates (scientific reprints) and one for letters; a small metal box holds pens, pencils, erasers, clips, steel tape, scissors, labels, pins, rubber bands, and so forth. Another compartment contains a three-by-five-inch card file. There are cubby-holes for envelopes, large separates, small separates, typewriter paper, carbon, a box for India ink and glue. The construction of the front makes room for a portable typewriter, drawing board, and T-square. There is a long narrow space for rolled charts and maps. Closed, this compact and complete box is forty-four inches long by eighteen by eighteen; loaded, it weighs between three and four hundred pounds. It was designed to rest on a low table or in an unused bunk. Its main value is compactness, completeness, and accessibility. We took it aboard the *Western Flyer*. There was no table for it to rest on. It did not fit in a bunk. It could not be put on the deck because of moisture. It ended up lashed to the rail on top of the deckhouse, covered with several layers of tarpaulin and roped on. Because of the roll of the boat it had to be tied down at all times. It took about ten minutes to remove the tarpaulin, untie the lashing line, open the cover, squeeze down between two crates of oranges, read the title of the wanted book upside down, remove it, close and lash and cover the box again. But if there had been a low table or a large bunk, it would have been perfect.

For many little errors like this, we have concluded that all collecting trips to fairly unknown regions should be made twice; once to make mistakes and once to correct them. Some of the greatest difficulty lies in the fact that previous collectors have never set down the equipment taken and its success or failure. We propose to rectify this in our account.

The library contained all the separates then available on the Panamic and Gulf fauna. Primary volumes such as Johnson and Snook, Ricketts and Calvin, Russell and Yonge, Flattely and Walton, Keep's *West Coast Shells*, Fisher's three-volume starfish monograph, the Rathbun brachyuran monograph, Schmitt's *Marine Decapod Crustacea of California*, Fraser's *Hydroids*, Barnhart's *Marine Fishes of Southern California*, *Coast Pilots* for the whole Pacific Coast; charts, both large and small scale, of the whole region to be covered.

The camera equipment was more than adequate, for it was never used. It included a fine German reflex and an 8-mm. movie camera with tripod, light meters, and everything. But we had no camera-man. During low tides we all collected; there was no time to dry hands and photograph at the collecting scene. Later, the anesthetizing, killing, preserving, and labeling of specimens were so important that we still took no pictures. It was an error in personnel. There should be a camera-man who does nothing but take pictures.

Our collecting material at least was good. Shovels, wrecking- and abalone-bars, nets, long-handled dip-nets, wooden fish-kits, and a number of seven-cell flashlights for night collecting were taken. Containers seemed to go endlessly into the hold of the *Western Flyer*. Wooden fish-kits with heads; twenty hard-fir barrels with galvanized hoops in fifteen- and thirty-gallon sizes; cases of gallon jars, quart, pint, eight-ounce, five-ounce, and two-ounce screw-cap jars; several gross of corked vials in four chief sizes, 100×33 mm, six-dram, four-dram, and two-dram sizes. There were eight two-and-a-half-gallon jars with screw caps. And with all these we ran short of containers, and before we were through had to crowd those we had. This was unfortunate, since many delicate animals should be preserved separately to prevent injury.

Of chemicals, we put into the boat a fifteen-gallon barrel of U.S.P. formaldehyde and a fifteen-gallon barrel of denatured alcohol. This was not nearly enough alcohol. The stock had to be replenished at Guaymas, where we bought ten gallons of pure sugar alcohol. We took two gallons of Epsom salts for anesthetization and again ran out and had to buy more in Guaymas. Menthol, chromic acid, and novocain, all for relaxing animals, were included in the chemical kit. Of preparing equipment, there were glass chiton plates and string, lots of rubber gloves, graduates, forceps, and scalpels. Our binocular microscope, Bausch & Lomb A.K.W., was fitted with a twelve-volt light, but on the rolling boat the light was so difficult to handle that we used a spot flashlight instead. We had galvanized iron nested trays of fifteen- to twenty-gallon capacity for gross hardening and preservation. We had enameled and glass trays for the laying out of specimens, and one small examination aquarium.

The medical kit had been given a good deal of thought. There were nembutal, butesin picrate for sunburn, a thousand two-grain quinine capsules, two-percent mercuric oxide salve for barnacle cuts, cathartics, ammonia, mercurochrome, iodine, alcaroid, and, last, some whisky for medicinal purposes. This did not survive our leave-taking, but since no one was ill on the whole trip, it may have done its job very well.

2

WHAT little time we were not on lists and equipment or in grudging sleep we went to the pier and looked at boats, watched them tied to their buoys behind the breakwater—the dirty boats and the clean painted boats, each one stamped with the personality of its owner. Here, where the discipline was as individual as the owners, every boat was different from every other one. If the stays were rusting and the deck unwashed, paint scraped off and lines piled carelessly, there was no need to see the master; we knew him. And if the lines were coiled and the cables greased and the little luxury of deer horns nailed to the crow's-nest, there was no need to see that owner either. There were deer horns on many of the crow's-nests, and when we asked why, we were told they brought good luck. Out of some ancient time, they brought good luck to these people, most of them out of Sicily, the horns grown sturdily on the structure of their race. If you ask, "Where does the idea come from?" the owner will say, "It brings good luck, we always put them on." And a thousand years ago the horns were on the masts and brought good luck, and probably when the ships of Carthage and Tyre put into the harbors of Sicily, the horns were on the mastheads and brought good luck and no one knew why. Out of some essential race soul the horns come, and not only the horns, but the boats themselves, so that to a man, to nearly all men, a boat more than any other tool he uses is a little representation of an archetype. There is an "idea" boat that is an emotion, and because the emotion is so strong it is probable that no other tool is made with so much honesty as a boat. Bad boats are built, surely, but not many of them. It can be argued that a bad boat cannot survive tide and wave and hence is not worth building, but the same might be said of a bad automobile on a rough road. Apparently the builder of a boat acts under a compulsion greater than himself. Ribs are strong by definition and feeling. Keels are sound, planking truly chosen and set. A man builds the best of himself into a boat—builds many of the unconscious memories of his ancestors. Once, passing the boat department of Macy's in New York, where there are duck-boats and skiffs and little cruisers, one of the authors discovered that as he passed each hull he knocked on it sharply with his knuckles. He wondered why he did it, and as he wondered, he heard a knocking behind him, and another man was rapping the hulls with *his* knuckles, the same tempo—three sharp knocks on each hull. During an hour's observation there no man or boy and few women passed who did not do the same thing. Can this have been an unconscious testing of the hulls? Many who passed could not have been in a boat, perhaps some of the little boys had never seen a boat, and yet everyone tested the hulls, knocked to see if they were sound, and did not even know he was doing it. The observer thought perhaps they and he would knock on any large wooden object that might give forth a resonant sound. He went to the piano department, icebox floor, beds, cedar-chests, and no one knocked on them—only on boats.

How deep this thing must be, the giver and the receiver again; the boat designed through millenniums of trial and error by the human consciousness, the boat which has no counterpart in nature unless it be a dry leaf fallen by accident in a stream. And Man receiving back from Boat a warping of his psyche so that the sight of a boat riding in the water clenches a fist of emotion in his chest. A horse, a beautiful dog, arouses sometimes a quick emotion, but of inanimate things only a boat can do it. And a boat, above all other inanimate things, is personified in man's mind. When we have been steering, the boat has seemed sometimes nervous and irritable, swinging off course before the correction could be made, slapping her nose into the quartering wave. After a storm she has seemed tired and sluggish. Then with the colored streamers set high and snapping, she is very happy, her nose held high and her stern bouncing a little like the buttocks of a proud and confident girl. Some have said they have felt a boat shudder before she struck a rock, or cry when she beached and the surf poured into her. This is not mysticism, but identification; man, building this greatest and most personal of all tools, has in turn received a boat-shaped mind, and the boat, a man-shaped soul. His spirit and the tendrils of his feeling are so deep in a boat that the identification is complete. It is very easy to see why the Viking wished his body to sail away in an unmanned ship, for neither could exist without the other; or, failing that, how it was necessary that the things he loved most, his women and his ship, lie with him and thus keep closed the circle. In the great fire on the shore, all three started at least in the same direction, and in the gathered ashes who could say where man or woman stopped and ship began?

This strange identification of man with boat is so complete that probably no man has even destroyed a boat by bomb or torpedo or shell without murder in his heart; and were it not for the sad trait of self-destruction that is in our species, he could not do it. Only the trait of murder which our species seems to have could allow us the sick, exultant sadness of sinking a ship, for we can murder the things we love best, which are, of course, ourselves.

We have looked into the tide pools and seen the little

animals feeding and reproducing and killing for food. We name them and describe them and, out of long watching, arrive at some conclusion about their habits so that we say, "This species typically does thus and so," but we do not objectively observe our own species as a species, although we know the individuals fairly well. When it seems that men may be kinder to men, that wars may not come again, we completely ignore the record of our species. If we used the same smug observation on ourselves that we do on hermit crabs we would be forced to say, with the information at hand, "It is one diagnostic trait of *Homo sapiens* that groups of individuals are periodically infected with a feverish nervousness which causes the individual to turn on and destroy, not only his own kind, but the works of his own kind. It is not known whether this be caused by a virus, some airborne spore, or whether it be a species reaction to some meteorological stimulus as yet undetermined." Hope, which is another species diagnostic trait—the hope that this may not always be—does not in the least change the observable past and present. When two crayfish meet, they usually fight. One would say that perhaps they might not at a future time, but without some mutation it is not likely that they will lose this trait. And perhaps our species is not likely to forgo war without some psychic mutation which at present, at least, does not seem imminent. And if one place the blame for killing and destroying on economic insecurity, on inequality, on injustice, he is simply stating the proposition in another way. We have what we are. Perhaps the crayfish feels the itch of jealousy, or perhaps he is sexually insecure. The effect is that he fights. When in the world there shall come twenty, thirty, fifty years without evidence of our murder trait, under whatever system of justice or economic security, then we may have a contrasting habit pattern to examine. So far there is no such situation. So far the murder trait of our species is as regular and observable as our various sexual habits.

3

IN THE time before our departure for the Gulf we sat on the pier and watched the sardine purse-seiners riding among the floating grapefruit rinds. A breakwater is usually a dirty place, as though the tampering with the shore line is obscene and impractical to the cleansing action of the sea. And we talked to our prospective crew. Tex, our engineer, was caught in the ways of the harbor. He was born in the Panhandle of Texas and early he grew to love Diesel engines. They are so simple and powerful, blocks of pure logic in shining metal. They appealed to some sense of neat thinking in Tex. He might be sentimental and illogical in some things, but he liked his engines to be true and logical. By an accident, possibly alcoholic, he came to the Coast in an old Ford and sat down beside the Bay, and there he discovered a wonderful thing. Here, combined in one, were the best Diesels to be found anywhere, and boats. He never recovered from his shocked pleasure. He could never leave the sea again, for nowhere else could he find these two perfect things in one. He is a sure man with an engine. When he goes below he is identified with his engine. He moves about, not seeing, not looking, but knowing. No matter how tired or how deeply asleep he may be, one miss of the engine jerks him to his feet and into the engine-room before he is awake, and we truly believe that a burned bearing or a cracked shaft gives him sharp pains in his stomach.

We talked to Tony, the master and part owner of the *Western Flyer*, and our satisfaction with him as master increased constantly. He had the brooding, dark, Slavic eyes and the hawk nose of the Dalmatian. He rarely talked or laughed. He was tall and lean and very strong. He had a great contempt for forms. Under way, he liked to wear a tweed coat and an old felt hat, as though to say, "I keep the sea in my head, not on my back like a Goddamn yachtsman." Tony has one great passion; he loves rightness and he hates wrongness. He thinks speculation a complete waste of time. To our sorrow, and some financial loss, we discovered that Tony never spoke unless he was right. It was useless to bet with him and impossible to argue with him. If he had not been right, he would never have opened his mouth. But once knowing and saying a truth, he became infuriated at the untruth which naturally enough was set against it. Inaccuracy was like an outrageous injustice to him, and when confronted with it, he was likely to shout and to lose his temper. But he did not personally triumph when his point was proven. An ideal judge, hating larceny, feels no triumph when he sentences a thief, and Tony, when he has nailed a true thing down and routed a wrong thing, feels good, but not righteous. He retires grumbling a little sadly at the stupidity of a world which can conceive a wrongness or for one moment defend one. He loves the leadline because it tells a truth on its markers; he loves the Navy charts; and until he went into the Gulf he admired the *Coast Pilot*. The *Coast Pilot* was not wrong, but things had changed since its correction, and Tony is uneasy in the face of variables. The whole relational thinking of modern physics was an obscenity to him and he refused to have anything to do with it. Parallels and compasses and the good Navy maps were things you could trust. A circle is true and a direction is set forever, a shining golden line across the mind. Later, in the mirage of the Gulf where visual distance is a highly variable matter, we wondered whether Tony's certainties were ever tipped. It did not seem so. His qualities made him a good master. He took no chances he could avoid, for his boat and his life and ours were no light things for him to tamper with.

We come now to a piece of equipment which still brings anger to our hearts and, we hope, some venom to our pen. Perhaps in self-defense against suit, we should say, "The outboard motor mentioned in this book is purely fictitious and any resemblance to outboard motors living or dead is coincidental." We shall call this contraption, for the sake of secrecy, a Hansen Sea-Cow—a dazzling little piece of machinery, all aluminum paint and touched here and there with spots of red. The Sea-Cow was built to sell, to dazzle the eyes, to splutter its way into the unwary heart. We took it along for the skiff. It was intended that it should push us ashore and back, should drive our boat into estuaries and along the borders of little coves. But we had not reckoned with one thing. Recently, industrial civilization has reached its peak of reality and has lunged forward into something that approaches mysticism. In the Sea-Cow factory where steel fingers tighten screws, bend and mold, measure and divide, some curious mathematick has occurred. And that secret so long sought has accidentally been found. Life has been created. The machine is at last stirred. A soul and a malignant mind have been born. Our Hansen Sea-Cow was not only a living thing but a mean, irritable, contemptible, vengeful, mischievous, hateful living thing. In the six weeks of our association we observed it, at first mechanically and then, as its living reactions became more and more apparent, psychologically. And we determined one thing to our satisfaction. When and if these ghoulish little motors learn to reproduce themselves the human species is doomed. For their hatred of us is so great that they will wait and plan and organize and one night, in a roar of little exhausts, they will wipe us out. We do not think that Mr. Hansen, inventor of the Sea-Cow, father of the outboard motor, knew what he was doing. We think the monster he created was as accidental and arbitrary as the beginning of any other life. Only one thing differentiates the Sea-Cow from the life that we know. Whereas the forms that are familiar to us are the results of billions of years of mutation and complication, life and intelligence emerged simultaneously in the Sea-Cow. It is more than a species. It is a whole new re-definition of life. We observed the following traits in it and we were able to check them again and again:

1. Incredibly lazy, the Sea-Cow loved to ride on the back of a boat, trailing its propeller daintily in the water while we rowed.

2. It required the same amount of gasoline whether it ran or not, apparently being able to absorb this fluid through its body walls without recourse to explosion. It had always to be filled at the beginning of every trip.

3. It had apparently some clairvoyant powers, and was able to read our minds, particularly when they were inflamed with emotion. Thus, on every occasion when we were driven to the point of destroying it, it started and ran with a great noise and excitement. This served the double purpose of saving its life and of resurrecting in our minds a false confidence in it.

4. It had many cleavage points, and when attacked with a screwdriver, fell apart in simulated death, a trait it had in com-

mon with opossums, armadillos, and several members of the sloth family, which also fall apart in simulated death when attacked with a screwdriver.

5. It hated Tex, sensing perhaps that his knowledge of mechanics was capable of diagnosing its shortcomings.

6. It completely refused to run: (a) when the waves were high, (b) when the wind blew, (c) at night, early morning, and evening, (d) in rain, dew, or fog, (e) when the distance to be covered was more than two hundred yards. But on warm, sunny days when the weather was calm and the white beach close by—in a word, on days when it would have been a pleasure to row—the Sea-Cow started at a touch and would not stop.

7. It loved no one, trusted no one. It had no friends.

Perhaps toward the end, our observations were a little warped by emotion. Time and again as it sat on the stern with its pretty little propeller lying idly in the water, it was very close to death. And in the end, even we were infected with its malignancy and its dishonesty. We should have destroyed it, but we did not. Arriving home, we gave it a new coat of aluminum paint, spotted it at points with new red enamel, and sold it. And we might have rid the world of this mechanical cancer!

4

IT WOULD be ridiculous to suggest that ours was anything but a makeshift expedition. The owner of a boat on short charter does not look happily on any re-designing of his ship. In a month or two we could have changed the *Western Flyer* about and made her a collector's dream, but we had neither the time nor the money to do it. The low-tide period was approaching. We had on board no permanent laboratory. There was plenty of room for one in the fish-hold, but the dampness there would have rusted the instruments overnight. We had no dark-room, no permanent aquaria, no tanks for keeping animals alive, no pumps for delivering sea water. We had not even a desk except the galley table. Microscopes and cameras were put away in an empty bunk. The enameled pans for laying out animals were in a large crate lashed to the net-table aft, where it shared the space with the two skiffs. The hatch cover of the fish-hold became laboratory and aquarium, and we carried sea water in buckets to fill the pans. Another empty bunk was filled with flashlights, medicines, and the more precious chemicals. Dip-nets, wooden collecting buckets, and vials and jars in their cases were stowed in the fish-hold. The barrels of alcohol and formaldehyde were lashed firmly to the rail on deck, for all of us had, I think, a horror-thought of fifteen gallons of U.S.P. formaldehyde broken loose and burst. One achieves a respect and a distaste for formaldehyde from working with it. Fortunately, none of us had a developed formalin allergy. Our small refrigerating chamber, powered by a two-cycle gasoline engine and designed to cool sea water for circulation to living animals, began the trip on top of the deckhouse and ended back on the net-table. This unit, by the way, was not very effective, the motor being jerky and not of sufficient power. But on certain days in the Gulf it did manage to cool a little beer or perhaps more than a little, for the crew fell in joyfully with our theory that it is unwise to drink unboiled water, and boiled water isn't any good. In addition, the weather was too hot to boil water, and besides the crew wished to test this perfectly sound scientific observation thoroughly. We tested it by reducing the drinking of water to an absolute minimum.

A big pressure tube of oxygen was lashed to a deck rail, its gauges and valves wrapped in canvas. Gradually, the boat was loaded and the materials put away, some never to be taken out again. It was agreed that we should all stand wheel-watch when we were running night and day; but once in the Gulf, and working at collecting stations, the hired crew should work the boat, since we would anchor at night and run only during the daytime.

Toward the end of the preparation, a small hysteria began to build in ourselves and our friends. There were hundreds of unnecessary trips back and forth. Some materials were stowed on board with such cleverness that we never found them again. Now the whole town of Monterey was becoming fevered and festive—but not because of our going. At the end of the sardine season, canneries and boat owners provide a celebration. There is a huge barbecue on the end of the pier with free beef and beer and salad for all comers. The sardine fleet is decorated with streamers and bunting and serpentine, and the boat with the biggest season catch is queen of a strange nautical parade of boats; and every boat is an open house, receiving friends of owners and of crew. Wine flows beautifully, and the parade of boats that starts with dignity and precision sometimes ends in a turmoil. This fiesta took place on Sunday, and we were to sail on Monday morning. The *Western Flyer* was decorated like the rest with red and blue bunting and serpentine. Master and crew refused to sail before the fiesta was over. We rode in the parade of boats, some of us in the crow's-nest and some on the house. With five thousand other people we crowded on the pier and ate great hunks of meat and drank beer and heard speeches. It was the biggest barbecue the sardine men had ever given, and the potato salad was served out of washtubs. The speeches rose to a crescendo of patriotism and good feeling beyond anything Monterey had ever heard.

There should be here some mention of the permits obtained from the Mexican government. At the time of our preparation, Mexico was getting ready for a presidential election, and the apparent issues were so complex as to cause apprehension that there might be violence. The nation was a little nervous, and it seemed to us that we should be armed with permits which clearly established us as men without politics or business interests. The work we intended to do might well have seemed suspicious to some patriotic customs official or soldier—a small boat that crept to uninhabited points on a barren coast, and a party which spent its time turning over rocks. It was not likely that we could explain our job to the satisfaction of a soldier. It would seem ridiculous to the military mind to travel fifteen hundred miles for the purpose of turning over rocks on the seashore and picking up small animals, very few of which were edible; and doing all this without shooting at anyone. Besides, our equipment might have looked subversive to one who had seen the war sections of *Life* and *Pic* and *Look*. We carried no firearms except a .22-caliber pistol and a very rusty ten-gauge shotgun. But an oxygen cylinder might look too much like a torpedo to an excitable rural soldier, and some of the laboratory equipment could have had a lethal look about it. We were not afraid for ourselves, but we imagined being held in some mud *cuartel* while the good low tides went on and we missed them. In our naïveté, we considered that our State Department, having much business with the Mexican government, might include a paragraph about us in one of its letters, which would convince Mexico of our decent intentions. To this end, we wrote to the State Department explaining our project and giving a list of people who would confirm the purity of our motives. Then we waited with a childlike faith that when a thing is stated simply and evidence of its truth is included there need be no mix-up. Besides, we told ourselves, we were American citizens and the government was our servant. Alas, we did not know diplomatic procedure. In due course, we had an answer from the State Department. In language so diplomatic as to be barely intelligible it gently disabused us. In the first place, the State Department was *not* our servant, however other departments might feel about it. The State Department had little or no interest in the collection of marine invertebrates unless carried on by an institution of learning, preferably with Dr. Butler as its president. The government never made such representations for private citizens. Lastly, the State Department hoped to God we would not get into trouble and appeal to it for aid. All this was concealed in language so beautiful and incomprehensible that we began to understand why diplomats say they are "studying" a message from Japan or England or Italy. We studied this letter for the better part of one night, reduced its sentences to words, built it up again, and came out with the above-mentioned gist. "Gist" is, we imagine, a word which makes the State Department shudder with its vulgarity.

There we were, with no permits and the imaginary soldier still upset by our oxygen tube. In Mexico, certain good friends worked to get us the permits; the consul-general in San Francisco wrote letters about us, and then finally, through a friend, we got in touch with Mr. Castillo Najera, the Mexican ambassador to Washington. To our wonder there came an immediate reply from the ambassador which said there was no reason why we should not go and that he would see the permits were issued immediately. His letter said just that. There was a little sadness in us when we read it. The ambassador seemed such a good man we felt it a pity that he had no diplomatic future, that he could never get anywhere in the world of international politics. We understood his letter the first time we read it. Clearly, Mr. Castillo Najera is a misfit and a rebel. He not only wrote clearly, but he kept his word. The permits came through quickly and in order. And we wish here and now to assure this gentleman that whenever the inevitable punishment for his logic and clarity falls upon him we will gladly help him to get a new start in some other profession.

When the permits arrived, they were beautifully sealed so that even a soldier who could not read would know that if we were not what we said we were, we were at least influential enough spies and saboteurs to be out of his jurisdiction.

And so our boat was loaded, except for the fuel tanks, which we planned to fill at San Diego. Our crew entered the contests at the sardine fiesta—the skiff race, the greased-pole walk, the water-barrel tilt—and they did not win anything, but no one cared. And late in the night when the feast had died out we slept ashore for the last time, and our dreams were cluttered with things we might have forgotten. And the beer cans from the fiesta washed up and down the shore on the little brushing waves behind the breakwater.

We had planned to sail about ten o'clock on March 11, but so many people came to see us off and the leave-taking was so pleasant that it was afternoon before we could think of going. The moment or hour of leave-taking is one of the pleasantest times in human experience, for it has in it a warm sadness without loss. People who don't ordinarily like you very well are overcome with affection at leave-taking. We said good-by again and again and still could not bring ourselves to cast off the lines and start the engines. It would be good to live in a perpetual state of leave-taking, never to go nor to stay, but to remain suspended in that golden emotion of love and longing; to be missed without being gone; to be loved without satiety. How beautiful one is and how desirable; for in a few moments one will have ceased to exist. Wives and fiancées were there, melting and open. How beautiful they were too; and against the hull of the boat the beer cans from the fiesta of yesterday tapped lightly like little bells, and the sea-gulls flew around and around but did not land. There was no room for them—too many people were seeing us off. Even a few strangers were caught in the magic and came aboard and wrung our hands and went into the galley. If our medicine chest had held out we might truly never have sailed. But about twelve-thirty the last dose was prescribed and poured and taken. Only then did we realize that not only were *we* fortified against illness, but that fifty or sixty inhabitants of Monterey could look forward to a long period of good health.

The day of charter had arrived. That instrument said we would leave on the eleventh, and the master was an honest man. We ejected our guests, some forcibly. The lines were cast off. We backed and turned and wove our way out among the boats of the fishing fleet. In our rigging the streamers, the bunting, the serpentine still fluttered, and as the breakwater was cleared and the wind struck us, we seemed, to ourselves at least, a very brave and beautiful sight. The little bell buoy on the reef at Cabrillo Point was excited about it too, for the wind had freshened and the float rolled heavily and the four clappers struck the bell with a quick tempo. We stood on top of the deckhouse and watched the town of Pacific Grove slip by and dark pine-covered hills roll back on themselves as though they moved, not we.

We sat on a crate of oranges and thought what good men most biologists are, the tenors of the scientific world—temperamental, moody, lecherous, loud-laughing, and healthy. Once in a while one comes on the other kind—what used in the university to be called a "dry-ball"—but such men are not really biologists. They are the embalmers of the field, the picklers who see only the preserved form of life without any of its principle. Out of their own crusted minds they create a world wrinkled with formaldehyde. The true biologist deals with life, with teeming boisterous life, and learns something from it, learns that the first rule of life is living. The dry-balls cannot possibly learn a thing every starfish knows in the core of his soul and in the vesicles between his rays. He must, so know the starfish and the student biologist who sits at the feet of living things, proliferate in all directions. Having certain tendencies, he must move along their lines to the limit of their potentialities. And we have known biologists who did proliferate in all directions: one or two have had a little trouble about it. Your true biologist will sing you a song as loud and off-key as will a blacksmith, for he knows that morals are too often diagnostic of prostatitis and stomach ulcers. Sometimes he may proliferate a little too much in all directions, but he is as easy to kill as any other organism, and meanwhile he is very good company, and at least he does not confuse a low hormone productivity with moral ethics.

The *Western Flyer* pushed through the swells toward Point Joe, which is the southern tip of the Bay of Monterey. There was a line of white which marked the open sea, for a strong north wind was blowing, and on that reef the whistling buoy rode, roaring like a perplexed and mournful bull. On the shore road we could see the cars of our recent friends driving along keeping pace with us while they waved handkerchiefs sentimentally. We were all a little sentimental that day. We turned the buoy and cleared the reef, and as we did the boat rolled heavily and then straightened. The north wind drove down on our tail, and we headed south with the big swells growing under us and passing, so that we seemed to be standing still. A squadron of pelicans crossed our bow, flying low to the waves and acting like a train of pelicans tied together, activated by one nervous system. For they flapped their powerful wings in unison, coasted in unison. It seemed that they tipped a wavetop with their wings now and then, and certainly they flew in the troughs of the waves to save themselves from the wind. They did not look around or change direction. Pelicans seem always to know exactly where they are going. A curious sea-lion came out to look us over, a tawny, crusty old fellow with rakish mustaches and the scars of battle on his shoulders. He crossed our bow too and turned and paralleled our course, trod water, and looked at us. Then, satisfied, he snorted and cut for shore and some sea-lion appointment. They always have them, it's just a matter of getting around to keeping them.

And now the wind grew stronger and the windows of houses along the shore flashed in the declining sun. The forward guy-wire of our mast began to sing under the wind, a deep and yet penetrating tone like the lowest string of an incredible bull-fiddle. We rose on each swell and skidded on it until it passed and dropped us in the trough. And from the galley ventilator came the odor of boiling coffee, a smell that never left the boat again while we were on it.

In the evening we came back restlessly to the top of the deckhouse, and we discussed the Old Man of the Sea, who might well be a myth, except that too many people have seen him. There is some quality in man which makes him people the ocean with monsters and one wonders whether they are there or not. In one sense they are, for we continue to see them. One afternoon in the laboratory ashore we sat drinking coffee and talking with Jimmy Costello, who is a reporter on the Monterey *Herald*. The telephone rang and his city editor said that the decomposed body of a sea-serpent was washed up on the beach at Moss Landing, half-way around the Bay. Jimmy was to rush over and get pictures of it. He rushed, approached the evil-smelling monster from which the flesh was dropping. There was a note pinned to its head which said, "Don't worry about it, it's a basking shark. [Signed] Dr. Rolph Bolin of the Hopkins Marine Station." No doubt that Dr. Bolin acted kindly, for he loves true things; but his kindness was a blow to the people of Monterey. They so wanted it to be a sea-serpent. Even we hoped it would be. When sometime a true sea-serpent, complete and undecayed, is found or caught, a shout of triumph will go through the world. "There, you see," men will say, "I knew they were there all the time. I just had a feeling they were there." Men really need sea-monsters in their personal oceans. And the Old Man of the Sea is one of these. In Monterey you can find many people who have seen him. Tiny Colletto has seen him close up and can draw a crabbed sketch of him. He is very large. He stands up in the water, three or four feet emerged above the waves, and watches an approaching boat until it comes too close, and then he sinks slowly out of sight. He looks somewhat like a tremendous diver, with large eyes and fur shaggily hanging from him. So far, he has not been photographed. When he is, probably Dr. Bolin will identify him and another beautiful story will be shattered. For this reason we rather hope he is never photographed, for if the Old Man of the Sea should turn out to be some great malformed sea-lion, a lot of people would feel a sharp personal loss—a Santa Claus loss. And the ocean would be none the better for it. For the ocean, deep and black in the depths, is like the low dark levels of our minds in which the dream symbols incubate and sometimes rise up to sight like the Old Man of the Sea. And even if the symbol vision be horrible, it is there and it is ours. An ocean without its unnamed monsters would be like a completely dreamless sleep. Sparky and Tiny do not question the Old Man of the Sea, for they have looked at him. Nor do we question him because we know he is there. We would accept the testimony of these boys sufficiently to send a man to his death for murder, and we know they saw this monster and that they described him as they saw him.

We have thought often of this mass of sea-memory, or sea-thought, which lives deep in the mind. If one ask for a description of the unconscious, even the answer-symbol will usually be in terms of a dark water into which the light descends only a short distance. And we have thought how the human fetus has, at one stage of its development, vestigial gill-slits. If the gills are a component of the developing human, it is not unreasonable to suppose a parallel or concurrent mind or psyche development. If there be a life-memory strong enough to leave its symbol in vestigial gills, the preponderantly aquatic symbols in the individual unconscious might well be indications of a group psyche-memory which is the foundation of the whole unconscious. And what things must be there, what monsters, what enemies, what fear of dark and pressure, and of prey! There are numbers of examples wherein even invertebrates seem to remember and to react to stimuli no longer violent enough to cause the reaction. Perhaps, next to that of the sea, the strongest memory in us is that of the moon. But moon and sea and tide are one. Even now, the tide establishes a measurable, although minute, weight differential. For example, the steamship *Majestic* loses about fifteen pounds of its weight under a full moon.* According to a theory of George Darwin (son of Charles Darwin), in pre-

*Marmer, *The Tide*, 1926, p. 26.

Cambrian times, more than a thousand million years ago, the tides were tremendous; and the weight differential would have been correspondingly large. The moon-pull must have been the most important single environmental factor of littoral animals. Displacement and body weight then must certainly have decreased and increased tremendously with the rotation and phases of the moon, particularly if the orbit was at that time elliptic. The sun's reinforcement was probably slighter, relatively.

Consider, then, the effect of a decrease in pressure on gonads turgid with eggs or sperm, already almost bursting and awaiting the slight extra pull to discharge. (Note also the dehiscence of ova through the body walls of the polychaete worms. These ancient worms have their ancestry rooted in the Cambrian and they are little changed.) Now if we admit for the moment the potency of this tidal effect, we have only to add the concept of inherited psychic pattern we call "instinct" to get an inkling of the force of the lunar rhythm so deeply rooted in marine animals and even in higher animals and in man.

When the fishermen find the Old Man rising in the pathways of their boats, they may be experiencing a reality of past and present. This may not be a hallucination; in fact, it is little likely that it is. The interrelations are too delicate and too complicated. Tidal effects are mysterious and dark in the soul, and it may well be noted that even today the effect of the tides is more valid and strong and widespread than is generally supposed. For instance, it has been reported that radio reception is related to the rise and fall of Labrador tides,* and that there may be a relation between tidal rhythms and the recently observed fluctuations in the speed of light.† One could safely predict that all physiological processes correspondingly might be shown to be influenced by the tides, could we but read the indices with sufficient delicacy.

It appears that the physical evidence for this theory of George Darwin is more or less hypothetical, not in fact, but by interpretation, and that critical reasoning could conceivably throw out the whole process and with it the biologic con-

---

*Science Supplement, Vol. 80, No. 2069, p. 7, Aug. 24, 1934.
†Science, Vol. 81, No. 2091, p. 101, Jan. 25, 1935.

notations, because of unknown links and factors. Perhaps it should read the other way around. The animals themselves would seem to offer a striking confirmation to the tidal theory of cosmogony. One is almost forced to postulate some such theory if he would account causally for this primitive impress. It would seem far-fetched to attribute the strong lunar effects actually observable in breeding animals to the present fairly weak tidal forces only, or to coincidence. There is tied up to the most primitive and powerful racial or collective instinct a rhythm sense or "memory" which affects everything and which in the past was probably more potent than it is now. It would at least be more plausible to attribute these profound effects to devastating and instinct-searing tidal influences active during the formative times of the early race history of organisms; and whether or not any mechanism has been discovered or is discoverable to carry on this imprint through the germ plasms, the fact remains that the imprint is there. The imprint is in us and in Sparky and in the ship's master, in the palolo worm, in mussel worms, in chitons, and in the menstrual cycle of women. The imprint lies heavily on our dreams and on the delicate threads of our nerves, and if this seems to come a long way from sea-serpents and the Old Man of the Sea, actually it has not come far at all. The harvest of symbols in our minds seems to have been planted in the soft rich soil of our pre-humanity. Symbol, the serpent, the sea, and the moon might well be only the signal light that the psycho-physiologic warp exists.

5

THE EVENING came down on us and as it did the wind dropped but the tall waves remained, not topped with whitecaps any more. A few porpoises swam near and looked at us and swam away. The watches changed and we ate our first meal aboard, the cold wreckage of farewell snacks, and when our watch was done we were reluctant to go down to the bunks. We put on heavier coats and hung about the long bench where the helmsman sat. The little light on the compass card and the port and starboard lights were our outmost boundaries. Then we passed Point Sur and the waves flattened out into a ground-swell and increased in speed. Tony the master said, "Of course, it's always that way. The point draws the waves." Another might say, "The waves come greatly to the point," and in both statements there would be a good primitive exposition of the relation between giver and receiver. This relation would be through waves; wave to wave to wave, each of which is connected by torsion to its inshore fellow and touches it enough, although it has gone before, to be affected by its torsion. And so on and on to the shore, and to the point where the last wave, if you think from the sea, and the first if you think from the shore, touches and breaks. And it is important where you are thinking from.

The sharp, painful stars were out and bright enough to make the few whitecaps gleam against the dark surrounding water. From the wheel the little flag-jack on the peak stood against the course and swung back and forth over the horizon stars, blotting out each one as it passed. We tried to cover a star with the flag-jack and keep it covered, but this was impossible; no one could do that, not even Tony. But Tony, who knew his boat so well, could feel the yaw before it happened, could correct an error before it occurred. This is no longer reason or thought. One achieves the same feeling on a horse he knows well; one almost feels the horse's impulse in one's knees, and knows, but does not know, not only when the horse will shy, but the direction of his jump. The landsman, or the man who has been long ashore, is clumsy with the wheel, and his steering in a heavy sea is difficult. One grows tense on the wheel, particularly if someone like Tony is watching sardonically. Then keeping the compass card steady becomes impossible and the swing, a variable arc from two to ten degrees. And as weariness creeps up it is not uncommon to forget which way to turn the wheel to make the compass card swing back where you want it. The wheel turns only two ways, left or right. The fact of the lag, and the boat swinging rapidly so that a slow correcting allows it to pass the course and err on the other side, becomes a maddening thing when Tony the magnificent sits beside you. He does not correct you, he doesn't even speak. But Tony loves the truth, and the course is the truth. If the helmsman is off course he is telling a lie to Tony. And as the course projects, hypothetically, straight off the bow and around the world, so the wake drags out behind, a tattler on the conduct of the steersman. If one should steer mathematically perfectly, which is of course impossible, the wake will be a straight line; but even if, when drawn, it may have been straight, it bends to currents and to waves, and your true effort is wiped out. There is probably a unified-field hypothesis available in navigation as in all things. The internal factors would be the boat, the controls, the engine, and the crew, but chiefly the will and intent of the master, sub-headed with his conditioning experience, his sadness and ambitions and pleasures. The external factors would be the ocean with its bordering land, the waves and currents and the winds with their constant and varying effect in modifying the influence of the rudder against the changing tensions exerted on it.

If you steer *toward an object*, you cannot perfectly and indefinitely steer directly at it. You must steer to one side, or run it down; but you can steer exactly at a compass point, indefinitely. That does not change. Objects achieved are merely its fulfillment. In going toward a headland, for example, you can steer directly for it while you are at a distance, only changing course as you approach. Or you may set your compass course for the point and correct it by vision when you approach. The working out of the ideal into the real is here—the relationship between inward and outward, microcosm to macrocosm. The compass simply represents the ideal, present but unachievable, and sight-steering a compromise with perfection which allows your boat to exist at all.

In the development of navigation as thought and emotion—and it must have been a slow, stumbling process frightening to its innovators and horrible to the fearful—how often must the questing mind have wished for a constant and unvarying point on the horizon to steer by. How simple if a star floated unchangeably to measure by. On clear nights such a star is there, but it is not trustworthy and the course of it is an arc. And the happy discovery of Stella Polaris—which, although it too shifts very minutely in an arc, is constant relatively—was encouraging. Stella Polaris will get you there. And so to the crawling minds Stella Polaris must have been like a very goddess of constancy, a star to love and trust.

What we have wanted always is an *unchangeable*, and we have found that only a compass point, a thought, an individual ideal, does not change—Schiller's and Goethe's *Ideal* to be worked out in terms of reality. And from such a thing as this, Beethoven writes a Ninth Symphony to Schiller's *Ode to Joy*.

A tide pool has been called a world under a rock, and so it might be said of navigation, "It is the world within the horizon."

Of steering, the external influences to be overcome are in the nature of oscillations; they are of short or long periods or both. The mean levels of the extreme ups and downs of the oscillations symbolize opposites in a Hegelian sense. No wonder, then, that in physics the symbol of oscillation, $\sqrt{-1}$, is fundamental and primitive and ubiquitous, turning up in every equation.

6

March 12

IN THE morning we had come to the Santa Barbara Channel and the water was slick and gray, flowing in long smooth swells, and over it, close down, there hung a little mist so that the sea-birds flew in and out of sight. Then, breaking the water as though they swam in an obscure mirror, the porpoises surrounded us. They really came to us. We have seen them change course to join us, these curious animals. The Japanese will eat them, but rarely will Occidentals touch them. Of our crew, Tiny and Sparky, who loved to catch every manner of fish, to harpoon any swimming thing, would have nothing to do with porpoises. "They cry so," Sparky said, "when they are hurt, they cry to break your heart." This is rather a difficult thing to understand; a dying cow cries too, and a stuck pig raises his protesting voice piercingly and few hearts are broken by those cries. But a porpoise cries like a child in sorrow and pain. And we wonder whether the general sea-man's real affection for porpoises might not be more compli-cated than the simple fear of hearing them cry. The nature of the animal might parallel certain traits in ourselves—the out-rageous boastfulness of porpoises, their love of play, their joy in speed. We have watched them for many hours, making de-signs in the water, diving and rising and then seeming to turn over to see if they are watched. In bursts of speed they hump their backs and the beating tails take power from the whole body. Then they slow down and only the muscles near the tails are strained. They break the surface, and the blow-holes, like eyes, open and gasp in air and then close like eyes before they submerge. Suddenly they seem to grow tired of playing; the bodies hump up, the incredible tails beat, and instantly they are gone.

The mist lifted from the water but the oily slickness re-mained, and it was like new snow for keeping the impressions of what had happened there. Near to us was the greasy mess where a school of sardines had been milling, and on it the feathers of gulls which had come to join the sardines and, having fed hugely, had sat on the water and combed them-selves in comfort. A Japanese liner passed us, slipping quickly through the smooth water, and for a long time we rocked in her wake. It was a long lazy day, and when the night came we passed the lights of Los Angeles with its many little dan-gling towns. The searchlights of the fleet at San Pedro combed the sea constantly, and one powerful glaring beam crept several miles and lay on us so brightly that it threw our shadows on the exhaust stack.

In the early morning before daylight we came into the har-bor at San Diego, in through the narrow passage, and we followed the lights on a changing course to the pier. All about us war bustled, although we had no war; steel and thunder, powder and men—the men preparing thoughtlessly, like dead men, to destroy things. The planes roared over in formation and the submarines were quiet and ominous. There is no play-fulness in a submarine. The military mind must limit its think-ing to be able to perform its function at all. Thus, in talking with a naval officer who had won a target competition with big naval guns, we asked, "Have you thought what happens in a little street when one of your shells explodes, of the families torn to pieces, a thousand generations influenced when you signaled *Fire?*" "Of course not," he said. "Those shells travel so far that you couldn't possibly see where they land." And he was quite correct. If he could really see where they land and what they do, if he could really feel the power in his dropped hand and the waves radiating out from his gun, he would not be able to perform his function. He himself would be the weak point of his gun. But by not seeing, by insisting that it be a problem of ballistics and trajectory, he is a good gunnery officer. And he is too humble to take the responsibility for thinking. The whole structure of his world would be endangered if he permitted himself to think. The pieces must stick within their pattern or the whole thing collapses and the design is gone. We wonder whether in the present pattern the pieces are not straining to fall out of line; whether the paradoxes of our times are not finally mounting to a conclusion of ridiculousness that will make the whole structure collapse. For the paradoxes are becoming so great that leaders of people must be less and less intelligent to stand their own leadership.

The port of San Diego in that year was loaded with explosives and the means of transporting and depositing them on some enemy as yet undetermined. The men who directed this mechanism were true realists. They knew an enemy would emerge, and when one did, they had explosives to deposit on him.

In San Diego we filled the fuel tanks and the water tanks. We filled the icebox and took on the last perishable foods, bread and eggs and fresh meat. These would not last long, for when the ice was gone only the canned goods and the foods we could take from the sea would be available. We tied up to the pier all day and a night; got our last haircuts and ate broiled steaks.

This little expedition had become tremendously important to us; we felt a little as though we were dying. Strangers came to the pier and stared at us and small boys dropped on our deck like monkeys. Those quiet men who always stand on piers asked where we were going and when we said, "To the Gulf of California," their eyes melted with longing, they wanted to go so badly. They were like the men and women who stand about airports and railroad stations; they want to go away, and most of all they want to go away from themselves. For they do not know that they would carry their globes of boredom with them wherever they went. One man on the pier who wanted to participate made sure he would be allowed to cast us off, and he waited at the bow line for a long time. Finally he got the call and he cast off the bow line and ran back and cast off the stern line; then he stood and watched us pull away and he wanted very badly to go.

Below the Mexican border the water changes color; it takes on a deep ultramarine blue—a washtub bluing blue, intense and seeming to penetrate deep into the water; the fishermen call it "tuna water." By Friday we were off Point Baja. This is the region of the sea-turtle and the flying fish. Tiny and Sparky put out the fishing lines, and they stayed out during the whole trip.

Sparky Enea and Tiny Colletto grew up together in Monterey and they were bad little boys and very happy about it. It is said lightly that the police department had a special detail to supervise the growth and development of Tiny and Sparky. They are short and strong and nearly inseparable. An impulse seems to strike both of them at once. Let Tiny make a date with a girl and Sparky make a date with another girl—it then becomes necessary for Tiny, by connivance and trickery, to get Sparky's girl. But it is all right, since Sparky has been moving mountains to get Tiny's girl.

These two shared a watch, and on their watches we often went strangely off course and no one ever knew why. The compass had a way of getting out of hand so that the course invariably arced inshore. These two rigged the fishing lines with feathered artificial squid. Where the tackle was tied to the stays on either side, they looped the line and inset automobile inner tubes. For the tuna strikes so hard that something must give, and if the line does not break, the jaws tear off, so great is the combination of boat speed and tuna speed. The inner tube solves this problem by taking up the strain of the first great strike until direction and speed are equalized.

When Sparky and Tiny had the watch they took care of the fishing, and when the rubber tubes snapped and shook, one of them climbed down to take in the fish. If it were a large one, or a sharp-fighting fish, hysterical shrieks came from the fisherman. Whereupon the one left at the wheel came down to help and the wheel swung free. We wondered if this habit might not have caused the wonderful course we sailed sometimes. It is not beyond reason that coming back to the wheel, arguing and talking, they might have forgotten the set course and made one up almost as good. "Surely," they might think, "that is kinder and better than waking up the master to ask the course again, and five or ten degrees isn't so important when you aren't going far." If Tony loved the truth for itself, he was more than counterbalanced by Sparky and Tiny. They have little faith in truth, or, for that matter, in untruth. The police who had overseen their growing up had given them a nice appreciation of variables; they tested everything to find out whether it were true or not. In a like manner they tested the compass for a weakness they suspected was in it. And if Tony should say, "You are way off course," they could answer, "Well, we didn't hit anything, did we?"

7

March 16

BY TWO P.M. we were in the region of Magdalena Bay. The sea was still oily and smooth, and a light lacy fog lay on the water. The flying fish leaped from the forcing bow and flew off to right and left. It seemed, although this has not been verified, that they could fly farther at night than during the day. If, as is supposed, the flight is terminated when the flying fins dry in the air, this observation would seem to be justified, for at night they would not dry so quickly. Again, the whole thing might be a trick of our eyes. Often we played the searchlight on a fish in flight. The strangeness of light may have made the flight seem longer.

Tiny is a natural harpooner; often he had stood poised on the bow, holding the lance, but thus far nothing had appeared except porpoises, and these he would not strike. But now the sea-turtles began to appear in numbers. He stood for a long time waiting, and finally he drove his lance into one of them. Sparky promptly left the wheel, and the two of them pulled in a small turtle, about two and a half feet long. It was a tortoise-shell turtle.* Now we were able to observe the tender hearts of our crew. The small arrow-harpoon had penetrated the fairly soft shell, then turned sideways in the body. They hung the turtle to a stay where it waved its flippers helplessly and stretched its old wrinkled neck and gnashed its parrot beak. The small dark eyes had a quizzical pained look and a quantity of blood emerged from the pierced shell. Suddenly remorse seized Tiny; he wanted to put the animal out of its pain. He lowered the turtle to the deck and brought out an ax. With his first stroke he missed the animal entirely and sank the blade into the deck, but on his second stroke he severed the head from the body. And now a strange and terrible bit of knowledge came to Tiny; turtles are very hard to kill. Cutting off the head seems to have little immediate effect. This turtle was as lively as it had been, and a large quantity of very red blood poured from the trunk of the neck. The flippers waved frantically and there was none of the constricting motion of a decapitated animal. We were eager to examine this turtle and we put Tiny's emotion aside for the moment. There were two barnacle bases on the shell and many hydroids which we preserved immediately. In the hollow beside the small tail were two pelagic crabs† of the square-fronted group, a male and a female; and from the way in which they hid themselves in the fold of turtle skin they seemed to be at home there. We were eager to examine the turtle's intestinal tract, both to find the food it had been eating and to look for possible tapeworms. To this end we sawed the shell open at the sides and opened the body cavity. From gullet to anus the digestive tract was crammed with small bright-red rock-lobsters‡; a few of those nearest the gullet were whole enough to preserve. The gullet itself was lined with hard, sharp-pointed spikes, not of bone, but of a specialized tissue hard enough to macerate the

* *Eretmochelys imbricata* (Linn.). Nelson, but usually known as *Chelone imbricata.*

† *Planes minutus* (Linn.).

‡ *Pleuroncodes planipes* Stimpson.

small crustacea the turtle fed on. A curious peristalsis of the gullet (still observable, since even during dissection the reflexes were quite active) brought these points near together in a grinding motion and at the same time passed the increasingly macerated material downward toward the stomach. A good adaptation to food supply by structure, or perhaps vice versa. The heart continued to beat regularly. We removed it and placed it in a jar of salt water, where it continued to pulse for several hours; and twenty-four hours later, when it had apparently stopped, a touch with a glass rod caused it to pulse several times before it relaxed again. Tiny did not like this process of dissection. He wants his animals to die and be dead when he chops them; and when we cut up the muscular tissue, intending to cook it, and even the little cubes of white meat responded to touch, Tiny swore that he would give up sea-turtles and he never again tried to harpoon one. In his mind they joined the porpoises as protected animals. Probably he identified himself with the writhing tissue of the turtle and was unable to see it objectively.

The cooking was a failure. We boiled the meat, and later threw out the evil-smelling mess. (Subsequently, we discovered that one has to know how to cook a turtle.) But the turtle shell we wished to preserve. We scraped it as well as we could and salted it. Later we hung it deep in the water, hoping the isopods would clean it for us, but they never did. Finally we impregnated it with formaldehyde, then let it dry in the sun, and after all that we threw it away. It was never pretty and we never loved it.

During the night we crossed a school of bonito,* fast, clean-cut, beautiful fish of the mackerel family. The boys on watch caught five of them on the lines and during the process we got quite badly off course. We tried to take moving pictures of the color and of the color-pattern change which takes place in these fish during their death struggles. In the flurry when they beat the deck with their tails, the colors pulse and fade and brighten and fade again, until, when they are dead, a new pattern is visible. We wished to take color photographs of many of the animals because of the impossibility of retain-

* *Sarda chiliensis* (Girard).

ing color in preserved specimens, and also because many animals, in fact most animals, have one color when they are alive and another when they are dead. However, none of us was expert in photography and we had a very mediocre success. The bonitos were good to eat, and Sparky fried big thick fillets for us.

That night we netted two small specimens of the northern flying fish.* Sparky, when we were looking at Barnhart's *Marine Fishes of Southern California*, saw a drawing of a lantern-fish entitled "*Monoceratias acanthias* after Gilbert" and he asked, "What's he after Gilbert for?"

This smooth blue water runs out of time very quickly, and a kind of dream sets in. Then a floating box cast overboard from some steamship becomes a fascinating thing, and it is nearly impossible not to bring the wheel over and go to pick it up. A new kind of porpoise began to appear, gray, where the northern porpoise had been dark brown. They were slim and very fast, the noses long and paddle-shaped. They move about in large schools, jumping out of the water and seeming to have a very good time. The abundance of life here gives one an exuberance, a feeling of fullness and richness. The playing porpoises, the turtles, the great schools of fish which ruffle the water surface like a quick breeze, make for excitement. Sometimes in the distance we have seen a school of jumping tuna, and as they threw themselves clear of the water, the sun glittered on them for a moment. The sea here swarms with life, and probably the ocean bed is equally rich. Microscopically, the water is crowded with plankton. This is the tuna water—life water. It is complete from plankton to gray porpoises. The turtle was complete with the little almost-commensal crab living under his tail and with barnacles and hydroids riding on his back. The pelagic rock-lobsters† littered the ocean with red spots. There was food everywhere. Everything ate everything else with a furious exuberance.

About five P.M. on the sixteenth, seventy miles north of Point Lazaro, we came upon hosts of the red rock-lobsters on the surface, brilliant red and beautiful against the ultramarine of the water. There was no protective coloration here—a

Cypselurus californicus.
†*Pleuroncodes.*

greater contrast could not have been chosen. The water seemed almost solid with the little red crustacea, called "*langustina*" by the Mexicans. According to Stimpson, on March 8, 1859, a number of them were thrown ashore at Monterey in California, many hundreds of miles from their usual range. It was probably during one of those queer cycles when the currents do amazing things. We idled our engine and crept slowly along catching up the *langustina* in dip-nets. We put them in white porcelain pans and took some color moving pictures of them—some of the few good moving pictures, incidentally, made during the whole trip. In the pans we saw that these animals do not swim rapidly, but rather wriggle and crawl through the water. Finally, we immersed them in fresh water and when they were dead, preserved them in alcohol, which promptly removed their brilliant color.

8

March 17

AT TWO A.M. we passed Point Lazaro, one of the reputedly dangerous places of the world, like Cedros Passage, or like Cape Horn, where the weather is always bad even when it is good elsewhere. There is a sense of relief when one is safely past these half-mythical places, for they are not only stormy but treacherous, and again the atavistic fear arises— the Scylla-Charybdis fear that made our ancestors people such places with monsters and enter them only after prayer and propitiation. It was only reasonably rough when we passed, and immediately south the water was very calm. About five in the morning we came upon an even denser concentration of the little red *Pleuroncodes*, and we stopped again and took a great many of them. While we netted the *langustina*, a skip-jack struck the line and we brought him in and had him for breakfast. During the meal we said the fish was *Katsuwonus pelamis*, and Sparky said it was a skipjack because he was eating it and he was quite sure he would not eat *Katsuwonus pelamis* ever. A few hours later we caught two small dolphins,* startlingly beautiful fish of pure gold, pulsing and fading and changing colors. These fish are very widely distributed.

We were coming now toward the end of our day-and-night running; the engine had never paused since we left San Diego except for idling the little time while we took the *langustina*. The coastline of the Peninsula slid along, brown and desolate and dry with strange flat mountains and rocks torn by dryness, and the heat shimmer hung over the land even in March. Tony had kept us well offshore, and only now we approached closer to land, for we would arrive at Cape San Lucas in the night, and from then on we planned to run only in the daytime. Some collecting stations we had projected, like Pulmo Reef and La Paz and Angeles Bay, but except for those, we planned to stop wherever the shore looked interesting. Even this little trip of ninety hours, though, had grown long, and we were glad to be getting to the end of it. The dry hills were red gold that afternoon and in the night no one left the top of the deckhouse. The Southern Cross was well above the horizon, and the air was warm and pleasant. Tony spent a long time in the galley going over the charts. He had been to Cape San Lucas once before. Around ten o'clock we saw the lighthouse on the false cape. The night was extremely dark when we rounded the end; the great tall rocks called "The Friars" were blackly visible. The *Coast Pilot* spoke of a light on the end of the San Lucas pier, but we could see no light. Tony edged the boat slowly into the dark harbor. Once a flashlight showed for a moment on the shore and then went out. It was after midnight, and of course there would be no light in a Mexican house at such a time. The searchlight on our deckhouse seemed to be sucked up by the darkness. Sparky on the bow with the leadline found deep water, and we moved slowly in, stopping and drifting and sounding. And then suddenly there was the beach, thirty feet away, with little waves breaking on it, and still we had eight fathoms on the lead. We backed away a little and dropped the anchor and waited until it took a firm grip. Then the engine stopped, and we sat for a long time on the deckhouse. The sweet smell of the land blew out to us on a warm wind, a smell of sand verbena and

* *Coryphaena equisetis* Linn.

grass and mangrove. It is so quickly forgotten, this land smell. We know it so well on shore that the nose forgets it, but after a few days at sea the odor memory pattern is lost so that the first land smell strikes a powerful emotional nostalgia, very sharp and strangely dear.

In the morning the black mystery of the night was gone and the little harbor was shining and warm. The tuna cannery against the gathering rocks of the point and a few houses along the edge of the beach were the only habitations visible. And with the day came the answer to the lightlessness of the night before. The *Coast Pilot* had not been wrong. There is indeed a light on the end of the cannery pier, but since the electricity is generated by the cannery engine, and since the cannery engine runs only in the daytime, so the light burns only in the daytime. With the arrived day, this light came on and burned bravely until dusk, when it went off again. But the *Coast Pilot* was absolved, it had not lied. Even Tony, who had been a little bitter the night before, was forced to revise his first fierceness. And perhaps it was a lesson to Tony in exact thinking, like those carefully worded puzzles in joke books; the *Pilot* said a light burned—it only neglected to say when, and we ourselves supplied the fallacy.

The great rocks on the end of the Peninsula are almost literary. They are a fitting Land's End, standing against the sea, the end of a thousand miles of peninsula and mountain. Good Hope is this way too, and perhaps we take some of our deep feelings of termination from these things, and they make our symbols. The Friars stood high and protective against an interminable sea.

Clavigero, a Jesuit monk, came to the Point and the Peninsula over two hundred years ago. We quote from the Lake and Gray translation of his history of Lower California,* page fifteen: "This Cape is its southern terminus, the Red River [Colorado] is the eastern limit, and the harbor of San Diego, situated at 33 degrees north latitude and about 156 degrees longitude, can be called its western limit. To the north and the northeast it borders on the countries of barbarous nations little known on the coasts and not at all in the interior. To

*Stanford University Press, 1937.

the west it has the Pacific Sea and on the east the Gulf of California, already called the Red Sea because of its similarity to the Red Sea, and the Sea of Cortés, named in honor of the famous conqueror of Mexico who had it discovered and who navigated it. The length of the Peninsula is about 10 degrees, but its width varies from 30 to 70 miles and more.

"The name, California," Clavigero goes on, "was applied to a single port in the beginning, but later it was extended to mean all the Peninsula. Some geographers have even taken the liberty of comprising under this denomination New Mexico, the country of the Apaches, and other regions very remote from the true California and which have nothing to do with it."

Clavigero says of its naming, "The origin of this name is not known, but it is believed that the conqueror, Cortés, who pretended to have some knowledge of Latin, named the harbor, where he put in, *'Callida fornax'* because of the great heat which he felt there; and that either he himself or some one of the many persons who accompanied him formed the name California from these two words. If this conjecture be not true, it is at least credible."

We like Clavigero for these last words. He was a careful man. The observations set down in his history of Baja California are surprisingly correct, and if not all true, they are at least all credible. He always gives one his choice. Perhaps his Jesuit training is never more evident than in this. "If you believe this," he says in effect, "perhaps you are not right, but at least you are not a fool."

Lake and Gray include an interesting footnote in their translation. "The famous corsair, Drake, called California 'New Albion' in honor of his native land. Father Scherer, a German Jesuit, and M. de Fer, a French geographer, used the name 'Carolina Island' to designate California, which name began to be used in the time of Charles II, King of Spain, when that Peninsula was considered an island, but these and other names were soon forgotten and that given it by the conqueror, Cortés, prevailed."

And in a second footnote, Lake and Gray continue, "We shall add the opinion of the learned ex-Jesuit, Don José Campoi, on the etymology of the name, 'California,' or 'Californias' as others say. This Father believes that the said name is composed of the Spanish word *'Cala'* which means a small cove of the sea, and the latin word *'fornix'* which means an arch; because there is a small cove at the cape of San Lucas on the western side of which there overhangs a rock pierced in such a way that in the upper part of that great opening is seen an arch formed so perfectly that it appears made by human skill. Therefore Cortés, noticing the cove and arch, and understanding Latin, probably gave to that port the name 'California' or *Cala-y-fornix*, speaking half Spanish and half Latin.

"To these conjectures we could add a third one, composed of both, by saying that the name is derived from *Cala*, as Campoi thinks, and *fornax*, as the author believes, because of the cove, and the heat which Cortés felt there, and that the latter might have called that place *Cala, y fornax*." This ends the footnote.

Our feeling about this, and all the erudite discussion of the origin of this and other names, is that none of these is true. Names attach themselves to places and stick or fall away. When men finally go to live in Antarctica it is unlikely that they will ever speak of the Rockefeller Mountains or use the names designated by breakfast food companies. More likely a name emerges almost automatically from a place as well as from a man and the relationship between name and thing is very close. In the naming of places in the West this has seemed apparent. In this connection there are two examples: in the Sierras there are two little mountains which were called by the early settlers "Maggie's Bubs." This name was satisfactory and descriptive, but it seemed vulgar to later and more delicate lovers of nature, who tried to change the name a number of times and failing, in usage at least, finally surrendered and called them "The Maggies," explaining that it was an Indian name. In the same way Dog ----- Point (and I am delicate only for those same nature lovers) has had finally to be called in print "The Dog." It does not look like a dog, but it does look like that part of a dog which first suggested its name. However, anyone seeing this point immediately reverts to the designation which was anatomically accurate and strangely satisfying to the name-giving faculty. And this name-giving faculty is very highly developed and deeply rooted in our atavistic magics. To name a thing has always been to make it familiar and therefore a little less dangerous to us. "Tree" the abstract may harbor some evil until it has a name, but once having a name one can cope with it. A tree is not dangerous, but the forest is. Among primitives sometimes evil is escaped by never mentioning the name, as in Malaysia, where one never mentions a tiger by name for fear of calling him. Among others, as even among ourselves, the giving of a name establishes a familiarity which renders the thing impotent. It is interesting to see how some scientists and philosophers, who are an emotional and fearful group, are able to protect themselves against fear. In a modern scene, when the horizons stretch out and your philosopher is likely to fall off the world like a Dark Ages mariner, he can save himself by establishing a taboo-box which he may call "mysticism" or "supernaturalism" or "radicalism." Into this box he can throw all those thoughts which frighten him and thus be safe from them. But in geographic naming it seems almost as though the place contributed something to its own name. As Tony says, "The point draws the waves"—we say, "The place draws the name." It doesn't matter what California means; what does matter is that with all the names bestowed upon this place, "California" has seemed right to those who have seen it. And the meaningless word "California" has completely routed all the "New Albions" and "Carolinas" from the scene.

The strangest case of nicknaming we know concerns a man whose first name is Copeland. In three different parts of the country where he has gone, not knowing anyone, he has been called first "Copenhagen" and then "Hagen." This has happened automatically. He is Hagen. We don't know what quality of Hagen-ness he has, but there must be some. Why not "Copen" or "Cope"? It is never that. He is invariably Hagen. This, we realize, has become mystical, and anyone who wishes may now toss the whole thing into his taboo-box and slam the lid down on it.

The tip of the Cape at San Lucas, with the huge gray Friars standing up on the end, has behind the rocks a little beach which is a small boy's dream of pirates. It seems the perfect place to hide and from which to dart out in a pinnace on the shipping of the world; a place to which to bring the gold bars and jewels and beautiful ladies, all of which are invariably carried by the shipping of the world. And this little beach must so have appealed to earlier men, for the names of pirates are still in the rock, and the pirate ships did dart out of here and did come back. But now in back of the Friars on the beach there is a great pile of decaying hammer-head sharks, the livers torn out and the fish left to rot. Some day, and that soon, the more mature piracy which has abandoned the pinnace for the coast gun will stud this point with gray monsters and will send against the shipping of the Gulf, not little bands of ragged men, but projectiles filled with TNT. And from that piracy no jewels or beautiful ladies will come back to the beach behind the rocks.

On that first morning we cleaned ourselves well and shaved while we waited for the Mexican officials to come out and give us the right to land. They were late in coming, for they had to find their official uniforms, and they too had to shave. Few boats put in here. It would not be well to waste the occasion of the visit of even a fishing boat like ours. It was noon before the well-dressed men in their sun helmets came down to the beach and were rowed out to us. They were armed with the .45-caliber automatics which everywhere in Mexico designate officials. And they were armed also with the courtesy which is unique in official Mexico. No matter what they do to you, they are nice about it. We soon learned the routine in other ports as well as here. Everyone who has or can borrow a uniform comes aboard—the collector of customs in a washed and shiny uniform; the business agent in a business suit having about him what Tiny calls "a double-breasted look"; then soldiers if there are any; and finally the Indians, who row the boat and rarely have uniforms. They come over the side like ambassadors. We shake hands all around. The galley has been prepared: coffee is ready and perhaps a drop of rum. Cigarettes are presented and then comes the ceremonial of the match. In Mexico cigarettes are cheap, but matches are not. If a man wishes to honor you, he lights your cigarette, and if you have given him a cigarette, he must so honor you. But having lighted your cigarette and his, the match is still burning and not being used. Anyone may now make use of this match. On a street, strangers who have been wishing for a light come up quickly and light from your match, bow, and pass on.

We were impatient for the officials, and this time we did not have to wait long. It developed that the Governor of the southern district had very recently been to Cape San Lucas and just before that a yacht had put in. This simplified matters, for, having recently used them, the officials knew exactly where to find their uniforms, and, having found them, they did not, as sometimes happens, have to send them to be laundered before they could come aboard. About noon they trooped to the beach, scattering the pigs and Mexican vultures which browsed happily there. They filled the rowboat until the gunwales just missed dipping, and majestically they came alongside. We conducted the ceremony of clearing with some dignity, for if we spoke to them in very bad Spanish, they in turn honored us with very bad English. They cleared us, drank coffee, smoked, and finally left, promising to come back. Much as we had enjoyed them, we were impatient, for the tide was dropping and the exposed rocks looked very rich with animal life.

All the time we were indulging in courtliness there had been light gunfire on the cliffs, where several men were shooting at black cormorants; and it developed that everyone in Cape San Lucas hates cormorants. They are the flies in a perfect ecological ointment. The cannery cans tuna; the entrails and cuttings of the tuna are thrown into the water from the end of the pier. This refuse brings in schools of small fish which are netted and used for bait to catch tuna. This closed and tight circle is interfered with by the cormorants, who try to get at the bait-fish. They dive and catch fish, but also they drive the schools away from the pier out of easy reach of the baitmen. Thus they are considered interlopers, radicals, subversive forces against the perfect and God-set balance on Cape San Lucas. And they are rightly slaughtered, as all radicals should be. As one of our number remarked, "Why, pretty soon they'll want to vote."

Finally we could go. We unpacked the Hansen Sea-Cow and fastened it on the back of the skiff. This was our first use of the Sea-Cow. The shore was very close and we were able just by pulling on the starter rope to spin the propeller enough to get us to shore. The Sea-Cow did not run that day but it seemed to enjoy having its flywheel spun.

The shore-collecting equipment usually consisted of a number of small wrecking bars; wooden fish-kits with handles; quart jars with screw caps; and many glass tubes. These tubes are invaluable for small and delicate animals: the chance of bringing them back uninjured is greatly increased if each individual, or at least only a few of like species, are kept in separate containers. We filled our pockets with these tubes. The soft animals must never be put in the same container with any of the livelier crabs, for these, when restrained or inhibited in any way, go into paroxysms of rage and pinch everything at random, even each other; sometimes even themselves.

The exposed rocks had looked rich with life under the lowering tide, but they were more than that: they were ferocious with life. There was an exuberant fierceness in the littoral here, a vital competition for existence. Everything seemed speeded-up; starfish and urchins were more strongly attached than in other places, and many of the univalves were so tightly fixed that the shells broke before the animals would let go their hold. Perhaps the force of the great surf which beats on this shore has much to do with the tenacity of the animals here. It is noteworthy that the animals, rather than deserting such beaten shores for the safe cove and protected pools, simply increase their toughness and fight back at the sea with a kind of joyful survival. This ferocious survival quotient excites us and makes us feel good, and from the crawling, fighting, resisting qualities of the animals, it almost seems that they are excited too.

We collected down the littoral as the water went down. We didn't seem to have time enough. We took samples of everything that came to hand. The uppermost rocks swarmed with Sally Lightfoots, those beautiful and fast and sensitive crabs. With them were white periwinkle snails. Below that, barnacles and Purpura snails; more crabs and many limpets. Below that many serpulids—attached worms in calcareous tubes with beautiful purple floriate heads. Below that, the multi-rayed starfish, *Heliaster kubiniji* of Xantus. With *Heliaster* were a few urchins, but not many, and they were so placed in crevices as to be hard to dislodge. Several resisted the steel bar to the extent of breaking—the mouth remaining tight to the rock while the shell fell away. Lower still there were to be seen swaying in the water under the reefs the dark gorgonians, or sea-fans. In the lowest surf-levels there was a brilliant gathering of the moss animals known as bryozoa; flatworms; flat crabs; the large sea-cucumber*; some anemones; many sponges of two types, a smooth, encrusting purple one, the other erect, white, and calcareous. There were great colonies of tunicates, clusters of tiny individuals joined by a common tunic and looking so like the sponges that even a trained worker must await the specialist's determination to know whether his find is sponge or tunicate. This is annoying, for the sponge being one step above the protozoa, at the bottom of the evolutionary ladder, and the tunicate near the top, bordering the vertebrates, your trained worker is likely to feel that a dirty trick has been played upon him by an entirely too democratic Providence.

We took many snails, including cones and murexes; a small red tectibranch (of a group to which the sea-hares belong); hydroids; many annelid worms; and a red pentagonal starfish.† There were the usual hordes of hermit crabs, but oddly enough we saw no chitons (sea-cradles), although the region seemed ideally suited to them.

We collected in haste. As the tide went down we kept a little ahead of it, wading in rubber boots, and as it came up again it drove us back. The time seemed very short. The incredible beauty of the tide pools, the brilliant colors, the swarming species ate up the time. And when at last the afternoon surf began to beat on the littoral and covered it over again, we seemed barely to have started. But the buckets and jars and tubes were full, and when we stopped we discovered that we were very tired.

Our collecting ends were different from those ordinarily entertained. In most cases at the present time, collecting is done by men who specialize in one or more groups. Thus, one man interested in hydroids will move out on a reef, and if his interest is sharp enough, he will not even see other life

* *Holothuria lubrica.*
† *Oreaster.*

forms about him. For him, the sponge is something in the way of his hydroids. Collecting large numbers of animals presents an entirely different aspect and makes one see an entirely different picture. Being more interested in distribution than in individuals, we saw dominant species and changing sizes, groups which thrive and those which recede under varying conditions. In a way, ours is the older method, somewhat like that of Darwin on the *Beagle*. He was called a "naturalist." He wanted to see everything, rocks and flora and fauna; marine and terrestrial. We came to envy this Darwin on his sailing ship. He had so much room and so much time. He could capture his animals and keep them alive and watch them. He had years instead of weeks, and he saw so many things. Often we envied the inadequate transportation of his time—the *Beagle* couldn't get about rapidly. She moved slowly along under sail. And we can imagine that young Darwin, probably in a bos'n's chair hung over the side, with a dip-net in his hands, scooping up jellyfish. When he went inland, he rode a horse or walked. This is the proper pace for a naturalist. Faced with all things he cannot hurry. We must have time to think and to look and to consider. And the modern process—that of looking quickly at the whole field and then diving down to a particular—was reversed by Darwin. Out of long long consideration of the parts he emerged with a sense of the whole. Where we wished for a month at a collecting station and took two days, Darwin stayed three months. Of course he could see and tabulate. It was the pace that made the difference. And in the writing of Darwin, as in his thinking, there is the slow heave of a sailing ship, and the patience of waiting for a tide. The results are bound up with the pace. We *could* not do this even if we could. We have thought in this connection that the speed and tempo and tone of modern writing might be built on the nervous clacking of a typewriter; that the brittle jerky thinking of the present might rest on the brittle jerky curricula of our schools with their urge to "turn them out." To turn them out. They use the phrase in speeches; turn them out to what? And the young biologists tearing off pieces of their subject, tatters of the life forms, like sharks tearing out hunks of a dead horse, looking at them, tossing them away. This is neither a good nor a bad method; it is simply the one of our time. We can look with longing back to Charles Darwin, staring into the water over the side of the sailing ship, but for us to attempt to imitate that procedure would be romantic and silly. To take a sailing boat, to fight tide and wind, to move four hundred miles on a horse when we could take a plane, would be not only ridiculous but ineffective. For we first, before our work, are products of our time. We might produce a philosophical costume piece, but it would be completely artificial. However, we can and do look on the measured, slow-paced accumulation of sight and thought of the Darwins with a nostalgic longing.

Even our boat hurried us, and while the Sea-Cow would not run, it had nevertheless infected us with the idea of its running. Six weeks we had, and no more. Was it a wonder that we collected furiously; spent every low-tide moment on the rocks, even at night? And in the times between low tides we kept the bottom nets down and the lines and dip-nets working. When the charter was up, we would be through. How different it had been when John Xantus was stationed in this very place, Cape San Lucas, in the sixties. Sent down by the United States Government as a tidal observer, but having lots of time, he collected animals for our National Museum. The first fine collections of Gulf forms came from Xantus. And we do not feel that we are injuring his reputation, but rather broadening it, by repeating a story about him. Speaking to the manager of the cannery at the Cape, we remarked on what a great man Xantus had been. Where another would have kept his tide charts and brooded and wished for the Willard Hotel, Xantus had collected animals widely and carefully. The manager said, "Oh, he was even better than that." Pointing to three little Indian children he said, "Those are Xantus's great-grandchildren," and he continued, "In the town there is a large family of Xantuses, and a few miles back in the hills you'll find a whole tribe of them." There were giants in the earth in those days.

We wonder what modern biologist, worried about titles and preferment and the gossip of the Faculty Club, would have the warmth and breadth, or even the fecundity for that matter, to leave a "whole tribe of Xantuses." We honor this man for all his activities. He at least was one who literally did proliferate in all directions.

Many people have spoken at length of the Sally Lightfoots. In fact, everyone who has seen them has been delighted with them. The very name they are called by reflects the delight of the name. These little crabs, with brilliant cloisonné carapaces, walk on their tiptoes. They have remarkable eyes and an extremely fast reaction time. In spite of the fact that they swarm on the rocks at the Cape, and to a less degree inside the Gulf, they are exceedingly hard to catch. They seem to be able to run in any one of four directions; but more than this, perhaps because of their rapid reaction time, they appear to read the mind of their hunter. They escape the long-handled net, anticipating from what direction it is coming. If you walk slowly, they move slowly ahead of you in droves. If you hurry, they hurry. When you plunge at them, they seem to disappear in little puffs of blue smoke—at any rate, they disappear. It is impossible to creep up on them. They are very beautiful, with clear brilliant colors, reds and blues and warm browns. We tried for a long time to catch them. Finally, seeing fifty or sixty in a big canyon of rock, we thought to outwit them. Surely we were more intelligent, if slower, than they. Accordingly, we pitted our obviously superior intelligence against the equally obvious physical superiority of Sally Lightfoot. Near the top of the crevice a boulder protruded. One of our party, taking a secret and circuitous route, hid himself behind this boulder, net in hand. He was completely concealed even from the stalk eyes of the crabs. Certainly they had not seen him go there. The herd of Sallys drowsed on the rocks in the lower end of the crevice. Two more of us strolled in from the seaward side, nonchalance in our postures and ingenuousness on our faces. One might have thought that we merely strolled along in a contemplation which severely excluded Sally Lightfoots. In time the herd moved ahead of us, matching our nonchalance. We did not hurry, they did not hurry. When they passed the boulder, helpless and unsuspecting, a large net was to fall over them and imprison them. But they did not know that. They moved along until they were four feet from the boulder, and then as one crab they turned to the right, climbed up over the edge of the crevice and down to the sea again.

Man reacts peculiarly but consistently in his relationship with Sally Lightfoot. His tendency eventually is to scream curses, to hurl himself at them, and to come up foaming with rage and bruised all over his chest. Thus, Tiny, leaping forward, slipped and fell and hurt his arm. He never forgot nor forgave his enemy. From then on he attacked Lightfoots by every foul means he could contrive (and a training in Monterey street fighting had equipped him well for this kind of battle). He hurled rocks at them; he smashed at them with boards; and he even considered poisoning them. Eventually we did catch a few Sallys, but we think they were the halt and the blind, the simpletons of their species. With reasonably well-balanced and non-neurotic Lightfoots we stood no chance.

We came back to the boat loaded with specimens, and immediately prepared to preserve them. The square, enameled pans were laid out on the hatch, the trays and bowls and watch-glasses (so called because at one time actual watch-crystals were used). The pans and glasses were filled with fresh sea water, and into them we distributed the animals by families—all the crabs in one, anemones in another, snails in another, and delicate things like flatworms and hydroids in others. From this distribution it was easier to separate them finally by species.

9

WHEN the catch was sorted and labeled, we went ashore to the cannery and later drove with Chris, the manager, and Señor Luis, the port captain, to the little town of San Lucas. It was a sad little town, for a winter storm and a great surf had wrecked it in a single night. Water had driven past the houses, and the streets of the village had been a raging river. "Then there were no roofs over the heads of the people," Señor Luis said excitedly. "Then the babies cried and there was no food. Then the people suffered."

The road to the little town, two wheel-ruts in the dust, tossed us about in the cannery truck. The cactus and thorny shrubs ripped at the car as we went by. At last we stopped in front of a mournful *cantina* where morose young men hung about waiting for something to happen. They had waited a long time—several generations—for something to happen, these good-looking young men. In their eyes there was a hopelessness. The storm of the winter had been discussed so often that it was sucked dry. And besides, they all knew the same things about it. Then we happened to them. The truck pulled up to the *cantina* door and we—strangers, foreigners—stepped out, as disorderly-looking a group as had ever come to their *cantina*. Tiny wore a Navy cap of white he had traded for, he said, in a washroom in San Diego. Tony still had his snap-brim felt. There were yachting caps and sweaters, and jeans stiff with fish blood. The young men stirred to life for a little while, but we were not enough. The flood had been much better. They relapsed again into their gloom.

There is nothing more doleful than a little *cantina*. In the first place it is inhabited by people who haven't any money to buy a drink. They stand about waiting for a miracle that never happens: the angel with golden wings who settles on the bar and orders drinks for everyone. This never happens, but how are the sad handsome young men to know it never will happen? And suppose it did happen and they were somewhere else? And so they lean against the wall; and when the sun is high they sit down against the wall. Now and then they go away into the brush for a while, and they go to their little homes for meals. But that is an impatient time, for the golden angel might arrive. Their faith is not strong, but it is permanent.

We could see that we did not greatly arouse them. The *cantina* owner promptly put his loudest records on the phonograph to force a gaiety into this sad place. But he had Carta Blanca beer and (at the risk of a charge that we have sold our souls to this brewery) we love Carta Blanca beer. There was no ice, no electric lights, and the gasoline lanterns hissed and drew the bugs from miles away. The cockroaches in their hordes rushed in to see what was up. Big, handsome cockroaches, with almost human faces. The loud music only made us sadder, and the young men watched us. When we lifted a split of beer to our lips the eyes of the young men rose with our hands, and even the cockroaches lifted their heads. We couldn't stand it. We ordered beer all around, but it was too late. The young men were too far gone in sorrow. They drank their warm beer sadly. Then we bought straw hats, for the sun is deadly here. There should be a kind of ridiculous joy in buying a floppy hat, but those young men, so near to tears, drained even that joy. Their golden angel had come, and they did not find him good. We felt rather as God would feel when, after all the preparation of Paradise, all the plannings for eternities of joy, all the making and tuning of harps, the street-paving with gold, and the writing of hosannas, at last He let in the bleacher customers and they looked at the heavenly city and wished to be again in Brooklyn. We told funny stories, knowing they wouldn't be enjoyed, tiring of them ourselves before the point was reached. Nothing was fun in that little *cantina*. We started back for the boat. I think those young men were glad to see us go; because once we were gone, they could begin to build us up, but present, we inhibited their imaginations.

At the bar Chris told us of a native liquor called *damiana*, made from an infusion of a native herb, and not much known outside of Baja California. Chris said it was an aphrodisiac, and told some interesting stories to prove it. We felt a scientific interest in his stories, and bought a bottle of *damiana*, intending to subject it to certain tests under laboratory conditions. But the customs officials of San Diego took it away from us, not because of its romantic aspect, but because it had alcohol in it. Thus we were never able to give it a truly scientific testing. We think we were going to use it on a white rat. Tiny said he didn't want any such stuff getting in his way when he felt lustful.

There doesn't seem to be a true aphrodisiac; there are excitants like cantharides, and physical aids to the difficulties of psychic traumas, like yohimbine sulphate; there are strong protein foods like *bêche-de-mer* and the gonads of sea-urchins, and the much over-rated oyster; even chiles, with their irritating qualities, have some effect, but there seems to be no true aphrodisiac, no sweet essence of that goddess to be taken in a capsule. A certain young person said once that she found sexual intercourse an aphrodisiac; certainly it is the only good one.

So many people are interested in this subject but most of them are forced to pretend they are not. A man, for his own ego's sake, must, publicly at least, be over-supplied with libido. But every doctor knows so well the "friend of the client" who needs help. He is the same "friend" who has gonorrhea, the same "friend" who needs the address of an abortionist. This elusive friend—what will we not do to help him out of his difficulties; the nights we spend sleepless, worrying about him! He is interested in an aphrodisiac; we must try to find him one. But the *damiana* we brought back for our "friend" possibly just now is in the hands of the customs officials in San Diego. Perhaps they too have a friend. Since we suggested the qualities of *damiana* to them, it is barely possible that this fascinating liquor has already been either devoted to a friend or even perhaps subjected to a stern course of investigation under laboratory conditions.

We have wondered about the bawdiness this book must have if it is to be true. Bawdiness, vulgarity—call it what you will—is such a relative matter, so much a matter of attitude. A man we know once long ago worked for a wealthy family in a country place. One morning one of the cows had a calf. The children of the house went down with him to watch her. It was a good normal birth, a perfect presentation, and the cow needed no help. The children asked questions and he answered them. And when the emerged head cleared through the sac, the little black muzzle appeared, and the first breath was drawn, the children were fascinated and awed. And this was the time for their mother to come screaming down on the vulgarity of letting the children see the birth. This "vulgarity" had given them a sense of wonder at the structure of life, while the mother's propriety and gentility supplanted that feeling with dirtiness. If the reader of this book is "genteel," then this is a very vulgar book, because the animals in a tide pool have two major preoccupations: first, survival, and second, reproduction. They reproduce all over the place. We could retire into obscure phrases or into Greek or Latin. This, for some reason, protects the delicate. In an earlier time biologists made their little jokes that way, as in the naming of the animals. But some later men found their methods vulgar. Verrill, in *The Actinaria of the Canadian Arctic Expeditions*, broke out in protest. He cries, "Prof. McMurrich has endeavored to restore for this species a name (*senilis*) used by Linnaeus for a small indeterminable species very imperfectly described in 1761. . . . The description does not in the least apply to this species. He described the thing as the size of the last joint of a finger, sordid, rough, with a sub-coriaceous tunic. Such a description could not possibly apply to this soft and smooth species . . . but it would be mere guesswork to say what species he had in view. . . . Moreover, aside from this uncertainty, most modern writers have rejected most of the Linnaean names of actinians on account of their obscenity or indecency. All this confusion shows the impossibility of fixing the name, even if it were not otherwise objectionable. It should be forgotten or ignored, like the generic names used by Linnaeus in 1761, and by some others of that period, for species of Actinia. Their indecent names were usually the Latinized forms of vulgar names used by fishermen, some of which are still in use among the fishermen of our own coasts, for similar things."

This strange attempt to "clean up" biology will have, we hope, no effect whatever. We at least have kept our vulgar sense of wonder. We are no better than the animals; in fact in a lot of ways we aren't as good. And so we'll let the book fall as it may.

We left the truck and walked through the sandy hills in the night, and in this latitude the sky seemed very black and the stars very white. Already the smell of the land was gone from our noses, for we were used to the smell of vegetation again. The beer was warm in us and pleasant, and the air had a liquid warmth that was really there without the beer, for we tested it later. In the brush beside the track there was a little heap of light, and as we came closer to it we saw a rough wooden cross lighted indirectly. The cross-arm was bound to the staff with a thong, and the whole cross seemed to glow, alone in the darkness. When we came close we saw that a kerosene can stood on the ground and that in it was a candle which threw its feeble light upward on the cross. And our companion told us how a man had come from a fishing boat, sick and weak and tired. He tried to get home, but at this spot he fell down and died. And his family put the little cross and the candle there to mark the place. And eventually they would put up a stronger cross. It seems good to mark and to remember for a little while the place where a man died. This is his one whole lonely act in all his life. In every other thing, even in his birth, he is bound close to others, but the moment of his dying is his own. And in nearly all of Mexico such places are marked. A grave is quite a different thing. Here one's family boasts, or lies, or excuses, in material of elegance and extravagance. But that is a family or a social matter, not the dead man's own at all. The unmarked cross and the secret light are his; almost a reflection of the last piercing loneliness that comes into a dying man's eyes.

From a few feet away the cross seemed to flicker unsubstantially with a small yellow light, seemed to be almost a memory while we saw it. And the man who tried to get home and crawled this far—we never knew his name but he stays in our memory too, for some reason—a supra-personal being, a slow, painful symbol and a pattern of his whole species which tries always from generation to generation, man and woman, which struggles always to get home but never quite makes it.

We came back to the pier and got into our little boat. The Sea-Cow of course would not start, it being night time, so we rowed out to the *Western Flyer*. Before we started, by some magic, there on the end of the pier stood the sad beautiful young men watching us. They had not moved; some jinni had picked them up and transported them and set them down. They watched us put out into the darkness toward our riding lights, and then we suppose they were whisked back again to the *cantina*, where the proprietor was putting the records away and feeling with delicate thumbs the dollar bills we had left. On the pier no light burned, for the engine had stopped at sundown. We went to bed; there was a tide to be got to in the morning.

On the beach at San Lucas there is a war between the pigs and the vultures. Sometimes one side dominates and sometimes the other. On occasion the swine feel a dynamism and demand *Lebensraum*, and in the pride of their species drive the vultures from the decaying offal. And again, when their thousand years of history is over, the vultures spring to arms, tear up treaties, and flap the pigs from the garbage. And on the beach there are certain skinny dogs, without any dynamisms whatever and without racial pride, who nevertheless manage to get the best snacks. They don't thrive on it—always they are meager and skinny and cowardly—but when the *Gauleiter* swine has just captured a fish belly, and before he can shout his second *"Sieg Heil!"* the dog has it.

10
March 18

THE tidal series was short. We wished to cover as much ground as possible, to establish as many collecting stations as we could, for we wanted a picture as nearly whole of the Gulf as possible. The next morning we got under way to run the short distance to Pulmo Reef, around the tip and on the eastern shore of the Peninsula. It was a brilliant day, the water riffled and very blue, the sandy beaches of the shore shining with yellow intensity. Above the beaches the low hills were dark with brush. Many people had come to Cape San Lucas, and many had described it. We had read a number of the accounts, and of course agreed with none of them. To a man straight off a yacht, it is a miserable little flea-bitten place, poor and smelly. But to one who puts in hungry, in a storm-beaten boat, it must be a place of great comfort and warmth. These are extremes, but the area in between them also has its multiform conditioning, and what we saw had our conditioning. Once we read a diary, written by a man who came through Panama in 1839. He had read about the place before he got there, but the account he read was about the old city, and in his diary, written after he had gone through, he set down a description of the city he had read about. He didn't know that the town in the book had been destroyed, and that the new one was not even in the same place, but he was not disturbed by these discrepancies. He knew what he would find there and he found it.

There is a curious idea among unscientific men that in scientific writing there is a common plateau of perfectionism. Nothing could be more untrue. The reports of biologists are the measure, not of the science, but of the men themselves. There are as few scientific giants as any other kind. In some reports it is impossible, because of inept expression, to relate the descriptions to the living animals. In some papers collecting places are so mixed or ignored that the animals mentioned cannot be found at all. The same conditioning forces itself into specification as it does into any other kind of observation, and the same faults of carelessness will be found in scientific reports as in the witness chair of a criminal court. It has seemed sometimes that the little men in scientific work assumed the awe-fullness of a priesthood to hide their deficiencies, as the witch-doctor does with his stilts and high masks, as the priesthoods of all cults have, with secret or unfamiliar languages and symbols. It is usually found that only the little stuffy men object to what is called "popularization," by which they mean writing with a clarity understandable to one not familiar with the tricks and codes of the cult. We have not known a single great scientist who could not discourse freely and interestingly with a child. Can it be that the haters of clarity have nothing to say, have observed nothing, have no clear picture of even their own fields? A dull man seems to be a dull man no matter what his field, and of course it is the right of a dull scientist to protect himself with feathers and robes, emblems and degrees, as do other dull men who are potentates and grand imperial rulers of lodges of dull men.

As we neared Pulmo Reef, Tony sent a man up the mast to the crow's-nest to watch for concealed rocks. It is possible to see deep into the water from that high place; the rocks seem to float suddenly up from the bottom like dark shadows. The water in this shallow area was green rather than blue, and the sandy bottom was clearly visible. We pulled in as close as was safe and dropped our anchor. About a mile away we could see the proper reef with the tide beginning to go down on it. On the shore behind the white beach was one of those lonely little *rancherias* we came to know later. Usually a palm or two are planted near by, and by these trees sticking up out of the brush one can locate the houses. There is usually a small corral, a burro or two, a few pigs, and some scrawny chickens. The cattle range wide for food. A dugout canoe lies on the beach, for a good part of the food comes from the sea. Rarely do you see a light from the sea, for the people go to sleep at dusk and awaken with the first light. They must be very lonely people, for they appear on shore the moment a boat anchors, and paddle out in their canoes. At Pulmo Reef the little canoe put off and came alongside. In it were two men and a woman, very ragged, their old clothes patched with the tatters of older clothes. The *serapes* of the men were so thin and threadbare that the light shone through them, and the woman's *rebozo* had long lost its color. They sat in the canoe holding to the side of the *Western Flyer*, and they held their greasy blankets carefully over their noses and mouths to protect themselves from us. So much evil the white man had brought to their ancestors: his breath was poisonous with the lung disease; to sleep with him was to poison the generations. Where he set down his colonies the indigenous people withered and died. He brought industry and trade but no prosperity, riches but no ease. After four hundred years of him these people have ragged clothes and the shame that forces the wearing of them; iron harpoons for their hands, syphilis and tuberculosis; a few of the white man's less complex neuroses, and a curious devotion to a God who was sacrificed long ago in the white man's country. They know the white man is poisonous and they cover their noses against him. They do find us fascinating. However, they sit on the rail for many hours watching us and waiting. When we feed them they eat and are courteous about it, but they did not come for food, they are not beggars. We give the men some shirts and they fold them and put them into the bow of the canoe, but they did not come for clothing. One of the men at last offers us a match-box in which are a few misshapen little pearls like small pale cancers. Five pesos he wants for the pearls, and he knows they aren't worth it. We give him a carton of cigarettes and take his pearls, although we do not want them, for they are ugly little things. Now these three should go, but they do not. They would stay for weeks, not moving nor talking except now and then to one another in soft little voices as gentle as whispers. Their dark eyes never leave us. They ask no questions. They seem actually to be dreaming. Sometimes we asked of the Indians the local names of animals we had taken, and then they consulted together. They seemed to live on remembered things, to be so related to the seashore and the rocky hills and the loneliness that they are these things. To ask about the country is like asking about themselves. "How many toes have you?" "What, toes? Let's see—of course, ten. I have known them all my life, I never thought to count them. Of course it will rain tonight, I don't know why. Something in me tells me I will rain tonight. Of course, I am the whole thing, now that I think about it. I ought to know when I will rain." The dark eyes, whites brown and stained, have curious red lights in the pupils. They seem to be a dreaming people. If finally you must escape their eyes, their timeless dreaming eyes, you have only to say, *"Adiós, señor,"* and they seem to start awake. *"Adiós,"* they say softly. *"Que vaya con Dios."* And they paddle away. They bring a hush with them, and when they go away one's own voice sounds loud and raw.

We loaded the smaller skiff with collecting materials: the containers and bars, tubes and buckets. We put the Sea-Cow on the stern and it made one of its few mistakes. It thought we were going directly to the beach instead of to the reef a mile away. It started up with a great roar and ran for a quarter of a mile before it became aware of its mistake. It was rarely fooled again. We rowed on to the reef.

Collecting in this region, we always wore rubber boots. There are many animals which sting, some severely, and at least one urchin which is highly poisonous. Some of the worms, such as *Eurythoë*, leave spines in the skin which burn unmercifully. And even a barnacle cut infects readily. It is impossible to wear gloves; one must simply be as careful as possible and look where the finger is going before it is put down. Some of the little beasts are incredibly gallant and ferocious. On one occasion, a moray eel not more than eight inches long lashed out from under a rock, bit one of us on the finger, and retired. If one is not naturally cautious, painful and bandaged hands very soon teach caution. The boots protect one's feet from nearly everything, but there is an urchin which has spines so sharp that they pierce the rubber and break off in the flesh, and they sting badly and usually cause infection.

Pulmo is a coral reef. It has often been remarked that reef-building corals seem to live only on the eastern sides of large land bodies, not on the western sides. This has been noticed many times, and even here at Pulmo the reef-building coral* occurs only on the eastern side of the Peninsula. This can have nothing to do with wave-shock or current, but must be governed by another of those unknown factors so ever-present and so haunting to the ecologist.

The complexity of the life-pattern on Pulmo Reef was even greater than at Cape San Lucas. Clinging to the coral, growing on it, burrowing into it, was a teeming fauna. Every piece of the soft material broken off skittered and pulsed with life— little crabs and worms and snails. One small piece of coral might conceal thirty or forty species, and the colors on the reef were electric. The sharp-spined urchins† gave us trouble immediately, for several of us, on putting our feet down injudiciously, drove the spines into our toes.

The reef was gradually exposed as the tide went down, and on its flat top the tide pools were beautiful. We collected as widely and rapidly as possible, trying to take a cross-section of the animals we saw. There were purple pendent gorgonians like lacy fans; a number of small spine-covered puffer fish which bloat themselves when they are attacked, erecting the spines; and many starfish, including some purple and gold cushion stars. The club-spined sea-urchins‡ were numerous in their rock niches. They seemed to move about very little, for their niches always just fit them, and have the marks of constant occupation. We took a number of the slim green and brown starfish§ and the large slim five-rayed starfish with plates bordering the ambulacral grooves.‖ There were numbers of barnacles and several types of brittle-stars. We took one huge, magnificent murex snail. One large hemispherical

* *Pocillopora capitata* Verrill.
† *Arbacia incisa.*
‡ *Eucidaris thouarsii.*
§ *Phataria unifascialis* Gray.
‖ *Pharia pyramidata.*

snail was so camouflaged with little plants, corallines, and other algae that it could not be told from the reef itself until it was turned over. Rock oysters there were, and oysters; limpets and sponges; corals of two types; peanut worms; sea-cucumbers; and many crabs, particularly some disguised in dresses of growing algae which made them look like knobs on the reef until they moved. There were many worms, including our enemy *Eurythoë*, which stings so badly. This worm makes one timid about reaching without looking. The coral clusters were violently inhabited by snapping shrimps, red smooth crabs,* and little fuzzy black and white spider crabs.† Autotomy in these crabs, shrimps, and brittle-stars is very highly developed. At last, under the reef, we saw a large fleshy gorgonian, or sea-fan, waving gently in the clear water, but it was deep and we could not reach it. One of us took off his clothes and dived for it, expecting at any moment to be attacked by one of those monsters we do not believe in. It was murky under the reef, and the colors of the sponges were more brilliant than in those exposed to greater light. The diver did not stay long; he pulled the large sea-fan free and came up again. And although he went down a number of times, this was the only one of this type of gorgonian he could find. Indeed, it was the only one taken on the entire trip.

The collecting buckets and tubes and jars were very full of specimens—so full that we had constantly to change the water to keep the animals alive. Several large pieces of coral were taken and kept submerged in buckets and later were allowed to lie in stale sea water in one of the pans. This is an interesting thing, for as the water goes stale, the thousands of little roomers which live in the tubes and caves and interstices of the coral come out of hiding and scramble for a new home. Worms and tiny crabs appear from nowhere and are then easily picked up.

The sea bottom inside the reef was of white sand studded with purple and gold cushion stars, of which we collected many. And lying on the sandy bottom were heads and knobs of another coral,‡ much harder and more regularly formed

* *Trapezia* spp.
† *Mithrax areolatus.*
‡ *Porites porosa* Verrill.

than the reef-building coral. The rush of collecting as much as possible before the tide re-covered the reef made us indiscriminate in our collecting, but in the long run this did not matter. For once on board the boat again we could re-collect, going over the pieces of coral and rubble carefully and very often finding animals we had not known were there.

El Pulmo was the only coral reef we found on the entire expedition, and the fauna and even the algae were rather specialized to it. No very great surf could have beaten it, for extremely delicate animals lived on its exposed top where they would have been crushed or washed away had strong seas struck them. And the competition for existence was as great as it had been at San Lucas, but it seemed to us that different methods were employed for frustrating enemies. Whereas at San Lucas speed and ferocity were the attributes of most animals, at Pulmo concealment and camouflage were largely employed. The little crabs wore masks of algae and bryozoa and even hydroids, and most animals had little tunnels or some protected place to run to. The softness of the coral made this possible, where the hard smooth granite of San Lucas had forbidden it. On several occasions we wished for diving equipment, but never more than here at Pulmo, for the under-cut shoreward side of the reef concealed hazy wonders which we could not get at. It is not satisfactory to hold one's breath and to look with unglassed eyes through the dim waters.

The water behind the reef was very warm. We abandoned our boots and, putting on tennis shoes to protect our feet from various stingers, we dived again and again for perfect knobs of coral.

Again we tried to start the Sea-Cow—and then rowed back to the *Western Flyer*. There we complained so bitterly to Tex, the engineer, that he took the evil little thing to pieces. Piece by piece he examined it, with a look of incredulity in his eyes. He admired, I think, the ingenuity which could build such a perfect little engine, and he was astonished at the concept of building a whole motor for the purpose of not running. Having put it together again, he made a discovery. The Sea-Cow would run perfectly out of water—that is, in a barrel of water with the propeller and cooling inlet submerged. Placed thus, the Sea-Cow functioned perfectly and got good mileage.

Immediately on arriving back at the *Western Flyer* we pulled up the anchor and got under way again. It was efficient that we preserve and label while we sailed as long as the sea was calm, and now it was very calm. The great collection from the reef required every enameled pan and glass dish we had. The killing and relaxing and preserving took us until dark, and even after dark we sat and made the labels to go into the tubes. As the jars filled and were labeled, we put them back in their corrugated-paper cartons and stowed them in the hold. The corked tubes were tested for leaks, then wrapped in paper toweling and stacked in boxes. Thus there was very small loss from breakage or leakage, and by labeling the same day as collecting, there had thus far been virtually no confusion in the tabulation of animals. But we knew already that we had made one error in planning: we had not brought nearly enough small containers. It is best to place an animal alone in a jar or a tube which accommodates him, but not too freely. The enormous numbers of animals we took strained our resources and containers long before we were through.

As we moved up the Gulf, the mirage we had heard about began to distort the land. While it is worse on the Sonora coast, it is sufficiently interesting on the Peninsula to produce a heady, crazy feeling in the observer. As you pass a headland it suddenly splits off and becomes an island and then the water seems to stretch inward and pinch it to a mushroom-shaped cliff, and finally to liberate it from the earth entirely so that it hangs in the air over the water. Even a short distance offshore one cannot tell what the land really looks like. Islands too far off, according to the map, are visible; while others which should be near by cannot be seen at all until suddenly they come bursting out of the mirage. The whole surrounding land is unsubstantial and changing. One remembers the old stories of invisible kingdoms where princes lived with ladies and dragons for company; and the more modern fairy-tales in which heroes drift in and out of dimensions more complex than the original three. We are open enough to miracles of course, but what must have been the feeling of the discovering Spaniards? Miracles were daily happenings to them. Perhaps to that extent their feet were more firmly planted on the ground. Subject as they were to the constant apparitions of saints, to the trooping of holy virgins into their dreams and reveries, perhaps mirages were commonplaces. We have seen many miraculous figures in Mexico. They are usually Christs which have supernaturally appeared on mountains or in caves and usually at times of crisis. But it does seem odd that the heavenly authorities, when they wished a miraculous image to appear, invariably chose bad Spanish wood-carving of the seventeenth century. But perhaps art criticism in heaven was very closely related to the sensibilities of the time. Certainly it would have been a little shocking to find an Epstein Christ under a tree on a mountain in Mexico, or a Brancusi bird, or a Dali *Descent from the Cross*.

It must have been a difficult task for those first sturdy Jesuit fathers to impress the Indians of the Gulf. The very air here is miraculous, and outlines of reality change with the moment. The sky sucks up the land and disgorges it. A dream hangs over the whole region, a brooding kind of hallucination. Perhaps only the shock of seventeenth-century wood-carving could do the trick; surely the miracle must have been very virile to be effective.

Tony grew restive when the mirage was working, for here right and wrong fought before his very eyes, and how could one tell which was error? It is very well to say, "The land is here and what blots it out is a curious illusion caused by light and air and moisture," but if one is steering a boat, he must sail by what he sees, and if air and light and moisture—three realities—plot together and perpetrate a lie, what is a realistic man to believe? Tony did not like the mirage at all.

While we worked at the specimens, the trolling lines were out and we caught another skipjack, large and fat and fast. As it came in on the line, one of us ran for the moving-picture camera, for we wanted to record on color film the changing tints and patterns of the fish's dying. But the exposure was wrong as usual, and we did not get it.

Near the moving boat swordfishes played about. They seemed to play in pure joy or exhibitionism. It is thought that they leap to clear themselves of parasites; they jump clear of the water and come crashing down, and sometimes they turn over in the air and flash in the sunshine. This afternoon, too, we saw the first specimens of the great manta ray (a giant skate), and we rigged the harpoons and coiled the line ready. One light harpoon just pierced a swordfish's tail, but he swished away, for the barb had not penetrated. And we did not turn and pursue the great rays, for we wished to anchor that night near Point Lobos on Espíritu Santo Island.

In the evening we came near to it, but as we prepared to anchor, the wind sprang up full on us, and Tony decided to run for the shelter of Pescadero Point on the mainland. The wind seemed to grow instantly out of the evening, and the sea with it. The jars and collecting pans were in danger of flying overboard. For half an hour we were very busy tying the equipment down and removing the flapping canvas we had stretched to keep the sun off our specimen pans. Under the powerful wind we crossed the channel which leads to La Paz, and saw the channel light—the first one we had seen since the big one on the false cape. This one seemed very strange in the Gulf. The waves were not high, but the wind blew with great intensity, making whitecaps rather than rollers, and only when we ran in under Pescadero Point did we drop the wind. We eased in slowly, sounding as we went. When the anchor was finally down we cooked and ate the skipjack, a most delicious fish. And after dinner a group action took place.

We carried no cook and dishwasher; it had been understood that we would all help. But for some time Tex had been secretly mutinous about washing dishes. At the proper times he had things to do in the engine-room. He might have succeeded in this crime, if he had ever varied his routine, but gradually a suspicion grew on us that Tex did not like to wash dishes. He denied this vigorously. He said he liked very much to wash dishes. He appealed to our reason. How would we like it, he argued, if we were forever in the engine-room, getting our hands dirty? There was danger down there too, he said. Men had been killed by engines. He was not willing to see us take the risk. We met his arguments with a silence that made him nervous. He protested then that he had once washed dishes from west Texas to San Diego without stopping, and that he had learned to love it so much that he didn't want to be selfish about it now. A circle of cold eyes surrounded him. He began to sweat. He said that later (he didn't say how much later) he was going to ask us for the privilege of washing all the dishes, but right now he had a little job to do in the engine-room. It was for the safety of the ship, he said. No one answered him. Then he cried, "My God, are you going to hang me?" At last Sparky spoke up, not unkindly, but inexorably. "Tex," he said, "you're going to wash 'em or you're going to sleep with 'em." Tex said, "Now just as soon as I do one little job there's nothing I'd rather do than wash four or five thousand dishes." Each of us picked up a load of dishes, carried them in, and laid them gently in Tex's bunk. He got up resignedly then and carried them back and washed them. He didn't grumble, but he was broken. Some joyous light had gone out of him, and he never did get the catsup out of his blankets.

That night Sparky worked at the radio and made contact with the fishing fleet that was operating in the region from Cedros Island and around the tip into the Gulf, fishing for tuna. Fishermen are no happier than farmers. It is difficult to see why anyone becomes a farmer or a fisherman. Dreadful things happen to them constantly: they lose their nets; the fish are wild; sea-lions get into the nets and tear their way out; snags are caught; there are no fish, and the price high; there are too many fish, and the price is low; and if some means could be devised so that the fish swam up to a boat, wriggled up a trough, squirmed their way into the fish-hold, and pulled ice over themselves with their own fins, the imprecations would be terrible because they had not removed their own entrails and brought their own ice. There is no happiness for fishermen anywhere. Cries of anguish at the injustice of the elements inundated the short-wave receiver as we lay at anchor.

The pattern of a book, or a day, of a trip, becomes a characteristic design. The factors in a trip by boat, the many-formed personality phases all shuffled together, changing a little to fit into the box and yet bringing their own lumps and corners, make the trip. And from all these factors your expedition has a character of its own, so that one may say of it, "That was a good, kind trip." Or, "That was a mean one." The character of the whole becomes defined and definite. We

ran from collecting station to new collecting station, and
when the night came and the anchor was dropped, a quiet
came over the boat and the trip slept. And then we talked and
speculated, talked and drank beer. And our discussions ranged
from the loveliness of remembered women to the complexities
of relationships in every other field. It is very easy to grow
tired at collecting; the period of a low tide is about all men
can endure. At first the rocks are bright and every moving
animal makes his mark on the attention. The picture is wide
and colored and beautiful. But after an hour and a half the
attention centers weary, the colors fade, and the field is likely
to narrow to an individual animal. Here one may observe his
own world narrowed down until interest and, with it, observation, flicker and go out. And what if with age this weariness
become permanent and observation dim out and not recover?
Can this be what happens to so many men of science? Enthusiasm, interest, sharpness, dulled with a weariness until finally
they retire into easy didacticism? With this weariness, this stul-
tification of the attention centers, perhaps there comes the
pained and sad memory of what the old excitement was like,
and regret might turn to envy of the men who still have it.
Then out of the shell of didacticism, such a used-up man
might attack the unwearied, and he would have in his hands
proper weapons of attack. It does seem certain that to a wea-
ried man an error in a mass of correct data wipes out all the
correctness and is a focus for attack; whereas the unwearied
man, in his energy and receptivity, might consider the little
dross of error a by-product of his effort. These two may balance and produce a purer thing than either in the end. These
two may be the stresses which hold up the structure, but it is
a sad thing to see the interest in interested men thin out and
weaken and die. We have known so many professors who once
carried their listeners high on their single enthusiasm, and
have seen these same men finally settle back comfortably into
lectures prepared years before and never vary them again. Perhaps this is the same narrowing we observe in relation to ourselves and the tide pool—a man looking at reality brings his
own limitations to the world. If he has strength and energy
of mind the tide pool stretches both ways, digs back to electrons and leaps space into the universe and fights out of the

moment into non-conceptual time. Then ecology has a synonym which is ALL.

It is strange how the time sense changes with different peoples. The Indians who sat on the rail of the *Western Flyer* had a different time sense—"time-world" would be the better term—from ours. And we think we can never get into them unless we can invade that time-world, for this expanding time seems to trail an expanding universe, or perhaps to lead it. One considers the durations indicated in geology, in paleontology, and, thinking out of our time-world with its duration between time-stone and time-stone, says, "What an incredible interval!" Then, when one struggles to build some picture of astro-physical time, he is faced with a light-year, a thought-deranging duration unless the relativity of all things intervenes and time expands and contracts, matching itself relatively to the pulsings of a relative universe.

It is amazing how the strictures of the old teleologies infect our observation, causal thinking warped by hope. It was said earlier that hope is a diagnostic human trait, and this simple cortex symptom seems to be a prime factor in our inspection of our universe. For hope implies a change from a present bad condition to a future better one. The slave hopes for freedom, the weary man for rest, the hungry for food. And the feeders of hope, economic and religious, have from these simple strivings of dissatisfaction managed to create a world picture which is very hard to escape. Man grows toward perfection; animals grow toward man; bad grows toward good; and down toward up, until our little mechanism, hope, achieved in ourselves probably to cushion the shock of thought, manages to warp our whole world. Probably when our species developed the trick of memory and with it the counterbalancing projection called "the future," this shock-absorber, hope, had to be included in the series, else the species would have destroyed itself in despair. For if ever any man were deeply and unconsciously sure that his future would be no better than his past, he might deeply wish to cease to live. And out of this therapeutic poultice we build our iron teleologies and twist the tide pools and the stars into the pattern. To most men the most hateful statement possible is, *"A thing is because it is."* Even those who have managed to drop the leading-strings of a

Sunday-school deity are still led by the unconscious teleology of their developed trick. And in saying that hope cushions the shock of experience, that one trait balances the directionalism of another, a teleology is implied, unless one know or feel or think that we *are* here, and that without this balance, hope, our species in its blind mutation might have joined many, many others in extinction. Dr. Torsten Gislén, in his fine paper on fossil echinoderms called "Evolutional Series toward Death and Renewal,"* has shown that as often as not, in his studied group at least, mutations have had destructive, rather than survival value. Extending this thesis, it is interesting to think of the mutations of our own species. It is said and thought there has been none in historical times. We wonder, though, where in man a mutation might take place. Man is the only animal whose interest and whose drive are outside himself. Other animals may dig holes to live in; may weave nests or take possession of hollow trees. Some species, like bees or spiders, even create complicated homes, but they do it with the fluids and processes of their own bodies. They make little impression on the world. But the world is furrowed and cut, torn and blasted by man. Its flora has been swept away and changed; its mountains torn down by man; its flat lands littered by the debris of his living. And these changes have been wrought, not because any inherent technical ability has demanded them, but because his desire has created that technical ability. Physiological man does not require this paraphernalia to exist, but the whole man does. He is the only animal who lives outside of himself, whose drive is in external things—property, houses, money, concepts of power. He lives in his cities and his factories, in his business and job and art. But having projected himself into these external complexities, he *is* them. His house, his automobile are a part of him and a large part of him. This is beautifully demonstrated by a thing doctors know—that when a man loses his possessions a very common result is sexual impotence. If then the projection, the preoccupation of man, lies in external things so that even his subjectivity is a mirror of houses and cars and grain elevators, the place to look for his mutation would be in the

Ark. f. zool. K. Svenska Vetens., Vol. 26 A, No. 16, Stockholm, Jan. 1934.

direction of his drive, or in other words in the external things he deals with. And here we can indeed readily find evidence of mutation. The industrial revolution would then be indeed a true mutation, and the present tendency toward collectivism, whether attributed to Marx or Hitler or Henry Ford, might be as definite a mutation of the species as the lengthening neck of the evolving giraffe. For it must be that mutations take place in the direction of a species drive or preoccupation. If then this tendency toward collectivization is mutation there is no reason to suppose it is for the better. It is a rule in paleontology that ornamentation and complication precede extinction. And our mutation, of which the assembly line, the collective farm, the mechanized army, and the mass production of food are evidences or even symptoms, might well correspond to the thickening armor of the great reptiles—a tendency that can end only in extinction. If this should happen to be true, nothing stemming from thought can interfere with it or bend it. Conscious thought seems to have little effect on the action or direction of our species. There is a war now which no one wants to fight, in which no one can see a gain—a zombie war of sleep-walkers which nevertheless goes on out of all control of intelligence. Some time ago a Congress of honest men refused an appropriation of several hundreds of millions of dollars to feed our people. They said, and meant it, that the economic structure of the country would collapse under the pressure of such expenditure. And now the same men, just as honestly, are devoting many billions to the manufacture, transportation, and detonation of explosives to protect the people they would not feed. And it must go on. Perhaps it is all a part of the process of mutation and perhaps the mutation will see us done for. We have made our mark on the world, but we have really done nothing that the trees and creeping plants, ice and erosion, cannot remove in a fairly short time. And it is strange and sad and again symptomatic that most people, reading this speculation which is *only* speculation, will feel that it is a treason to our species so to speculate. For in spite of overwhelming evidence to the contrary, the trait of hope still controls the future, and man, not a species, but a triumphant race, will approach perfection, and, finally, tearing himself free, will march up the stars and take his place where, because of his power and virtue, he belongs: on the right hand of the $\sqrt[\pi]{-1}$. From which majestic seat he will direct with pure intelligence the ordering of the universe. And perhaps when that occurs—when our species progresses toward extinction or marches into the forehead of God—there will be certain degenerate groups left behind, say, the Indians of Lower California, in the shadows of the rocks or sitting motionless in the dugout canoes. They may remain to sun themselves, to eat and starve and sleep and reproduce. Now they have many legends as hazy and magical as the mirage. Perhaps then they will have another concerning a great and godlike race that flew away in four-motored bombers to the accompaniment of exploding bombs, the voice of God calling them home.

Nights at anchor in the Gulf are quiet and strange. The water is smooth, almost solid, and the dew is so heavy that the decks are soaked. The little waves rasp on the shell beaches with a hissing sound, and all about in the darkness the fishes jump and splash. Sometimes a great ray leaps clear and falls back on the water with a sharp report. And again, a school of tiny fishes whisper along the surface, each one, as it breaks clear, making the tiniest whisking sound. And there is no feeling, no smell, no vibration of people in the Gulf. Whatever it is that makes one aware that men are about is not there. Thus, in spite of the noises of waves and fishes, one has a feeling of deadness and of quietness. At anchor, with the motor stopped, it is not easy to sleep, and every little sound starts one awake. The crew is restless and a little nervous. If a dog barks on shore or a cow bellows, we are reassured. But in many places of anchorage there were utterly no sounds associated with man. The crew read books they have not known about—Tony reads *Studs Lonigan* and says he does not like to see such words in print. And we are reminded that we once did not like to hear them spoken because we were not used to them. When we became used to hearing them, they took their place with the simple speech-sounds of the race of man. Tony read on in *Studs Lonigan*, and the shock of the new words he had not seen printed left him and he grew into the experience of Studs. Tiny read the book too. He said, "It's like something that happened to me."

Sometimes in the night a little breeze springs up and the boat tugs experimentally at the anchor and swings slowly around. There is nothing so quiet as a boat when the motor has stopped; it seems to lie with held breath. One gets to longing for the deep beat of the cylinders.

II

March 20

WE HAD MARKED the southern end of Espíritu Santo Island as our next collecting stop. This is a long narrow island which makes the northern side of the San Lorenzo Channel. It is mountainous and stands high and sheer from the blue water. We wanted particularly to collect there so that we could contrast the fauna of the eastern tip of this island with that of the secluded and protected bay of La Paz. Throughout we attempted to work in stations in the same area which nevertheless contrasted conditions for living, such as wave-shock, bottom, rock formation, exposure, depth, and so forth. The most radical differences in life forms are discovered in this way.

Early in the morning we sailed from our shelter under Pescadero Point and crossed the channel again. It was a very short run. There were many manta rays cruising slowly near the surface, with only the tips of their "wings" protruding above the water. They seemed to hover, and when we approached too near, they disappeared into the blue depths. Their effortless speed is astonishing. On the lines we caught two yellowfin tunas,* speedy and efficient fish. They struck the line so hard that it is impossible to see why they did not tear their heads off.

We anchored near a bouldery shore. This would be the first

---

* *Neothunnus macropterus.*

station in the Gulf where we would be able to turn over rocks, and a new ecological set-up was indicated by the fact that the small boulders rested in sand.

This time everyone but Tony went ashore. Sparky and Tiny were already developing into good collectors, and now Tex joined us and quickly became excited in the collecting. We welcomed this help, for in general work, what with the shortness of the time and the large areas to be covered, the more hands and eyes involved, the better. Besides, these men who lived by the sea had a great respect for the sea and all its inhabitants. Association with the sea does not breed contempt.

The boulders on this beach were almost a perfect turning-over size—heavy enough to protect the animals under them from grinding by the waves, and light enough to be lifted. They were well coated with short algae and bedded in very coarse sand. The dominant species on this beach was a sulphury cucumber,* a dark, almost black-green holothurian which looks as though it were dusted with sulphur. As the tide dropped on the shallow beach we saw literally millions of these cucumbers. They lay in clusters and piles between the rocks and under the rocks, and as the tide went down and the tropical sun beat on the beach, many of them became quite dry without apparent injury. Most of these holothurians were from five to eight inches long, but there were great numbers of babies, some not more than an inch in length. We took a great many of them.

Easily the second most important animal of this shore in point of quantity was the brittle-star. We had read of their numbers in the Gulf and here they were, mats and clusters of them, giants under the rocks. It was simple to pick up a hundred at a time in black, twisting, squirming knots. There were five species of them, and these we took in large numbers also, for in preservation they sometimes cast off their legs or curl up into knots, and we wished to have a number of perfect specimens. Starfish were abundant here and we took six varieties. The difference between the brittle-star and the starfish is interestingly reflected in the scientific names—"Ophio" is

---

* *Holothuria lubrica.*

a Greek root signifying "serpent"—the round compact body and long serpent-like arms of the brittle-star are suggested in the generic name "ophiuran," while the more truly star-like form of the starfish is recognizable in the Greek root "aster," which occurs in so many of its proper names, "Heliaster," "Astrometis," etc. We found three species of urchins, among them the very sharp-spined and poisonous *Centrechinus mexicanus*; approximately ten different kinds of crabs, four of shrimps, a number of anemones of various types, a great number of worms, including our enemy *Eurythoë*, which seems to occur everywhere in the Gulf, several species of naked mollusks, and a good number of peanut worms. The rocks and the sand underneath them were heavily populated. There were chitons and keyhole limpets, a number of species of clams, flatworms, sponges, bryozoa, and numerous snails.

Again the collecting buckets were very full, but already we had begun the elimination of animals to be taken. On this day we took enough of the sulphury cucumbers and brittle-stars for our needs. These were carefully preserved, but when found again at a new station they would simply be noted in the collecting record, unless some other circumstance such as color change or size variation prevailed. Thus, as we proceeded, we gradually stopped collecting certain species and only noted them as occurring.

On board the *Western Flyer*, again we laid out the animals in pans and prepared them for anesthetization. In one of the sea-cucumbers we found a small commensal fish* which lived well inside the anus. It moved in and out with great ease and speed, resting invariably head inward. In the pan we ejected this fish by a light pressure on the body of the cucumber, but it quickly returned and entered the anus again. The pale, colorless appearance of this fish seemed to indicate that it habitually lived there.

It is interesting to see how areas are sometimes dominated by one or two species. On this beach the yellow-green cucumber was everywhere, with giant brittle-stars a close second. Neither of these animals has any effective offensive property as far as we know, although neither of them seems to be a

---

* *Encheliophiops hancocki* Reid.

delicacy enjoyed by other animals. There does seem to be a balance which, when passed by a certain species, allows that animal numerically to dominate a given area. When this threshold of successful reproduction and survival is crossed, the area becomes the special residence of this form. Then it seems other animals which might be either hostile or perhaps the prey of the dominating animal would be wiped out or would desert the given area. In many cases the arrival and success of a species seem to be by chance entirely. In some northern areas, where the ice of winter yearly scours and cleans the rocks, it has been noted that summer brings some-times one dominant species and sometimes another, the suc-cess factor seeming to be prior arrival and an early start.* With marine fauna, as with humans, priority and possession appear to be vastly important to survival and dominance. But some-times it is found that the very success of an animal is its down-fall. There are examples where the available food supply is so exhausted by the rapid and successful reproduction that the animal must migrate or die. Sometimes, also, the very by-products of the animals' own bodies prove poisonous to a too great concentration of their own species.

It is difficult, when watching the little beasts, not to trace human parallels. The greatest danger to a speculative biologist is analogy. It is a pitfall to be avoided—the industry of the bee, the economics of the ant, the villainy of the snake, all in human terms have given us profound misconceptions of the animals. But parallels are amusing if they are not taken too seriously as regards the animal in question, and are downright valuable as regards humans. The routine of changing domi-nation is a case in point. One can think of the attached and dominant human who has captured the place, the property, and the security. He dominates his area. To protect it, he has police who know him and who are dependent on him for a living. He is protected by good clothing, good houses, and good food. He is protected even against illness. One would say that he is safe, that he would have many children, and that his seed would in a short time litter the world. But in his fight for dominance he has pushed out others of his species who

*Gislén, T., "Epibioses of the Gullmar Fjord II." 1930, p. 157. Kristinebergs Zool. Sta. 1877–1927, *Skrift. ut. av K. Svenska Vetens.* N:r 4.

were not so fit to dominate, and perhaps these have become wanderers, improperly clothed, ill fed, having no security and no fixed base. These should really perish, but the reverse seems true. The dominant human, in his security, grows soft and fearful. He spends a great part of his time in protecting himself. Far from reproducing rapidly, he has fewer children, and the ones he does have are ill protected inside themselves because so thoroughly protected from without. The lean and hungry grow strong, and the strongest of them are selected out. Having nothing to lose and all to gain, these selected hungry and rapacious ones develop attack rather than defense techniques, and become strong in them, so that one day the dominant man is eliminated and the strong and hungry wanderer takes his place.

And the routine is repeated. The new dominant entrenches himself and then softens. The turnover of dominant human families is very rapid, a few generations usually sufficing for their rise and flowering and decay. Sometimes, as in the case of Hearst, the rise and glory and decay take place in one generation and nothing is left. One dominant thing sometimes does survive and that is not even well defined; some quality of the spirit of an individual continues to dominate. Whereas the great force which was Hearst has died before the death of the man and will soon be forgotten except perhaps as a ridiculous and vulgar fable, the spirit and thought of Socrates not only survive, but continue as living entities.

There is a strange duality in the human which makes for an ethical paradox. We have definitions of good qualities and of bad; not changing things, but generally considered good and bad throughout the ages and throughout the species. Of the good, we think always of wisdom, tolerance, kindliness, generosity, humility; and the qualities of cruelty, greed, self-interest, graspingness, and rapacity are universally considered undesirable. And yet in our structure of society, the so-called and considered good qualities are invariable concomitants of failure, while the bad ones are the cornerstones of success. A man—a viewing-point man—while he will love the abstract good qualities and detest the abstract bad, will nevertheless envy and admire the person who through possessing the bad qualities has succeeded economically and socially, and will hold in contempt that person whose good qualities have caused failure. When such a viewing-point man thinks of Jesus or St. Augustine or Socrates he regards them with love because they are the symbols of the good he admires, and he hates the symbols of the bad. But actually he would rather be successful than good. In an animal other than man we would replace the term "good" with "weak survival quotient" and the term "bad" with "strong survival quotient." Thus, man in his thinking or reverie status admires the progression toward extinction, but in the unthinking stimulus which really activates him he tends toward survival. Perhaps no other animal is so torn between alternatives. Man might be described fairly adequately, if simply, as a two-legged paradox. He has never become accustomed to the tragic miracle of consciousness. Perhaps, as has been suggested, his species is not set, has not jelled, but is still in a state of becoming, bound by his physical memories to a past of struggle and survival, limited in his futures by the uneasiness of thought and consciousness.

Back on the *Western Flyer*, Sparky cooked the tuna in a sauce of tomatoes and onions and spices and we ate magnificently. Each rock turned over had not been heavy, but we had turned over many tons of rocks in all. And now the work with the animals had to go on, the preservation and labeling. But we rested and drank a little beer, which in this condition of weariness is rest itself.

While we were eating, a boat came alongside and two Indians climbed aboard. Their clothing was better than that of the poor people of the day before. They were, after all, within a day's canoe trip of La Paz, and some of the veneer of that city had stuck to them. Their clothing was patched and ragged, but at least not falling apart from decay. We asked Sparky and Tiny to bring them a little wine, and after two glasses they became very affable, making us think of the intolerance of the Indian for alcohol. Later it developed that Sparky and Tiny had generously laced the wine with whisky, which proved just the opposite about the Indians' tolerance for alcohol. None of us could have drunk two tumblers, half whisky and half wine, but these men did and became gay and companionable. They were barefoot and carried the iron harpoons of the region, and in the bottom of their canoe lay a huge fish.

Their canoe was typical of the region and was interesting. There are no large trees in the southern part of the Peninsula, hence all the canoes come from the mainland, most of them being made near Mazatlán. They are double-ended canoes carved from a single log of light wood, braced inside with struts. Sometimes a small sail is set, but ordinarily they are paddled swiftly by two men, one at either end. They are seaworthy and fast. The wood inside and out is covered with a thin layer of white or blue plaster, waterproof and very hard. This is made by the people themselves and applied regularly. It is not a paint, but a hard, shell-like plaster, and we could not learn how it is made although this is probably well known to many people. Equipped with one of these canoes, an iron harpoon, a pair of trousers, shirt, and hat, a young man is fairly well set up in life. In fact, the acquiring of a Nayarit canoe will probably give a young man so much security in his own eyes and make him so desirable in the eyes of others that he will promptly get married.

It is said so often and in such ignorance that Mexicans are contented, happy people. "They don't want anything." This, of course, is not a description of the happiness of Mexicans, but of the unhappiness of the person who says it. For Americans, and probably all northern peoples, are all masses of wants growing out of inner insecurity. The great drive of our people stems from insecurity. It is often considered that the violent interest in little games, the mental rat-mazes of contract bridge, and the purposeful striking of little white balls with sticks, comes from an inner sterility. But more likely it comes from an inner complication. Boredom arises not so often from too little to think about, as from too much, and none of it clear nor clean nor simple. Bridge is a means of forgetting the thousands of little irritations of a mind overcrowded with anarchy. For bridge has a purpose, that of taking as many tricks as possible. The end is clear and very simple. But nothing in the lives of bridge-players is clean-cut, and no ends are defined. And so they retire into some orderly process, even in a game, from the messy complication of their lives. It is possible, although we do not know this, that the poor Mexican Indian is a little less messy in his living, having a baby, spearing a fish, getting drunk, backing a political candidate;

each one of these is a clear, free process, ending in a result. We have thought of this in regard to the bribes one sometimes gives to Mexican officials. This is universally condemned by Americans, and yet it is a simple, easy process. A bargain is struck, a price named, the money paid, a graceful compliment exchanged, the service performed, and it is over. He is not your man nor you his. A little process has been terminated. It is rather like the old-fashioned buying and selling for cash or produce.

We find we like this cash-and-carry bribery as contrasted with our own system of credits. With us, no bargain is struck, no price named, nothing is clear. We go to a friend who knows a judge. The friend goes to the judge. The judge knows a senator who has the ear of the awarder of contracts. And eventually we sell five carloads of lumber. But the process has only begun. Every member of the chain is tied to every other. Ten years later the son of the awarder of contracts must be appointed to Annapolis. The senator must have traffic tickets fixed for many years to come. The judge has a political lien on your friend, and your friend taxes you indefinitely with friends who need jobs. It would be simpler and cheaper to go to the awarder of contracts, give him one-quarter of the price of the lumber, and get it over with. But that is dishonest, that is a bribe. Everyone in the credit chain eventually hates and fears everyone else. But the bribe-bargain, having no enforcing mechanism, promotes mutual respect and a genuine liking. If the accepter of a bribe cheats you, you will not go to him again and he will soon have to leave the public service. But if he fulfills his contract, you have a new friend whom you can trust.

We do not know whether Mexicans are happier than we; it is probable that they are exactly as happy. However, we do know that the channels of their happiness or unhappiness are different from ours, just as their time sense is different. We can invade neither, but it is some gain simply to know that it is so.

As the men on our deck continued with what we thought was wine and they probably considered some expensive foreign beverage (it must have tasted bad enough to be very foreign and very expensive), they uncovered a talent for speech we have often noticed in these people. They are natural orators, filling their sentences with graceful forms, with similes and elegant parallels. Our oldest man delivered for us a beautiful political speech. He was an ardent admirer of General Almazán, who was then a candidate for the Mexican presidency. Our Indian likened the General militarily to the god of war, but whether Mars, or Huitzilopochtli, he did not say. In physical beauty the General stemmed from Apollo, not he of the Belvedere, but an earlier, sturdier Apollo. In kindness and forethought and wisdom Almazán was rather above the lesser deities. Our man even touched on the General's abilities in bed, although how he knew he did not say. We gathered, though, that the General was known and well thought of in this respect by his total feminine constituency. "He is a strong man," said our orator, holding himself firmly upright by the port stay. One of us interposed, "When he is elected there will be more fish in the sea for the poor people of Mexico." And the orator nodded wisely. "That is so my friend," he said. It was later that we learned that General Camacho, the other candidate, had many of the same beautiful qualities as General Almazán. And since he won, perhaps he had them more highly developed. For political virtues always triumph, and when two such colossi as these oppose each other, one can judge their relative excellences only by counting the vote.

We had known that sooner or later we must develop an explanation for what we were doing which would be short and convincing. It couldn't be the truth because that wouldn't be convincing at all. How can you say to a people who are preoccupied with getting enough food and enough children that you have come to pick up useless little animals so that perhaps your world picture will be enlarged? That didn't even convince us. But there had to be a story, for everyone asked us. One of us had once taken a long walking trip through the southern United States. At first he had tried to explain that he did it because he liked to walk and because he saw and felt the country better that way. When he gave this explanation there was unbelief and dislike for him. It sounded like a lie. Finally a man said to him, "You can't fool me, you're doing it on a bet." And after that, he used this explanation, and everyone liked and understood him from then on. So with these men we developed our story and stuck to it thereafter. We were collecting curios, we said. These beautiful little animals and shells, while they abounded so greatly here as to be valueless, had, because of their scarcity in the United States, a certain value. They would not make us rich but it was at least profitable to take them. And besides, we liked taking them. Once we had developed this story we never had any more trouble. They all understood us then, and brought us what they thought were rare articles for the collection. They considered that we might get very rich. Thank heaven they do not know that when at last we came back to San Diego the customs fixed a value on our thousands of pickled animals of five dollars. We hope these Indians never find it out; we would go down steeply in their estimations.

Our men went away finally a trifle intoxicated, but not forgetting to take an armload of empty tomato cans. They value tin cans very highly.

It would not have done to sail for La Paz harbor that night, for the pilot has short hours and any boat calling for him out of his regular hours must pay double. But we wanted very much to get to La Paz; we were out of beer and already the water in our tanks was stale-tasting. It had seemed to us that it was stale when we put it in and time did not improve it. It isn't likely that we would have died of thirst. The second or third day would undoubtedly have seen us drinking the unpleasant stuff. But there were other reasons why we longed for La Paz. Cape San Lucas had not really been a town, and our crew had convinced itself that it had been a very long time out of touch with civilization. In civilization we think they included some items which, if anything, are attenuated in highly civilized groups. In addition, there is the genuine fascination of the city of La Paz. Everyone in the area knows the greatness of La Paz. You can get anything in the world there, they say. It is a huge place—not of course so monstrous as Guaymas or Mazatlán, but beautiful out of all comparison. The Indians paddle hundreds of miles to be at La Paz on a feast day. It is a proud thing to have been born in La Paz, and a cloud of delight hangs over the distant city from the time when it was the great pearl center of the world. The robes of the Spanish kings and the stoles of bishops in Rome were stiff with the pearls from La Paz. There's a magic-carpet sound to the name, anyway. And it is an old city, as cities in the West are old, and very venerable in the eyes of Indians of the Gulf. Guaymas is busier, they say, and Mazatlán gayer, perhaps, but La Paz is *antigua*.

The Gulf and Gulf ports have always been unfriendly to colonization. Again and again attempts were made before a settlement would stick. Humans are not much wanted on the Peninsula. But at La Paz the pearl oysters drew men from all over the world. And, as in all concentrations of natural wealth, the terrors of greed were let loose on the city again and again. An event which happened at La Paz in recent years is typical of such places. An Indian boy by accident found a pearl of great size, an unbelievable pearl. He knew its value was so great that he need never work again. In his one pearl he had the ability to be drunk as long as he wished, to marry any one of a number of girls, and to make many more a little happy too. In his great pearl lay salvation, for he could in advance purchase masses sufficient to pop him out of Purgatory like a squeezed watermelon seed. In addition he could shift a number of dead relatives a little nearer to Paradise. He went to La Paz with his pearl in his hand and his future clear into eternity in his heart. He took his pearl to a broker and was offered so little that he grew angry, for he knew he was cheated. Then he carried his pearl to another broker and was offered the same amount. After a few more visits he came to know that the brokers were only the many hands of one head and that he could not sell his pearl for more. He took it to the beach and hid it under a stone, and that night he was clubbed into unconsciousness and his clothing was searched. The next night he slept at the house of a friend and his friend and he were injured and bound and the whole house searched. Then he went inland to lose his pursuers and he was waylaid and tortured. But he was very angry now and he knew what he must do. Hurt as he was he crept back to La Paz in the night and he skulked like a hunted fox to the beach and took out his pearl from under the stone. Then he cursed it and threw it as far as he could into the channel. He was a free man again with his soul in danger and his food and shelter insecure. And he laughed a great deal about it.

This seems to be a true story, but it is so much like a parable that it almost can't be. This Indian boy is too heroic, too wise. He knows too much and acts on his knowledge. In every way, he goes contrary to human direction. The story is probably true, but we don't believe it; it is far too reasonable to be true.

La Paz, the great city, was only a little way from us now, we could almost see its towers and smell its perfume. And it was right that it should be so hidden here out of the world, inaccessible except to the galleons of a small boy's imagination.

While we were anchored at Espíritu Santo Island a black yacht went by swiftly, and on her awninged after-deck ladies and gentlemen in white clothing sat comfortably. We saw they had tall cool drinks beside them and we hated them a little, for we were out of beer. And Tiny said fiercely, "Nobody but a pansy'd sail on a thing like that." And then more gently, "But I've never been sure I ain't queer." The yacht went down over the horizon, and up over the horizon climbed an old horror of a cargo ship, dirty and staggering. And she stumbled on toward the channel of La Paz; her pumps must have been going wide open. Later, at La Paz, we saw her very low in the water in the channel. We said to a man on the beach, "She is sinking." And he replied calmly, "She always sinks."

On the *Western Flyer*, vanity had set in. Clothing was washed unmercifully. The white tops of caps were laundered, and jeans washed and patted smooth while wet and hung from the stays to dry. Shoes were even polished and the shaving and bathing were deafening. The sweet smell of unguents and hair oils, of deodorants and lotions, filled the air. Hair was cut and combed; the mirror over the washstand behind the deck-house was in constant use. We regarded ourselves in the mirror with the long contemplative coy looks of chorus girls about to go on stage. What we found was not good, but it was the best we had. Heaven knows what we expected to find in La Paz, but we wanted to be beautiful for it.

And in the morning, when we got under way, we washed the fish blood off the decks and put away the equipment. We coiled the lines in lovely spirals and washed all the dishes. It seemed to us we made a rather gallant show, and we hoped that no beautiful yacht was anchored in La Paz. If there were a yacht, we would be tough and seafaring, but if no such contrast was available some of us at least proposed to be not a little jaunty. Even the least naïve of us expected Spanish ladies in high combs and mantillas to be promenading along the beach. It would be rather like the opening scene of a Hollywood production of *Life in Latin America*, with dancers in the foreground and cabaret tables upstage from which would rise a male chorus to sing "I met my love in La Paz— satin and Latin she was."

We assembled on top of the deckhouse, the *Coast Pilot* open in front of us. Even Tony had succumbed; he wore a gaudy white seaman's cap with a gold ornament on the front of it which seemed to be a combination of field artillery and submarine service, except that it had an arrow-pierced heart superimposed on it.

We have so often admired the literary style and quality of the *Coast Pilot* that it might be well here to quote from it. In the first place, the compilers of this book are cynical men. They know that they are writing for morons, that if by any effort their descriptions can be misinterpreted or misunderstood by the reader, that effort will be made. These writers have a contempt for almost everything. They would like an ocean and a coastline unchanging and unchangeable; lights and buoys that do not rust and wash away; winds and storms that come at specified times; and, finally, reasonably intelligent men to read their instructions. They are gratified in none of these desires. They try to write calmly and objectively, but now and then a little bitterness creeps in, particularly when they deal with Mexican lights, buoys, and port facilities. The following quotation is from H. O. No. 84, "Sailing Directions for the West Coasts of Mexico and Central America, 1937, Corrections to January 1940," page 125, under "La Paz Harbor."

La Paz Harbor is that portion of La Paz Channel between the eastern end of El Mogote and the shore in the vicinity of La Paz. El Mogote is a low, sandy, bush-covered peninsula, about 6 miles long, east and west, and 1½ miles wide at its widest part, that forms the northern side of Ensenada de Anpe, a large lagoon. This lagoon lies in a low plain that is covered with a thick growth of trees, bushes, and cactus. The water is shoal over the greater part of the lagoon, but a channel in which there are depths of 2 to 4 fathoms leads from La Paz Harbor to its northwestern part.

La Paz Harbor is ½ to ¾ mile wide, but it is nearly filled with shoals through which there is a winding channel with depths of 3 to 4 fathoms. A shoal with depths of only 1 to 8 feet over it extends northward from the eastern end of El Mogote to within 400 yards of Prieta Point and thus protects La Paz Harbor from the seas caused by northwesterly winds.

La Paz Channel, leading between the shoal just mentioned and the mainland, and extending from Prieta Point to abreast the town of La Paz, has a length of about 3½ miles and a least charted depth of 3¼ fathoms, but this depth can not be depended upon. Vessels of 13-foot draft may pass through the channel at any stage of the tide. The channel is narrow, with steep banks on either side, the water in some places shoaling from 3 fathoms to 3 to 4 feet within a distance of 20 yards. The deep water of the channel and the projecting points of the shoals on either side can readily be distinguished from aloft. In 1934 the controlling depth in the channel was reported to be 16 feet.

A 9-foot channel, frequently used by coasters, leads across the shoal bank and into La Paz Channel at a position nearly 1 mile south-southeastward of Prieta Point. Caymancito Rock, on the eastern side of La Paz Channel, bearing 129°, leads through this side channel.

Beacons —Off Prieta Point, at the entrance to the channel leading to La Paz, there are three beacons consisting of lengths of 3-inch pipe driven into the bottom and extending only a few feet above the surface of the water. They are difficult to make out at high tide in the daytime, and are not lighted at night [here the hatred creeps in subtly].

Light Beacons —Three pairs of concrete range beacons, from each of which a light is shown, mark La Paz Channel. The outer range is situated on the shore near the entrance to the channel, about 1 mile southeastward of Prieta Point; the middle range is on a hillside about ¼ mile south-southeastward of Caymancito Rock; and the inner range is situated about ¾ mile northeastward of the municipal pier at La Paz. . . .

Harbor Lights —A light is shown from a wooden post 18 feet high and another from a post 20 feet high on the north and south ends, respectively, of the T-head of the municipal pier at La Paz. . . .

Anchorage —Vessels waiting for a pilot can anchor southward of

Prieta Point in depths of 7 to 10 fathoms. Anchorage can also be taken northward of El Mogote, but it is exposed to wind and sea. . . .

The best berth off the town is 200 to 300 yards westward of the pier in a depth of about 3½ fathoms, sand. . . .

Pilotage is compulsory for all foreign merchant vessels. Pilots come out in a small motor launch carrying a white flag on which is the letter P, and board incoming vessels in the vicinity of Prieta Point. Although pilots will take vessels in at night, it is not advisable to attempt to enter the harbor after dark.

This is a good careful description by men whose main drive is toward accuracy, and they must be driven frantic as man and tide and wave undermine their work. The shifting sands of the channel; the three-inch pipe driven into the bottom; the T-head municipal pier with its lights on wooden posts, none of which has been there for some time; and, last, their conviction that the pilots cannot find the channel at night, make for their curious, cold, tactful statement. We trust these men. They are controlled, and only now and then do their nerves break and a cry of pain escape them thus, in the "Supplement" dated 1940:

Page 109, Line 1, for *"LIGHTS"* read *"LIGHT"* and for *"TWO LIGHTS ARE"* read *"WHEN THE CANNERY IS IN OPERATION, A LIGHT IS."*

Or again:

Page 149, Line 2, after *"line"* add: *"two piers project inward from this mole, affording berths for vessels and, except alongside these two piers, the mole is foul with debris and wrecked cranes."*

These coast pilots are constantly exasperated; they are not happy men. When anything happens they are blamed, and their writing takes on an austere tone because of it. No matter how hard they work, the restlessness of nature and the carelessness of man are always two jumps ahead of them.

We ran happily up under Prieta Point as suggested, and dropped anchor and put up the American flag and under it the yellow quarantine flag. We would have liked to fire a gun, but we had only the ten-gauge shotgun, and its hammer was rusted down. It was only for a show of force anyway; we had never intended it for warlike purposes. And then we sat and waited. The site was beautiful—the highland of Prieta Point and a tower on the hillside. In the distance we could see the beach of La Paz, and it really looked like a Hollywood production, the fine, low buildings close down to the water and trees flanking them and a colored bandstand on the water's edge. The little canoes of Nayarit sailed by, and the sea was ruffled with a fair breeze. We took some color motion pictures of the scene, but they didn't come out either.

After what seemed a very long time, the little launch mentioned in the *Coast Pilot* started for us. But it had no white flag with the letter "P." Like the municipal pier, that was gone. The pilot, an elderly man in a business suit and a dark hat, came stiffly aboard. He had great dignity. He refused a drink, accepted cigarettes, took his position at the wheel, and ordered us on grandly. He looked like an admiral in civilian clothes. He governed Tex with a sensitive hand—a gentle push forward against the air meant "ahead." A flattened hand patting downward signified "slow." A quick thumb over the shoulder, "reverse." He was not a talkative man, and he ran us through the channel with ease, hardly scraping us at all, and signaled our anchor down 250 yards westward of the municipal pier—if there had been one—the choicest place in the harbor.

La Paz grew in fascination as we approached. The square, iron-shuttered colonial houses stood up right in back of the beach with rows of beautiful trees in front of them. It is a lovely place. There is a broad promenade along the water lined with benches, named for dead residents of the city, where one may rest oneself.

Soon after we had anchored, the port captain, customs man, and agent came aboard. The captain read our papers, which complimented us rather highly, and was so impressed that he immediately assigned us an armed guard—or, rather, three shifts of armed guards—to protect us from theft. At first we did not like this, since we had to pay these men, but we soon found the wisdom of it. For we swarmed with visitors from morning to night; little boys clustered on us like flies, in the rigging and on the deck. And although we were infested and crawling with very poor people and children, we lost nothing;

and this in spite of the fact that there were little gadgets lying about that any one of us would have stolen if we had had the chance. The guards simply kept our visitors out of the galley and out of the cabin. But we do not think they prevented theft, for in other ports where we had no guard nothing was stolen.

The guards, big pleasant men armed with heavy automatics, wore uniforms that were starched and clean, and they were helpful and sociable. They ate with us and drank coffee with us and told us many valuable things about the town. And in the end we gave each of them a carton of cigarettes, which seemed valuable to them. But they were the reverse of what is usually thought and written of Mexican soldiers—they were clean, efficient, and friendly.

With the port captain came the agent, probably the finest invention of all. He did everything for us, provisioned us, escorted us, took us to dinner, argued prices for us in local stores, warned us about some places and recommended others. His fee was so small that we doubled it out of pure gratitude.

As soon as we were cleared, Sparky and Tiny and Tex went ashore and disappeared, and we did not see them until late that night, when they came back with the usual presents: shawls and carved cow-horns and colored handkerchiefs. They were so delighted with the exchange (which was then six pesos for a dollar) that we were very soon deeply laden with curios. There were five huge stuffed sea-turtles in one bunk alone, and Japanese toys, combs from New England, Spanish shawls from New Jersey, machetes from Sheffield and New York; but all of them, from having merely lived a while in La Paz, had taken on a definite Mexican flavor. Tony, who does not trust foreigners, stayed aboard, but later even he went ashore for a while.

The tide was running out and the low shore east of the town was beginning to show through the shallow water. We gathered our paraphernalia and started for the beach, expecting and finding a fauna new to us. Here on the flats the water is warm, very warm, and there is no wave-shock. It would be strange indeed if, with few exceptions of ubiquitous animals, there should not be a definite change. The base of this flat was of rubble in which many knobs and limbs of old coral were imbedded, making an easy hiding place for burrowing animals. In rubber boots we moved over the flat uncovered by the dropping tide; a silty sand made the water obscure when a rock or a piece of coral was turned over. And as always when one is collecting, we were soon joined by a number of small boys. The very posture of search, the slow movement with the head down, seems to draw people. "What did you lose?" they ask.

"Nothing."

"Then what do you search for?" And this is an embarrassing question. We search for something that will seem like truth to us; we search for understanding; we search for that principle which keys us deeply into the pattern of all life; we search for the relations of things, one to another, as this young man searches for a warm light in his wife's eyes and that one for the hot warmth of fighting. These little boys and young men on the tide flat do not even know that they search for such things too. We say to them, "We are looking for curios, for certain small animals."

Then the little boys help us to search. They are ragged and dark and each one carries a small iron harpoon. It is the toy of La Paz, owned and treasured as tops or marbles are in America. They poke about the rocks with their little harpoons, and now and then a lazing fish which blunders too close feels the bite of the iron.

There is a small ghost shrimp which lives on these flats, an efficient little fellow who lives in a burrow. He moves very rapidly, and is armed with claws which can pinch painfully. He retires backward into his hole, so that to come at him from above is to invite his weapons. The little boys solved the problem for us. We offered ten centavos for each one they took. They dug into the rubble and old coral until they got behind the ghost shrimp in his burrow, then, prodding, they drove him outraged from his hole. Then they banged him good to reduce his pinching power. We refused to buy the banged-up ones—they had to get us lively ones. Small boys are the best collectors in the world. Soon they worked out a technique for catching the shrimps with only an occasionally pinched finger, and then the ten-centavo pieces began running out, and an increasing cloud of little boys brought us specimens. Small boys have such sharp eyes, and they are quick to notice deviation. Once they know you are generally curious, they bring amazing things. Perhaps we only practice an extension of their urge. It is easy to remember when we were small and lay on our stomachs beside a tide pool and our minds and eyes went so deeply into it that size and identity were lost, and the creeping hermit crab was our size and the tiny octopus a monster. Then the waving algae covered us and we hid under a rock at the bottom and leaped out at fish. It is very possible that we, and even those who probe space with equations, simply extend this wonder.

Among small-boy groups there is usually a stupid one who understands nothing, who brings dull things, rocks and pieces of weed, and pretends that he knows what he does. When we think of La Paz, it is always of the small boys that we think first, for we had many dealings with them on many levels.

The profile of this flat was easy to get. The ghost shrimps, called *"langusta,"* were quite common; our enemy the stinging worm was about, to make us careful of our fingers; the big brittle-stars were there under the old coral, but not in such great masses as at Espíritu Santo. A number of sponges clung to the stones, and small decorated crabs skulked in the interstices. Beautiful purple polyclad worms crawled over lawns of purple tunicates; the giant oyster-like hacha* was not often found, but we took a few specimens. There were several growth forms of the common corals†; the larger and handsomer of the two slim asteroids‡; anemones of at least three types; some club urchins and snails and many hydroids.

Some of the exposed snails were so masked with forests of algae and hydroids that they were invisible to us. We found a worm-like fixed gastropod,§ many bivalves, including the long peanut-shaped boring clam‖; large brilliant-orange nudibranchs; hermit crabs; mantids; flatworms which seemed to flow over the rocks like living gelatin; sipunculids; and many

---

* *Pinna* sp.
† *Porites.*
‡ *Phataria.*
§ *Aletes*, or similar.
‖ *Lithophaga plumula*, or similar.

limpets. There were a few sun-stars, but not so many or so large as they had been at Cape San Lucas.

The little boys ran to and fro with full hands, and our buckets and tubes were soon filled. The ten-centavo pieces had long run out, and ten little boys often had to join a club whose center and interest was a silver peso, to be changed and divided later. They seemed to trust one another for the division. And certainly they felt there was no chance of their being robbed. Perhaps they are not civilized and do not know how valuable money is. The poor little savages seem not to have learned the great principle of cheating one another.

The population of small boys at La Paz is tremendous, and we had business dealings with a good part of it. Hardly had we returned to the *Western Flyer* and begun to lay out our specimens when we were invaded. Word had spread that there were crazy people in port who gave money for things a boy could pick up on the rocks. We were more than invaded—we were deluged with small boys bearing specimens. They came out in canoes, in flatboats, some even swam out, and all of them carried specimens. Some of the things they brought we wanted and some we did not want. There were hurt feelings about this, but no bitterness. Battalions of boys swarmed back to the flats and returned again. The second day little boys came even from the hills, and they brought every conceivable living thing. If we had not sailed the second night they would have swamped the boat. Meanwhile, in our dealings on shore, more small boys were involved. They carried packages, ran errands, directed us (mostly wrongly), tried to anticipate our wishes; but one boy soon emerged. He was not like the others. His shoulders were not slender, but broad, and there was a hint about his face and expression that seemed Germanic or perhaps Anglo-Saxon. Whereas the other little boys lived for the job and the payment, this boy created jobs and looked ahead. He did errands that were not necessary, he made himself indispensable. Late at night he waited, and the first dawn saw him on our deck. Further, the other small boys seemed a little afraid of him, and gradually they faded into the background and left him in charge.

Some day this boy will be very rich and La Paz will be proud of him, for he will own the things other people must buy or rent. He has the look and the method of success. Even the first day success went to his head, and he began to cheat us a little. We did not mind, for it is a good thing to be cheated a little; it causes a geniality and can be limited fairly easily. His method was simple. He performed a task, and then, getting each of us alone, he collected for the job so that he was paid several times. We decided we would not use him any more, but the other little boys decided even better than we. He disappeared, and later we saw him in the town, his nose and lips heavily bandaged. We had the story from another little boy. Our financial wizard told the others that he was our sole servant and that we had said that they weren't to come around any more. But they discovered the lie and waylaid him and beat him very badly. He wasn't a very brave little boy, but he will be a rich one because he wants to. The others wanted only sweets or a new handkerchief, but the aggressive little boy wishes to be rich, and they will not be able to compete with him.

On the evening of our sailing we had rather a sad experience with another small boy. We had come ashore for a stroll, leaving our boat tied to a log on the beach. We walked up the curiously familiar streets and ended, oddly enough, in a bar to have a glass of beer. It was a large bar with high ceilings, and nearly deserted. As we sat sipping our beer we saw a ferocious face scowling at us. It was a very small, very black Indian boy, and the look in his eyes was one of hatred. He stared at us so long and so fiercely that we finished our glasses and got up to go. But outside he fell into step with us, saying nothing. We walked back through the softly lighted streets, and he kept pace. But near the beach he began to pant deeply. Finally we got to the beach and as we were about to untie the skiff he shouted in panic, *"Cinco centavos!"* and stepped back as from a blow. And then it seemed that we could see almost how it was. We have been the same way trying to get a job. Perhaps the father of this little boy said, "Stupid one, there are strangers in the town and they are throwing money away. Here sits your father with a sore leg and you do nothing. Other boys are becoming rich, but you, because of your sloth, are not taking advantage of this miracle. Señor Ruiz had a cigar this afternoon and a glass of beer at the *cantina* because his fine son is not like you. When have you known me, your father, to have a cigar? Never. Now go and bring back some little piece of money."

Then that little boy, hating to do it, was burdened with it nevertheless. He hated us, just as we have hated the men we have had to ask for jobs. And he was afraid, too, for we were foreigners. He put it off as long as he could, but when we were about to go he had to ask and he made it very humble. Five centavos. It did seem that we knew how hard it had been. We gave him a peso, and then he smiled broadly and he looked about for something he could do for us. The boat was tied up, and he attacked the water-soaked knot like a terrier, even working at it with his teeth. But he was too little and he could not do it. He nearly cried then. We cast off and pushed the boat away, and he waded out to guide us as far as he could. We felt both good and bad about it; we hope his father bought a cigar and an *aguardiente*, and became mellow and said to a group of men in that little boy's hearing, "Now you take Juanito. You have rarely seen such a good son. This very cigar is a gift to his father who has hurt his leg. It is a matter of pride, my friends, to have a son like Juanito." And we hope he gave Juanito, if that was his name, five centavos to buy an ice and a paper bull with a firecracker inside.

No doubt we were badly cheated in La Paz. Perhaps the boatmen cheated us and maybe we paid too much for supplies—it is very hard to know. And besides, we were so incredibly rich that we couldn't tell, and we had no instinct for knowing when we were cheated. Here we were rich, but in our own country it was not so. The very rich develop an instinct which tells them when they are cheated. We knew a rich man who owned several large office buildings. Once in reading his reports he found that two electric-light bulbs had been stolen from one of the toilets in one of his office buildings. It hurt him; he brooded for weeks about it. "Civilization is dying," he said. "Whom can you trust any more? This little theft is an indication that the whole people is morally rotten."

But we were so newly rich that we didn't know, and besides we were a little flattered. The boatmen raised their price as soon as they saw the Sea-Cow wouldn't work, but as they said, times are very hard and there is no money.

12

March 22

T HIS was Good Friday, and we scrubbed ourselves and put on our best clothes and went to church, all of us. We were a kind of parade on the way to church, feeling foreign and out of place. In the dark church it was cool, and there were a great many people, old women in their black shawls and Indians kneeling motionless on the floor. It was not a very rich church, and it was old and out of repair. But a choir of small black children made the Stations of the Cross. They sang music that sounded like old Spanish madrigals, and their voices were shrill and sharp. Sometimes they faltered a little bit on the melody, but they hit the end of each line shrieking. When they had finished, a fine-looking young priest with a thin ascetic face and the hot eyes of fervency preached from over their heads. He filled the whole church with his faith, and the people were breathlessly still. The ugly bloody Christs and the simpering Virgins and the over-dressed saints were suddenly out of it. The priest was purer and cleaner and stronger than they. Out of his own purity he seemed to plead for them. After a long time we got up and went out of the dark cool church into the blinding white sunlight.

The streets were very quiet on Good Friday, and no wind blew in the trees, the air was full of the day—a kind of hush, as though the world awaited a little breathlessly the dreadful experiment of Christ with death and Hell; the testing in a furnace of an idea. And the trees and the hills and the people seemed to wait as a man waits when his wife is having a baby, expectant and frightened and horrified and half unbelieving.

There is no certainty that the Easter of the Resurrection will really come. We were probably literarily affected by the service and the people and their feeling about it, the crippled and the pained who were in the church, the little half-hungry children, the ancient women with eyes of patient tragedy who stared up at the plaster saints with eyes of such pleading. We liked them and we felt at peace with them. And strolling slowly through the streets we thought a long time of these people in the church. We thought of the spirits of kindness which periodically cause them to be fed, a little before they are dropped back to hunger. And we thought of the good men who labored to cure them of disease and poverty.

And then we thought of what they are, and we are—products of disease and sorrow and hunger and alcoholism. And suppose some all-powerful mind and will should cure our species so that for a number of generations we would be healthy and happy? We are the products of our disease and suffering. These are factors as powerful as other genetic factors. To cure and feed would be to change the species, and the result would be another animal entirely. We wonder if we would be able to tolerate our own species without a history of syphilis and tuberculosis. We don't know.

Certain communicants of the neurological conditioning religions practiced by cowardly people who, by narrowing their emotional experience, hope to broaden their lives, lead us to think we would not like this new species. These religionists, being afraid not only of pain and sorrow but even of joy, can so protect themselves that they seem dead to us. The new animal resulting from purification of the species might be one we wouldn't like at all. For it is through struggle and sorrow that people are able to participate in one another—the heartlessness of the healthy, well-fed, and unsorrowful person has in it an infinite smugness.

On the water's edge of La Paz a new hotel was going up, and it looked very expensive. Probably the airplanes will bring week-enders from Los Angeles before long, and the beautiful poor bedraggled old town will bloom with a Floridian ugliness.

Hearing a burst of chicken voices, we looked over a mud wall and saw that there were indeed chickens in the yard behind it. We asked then of a woman if we might buy several. They could be sold, she said, but they were not what one calls "for sale." We entered her yard. One of the proofs that they were not for sale was that we had to catch them ourselves. We picked out two which looked a little less muscular than the others, and went for them. Whatever has been said, true or not, of the indolence of the Lower Californian is entirely untrue of his chickens. They were athletes, highly trained both in speed and in methods of escape. They could run, fly, and, when cornered, disappear entirely and re-materialize in another part of the yard. If the owner did not want to catch them, that hesitancy was not shared by the rest of La Paz. People and children came from everywhere; a mob collected, first to give excited advice and then to help. A pillar of dust arose out of that yard. Small boys hurled themselves at the chickens like football-players. We were bound to catch them sooner or later, for as one group became exhausted, another took up the chase. If we had played fair and given those chickens rest periods, we would never have caught them. But by keeping at them, we finally wore them down and they were caught, completely exhausted and almost shorn of their feathers. Everyone in the mob felt good and happy then and we paid for the chickens and left.

On board it was Sparky's job to kill them, and he hated it. But finally he cut their heads off and was sick. He hung them over the side to bleed and a boat came along and mashed them flat against our side. But even then they were tough. They had the most highly developed muscles we have ever seen. Their legs were like those of ballet dancers and there was no softness in their breasts. We stewed them for many hours and it did no good whatever. We were sorry to kill them, for they were gallant, fast chickens. In our country they could easily have got scholarships in one of our great universities and had collegiate careers, for they had spirit and fight and, for all we know, loyalty.

On the afternoon tide we were to collect on El Mogote, a low sandy peninsula with a great expanse of shallows which would be exposed at low tide. The high-tide level was defined by a heavy growth of mangrove. The area was easily visible from our anchorage, and the sand was smooth and not filled with rubble or stones or coral. A tall handsome boy of about nineteen had been idling about the *Western Flyer*. He had his own canoe, and he offered to paddle us to the tide flats. This boy's name was Raúl Velez; he spoke some English and was of great service to us, for his understanding was quick and he helped valuably at the collecting. He told us the local names of many of the animals we had taken; "cornuda" was the hammer-head shark; "barco," the red snapper; "caracol," and also "burral," all snails in general, but particularly the large conch. Urchins were called "erizo" and sea-fans, "abanico." "Bromas" were barnacles and "hacha" the pinna, or large clam.

The sand flats were very interesting. We dug up a number of Dentaliums of two species, the first we had found. These animals, which look like slender curved teeth, belong to a small class of mollusks, little known popularly, called "tooth shells."

On the shallow bottom, attached to very small stones, we found little anemones of three types. There were also sand anemones,* in long filthy-looking gray cases when they were dug out. But when they were imbedded in the bottom and expanded, they looked like lovely red and purple flowers. A great number of small black cucumbers of a type we had not taken crawled on the bottom, as well as one large pepper-and-salt cucumber. We found many heart-urchins, two species of the ordinary ophiurans (brittle-stars), and one burrowing ophiuran. Sponges and tunicates were fastened to the insecure footing of very small stones, but since there is probably very little churning of water on the tide flats, they were safe enough. There were flat worms of several species; stinging worms, peanut worms, echiuroid worms, and what in the collecting notes are listed rather tiredly as "worms." We took one specimen of the sea-whip, a rather spectacular colony of animals looking exactly like a long white whip. The lower portion is a horny stalk and the upper part consists of zooids carrying on their own life processes but connected by a series of canals which unite their body cavities with the main stalk.

As the tide came up we moved upward in the intertidal toward the mangrove trees, and the foul smell of them reached us. They were in bloom, and the sharp sweet smell of their flowers, combined with the filthy odor of the mud about their roots, was sickening. But they are fascinating to look into. Huge hermit crabs seem to live among their stilted roots; the black mud, product of the root masses, swarms as a meeting place for land and sea animals. Flies and insects in great numbers crawl and buzz about the mud, and the scav-

---

* *Cerianthus.*

enging hermit crabs steal secretly in and out and even climb into the high roots.

We suppose it is the combination of foul odor and the impenetrable quality of the mangrove roots which gives one a feeling of dislike for these salt-water-eating bushes. We sat quietly and watched the moving life in the forests of the roots, and it seemed to us that there was stealthy murder everywhere. On the surf-swept rocks it was a fierce and hungry and joyous killing, committed with energy and ferocity. But here it was like stalking, quiet murder. The roots gave off clicking sounds, and the odor was disgusting. We felt that we were watching something horrible. No one likes the mangroves. Raúl said that in La Paz no one loved them at all.

On the level flats the tide covers the area very quickly. We waded out to a wrecked boat lying turned over on the sand, and took a number of barnacles from the rotten wood and even from the rusted engine. It was a good rich collecting day, and it had been a curiously emotional day beginning with the church. Sometimes one has a feeling of fullness, of warm wholeness, wherein every sight and object and odor and experience seems to key into a gigantic whole. That day even the mangrove was part of it. Perhaps among primitive peoples the human sacrifice has the same effect of creating a wholeness of sense and emotion—the good and bad, beautiful, ugly, and cruel all welded into one thing. Perhaps a whole man needs this balance. And we had been as excited at finding the Dentaliums as though they had been nuggets of gold.

Raúl had a La Paz harpoon in his canoe, and we bought it from him, hoping to bring it home. It was a shaft of iron with a ring on one end for the line and a point and hinged barb at the other. A little circle of cord holds the barb against the shaft until the friction of the flesh of the victim pushes the cord free and allows the barb to open out inside the flesh. We wanted to keep this harpoon, but we lost it in a manta ray later. At this reading, there are many manta rays in the Gulf cruising about with our harpoons in their hides.

We also wanted one of the Nayarit canoes to take back, for they are light and of shallow draft, ideal for collecting in the lagoons and seaworthy even in rough water. But no one would sell a canoe. They came from too far away and were too well loved. Some very old ones were solid with braces and patches.

It was dusk when we came back to the *Western Flyer*, and the deck was filled with waiting little boys holding mashed and mangled specimens of all kinds. We bought what we needed and then we bought a lot of things we didn't need. The boys had waited a long time for us, under the stern eye of our military man. And it was interesting to see how our soldier loved the ragged little boys of La Paz. When they got out of hand or ran too fast over the deck, he cautioned them, but there was none of the bluster of the policeman. And had we not been just to the little boys, he would have joined them; for they were his people and our great wealth would not have deflected him from them. He wore his automatic, but it was only a badge with no show of force about it, and when he entered the galley or sat down with us he removed the gun belt and hung it up. We liked the tone of voice he used on the boys. It had dignity and authority but no bullying quality, and the boys of the town seemed to respect him without fearing him.

Once when a little boy practiced the most ancient trick in the list of boy skulduggery—that of removing a specimen and selling it again—the soldier spoke to him shortly with contempt, and that boy lost his standing and even his friends.

One boy had, on a light harpoon, a fish which looked something like the puffers—a gray and black fish with a large flat head. When we wished to buy it he refused, saying that a man had commissioned him to get this fish and he was to receive ten centavos for it because the man wanted to poison a cat. This was the *botete*, and our first experience with it. It is thought in La Paz that the poison concentrates in the liver and this part is used for poisoning small animals and even flies. We did not make this test, but we found *botete* everywhere in the warm shallow waters of the Gulf. Probably he is the most prevalent fish of all in lagoons and eel-grass flats. He lies on the bottom, and his marking makes him nearly invisible. Sometimes he lies in a small cleared place in eel-grass or in a slight depression on the silt bottom which indicates, but does not prove, that he has a fairly permanent resting-place to which he returns. When one is wading in the shallows, *botete* lies quiet until he is nearly stepped on before he streaks away, drawing a cloud of disturbed mud after him.

In the press of collecting and preserving, we neglected to dissect the stomach of this fish, so we do not know what he eats.

The literature on *botete* is scattered and hard to come by. Members of his genus, having his poisonous qualities, are distributed all over the world where there are shallows of warm water. Since this fish is very dangerous to eat and is so widely found, it is curious that so little has been written about it. Eating him almost invariably causes death in agony. If he were rare, it would be understandable why he has been so little discussed. But more has been written about some of the seldom-seen fishes of the great depths than of this deadly little *botete*. We were fascinated with him and took a number of specimens. Following are some of the few reports available on his nature and misdemeanors. We still do not know whether he kills flies.

From Herre* we learn that "In at least two or three of the sub-orders the flesh nearly always is not only thin, hard, often bitter and usually unpalatable, but also contains poisonous alkaloids. These produce the disease known as ciguatera, in which the nervous system is attacked and violent gastric disturbances, paralysis, and death may follow."

On page 423 he discusses the Balistidae, or trigger-fish such as the Gulf puerco: "Although seen in fish markets throughout the Orient, none of the Balistidae are much used as human food. In some localities of the Philippines, those of moderate size are eaten, but their sale here should be forbidden as their flesh is always more or less poisonous. In such places as Cuba and Mauritius they are not allowed in the markets as they are known to cause ciguatera.

"Francis Day says (*Fishes of India*, 1878, p. 686): 'Dr. Meunier, at Mauritius, considers that the poisonous flesh acts primarily on the nervous tissue of the stomach, causing violent spasms of that organ and, shortly afterwards, of all the muscles of the body. The frame becomes wracked with spasms, the

*"Poisonous and Worthless Fishes: An Account of the Philippine Plectognaths," *Phil. Journ. Sci.*, Vol. 25 (4), p. 415.

tongue thickened, the eye fixed, the breathing laborious, and the patient expires in a paroxysm of extreme suffering. The first remedy to be given is a strong emetic, and subsequently oils and demulcents to allay irritability.'

"In his account of the backboned animals of Abyssinia Rüppel states that *Balistes flavomarginatus* is very common in the Red Sea at Djetta, where it is often brought to market, although only pilgrims who do not know the quality of the flesh will buy it. He goes on to say that as a whole the Balistidae not only have a bad taste, but also are unwholesome as food."

Referring to the Tetraodontidae, page 479, Herre uses the name *batete*, or *botete*, as used in most Philippine languages. "This dangerous group of fishes," he says, "is widely distributed in warm seas all over the world and is common throughout the Philippines. Although most people are more or less aware of the poisonous properties of the flesh, it is eaten in practically every Philippine fishing village and not a year goes by without several deaths from this cause.

"A Japanese investigator (I have been unable to obtain a copy of his paper, which appeared in *Archiv für Pathologie und Pharmacologie*) has studied carefully the alkaloid present in the flesh of the Tetraodontidae and finds it to be very near to muscarine, the active poisonous principle of *Amanita muscaria* and other fungi. It is a tasteless, odorless, and very poisonous crystalline alkaloid."

He goes on to state that the natives consider the gall-bladder, the milt, and the eggs to be particularly poisonous. But in La Paz it was the liver which was thought to be the most poisonous part. Only the liver was used to poison animals and flies, although this might be because the liver was more attractive as bait than other portions.

Herre continues on page 488 concerning *Tetraodon*: "The *Medical Journal of Australia* under the date of December 1, 1923, tells of two Malays who ate of a species of Tetraodon although warned of the danger. They ate at noon with no serious effects, but on eating some for supper they were taken violently ill, one dying in an hour, the other about three hours later." Of the Diodontidae, page 503 (the group to which the puffer fish belong): "The fishes of this family have a well-deserved reputation for being poisonous and their flesh should never be eaten."

Botete is sluggish, fairly slow, unarmored, and not very clever at either concealment, escape, or attack. It is amusing but valueless to speculate anthropomorphically in the chicken-egg manner regarding the relationship between his habits and his poison. Did he develop poison in his flesh as a protection in lieu of speed and cleverness, or being poisonous and quite unattractive, was he able to "let himself go," to abandon speed and cleverness? The protected human soon loses his power of defense and attack. Perhaps *botete*, needing neither brains nor tricks nor techniques to protect himself except from a man who wants to poison a cat, has become a frump.

In the evening Tiny returned to the *Western Flyer*, having collected some specimens of *Phthirius pubis*, but since he made no notes in the field, he was unable or unwilling to designate the exact collecting station. His items seemed to have no unusual qualities but to be members of the common species so widely distributed throughout the world.

We were to sail in the early morning, and that night we walked a little in the dim-lighted streets of La Paz. And we wondered why so much of the Gulf was familiar to us, why this town had a "home" feeling. We had never seen a town which even looked like La Paz, and yet coming to it was like returning rather than visiting. Some quality there is in the whole Gulf that trips a trigger of recognition so that in fantastic and exotic scenery one finds oneself nodding and saying inwardly, "Yes, I know." And on the shore the wild doves mourn in the evening and then there comes a pang, some kind of emotional jar, and a longing. And if one followed his whispering impulse he would walk away slowly into the thorny brush following the call of the doves. Trying to remember the Gulf is like trying to re-create a dream. This is by no means a sentimental thing, it has little to do with beauty or even conscious liking. But the Gulf does draw one, and we have talked to rich men who own boats, who can go where they will. Regularly they find themselves sucked into the Gulf. And since we have returned, there is always in the backs of our minds the positive drive to go back again. If it were lush and rich, one could understand the pull, but it is fierce and hostile and sullen. The stone mountains pile up to the sky and there is little fresh water. But we know we must go back if we live, and we don't know why.

Late at night we sat on the deck. They were pumping water out of the hold of the trading boat, preparing her to float and flounder away to Guaymas for more merchandise. But La Paz was asleep; not a soul moved in the streets. The tide turned and swung us around, and in the channel the ebbing tide whispered against our hull and we heard the dogs of La Paz barking in the night.

13

March 23

WE SAILED in the morning. The mustached old pilot came aboard and steered us out, then bowed deeply and stepped into the launch which had followed us. The sea was calm and very blue, almost black-blue, as we turned northward along the coast. We wished to stop near San José Island as our next collecting station. It was good to be under way again and good to be out from under the steady eyes of those ubiquitous little boys who waited interminably for us to do something amusing.

In mid-afternoon we came to anchorage at Amortajada Bay on the southwest tip of San José Island. A small dark islet had caught our attention as we came in. For although the day was bright this islet, called Cayo on the map, looked black and mysterious. We had a feeling that something strange and dark had happened there or that it was the ruined work of men's hands. Cayo is only a quarter of a mile long and a hundred yards wide. Its northern end is a spur and its southern end a flat plateau about forty feet high. Even in the distance it had a quality which we call "burned." One knows there will be few animals on a "burned" coast; that animals will not like it, will not be successful there. Even the algae will be like lost colonists. Whether or not this is the result of a deadly chemistry we cannot say. But we can say that it is possible, after long collecting, to recognize a shore which is "burned" even if it is so far away that details cannot be seen.

Cayo lay about a mile and a half from our anchorage and seemed to blacken even the air around it. This was the first time that the Sea-Cow could have been of great service to us. It was for just such occasions that we had bought it. We were kind to it that day—selfishly of course. We said nice things about it and put it tenderly on the stern of the skiff, pretending to ourselves that we expected it to run, that we didn't dream it would not run. But it would not. We rowed the boat—and the Sea-Cow—to Cayo Islet. There is so much that is strange about this islet that we will set much of it down. It is nearly all questions, but perhaps someone reading this may know the answers and tell us. There is no landing place; all approaches are strewn with large sea-rounded boulders which even in fairly still water would beat the bottom out of a boat. On its easterly side, the one we approached, a cliff rises in back of a rocky beach and there are a number of shallow caves in the cliffside. Set in the great boulders in the intertidal zone there are large iron rings and lengths of big chain, but so rusted and disintegrated that they came off in our hands. Also, set in the cliff six to eight feet above the beach, are other iron rings with loops eight inches in diameter. They look very old, but the damp air of the Gulf and the rapid oxidation caused by it make it impossible to say exactly how old they are. In the shallow caves in the cliff there were evidences of many fires' having been built, and piled about the fireplaces, some old and some fresh, were not only thousands of clam-shells but turtle-shells also, as though these animals had been brought here to be smoked. A heap of fairly fresh diced turtle-meat lay beside one of the fireplaces. The mysterious quality of all this lies here. There are no clams in this immediate vicinity and turtles do not greatly abound. There is no wood whatever on the island with which to build fires; it would have to be brought here. There is no water whatever. And once arrived, there is no anchorage. Why people would bring clams and turtles and wood and water to an islet where there was no protection we do not know. A mile and a half away they could have beached easily and have found both wood and water. It is a riddle we cannot answer, just as we can think of no reason for the big iron rings. They could not have been for fastening a big boat to, since there is no safe water for a boat to lie in and no cove protection from wind and storm. We are very curious about this. We climbed the cliff by a trail that was well beaten in a crevice and on the flat top found a sparse growth of brown grass and some cactus. Nothing more. On the southernmost end of the cliff sat one large black crow who shrieked at us with dislike, and when we approached flew off and disappeared in the direction of San José Island.

The cliffs were light buff in color, and the grass light brown. It is impossible to say why distance made Cayo look black. Boulders and fixed stones of the reef were of a reddish igneous rock and the island, like the whole region, was volcanic in origin.

Collecting on the rocks we found, as we knew we would, a sparse and unhappy fauna. The animals were very small. *Heliaster*, the sun-star of which there were a few, was small and pale in color. There were anemones, a few sea-cucumbers, and a few sea-rabbits. The one animal which seemed to like Cayo was Sally Lightfoot. These beautiful crabs crawled on the rocks and dominated the life of the region. We took a few *Aletes* (worm-like snails) and some serpulid worms, two or three types of snails, and a few isopods and beach-hoppers.

The tide came up and endangered our boat, which we had balanced on top of a boulder, and we rowed back toward the *Western Flyer*, one of us in the stern pulling with a quiet fury on the starting rope of the Sea-Cow. We wished we had left it dangling by its propeller on one of the cliff rings, and its evil and mysterious magneto would have liked that too.

As soon as we pulled away, Cayo looked black again, and we hope someone can tell us something about this island.

Back on the *Western Flyer* we asked Tex to take the Sea-Cow apart down to the tiniest screw and to find out in truth, once for all, whether its failure were metaphysical or something which could be fixed. This he did, under a deck-light. When he put it together and attached it to the boat, it ran perfectly and he went for a cruise with it. Now at last we felt we had an outboard motor we could depend on.

We were anchored quite near San José Island and that night we were visited by little black beetle-like flies which bit and left a stinging, itching burn. Covering ourselves did not help, for they crawled down inside our bedding and bit us unmercifully. Being unable to sleep, we talked and Tiny told us a little of his career, which, if even part of it is true, is one of the most decoratively disreputable sagas we have ever heard. It is with sadness that we do not include some of it, but certain members of the general public are able to keep from all a treatise on biology unsurpassed in our experience. The great literature of this kind is kept vocal by the combined efforts of Puritans and postal regulations, and so the saga of Tiny must remain unwritten.

14

March 24, Easter Sunday

T HE BEACH was hot and yellow. We swam, and then walked along on the sand and went inland along the ridge between the beach and a large mangrove-edged lagoon beyond. On the lagoon side of the ridge there were thousands of burrows, presumably of large land-crabs, but it was hopeless to dig them out. The shores of the lagoon teemed with the little clicking bubbling fiddler crabs and estuarian snails. Here we could smell the mangrove flowers without the foul root smell, and the odor was fresh and sweet, like that of new-cut grass. From where we waded there was a fine picture, still reflecting water and the fringing green mangroves against the burnt red-brown of the distant mountains, all like some fantastic Doré drawing of a pressed and embattled heaven. The air was hot and still and the lagoon rippleless. Now and then the surface was ringed as some lagoon fish came to the air. It was a curious quiet resting-place and perhaps because of the quiet we heard in our heads the children singing in the church at La Paz. We did not collect strongly or very efficiently, but rather we half dozed through the day, thinking of old things, each one in himself. And later we discussed manners of thinking and methods of thinking, speculation which is not stylish any more. On a day like this the mind goes outward and touches in all directions. We discussed intellectual methods and approaches, and we thought that through inspection of thinking technique a kind of purity of approach might be consciously achieved—that non-teleological or "is" thinking might be substituted in part for the usual cause-effect methods.

The hazy Gulf, with its changes of light and shape, was rather like us, trying to apply our thoughts, but finding them always pushed and swayed by our bodies and our needs and our satieties. It might be well here to set down some of the discussions of non-teleological thinking.

During the depression there were, and still are, not only destitute but thriftless and uncareful families, and we have often heard it said that the county had to support them because they were shiftless and negligent. If they would only perk up and be somebody everything would be all right. Even Henry Ford in the depth of the depression gave as his solution to that problem, "Everybody ought to roll up his sleeves and get to work."

This view may be correct as far as it goes, but we wonder what would happen to those with whom the shiftless would exchange places in the large pattern—those whose jobs would be usurped, since at that time there was work for only about seventy percent of the total employable population, leaving the remainder as government wards.

This attitude has no bearing on what might be or could be if so-and-so happened. It merely considers conditions "as is." No matter what the ability or aggressiveness of the separate units of society, at that time there were, and still there are, great numbers necessarily out of work, and the fact that those numbers comprised the incompetent or maladjusted or unlucky units is in one sense beside the point. No causality is involved in that; collectively it's just "so"; collectively it's related to the fact that animals produce more offspring than the world can support. The units may be blamed as individuals, but as members of society they cannot be blamed. Any given individual very possibly may transfer from the underprivileged into the more fortunate group by better luck or by improved aggressiveness or competence, but all cannot be so benefited whatever their strivings, and the large population will be unaffected. The seventy-thirty ratio will remain, with merely a reassortment of the units. And no blame, at least no social fault, imputes to these people; they are where they are "because" natural conditions are what they are. And so far as we selfishly are concerned we can rejoice that they, rather than we, represent the low extreme, since there must be one.

So if one is very aggressive he will be able to obtain work even under the most sub-normal economic conditions, but only because there are others, less aggressive than he, who serve in his stead as potential government wards. In the same way, the sight of a half-wit should never depress us, since his extreme, and the extreme of his kind, so affects the mean standard that we, hatless, coatless, often bewhiskered, thereby will be regarded only as a little odd. And similarly, we cannot justly approve the success manuals that tell our high school graduates how to get a job—there being jobs for only half of them!

This type of thinking unfortunately annoys many people. It may especially arouse the anger of women, who regard it as cold, even brutal, although actually it would seem to be more tender and understanding, certainly more real and less illusionary and even less blaming, than the more conventional methods of consideration. And the value of it as a tool in increased understanding cannot be denied.

As a more extreme example, consider the sea-hare *Tethys*, a shell-less, flabby sea-slug, actually a marine snail, which may be seen crawling about in tidal estuaries, somewhat resembling a rabbit crouched over. A California biologist estimated the number of eggs produced by a single animal during a single breeding season to be more than 478 million. And the adults sometimes occur by the hundred! Obviously all these eggs cannot mature, all this potential cannot, *must not*, become reality, else the ocean would soon be occupied exclusively by sea-hares. There would be no kindness in that, even for the sea-hares themselves, for in a few generations they would overflow the earth; there would be nothing for the rest of us to eat, and nothing for them unless they turned cannibal. On the average, probably no more than the biblical one or two attain full maturity. Somewhere along the way all the rest will have been eaten by predators whose life cycle is postulated upon the presence of abundant larvae of sea-hares and other forms as food—as all life itself is based on such a postulate. Now picture the combination mother-father sea-hare (the animals are hermaphroditic, with the usual cross-fertilization) parentally blessing its offspring with these words: "Work hard and be aggressive, so you can grow into a nice husky *Tethys* like your ten-pound parent." Imagine it, the hypocrite, the illusionist, the Pollyanna, the genial liar, saying that to its millions of eggs *en masse*, with the dice loaded at such a ratio! Inevitably, 99.999 percent are destined to fall by the wayside. No prophet could foresee which specific individuals are to survive, but the most casual student could state confidently that no more than a few are likely to do so; any given individual has *almost* no chance at all—but still there is the "almost," since the race persists. And there is even a semblance of truth in the parent sea-hare's admonition, since even here, with this almost infinitesimal differential, the race is still to the swift and/or to the lucky.

What we personally conceive by the term "teleological thinking," as exemplified by the notion about the shiftless unemployed, is most frequently associated with the evaluating of causes and effects, the purposiveness of events. This kind of thinking considers changes and cures—what "should be" in the terms of an end pattern (which is often a subjective or an anthropomorphic projection); it presumes the bettering of conditions, often, unfortunately, without achieving more than a most superficial understanding of those conditions. In their sometimes intolerant refusal to face facts as they are, teleological notions may substitute a fierce but ineffectual attempt to change conditions which are assumed to be undesirable, in place of the understanding-acceptance which would pave the way for a more sensible attempt at any change which might still be indicated.

Non-teleological ideas derive through "is" thinking, associated with natural selection as Darwin seems to have understood it. They imply depth, fundamentalism, and clarity—seeing beyond traditional or personal projections. They consider events as outgrowths and expressions rather than as results; conscious acceptance as a desideratum, and certainly as an all-important prerequisite. Non-teleological thinking concerns itself primarily not with what should be, or could be, or might be, but rather with what actually "is"—attempting at most to answer the already sufficiently difficult questions *what* or *how*, instead of *why*.

An interesting parallel to these two types of thinking is afforded by the microcosm with its freedom or indeterminacy, as contrasted with the morphologically inviolable pattern of the macrocosm. Statistically, the electron is free to go where it will. But the destiny pattern of any aggregate, comprising uncountable billions of these same units, is fixed and certain, however much that inevitability may be slowed down. The eventual disintegration of a stick of wood or a piece of iron through the departure of the presumably immortal electrons is assured, even though it may be delayed by such protection against the operation of the second law of thermodynamics as is afforded by painting and rustproofing.

Examples sometimes clarify an issue better than explanations or definitions. Here are three situations considered by the two methods.

A. *Why are some men taller than others?*

Teleological "answer": because of the underfunctioning of the growth-regulating ductless glands. This seems simple enough. But the simplicity is merely a function of inadequacy and incompleteness. The finality is only apparent. A child, being wise and direct, would ask immediately if given this answer: "Well, why do the glands underfunction?" hinting instantly towards non-teleological methods, or indicating the rapidity with which teleological thinking gets over into the stalemate of first causes.

In the non-teleological sense there can be no "answer." There can be only pictures which become larger and more significant as one's horizon increases. In this given situation, the steps might be something like this:

(1) Variation is a universal and truly primitive trait. It occurs in any group of entities—razor blades, measuring-rods, rocks, trees, horses, matches, or men.

(2) In this case, the apropos variations will be towards short-

ness or tallness from a mean standard—the height of adult men as determined by the statistics of measurements, or by common-sense observation.

(3) In men varying towards tallness there seems to be a constant relation with an underfunctioning of the growth-regulating ductless glands, of the sort that one can be regarded as an index of the other.

(4) There are other known relations consistent with tallness, such as compensatory adjustments along the whole chain of endocrine organs. There may even be other factors, separately not important or not yet discovered, which in the aggregate may be significant, or the integration of which may be found to wash over some critical threshold.

(5) The men in question are taller "because" they fall in a group within which there are the above-mentioned relations. In other words, "they're tall because they're tall."

This is the statistical, or "is," picture to date, more complex than the teleological "answer"—which is really no answer at all—but complex only in the sense that reality is complex; actually simple, inasmuch as the simplicity of the word "is" can be comprehended.

Understandings of this sort can be reduced to this deep and significant summary: "It's so because it's so." But exactly the same words can also express the hasty or superficial attitude. There seems to be no explicit method for differentiating the deep and participating understanding, the "all-truth" which admits infinite change or expansion as added relations become apparent, from the shallow dismissal and implied lack of further interest which may be couched in the very same words.

B. *Why are some matches larger than others?*

Examine similarly a group of matches. At first they seem all to be of the same size. But to turn up differences, one needs only to measure them carefully with calipers or to weigh them with an analytical balance. Suppose the extreme comprises only a .001 percent departure from the mean (it will be actually much more); even so slight a differential we know can be highly significant, as with the sea-hares. The differences will group into plus-minus variations from a hypothetical mean to which not one single example will be found exactly to conform. Now the ridiculousness of the question becomes apparent. There is no *particular* reason. It's just so. There may be in the situation some factor or factors more important than the others: owing to the universality of variation (even in those very factors which "cause" variation), there surely *will* be, some even predominantly so. But the question as put is seen to be beside the point. The good answer is: "It's just in the nature of the beast." And this needn't imply belittlement; to have understood the "nature" of a thing is in itself a considerable achievement.

But if the size variations should be quite obvious—and especially if uniformity were to be a desideratum—then there might be a particularly dominant "causative" factor which could be searched out. Or if a person must have a stated "cause"—and many people must, in order to get an emotional understanding, a sense of relation to the situation and to give a name to the thing in order to "settle" it so it may not bother them any more—he can examine the automatic machinery which fabricates the products, and discover in it the variability which results in variation in the matches. But in doing so, he will become involved with a larger principle or pattern, the universality of variation, which has little to do with causality as we think of it.

C. *Leadership*.

The teleological notion would be that those in the forefront are leaders in a given movement and actually direct and consciously lead the masses in the sense that an army corporal orders "Forward march" and the squad marches ahead. One speaks in such a way of church leaders, of political leaders, and of leaders in scientific thought, and of course there is some limited justification for such a notion.

Non-teleological notion: that the people we call leaders are simply those who, at the given moment, are moving in the direction behind which will be found the greatest weight, and which represents a future mass movement.

For a more vivid picture of this state of affairs, consider the movements of an ameba under the microscope. Finger-like processes, the pseudopodia, extend at various places beyond the confines of the chief mass. Locomotion takes place by means of the animal's flowing into one or into several adjacent pseudopodia. Suppose that the molecules which "happened" to be situated in the forefront of the pseudopodium through which the animal is progressing, or into which it will have flowed subsequently, should be endowed with consciousness and should say to themselves and to their fellows: "We are directly leading this great procession, our leadership 'causes' all the rest of the population to move this way, the mass follows the path we blaze." This would be equivalent to the attitude with which we commonly regard leadership.

As a matter of fact there are three distinct types of thinking, two of them teleological. Physical teleology, the type we have been considering, is by far the commonest today. Spiritual teleology is rare. Formerly predominant, it now occurs metaphysically and in most religions, especially as they are popularly understood (but not, we suspect, as they were originally enunciated or as they may still be known to the truly adept). Occasionally the three types may be contrasted in a single problem. Here are a couple of examples:

(1) Van Gogh's feverish hurrying in the Arles epoch, culminating in epilepsy and suicide.

Teleological "answer": Improper care of his health during times of tremendous activity and exposure to the sun and weather brought on his epilepsy out of which discouragement and suicide resulted.

Spiritual teleology: He hurried because he innately foresaw his imminent death, and wanted first to express as much of his essentiality as possible.

Non-teleological picture: Both the above, along with a good many other symptoms and expressions (some of which could probably be inferred from his letters), were parts of his essentiality, possibly glimpsable as his "lust for life."

(2) The thyroid-neurosis syndrome.

Teleological "answer": Over-activity of the thyroid gland irritates and over-stimulates the patient to the point of nervous breakdown.

Spiritual teleology: The neurosis is causative. Something psychically wrong drives the patient on to excess mental irritation which harries and upsets the glandular balance, especially the thyroid, through shock-resonance in the autonomic system, in the sense that a purely psychic shock may spoil one's appetite, or may even result in violent illness. In this connection, note the army's acceptance of extreme homesickness as a reason for disability discharge.

Non-teleological picture: Both are discrete segments of a vicious circle, which may also include other factors as additional more or less discrete segments, symbols or maybe parts of an underlying but non-teleological pattern which comprises them and many others, the ramifications of which are n, and which has to do with causality only reflectedly.

Teleological thinking may even be highly fallacious, especially where it approaches the very superficial but quite common *post hoc, ergo propter hoc* pattern. Consider the situation with reference to dynamiting in a quarry. Before a charge is set off, the foreman toots warningly on a characteristic whistle. People living in the neighborhood come to associate the one with the other, since the whistle is almost invariably followed within a few seconds by the shock and sound of an explosion for which one automatically prepares oneself. Having experienced this many times without closer contact, a very naïve and unthinking person might justly conclude not only that there was a cause-effect relation, but that the whistle actually caused the explosion. A slightly wiser person would insist that the explosion caused the whistle, but would be hard put to explain the transposed time element. The normal adult would recognize that the whistle no more caused the explosion than the explosion caused the whistle, but that both were parts of a larger pattern out of which a "why" could be postulated for both, but more immediately and particularly for the whistle. Determined to chase the thing down in a cause-effect sense, an observer would have to be very wise indeed who could follow the intricacies of cause through more fundamental cause to primary cause, even in this largely man-made series about which we presumably know most of the motives, causes, and ramifications. He would eventually find himself in a welter of thoughts on production, and ownership of the means of production, and economic whys and wherefores about which there is little agreement.

The example quoted is obvious and simple. Most things are

far more subtle than that, and have many of their relations and most of their origins far back in things more difficult of access than the tooting of a whistle calculated to warn by-standers away from an explosion. We know little enough even of a man-made series like this—how much less of purely natural phenomena about which also there is apt to be teleological pontificating!

Usually it seems to be true that when even the most definitely apparent cause-effect situations are examined in the light of wider knowledge, the cause-effect aspect comes to be seen as less rather than more significant, and the statistical or relational aspects acquire larger importance. It seems safe to assume that non-teleological is more "ultimate" than teleological reasoning. Hence the latter would be expected to prove to be limited and constricting except when used provisionally. But while it is true that the former is more open, for that very reason its employment necessitates greater discipline and care in order to allow for the dangers of looseness and inadequate control.

Frequently, however, a truly definitive answer seems to arise through teleological methods. Part of this is due to wish-fulfillment delusion. When a person asks "Why?" in a given situation, he usually deeply expects, and in any case receives, only a relational answer in place of the definitive "because" which he thinks he wants. But he customarily accepts the actually relational answer (it couldn't be anything else unless it comprised the whole, which is unknowable except by "living into") as a definitive "because." Wishful thinking probably fosters that error, since everyone continually searches for absolutisms (hence the value placed on diamonds, the most permanent physical things in the world) and imagines continually that he finds them. More justly, the relational picture should be regarded only as a glimpse—a challenge to consider also the rest of the relations as they are available—to envision the whole picture as well as can be done with given abilities and data. But one accepts it instead of a real "because," considers it settled, and, having named it, loses interest and goes on to something else.

Chiefly, however, we seem to arrive occasionally at definitive answers through the workings of another primitive principle:

the universality of quanta. No one thing ever merges gradually into anything else; the steps are discontinuous, but often so very minute as to seem truly continuous. If the investigation is carried deep enough, the factor in question, instead of being graphable as a continuous process, will be seen to function by discrete quanta with gaps or synapses between, as do quanta of energy, undulations of light. The apparently definitive answer occurs when causes and effects both arise on the same large plateau which is bounded a great way off by the steep rise which announces the next plateau. If the investigation is extended sufficiently, that distant rise will, however, inevitably be encountered; the answer which formerly seemed definitive now will be seen to be at least slightly inadequate and the picture will have to be enlarged so as to include the plateau next further out. Everything impinges on everything else, often into radically different systems, although in such cases faintly. We doubt very much if there are any truly "closed systems." Those so called represent kingdoms of a great continuity bounded by the sudden discontinuity of great synapses which eventually must be bridged in any unified-field hypothesis. For instance, the ocean, with reference to waves of water, might be considered as a closed system. But anyone who has lived in Pacific Grove or Carmel during the winter storms will have felt the house tremble at the impact of waves half a mile or more away impinging on a totally different "closed" system.

But the greatest fallacy in, or rather the greatest objection to, teleological thinking is in connection with the emotional content, the belief. People get to believing and even to professing the apparent answers thus arrived at, suffering mental constrictions by emotionally closing their minds to any of the further and possibly opposite "answers" which might otherwise be unearthed by honest effort—answers which, if faced realistically, would give rise to a struggle and to a possible rebirth which might place the whole problem in a new and more significant light. Grant for a moment that among students of endocrinology a school of thought might arise, centering upon some belief as to etiology—upon the belief, for instance, that all abnormal growth is caused by glandular imbalance. Such a clique, becoming formalized and powerful, would tend, by scorn and opposition, to wither any contrary view which, if untrammeled, might discover a clue to some opposing "causative" factor of equal medical importance. That situation is most unlikely to arise in a field so lusty as endocrinology, with its relational insistence, but the principle illustrated by a poor example is thought nevertheless to be sound.

Significant in this connection is the fact that conflicts may arise between any two or more of the "answers" brought forth by either of the teleologies, or between the two teleologies themselves. But there can be no conflict between any of these and the non-teleological picture. For instance, in the condition called hyperthyroidism, the treatments advised by believers in the psychic or neurosis etiology very possibly may conflict with those arising out of a belief in the purely physical cause. Or even within the physical teleology group there may be conflicts between those who believe the condition due to a strictly thyroid upset and those who consider causation derived through a general imbalance of the ductless glands. But there can be no conflict between any or all of these factors and the non-teleological picture, because the latter includes them—evaluates them relationally or at least attempts to do so, or maybe only accepts them as time-place truths. Teleological "answers" necessarily must be included in the non-teleological method—since they are part of the picture even if only restrictedly true—and as soon as their qualities of relatedness are recognized. Even erroneous beliefs are real things, and have to be considered proportional to their spread or intensity. "All-truth" must embrace all extant apropos errors also, and know them as such by relation to the whole, and allow for their effects.

The criterion of validity in the handling of data seems to be this: that the summary shall say in substance, significantly and understandingly, "It's so because it's so." Unfortunately the very same words might equally derive through a most superficial glance, as any child could learn to repeat from memory the most abstruse of Dirac's equations. But to know a thing emergently and significantly is something else again, even though the understanding may be expressed in the self-same words that were used superficially. In the following example* note the deep significance of the emergent as contrasted with the presumably satisfactory but actually incorrect original naïve understanding. At one time an important game bird in Norway, the willow grouse, was so clearly threatened with extinction that it was thought wise to establish protective regulations and to place a bounty on its chief enemy, a hawk which was known to feed heavily on it. Quantities of the hawks were exterminated, but despite such drastic measures the grouse disappeared actually more rapidly than before. The naïvely applied customary remedies had obviously failed. But instead of becoming discouraged and quietistically letting this bird go the way of the great auk and the passenger pigeon, the authorities enlarged the scope of their investigations until the anomaly was explained. An ecological analysis into the relational aspects of the situation disclosed that a parasitic disease, coccidiosis, was epizootic among the grouse. In its incipient stages, this disease so reduced the flying speed of the grouse that the mildly ill individuals became easy prey for the hawks. In living largely off the slightly ill birds, the hawks prevented them from developing the disease in its full intensity and so spreading it more widely and quickly to otherwise healthy fowl. Thus the presumed enemies of the grouse, by controlling the epizootic aspects of the disease, proved to be friends in disguise.

In summarizing the above situation, the measure of validity wouldn't be to assume that, even in the well-understood factor of coccidiosis, we have the real "cause" of any beneficial or untoward condition, but to say, rather, that in this phase we have a highly significant and possibly preponderantly important relational aspect of the picture.

However, many people are unwilling to chance the sometimes ruthless-appearing notions which may arise through non-teleological treatments. They fear even to use them in that they may be left dangling out in space, deprived of such emotional support as had been afforded them by an unthinking belief in the proved value of pest control in the conser-

*Abstracted from the article on ecology by Elton, *Encyclopaedia Britannica*, 14th Edition, Vol. VII, p. 916.

vation of game birds; in the institutions of tradition; religion; science; in the security of the home or the family; or in a comfortable bank account. But for that matter emancipations in general are likely to be held in terror by those who may not yet have achieved them, but whose thresholds in those respects are becoming significantly low. Think of the fascinated horror, or at best tolerance, with which little girls regard their brothers who have dispensed with the Santa Claus belief; or the fear of the devout young churchman for his university senior who has grown away from depending on the security of religion.

As a matter of fact, whoever employs this type of thinking with other than a few close friends will be referred to as detached, hard-hearted, or even cruel. Quite the opposite seems to be true. Non-teleological methods more than any other seem capable of great tenderness, of an all-embracingness which is rare otherwise. Consider, for instance, the fact that, once a given situation is deeply understood, no apologies are required. There are ample difficulties even to understanding conditions "as is." Once that has been accomplished, the "why" of it (known now to be simply a relation, though probably a near and important one) seems no longer to be preponderantly important. It needn't be condoned or extenuated, it just "is." It is seen merely as part of a more or less dim whole picture. As an example: A woman near us in the Carmel woods was upset when her dog was poisoned—frightened at the thought of passing the night alone after years of companionship with the animal. She phoned to ask if, with our windows on that side of the house closed as they were normally, we could hear her ringing a dinner bell as a signal during the night that marauders had cut her phone wires preparatory to robbing her. Of course that was, in fact, an improbable contingency to be provided against; a man would call it a foolish fear, neurotic. And so it was. But one could say kindly, "We can hear the bell quite plainly, but if desirable we can adjust our sleeping arrangements so as to be able to come over there instantly in case you need us," without even stopping to consider whether or not the fear was foolish, or to be concerned about it if it were, correctly regarding all that as secondary. And if the woman had said apologetically, "Oh, you must forgive me; I know my fears are foolish, but I am so upset!" the wise reply would have been, "Dear person, nothing to forgive. If you have fears, they *are*; they are real things and to be considered. Whether or not they're foolish is beside the point. *What* they are is unimportant alongside the fact *that* they are." In other words, the badness or goodness, the teleology of the fears, was decidedly secondary. The whole notion could be conveyed by a smile or by a pleasant intonation more readily than by the words themselves. Teleological treatment which one might have been tempted to employ under the circumstances would first have stressed the fact that the fear was foolish—would say with a great show of objective justice, "Well, there's no use in *our* doing anything; the fault is that *your* fear is foolish and improbable. Get over that" (as a judge would say, "Come into court with clean hands"); "then if there's anything *sensible* we can do, we'll see," with smug blame implied in every word. Or, more kindly, it would try to reason with the woman in an attempt to help her get over it—the business of propaganda directed towards change even before the situation is fully understood (maybe as a lazy substitute for understanding). Or, still more kindly, the teleological method would try to understand the fear causally. But with the non-teleological treatment there is only the love and understanding of instant acceptance; after that fundamental has been achieved, the next step, if any should be necessary, can be considered more sensibly.

Strictly, the term non-teleological thinking ought not to be applied to what we have in mind. Because it involves more than thinking, that term is inadequate. *Modus operandi* might be better—a method of handling data of any sort. The example cited just above concerns feeling more than thinking. The method extends beyond thinking even to living itself; in fact, by inferred definition it transcends the realm of thinking possibilities, it postulates "living into."

In the destitute-unemployed illustration, thinking, as being the evaluatory function chiefly concerned, was the point of departure, "the crust to break through." There the "blame approach" considered the situation in the limited and inadequate teleological manner. The non-teleological method included that viewpoint as correct but limited. But when it came to the feeling aspects of a human relation situation, the non-teleological method would probably ameliorate the woman's fears in a loving, truly mellow, and adequate fashion, whereas the teleological would have tended to bungle things by employing the limited and sophisticated approach.

Incidentally, there is in this connection a remarkable etiological similarity to be noted between cause in thinking and blame in feeling. One feels that one's neighbors are to be blamed for their hate or anger or fear. One thinks that poor pavements are "caused" by politics. The non-teleological picture in either case is the larger one that goes beyond blame or cause. And the non-causal or non-blaming viewpoint seems to us very often relatively to represent the "new thing," the Hegelian "Christ-child" which arises emergently from the union of two opposing viewpoints, such as those of physical and spiritual teleologies, especially if there is conflict as to causation between the two or within either. The new viewpoint very frequently sheds light over a larger picture, providing a key which may unlock levels not accessible to either of the teleological viewpoints. There are interesting parallels here: to the triangle, to the Christian ideas of trinity, to Hegel's dialectic, and to Swedenborg's metaphysic of divine love (feeling) and divine wisdom (thinking).

The factors we have been considering as "answers" seem to be merely symbols or indices, relational aspects of things— of which they are integral parts—not to be considered in terms of causes and effects. The truest reason for anything's being so is that it *is.* This is actually and truly a reason, more valid and clearer than all the other separate reasons, or than any group of them short of the whole. Anything less than the whole forms part of the picture only, and the infinite whole is unknowable except by *being* it, by living into it.

A thing may be *so* "because" of a thousand and one reasons of greater or lesser importance, such as the man oversized because of glandular insufficiency. The integration of these many reasons which are in the nature of relations rather than reasons is that he *is.* The separate reasons, no matter how valid, are only fragmentary parts of the picture. And the whole necessarily includes all that it impinges on as object and subject, in ripples fading with distance or depending upon the original intensity of the vortex.

The frequent allusions to an underlying pattern have no implication of mysticism—except inasmuch as a pattern which comprises infinity in factors and symbols might be called mystic. But infinity as here used occurs also in the mathematical aspects of physiology and physics, both far away from mysticism as the term is ordinarily employed. Actually, the underlying pattern is probably nothing more than an integration of just such symbols and indices and mutual reference points as are already known, except that its power is n. Such an integration might include nothing more spectacular than we already know. But, equally, it *could* include anything, even events and entities as different from those already known as the vectors, tensors, scalars, and ideas of electrical charges in mathematical physics are different from the mechanical-model world of the Victorian scientists.

In such a pattern, causality would be merely a name for something that exists only in our partial and biased mental reconstructings. The pattern which it indexes, however, would be real, but not intellectually apperceivable because the pattern goes everywhere and is everything and cannot be encompassed by finite mind or by anything short of life—which it is.

The psychic or spiritual residua remaining after the most careful physical analyses, or the physical remnants obvious, particularly to us of the twentieth century, in the most honest and disciplined spiritual speculations of medieval philosophers, all bespeak such a pattern. Those residua, those most minute differentials, the 0.001 percentages which suffice to maintain the races of sea animals, are seen finally to be the most important things in the world, not because of their sizes, but because they are everywhere. The differential is the true universal, the true catalyst, the cosmic solvent. Any investigation carried far enough will bring to light these residua, or rather will leave them still unassailable as Emerson remarked a hundred years ago in "The Oversoul"—will run into the brick wall of the *impossibility* of perfection while at the same time insisting on the *validity* of perfection. Anomalies especially testify to that framework; they are the commonest intellectual vehicles for breaking through; all are solvable in the sense that any *one* is understandable, but that one leads with the power *n* to still more and deeper anomalies.

This deep underlying pattern inferred by non-teleological thinking crops up everywhere—a relational thing, surely, relating opposing factors on different levels, as reality and potential are related. But it must not be considered as causative, it simply exists, it *is*, things are merely expressions of it as it is expressions of them. And they *are* it, also. As Swinburne, extolling Hertha, the earth goddess, makes her say: "Man, equal and one with me, man that is made of me, man that is I," so all things which are *that*—which is all—equally may be extolled. That pattern materializes everywhere in the sense that Eddington finds the non-integer *q* "number" appearing everywhere, in the background of all fundamental equations,* in the sense that the speed of light, constant despite compoundings or subtractions, seemed at one time almost to be conspiring against investigation.

The whole is necessarily everything, the whole world of fact and fancy, body and psyche, physical fact and spiritual truth, individual and collective, life and death, macrocosm and microcosm (the greatest quanta here, the greatest synapse between these two), conscious and unconscious, subject and object. The whole picture is portrayed by *is*, the deepest word of deep ultimate reality, not shallow or partial as reasons are, but deeper and participating, possibly encompassing the Oriental concept of *being*.

And all this against the hot beach on an Easter Sunday, with the passing day and the passing time. This little trip of ours was becoming a thing and a dual thing, with collecting and eating and sleeping merging with the thinking-speculating activity. Quality of sunlight, blueness and smoothness of water, boat engines, and ourselves were all parts of a larger whole and we could begin to feel its nature but not its size.

* *The Nature of the Physical World*, pp. 208–10.

15

ABOUT noon we sailed and moved out of the shrouded and quiet Amortajada Bay and up the coast toward Marcial Reef, which was marked as our next collecting station. We arrived in mid-afternoon and collected on the late tide, on a northerly pile of boulders, part of the central reef. This was just south of Marcial Point, which marks the southern limit of Agua Verde Bay.

It was not a good collecting tide, although it should have been according to the tide chart. The water did not go low enough for exhaustive collecting. There were a few polyclads which here were high on the rocks. We found two large and many small chitons—the first time we had discovered them in numbers. There were many urchins visible but too deep below the surface to get to. Swarms of larval shrimps were in the water swimming about in small circles. The collecting was not successful in point of view of numbers of forms taken.

That night we rigged a lamp over the side, shaded it with a paper cone, and hung it close down to the water so that the light was reflected downward. Pelagic isopods and mysids immediately swarmed to the illuminated circle until the water seemed to heave and whirl with them. The small fish came to this horde of food, and on the outer edges of the light ring large fishes flashed in and out after the small fishes. Occasionally we interrupted this mad dance with dip-nets, dropping the catch into porcelain pans for closer study, and out of the nets came animals small or transparent that we had not noticed in the sea at all.

Having had no good tide at Marcial Reef, we arose at four o'clock the following morning and went in the darkness to collect again. We carried big seven-cell focusing flashlights. In some ways they make collecting in the dark, in a small area at least, more interesting than daytime collecting, for they limit the range of observation so that in the narrowed field one is likely to notice more detail. There is a second reason for our preference for night collecting—a number of animals are more active at night than in the daytime and they seem to be not much disturbed or frightened by artificial light. This time we had a very fair tide. The light fell on a monster highly colored spiny lobster in a crevice of the reef. He was blue and orange and spotted with brown. The taking of him required caution, for these big lobsters are very strong and are so armed with spikes and points that in struggling with one the hands can be badly cut. We approached with care, bent slowly down, and then with two hands grabbed him about the middle of the body. And there was no struggle whatever. He was either sick or lazy or hurt by the surf, and did not fight at all.

The cavities in Marcial Reef held a great many club-spined urchins and a number of the sharp-spined purple ones which had hurt us before. There were numbers of sea-fans, two of the usual starfish and a new species* which later we were to find common farther north in the Gulf. We took a good quantity of the many-rayed sun-stars, and a flat kind of cucumber which was new to us.† This was the first time we had collected at night, and under our lights we saw the puffer fish lazily feeding near the surface in the clear water. On the bottom, the brittle-stars, which we had always found under rocks, were crawling about like thousands of little snakes. They rarely move about in the daylight. Wherever the sharp, powerful rays of the flashlight cut into the water we could see the moving beautiful fish and the bottoms alive with busy feeding invertebrates. But collecting with a flashlight is difficult unless it is arranged that two people work together—one to hold the light and the other to take the animals. Also, from constant wetting in salt water the life of a flashlight is very short.

The one huge and beautiful lobster was the prize of this trip. We tried to photograph him on color film and as usual something went wrong but we got a very good likeness of one end of him, which was an improvement on our previous pictures. In most of our other photographs we didn't get either end.

We took several species of chitons and a great number of tunicates. There were several turbellarian flatworms, but these are so likely to dissolve before they preserve that we had great difficulties with them. There were in the collecting pans several species of brittle-stars, numbers of small crabs and snapping shrimps, plumularian hydroids, bivalves of a number of

* *Othilia tenuispinus.*
†Probably *Stichopus fuscus*—the specimen has since been lost sight of.

species, snails, and some small sea-urchins. There were worms, hermit crabs, sipunculids, and sponges. The pools too had been thick with pelagic larval shrimps, pelagic isopods—tiny crustacea similar to sow-bugs—and tiny shrimps (mysids). In this area the water seemed particularly peopled with small pelagic animals—"bugs," so the boys said. Everywhere there were bugs, flying, crawling, and swimming. The shallow and warm waters of the area promoted a competitive life that was astonishing.

After breakfast we pulled up the anchor and set out again northward. The pattern of the technique of the trip had by now established itself almost as a habit with us; collecting, running to a new station, collecting again. The water was intensely blue on this run, and the fish were very many. We could see the splashing of great schools of tuna in the distance where they beat the water to spray in their millions. The swordfish leaped all about us, and someone was on the bow the whole time trying to drive a light harpoon into one, but we never could get close enough. Cast after cast fell short.

We preserved and labeled as we went, and the water was so smooth that we had no difficulty with delicate animals. If the boat rolls, retractile animals such as anemones and sipunculids are more than likely to draw into themselves and refuse to relax under the Epsom-salts treatment, but this sea was as smooth as a lawn, and our wake fanned out for miles behind us.

The fish-lines on the stays snapped and jerked and we brought in skipjack, Sparky's friend of the curious name, and the Mexican sierra. This golden fish with brilliant blue spots is shaped like a trout. In size it ranges from fifteen inches to two feet, is slender and a very rapid swimmer. The sierra does not seem to travel in dense, surface-beating schools as the tuna does. Although it belongs with the mackerel-like forms, its meat is white and delicate and sweet. Simply fried in big hunks, it is the most delicious fish of all.

16

March 25

ABOUT NOON we arrived at Puerto Escondido, the Hidden Harbor, a place of magic. If one wished to design a secret personal bay, one would probably build something very like this little harbor. A point swings about, making a small semicircular bay fringed with bright-green mangroves, and only when one has turned inside this outer bay can one see that there is a second, secret bay beyond—a long narrow bay with an entrance not more than fifty feet wide at flood. The charts gave three fathoms at the center of the entrance, but the tide run was so furious that we did not attempt to take the *Western Flyer* in, but anchored in back of the first point, called Piedra de la Marina. Here we had more than ten fathoms, and Tony felt better about it.

In the distance, and from the south, a canoe came up the coast with a small sail set. The Indians move great distances in their tiny boats. As soon as the anchor was out, we dropped the fishing lines and immediately hooked several hammerhead sharks and a large red snapper. The air here was hot and filled with the smell of mangrove flowers. The little outer bay was our first collecting station, a shallow warm cove with a mud bottom and edged with small boulders, smooth and unencrusted with algae. On the bottom we could see long snake-like animals, gray with black markings, with purplish-orange floriate heads like chrysanthemums. They were about three feet long and new to us. Wading in rubber boots, we captured some of them and they proved to be giant synaptids.* They were strange and frightening to handle, for they stuck to anything they touched, not with slime but as though they were coated with innumerable suction-cells. On being taken from the water, they collapsed to skin, for their bodily shape is maintained by the current of water which they draw through themselves. When lifted out, this water escapes and they hang as limp as unfilled sausage skins. Since they were new and fascinating to us, we took many specimens, maneu-

---

*A worm-like sea-cucumber, *Euapta godeffroyi*.

vering them gently to the surface and then sliding them into submerged wooden collecting buckets to prevent them from dropping their water. On the bottom they crawled about, their flower-heads moving gently, while the current of water passing through their bodies drew food into their stomachs. When we took them on board, we found they had to a high degree the habit of a number of holothurians: eviscerating. These *Euapta* were a nervous lot. We tried to relax them with Epsom salts so that we might kill them with their floriate heads extended, but the salts, no matter how carefully administered, caused the heads to retract, and soon afterwards they threw their stomachs out into the water. The word "stomach" is used here inadvisedly, for what they actually disgorge is the intestinal tract and respiratory tree.

We intoxicated them with pure oxygen and then tried the salts, but with the same result. Finally, by administering the salts in minute quantities and very slowly, we were able to preserve some uneviscerated specimens, but none with the head extended. The color motion pictures of the living animals, while not very good, at least showed the color and shape and movement of the extended heads. Again we got photographs of only one end, but this time the more important end, the floriate head.

In the little shallow bay there were many bright-green gars, or needle-fish, but they were too fast for our dip-nets and we were unable to take them. *Botete*, the poison fish, was here also in great numbers, and the boys took some of them with a light seine. We found here two new starfishes and many *Cerianthus* anemones.

While we were collecting on the shore, Tiny rowed about in the little skiff in slightly deeper water. He carried a light three-pronged spear with which he picked up an occasional cushion star from the bottom. We heard him shout, and looked up to see a giant manta ray headed for him, the tips of the wings more than ten feet apart. It was rare to see them in such shallow water. As it passed directly under his boat we yelled at him to spear it, since he wanted to so badly, but he simply sat in the bottom of the boat, gazing after the retreating ray, weakly swearing at us. For a long time he sat there quietly, not quite believing what he had seen. This great fish

could have flicked Tiny and boat and all into the air with one
flap of its wing. Tiny wanted to sit still and think for a long
time and he did. For an hour afterward he could only repeat,
"Did you see that Goddamned thing!" And from that moment it became Tiny's ambition to catch and kill one of the
giant rays.

The canoe which had been sailing up the coast came alongside and a man and a little boy boarded us. They had with
them what they called "abalon"—not true abalones, but gigantic fixed scallops, very good for food. They had also some
of the hacha, the huge fan-shaped clam; pearl oysters, which
are growing rare; and several huge conchs. We bought from
the man what he had and asked him to get us more of the
large shellfish. We might look for weeks for animals he could
go to directly. Everywhere it is the same: if an animal is good
to eat or poisonous or dangerous the natives of the place will
know about it and where it lives. But if it have none of these
qualities, no matter how highly colored or beautiful, he may
never in his life have seen it.

On the stone-bordered sandspit which is the southern block
to the true inner Puerto Escondido there was a new stone
building not quite finished, with no one about it. Around the
point there now came a large rowboat pushed by a fast outboard motor of a species distinct from the Sea-Cow, for it
seemed controlled and dominated by its master. In this boat
there were several Indians and three men dressed in riding
breeches and hiking boots. They came aboard and introduced
themselves as Leopoldo Pérpuly, who owned a ranch on the
edge of Puerto Escondido, Gilbert Baldibia, a school-teacher
from Loreto, and Manuel Madinabeitia C., of the customs
service, also of Loreto. These last two were on a vacation and
hunting trip. They were strong, fine-looking men wearing the
ever-present .45-caliber automatics of the government service.
We served them canned fruit salad and discussed with them
the country we had covered, and they asked us to go hunting
the *borrego*, or big-horn sheep, with them, starting that afternoon and getting back the next day. We were to go into the
tremendous and desolate stone mountains to camp and hunt.
We accepted immediately, and went with them to the little
ranch set back half a mile from Puerto Escondido. We didn't

want to kill a big-horn sheep, but we wanted to see the country. As it turned out, none of them—the rancher, the teacher, or the customs man—had any intention of killing a big-horn sheep.

The little ranch was set deep in the brush. It was watered by deep wells of brackish brown water out of which endless chains of buckets emerged at the insistence of mules which turned the windlass. This rancher in the desert has dug sixty-foot wells, and he is raising tomatoes and he has planted many grapevines. But so dry is the earth that a few weeks without the rising buckets would destroy all his work. The houses of the ranch were simply roofs and low walls of woven palm, enough to keep out the wind but no obstruction to the air. The floors were of swept hard-packed earth, and there was an air of comfort about the place. The Indian workmen worked very slowly, and the babies peeked out of the woven houses at us. We were to ride to the mountains on mules and one small horse while two Indian men walked ahead. We were sorry for them until we discovered that their main irritation lay in the fact that horses and mules are so slow. Often they disappeared ahead of us, and we found them later sitting beside the trail waiting for us. The line of us started out on a clear but unfinished road that was eventually to go to Loreto. The thick and thorny brush and cactus had been grubbed, but no scraping had been done yet. It was a fantastic country; heavy xerophytic plants: cacti, mimosa, and thorned bushes and trees crackled with the heat. There were the lichens which bleed bright red when they are broken and were once a source of dye before the anilines were developed. There were poison bushes which we were warned about, for if one touches them and then rubs one's eyes, blindness ensues. We learned some of the uses of plants of this country; maidenhair fern, we were told, is boiled to an infusion and given to women after childbirth. It is said that no hemorrhage can follow this treatment. We rode over a rolling, rocky, desolate country, then left the cleared, some-day road and turned up a trail toward the stone mountains, steep and slippery with shale. And here our Indians were even more impatient, for the mules went more slowly while the Indians did not change gait for the steep places.

"My mule was a complainer. For a while I thought he simply didn't like me, but I believe now that he had a sour eye for the world. With every step he groaned with pain so convincingly that once I removed the saddle to see whether he might not be saddled-burned. He did not grunt, but drew from deep in his belly great groans of an agonized soul left to molder in Purgatory. It is impossible to see why he did this, for certainly no Mexican would believe him and he had never carried one of the more sentimental northern race before. I was heart-broken for him, but not sufficiently to get off and walk. We both suffered up the trail, he with pain and I with sorrow for him." (Extract from the personal journal of one of us.)

The trail cut back on itself again and again, and the bare mountains towered high and brooding over us. Far below we could see the brilliant blue water of the Gulf with a fantastic mirage cast over it.

There was in our party one horse, a spindle-legged, small-buttocked little animal with eyes haunted by social inadequacy; one horse in a society of mules, and a gelding at that. We thought how often one mule is surrounded by socially dominant horses, all grace and prance, conscious of their power and loveliness. In this pattern the mule has developed his anti-social self-sufficiency. He knows he can out-think a horse and he is pretty sure he can out-think a human. In both respects he is correct. And so your socially outcast mule dwells inward in sneering intellectuality; his mental pattern, conditioned by centuries of this cynical intellectualism, is set, and he is complete, sullen, treacherous, loving no one, selfish and self-centered. But this horse, having no such background, was unable to make the change in one generation. Surrounded by mules, he sorrowed and his spirit broke and his eyes were sad. The stiffening was gone from his ears and his mouth hung open. He slunk ashamedly along behind the mules. Stripped of his regalia and his titles, he was a pitiful thing. Refugee princes usually become waiters, but this poor horse was not even able to be a waiter, let alone a horse. And just as one is irritated by a grand duke if he has no robes and garters and large metal-and-enamel decorations, so we found ourselves disliking this poor horse; and he knew it and it didn't help him.

We came at last to a trail of broken stone and rubble so steep that the mules could not carry us any more. We dismounted and crawled on all fours, and we don't know how the mules got up. After a short climb we emerged on a level place in a deep cleft in the granite mountains. In this cleft a tiny stream of water fell hundreds of feet from pool to pool. There were palm trees and wild grapevines and large ferns, and the water was cool and sweet. This little stream, coming from so high up in the mountains and falling so far, never had the final dignity of reaching the ocean. The desert sucked it down and the heat dried it up and on the level it disappeared in a light mist of frustration. We sat beside a pool of the waterfall and our Indians made coffee for us and unpacked a lunch, and one item of this lunch was so delicious that we have wanted it again. It is made in this way: a warm tortilla is laid down and spread with well-cooked beans, and another tortilla laid on top and spread, and another, until it is ten or twelve layers thick. Then it is wrapped in cloth. Before eating it one slices downward through the layers as with a cake. It is a fine dish and very filling. While we ate, the Indians made our beds on the ground, and we fired a few shots at a rock across the canyon. Then it was dark and we lay in our blankets and talked, and here we suffered greatly. For the funny stories began. We suppose they weren't clean stories, but we couldn't be sure. Nearly every one began, "Once there was a school-teacher with large black eyes—very sympathetic—" *"Muy simpática"* has a slightly different connotation from that of "sympathetic," for sympathy is a passive state of receptivity, but to be *"simpática"* is to be more active or co-operative, even sometimes a little forward. At any rate, this *"simpática"* school-teacher invariably had as one of her students "a tall strong boy, *con cojones, pero cojones*"—this last with a gesture easily seen in the firelight. The stories progressed until they came to the snappers; we leaned forward studiously intent, but the snappers were either so colloquial that we could not understand them or so filled with the laughter of the teller that we couldn't make out the words. Story after story was told, and we didn't get a single snapper, not one. Our suspicions were aroused of course. We knew something was bound to happen when a school-teacher *"muy simpática"* asks a large boy *"con cojones"* to stay after school, but whether it ever did or not we do not know.

It grew cold in the night, and the mosquitoes were unmerciful. In this sparsely populated country human blood must be a rarity. We were a seldom-found dessert to them, and they whooped and screamed and attacked, power-diving and wheeling up and diving again. The visibility was good, and we made excellent targets. Only when it became bitterly cold did they go away.

We have noticed many times how lightly Mexican Indians sleep. Often in the night they awaken to smoke a cigarette and talk softly together for a while, and then go to sleep again rather like restless birds, which sing a little in the dark, dreaming that it is already day. Half a dozen times a night they may awaken thus, and it is pleasant to hear them, for they talk very quietly as though they were dreaming.

When the dawn came, our Indians made coffee for us and we ate more of the lunch. Then, with some ceremony, the ranch-owner presented a Winchester .30-30 carbine with a broken stock to those Indians, and they set off straight up the mountainside. This, our first hunt for the *borrego*, or big-horn sheep, was the nicest hunting we have ever had. We did not raise a hand in our own service during the entire trip. Besides, we do not like to kill things—we do it when it is necessary, but we take no pleasure in it; and those fine Indians did it for us—the hunting, that is—while we sat beside the little waterfall and discussed many things with our hosts—how all Americans are rich and own new Fords; how there is no poverty in the United States and everyone sees a moving picture every night and is drunk as often as he wishes; how there are no political animosities; no need; no fear; no failure; no unemployment or hunger. It was a wonderful country we came from and our hosts knew all about it and told us. We could not spoil such a dream. After each one of his assurances we said, *"Cómo no?"* which is the most cautious understatement in the world, for *"Cómo no?"* means nothing at all. It is a polite filler between two statements from your companion. And we sat in that cool place and looked out over the hot desert country to the blue Gulf. In a couple of hours our Indians came back; they had no *borrego*, but one of them had a pocketful of droppings. It was time by now to start back to the boat. We intend to do all our future hunting in exactly this way. The ranch-owner said a little sadly, "If they had killed one we could have had our pictures taken with it," but except for that loss, there was no loss, for none of us likes to have the horns of dead animals around.

We had sat beside the little pool and watched the tree-frogs and the horsehair worms and the water-skaters, and had wondered how they got there, so far from other water. It seemed to us that life in every form is incipiently everywhere waiting for a chance to take root and start reproducing; eggs, spores, seeds, bacilli—everywhere. Let a raindrop fall and it is crowded with the waiting life. Everything is everywhere; and we, seeing the desert country, the hot waterless expanse, and knowing how far away the nearest water must be, say with a kind of disbelief, "How did they get clear here, these little animals?" And until we can attack with our poor blunt weapon of reason that causal process and reduce it, we do not quite believe in the horsehair worms and the tree-frogs. The great fact is that they are there. Seeing a school of fish lying quietly in still water, all the heads pointing in one direction, one says, "It is unusual that this is so"—but it isn't unusual at all. We begin at the wrong end. They simply lie that way, and it is remarkable only because with our blunt tool we cannot carve out a human reason. Everything is potentially everywhere—the body is potentially cancerous, phthisic, strong to resist or weak to receive. In one swing of the balance the waiting life pounces in and takes possession and grows strong while our own individual chemistry is distorted past the point where it can maintain its balance. This we call dying, and by the process we do not give nor offer but are taken by a multiform life and used for its proliferation. These things are balanced. A man is potentially all things too, greedy and cruel, capable of great love or great hatred, of balanced or unbalanced so-called emotions. This is the way he is—one factor in a surge of striving. And he continues to ask "why" without first admitting to himself his cosmic identity. There are colonies of pelagic tunicates* which have taken a shape like the

* *Pyrosoma giganteum.*

finger of a glove. Each member of the colony is an individual animal, but the colony is another individual animal, not at all like the sum of its individuals. Some of the colonists, girdling the open end, have developed the ability, one against the other, of making a pulsing movement very like muscular action. Others of the colonists collect the food and distribute it, and the outside of the glove is hardened and protected against contact. Here are two animals, and yet the same thing—something the early Church would have been forced to call a mystery. When the early Church called some matter "a mystery" it accepted that thing fully and deeply as *so*, but simply not accessible to reason because reason had no business with it. So a man of individualistic reason, if he must ask, "Which is the animal, the colony or the individual?" must abandon his particular kind of reason and say, "Why, it's two animals and they aren't alike any more than the cells of my body are like me. I am much more than the sum of my cells and, for all I know, they are much more than the division of me." There is no quietism in such acceptance, but rather the basis for a far deeper understanding of us and our world. And now this is ready for the taboo-box.

It is not enough to say that we cannot know or judge because all the information is not in. The process of gathering knowledge does not lead to knowing. A child's world spreads only a little beyond his understanding while that of a great scientist thrusts outward immeasurably. An answer is invariably the parent of a great family of new questions. So we draw worlds and fit them like tracings against the world about us, and crumple them when they do not fit and draw new ones. The tree-frog in the high pool in the mountain cleft, had he been endowed with human reason, on finding a cigarette butt in the water might have said, "Here is an impossibility. There is no tobacco hereabouts nor any paper. Here is evidence of fire and there has been no fire. This thing cannot fly nor crawl nor blow in the wind. In fact, this thing cannot be and I will deny it, for if I admit that this thing is here the whole world of frogs is in danger, and from there it is only one step to anti-frogicentricism." And so that frog will for the rest of his life try to forget that something that is, is.

On the way back from the mountain one of the Indians

offered us his pocketful of sheep droppings, and we accepted only a few because he did not have many and he probably had relatives who wanted them. We came back through heat and dryness to Puerto Escondido, and it seemed ridiculous to us that the *Western Flyer* had been there all the time. Our hosts had been kind to us and considerate as only Mexicans can be. Furthermore, they had taught us the best of all ways to go hunting, and we shall never use any other. We have, however, made one slight improvement on their method: we shall not take a gun, thereby obviating the last remote possibility of having the hunt cluttered up with game. We have never understood why men mount the heads of animals and hang them up to look down on their conquerors. Possibly it feels good to these men to be superior to animals, but it does seem that if they were sure of it they would not have to prove it. Often a man who is afraid must constantly demonstrate his courage and, in the case of the hunter, must keep a tangible record of his courage. For ourselves, we have had mounted in a small hardwood plaque one perfect *borrego* dropping. And where another man can say, "There was an animal, but because I am greater than he, he is dead and I am alive, and there is his head to prove it," we can say, "There was an animal, and for all we know there still is and here is the proof of it. He was very healthy when we last heard of him."

After the dryness of the mountain it was good to come back to the sea again. One who was born by the ocean or has associated with it cannot ever be quite content away from it for very long.

Sparky made us a great dish of his spaghetti, the veritable Enea spaghetti, and we ate until we were bloated with it.

Now our equipment began to show its weaknesses. The valve of the oxygen cylinder gave trouble owing to the humidity. The little ice-plant was not powerful enough, and where it should have cooled sea water for us, it was all it could do to keep the beer chilled. Besides, it broke down very often.

By now, some animals began to emerge as ubiquitous. *Heliaster kubiniji*, the sun-star, was virtually everywhere, but we did observe that the farther up the Gulf we went, the smaller he became. *Eurythoë*, the stinging worm, occurred wherever there were loosely imbedded rocks or coral under which he could hide. In this connection it is interesting that in the description of this worm in Chamberlin,* the one descriptive item completely ignored is the one most important to the collector—that he stings like the devil, his hair-like fringe breaking off in the hands and leaving a burn which does not disappear for a long time. Tiny, who is able to translate experience readily into emotion, found that anger did not overcome *Eurythoë*, and he grew to have the greatest respect for the worm, even to the point of adopting the usual collector's caution of never putting the hands where one hasn't looked first.

The purple sharp-spined urchin† occurred wherever there was rock or reef exposed to wave-shock or fast-scouring currents. There were the usual barnacles and limpets on the rocks high up in the littoral wherever their pattern of alternating water and air was available. Anemones, the small bunodid forms, were everywhere too. And, of course, the porcelain crabs, hermit crabs, and sea-cucumbers.

We had taken a great many animals and, as compared with the work of some expensive, well-equipped, well-manned expeditions, our results began to cause us to wonder what methods were used by those collectors. For instance, the best reports to date (with the possible exception of the Hancock Expedition reports—and these are so expensive and rare that an amateur cannot afford them, and even university libraries do not always have them) are those of a well-known scientific expedition into the Gulf, about thirty years ago. There were eight naturalists aboard a specially built and equipped steamboat, with a complete and well-trained crew. In two months out of San Francisco they occupied thirty-five stations and took a total of 2351 individuals of 118 species of echinoderms both from deep water (including dredge hauls down to 1760 fathoms) and from along shore, and in two great faunal provinces. Only 39 species were from shallow water; 31 of these, in about 387 individuals, were from the Gulf. Already, in only nine days of Gulf collecting, in the one zoogeographical province and entirely along shore, we had taken almost double their 31 Gulf echinoderm species—the only group we had so

*"The Annelida Polychaeta," 1919, p. 28.
†*Arbacia incisa.*

far tabulated—and had begun to restrain our enthusiasm owing to the lack of containers. We worked hard, but not beyond reason, and our wonder is caused not by the numbers we took, but by the small numbers they did. We had time to play and to talk, and even to drink a little beer. (We took 2160 individuals of two species of beer.)

The shores of the Gulf, so rich for the collector, must still be fairly untouched (again except for the largely unreported Hancock collections). We had not the time for the long careful collecting which is necessary before the true picture of the background of life can be established. We rushed through because it was all we could afford, but our results seem to indicate that energy and enthusiasm can offset lack of equipment and personnel.

17

March 27

WE HAD collected extensively on the outer parts of Puerto Escondido, but not in the inner bay itself. At five-thirty A.M. Mexican time, we set out to circle this inner bay in the little skiff. It was dark when we started, and we used the big flashlights for collecting. There was a good low tide, and we moved slowly along the shore, one rowing while the other inspected the bottom with the light. There was no ripple to distort the surface. The eastern shore was dominated by the big, flat, chocolate-brown holothurian.* They moved slowly along, feeding on the bottom, many hundreds of them. They far overshadowed in number any other animals in this area. There were many of the ruffled clams† with hard, thick, wavy shells. The under-rock fauna was not very rich. The eastern and northern shores were littered with shattered rock, recently enough splintered so that the edges were still sharp, and in this quiet bay no waves would have ground the edges

* *Stichopus fuscus.*
† *Carditamera affinis.*

smooth. Mangroves bordered a great part of the bay, and the spicy smell of their flowers was strong and pleasant. A few of the giant, snake-like synaptids that we had taken in the outer bay waved and moved on the bottom. As we rounded toward the westerly side of the bay, we came to sand flats and a change of fauna, for the big brown cucumbers did not live here. The dawn came as we moved along the sand flats. Two animals were at the waterside, about as large as small collies, dark brown, with a cat-like walk. In the half-light we could not see them clearly, and as we came nearer they melted away through the mangroves. Possibly they were something like giant civet-cats. They had undoubtedly been fishing at the water's edge. On the smooth sand bottom of this area there were clusters of knobbed, green coral (probably *Porites porosa* —no samples were gathered), but except for *Cerianthus* and a few bivalves this bottom was comparatively sterile.

Rounding the southern end of the bay, we came again to the single narrow entrance where the water was rushing in on the returning tide, and here, suddenly, the area was incredibly rich in fauna. Here, where the water rushes in and out, bringing with it food and freshness, there was a remarkable gathering. Beautiful red and green cushion stars littered the rocky bottom. We found clusters of a solitary soft coral-like form[*] in great knobs and heads in one restricted location on the rocks. Caught against the rocks by the current was a very large pelagic coelenterate, in appearance like an anemone with long orange-pink tentacles, apparently not retractable. On picking him up we were badly stung. His nettle-cells were vicious, stinging even through the calluses of the palms, and hurting like a great many bee-stings. At this entrance also we took several giant sea-hares,[†] a number of clams, and one small specimen of the clam-like hacha. For hours afterwards the sting of the anemone remained. So very many things are poisonous and hurtful in these Gulf waters: urchins, sting-rays, morays, heart-urchins, this beastly anemone, and many more. One becomes very timid after a while. Barnacle-cuts, which

[*]In superficial appearance it was identical with the figures of the West Indies *Zoanthus pulchellus* illustrated in Duerden's "Actinians of Porto Rico," 1902, *U. S. Fish Comm. Bulletin* for 1900, Vol. 2, pp. 321–74.

[†]*Dolabella californica.*

are impossible to avoid, cause irritating sores. The fingers and palms become cross-hatched with cuts, and then very quickly, possibly owing to the constant soaking in salt water and the regular lifting of rocks, the hands become covered with a hard, almost horny, callus.

The Puerto Escondido station was one of the richest we visited, for it combined many kinds of environment in a very small area; sand bottom, stone shore, boulders, broken rock, coral, still, warm, shallow places, and racing tide. It is highly probable that careful and extended collecting would show that individuals of species of a very respectable proportion of the total Panamic fauna could be found in this tiny world. Barring surf-battered reef, every probable environment occurs within these few acres—a textbook exhibit for ecologists.

We took rock isopods, sponges, tunicates, turbellarians, chitons, bivalves, snails, hermit crabs, and many other crabs, Heteronereids and mysids pelagic at night, small ophiurans, limpets, and worms and even listed in our collecting notes for the day the horsehair worms from the little waterfall in the mountains.* We took six to eight species of cucumbers and eleven of starfish at this one station.

When we came back from the early morning collecting we sailed immediately for the port of Loreto. We were eager to see this town, for it was the first successful settlement on the Peninsula, and its church is the oldest mission of all. Here the inhospitability of Lower California had finally been conquered and a colony had taken root in the face of hunger and mishap. From the sea, the town was buried in a grove of palms and greenery. We dropped anchor and searched the shore with our glasses. A line of canoes lay on the beach and a group of men sat on the sand by the canoes and watched us; comfortable, lazy-looking men in white clothes. When our anchor dropped they got up and made for the town. Of course, they had to find their uniforms, and since Loreto was not very often visited and since the Governor had *not* recently been there, this may not have been so easy. There may have been some scurrying of errand-bound children from house to house, looking for tunics or belts or borrowing clean shirts. Señor the official

---

Chorodes sp., probably *C. occidentalis* Montgomery, according to J. T. Lucker of the U. S. National Museum, their No. 159124.

had to shave and scent himself and dress. It all takes time, and the boat in the harbor will wait. It didn't look like much of a boat anyway, but at least it was a boat.

One fine thing about Mexican officials is that they greet a fishing boat with the same serious ceremony they would afford the *Queen Mary*, and the *Queen Mary* would have to wait just as long. This made us feel very good and not rebellious about the port fees—absent in this case! We came to them and they made us feel, not like stodgy people in a purse-seiner but like ambassadors from Ultra-Marina bringing letters of greeting out of the distances. It is no wonder that we too scurried for clean shirts, that Tony put on his master's cap, and Tiny polished the naval insignia on his, which he had come by no doubt honorably in a washroom in San Diego. We were not smart, not very alert, but we were clean and we smelled rather delicious. Sparky sprinkled us with shaving lotion and we filled the air with an odor of flowers. If the *brazo*, the double embrace, should be indicated by any feeling of uncontrollable good-will, we were ready.

The men came back to the beach in their uniforms, paddled out, and we passed the ceremony of induction. Loreto was asleep in the sunshine, a lovely town, with gardens in every yard and only the streets white and hot. The young males watched us from the safe shade of the *cantina* and passed greetings as we went by, and a covey of young girls grew tight-faced and rushed around a corner and giggled. How strange we were in Loreto! Our trousers were dark, not white; the silly caps we wore were so outlandish that no store in Loreto would think of stocking them. We were neither soldiers nor sailors—the little girls just couldn't take it. We could hear their strangled giggling from around the corner. Now and then they peeked back around the corner to verify for themselves our ridiculousness, and then giggled again while their elders hissed in disapproval. And one woman standing in a lovely garden shaded with purple bougainvillaea explained, "Everyone knows what silly things girls are. You must forgive their ill manners; they will be ashamed later on." But we felt that the silly girls had something worthwhile in their attitude. They were definitely amused. It is often so, particularly in our country, that the first reaction to strangeness is fear and hatred; we much preferred the laughter. We don't think it was even unkind—they'd simply never seen anything so funny in their lives.

As usual, a good serious small boy attached himself to us. It would be interesting to see whether a nation governed by the small boys of Mexico would not be a better, happier nation than those ruled by old men whose prejudices may or may not be conditioned by ulcerous stomachs and perhaps a little drying up of the stream of love.

This small boy could have been an ambassador to almost any country in the world. His straight-seeing dark eyes were courteous, yet firm. He was kind and dignified. He told us something of Loreto; of its poverty, and how its church was tumbled down now; and he walked with us to the destroyed mission. The roof had fallen in and the main body of the church was a mass of rubble. From the walls hung the shreds of old paintings. But the bell-tower was intact, and we wormed our way deviously up to look at the old bells and to strike them softly with the palms of our hands so that they glowed a little with tone. From here we could look down on the low roofs and into the enclosed gardens of the town. The white sunlight could not get into the gardens and a sleepy shade lay in them.

One small chapel was intact in the church, but the door to it was barred by a wooden grille, and we had to peer through into the small, dark, cool room. There were paintings on the walls, one of which we wanted badly to see more closely, for it looked very much like an El Greco, and probably was *not* painted by El Greco. Still, strange things have found their way here. The bells on the tower were the special present of the Spanish throne to this very loyal city. But it would be good to see this picture more closely. The Virgin Herself, Our Lady of Loreto, was in a glass case and surrounded by the lilies of the recently past Easter. In the dim light of the chapel she seemed very lovely. Perhaps she is gaudy; she has not the look of smug virginity so many have—the "I-am-the-Mother-of-Christ" look—but rather there was a look of terror in her face, of the Virgin Mother of the world and the prayers of so very many people heavy on her.

To the people of Loreto, and particularly to the Indians of

the outland, she must be the loveliest thing in the world. It doesn't matter that our eyes, critical and thin with *good taste*, should find her gaudy. And actually we did not. We too found her lovely in her dim chapel with the lilies of Easter around her. This is a very holy place, and to question it is to question a fact as established as the tide. How easily and quickly we slide into our race-pattern unless we keep intact the stiff-necked and blinded pattern of the recent intellectual training.

We threw it over, and there wasn't much to throw over, and we felt good about it. This Lady, of plaster and wood and paint, is one of the strong ecological factors of the town of Loreto, and not to know her and her strength is to fail to know Loreto. One could not ignore a granite monolith in the path of the waves. Such a rock, breaking the rushing waters, would have an effect on animal distribution radiating in circles like a dropped stone in a pool. So has this plaster Lady a powerful effect on the deep black water of the human spirit. She may disappear and her name be lost, as the Magna Mater, as Isis, have disappeared. But something very like her will take her place, and the longings which created her will find somewhere in the world a similar altar on which to pour their force. No matter what her name is, Artemis, or Venus, or a girl behind a Woolworth counter vaguely remembered, she is as eternal as our species, and we will continue to manufacture her as long as we survive.

We came back slowly through the deserted streets of Loreto, and we walked quietly laden with submergence in a dim chapel.

A few supplies went aboard, and we pulled up the anchor and moved northward again. On the way we caught a Mexican sierra and another fish, apparently a cross between a yellow-fin tuna* and an albacore.† Tiny and Sparky, who have fished in tuna water a good deal, say that this cross is often found and taken, although never in numbers.

We sailed north and found anchorage on the northern end

---

* *Neothunnus macropterus.*
† *Germo alalunga.*

of Coronado Island, and went immediately to collect on a long, westerly-extending point. This reef of water-covered stones was not very rich. In high boots we moved slowly about, turning over the flattened algae-covered boulders. We found here many solitary corals,* and with great difficulty took some of them. They are very hard, and shatter easily when they are removed. If one could saw out the small section of rock to which they are fastened, it would be easy to take them. The next best method is to use a thin, very sharp knife and, by treating them as delicately as jewels, to remove them from their hard anchorage. Even with care, only about one in five is unbroken. Here also we found clustered heads of hard zoanthidean anemones of two types, one much larger than the other. We found a great number of large hemispherical yellow sponges which were noted in the collecting reports as "strikingly similar to the Monterey Bay *Tethya aurantia* or *Geodia*"—a similarity partly explainable by the fact that they turned out to be *Tethya aurantia* and a species of *Geodia*! Our collecting included the usual assortment of creatures, ranging from the crabs which plant algae on their backs for protection to the bryozoa which look more like moss than animals. With all these, the region was still not rich, but "burned," and again we felt the thing which had been at the strange Cayo Islet, a resentment of the shore toward animal life, an inhospitable quality in the stones that would make an animal think twice about living there.

It is so strange, this burned quality. We have seen places which seemed hostile to human life, too. There are parts of the coast of California which do not like humans. It is as though they were already inhabited by another and invisible species which resented humans. Perhaps such places are "burned" for us; perhaps a petrologist could say why. Might there not be a mild radio-activity which made one nervous in such a place so that he would say, trying to put words to his feeling, "This place is unfriendly. There is something here that will not tolerate my kind"? While some radio-activities have been shown to encourage not only life but mutation (note

* *Astrangia pederseni.*

experimentation with fruit-flies), there might well be some other combinations which have an opposite effect.

Little fragments of seemingly unrelated information will sometimes accumulate in a process of speculation until a tenable hypothesis emerges. We had come on a riddle in our reading about the Gulf and now we were able to see this riddle in terms of the animals. There is an observable geographic differential in the fauna of the Gulf of California. The Cape San Lucas–La Paz area is strongly Panamic. Many warm-water mollusks and crustaceans are not known to occur in numbers north of La Paz, and some not even north of Cape San Lucas. But the region north of Santa Rosalia, and even of Puerto Escondido, is known to be inhabited by many colder-water animals, including *Pachygrapsus crassipes*, the commonest California shore crab, which ranges north as far as Oregon. These animals are apparently trapped in a blind alley with no members of their kind to the south of them.

The problem is: "How did they get there?" In 1895 Cooper* advanced an explanation. He remarks, referring to the northern part of the Gulf: "It appears that the species found there are more largely of the temperate fauna, many of them being identical with those of the same latitude on the west [outer] coast of the Peninsula. This seems to indicate that the dividing ridge, now three thousand feet or more in altitude, was crossed by one or more channels within geologically recent times."

This differential, which we ourselves saw, has been remarked a number of times in the literature of the region, especially by conchologists. Eric Knight Jordan, son of David Starr Jordan, an extremely promising young paleontologist who was killed some years ago, studied the geological and present distribution of mollusks along the west coast of Lower California. He says†: "Two distinct faunas exist on the west coast of Lower California. The southern Californian *now*

---

*"Catalogue of Marine Shells . . . on Eastern Shore of Lower California . . . ," *Proc. Calif. Acad. Sci.*, Vol. 5 (2), p. 37.

†"Quarternary and Recent Molluscan Faunas of the West Coast of Lower California," *Bull. South Calif. Acad. Sci.*, Vol. 23 (5), p. 146.

ranges southward from Point Conception to Cedros Island . . . probably extends a little farther. . . . The fauna of the Gulf of California ranges to the north on the west coast of the Peninsula approximately to Scammon's Lagoon, which is a little farther up than Cedros Island." Present geographical ranges are given for 124 species, collected in lower Quaternary beds at Magdalena Bay, all of which occur living today, but farther to the north. Two pages later he remarks: "It . . . appears that when these Quaternary beds were laid down there was a southward displacement of the isotherms sufficient to carry the conditions today prevailing at Cedros down as far as the latitude of Magdalena Bay."

Having reviewed the literature, we can confirm the significance of the Cedros Island complex as a present critical horizon (as Carpenter did eighty years ago) where the north and south fauna to some extent intermingle. Apparently this is the very condition that obtained at Magdalena Bay or southward when the lower Quaternary beds were being laid down. The present Magdalena Plain, extending to La Paz on the Gulf side, was at that time submerged. Then it was cold enough to permit a commingling of cold-water and warm-water species at that point. The hypothesis is tenable that when the isotherms retreated northward, the cold-water forms were no longer able to inhabit southern Lower California shores, which included the then Gulf entrance. In these increasingly warm waters they would have perished or would have been pushed northward, both along the outside coast, where they could retreat indefinitely, and into the Gulf. In the latter case the migrating waves of competing animals from the south, which were invading the Gulf and spilling upward, would have pocketed the northern species in the upper reaches, where they have remained to this day. These animals, hemmed in by tropical waters and fortunate competitors, have maintained themselves for thousands of years, though in the struggle they have been modified toward pauperization.

This hypothesis would seem to offset Cooper's assumption of a channel through ridges some 350 miles to the north which show no signs of Quaternary submergence.

It is interesting that a paleontologist, working in one area, should lay the groundwork for a very reasonable hypothesis concerning the distribution of animals in another. It is, however, only one example among many of the obliqueness of investigation and the accident quotient involved in much investigation. The literature of science is filled with answers found when the question propounded had an entirely different direction and end.

There is one great difficulty with a good hypothesis. When it is completed and rounded, the corners smooth and the content cohesive and coherent, it is likely to become a thing in itself, a work of art. It is then like a finished sonnet or a painting completed. One hates to disturb it. Even if subsequent information should shoot a hole in it, one hates to tear it down because it once was beautiful and whole. One of our leading scientists, having reasoned a reef in the Pacific, was unable for a long time to reconcile the lack of a reef, indicated by soundings, with the reef his mind told him was there. A parallel occurred some years ago. A learned institution sent an expedition southward, one of whose many projects was to establish whether or not the sea-otter was extinct. In due time it returned with the information that the sea-otter was indeed extinct. One of us, some time later, talking with a woman on the coast below Monterey, was astonished to hear her describe animals living in the surf which could only be sea-otters, since she described accurately animals she couldn't have known about except by observation. A report of this to the institution in question elicited no response. It had extincted sea-otters and that was that. It was only when a reporter on one of our more disreputable newspapers photographed the animals that the public was informed. It is not yet known whether the institution of learning has been won over.

This is not set down in criticism; it is no light matter to make up one's mind about anything, even about sea-otters, and once made up, it is even harder to abandon the position. When a hypothesis is deeply accepted it becomes a growth which only a kind of surgery can amputate. Thus, beliefs persist long after their factual bases have been removed, and practices based on beliefs are often carried on even when the beliefs which stimulated them have been forgotten. The practice must follow the belief. It is often considered, particularly by reformers and legislators, that law is a stimulant to action or an inhibitor of action, when actually the reverse is true. Successful law is simply the publication of the practice of the majority of units of a society, and by it the inevitable variable units are either driven to conform or are eliminated. We have had many examples of law trying to be the well-spring of action; our prohibition law showed how completely fallacious that theory is.

The things of our minds have for us a greater toughness than external reality. One of us has a beard, and one night when this one was standing wheel-watch, the others sat in the galley drinking coffee. We were discussing werewolves and their almost universal occurrence in regional literature. From this beginning, we played with a macabre thought, "The moon will soon be full," we said, "and he of the beard will begin to feel the pull of the moon. Last night," we said, "we heard the scratch of claws on the deck. When you see him go down on all fours, when you see the red light come into his eyes, then look out, for he will slash your throat." We were delighted with the game. We developed the bearded one's tendencies, how his teeth, the canines at least, had been noticeably longer of late, how for the past week he had torn his dinner apart with his teeth. It was night as we talked thus, and the deck was dark and the wind was blowing. Suddenly he appeared in the doorway, his beard and hair blown, his eyes red from the wind. Climbing the two steps up from the galley, he seemed to arise from all fours, and everyone of us started, and felt the prickle of erecting hairs. We had actually talked and thought ourselves into this pattern, and it took a while for it to wear off.

These mind things are very strong; in some, so strong as to blot out the external things completely.

18

March 28

AFTER the collecting on Coronado Island, on the twenty-seventh, and the preservation and labeling, we found that we were very tired. We had worked constantly. On the morning of the twenty-eighth we slept. It was a good thing, we told ourselves; the eyes grow weary with looking at new things; sleeping late, we said, has its genuine therapeutic value; we would be better for it, would be able to work more effectively. We have little doubt that all this was true, but we wish we could build as good a rationalization every time we are lazy. For in some beastly way this fine laziness has got itself a bad name. It is easy to see how it might have come into disrepute, if the result of laziness were hunger. But it rarely is. Hunger makes laziness impossible. It has even become sinful to be lazy. We wonder why. One could argue, particularly if one had a gift for laziness, that it is a relaxation pregnant of activity, a sense of rest from which directed effort may arise, whereas most busyness is merely a kind of nervous tic. We know a lady who is obsessed with the idea of ashes in an ashtray. She is not lazy. She spends a good half of her waking time making sure that no ashes remain in any ashtray, and to make sure of keeping busy she has a great many ashtrays. Another acquaintance, a man, straightens rugs and pictures and arranges books and magazines in neat piles. He is not lazy, either; he is very busy. To what end? If he should relax, perhaps with his feet up on a chair and a glass of cool beer beside him—not cold, but cool—if he should examine from this position a rumpled rug or a crooked picture, saying to himself between sips of beer (preferably Carta Blanca beer), "This rug irritates me for some reason. If it were straight, I should be comfortable; but there is only one straight position (and this is, of course, only my own personal discipline of straightness) among all possible positions. I am, in effect, trying to impose my will, my insular sense of rightness, on a rug, which of itself can have no such sense, since it seems equally contented straight or crooked. Suppose I should try to straighten people," and here he sips deeply. "Helen C., for instance, is not neat, and Helen C."—here he goes into a reverie—"how beautiful she is with her hair messy, how lovely when she is excited and breathing through her mouth." Again he raises his glass, and in a few minutes he picks up the telephone. He is happy; Helen C. may be happy; and the rug is not disturbed at all.

How can such a process have become a shame and a sin? Only in laziness can one achieve a state of contemplation which is a balancing of values, a weighing of oneself against the world and the world against itself. A busy man cannot find time for such balancing. We do not think a lazy man can commit murders, nor great thefts, nor lead a mob. He would be more likely to think about it and laugh. And a nation of lazy contemplative men would be incapable of fighting a war unless their very laziness were attacked. Wars are the activities of busy-ness.

With such a background of reasoning, we slept until nine A.M. And then the engines started and we moved toward Concepción Bay. The sea, with the exception of one blow outside of La Paz, had been very calm. This day, a little wind blew over the ultramarine water. The swordfish in great numbers jumped and played about us. We set up our lightest harpoon on the bow with a coil of cotton line beside it, and for hours we stood watch. The helmsman changed course again and again to try to bring the bow over a resting fish, but they seemed to wait until we were barely within throwing range and then they sounded so quickly that they seemed to snap from view. We made many wild casts and once we got the iron in, near the tail of a monster. But he flicked his tail and tore it out and was gone. We could see schools of leaping tuna all about us, and whenever we crossed the path of a school, our lines jumped and snapped under the strikes, and we brought the beautiful fish in.

We had set up a salt barrel near the stern, and we cut the fish into pieces and put them into brine to take home. It developed after we got home that several of us had added salt to the brine and the whole barrel was hopelessly salty and inedible.

As we turned Aguja Point and headed southward into the deep pocket of Concepción Bay, we could see Mulege on the northern shore—a small town in a blistering country. We had no plan for stopping there, for the story is that the port charges are mischievous and ruinous. We do not know that this is so, but it is repeated about Mulege very often. Also, there may be malaria there. We had been following the trail of malaria for a long time. At the Cape they said there was no malaria there but at La Paz it was very serious. At La Paz, they said it was only at Loreto. At Loreto they declared that Mulege was full of it. And there it must remain, for we didn't stop at Mulege; so we do not know what the Mulegeños say about it. Later, we picked up the malaria on the other side, ran it down to Topolobambo, and left it there. We would say offhand, never having been to either place, that the malaria is very bad at Mulege and Topolobambo.

A strong, north-pointing peninsula is the outer boundary of Concepción Bay. At the mouth it is three and a quarter miles wide and it extends twenty-two miles southward, varying in width from two to five miles. The eastern shore, along which we collected, is regular in outline, with steep beaches of sand and pebbles and billions of bleaching shells and many clams and great snails. From the shore, the ascent is gradual toward mountains which ridge the little peninsula and protect this small gulf from the Gulf of California. Along the shore are many pools of very salty water, where thousands of fiddler crabs sit by their moist burrows and bubble as one approaches. The beach was beautiful with the pink and white shells of the murex.* Sparky found them so beautiful that he collected a washtubful of them and stored them in the hold. And even then, back in Monterey, he found he did not have enough for his friends.

Behind the beach there was a little level land, sandy and dry and covered with cactus and thick brush. And behind that, the rising dry hills. Now again the wild doves were calling among the hills with their song of homesickness. The quality of longing in this sound, the memory response it sets up, is curious and strong. And it has also the quality of a dying day. One wishes to walk toward the sound—to walk on and on toward it, forgetting everything else. Undoubtedly there are sound symbols in the unconscious just as there are visual symbols—sounds that trigger off a response, a little spasm of fear, or a quick lustfulness, or, as with the doves, a nostalgic sadness. Perhaps in our pre-humanity this sound of doves was a signal that the day was over and a night of terror due—a night which perhaps this time was permanent. Keyed to the visual

* *Phyllonotus bicolor.*

symbol of the sinking sun and to the odor symbol of the cooling earth, these might all cause the little spasm of sorrow; and with the long response-history, one alone of these symbols might suffice for all three. The smell of a musking goat is not in our experience, but it is in some experience, for smelled faintly, or in perfume, it is not without its effect even on those who have not smelled the passionate gland nor seen the play which follows its discharge. But some great group of shepherd peoples must have known this odor and its result, and must, from the goat's excitement, have taken a very strong suggestion. Even now, a city man is stirred deeply when he smells it in the perfume on a girl's hair. It may be thought that we produce no musk nor anything like it, but this we do not believe. One has the experience again and again of suddenly turning and following with one's eyes some particular girl among many girls, even trotting after her. She may not be beautiful, indeed, often is not. But what are the stimuli if not odors, perhaps above or below the conscious olfactory range? If one follows such an impulse to its conclusion, one is not often wrong. If there be visual symbols, strong and virile in the unconscious, there must be others planted by the other senses. The sensitive places, ball of thumb, ear-lobe, skin just below the ribs, thigh, and lip, must have their memories too. And smell of some spring flowers when the senses thaw, and smell of a ready woman, and smell of reptiles and smell of death, are deep in our unconscious. Sometimes we can say truly, "That man is going to die." Do we smell the disintegrating cells? Do we see the hair losing its luster and uneasy against the scalp, and the skin dropping its tone? We do not know these reactions one by one, but we say, that man or cat or dog or cow is going to die. If the fleas on a dog know it and leave their host in advance, why do not we also know it? Approaching death, the pre-death of the cells, has informed the fleas and us too.

The shallow water along the shore at Concepción Bay was littered with sand dollars, two common species* and one†

*Encope californica and E. grandis.
†Clypeaster rotundus.

very rare. And in the same association, brilliant-red sponge arborescences* grew in loose stones in the sand or on the knobs of old coral. These are the important horizon markers. On other rocks, imbedded in the sand, there were giant hachas, clustered over with tunicates and bearing on their shells the usual small ophiurans and crabs. One of the masked rock-clams had on it a group of solitary corals. Close inshore were many brilliant large snails, the living animals the shells of which had so moved Sparky. In this area we collected from the skiff, leaning over the edge, bringing up animals in a dip-net or spearing them with a small trident, sometimes jumping overboard and diving for a heavier rock with a fine sponge growing on it.

The ice we had taken aboard at La Paz was all gone now. We started our little motor and ran it for hours to cool the ice-chest, but the heat on deck would not permit it to drop the temperature below about thirty-eight degrees F., and the little motor struggled and died often, apparently hating to run in such heat. It sounded tired and sweaty and disgusted. When the evening came, we had fried fish, caught that day, and after dark we lighted the deck and put our reflecting lamp over the side. We netted a serpent-like eel, thinking from its slow, writhing movement through the water that it might be one of the true viperine sea-snakes which are common farther south. Also we captured some flying fish.

We used long-handled dip-nets in the lighted water, and set up the enameled pans so that the small pelagic animals could be dropped directly into them. The groups in the pans grew rapidly. There were *heteronereis* (the free stages of otherwise crawling worms who develop paddle-like tails upon sexual maturity). There were swimming crabs, other free-swimming annelids, and ribbon-fish which could not be seen at all, so perfectly transparent were they. We should not have known they were there, if they had not thrown faint shadows on the bottom of the pans. Placed in alcohol, they lost their transparency and could easily be seen. The pans became crowded with little skittering animals, for each net brought in many species. When the hooded light was put down very near the

Tedania ignis.

water, the smallest animals came to it and scurried about in a dizzying dance so rapidly that they seemed to draw crazy lines in the water. Then the small fishes began to dart in and out, snapping up this concentration, and farther out in the shadows the large wise fishes cruised, occasionally swooping and gobbling the small fishes. Several more of the cream-colored spotted snake-eels wriggled near and were netted. They were very snake-like and they had small bright-blue eyes. They did not swim with a beating tail as fishes do, but rather squirmed through the water.

While we worked on the deck, we put down crab-nets on the bottom, baiting them with heads and entrails of the fish we had had for dinner. When we pulled them up they were loaded with large stalk-eyed snails* and with sea-urchins having long vicious spines.† The colder-water relatives of both these animals are very slow-moving, but these moved quickly and were completely voracious. A net left down five minutes was brought up with at least twenty urchins in it, and all attacking the bait. In addition to the speed with which they move, these urchins are clever and sensitive with their spines. When approached, the long sharp little spears all move and aim their points at the approaching body until the animal is armed like a Macedonian phalanx. The main shafts of the spines were cream-yellowish-white, but a half-inch from the needle-points they were blue-black. The prick of one of the points burned like a bee-sting. They seemed to live in great numbers at four fathoms; we do not know their depth range, but their physical abilities and their voraciousness would indicate a rather wide one. In the same nets we took several dromiaceous crabs, reminiscent of hermits, which had adjusted themselves to life in half the shell of a bivalve, and had changed their body shapes accordingly.

It is probable that no animal tissue ever decays in this water. The furious appetites which abound would make it unlikely that a dead animal, or even a hurt animal, should last more than a few moments. There would be quick death for the quick animal which became slow, for the shelled animal which opened at the wrong time, for the fierce animal which grew

---

Strombus spp.

†*Astropyga pulvinata.*

timid. It would seem that the penalty for a mistake or an error would be instant death and there would be no second chance.

It would have been good to keep some of the sensitive urchins alive and watch their method of getting about and their method of attack. Indeed, we will never go again without a full-sized observation aquarium into which we can put interesting animals and keep them for some time. The aquaria taken were made with polarized glass. Thus, the fish could look out but we could not look in. This, it turned out, was an error on our part.

There are three ways of seeing animals: dead and preserved; in their own habitats for the short time of a low tide; and for long periods in an aquarium. The ideal is all three. It is only after long observation that one comes to know the animal at all. In his natural place one can see the normal life, but in an aquarium it is possible to create abnormal conditions and to note the animal's adaptability or lack of it. As an example of this third method of observation, we can use a few notes made during observation of a small colony of anemones in an aquarium. We had them for a number of months.

In their natural place in the tide pool they are thick and close to the rock. When the tide covers them they extend their beautiful tentacles and with their nettle-cells capture and eat many micro-organisms. When a powerful animal, a small crab for example, touches them, they paralyze it and fold it into the stomach, beginning the digestive process before the animal is dead, and in time ejecting the shell and other indigestible matter. On being touched by an enemy, they fold in upon themselves for protection. We brought a group of these on their own stone into the laboratory and placed them in an aquarium. Cooled and oxygenated sea water was sprayed into the aquarium to keep them alive. Then we gave them various kinds of food, and found that they do not respond to simple touch-stimulus on the tentacles, but have something which is at least a vague parallel to taste-buds, whatever may be the chemical or mechanical method. Thus, protein food was seized by the tentacles, taken and eaten without hesitation; fat was touched gingerly, taken without enthusiasm to the stomach, and immediately rejected; starches were not taken at all— the tentacles touched starchy food and then ignored it.

Sugars, if concentrated, seemed actually to burn them so that the tentacles moved away from contact. There did really appear to be a chemical method of differentiation and choice. We circulated the same sea water again and again, only cooling and freshening it. Pure oxygen, introduced into the stomach in bubbles, caused something like drunkenness; the animal relaxed and its reaction to touch was greatly slowed, and sometimes completely stopped for a while. But the reaction to chemical stimulus remained active, although slower. In time, all the microscopic food was removed from the water through constant circulation past the anemones, and then the animals began to change their shapes. Their bodies, which had been thick and fat, grew long and neck-like; from a normal inch in length, they changed to three inches long and very slender. We suspected this was due to starvation. Then one day, after three months, we dropped a small crab into the aquarium. The anemones, moving on their new long necks, bent over and attacked the crab, striking downward like slow snakes. Their normal reaction would have been to close up and draw in their tentacles, but these animals had changed their pattern in hunger, and now we found that when touched on the body, even down near the base, they moved downward, curving on their stalks, while their tentacles hungrily searched for food. There seemed even to be competition among the individuals, a thing we have never seen in a tide pool among anemones. This versatility had never been observed by us and is not mentioned in any of the literature we have seen.

The aquarium is a very valuable extension of shore observation. Quick-eyed, timid animals soon become used to having humans about, and quite soon conduct their business under lights. If we could have put our sensitive urchins in an aquarium, we could have seen how it is that they move so rapidly and how they are stimulated to aim their points at an approaching body. But we preserved them, and of course they lost color and dropped many of their beautiful sharp spines. Also, we could have seen how the great snails are able to consume animal tissue so quickly. As it is, we do not know these things.

19

March 29

TIDES had been giving us trouble, for we were now far enough up the Gulf so that the tidal run had to be taken into time consideration. In the evening we had set up a flagged stake at the waterline, so that with glasses we could see from the deck the rise and fall of the tide in relation to the stick. At seven-thirty in the morning the tide was going down from our marker. We had abandoned our tide charts as useless by now, and since we stayed such a short time at each station we could not make new ones. The irregular length of our jumps made it impossible for us to forecast with accuracy from a preceding station. Besides all this, a good, leisurely state of mind had come over us which had nothing to do with the speed and duration of our work. It is very possible to work hard and fast in a leisurely manner, or to work slowly and clumsily with great nervousness.

On this day, the sun glowing on the morning beach made us feel good. It reminded us of Charles Darwin, who arrived late at night on the *Beagle* in the Bay of Valparaiso. In the morning he awakened and looked ashore and he felt so well that he wrote, "When morning came everything appeared delightful. After Tierra del Fuego, the climate felt quite delicious, the atmosphere so dry and the heavens so clear and blue with the sun shining brightly, that all nature seemed sparkling with life."* Darwin was not saying how it was with Valparaiso, but rather how it was with him. Being a naturalist, he said, "All nature seemed sparkling with life," but actually it was he who was sparkling. He felt so very fine that he can, in these charged though general adjectives, translate his ecstasy over a hundred years to us. And we can feel how he stretched his muscles in the morning air and perhaps took off his hat— we hope a bowler—and tossed it and caught it.

On this morning, we felt the same way at Concepción Bay. "Everything appeared delightful." The tiny waves slid up and down the beach, hardly breaking at all; out in the Bay the

* *Voyage of the Beagle*, Chap. 12, July 23.

pelicans were fishing, flying along and then folding their wings and falling in their clumsy-appearing dives, which nevertheless must be effective, else there would be no more pelicans.

By nine A.M. the water was well down, and by ten seemed to have passed low and to be flowing again. We went ashore and followed the tide down. The beach is steep for a short distance, and then levels out to a gradual slope. We took two species of cake urchins which commingled at one-half to one and one-half feet of water at low tide. The ordinary cake urchin here, with holes, is *Encope californica* Verrill. The grotesquely beautiful keyhole sand dollar* was very common here. Finally, there was a rare member of the same group,† which we collected unknowingly, and turned out only three individuals of the species when the animals were separated on deck. A little deeper, about two feet submerged, at low tide, a species of cucumber new to us was taken, a flat, sand-encrusted fellow.‡ Giant heart-urchins§ in some places were available in the thousands. They ranged between two feet and three feet below the surface at low water, and very few were deeper. The greatest number occurred at three feet.

The shore line here is much like that at Puget Sound: in the high littoral is a foreshore of gravel to pebbles to small rocks; in the low littoral, gravelly sand and fine sand with occasional stones below the low tide level. In this zone, with a maximum at four feet, were heavy groves of algae, presumably *Sargassum*, lush and tall, extending to the surface. Except for the lack of eel-grass, it might have been Puget Sound. We took giant stalk-eyed conchs,‖ several species of holothurians and *Cerianthus*, the sand anemone whose head is beautiful but whose encased body is very ugly, like rotting gray cloth. Tiny christened *Cerianthus* "sloppy-guts," and the name stuck. By diving, we took a number of hachas, the huge mussel-like clams. Their shells were encrusted with sponges and tunicates under which small crabs and snapping shrimps hid themselves. Large scalloped limpets also were attached to the

---

* *Encope grandis* L. Agassiz.
† *Clypeaster rotundus* (A. Agassiz).
‡ *Holothuria inhabilis.*
§ *Meoma grandis.*
‖ *Strombus galeatus.*

shells of the hachas. This creature closes itself so tightly with its big adductor muscle that a knife cannot penetrate it and the shell will break before the muscle will relax. The best method for opening them is to place them in a bucket of water and, when they open a little, to introduce a sharp, thin-bladed knife and sever the muscle quickly. A finger caught between the closing shells would probably be injured. In many of the hachas we found large, pale, commensal shrimps† living in the folds of the body. They are soft-bodied and apparently live there always.

About noon we got under way for San Lucas Cove, and as usual did our preserving and labeling while the boat was moving. Some of the sand dollars we killed in formalin and then set in the sun to dry, and many more we preserved in formaldehyde solution in a small barrel. We had taken a great many of them. Sparky had, by now, filled several sacks with the fine white rose-lined murex shells, explaining, as though he were asked for an explanation, that they would be nice for lining a garden path. In reality, he simply loved them and wanted to have them about.

We passed Mulege, that malaria-ridden town, that town of high port fees—so far as we know—and it looked gay against the mountains, red-roofed and white-walled. We wished we were going ashore there, but the wall of our own resolve kept us out, for we had said, "We will *not* stop at Mulege," and having said it, we could not overcome our own decision. Sparky and Tiny looked longingly at it as we passed; they had come to like the quick excursions into little towns: they found that their Italian was understood for any purposes they had in mind. It was their practice to wander through the streets, carrying their cameras, and in a very short time they had friends. Tony and Tex were foreigners, but Tiny and Sparky were very much at home in the little towns—and they never inquired whose home. This was not reticence, but rather a native tactfulness.

Now that we were engaged in headland navigating, Tiny's and Sparky's work at the wheel had improved, and except when they chased a swordfish (which was fairly often) we were

---

Pontonia pinnae.

not off course more than two or three times during their watch. They had abandoned the compass with relief and blue water was no longer thrust upon them.

At about this time it was discovered that Tex was getting fat, and inasmuch as he was to be married soon after his return, we decided to diet him and put him in a marrying condition. He protested feebly when we cut off his food, and for three days he sneaked food and stole food and cozened us out of food. During the three days of his diet, he probably ate twice as much as he did before, but the idea that he was starving made him so hungry that at the end of the third day he said he couldn't stand it any longer, and he ate a dinner that nearly killed him. Actually, with his thefts of food he had picked up a few pounds during his diet, but always afterwards he shuddered at the memory of those three days. He said, "A man doesn't feel his best when he is starving" and he asked what good it would do him to be married if he were weak and sick.

At five P.M. on March 29 we arrived at San Lucas Cove and anchored outside. The cove, a deep salt-water lagoon, guarded by a large sandspit, has an entrance that might have been deep enough for us to enter, but the current is strong and there were no previous soundings available. Besides, Tony was nervous about taking his boat into such places. There was another reason for anchoring outside; in the open Gulf where the breeze moves there are no bugs, while if one anchors in still water near the mangroves little visitors come and spend the night. There is one small, beetle-like black fly which crawls down into bed with you and has a liking for very tender places. We had suffered from this fellow when the wind blew over the mangroves to us. This bug hates light, but finds security and happiness under the bedding, nestling over one's kidneys, munching contentedly. His bite leaves a fiery itch; his collective soul is roasting in Hell, if we have any influence in the court of Heaven. After one experience with him, we anchored always a little farther out.

When we came to San Lucas, the tide was flowing and the little channel was a mill-race. It would be necessary to wait for the morning tide. We were eager to see whether on this sand-bar, so perfectly situated, we could not find amphioxus, that most primitive of vertebrates. As we dropped anchor a large shark cruised about us, his fin high above the water. We shot at him with a pistol and one shot went through his fin. He cut away like a razor blade and we could hear the hiss of the water. What incredible speed sharks can make when they hurry! We wonder how their greatest speed compares with that of a porpoise. The variations in speed among individuals of these fast-swimming species must be very great too. There must be incredible sharks, like Man o' War or Charlie Paddock, which make other sharks seem slow.

That night we hung the light over the side again and captured some small squid, the usual *heteronereis*, a number of free-swimming crustacea, quantities of crab larvae and the transparent ribbon-fish again. The boys developed a technique for catching flying fish: one jabbed at it with a net, making it fly into the net of another. But even in the nets they were not caught, for they struggled and fluttered away with ease. That night we had a mild celebration of some minor event which did not seem important enough to remember. The pans of animals were still lying on the deck and one of our members, confusing Epsom salts with cracker-crumbs, tried to anesthetize a large pan of holothurians with cracker-meal. The resulting thick paste seemed to have no narcotic qualities whatever.

Late, late in the night we recalled that Horace says fried shrimps and African snails will cure a hangover. Neither was available. And we wonder whether this classical remedy for a time-bridging ailment has been prescribed and tried since classical times. We do not know what snail he refers to, or whether it is a marine snail or an escargot. It is too bad that such imaginative remedies have been abandoned for the banalities of anti-acids, heart stimulants, and analgesics. The Bacchic mystery qualified and nullified by a biochemistry which is almost but not quite yet a mystic science. Horace suggests that wine of Cos taken with these shrimps and snails guarantees the remedy. Perhaps it would. In that case, his remedy is in one respect like those unguents used in witchcraft which combine such items as dried babies' brains, frog-eyes, lizards' tongues, and mold from a hanged man's skull with a quantity of good raw opium, and thus serve to stimulate the imagination and the central nervous system at the same time. In our pained discussion at San Lucas Cove we found we had no snails nor shrimps nor wine of Cos. We tore the remedy down to its fundamentals, and decided that it was a good strong dose of proteins and alcohol, so we substituted a new compound—fried fish and a dash of medicinal whisky—and it did the job.

The use of euphemism in national advertising is giving the hangover a bad name. "Over-indulgence" it is called. There is a curious nastiness about over-indulgence. We would not consider over-indulging. The name is unpleasant, and the word "over" indicates that one shouldn't have done it. Our celebration had no such implication. We did *not* drink too much. We drank just enough, and we refuse to profane a good little time of mild inebriety with that slurring phrase "over-indulgence."

There was a reference immediately above to the medicine chest. On leaving Monterey, it may be remembered, we had exhausted the medicine, but no sooner had we put to sea when it was discovered that each one of us, with the health of the whole party in mind, had laid in auxiliary medicine for emergencies. We had indeed, when the good-will of all was assembled, a medicine chest which would not have profaned a fair-sized bar. And the emergencies did occur. Who is to say that an emergency of the soul is not worse than a bad cold? What was good enough for Li-Po was good enough for us. There have been few enough immortals who did not love wine; offhand we cannot think of any and we do not intend to try very hard. The American Indians and the Australian Bushmen are about the only great and intellectual peoples who have not developed an alcoholic liquor and a cult to take care of it. There are, indeed, groups among our own people who have abandoned the use of alcohol, due no doubt to Indian or Bushman blood, but we do not wish to claim affiliation with them. One can imagine such a specimen of Bushman reading this journal and saying, "Why, it was all drinking—beer—and at San Lucas Cove, whisky." So might a night-watchman cry out, "People sleep all the time!" So might a blind man complain, "Among some people there is a pernicious and wicked practice called 'seeing.' This eventually causes death and should be avoided." Actually, with few tribal exceptions, our race has a triumphant alcoholic history and no definite symptoms of degeneracy can be attributed to it. The theory that alcohol is a poison was too easily and too blindly accepted. So it is to some individuals; sugar is poison to others and meat to others. But to the race in general, alcohol has been an anodyne, a warmer of the soul, a strengthener of muscle and spirit. It has given courage to cowards and has made very ugly people attractive. There is a story told of a Swedish tramp, sitting in a ditch on Midsummer Night. He was ragged and dirty and drunk, and he said to himself softly and in wonder, "I am rich and happy and perhaps a little beautiful."

20

March 30

AT EIGHT-THIRTY in the morning the tide was ebbing, uncovering the sand-bar and a great expanse of tidal sandflat. This flat was made up to a large extent of the broken shells of mollusks. In digging, we found many small clams and a few smooth *Venus*-like clams. We took one very large male fiddler crab. "Sloppy-guts," the *Cerianthus*, was very common here. There were numbers of hermit crabs and many of the swimming crabs with bright-blue claws. These crabs* are eaten by Mexicans and are delicious. They swim very rapidly through the water. When we pursued them to the shallows they tried to escape for a time, but soon settled to the bottom and raised their claws to a position not unlike that of a defensive boxer. Their pinch was very painful. When captured and put into a collecting bucket they vented their fury on one another; pinched-off legs and claws littered the buckets on our return. These crabs do not seem to come out of the water as the grapsoids do. Removed from the water, they very soon weaken and lose their fight. Moreover, they do not die as

* *Callinectes bellicosus.*

rapidly in fresh water as do most other crabs. Perhaps, living in the lagoons which sometimes must be almost brackish, they have achieved a tolerance for fresh water greater than that of other crabs; greater indeed, although it is not much of a trick, than that of a certain biologist who shall be nameless.

This varying threshold of tolerance is always an astonishing thing.

Amphioxus ordinarily lives on the seaward side of a sand-bar and in sub-tidal water; or, at least, in sand bared by only the lowest of tides. We dug for them here and took only a few weak ones. It was not a very low tide and these were very possibly stragglers. It is probable that an extremely low tide would expose a level in which a great many of them live. The capture of these animals is exciting and requires speed. They are perfectly streamlined and partly transparent. Also, they are extremely nervous. Sometimes if the sand is struck with a shovel they will jump out and then frantically wriggle to get under the sand again—which they readily do. They are able to move through sand and even under it with great rapidity. We turned over the sand and leaped at them before they could escape. There used to be very many of them at Balboa Beach in Southern California, but channel dredging and perhaps the great number of motor boats have made them rare. And they are very interesting animals, being almost the dividing point between vertebrates and invertebrates. Usually one to three inches long and shuttle-shaped, they are perfectly built to slip through the sand without resistance.

The bar was rich with clams, many small *Chione*, and some small razor clams. We extracted the *Cerianthus* from their sloppy casings and found a great many tiny commensal sipunculid worms* in the smooth inner linings of the cases. These were able to extend themselves so far that they seemed like hairs, or to retract until they were like tiny peanuts. We did not find commensal pea crabs in the linings, as we had thought we would.

San Lucas Cove is nearly slough-like. The water gets very warm and probably very stale. It is exposed to a deadly sun and is so shallow that the water is soupy. This very quality of

* *Phascolosoma hesperum.*

probable high salinity and warmth made it very difficult to preserve the *Cerianthus* in an expanded state. The small bunodids are easily anesthetized in Epsom salts, but *Cerianthus*, after six to eight hours of concentrated Epsom-salts solution, and even standing in pans under the hot sun, were able to retract rapidly and violently by expelling water from the aboral pore when the preserving liquid touched them. Sooner or later we will find the perfect method for anesthetizing anemones, but it has not yet been found. There is hope that cold may work as the anesthetic, if we can force absorption of formalin while the animals are relaxed with dry ice. But a great deal of experimenting is necessary, for if too cold they do not receive the formalin, and if too warm they retract on contact with it.

Back on board at about eleven-thirty we sailed for San Carlos Bay. We did not plan to stop at Santa Rosalia. It is a fairly large town which has long been supported by copper mines in the neighborhood, under the control of a French company. A little feeling of hurry was creeping upon us, for by now we had begun to see the magnitude of the job we had undertaken, and to realize that with the limited time and the more than limited equipment and personnel, we could not make much of a job of it. Our time was going fast. Much as Sparky and Tiny wished to continue their research and shore collecting at Santa Rosalia, we sailed on past it. And it looked, from the sea at least, to be less Mexican than other towns. Perhaps that was because we knew it was run by a French company. A Mexican town grows out of the ground. You cannot conceive its never having been there. But Santa Rosalia looked "built." There were industrial works of large size visible, loading trestles, and piles of broken rock. The mountains rose behind the town, burned almost white, and the green about the houses and the red roofs were in startling contrast. Sparky had the wheel as we went by, and his left hand was heavy. It required a definite effort of will for him to keep the course off shore.

At about six P.M. we came to San Carlos Bay, a curious landlocked curve with an inner shallow bay. There is good anchorage for small craft in the outer bay, with five to seven fathoms of water. The inner bay, or lagoon, has a sand beach on all sides. We intended to collect on the heavy boulders on the inner, or eastern, shore. There might be, we thought, a contrasting fauna to that of the tide flats of morning. This beach was piled high with rotting seaweed, left by some fairly recent storm perhaps. Or possibly this beach is at the end of some current-cycle, so that a high tide deposits great amounts of torn weed. There is such a beach at San Antonio del Mar on the western shore of Lower California, about sixty miles south of Ensenada. The debris from ships from hundreds of miles around is piled on this beach—mountains of sea-washed boxes and crates, logs and lumber, great whitened piles of it, mixed in with bottles and cans and pieces of clothing. It is the termination of some great sweeping in the Pacific.

Here at San Carlos there was little human debris; so very few boats pass up the Gulf this far and the people so prize planed wood and cans that such things would be picked up very quickly. In the decaying weed were myriads of flies and beach-hoppers working on this endless food supply. But in spite of their incredible numbers, we were able to catch only a few of the hoppers; they were too fast for us. Again we felt that here in the Gulf a little extra is added to the protection of animals. They are extra-fast, they are extra-armored, they seem to sting and pinch and bite worse than animals in other places. In the sand we found some clams rather like the Pismo clams of California, but shiny brown to black; also some ribbed mussel-like clams.* On the rocks we took two species of chitons and some new snails and crabs. There were blue, sharp-spined urchins and a number of flatworms. The flatworms are hard to catch, for they flow over the rocks like quicksilver. Also they are impossible to preserve well; many of them simply dissolve in the preservative, while others roll up tightly. *Heliaster*, the sun-star, was here, but he had continued to shrink and was quite small this far up in the Gulf. Under the sand there were a great number of heart-urchins.

That night, using the shaded lamp hung over the side, we had a great run of transparent fish, including a type we had not seen before. We took another squid, a larval mantis-shrimp, and the usual *heteronereis* and crustacea.

Carditamera affinis.

21

March 31

THE TIDE was very poor this morning, only two and a half to three feet below the uppermost line of barnacles. We started about ten o'clock and had a little collecting under water, but soon the wind got up and so ruffled the surface that we could not see what we were doing. To a certain extent this was a good thing. Not being able to get into the low littoral, where no doubt the spectacular spiny lobsters would have distracted us, we were able to make a more detailed survey of the upper region. One fact increasingly emerged: the sulphury-green and black cucumber* is the most ubiquitous shore animal of the Gulf of California, with *Heliaster*, the sunstar, a close second. These two are found nearly everywhere. In this region at San Carlos, Sally Lightfoot lives highest above the ordinary high tide, together with a few *Ligyda occidentalis*, a cockroach-like crustacean. Attached to the rocks and cliffsides, high up and fully exposed to this deadly sun, were barnacles and limpets, so placed that they must experience only occasional immersion, although they may be often dampened by spray. Under rocks and boulders, in the next association lower down, were the mussel-like ruffled clams and the brown chitons, many cucumbers, a few *Heliasters*, and only two species of brittle-stars—another common species, *Ophiothrix spiculata*, we did not find here although we had seen it everywhere else. In this zone verrucose anemones were growing under overhangs on the sides of rocks and in pits in the rocks. There were also a few starfish†; garbanzo clams were attached to the rock undersides by the thousands together with club urchins. Farther down in a new zone was a profusion of sponges of a number of species, including a beautiful blue sponge. There were octopi‡ here, and one species of chiton; there were many large purple urchins, although no specimens were taken, and heart-urchins in the sand and be-

---

Holothuria lubrica.
†*Astrometis sertulifera.*
‡*Octopus bimaculatus.*

tween the rocks. There were some sipunculids and a great many tunicates.

We found extremely large sponges, a yellow form (probably *Cliona*) superficially resembling the Monterey *Lissodendoryx noxiosa*, and a white one, *Steletta*, of the wicked spines. There were brilliant-orange nudibranchs, giant terebellid worms, some shell-less air-breathing (pulmonate) snails, a ribbon-worm, and a number of solitary corals. These were the common animals and the ones in which we were most interested, for while we took rarities when we came upon them in normal observation, our interest lay in the large groups and their associations—the word "association" implying a biological assemblage, all the animals in a given habitat.

It would seem that the commensal idea is a very elastic thing and can be extended to include more than host and guest; that certain kinds of animals are often found together for a number of reasons. One, because they do not eat one another; two, because these different species thrive best under identical conditions of wave-shock and bottom; three, because they take the same kinds of food, or different aspects of the same kinds of food; four, because in some cases the armor or weapons of some are protection to the others (for instance, the sharp spines of an urchin may protect a tide-pool johnny from a larger preying fish); five, because some actual commensal partition of activities may truly occur. Thus the commensal tie may be loose or very tight and some associations may partake of a real thigmotropism.

Indeed, as one watches the little animals, definite words describing them are likely to grow hazy and less definite, and as species merges into species, the whole idea of definite independent species begins to waver, and a scale-like concept of animal variations comes to take its place. The whole taxonomic method in biology is clumsy and unwieldy, shot through with the jokes of naturalists and the egos of men who wished to have animals named after them.

Originally the descriptive method of naming was not so bad, for every observer knew Latin and Greek well and was able to make out the descriptions. Such knowledge is fairly rare now and not even requisite. How much easier if the animals bore numbers to which the names were auxiliary! Then, one knowing that the phylum Arthropoda was represented by the roman figure *VI*, the class Crustacea by a capital *B*, order by arabic figure *13*, and genus and species by a combination of small letters, would with little training be able to place the animals in his mind much more quickly and surely than he can now with the descriptive method tugged bodily from a discarded antiquity.

As we ascended the Gulf it became more sparsely inhabited; there were fewer of the little heat-struck *rancherias*, fewer canoes of fishing Indians. Above Santa Rosalia very few trading boats travel. One would be really cut off up here. And yet here and there on the beaches we found evidences of large parties of fishermen. On one beach there were fifteen or twenty large sea-turtle shells and the charcoal of a bonfire where the meat had been cooked or smoked. In this same place we found also a small iron harpoon which had been lost, probably the most valued possession of the man who had lost it. These Indians do not seem to have firearms; probably the cost of them is beyond even crazy dreaming. We have heard that in some of the houses are the treasured weapons of other times, muskets, flintlocks, old long muzzle-loaders kept from generation to generation. And one man told us of finding a piece of Spanish armor, a breastplate, in an Indian house.

There is little change here in the Gulf. We think it would be very difficult to astonish these people. A tank or a horseman armed cap-a-pie would elicit the same response—a mild and dwindling interest. Food is hard to get, and a man lives inward, closely related to time; a cousin of the sun, at feud with storm and sickness. Our products, the mechanical toys which take up so much of our time, preoccupy and astonish us so, would be considered what they are, rather clever toys but not related to very real things. It would be interesting to try to explain to one of these Indians our tremendous projects, our great drives, the fantastic production of goods that can't be sold, the clutter of possessions which enslave whole populations with debt, the worry and neuroses that go into the rearing and educating of neurotic children who find no place for themselves in this complicated world; the defense of the country against a frantic nation of conquerors, and the necessity for becoming frantic to do it; the spoilage and wastage and death necessary for the retention of the crazy thing; the science which labors to acquire knowledge, and the movement of people and goods contrary to the knowledge obtained. How could one make an Indian understand the medicine which labors to save a syphilitic, and the gas and bomb to kill him when he is well, the armies which build health so that death will be more active and violent. It is quite possible that to an ignorant Indian these might not be evidences of a great civilization, but rather of inconceivable nonsense.

It is not implied that this fishing Indian lives a perfect or even a very good life. A toothache may be to him a terrible thing, and a stomachache may kill him. Often he is hungry, but he does not kill himself over things which do not closely concern him.

A number of times we were asked, Why do you do this thing, this picking up and pickling of little animals? To our own people we could have said any one of a number of meaningless things, which by sanction have been accepted as meaningful. We could have said, "We wish to fill in certain gaps in the knowledge of the Gulf fauna." That would have satisfied our people, for knowledge is a sacred thing, not to be questioned or even inspected. But the Indian might say, "What good is this knowledge? Since you make a duty of it, what is its purpose?" We could have told our people the usual thing about the advancement of science, and again we would not have been questioned further. But the Indian might ask, "Is it advancing, and toward what? Or is it merely becoming complicated? You save the lives of children for a world that does not love them. It is our practice," the Indian might say, "to build a house before we move into it. We would not want a child to escape pneumonia, only to be hurt all its life." The lies we tell about our duty and our purposes, the meaningless words of science and philosophy, are walls that topple before a bewildered little "why." Finally, we learned to know why we did these things. The animals were very beautiful. Here was life from which we borrowed life and excitement. In other words, we did these things because it was pleasant to do them.

We do not wish to intimate in any way that this hypothetical

Indian is a noble savage who lives in logic. His magics and his techniques and his teleologies are just as full of nonsense as ours. But when two people, coming from different social, racial, intellectual patterns, meet and wish to communicate, they must do so on a logical basis. Clavigero discusses what seems to our people a filthy practice of some of the Lower California Indians. They were always hungry, always partly starved. When they had meat, which was a rare thing, they tied pieces of string to each mouthful, then ate it, pulled it up and ate it again and again, often passing it from hand to hand. Clavigero found this a disgusting practice. It is rather like the Chinese being ridiculed for eating twenty-year-old eggs who said, "Your cheese is rotten milk. You like rotten milk—we like rotten eggs. We are both silly."

Costume on the *Western Flyer* had degenerated completely. Shirts were no longer worn, but the big straw hats were necessary. On board we went barefoot, clad only in hats and trunks. It was easy then to jump over the side to freshen up. Our clothes never got dry; the salt deposited in the fibers made them hygroscopic, always drawing the humidity. We washed the dishes in hot salt water, so that little crystals stuck to the plates. It seemed to us that the little salt adhering to the coffee pot made the coffee delicious. We ate fish nearly every day: bonito, dolphin, sierra, red snappers. We made thousands of big fat biscuits, hot and unhealthful. Twice a week Sparky created his magnificent spaghetti. Unbelievable amounts of coffee were consumed. One of our party made some lemon pies, but the quarreling grew bitter over them; the thievery, the suspicion of favoritism, the vulgar traits of selfishness and perfidy those pies brought out saddened all of us. And when one of us who, from being the most learned should have been the most self-controlled, took to hiding pie in his bed and munching it secretly when the lights were out, we decided there must be no more lemon pie. Character was crumbling, and the law of the fang was too close to us.

One thing had impressed us deeply on this little voyage: the great world dropped away very quickly. We lost the fear and fierceness and contagion of war and economic uncertainty. The matters of great importance we had left were not important. There must be an infective quality in these things. We had lost the virus, or it had been eaten by the anti-bodies of quiet. Our pace had slowed greatly; the hundred thousand small reactions of our daily world were reduced to very few. When the boat was moving we sat by the hour watching the pale, burned mountains slip by. A playful swordfish, jumping and spinning, absorbed us completely. There was time to observe the tremendous minutiae of the sea. When a school of fish went by, the gulls followed closely. Then the water was littered with feathers and the scum of oil. These fish were much too large for the gulls to kill and eat, but there is much more to a school of fish than the fish themselves. There is constant vomiting; there are the hurt and weak and old to cut out; the smaller prey on which the school feeds sometimes escape and die; a moving school is like a moving camp, and it leaves a camp-like debris behind it on which the gulls feed. The sloughing skins coat the surface of the water with oil.

At six P.M. we made anchorage at San Francisquito Bay. This cove-like bay is about one mile wide and points to the north. In the southern part of the bay there is a pretty little cove with a narrow entrance between two rocky points. A beach of white sand edges this cove, and on the edge of the beach there was a poor Indian house, and in front of it a blue canoe. No one came out of the house. Perhaps the inhabitants were away or sick or dead. We did not go near; indeed, we had a strong feeling of intruding, a feeling sharp enough even to prevent us from collecting on that little inner bay. The country hereabouts was stony and barren, and even the brush had thinned out. We anchored in four fathoms of water on the westerly side of the bay, then went ashore immediately and set up our tide stake at the water's edge, with a bandanna on it so we could see it from the boat. The wind was blowing and the water was painfully cold. The tide had dropped two feet below the highest line of barnacles. Three types of crabs* were common here. There were many barnacles and great limpets and two species of snails, *Tegula* and a small *Purpura*. There were many large smooth brown chitons, and a few bristle-chitons. Farther down under the rocks were great anas-

---

* *Pachygrapsus crassipes, Geograpsus lividus*, and, under the rocks, *Petrolisthes nigrunguiculatus*, a porcelain crab.

tomosing masses of a tube-worm with rusty red gills,* some tunicates, *Astrometis*, and the usual holothurians.

Tiny found the shell of a fine big lobster,† newly cleaned by isopods. The isopods and amphipods in their millions do a beautiful job. It is common to let them clean skeletons designed for study. A dead fish is placed in a jar having a cap pierced with holes just large enough to permit the entrance of the isopods. This is lowered to the bottom of a tide pool, and in a very short time the skeleton is clean of every particle of flesh, and yet is articulated and perfect.

The wind blew so and the water was so cold and ruffled that we did not stay ashore for very long. On board, we put down the baited bottom nets as usual to see what manner of creatures were crawling about there. When we pulled up one of the nets, it seemed to be very heavy. Hanging to the bottom of it on the outside was a large horned shark.‡ He was not caught, but had gripped the bait through the net with a bulldog hold and he would not let go. We lifted him unstruggling out of the water and up onto the deck, and still he would not let go. This was at about eight o'clock in the evening. Wishing to preserve him, we did not kill him, thinking he would die quickly. His eyes were barred, rather like goat's eyes. He did not struggle at all, but lay quietly on the deck, seeming to look at us with a baleful, hating eye. The horn, by the dorsal fin, was clean and white. At long intervals his gill-slits opened and closed but he did not move. He lay there all night, not moving, only opening his gill-slits at great intervals. The next morning he was still alive, but all over his body spots of blood had appeared. By this time Sparky and Tiny were horrified by him. Fish out of water should die, and he didn't die. His eyes were wide and for some reason had not dried out, and he seemed to regard us with hatred. And still at intervals his gill-slits opened and closed. His sluggish tenacity had begun to affect all of us by this time. He was a baleful personality on the boat, a sluggish, gray length of hatred, and the blood spots on him did not make him more pleasant. At noon we put him into the formaldehyde tank,

* *Salmacina.*
† Apparently the northern *Panulirus interruptus.*
‡ *Gyropleurodus* of the Heterodontidae.

and only then did he struggle for a moment before he died. He had been out of the water for sixteen or seventeen hours, had never fought or flopped a bit. The fast and delicate fishes like the tunas and mackerels waste their lives out in a complete and sudden flurry and die quickly. But about this shark there was a frightful quality of stolid, sluggish endurance. He had come aboard because he had grimly fastened on the bait and would not release it, and he lived because he would not release life. In some earlier time he might have been the basis for one of those horrible myths which abound in the spoken literature of the sea. He had a definite and terrible personality which bothered all of us, and, as with the sea-turtle, Tiny was shocked and sick that he did not die. This fish, and all the family of the Heterodontidae, ordinarily live in shallow, warm lagoons, and, although we do not know it, the thought occurred to us that sometimes, perhaps fairly often, these fish may be left stranded by a receding tide so that they may have developed the ability to live through until the flowing tide comes back. The very sluggishness in that case would be a conservation of vital energy, whereas the beautiful and fragile tuna make one frantic rush to escape, conserving nothing and dying immediately.

Within our own species we have great variation between these two reactions. One man may beat his life away in furious assault on the barrier, where another simply waits for the tide to pick him up. Such variation is also observable among the higher vertebrates, particularly among domestic animals. It would be strange if it were not also true of the lower vertebrates, among the individualistic ones anyway. A fish, like the tuna or the sardine, which lives in a school, would be less likely to vary than this lonely horned shark, for the school would impose a discipline of speed and uniformity, and those individuals which would not or could not meet the school's requirements would be killed or lost or left behind. The over-fast would be eliminated by the school as readily as the over-slow, until a standard somewhere between the fast and slow had been attained. Not intending a pun, we might note that our schools have to some extent the same tendency. A Harvard man, a Yale man, a Stanford man—that is, the ideal—is as easily recognized as a tuna, and he has, by a process of elimination, survived the tests against idiocy and brilliance. Even in physical matters the standard is maintained until it is impossible, from speech, clothing, haircuts, posture, or state of mind, to tell one of these units of his school from another. In this connection it would be interesting to know whether the general collectivization of human society might not have the same effect. Factory mass production, for example, requires that every man conform to the tempo of the whole. The slow must be speeded up or eliminated, the fast slowed down. In a thoroughly collectivized state, mediocre efficiency might be very great, but only through the complete elimination of the swift, the clever, and the intelligent, as well as the incompetent. Truly collective man might in fact abandon his versatility. Among school animals there is little defense technique except headlong flight. Such species depend for survival chiefly on tremendous reproduction. The great loss of eggs and young to predators is the safety of the school, for it depends for its existence on the law of probability that out of a great many which start some will finish.

It is interesting and probably not at all important to note that when a human state is attempting collectivization, one of the first steps is a frantic call by the leaders for an increased birth rate—replacement parts in a shoddy and mediocre machine.

Our interest had been from the first in the common animals and their associations, and we had not looked for rarities. But it was becoming apparent that we were taking a number of new and unknown species. Actually, more than fifty species undescribed at the time of capture will have been taken. These will later have been examined, classified, described, and named by specialists. Some of them may not be determined for years, for it is one of the little by-products of the war that scientific men are cut off from one another. A Danish specialist in one field is unable to correspond with his colleague in California. Thus some of these new animals may not be named for a long time. We have listed in the Appendix those already specified and indicated in so far as possible those which have not been worked on by specialists.

Dr. Rolph Bolin, ichthyologist at the Hopkins Marine Station, found in our collection what we thought to be a new

species of commensal fish which lives in the anus of a cucumber, flipping in and out, possibly feeding on the feces of the
host but more likely merely hiding in the anus from possible
enemies. This fish later turned out to be an already named
species, but, carrying on the ancient and disreputable tradition
of biologists, we had hoped to call it by the euphemistic name
Proctophilus winchellii.

There are some marine biologists whose chief interest is in
the rarity, the seldom seen and unnamed animal. These are
often wealthy amateurs, some of whom have been suspected
of wishing to tack their names on unsuspecting and unresponsive invertebrates. The passion for immortality at the expense of a little beast must be very great. Such collectors
should to a certain extent be regarded as in the same class
with those philatelists who achieve a great emotional stimulation from an unusual number of perforations or a misprinted
stamp. The rare animal may be of individual interest, but he
is unlikely to be of much consequence in any ecological picture. The common, known, multitudinous animals, the red
pelagic lobsters which litter the sea, the hermit crabs in their
billions, scavengers of the tide pools, would by their removal
affect the entire region in widening circles. The disappearance
of plankton, although the components are microscopic, would
probably in a short time eliminate every living thing in the sea
and change the whole of man's life, if it did not through a
seismic disturbance of balance eliminate all life on the globe.
For these little animals, in their incalculable numbers, are
probably the base food supply of the world. But the extinction
of one of the rare animals, so avidly sought and caught and
named, would probably go unnoticed in the cellular world.

Our own interest lay in relationships of animal to animal.
If one observes in this relational sense, it seems apparent that
species are only commas in a sentence, that each species is at
once the point and the base of a pyramid, that all life is relational to the point where an Einsteinian relativity seems to
emerge. And then not only the meaning but the feeling about
species grows misty. One merges into another, groups melt
into ecological groups until the time when what we know as
life meets and enters what we think of as non-life: barnacle
and rock, rock and earth, earth and tree, tree and rain and

air. And the units nestle into the whole and are inseparable from it. Then one can come back to the microscope and the tide pool and the aquarium. But the little animals are found to be changed, no longer set apart and alone. And it is a strange thing that most of the feeling we call religious, most of the mystical outcrying which is one of the most prized and used and desired reactions of our species, is really the understanding and the attempt to say that man is related to the whole thing, related inextricably to all reality, known and unknowable. This is a simple thing to say, but the profound feeling of it made a Jesus, a St. Augustine, a St. Francis, a Roger Bacon, a Charles Darwin, and an Einstein. Each of them in his own tempo and with his own voice discovered and reaffirmed with astonishment the knowledge that all things are one thing and that one thing is all things—plankton, a shimmering phosphorescence on the sea and the spinning planets and an expanding universe, all bound together by the elastic string of time. It is advisable to look from the tide pool to the stars and then back to the tide pool again.

22

April 1

WITHOUT the log we should have lost track of the days of the week, were it not for the fact that Sparky made spaghetti on Thursdays and Sundays. We think he did this by instinct, that he could come out of a profound amnesia, and if he felt an impulse to make spaghetti, it would be found to be either Thursday or Sunday. On Monday we sailed for Angeles Bay, which was to be our last station on the Peninsula. The tides were becoming tremendous, and while the tidal bore of the Colorado River mouth was still a long way off, Tony was already growing nervous about it. During the trip between San Francisquito and Angeles Bay, we worried again over the fact that we were not taking photographs. As has been said, no one was willing to keep his hands dry long enough to use the cameras. Besides, none of us knew much about cameras. But it was a constant source of bad conscience to us.

On this day it bothered us so much that we got out the big camera and began working out its operation. We figured everything except how to put the shutter curtain back to a larger aperture without making an exposure. Several ways were suggested and, as is often the case when more than one method is possible, an argument broke out which left shutters and cameras behind. This was a good one. Everyone except Sparky and Tiny, who had the wheel, gathered on the hatch around the camera, and the argument was too much for the steersmen. They sent down respectful word that either we should bring the camera up where they could hear the argument, or they would abandon their posts. We suggested that this would be mutiny. Then Sparky explained that on an Italian fishing boat in Monterey mutiny, far from being uncommon, was the predominant state of affairs, and that he and Tiny would rather mutiny than not. We took the camera up on the deckhouse and promptly forgot it in another argument.

Except for a completely worthless lot of 8-mm. movie film, this was the closest we came to taking pictures. But some day we shall succeed.

Angeles Bay is very large—twenty-five square miles, the *Coast Pilot* says. It is land-locked by fifteen islands, between several of which there is entrance depth. This is one of the few harbors in the whole Gulf about which the *Coast Pilot* is willing to go out on a limb. The anchorage in the western part of the bay, it says, is safe from all winds. We entered through a deep channel between Red Point and two small islets, pulled into eight fathoms of water near the shore, and dropped our anchor. The *Coast Pilot* had not mentioned any settlement, but here there were new buildings, screened and modern, and on a tiny airfield a plane sat. It was an odd feeling, for we had been a long time without seeing anything modern. Our feeling was more of resentment than of pleasure. We went ashore about three-thirty in the afternoon, and were immediately surrounded by Mexicans who seemed curious and excited about our being there. They were joined by three Americans who said they had flown in for the fishing, and they too seemed very much interested in what we wanted until they were convinced it was marine animals. Then they and the Mexicans left us severely alone. Perhaps we had been hearing too many rumors: it was said that many guns were being run over the border for the trouble that was generally expected during the election. The fishermen did not look like fisher-men, and Mexicans and Americans were *too* interested in us until they discovered what we were doing and too uninter-ested after they had found out. Perhaps we imagined it, but we had a strong feeling of secrecy about the place. Maybe there really were gold mines there and new buildings for re-cent development. A road went northward from there to San Felipe Bay, we were told. The country was completely parched and desolate, but half-way up a hill we could see a green spot where a spring emerged from a mountain. It takes no more than this to create a settlement in Lower California.

We went first to collect on a bouldery beach on the western side of the bay, and found it fairly rich in fauna. The highest rocks were peopled by anemones, cucumbers, sea-cockroaches and some small porcellanids. There were no Sally Lightfoots visible, in fact no large crabs at all, and only a very few small members of *Heliaster*. The dominant animal here was a soft marine pulmonate which occurred in millions on and under the rocks. We took several hundred of them. There were some chitons, both the smooth brown *Chiton virgulatus* and the fuzzy *Acanthochitona exquisitus*. We saw fine big clusters of the minute tube-worm, *Salmacina*, and there were a great many flatworms oozing along on the undersides of the rocks like drops of spilled brown sirup. Under the rocks we found two octopi, both *Octopus bimaculatus*. They are very clever and active in escaping, and when finally captured they grip the hand and arm with their little suckers, and, if left for any length of time, will cause small blood blisters or, rather, what in another field are called "monkey bites." Under the water and apparently below the ordinary tidal range were brilliant-yellow *Geodia* and many examples of another sponge of mag-nificent shape and size and color. This last (erect colonies of the cosmopolitan *Cliona celata*, more familiar as a boring sponge) was a reddish pink and stood high and vase-like, some of them several feet in diameter. Most of them were perfectly regular in shape. We took a number of them, dried some out of formaldehyde, and preserved others. The algal zonation on this slope was sharp and apparent—a *Sargassum* was submerged two or three feet at ebb. The rocks in the intertidal were perfectly smooth and bare but below this *Sargassum johnstonii*, in deeper water, there was a great zone of flat, frond-like alga, *Padina durvillaei*.* The wind rippled the surface badly but when an occasional lull came we could look down into this deeper water. It did not seem rich in life except for the algae, but then we were unable to turn over the rocks on the bottom.

While we collected, our fishermen rowed aimlessly about, and in our suspicious state of mind they seemed to be more anxious to appear to be fishing than actually to be fishing. We have little doubt that we were entirely wrong about this, but the place breathed suspicion, and no other place had been like that.

We went back on board and deposited our catch, then took the skiff to the sand flats on the northern side of the bay. It was a hard, compact mud sand with a long shallow beach, and it was heavy and difficult to dig into. We took there a number of *Chione* and *Tivela* clams and one poor half-dead amphioxus. Again the tide was not low enough to reach the real habitat of amphioxus, but if there was one stray in the high area, there must be many to be taken on an extremely low tide. We found a number of long turreted snails carrying commensal anemones on their shells. On this flat there were a number of imbedded small rocks, and these were rich with animals. There were rock-oysters on them and large highly ornamented limpets and many small snails. Tube-worms clustered on these rocks with pea crabs commensal in the tubes. One fair-sized octopus (not *bimaculatus*) had his home under one of these rocks. These small stones must have been havens in the shifting sands for many animals. The fine mud-like sand would make locomotion difficult except for specially equipped animals, and the others clustered to the rocks where there was footing and security.

The tide began to flow rapidly and the winds came up and we went back to the *Western Flyer*. When we were on board

*Determinations by Dr. E. Yale Dawson of the Department of Botany, University of California.

we saw a ship entering the harbor, a big green sailing schooner with her sails furled, coming in under power. She did not approach us, but came to anchorage about as far from us as she could. She was one of those incredible Mexican Gulf craft; it is impossible to say how they float at all and, once floating, how they navigate. The seams are sprung, the paint blistered away, ironwork rusted to lace, decks warped and sagging, and, it is said, so dirty and bebugged that if the cockroaches were not fed, or were in any way frustrated or insulted, they would mutiny and take the ship—and, as one Mexican sailor said, "probably sail her better than the master."

Once the anchor of this schooner was down there was no further sign of life on her and there was no sign of life from the buildings ashore either. The little plane sat in its runway and the houses seemed vacant. We had been asked how long we would remain and had said, until the next morning. Now we felt, curiously enough, that we were interfering with something, that some kind of activity would start only when we left. Again, we were probably all wrong, but it is strange that every one of us caught a sinister feeling from the place. Unless the wind was up, or the anchorage treacherous, we ordinarily kept no anchor watch, but this night the boys got up a number of times and were restless. As with the werewolf, we were probably believing our own imaginations. For a short time in the evening there were lights ashore and then they went out. The schooner did not even put up a riding light, but lay completely dark on the water.

23

April 2

WE STARTED EARLY and moved out through the channel to the Gulf. It was not long before we could make out Sail Rock far ahead, with Guardian Angel Island to the east of it. Sail Rock looks exactly like a tall Marconi sail in the distance. It is a high, slender pyramid, so whitened with guano that it catches the light and can be seen for a great distance.

Because of its extreme visibility it must have been a sailing point for many mariners. It is more than 160 feet high, rises to a sharp point, and there is deep water close in to it. With lots of time, we would have collected at its base, but we were aimed at Puerto Refugio, at the upper end of Guardian Angel Island. We did take some of our usual moving pictures of Sail Rock, and they were even a little worse than usual, for there was laundry drying on a string and the camera was set up behind it. When developed, the film showed only an occasional glimpse of Sail Rock, but a very lively set of scenes of a pair of Tiny's blue and white shorts snapping in the breeze. It is impossible to say how bad our moving pictures were—one film laboratory has been eager to have a copy of the film, for it embodies in a few thousand feet, so they say, every single thing one should not do with a camera. As an object lesson to beginners they think it would be valuable. If we took close-ups of animals, someone was in the light; the aperture was always too wide or too narrow; we made little jerky pan shots back and forth; we have one of the finest sequences of unadorned sky pictures in existence—but when there was something to take about which we didn't care, we got it perfectly. We dare say there is not in the world a more spirited and beautiful picture of a pair of blue and white shorts than that which we took passing Sail Rock.

The long, snake-like coast of Guardian Angel lay to the east of us; a desolate and fascinating coast. It is forty-two miles long, ten miles wide in some places, waterless and uninhabited. It is said to be crawling with rattlesnakes and iguanas, and a persistent rumor of gold comes from it. Few people have explored it or even gone more than a few steps from the shore, but its fine harbor, Puerto Refugio, indicates by its name that many ships have clung to it in storms and have found safety there. Clavigero calls the island both "Angel de la Guardia" and "Angel Custodio," and we like this latter name better.

The difficulties of exploration of the island might be very great, but there is a drawing power about its very forbidding aspect—a Golden Fleece, and the inevitable dragon, in this case rattlesnakes, to guard it. The mountains which are the backbone of the island rise to more than four thousand feet in some places, sullen and desolate at the tops but with heavy brush on the skirts. Approaching the northern tip we encountered a deep swell and a fresh breeze. The tides are very large here, fourteen feet during our stay, and that not an extreme tide at all. It is probable that a seventeen-foot tide would not be unusual here. Puerto Refugio is really two harbors connected by a narrow channel. It is a safe, deep anchorage, the only danger lying in the strength and speed of the tidal current, which puts a strain on the anchor tackle. It was so strong, indeed, that we were not able to get weighted nets to the bottom; they pulled out sideways in the water and sieved the current of weed and small animals, so that catch was fairly worthwhile anyway.

We took our time getting firm anchorage, and at about three-thirty P.M. rowed ashore toward a sand and rubble beach on the southeastern part of the bay. Here the beach was piled with debris: the huge vertebrae of whales scattered about and piles of broken weed and skeletons of fishes and birds. On top of some low bushes which edged the beach there were great nests three to four feet in diameter, pelican nests perhaps, for there were pieces of fish bone in them, but all the nests were deserted—whether they were old or it was out of season we do not know. We are so used to finding on the beaches evidence of man that it is strange and lonely and frightening to find no single thing that man has touched or used. Tiny and Sparky made a small excursion inland, not over several hundred yards from the shore, and they came back subdued and quiet. They had not seen any rattlesnakes, nor did they want to. The beach was alive with hoppers feeding on the refuse, but the coarse sand was not productive of other animal life. The tide was falling, and we walked around a rocky point to the westward and came into a bouldery flat where the collecting was very rich. The receding water had left many small tide pools. The smoothness of the rocks indicated a fairly strong surf; they were dangerously slippery, and Sally Lightfoots and *Pachygrapsus* both scuttled about. As we moved out toward the entrance of the harbor, the boulders became larger and smoother, and then there was a sudden change to unbroken reef, and the smooth rocks gave way to barnacle- and weed-covered stones. The tide was down about ten feet now, exposing the lower tide pools, rich and beautiful with sponges and corals and small pleasant algae. We tried to cover as much territory as possible, but again and again found ourselves fascinated by some small and perfect pool, like a set stage, peopled with broken-back shrimps and small masked crabs.

The point itself was jagged volcanic rock in which there were high mysterious caves. Entering one, we noticed a familiar smell, and a moment later recognized it. For the sound of our voices alarmed myriads of bats, and their millions of squeaks sounded like rushing water. We threw stones in to try to dislodge some, but they would not brave the daylight, and only squeaked more fiercely.

As evening approached, it grew quite cold. Our hands were torn from the long collecting day and we were glad when it was too dark to work any more. We had taken great numbers of animals. There was an echiuroid worm with a spoon-shaped proboscis, found loose under the rocks; many shrimps; an encrusting coral (*Porites* in a new guise); many chitons, some new; and several octopi. The most obvious animals were the same marine pulmonates we had found at Angeles Bay, and these must have been strong and tough, for they were in the high rocks, fairly dry and exposed to the killing sun. The rocky ledge was covered with barnacles. The change in animal sizes on different levels was interesting. In the high-up pools there were small animals, mussels, snails, hermits, limpets, barnacles, sponges; while in the lower pools, the same species were larger. Among the small rocks and coarse gravel we found a great many stinging worms and a type of ophiuran new to us—actually it turned out to be the familiar *Ophionereis* in its juvenile stage. These high tide pools can be regarded as nurseries for more submerged zones. There were urchins, both club- and sharp-spined, and, in the sand, a few heart-urchins. The caverns under the rocks, exposed by the receding tide, were beautiful with many species of sponge, some pure white, some blue, and some purple, encrusting the rock surface. These under-rock caverns were as beautiful as those near Point Lobos in Central California. It was a long job to lay out and list the animals taken; meanwhile the crab-nets meant for the bottom were straining the current. In them we caught a number of very short fat stinging worms (*Chloeia viridis*), a species we had not seen before, probably a deep-water form torn loose by the strength of the current. With a hand-net we took a pelagic nudibranch, *Chioraera leonina*, found also in Puget Sound. The water swirled past the boat at about four miles an hour and we kept the dip-nets out until late at night. This was a strange collecting place. The water was quite cold, and many of the members of both the northern and the southern fauna occurred here. In this harbor there were conditions of stress, current, waves, and cold which seemed to encourage animal life. And it is reasonable that this should be so, for active, churning water means not only a strong oxygen content, but the constant movement of food. And in addition, the very difficulties involved in such a position—necessity for secure footing, crowding, and competition—seem to encourage a ferocity and a tenacity in the animals which go past survival and into successful reproduction. Where there is little danger, there seems to be little stimulation. Perhaps the pattern of struggle is so deeply imprinted in the genes of all life conceived in this benevolently hostile planet that the removal of obstacles automatically atrophies a survival drive. With warm water and abundant food, the animals may retire into a sterile sluggish happiness. This has certainly seemed true in man. Force and cleverness and versatility have surely been the children of obstacles. Tacitus, in the *Histories*, places as one of the tactical methods advanced to be used against the German armies their exposure to a warm climate and a soft rich food supply. These, he said, will ruin troops quicker than anything else. If these things are true in a biologic sense, what is to become of the fed, warm, protected citizenry of the ideal future state?

The classic example of the effect of such protection on troops is that they invariably lost discipline and wasted their energies in weak quarrelsomeness. They were never happy, never contented, but always ready to indulge in bitter and bloody personal quarrels. Perhaps this has no emphasis. So far there has been only one state that we know of which protected its people *without* keeping them constantly alert and organized against a real or imaginary outside enemy. This was the pre-Pizarro Inca state, whose people were so weakened that a little band of fierce, hard-bitten men was able to overcome the whole nation. And of them the converse is also true. When the food supply was wasted and destroyed by the Spaniards, when the fine economy which had distributed clothing and grain was overturned, only then, in their hunger and cold and misery, did the Peruvian people become a dangerous striking force. We have little doubt that a victorious collectivist state would collapse only a little less quickly than a defeated one. In fact, a bitter defeat would probably keep a fierce conquest-ideal alive much longer than a victory, for men can fight an enemy much more successfully than themselves.

Islands have always been fascinating places. The old story-tellers, wishing to recount a prodigy, almost invariably fixed the scene on an island—Faëry and Avalon, Atlantis and Cipango, all golden islands just over the horizon where anything at all might happen. And in old days at least it was rather difficult to check up on them. Perhaps this quality of potential prodigy still lives in our attitude toward islands. We want very much to go back to Guardian Angel with time and supplies. We wish to go over the burned hills and snake-ridden valleys, exposed to heat and insects, venom and thirst, and we are willing to believe almost anything we hear about it. We believe that great gold nuggets are found there, that unearthly animals make their homes there, that the mountain sheep, which is said never to drink water, abounds there. And if we were told of a race of troglodytes in possession, we should think twice before disbelieving. It is one of the golden islands which will one day be toppled by a mining company or a prison camp.

Thus far, there had been no illness on board the *Western Flyer*. Tiny drooped a little at Puerto Refugio and confessed that he didn't feel very well, and we held a consultation on him in the galley, explaining to him that consultation was more pleasant to us, as well as to him, than autopsy. After a great many questions, some of which might have been considered personal but which Tiny used as a vehicle for outrageous boasting, we concocted a remedy which might have cured almost anything—which was apparently what he had. Tiny emerged on deck some hours later, shaken but smiling. He said that what he had been considering love had turned out to be simple flatulence. He said he wished all his romantic problems could be solved as easily.

It was now a long time since Sparky and Tiny had been able to carry out the good-will they felt toward Mexico, and they grew a little anxious about getting to Guaymas. There was no actual complaining, but they spoke tenderly of their intentions. Tex was inhibited in his good-will by his engagement to be married, which he wouldn't mention any more for fear we would diet him again. As for Tony, the master, he had no nerves, but the problems of finding new and unknown anchorages seemed to fascinate him. Tony would have made a great exploration captain. There would be few errors in judgment where he was concerned. The others of us were very busy all the time. We mention the health of the crew because we truly believe that the physical condition, and through it the mind, has reins on the actual collecting of animals. A man with a sore finger may not lift the rock under which an animal lives. We are likely to see more through our indigestion than through our eyes, and it seems to us that the ulcer-warped viewpoint is very often evident in animal descriptions. The man best fitted to observe animals, to understand them emotionally as well as intellectually, would be a hungry and libidinous man, for he and the animals would have the same preoccupations. Perhaps we fulfilled these requirements as well as most.

24

April 3

WE SAILED around the northern tip of Guardian Angel and down its eastern coast. The water was clear and blue, and a large swell flowed past us. About noon we moved through a great group of Zeppelin-shaped jellyfish, ctenophores or possibly siphonophores. They were six to ten inches long, and the sea was littered with them. We slowed down and tried to scoop them up, but the tension of their bodies was not sufficient to hold them together out of water. They broke up and slithered in pieces through the dip-nets. Soon after, a school of whales went by, one of them so close that the spray from his blow-hole came over our deck. There is nothing so evil-smelling as a whale anyway, and a whale's breath is frightfully sickening. It smells of complete decay. Perhaps the droplets were left on the boat, for it seemed to us that we could smell him for a long time after he had gone by. The great schools of tuna, so evident in the Lower Gulf, were not seen here, but a few seals lazed through the water, and on one or two occasions we nearly ran over one asleep on the surface. We felt deeply the loneliness of this sea; no ships, no boats, no canoes, no little ranches on the shore nor villages. Now we would have welcomed a fishing Indian to come aboard and eat canned fruit salad, but this is a deserted sea.

The queer shoulder of Tiburón showed to the southeast of us, and we ran down on it with the wind behind us and probably the tidal current too, for we made great speed. We went down the western coast of Tiburón and watched its high cliffs through the glasses. The cliffs are fairly sheer, and the mountains are higher than those on Guardian Angel Island. This is the island where the Seri Indians come during parts of the year. It is said of them that they are or have been cannibals, a story which has been firmly denied again and again. It is certain that they have killed many strangers, but whether or not they have eaten them does not seem to be documented. Cannibalism is a fascinating subject to most people, and in some way a sin. Possibly the deep feeling is that if people learn to eat one another the food supply would be so generous and so available that no one would be either safe or hungry. It is very curious the amount of hatred and fear that cannibalism inspires. These poor Seri Indians would not be so much feared for their murdering habits, but if in their hunger they should cut a steak from an American citizen a panic arises. Swift's quite reasonable suggestion concerning a possible use for Irish babies aroused a storm of emotionalism out of all proportion to its feasibility. There were not, it is thought, enough well-conditioned babies at that time to have provided anything like an adequate food supply. Swift without a doubt meant it only as an experiment. If it had been successful, there would have been time enough then to think of raising more babies. It has generally been found that starvation is the greatest single cause for cannibalism. In other words, people will not eat each other if they can get anything else. To some extent this reluctance must be caused by an unpleasant taste in human flesh, the result no doubt of our rather filthy eating habits. This need not be a future deterrent, for, if other barriers are removed, such as a natural distaste for eating relatives, or a man's gallant dislike for eating women, who in turn are inhibited by a romantic tendency—if all these difficulties should be solved it would be easy enough to improve the flavor of human flesh by special diets before slaughter and carefully prepared sauces and condiments afterwards. If this should occur, the Seri Indians, if indeed they do be cannibals, far from being loaded with our hatred, must be considered pioneers in a new field and honored as such.

Clavigero, in his *History of* [Lower] *California*,* has an account of these Seris.

The vessel, *San Javier* [he says], which had left Loreto in September 1709 with three thousand *scudi* to buy provisions in Yaqui, was carried 180 miles above the port of its destination by a furious storm and grounded on the sand. Some of the people were drowned; the rest saved themselves in the small boat; but after landing they were exposed to another not less serious danger because that coast was inhabited by the Seríes who were warlike gentiles and implacable enemies of the Spaniards. For this reason they hastened to bury the money and all the possessions which were on the boat; and after embarking again in the small boat they continued with a thousand dangers and hardships to Yaqui, from where they sent the news to Loreto. In a little while the Seríes came to the place where the Spaniards had buried those possessions, and they dug them up and carried them away. They even removed the rudder from the vessel and they destroyed it in order to get the nails.

As soon as Father Salvatierra learned of that misfortune, he left in the unseaworthy vessel, the *Rosario*, and went to the port of Guaymas. From there he sent this vessel to the place where the *San Javier* was grounded, and he himself went with fourteen Yaqui Indians in that direction over a very bad road which absolutely lacked potable water, and for this reason they suffered great thirst for two days. During the two months which he lived there, exposed to hunger and

*Lake and Gray translation, 1937, pp. 217–18.

hardships and to the great danger of all their lives (while the vessel was being repaired), he won the good-will of the Seris in such manner that he not only recovered all the cargo of the boat which they had stolen but induced them also to make peace with the Pimas, who were Christian neighbors of theirs and enemies whom they most hated. He baptized many of their children, he catechized the adults and inspired so much affection in them for Christianity that they immediately wanted a missionary to instruct them regularly and to baptize them and govern them in all respects.

So the dominating sweetness of the character of Father Salvatierra, aided by the grace of the Master, triumphed over the ferocity of those barbarians who were so feared, not only by the other Indians, but also by the Spaniards. He wept tenderly on seeing their unexpected docility and their good inclinations, thanking God for having had that much good come from the misfortune of the vessel.

The "dominating sweetness" of the character of Father Salvatierra did not, however, change them completely, for they have gone right on killing people until recently. In this account it is also interesting to notice Clavigero's statement that Father Salvatierra took the "unseaworthy" *Rosario*. In the long record of wrecks blowing off course, of marine disaster of every kind, it was wonderful how they were able to judge whether or not a ship was unseaworthy. A little reading of contemporary records of voyaging by these priestly and soldierly navigators indicates that they put more faith in prayer than in the compass. We think the present-day navigators of the Gulf have learned their seamanship in the same school. Some of the ships we saw at Guaymas and La Paz floated in violation of every law of physics. There must be in Heaven a small pilot-house where a worried and distraught St. Christopher spends a good deal of his time looking after the shipping of the Gulf of California with a handful of miracles.

Tiburón looked red to us, and the brush seemed stronger and greener than any we had seen in a long time. In some of the creases between the hills there were growths of small ground-hugging trees like our scrub-oaks. What they were, of course, we do not know. About five-thirty in the afternoon we rounded Red Bluff Point on the southwesterly corner of Tiburón and came to anchor in the lee of the long point, protected from northerly winds. The "corner" of the island is a chosen word, for Tiburón is a rough square lying plumb with the points of the compass. We searched the shore for Seris and saw none. In our usual condition of hunger, it would have been a toss-up whether Seris ate us or we ate Seris. The one who got in the first bite would have had the dinner, but we never did see a Seri.

The coast at this station was interesting; off Red Bluff Point low flat rocks shelved gradually seaward—fine collecting rocks, with many of the pot-holes which make such beautiful natural aquaria at low tide. Southward of this were long reef-like stone fingers extending outward, with shallow sand-bottom baylets between them, almost like boat slips. Next to this was a bouldery beach with stones imbedded in sand; and finally a coarse sand beach. Here again was nearly every kind of environment except mud-flat and lagoon. We began our collecting on the reef, and found the little pot-holes lovely with hydroids and coral and colored sponge and little bright algae. There were many broken-back shrimps in these pools, difficult little fellows to catch, for they are so transparent as to be almost invisible and they move with great speed by flipping their tails like lobsters. Only their stomachs and flickering gills are visible, and one can watch their insides work as though they were little glass models. We caught many of them by working our hands very slowly under them and raising them gradually to the surface.

On the reef, there were the usual *Heliasters*, anemones, and cucumbers, urchins, and a great number of giant snails,* of which we collected many hundreds. High up in the intertidal were many *Tegula*-like snails of the kind we found at Cape San Lucas, although here the water was clear and very cold whereas at Cape San Lucas it had been warm. There were very few Sally Lightfoots here; *Pachygrapsus*, the northern crabs, had taken their place. We took abundant solitary corals and laid in a large supply of plumularian hydroids, gathered carefully and preserved so that they might not be crushed or broken. These animals, in appearance at least, are so like plants that they indicate to the imagination a bridge between flora and fauna, just as some plants, like the tropical sensitive plants

* *Callopoma fluctuosum.*

and the insect-eating plants, indicate by their apparent nervous and muscular versatility an approach from the other side.

On the reef, we took a number of barnacles, many *Phataria* and *Linckia*, sponges, and tunicates. Moving from the reef to the stone fingers, we saw and captured a most attenuated spider crab,* all legs and little body. On the sand bottom between the fingers were many sting-rays lying quietly, and near the edge of one little harbor there were two in copulation, male (or female) lying on its back with its mate on top of it and the heads together. We wanted these two, and so after a moment in which we toughened the fibers of our romantic feelings, we put a light harpoon through both of them at once and brought them up, angry and disillusioned. We had hoped that they might remain fastened so that they might be preserved in coition, but their softer feelings were offended and they disengaged.

Meanwhile Tiny, moving in the little slip-like bays with the skiff, harpooned several more sting-rays. On the beach we took several sand-living cucumbers, and in the bottom of a mud pool searched long and unsuccessfully for a furry crab which had been seen scuttling into its burrow. This was a rich field for collecting, but the horizon markers were true to their position in the Gulf, and except for the profusion on Red Bluff Point reef, where the footing was excellent, there was nothing novel.

When it grew dark, we turned on the deck lights and saw numbers of a barracuda-like fish coming to eat the small fishes that gathered to the light. We put a fish-line on a small trident spear and began throwing it at them. About every tenth cast we struck one and brought him to the deck. And now a curious thing happened. From the shore came a swarm of very large bats. Their bodies were small but they had a twelve- to fifteen-inch wing-spread. They circled restlessly around the boat, although there were no insects about. Sparky was on the rail, spearing barracuda, and he is very much afraid of bats. Suddenly one swooped near him, and he struck at it with the harpoon. By one of those strange accidents, the barbs went into the bat and captured it, and now four or five more dived

---

* *Stenorhynchus debilis.*

straight at Sparky's head and he dropped the harpoon and ran for the galley. The dead bat fell over the side into the water, where we later picked it up.

Then an even stranger thing happened. As though at a signal, every bat of the hundreds suddenly turned and flew away to shore and not another one was seen. We have not yet a report on the one taken, so we do not know what kind of bats they were. There are reports of fish-eating bats, and these may have been that kind. We warned Sparky seriously to keep very quiet about the incident. "Sparky," we said, "we know that your reputation for truthfulness in Monterey is as good as most. In other words, it is not above reproach. If we were you, when you get back to Monterey, we would never mention to anyone that we had harpooned a bat. We would make up stories and adventures, but there is no reason for straining an already shaky reputation." Sparky promised he would never tell, but back in Monterey he couldn't resist and, just as we supposed, a roar of laughter went up. In Monterey they said, "You know what that Sparky said? He swears he harpooned a bat."

And as punishment to Sparky, when we were questioned we said, "Bat? What bat?" Sparky is a little touchy about the whole subject, and he dislikes bats very intensely now.

Meanwhile we had twelve of the barracuda-like fish. We preserved some of them but did not try to eat any. The sierras and tuna were too delicious to justify making experiments with strong fish.

The mountains of Tiburón were very black against the stars and the sea was calm. On the deck, Tiny made a little noise washing a shirt, for we were not far from Guaymas and Tiny was growing anxious. We discussed bats, and the horror they create in people and the myths about them—in his *Caribbean Treasure*, page 56, Ivan Sanderson makes some very interesting remarks about vampire bats as carriers of rabies, and their whole tie-in with the vampire tradition, so intimately related to werewolfism in the popular mind. A man with rabies, one might infer, could well be the werewolf which occurs all over the world, and vampire and werewolf very often go together. It is a fascinating speculation, and surely the unreasoning and almost instinctive fear of bats might indicate another of those memory-like patterns, some horrible recollection of the evil bats can do.

We find after reading many scientific and semi-scientific accounts of exploration that we have two strong prejudices: the first of these arises where there is a woman aboard—the wife of one of the members of the party. She is never called by her name or referred to as an equal. In the account she emerges as "the shipmate," the "skipper," the "pal." She is nearly always a stringy blonde with leathery skin who is included in all photographs to give them "interest." Our second prejudice concerns a hysteria of love which manifests itself in an outcry against parting and is usually written in Spanish. This outburst comes at the end of the book. It goes, "And so——." Always, "and so," for some reason. "And so we said good-by to Tiburón, vowing to come back again. *Adiós, Tiburón, amigo,* friend." For some reason this stringy shipmate and this rush of emotion are slightly obscene to us. And so we said good-by to Tiburón and trucked on down toward Guaymas.

25

April 4

THE TROLLING JIGS picked up two fine sierras on the way. Our squid jigs had gone to pieces from much use, and had to be repaired with white chicken feathers. We were under way all day, and toward evening began to see the sport-fishing boats of Guaymas with their cargoes of sportsmen outfitted with equipment to startle the fish into submission. And the sportsmen were mentally on tiptoe to out-think the fish— which they sometimes do. We thought it might be fun some time to engage in this intellectual approach toward fishing, instead of our barbarous method of throwing a line with a chicken-feather jig overboard. These fishermen in their swivel fishing chairs looked comfortable and clean and pink. We had been washing our clothes in salt water, and we felt sticky and salt-crusted; and, being less comfortable and clean than the sportsmen, we built a whole defense of contempt. With no effort at all on their part we had a good deal of dislike for them. It is probable that Sparky and Tiny had a true contempt, uncolored by envy, for they are descended from many generations of fishermen who went out for fish, not splendor. But even they might have liked sitting in a swivel chair holding a rod in one hand and a frosty glass in the other, blaming a poor day on the Democrats, and offering up prayers for good fishing to Calvin Coolidge.

We could not run for Guaymas that night, for the pilot fees rise after hours and we were getting a little low on money. Instead, about six P.M. we rounded Punta Doble and put into Puerto San Carlos. This is another of those perfect little harbors with narrow rocky entrances. The entrance is less than eight hundred yards wide, and steep rocks guard it. Once inside, there is anchorage from five to seven fathoms. The head of the bay is bordered by a sand beach, changing to boulders near the entrance. There was still time for collecting.

We went to the bouldery beach and took some snails new to us and two echiuroids. But nothing on or under the rocks was different from the Tiburón animals. The water was warm here and it was soupy with shrimps, of which we took a number in a dip-net. We made a quick survey of the area, for darkness was coming. As soon as it was dark we began to hear strange sounds in the water around the *Western Flyer*—a periodic hissing and many loud splashes. We went to the deckhouse and turned on the searchlight. The bay was swarming with small fish, apparently come to eat the shrimps. Now and then a school of six- to ten-inch fish would drive at the little fish with such speed and in such numbers that they made the sharp hissing we had heard, while farther off some kind of great fish leaped and splashed heavily. Without a word, Sparky and Tiny got out a long net, climbed into the skiff, and tried to draw their net around a school of fish. We shouted at them, asking what they would do with the fish if they caught them, but they were deaf to us. The numbers of fish had set off a passion in them—they were fishermen and the sons of fishermen—let businessmen dispose of the fish; their job was to catch them. They worked frantically, but they could not encircle a school, and soon came back exhausted.

Meanwhile, the water seemed almost solid with tiny fish,

one and one-half to two inches long. Sparky went to the galley and put the biggest frying pan on the fire and poured olive oil into it. When the pan was very hot he began catching the tiny fish with the dip-nets, a hundred or so in each net. We passed the nets through the galley window and Sparky dumped them into the frying pan. In a short time these tiny fish were crisp and brown. We drained, salted, and ate them without any cleaning at all and they were delicious. Probably no fresher fish were ever eaten, except perhaps by the Japanese, who are said to eat them alive, and by college boys, who are photographed doing it. Each fish was a curled, brown, crisp little bite, delicate and good. We ate hundreds of them. Afterwards we went back to the usual night practice of netting the pelagic animals which came to the light. We took shrimps and larval shrimps, numbers of small swimming crabs, and more of the transparent fish. All night the hissing rush and splash of hunters and hunted went on. We had never been in water so heavily populated. The light, piercing the surface, showed the water almost solid with fish—swarming, hungry, frantic fish, incredible in their voraciousness. The schools swam, marshaled and patrolled. They turned as a unit and dived as a unit. In their millions they followed a pattern minute as to direction and depth and speed. There must be some fallacy in our thinking of these fish as individuals. Their functions in the school are in some as yet unknown way as controlled as though the school were one unit. We cannot conceive of this intricacy until we are able to think of the school as an animal itself, reacting with all its cells to stimuli which perhaps might not influence one fish at all. And this larger animal, the school, seems to have a nature and drive and ends of its own. It is more than and different from the sum of its units. If we can think in this way, it will not seem so unbelievable that every fish heads in the same direction, that the water interval between fish and fish is identical with all the units, and that it seems to be directed by a school intelligence. If it is a unit animal itself, why should it not so react? Perhaps this is the wildest of speculations, but we suspect that when the school is studied as an animal rather than as a sum of unit fish, it will be found that certain units are assigned special functions to perform; that weaker or slower

units may even take their places as placating food for the predators for the sake of the security of the school as an animal.
In the little Bay of San Carlos, where there were many schools
of a number of species, there was even a feeling (and "feeling"
is used advisedly) of a larger unit which was the interrelation
of species with their interdependence for food, even though
that food be each other. A smoothly working larger animal
surviving within itself—larval shrimp to little fish to larger fish
to giant fish—one operating mechanism. And perhaps *this*
unit of survival may key into the larger animal which is the
life of all the sea, and this into the larger of the world. There
would seem to be only one commandment for living things:
Survive! And the forms and species and units and groups are
armed for survival, fanged for survival, timid for it, fierce for
it, clever for it, poisonous for it, intelligent for it. This commandment decrees the death and destruction of myriads of
individuals for the survival of the whole. Life has one final
end, to be alive; and all the tricks and mechanisms, all the
successes and all the failures, are aimed at that end.

26

April 5

WE SAILED in the morning on the short trip to Guaymas.
It was the first stop in a town that had anything like
communication since we had left San Diego. The world and
the war had become remote to us; all the immediacies of our
usual lives had slowed up. Far from welcoming a return, we
rather resented going back to newspapers and telegrams and
business. We had been drifting in some kind of dual world—
a parallel realistic world; and the preoccupations of the world
we came from, which are considered realistic, were to us filled
with mental mirage. Modern economies; war drives; party af-
filiations and lines; hatreds, political, and social and racial, cannot survive in dignity the perspective of distance. We could
understand, because we could feel, how the Indians of the
Gulf, hearing about the great ant-doings of the north, might

shake their heads sadly and say, "But it is crazy. It would be nice to have new Ford cars and running water, but not at the cost of insanity." And in us the factor of time had changed: the low tides were our clock and the throbbing engine our second hand.

Now, approaching Guaymas, we were approaching an end. We planned only two or three collecting stations beyond, and then the time of charter-end would be crowding us, and we would have to run for it to be back when the paper said we would. The charter at least fixed our place in time. And already our crew was trying to think of ways to come back to the Gulf. This trip had been like a dreaming sleep, a rest from immediacies. And in our contacts with Mexican people we had been faced with a change in expediencies. Perhaps—even surely—these people are expedient, but on some other plane than our ordinary one. What they did for us was without hope or plan of profit. We suppose there must have been some kind of profit involved, but not the kind we are used to, not of material things changing hands. And yet some trade took place at every contact—something was exchanged, some unnamable of great value. Perhaps these people are expedient in the unnamables. Maybe they bargain in feelings, in pleasures, even in simple contacts. When the Indians came to the *Western Flyer* and sat timelessly on the rail, perhaps they were taking something. We gave them presents, but it is sure they had not come for presents. When they helped us, it was with no idea of material payment. There were material prices for material things, but one couldn't buy kindness with money, as one can in our country. It was so in every contact, and they were so used to the spiritual transaction that they had difficulty translating material things into money. If we wanted to buy a harpoon, there was difficulty immediately. What was the price? An Indian had paid three pesos for the harpoon several years ago. Obviously, since that had been paid, that was the price. But he had not yet learned to give time a money value. If he had to go three days in a canoe to get another harpoon, he could not add his time to the price, because he had never thought of time as a medium of exchange. At first we tried to explain the feeling we all had that time is a salable article, but we had to give it up. Time, these Indians said, went on.

If one could stop time, or take it away, or hoard it, then one might sell it. One might as well sell air or heat or cold or health or beauty. And we thought of the great businesses in our country—the sale of clean air, of heat and cold, the scrabbling bargains in health offered over the radio, the boxed and bottled beauty, all for a price. This was not bad or good, it was only different. Time and beauty, they thought, could not be captured and sold, and we knew they not only *could* be, but that time could be warped and beauty made ugly. And again it was not good or bad. Our people would pay more for pills in a yellow box than in a white box—even the refraction of light had its price. They would buy books because they should rather than because they wanted to. They bought immunity from fear in salves to go under their arms. They bought romantic adventure in bars of tomato-colored soaps. They bought education by the foot and hefted the volumes to see that they were not short-weighted. They purchased pain, and then analgesics to put down the pain. They bought courage and rest and had neither. And they are vastly amused at the Indian who, with his silver, bought Heaven and ransomed his father from Hell. These Indians were far too ignorant to understand the absurdities merchandising can really achieve when it has an enlightened people to work on.

One can go from race to race. It is coming back that has its violation. As we feel greatness, we feel that these people are very great. It seems to us that the repose of an Indian woman sitting in the gutter is beyond our achievement. But even these people wish for our involvement in temporal and material things. Once we thought that the bridge between cultures might be through education, public health, good housing, and through political vehicles—democracy, Nazism, communism—but now it seems much simpler than that. The invasion comes with good roads and high-tension wires. Where those two go, the change takes place very quickly. Any of the political forms can come in once the radio is hooked up, once the concrete highway irons out the mountains and destroys the "localness" of a community. Once the Gulf people are available to contact, they too will come to consider clean feet more important than clean minds. These are the factors of civilization and their paths, good roads, high-voltage wires, and possibly canned foods. A local 110-volt power unit and a winding dirt road may leave a people for a long time untouched, but high-voltage operating day and night, the network of wires, will draw the people into the civilizing web, whether it be in Asiatic Russia, in rural England, or in Mexico. That *Zeitgeist* operates everywhere, and there is no escape from it.

Again, this is not to be considered good or bad. To us, a little weary of the complication and senselessness of a familiar picture, the Indian seems a rested, simple man. If we should permit ourselves to remain in ignorance of his complications, then we might long for his condition, thinking it superior to ours. The Indian on the other hand, subject to constant hunger and cold, mourning a grandfather and set of uncles in Purgatory, pained by the aching teeth and sore eyes of malnutrition, may well envy us our luxury. It is easy to remember how, when we were in the terrible complication of childhood, we longed for easy and uncomplicated adulthood. Then we would have only to reach into our pockets for money, then all problems would be ironed out. The ranch-owner had said, "There is no poverty in your country and no misery. Everyone has a Ford."

We arrived early at Guaymas, passed the usual tests of customs, got our mail at the consulate, and then did the various things of the port. Some of those things are amusing, but they are out of drawing for this account. Guaymas was already in the pathway of the good highway; it was no longer "local." At La Paz and Loreto the Gulf and the town were one, inextricably bound together, but here at Guaymas the railroad and the hotel had broken open that relationship. There were gimcracks for tourists everywhere. This is no criticism of the change, but Guaymas seems to us to be outside the boundaries of the Gulf. We had good treatment there, met charming people, did good and bad things, and left with reluctance.

27

April 8

W E SAILED out on Monday, a little tattered and a little tired. Captain Corona, pilot and shrimp-boat owner, who had been kind and hospitable to us, piloted us out and stopped one of his incoming boats for us to inspect. It was a poor small boat, and had not much of a catch of shrimps. Everyone in this neighborhood had complained of the Japanese shrimpers who were destroying the shrimp fisheries. We determined to pay them a visit on the next day. The moment we dropped the pilot, just outside of Guaymas, the Gulf was local again and part of the design it had put in our heads. The mirage was over the land and the sea was very blue. We sailed only a short distance and dropped our anchor in a little cove opposite the Pajaro Island light. That night we caught a number of fish that looked and felt like catfish. Tex skinned them and prepared them, and we did not eat them. A little gloom hung over all of us; Sparky and Tiny had fallen in love with Guaymas and planned to go back there and live forever. But Tex and Tony were gloomy and a little homesick.

We were awakened well before daylight by the voices of men paddling out for the day's fishing, and it was with some relief that we pulled up our anchor and started out to continue the work we had come to do. The day was thick with haze, the sun came through it hot and unpleasant, and the water was oily and at the same time choppy. The sticky humidity was on us.

In about an hour we came to the Japanese fishing fleet. There were six ships doing the actual dredging while a large mother ship of at least 10,000 tons stood farther offshore at anchor. The dredge boats themselves were large, 150 to 175 feet, probably about 600 tons. There were twelve boats in the combined fleet including the mother ship, and they were doing a very systematic job, not only of taking every shrimp from the bottom, but every other living thing as well. They cruised slowly along in echelon with overlapping dredges, literally scraping the bottom clean. Any animal which escaped must have been very fast indeed, for not even the sharks got away.

Why the Mexican government should have permitted the complete destruction of a valuable food supply is one of those mysteries which have their ramifications possibly back in pockets it is not well to look into.

We wished to go aboard one of the dredge boats. Tony put the *Western Flyer* ahead of one of them, and we dropped the skiff over the side and got into it. It was not a friendly crew that looked at us over the side of the iron dredge boat. We clung to the side, almost swamping the skiff, and passed our letter from the Ministry of Marine aboard. Then we hung on and waited. We could see the Mexican official on the bridge reading our letter. And then suddenly the atmosphere changed to one of extreme friendliness. We were helped aboard and our skiff was tied alongside.

The cutting deck was forward, and the great dredge loads were dumped on this deck. Along one side there was a long cutting table where the shrimps were beheaded and dropped into a chute, whether to be immediately iced or canned, we do not know. But probably they were canned on the mother ship. The dredge was out when we came aboard, but soon the cable drums began to turn, bringing in the heavy purse-dredge. The big scraper closed like a sack as it came up, and finally it deposited many tons of animals on the deck—tons of shrimps, but also tons of fish of many varieties: sierras; pompano of several species; of the sharks, smooth-hounds and hammer-heads; eagle rays and butterfly rays; small tuna; cat-fish; *puerco*—tons of them. And there were bottom-samples with anemones and grass-like gorgonians. The sea bottom must have been scraped completely clean. The moment the net dropped open and spilled this mass of living things on the deck, the crew of Japanese went to work. Fish were thrown overboard immediately, and only the shrimps kept. The sea was littered with dead fish, and the gulls swarmed about eating them. Nearly all the fish were in a dying condition, and only a few recovered. The waste of this good food supply was appalling, and it was strange that the Japanese, who are usually so saving, should have done it. The shrimps were shoveled into baskets and delivered to the cutting table. Meanwhile the dredge had gone back to work.

With the captain's permission, we picked out several representatives of every fish and animal we saw. A stay of several days on the boat would have been the basis of a great and complete collection of every animal living at this depth. Even going over two dredgeloads gave us many species. The crew, part Mexican and part Japanese, felt so much better about us by now that they brought out their treasures and gave them to us: bright-red sea-horses and brilliant sea-fans and giant shrimps. They presented them to us, the rarities, the curios which had caught their attention.

At intervals a high, chanting cry arose from the side of the ship and was taken up and chanted back from the bridge. From the upper deck a slung cat-walk extended, and on it the leadsman stood, swinging his leadline, bringing it up and swinging it out again. And every time he read the markers he chanted the depth in Japanese in a high falsetto, and his cry was repeated by the helmsman.

We went up on the bridge, and as we passed this leadsman he said, "Hello." We stopped and talked to him a few moments before we realized that that was the only English word he knew. The Japanese captain was formal, but very courteous. He spoke neither Spanish nor English; his business must all have been done through an interpreter. The Mexican fish and game official stationed aboard was a pleasant man, but he said that he had no great information about the animals he was overseeing. The large shrimps were *Penaeus stylirostris*, and one small specimen was *P. californiensis*.

The shrimps inspected all had the ovaries distended and apparently, as with the Canadian *Pandalus*, this shrimp had the male-female succession. That is, all the animals are born male, but all become females on passing a certain age. The fish and game man seemed very eager to know more about his field, and we promised to send him Schmitt's fine volume on *Marine Decapod Crustacea of California* and whatever other publications on shrimps we could find.

We liked the people on this boat very much. They were good men, but they were caught in a large destructive machine, good men doing a bad thing. With their many and large boats, with their industry and efficiency, but most of all with their intense energy, these Japanese will obviously soon clean out the shrimps of the region. And it is not true that a species thus attacked comes back. The disturbed balance often gives a new species ascendancy and destroys forever the old relationship.

In addition to the shrimps, these boats kill and waste many hundred of tons of fish every day, a great deal of which is sorely needed for food. Perhaps the Ministry of Marine had not realized at that time that one of the good and strong food resources of Mexico was being depleted. If it has not already been done, catch limits should be imposed, and it should not be permitted that the region be so intensely combed. Among other things, the careful study of this area should be undertaken so that its potential could be understood and the catch maintained in balance with the supply. Then there might be shrimps available indefinitely. If this is not done, a very short time will see the end of the shrimp industry in Mexico.

We in the United States have done so much to destroy our own resources, our timber, our land, our fishes, that we should be taken as a horrible example and our methods avoided by any government and people enlightened enough to envision a continuing economy. With our own resources we have been prodigal, and our country will not soon lose the scars of our grasping stupidity. But here, with the shrimp industry, we see a conflict of nations, of ideologies, and of organisms. The units of the organisms are good people. Perhaps we might find a parallel in a moving-picture company such as Metro-Goldwyn-Mayer. The units are superb—great craftsmen, fine directors, the best actors in the profession— and yet due to some overlying expediency, some impure or decaying quality, the product of these good units is sometimes vicious, sometimes stupid, sometimes inept, and never as good as the men who make it. The Mexican official and the Japanese captain were both good men, but by their association in a project directed honestly or dishonestly by forces behind and above them, they were committing a true crime against nature and against the immediate welfare of Mexico and the eventual welfare of the whole human species.

The crew helped us back into our skiff, handed our buckets of specimens down to us, and cast us off. And Tony, who had been cruising slowly about, picked us up in the *Western Flyer*. We had taken perhaps a dozen pompano as specimens when hundreds were available. Sparky was speechless with rage that we had brought none back to eat, but we had forgotten that. We set our course southward toward Estero de la Luna—a great inland sea, the borders of which were dotted lines on our maps. Here we expected to find a rich estuary fauna. In the scoop between Cape Arco and Point Lobos there is a fairly shallow sea which makes a deep ground-swell. It was Tiny up forward who noticed the great numbers of manta rays and suggested that we hunt them. They were monsters, sometimes twelve feet between the "wing" tips. We had no proper equipment, but finally we rigged one of the arrow-tipped harpoons on a light line. This harpoon was a five-inch bronze arrow slotted on an iron shaft. After the stroke, the arrow turns sideways in the flesh and the shaft comes out and floats on its wooden handle. The line is fastened to the arrow itself.

The huge rays cruised slowly about, the upturned tips of the wings out of water. Sparky went to the crow's-nest, where he could look down into the water and direct the steersman. A hundred feet from one of the great fish we cut the engine and coasted down on it. It lay still on the water. Tiny poised prettily on the bow. When we were right on it, he drove the harpoon into it. The monster did not flurry, it simply faded for the bottom. The line whistled out to its limit, twanged like a violin string, and parted. A curious excitement ran through the boat. Tex came down and brought out a one-and-one-half-inch hemp line. He ringed this into a new harpoon-head, and again Tiny took up his position, so excited that he had his foot in a bight of the line. Luckily, we noticed this and warned him. We coasted up to another ray—Tiny missed the stroke. Another, and he missed again. The third time, his arrow drove home, the line sang out again, two hundred feet of it. Then it came to the end where it was looped over a bitt, vibrated for a moment, and parted. The breaking strain of this rope was enormous. But we were doing it all wrong and we knew it. A ton and a half of speeding fish is not to be brought up short. We should have thrown a keg overboard with the line and let the fish fight the keg's buoyancy until exhausted. But we were not equipped. Tiny was almost hysterical by this time. Tex brought a three-inch line with an extremely high breaking strain. We had no more arrow harpoons. Tex made his hawser fast to a huge trident spear. When he finished, the assembly was so heavy that one man could hardly lift it. This time, Tex took the harpoon. He did not waste his time with careless strokes; he waited until the bow was right over one of the largest rays, then drove his spear down with all his strength. The heavy hawser ran almost smoking over the rail. Then it came to the bitt and struck with a kind of groaning cry, quivered, and went limp. When we pulled the big harpoon aboard, there was a chunk of flesh on it. Tiny was heart-broken. The wind came up now and so ruffled the water that we could not see the coasting monsters any more. We tried to soothe Tiny.

"What could we do with one if we caught it?" we asked.

Tiny said, "I'd like to pull it up with the boom and hang it right over the hatch."

"But what could you do with it?"

"I'd hang it there," he said, "and I'd have my picture taken with it. They won't believe in Monterey I speared one unless I can prove it."

He mourned for a long time our lack of foresight in failing to bring manta ray equipment. Late into the night Tex worked, making with file and emery stone a new arrow harpoon, but one of great size. This he planned to use with his three-inch hawser. He said the rope would hold fifteen to twenty tons, and this arrow would not pull out. But he never had a chance to prove it; we did not see the rays in numbers any more.

We came to anchorage that night south of Lobos light and about five miles from the entrance to Estero de la Luna. In this shallow water Tony did not like to go closer for fear of stranding. It was a strange and frightening night, and no one knew why. The water was glassy again and the deck soaked with humidity. We had a curious feeling that a stranger was aboard, some presence not seen but felt, a dark-cloaked person who was with us. We were all nervous and irritable and frightened, but we could not find what frightened us. Tex worked on the Sea-Cow and got it to running perfectly, for we wanted to use it on the long run ashore in the morning. We had checked the tides in Guaymas; it was necessary to leave before daylight to get into the estuary for the low tide.

In the night, one of us had a nightmare and shouted for help and the rest of us were sleepless. In the darkness of the early morning, only two of us got up. We dressed quietly and got our breakfast. The light on Lobos Point was flashing to the north of us. The decks were soaked with dew. Climbing down to the skiff, one of us fell and wrenched his leg. True to form, the Sea-Cow would not start. We set off rowing toward the barely visible shore, fixing our course by Lobos Light. A little feathery white shape drifted over the water and it was joined by another and another, and very soon a dense white fog covered us. The *Western Flyer* was lost and the shore blotted out. With the last flashing of the Lobos light we tried to judge the direction of the swell to steer by, and then the light was gone and we were cut off in this ominous glassy water. The air turned steel-gray with the dawn, and the fog was so thick that we could not see fifteen feet from the boat. We rowed on, remembering to quarter on the direction of the swells. And then we heard a little vicious hissing as of millions of snakes, and we both said, "It's the *cordonazo*." This is a quick fierce storm which has destroyed more ships than any other. The wind blows so that it clips the water. We were afraid for a moment, very much afraid, for in the fog, the *cordonazo* would drive our little skiff out into the Gulf and swamp it. We could see nothing and the hissing grew louder and had almost reached us.

It seems to be this way in a time of danger. A little chill of terror runs up the spine and a kind of nausea comes into the throat. And then that disappears into a kind of dull "what the hell" feeling. Perhaps this is the working of some mind-to-gland-to-body process. Perhaps some shock therapy takes control. But our fear was past now, and we braced ourselves to steady the boat against the impact of the expected wind. And at that moment the bow of the skiff grounded gently, for it was not wind at all that hissed, but little waves washing strongly over an exposed sand-bar. We climbed out, hauled the boat up, and sat for a moment on the beach. We had been badly frightened, there is no doubt of it. Even the sleepy dullness which follows the adrenal drunkenness was there. And while we sat there, the fog lifted, and in the morning light we could see the *Western Flyer* at anchor offshore, and we had

landed only about a quarter of a mile from where we had intended. The sun broke clear now, and true to form when there
was neither danger nor much work the Sea-Cow started easily
and we rounded the sand-hill entrance of the big estuary. Now
that the sun was up, we could see why there were dotted lines
on the maps to indicate the borders of the *estero*. It was endless—there were no borders. The mirage shook the horizon
and draped it with haze, distorted shapes, twisted mountains,
and made even the bushes seem to hang in the air. Until every
foot of such a shore is covered and measured, the shape and
extent of these estuaries will not be known.

Inside the entrance of the estuary a big canoe was anchored
and four Indians were coming ashore from the night's fishing.
They were sullen and unsmiling, and they grunted when we
spoke to them. In their boat they had great thick mullet-like
fish, so large that it took two men to carry each fish. They
must have weighed sixty to one hundred pounds each. These
Indians carried the fish through an opening in the brush to a
camp of which we could see only the smoke rising, and they
were definitely unfriendly. It was the first experience of this
kind we had had in the Gulf. It wasn't that they didn't like
us—they didn't seem to like each other.

The tide was going down in the estuary, making a boiling
current in the entrance. Biologically, the area seemed fairly
sterile. There were numbers of small animals, several species
of large snails and a number of small ones. There were burrowing anemones* with transparent, almost colorless tentacles
spread out on the sand bottom. And there were the flower-
like *Cerianthus* in sand-tubes everywhere. On the bottom
were millions of minute sand dollars of a new type, brilliant
light green and having holes and fairly elongate spines. Farther
inside the estuary we took a number of small heart-urchins
and a very few larger ones. On the sand bottoms there were
large burrows, but dig as we would, we could never find the
owners. They were either very quick or very deep, but even
under water their burrows were always open and piles of
debris lay about the entrances. Some large crustacean, we
thought, possibly of the fiddler crab clan.

Harenactis.

The commonest animal of all was the enteropneust, an "acorn-tongued" worm presumably about three feet long that we had found at San Lucas Cove and at Angeles Bay. There were hundreds of their sand-castings lying about. We were not convinced that with all our digging we had got the whole animal even once (and the specialist subsequently confirmed our opinion with regret!).

Deep in the estuary we took several large beautifully striped *Tivela*-like clams and a great number of flat pearly clams. There were hundreds of large hermit crabs in various large gastropod shells. We found a single long-armed sand-burrowing brittle-star which turned out to be *Ophiophragmus marginatus*, and our listing of it is the only report on record since Lütken, in Denmark, erected the species from Nicaraguan material nearly a hundred years ago. In the uneasy footing of the sand, every stick and large shell and rock was encrusted with barnacles; even one giant swimming crab carried a load of barnacles on his back.

The wind had been rising a little as we collected, rippling the water. We cruised about in the shallows trying to see the bottom. There were great numbers of sand sharks darting about, but the bottom was clean and sterile and not at all as well populated as we would have supposed. The mirage grew more and more crazy. Perhaps these sullen Indians were bewildered in such an uncertain world where nothing half a mile away could maintain its shape or size, where the world floated and trembled and flowed in dream forms. And perhaps the reverse is true. Maybe these Indians dream of a hard sharp dependable world as an opposite of their daily vision.

We had not taken riches in this place. When the tide turned we started back for the *Western Flyer*. Perhaps the Sea-Cow too had been frightened that morning, for it ran steadily. But the tide was so strong that we had to help it with the oars or it would not have been able to hold its own against the current. It took two hours of oars and motor to get back to the *Western Flyer*.

We felt that this had not been a good nor a friendly place. Some quality of evil hung over it and infected us. We were not at all sorry to leave it. Everyone on board was quiet and uneasy until we pulled up the anchor and started south for

Agiabampo, which was, we thought, to be our last collecting station.

It was curious about this Estero de la Luna. It had been a bad place—bad feelings, bad dreams, and little accidents. The look and feel of it were bad. It would be interesting to know whether others have found it so. We have thought how places are able to evoke moods, how color and line in a picture may capture and warp us to a pattern the painter intended. If to color and line in accidental juxtaposition there should be added odor and temperature and all these in some jangling relationship, then we might catch from this accident the un-ease we felt in the *estero*. There is a stretch of coast country below Monterey which affects all sensitive people profoundly, and if they try to describe their feeling they almost invariably do so in musical terms, in the language of symphonic music. And perhaps here the mind and the nerves are true indices of the reality neither segregated nor understood on an intellec-tual level. Boodin remarks the essential nobility of philosophy and how it has fallen into disrepute. "Somehow," he says, "the laws of thought must be the laws of things if we are going to attempt a science of reality. Thought and things are part of one evolving matrix, and cannot ultimately conflict."*

And in a unified-field hypothesis, or in life, which is a uni-fied field of reality, everything is an index of everything else. And the truth of mind and the way mind is must be an index of things, the way things are, however much one may stand against the other as an index of the second or irregular order, rather than as a harmonic or first-order index. These two types of indices may be compared to the two types of waves, for indices are symbols as primitive as waves. The first wave-type is the regular or cosine wave, such as tide or undulations of light or sound or other energy, especially where the output is steady and unmixed. These waves may be progressive—in-creasing or diminishing—or they can seem to be stationary, although deeply some change or progression may be found in all oscillation. All terms of a series must be influenced by the torsion of the first term and by the torsion of the end, or change, or stoppage of the series. Such waves as these may be

---

* *A Realistic Universe*, p. xviii. 1931. Macmillan, New York.

predictable as the tide is. The second type, the irregular for the while, such as graphs of rainfall in a given region, falls into means which are the functions of the length of time during which observations have been made. These are unpredictable individually; that is, one cannot say that it will rain or not rain tomorrow, but in ten years one can predict a certain amount of rainfall and the season of it. And to this secondary type mind might be close by hinge and "key-in" indices.

We had had many discussions at the galley table and there had been many honest attempts to understand each other's thinking. There are several kinds of reception possible. There is the mind which lies in wait with traps for flaws, so set that it may miss, through not grasping it, a soundness. There is a second which is not reception at all, but blind flight because of laziness, or because some pattern is disturbed by the processes of the discussion. The best reception of all is that which is easy and relaxed, which says in effect, "Let me absorb this thing. Let me try to understand it without private barriers. When I have understood what you are saying, only then will I subject it to my own scrutiny and my own criticism." This is the finest of all critical approaches and the rarest.

The smallest and meanest of all is that which, being frightened or outraged by thinking outside or beyond its pattern, revenges itself senselessly; leaps on a misspelled word or a mispronunciation, drags tricky definition in by the scruff of the neck, and, ranging like a small unpleasant dog, rags and tears the structure to shreds. We have known a critic to base a vicious criticism on a misplaced letter in a word, when actually he was venting rage on an idea he hated. These are the suspicious ones, the self-protective ones, living lives of difficult defense, insuring themselves against folly with folly—stubbornly self-protective at too high a cost.

Ideas are not dangerous unless they find seeding place in some earth more profound than the mind. Leaders and would-be leaders are so afraid that the *idea* "communism" or the *idea* "Fascism" may lead to revolt, when actually they are ineffective without the black earth of discontent to grow in. The strike-raddled businessman may lean toward strikeless Fascism, forgetting that it also eliminates him. The rebel may yearn violently for the freedom from capitalist domination expected in a workers' state, and ignore the fact that such a state is free from rebels. In each case the idea is dangerous only when planted in unease and disquietude. But being so planted, growing in such earth, it ceases to be idea and becomes emotion and then religion. Then, as in most things teleologically approached, the wrong end of the animal is attacked. Lucretius, striking at the teleology of his time, was not so far from us. "I shall untangle by what power the steersman nature guides the sun's courses, and the meanderings of the moon, lest we, percase, should fancy that of own free will they circle their perennial courses round, timing their motions for increase of crops and living creatures, or lest we should think they roll along by any plan of gods. For even *those* men who have learned full well that godheads lead a long life free of care, if yet meanwhile they wonder by what plans things can go on (and chiefly yon high things observed o'erhead on the ethereal coasts), again are hurried back unto the fears of old religion and adopt again harsh masters, deemed almighty,—wretched men, unwitting what can be and what cannot, and by what law to each its scope prescribed, its boundary stone that clings so deep in Time.''*

In the afternoon we sailed down the coast carefully, for the sand-bars were many and some of them uncharted. It was a shallow sea again, and the blueness of deep water had changed to the gray-green of sand and shallows. Again we saw manta rays, but not on the surface this day, and the hunt had gone out of us. Tex did not even get out his new harpoon. Perhaps the crew were homesick now. They had seen Guaymas, they were bloated with stories, and they wanted to get back to Monterey to tell them. We would stop at no more towns, see no more people. The inland water of Agiabampo was our last stop, and then quickly home. The shore was low and hot and humid, covered with brush and mangroves. The sea was sterile, or populated with sharks and rays. No algae adhered to the sand bottom, and we were sad in this place after the booming life of the other side. We sailed all afternoon and it

*Lucretius, *On the Nature of Things*, W. E. Leonard translation, Everyman's Library, 1921, p. 190.

was evening when we came to anchorage five miles offshore in the safety of deeper water. We would edge in with the lead-line in the morning.

28

April 11

AT TEN O'CLOCK we moved toward the northern side of the entrance of Agiabampo estuary. The sand-bars were already beginning to show with the lowering tide. Tiny used the leadline on the bow while Sparky was again on the crow's-nest where he could watch for the shallow water. Tony would not approach closer than a mile from the entrance, leaving as always a margin of safety.

When we anchored, five of us got into the little skiff, filling it completely. Any rough water would have swamped us. Sparky and Tiny rowed us in, competing violently with each other, which gave a curious twisting course to the boat.

Agiabampo is a great lagoon with a narrow seaward entrance. There is a little town ten miles in on the northern shore which we did not even try to reach. The entrance is intricate and obstructed with many shoals and sand-bars. It would be difficult without local knowledge to bring in a boat of any draft. We moved in around the northern shore; there were dense thickets of mangrove with little river-like entrances winding away into them. We saw great expanses of sand flat and the first extensive growth of eel-grass we had found.* But the eel-grass, which ordinarily shelters a great variety of animal life, was here not very rich at all. We saw the depressions where *botete*, the poison fish, lay. And there were great numbers of sting-rays, which made us walk very carefully, even in rubber boots, for a slash with the tail-thorn of a sting-ray can easily pierce a boot.

The sand banks near the entrance were deeply cut by cur-

*The true *Zostera marina* according to Dr. Dawson, botanist at the University of California, who remarks that it had not been reported previously so far south.

rents. High in the intertidal many grapsoid crabs* lived in slanting burrows about eighteen inches deep. There were a great many of the huge stalk-eyed conchs and the inevitable big hermit crabs living in the cast-off conch shells. Farther in, there were numbers of *Chione* and the blue-clawed swimming crabs. They seemed even cleverer and fiercer here than at other places. Some of the eel-grass was sexually mature, and we took it for identification. On this grass there were clusters of snail eggs, but we saw none of the snails that had laid them. We found one scale-worm,† a magnificent specimen in a *Cerianthus*-like tube. There were great numbers of tube-worms in the sand. The wind was light or absent while we collected, and we could see the bottom everywhere. On the exposed sand-bars birds were feeding in multitudes, possibly on the tube-worms. Along the shore, oyster-catchers hunted the burrowing crabs, diving at them as they sat at the entrances of their houses. It was not a difficult collecting station; the pattern, except for the eel-grass, was by now familiar to us although undoubtedly there were many things we did not see. Perhaps our eyes were tired with too much looking.

As soon as the tide began its strong ebb we got into the skiff and started back to the *Western Flyer*. Collecting in narrow-mouthed estuaries, we are always wrong with the currents, for we come in against an ebbing tide and we go out against the flow. It was heavy work to defeat this current. The Sea-Cow gave us a hand and we rowed strenuously to get outside.

That night we intended to run across the Gulf and start for home. It was good to be running at night again, easier to sleep with the engine beating. Tiny at the wheel inveighed against the waste of fish by the Japanese. To him it was a waste complete, a loss of something. We discussed the widening and narrowing picture. To Tiny the fisherman, having as his function not only the catching of fish but the presumption that they would be eaten by humans, the Japanese were wasteful. And in that picture he was very correct. But all the fish actually were eaten; if any small parts were missed by the birds they were taken by the detritus-eaters, the worms and cucum-

*Ocypode occidentalis.
†Polyodontes oculea.

bers. And what they missed was reduced by the bacteria. What was the fisherman's loss was a gain to another group. We tried to say that in the macrocosm nothing is wasted, the equation always balances. The elements which the fish elaborated into an individuated physical organism, a microcosm, go back again into the undifferentiated macrocosm which is the great reservoir. There is not, nor can there be, any actual waste, but simply varying forms of energy. To each group, of course, there must be waste—the dead fish to man, the broken pieces to gulls, the bones to some and the scales to others—but to the whole, there is no waste. The great organism, Life, takes it all and uses it all. The large picture is always clear and the smaller can be clear—the picture of eater and eaten. And the large equilibrium of the life of a given animal is postulated on the presence of abundant larvae of just such forms as itself for food. Nothing is wasted; "no star is lost."

And in a sense there is no over-production, since every living thing has its niche, *a posteriori*, and God, in a real, non-mystical sense, sees every sparrow fall and every cell utilized. What is called "over-production" even among us in our manufacture of articles is only over-production in terms of a status quo, but in the history of the organism, it may well be a factor or a function in some great pattern of change or repetition. Perhaps some cells, even intellectual ones, must be sickened before others can be well. And perhaps with us these production climaxes are the therapeutic fevers which cause a rush of curative blood to the sickened part. Our history is as much a product of torsion and stress as it is of unilinear drive. It is amusing that at any given point of time we haven't the slightest idea of what is happening to us. The present wars and ideological changes of nervousness and fighting seem to have direction, but in a hundred years it is more than possible it will be seen that the direction was quite different from the one we supposed. The limitation of the seeing point in time, as well as in space, is a warping lens.

Among men, it seems, historically at any rate, that processes of co-ordination and disintegration follow each other with great regularity, and the index of the co-ordination is the measure of the disintegration which follows. There is no mob like a group of well-drilled soldiers when they have thrown off their discipline. And there is no lostness like that which comes to a man when a perfect and certain pattern has dissolved about him. There is no hater like one who has greatly loved.

We think these historical waves may be plotted and the harmonic curves of human group conduct observed. Perhaps out of such observation a knowledge of the function of war and destruction might emerge. Little enough is known about the function of individual pain and suffering, although from its profound organization it is suspected of being necessary as a survival mechanism. And nothing whatever is known of the group pains of the species, although it is not unreasonable to suppose that they too are somehow functions of the surviving species. It is too bad that against even such investigation we build up a hysterical and sentimental barrier. Why do we so dread to think of our species as a species? Can it be that we are afraid of what we may find? That human self-love would suffer too much and that the image of God might prove to be a mask? This could be only partly true, for if we could cease to wear the image of a kindly, bearded, interstellar dictator, we might find ourselves true images of his kingdom, our eyes the nebulae, and universes in our cells.

The safety-valve of all speculation is: *It might be so.* And as long as that *might* remains, a variable deeply understood, then speculation does not easily become dogma, but remains the fluid creative thing it might be. Thus, a valid painter, letting color and line, observed, sift into his eyes, up the nerve trunks, and mix well with his experience before it flows down his hand to the canvas, has made his painting say, "It might be so." Perhaps his critic, being not so honest and not so wise, will say, "It is not so. The picture is damned." If this critic could say, "It is not so with me, but that might be because my mind and experience are not identical with those of the painter," that critic would be the better critic for it, just as that painter is a better painter for knowing he himself is in the pigment.

We tried always to understand that the reality we observed was partly us; the speculation, our product. And yet if somehow, "The laws of thought must be the laws of things," one can find an index of reality even in insanity.

• • •

We sailed a compass course in the night and before daylight a deep fog settled on us. Tony stopped the engine and let us drift, and the dawn came with the thick fog still about us. Tiny and Sparky had the watch, and as the dawn broke, they heard surf and reported it. We came out of our bunks and went up on the deckhouse just as the fog lifted. There was an island half a mile away. Then Tony said, "Did you keep the course I gave you?" Tiny insisted that they had, and Tony said, "If that is so, you have discovered an island, and a big one, because the chart shows no island here." He went on delicately, "I want to congratulate you. We'll call it 'Colletto and Enea Island.'" Tony continued silkily, "But you know Goddamn well you didn't keep the course. You know you forgot, and are a good many miles off course." Sparky and Tiny did not argue. They never claimed the island, nor mentioned it again. It developed that it was Espíritu Santo Island, and would have been a prize if they had discovered it, but some Spaniards had done that several hundred years before.

San Gabriel Bay was near us, its coral sand dazzlingly white, and a good reef projecting and a mangrove swamp along part of the coast. We went ashore for this last collecting station. The sand was so white and the water so clear that we took off our clothes and plunged about. The animals here had been affected by the white sand. The crabs were pale and nearly white, and all the animals, even the starfish, were strangely colored. There were stretches of this blinding sand alternating with bouldery reef and mangrove. In the center of the little bay, a fine big patch of green coral almost emerged from the water. It was green and brown coral in great heads, and there were *Phataria* and many club-spined urchins on the heads. There were multitudes of the clam *Chione* just under the surface of the sand, very hard to find until we discovered that every clam had a tiny veil of pale-green algae growing on the front of each valve and sticking up above the sand. Then we took a great number of them.

Near the beds of clams lived heart-urchins with vicious spines.* These too were buried in the sand, and to dig for the

_____
*Lovenia cordiformis.

clams was to be stabbed by the heart urchins, and to be stung badly. There were many hachas here with their clustered colonies of associated fauna. We found solitary and clustered zoanthidean anemones, possibly the same we had been seeing in many variations. We found light-colored *Callinectes* crabs and one of the long snake-like sea-cucumbers* such as the ones we had taken at Puerto Escondido. On the rocky reef there were anemones, limpets, and many barnacles. The most common animal on the reef was a membranous tube-worm† with tentacles like a serpulid's. These tentacles were purple and brown, but when approached they were withdrawn and the animal became sand-colored. The mangrove region here was rich. The roots of the trees, impacted with rocks, maintained a fine group of crabs and cucumbers. Two large, hairy grapsoid crabs‡ lived highest in the littoral. They were very fast and active and difficult to catch, and when caught, battled fiercely and ended up by autotomizing.

There was also a *Panopeus*-like crab, *Xanthodius hebes*, but dopey and slow. We found great numbers of porcelain crabs and snapping shrimps. There were barnacles on the reef and on the roots of the mangroves; two new ophiurans and a large sea-hare, besides a miscellany of snails and clams. It was a rich haul, this last day. The sun was hot and the sand pleasant and we were comfortable except for mosquito bites. We played in the water a long time when we were tired of collecting.

When once the engine started now, it would not stop until we reached San Diego. We were reluctant to go back. This balance in time is one of the very few occasions when we have the right of "yes" and "no," and even now the cards were stacked against "yes."

At last we picked up the collecting buckets and the little crowbars and all the tubes, and we rowed slowly back to the *Western Flyer*. Even then, we had difficulty in starting. Someone was overboard swimming in the beautiful water all the time. Tony and Tex, who had been eager to get home, were reluctant now that it was upon them. We had all felt the pattern of the Gulf, and we and the Gulf had established another

* *Euapta godeffroyi.*
† *Megalomma mushaensis.*
‡ *Geograpsus* and *Goniopsis.*

pattern which was a new thing composed of it and us. At last, and with sorrow, Tex started the engine and the anchor came up for the last time.

All afternoon we stowed and lashed equipment, set the corks in hundreds of glass tubes and wrapped them in paper toweling, screwed tight the caps of jars, tied down the skiffs, and finally dropped the hatch cover in place. We covered the bookcase with triple tarpaulin, and one last time overcame the impulse to throw the Sea-Cow overboard. Then we were under way, sailing southward toward the Cape. The swordfish jumped in the afternoon light, flashing like heliographs in the distance. We took back our old watches that night, and the engine drummed happily and drove us through a calm sea. In the morning the tip of the Peninsula was on our right. Behind us the Gulf was sunny and calm, but out in the Pacific a heavy threatening line of clouds hung.

Then a crazy literary thing happened. As we came opposite the Point there was one great clap of thunder, and immediately we hit the great swells of the Pacific and the wind freshened against us. The water took on a gray tone.

29

April 13

A T THREE A.M. Pacific time we passed the light on the false cape and made our new course northward, and the sky was gray and threatening and the wind increased. The Gulf was blotted out for us—the Gulf that was thought and work and sunshine and play. This new world of the Pacific took hold of us and we thought again of an unseen person on the deckhouse, some kind of symbol person—to a sailor, a ghost, a premonition, a feeling in human form.

We could not yet relate the microcosm of the Gulf with the macrocosm of the sea. As we went northward the gray waves rolled up and the *Western Flyer* stubbed her nose into them and the white spray flew over us. The day passed and a new night came and the sea grew more stern. Now we plunged like a nervous horse, and no step could be taken without a steadying hand. The galley was in confusion, for a can of olive oil had leaped from its stand and flooded the floor. On the stove, the coffee pot slipped back and forth between its bars.

Over the surface of the heaving sea the birds flew landward, zigzagging to cover themselves in the wave troughs from the wind. The man at the wheel was the lucky one, for he had a grip against the pitching. He was closest to the boat and to the rising storm. He was the receiver, but also he was the giver and his hand was on the course.

What was the shape and size and color and tone of this little expedition? We slipped into a new frame and grew to be a part of it, related in some subtle way to the reefs and beaches, related to the little animals, to the stirring waters and the warm brackish lagoons. This trip had dimension and tone. It was a thing whose boundaries seeped through itself and beyond into some time and space that was more than all the Gulf and more than all our lives. Our fingers turned over the stones and we saw life that was like our life.

On the deckhouse we held the rails for support, and the blunt nose of the boat fought into the waves and the gray-green water struck us in the face. Some creative thing had happened, a real tempest in our small teapot minds. But boiling water still produces steam, whether in a watch-glass or in a turbine. It is the same stuff—weak and dissipating or explosive, depending on its use. The shape of the trip was an integrated nucleus from which weak strings of thought stretched into every reachable reality, and a reality which reached into us through our perceptive nerve trunks. The laws of thought seemed really one with the laws of things. There was some quality of music here, perhaps not to be communicated, but sounding clear and huge in our minds. The boat plunged and shook herself, and rivers of swirling water ran down the scuppers. Below in the hold, packed in jars, were thousands of little dead animals, but we did not think of them as trophies, as things cut off from the tide pools of the Gulf, but rather as drawings, incomplete and imperfect, of how it had been there. The real picture of how it had been there and how we had been there was in our minds, bright with sun and wet with sea water and blue or burned, and the whole crusted over with exploring thought. Here was no service to science, no naming of unknown animals, but rather—we simply liked it. We liked it very much. The brown Indians and the gardens of the sea, and the beer and the work, they were all one thing and we were that one thing too.

The *Western Flyer* hunched into the great waves toward Cedros Island, the wind blew off the tops of the whitecaps, and the big guy wire, from bow to mast, took up its vibration like the low pipe on a tremendous organ. It sang its deep note into the wind.

Glossary
of Terms as Used in This Work

ABORAL. The upper surface of a starfish, brittle-star, or sea-urchin, as opposed to the under or oral surface whereon the mouth is situated.

ALGAE. Simple plants, often unicellular; the higher forms include the seaweeds.

AMBULACRAL GROOVE. A furrow bisecting the underside of the rays of starfish through which the tube feet are protruded.

AMPHIPOD. Literally, "paired-legs." Minute shrimp-like crustaceans, laterally compressed; the beach hoppers, sand fleas, skeleton shrimps, etc.

ANASTOMOSING. Dictionary definition: "Union or intercommunication of any system or network of lines, branches, streams, or the like."

ASSOCIATION. An assemblage of animals having ecologically similar requirements.

ATOKOUS. The sexually immature stage of certain polychaet worms.

AUTOTOMY. Reflex, or seemingly voluntary, separation of a part or a limb from the body, followed by regeneration.

BUNODID ANEMONE. One of a family of sea-anemones characterized by a bumpy or warty body wall.

CALCAREOUS. Containing deposits of calcium carbonate; calcification.

CERATA. Dorsal projections which take the place of gills.

COMMENSAL. An organism living in, with, or on another, generally partaking of the same food.

COSINE WAVE. A wave graphically represented by a curving line, the peaks and troughs of which are equal and complementary.

CTENOPHORE. A type of jellyfish characterized by the possession of meridional rows of vibrating plates which propel and orient the animal.

DACTYL. Term applied to the last joint of a crustacean leg.

DEHISCENCE. A bursting discharge, usually of eggs or sperm.

DROWNED CORAL FLAT. A flat containing coral, some heads of which have been suffocated by sand.

ECHIUROID. A worm-like animal related to the sipunculids, in which the body is variably sac-like, usually with thin skin, and having often a spoon-shaped proboscis.

ECOLOGY. The study of the mutual relations between an organism and its physical and sociological environment.

ELYTRA. Shield-like scales of certain worms.

ENDEMIC. Dictionary example: "An *endemic disease* is one which is constantly present to a greater or less degree in any place, as distinguished from an *epidemic disease*, which prevails widely at some time, or periodically. . . ."

EPITOKOUS. Sexually mature stage in polychaet worms, characterized by changes of the posterior end which enable normally crawling worms to be free-swimming.

ETIOLOGY. Dictionary definition: "1. The science, doctrine, or demonstration of causes, especially the investigation of the causes of any disease. 2. The assignment of a cause or reason; as, the *etiology* of a historical custom."

FLORIATE. Flower-like.

GASTROPOD. Literally, "stomach-foot." Belonging to a group of animals comprising the snails, slugs, sea-hares, etc.

GYMNOBLAST. Belonging to a group

(of hydroids) in which the polyps lack the skeletal cups of other hydroids into which the soft parts can be withdrawn.

HOLOTHURIAN. Sea-cucumber. One of a group of echinoderms, or spiny-skinned animals, some varieties of which, under the commercial name *bêche-de-mer* or *trepang*, are used by the Chinese for food.

HYDROID. A small, plant-like, usually colonial animal.

INTERTIDAL. See *Littoral*.

INTROVERT. A closed tubular pocket capable of being unrolled and extended inside out.

ISOPOD. Literally, "same legs." Usually small crustaceans in which all the legs are similar, comprising the pill-bugs, sow-bugs, and many marine forms.

ISOTHERM. A line joining or marking equal temperatures.

LITTORAL. Region of the shore bounded by its highest normal submergence at high tide and most extreme emergence at low tide. Intertidal.

MUTATION. In the life history of a species, the sudden appearance of a new trait that breeds true and becomes eventually one of the characters of the species or of the new species thus formed.

MYSIDS. Usually minute crustacea, called "opossum shrimps" because of their possession of marsupial plates within which the young develop.

NUDIBRANCH. Literally, "naked gill." One of a group of shell-less gastropods, often brilliantly colored and of delicately beautiful form.

OPHIURAN. Brittle-star or serpent-star. Members of one of the five classes of echinoderms or spiny-skinned animals.

PAPILLA. Small elevation; in holothurians, modified tube feet not used for locomotion.

PELAGIC. Free-floating at or near the surface of the sea.

PLANKTON. Generally microscopic plant and animal life floating or weakly swimming in the upper layer of a body of water.

POLYCHAETS. Usually elongate worms characterized by the possession of abundant chaetae or bristles.

POLYCLADS. Flatworms in which the intestinal tract has extensive ramifications.

POLYP. An invertebrate having a hollow cylindrical body, closed and attached at one end and opening at the other by a central mouth surrounded by tentacles. May be an individual (as an anemone) or a member of a colony (as a coral polyp).

PORCELLANIDS. Crabs of the family Porcellanidae, often called porcelain crabs because of the carapace texture of typical examples.

QUATERNARY, OR RECENT. The latest of the epochs into which geologists divide the history of the earth. Late Quaternary includes the present time.

RESPIRATORY TREE. The respiratory organ of holothurians; so named because it resembles a tree inside out. Fresh water is taken in at what corresponds to the trunk and penetrates to the delicate branches, which provide great absorption area in proportion to the volume.

SCALAR. Mathematical term. An abstract quantity having magnitude but not direction, such as volume, mass, weight, time, electrical charge, and always indicated by a real number.

SERPULID. A polychaet worm which builds a calcareous tube, usually coiled.

SESSILE. Attached, therefore not moving.

SIPHONOPHORE. A type of jellyfish. The Portuguese man-o'-war and other spectacular forms belong to this group.

SIPUNCULIDS. Worm-like animals characterized (among other things) by the possession of an introvert, and of rough, cuticle-like skin. Capable of great expansion; contracted, some of them merit the name peanut worm.

SYNDROME. A group of signs and symptoms occurring together and characterizing a disease.

SYNONYMY. The various names used to designate a given species or group.

TAXONOMY. A sub-science of biology concerned with the classification of animals according to natural relationships and with the rules governing the system of nomenclature.

TECTIBRANCHS. A group of sometimes shell-less gastropods to which belong the sea-hares and bubble-shells.

TELEOLOGY. The assumption of predetermined design, purpose, or ends in Nature by which an explanation of phenomena is postulated.

TENSOR. A mathematical term for the stretching factor which is necessary to change one vector, or force, into another vector having a different amount of force and direction. (Thus, if one imagines a given force *A* traveling south at 40 miles an hour, and another force *B* traveling southeast at 60 miles an hour, mathematically to translate force *A* into force *B*, the factor which changes one into the other must have not only force and direction, but stretching power, to pull *A* equal to *B*, and that factor is called the *tensor*.) Tensor is

the quantity necessary in Einsteinian physics to translate vectors from one set of co-ordinates (frame of reference) to another.

TEREBELLID WORM. A polychaet worm which builds a sandy or pebbly tube, cemented usually to the underside of rocks by its own mucus.

THIGMOTROPISM. An innate tendency to seek enclosing contact with a solid or rigid surface, as in a burrow.

TROPISM. Innate involuntary movement of an organism or any of its parts toward (positive) or away from (negative) a stimulus.

TURBELLARIAN WORMS. The large group of flatworms to which the polyclads belong.

UBIQUITOUS. Occurring everywhere (though not necessarily abundantly) in the total area under consideration.

VECTOR. A mathematical term for an abstract quantity such as velocity, acceleration, or force, having *both* magnitude and direction. It may also have position in space, but this is not necessary. A vector is symbolized or represented by an arrow.

XEROPHYTIC. Plants structurally adapted to withstand drought.

ZOOID. Individual member of a colony or compound organism, having more or less independent life of its own.

Index

THE HARVEST GYPSIES

STARVATION UNDER THE ORANGE TREES

(Collected as *Their Blood Is Strong*)

The Harvest Gypsies

AT THIS SEASON of the year, when California's great crops are coming into harvest, the heavy grapes, the prunes, the apples and lettuce and the rapidly maturing cotton, our highways swarm with the migrant workers, that shifting group of nomadic, poverty-stricken harvesters driven by hunger and the threat of hunger from crop to crop, from harvest to harvest, up and down the state and into Oregon to some extent, and into Washington a little. But it is California which has and needs the majority of these new gypsies. It is a short study of these wanderers that these articles will undertake. There are at least 150,000 homeless migrants wandering up and down the state, and that is an army large enough to make it important to every person in the state.

To the casual traveler on the great highways the movements of the migrants are mysterious if they are seen at all, for suddenly the roads will be filled with open rattletrap cars loaded with children and with dirty bedding, with fire-blackened cooking utensils. The boxcars and gondolas on the railroad lines will be filled with men. And then, just as suddenly, they will have disappeared from the main routes. On side roads and near rivers where there is little travel the squalid, filthy squatters' camp will have been set up, and the orchards will be filled with pickers and cutters and driers.

The unique nature of California agriculture requires that these migrants exist, and requires that they move about. Peaches and grapes, hops and cotton cannot be harvested by a resident population of laborers. For example, a large peach orchard which requires the work of 20 men the year round will need as many as 2000 for the brief time of picking and packing. And if the migration of the 2000 should not occur, if it should be delayed even a week, the crop will rot and be lost.

Thus, in California we find a curious attitude toward a group that makes our agriculture successful. The migrants are needed, and they are hated. Arriving in a district they find the dislike always meted out by the resident to the foreigner, the outlander. This hatred of the stranger occurs in the whole range of human history, from the most primitive village form to our own highly organized industrial farming. The migrants are hated for the following reasons, that they are ignorant and dirty people, that they are carriers of disease, that they increase the necessity for police and the tax bill for schooling in a community, and that if they are allowed to organize they can, simply by refusing to work, wipe out the season's crops. They are never received into a community nor into the life of a community. Wanderers in fact, they are never allowed to feel at home in the communities that demand their services.

Let us see what kind of people they are, where they come from, and the routes of their wanderings. In the past they have been of several races, encouraged to come and often imported as cheap labor; Chinese in the early period, then Filipinos, Japanese and Mexicans. These were foreigners, and as such they were ostracized and segregated and herded about.

If they attempted to organize they were deported or arrested, and having no advocates they were never able to get a hearing for their problems. But in recent years the foreign migrants have begun to organize, and at this danger signal they have been deported in great numbers, for there was a new reservoir from which a great quantity of cheap labor could be obtained.

The drouth in the middle west has driven the agricultural populations of Oklahoma, Nebraska and parts of Kansas and Texas westward. Their lands are destroyed and they can never go back to them.

Thousands of them are crossing the borders in ancient rattling automobiles, destitute and hungry and homeless, ready to accept any pay so that they may eat and feed their children. And this is a new thing in migrant labor, for the foreign workers were usually imported without their children and everything that remains of their old life with them.

They arrive in California usually having used up every resource to get here, even to the selling of the poor blankets and utensils and tools on the way to buy gasoline. They arrive bewildered and beaten and usually in a state of semi-starvation, with only one necessity to face immediately, and that is to find work at any wage in order that the family may eat.

And there is only one field in California that can receive them. Ineligible for relief, they must become migratory field workers.

Because the old kind of laborers, Mexicans and Filipinos, are being deported and repatriated very rapidly, while on the other hand the river of dust bowl refugees increases all the time, it is this new kind of migrant that we shall largely consider.

The earlier foreign migrants have invariably been drawn from a peon class. This is not the case with the new migrants.

They are small farmers who have lost their farms, or farm hands who have lived with the family in the old American way. They are men who have worked hard on their own farms and have felt the pride of possessing and living in close touch with the land.

They are resourceful and intelligent Americans who have gone through the hell of the drouth, have seen their lands wither and die and the top soil blow away; and this, to a man who has owned his land, is a curious and terrible pain.

And then they have made the crossing and have seen often the death of their children on the way. Their cars have broken down and been repaired with the ingenuity of the land man.

Often they patched the worn-out tires every few miles. They have weathered the thing, and they can weather much more for their blood is strong.

They are descendants of men who crossed into the middle west, who won their lands by fighting, who cultivated the prairies and stayed with them until they went back to desert.

And because of their tradition and their training, they are not migrants by nature. They are gypsies by force of circumstances.

In their heads, as they move wearily from harvest to harvest, there is one urge and one overwhelming need, to acquire a little land again, and to settle on it and stop their wandering. One has only to go into the squatters' camps where the families live on the ground and have no homes, no beds and no equipment; and one has only to look at the strong purposeful faces, often filled with pain and more often, when they see the corporation-held idle lands, filled with anger, to know that this new race is here to stay and that heed must be taken of it.

It should be understood that with this new race the old methods of repression, of starvation wages, of jailing, beating and intimidation are not going to work; these are American people. Consequently we must meet them with understanding and attempt to work out the problem to their benefit as well as ours.

It is difficult to believe what one large speculative farmer has said, that the success of California agriculture requires that we create and maintain a peon class. For if this is true, then California must depart from the semblance of democratic government that remains here.

The names of the new migrants indicate that they are of English, German and Scandanavian descent. There are Munns, Holbrooks, Hansens, Schmidts.

And they are strangely anachronistic in one way: Having been brought up in the prairies where industrialization never penetrated, they have jumped with no transition from the old agrarian, self-containing farm where nearly everything used was raised or manufactured, to a system of agriculture so industrialized that the man who plants a crop does not often see, let alone harvest, the fruit of his planting, where the migrant has no contact with the growth cycle.

And there is another difference between their old life and the new. They have come from the little farm districts where democracy was not only possible but inevitable, where popular government, whether practiced in the Grange, in church organization or in local government, was the responsibility of every man. And they have come into the country where, because of the movement necessary to make a living, they are not allowed any vote whatever, but are rather considered a properly unpriviledged class.

Let us see the fields that require the impact of their labor and the districts to which they must travel. As one little boy in a squatters' camp said, "When they need us they call us migrants, and when we've picked their crop, we're bums and we got to get out."

There are the vegetable crops of the Imperial Valley, the lettuce, cauliflower, tomatoes, cabbage to be picked and packed, to be hoed and irrigated. There are several crops a year to be harvested, but there is not time distribution sufficient to give the migrants permanent work.

The orange orchards deliver two crops a year, but the picking season is short. Farther north, in Kern County and up the San Joaquin Valley, the migrants are needed for grapes, cotton, pears, melons, beans and peaches.

In the outer valley, near Salinas, Watsonville and Santa Clara there are lettuce, cauliflowers, artichokes, apples, prunes, apricots. North of San Francisco the produce is of grapes, deciduous fruits and hops. The Sacramento Valley needs masses of migrants for its asparagus, its walnuts, peaches, prunes, etc. These great valleys with their intensive farming make their seasonal demands on migrant labor.

A short time, then, before the actual picking begins, there is the scurrying on the highways, the families in open cars hurrying to the ready crops and hurrying to be first at work. For it has been the habit of the growers associations of the state to provide by importation, twice as much labor as was necessary, so that wages might remain low.

Hence the hurry, for if the migrant is a little late the places may all be filled and he will have taken his trip for nothing. And there are many things that may happen even if he is in time. The crop may be late, or there may occur one of those situations like that at Nipomo last year when twelve hundred workers arrived to pick the pea crop only to find it spoiled by rain.

All resources having been used to get to the field, the migrants could not move on; they stayed and starved until government aid tardily was found for them.

And so they move, frantically, with starvation close behind them. And in this series of articles we shall try to see how they live and what kind of people they are, what their living standard is, what is done for them and to them, and what their problems and needs are. For while California has been successful in its use of migrant labor, it is gradually building a human structure which will certainly change the State, and may, if handled with the inhumanity and stupidity that have characterized the past, destroy the present system of agricultural economics.

CHAPTER 2

THE SQUATTERS' CAMPS are located all over California. Let us see what a typical one is like. It is located on the banks of a river, near an irrigation ditch or on a side road where a spring of water is available. From a distance it looks like a city dump, and well it may, for the city dumps are the sources for the material of which it is built. You can see a litter of dirty rags and scrap iron, of houses built of weeds, of flattened cans or of paper. It is only on close approach that it can be seen that these are homes.

Here is a house built by a family who have tried to maintain a neatness. The house is about 10 feet by 10 feet, and it is built completely of corrugated paper. The roof is peaked, the walls are tacked to a wooden frame. The dirt floor is swept clean, and along the irrigation ditch or in the muddy river the wife of the family scrubs clothes without soap and tries to rinse out the mud in muddy water. The spirit of this family is not quite broken, for the children, three of them, still have clothes, and the family possesses three old quilts and a soggy, lumpy mattress. But the money so needed for food cannot be used for soap nor for clothes.

With the first rain the carefully built house will slop down into a brown, pulpy mush; in a few months the clothes will fray off the children's bodies while the lack of nourishing food will subject the whole family to pneumonia when the first cold comes.

Five years ago this family had fifty acres of land and a thousand dollars in the bank. The wife belonged to a sewing circle and the man was a member of the grange. They raised chickens, pigs, pigeons and vegetables and fruit for their own use; and their land produced the tall corn of the middle west. Now they have nothing.

If the husband hits every harvest without delay and works the maximum time, he may make four hundred dollars this year. But if anything happens, if his old car breaks down, if he is late and misses a harvest or two, he will have to feed his whole family on as little as one hundred and fifty.

But there is still pride in this family. Wherever they stop they try to put the children in school. It may be that the children will be in a school for as much as a month before they are moved to another locality.

Here, in the faces of the husband and his wife, you begin to see an expression you will notice on every face; not worry, but absolute terror of the starvation that crowds in against the borders of the camp. This man has tried to make a toilet by digging a hole in the ground near his paper house and surrounding it with an old piece of burlap. But he will only do things like that this year.

He is a newcomer and his spirit and his decency and his sense of his own dignity have not been quite wiped out. Next year he will be like his next door neighbor.

This is a family of six; a man, his wife and four children. They live in a tent the color of the ground. Rot has set in on the canvas so that the flaps and the sides hang in tatters and are held together with bits of rusty baling wire. There is one bed in the family and that is a big tick lying on the ground inside the tent.

They have one quilt and a piece of canvas for bedding. The sleeping arrangement is clever. Mother and father lie down together and two children lie between them. Then, heading the other way, the other two children lie, the littler ones. If the mother and father sleep with their legs spread wide, there is room for the legs of the children.

There is more filth here. The tent is full of flies clinging to the apple box that is the dinner table, buzzing about the foul clothes of the children, particularly the baby, who has not been bathed nor cleaned for several days.

This family has been on the road longer than the builder of the paper house. There is no toilet here, but there is a clump of willows nearby where human faeces lie exposed to the flies—the same flies that are in the tent.

Two weeks ago there was another child, a four year old boy. For a few weeks they had noticed that he was kind of lackadaisical, that his eyes had been feverish.

They had given him the best place in the bed, between father and mother. But one night he went into convulsions and died, and the next morning the coroner's wagon took him away. It was one step down.

They know pretty well that it was a diet of fresh fruit, beans and little else that caused his death. He had no milk for months. With this death there came a change of mind in his family. The father and mother now feel that paralyzed dullness with which the mind protects itself against too much sorrow and too much pain.

And this father will not be able to make a maximum of four hundred dollars a year any more because he is no longer alert; he isn't quick at piece-work, and he is not able to fight clear of the dullness that has settled on him. His spirit is losing caste rapidly.

The dullness shows in the faces of this family, and in addition there is a sullenness that makes them taciturn. Sometimes they still start the older children off to school, but the ragged little things will not go; they hide in ditches or wander off by themselves until it is time to go back to the tent, because they are scorned in the school.

The better-dressed children shout and jeer, the teachers are quite often impatient with these additions to their duties, and the parents of the "nice" children do not want to have disease carriers in the schools.

The father of this family once had a little grocery store and his family lived in back of it so that even the children could wait on the counter. When the drouth set in there was no trade for the store any more.

This is the middle class of the squatters' camp. In a few months this family will slip down to the lower class.

Dignity is all gone, and spirit has turned to sullen anger before it dies.

The next door neighbor family of man, wife and three children of from three to nine years of age, have built a house by driving willow branches into the ground and wattling weeds, tin, old paper and strips of carpet against them.

A few branches are placed over the top to keep out the noonday sun. It would not turn water at all. There is no bed.

Somewhere the family has found a big piece of old carpet. It is on the ground. To go to bed the members of the family lie on the ground and fold the carpet up over them.

The three year old child has a gunny sack tied about his middle for clothing. He has the swollen belly caused by malnutrition.

He sits on the ground in the sun in front of the house, and

the little black fruit flies buzz in circles and land on his closed eyes and crawl up his nose until he weakly brushes them away.

They try to get at the mucous in the eye-corners. This child seems to have the reactions of a baby much younger. The first year he had a little milk, but he has had none since.

He will die in a very short time. The older children may survive. Four nights ago the mother had a baby in the tent, on the dirty carpet. It was born dead, which was just as well because she could not have fed it at the breast; her own diet will not produce milk.

After it was born and she had seen that it was dead, the mother rolled over and lay still for two days. She is up today, tottering around. The last baby, born less than a year ago, lived a week. This woman's eyes have the glazed, far-away look of a sleep walker's eyes.

She does not wash clothes any more. The drive that makes for cleanliness has been drained out of her and she hasn't the energy. The husband was a share-cropper once, but he couldn't make it go. Now he has lost even the desire to talk.

He will not look directly at you, for that requires will, and will needs strength. He is a bad field worker for the same reason. It takes him a long time to make up his mind, so he is always late in moving and late in arriving in the fields. His top wage, when he can find work now, which isn't often, is a dollar a day.

The children do not even go to the willow clump any more. They squat where they are and kick a little dirt. The father is vaguely aware that there is a culture of hookworm in the mud along the river bank. He knows the children will get it on their bare feet.

But he hasn't the will nor the energy to resist. Too many things have happened to him. This is the lower class of the camp.

This is what the man in the tent will be in six months; what the man in the paper house with its peaked roof will be in a year, after his house has washed down and his children have sickened or died, after the loss of dignity and spirit have cut him down to a kind of sub-humanity.

Helpful strangers are not well-received in this camp. The local sheriff makes a raid now and then for a wanted man, and if there is labor trouble the vigilantes may burn the poor houses. Social workers, survey workers have taken case histories.

They are filed and open for inspection. These families have been questioned over and over about their origins, number of children living and dead.

The information is taken down and filed. That is that. It has been done so often, and so little has come of it.

And there is another way for them to get attention. Let an epidemic break out, say typhoid or scarlet fever, and the country doctor will come to the camp and hurry the infected cases to the pest house. But malnutrition is not infectious, nor is dysentery, which is almost the rule among the children.

The county hospital has no room for measles, mumps, whooping cough; and yet these are often deadly to hunger-weakened children. And although we hear much about the free clinics for the poor, these people do not know how to get the aid and they do not get it. Also, since most of their dealings with authority are painful to them, they prefer not to take the chance.

This is the squatters' camp. Some are a little better, some much worse. I have described three typical families. In some of the camps there are as many as three hundred families like these. Some are so far from water that it must be bought at five cents a bucket.

And if these men steal, if there is developing among them a suspicion and hatred of well-dressed, satisfied people, the reason is not to be sought in their origin nor in any tendency to weakness in their character.

CHAPTER 3

WHEN in the course of the season the small farmer has need of an influx of migrant workers he usually draws from the squatters' camps. By small farmer I mean the owner of the five to 100-acre farm, who operates and oversees his own farm.

Farms of this size are the greatest users of labor from the

notorious squatters' camps. A few of the small farms set aside little pieces of land where the workers may pitch their shelters. Water is furnished, and once in a while a toilet. Rarely is there any facility for bathing. A small farm cannot afford the outlay necessary to maintain a sanitary camp.

Furthermore, the small farmers are afraid to allow groups of migrants to camp on their land, and they do not like the litter that is left when the men move on. On the whole, the relations between the migrants and the small farmers are friendly and understanding.

In many of California's agricultural strikes the small farmer has sided with the migrant against the powerful speculative farm groups. The workers realize that the problem of the small farmer is not unlike their own. We have the example in the San Joaquin Valley two years ago of a small farmer who sided with the workers in the cotton strike.

The speculative farm group, which is closely tied up with the power companies, determined to force this farm from opposition by cutting off the power necessary for irrigation.

But the strikers surrounded and held the power pole and refused to allow the current to be cut off. Incidents of this nature occur very frequently.

The small farmer, then, draws his labor from the squatters' camps and from the state and Federal camps, which will be dealt with later.

On the other hand the large farms very often maintain their camps for the laborers.

The large farms in California are organized as closely and are as centrally directed in their labor policy as are the industries and shipping, the banking and public utilities.

Indeed such organizations as Associated Farmers, Inc. have as members and board members officials of banks, publishers of newspapers and politicians; and through close association with the State Chamber of Commerce they have interlocking associations with shipowners' associations, public utilities corporations and transportation companies.

Members of these speculative farm organizations are of several kinds—individual absentee owners of great tracts of land, banks that have acquired lands by foreclosure, for example the tremendous Bank of America holdings in the San Joaquin

Valley, and incorporated farms having stockholders, boards of directors and the usual corporation approach.

These farms are invariably run by superintendents whose policies with regard to labor are directed from above. But the power of these organizations extends far beyond the governing of their own lands.

It is rare in California for a small farmer to be able to plant and mature his crops without loans from banks and finance companies. And since these banks and finance companies are at once members of the powerful growers' associations, and at the same time the one source of crop loans, the force of their policies on the small farmer can readily be seen. To refuse to obey is to invite foreclosure or a future denial of the necessary crop loan.

These strong groups, then, do not necessarily represent the general feeling toward labor; but being able to procure space in newspapers and on the radio, they are able not only to represent themselves as the whole body of California farmers, but are actually able to impose their policies on a great number of the small farms.

The ranches operated by these speculative farmers usually have houses for their migrant laborers, houses for which they charge a rent of from three to 15 dollars a month.

On most of the places it is not allowed that a worker refuse to pay the rent. If he wants to work, he must live in the house, and the rent is taken from his first pay.

Let us see what this housing is like, not the $15 houses which can only be rented by field bosses (called pushers), but the three to five dollar houses forced on the laborers.

The houses, one-room shacks usually about 10 by 12 feet, have no rug, no water, no bed. In one corner there is a little iron wood stove. Water must be carried from a faucet at the end of the street.

Also at the head of the street there will be either a dug toilet or a toilet with a septic tank to serve 100 to 150 people. A fairly typical ranch in Kern County had one bath house with a single shower and no heated water for the use of the whole block of houses, which had a capacity of 400 people.

The arrival of the migrant on such a ranch is something like this—he is assigned a house for his family; he may have from three to six children, but they must all live in the one room. He finds the ranch heavily policed by deputized employes.

The will of the ranch owner, then, is law; for these deputies are always on hand, their guns conspicuous. A disagreement constitutes resisting an officer. A glance at the list of migrants shot during a single year in California for "resisting an officer" will give a fair idea of the casualness of these "officers" in shooting workers.

The new arrival at the ranch will probably be without funds. His resources have been exhausted in getting here. But on many of the great ranches he will find a store run by the management at which he can get credit.

Thus he must work a second day to pay for his first, and so on. He is continually in debt. He must work. There is only one piece of property which is worth attaching for the debt, and that is his car; and while single men are able to get from harvest to harvest on the railroads and by hitch-hiking, the man with a family will starve if he loses his car. Under this threat he must go on working.

In the field he will be continually attended by the "pusher," the field boss, and in many cases a pacer. In picking, a pacer will be a tree ahead of him. If he does not keep up, he is fired. And it is often the case that the pacer's row is done over again afterwards.

On these large ranches there is no attempt made for the relaxation or entertainment of the workers. Indeed any attempt to congregate is broken up by the deputies for it is feared that if they are allowed to congregate they will organize, and that is the one thing the large ranches will not permit at any cost.

The attitude of the employer on the large ranch is one of hatred and suspicion, his method is the threat of the deputies' guns.

The workers are herded about like animals. Every possible method is used to make them feel inferior and insecure. At the slightest suspicion that the men are organizing they are run from the ranch at the points of guns.

The large ranch owners know that if organization is ever effected there will be the expense of toilets, showers, decent living conditions and a raise in wages.

The attitude of the workers on the large ranch is much that of the employer, hatred and suspicion. The worker sees himself surrounded by force. He knows that he can be murdered without fear on the part of the employer, and he has little recourse to law.

He has taken refuge in a sullen, tense quiet. He cannot resist the credit that allows him to feed his family, but he knows perfectly well the reason for the credit.

There are a few large ranches in California which maintain "model houses" for the workers, neatly painted buildings with some conveniences.

These ranches usually charge a rent of $5 a month for a single-room house and pay 33 1/3 per cent less than the prevailing wage.

The labor policy of these absentee-directed large farms has created the inevitable result. Usually there are guards at the gates, the roads are patrolled, permission to inspect the premises is never given.

It would almost seem that having built the repressive attitude toward the labor they need to survive, the directors were terrified of the things they have created.

This fear dictates an increase of the repressive method, a greater number of guards and a constant suggestion that the ranch is armed to fight.

Here, as in the squatters' camps, the dignity of the men is attacked. No trust is accorded them. They are surrounded as though it were suspected that they would break into revolt at any moment. It would seem that a surer method of forcing them to revolt could not be devised.

This repressive method results inevitably in flares of disorganized revolt which must be put down by force and by increased intimidation.

The large growers' groups have found the law inadequate to their uses; and they have become so powerful that such charges as felonious assault, mayhem and inciting to riot, kidnaping and flogging cannot be brought against them in the controlled courts.

The attitude of the large growers' associations toward labor is best stated by Mr. Hugh T. Osburne, a member of the Board of Supervisors of Imperial County and active in the

Imperial Valley Associated Farmers group. Before the judiciary committee of the California Assembly he said:

"In Imperial Valley we don't need this criminal syndicalism law. They have got to have it for the rest of the counties that don't know how to handle these matters. We don't need it because we have worked out our own way of handling these things. We won't have another of these trials. We have a better way of doing it. Trials cost too much."

"The better way," as accepted by the large growers of the Imperial Valley, includes a system of terrorism that would be unusual in the Fascist nations of the world. The stupid policy of the large grower and the absentee speculative farmer in California has accomplished nothing but unrest, tension and hatred. A continuation of this approach constitutes a criminal endangering of the peace of the state.

CHAPTER 4

THE FEDERAL GOVERNMENT, realizing that the miserable condition of the California migrant agricultural worker constitutes an immediate and vital problem, has set up two camps for the moving workers and contemplates eight more in the immediate future. The development of the camps at Arvin and at Marysville makes a social and economic study of vast interest.

The present camps are set up on leased ground. Future camps are to be constructed on land purchased by the Government. The Government provides places for tents. Permanent structures are simple, including washrooms, toilets and showers, an administration building and a place where the people can entertain themselves. The equipment at the Arvin camp, exclusive of rent of the land, costs approximately $18,000.

At this camp, water, toilet paper and some medical supplies are provided. A resident manager is on the ground. Campers are received on the following simple conditions: (1) That the men are bona fide farm people and intend to work, (2) that they will help to maintain the cleanliness of the camp and

(3) that in lieu of rent they will devote two hours a week towards the maintenance and improvement of the camp.

The result has been more than could be expected. From the first, the intent of the management has been to restore the dignity and decency that had been kicked out of the migrants by their intolerable mode of life.

In this series the word "dignity" has been used several times. It has been used not as some attitude of self-importance, but simply as a register of a man's responsibility to the community.

A man herded about, surrounded by armed guards, starved and forced to live in filth loses his dignity; that is, he loses his valid position in regard to society, and consequently his whole ethics toward society. Nothing is a better example of this than the prison, where the men are reduced to no dignity and where crimes and infractions of rule are constant.

We regard this destruction of dignity, then, as one of the most regrettable results of the migrant's life since it does reduce his responsibility and does make him a sullen outcast who will strike at our Government in any way that occurs to him.

The example at Arvin adds weight to such a conviction. The people in the camp are encouraged to govern themselves, and they have responded with simple and workable democracy.

The camp is divided into four units. Each unit, by direct election, is represented in a central governing committee, an entertainment committee, a maintenance committee and a Good Neighbors committee. Each of these members is elected by the vote of his unit, and is recallable by the same vote.

The manager, of course, has the right of veto, but he practically never finds it necessary to act contrary to the recommendations of the committee.

The result of this responsible self-government has been remarkable. The inhabitants of the camp came there beaten, sullen and destitute. But as their social sense was revived they have settled down. The camp takes care of its own destitute, feeding and sheltering those who have nothing with their own poor stores. The central committee makes the laws that govern the conduct of the inhabitants.

In the year that the Arvin camp has been in operation there

has not been any need for outside police. Punishments are the restrictions of certain privileges such as admission to the community dances, or for continued anti-social conduct, a recommendation to the manager that the culprit be ejected from the camp.

A works committee assigns the labor to be done in the camp, improvements, garbage disposal, maintenance and repairs. The entertainment committee arranges for the weekly dances, the music for which is furnished by an orchestra made up of the inhabitants.

So well do they play that one orchestra has been lost to the radio already. This committee also takes care of the many self-made games and courts that have been built.

The Good Neighbors, a woman's organization, takes part in quilting and sewing projects, sees that destitution does not exist, governs and watches the nursery, where children can be left while the mothers are working in the fields and in the packing sheds. And all of this is done with the outside aid of one manager and one part-time nurse. As experiments in natural and democratic self-government, these camps are unique in the United States.

In visiting these camps one is impressed with several things in particular. The sullen and frightened expression that is the rule among the migrants has disappeared from the faces of the Federal camp inhabitants. Instead there is a steadiness of gaze and a self-confidence that can only come of restored dignity.

The difference seems to lie in the new position of the migrant in the community. Before he came to the camp he had been policed, hated and moved about. It had been made clear that he was not wanted.

In the Federal camps every effort of the management is expended to give him his place in society. There are no persons on relief in these camps.

In the Arvin camp the central committee recommended the expulsion of a family which applied for relief. Employment is more common than in any similar group for, having something of their own, these men are better workers. The farmers in the vicinity seem to prefer the camp men to others.

The inhabitants of the Federal camps are no picked group. They are typical of the new migrants. They come from

Oklahoma, Arkansas and Texas and the other drouth states. Eighty-five per cent of them are former farm owners, farm renters or farm laborers. The remaining 15 per cent includes painters, mechanics, electricians and even professional men.

When a new family enters one of these camps it is usually dirty, tired and broken. A group from the Good Neighbors meets it, tells it the rules, helps it to get settled, instructs it in the use of the sanitary facilities; and if there are insufficient blankets or shelters, furnishes them from its own stores.

The children are bathed and cleanly dressed and the needs of the future canvassed. If the children have not enough clothes the community sewing circle will get busy immediately. In case any of the family are sick the camp manager or the part-time nurse is called and treatment is carried out.

These Good Neighbors are not trained social workers, but they have what is perhaps more important, an understanding which grows from a likeness of experience. Nothing has happened to the newcomer that has not happened to the committee.

A typical manager's report is as follows:

"New arrivals. Low in foodstuffs. Most of the personal belongings were tied up in sacks and were in a filthy condition. The Good Neighbors at once took the family in hand, and by 10 o'clock they were fed, washed, camped, settled and asleep."

These two camps each accommodate about 200 families. They were started as experiments, and the experiments have proven successful. Between the rows of tents the families have started little gardens for the raising of vegetables, and the plots, which must be cared for after a 10 or 12-hours' day of work, produce beets, cabbages, corn, carrots, onions and turnips. The passion to produce is very great. One man, who has not yet been assigned his little garden plot, is hopefully watering a jimpson weed simply to have something of his own growing.

The Federal Government, through the Resettlement Administration, plans to extend these camps and to include with them small maintenance farms. These are intended to solve several problems.

They will allow the women and children to stay in one place, permitting the children to go to school and the women to maintain the farms during the work times of the men. They will reduce the degenerating effect of the migrants' life, they will reinstil the sense of government and possession that have been lost by the migrants.

Located near to the areas which demand seasonal labor, these communities will permit these subsistence farmers to work in the harvests, while at the same time they stop the wanderings over the whole state. The success of these Federal camps in making potential criminals into citizens makes the usual practice of expending money on tear gas seem a little silly.

The greater part of the new migrants from the dust bowl will become permanent California citizens. They have shown in these camps an ability to produce and to co-operate. They are passionately determined to make their living on the land. One of them said, "If it's work you got to do, mister, we'll do it. Our folks never did take charity and this family ain't takin' it now."

The plan of the Resettlement Administration to extend these Federal camps is being fought by certain interests in California. The arguments against the camps are as follows:

That they will increase the need for locally paid police. But the two camps already carried on for over a year have proved to need no locally paid police whatever, while the squatters' camps are a constant charge on the sheriff's offices.

The second argument is that the cost of schools to the district will be increased. School allotments are from the state and governed by the number of pupils. And even if it did cost more, the communities need the work of these families and must assume some responsibility for them. The alternative is a generation of illiterates.

The third is that they will lower the land values because of the type of people inhabiting the camps. Those camps already established have in no way affected the value of the land and the people are of good American stock who have proved that they can maintain an American standard of living. The cleanliness and lack of disease in the two experimental camps are proof of this.

The fourth argument, as made by the editor of The Yuba City Herald, a self-admitted sadist who wrote a series of incendiary and subversive editorials concerning the Marysville camp, is that these are the breeding places for strikes.

Under pressure of evidence the Yuba City patriot withdrew his contention that the camp was full of radicals. This will be the argument used by the speculative growers' associations. These associations have said in so many words that they require a peon class to succeed. Any action to better the condition of the migrants will be considered radical to them.

CHAPTER 5

MIGRANT FAMILIES in California find that unemployment relief, which is available to settled unemployed, has little to offer them. In the first place there has grown up a regular technique for getting relief; one who knows the ropes can find aid from the various state and Federal disbursement agencies, while a man ignorant of the methods will be turned away.

The migrant is always partially unemployed. The nature of his occupation makes his work seasonal. At the same time the nature of his work makes him ineligible for relief. The basis for receiving most of the relief is residence.

But it is impossible for the migrant to accomplish the residence. He must move about the country. He could not stop long enough to establish residence or he would starve to death. He finds, then, on application, that he cannot be put on the relief rolls. And being ignorant, he gives up at that point.

For the same reason he finds that he cannot receive any of the local benefits reserved for residents of a county. The county hospital was built not for the transient, but for residents of the county.

It will be interesting to trace the history of one family in relation to medicine, work relief and direct relief. The family consisted of five persons, a man of 50, his wife of 45, two boys, 15 and 12, and a girl of six. They came from Oklahoma, where the father operated a little ranch of 50 acres of prairie.

When the ranch dried up and blew away the family put its moveable possessions in an old Dodge truck and came to Cal-

ifornia. They arrived in time for the orange picking in Southern California and put in a good average season.

The older boy and the father together made $60. At that
time the automobile broke out some teeth of the differential
and the repairs, together with three second-hand tires, took
$22. The family moved into Kern County to chop grapes and
camped in the squatters' camp on the edge of Bakersfield.

At this time the father sprained his ankle and the little girl
developed measles. Doctors' bills amounted to $10 of the
remaining store, and food and transportation took most of
the rest.

The 15-year-old boy was now the only earner for the family.
The 12-year-old boy picked up a brass gear in a yard and took
it to sell.

He was arrested and taken before the juvenile court, but
was released to his father's custody. The father walked in to
Bakersfield from the squatters' camp on a sprained ankle because the gasoline was gone from the automobile and he
didn't dare invest any of the remaining money in more gasoline.

This walk caused complications in the sprain which laid him
up again. The little girl had recovered from measles by this
time, but her eyes had not been protected and she had lost
part of her eyesight.

The father now applied for relief and found that he was
ineligible because he had not established the necessary residence. All resources were gone. A little food was given to the
family by neighbors in the squatters' camp.

A neighbor who had a goat brought in a cup of milk every
day for the little girl.

At this time the 15-year-old boy came home from the fields
with a pain in his side. He was feverish and in great pain.

The mother put hot cloths on his stomach while a neighbor
took the crippled father to the county hospital to apply for
aid. The hospital was full, all its time taken by bona fide local
residents. The trouble described as a pain in the stomach by
the father was not taken seriously.

The father was given a big dose of salts to take home to
the boy. That night the pain grew so great that the boy became unconscious. The father telephoned the hospital and

found that there was no one on duty who could attend to his case. The boy died of a burst appendix the next day.

There was no money. The county buried him free. The father sold the Dodge for $30 and bought a $2 wreath for the funeral. With the remaining money he laid in a store of cheap, filling food—beans, oatmeal, lard. He tried to go back to work in the fields. Some of the neighbors gave him rides to work and charged him a small amount for transportation.

He was on the weak ankle too soon and could not make over 75¢ a day at piece-work, chopping. Again he applied for relief and was refused because he was not a resident and because he was employed. The little girl, because of insufficient food and weakness from measles, relapsed into influenza.

The father did not try the county hospital again. He went to a private doctor who refused to come to the squatters' camp unless he were paid in advance. The father took two days' pay and gave it to the doctor who came to the family shelter, took the girl's temperature, gave the mother seven pills, told the mother to keep the child warm and went away. The father lost his job because he was too slow.

He applied again for help and was given one week's supply of groceries.

This can go on indefinitely. The case histories like it can be found in their thousands. It may be argued that there were ways for this man to get aid, but how did he know where to get it? There was no way for him to find out.

California communities have used the old, old methods of dealing with such problems. The first method is to disbelieve it and vigorously to deny that there is a problem. The second is to deny local responsibility since the people are not permanent residents. And the third and silliest of all is to run the trouble over the county borders into another county. The floater method of swapping what the counties consider undesirables from hand to hand is like a game of medicine ball.

A fine example of this insular stupidity concerns the hookworm situation in Stanislaus County. The mud along water courses where there are squatters living is infected. Several business men of Modesto and Ceres offered as a solution that the squatters be cleared out. There was no thought of isolating the victims and stopping the hookworm.

The affected people were, according to these men, to be run out of the county to spread the disease in other fields. It is this refusal of the counties to consider anything but the immediate economy and profit of the locality that is the cause of a great deal of the unsolvable quality of the migrants' problem. The counties seem terrified that they may be required to give some aid to the labor they require for their harvests.

According to several Government and state surveys and studies of large numbers of migrants, the maximum a worker can make is $400 a year, while the average is around $300, and the large minimum is $150 a year. This amount must feed, clothe and transport whole families.

Sometimes whole families are able to work in the fields, thus making an additional wage. In other observed cases a whole family, weakened by sickness and malnutrition, has worked in the fields, making less than the wage of one healthy man. It does not take long at the migrants' work to reduce the health of any family. Food is scarce always, and luxuries of any kind are unknown.

Observed diets run something like this when the family is making money:

Family of eight—Boiled cabbage, baked sweet potatoes, creamed carrots, beans, fried dough, jelly, tea.

Family of seven—Beans, baking-powder biscuits, jam, coffee.

Family of six—Canned salmon, cornbread, raw onions.

Family of five—Biscuits, fried potatoes, dandelion greens, pears.

These are dinners. It is to be noticed that even in these flush times there is no milk, no butter. The major part of the diet is starch. In slack times the diet becomes all starch, this being the cheapest way to fill up. Dinners during lay-offs are as follows:

Family of seven—Beans, fried dough.

Family of six—Fried cornmeal.

Family of five—Oatmeal mush.

Family of eight (there were six children)—Dandelion greens and boiled potatoes.

It will be seen that even in flush times the possibility of

remaining healthy is very slight. The complete absence of milk for the children is responsible for many of the diseases of malnutrition. Even pellagra is far from unknown.

The preparation of food is the most primitive. Cooking equipment usually consists of a hole dug in the ground or a kerosene can with a smoke vent and open front.

If the adults have been working 10 hours in the fields or in the packing sheds they do not want to cook. They will buy canned goods as long as they have money, and when they are low in funds they will subsist on half-cooked starches.

The problem of childbirth among the migrants is among the most terrible. There is no prenatal care of the mothers whatever, and no possibility of such care. They must work in the fields until they are physically unable or, if they do not work, the care of the other children and of the camp will not allow the prospective mothers any rest.

In actual birth the presence of a doctor is a rare exception. Sometimes in the squatters' camps a neighbor woman will help at the birth. There will be no sanitary precautions nor hygienic arrangements. The child will be born on newspapers in the dirty bed. In case of a bad presentation requiring surgery or forceps, the mother is practically condemned to death. Once born, the eyes of the baby are not treated, the endless medical attention lavished on middle-class babies is completely absent.

The mother, usually suffering from malnutrition, is not able to produce breast milk. Sometimes the baby is nourished on canned milk until it can eat fried dough and cornmeal. This being the case, the infant mortality is very great.

The following is an example: Wife of family with three children. She is 38; her face is lined and thin and there is a hard glaze on her eyes. The three children who survive were born prior to 1929, when the family rented a farm in Utah. In 1930 this woman bore a child which lived four months and died of "colic."

In 1931 her child was born dead because "a han' truck fulla boxes run inta me two days before the baby come." In 1932 there was a miscarriage. "I couldn't carry the baby 'cause I was sick." She is ashamed of this. In 1933 her baby lived a week. "Jus' died. I don't know what of." In 1934 she had no pregnancy. She is also a little ashamed of this. In 1935 her baby lived a long time, nine months.

"Seemed for a long time like he was gonna live. Big strong fella it seemed like." She is pregnant again now. "If we could get milk for um I guess it'd be better." This is an extreme case, but by no means an unusual one.

CHAPTER 6

THE HISTORY of California's importation and treatment of foreign labor is a disgraceful picture of greed and cruelty. The first importations of large groups consisted of thousands of Chinese, brought in as cheap labor to build the transcontinental railroads. When the roads were completed a few of the Chinese were retained as section hands, but the bulk went as cheap farm labor.

The traditional standard of living of the Chinese was so low that white labor could not compete with it. At the same time the family organizations allowed them to procure land and to make it produce far more than could the white men. Consequently white labor began a savage warfare on the coolies.

Feeling against them ran high and culminated in riots which gradually drove the Chinese from the fields, while immigration laws closed the borders to new influxes.

The Japanese were the next people encouraged to come in as cheap labor, and the history of their activities was almost exactly like that of the Chinese: A low standard of living which allowed them to accumulate property while at the same time they took the jobs of white labor.

And again there were riots and land laws and closed borders. The feeling against the Japanese culminated in the whole "yellow peril" literature which reached its peak just before the war. The Japanese as a threat to white labor were removed. Some of them had acquired land, some went to the cities, and large numbers of them were moved or deported. The Japanese farm laborers, although unorganized, developed a kind of spontaneous organization which made them less tractable than the Chinese had been.

But, as usual, the nature of California's agriculture made the owners of farm land cry for peon labor. In the early part of the century another source of cheap labor became available.

Mexicans were imported in large numbers, and the standard of living they were capable of maintaining depressed the wages of farm labor to a point where the white could not compete. By 1920 there were 80,000 foreign-born Mexicans in California. The opening of the intensive farming in the Imperial Valley and Southern California made necessary the use of this cheap labor.

And at about this time the demand for peon labor began to come more and more from the large growers and the developing shipper-growers. When the imposition of a quota was suggested, the small farmers (five to 20 acres) had no objection to the restriction, and 66 per cent were actively in favor of the quota.

The large grower, on the other hand, was opposed to the quota. Seventy-eight per cent were openly opposed to any restriction on the importation of peon labor. With the depression, farm wages sank to such a low level in the southern part of the state that white labor could not exist on them. Fourteen cents an hour became the standard wage.

To the large grower the Mexican labor offered more advantages than simply its cheapness. It could be treated as so much scrap when it was not needed. Any local care for the sick and crippled could be withheld; and in addition, if it offered any resistance to the low wage or the terrible living conditions, it could be deported to Mexico at Government expense.

Recently, led by the example of the workers in Mexico, the Mexicans in California have begun to organize. Their organization in Southern California has been met with vigilante terrorism and savagery unbelievable in a civilized state.

Concerning these repressive activities of the large growers, a special commission's report to the National Labor Board has this to say: "Fundamentally, much of the trouble with Mexican labor in the Imperial Valley lies in the natural desire of the workers to organize.

"Their efforts have been thwarted or rendered ineffective by a well-organized opposition against them. . . . We uncovered sufficient evidence to convince us that in more than one instance the law was trampled under foot by representative citizens of Imperial Valley and by public officials under oath to support the law."

The report lists a number of such outrages. "Large numbers of men and women arrested but not booked . . . intimidation used to force pleas of guilty to felonious charges . . . bail was set so large that release was impossible." This report further says: "In our opinion, regular peace officers and civilians displayed pistols too freely, and the police unwarrantedly used tear gas bombs.

"We do not understand why approximately 80 officers found it necessary to gas an audience of several hundred men and women and children in a comparatively small one-story building while searching for three 'agitators.' "

The right of free speech, the right of assembly and the right of jury trial are not extended to Mexicans in the Imperial Valley.

This treatment of Mexican labor, together with the deportation of large groups and the plan of the present Mexican government for repatriating its nationals, is gradually withdrawing Mexican labor from the fields of California. As with the Chinese and Japanese, they have committed the one crime that will not be permitted by the large growers.

They have attempted to organize for their own protection. It is probable that Mexican labor will not long be available to California agriculture.

The last great source of foreign labor to be furnished the California grower has been the Filipino. Between 1920 and 1929, 31,000 of these little brown men were brought to the United States, and most of them remained in California, a new group of peon workers.

They were predominantly young, male and single. Their women were not brought with them. The greatest number of them found agricultural employment in Central and Northern California. Their wages are the lowest paid to any migratory labor.

As in the case of the Mexicans, Japanese and Chinese, the Filipinos have been subjected to racial discrimination.

They are unique in California agriculture. Being young,

male and single, they form themselves into natural groups of five, six, eight; they combine their resources in the purchase of equipment, such as autos. Their group life constitutes a lesson in economy.

A labor co-ordinator of SRA has said, "They often subsist for a week on a double handful of rice and a little bread."

These young men were not permitted to bring their women. At the same time the marriage laws of California were amended to include persons of the Malay race among those peoples who cannot intermarry with whites. Since they were young and male, the one outlet for their amorous energies lay in extra-legal arrangements with white women.

This not only gained for them a reputation for immorality, but was the direct cause of many race riots directed against them.

They were good workers, but like the earlier immigrants they committed the unforgivable in trying to organize for their own protection. Their organization brought on them the usual terrorism.

A fine example of this was the vigilante raid in the Salinas Valley last year when a bunk house was burned down and all the possessions of the Filipinos destroyed.

In this case the owner of the bunk house collected indemnity for the loss of his property. Although the Filipinos have brought suit, no settlement has as yet been made for them.

But the Filipino is not long to be a factor in California agriculture. With the establishment of the Philippine Islands as an autonomous nation, the 35,000 Filipinos in California have suddenly become aliens.

The Federal Government, in co-operation with the Philippine government, has started a campaign to repatriate all of the Filipinos in California. It is only a question of time before this is accomplished.

The receding waves of foreign peon labor are leaving California agriculture to the mercies of our own people. The old methods of intimidation and starvation perfected against the foreign peons are being used against the new white migrant workers. But they will not be successful.

Consequently California agriculture must begin some kind of stock-taking, some reorganization of its internal economy. Farm labor in California will be white labor, it will be American labor, and it will insist on a standard of living much higher than that which was accorded the foreign "cheap labor."

Some of the more enlightened of the large growers argue for white labor on the ground "that it will not go on relief as readily as the Mexican labor has."

These enthusiasts do not realize that the same pride and self-respect that deters white migrant labor from accepting charity and relief, if there is an alternative, will also cause the white American labor to refuse to accept the role of field peon, with its attendant terrorism, squalor and starvation.

Foreign labor is on the wane in California, and the future farm workers are to be white and American. This fact must be recognized and a rearrangement of the attitude toward and treatment of migrant labor must be achieved.

CHAPTER 7

FROM ALMOST daily news stories, from a great number of Government reports available to anyone who is interested, and from this necessarily short series of articles, it becomes apparent that some plan must be contrived to take care of the problem of the migrants. If for no humanitarian reason, the need of California agriculture for these people dictates the necessity of such a plan. A survey of the situation makes a few suggestions obvious. The following are offered as a partial solution of the problem:

Since the greatest number of the white American migrants are former farm owners, renters or laborers, it follows that their training and ambition have never been removed from agriculture. It is suggested that lands be leased; or where it is possible, that state and Federal lands be set aside as subsistence farms for migrants. These can be leased at a low rent or sold on long time payments to families of migrant workers.

Blocks of these subsistence farms should be located in regions which require an abundance of harvest labor. Small houses should be erected and the families settled, schools located so that the children can be educated. People who take these farms should be encouraged and helped to produce for their own subsistence fruits, vegetables and livestock—pigs, chickens, rabbits, turkeys and ducks.

Crops should be so arranged that they do not conflict with the demand for migratory labor. When the seasonal demand is on, the whole family should not be moved, but only the employable men. The subsistence farm could be managed during the harvest season by the women, the growing children and such unemployables as the old and the partially crippled.

In these communities a spirit of co-operation and self-help should be encouraged so that by self-government and a returning social responsibility these people may be restored to the rank of citizens. The expense of such projects should be borne by the Federal Government, by state and county governments, so that the community which requires the greatest number of seasonal workers should contribute to their well-being.

The cost of such ventures would not be much greater than the amount which is now spent for tear gas, machine guns and ammunition, and deputy sheriffs. Each of these subsistence districts should have assigned to it a trained agriculturist to instruct the people in scientific farming; and a spirit of co-operation should be encouraged so that certain implements such as tractors and other farm equipment might be used by the whole unit. Through the school or through the local board of health, medical attention should be made available, and instruction in sanitary measures carried on and enforced. By establishing these farms the problem of food during the five or six-month unemployment season would be solved, the degenerating influence of family moving would be removed and the education of the children would be assured.

There should be established in the state a migratory labor board with branches in the various parts of the state which require seasonal labor. On this board labor should be represented.

Local committees should, before the seasonal demand for labor, canvass the district, discover and publish the amount of labor needed and the wage to be paid.

Such information should then be placed in the hands of the

subsistence farms and of the labor unions, so that the harvest does not become a great, disorganized gold rush with twice and three times as much labor applying as is needed.

It has long been the custom of the shipper-grower, the speculative farmer and the corporation farm to encourage twice as much labor to come to a community as could possibly be used. With an over-supply of labor, wages could be depressed below any decent standard. Such a suggested labor board (if it had a strong labor representation) would put a stop to such tactics.

Agricultural workers should be encouraged and helped to organize, both for their own protection, for the intelligent distribution of labor and for their self-government through the consideration of their own problems.

The same arguments are used against the organizing of agricultural labor as were used 60 years ago against the organizing of the craft and skilled labor unions. It was argued then that industry could not survive if labor were organized. It is argued today that agriculture cannot exist if farm labor is organized. It is reasonable to believe that agriculture would suffer no more from organization than industry has.

It is certain that until agricultural labor is organized, and until the farm laborer is represented in the centers where his wage is decided, wages will continue to be depressed and living conditions will grow increasingly impossible until from pain, hunger and despair the whole mass of labor will revolt.

The attorney-general, who has been given power in such matters, should investigate and trace to its source any outbreak of the vigilante terrorism which is the disgrace of California. Inspiration for such outbreaks is limited to a few individuals.

It should be as easy for an unbought investigation to hunt them down as it was for the Government to hunt down kidnapers. Since a government is its system of laws, and since armed vigilantism is an attempt to overthrow that system of laws and to substitute a government by violence, prosecution could be carried out on the grounds of guilt under the criminal syndicalism laws already on our statute books.

These laws have been used only against workers. Let them be equally used on the more deadly fascistic groups which preach and act the overthrow of our form of government by force of arms.

If these three suggestions could be carried out, a good part of the disgraceful condition of agricultural labor in California might be alleviated.

If, on the other hand, as has been stated by a large grower, our agriculture requires the creation and maintenance at any cost of a peon class, then it is submitted that California agriculture is economically unsound under a democracy.

And if the terrorism and reduction of human rights, the floggings, murder by deputies, kidnapings and refusal of trial by jury are necessary to our economic security, it is further submitted that California democracy is rapidly dwindling away. Fascistic methods are more numerous, more powerfully applied and more openly practiced in California than any other place in the United States.

It will require a militant and watchful organization of middle-class people, workers, teachers, craftsmen and liberals to fight this encroaching social philosophy, and to maintain this state in a democratic form of government.

The new migrants to California from the dust bowl are here to stay. They are of the best American stock, intelligent, resourceful; and, if given a chance, socially responsible.

To attempt to force them into a peonage of starvation and intimidated despair will be unsuccessful. They can be citizens of the highest type, or they can be an army driven by suffering and hatred to take what they need. On their future treatment will depend which course they will be forced to take.

The San Francisco News,
October 5–12, 1936

Starvation Under the Orange Trees

THE SPRING is rich and green in California this year. In the fields the wild grass is ten inches high, and in the orchards and vineyards the grass is deep and nearly ready to be plowed under to enrich the soil. Already the flowers are starting to bloom. Very shortly one of the oil companies will be broadcasting the locations of the wild-flower masses. It is a beautiful spring.

There has been no war in California, no plague, no bombing of open towns and roads, no shelling of cities. It is a beautiful year. And thousands of families are starving in California. In the county seats the coroners are filling in "malnutrition" in the spaces left for "causes of death." For some reason, a coroner shrinks from writing "starvation" when a thin child is dead in a tent.

For it's in the tents you see along the roads and in the shacks built from dump heap material that the hunger is, and it isn't malnutrition. It is starvation. Malnutrition means you go without certain food essentials and take a long time to die, but starvation means no food at all. The green grass spreading right into the tent doorways and the orange trees are loaded. In the cotton fields, a few wisps of the old crop cling to the black stems. But the people who picked the cotton, and cut the peaches and apricots, who crawled all day in the rows of lettuce and beans are hungry. The men who harvested the crops of California, the women and girls who stood all day and half the night in the canneries, are starving.

It was so two years ago in Nipomo, it is so now, it will continue to be so until the rich produce of California can be grown and harvested on some other basis than that of stupidity and greed.

What is to be done about it? The Federal Government is trying to feed and give direct relief, but it is difficult to do quickly for there are forms to fill out, quesions to ask, for fear someone who isn't actually starving may get something. The state relief organizations are trying to send those who haven't been in the state for a year back to the states they came from.

The Associated Farmers, which presumes to speak for the farms of California and which is made up of such earth stained toilers as chain banks, public utilities, railroad companies and those huge corporations called land companies, this financial organization in the face of the crisis is conducting Americanism meetings and bawling about reds and foreign agitators. It has been invariably true in the past that when such a close knit financial group as the Associated Farmers becomes excited about our ancient liberties and foreign agitators, some one is about to lose something.

A wage cut has invariably followed such a campaign of pure Americanism. And of course any resentment of such a wage cut is set down as the work of foreign agitators. Anyway that is the Associated Farmers contribution to the hunger of the men and women who harvest their crops.

The small farmers, who do not belong to the Associated Farmers and cannot make the use of the slop chest, are helpless to do anything about it. The little store keepers at cross roads and in small towns have carried the accounts of the working people until they are near to bankruptcy.

And there are one thousand families in Tulare County, and two thousand families in Kings, fifteen hundred families in Kern, and so on. The families average three persons, by the way. With the exception of a little pea picking, there isn't going to be any work for nearly three months.

There is sickness in the tents, pneumonia and measles, tuberculosis. Measles in a tent, with no way to protect the eyes, means a child with weakened eyes for life. And there are varied diseases attributable to hunger, rickets and the beginning of pellagra.

The nurses in the county, and there aren't one-tenth enough of them, are working their heads off, doing a magnificent job and they can only begin to do the work. The corps includes nurses assigned by the federal and state public health services, school nurses and county health nurses, and a few nurses furnished by the Council of Women for Home Missions, a national church organization. I've seen them, red-eyed, weary from far too many hours, and seeming to make no impression in the illness about them.

It may be of interest to reiterate the reasons why these people are in the state and the reason they must go hungry. They are here because we need them. Before the white American migrants were here, it was the custom in California to import great numbers of Mexicans, Filipinos, Japanese, to keep them segregated, to herd them about like animals, and, if there were any complaints, to deport or to imprison the leaders. This system of labor was a dream of heaven to such employers as those who now fear foreign agitators so much.

But then the dust and the tractors began displacing the sharecroppers of Oklahoma, Texas, Kansas and Arkansas. Families who had lived for many years on the little "cropper lands" were dispossessed because the land was in the hands of the banks and finance companies, and because these owners found that one man with a tractor could do the work of ten sharecropper families.

Faced with the question of starving or moving, these dispossessed families came west. To a certain extent they were actuated by advertisements and hand bills distributed by labor contractors from California. It is to the advantage of the corporate farmer to have too much labor, for then wages can be cut. Then people who are hungry will fight each other for a job rather than the employer for a living wage.

It is possible to make money for food and gasoline for at least nine months of the year if you are quick on the get away, if your wife and children work in the fields. But then the dead three months strikes, and what can you do then? The migrant cannot save anything. It takes everything he can make to feed his family and buy gasoline to go to the next job. If you don't believe this, go out in the cotton fields next year. Work all day and see if you have made thirty-five cents. A good picker makes more, of course, but you can't.

The method of concentrating labor for one of the great crops is this. Handbills are distributed, advertisements are printed. You've seen them. Cotton pickers wanted in Bakersfield or Fresno or Imperial Valley. Then all the available migrants rush to the scene. They arrive with no money and little food. The reserve has been spent getting there.

If wages happen to drop a little, they must take them anyway. The moment the crop is picked, the locals begin to try to get rid of the people who have harvested their crops. They want to run them out, move them on.

The county hospitals are closed to them. They are not eligible to relief. You must be eligible to eat. That particular locality is through with them until another crop comes in.

It will be remembered that two years ago some so-called agitators were tarred and feathered. The population of migrants left the locality just as the hops were ripe. Then the howling of the locals was terrible to hear. They even tried to get the army and the CCC ordered to pick their crops.

About the fifteenth of January the dead time sets in. There is no work. First the gasoline gives out. And without gasoline a man cannot go to a job even if he could get one. Then the food goes. And then in the rains, with insufficient food, the children develop colds because the ground in the tents is wet.

I talked to a man last week who lost two children in ten days with pneumonia. His face was hard and fierce and he didn't talk much.

I talked to a girl with a baby and offered her a cigaret. She took two puffs and vomited in the street. She was ashamed. She shouldn't have tried to smoke, she said, for she hadn't eaten for two days.

I heard a man whimpering that the baby was sucking but nothing came out of the breast. I heard a man explain very shyly that his little girl couldn't go to school because she was too weak to walk to school and besides the school lunches of the other children made her unhappy.

I heard a man tell in a monotone how he couldn't get a doctor while his oldest boy died of pneumonia but that a doctor came right away after it was dead. It is easy to get a doctor to look at a corpse, not so easy to get one for a live person. It is easy to get a body buried. A truck comes right out and takes it away. The state is much more interested in how you die than in how you live. The man who was telling about it had just found that out. He didn't want to believe it.

Next year the hunger will come again and the year after

that and so on until we come out of this coma and realize that our agriculture for all its great produce is a failure.

If you buy a farm horse and only feed him when you work him, the horse will die. No one complains of the necessity of feeding the horse when he is not working. But we complain about feeding the men and women who work our lands. Is it possible that this state is so stupid, so vicious and so greedy that it cannot feed and clothe the men and women who help to make it the richest area in the world? Must the hunger become anger and the anger fury before anything will be done?

Monterey Trader, April 15, 1938

CHRONOLOGY

NOTE ON THE TEXTS

NOTES

Chronology

1902   Born John Ernst Steinbeck on February 27 in Salinas, Cal-
        ifornia; the third child and only son (sisters are Esther,
        b. 1892, and Beth, b. 1894) of Olive Hamilton Steinbeck,
        a former schoolteacher, and John Ernst Steinbeck, mana-
        ger of a flour mill. (Paternal grandfather, John Adolph
        Grossteinbeck, a German cabinetmaker from Düsseldorf,
        moved to Jerusalem with his brother Frederic in 1854 and
        married Almira Dickson, daughter of Sarah Eldridge Dick-
        son and evangelist Walter Dickson, Americans who had
        gone to the Holy Land to convert the Jews. After Arab
        raiders killed Frederic and raped Sarah Dickson and her
        daughter, Mary, in 1858, John and Almira came to the
        United States, where they used the name Steinbeck. They
        settled in New England and then in Florida, where John
        Ernst Steinbeck was born, before moving to California af-
        ter the Civil War. Maternal grandfather, Samuel Hamilton,
        born in northern Ireland, immigrated to the United States
        at age 17 and settled in New York City, where he married
        Elizabeth Fagen, an American of northern Irish ancestry;
        they soon moved to California, where Hamilton home-
        steaded a ranch and was a skilled blacksmith.)

1903–9 Spends summers by the sea in Pacific Grove near Monterey
        and on uncle Tom Hamilton's ranch near King City. Sister
        Mary is born in 1905. Steinbeck enjoys roaming in fields
        and along seashore; from father learns to love gardening.
        Receives a red Shetland pony named Jill from family in
        1906, and cares for her himself. Home is full of books;
        parents and older sisters read out loud to him, and he
        becomes acquainted at an early age with novels of Robert
        Louis Stevenson and Walter Scott, the Bible, Greek myths,
        The Pilgrim's Progress, and *Paradise Lost*. Begins reading
        books himself and especially enjoys Sir Thomas Malory's
        Le Morte d'Arthur (later writes, "The Bible and Shake-
        speare and *Pilgrim's Progress* belonged to everyone. But
        this was mine—secretly mine . . . Perhaps a passionate
        love for the English language opened to me from this one
        book"). Attends public schools in Salinas; does well in
        school and skips fifth grade. Enjoys reading Mark Twain
        and Jack London. Often cared for by older sisters while
        mother takes active part in town affairs.

1910 When the mill is closed in Salinas, father decides against taking job offer with a company farther north because it would mean uprooting the family. Father opens a feed and grain store which fails, and works briefly as accountant for sugar refinery before being appointed treasurer of Monterey County (holds position, through continual reelection, until shortly before his death).

1918 In junior year of high school Steinbeck develops pleural pneumonia and nearly dies; nursed by mother on ranch farther south in Salinas Valley. Writes stories and reads them out loud to close friends.

1919–24 Graduates from Salinas High School. Begins sporadic attendance at Stanford University in October as an English major. Meets Carlton "Dook" Sheffield and Carl Wilhelmson, who become lifelong friends. In spring 1920 undergoes operation for acute appendicitis. After working as surveyor in mountains above Big Sur, works in the summer as carpenter's helper at Spreckels Sugar Mill (continues to work over the next several years at the mill and on its many sugar beet ranches, where his duties include running chemical tests on sugar beets and supervising day laborers). Returns to Stanford full-time in January 1923; studies English versification with William Herbert Carruth in spring 1923, and enrolls for summer study at Stanford-affiliated Hopkins Marine Station in Pacific Grove, where he takes courses in English and zoology. Studies creative writing with Edith Mirrielees at Stanford for two terms in 1924. Influenced by philosophy lectures of Harold Chapman Brown. Publishes stories "Fingers of Cloud: A Satire on College Protervity" and "Adventures in Arcademy: A Journey into the Ridiculous" in the February and June issues of *The Stanford Spectator*, student literary magazine.

1925–26 Leaves Stanford without a degree in June 1925, having completed less than three years of coursework. After working during the summer as caretaker of a lodge near Lake Tahoe, sails on a freighter by way of the Panama Canal to New York City. Settles in Brooklyn (moves to Gramercy Park area of Manhattan in 1926). Works as laborer on the construction of Madison Square Garden and as reporter for the *New York American*. Submits short stories to Robert M. McBride & Company, New York publishing firm, which rejects them. Returns to California by freighter in summer 1926, working as assistant steward in return for passage. Hired in the fall to work as caretaker of Lake Tahoe estate of Mrs. Alice Brigham.

1927   Lives alone on Brigham estate during winter. Story "The Gifts of Iban" appears in *The Smoker's Companion* in March under pseudonym "John Stern." Works with close friend Webster (Toby) Street on Street's play "The Green Lady" (material becomes the basis for *To a God Unknown*).

1928   Finishes first novel, *Cup of Gold*, in January. Leaves care-taker job in May and begins work at fish hatchery in Tahoe City in June. Meets Carol Henning, a tourist visiting the hatchery, during summer. Fired from hatchery job for wrecking superintendent's truck. In September moves to San Francisco, where he lives in "a dark little attic" on Powell Street and gets job as warehouse worker for com-pany owned by sister Mary's husband, Bill Dekker.

1929   With help of college acquaintance Amasa (Ted) Miller, *Cup of Gold* is accepted for publication by Robert M. McBride. Gives up warehouse job and with father's finan-cial help spends most of year writing in Pacific Grove and Palo Alto (father frequently sends money during the next several years). *Cup of Gold* published in August. Moves back to San Francisco in the fall and shares an apartment with Carl Wilhelmson.

1930   Marries Carol Henning in January. They stay briefly with Dook Sheffield and his wife in Eagle Rock, near Los An-geles, and then, successively, in a shack and two rented houses in the vicinity, before moving in September to family's three-room cottage in Pacific Grove where they live rent-free and feed themselves in part through fish-ing and raising vegetables. Manuscript of *To a God Un-known* rejected by Robert M. McBride. Meets marine biologist Edward F. Ricketts, owner of Pacific Biological Laboratory, who becomes close friend and major intel-lectual influence. Writes experimental novella "Dissonant Symphony" and, under pseudonym Peter Pym, crime novel "Murder at Full Moon"; neither is accepted for pub-lication, and he later destroys manuscript of "Dissonant Symphony."

1931   Works on series of related stories, *The Pastures of Heaven*.
            Begins lifelong association with New York literary agency
            McIntosh & Otis (agent Elizabeth Otis becomes close
            friend).

1932   *The Pastures of Heaven* accepted for publication by Cape
            and Smith in February. Through Ricketts, becomes ac-
            quainted with religious scholar Joseph Campbell. Carol
            works part-time as bookkeeper-secretary at Ricketts' lab-
            oratory in spring and summer; after she loses job because
            Ricketts cannot afford to pay her, Steinbeck and Carol
            move to Montrose area, north of Eagle Rock, staying with
            the Sheffields until they find a house to rent. Following
            bankruptcy of Cape and Smith, *The Pastures of Heaven*
            published by Brewer, Warren, and Putnam (where Cape
            and Smith editor Robert O. Ballou had moved).

1933   Despite father's financial help, Steinbeck and Carol are un-
            able to make ends meet and are forced in February to give
            up the Montrose house. Mother becomes seriously ill in
            March, and after being hospitalized, suffers massive stroke;
            Steinbeck and Carol move to family home in Salinas.
            Steinbeck spends most of his time taking care of his
            mother at hospital and, after her release in June, at home.
            Writes the first of the four stories later joined together as
            The Red Pony. Father collapses in August and remains in-
            capacitated for nearly a year; cared for by Carol at Pacific
            Grove cottage while Steinbeck spends much time in Sali-
            nas caring for mother. *To a God Unknown* published in
            September by Robert O. Ballou under his own imprint.
            During summer and fall completes first draft of *Tortilla
            Flat*, partly based on anecdotes told to him by Susan Gre-
            gory, a high school Spanish teacher in Monterey. Meets
            journalist Lincoln Steffens and his wife, Ella Winter, who
            are living in Carmel (continues to visit them until Steffens'
            death in 1936). "The Red Pony" (later titled "The Gift")
            and "The Great Mountains" appear in *North American
            Review*, November–December (both later become part of
            The Red Pony).

1934   Mother dies in February. Steinbeck and Carol live with
            father in Pacific Grove cottage, until arrangements are
            made for father to move back into Salinas home with care-
            takers in March. Steinbeck meets fugitive labor organizers

Cicil McKiddy and Carl Williams in Seaside, California; interviews them about their involvement with 1933 cotton workers' strike in the San Joaquin Valley, organized by Communist-led Cannery and Agricultural Workers' Industrial Union, and about strike leader Pat Chambers. Manuscript of *Tortilla Flat* rejected by Robert O. Ballou and by Louis Kronenberger at Knopf. During summer completes nine short stories, eight of which are later collected in *The Long Valley*. Begins writing *In Dubious Battle*, based in part on interviews with McKiddy and Williams, in August. *Tortilla Flat* is accepted for publication by Pascal Covici of Covici-Friede. Enunciates "aggregation" theory of groups in unpublished essay "Argument of Phalanx": "Men are not final individuals but units in the greater beast, the phalanx . . . The nature of the phalanx is not the sum of the natures of unit-men, but a new individual having emotions and ends of its own, and these are foreign and incomprehensible to unit-men."

1935   *In Dubious Battle* accepted by Covici-Friede. Father dies in May. *Tortilla Flat*, published in May, becomes Steinbeck's first commercially successful book. Forms friendship with Joseph Henry Jackson, book reviewer for *San Francisco Chronicle*. Meets Pascal Covici for the first time in August. With royalties from *Tortilla Flat*, travels with Carol to Mexico in September; they rent an apartment in Mexico City (writes to friend: "This well of just pure life is charging us up again"). Meets painter Diego Rivera. Learns that film rights for *Tortilla Flat* have been sold to Paramount for $4,000. Returns to United States at year's end, traveling to New York to sign Paramount contract and then to Pacific Grove before Christmas.

1936   *In Dubious Battle* published by Covici-Friede in January. Begins work on children's book (project eventually leads him to write *Of Mice and Men*); much of manuscript is destroyed by his dog in May. Visited by John O'Hara, who had contracted to write a dramatic adaptation (eventually abandoned) of *In Dubious Battle*; O'Hara becomes lifelong friend. In May begins to build house in Los Gatos, north of Monterey. Goes on six-day trip with Ricketts collecting octopuses along Baja California coast. Moves into Los Gatos house, completed at end of July. Completes *Of Mice and Men* in August. Commissioned by *San Francisco*

News to write articles on migrant farm workers; after meeting with federal officials at Resettlement Administration in San Francisco, tours San Joaquin Valley in bakery truck, accompanied by former preacher Eric H. Thomsen, regional director of federal migrant camp program. At Arvin Sanitary Camp ("Weedpatch") in Kern County, meets camp director Tom Collins, and from his conversation and written reports on migrant workers gathers material later incorporated into *The Grapes of Wrath*. Articles published as "The Harvest Gypsies" in seven installments in October. Begins researching and writing novel about migrants (later referred to as "The Oklahomans"). Limited editions of *Nothing So Monstrous* (excerpt from *The Pastures of Heaven*, with a new epilogue) and *Saint Katy the Virgin* published by Covici-Friede.

1937 *Of Mice and Men* published in March; becomes a bestseller and Book-of-the-Month Club selection. Sails in March with Carol through Panama Canal to Philadelphia; after two-and-a-half-week stay in New York, they travel to Denmark, Sweden, Finland, and the Soviet Union, returning to New York in July. Works with director George S. Kaufman on dramatic adaptation of *Of Mice and Men*. Visits Farm Security Administration office in Washington, D.C., and talks with deputy administrator Dr. Will Alexander. Stories "The Promise," "The Gift," and "The Great Mountains" published as *The Red Pony* in a limited edition by Covici-Friede. Travels in California in October doing research on migrants; joined at migrant camp in Gridley by Tom Collins, who accompanies him on rest of trip. *Of Mice and Men* opens on Broadway November 23, starring Wallace Ford and Broderick Crawford; it runs for 207 performances (Steinbeck never sees the production).

1938 Dramatic adaptation of *Tortilla Flat* by Jack Kirkland opens on Broadway in January (closes after four performances). Meets documentary filmmaker Pare Lorentz. Makes two trips to San Joaquin Valley in February and March, where he joins Tom Collins in investigating condition of migrant workers in the wake of devastating floods in Visalia. Article based on trips is rejected by *Life*. Invited by Lorentz, travels to Hollywood where he meets film directors King Vidor, Lewis Milestone, and Mervyn Le Roy and actor James Cagney. Article published in April as

"Starvation Under the Orange Trees" in the *Monterey Trader*. *Their Blood Is Strong*, expanded version of "The Harvest Gypsies," published as pamphlet by Simon J. Lubin Society of California to raise money for migrant workers. In May abandons unfinished satirical novel ("L'Affaire Lettuceberg") about vigilantes, suggested by brutal Salinas lettuce strike of September 1936. Learns that *Of Mice and Men* has won the New York Drama Critics' Circle Award as best play of 1937. In late May begins 100-day period of work on novel that becomes *The Grapes of Wrath*. Keeps journal of novel's composition (published posthumously in 1989 as *Working Days*); of the title, suggested by Carol, Steinbeck writes: "I like it because it is a march and this book is a kind of march—because it is in our own revolutionary tradition and because in reference to this book it has a large meaning." Visited unexpectedly by Charlie Chaplin, who is living in Pebble Beach, near Carmel, and they establish friendship. Purchases 47-acre ranch (the "Old Biddle Ranch") outside Los Gatos; begins construction of new house on property in September. In July, Covici-Friede goes bankrupt and Pascal Covici joins Viking Press as senior editor; short story collection *The Long Valley* is published by Viking in September and sells well. (Viking becomes the publisher of all of Steinbeck's subsequent books.) Physically exhausted, completes manuscript of *The Grapes of Wrath* in November.

1939   Suffers for most of the year from sometimes crippling leg pain. Elizabeth Otis, his agent, urges him to make changes in the language of *The Grapes of Wrath*; during two days of intensive work agrees to some revisions. Later writes to Covici, "This book wasn't written for delicate ladies. If they read it at all they're messing in something not their business. I've never changed a word to fit the prejudices of a group and I never will." Argues further with Covici over proposal to change the novel's ending: "You know that I have never been touchy about changes, but I have too many thousands of hours on this book, every incident has been too carefully chosen and its weight judged and fitted. The balance is there. One other thing—I am not writing a satisfying story. I've done my damndest to rip a reader's nerves to rags, I don't want him satisfied." In March hears rumor that he is being investigated by the FBI; worries about possible violence against him by Associated Farmers organization. *The Grapes of Wrath*, published in April by Viking with large advance sale, becomes the number one national bestseller; screen rights are sold for $75,000. Novel is banned or burned in Buffalo, New York, East St. Louis, Illinois, and Kern County, California, is denounced in Congress by Oklahoma representative Lyle Boren, and is the subject of a protest meeting at the Palace Hotel in San Francisco. Steinbeck is overwhelmed by flood of public attention and correspondence. Travels to Chicago in April to work with Pare Lorentz on *The Fight for Life*, documentary about Chicago Maternity Center. Rents apartment in Hollywood in June. Through old friend Max Wagner, now working in Hollywood, meets singer Gwendolyn ("Gwyn") Conger, and begins affair with her. Forms friendships with songwriter Frank Loesser and his wife, Lynn Loesser, actor Burgess Meredith, Nunnally Johnson (screenwriter for *The Grapes of Wrath*), and writer Robert Benchley. Difficulties with Carol lead to temporary separation; they reconcile and go on car trip in Pacific Northwest, visiting Vancouver in company with composer John Cage and his wife, Xenia. Travels with Carol in September to Chicago, visiting Lorentz and science writer Paul de Kruif in connection with *The Fight for Life*. Plans to devote himself to study of science and to write science textbooks in collaboration with Ricketts; spends much time at Ricketts' laboratory, and makes marine collecting trips with him in San Francisco Bay area. In December sees previews of John Ford's film version of *The Grapes of Wrath* ("No punches were pulled—in fact . . . it is a harsher thing than the book") and Lewis Milestone's film of *Of Mice and Men* ("Milestone has done a curious lyrical thing. It hangs together and is underplayed").

1940   In March, embarks with Ricketts, Carol, and small crew on marine collecting expedition in Gulf of California on boat *Western Flyer*, returning to Monterey April 20. Writes Eleanor Roosevelt, thanking her for remarking after her visit to a migrant workers camp in April that she had "never believed that *The Grapes of Wrath* was exaggerated." Wins Pulitzer Prize for *The Grapes of Wrath* (gives prize money to friend Ritchie Lovejoy to enable him to complete a novel). Impressed by singer Woody Guthrie, who records "The Ballad of Tom Joad," based on *The*

Grapes of Wrath. Travels with Carol to Mexico in May to work on script for *The Forgotten Village*, an independent feature film produced and directed by Herbert Kline, about the struggle to bring modern medicine to a remote village. Meets with Lewis Milestone in Hollywood about film version of *The Red Pony.* Disturbed by influence of German propaganda in Latin America, writes to President Franklin D. Roosevelt, who receives him for brief visit in which Steinbeck proposes the formation of a propaganda office focusing on the Western Hemisphere. Visits Roosevelt again in September and proposes scheme to undermine Axis powers by distributing counterfeit German money in occupied countries of Europe. Takes flying lessons. Returns to Mexico in October to work on *The Forgotten Village.*

1941   Buys small house on Eardley Street in Monterey. Tells Carol in April about affair with Gwyn Conger. Separates from Carol at end of April; lives in Eardley Street house. *The Forgotten Village,* book version of film script, illustrated with stills, published in May. Works on book about Gulf of California trip, describing it to Pascal Covici as "a new kind of writing," and completes manuscript in July. Sells Los Gatos ranch at end of August. Works on screenplay for *The Red Pony.* In autumn moves to East Coast with Gwyn; they stay in a house on Burgess Meredith's farm in Suffern, New York, before moving in November into Bedford Hotel in Manhattan. Writes radio speeches for Foreign Information Service under direction of Robert E. Sherwood; travels frequently between New York and Washington. *Sea of Cortez: A Leisurely Journey of Travel and Research,* narrative by Steinbeck with a detailed scientific appendix by Ricketts, published in December. Film of *The Forgotten Village* banned for indecency by New York State Board of Censors because of scenes of childbirth and breast-feeding (ban lifted after public hearing).

1942   *The Moon Is Down,* set in occupied Norway, published in March; opens as play on Broadway in April. Moves into rented house at Sneden's Landing in Rockland County, New York, in April. Becomes friendly with playwright Maxwell Anderson, singer Burl Ives, and radio comedian Fred Allen. Sells film rights to *The Moon Is Down.* Appointed special consultant to the Secretary of War and accepts assignment from the Army Air Forces to write book about the training of bomber crews. Visits 20 air bases across the United States with photographer John Swope; their work is published as *Bombs Away: The Story of a Bomber Team*. Rents house in Sherman Oaks, California, in September to work on film based on *Bombs Away*, but production is plagued by difficulties and film is never made. With old friend Jack Wagner (brother of Max Wagner), writes script for film *A Medal for Benny*. Film of *Tortilla Flat*, directed by Victor Fleming and starring Spencer Tracy, released.

1943   Writes novella (unpublished) as basis for film *Lifeboat*, directed by Alfred Hitchcock. Moves into apartment on East 51st Street in New York City with Gwyn. Divorce from Carol becomes final on March 18. Marries Gwyn on March 29 in New Orleans. Accredited as war correspondent for New York *Herald Tribune*, following intensive security investigation by army counterintelligence. Travels to England on troop ship in June; meets photographer Robert Capa, renews acquaintance with foreign correspondent William L. Shirer, and spends time with Burgess Meredith. Receives clearance in early August to go to North Africa; travels in Algeria and Tunisia, writing reports and working on an army film project. Sails on PT boat from Tunisia to Sicily as part of special operations unit commanded by actor Douglas Fairbanks Jr. that carries out coastal raids designed to harass and mislead the Germans. Reports from Salerno beachhead in Italy in mid-September. Rejoins Fairbanks' unit and participates in operations, including capture of Italian island of Ventotene. After a few weeks in London returns to New York City in early October, suffering from effects of combat, including burst eardrums and partial amnesia. Begins *Cannery Row* in November. *The Portable Steinbeck*, edited by Pascal Covici, published by Viking Press. Film of *The Moon Is Down*, directed by Irving Pichel, released.

1944   Sees screening of Hitchcock's *Lifeboat*; angered by changes in his original story and tries unsuccessfully to have his name removed from the credits. Travels with Gwyn to Mexico by way of Chicago and New Orleans in mid-January. Begins to develop film project *The Pearl* (based on Mexican folktale briefly recounted in *Sea of Cortez*), to be directed by Emilio Fernandez. Returns to New York in March. Has busy social life with friends, including Robert Capa and John O'Hara; meets Ernest Hemingway but is dismayed by his boorish behavior. Discusses plans for a musical comedy, "The Wizard of Maine," with Frank Loesser. Receives Academy Award nomination for best original story for *Lifeboat*. Finishes *Cannery Row* in July, with central character modeled on Ricketts. Writes to Dook Sheffield about the book: "One thing—it never mentions the war—not once . . . The crap I wrote over seas had a profoundly nauseating effect on me. Among other unpleasant things modern war is the most dishonest thing imaginable." Son Thom born August 2. In October moves back to California, settling in Soto House, large 19th-century adobe house near waterfront in Monterey.

1945   *Cannery Row* published; it sells well despite poor reviews. Completes draft of novella *The Pearl* and goes to Mexico with Gwyn in February to work with Fernandez on the film; they return in mid-March. Troubled by resentment he has experienced in Monterey, writes to Covici: "You remember how happy I was to come back here. It really was a home coming. Well there is no home coming nor any welcome. What there is is jealousy and hatred and the knife in the back . . . Our old friends won't have us back . . . And the town and the region—that is the people of it—just pure poison." Returns to Mexico in April with Jack Wagner, followed by Gwyn and Thom; works on shooting script for *The Pearl* in luxurious rented house in Cuernavaca. Does research in Mexican archives for proposed film about Emiliano Zapata. With Jack Wagner, receives Academy Award nomination for best original story for *A Medal for Benny* (directed by Irving Pichel). Begins to work on *The Wayward Bus*. Gwyn leaves Mexico for New York because of ill health; Steinbeck visits her there for over a month, then returns to Cuernavaca in October for filming of *The Pearl*. Having sold Monterey house, Steinbeck and Gwyn buy pair of adjacent brownstones on East 78th Street in New York City; he drives back to New York in early December.

1946   Settles into new home. (Rents out second brownstone to Nathaniel Benchley and wife, Marjorie, who become close friends of Steinbeck and Gwyn.) Son John born June 12. After difficult pregnancy, Gwyn continues to be in poor health. Steinbeck returns to Mexico in August for further work on film of *The Pearl*. After finishing *The Wayward Bus*, sails to Europe with Gwyn in October, visiting Sweden, Denmark, Norway, and France. Awarded King Haakon Liberty Cross in Norway for *The Moon Is Down*.

1947 Works on play "The Last Joan" (abandoned by April). *The Wayward Bus* published in February. Amid marital difficulties Gwyn goes to California for a month. With Robert Capa, Steinbeck plans trip to Russia for the New York *Herald Tribune*. Hospitalized after seriously injuring knee and foot when second-story railing in apartment breaks. Still walking with a cane, travels to France in June with Gwyn and Capa; after Gwyn returns home in July, goes on with Capa for brief stay in Sweden before proceeding to Soviet Union; visits Moscow, Stalingrad, Ukraine, and Georgia; returns by way of Prague and Budapest. Begins research for novel *The Salinas Valley* (later *East of Eden*). *The Pearl* published in November.

1948 Invests in World Video, television venture which collapses after a few months. Film of *The Pearl* released in the United States. Goes to Monterey for several weeks in February to research *East of Eden*. *A Russian Journal*, with text by Steinbeck and photographs by Capa, published in April. Hospitalized in April for removal of varicose veins. Ed Ricketts is severely injured in automobile accident on May 7 and dies on May 11; Steinbeck writes to friend Bo Beskow, "there died the greatest man I have known and the best teacher. It is going to take a long time to reorganize my thinking and my planning without him." After returning from funeral in Monterey, is told by Gwyn that she wants a divorce; moves into Bedford Hotel. Spends much of summer in Mexico, researching screenplay for *Viva Zapata!*, to be directed by Elia Kazan. Returns to California in September, settling again in Pacific Grove house. Divorce becomes final in October. Devotes himself to gardening and home repairs; drinks heavily, and suffers from deep depression. Travels to Mexico in November with Kazan. Learns in December that he has been elected to the American Academy of Arts and Letters.

1949   Film of *The Red Pony*, directed by Lewis Milestone and
        with screenplay by Steinbeck, released. Returns briefly to
        Mexico in February. Over Memorial Day weekend meets
        Elaine Scott, wife of actor Zachary Scott; sees her fre-
        quently thereafter while working in Hollywood on *Zapata*
        screenplay. Sons come to stay for two months in summer,
        first in series of annual visits mandated by custody agree-
        ment. Begins work on *Everyman* (later *Burning Bright*),
        play in novella form. Finishes draft of *Viva Zapata!* screen-
        play. Elaine Scott files for divorce; Steinbeck moves to
        New York City and Elaine joins him there with her daugh-
        ter Waverly; they settle in large apartment on East 52nd
        Street.

1950   Finishes *Burning Bright* in January. Leads active social life,
        meeting Elaine's many friends in the theater (she had pre-
        viously worked as stage manager and in casting for the
        Theatre Guild and as stage manager for the original pro-
        duction of *Oklahoma!*). In February works with Kazan in
        Los Angeles on *Zapata*. Travels with Elaine to Texas in
        the spring to meet her family in Fort Worth (her father,
        Waverly Anderson, is a prominent oilman). Rents house
        for summer in Rockland County, near Burgess Meredith,
        Maxwell Anderson, and cartoonist Bill Mauldin. *Burning
        Bright*, produced by Richard Rodgers and Oscar Ham-
        merstein II and starring Kent Smith and Barbara Bel Ged-
        des, opens on Broadway in October to generally poor
        reviews; novel version published in November. Resumes
        work on *East of Eden*. Marries Elaine on December 28,
        and they honeymoon in Bermuda.

1951   Writes in *East of Eden* journal addressed to Pascal Covici:
        "The form will not be startling, the writing will be spare
        and lean, the concepts hard, the philosophy old and yet
        new born. In a sense it will be two books—the story of
        my county and the story of me." Steinbeck and Elaine
        move in February into brownstone on East 72nd Street
        (their home for the next 13 years). Summers in Nantucket
        with Elaine and sons. *The Log from the Sea of Cortez*, edi-
        tion of the narrative portion of *Sea of Cortez*, with new
        introductory memoir "About Ed Ricketts," published in
        September. Completes draft of *East of Eden* in November.

1952   Renews acquaintance with playwright Arthur Miller, with
            whom he forms close friendship. *Viva Zapata!* released.
            Travels from March to September in Morocco, Algeria,
            Spain, France, Switzerland, Italy, England, Scotland, and
            Ireland, writing articles for *Collier's*, with Elaine collabo-
            rating as photographer. Attacked by Italian Communist
            newspaper *L'Unità* while in Rome for failure to denounce
            U.S. policy in Korea, and writes lengthy retort (incident
            recounted in *Collier's* article "Duel Without Pistols").
            East of Eden is published in September; receives mixed
            reviews but sells well. Writes and delivers on-camera intro-
            duction to omnibus film *O. Henry's Full House*. Writes
            speeches for supporters of Adlai Stevenson's presidential
            campaign.

1953   Travels with Elaine and writer Barnaby Conrad to the Vir-
            gin Islands, for first of nine annual Caribbean vacations.
            Receives Academy Award nominations for best story and
            best screenplay for *Viva Zapata!* Collaborates with Cy
            Feuer and Ernest Martin, who are to produce musical *Bear
            Flag*, a continuation of *Cannery Row*; works on novel de-
            rived from idea for the musical, later titled *Sweet Thursday*.
            In September rents cottage in Sag Harbor, Long Island,
            where he consults with neighbor Ernest Martin on prog-
            ress of musical. Suffers from depression and consults psy-
            chologist Gertrudis Brenner.

1954   During Virgin Islands vacation enjoys company of econ-
            omist John Kenneth Galbraith and his wife, Catherine.
            Richard Rodgers and Oscar Hammerstein take over both
            writing and production of *Bear Flag* (now titled *Pipe
            Dream*). Sails with Elaine to Europe in March; they travel
            in Portugal and Spain, and in May begin four-month stay
            in Paris; suffers minor stroke on his way to Paris. Shocked
            by news that Robert Capa has been killed by a land mine
            in Vietnam. *Sweet Thursday* published in June. Travels to
            Munich to visit facilities of Radio Free Europe; writes
            statement on freedom of expression for broadcast behind
            the Iron Curtain. Writes weekly articles for literary sup-
            plement of *Le Figaro*; honored at dinner given by the Aca-
            démie Française. Leaves Paris in September to travel in
            England (where he meets editor Malcolm Muggeridge
            and agrees to contribute occasional pieces to *Punch*),

southern France, Italy, and Greece; returns with Elaine to America in December on the *Andrea Doria*.

1955   Invites William Faulkner to dinner in New York, but Faulkner drinks heavily and is uncommunicative (later they become friendly). Buys house in Sag Harbor, Long Island. Film of *East of Eden*, directed by Elia Kazan, with screenplay by Paul Osborn based on the novel's final segment, opens in March. Joins staff of *Saturday Review* as "Editor-at-Large" (contributes 17 articles and editorials by 1960). *Pipe Dream* opens on Broadway in September.

1956   Flies with Elaine to Trinidad in January. Covers Democratic and Republican political conventions in Chicago and San Francisco for Louisville *Courier-Journal* and its syndicated papers. Meets Adlai Stevenson, who becomes close friend; again contributes speech material to Stevenson campaign. Beginning in November serves on writers' committee (chaired by William Faulkner) of government-sponsored People to People program. Finishes comic novel *The Short Reign of Pippin IV* in November. Begins version of Sir Thomas Malory's *Morte d'Arthur* in modern English (never completed; it is published posthumously in 1976 as *The Acts of King Arthur and His Noble Knights*). Collection of essays in French written for *Le Figaro Littéraire* and other magazines published in Paris as *Un Américain à New York et à Paris*.

1957   Reads Malory intensively; does medieval research in Morgan Library in New York, assisted and advised by bookstore manager Chase Horton. Writes defense of Arthur Miller, then standing trial for contempt of Congress as a result of House Un-American Activities Committee investigation: "The Congress is truly on trial along with Arthur Miller . . . I feel profoundly that our country is better served by individual courage and morals than by the safe and public patriotism which Dr. Johnson called 'the last refuge of scoundrels.' " Sails in March to Italy with Elaine and sister Mary Dekker, partly under auspices of United States Information Agency, staying mostly in Florence and Rome. Continues Arthurian research, including investigation of Thomas Malory's life. Writes about the trip for Louisville *Courier-Journal*. *The Short Reign of Pippin IV* published in April. After leaving Italy, travels in France,

England, Denmark, and Sweden. Meets leading Malory scholar Eugène Vinaver in Manchester, England, and sees Dag Hammarskjöld and Soviet novelist Mikhail Sholokhov in Stockholm. Flies to Tokyo in September with John Hersey and John Dos Passos to attend P.E.N. conference; becomes ill with severe influenza shortly after arrival.

1958   Travels to the Bahamas with Burgess Meredith and others as part of unsuccessful treasure salvage project. Spends June in England with Elaine. Sees Vinaver again and meets playwright Robert Bolt; continues Malory research. Works on novella "Don Keehan," based on *Don Quixote* (eventually abandoned). *Once There Was a War*, collection of war dispatches from 1943, published in September.

1959   Sails with Elaine to England in February; meets novelist Erskine Caldwell on board ship. Spends next eight months in rented cottage near Bruton, Somerset. Works on Malory project. Discouraged by unsympathetic response of Elizabeth Otis and Chase Horton to Malory book. In August goes on motor trip through Wales. Returns to United States in October. Suffers an undiagnosed attack (possibly from a small stroke) and is briefly hospitalized. Letter to Adlai Stevenson on destructive aspects of American affluence creates controversy when it is published in the press ("If I wanted to destroy a nation, I would give it too much, and I would have it on its knees, miserable, greedy, and sick").

1960   Puts aside Malory book, intending to return to it later. Begins novel eventually titled *The Winter of Our Discontent* in March; completes first draft in mid-July. Becomes involved in unsuccessful effort to draft Adlai Stevenson for Democratic presidential nomination. In September sets out on eleven-week journey ("Operation Windmills") with dog Charley across America, in pick-up truck he names Rocinante. Travels through New England, the Great Lakes region, and the Dakotas to the West Coast, where he is joined temporarily by Elaine in Seattle, then returns to New York by way of California, Texas, and Louisiana.

1961   Attends inauguration of President John F. Kennedy. Continues working on *Travels with Charley*, account of his cross-country journey, in February during vacation on Barbados. Sons Thom and John move in permanently with Steinbeck and Elaine because of difficulties with Gwyn. Accompanies Mohole expedition off the Mexican coast and writes account that appears in *Life* in April (project attempted to drill hole through the oceanic crust into the earth's mantle). *The Winter of Our Discontent* published in spring; Steinbeck is depressed by reviews, "even the favorable ones." In September begins ten-month stay in Europe with wife, sons, and their tutor, future playwright Terrence McNally. On arrival in London shocked by news of death of Dag Hammarskjöld in plane crash. Tours England, Wales, and Scotland in rented car, and after brief stay in Paris continues on through southern France to Italy; in Milan, at end of November, suffers attack (either a small stroke or heart attack). Family spends Christmas in Rome.

1962   Stays on Capri with Elaine, recuperating for several months, while sons travel with McNally. Pays tribute to his Stanford creative writing teacher Edith Mirrielees in preface to Viking reissue of her book *Story Writing*. Resumes travels in Italy and Greece in April; gives speech to Greek students at American College in Athens. *Travels with Charley in Search of America* published in midsummer. Through McNally meets playwright Edward Albee, with whom he forms friendship. Learns on October 25 that he has won Nobel Prize for Literature. Writes to Swedish friend Bo Beskow: "I suppose you know of the attack on the award to me not only by Time Magazine with which I have had a long-time feud but also from the cutglass critics, that grey priesthood which defines literature and has little to do with reading. They have never liked me and now are really beside themselves with rage." Travels to Stockholm for award ceremonies; makes short visit to London.

1963   Attends honorary dinner in New York for longtime friend Carl Sandburg in January. Moves with Elaine out of brownstone into high-rise apartment on same block in March. Dog Charley dies in April. Undergoes surgery for detached retina in June; while recuperating in hospital, visited regularly and read to by John O'Hara. At the suggestion of President Kennedy, makes two-month cultural exchange visit to Eastern Europe; in October travels with

Elaine to Finland, the Soviet Union (including visits to Ukraine, Armenia, and Georgia), Poland, Austria, Hungary, Czechoslovakia, and West Germany. Tour joined (as Steinbeck had requested) by Edward Albee in Moscow. Steinbeck publicly protests pirating of Western books in the Soviet Union; sees Soviet writers including Ilya Ehrenburg, Victor Nekrasov, and Yevgeny Yevtushenko, and visits grave of Boris Pasternak despite official interference. Spends time with Erskine Caldwell, also staying in Moscow. Learns in Warsaw of assassination of President Kennedy. In West Berlin meets German writers Günter Grass and Uwe Johnson. Travels with Elaine to Washington in December for State Department debriefing; they attend private dinner with President Lyndon Johnson and Lady Bird Johnson (Elaine had known Lady Bird at University of Texas), establishing friendship.

1964   Asked by Jacqueline Kennedy to write book about John F. Kennedy; has long correspondence with her, but declines project. Estranged from sons, who return to live with Gwyn and bring suit with her for additional child support (large increase denied by New York Family Court in April). Spends Easter in Rome with Elaine. Begins work on text originally designed to accompany collection of photographs of America (eventually published as essay collection *America and Americans*). Helps write Lyndon Johnson's speech accepting the Democratic presidential nomination. Receives Presidential Medal of Freedom in September. Resumes work on Malory book. Pascal Covici dies October 14; Steinbeck speaks at memorial service along with Arthur Miller and Saul Bellow. Attends reunion with relatives in Watsonville, California. Works on President Johnson's inaugural address. Spends Christmas in County Galway, Ireland, with film director John Huston.

1965   Spends several weeks in London and Paris in early January; in Paris learns of sister Mary Dekker's death. Asked by President Johnson to make trip to Vietnam as special emissary, but declines. Writes to Elizabeth Otis proposing publication of journal written during composition of *East of Eden* (published posthumously in 1969 as *Journal of a Novel*). Begins regular column for *Newsday* (it runs, with some interruptions, from November 1965 to May 1967).

Travels with Elaine to England in December; accompanied by Eugène Vinaver and his wife on tour of libraries in northern England. Spends Christmas with John Huston in Ireland.

1966   Travels with Elaine to Israel in February for *Newsday*, visits graves of relatives there. Appointed by President Johnson to council of the National Endowment for the Arts in April. *America and Americans* published. Son John finishes basic training and asks father's help in getting assigned to serve with American forces in Vietnam; Steinbeck writes, "I was horrified when you asked me to get you orders to go out, but I couldn't have failed you there . . . But if I had had to request that you *not* be sent, I think I would have been far more unhappy." Writes to Lyndon Johnson in May in support of his Vietnam policy. After *The New York Times* publishes poem by Yevtushenko attacking Steinbeck's failure to oppose the Vietnam War, Steinbeck writes public letter describing war as "Chinese-inspired" and criticizing the Soviet Union for arming North Vietnam. Makes unsuccessful attempt to start new novel, "A Piece of It Fell on My Tail." Sees Yevtushenko, who is on reading tour of America, in November; they are partially reconciled. In December goes to Southeast Asia as reporter for *Newsday* with Elaine; met in Saigon by son John. Over six-week period tours wide area of South Vietnam, frequently going on combat missions and reporting sympathetically on American war effort.

1967   Visits Thailand, Laos, Indonesia, Hong Kong, where he suffers slipped disk, and Japan; returns home in April. Spends weekend at White House in May, and at President Johnson's request discusses his journey with Vice-President Hubert Humphrey, Secretary of State Dean Rusk, and Secretary of Defense Robert McNamara. Suffers debilitating pain as a result of back injury, and in October enters hospital for surgery. While awaiting operation, learns of son John's arrest in Washington, D.C., in connection with marijuana found in his apartment; John visits his father in hospital, but rejects offer of legal assistance. (While still in the army, John had written a magazine article about widespread marijuana use among soldiers in Vietnam; following his arrest, his comments on the subject are given wide press exposure; he is acquitted of the drug charge in mid-December.) Steinbeck undergoes successful back operation and spinal fusion on October 23; released from hospital in early December. Flies to Grenada with Elaine for Christmas.

1968   After a month in Grenada, recuperates in New York apartment. Goes to Sag Harbor in spring. Suffers minor stroke on Memorial Day weekend in Sag Harbor, followed by heart attack later in July. Enters New York Hospital July 17, and suffers another heart attack while there. Leaves hospital and returns to Sag Harbor in August. Writes to Elizabeth Otis: "I am pretty sure by now that the people running the war have neither conception nor control of it . . . I know we cannot win this war, nor any war for that matter." Returns to city apartment in November. Dies at home of cardiorespiratory failure at 5:30 P.M.. on December 20. Funeral service is held at St. James Episcopal Church on Madison Avenue. Elaine takes ashes to Pacific Grove; after family service at Point Lobos on December 26, they are later buried in the family plot in Garden of Memories Cemetery, Salinas.

Note on the Texts

This volume contains the following works by John Steinbeck: the short-story collection *The Long Valley* (1938), the novel *The Grapes of Wrath* (1939), the nonfiction work *The Log from the Sea of Cortez* (1951, but originally published in 1941 as part of *Sea of Cortez*), and the investigative articles "The Harvest Gypsies" (published as a series in 1936) and "Starvation Under the Orange Trees" (1938).

The stories collected in *The Long Valley* were written (with the exception of "St. Katy the Virgin") between the spring of 1933 and the late summer of 1934, and except for "Flight" had all appeared previously in periodicals, as follows: "The Chrysanthemums," *Harper's Magazine*, October 1937; "The White Quail," *The North American Review*, March 1935; "The Snake," *The Monterey Beacon*, June 22, 1935; "Breakfast," *Pacific Weekly*, November 9, 1936; "The Raid," *The North American Review*, October 1934; "The Harness," *Atlantic Monthly*, June 1938; "The Vigilante," *Esquire*, October 1936; "Johnny Bear," *Esquire*, September 1937; "The Murder," *The North American Review*, April 1934; "The Red Pony, I: The Gift," *The North American Review*, November 1933; "The Red Pony, II: The Great Mountains," *The North American Review*, December 1933; "The Red Pony, III: The Promise," *Harper's Magazine*, August 1937; "The Leader of the People," *Argosy* (London), August 1936. "St. Katy the Virgin" had been written earlier than the others; Steinbeck had sent it to his agents McIntosh and Otis as early as the spring of 1932, and it was published by Covici-Friede in a limited edition of 199 copies as a Christmas gift book in December 1936. Steinbeck made a few revisions and alterations in these stories prior to their publication as a collection. *The Long Valley* was originally to have been published by Covici-Friede, but after the company went bankrupt and Steinbeck's editor, Pascal Covici, moved to Viking Press as a senior editor, it was published by Viking in September 1938. The text printed here is that of the first printing of the first edition.

Steinbeck began work on the manuscript of what would become *The Grapes of Wrath* at the end of May 1938 and completed the book by the beginning of December 1938. The book was written under difficult circumstances—Steinbeck and his wife, Carol, were living in a house undergoing construction, and during the course of the writing both suffered from exhaustion and a variety of physical ailments. Covici was enthusiastic about the book and planned a large first printing; others at Viking, however, were distressed by some of the language and feared that the novel would be banned in parts of the country. In early January 1939, Steinbeck's agent, Elizabeth Otis, visited him in Los Gatos and, in what he described as "two terrible days," attempted to win his agreement to a number of editorial changes, with mixed success. The alterations reluctantly agreed upon by the exhausted Steinbeck were telegraphed back to Viking the day before the typescript was due to be sent to the printer. The book was published in April 1939 in a first printing of 50,000 copies, and it became a tremendous bestseller.

The text of *The Grapes of Wrath* printed here is that of the first printing of the first edition, corrected with reference to the original manuscript, typescript, and galleys. (In addition, Roy Simmonds' collation of the manuscript against the first edition was consulted; see Roy S. Simmonds, "The Original Manuscript," in "*The Grapes of Wrath*, A Special Issue," *San Jose Studies*, Vol. XVI, no. 1, Winter 1990.) Steinbeck thought of his manuscript as a first draft and Carol's typed version as a second draft; he expected that there would be yet another draft before the book was ready for publication, but Covici decided that the typed second draft was acceptable. Steinbeck worked with Carol when she typed and oversaw some minor revisions along the way; he trusted her to insert appropriate paragraphing and punctuation when they were missing in the manuscript. Although Steinbeck made some corrections on the typescript, he did not compare the text with his manuscript, and his proofreading of the typescript appears to have been perfunctory and hurried.

The present text corrects errors made by Carol in transcribing Steinbeck's manuscript, such as the accidental omission of whole lines and the misreading or mistyping of some words. In addition, the original wording has been restored at places where the Viking staff thought it would be found objectionable and softened it. These changes are listed at the end of this note.

The narrative text of *The Log from the Sea of Cortez* (New York: Viking Press, 1951) was first published in 1941 as part of *Sea of Cortez* (New York: Viking Press); that volume, which listed Steinbeck and his friend Edward Ricketts as co-authors, also included a lengthy catalogue of the findings of the marine biological expedition in which the two participated in the Gulf of California, March–April 1940. In writing the log, Steinbeck drew heavily on Ricketts' journal of the expedition, and both men regarded the book as a truly collaborative work. A joint memo to Pascal Covici, drafted by Ricketts, describes the writing process as follows: "Originally, a journal of the trip was to have been kept by both of us, but this record was found to be a natural expression of only one of us. This journal was subsequently used by the other chiefly as a reminder of what actually had taken place, but in several cases parts of the original field notes were incorporated into the final narrative, and in one case a large section was lifted verbatim from the other unpublished work. This was then passed back to the other for comment, completion of certain chiefly technical details, and corrections. And then the correction was passed back again." (See *The Outer Shores: From the Papers of Edward F. Ricketts*, edited by Joel W. Hedgpeth; Eureka, CA: Mad River Press, 1978.)

Ricketts died in an automobile accident in May 1948, and when Steinbeck's portion of *Sea of Cortez* was reissued separately in 1951, it was introduced by the memoir "About Ed Ricketts." In the 1951 edition, the text of the log itself was reprinted from the original 1941 edition, with a few corrections of minor typographical errors. The text printed here is that of the first edition of *The Log from the Sea of Cortez*.

"The Harvest Gypsies" was originally published as a series of seven articles in the *San Francisco News*, October 5–12, 1936. When told that some migrant workers objected to the term "harvest gypsies," Steinbeck responded in a letter to the *News*: "The title was used ironically, since it is ironical that a huge group of workers should, through the injustice and bad planning of our agricultural system, be forced into a gypsy life. Certainly I had no intention of insulting a people who are already insulted beyond endurance." The articles were subsequently issued in 1938 as a pamphlet by the Simon J. Lubin Society, with the title *Their Blood Is Strong*; there is no evidence that Steinbeck was directly involved in the preparation of this pamphlet, beyond adding at the end (under the heading "Epilogue: Spring 1938") the article "Starvation Under the Orange Trees" from the *Monterey Trader* of April 15, 1938. The texts printed here are those of the original newspaper versions.

This volume presents the texts of the original printings chosen for inclusion here, but it does not attempt to reproduce features of their typographic design, such as display capitalization of chapter openings. The texts are printed without change, except for the correction of typographical errors and the restoration of the original wording of *The Grapes of Wrath* where it was mistyped by Carol Steinbeck or censored by the Viking staff. Spelling, punctuation, and capitalization are often expressive features, and they are not altered, even when inconsistent or irregular.

The following two lists record, by page and line number, the changes (other than corrections of typographical errors) incorporated into the text of *The Grapes of Wrath* in this volume. The first list reports the transcription errors that have been corrected; the second list reports the places where censored passages have been restored. In each item, the reading of the present text comes first, followed by that of the first edition.

Transcription errors in *The Grapes of Wrath*: 235.33–35, man . . . How] man. How 242.29, enslaved] ensnared 254.38, three] the 256.32, child] child's 256.38–40, Tommy?" . . . "Two] Tommy?" ¶ "Two 257.22–24, house . . . an'] house, an' 258.33, a couple-three] couple-three 259.24, han'] hand 260.11–13, went. Bought . . . wasn't] went. They wasn't 260.34–35, own words] words 262.22–23, said . . . Salt,] said. Salt, 262.35, wherever] where 263.28, Casy . . . You're] Casy. "You're 264.33, preacher] preachin' 265.1–2, knife . . . and] knife and 265.33, wasn't] was 269.14, "You'd be] "You're 277.34, even give] give 280.11, come an'] come and 281.34–35, killer.' In . . . 'You] killer.' You 296.1–3, An' there . . . An' that] An' that 310.21, film] flour 316.32, an'] and 322.10, go." . . . "Hardly] go. Hardly 327.10–11, spareribs . . . wasn't] spareribs. ¶ "I wasn't 332.28, That] The 340.29, git] get 342.7–8, loose . . . "Need] loose. "Need 347.27, "I—I] "I 359.16, really truly] really 361.18–20, jar . . . screwed] jar and Tom screwed 364.24–25, He . . . An'] An' 364.28–29, cried. "Why no!" ¶ "Oh] cried. ¶ "Why, no. Oh 365.26, 'em] cars 367.39, barely] hardly 374.19, from . . . mouth] from the mouth 375.10, know . . . syphilis] know—she has syphilis 383.6, They] Then 387.24, it . . . got] it. We got 387.33, idear] idea 387.40, you'll all] you'll 388.33, s'pose] suppose 392.34, "Ready] "Reach 395.1, comin'] gonna come 395.8, kinda folks] kinda fences 402.19, black patches] patches 403.13, dusk] dark 412.15–16, An' he'll . . . look] An' he'll look 413.12–13, fellas] folks 414.33, fust] first 416.3, then] they 420.19, as a] as—as a 449.31, I . . . you] I can't tell you. I can't tell you 456.12, ferociously] frantically 464.11–12, through . . . holdings] through their holdings 465.17, side] sides 467.3, moved cautiously] moved 470.3, kid] kids 473.24, wanta] want ta 478.38, wanta] want ta 479.25–26, was a-braggin' . . . High] was a braggin'. High 479.27, says] say 483.13, wanta] want ta 492.22, wanta] want ta 493.14–19, moment . . . "I] moment. "O.K.," he said. "I 494.38, gonna] goin' to 500.29, wanta] want ta 500.32, shush?] shh? 508.39, wanta] want ta 510.11, farmed] formed 520.38–40, rent." . . . hell!"] rent." ¶ "Rent, hell!" 522.24, sheds] shade trees 523.27, wage] rate 539.6, play . . . She] play." She 541.16, An'—did them] An'—them 544.2, roofed] unroofed 545.39, Four been] Four 546.37, No,"] Nor," 553.15, on] of 553.37, But] But now 555.12, go] to 557.14, spoiled him . . . somepin] spoiled somepin 557.34, if . . . rich] if I was rich, if I was rich   558.30, back . . . A girl] back—a girl   584.24, woman you're] woman, you're   584.34–35, beat . . . He's] beat. He's   585.13, joke fell from] job fell on   590.33, "Gits] "Gets   592.23, unit.] units.   603.38, wanta] want ta   607.22, waved] moved   614.1, path] patch   619.14–15, ain't doin'] didn't do   648.31–32, over an'] over   654.23, playin' it] playin'   657.37, wage] rate   664.4–7, Sharon. "You shouldn't . . . "You got] Sharon. She said, "You got   671.17, night] night the   676.9, gonna] goin' to   676.28, outa] inta   682.24–27, "Shucks!" . . . yawned.] "Shucks!" Ruthie yawned.

Censored passages in *The Grapes of Wrath*: 233.4, you . . . wasn't] you. They wasn't   233.8, out . . . 'em."] out in the grass."   247.5–6, no skin . . . ass.] nothing.   270.21, shit] crap   293.22, fuck] mess   298.20, fuckin'] messin'   336.34, Horseshit!] Baloney!   337.9, fuck] jump   375.5, Joan Crawford] So-and-So   401.9, shit] crap   408.30, shit] talk   412.40, fucked] fooled   417.21, shit] foul   431.11, ass] tail   451.31, up his ass] in his ear   464.15, fat-assed deputy] deputy   500.20, balls] overhalls   509.1, fat-ass deputies] deputies   515.35, fat-ass cops] cops   576.27, their ass] 'em.

The following is a list of typographical errors corrected, cited by page and line number: 7.25–26, chysanthemum; 13.10, chrysantheums; 31.16., 'Si,; 31.25, denin; 64.6, on on; 100.14, Nothing; 112.25, elbow,; 118.10, His; 123.37, "And; 150.35, Bill; 151.19, fittted; 158.28, furiously,; 163.11, Judy; 169.40, know?"; 225.23, forty-year old; 248.20, It; 271.8, said,; 272.12, Casey; 274.23, Start' em; 283.16, wouldn't; 283.21, couldn't; 287.20, a'plenty; 289.4–5, goin' without; 290.22, a' they; 294.34, Don't; 347.13, look; 354.17, mattresses; 357.22, hundred; 396.23, don't; 398.24, idea; 399.29, eyes; 412.20, "When; 420.29, go; 467.38, here here; 481.37, don't; 486.7, 'em; 494.6, Mike. is; 498.31, thinkin'.'; 498.40, out?'; 502.2, Tom,; 502.27, "Thank; 519.38, want to; 539.25, An; 540.21, it."; 545.38, tol',; 550.29, don't; 551.24, child; 560.4, don't; 589.32, Willy; 605.5, "O.K."; 611.11, jes'; 626.21, Don't . . . Don't; 627.11, sin now.; 627.21, on'; 637.28, headlight; 640.11, work, I; 640.36, Don' let; 662.28, matches,; 672.7, on the nose; 677.3, about him; 683.27, 'an; 688.35, where'; 689.6, don't; 715.21, wating; 725.14, It's; 769.11, US.P.; 797.39, Xanthus; 901.29, is of; 912.21, mave; 946.20, April 22; 975.28a, AUTONOMY; 987.2a, Xanthus; 996.35, anythings happen; 1010.36, possession; 1025.38, are rive.

Notes

In the notes below, the reference numbers denote page and line of this volume (the line count includes headings). No note is made for material included in standard desk-reference books such as Webster's *Collegiate*, *Biographical*, and *Geographical* dictionaries. For references to other studies and further biographical background than is contained in the Chronology, see Jackson J. Benson, *The True Adventures of John Steinbeck, Writer* (New York: Viking Press, 1984); *Steinbeck: A Life in Letters* (New York: Viking Press, 1975), edited by Elaine Steinbeck and Robert Wallsten; John Steinbeck, *Working Days: The Journals of The Grapes of Wrath, 1938–1941* (New York: Viking Penguin, 1989), edited by Robert DeMott; Thomas Fensch, *Steinbeck and Covici: The Story of a Friendship* (Middlebury, VT: Paul S. Eriksson, 1979); Jay Parini, *John Steinbeck: A Biography* (New York, Henry Holt, 1995); Roy Simmonds, *John Steinbeck: The War Years, 1939–1945* (Lewisburg, PA: Bucknell University Press; London: Associated University Press, 1996); Robert DeMott, *Steinbeck's Typewriter: Essays on Creative Dimensions of His Art* (Troy, NY: Whitston Publishing, 1996); Robert DeMott, *Steinbeck's Reading: A Catalogue of Books Owned and Borrowed* (New York & London: Garland Publishing, 1984); Peter Lisca, *The Wide World of John Steinbeck* (New Brunswick, NJ: Rutgers University Press, 1958; new edition, New York: Gordian Press, 1981); Tetsumaro Hayashi, *A New Steinbeck Bibliography, 1929–1971* and *A New Steinbeck Bibliography: 1971–1981* (Metuchen, NJ: Scarecrow Press, 1973 & 1983); *Conversations with John Steinbeck* (Jackson & London: University Press of Mississippi, 1988), edited by Thomas Fensch; and *Letters to Elizabeth: A Selection of Letters from John Steinbeck to Elizabeth Otis* (San Francisco: Book Club of California, 1978), edited by Florian J. Shasky and Susan F. Riggs.

THE LONG VALLEY

31.29   *dulces*]   Spanish: sweets.

32.20   *metate*]   Spanish: grinding stone.

34.37   *'Qui 'st 'l caballo*]   Spanish: *Aquí está el caballo*, Here is the horse.

61.15–16   *Come . . . Baby*]   "My Melancholy Baby" (1912), song by George A. Norton and Ernie Burnett.

97.1   Blind Tom]   Thomas Greene Bethune (1849–1908), pianist and composer born in slavery in Columbus, Georgia. Bethune was a child prodigy and amazed audiences with his musical and verbal recall and his ability to mimic natural and instrumental sounds; he could perform more than 700 pieces from memory. His white managers encouraged him to create an impression of idiocy in his public performances.

127.13   APAGE SATANAS!] Latin: Get thee hence, Satan!

THE GRAPES OF WRATH

207.1   THE GRAPES OF WRATH] The title, which was suggested by Steinbeck's wife, Carol, is taken from the second stanza of Julia Ward Howe's "The Battle Hymn of the Republic," first published in the *Atlantic Monthly*, February, 1862: "Mine eyes have seen the glory of the coming of the Lord; / He is trampling out the vintage where the grapes of wrath are stored . . . " In a letter to his agent, Elizabeth Otis, Steinbeck wrote that he liked Howe's song "because it is a march and this book is a kind of march—because it is in our own revolutionary tradition and because in reference to this book it has a large meaning. And I like it because people know the Battle Hymn who don't know the Star Spangled Banner." He instructed Viking Press to print the "Battle Hymn" on the endpapers of the first edition.

208.5   TOM] Thomas Collins, a federal relief camp specialist working for the Farm Security Administration, who facilitated much of Steinbeck's research on and field work among the migrant workers in California's Central Valley.

222.32   McAlester] Location of the Oklahoma State Penitentiary, which opened in 1908.

241.6–7   fatted calf . . . Scripture] Cf. Luke 15:11–32.

245.5   angry . . . go.] Steinbeck had written originally in the typescript: "angry. That's socialism, that's bolshivism! That is an attack on the sacred rights of property."

269.6   Rosasharn] Rose of Sharon; the name comes from The Song of Solomon, 2:1: "I am the rose of Sharon, and the lily of the valleys."

274.27   Hymie] Steinbeck noted on the galleys to his editor: "Probably a corruption of 'high sign' but it's good."

290.18   Purty Boy Floyd] Charles Arthur "Pretty Boy" Floyd (1901–34), notorious outlaw born in Sallisaw, Oklahoma, and frequently regarded as a Robin Hood–like figure. He died in a shootout with law enforcement agents in a cornfield near East Liverpool, Ohio.

293.23   McCoy blood] The McCoy clan of Pike County, Kentucky, engaged in a violent feud with the Hatfields of Logan County, West Virginia, from 1878 to 1890, during which a dozen people were killed on both sides.

301.11   guayule] *Parthenium argentatum*, a desert shrub containing rubber, native to the north central plateau of Mexico and the Big Bend area of Texas. In the 1930s and early 1940s attempts were made to produce rubber on a large scale by harvesting this plant.

303.31   *Pilgrim's Progress*] John Bunyan's *The Pilgrim's Progress from This World to That Which Is To Come* (1678–84).

305.35–36   *The Winning of Barbara Worth*] Novel (1911) by Harold Bell Wright.

310.34   snipes] Discarded stubs of cigars or cigarettes.

357.34   Floyd] See note 290.18.

361.7–8   " 'An' Lot . . . my Lord.' "] Cf. Genesis 19:18.

361.15–16   'Blessed . . . covered.'] Psalm 32:1.

362.25   'All that lives is holy.'] Cf. William Blake, *The Marriage of Heaven and Hell* (1790): "Everything that lives is holy." Blake repeats the line in *America: A Prophecy* and *Visions of the Daughters of Albion* (both 1793).

372.9   "Ti-pi-ti-pi-tin," . . . the Memory,"] "Ti-Pi-Tin" (1938), popular Mexican song with music based on motifs from Chabrier and Lalo and lyrics by Maria Grever; "Thanks for the Memory," song by Leo Robin and Ralph Rainger, featured in the film *The Big Broadcast of 1938*.

372.27   IITYWYBAD?] Steinbeck noted on the galleys to his editor: "If I Tell You Will You Buy A Drink. (Get it?)"

429.28–29   newspaper fella near the coast] Newspaper publisher William Randolph Hearst (1863–1951), who in 1919 began building a private castle on 240,000 acres adjacent to the Pacific Ocean at San Simeon, California.

460.16   Well . . . yourn.] In the typescript, this was followed by a paragraph Steinbeck later crossed out: "Hearst got a million acres, they say, an' the old houses all burned down 'fear somebody'd live in 'em."

462.35–36   fella . . . in a wagon] Land and cattle baron Henry Miller (also known as Heinrich Alfred Kreiser; 1827–1916) fraudulently received patents to thousands of acres of alleged swamplands after testifying to land officers that the land was traversable only by rowboat, when in fact the boat was mounted on a wagon and towed by horses.

464.25   black-tongue] Pellagra.

476.33   Durham] Bull Durham tobacco.

510.25   people.] In the typescript, this was followed by a paragraph Steinbeck later crossed out: "Once the Germans in their hordes came to the rich margin of Rome; and they came timidly, saying 'we have been driven give us land.' And the Romans armed the frontier and built forts against the hordes of need. And the legions patrolled the borders, cased in metal, armed with the best steel. And the barbarians came, naked, across the border, humbly, humbly. They received the swords in their breasts and marched on; and their dead bore down the swords and the barbarians marched on and took the land. And they were driven by their need, and they conquered with their need. In battle the women fought in the line, and the yellow-haired children lay in the grass with knives to hamstring the legionaries, to snick through the hamstrings of the horses. But the legions had no needs, no wills, no force. And the best trained, best armed troops in the world went down before the hordes of need."

517.17–519.39   It was . . . on."]   This passage is based on Steinbeck's short story "Breakfast" in *The Long Valley*.

523.14–18   Farmers' Association . . . Bank of the West]   Carol responded on the galleys to a query from Steinbeck's editor, who was concerned about possible libel: "Real names are Associated Farmers & Bank of America." Steinbeck added: "probably shoot me as it is!"

532.16   frawny]   Steinbeck wrote on the galleys to his editor: "Beautiful word—means sweat and dust mixed."

565.39   "Down Home Blues,"]   Words and music by Tom Delaney; first recorded by Ethel Waters.

577.12–13   what happened in Akron, Ohio]   On February 17, 1936, workers struck at Goodyear Tire and Rubber Company in Akron, in response to layoffs and increased working hours. The Akron Central Labor Union leaders called for a general strike if authorities used force to uphold a restraining order against mass picketing. When a Law and Order League was formed among local citizens, the Union began regular military-type drills to prepare for vigilante attacks. In March 1936 Goodyear recognized the union, reinstated the laid-off workers, and cut the work-day hours back from eight to six.

599.33   Happy Hooligan]   Kindly hobo featured in the comic strip of the same name, drawn by Frederick B. Opper from 1890 to 1932, and syndicated in Hearst newspapers.

643.27   cotton-pickin' machine]   John and Mack Rust designed and built a horse-drawn mechanical harvester, the Rust Cotton Picker, in 1928, and experimented with several mechanized versions of it. In 1937 an improved tractor model picked 13 bales of cotton in one day; however, because of the availability of cheap labor in the Depression such machines did not become widely used until the 1940s.

655.2–5   'Two are better . . . to help him up.']   Cf. Ecclesiastes 4:9–12.

655.7–10   'Again, if two lie . . . not quickly broken.']   Deuteronomy 15:11.

655.40   young Floyd]   See note 290.18.

THE LOG FROM THE SEA OF CORTEZ

693.2–3   THE LOG . . . CORTEZ]   *Sea of Cortez: With a Scientific Appendix Comprising Materials for a Source Book on the Marine Animals of the Panamic Faunal Province* (1940) was published with Steinbeck and Edward Ricketts listed as co-authors. When the narrative portion of the original book, written by Steinbeck but closely based on Ricketts' journal of their 1940 collecting trip to the Sea of Cortez, was published by Viking in 1951 as *The Log from the Sea of Cortez*, Steinbeck was credited as sole author.

697.2   one day in April 1948]   Ricketts' accident occurred May 7, 1948; he died May 11, 1948, three days short of his 53rd birthday.

701.15   Born in Chicago]   Edward Flanders Ricketts was born May 14, 1897; he studied a year at Illinois State Normal University, then, after serving in the army, 1918–19, attended the University of Chicago from 1919 to 1922 without obtaining a degree. He arrived on the Monterey Peninsula in 1923, where he started Pacific Biological Laboratories with Alfred E. Galigher.

704.5   the fire]   The fire which destroyed Pacific Biological Laboratories, and the Del Mar Canning Company next door, occurred November 25, 1936; Ricketts rebuilt the laboratories on the same site.

711.21   a short story]   "The Snake," in *The Long Valley.*

719.29   Lotus Eaters]   The Lotophagoi, a mythical people featured in Homer's *Odyssey*; they inhabit the north coast of Africa and live on the fruit of the lotus plant, which induces forgetfulness and contented indolence. They were later the subject of Tennyson's poem "The Lotus-Eaters" (1832).

729.15   *Black Marigolds*]   Translations of Sanskrit poetry (1919) by Edward Powys Mathers.

735.16   Welsh tale]   The magician Math conjures Blodenwedd out of flowers for Lleu Llaw Gyffes in the fourth tale of the ancient Welsh *Mabinogion* cycle, compiled in the 14th and 15th centuries.

737.24–25   philosophy of "breaking through,"]   In 1940 Ricketts wrote an essay, "The Philosophy of 'Breaking Through,' " never published in his lifetime. The title is taken from the 1925 poem "Roan Stallion" by Robinson Jeffers (1887–1962): "Humanity is the mold to break away from, the crust to break / through . . . "

741.26   *Studs Lonigan*]   Trilogy by James T. Farrell consisting of the novels *Young Lonigan* (1932), *The Young Manhood of Studs Lonigan* (1934), and *Judgment Day* (1935).

754.17   *Coast Pilot*]   Steinbeck and Ricketts used the 430-page *Sailing Directions for the West Coasts of Mexico and Central America*, published in 1937 by the U.S. Navy Hydrographic Office.

754.20–21   Clavigero]   Francisco Javier Clavigero (1731–87), Mexican-born Jesuit whose *Storia del California* was first published posthumously in Italian in 1789; an English translation by Sara E. Lake and A. A. Gray was published by Stanford University Press in 1937 as *The History of (Lower) California*.

760.8–13   Johnson and Snook . . . *Southern California*]   The volumes referred to are Myrtle Elizabeth Johnson and Harry James Snook, *Seashore Animals of the Pacific Coast* (New York: Macmillan, 1935); Edward F. Ricketts and Jack Calvin, *Between Pacific Tides* (Stanford: Stanford University Press, 1939); F. S. Russell and C. M. Yonge, *The Seas: Our Knowledge of Life in the Sea and How It Is Gained* (London: Frederick Warne, 1936); F. W. Flattley and C. L. Walton, *The Biology of the Sea-Shore* (London: Macmillan, 1936); Josiah Keep, *West Coast Shells*, revised by Joshua Bailey (Stanford: Stanford University Press, 1935); W. K. Fisher, *Asteroidea of the North Pacific and Adjacent Waters*, published in three issues of *Bulletin of the United States National Museum* (1911, 1928, 1930); Mary J. Rathbun's four-part monograph, which appeared under four different titles in *The Bulletin of the United States National Museum* (vol. 97, 1918; vol. 129, 1925; vol. 152, 1930; vol. 166, 1937); Waldo L. Schmitt, *The Marine Decapod Crustacea of California* (Berkeley: University of California Press, 1921); C. McLean Fraser, *Hydroids of the Pacific Coast of Canada and the United States* (Toronto: University of Toronto Press, 1937); Percy Spencer Barnhart, *Marine Fishes of Southern California* (Berkeley: University of California Press, 1936).

760.40   U.S.P.]   United States Pharmocopeia.

771.4   *cuartel*]   Spanish: dwelling.

789.3   Stimpson]   William Stimpson (1832–72), author of *Researches Upon the Hydrobina and Allied Forms; Chiefly Made Upon Materials in the Museum of the Smithsonian Institutions* (1865).

789.24   Scylla-Charybdis]   In Greek mythology, mariners had to steer a course between the cave of the sea-monster Scylla and the whirlpool Charybdis.

792.17   '*Callida fornax*']   Latin: hot oven.

797.39   Xantus]   Janos Xantus (1825–94), ornithologist, was born in Hungary, and in 1850 escaped to America after being imprisoned for anti-Austrian activities; he worked as a topographer for the railroads and later participated in a number of expeditions in California and the Pacific during which he discovered many new species of birds. His account of Baja California was published in Hungarian in 1860. After serving as U.S. consul in Mexico, he returned to Hungary in 1864.

806.3   Verrill]   Addison Emery Verrill (1839–1926), American zoologist and naturalist.

808.1   *Lebensraum*]   German: living space.

808.8–9   *Gauleiter*]   A Nazi party "area commander."

808.34   the town . . . destroyed]   The old city of Panama was destroyed by the pirate Henry Morgan in 1671, and was subsequently rebuilt five miles west of its original site.

822.23–24   Congress . . . our people]   In June 1932, Congress voted down a request for full bonus payment to 17,000 unemployed World War I veterans known as the Bonus Army, who had camped in sight of the Capitol.

823.4 $\sqrt[\pi]{-1}$]   This expression indicates that the πth root of (-1) is to be taken; but since π is not an integer, there is no solution to this formula.

823.33   *Studs Lonigan*]   See note 741.26.

832.4–5   General Almazan]   Juan Andreu Almazan, a conservative land-owner, lost to General Avila Camacho, candidate of the Party of the Mexican Revolution, in the 1940 election.

832.7   Huitzilopochtli]   Aztec war god.

832.33   One of us . . . walking trip]   See Edward Ricketts, "Vagabonding Through Dixie," *Travel* 45 (June 1925).

834.12   An event which happened at La Paz]   This story was the basis for Steinbeck's novella *The Pearl* (1947).

854.16   *Phthirius pubis*]   Latin: genital crabs.

861.10   Pollyanna]   Optimistic heroine of Eleanor Hodgman Porter's 1913 novel of the same name.

865.20   Van Gogh . . . Arles epoch]   Van Gogh produced over 300 paint-ings, drawings, and watercolors during the 15 months he spent in Arles (Feb-ruary 1888–May 1889).

866.14   *post hoc, ergo propter hoc*]   Latin: after that, therefore because of that.

872.37   "crust . . . break through"]   See note 737.24–25.

874.37–38   as Emerson . . . "The Oversoul"]   Cf. Emerson, "The Over-Soul," *Essays: First Series* (1841): "The philosophy of six thousand years has not searched the chambers and magazines of the soul. In its experiments there has always remained, in the last analysis, a residuum it could not resolve."

875.10–11   Swinburne, extolling Hertha]   Algernon Charles Swinburne addresses in the ancient Germanic earth-goddess Hertha in *Songs Before Sun-rise* (1871).

884.32   *con cojones, pero cojones*]   Spanish: with balls, I mean balls.

889.23–24   Hancock Expedition] Detailed reports of Pacific Coast collecting expeditions carried out in the 1930s by the University of Southern California's Allan Hancock Foundation for Marine Research, founded in 1905 by George Allan Hancock (1876–1965).

889.26–27   a well-known . . . thirty years ago.] The scientific expedition of the U.S. Fish Commission steamer *Albatross* from San Francisco to Angel de la Guardia in 1911; C.H. Townsend's report "Voyage of the *Albatross* to the Gulf of California in 1911" was published in *Bulletin of the American Museum of Natural History*, Volume 25 (1916).

892.24–25   first successful . . . Peninsula] Loreto was founded in 1697 by the Jesuit priest Juan Maria Salvatierra.

897.29   Eric Knight Jordan] Jordan was killed in an automobile accident in 1926 at the age of 22; his scientific papers were collected in *The Pleistocene Fauna of Magdalena Bay, Lower California* (1936).

898.15   Carpenter] Philip P. Carpenter, "Report on the Present State of Our Knowledge with Regard to the Mollusca of the West Coast of North America," in *Report of the Meeting of the British Association for the Advancement of Science* (1857). In their Annotated Phyletic Catalogue in the 1941 edition of *Sea of Cortez*, Steinbeck and Ricketts describe this as "the most important single paper encountered in these investigations; the product, obviously, of a disciplined, humble, and competent mind . . . Like most of Darwin's writings, and like the monographs of Fisher, Rathbun, and Schmitt today, this transcends its time and subject matter and achieves a quality of universalness."

913.9–10   Man o' War . . . Charlie Paddock] Man o' War, renowned stallion who set five world racing records; Charles Paddock, American runner who won silver medals at the 1920 and 1924 Olympics.

913.25–26   Horace says . . . hangover.] Cf. *Satires*, II, 4: "Shrimps that are fried give relief after overindulgence in drinking; / African snails do the same." (Translated by Charles E. Passage.)

923.27   One of our party] Steinbeck's wife, Carol.

928.7   *Proctophilus winchellii*] The reference is to gossip columnist Walter Winchell (1897–1972).

933.33   Marconi sail] A triangular sail set on a tall mast.

938.13   Avalon] In Arthurian romance, the magical island to which Arthur is borne for the healing of his wounds after his final encounter with Mordred.

938.13–14   Cipango] Archaic European term for Japan.

940.34–36   Swift's . . . Irish babies] Jonathan Swift's *A Modest Proposal, for preventing the Children of poor People in Ireland, from being a Burden to their Parents or Country; and for making them beneficial to the publick* (1729).

945.32–33   *Caribbean Treasure*] Published by Viking in 1939.

962.18   Boodin] Swedish-born philosopher John Elof Boodin (1869–1950), who studied at Harvard under William James and Josiah Royce and later taught at the universities of Kansas and California; his writings include *Time and Reality* (1904) and *A Realistic Universe* (1916).

967.16   "no star is lost."] Cf. Adelaide Ann Procter (1825–64), "A Legend of Provence": "No star is ever lost we once have seen, / We always may be what we might have been."

THE HARVEST GYPSIES

994.28   the Grange] Local unit of American agrarian movement called the National Grange of the Patrons of Husbandry, founded in 1867 to serve the social, educational, political, and cooperative agricultural needs of farmers.

1001.15–16   San Joaquin Valley . . . cotton strike] A 24-day strike began on October 4, 1933, in Corcoran, California, when cotton-picking wages were lowered to 60 cents per hundred pounds. After at least three strikers were killed by ranchers, the strike ended when a compromise price of 75 cents per hundred pounds was negotiated. Steinbeck drew on details of the strike for his 1936 novel *In Dubious Battle.*

1001.31   Associated Farmers, Inc.] Organization of California's large growers and corporate farmers founded in 1934 to combat farm labor strikes, to lobby for anti-picketing ordinances and to shift unemployment relief administration from state to county level, and to oppose efforts by the American Communist Party's Cannery and Agricultural Workers Industrial Union (founded 1932) to organize farm laborers in California.

1005.3–4   criminal syndicalism law] California's Criminal Syndicalism Law went into effect April 30, 1919. It punished those espousing "any doctrine or precept advocating, teaching or aiding and abetting the commission of crime, sabotage . . . or unlawful acts of force and violence or unlawful methods of terrorism as a means of accomplishing a change in industrial ownership or control, or affecting any political change." Violators could be charged with a felony, punishable by imprisonment for not less than one nor more than fourteen years.

1005.17–20   THE FEDERAL GOVERNMENT . . . two camps] President Franklin D. Roosevelt created the Resettlement Administration in April 1935; it oversaw various New Deal land use and relief policy agencies and was responsible for setting up the first demonstration federal migratory labor camps at Arvin and Marysville. The 20-acre Arvin site in Kern County, opened on December 13, 1935, was divided into 12 blocks with eight tent sites in each, and could accommodate 96 families at a time. As of September 1, 1937, the RA was renamed Farm Security Administration (FSA) and placed under direct control of the Department of Agriculture. Though 25 demonstration camps were planned, only 15 were actually finished or under construction in California by 1940.

1009.39–40   Yuba City Herald] A front-page story with the headline "Migrant Camp Is Red Hotbed" appeared in the *Yuba City Herald* for July 9, 1936. It read in part: "The Federal migrant camp in the city of Marysville is becoming a Red hotbed, a breeding place for the fomenting of strikes to destroy the peach crops of Sutter, Yuba, and Butte counties. The U.S. government is sheltering these Reds at night, providing them with roofs, beds and living accommodations . . . The Marysville City Government can either keep that migrant camp cleared of Reds or the ranchers will level it to the ground."

1015.20–22   riots . . . immigration laws] The U.S. signed the Burlingame Treaty of 1868 with China in order to make official the ability of the U.S. to regulate Chinese immigration. Following this treaty, the so-called Chinese Exclusion Acts (1882–1904) were passed to further limit Chinese immigration into the U.S.

1016.13–14   quota was suggested] Steinbeck refers to the Congressional debate over the Box bill (1925) and the Harris bill (1926), both designed to establish a quota system for Mexican immigration, and both defeated in large degree through the opposition of California growers.

1016.37–38   desire . . . to organize] In November 1927, a Confederation of Mexican Labor Unions was organized in Los Angeles, and five months later the Mexican Labor Union of Imperial Valley was established among cantaloupe pickers. Both unions were severely dealt with by the corporate growers.

1018.5   SRA] California State Emergency Relief Administration.

1018.20–23   vigilante raid . . . Salinas Valley] In August 1934, 3,000 Filipino lettuce pickers went on strike near Salinas, but were summarily dealt with by a force of special deputies.

1018.27–28   establishment . . . autonomous nation] The Tydings-McDuffie Philippine Island Independence Act, passed on March 24, 1934, opened the way to deportation of resident Filipinos already in the U.S. and exclusion of further Filipino immigration to America.

STARVATION UNDER THE ORANGE TREES

1023.1   *Starvation Under the Orange Trees*] This article, published in the *Monterey Trader*, April 15, 1938, was included as the final chapter of *Their Blood Is Strong* under the title *Epilogue: Spring 1938*. In the *Trader*, it was accompanied by an editorial note which read in part: "It is the desire of the author to dedicate this article to his friends, the migratory workers who harvest California crops. He will not accept personal payment in any form for this piece of writing. If any money, either direct payment or donations from persons who read this, is forthcoming, it is his desire that such contributions be made to a fund under responsible management and distributed therefrom to assist worthy families among the group."

1026.11   CCC]   Civilian Conservation Corps.

CATALOGING INFORMATION

Steinbeck, John, 1902–1968.
    The grapes of wrath & other writings, 1936–1941 / John
Steinbeck.
        p.   cm. — (The library of America ; 86)
    Contents: The long valley — The grapes of wrath — The
log from the Sea of Cortez — The harvest gypsies.

    1. Salinas River Valley (Calif.)—Social life and customs—
Fiction. 2. Migrant agricultural laborers—California—
Fiction. 3. California, Gulf of (Mexico)—Description and
travel. 4. Marine invertebrates—Mexico—California, Gulf
of. 5. Migrant agricultural laborers—California—Social
conditions.   I. Title.   II. Series.
PS3537.T3234A6   1996
813'.52—dc20   96-3725
ISBN 1–883011–15–9   CIP

THE LIBRARY OF AMERICA SERIES

This book is set in 10 point Linotron Galliard,
a face designed for photocomposition by Matthew Carter
and based on the sixteenth-century face Granjon. The paper is
acid-free Ecusta Nyalite and meets the requirements for permanence
of the American National Standards Institute. The binding
material is Brillianta, a woven rayon cloth made by
Van Heek-Scholco Textielfabrieken, Holland.
The composition is by The Clarinda
Company. Printing and binding by
R.R.Donnelley & Sons Company.
Designed by Bruce Campbell.

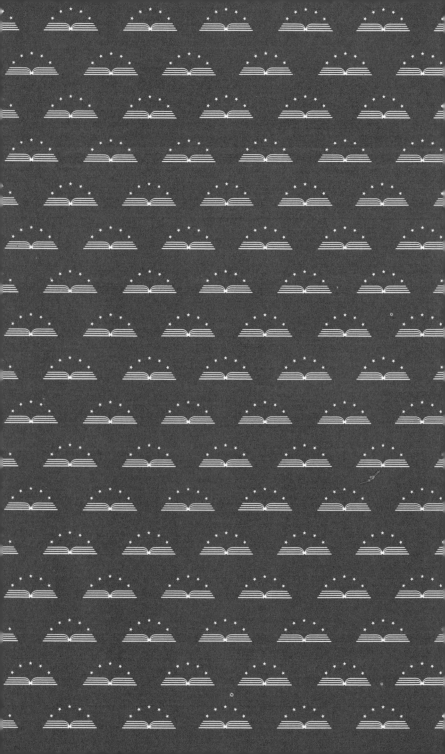